THE
OXFORD COMPANION
TO
FRENCH
LITERATURE

THE
OXFORD COMPANION
TO
FRENCH
LITERATURE

COMPILED AND EDITED BY

SIR PAUL HARVEY

AND

J. E. HESELTINE

OXFORD

AT THE CLARENDON PRESS

Oxford University Press, Amen House, London E.C.4

GLASGOW NEW YORK TORONTO MELBOURNE WELLINGTON
BOMBAY CALCUTTA MADRAS KARACHI KUALA LUMPUR
CAPE TOWN IBADAN NAIROBI ACCRA

70741

FIRST PUBLISHED 1959
REPRINTED 1959

PRINTED IN GREAT BRITAIN

PREFACE

AN Oxford Companion to French Literature was first spoken of in
1934. The lines it might, and in the event very closely did, follow were
mapped out by the late Sir Paul Harvey, whose volume on English
Literature had inaugurated the *Oxford Companions* series, and whom the
Clarendon Press at once invited to undertake the new compilation. At
first he refused, with characteristic diffidence and perhaps already with
some intimations of mortality, but he could not indefinitely withstand
the persuasive enthusiasm of Mr. Kenneth Sisam, then Assistant Secretary, and from 1942 to 1948 Secretary, to the Delegates of the Press.
He yielded, and by 1936 had set to work, but within self-imposed
limits: he would not undertake more than the period which began with
the emergence of the vernacular and the earliest traces of a French
literature, and which ended in the 18th century. A collaborator had to
be found, and the Revolutionary and post-Revolutionary periods were
ultimately entrusted to myself.

During the 1939-45 war Sir Paul Harvey managed to continue his
task. He found in it, he said, an anodyne; and at the end of 1947 he sent
his completed manuscript to Oxford for safe keeping. His 'manuscript',
collected in neatly-docketed, cardboard-backed bundles, consisted of
several thousand 6 by 4 inch slips of rather thick white paper, varied
by large sheets of bright, very thin, yellow paper, of the kind known as
'flimsy', which he had folded intricately to match the slips in size. Slips
and flimsy alike were closely written in a fine, graceful hand, little less
legible in his last years than it had been in the days of the *Companion to
English Literature*. In December 1948 he died, and I was told that
responsibility for the finished book must now be mine. To one who
had been left loose to wander, with little sense of pressure, over a mere
century and a half the prospect was stern, but the order came from
a Press that is the kindest of taskmasters.

This French *Companion* resembles its English precursor in devoting
most space to authors and to specific works (between them these form
the largest group of entries), or to the explanation of allusions. The
term 'author' comprises not only creative writers but also—though
here the net has been less widely flung—critics, historians, religious
writers, philosophers, savants, and scientists. Allusions and terms of frequent occurrence, which are not limited, as in the English *Companion*,

to those turning on proper names, find their explanation in articles on
(*a*) historical figures, places, and events, these being selected less for
their intrinsic importance than for their significance in, and in relation
to, literature, and the frequency with which references to them occur;
or (*b*) literary characters, those fictitious personages who, having never
existed, have so often achieved an immortality denied to their flesh-and-
blood contemporaries; or (*c*) artists, musicians, statesmen, saints, social
reformers, and eccentrics, a heterogeneous collection who are much in
the background of French literature and have at times definitely influenced it. There is no explanation of purely mythological allusions,
since these belong as much to English as to French literature.

In one respect the resemblance is, rather, to the *Companion to Classical
Literature*, for a considerable number of general articles, or surveys,
have been included, devoted mainly to phases or aspects of French
literary life and history, and the continually changing background of
movements, influences, and enthusiasms.

The terminal date at first envisaged was the outbreak of the 1914–18
war, with exceptional glances at the literature of the twenties. My share
of the task had to be interrupted for over seven years in 1939, and when
I resumed the terminal date was moved forward to, roughly, the outbreak of the 1939–45 war, with again the occasional later exception:
some necessary additions were made to the works listed under authors
already included; a few younger authors were admitted (whose reputations had in most cases been consolidated rather than freshly made after
1939); a very few post-war movements could not well be left out; and
from the point of view of social and constitutional background the
Fourth Republic could not go unremarked, however precarious its
existence might seem. But the aim was none the less to preserve the
distinction between a 'Companion to French Literature' and a 'Guide
to Contemporary French Authors', and to leave the post-1939 years
and the events, personages, and activities, or the attitudes, literary and
political, which belong to them, as much as possible untouched. The
Resistance Movement, for example, and its clandestine literature, have
not been covered.

The division of labour between Sir Paul Harvey and myself was
chronological, and clear from the beginning. In articles for which we
were jointly responsible the practice was for him to carry the story
to the end of his period, leaving me to continue and, if necessary, to
adapt and remodel for the sake of perspective. He made one excursion
into the 19th century at my request, and to my great relief, and wrote

the article on Bergson; and after he died I had to supply a few additional articles, mostly of a general character.

As it now stands, the volume contains some 6,000 articles, in alphabetical order, and liberally cross-referenced to make finding easy in a language in which a preposition, or the definite or indefinite article, may be an integral part of a name or of the title of a book. The articles vary in length from one, two, or three lines (cross-references or the briefest factual descriptions, little more than labels) to several columns. Length does not necessarily denote importance. Some authors died young, having written little, though they rivalled their longer-lived fellows in greatness. Some lived to a vast age and never stopped writing. (Some, even, never stopped writing great works, and compilers faced with their output must quail before the task of selection.) Some remain only by their associations or their manner of life, yet such are their personalities that they rebel against too hasty dispatch.

It is impossible to enumerate all the sources utilized in the work of compilation. Original works, memoirs, and correspondence were consulted as much as possible, and here the many excellent annotated editions of French authors which exist were of great service. Standard books of reference and histories of literature, journals and periodicals, biographical and bibliographical manuals, such as those mentioned in Appendix I or in the later section of the article on 'Dictionaries and Encyclopedias', were in constant use. So, too, were critical studies of individual authors and groups, or of the background from which they sprang; especially so for the later period, for much of the information about late 19th- and still more about 20th-century authors was obtained by a laborious piecemeal process before the many histories and studies of contemporary French literature which are now available had appeared.

I am woefully conscious of what the book suffered in its later stages by the loss of Sir Paul Harvey's scholarly editing and fine critical sense. If I dare to hope that my inadequacies are less glaring than they might otherwise have been it is because help and advice have come from so many quarters, and with such generosity. A number of articles were submitted in manuscript (some while Sir Paul Harvey was still alive) to specialists, and were altered or remodelled when necessary in the light of their comments. These advisers, whose help is gratefully recorded, include: Professor J. J. Seznec; Professor E. Vinaver; Professor H. H. Price; Dr. C. T. Onions; Dr. L. J. Beck; Dr. Brian Chapman; Mr. W. E. Collin, of the University of Western Ontario; Miss Flora

Hamilton; Mr. J. D. A. Thompson, of the Ashmolean Museum; and, lastly, Mr. R. C. Cobb, Lecturer in History at the University College of Wales, who went through some hundreds of articles with a historian's eye but also with an appreciation of the argument that they were intended as no more than annotations of literature.

A further, general, acknowledgement must suffice for the many other people whose suggestions were welcomed in the earlier stages; with an exception allowed for mention of help and kindness received in Paris from M. Louis Cazamian, sometime Professor of English Language and Literature at the Sorbonne, an *anglicisant* who has made more than one loving return to his native literature, and from M. René Lalou, critic and historian of contemporary French literature; and in Oxford from Professor Henri Fluchère, the Director of the Maison Française.

Once the work had been set up in type the proofs were read from A to Z in galley by Dr. Enid Starkie and by Dr. R. A. Sayce. In theory, the one was concerned with her particular province of French literature, the 19th and 20th centuries, and the other with the 16th to 18th centuries. In practice, both showed an enthusiasm that knew no bounds of centuries, and the book profited at all turns by their criticism and their suggestions for further, or more detailed, articles; also, it must be gratefully confessed, by their correction of some sad mis-statements. I must particularly acknowledge Dr. Starkie's authoritative criticism of articles such as those on Baudelaire, Rimbaud, and the various 19th- and 20th-century movements in French literature, also her many stimulating reminders of the connexion between writers and musicians. Dr. Sayce gave invaluable help in a field which was not my own and in which the picture had sometimes to be altered in the light of recent scholarship; and I owe him an admiring debt for his insistence on accuracy, as well as personal thanks for his unflagging patience and his willingness to be quizzed and pestered.

The proofs were also read, in page form, and with an eye to the medieval period, by Professor A. Ewert, who must be thanked not only for advice, but for restraining his comments to an indispensable and invariably helpful minimum.

It lay with me finally to make the corrections and additions recommended by these experts, or to decide not to make them. I hope I may be forgiven for disregarding some of their suggested additions. The book's period of gestation was already overlong; and there is much to be said for stopping short of those compilers who, in the words of Chamfort, 'ressemblent à ceux qui mangent des cerises ou des huîtres, choisissant d'abord les meilleures, et finissant par tout manger'. For the errors that remain I am responsible.

Sir Paul Harvey would, I know, have wished to express his constant indebtedness to the London Library. My own first debts of gratitude were to the officials and staffs of the Reading Rooms at the British Museum and the Bibliothèque Nationale, and to Mlle L.-N. Malclès, Conservateur at the Bibliothèque de la Sorbonne. In recent years I have to thank Mr. D. M. Sutherland, the Librarian of the Taylor Institution, and Mr. R. C. Maasz, Assistant Librarian, who gave information and advice on countless occasions, regardless of other calls on their time; also those young members of the staff whose help took the form of fetching and removing books that might only be wanted for five minutes (for a work of compilation entails a formidable amount of lifting and carrying). At this point, too, I must, gratefully and most respectfully, mention help received during the final stages of the proofs from a stern representative of the Printer, who wielded a blue pencil and filled the margins with queries.

Three very special acknowledgements shall end the list. The first is to Mr. Kenneth Sisam, to whom the *Companion* largely owes its inception, and to whose influence in persuading Sir Paul Harvey to undertake it I have already referred. The second is to Mr. D. M. Davin, the present Assistant Secretary to the Delegates, who took the book under his wing when Mr. Sisam retired. No one but myself can realize what I owe to these two. They were my masters, helpers, counsellors, safety-valves, and friends, unfailing dispensers of sympathy and encouragement. Both of them read and advised on articles (Mr. Davin read much of what Sir Paul Harvey wrote, and practically all that I wrote, in manuscript), and both were magicians, who could dissolve difficulties and transform despondency into eagerness.

And the third? It is to some living and many dead authors encountered in the course of this work, those who turned what seemed at times like a crucifixion into a voyage of discovery; who perhaps delayed progress, for they insisted on being read; and who time and again forced a jaded compiler to forget a world hungry for reference books and to dwell, rather, with beauty and truth—and often, blessedly, to laugh.

JANET E. HESELTINE

June 1958

ABBREVIATIONS

adv.	adverb	N.T.	New Testament
anon.	anonymously	*O.E.D.*	*Oxford English Dictionary*
augm.	augmented	O.T.	Old Testament
b.	born	p., pp.	page, pages
c., cent.	century	para., paras.	paragraph, paragraphs
c.	*circa*, about	plur.	plural
cf.	*confer*, compare	pop. L.	popular Latin
d.	died	posth.	posthumous(ly)
ed., edit.	edited, edition	prod.	produced
e.g.	*exempli gratia*, for example	pron.	pronounced
Eng.	English	pseud.	pseudonym
esp.	especially	q.v.	*quod vide*, which see
f.	founded	qq.v.	*quae vide*, both which, or all
fl.	*floruit*, flourished		which, see
fr.	from	ref.	refrain [music]
Gk.	Greek	ser.	series
i.e.	*id est*, that is	syn.	synonym
L., Lat.	Latin	tr.	translated
L.L.	Late Latin	*v.*	*vide*, see
Med. L.	Medieval Latin	vol., vols.	volume, volumes
N.R.F.	*Nouvelle Revue Française*		

A

Abailard, see *Abélard*.

Abbaye, L', an old house at Créteil, near Paris, leased in autumn 1906 by a group of young writers and artists—René Arcos, Georges Duhamel, Albert Gleizes, Henri Martin-Barzun, who provided most of the financial backing, Charles Vildrac (qq.v.). They proposed to live as a community, supporting themselves on the produce of the garden and by printing and selling books, their own and any others entrusted to them. Other writers (e.g. Jules Romains), painters, and musicians joined them or came at weekends; and the house was a centre of artistic activity for fourteen months. Lack of funds ended the venture, which forms the subject of Duhamel's novel *Le Désert de Bièvres* (1937).

L'Abbaye was not a poetical 'school'. Its artistic spirit was from the beginning strongly individualistic, though a team spirit prevailed for the work of the printing-press, to which all had undertaken to give four or five hours daily. But the fact that the Abbaye press issued the *Vie unanime* of Jules Romains, and that some of the poets of the community were afterwards classed with Romains as *unanimistes*, has led to its being associated with the movement known as *Unanimisme* (q.v.).

Abbaye, Prison de l', founded 1522, was attached to the Abbaye Saint-Germain-des-Prés, in Paris. It served first as a place of confinement for young nobles of disorderly habits, later for military, then for political, offenders. During the Revolution the notorious September massacres (1792) began in this prison. It was demolished in 1854.

Abbaye-aux-bois, see *Récamier, Mme*.

Abbaye de Saint-Denis, see *Saint-Denis*.

Abbaye de Saint-Victor, see *Saint-Victor*.

Abbaye de Thélème, see *Thélème*.

Abbé, a term denoting in the Middle Ages the head of a monastery (*abbas*). Later it was also used to signify any ecclesiastic, not necessarily in priest's orders. Many authors mentioned in this book, such as Chaulieu,

bore this designation while leading a purely worldly life.

Abbé Constantin, L' (1882), by Ludovic Halévy (q.v.), a light-hearted, rosy-hued, very sentimental novel of country life in which—a contrast to some more bleakly naturalistic novels of the period—all the characters are fundamentally good and kind. The gentle, elderly priest is beloved by his flock; the Americans who buy the local great property use their wealth to benefit the countryside; and the nearest approach to violence is shown by the young American heroine who has to force her proud but poor adorer to accept her proposal of marriage.

Abbé Tigrane, L' (1873), a novel by Ferdinand Fabre (q.v.), describes the quarrels and intrigues among the clergy of a country diocese when their bishop dies and a successor has to be appointed. It reflects the controversies which agitated clerical circles in 19th-century France as to the limits of Vatican control over the Church.

Abbesse de Jouarre, L', one of Renan's *Drames philosophiques* (q.v.).

Abélard or **Abailard,** PIERRE (1079–1142), a Breton, born near Nantes, celebrated as a disputant in logic and as one of the founders of scholastic theology. He was first a pupil of the great Nominalist Roscellinus, then studied in the Cathedral school of Paris under the Realist Guillaume de Champeaux, whose philosophical doctrine he proceeded, in spite of his youth, to combat successfully. He taught first at the Cathedral school and after 1106 at the school of Sainte-Geneviève. He later turned to theology and again attained distinction, treating his subject in a spirit of rational inquiry which brought upon him charges of heresy. But his popular fame rests principally on a tragic love affair. He seduced Héloïse (1101–64), the niece of a canon of Notre-Dame, one Fulbert, in whose house he lodged, a woman of high character and much learning, to whom he gave lessons. Although they were secretly married after she had given birth to a child, the affair ended in a cruel revenge by Fulbert (who caused Abélard to be castrated by hired ruffians), in the separation of the lovers, and in a famous correspondence. Abélard was much persecuted for his alleged heresy, especially by St. Bernard (q.v.), was driven in search of refuge from one monastery to another, was twice sentenced to imprisonment, and ended his days in retirement in the monastery of Cluny, under the protection of its good abbot, Peter the Venerable.

The correspondence referred to above is in Latin and has been frequently translated, but the authenticity of the text, at least in parts, has been suspected. It consists of eight letters. The first, written from the monastery of Saint-Gildas in Brittany, where Abélard spent the years 1128–34, is addressed to a friend. In this he relates with extreme candour and detail the story of his life, of his conflicts theological and philosophical, of his relations with Héloïse, and of his subsequent sufferings. This letter, having come into the hands of Héloïse, now head of the convent of the Paraclete (founded by Abélard and handed over to her), induces her to write to him, reproaching him for his neglect of her, recalling their former passion, and entreating in poignant terms that he will write to her. Abélard replies somewhat coldly, exhorting her to prayer and piety. A second letter from Héloïse in the same strain as the first draws from Abélard a less austere reply, with many words of encouragement and consolation. Héloïse, yielding obedience to his injunctions, now asks for guidance in the regulation of her convent, and receives from Abélard two long letters of direction, discussing with abundant citations from the Scriptures and the Fathers each point in the discipline appropriate to a nunnery, and prescribing the rules to be followed.

Abencérage, see *Aventures du dernier Abencérage.*

Ablancourt, NICOLAS PERROT D' (1606–64), born at Châlons-sur-Marne, translator and man of letters, noted for the excellence of his style; a friend of Patru (q.v.). The freedom of his method of translating caused Ménage to call his version of Lucian 'la belle infidèle'. His translations also included works of Thucydides, Xenophon, Arrian, Caesar, Cicero, and Tacitus.

About, EDMOND (1828–85), journalist (one of the most brilliant of his generation) and novelist. His publications included: *Causeries* (1865 and 1866), collected articles on social and religious questions; *Le Roman d'un brave homme* (1880), a successful novel; and several witty short stories which still make entertaining reading (*Les Mariages de Paris*, 1856; *Le Roi des montagnes*, 1857; *L'Homme à l'oreille cassée*, 1862; *Le Nez d'un notaire*, 1862; *Les Mariages de province*, 1868). His wit often had a moral in its tail.

Abrantès, JEAN-ANDOCHE JUNOT, DUC D' (1771–1813), nicknamed 'La Tempête' because of his dash and bravery, joined the Revolutionary armies in 1792, came to Bonaparte's notice at the siege of Toulon (1793) and campaigned with him in Italy and Egypt, becoming his A.D.C. He was sent to Lisbon as Ambassador in 1805 but rejoined the *Grande Armée* (q.v.) and distinguished himself at Austerlitz. He was also Military Governor of Paris. In 1807 he led the invasion of Portugal and captured Lisbon, when Napoleon created him duc d'Abrantès and Governor of Portugal. He fell from favour when, after the defeat of Vimeiro (q.v.), he signed the Convention of Cintra which led to the French evacuation of Portugal. He fought again in Spain and Germany, and in Russia in 1812, and in 1813 was sent to govern the Illyrian Provinces. While he was there his reason gave way and soon afterwards he committed suicide.

Abrantès, LAURE PERMON, DUCHESSE D' (1785–1838), born at Montpellier, knew the Bonaparte family almost from childhood because her mother was a Corsican and a friend of Mme Letizia Bonaparte, Napoleon's mother (see *Bonaparte family*; *Madame Mère*). After her marriage to General Junot, later duc d'Abrantès (see above), she became a lady-in-waiting to Napoleon's mother and was herself a leader of society. Her husband's death left her very badly off and she took to writing for a living. Her novels are forgotten but her *Mémoires historiques sur Napoléon, la Révolution, le Directoire . . . et la Restauration* (1831–5), also (1836) of the first years of Louis-Philippe's reign, are full of interest. With the perhaps even more interesting conversation pieces of her *Histoire des salons de Paris* (1836–8) they give an excellent, racy, if not always wholly reliable, picture of court, military, diplomatic, and literary society of the period.

Académie. For *Académie* in the sense of a literary, scientific, or artistic society see the following ten articles. See also *Literary academies*, and cf. *Institut de France*.

For *Académie* in the sense of an administrative region for educational purposes see *Université de France*.

Académie de Poésie et de Musique, see *Baïf*.

Académie des Beaux-Arts, see *Académie royale de Peinture et Sculpture*.

Académie des Inscriptions et Belles-Lettres, founded by Colbert in 1663 and directed to the encouragement of historical and archaeological learning. Its original purpose was the provision of appropriate mottoes for inscription on royal buildings. Charles Perrault and Chapelain (qq.v.) were among its first members. It is one of the five constituent bodies of the *Institut de France* (q.v.).

Académie des Sciences, founded by Colbert in 1666 (reorganized in 1699), for the study of mathematics, physics, and natural history (see under *Fontenelle*). It is one of the five constituent bodies of the *Institut de France* (q.v.).

Académie des Sciences morales et politiques, directed to the study of philosophy, political economy, law, &c., came into being in 1795 as one of the three classes of the *Institut national* created by the *Convention nationale*. Since 1832, with the title of '*académie*', it has been one of the five constituent bodies of the *Institut de France* (q.v.).

Académie du Palais, created by Henri III for the discussion of questions of philosophy and ethics. It included some of the most learned men in the kingdom, such as Ronsard, Pontus de Tyard, Desportes, Pibrac, Agrippa d'Aubigné. It was a successor of the *Académie de poésie* of Baïf (q.v.), and the short-lived precursor of the *Académie française*.

Académie française, L'. This had its origin in a group of men of letters, among them Conrart, Gombault, Godeau, Chapelain (qq.v.), who used to meet *c.* 1630 in Paris, at Conrart's house, to discuss literary and other questions. Their meetings were, by agree-

ment, secret, but in 1634 Richelieu heard of them and persuaded the group to become an official body, forty in number. The letters patent of the *Académie française*—the name adopted—were approved in 1635 but not registered by the *parlement* until 1637. The members included some of the most distinguished writers of the day, and critics and grammarians such as Chapelain and Vaugelas, but in general they were persons of literary taste rather than of literary eminence. They continued to meet in private houses until 1672 when they were installed in the Louvre. (Pellisson's *Histoire de l'Académie française jusqu'en 1652* (1653), continued, 'jusqu'à l'année 1700', by l'abbé d'Olivet (1729), gives an excellent description of the early phases of its existence.)

(2) The *Académie*'s purpose was to perfect the French language, and to this end they began the compilation of a Dictionary, in which work the authority of Vaugelas (q.v.) had especial weight. Progress was hindered at the outset when Richelieu imposed on the *Académie* the invidious duty of passing judgement on Corneille's *Le Cid*, a task performed with moderation and discretion (see *Corneille*; *Richelieu*). It became still slower after Richelieu and Vaugelas died (1650); and the first edition was not published till 1694. The Dictionary contained only the language of polite society: technical terms were excluded. As an 'element of relative fixity' in the language (P. de Julleville) it undergoes continual revision. (For later editions see *Dictionaries and Encyclopedias*, under date 1694.) A *Grammar*, a *Rhetoric*, and a *Poetic* were also originally contemplated to supplement the Dictionary (cf. *Grammaire de l'Académie française*).

(3) The main tendency of the *Académie* in the early 18th century was to defend consecrated rules and models and to discourage literary innovations. In the latter half of the century the *philosophes* obtained a footing and finally a majority, which included nearly all their leaders, and the *Académie* became a leading organ of opinion. Its career was interrupted by the Revolution, and in 1793 it was suppressed by decree of the *Convention nationale*. It was re-established in substance in 1803, when Napoleon reorganized the *Institut de France* (q.v., founded 1795), making the second *classe*, or Division, one of French Language and Literature, with a membership

of forty, elected by themselves. These forty included some former *académiciens*. They adopted the practices of the original body and soon spoke of themselves as the *Académie française*. After the Restoration the name was officially restored and the *Académie* was promoted first, because the most ancient in original order of creation, of the *classes* of the *Institut* (Royal ordinance of 1816). In 1805 it had moved to its present quarters in the Palais Mazarin, on the Quai de Conti.

(4) In the thirties the *Académie* was hostile to the Romantic Movement, but it yielded eventually to public opinion and admitted, for example, Lamartine (1829), Hugo (1841), and Vigny (1845). At one time or another it has been the target of much wit, both good-natured and bitter, but membership is a distinction to which even the most unorthodox writers aspire as they grow older. The distinction is not confined solely to persons eminent in literature: savants, clerics, soldiers, diplomats have all been members: but women are not eligible. Besides those already mentioned its members have included Corneille, Perrault, Racine, Boileau, Fontenelle, La Bruyère, Voltaire, Chateaubriand, Sainte-Beuve, Renan, Taine, Pasteur, Bergson, Joffre, Valéry. And a list of the great figures of French literature who were not members includes Molière, Diderot, Balzac, Flaubert.

(5) When a seat in the *Académie* falls vacant (almost never for any reason but that of death) the vacancy is declared. Aspirants to the empty *fauteuil* then write separately to each *académicien* notifying their wish to stand for election. It is usual, also, to make a round of formal visits, but it is against the rules for any *académicien* to pledge his support to an intending candidate. Election is secret, by ballot. The public are admitted to the formal reception of new members. On these occasions the new *académicien* wears the famous *habit vert*, a uniform that has persisted with little change since its introduction by Consular decree in 1801 as the dress of members of the *Institut*: its main features are the green palm leaves embroidered on the coat and down the trousers, the *bicorne*, or two-pointed hat (like an admiral's), and the sword. He is sponsored by two *académiciens* and must pronounce a *discours de réception* in the form of a eulogy of the *Académie* and of his predecessor. The formal response,

in its turn, pronounced by the acting *Directeur*, is in effect a biography of the new member and enumerates his publications and achievements. The custom of the formal *discours de réception* originated with Patru (q.v.).

(6) A number of prizes, literary and charitable, are within the adjudication of the *Académie* (see *Prix littéraires*).

Académie Goncourt, a literary society founded by the will of Edmond de Goncourt (q.v., died 1896). It was recognized as a public body, and began to function, in 1903. Membership consists of ten men, or women, of letters whose chief duty is to select annually, for the award of a money prize (the *Prix Goncourt*), the best imaginative prose work in French, and preferably a novel, published during the preceding year. (The first woman member was Judith Gautier, q.v.) The will directed that the members should meet monthly over dinner at a restaurant. After 1912 the dinner became a lunch, and voting now takes place, and the award is announced, after the November reunion. Some of the foundation members, the first President, Alphonse Daudet, among them, died before the *Académie Goncourt* began to function. It is not possible to be a member of both the *Académie française* and the *Académie Goncourt*.

Novels which have won the *Prix Goncourt* include Proust's *A l'ombre des jeunes filles en fleurs* (1919) and Malraux's *La Condition humaine* (1933).

Académie nationale de Musique, the official title of the *Théâtre de l'Opéra*, the home of grand opera in Paris. It began (1671) under the directorship of the poet Pierre Perrin (q.v.) as the *Académie des opéras*. Perrin was soon (1672) ousted by Lulli (q.v.), who obtained the king's *privilège* and in 1673, after the death of Molière, established his *Académie royale de musique* in the hall of the Palais-Royal. It had to move more than once, either because of fire and destruction or (in 1794) by order of the Revolutionary Government. The construction of the present edifice in the Place de l'Opéra was begun under the Second Empire, and the *Académie nationale de musique* (last of some seventeen changes of title) was installed there on 5 January 1875. It is subsidized by the State

Académie royale de Peinture et Sculpture, founded by Mazarin (q.v.) in 1648, brought French art for a time under central direction. Le Brun (q.v.) was its first director. It was one of the five *académies* which were suppressed in 1793 and then absorbed into the *Institut des sciences et des lettres* created in 1795 (cf. *Institut de France*). At the reorganization of the *Institut* in 1816 it recovered its separate identity as *Académie des beaux-arts*. Associated with it is the *École nationale supérieure des beaux-arts*, the official training school for painters, sculptors, engravers, &c. The *Grand Prix de Rome*, the most famous of many prizes at the disposal of the *École des beaux-arts*, goes back to the *École de Rome*, an offshoot of the earlier *Académie*, founded in 1666 for the study of Italian art in Italy.

Acadie, roughly the present-day Canadian province of Nova Scotia, was discovered in 1497 by the Cabots (John Cabot, or Giovanni Caboto, an Italian navigator in the service of Henry VII, and his son Sebastian), who had sailed earlier in the year from Bristol to try and find the North-West passage to India. It was given the name 'Acadie' in 1524 by Giovanni Verazzani, a Florentine navigator in the service of François Ier, who took possession of it (and of Newfoundland, then named 'Terre-Neuve') for France. Some French settlers established themselves there as early as 1598, but the French occupation was continually disputed by the English. Louis XIV abandoned the French claim to the territory (both Acadie and Terre-Neuve) at the Peace of Utrecht (1713), which ended the Wars of the Spanish Succession. Many of the French settlers (the *habitants*) still refused to acknowledge British sovereignty, with the result that they were deported in 1755. (The story comes into Longfellow's *Evangeline*.) The British were finally confirmed in possession of the whole of French Canada by the Treaty of Paris (1763), which ended the Seven Years War.

Accusateur public, L', a counter-Revolutionary journal founded soon after the Terror (1794) by Richer-Sérizy, a journalist of violently Royalist leanings. It was suppressed in 1797 (see *Press, Development of,* para. 7) and its editor was deported.

Achard, MARCEL (1899–), contemporary playwright, author of a successful adaptation of Jonson's *Silent Woman* (*La Femme silen-* *cieuse,* 1926) and of comedies which are a happy mixture of burlesque, pantomime, and unexpected pathos, e.g. *Voulez-vous jouer avec moâ?* (1924); *Marlborough s'en va-t-en guerre* (1924); *La Vie est belle* (1928); *Jean de la lune* (1929); *Le Corsaire* (1938); *Nous irons à Valparaiso* (1948).

Achery, LUC D' (1609–85), a learned Benedictine monk, author with Mabillon (q.v.) of *Acta sanctorum* of the order of St. Benedict; also of *Veterum aliquot scriptorum . . . spicilegium* (1655–77).

Ackermann, LOUISE CHOQUET, MME (1813–90), minor poetess of French birth, wife of Paul Ackermann, a German poet and philologist. The best of her somewhat pessimistically philosophical verse (originally contributed to *Le Parnasse contemporain,* q.v.) is contained in her *Premières poésies* (1874).

Acomat, a leading character in Racine's *Bajazet* (q.v.).

Acte additionnel aux constitutions de l'Empire (1815), an act embodying the new liberal constitution hurriedly drafted for Napoleon by Benjamin Constant (q.v.) during the Hundred Days. It provided for liberty of the Press, ministerial responsibility, and parliamentary government. Napoleon inaugurated it officially on 1 June 1815 at a ceremony on the Champ-de-Mars. With the return of Louis XVIII after Waterloo and Napoleon's second abdication, the Charter of 1814 (see *Charte*) again became operative.

Acte gratuit, a gratuitous or inconsequent action performed on impulse, possibly to gratify a desire for sensation. The term occurs in the writings of André Gide (q.v.), part of whose doctrine of individualist morality is that in order to learn how to keep our desires in check we should first yield to them without inhibition. A typical Gidian *acte gratuit* occurs in his tale *Les Caves du Vatican*. The chief character, Lafcadio, takes a dislike to his one companion on a railway journey, his starched collar, his continual fidgeting with the electric light. On a sudden impulse he decides to throw him out of the train if, before he can count twelve, he sees a light through the window. As he reaches the number ten he does spot one and thereupon with a couple of violent shoves sends

wrote regularly on history, politics, and philosophy for reviews. Liszt was her lover between 1830 and 1840, and the father of her daughter Cosima, who married Wagner. She left interesting *Souvenirs* (1877) of the Faubourg Saint-Germain society and of literary and musical circles and salons under the Bourbon and the Orleans monarchies.

Agrégation, agrégé. The *concours d'agrégation* is a yearly competitive examination—open to candidates who have already secured their ordinary university degree (*licence*)—for appointment to a strictly limited number of teaching posts (history, mathematics, philosophy, &c.) in lycées (q.v.). The *professeurs agrégés* so recruited are more highly paid than their fellow *professeurs licenciés*. The title '*agrégé*' has come with time to signify the possession of a very valuable degree. (See also *École normale supérieure*.)

Aguesseau, HENRI-FRANÇOIS D', see *Daguesseau*.

Aicard, JEAN (1848–1921), novelist and poet, is remembered for his descriptions of Provençal life and childhood, e.g. in *Le Roi de Camargue* (1890), *Maurin des Maures* (1907), *L'Illustre Maurin* (1908), *Les Poèmes de Provence* (1874), *La Chanson de l'enfant* (1875), *Le Livre des petits* (1886).

Aigle de Meaux, L', see *Bossuet*.

Aiglon, L' (1900), a poetic drama by Edmond Rostand (q.v.).

The hero is Napoleon's son, who was known as the duc de Reichstadt after the fall of the Empire and kept in semi-captivity at the castle of Schönbrunn, near Vienna. Rostand represents him as tortured by dreams of glory which he has no means of realizing. This was one of Bernhardt's (q.v.) most famous parts.

Aignelet, a character in *Pathelin* (q.v.).

Aimeri de Narbonne, one of the finest examples, belonging to the cycle of *Garin de Monglane* (q.v.), of the *chanson de geste* (q.v.). It was written in the early 13th century probably by Bertrand de Bar-sur-Aube (q.v.), in nearly 5,000 rhyming decasyllabic lines. In it are recounted the taking of Narbonne by Aimeri, son of Ernaut de Beaulande and grandson of Garin de Monglane, on the order of Charlemagne after the battle of Roncevaux; the courting of Ermenjart, sister of the king of Lombardy; further battles with the Saracens; and the marriage festivities. The poem shows a variety, nobility, and charm of style which have earned it a high place among medieval epics. Victor Hugo was inspired by it to write his *Aymerillot* in the *Légende des siècles*.

Aimerides, see *Garin de Monglane*.

Aiol, a *chanson de geste* (q.v.) of the 12th–13th century in two parts, the first in decasyllables, the second in alexandrines, recounting how the hero obtains the reinstatement of his father, who has been banished through the intrigues of the traitor Macaire from the court of King Louis, the son of Charlemagne.

Aïssé, MADEMOISELLE (c. 1694–1733), a Circassian slave bought as a child by M. de Ferriol (d. 1722), French ambassador at Constantinople. She was brought to France and educated there, and entered Parisian society, where her beauty and charm won the admiration, among others, of the Regent. Her *Lettres*, which are marked by simplicity and sincerity, throw light on some of the social personages of the day, such as Mme du Deffand. It was Mlle Aïssé who wrote: 'Il n'y a point de héros pour son valet de chambre.'

Akakia, see *Diatribe*.

Alacoque, MARIE (1647–90), a mystical nun of the order of the Visitation who founded the worship of the Sacred Heart of Jesus. She was canonized in 1920.

Alain, pen-name of Émile-Auguste Chartier (q.v.), 1868–1951.

Alain-Fournier, see *Fournier, Henri-Alban*.

'A la lanterne!' Before the 19th century Paris streets were lit by lamps hung from brackets fixed to the stone walls of houses. The 'lanterne de la Grève', a bracket above a grocer's shop in the Place de la Grève (q.v.) by the Hôtel de Ville, served for several summary executions after the fall of the Bastille (14 July 1789), hence the cry 'A la lanterne!'

A la recherche du temps perdu (1913–27), by Marcel Proust (q.v.), a novel in seven separately entitled but interrelated sections (see § iv below).

i. GENERAL

(1) The novel is reminiscent in character, told in the first person by the chief personage 'Marcel' (who bears considerable resemblance to Proust himself though the work is not an autobiography). It evolves on several planes at once, and a point important for appreciation is Marcel's dual approach to his task as Narrator. He is Marcel the central character, whose life we follow from childhood and see interpenetrated by the lives of the other characters. In this role he accepts experiences and contacts as they arrive, successively, with no inkling of their future significance. But he is at the same time Marcel the middle-aged Narrator, viewing and fully comprehending the same sensations, and the significance they were to have for himself and others, in retrospect ('sentant au fond de moi des terres reconquises sur l'oubli') and so, *recovering* time. When, and only when, we reach the concluding volume (*Le Temps retrouvé*, pt. ii) the reason for this dual standpoint in time becomes clear. Then, too, the long, complex novel takes shape as the concrete framework for an innermost plot—Marcel's awakening to his vocation as a creative writer.

(2) As a whole the work is undeniably difficult—though richly repaying—to read, partly because of Proust's brilliantly metaphorical thinking, partly because of his long, cumulative, many-faceted sentences. In the earlier volumes the style is also highly poetical and evocative. The concluding volumes, which Proust was rewriting up to the time of his death, have many repetitions and obscurities.

ii. THE INNER PLOT

(3) As child, adolescent, and grown man, Marcel observes the world of which he is the centre. He experiences—vicariously or in himself—anticipation, disillusionment, ecstasy, and passion. He is at times vaguely, at certain nearly transcendental moments urgently, aware of a reality, an essence, which is waiting to be captured. The transcendental moments have usually occurred when a trivial sensation or act (the taste of a sweet cake, a 'madeleine', sopped in tea,

the act of stooping to unfasten his shoe) has served as a stimulus to his 'involuntary' memory and illumined whole stretches of the past, registered hitherto only by his unconscious perceptions. More or less constantly, too, throughout life, and usually at moments of heightened aesthetic perception (for instance, when listening to music), he has played with the idea of writing. Sometimes this is little but a dilettante ambition. Sometimes it is an urge to clarify his own sensations, a warning whose import he does not fully seize that writing, for him, is the way to reality. He rebels unconsciously against the difficulties of creation: and a day comes in middle age when he decides finally that he will never write.

(4) Just at this time (we are in *Le Temps retrouvé*, pt. ii) he returns to Paris after an absence of several years which, except for a brief visit in 1914 and a rather longer stay in 1916, has covered the 1914–18 war, and makes his way to an afternoon reception. As he waits in an ante-room for some music to finish before he is announced, three trivial incidents are the stimuli in rapid succession for three supreme flashes of involuntary memory. He experiences, all over again, the sensations of moments of the past when he had been exceptionally aware of an intangible reality. And suddenly, as he reflects on this identity of past and present sensations, he penetrates to the essence. Reality, he sees, is the spiritual significance of all that we experience in our lives. Events, emotions, our reactions to all of these, are successive, as are our relations with and judgements of the people in our lives. But reality, this essence which can be disengaged from events, emotions, and contacts, transcends time and is universal, common to past and present alike. We seize it when flashes of involuntary memory (which links past and present by sensation and imagery rather than by conscious recollection) sharpen our perceptions by nullifying our sense of time as a dimension within which life's phases succeed each other.

(5) From this Marcel goes on to realize that this *essence* awaits the expression that the writer, and the writer alone, can give it 'par le lien indescriptible d'une alliance de mots'. Writing, he sees, so far from being an ambition that he will renounce, is the vocation for which his whole life has been a preparation.

His urgent task now—for he is ill and may soon die—is to seek, in the depths of his own consciousness, the 'vraie vérité' of his life and convert it by writing into its spiritual equivalent.

(6) At this point he lets himself be announced. In the main room he finds a company known to him since, or through contacts of, childhood. All are witnesses, physically and in their social aspect, to time's disintegrating and transforming action. Here, he sees, in this visible link between past and present, is the concrete framework for the book he is to write; for such a book cannot be constructed solely out of essences. He will resurrect his life and the lives of those people whose story has at various points been interwoven with his own. His book will not be written for its narrative value: the study of these persons' relations to himself and to one another, and to the events and passions of their lives, will be his means of reaching, and so of conveying, an understanding of the true significance of life itself and of the emotions—love, suffering, jealousy, and forgetting—of which life is made up. To succeed he must make use of a psychology which, like the memory on which he will rely to resurrect the past, can at any moment flash the past into the present without modification, as if it were the present.

(7) At what point in his life shall his book begin? A few moments ago, while waiting in the anteroom for the music to finish, he had noticed George Sand's *François le champi* (q.v.) on the bookshelves. It recalled an evening in childhood significant for the development of his own personality. His mother had come very late, when he had almost given up hope, to kiss him goodnight and had stayed and read him to sleep with *François le champi*. That evening, he determines, shall be the starting-point for his recovery of time, and of reality. The whole of *A la recherche du temps perdu*, which does, in fact, after an introductory chapter, begin with this particular evening of Marcel's childhood (*Du Côté de chez Swann*, pt. i. *Combray*), has led up to this moment; and with the choice the novel ends.

iii. The Framework

(8) The child Marcel comes from Paris regularly with his parents to spend holidays with relations at Combray (q.v.), a country town. He is a day-dreamer, sensitive and delicate (cf. Proust himself), and he is cherished by an adored and adoring mother and grandmother. We follow his developing interests, and as time passes and his social circle widens, we study, as he studies it, Parisian society of the late 19th and early 20th century. He belongs by birth to the wealthy, cultivated bourgeoisie, but he also makes friends, and is welcomed, in the seemingly impenetrable circles dominated by the Guermantes aristocracy. Twice he spends the summer at Balbec (q.v.), a seaside resort, once during adolescence with his grandmother, and again in early manhood after her death. In boyhood he loves Gilberte (q.v.) Swann. Later he fancies himself in love with the duchesse de Guermantes (q.v.). His unhappy love for Albertine (q.v.), whom he first meets at Balbec, lasts several years and turns to disillusion and oblivion. We end with him in middle age, at the afternoon reception described in *Le Temps retrouvé*, pt. ii (and see para. 4 above). This point is reached by way of many digressions, as when he pauses to emphasize the link between a past momentarily recaptured and the present from which he writes; or when he pursues subsidiary themes which are both integral to the structure of the novel and of interest in themselves, e.g. 'involuntary' memory, love (and particularly love in the form of inversion), jealousy, painting, literature, music, architecture, society and the social hierarchy. As the characters (well over 200) evolve we find that sometimes, as in life itself, the smallest incident has served to deflect the course of their lives or to make their paths converge.

(9) No brief summary of this long work can follow its ramifications, but the chief characters, other than those mentioned above, and their place in the framework, are described under separate headings (see *Bergotte*; *Bloch*; *Charlus*; *Elstir*; *Françoise*; *Norpois*; *Odette*; *Saint-Loup*; *Swann*; *Verdurin*; *Villeparisis*; *Vinteuil*).

iv. Publication

(10) After Proust had finished his novel in its first form, in 1912, he contemplated publication in one volume with the title *A la recherche du temps perdu*. It was too long for this, and three volumes were then envisaged. The first, *Du Côté de chez Swann*,

was published (by Grasset, at Proust's expense) in 1913. The remaining two were announced, with the titles *Le Côté de Guermantes* and *Le Temps retrouvé*. The war of 1914–18—which Proust felt intensely but which provided a wealth of fresh material for his theme of Time's disintegrating action upon society—interrupted publication, but this was resumed in 1917, by the publishing house of the *Nouvelle Revue Française* (q.v.). By then Proust had revised and enlarged his manuscript to such an extent (a practice which he followed until his death in 1922) that further subdivision was continually necessary.

(ii) The work as published by the NRF now became: *Du Côté de chez Swann* (1917, I vol., reissued 1919, 2 vols.); *A l'ombre des jeunes filles en fleurs* (1918, I vol., later 2 and then 3 vols.); *Le Côté de Guermantes*, pt. i (1920, I vol.); *Le Coté de Guermantes*, pt. ii with *Sodome et Gomorrhe*, pt. i [28 pages at the end] (1921, I vol.); *Sodome et Gomorrhe*, pt. ii (1922, 3 vols.) [the last section published during Proust's life-time]; *La Prisonnière* [*Sodome et Gomorrhe*, pt. iii] (1923, 2 vols.); *Albertine disparue* (1925, 2 vols.); *Le Temps retrouvé*, pts. i and ii (1927, 2 vols.). An English translation, *Remembrance of Things Past*, which captures the style and spirit of the original with remarkable sensitiveness, was published between 1922 and 1931. The translators were C. K. Scott-Moncrieff and (the last section only) Stephen Hudson. The section-titles, in translation, were: 'Swann's way'; 'Within a budding grove'; 'The Guermantes way'; 'Cities of the plain'; 'The captive'; 'The sweet cheat gone'; 'Time regained'.

Albatros, L', a well-known poem by Baudelaire (q.v.), in bk. i ('Spleen et Idéal') of *Les Fleurs du mal*.

Albertine disparue (1925, posth., 2 vols.), the sixth section of Proust's novel *A la recherche du temps perdu* (q.v.). Proust's original choice of title appears to have been *La Fugitive*, as a contrast to *La Prisonnière*. This had to be abandoned but was revived in the Pléiade edition (1954) of *A la recherche* .... In explaining the circumstances the editors say that it is doubtful whether Proust ever accepted the title *Albertine disparue*.

Albertine Simonet is one of the young girls whom Marcel (the Narrator of the novel) meets on his first holiday at Balbec. On a second stay, some years later, he is about to terminate an affair with her when a slight incident seems to confirm his suspicions of her Lesbianism and rekindles his love. He takes her to live with him at his flat in Paris and keeps her virtually a prisoner. He is alternately anxious and reluctant to marry her, for his love feeds on jealousy and withers when suspicion is stilled. Albertine runs away and is killed when out riding. Marcel's love fades gradually and painfully into oblivion.

Earlier 'Albertine' sections of the novel are: *A l'ombre des jeunes filles en fleurs*; *Sodome et Gomorrhe*, ii; *La Prisonnière*.

Albert Savarus, one of the 'Scènes de la vie privée' of Balzac's *Comédie humaine*.

Albertus ou l'Âme et le Péché (1832), a fantastic, but not too serious, poem by Théophile Gautier about a young poet of Leyden who offers his soul to the devil for love. The clock strikes midnight, and the flesh shrivels from the bones of the radiant creature in the poet's arms, leaving a loathsome sorceress. She whisks him off to a witches' Sabbath presided over by the devil. The devil sneezes. The poet says 'God bless you'. The shrieking company dissolves. Next morning a hideously mutilated corpse is found in the outskirts of Rome. The descriptions, and the sorceress's cat (who can turn himself into Don Juan at will) make lively reading.

Albigeois (Albigenses), sectarians living in Languedoc, taking their name from the town of Albi (though Toulouse was rather the centre of the movement). They became conspicuous in the 12th century for their piety and virtue in the midst of a dissolute society, and had the support of the nobles and even the bishops of the region. They censured the corruptions of the papacy and were accused of holding Manichean doctrines. Pope Innocent III launched a crusade against them, which was conducted with great cruelty by Simon de Montfort (1209–13) and resulted in the fall of Count Raymond of Toulouse, their leader, who was supported by Peter II of Aragon. Thus began the subjection of the 'princes of the Midi' to the central government in Paris, bringing to an end the literature which they had fostered (see *Troubadours*). There is an interesting passage on the Albigenses in Bridges, *The Testament of Beauty*, iii. 680 ff.

Album de vers anciens, 1890–1900, see *Valéry, Paul.*

Alcaforado (Alcaforada), MARIANNA, see *Lettres portugaises.*

Alceste, the hero of Molière's *Le Misanthrope* (q.v.).

Alceste, an opera. Quinault's *Alceste* (1674) was set to music by Lulli (qq.v.). The French libretto for the adapted form of Gluck's (q.v.) *Alceste* (originally in Italian) performed in Paris in 1776 was by Durollet [Duroullet], q.v.

Alcionée, a tragedy by Du Ryer, probably produced about 1637, published in 1640.

The scene is Sardis. Alcionée loves Lydie, the king's daughter, but his humble birth precludes their marriage. He has therefore taken up arms against the king, reduced him to terms, and obtained from him the promise of her hand. But now Lydie, divided between love of Alcionée and pride of rank, decides to reject her lover. Alcionée, in despair at her refusal, at first decides to go into exile; but, finding it impossible to live separated from his lady, seeks a solution in suicide and is carried dying to the feet of the now repentant Lydie.

Alcuin (*c.* 730–*c.* 804), a Northumbrian theologian, and director of the school at York, was on a mission to Rome when he met Charlemagne at Parma and consented to go to France (782) to preside over the academy of the palace (a sort of learned society attached to Charlemagne's court, *see École palatine*). Through his influence, with the encouragement of Charlemagne, schools were founded and a system of education was introduced. He enriched his abbey at Tours, to which he went in 796, with a library, a scriptorium (for copying manuscripts), and a school. He wrote many educational and theological works in Latin, and the rise of intellectual culture after the dark Merovingian period was largely his work.

Aldomen, see *Senancour.*

Alecis, GUILLAUME, see *Alexis, Guillaume.*

Alembert, JEAN LE ROND D' (1717–83), natural son of Mme de Tencin (q.v.), exposed as an infant by her on the steps of the church of Saint-Jean-le-Rond, whence his Christian name. He was a *philosophe* and also a distinguished mathematician, who advanced the sciences of dynamics and astronomy (his *Traité de dynamique* was written when he was twenty-six). In philosophy he was a sceptic or agnostic and an ardent opponent of religion and the priesthood. He collaborated in the preparation of the *Encyclopédie* as Diderot's principal assistant until 1758, when he abandoned his part in the direction of the enterprise, discouraged by the vexations it entailed. Apart from the remarkable *Discours préliminaire* to the *Encyclopédie* (q.v.) and the article in that work on *Genève* (1757), which created a storm by its praise of the doctrines and practice of the Genevan pastors, he published little of importance, except scientific works (*Mélanges de littérature, d'histoire, et de philosophie*, 1753; second edition 1758). But he exercised influence as a member of the *Académie française* (from 1754), as a frequenter of literary *salons*, and through his European reputation. As perpetual secretary of the *Académie* (from 1772) he wrote a series of *éloges* on the academicians who had died between 1700 and 1772. He was a close friend of Mlle de Lespinasse (q.v.). He refused the invitations of the Empress Catharine and of Frederick II to settle in their respective countries, but spent three months at the court of the latter in 1763. Hume left him a legacy of £200. (For *Le Rêve de d'Alembert* see *Diderot*, para. 2.)

Alexandre de Bernay, surnamed **de Paris**, see *Alexandre le Grand* (1) and *Alexandrin*.

Alexandre le Grand

(1) A cycle of poems based on an Alexandrian Greek original of the 2nd century, translated into Latin in the 4th century. A later popular epitome of this translation was used for a version (in the dialect of the Dauphiné) by Albéric de Besançon, or Pisançon (near Valence), or Briançon, early in the 12th century. Only fragments remain. It was the first vernacular poem (recalling the *chansons de geste* but in eight-syllabled lines) on a classical rather than a national subject. Another version, in ten-syllabled lines and also, it would seem, belonging to the first half of the 12th century, may have appeared in Poitou.

Other poets, among them Alexandre de Bernay (q.v.), rehandled the material at the end of the century, using a line of twelve syllables which was later known, because of this, as the *alexandrin* (q.v.). This composite work is known as the *Roman d'Alexandre*. Oriental influence is marked in the descriptions of sumptuous palaces, strange scenery, rich clothing, and precious stones, and in the adventures which befall the hero. Liberality, much esteemed during this epoch, is the hero's most distinguishing characteristic.

The story was amplified about the same time by two poets, who produced the *Vengeance d'Alexandre*; and the same subject is treated in the 13th-century English metrical romance of *King Alisaunder*.

(2) A tragedy by Racine, produced in 1665, his second play.

Alexander the Great has reached the banks of the Hydaspes in his endeavour to conquer India. He is confronted by two Indian kings, Porus and Taxile, and a queen, Axiane, whom both the kings love, and who excites them against Alexander. But while the brave Porus is eager for battle, Taxile, encouraged by his sister Cléophile, who is loved by Alexander, betrays his ally Porus and comes to terms with the invader. Porus is defeated, and the victorious Alexander proposes to reward Taxile with the hand of Axiane; but she repulses the traitor with indignation. Taxile in despair rushes to the battlefield, where Porus is still holding out with a few soldiers, and confronts his rival. Porus kills Taxile and, satisfied with his revenge, surrenders to Alexander. The latter, struck by the proud courage of Porus, restores his kingdom to him and gives him Axiane.

Alexandrin, in French prosody, a line of twelve syllables. It is found for the first time in the *Pèlerinage de Charlemagne* (late 11th or early 12th century) and was used deliberately as the line appropriate to epic poetry in the *Roman d'Alexandre* (q.v., late 12th century), whence its name. During the 13th century it ousted the ten-syllabled line as the accepted metre of the *chansons de geste* (q.v.). In the 15th century it fell into disuse but was revived towards the middle of the 16th century by Ronsard and the poets of the *Pléiade* (q.v.), who used it also in lyric poetry. It became the standard metre of tragedy and, from the 17th century, of

comedy, as well as the metre in which more than half of French poetry since that time has been written. It was subjected to very strict rules by the 17th-century arbiters of French poetry, notably Boileau (q.v.), but these were considerably eased during the 19th century, first by Victor Hugo and other poets of the Romantic Movement, and later by the Symbolists. (See also *Alternance des rimes*; *Enjambement*; *Tragiques, Les*.)

Alexis, or **Alecis,** GUILLAUME (*c.* 1425–86), a monk of the Abbaye de Lire in Normandy, author, among other edifying works, of two poems which had a great vogue, *Les Faintises du monde*, a lively work of proverbial philosophy, and *Le Blason de faulses amours*, on the dangers of illicit passion; the latter was imitated by La Fontaine in his *Janot et Catin* (*Œuvres diverses*).

Alexis, PAUL (1847–1901), novelist and dramatist, one of the *naturalistes* (see *Naturalisme*), and a friend of Zola (q.v.), contributed the short story *Après la bataille* to *Les Soirées de Médan* (q.v.) and published collections of tales, including *La Fin de Lucie Pellegrin* (1880) and *Le Besoin d'aimer* (1885). With Oscar Méténier (1859–1913) he collaborated in writing for the stage, notably dramatizations of *Les Frères Zemganno* (1890, by E. de Goncourt) and *Charles Demailly* (1893, by E. and J. de Goncourt, qq.v.).

Alexis, Vie de Saint, by an unknown author, one of the most remarkable of early French literary texts, composed about 1040, in 125 stanzas of five assonanced decasyllabic lines. Amplified versions of the poem were produced in the 12th, 13th, and 14th centuries.

Alexis is the son of a noble Roman; on the night of his marriage he renounces the world, leaves his bride, and devotes himself to a life of religion in complete poverty, first for seventeen years at Edessa, in Syria, until his saintliness is revealed by an image of the Virgin. Then he returns, without making himself known, to his father's house, where he is given shelter and for another seventeen years continues his miserable but saintly existence. Feeling the approach of death he inscribes on a piece of parchment the story of his life, and his identity is recognized after his death. The characters of the saint, his wife, and his parents are depicted with great literary skill.

Aliboron, Maître, a name of unknown derivation given in the Middle Ages to a person of versatility and consequence. Later the expression came to signify a foolish person, and was even used of a donkey (La Fontaine, *Fables,* i. 13). A poem of the end of the 15th century, having somewhat the character of a dramatic monologue and entitled *Les Dits de Maistre Aliborum qui de tout se mesle,* gives a description of this personage.

Aliscans, a *chanson de geste* (q.v.) of the late 12th or early 13th century. It is a rehandling of the *Chanson de Guillaume* (q.v.).

Alissa, the chief character in Gide's *La Porte étroite* (q.v.).

Allain, MARCEL, see *Fantomas.*

Allainval, LÉONOR-J.-C. SOULAS D' (1700–53), dramatist, author of *L'Embarras des richesses* (1725) and *L'École des bourgeois* (q.v., 1728), notable comedies of manners, of the period between Lesage and Beaumarchais.

Allais, ALPHONSE (1885–1905), a humorist of the nineties, author of light verse, often in monologue form (cf. *Charles Cros,* like whom, too, he was an early experimenter in colour photography); of tales and sketches, e.g. *Le Parapluie de l'Escouade* (1894), *On n'est pas des bœufs* (1896); and of *L'Affaire Blaireau* (1899), a novel. He was associated with the early days of the Chat-Noir (q.v.) cabaret.

Allart, HORTENSE [Mme Hortense Allart de Meritens] (1801–79), born in Milan of French parents, is remembered as a figure in the literary life of mid-19th-century Paris, mistress of, among others, Chateaubriand, and of Sainte-Beuve, with whom she carried on an interesting correspondence. In 1873, under the pseudonym 'Mme de Saman', she published an autobiographical novel *Les Enchantements de Prudence.*

Alliance, La Sainte (the Holy Alliance), an alliance formed in 1815, after the fall of Napoleon, between Russia, Austria, and Prussia. The rulers of these countries bound themselves to let their conduct of their own, and their relations with other, peoples be animated solely by a spirit of mutual helpfulness and Christian fraternity, according to the precepts of Holy Scripture. The Czar Alexander I, at that time traversing a phase of mysticism, is said to have been responsible for the semi-religious character of the alliance, to which Great Britain refused to be a party. Some European sovereigns, including Louis XVIII, adhered to it *par politesse.* Castlereagh termed it 'a piece of sublime mysticism and nonsense', Metternich 'un monument vide et sonore'. It had dissolved by 1825. (Cf. *Krüdener, Mme de.*)

Alliance française, L', a body 'pour la propagation de la langue française dans les colonies et à l'étranger', founded in 1883 and recognized as being of public utility. In the French colonies and in foreign countries it maintains or helps to support schools, libraries, or other organizations for the study of French. At the Headquarters branch in Paris it runs special French courses for foreigners. Its funds are drawn from a practically world-wide membership.

Allobroges, early inhabitants of SE. Gaul (the parts known later as Dauphiné and Savoie).

Almaviva, COMTE, a character in Beaumarchais's *Le Barbier de Séville, Le Mariage de Figaro* (qq.v.), and *La Mère coupable.*

A l'ombre des jeunes filles en fleurs (1919), the second section of Proust's novel *A la recherche du temps perdu* (q.v.).

Alternance des rimes, in French prosody, principles (dating for the most part from the 16th century) which govern the alternation of masculine and feminine rhymes (q.v.). They were fairly generally accepted till the second half of the 19th century, when the Symbolists (see *Symbolisme*) began to ignore them. In modern times they have been much less closely observed. One of the most firmly held was that in Alexandrine verse (see *Alexandrin*) a couplet ending with a masculine rhyme should be followed by a couplet ending with a feminine rhyme, or vice versa. This alternation of masculine and feminine couplets was called *rimes plates* or *rimes suivies.* (See also *Rimes croisées, Rime embrassées, Rimes mêlées.*)

Alzire ou les Américains, a tragedy by Voltaire, produced in 1736.

The scene is the city of Lima. Alvarez, a humane Spanish governor of Peru, has just transferred his office to his son Gusman, a fierce and cruel conqueror of the Indians. Gusman marries Alzire, daughter of Montèze, a conquered chief, her reluctant consent having been obtained by her father; for although she and her father have become Christians, she has remained faithful to the memory of Zamore, an Indian chief, long presumed dead, to whom her hand was promised. Now Zamore, who has survived cruel tortures inflicted on him by Gusman, appears in Lima and reveals himself to Alvarez as the Indian who had once saved his life. He then gains access to Alzire and is thunderstruck to learn that she has become the bride of the tyrant. At this juncture Gusman enters and discovers that the enemy whom his wife loved is still alive. Maddened with jealousy he orders Zamore to execution, but Zamore escapes, and disguised as a Spanish soldier penetrates to the council chamber where he mortally stabs Gusman. The council decide on the death of Zamore and Alzire, unless Zamore accepts conversion to the Christian faith. Zamore and Alzire proudly refuse the concession. Gusman, however, his eyes opened to his own barbarity by the approach of death, pardons his assassin and delivers Alzire to her lover. Zamore is converted to a religion which has inspired so striking an example of repentance and generosity.

Amadas et Idoine, a *roman d'aventure* of the first half of the 13th century, the story of the trials and success of a squire of low degree; it shows considerable power and originality.

Amadis de Gaule, the title of certain Spanish romances of the 15th century, perhaps translated from a Portuguese original of the 14th century, relating the feats and marvellous adventures of Amadis, an imaginary knight, the flower of chivalry, son of Perion, king of Gaul (= ? Wales), and of his descendants. Eight books of a French prose version of these romances were published by Herberay des Essarts (q.v.) in 1540–8 and the translation was continued by others (of the 22nd–24th books as late as 1615). The element of gallantry and the scenes of sensual or exalted love were developed in the French version and the work was regarded by judges so different as Brantôme and La Noue as pernicious to

youth. Nevertheless it was very popular and prepared the way for the heroic romances of Mlle de Scudéry, Gomberville, &c. Quinault's (q.v.) *Amadis de Gaule*, with music by Lulli (q.v.), was performed in 1684.

Amant rendu cordelier à l'observance d'amours, L', a poem of 1872 lines composed about 1440, often attributed, probably wrongly, to Martial d'Auvergne, treating in the form of a vision of the code of gallantry.

Amants, Les (1895), a play by Maurice Donnay (q.v.).

Amants de Venise, Les (1902), by Charles Maurras (q.v.), a study of some months in the lives of George Sand and Alfred de Musset (qq.v.).

Amants magnifiques, Les, a *comédie-ballet* in prose by Molière, produced in 1670.

The very slight plot serves largely as a pretext for the music, songs, and dances of the interludes. Two princes are suitors for the hand of a princess, but she prefers to them a humble warrior. Some similarity was seen between this theme and the case of Mademoiselle, grand-daughter of Henri IV, who loved Lauzun. The play contains some satire of astrologers. The subject was chosen by the king.

Amaury, the narrator and chief character of Sainte-Beuve's novel *Volupté* (q.v.).

Amboise, Conjuration d', a conspiracy formed in 1560 by the Sieur de la Renaudie and his Huguenot supporters to wrest the power from the government of the Guises (under the young king François II) by a *coup de main* at Amboise. The conspiracy failed and a cruel repression followed. The bodies of La Renaudie and the chief conspirators were hung from the balconies of Amboise. The young Agrippa d'Aubigné passing under them with his father was required by him to swear to avenge them.

Ambroise d'Évreux, a Norman *jongleur* of the end of the 12th century, who wrote a metrical *Estoire de la guerre sainte* (12,000 octosyllabic lines) or history of the third Crusade, in which he had taken part. The poem celebrates the sufferings of humbler pilgrims, as well as the gallant deeds of

Richard Cœur de Lion (his king) and other knights, and is a sincere piece of historical writing.

Âmes du purgatoire, Les, a short story by Prosper Mérimée (q.v.), first published in 1836; the exploits of Don Juan de Marana.

Ami des hommes, L'. The elder Mirabeau (q.v.), was so called after the title of one of his books.

Ami du peuple, L' (originally Le Publiciste parisien), a violently sensationalist daily, founded by Marat (q.v.) in September 1789 and widely read by the people. It was frequently suppressed and from March 1793, after many changes of name, became Le Publiciste de la République française. The last number appeared on 14 July 1793, the day after Marat was assassinated. The title Ami du peuple was so popular that it was revived for papers founded subsequently in the Revolutionary era and again in 1871 during the Commune (q.v.).

Ami du Roi, des Français, de l'ordre et surtout de la vérité, L'. Two journals of this name, both Royalist and to some extent continuations and transformations of Élie Fréron's (q.v.) Année littéraire, existed between 1790 and 1792. One (June 1790–Aug. 1792) was conducted by Montjoye (1730–1816). The other (Sept. 1790–May 1792) was conducted by the abbé Thomas Royou (1741–92), Fréron's brother-in-law, who was almost as violent and vindictive a Royalist as Marat (q.v.) was a Revolutionary. It became the official organ of the émigrés and the clergy and was denounced by the Assemblée législative in May 1792.

Amiel, DENYS (1884–), playwright. His tragicomedies of everyday life, written alone or in collaboration with André Obey (q.v.), include: La Souriante Madame Beudet (1921), Le Voyageur (1923), Le Couple (1923), M. et Mme Un Tel (1926), L'Engrenage (1927).

Amiel, HENRI-FRÉDÉRIC (1821–81), diarist and critic, of French Protestant ancestry, spent most of his life as a professor (Aesthetics, then Philosophy) at the university of Geneva, his birthplace. He became known to a wider circle after his death, when fragments of a diary kept by him from 1847 onwards were published (Fragments d'un journal intime, 1883–7, re-edited and augmented 1923

and 1927; Philine, further fragments, 1927). In this remarkable piece of introspective literature the note was struck at the beginning: 'Je ne suis pas libre, car je n'ai pas la force d'exécuter ma volonté'; and after thirty years of observing and analysing himself, his creative impotence, and his inability to adopt a determined attitude towards existence he was still saying 'Agir est mon supplice', and 'Je regarde couler ma vie, comme un blessé regarde couler le sang de ses veines'. Other passages show his delicate perceptions and rare intellectual and critical ability. His Essais critiques were edited in 1932 and Lettres à sa famille, ses amis, ses amies, 1837–49 in 1935. The first English translation of his Journal, by Mrs. Humphry Ward, was published in 1885.

Amiens, La Paix d' (27 March 1802). The Peace of Amiens, between France and Great Britain, ended the Second Coalition (q.v., and see Lunéville). Many thousands of English tourists profited by the welcome general peace in Europe, the first since 1792, and lasting only till 1803, to visit Paris. It was by this treaty that the royal title of France, borne by English kings since Edward III, was dropped.

Ami Fritz, L' (1864), by the collaborators Erckmann–Chatrian (q.v.), a genial, sentimental tale of Alsace and of a confirmed bachelor who falls in love in the end. It was successfully dramatized in 1877.

Amis de la constitution, Société des, see Jacobins.

Amis des droits de l'homme et du citoyen, Société des, see Cordeliers.

Amis et Amile, a 12th-century metrical romance in the form of a chanson de geste (q.v.), which was brought into connexion with the Charlemagne cycle, though its source is oriental. There is an English version, Amis and Amiloun, of the 13th century.

It is the story of the incomparable devotion of two friends, one of whom, Amile, surreptitiously takes the place of the other in a trial by combat, and for this piece of unselfish deception is punished with leprosy. To cure Amile of the leprosy Amis, at the bidding of Heaven, sacrifices his own two children; but later, going to see their dead bodies, finds them sleeping.

This story is also the theme of one of the *Miracles de Notre Dame par personnages* (see *Miracles*).

Amour, see *De l'amour*.

Amour courtois, a medieval conception of love which was elaborated in the courts of Southern France and is first traced in the lyric poetry of the troubadours. From the south it penetrated to the nobility of the centre (to the court of Champagne in particular) and is seen fully developed in the poems of Chrétien de Troyes (q.v.), in its extreme form in his *Lancelot*. As expressed by the more refined and subtle among the *troubadours* and *trouvères*, it is a disciplined and reasonable passion, directed to a worthy object, a beautiful and virtuous woman; such a love is a service which ennobles, for the lover must win his lady by his prowess, courtesy, and patience. It is therefore an ordeal which the lover welcomes. The consequent exaltation of woman is in strong contrast to the brutal indignities that she is frequently represented as suffering in the *chansons de geste* (q.v.). This courtly love was governed by a code of conduct, which was fully set forth in a Latin work of the early 13th century, *De arte honeste amandi*, by Andreas Capellanus [André le Chapelain], translated in the same century into both prose and verse by Drouart de la Vache. But the chief work inspired by the notion of *amour courtois* was the earlier portion of the *Roman de la rose* (q.v.).

Amour de Dieu, Traité de l' (1616), by St. François de Sales, a devotional work; see *François de Sales, Saint*.

Amoureuse, L' (1891), a drama by Georges de Porto-Riche (q.v.).

In a fit of nervous exasperation Étienne Fériaud, a scientist, advises his wife to take a lover and leave him in peace. She does so, her choice falling on her husband's friend Pascal Delannoy. The play is a study of three unhappy people—Étienne, who suspects what has happened; Pascal, who is ashamed; and Germaine, who still loves her husband.

Amour médecin, L', a *comédie-ballet* in prose by Molière, produced in 1665 at Versailles, a light impromptu written, rehearsed, and acted within five days of its order by the king.

Sganarelle, a selfish bourgeois, devoted to his daughter Lucinde, will do anything for her except let her be married and so lose her and her dowry. Being thus crossed in her love for Clitandre, Lucinde falls into a melancholy. Her maid devises a stratagem. Lucinde feigns illness. Four doctors are called in, disagree, and do nothing. Then Clitandre, dressed up as a physician, is introduced by the maid. His method is to cure through the mind. Lucinde longs for marriage, and her mind must be cured by an imaginary marriage which he will perform. Sganarelle, duly impressed, lends himself to the cheat, only to find too late that the marriage agreement he has signed is a binding one.

It is said that Molière, in this play, strong in the king's protection, caricatured the principal doctors of the court.

Amour peintre, L', see *Sicilien, Le*.

Amours, see *Ronsard*.

Amours de Psyché et de Cupidon, Les (1669), see *La Fontaine*.

Amours du Chevalier de Faublas, Les (1789–90), a novel by Louvet de Couvray (q.v.), typical of many frivolous, licentious novels of its time, and still mentioned. Faublas, the amiable hero, is the victim of his own charms. His amorous adventures, recounted with a certain lively force, begin with his entry into society at the age of sixteen. He loves several women by the way and three in particular. A jealous husband and a despairing suicide reduce the three to one. The novel ends on a moral note: Faublas, who had hoped to settle down with his remaining love, is haunted by the avenging phantoms of the other two and goes mad.

Amours jaunes, Les, see *Corbière, Tristan*.

Amour tyrannique, L', see *Scudéry, Georges de*.

Ampère, ANDRÉ-MARIE (1775–1836), the mathematician and physicist, born at Lyons, whose discoveries in electrodynamics and electromagnetics led to later work on electric telegraphy. His *Essai sur la philosophie des sciences* (1834–44) is less specialized than his other scientific writings; and his posthumously published *Journal et correspondance* has both interest and charm for the lay reader.

Ampère, JEAN-JACQUES, son of the foregoing (1800–64), man of letters and historian, a professor at the *Collège de France* (q.v.), was the generous friend and adviser of many of his literary contemporaries. His works include: *Histoire littéraire de la France avant le xiie siècle* (1839–40); *Histoire romaine à Rome* (1858).

Amphitryon, a comedy by Molière in irregular verse (see *Vers libres*), produced in 1668, based on the *Amphitruo* of Plautus. Molière imitated some passages in Rotrou's (q.v.) *Les Sosies* on the same subject.

The scene is Thebes. Amphitryon, a Theban general, is returning from a successful campaign and sends his servant Sosie to announce his arrival to his wife Alcmène. But Jupiter, enamoured of Alcmène, has assumed the features of Amphitryon and introduced himself to her on the preceding night as her victorious husband. Mercury, in attendance on Jupiter, has similarly assumed the appearance of Sosie, and when the latter arrives, claims to be the real Sosie and drives him off. The comedy consists in the complications arising from the presence at Amphitryon's palace of two indistinguishable Amphitryons and two indistinguishable Sosies, the confusion in the minds of their respective wives, and the final confrontation of the two Amphitryons. Nor does Sosie know which is his real master: when he hears Jupiter inviting Amphitryon's friends to dinner, he thinks the doubt resolved, for

Le véritable Amphitryon
Est l'Amphitryon où l'on dîne,

a trait borrowed from Rotrou and the origin of the association of Amphitryon with gastronomy. At last Jupiter explains the cheat, turning it into a neat compliment to Amphitryon and Alcmène, which provokes Sosie's remark, now proverbial,

Le Seigneur Jupiter sait dorer la pilule.

Dryden's *Amphitryon* (1690) is adapted from this play and from Plautus. In modern times the same story is handled with wit and felicity in *Amphitryon 38,* by Giraudoux (q.v.).

Amphitryon 38, see above.

Amyot, JACQUES (1513–93), humanist, born at Melun of humble parentage. He was for some ten years (till 1543) a teacher at the university of Bourges, then became known to François Ier, from whom he received an abbacy. He visited Italy more than once, was appointed tutor to two of the sons of Henri II (the future Charles IX and Henri III), and under the former became Grand Almoner and Bishop of Auxerre. He is famous as the translator into admirable French of Plutarch's *Lives* (1559) and *Moralia* (1572), of seven books of Diodorus Siculus (1554), as well as of the *Theagenes and Chariclea* of Heliodorus (1547 and 1559) and the *Daphnis and Chloe* of Longus (1559). Amyot is important not only because he raised the quality of French prose but as having popularized by his Plutarch the wisdom of the ancients. Many passages from this translation are included by Montaigne in his *Essais*. North's translation of Plutarch's *Lives*, from which Shakespeare drew the plot of his Roman plays, was from Amyot's French version.

Anacharsis en Grèce, Voyage du jeune, see *Barthélemy, abbé J.-J.*

Anarchisme, see *Literary Isms*.

Anastasie, a nickname for the Censorship, apparently first applied during the Second Empire (1852–70, q.v.). 'Dame Censure', or 'Anastasie', was sometimes caricatured as an old hag with an owl on her shoulder and a large pair of scissors under one arm; or as a crow, whose large beak was formed by the blades of a pair of scissors. A biography of Censure (Anastasie), in fact a short, amusing history of the origin and development of literary and dramatic censorship, was given in the July 1874 issue of *Trombinoscope*, collections of irreverent satirical sketches and caricatures of contemporary personalities and institutions (1872–6).

'Anastasie' was a frequent name in vaudeville for the character of the ugly old maid.

Ancelot, JACQUES-ARSÈNE (1794–1854) and his wife Marguerite-Louise-Virginie, *née* Chardon (1792–1875), a well-known couple in the literary life of Paris during the Restoration, the July Monarchy, and well into the Second Empire. He wrote over sixty tragedies, comedies, and vaudevilles, now forgotten, though one early tragedy, *Louis XI* (1819), brought him sudden, short-lived fame and a royal pension, and his vaudevilles bolstered up the family finances. He also, after long perseverance, succeeded in becoming a member of the *Académie française* (q.v.). He is most often remembered as his wife's husband. Mme Ancelot was a pushing but amiable and kind-hearted woman whose salon was one of the best known and most influential in Paris, in its heyday, perhaps, during the July Monarchy (1831–48). It is frequently mentioned in correspondence and memoirs—by Mérimée and Stendhal (qq.v.) among others. She put the best of her energies into collecting celebrities but she also had some success with her paint-brush (many pictures of her salon and its frequenters at various dates) as well as with her pen, for she, too, wrote vaudevilles; and she left two books which are still read: *Salons de Paris, foyers éteints* (1858) and *Un salon de Paris, 1824–1864* (1866).

Ancey, GEORGES (1860–1917), a dramatist associated with the early days of the *Théâtre Libre* (q.v.). His comedies contained a farcical element, more bitter than gay (*M. Lamblin*, 1888; *Les Inséparables*, 1889; *L'École des veufs*, 1889; *La Dupe*, 1891; *Ces Messieurs*, 1901, and, another version, 1903).

Ancien régime, L', the term applied to the system of government, or the political structure, of pre-Revolutionary France.

Ancien régime, L', see *Tocqueville.*

Anciens et des modernes, Parallèle des, see *Perrault.*

Anciens et des modernes, Querelle des, see *Querelle.*

Anciens et les modernes, ou La Toilette de Mme de Pompadour, Les, title of a dialogue by Voltaire (q.v.).

Ancre, MARÉCHAL D', see *Concini.*

André Cornélis (1887) by Paul Bourget, a novel of psychological analysis. The hero is thrown into a state of anguish and indecision by the discovery that his father, who was thought to have died a natural death, was in fact murdered by the man who is now his stepfather and whom his mother, innocent of all that happened, adores. He confronts his stepfather and asks him to commit suicide. When the stepfather refuses he stabs him. The stepfather dies but manages first to scrawl a note, found by his wife, saying that he is suffering from an incurable disease and has preferred a speedy death. André's

anguish and indecision are no less, for his dilemma now is, shall he disclose the secret or shall he leave his mother in peace to worship her dead?

Andrieux, FRANÇOIS (1759–1833), advo-cate, judge, professor of literature at the *Collège de France* and Perpetual Secretary of the *Académie française* from 1829, also wrote several comedies, including *Les Étourdis* (1787), *Le Trésor* (1804), *Le Vieux Fat* (1810). They were feeble, but won him official recognition during his lifetime.

Andromaque, a tragedy by Racine, pro-duced in 1667. Based on the Greek legend of the fate of Andromache after the fall of Troy, it differs from this in representing Andromache merely as the widow of Hector and mother of Astyanax (who in the play has survived), and not also as the mother of Molossus by Pyrrhus, son of Achilles.

The scene is in Epirus, where Pyrrhus is king. Hermione, daughter of Menelaus, is betrothed to Pyrrhus and jealous of An-dromache, his captive. Pyrrhus neglects Hermione and loves Andromache, who, faithful to the memory of Hector, hates her new lover. Orestes is sent by the Greek States to demand the death of Astyanax, whom, as son of the great Hector, they dread. He comes to Epirus, and having long loved Hermione, hopes to carry her off. To bend Andromache to his will Pyrrhus threatens to surrender her son to the Greeks. Andro-mache vacillates between hatred of Pyrrhus and terror for her child; Pyrrhus, between love for Andromache and cruel anger against her; Hermione, between love for Pyrrhus and resentment at his neglect. Finally Andro-mache consents to marry Pyrrhus and thus secure his vow to protect her son, but designs to kill herself thereafter. Hermione, in-furiated at news of the intended marriage, consents to fly with Orestes, but demands first the death of Pyrrhus, and this Orestes reluctantly promises her. But when he comes announcing that Pyrrhus is dead, Hermione by a revulsion of feeling turns fiercely against him for having killed the man she loves, rushes away, and kills herself on the body of Pyrrhus. Orestes goes mad.

Andromaque was parodied in 1668 in *La Folle Querelle* by an author and critic named Subligny. It has been described (by Jules

Lemaître) as the first appearance in tragedy of psychological realism and passionate love.

Andromède (1650), a spectacle-play by Pierre Corneille (q.v.). Much of its success was due to its production and scenic effects by the Italian master of theatre machinery, Giacomo Torelli (1608–78), who was brought to Paris by Louis XIV in 1645 and remained there till 1662.

Aneau, BARTHÉLEMY, called ANNULUS (*c.* 1500–65), was from 1529 a teacher of rhetoric at the Collège de la Trinité at Lyons. He was suspected of Protestantism and murdered during a people's uprising. His works include a *Mystère de la Nativité* (1539), performed by his pupils; *Picta Poesis* (1552), Greek and Latin emblem verses (which he translated into French the same year); a translation of More's *Utopia*; and, almost certainly, *Le Quintil Horatian,* criticizing Du Bellay's *Défense.*

Âne mort et La Femme guillotinée, L', see *Janin, Jules-Gabriel.*

Angélique, a character in Molière's *George Dandin.*

Angélique de Saint-Jean, La Mère, see *Arnauld d'Andilly, Angélique.*

Angélique de Sainte-Madeleine, La Mère (remembered as *la Mère Angélique*), see *Arnauld, Jacqueline-Marie-Angélique.*

Angellier, AUGUSTE (1848–1911), poet, born at Dunkirk, gave some years to journalism, then became Professor of English at the University of Lille. He was best known by the sonnet-sequence *A l'amie perdue* (1896. Two people meet, love, are not free to marry, part. The emotion expressed, if deep, is not violent). His other works include *Le Chemin des saisons* (1903, nature poems) and various series of poems entitled *Dans la lumière antique* (1905–11); also an *Étude sur la vie et les œuvres de Robert Burns* (1892).

Angelo (1835), a prose drama by Victor Hugo. Tisbe, a courtesan, mistress of Angelo the *podestà* (governor) of Brescia, loves and believes herself loved by Rodolpho. She discovers that he has for years been the lover of Angelo's wife Catarina. But vengeance is impossible, for she learns at the same time that Catarina, when a child, had been instrumental in saving her (Tisbe's) mother from

the gallows. Now Angelo discovers that his wife has a lover, and plots to murder her with a poison that Tisbe is to procure. Tisbe contrives to substitute a strong narcotic which renders Catarina dead to all appearances for twelve hours. Rodolpho appears in the vault to which the 'corpse' has been carried. He accuses Tisbe of murder and stabs her. Catarina wakens, and the dying Tisbe plots escape for the lovers.

Angennes, JULIE D', see *Rambouillet, Hôtel de: Guirlande de Julie.*

Ange Pitou (1853), an historical novel of the Revolution, by Dumas *père* (q.v.), one of his best romances. It has excellent pictures of the early days of the Revolution, both in the country and in Paris.

Anglo-Norman or **Anglo-French,** that form of the French language which became current in Great Britain and Ireland as a consequence of the Norman Conquest and of the resulting immigration of French people and the intercommunication between France and this country during the succeeding two hundred years. It was mainly the language of the superior classes, but there is evidence (as in the vocabulary of modern English dialects) that it penetrated to the lower grades. Its basis was the French of Normandy, but it had from the outset an admixture of other elements. Typical Normanisms are *garden* and *war* (contrast central French *jardin* and *guerre*) and dialectal variation is preserved in our *chattel* and *cattle*. Through isolation from the Continent and contact with English, its grammar, orthography, and pronunciation were greatly altered; thus, it anticipated Continental French in discarding the distinctive nominative form in nouns, it extended the infinitive ending -*er* of the first conjugation, and reduced many diphthongs to simple vowels; some notable features of its representation of vowel sounds are shown in *launch, haunt, people, jeopardy, rule.* Heterogeneous in structure and largely individual in usage, it degenerated rapidly, and its decline during the late thirteenth and the fourteenth centuries led to its extinction as a literary and colloquial medium. This insular French was the vehicle of an extensive literature from *c.* 1120 (Philippe de Thaon) to *c.* 1400 (Gower); but latterly it had been much affected by the standard French of

France. The literature written in this language and the authors who wrote it are known as Anglo-Norman. The term is also used in a looser sense of writers such as Wace (q.v.), canon of Bayeux, who wrote his *Roman de Brut* for Queen Eleanor of England, using English sources, and his *Roman de Rou* for her husband Henry II.

Anglo-Norman literature, which was at its peak in the 12th century, treated especially historical subjects (it is notable that chronicles in the vernacular appear earlier in England than in France) and religious and moral themes. Typical works are a *Voyage of St. Brendan* (q.v.), translations of Biblical books, *bestiaires*, the *Chasteau d'amour*, an allegorical poem in praise of the Virgin Mary by Robert Grosseteste, bishop of Lincoln and first chancellor of Oxford University (1175–1253). There were also a number of tales relating to the adventures of knights of the Round Table (for instance works now lost on Perceval and Ivain or Ywain), and quasi-historical romances, such as *Horn, Havelok, Beuves de Haumtone, Ipomédon*, and *Guy de Warewic* (qq.v.); also the Norman-French original of the 14th-century English *Richard Coer de Lyon*. Except *Horn* and *Beuves de Haumtone* (which are in monorhyme stanzas), these poems were written in couplets of short verses. Many French writers, notably Chrétien de Troyes (q.v.), found inspiration in this quasi-historical material.

The important mystery play *Adam* (see *Religious Writings*) was written in Anglo-Norman eight-syllabled verse, in England. The early version of the Books of Kings, though perhaps not in Anglo-Norman, was written in England. The great French national epic, the *Chanson de Roland* itself, has survived in the manuscript, preserved at Oxford, of an Anglo-Norman scribe. The language continued in commercial and official use into the 15th century; it survived in the conventionalized form of Law French till about 1700, and a relic of this remains in the formula *Le roi le veult*, used by the sovereign in giving assent to an act of parliament, as well as in many legal phrases.

Angot, Mme, the popular type of a woman of the lower classes who has become suddenly enriched and retains the coarseness of taste and language of her previous condition. The name comes from the comic opera *Madame Angot ou la Poissarde parvenue* (1796) by Antoine-François-Ève, called Maillot or Demaillot (1747–1814), which was popular during the Directoire and which had successors in the even more celebrated operetta *La Fille de Madame Angot* (1872), with music by Alexandre-Charles Lecocq (1832–1918), and the comedy *La Petite Fille de Madame Angot* (1934) by the contemporary author Clément Vautel (1876).

Angoulême, DUCHESSE DE, see *Orpheline du Temple*.

Angoulevent, jester to Henri IV.

Angoysses douloureuses qui procèdent d'amours, see *Crenne*.

Annales de la littérature et des arts, Les (1820–9), a literary review, published work by young Romantic writers. Charles Nodier (q.v.) contributed literary criticism.

Annales patriotiques et littéraires, Les, or *La Tribune des hommes libres* (1789–97), a journal devoted to politics, commerce, and literature, and better remembered by the name it eventually bore: *Les Annales politiques et littéraires*. It was founded and edited by L.-S. Mercier (q.v.), author of the *Tableau de Paris*, and was widely read among the Jacobins (q.v.) in the provinces.

Annales philosophiques, Les, one of the early, and best remembered, French literary and philosophical reviews (fortnightly). It bore this name only from 1800 to 1801, but under various titles and with various intervals of suppression it existed from its foundation in 1796 (as *Les Annales religieuses*) until 1859, when it became a daily, of political, literary, and general interest.

Annales politiques, civiles et littéraires du dix-huitième siècle, Les, more often referred to shortly as *Les Annales politiques*, a periodical of political, economic, and literary interest, founded 1777 in London by Linguet (1736–94), an able but arrogant advocate and political journalist who had been disbarred and obliged to leave France on account of the caustic violence of his writings. His journal, though it circulated in France, could not be published there till 1790. Between 1780 and 1783 it was continued in Geneva by Mallet du Pan (q.v.) while Linguet, who had returned to France and been arrested, was a prisoner in the Bastille. After his release Linguet resumed control, first from London and then (1790) in Paris. He ceased publication after the fall of the monarchy (1792) and was himself executed under the Terror. This journal created a stir because of Linguet's virulent articles. While conducted by Mallet du Pan it was noted for the fairness of its political comment.

Annales politiques et littéraires, Les, see *Annales patriotiques et littéraires.*

Annales romantiques, Les (1823–36), a periodical publication, twelve volumes in all, issued in the form of a miscellany to evade the censorship restrictions (see *Press, Development of,* para. 9). It was one of the organs of the Romantic Movement (see *Romantisme*). The first volume was entitled *Tablettes romantiques.*

Anneau d'améthyste, L', see *Bergeret, M.*

Anne d'Autriche [Anne of Austria] (1602–66), consort of Louis XIII, mother of Louis XIV, and regent during the latter's minority. Her father was Philip III of Spain.

Année littéraire, L', one of the first periodical reviews to devote considerable space to literary criticism. It was conducted in the first place (1754–75) by Élie Fréron (q.v.), and after his death continued (until 1790) by other hands, notably his son Stanislas Fréron (see *Orateur du peuple*), his brother-in-law the abbé Royou (see *Ami du roi*), and the critic J.-L. Geoffroy (q.v.). For most of the time it appeared at ten-day intervals and until the end it supported the Monarchy and the Church.

Année philosophique, L', one of two well-known periodicals founded (1867) by Renouvier (q.v.).

Année terrible, L' (1872), by Victor Hugo, poems descriptive of or inspired by the events of 1870–1; not his finest verse.

Annonce faite à Marie, L' (1912), by Claudel (q.v.), a medieval mystery in four acts and a prologue.

Anne Vercors departs on a pilgrimage leaving Jacques Hury, a labourer, to look after his wife and his two daughters—the violent, jealous Mara (in love with Jacques) and the gentle, innocent Violaine, to whom

Jacques is betrothed. Violaine talks with the leper Pierre de Craon. She is seen by Mara to kiss him, moved by pity and the mystical belief that by so doing she may heal him. On her wedding eve she shows Jacques the marks of the leprosy which has now attacked her. (Pierre, we learn later, has in fact been cured.) Jacques, influenced by Mara's tales, refuses to believe in Violaine's innocence and she leaves home. Jacques marries Mara.

Eight years later, on Christmas Eve, the distraught Mara brings the corpse of her infant son to the cave where Violaine, now blinded with disease, and a pauper, has taken refuge. At Violaine's request she reads the Christmas Office while Violaine holds the corpse. A miracle happens. A heavenly choir, heard only by Violaine, joins in the prayer; and when Violaine returns a living infant to her sister the eyes it opens are blue, like her own.

Anonyme de Béthune, see *History (Medieval period).*

Anouilh, JEAN (1910–), born in Bordeaux, contemporary playwright, has had much success in England as well as in France. Published collections of his works are of two kinds—*Pièces roses* (1945 and later collections) and *Pièces noires* (1945 and later) because, like Shaw's *Plays Pleasant and Unpleasant,* they deal with the lighter or the darker side of life. The *Pièces roses* include: *Le Bal des voleurs, Le Rendez-vous de Senlis, Léocadia.* The *Pièces noires* include: *La Sauvage, Le Voyageur sans bagage, Eurydice* (a modern treatment of the story of Orpheus and Eurydice in which Orpheus is a café violinist, Eurydice one of a company of seedy actors, and Death a commercial traveller); also two modern versions of classical themes, *Antigone* and *Médée,* which, though played in modern dress, preserve some of the conventions and the firmness of dialogue of classical tragedy. The action takes place off-stage and there is a chorus. Another collection by this author, *Pièces brillantes,* was published in 1951.

Anquetil-Duperron, ABRAHAM-HYA-CINTHE (1731–1805), celebrated French orientalist, born in Paris. At the age of twenty-three he set off for India, with little more than two shirts, the Bible in Hebrew, the essays of Montaigne, and a map for baggage, determined to discover the sacred writings of the Parsees. He met with numerous adventures and hardships, but in 1762 reached Paris again with a priceless collection of 180 manuscripts which he deposited at the *Bibliothèque nationale* (then the *Bibliothèque du roi*). He spent the remainder of his life deciphering, commenting, and translating these. His translation of the Zend Avesta (1771, with a preface giving the story of his Indian journey), although superseded by later work, opened a new era in oriental studies. He was a scholar of great single-mindedness and austerity who found solace and escape in his studies when the Revolution brought hardship and disillusionment. He lived into old age, without wife, children, or servants, 'privé de tous les biens, exempt aussi de tous les liens de ce monde; seul, absolument libre, et pourtant très ami de tous les hommes', despising worldly temptations, and awaiting his end with tranquillity and 'une âme allègre'.

Anseïs de Carthage, a *chanson de geste* (q.v.) of the late 12th or early 13th century, one of the Charlemagne cycle.

Charlemagne has conquered Spain and placed it under a Christian king. This king, by an outrage to the daughter of one of his chief vassals, provokes the latter to lead the Moors from Africa into Spain. (Cf. the Spanish legend of Roderick and Julian.)

Anthinéa (1901), by Charles Maurras (q.v.), travel essays.

Antier, BENJAMIN, dramatist, see *Macaire, Robert*.

Antin, LOUIS-ANTOINE, DUC D' (1665–1736), son of the marquis de Montespan, an assiduous courtier but a failure as a soldier (he was disgraced after Ramillies). He was restored to favour, succeeded Mansart as director of buildings, and later was a member of the council of regency. He left memoirs.

Antioche, Chanson d', a poem in monorhyme stanzas of alexandrines composed early in the 13th century by Graindor de Douay. It recounts the incidents of the First Crusade (1096–9) prior to the capture of Jerusalem, including the disastrous end of the expedition of Peter the Hermit and culminating in the siege and occupation of Antioch. Graindor completed the story in a further poem, the *Conquête de Jérusalem*. The two

works were probably based on Latin records of the Crusade but falsify some of the facts, and only the passages dealing with the sieges of the two cities are of some historical interest. The poems are of only moderate literary merit; the author probably had before him an earlier verse narrative now lost, by a certain Richard le Pèlerin.

With the poems on Godefroi de Bouillon (see *Chevalier au Cygne*) these narratives form the *Cycle de la Croisade* (see *Cycle*).

Antiquité dévoilée, L', see *Boulanger, Nicolas-Antoine*.

Antiquités de Rome, see *Du Bellay*.

Antoine, ANDRÉ-LÉONARD (1858–1943), theatre-director, born in Limoges, lived in Paris and had to earn his living from the age of thirteen. He had a passion for the theatre and joined a dramatic club, the *Cercle gaulois*. His fellow members did not share his enthusiasm for dramatic innovations so in 1877 he adventurously threw up his job with the Paris Gas Company and used his meagre savings to found the *Théâtre Libre* (q.v.). He produced plays by young authors, experimented with new methods of production and acting, and in seven years' time had accumulated one million francs of debts but practically revolutionized stage conventions. In after years he was director of other theatres in Paris, including the (then) Odéon (q.v.). His published works include: *Mes Souvenirs sur le Théâtre Libre* (1921), reminiscences, and *Le Théâtre* (1932), a history of the French stage since 1859.

Antony (1831), a drama by Dumas *père*. Adèle d'Hervey, the weak, misunderstood wife of an army officer, succumbs to the sadistic charms of Antony, a wealthy but nameless orphan. Antony comes at night to persuade her to flee with him, urging that their passion transcends wifely or maternal ties. At this moment Colonel d'Hervey appears. The inimitable Antony stabs Adèle and turning to the husband says, 'Elle me résistait, je l'ai assassinée!' He has saved Adèle's honour and made sure that no one else will have what he has been denied.

This drama may seem ridiculous nowadays but it contained much that was then novel—the Romantic hero, the 'outsider' deprived of his due place in society; the 'femme incomprise', and the idea that passions do not only move people in exalted situations. It has thus a definite place in the evolution of the modern theatre.

Aphrodite, see *Louÿs, Pierre.*

Apollinaire, GUILLAUME, the name taken by Wilhelm Apollinaris Kostrowitzky (1880–1918), poet. He was born in Rome, said to be the natural child of a Polish mother. After an education in the South of France he came to Paris (1898) and worked in a bank. From 1903 he supported himself by literary journalism, edited small reviews, and became a leading figure in younger literary and artistic circles, especially those of the *Futuristes* and *Cubistes* (qq.v.). He believed that modern poets should adventure into new fields of poetic fancy, develop a seeing eye for the exciting resemblances of apparently disparate things, and strive to endow 'mille phantasmes impondérables' with reality. *L'Enchanteur pourrissant* (1909, essays) was his first separately published work but his reputation stands, and has grown, by the poems of *Alcools* (1913) and *Calligrammes* (1918). He used no punctuation in his verse and at times experimented with pictorial typography. For instance, *Il pleut,* a poem (in *Calligrammes*) in traditional form, is printed with the letters trickling down the page (cf., in French, Rabelais's *epilenie,* or song in honour of Bacchus, printed in the shape of a bottle (Bk. iv, ch. xlv)).

Apollinaire died of injuries received early in the 1914–18 war. His other works include: *L'Hérésiarque et Cie* (1910), short stories, and *Les Mamelles de Tirésias* (1918), called by the author a 'drame surréaliste' (said to be the earliest use of the word '*surréaliste*') because it proceeds on the principle of 'l'usage raisonnable des invraisemblances'. (It has been very successfully turned into a light opera by the contemporary French composer Francis Poulenc.)

Apologie pour Hérodote, see *Estienne.*

Appel au soldat, L' (1900), Part II of the trilogy *Le Roman de l'énergie nationale* by Maurice Barrès (q.v.). It is mainly concerned with the Boulangist movement (see *Boulanger*).

Approximations, see *Du Bos, Charles.*

Après-midi d'un faune, L' (1876), by Mallarmé (q.v.), one of his most famous poems (cf. *Debusssy*).

Aquinas, see *Thomas Aquinas, Saint.*

A quoi rêvent les jeunes filles?, one of the most perfect of Alfred de Musset's short comedies (in verse), was first published in *Un Spectacle dans un fauteuil* (1832, q.v.).

The Duke Laertes wishes to marry his twin daughters Ninon and Ninette to Silvio and Irus. He knows that youth sees no charm in a husband who comes provided only with a father's blessing and a wedding-ring, so he schemes for the youthful suitors to appear with an accompaniment of serenades, anonymous love-letters, midnight assignations, even a duel, such as must satisfy the most romantic of girlish dreams.

This comedy reveals a quality of gay, tender lyricism that has sometimes caused Musset to be compared to Shakespeare: and it is typical of his gift for capturing the spirit of youth, its gaiety, wistfulness, and evanescence.

Arago, FRANÇOIS (1786–1853), scientist, born near Perpignan, finished his education at the *École polytechnique* (q.v.) in Paris. From 1809 he was on the staff of the Observatoire, later becoming its director. He was also Perpetual Secretary of the *Académie des sciences* (from 1830), and founder (1816) of the *Annales de chimie et de physique,* one of the foremost French scientific journals. He was a distinguished lecturer with a remarkable gift of clear exposition of scientific subjects, hence the uninterrupted success of his public lectures on astronomy, delivered between 1812 and 1845.

But Arago's career, after 1830, was also political. He was one of the great figures of the 1848 Revolution, and with Lamartine helped to form the Provisional Government. As Minister of Marine at this time he was largely responsible for the abolition of slavery in the French colonies. His political career ended with the June insurrection (see *Republics,* para. 2). A sign of the esteem in which he was held is the fact that although he refused (1852) to swear allegiance to the government of Louis-Napoléon he was not removed from his Directorship of the Observatoire.

Besides many scientific works he left

Mélanges and, most interesting of all for the general reader, memoirs in the form of an autobiography of his early years (*Histoire de ma jeunesse*, 1854), a stirring tale of his adventures on a scientific mission in Spain, his imprisonment as a spy, and subsequent escape.

Aragon, LOUIS (1897–), novelist and poet, one of the founders of *Surréalisme* (q.v.) in literature, broke with this movement when he joined the Communist Party. Among his novels, *Le Paysan de Paris* (1926) takes, more than anything else, the continually renewed marvel of Paris itself as theme. *Les Cloches de Bâle* (1935) and *Les Beaux Quartiers* (1936) are pictures, against the political background of France before the 1914–18 war, of life in Paris and in a small town in the Midi. The life, viewed from a Marxist standpoint, is largely corrupt, vitiated, 'bourgeois', and capitalist. Two later novels, *Les Voyageurs de l'impériale* (1943) and *Aurélien* (1944), are situated in the inter-war years. Poems of Aragon's surrealist period are collected in *Feu de joie* (1920) and *Mouvement perpétuel* (1926). The love and patriotic poems of *Le Crève-cœur* (1940) and *Les Yeux d'Elsa* (1942), which continue the tradition of the *chanson*, belong to the war years when he was a member of the Resistance movement. His *Traité du style* (1928) is an exposition of surrealist theories, not an essay on style.

Aramis, one of the heroes of *Les Trois Mousquetaires* (q.v.) by Dumas *père*.

Arbres de liberté. During the Revolution trees were erected temporarily, or definitely planted, in the provinces and in parts of Paris, as symbols of liberty and fraternity. They also, after a decree of the *Convention* of 23 January 1794 (3 pluviôse An II) directing that one should be planted and cared for in every *commune* (roughly the equivalent of a village), commemorated the constitution of 1793. The young trees were hung with ribbons, borne in procession, and planted in the presence of local notabilities. The practice seems to have been adopted in reminiscence of May Day and May Tree rejoicings, and the fact that the species most often chosen was a poplar (fr. Latin *populus*) may have been one of the many contemporary manifestations of neoclassical symbolism.

The first trees of Liberty are said to have been planted in 1792 at Lille and Auxerre. A great many died or were destroyed during the Napoleonic era but there were survivors, e.g. a tree which still flourishes at Bayeux. For a time, again, trees of Liberty were a feature of the 1848 revolution, though in Paris more than the provinces.

Arc de Triomphe, L', in Paris, the most famous, though not the most beautiful architecturally, of the triumphal arches erected in France, on the ancient Roman model, to celebrate military glory. Begun in 1806, it was completed in 1836 and stands magnificently, against the setting sun, at the head of the Avenue des Champs-Élysées. The procession bearing Napoleon's ashes across Paris, when they were brought back from St. Helena in 1840, was one of the first of many that have filed past it (see *Légende napoléonienne*). After the 1914–18 war France's Unknown Soldier was buried beneath it, since when a torch, the 'flamme du souvenir', has been kept continuously alight above the memorial flagstone.

Another *arc de triomphe* in Paris, on the west side of the Place du Carrousel, commemorates Napoleon's great military achievements of 1805.

Archives de philosophie, a philosophical journal (1923–38 and 1950–). It appears at irregular intervals and usually consists of monographs on the same or divers subjects, with one section devoted to bibliography.

Archives nationales, Les, the French equivalent of our Public Record Office, a central depot for documents relating to the political and administrative history of France. Before the Revolution various monarchs, notably Louis XIV, had interested themselves in the conservation of royal archives and there were also collections of documents concerning the Army and the Navy. Centralization was effected by a decree (1793) of the French Revolutionary Government, and from 1808 the home of the *Archives nationales* became the Hôtel de Soubise, one of the splendid early 18th-century residences of Paris, of great architectural interest. To this in 1927 was added the neighbouring and equally splendid Hôtel de Rohan. It was in this *hôtel*, in his small study the *Cabinet des Singes*, so called because decorated in the Chinese manner, that the Cardinal de Rohan was arrested at the time of the *Affaire du collier* (see *Collier, L'Affaire du*). (The House of Soubise was a branch of the House of Rohan.)

Archives philosophiques, Les (1817–18), a literary and philosophical review, the organ of the *doctrinaires* (q.v.), was edited by Royer-Collard and Guizot (qq.v.).

Arcos, RENÉ (1881–), *unanimiste* (see *Unanimisme*) poet, born in Paris, was an original member of the Abbaye (q.v.) community. His poetical works, characterized by faith in mankind's progress towards happiness, include *L'Âme essentielle* (1902), *La Tragédie des espaces* (1908), *Ce qui naît* (1910), *L'Île perdue* (1913), *Le Sang des autres* (1918, containing one of his best poems, *Les Morts sont tous d'un seul côté*), &c. *Pays du soir* (1918) and *Autrui* (1926) are novels.

A rebours (1884), a novel by J.-K. Huysmans (q.v.). The hero, Des Esseintes, the effete survivor of a worn-out family, tries to overcome his profound ennui by leading a life elaborately opposed to the banal existence of ordinary men. But no experiments, whether with exotic furnishings, perfumes, or pleasures, can stir this hyper-aesthete to enthusiasm. In the end, owing to his perverse manner of life, his original neurasthenia is complicated by acute biliousness. When this has been cured he returns to Paris and touches the lowest depths of pessimism. But as the work ends he is turning to religion as a last resource.

The book owed much to its appearance at the time when the *esprit décadent* (q.v.) was merging into *Symbolisme* (q.v.). It has a retrospective importance as a compendium of *fin-de-siècle* tastes and interests, for which English comparisons might be found in Wilde's *Picture of Dorian Gray*, or the quarterly *Yellow Book*, or the aesthetic movement burlesqued in Gilbert and Sullivan's *Patience*. If at one moment the weary Des Esseintes bought a tortoise and had its shell encrusted with jewels so that its slow, scintillating progress might deaden the too, too brilliant tones of his carpet, at another he found his greatest pleasure in reading Mallarmé (q.v.), then barely known, and dreamed of the perfect evocative prose in which an adjective would be 'posé d'une

si ingénieuse et d'une si définitive façon qu'il ne pourrait être légalement dépossédé de sa place, ouvrirait de telles perspectives que le lecteur pourrait rêver, pendant des semaines entières, sur son sens, tout à la fois précis et multiple'. (Mallarmé returned the compliment by writing *Prose pour des Esseintes*, q.v.)

Arène, PAUL (1843–96), novelist and poet of Provençal life. His works include: *Jean des figues* (1868), a novel which at one stage describes the milieu of the *Décadents* (see *Esprit décadent*); *La Gueuse parfumée, récits provençaux* (1876); *Au bon soleil* (1881); *Le midi rouge* (1895); the posthumously published *Contes de Provence* (1920); and *Le Parnassiculet contemporain* (1867), see *Pastiche*.

Argan, the *malade imaginaire* in Molière's play of that name.

Argens, JEAN-BAPTISTE, MARQUIS D' (1704–71), *philosophe* and man of letters, friend and chamberlain of Frederick II of Prussia, and author of *Lettres juives* (1736) written in the assumed character of a Jewish visitor to France, pungently criticizing the customs and in particular the religious institutions of that country.

Argenson, MARC-PIERRE, COMTE D' (1694–1764), younger brother of the following, held a variety of offices, including those of Minister of War and of *directeur de la librairie* (see *Librairie*), the latter from 1737 to 1740. He (among others) is said to have been depicted in Gresset's *Le Méchant*; and when Desfontaines (q.v.), in defence of a scandalous pamphlet, pleaded, 'Monseigneur, il faut bien que je vive', he replied dryly,' Je n'en vois pas la nécessité.' *L'Encyclopédie* (q.v.) was dedicated to him.

Argenson, RENÉ-LOUIS VOYER, MARQUIS D' (1694–1757), minister of foreign affairs (1744–7) under Louis XV. He was the elder son of a famous lieutenant of police of the latter years of Louis XIV, and a man of original and enlightened views who in his earlier years (1724–31) was an active member of the *Club de l'entresol* (q.v.). He was an ardent believer in free trade. His *Considérations sur le gouvernement ancien et présent de la France*, imperfectly published in 1764, and previously much read in manuscript, were approved by Voltaire and quoted by Rousseau in his *Contrat social*. The true title, which defines the subject, was *Jusques où la démocratie peut être admise dans le gouvernement monarchique*. D'Argenson was present at the battle of Fontenoy (as was also his brother Marc-Pierre, see above). His *Relation* of it, published by Voltaire in the *Commentaire historique*, 1776, is well known. He also left *Essais* (in the style of Montaigne) and *Mémoires*, which reveal the naïve self-confidence and pertinacity with which he pursued his ambition to be minister, his sound views on political reform, and a certain prophetic spirit.

Argent, L' (1891), one of Zola's later *Rougon-Macquart* (q.v.) novels. Aristide Saccard, whose grandiose speculative mania had once already brought him to ruin (see *La Curée*), rises dramatically to the surface again. He founds a joint-stock company (involving disastrous competition with the Jewish banker Gundermann) for exploitation and development in the Near East. It is a sort of South Sea Bubble; the shares rocket up; and the inevitable crash entails the usual pitiful tragedies. In Saccard's nature every instinct, degraded, brutal, perverse or, upon occasion, good, yields to his passion for speculation and the power that money can give. Even in his cell, awaiting trial for fraudulent conversion of funds, he is planning still vaster financial conquests. Only Sigismond Busch, the invalid disciple of Karl Marx, can disturb him by expounding anti-capitalistic doctrines. The launching of the vast speculative *Banque universelle*, the feverish atmosphere and manipulation of the Stock Exchange, with accompanying corruption and political intrigue, are described with impressionistic mastery of detail.

Argenton, MONSIEUR D', see *Commines*.

Aricie, a character in *Phèdre* (q.v.), by Racine. She is loved by Hippolyte.

Arimène, a pastoral play by Nicolas de Montreux, performed at Nantes in 1596 with great splendour. It is a complicated story of thwarted love and threatened suicide, with magic superadded. Arimène loves Alphise, but she loves Floridor, who has rescued her from a savage. Arimène in turn is loved by Clorise, who is loved by Cloridan. A magician, also enamoured of Alphise, petrifies her and Floridor. But all is set right in the end.

Ariste, a character in many plays, but chiefly remembered as Chrysale's brother in Molière's *Les Femmes savantes* (q.v.).

Aristocratisme, see *Literary Isms*.

Aristote, Lai d', see *Lai d'Aristote*.

Arlequin or **Harlequin,** from the Italian *Arlecchino* (perhaps to be identified with the medieval demon *Hellequin*, Germ. *Erlkönig*), a character of old Italian comedy. Florian relates the legend of his origin thus: a little negro orphan abandoned in the streets of Bergamo was succoured by three boys, sons of drapers, who, to clothe him, each stole from the paternal store a piece of cloth of a different colour (hence his particoloured dress), and provided him with a wooden sword. The name was assumed by an Italian actor, according to Malherbe born *c.* 1558, whom Marie de Médicis invited to France with his family in 1613. Arlequin became a protean character in comedy and *opéra-comique*, in the hands of Regnard, Dufresny, Le Sage, Piron, Marivaux, &c., at once credulous and sly, blundering and witty. In Florian's *arlequinades* he becomes the simple good-natured hero of the *comédie bourgeoise*. For 'Arlequin-Deucalion' see *Piron*. He also figures as 'Arlequin-Cartouche' (see *Cartouche*) and 'Arlequin traitant' (i.e. revenue-farmer), and even in the dispute between Jesuits and Jansenists.

Arlequin poli par l'amour (1720), a comedy by Marivaux (q.v.).

Arlésienne, L', see *Daudet, A.*; *Bizet*.

Arlincourt, VICTOR-PRÉVOST, VICOMTE D' (1789–1856), novelist, born near Versailles, was nicknamed 'le vicomte inversif' because he wrote in a style packed with inversions. His first novel *Le Solitaire* (1821) was a best-seller, translated into six languages. The hero, a miraculously resurrected Charles the Bold, is a gloomy hermit who has retired to a mountain-top to expiate innumerable fearful crimes, and only sallies forth to perform incredible rescues or steal the heroine's blue hair-ribbons. The heroine, Élodie, is a tender virgin who can accept the fact that the hero has murdered her father, seduced her cousin, and wrecked her uncle's happiness, but cannot face love without a wedding-ring. His other novels, feeble imitations of the first, include *Ipsiboë* (1823) and *L'Étranger* (1825).

Armagnacs, the party which during the reign of Charles VI, when the king was incapacitated by madness, supported the house of Orleans against the house of Burgundy (Jean II had made his fourth son duke of Burgundy); so named from Bernard d'Armagnac, a leader of the party, and member of a family of Aquitaine which had been a centre of opposition to the English. The dissension between Armagnacs and Burgundians (*c.* 1410–18) greatly favoured the operations of the English under Henry V, who received help from the Burgundians. The Armagnacs were the aristocratic, the Burgundians the popular party. The two names in conjunction are used proverbially of irreconcilable enemies.

Armance (1827), the first of Stendhal's (q.v.) novels to be published. The sub-title is 'Quelques scènes d'un salon de Paris en 1827'.

Armande, one of the *femmes savantes* in Molière's comedy of that name (q.v.).

Armée, La Grande. This is now usually taken to mean the army with which Napoleon invaded Russia in 1812.

Napoleon raised four armies between 1803 and 1814, each profoundly different. The first was the army raised and trained with the intention, later abandoned, of invading England. It was known as *la Grande Armée* or *l'Armée de l'Angleterre* and was concentrated round Boulogne (*le camp de Boulogne*) between 1803 and 1805. It was wholly French in composition and 'l'un des plus parfaits instruments de guerre qui aient jamais existé dans l'histoire' (Lavisse, *Hist. de France contemp.* iii. 379). It fought in Austria, Prussia, and Poland, and then in Spain, where it disintegrated. In 1809 Napoleon raised another army, composed partly of hastily levied French recruits and partly of allied contingents. It was of much poorer quality and won its victories at great cost. The third army, *l'armée de Russie*, was international in composition, raised and trained expressly with a view to the Russian campaign, and was defeated. The fourth, used by Napoleon in the campaign of 1813 and

1814, was much more wholly French than its two immediate predecessors and is said by Lavisse to have borne a resemblance to the Revolutionary armies.

Armée des émigrés, L' (sometimes also called *l'armée des princes*), the royalist army formed towards the end of 1791 by the princes of the blood royal who had left France after the outbreak of the Revolution. At first it consisted mainly of former officers of the pre-Revolutionary French army, but as time passed an increasing number of civilian *émigrés* joined it. The comte de Provence, brother of Louis XVI and later to become Louis XVIII, who had set up what was virtually a small court at Coblentz, was commander-in-chief, but while they were being organized the forces were mainly concentrated at Worms, the headquarters of the prince de Condé (see *Bourbon*). By 1792 the *armée des émigrés* was attached to the coalition (q.v.) forces and divided into three corps under the command of Prussian or Austrian generals. The comte de Provence and his younger brother the comte d'Artois (later Charles X) led the first corps, the *armée du centre*, about 10,000 strong. It endured defeat and terrible suffering with the Prussians at Valmy (q.v.) and was soon afterwards disbanded. Chateaubriand fought with this corps. The third corps, about 4,000–5,000 strong, led by the duc de Bourbon under Austrian command, was disbanded after the defeat of the Austrians at Jemmapes (q.v.). It suffered much less hardship than the *armée du centre*. The second corps, the *armée de Condé*, about 5,000 strong, remained in being for much longer. At first it moved from one place to another without any fighting. Between 1793 and 1801 it owed its continued existence to funds provided variously by Austria, Russia, and England. It fought as a division of the Austrian army in Alsace, was for a time in Russia, and was then again absorbed into the Austrian army, fighting against the French Republican armies in Austria and Bavaria, on the Rhine, and in Italy. It was disbanded early in 1801 after the Treaty of Lunéville (q.v.).

Armide (1686), title of an opera by Lulli (q.v.) of which Quinault (q.v.) wrote the libretto, regarded as their masterpiece. It is also the title of a famous opera by Gluck (q.v., 1777), and he, too, used Quinault's libretto. The subject is taken from Tasso's *Jerusalem delivered*.

Arnaud, FRANÇOIS-THOMAS DE BACULARD D' (1718–1805), dramatist and novelist, author of *Coligny* (tragedy, 1740), *Le Comte de Comminges* (a very successful horrific drama, 1764; the scene is the crypt in which Trappist monks are buried; cordials were provided by the management for spectators who were overcome by the horrors); and *Les Épreuves du sentiment* (1772–81), *Les Délassements de l'homme sensible* (1783–93), romances. He also wrote a religious poem, *Les Lamentations de Jérémie*, which provoked the following epigram by Voltaire:

> Savez-vous pourquoi Jérémie
> A tant pleuré pendant sa vie?
> C'est qu'en prophète il prévoyait
> Que Baculard le traduirait.

Arnaud, L'ABBÉ FRANÇOIS (1721–84), man of letters, linguist, and wit, was joint editor, with Suard (q.v.), of journals such as the *Gazette littéraire de l'Europe* which published translations or abstracts of foreign works (literary, scientific, &c.). His *Œuvres* were published in 1808. (See also *Gluck*.)

Arnauld, ANTOINE (1612–94), known as *le Grand Arnauld*, twentieth, and youngest surviving, son of Antoine Arnauld (c. 1560–1619, a famous advocate who pleaded against the Jesuits in 1594), and the most celebrated member of a distinguished family of Auvergne which gave many of its sons and daughters to Port-Royal (q.v.), including three abbesses. He was an ardent theologian and controversialist, pupil of Saint-Cyran (see *Du Vergier de Hauranne*), a defender of Jansenism, and an opponent of the Jesuits. He was author of *La Fréquente Communion* (1643), an eloquent protest against the idea that the profligate could atone for continued sin by frequent communion without repentance. His *Seconde Lettre à un duc et pair* in the Jansenist controversy was condemned by the Sorbonne in 1656 and Arnauld went into hiding. From this he emerged in 1669 (during the period of ecclesiastical peace established by Clement IX) and wrote, among many religious and controversial works, *La Perpétuité de la foi de l'Église catholique touchant l'Eucharistie* (1669–76, with Pierre Nicole, q.v.), against the Protestant doctrine of the Eucharist. In 1679 he had again to go into exile, where he died. With the assistance of Nicole he prepared the *Logique* of Port-Royal (originally for the young duc de Chevreuse), among other educational works. In his last years he wrote against Malebranche (*Traité des vraies et fausses idées*, 1683), and also against William III in favour of the rights of James II; also *Réflexions sur l'éloquence des prédicateurs*. [NOTE. Pascal's (q.v.) *Lettres Provinciales* were occasioned by the Sorbonne's attacks on Arnauld.]

Arnauld, JACQUELINE - MARIE - ANGÉLIQUE (1591–1661), *la Mère Angélique de Sainte-Madeleine*, sister of le Grand Arnauld (above), was installed in 1602, at the age of eleven, as abbess of the convent of Port-Royal (q.v.), which she reformed. La Mère Angélique de Saint-Jean (see *Arnauld d'Andilly, Angélique*) was her niece. Her letters have been published.

Arnauld, JEANNE-CATHERINE-AGNÈS (1594–1671), *la Mère Agnès de Saint-Paul*, sister of le Grand Arnauld and la Mère Angélique (above), was abbess of Port-Royal for six years from 1636. Her letters have been published.

Arnauld d'Andilly, ANGÉLIQUE (1624–84), *la Sœur*—later *la Mère*—*Angélique de Saint-Jean*, niece of the three foregoing and daughter of the following, was abbess of Port-Royal des Champs for six years from 1678. She was mistress of the novices at Port-Royal de Paris (see *Port-Royal*) in 1664 when the Archbishop of Paris broke up the community and had twelve of the most recalcitrant nuns (herself included) removed to other convents (and later reunited at Port-Royal des Champs), where they were placed in solitary confinement and deprived of the Sacraments. (The drama *Port-Royal*, 1954, by H. de Montherlant, takes place on the day of their removal.) She suffered great moral and spiritual anguish during this period, described in her moving *Relation de captivité* (published 1760).

Arnauld d'Andilly, ROBERT (1589–1674), eldest brother of le Grand Arnauld (see *Arnauld, Antoine*), was employed in the administrative service, particularly of the army, under Richelieu. In 1646 he retired and became one of the solitaries of Port-Royal. He translated the *Confessions* of St.

Augustine, Josephus's *History of the Jews and of the Jewish Wars*, and *Vies des Saints Pères des déserts,* and left *Mémoires,* concerned in the main with his life before his retirement, for the education of his grandchildren. He was father of la Mère Angélique de Saint-Jean (see the foregoing) and of Simon, marquis de Pomponne (d. 1695), also minister for foreign affairs (1671–9) under Louis XIV, and a great friend of Mme de Sévigné. He received high praise for his character and ability as Timante in the 6th volume of Mlle de Scudéry's *Clélie.*

Arnault, ANTOINE-VINCENT (1766–1834) is perhaps best remembered as the author of *La Feuille,* a short poem sometimes included in anthologies and first published in his *Fables* (1812–16), a collection of mainly satirical verse. He also wrote tragedies, now forgotten—*Marius à Minturnes* (1791), *Blanche et Montcassin ou les Vénitiens* (1798), &c. After the Restoration he was for some time suspended from the *Académie française* because of his fidelity to Napoleon.

Arnolphe, the chief character in Molière's *École des femmes* (q.v.).

Arnould, MADELEINE-SOPHIE (1764–1803), a famous operatic singer and actress between 1757 and 1778, also renowned for her beauty and wit. She sang in operas by Rameau and Gluck. She was praised by Garrick.

Arouet, see *Voltaire.*

Arras, *chef-lieu* of the *département* of Pas-de-Calais, once the capital of Artois (q.v.); a literary centre in the 13th century. It was a rich town, the home of a *puy* or confraternity which encouraged every form of poetry, and of a number of poets, of whom Jean Bodel and Adam de la Halle (qq.v.) are the most famous.

Arrêts d'amour, Les Cinquante et un, see *Martial d'Auvergne.*

Ars, LE CURÉ D', i.e. Saint Jean-Baptiste-Marie Vianney (1786–1859). He was priest of the country parish of Ars, near Bourg (Ain), from 1818 until his death, and in 1925 was canonized as the model and patron of parish priests. His house at Ars is now a place of pilgrimage.

Arsenal, see *Bibliothèque de l'Arsenal.*

Arsène Guillot, a short story by Mérimée (q.v.), first published in 1844.

Arsinoé, a character in Molière's *Le Misanthrope* (q.v.); also in Corneille's *Nicomède* (q.v.).

Art, L' [i.e. the art of poetry], a poem (1852) by Théophile Gautier, a precursor of the *Parnassiens* (q.v.). See under *Émaux et Camées.*

Art, Théâtre d', see *Œuvre, Théâtre de l'.*

Art d'être grand-père, L' (1877), one of the collections of Victor Hugo's later years, lyrics of family life and love.

Art de vérifier les dates des faits historiques, des chartes, des chroniques et anciens monuments depuis la naissance de Jésus-Christ, par le moyen d'une table chronologique . . . , avec un calendrier perpétuel, L'. This vast work of erudition, far more than a dictionary of dates, was compiled by Dom Maurice d'Antine and several of his fellow Benedictines of the *Congrégation de Saint-Maur* (q.v.). It was first published (1 vol.) in 1750. There were revised and augmented editions in 1770, 1783–92. An *Art de vérifier les dates avant l'ère chrétienne* was added in 1820, also (1821–44) an *Art de vérifier les dates depuis l'année 1770 jusqu'à nos jours* (1827).

Art poétique, L', a didactic poem by Boileau, in four cantos, published in 1674, modelled on the *Ars Poetica* of Horace.

The first canto is on the general principles of poetic composition, the need for good sense, clear thought, fidelity to nature, nobility of style, observance of the rules of the caesura and the hiatus, &c. The second is concerned with specific types of poem, the idyll, the elegy, the ode, &c., holding up the authors of classical antiquity as models for imitation; the third with tragedy and comedy, and incidentally the unities:

> Qu'en un Lieu, qu'en un Jour, un seul Fait accompli
> Tienne jusqu'à la fin le Théâtre rempli.

He also treats of the epic, condemning the use of national and Christian themes as advocated by Desmarets de Saint-Sorlin (q.v.), at a time when Milton had recently published his *Paradise Lost*. The fourth canto contains general advice to the author, showing a high sense of the dignity of the man of letters; for the poet cannot reach eminence without nobility of character: 'Le vers se sent toujours des bassesses du cœur.' The work is thus a summary of the teaching of Boileau's *Satires*, and of the doctrines of the contemporary classical writers.

Art poétique, a poem by Verlaine (q.v.), written 1871–3 and printed in *Jadis et Naguère* (1885). It was one influence in the development of the Symbolist movement.

Art poétique (1907), by Claudel (q.v.), a collection of essays on poetry and poetic form.

Art pour l'art, L'. This expression appears in an entry of 1804, apropos of Kant's Aesthetic, in Benjamin Constant's *Journal intime*. It was—according to the *Cours de philosophie* edited (1836) from notes made by his students—used by Victor Cousin in 1818 in his Sorbonne lectures on the Nature of Art and the Ideal of Beauty. ('Il faut de la religion pour la religion, de la morale pour la morale, comme de l'art pour l'art . . . le beau ne peut être la voie ni de l'utile, ni du bien, ni du saint; il ne conduit qu'à lui-même.') Théophile Gautier's prefaces to *Albertus* (1832) and *Mademoiselle de Maupin* (1835), qq.v., though not in so many words employing the phrase 'l'art pour l'art', were manifestoes of the theory. The duty, as he saw it, of creative artists and critics alike was to realize that the achievement of formal Beauty was the sole purpose of a work of art, that aesthetic—and never ulterior—value was what counted.

The phrase itself became the rallying-cry of, for example, Gautier, Baudelaire, Théodore de Banville, Flaubert, in their fight for liberty in art. It acquired the further significance that beauty in a work of art was a matter of perfect expression and of the absolute, indissoluble unity of form and content. In poetry this led to 'l'horrible artistement exprimé' and 'la douleur rythmée et cadencée' of Baudelaire's *Fleurs du mal*, and to the impassive, descriptive verse of the *Parnassiens* (e.g. Gautier's *Émaux et Camées*, Heredia's *Les Trophées*, Leconte de Lisle's *Poèmes*); while in the novel the outcome was the movement known as *le réalisme*

(q.v.), and in some cases, notably Flaubert, a passionate devotion to style. (Cf. *French Influence on English Literature*, para. 8.)

Artaban, the hero of the *Cléopâtre* of La Calprenède (q.v.), proverbial for his pride: *Fier comme Artaban.*

Artagnan, Mémoires de M. d', by Courtilz de Sandras (q.v.), is the source of Dumas *père*'s *Les Trois Mousquetaires* (q.v.), one of whom is called D'Artagnan.

Artamène, see *Grand Cyrus, Le.*

Arthénice, anagram of 'Catherine', the name by which Mme de Rambouillet (q.v.) was known in her circle.

Arthurian romances, see *Romans bretons*; *Perceval*; *Lancelot.*

Artois, a former province of Northern France, comprising most of the present-day department of the Pas-de-Calais. The title of comte d'Artois was borne by several princes of the blood, notably by Charles-Philippe, brother of Louis XVI and Louis XVIII, who became King of France (Charles X, q.v.) in 1824.

Arvers, FÉLIX (1806–50), poet and dramatist, born in Paris, frequented the salon of Charles Nodier (q.v.). He keeps his place in French literature by one sonnet, *Mon âme a son secret, ma vie a son mystère*, included in his collection *Mes Heures perdues* (1833). It is said to have been addressed to Nodier's daughter Marie.

Asmodée, the devil in Lesage's novel *Le Diable boiteux* (q.v.).

Asmodée (1938), a play (his first) by François Mauriac (q.v.).

Aspremont, a *chanson de geste* of the late 12th or early 13th century, one of the Charlemagne cycle. It deals with the emperor's legendary liberation of Rome and Italy from the Saracens.

Assemblée constituante, L' (or Assemblée nationale constituante), the name adopted on 9 July 1789 by the representative body, composed of the *Tiers État* (q.v.), a majority of the clergy, and a minority of the nobles, which developed out of the *Assemblée* *nationale* and undertook to frame a constitution for the country. It voted the constitution of 1791. On 1 October 1791 it was succeeded by the *Assemblée législative* (see *Revolutions, Ia*).

Since the Assembly of 1789 France has had other constituent assemblies and other constitutions. At the elections for the *Assemblée constituante* of 1848, after the February Revolution, universal (manhood) suffrage was employed in France for the first time. The Constitution of the Fourth Republic (the 14th constitution in French history, promulgated on 27 October 1946) extended the suffrage to women.

Assemblée législative, L', the second of the national assemblies of the Revolution, succeeded the *Assemblée constituante* on 1 October 1791 and was replaced by the *Convention nationale* (qq.v.) on 21 September 1792. It voted the war against Austria and imprisoned Louis XVI.

Assemblée nationale

(*a*) The name taken by the Tiers État (q.v.) on 17 June 1789. Three weeks later it became the *Assemblée nationale constituante* or *Assemblée constituante* (q.v.).

(*b*) There were again *assemblées nationales* in 1848 and 1871 (lasting till 1875) which resembled the first body.

(*c*) Under the Third Republic (1875–1940) the title *Assemblée nationale* was used to denote a joint session of Senators and Deputies (i.e. the upper and lower Houses) sitting to elect a President of the Republic or to revise the Constitution. (In this connexion see *Republics*, para. 9.)

(*d*) With the Fourth Republic, the *Assemblée nationale* (which replaced the former *Chambre des Députés*) became one of the two elected bodies constituting the Parliament and the only one with legislative powers (the other being the *Conseil de la République*, q.v.; and see also *Député*; *Palais Bourbon*; *Republics*; *Revolutions*.)

Assemblée nationale, L', an opposition daily paper, founded after the February Revolution (1848) by former officials of Louis-Philippe's government, had many readers. It was frequently suspended during the Second Empire, changed its name to *Le Spectateur*, and was finally suppressed in 1858.

Assignats. In the first instance (1790) these were interest-bearing bonds issued by the *Assemblée constituante* in an attempt to secure revenue. Their security was the *biens nationaux* (substantially the nationalized Church and, later, Crown property) to which holders were to have a preferential right of exchange, the theory being that as the assignats returned to the State the whole issue would be cancelled. Later, the assignats became paper currency pure and simple, bearing no interest, constantly over-issued, and continually depreciating. The assignats in circulation were liquidated, at a bankruptcy value, in December 1796, and the plate from which they were engraved was destroyed.

Assises de Jérusalem, also known as the *Lettres du Sépulcre* from the place of their custody, the code of law of the kingdom of Jerusalem arranged for Godefroi de Bouillon (q.v.) *c.* 1099. The original text was lost when Saladin recaptured Jerusalem in 1187, but a new *Assise* was subsequently compiled.

Assommoir, L' (1877), by Émile Zola, one of the best of his *Rougon-Macquart* (q.v.) novels. Gervaise—daughter of Antoine Macquart and grand-daughter of Adèle Rougon —has come to Paris with her lover Lantier and their two children. She works in a laundry. Lantier is an idler. He deserts her and she marries Coupeau, a zinc-roofer. For a time the two lead a contented, industrious, not unprosperous life. Gervaise starts a laundry on borrowed money. It flourishes, but Coupeau has an accident and after a long convalescence he becomes lazy and a drunkard, squandering the household earnings in the *assommoir* (drinking-shop) of the *Père* Colombe. Gervaise too becomes indolent and greedy and her inherited tendency to drunkenness soon shows itself. The couple's downward trend has begun. Lantier reappears and remains, contentedly forming a *ménage à trois* with the couple until their increasing poverty can no longer provide him with ease and good living. The laundry fails, and husband and wife sink to besotted, bestial poverty. Coupeau dies of delirium tremens. Gervaise drags out an imbecile existence a few months longer.

The picture of working-class life, though it dwells mainly on brutality and degradation, is powerful and relentlessly drawn.

The book is also a notable example of Zola's care to intensify his naturalistic atmosphere, by describing life through the eyes of his characters, using the vocabulary that they would use, and making no artistic distinction between dialogue and narrative. Some of the descriptions remain in the memory, such as the *jeunes filles en fleurs* (à la Zola!), a band of vicious young girls from the slums, decked up in their Sunday finery, and patrolling the outer boulevards, arms linked and eyes roving; or the account of the wedding-day of Gervaise and Coupeau, when the whole party are forced to spend a wet afternoon at the Louvre until they can return home to an enormous wedding dinner.

Assonance, agreement in the last accented vowel of two or more metrical lines, but not in the consonants that follow or precede it (e.g. *tombe, onde*). This partial form of rhyme is characteristic of the *Chansons de geste* (q.v.) in their early form. It was reintroduced by the Symbolists (see *Symbolisme*), since when it is to be found frequently in modern poetry. (Cf. *Consonance*.)

Assouci, CHARLES COYPEAU, SIEUR D' (1605–75), burlesque writer, author of *Aventures burlesques* (a mocking account of incidents of his own life) and of a poor parody of Ovid.

Astrate, Roi de Tyr, a tragedy by Quinault, produced in 1664.

Élise has usurped the throne of Tyre, killing the legitimate king and two of his sons. A third son has escaped. Astrate, a young man who loves the queen and is loved by her, at the moment when he receives from her the royal ring, discovers that he is the son and brother of her murdered victims.

Astrée, L', a prose romance by Honoré d'Urfé, published in four parts, 1607–27. The fourth part was published posthumously by Balthazar Baro (q.v.), who in 1628 added a conclusion based on the author's notes and confidences.

The many stories and episodes in this work are supposed to occur on the banks of the little river Lignon (in the Forez district of the Lyonnais) in the 5th century, at a time when the barbarians were invading Gaul but when this region, under Queen Amasis, is depicted as free from their incursions. In its main features *L'Astrée* is a sentimental romance,

agreeably told, though somewhat insipid, diffuse, and overloaded with witty conceits for the modern taste, combining elements of history, adventure, chivalry, and pastoral life, and interspersed with madrigals and sonnets. It sets forth an ideal of polite and distinguished living, in which men and women of the world are shown in the guise of shepherds and shepherdesses. It depicts love as an honourable sentiment, of which virtue, modesty, and constancy are the leading characteristics, and displays the variety of its effects and of its conflicts with duty, honour, and so forth. The problems it raises are discussed in numerous conversations.

The principal substance of the plot is the love of the shepherd Céladon for the shepherdess Astrée. Suspecting him of infidelity she dismisses him; whereupon he throws himself into the river, but is rescued by three 'nymphs' of the queen's court. Their coquetries, however, he resists. But he dares not return to his mistress (except disguised as the daughter of a Druid) until she has revoked his dismissal, which (in the conclusion added by Balthazar Baro) she finally does, after both have been exposed to great dangers and Céladon has been wounded in an attack by the traitor Polémas on the kingdom of Amasis. The test of her lover's fidelity has been extended over several volumes, in the course of which the reader has also been told the story of the loves of Sylvandre (a saner and more robust lover than Céladon) and the virtuous Diane, of the inconstancy of Hylas (the lively champion of infidelity), and of the difficulties and adventures of a multitude of other couples, skilfully woven into the general scheme. The various stories are said to have some foundation in fact.

The work was ridiculed in Sorel's (q.v.) *Berger extravagant* (1627), but was nevertheless immensely popular, provided plots for many dramas, and contributed (with the Hôtel de Rambouillet) to improve the moral tone of society.

Astyanax, a character in Racine's *Andromaque* (q.v.).

Atala, ou les Amours de deux sauvages dans le désert (1801), a tale by Chateaubriand. The scene is Louisiana, in the 18th century.

Chactas, an aged Indian, tells his life-story to René, a young French exile (cf. *René*). As a young man he had been captured by a hostile tribe and saved by the maiden Atala, a Christian convert. The two fled and after long wandering arrived at a hermitage established by the missionary Père Aubry. Atala would gladly have consented to marry Chactas but for her mother's dying vow that she should take the veil. Too weak to fulfil the vow, yet too weak to resist her love for Chactas, she took poison, opening her heart to Chactas on her deathbed. (The scene when Chactas and Père Aubry bury Atala in the forest, near a mountain torrent, is one of Chateaubriand's most beautiful descriptive passages.) In after years, revisiting the spot, Chactas learnt from some passing Indians that Père Aubry had been murdered. His remains lay beside those of Atala.

Atala, like *René*, was originally intended by Chateaubriand to form part of *Les Natchez* (q.v.). Instead, he included both tales in *Le Génie du christianisme* (q.v.) but detached *Atala* and published it in advance.

Atalide, a character in Racine's *Bajazet* (q.v.).

Atelier, Théâtre de l', one of the foremost experimental theatres in Paris during the years before the 1939–45 war. It was run by Charles Dullin (1885–1949), one of the original company of the famous *Théâtre du Vieux-Colombier* (q.v.), who later assembled and trained his own company.

Ateliers nationaux. Under a national scheme instituted by the Provisional Government in 1848, after the February Revolution, unemployed men were taken on and, regardless of their former trades, set to work to level the Champ-de-Mars (q.v.). Their numbers, and the purposeless employment, made this a ruinous proceeding and in June 1848 the *ateliers nationaux* were abolished by decree of the *Assemblée constituante*. The distress and disillusionment caused by this action brought discontent (which had been mounting steadily) to a head and an insurrection followed, with four days of bitter street fighting (*les journées de juin*). It was repressed, with harsh reprisals, by General Cavaignac (1802–57), then War Minister (see *Révolution du 24 février, 1848; Republics*).

Athalie, a tragedy by Racine, his last drama, performed in 1691 by the young ladies of Saint-Cyr, but not produced in public until 1716, after the author's death. It is based on the story of Athaliah and Joash in 2 Kings xi and 2 Chronicles xxii–xxiii. It includes songs by a chorus of young girls of the tribe of Levi. It is regarded as a model of classical tragedy, and Sainte-Beuve (article on Sénecé) makes appreciation of it the touchstone of sound taste.

The scene is the Temple at Jerusalem. The impious Athaliah, widow of Jehoram and a worshipper of Baal, is queen of Judah, having, after the slaying of her son Ahaziah (in French Ochozias) by Jehu, destroyed all the children of the house of David. But one of them, the child Jehoash or Joash (Joas), has been saved by Jehoseba (Josabeth), his aunt, wife of the high priest Jehoiada(Joad), and for eight years has been secretly brought up in the Temple. The day has come on which Jehoiada purposes to proclaim him king. Athaliah, disturbed by an ominous dream, profanes the Temple by her presence, and recognizes in the young Joash the youth who in her dream menaced her life. She seeks in vain to discover his parentage, and suspicious of his origin demands his surrender, under threat of destruction of the Temple. Joash is presented to the Levites in the Temple and joyfully acclaimed. Athaliah is lured into the holy precinct, and is suddenly confronted with Joash, seated on the throne, surrounded by the Levites. News is brought that he has been proclaimed to the people and received with joy and thanksgiving, and that the Temple is free of its enemies. Athaliah, confessing the victory of the God of the Jews, is hauled off to death.

Athénée, L', or **Athénée royal,** see *Lycée*.

Athénée, Théâtre de l', the theatre in Paris with which the actor-producer Louis Jouvet (1887–1951, q.v.) was associated.

Athos, one of the heroes of *Les Trois Mousquetaires* (q.v.) by Dumas *père*.

Atlas linguistique de la France, see *Gilliéron, Jules*.

Attaque au moulin, L' (1880), a short story by Zola; see under *Soirées de Médan, Les*.

Attila, a tragedy by Corneille, produced in 1667. It suffered by comparison with Racine's *Andromaque* (q.v.), produced in the same year, and was one of the author's least successful plays.

Attila, the victorious king of the Huns, is hesitating between marriage with the proud Honorie, sister of the emperor Valentinian, and with Ildione, sister of the king of France. He learns that he has rivals in the persons of two conquered kings whom he drags with him in his suite. While menacing the lives of both, he offers to each the princess that he loves on condition that he will slay the other king. His murderous career is interrupted by his sudden death.

Atys (1676), an opera, by Quinault with music by Lulli (qq.v.).

Aubanel, THÉODORE (1829–86), poet, one of the *félibres* (q.v.). His works, written in Provençal, include, notably, the love-poems of *La Miougrano entraduberto* [*La Grenade entr'ouverte*] (1860). One of his plays, *Lou Pan dou pecat*, was produced in translation in Paris (*Le Pain du péché*, 1891).

Aube, see *Chansons à personnages.*

Auber, DANIEL-FRANÇOIS-ESPRIT (1782–1871), born at Caen, lived and died in Paris, was a well-known composer of light opera (in which the influence of Rossini has been noted) and for many years the musical partner of the dramatist Scribe (q.v.). In 1842 he succeeded Cherubini as head of the Paris *Conservatoire de musique.*

Auberée, a typical *fabliau* (q.v.). The substance of the story is found also in oriental collections of tales.

A young man is prevented from marrying the lady he loves, and to his despair she becomes the wife of a widower. An obliging seamstress, Auberée, engages to bring about a meeting between the lover and the lady. She borrows the former's fine cloak and hides in it a needle and a thimble, and calling upon the lady while her husband is out, contrives to conceal the cloak under the coverlet of their bed. The husband returning finds the cloak in the bed, and, inferring that his wife has been unfaithful to him, without more ado turns her out of doors. Here she is met by the seamstress, who, professing to give her shelter till the husband's delusion

shall be passed, takes the lady to her house, where the gallant joins her. To reassure the husband Auberée causes him to find his wife in a church in an edifying posture of prayer; and by lamenting that she has mislaid in some house a cloak that she was mending, and her needle and thimble withal, provides the explanation of the presence of the incriminating cloak. She thus brings the episode to an issue satisfactory to the various parties.

Auberge des Adrets, L' (first prod. 1823), a melodrama, see *Macaire, Robert.*

Auberge rouge, L,' one of the 'Études philosophiques' in Balzac's *Comédie humaine* (q.v.).

Aubert de La Chesnaye des Bois, FRANÇOIS-ALEXANDRE, see *Dictionaries and Encyclopedias,* under date 1767.

Aubignac, FRANÇOIS HÉDELIN, ABBÉ D' (*c.* 1604–*c.* 1673), author of indifferent dramas and other works, and of a *Pratique du théâtre* (1657) in which, besides giving valuable information on the 17th-century theatre in France, he vigorously defended the rule of the unities, as founded not on authority but on reason, and required by verisimilitude. It may be noted that he questioned the existence of Homer as a single poet. Some of his epigrams are directed against Corneille.

Aubigné, AGRIPPA D' (1552–1630), born in Saintonge, a man of heroic spirit and an ardent Protestant, sworn by his father to the support of the cause from his youth (see *Amboise*). He studied at Geneva under Théodore de Bèze (q.v.), and from 1573 served Henri de Navarre as soldier, diplomatist, and councillor. He left the court after the death of Henri IV and settled at Geneva, where he wrote the greater part of his works. His early poems (*Printemps*, not published until 1874) celebrated Diane Salviati, the niece of Ronsard's Cassandre, in verses marked with Italian affectation. His later works show religious enthusiasm. His chief poem, *Les Tragiques* (q.v.), was conceived about 1577, when he was recovering from a wound received in battle; it is a fierce denunciation of the evils he sees about him and of the enemies of the Reformation, tinged with the sombre spirit of the Old Testament prophets. It was published in

1616. D'Aubigné also wrote an *Histoire universelle* of the period 1550–1601, published in 1616–20, which centres in Henri IV and the Calvinist party, and is written with an effort at impartiality; it is of value as an historical narrative, but apart from some dramatic passages makes obscure and laborious reading. Besides this he wrote the *Aventures du baron de Fæneste* (q.v.), a satirical attack on papistry (1617); the *Confession de Sancy*, the imaginary confession of base motives by an apostate from the reformed religion; and an autobiography (*Sa vie à ses enfants*). D'Aubigné was grandfather of Mme de Maintenon (q.v.).

Au bonheur des dames (1883), one of Zola's *Rougon-Macquart* (q.v.) novels. Octave Mouret, a Provençal, son of François and Marthe Mouret (see *Conquête de Plassans, La*), and full of enthusiasm and commercial vision, acquires control of a moderately prosperous draper's shop in Paris. He exploits his success with women, and his understanding of the Second Empire craze for luxury and building development, and transforms the shop into an enormous, sensationally successful, department store, ruining small competitors mercilessly by the way. In its description of the transformation process, and of the machine at work, with publicity drives and adventurous commercial organization, the book at times recalls Balzac (e.g. *César Birotteau*, q.v.). Human interest is supplied by the intrigues of the staff and by Mouret's relations with one of his saleswomen, whose quiet charm and unwavering honesty defeat his hitherto all-conquering toughness.

Aubusson, in the Creuse, a department of central France, the site of a celebrated manufactory of carpets, dating from the 15th century.

Aubusson, PIERRE D' (1423–1503), Grand Master of the Knights of St. John from 1476, successfully conducted the defence of Rhodes in a famous siege by the Turks in 1480.

Aucassin et Nicolette, a *chante-fable* (i.e. prose narrative interspersed with verse, in this case of seven syllables) by an unknown author probably of the early 13th century, telling with exquisite delicacy the story of the loves of a youth and a maid in a world of mingled reality and fantasy. The work survived in a single manuscript rediscovered in 1752.

Aucassin is the young son of the lord of Beaucaire in Provence. Nicolette is a captive girl bought from the Saracens by one of the lord's vassals. Aucassin is deeply in love with Nicolette, but his parents will not hear of so unworthy a union and cause Nicolette's master to imprison her. Aucassin is so overcome by his love that he will not even fight for the defence of his father's castle until he is promised a brief word with her and a single kiss. But the father repudiates his pledge and Aucassin also is imprisoned. Nicolette escapes by night and sings outside Aucassin's prison of her love for him, till a friendly warder warns her of the approach of her enemies. She takes refuge in the forest and is thought to be lost or killed. The lord of Beaucaire releases Aucassin and tries to comfort him in his sorrow, but Aucassin sets out in search of Nicolette and eventually finds her. Together they escape to the coast and take ship to the strange and fabulous castle of Torelore, where they spend three years in happiness, until Saracens attack the castle and carry off the inhabitants. Nicolette is brought to Carthage, where the king recognizes her as his lost daughter. Aucassin is wrecked near Beaucaire and, his father now being dead, becomes lord of the place. Nicolette, threatened with marriage to a Saracen king, makes her way to Beaucaire disguised as a minstrel, and is reunited to her lover.

The charm of the work lies principally in the freshness and vividness of the scenes and characters it presents, e.g. Nicolette leaning out of her prison window, her descent from it in the moonlight, her talk with the shepherd boys in the forest, the sturdy ploughboy reproving Aucassin for his lack of spirit; Aucassin refusing to go to heaven without Nicolette, Nicolette as a minstrel, singing before Aucassin of their love.

Aude, in the *Chanson de Roland* (q.v.) and other *chansons de geste* (q.v.), the sister of Olivier and affianced to Roland. She dies of grief at the feet of Charlemagne when she learns the death of Roland.

Aude, LE CHEVALIER JOSEPH (1755–1841), a now forgotten author of farces and vaudevilles, and some time secretary to Buffon (q.v.), exploited the character Cadet Roussel, for long a type of well-meaning but pretentious nincompoop (*Cadet Roussel ou le Café des aveugles*, 1793; *Cadet Roussel barbier à la Fontaine des Innocents*, 1798, &c.). The 'Cadet Rousselle' of a song—author unknown—popular among the Revolutionary armies possessed three of everything, e.g.

> Cadet Rousselle a trois maisons,
> Qui n'ont ni poutres ni chevrons.
> C'est pour loger les hirondelles,

&c., and may have originated in a real personage named Roussel, an eccentric of Auxerre. He lived in one part of a house of which the other part was occupied by Restif de la Bretonne (q.v.).

Audefroi le bastard (13th century), a poet of Arras (q.v.), author of *romances* (q.v.) and other songs.

Au-dessus de la mêlée (1915), see under *Rolland, Romain.*

Audiberti, JACQUES (1899–   ), contemporary poet, author of the collections *Race des hommes* (1937), *Des tonnes de semences* (1941), *La Nouvelle Origine* (1942), *Toujours* (1944), *Vive guitare* (1950); also novelist (*Abraxas*, 1938; *Carnage*, 1942, &c.) and playwright (*Quoat-Quoat*, 1946; *Le Mal court*, 1947; *Pucelle*, 1950, &c.).

Audoux, MARGUERITE (1863–1937), born at Sancoins, near Nevers, and early parentless, was placed by the Public Assistance authorities as a farm worker. In 1881 she came to Paris, became a dressmaker, and wrote when she had time. A chance meeting led to literary friendships and the publication (with a preface by Octave Mirbeau, q.v.) of *Marie-Claire* (1910), an autobiographical novel written with great simplicity. *L'Atelier de Marie-Claire* (1920) continued the story.

Auerstadt, in Saxony, near Leipzig, where the French under Davout defeated the Prussians (14 October 1806) in Napoleon's campaign against the Fourth Coalition (q.v.). Jena (q.v.) followed.

Augé, CLAUDE, see *Dictionaries and Encyclopedias* under date 1865–76.

Auger, LOUIS-SIMON (1772–1829), man of letters, wrote essays and criticism of a con-ventional character, collected in *Mélanges philosophiques et littéraires* (1828). He edited many French classics.

Augereau, PIERRE-FRANÇOIS-CHARLES, one of Napoleon's marshals (see *Maréchal de l'Empire*).

Augier, ÉMILE (1820–89), dramatist, a grandson of Pigault-Lebrun (q.v.), was, like Ponsard (q.v.), a leader of the *école du bon sens* in the theatre, i.e. the reaction against the exaggerations of the Romantic Drama. His greatest successes were solid, well-constructed, conventional plays of bourgeois life which upheld the virtues of honesty, common sense, and wedded love. They included the well-known *Gendre de M. Poirier* (1854, prose, in collaboration with Jules Sandeau, q.v.); *Les Lionnes pauvres* (1858); *Maître Guérin* (1865); *Les Effrontés* (1861, prose), which satirized the Second Empire passion for money and speculation; and *Le Fils de Giboyer* (1862, prose). This, his greatest success, attacked contemporary efforts to mix religion and politics. Its hard-hitting satire provoked great indignation. His first two plays, in verse, were *L'Aventurière* (1848, q.v.) and *Gabrielle* (1850), the latter remembered for its banality.

Augustinus, see *Jansenius.*

Au jardin de l'Infante (1893), poems by Albert Samain (q.v.).

Aulard, ALPHONSE (1849–1928), historian of the French Revolution, noted for his studies of Danton (who was for him the hero of the Revolution), the *Jacobins*, the *Convention nationale*, the *Comité de salut public*, &c. His works include: *Études et leçons sur la Révolution française* (1893–1921) and *Histoire politique de la Révolution française* (1901).

Aulnoy (pron. as if *Onoy*), MARIE-CATHERINE, COMTESSE D' (c. 1650–1705), remembered as the author of fairy-tales (1698), among them the stories of the *Yellow Dwarf* and the *White Cat*, which have retained their popularity. She also wrote *Mémoires de la Cour d'Espagne* and some romances.

Aurélia, ou le rêve et la vie (1855), by Gérard de Nerval (q.v.), a remarkable description of his experiences while mentally deranged.

Aurore, L', a pro-Dreyfus (q.v.) daily paper founded in 1897 and remembered for its association with Clemenceau, its political editor, and Zola (see *J'accuse*).

Austerlitz, in Moravia (now Czecho-slovakia, then part of the Austrian Empire), where Napoleon in one of his most striking victories (2 Dec. 1805) defeated the Austro-Russian armies led by their Emperors (cf. *Pressburg*). On the morning of the battle Napoleon left his tent at four o'clock but the country was thickly enveloped in fog and remained so for several hours. When at length the sun—'le soleil d'Austerlitz'—broke through, 'and fields and mist were aglow with dazzling light . . . he drew the glove from his shapely white hand, made a signal with it to the marshals, and ordered the action to begin' [*War and Peace*, bk. iii, ch. xiv]. His proclamation to his soldiers after the battle ended with the words: 'Il vous suffira de dire: "J'étais à Austerlitz", pour que l'on vous réponde "Voilà un brave!"'

Austrasia, see *Mérovingiens*.

Autobiographies, see *Memoirs*.

Auton, JEAN D', see *Jean d'Auton*.

Autran, JOSEPH (1813–77), man of letters, born, and for many years town librarian, at Marseilles, wrote poetry influenced by Lamartine—*La Mer* (1835), *Ludibria Ventis* (1838), *Laboureurs et soldats* (1854), &c.—and a number of dramatic works. The best of these was a tragedy, *La Fille d'Eschyle* (1848).

Autrichienne, L', a nickname for Marie-Antoinette (q.v.).

Autun, Évêque d', a term sometimes used to designate Talleyrand (q.v.), who was appointed to the bishopric in 1788 before he embarked on his political career.

Aux flancs du vase (1898), poems by Albert Samain (q.v.).

Avant-garde, Théâtre(s) d', see *Theatres and theatre companies*.

Avare, L', a prose comedy by Molière, produced in 1668, based on the *Aulularia* of Plautus.

Harpagon, a rich miser, has a daughter, Élise, whom he wishes to marry to another old man, Anselme, because the latter is willing to take her without a dowry. He himself proposes to marry a young lady, Mariane, hoping to get a dowry with her. But his son Cléante already loves Mariane. Valère, a young man in love with Élise, takes service with Harpagon in the guise of a steward, hoping to further his suit. Cléante, determined to win Mariane from his father, obtains possession of a box containing part of Harpagon's treasure, and the old miser is distraught by its loss. Suspicion is thrown on Valère, who, by an amusing misunderstanding, thinks that he is being charged with designs on Élise, admits his guilt, and pleads the allurement of her 'beaux yeux' ('Les beaux yeux de ma cassette!' exclaims Harpagon). Finally the matter is cleared up. Harpagon surrenders his daughter to Valère, who is discovered to be the lost son of Anselme, and, in consideration of the return of his treasure, consents to his son's marriage with Mariane. But in his last words he stipulates that he is to be put to no expense.

In this grim comedy Molière showed how avarice not only kills all sense of dignity and paternal affection in the miser himself, but also provokes disrespect and revolt in his children. Nevertheless it was censured as immoral by J.-J. Rousseau.

A vau l'eau (1882), a long-short story by J.-K. Huysmans (q.v.).

M. Folantin, an elderly, impecunious civil servant, lives alone, bullied by concierges and charwomen. In the evenings he samples cheap restaurants. His drab expeditions and the nauseating food he encounters are described in minute detail. This tale was said by the critic Remy de Gourmont to be typical of all Huysmans's works: 'En chacun . . . il s'agit d'un monsieur qui s'ennuie, cherche à améliorer sa vie et n'y parvient pas.'

Avenir, L', a journal with the motto 'Dieu et Liberté', was founded in 1830 by the reformer Lamennais, with the assistance of Lacordaire and Montalembert (qq.v.), to promote ideals of spiritual and political liberty and the establishment of a Christian democracy. It lasted till 1832, its career being bound up with that of Lamennais himself.

Avenir de la science, L', by Ernest Renan (q.v.), was not published till 1890 but he wrote it some forty years earlier, after his break with orthodox religion and largely to take stock of his own mental attitude. He urged the need for more, and more specialized, study of the philosophical sciences as a means of arriving at ultimate truth. For instance, he suggested, the evolution of human thought and beliefs was to be traced through the study of comparative philology and comparative religion. He also, in this book, roughed out his idea for his great work (1863–83) on *Les Origines du Christianisme*.

Avenir de l'intelligence, L' (1905), by Charles Maurras (q.v.), essays.

Avent. Two 17th-century preachers, Bourdaloue and Massillon (qq.v.), delivered notable Advent sermons (later printed), Bourdaloue between 1670 and 1693, and Massillon in 1699.

Aventures de Jérôme Bardini, Les (1930), a novel by Jean Giraudoux (q.v.).

Aventures du baron de Fæneste, Les, see *Fæneste.*

Aventures du dernier Abencérage, Les (1826), by Chateaubriand, a short tale of honour, chivalry, and fidelity set in 16th-century Spain after the Moors have been driven out by the Spaniards. The noble, but infidel, Aben-Hamet, last of the tribe of the Abencérages who had formerly ruled in Granada, loves and is loved by Bianca, a Christian, daughter of the Spanish governor of Granada. Religion, and a long history of blood and cruelty between the two families, are inseparable barriers to their union and the two must live out their lives apart. *He* returns to the African desert and gradually disappears from man's ken, but in the cemetery by ruined Carthage *le tombeau du dernier Abencérage* can still (says Chateaubriand) be seen. *She* grows old in Granada, with memories for company. Shortly after 1814 Chateaubriand read this tale in Madame Récamier's *salon* to a company which included Mme de Staël, Wellington, Bernadotte, and other leading figures of European society.

Aventures du Roi Pausole, Les (1900), a novel by Pierre Louÿs (q.v.).

Aventurière, L' (1848), a comedy (5 acts, verse) by Émile Augier (q.v.). The scene is 16th-century Padua.

Monte Prado, an elderly noble, will hear nothing against Clorinde, an adventuress, and insists on marrying her, even at the cost of disgracing his name and so making it impossible for the young lovers Célie (his daughter) and Horace (his nephew) to marry. His son Fabrice returns in disguise after many years' absence. Célie and Horace arouse his pity and making himself known to them he engineers a plot by which his father's eyes are opened to Clorinde's real profession. Thus all ends well for the young pair. Yet the ending has a deeper note. In the final scenes Clorinde shows qualities of self-sacrifice which fill Fabrice with respect for the only sincere love he has ever known. Perhaps, after all, Monte Prado would have found himself married to a loving and dutiful wife who asked nothing better than to settle down to a dull, honest, and respectable existence.

Averroès et l'Averroïsme (1852), by Renan (q.v.), his doctoral thesis.

Aveugle, L' (i.e. Homer), a famous poem by André Chénier (q.v.).

Aveugle et le Boiteux, L', a *moralité* by André de la Vigne, performed in 1496, as a companion piece to the mystery of Saint Martin. Two beggars, one blind, the other lame, implore compassion. But they are in reality idle, drunken rascals. They confide in one another that their infirmities are a welcome source of income. But they are disconcerted by the news of the miracles of healing wrought by the body of Saint Martin. They resolve to flee, the lame man on the back of the blind man; but they meet the saint's procession and are cured. The blind man is delighted by the recovery of his sight, the lame man decides to feign his old infirmity and other claims to pity.

Aveugles de Compiègne, Les Trois, a typical *fabliau* (q.v.). Three blind men are trudging along the road from Compiègne to Senlis. A merry scholar who comes along says to them 'Here is a bezant for the three of you', but gives nothing, and each of the vagrants thinks that one of the others has received the lavish alms. At an inn, observed by the scholar, they enjoy a sumptuous repast, and only when it comes to settling the score do they discover that none has the money. They quarrel and fight, to the diversion of the scholar, who however takes pity and tells the landlord that he will pay, or the priest for him. Scholar and landlord go to the church, where the former takes the priest aside: 'Sir, this good man, your parishioner, is possessed. Here is tenpence: read the Gospel over his head.' 'Wait till I've said my mass and I'll settle your affair', says the priest to the landlord, who, re-assured, waits patiently; meanwhile the scholar makes off. When the mass is finished, the landlord is bidden to kneel. In vain he protests that he wants, not exorcism, but his money. This is put down to his delusions. His resistance is overcome and he is forced to undergo the ceremony.

Aveugles, Lettre sur les, see *Lettre.*

Avignon, the capital, originally, of the marquisate of Provence, constituted itself a republic at the end of the 12th century to escape the domination of the counts of Toulouse. It was captured by Louis VIII in 1226 and ceded to the Count of Provence. From 1309 to 1378 it was the residence of seven popes in succession, and from 1378 to 1408 of two anti-popes. The town had been sold to Clement VI (one of the above popes) in 1348 by Joanna I of Naples, countess of Provence. It remained a papal possession till 1791. The town is famous also for its connexion with Petrarch, who migrated there in 1313 and there first saw Laura. (Cf. *Vaucluse.*)

Avril, see *Belleau.*

Axël (1890), a drama of Wagnerian character by Villiers de l'Isle-Adam (q.v.), appeared first in Symbolist reviews. The plot evolves round a treasure said to be hidden in the secret vaults of Auërsperg, an ancient castle isolated in a German forest. The time is *c.* 1828. The scene turns from a nunnery in Flanders to the castle. Axël, the young lord of Auërsperg, fearful of arousing harmful passions, discourages interest in the treasure. Kaspar, a relative, abuses Axël's hospitality by trying to fathom the truth of the legend. The two fight a duel. Axël kills his opponent, but now visions of the treasure tempt him. At night in the family vault he

surprises Sara, an escaped novice whose readings in Rosicrucian books have given her the clue to the secret. (Her dramatic refusal to take the vows and her escape from the nunnery form Part I of the drama.) She has just worked the charm by which the walls and floor of the vault recede and cascades of gold and jewels pour from every side. She attempts to kill Axël. He disarms her, but raising the weapon in his turn is overcome by her rare beauty, as she by his. The two remain, talking of their sudden passion. Sara paints a future in which, thanks to the power the treasure will confer on them, no desire need remain unfulfilled, no corner of the world unexplored. But Axël persuades her that life has no further joys to equal this night of anticipation. The day dawns, and from a jewelled cup found among the treasure the lovers drink swift death. This play's symbolic value and its influence on later literature have been increasingly recognized by modern critics.

Aymé, MARCEL (1902–), contemporary author of novels, e.g. *Aller Retour* (1928), *La Jument verte* (1933), *Le Moulin de la Sourdine* (1936); and, since the 1939–45 war, of plays, e.g. *Lucienne et le Boucher* (1948). He is, in addition, a particularly happy writer of children's stories, e.g. *Les Contes du chat perché* (1934).

Aymon, Les Quatre Fils, the four brothers whose exploits are described in *Renaud de Montauban* (q.v.), a *chanson de geste.* The later, very popular, prose version of this tale was called *Les Quatre Fils Aymon* (see *Bibliothèque bleue*).

Azincourt, in medieval times AGINCOURT, a village in Northern France, not far from Arras. At the battle of Agincourt, on 25 October 1415, St. Crispin's Day, Henry V of England defeated a very much larger French army led by le connétable d'Albret. (The *Maison* d'Albret, a Gascon duchy, was united to the crown of France in 1607 by Henri IV, q.v.)

Aziyadé (1879), a novel by Pierre Loti (q.v.).

B

Babeuf, FRANÇOIS-ÉMILE (1760–97), who called himself 'Caius-Gracchus, Tribun du peuple', was a Revolutionary politician and journalist whose ideas of State control and organization of property, employment, and the individual were an interesting anticipation of present-day communistic theories. He himself had bitter personal experience of poverty, oppression, and hunger. Between 1789 and 1795 both in his native province (Picardy) and in Paris his red-hot devotion to Revolutionary principles often landed him in trouble. By 1796 he was convinced that the events of the last seven years had only resulted in the rise of a new dominating class. He engineered a conspiracy, which narrowly missed success, to overthrow the Directoire and frame a new constitution more akin to the original ideals of the Revolution. It was betrayed and its leaders were arrested. Babeuf was taken in a cage to Vendôme and sentenced to death (but committed suicide) after a long trial at which he spoke movingly and impressively in defence of freedom of speech and action, of equality, and the sovereign rights of the people. Thirty of his followers ('Babouvistes') were executed and many more deported or sent to penal servitude. In 1828 one of his fellow conspirators, Michel Buonarotti (1761–1837), who had been deported and later lived in Geneva, Belgium, and Paris, published *La Conspiration pour l'égalité*, which reawakened interest in Babeuf and did much to stimulate the romantic socialism of the 1830's.

The *Journal de la liberté de la presse*, later entitled *Le Tribun du peuple*, was a paper edited by Babeuf in Paris between August 1794 and April 1796.

Babouc, Le Monde comme il va, Vision de, a philosophic tale by Voltaire, probably composed in 1747 at Sceaux, published in 1748, a revised edition in 1749, with the title *Babouc, ou le Monde comme il va*. It illustrates the author's earlier, more optimistic philosophy.

Ituriel, one of the spirits that preside over the empires of the world, angered at the follies and excesses of the Persians, sends the Scythian Babouc on a mission to Persepolis, to report on all that he sees there, so that it may be decided whether the city shall be exterminated or corrected. Babouc is filled alternately with disgust and admiration at what he sees: instances of cruelty, superstition, licentiousness, venality on the one hand; of bravery, learning, fidelity, generosity on the other. On his report Ituriel decides to 'laisser aller le monde comme il va, car, dit-il, si tout n'est pas bien, tout est passable'.

Babouvistes, followers of Babeuf (q.v.).

Bacbuc, see *Pantagruel* (*Cinquième livre*).

Baccalauréat, the state examination taken by pupils at the end of their secondary school education, a necessary first step to university studies and most forms of professional career. It is, roughly, the equivalent of the General Certificate of Education. The slang term is *bachot*.

Bachaumont, FRANÇOIS DE (1624–1702), a wit and man of pleasure, a versifier in a modest way, author with Chapelle (q.v.) of the lively *Voyage en Provence et Languedoc* (1656).

Bachaumont, LOUIS PETIT DE (1690–1771), publicist, author of *Mémoires secrets pour servir à l'histoire de la république des lettres en France depuis 1762*, containing daily records of incidents, art, fashion, opinions, and general literary intelligence, published in 1777, after his death. They were continued until 1787 by other hands, and are of some historical value.

Bachelier de Salamanque, Le (1736), a novel, his last, by Lesage (q.v.).

Bachot, see *Baccalauréat*.

Backer, GEORGE DE, see *Dictionaries and Encyclopedias*, under date 1718.

Baculard d'Arnaud, see *Arnaud*.

Badebec, in Rabelais, the wife of Gargantua, died in giving birth to Pantagruel (qq.v.).

Badinguet, a nickname for Prince Louis-Napoléon Bonaparte (afterwards Napoléon III, q.v.). It refers to his escape from the fortress of Ham in 1846, disguised as a workman of this name.

Bague d'Annibal, La (1843), an early novel by Jules Barbey d'Aurevilly (q.v.).

Baïf, JEAN-ANTOINE DE (1532–89), poet, born at Venice, where his father Lazare de Baïf (q.v.) was ambassador. He was one of the members of the *Pléiade* (q.v.), a man whose poetical talent was not equal to his great learning. He wrote works of many kinds, including love poems, epitaphs, adaptations from Greek and Latin dramatists, and a translation of the Psalms, employing alexandrines, decasyllabics, and verses of shorter measure with ease and fluency, but without taste and judgement. His comedy *Le Brave ou Taillebras*, adapted from the *Miles Gloriosus* of Plautus, in octosyllabic verse, was performed in 1567. He also adapted *L'Eunuque* from Terence (published 1573) and the *Antigone* of Sophocles. His most important work was his *Mimes* (1581), a miscellany of moral and satirical pieces. He was an experimenter in matters of language and versification, trying to introduce quantitative verse and phonetic spelling. He founded, in 1570, under the patronage of Charles IX, an 'Académie de poésie et de musique', but it was brought to an end after a few months by the civil war.

Baïf, LAZARE DE (1485–1547), French ambassador in Italy under Henri II, translated the *Electra* of Sophocles (1537) into alexandrines, one of the earliest steps towards the introduction of tragedy (in its 16th-century form) in France. He was father of Jean-Antoine de Baïf.

Baillet, ADRIEN (1649–1706), an erudite and assiduous compiler (e.g. *Jugements des savants sur les principaux ouvrages des auteurs*, 1685 and 1686, 9 vols., reaching half-way through the second of six sections contemplated; *Des Enfants devenus célèbres par leurs études et par leurs écrits*, 1688); author, also, of a *Vie de Descartes* (1691) still considered useful; and of various devotional works. He was ascetic to a degree: slept little (and then seldom undressed), ate once a day, drank no wine, never had a fire to warm himself when he was alone, doctored his indifferent health solely with hot or cold water and vinegar; and only once a week (on Mondays) exchanged the companionship of his studies or of other scholars for a little fresh air.

Bailli, Sénéchal. The kingdom of France was divided into *gouvernements*, and the *gouvernements* into *bailliages* (in Northern France) or *sénéchaussées* (in Southern). The *bailli* or *sénéchal* was the judge representing the king in the latter areas. His jurisdiction was subordinate to that of the *parlements* (q.v.).

Bailly, SYLVAIN (1736–93), a distinguished astronomer and man of letters, author of a notable history of astronomy (1775–87). During the Revolution he was for a month president of the *Assemblée nationale*, then mayor of Paris. He was guillotined in 1793. As he waited in the cold rain during the preparations for his execution, someone said to him, 'Tu trembles, Bailly'; to which he replied simply, 'Oui, mon ami, mais c'est de froid.'

Bainville, JACQUES (1879–1936), popular historian, author of an *Histoire de France* (1924), also of one of the outstanding modern studies of Napoleon (1931); and of *Histoire de deux peuples. La France et l'Empire Allemand* (1915) and *Histoire de trois générations, 1815–1918* (1918), two works of political history in which Franco-German relations are studied and the part played by internal policy in France in determining her conduct of foreign affairs. This author was one of the chief contributors to the Monarchist *Action française* (q.v.) and his writings were not wholly free from political bias.

Baiser au lépreux, Le (1922), a novel by François Mauriac (q.v.).

Bajazet, a tragedy by Racine, produced in 1672, founded on an actual occurrence at Constantinople in 1638.

The scene is Constantinople. The sultan Amurath is absent at the siege of Babylon. He has left his brother Bajazet imprisoned in the seraglio at Constantinople. Acomat, the grand vizier, knowing himself suspected by Amurath, plots to overthrow him, and for this purpose favours the love of the sultana Roxane for Bajazet. She is to release Bajazet, marry him, and place him on the throne. The supposed love of Bajazet for Atalide, a young Ottoman princess, serves as a pretext for their interviews. But Bajazet has deceived both Acomat and Roxane: he and Atalide really love one another, and he has pretended to respond to the passion of Roxane only to gain his freedom. When Roxane demands an immediate marriage, he temporizes. Roxane becomes suspicious, and her fury breaks out when a letter found in Atalide's possession reveals his perfidy. An order arrives from Amurath for the execution of Bajazet, and Roxane abandons him to the mutes, who strangle him. But the sultan, who has learnt of Roxane's infidelity, has ordered her death also, and this follows. Atalide kills herself on her lover's body.

Balafré, Le, a nickname given to two members of the house of Guise (q.v.): François the second duke (1519–63) and Henri his son, the third duke (1550–88). The word means 'scarred on the face'.

Balbec, the seaside resort where Marcel, in Proust's *A la recherche du temps perdu* (q.v.), stays on two occasions and where he meets Albertine (q.v.). It figures notably in the sections *A l'ombre des jeunes filles en fleurs* and *Sodome et Gomorrhe*. The model for it was Cabourg, in Normandy, where Proust himself used to stay.

Bal Bullier, see *Bals populaires*.

Bal de Sceaux, Le, one of the 'Scènes de la vie privée' in Balzac's *Comédie humaine* (q.v.).

Bal des pendus, Le, a poem by Rimbaud (q.v.).

Bal du comte d'Orgel, Le (1924), a novel by Raymond Radiguet (q.v.).

Ballade, a poem consisting either of three *dizains* (ten-lined stanzas) of ten-syllabled lines with an *envoi* (q.v.) of five lines, or of three *huitains* (eight-lined stanzas) of eight-syllabled lines with an *envoi* of four lines. The rhyme-scheme for the ballade in *dizains* is:

ababbccdcD, three times, followed by ccdcD.

For the ballade in *huitains* it is:

ababbcbC, three times, followed by bcbC.

In both types the last line of the first stanza is repeated as the last line of the other two

stanzas and of the *envoi*, thus (as indicated by the capital letters in the rhyme-scheme) forming the refrain.

There are occasional departures from the regular forms. Villon (q.v.), for instance, sometimes wrote ballades with *huitains* of ten-syllabled lines. Villon was the greatest writer of ballades, but there are good examples in Marot and later poets.

The *Double ballade* is composed of six *dizains* or six *huitains* similar to the above, usually without *envoi*.

Ballade des dames du temps jadis, see *Villon*.

Ballade des pendus, by Villon (q.v.), composed when he was under sentence of death in 1463.

Ballanche, PIERRE-SIMON (1776–1847), Christian philosopher (cf. his contemporaries *Joseph de Maistre* and *Bonald*), born in Lyons. He gave up publishing for travel and eventually settled in Paris. His mystical conceptions of universal religion, of 'harmonies', and of poetry as the expression of the universal mind, had some influence on 19th-century thought. His writings, poetical but obscure, included *Du Sentiment considéré dans ses rapports avec la littérature et les arts* (1801), in some degree a forerunner of Chateaubriand's *Génie du Christianisme* (q.v.); *Antigone* (1814); *Essai sur les institutions sociales dans leurs rapports avec les idées nouvelles* (1818); *Essais de palingénésie sociale* (1827). The last, in two volumes (*Prolégomènes* and *Orphée*), is a philosophical epic in prose, inspired by the myth of Atlantis as told by Plato in the *Timaeus*. Ballanche was a friend of Joubert and of Mme Récamier (qq.v.).

Ballet, introduced into France from Italy in the time of Catherine de Médicis, had a great vogue at court in the 17th century. It was developed by Benserade (q.v.), who excelled in the rhymed commentaries and epigrams which he added to the pantomimic dances. From this Molière evolved the *comédie-ballet* (q.v.).

Ballette, see *Chansons à danser*.

Bals populaires, public dance-halls and places of amusement, sometimes out of doors, more often on the premises of cafés or drinking-shops. Forerunners of the modern night club, *café-concert*, *café-chantant*, or *dancing*, they were dotted all over Paris in the years between the Revolution and the end of the Second Empire, and catered for various classes, from nobles to ragpickers. There are many references to them in novels, e.g. Balzac, Murger's *Vie de Bohème*, Zola's *L'Assommoir*, or in light comedies and vaudevilles of the Restoration and July Monarchy periods; and the different types are described in, for example, Taine's *Graindorge* (q.v.). They had mostly disappeared before the end of the 19th century. One of the few to be remembered by name was the *Bal Bullier*, which formed part of the Closerie des Lilas, a café on the boulevard Montparnasse. 'Bullier' was the name of the proprietor. In Henry James's *The American* it was the dream of the young marquise de Bellegarde, hidebound by propriety and the shades of her ancestors, to go to the Bal Bullier, 'the ball in the Latin Quarter, where the students dance with their mistresses'.

Balsamo, JOSEPH, see *Cagliostro*.

Baluze, ÉTIENNE (1630–1718), a man of great erudition, employed by Colbert as librarian. Editor of the *Capitulaires* or edicts of the Carolingian kings, &c.

Balzac, HONORÉ [self-styled 'DE'] (1799–1850), one of the great novelists of all literature, author of *La Comédie humaine* (q.v.), came of Midi peasant stock through his grandfather, whose surname had originally been 'Balssa', and of Parisian stock through his mother. He was born at Tours, where his father had an employment to do with army supplies. At the Collège des Oratoriens at Vendôme (1807–13) he seemed a loutish, far from brilliant pupil, but he was, in secret, devouring the school library so rapidly that he had a breakdown. (This period of his life provided material for his tale of a youthful prodigy, *Louis Lambert*, q.v.) By 1814 his father was employed in Paris and Balzac went to a private school. Then, in a lawyer's office, he acquired the sound knowledge of law and the ways of lawyers which pervades his work. At the same time, at the Sorbonne, he followed the lectures to which Cousin, Guizot, and Villemain (qq.v.) were drawing large audiences. In 1819 his parents agreed to his forsaking law for literature, and gave him a meagre allowance. On this he scraped along

in a garret and wrote poems, history, a tragedy (*Cromwell*), all equally bad. In 1820 his parents made him return home to Villeparisis, near Paris, where they had retired. Between then and 1825 he published several bad, sensational novels under pseudonyms (see *Saint-Aubin, Horace de*) but earned neither fame nor money. Then, once more on his own in Paris, he devoted himself to grandiose, often harebrained, commercial schemes in the hope of winning fortune and freedom to write. But in spite of financial help from Mme de Berny ('la Dilecta', the first of many women friends) he was, at the age of twenty-nine, over 100,000 francs in debt. His enduring mania for speculation and his equally strong collector's passion date from these years: the two were to prevent him from ever getting clear of debt. Undaunted by failure he returned to his pen and within five months had produced *Les Chouans* (1829, q.v.). This, the first novel to be published under his own name, and his first success, showed his great gift for setting a scene with living figures, acting from plausible motives. He had at last got into his stride. His output became prodigious—some ninety-one novels and tales between 1829 and 1848 over and above the increasing demands of regular journalism. Thenceforward his life-history was that of his writing, of his continual speculative enterprises and financial crises (often necessitating ingenious escapes from creditors), and of his friendships with women. In 1832, shortly after the publication of *La Peau de chagrin* (q.v.), a letter of admiration and criticism reached him from Poland, signed 'L'Étrangère'. This began a long correspondence and —without hindering others—a liaison with Mme Hanska (1801–82), a wealthy Polish countess. The outcome, in the year 1850, was marriage, after Mme Hanska had been eight years a widow, and too late for her money to be of use: Balzac, whose powers had been failing for some time, had only a few months to live.

As early as 1834 Balzac contemplated grouping his novels and tales as sections of one composite whole, to be issued under a collective title which would indicate purpose and scope. This intention became fact with the 1842–8 collected edition (17 vols.), in which the order and grouping of the separate works was his. There were three main groups: *Études de mœurs, Études philosophiques, Études analytiques*. The system of classification, with the repetition of the word 'étude', implied a scientific basis for the work and shows Balzac a true child of an age in which Geoffroy Saint-Hilaire was breaking new ground in natural science. (Balzac's interest, frequently evident, in Mesmer, Gall, Lavater, Swedenborg, &c., may also be mentioned.)

To the whole work he gave the title *La Comédie humaine*, possibly in imitation of Dante's *Divine Comedy*, and said of it: 'Une génération est un drame à quatre ou cinq mille personnages saillants. Ce drame, c'est mon livre.' *La Comédie humaine* is a panorama of French society during the Consulate, the Empire, the Restoration, and the July Monarchy. Throughout the various volumes the characters—more than two thousand in all—appear and reappear at different stages of their existence and, like the actors in a stock company, take now principal now minor parts. The framework of the whole is genealogical and geographical, perhaps geological too, for all strata of society and all professions are represented. The underlying theme is that money can do everything. Restraints of religion, or of monarchical or parental authority, have vanished, leaving self-interest as the supreme motive of human conduct. The way to success is paved with money, and whoever wishes to acquire wealth must play a dangerous game in which the stakes are wealth or disgrace.

For the separate works which make up the *Comédie humaine*, with dates, and the groups into which they fall, see *Comédie humaine*. Here it may be noted that some of Balzac's most famous studies of Parisian and provincial life fall into the group of *Études de mœurs*, e.g. *Eugénie Grandet, La Cousine Bette, Le Cousin Pons, Le Père Goriot*, and the whole series of tales through which Vautrin, the master criminal, makes his sinister way.

Balzac's genius consists in: his dynamic, unflagging, creative vigour; his superabundant imagination, which has in it a fantastic, visionary strain all the more forcible for being allied to remarkable powers of realistic observation and delineation of character (his most sensational incidents read like something that must have happened or might easily happen, and in his care for *documentation* he is a precursor of

le réalisme, q.v.); his masterly portrayal of passions which, if not always vicious in themselves, have a devastating effect upon men's lives, e.g. avarice (*Eugénie Grandet*), jealousy (*La Cousine Bette*), exaggerated paternal affection (*Le Père Goriot*), insensate devotion to science (*La Recherche de l'absolu*); his grasp of such widely differing subjects as geology, architecture, mysticism, and finance, and his acute business sense, e.g. when he describes *le père* Grandet's monetary affairs (*Eugénie Grandet*) or the launching of César Birotteau's hair-oil and the complicated arrangements for marketing and publicity (*Histoire de la grandeur et de la décadence de César Birotteau*), or discusses the most profitable manner of working the Mortsauf property (*Le Lys dans la vallée*). His descriptive powers are at their most characteristic in long, cumulative portraits. His style has none of the limpidity, harmony, or rhythm of the great French stylists: it hammers its way to comprehensive expression through the vast resources of his thought, and becomes 'le style nécessaire, fatal et mathématique de son idée' (Th. Gautier). His greatness as a novelist can be measured by the fact that the characters he created are discussed and used as types for comparison as if they had actually existed. He himself is said to have interrupted a friend recounting some family trouble with 'Revenons à la réalité. Avec qui marierons-nous Eugénie Grandet?' Paul Bourget said of him: 'Balzac semble avoir moins observé la société de son époque qu'il n'a contribué à en former une.'

His practice in writing was extravagant in cost (because his bills for printers' corrections exceeded what he made from his books) and in labour. He worked from ten to fourteen hours daily, often going to bed at six in the evening and rising at midnight to write till the following mid-day, subsisting meanwhile on strong black coffee brewed by himself. His first draft for the printer was little but a skeleton. On the proofs he enlarged this till the pages were a labyrinth of erasures, emendations, and insertions. He then called for fresh proofs and might repeat the process several times, till the printers detested working on his copy. The first draft of *Le Médecin de campagne* was written in seventy-two hours, but the subsequent rewriting took sixty nights.

Besides the pseudonymous novels and the

Comédie humaine Balzac wrote the *Contes drolatiques* (1832–7), imitations of Rabelais, written for recreation, and he contributed historical and political articles to periodicals. In his last years, hoping to save his fortunes from wreck, he turned to the drama, with *Vautrin* (1840), based on the Vautrin of his novels; *Les Ressources de Quinola* (1842); *La Marâtre* (1848), and *Le Faiseur*, a 5-act comedy which was adapted, renamed *Mercadet* (q.v.), and produced after his death. *Lettres à l'Étrangère* (1899–1906, 2 vols.) are his correspondence with Mme Hanska.

Balzac, JEAN-LOUIS GUEZ DE (1594–1654), essayist and stylist, a gentleman of the province of Angoumois, for some time in the service of the duc d'Épernon, governor of that province, and then of the cardinal de Valette, whose agent he was in Rome. He retired to his estate of Balzac in 1624, where he spent the greater part of the remainder of his life in an affectation of antique wisdom. He is remembered as having perfected French prose in the same manner that Malherbe perfected French verse, making it orderly and lucid, constructing the eloquent period (based on assiduous study of the Latin authors, especially Cicero), and thus preparing the way for Pascal and Bossuet. The matter of his writings is of less importance than the form, for they were among the first pieces of deliberate French prose composition. He expressed sound, if somewhat pessimistic, opinions (some of them commonplaces from ancient authors) on ethics, politics, and literature; but he also shows love of rustic scenery and he can give an agreeable turn to his wisdom. His *Le Prince* (on the political situation of France under Louis XIII, with a flattering portrait of the king) appeared in 1631; *Le Barbon* (a satire) in 1648; *Socrate chrétien* (a series of dialogues and discourses on religious subjects) in 1652; his *Entretiens*, mostly on literary subjects, collected (after his death) in 1657; and *Aristippe*, his favourite work, on wisdom in political administration (also published posthumously) in 1658. The first collection of his *Lettres* (elaborate dissertations) appeared in 1624. His writings were much admired by his contemporaries and he was made a member of the *Académie française*, but attended its meetings only once.

Bamboche, from *Bamboccio* (cripple), nick-name of Pieter van Laar (1613–74?), Dutch painter of scenes of humble life, whence *bambochade* for genre pictures of this kind. The brothers Le Nain (q.v.) were distinguished for works of this character.

Banc d'œuvre, a special pew in church, a privilege accorded only to the nobility, in pre-Revolutionary France.

Bandello, MATTEO (1480?–1562), an Italian, nephew of a celebrated theologian, and himself also a Dominican, born and brought up in Italy. As a result of the vicissitudes of war and fortune he passed into the service of France and finally settled at Agen. He was made a bishop but devoted himself mainly to writing (in Italian) tales much influenced by Boccaccio. These were the *Novelle* later translated by Belleforest and Boaistuau (qq.v.). In English literature Bandello, or Bandello via Belleforest, was one of the sources of Geoffrey Fenton's *Tragical Discourses* (1567) and Painter's *Palace of Pleasure* (1566–7), and an influence on Elizabethan drama (the source, for instance, of *Romeo and Juliet*).

Ban et de l'arrière-ban, Appel du, under feudal custom, the summoning of the king's vassals and the population at large to the king's support in an emergency; a sort of levy in mass. All possessed of a fief were required to attend the king on horseback, gratis, for three months.

Banquet, Le, a small literary review which ran for eight numbers in 1892. It was founded and written, on a very high level of promise and excellence, by former pupils of the Lycée Condorcet, among whom were Marcel Proust and Léon Blum.

Banquets. In July 1847 the Opposition party circumvented the law against public meetings by organizing political banquets at which speakers, among whom the poet Lamartine was one of the most popular, agitated for liberal and electoral reform. The Government's refusal to allow one of these banquets to be held (on 22 Feb. 1848) provoked manifestations which grew unexpectedly serious and developed into the February Revolution (see *Revolutions*; *Republics*, paras. 2, 3; and cf. the description in Flaubert's *Éducation sentimentale*).

Banville, THÉODORE FAULLAIN DE (1823–91), poet, dramatist, and man of letters. His verse charmed by its delicately lyrical quality and its mixture of sentiment and irony; and he had a great command of language and rhythm, as well as a remarkable facility for rhyming. His first collection was *Les Cariatides* (1842). In *Les Stalactites* (1846), *Le Sang de la coupe* (1857), and *Les Exilés* (1867), his best work, perfection of form and choice of subject show him to have been a precursor of the *Parnassiens* (q.v.); and he was, in 1866, one of the thirty-seven contributors to *Le Parnasse contemporain*. *Odes funambulesques* (1857) was a collection of light, often topical verse, full of fantasy and witty rhymes. In *Trente-six ballades joyeuses à la manière de François Villon* (1873) and the *Rondels à la manière de Charles d'Orléans* (in *Poésies*, 1875) he employed forms long disused, e.g. the rondel, villanelle, triolet. His other collections of poems included *Roses de Noël* (1878), *Sonnailles et clochettes* (1890), *Dans la fournaise* (1892), &c. His most successful comedies were *Gringoire* (1866) and *Riquet à la houppe* (1885). He also wrote tales of Parisian life, e.g. *Esquisses parisiennes* (1859), *Contes bourgeois* (1891); and a *Petit traité de poésie française* (1872), still one of the most useful expositions of the French art of versification. One chapter is notable for its brevity: 'Licences poétiques. Il n'y en a pas.'

Baour-Lormian, MARIE-FRANÇOIS (1770–1854), author of occasional verse and of conventional tragedies, e.g. *Omasis ou Joseph en Égypte* (1807), *Mahomet* (1811); an adversary of the Romantics (see *Romantisme*). He translated Ossian (1801) and Tasso (*Jérusalem délivrée*, 1795).

Barante, GUILLAUME-PROSPER BRUGIÈRE, BARON DE (1782–1866), born at Riom (Auvergne), historian, also literary critic and, for some time, diplomat. In his famous *Histoire des Ducs de Bourgogne de la Maison de Valois* (1824–6), based on chronicles of the 15th century, he aimed at presenting history in the form of objectively written narrative, with all the interest of a historical novel. His other works included a *Tableau de la littérature française au XVIIIᵉ siècle* (1809). In youth he was a devoted admirer of Mme de Staël (q.v.).

Barbe-Bleue, Perrault's (q.v.) tale of Bluebeard. See also *Retz* (or *Rais*), *Gilles de*.

Barberine, a comedy (prose) by Alfred de Musset (q.v.), a revised and augmented version (three acts instead of two, and more characters) of his earlier *La Quenouille de Barberine*. The latter, first published in the *Revue des Deux Mondes* of 1 August 1835, had been included in the first edition (1840) of *Comédies et Proverbes* and in subsequent re-editions down to 1851. Musset rewrote it in 1850 with a view to its production by the Comédie-Française but it was not then accepted. He published this rewritten version, called *Barberine*, in the 1853 edition of *Comédies et Proverbes*. (It was produced at the Comédie-Française in 1882.) The subject—an absent husband uses a magic mirror to test his wife's fidelity—was taken from one of Bandello's (q.v.) *Novelle*. The action takes place in Bohemia and Hungary.

Barbey d'Aurevilly, JULES-AMÉDÉE (1808–89), poet to begin with, better remembered as novelist and critic, was born at Saint-Sauveur-le-Vicomte (Normandy). He was at school in Paris, then lived there more or less continuously from 1833, after studying law at Caen (where he had some contact with the British consul, the decayed Beau Brummell). He made his living by journalism; and his writings, and his arrogant, tempestuous, posturing, and flamboyantly romantic character, make him an interesting minor figure of 19th-century French literature. Latterly he had many disciples among younger writers (to whom he was 'Le Connétable', or 'Le Connétable des Lettres'), and his reputation has grown since his death.

After the early *L'Amour impossible* (1841) and *La Bague d'Annibal* (1843) he wrote two novels of exceptional merit—*L'Ensorcelée* (1854, q.v.) and *Le Chevalier des Touches* (1864, q.v.)—as well as others—*Une Vieille Maîtresse* (1851, q.v.), *Un Prêtre marié* (1865), *Les Diaboliques* (1874, q.v., short stories), *Une Histoire sans nom* (1882), *Ce qui ne meurt pas* (1884), *Une Page d'histoire* (1886) —which were extravagant, at times ridiculous, in character. In all of them he excelled at conveying the atmosphere of the lonely, wild Cotentin country in which they were set—the country of his childhood, steeped in Royalist traditions and memories of the *Chouannerie* (q.v.). He was also literary or dramatic critic on several papers, including the *Constitutionnel* (where he succeeded Sainte-Beuve, q.v.) and his collected articles fill several volumes—*Le Théâtre contemporain* (1887–9, 3 vols.; 1892; 1896); *Les Œuvres et les Hommes* (1860–1909, 4 series, 26 vols.), studies of 19th-century literature, history, and thought. His vigorous, paradoxical criticism was often far-seeing in its appraisements, but often impaired by his passionate likes and dislikes and by his militantly Royalist and Catholic attitude. His other works included *Du Dandysme et de G. Brummell* (1845), one dandy seen by another; and a form of journal entitled *Memoranda*, published at intervals during his lifetime.

Barbier, ANTOINE-ALEXANDRE, see *Dictionaries and encyclopedias*, under date 1806–9.

Barbier, AUGUSTE (1805–82), minor poet and satirist, born in Paris, made a sudden reputation with *La Curée*, a verse-satire on the place-hunters who sought to profit by the July Revolution (q.v.). It was printed in the *Revue des Deux Mondes* of August 1830 and included later in *Ïambes* (1832), satires again, eloquent, indignant condemnation of contemporary evils. *L'Idole*, in this collection, was a denunciation of Napoleon (at a time when the *Légende napoléonienne*, q.v., was developing). Barbier's later works include *Il Pianto* (1833), poems of Italy, lamenting her former glories, and *Lazare* (1837), which contains some melancholy impressions of the English scene and English industrialism. But he outlived his success.

Barbier, EDMOND-JEAN-FRANÇOIS (1689–1771), an advocate, was author of a *Journal historique et anecdotique* for the period 1718–63, i.e. the greater part of the reign of Louis XV, containing some valuable information.

Barbier de Séville, Le, a comedy in prose by Beaumarchais, produced in 1775. The play, in five acts, was at first a failure; the author reduced it to four, whereupon it met with brilliant success.

Bartholo, a doctor and an old curmudgeon, has a ward Rosine, whom he keeps imprisoned and, against her will, intends to marry. Bazile, Rosine's music-master, an insidious villain, aids Bartholo in his designs. The comte Almaviva, a young Spanish grandee, has seen Rosine and has fallen in love with her and she with him, though she does not know who he is. The play is concerned with the devices by which, with the aid of the resourceful Figaro (formerly his servant, now a barber), Almaviva succeeds in marrying Rosine, in spite of the jealous precautions of Bartholo and under his very nose.

Barbizon, a village to the west of the Forêt de Fontainebleau, famous since the early 19th century, and particularly *c.* 1850, as an artists' colony. Among the best-known artists of the Barbizon School were Jean-Baptiste Corot (1796–1875) and Théodore Rousseau (1812–67). Artist life at Barbizon is depicted in, for example, the Goncourts' novel *Manette Salomon* (q.v.).

Barbusse, HENRI (1874–1935), novelist and journalist, made his name with *Le Feu: journal d'une escouade* (1916), one of the most widely read novels of the 1914–18 war. Its sketches of daily life in the trenches, behind the lines, on leave, in the attack, were written with a realism unusual in previous war novels. Barbusse had begun by writing poetry, e.g. *Pleureuses* (1895). *Les Suppliants* (1903) and *L'Enfer* (1908) were novels. After *Clarté* (1919), another war novel, his writings were mainly political, of a pacifist and socialist character, e.g. *La Lueur dans l'abîme* (1920, essays), *Paroles d'un combattant* (1920), &c.

Barclay, JOHN (1582–1621), a Scot, born in France, who wrote in Latin and is remembered specially by two works—*Argenis* (1621), an allegorical satire (much enjoyed by Richelieu), in effect a history of the reigns of Henri III and Henri IV, and the earlier *Euphormionis Lusinini Satyricon* (in two parts: 1602, London; 1603, Paris), likewise allegorical, directed against the Jesuits. Barclay's father William Barclay, an eminent jurist, was a native of Aberdeen who had studied, and remained to teach, law in France. Barclay himself lived for a time in England and was employed on editorial work by James VI and I. He died in Rome.

Bargone, ÉDOUARD, see *Farrère, Claude*.

Barlaam et Josaphat, a medieval religious romance based on a Greek original, and interesting as a christianized version of the story of Buddha. There are three 13th-century French poems on the subject (one anonymous, one by an Anglo-Norman named Chardri, and one by Gui de Cambrai). English versions (*Barlaam and Josaphat*) are included in 14th-century collections of legends.

Josaphat is the son of an Indian king, at first secluded from the world by his father; but at last, gaining his liberty, he is converted to Christianity by Barlaam, a holy man. He in turn converts his father, and abandoning the kingdom when he succeeds to it, dies a hermit.

Barnabooth, see *Larbaud, Valéry*.

Barnave, ANTOINE - PIERRE - JOSEPH - MARIE (1761–93), originally an advocate at Grenoble, his birthplace, was one of the great orators of the Revolution, at times an adversary of Mirabeau (q.v.). He was one of three members of the *Assemblée constituante* (q.v.) sent to Varennes (q.v.) in June 1791 to bring the Royal family back to Paris. Thereafter he became increasingly suspect as a Royalist. He was arrested, tried, condemned to death, and guillotined.

Baro, BALTHAZAR (17th c.), dramatist and novelist, author of forgotten tragi-comedies, &c. He was d'Urfé's secretary and wrote from d'Urfé's notes the conclusion of the latter's romance *L'Astrée* (q.v.).

Baron, MICHEL BOYRON, *known as* (1653–1729), actor and comic dramatist, a disciple of Molière. His best comedy was *L'Homme à bonnes fortunes* (1686), the exposure of an arrogant Lothario, named Moucade. His *L'Andrienne* is a good adaptation from Terence.

Baronius, CESARE, CARDINAL (1538–1607), an Italian church historian, appointed by Clement VIII Librarian of the Vatican in 1596, author of important *Annales ecclesiastici* to the year 1198. He was Superior of the congregation of the Oratory (see *Oratoire*) in succession to St. Philip Neri, its founder. Henri IV writes to him (7 June 1599) with great respect.

Barras, PAUL - JEAN - FRANÇOIS - NICOLAS, VICOMTE DE (1755–1829), came of an old Provençal family and had served in the army in India before taking (successfully) to Revolutionary politics (as a means, it is said, of escaping from his debts, for he was

throughout his career extravagant and sensual, a man of pleasure). He was present at the fall of the Bastille (q.v.), voted for the abolition of the monarchy and the death of Louis XVI in 1792, was a member of the *comité du salut public* (q.v.), helped to overthrow Robespierre (1794), and thereafter was a prominent *Thermidorien* (see *Réaction thermidorienne*) and one of the five members of the *Directoire* (q.v.). During this time he was a protector of the young General Bonaparte, who married his one-time mistress the vicomtesse de Beauharnais (q.v.). He retired into private life when Bonaparte became First Consul (1799, see *Dix-huit Brumaire, Le*).

Barrault, JEAN-LOUIS (1910–   ), actor and producer, founded the *Compagnie Jean-Louis Barrault–Madeleine Renaud* in 1947 with his wife, herself an actress. Their theatre, where some of the most interesting acting and productions of the modern French stage could be seen (until they had to leave it in 1956), was the Théâtre Marigny. Barrault's *Réflexions sur le théâtre* were published in 1945.

Barrès, MAURICE (1862–1923), novelist, essayist, and politician, born at Charmes-sur-Moselle (Lorraine), studied law at Nancy, then went to Paris, and made his literary beginnings about 1884, when he founded a short-lived review, *Taches d'encre*. In 1888, *Huit jours chez M. Renan*, imaginary conversations on an impertinently ironic note, won him both praise and blame, and before long he was in the first rank of authors. At this time, when he made many disciples among other writers, he was a somewhat dilettante, sceptical aesthete, impatient of discipline, always concerned to experience new sensations and develop his personality. He exalted this *culte du moi* in novels (partly essays), *Sous l'œil des barbares* (1888), *Un Homme libre* (1889), and *Le Jardin de Bérénice* (1891); also in travel impressions, *Du sang, de la volupté et de la mort* (1894, Spain), *Amori et dolori sacrum: La Mort de Venise* (1902), &c. But his patriotic conscience had been stirred by the Boulangist movement (see *Boulanger*) and he had entered politics as Deputy for Nancy in 1889. With his political evolution he came to see the individual as dependent on the group. True development of the self, he now held, demanded consciousness on the individual's part of being one of, and with, his race, allied by ties of blood to the soil of his forefathers. A young Frenchman could most fitly serve his country in his native province, where environment, tradition, and inherited cultural and social instincts would foster his capabilities. It was for national education to encourage this point of view, rather than to force the youth of the country into becoming apostles of pure reason, citizens of an abstract 'humanity', for whom racial and regional ties were non-existent and France, the Republic, was merely an administrative fiction. This form of mystico-nationalism inspired another trilogy, *Le Roman de l'énergie nationale*: I. *Les Déracinés* (1897, q.v.), II. *L'Appel au soldat* (1900), III. *Leurs figures* (1902); the essays of *Les Amitiés françaises* (1902); and *Les Bastions de l'Est*, two patriotic novels of Alsace-Lorraine: i. *Au service de l'Allemagne* (1905) and ii. *Colette Baudoche* (1909). They also, added to his anti-Dreyfus (q.v.) attitude during *l'affaire*, caused Barrès to be regarded as a reactionary and considerably lessened his influence.

During the 1914–18 war and for some time afterwards Barrès, who was president of the *Ligue des patriotes*, wrote daily patriotic articles in the *Écho de Paris* (published in book form as *Chronique de la Grande Guerre*, 1920–4, 14 vols.). His other works included the two novels *La Colline inspirée* (1913, q.v.) and *Un Jardin sur l'Oronte* (1922, a return to the more sensuous manner of his earliest works). *Mes Cahiers* (1929–38, 11 vols., posth.) is the interesting journal he kept from 1896 to 1918.

Barricades. These were rough street blocks used by the people of Paris in times of up-risings and civil strife. They could be im-provised speedily from empty barrels (*barriques*, hence the name), uprooted paving-stones, overturned vehicles, &c. In narrow streets they were very effective against the passage of troops and were good cover for an ill-armed defence. While the troops were struggling to remove them the people could add to the confusion by firing, or by raining heavy objects, from furniture to iron stew-pots, from their windows. The cry 'Aux barricades!' became a typical call to desperate measures against authority and the barricades themselves a symbol of a revolutionary city populace in arms. For the *Journées des*

barricades of 12 May 1588 and 27 August 1648 see *Ligue, La*, and *Fronde, La*.

Barrière, THÉODORE (1823–77), dramatist, wrote both farce and drama. His characters were types of stupidity, egoism, or malice: *Les Filles de marbre* (1853), courtesans of a very different type from the romanticized Marguerite of *La Dame aux camélias* (q.v.); *Les Faux Bonshommes* (1856), in collaboration with E. Capendu (1826–68); *Les Jocrisses de l'amour* (1865), in collaboration with Lambert-Thiboust (1826–67).

Barruel-Bauvert, L'ABBÉ ANTOINE-JOSEPH (1756–1817), a writer in defence of religious orthodoxy against the *philosophes* (*Les Helviennes*, 1781), and a defender of Louis XVI and the nobility.

Barthélemy, L'ABBÉ JEAN-JACQUES (1716–95), born in Provence, a learned antiquarian and numismatist, and a man of modest and amiable character. A sojourn of two years in Italy (1755–7) in the suite of the French ambassador, later known as the duc de Choiseul, his patron, suggested to him the idea of his *Voyage du jeune Anacharsis en Grèce* (1788), on the composition of which he spent thirty years. It relates the imaginary visit of a young Scythian to Greece in the time of Philip of Macedon (4th century B.C.), and is a popular reconstruction of the Greek civilization of that period, somewhat superficial in character. It brings on the stage various eminent personages, such as Epaminondas, Xenophon at Scillus, and the youthful Alexander. The work, which is agreeably written, was highly successful, and Barthélemy was admitted to the *Académie* in 1789.

Bartholo, a character in Beaumarchais's *Barbier de Séville* and *Mariage de Figaro* (qq.v.).

Bartholomew, Massacre of Saint, see *Saint-Barthélemy*.

Bartole or **Bartolus** (1314–57), a famous Italian jurist, author of commentaries on the *Corpus Juris* of Justinian. He is frequently referred to in early French literature, e.g. by Rabelais.

'Baruch ?, Avez-vous lu', allusion to a saying of La Fontaine who, having chanced to read the prayer of the Jews in the book of Baruch and being greatly struck with its beauty, went about asking all and sundry, 'Avez-vous lu Baruch?' Used proverbially of a sudden and striking discovery.

Barzun, HENRI-MARTIN (1881–), author of the verses collected in *La Terrestre Tragédie* (1907) and, after founding the *Simultanéiste* movement (see *Literary Isms*), of 'La Trilogie des forces' (1908–14), collections intended to illustrate his theories. He was associated with the early days of the Abbaye (q.v.) Group.

Bashkirtseff, MARIE (1860–84), a Russian whose diary (written in French) is one of the remarkable *journaux intimes* of the 19th century. She came, aged twelve, to Nice with her mother, grandfather, aunt, and other relatives, as well as governesses and family appendages. (Her parents were separated, but amicable relations with the father on his property in Russia were maintained.) The little party lived in Nice, in Rome, and from 1877 in Paris, in a succession of hotels and furnished houses, until Marie, always its centre, died in 1884 of consumption. In the diary, begun in Nice in 1873 and broken off eleven days before her death, the writer revealed herself 'tout entière', at first for her own benefit but before long intentionally as a means of leaving her imprint on posterity. She recorded her experiences, her life of (at times precarious) luxury, her enjoyment of this but at the same time her rebellion against its meaninglessness and her determination to educate herself to a higher level (which she fulfilled in no small degree), her arrogance, her romantic fancies and day-dreaming, and her ambition, especially to win fame as a painter: she worked during her last years at the well-known Académie Julian, so feverishly and desperately that she hastened her own end. She described, too, her continual struggles with encroaching malady, and in the final, moving, pages her realization that no doctors or treatment could save her.

Basiliade, La, see *Morelly.*

Basnage de Beauval, HENRI (1656–1710), Protestant scholar and compiler, settled in Holland after the Revocation of the Edict of Nantes. He issued a periodical collection, *Histoire des ouvrages des savants* (Rotterdam, 1687–1709, 12 vols.), a continuation of Bayle's (q.v.) *Nouvelles de la République des*

Lettres. He was also responsible for the augmented edition of Furetière's (q.v.) *Dictionnaire,* of which the *Dictionnaire de Trévoux* (1704) was practically a reprint (see *Dictionaries and Encyclopedias* under dates 1690 and 1704).

Basnage de Beauval, JACQUES (1653–1723), Protestant scholar and compiler, brother of the above, also settled in Holland after the Revocation of the Edict of Nantes and is said to have had a hand in the *Histoire des ouvrages des savants.*

Basoche (from L. *basilica* in the sense of tribunal), the name given to associations of attorneys', registrars' and law clerks, formed in Paris and the provinces for mutual protection and amusement. In Paris the chief societies were, (1) the *Basoche du Parlement* (the High Court of Justice), formed about the year 1303, and known as the *Royaume de la Basoche*; it had a king, a chancellor, a vice-chancellor, and other officials and exercised a certain jurisdiction over its members; (2) the *Basoche du Châtelet* (the Court of Criminal Justice); and (3) the *Empire de Galilée* (for those attached to the *Cour des Comptes* or Audit Office). They assembled at stated times, such as the beginning of July, when they were obliged by statute to present themselves at a *montre,* or general review. On these occasions they performed pantomimes or *tableaux vivants,* and, as time went on, dialogues, farces, and moralities, often written by their own members and usually satirizing the world of the judicature, from which these members were drawn. On the *jours gras* of Carnival they pleaded the burlesque law-suits known as 'causes grasses', which gave scope for satire. Except during the reign of Louis XII (1498–1515) who, either from easy nature or to serve his own political ends, encouraged their audacities, this fondness for satire brought the *Basochiens* into disrepute with the Court and the authorities, and their performances were often heavily censored and for periods prohibited altogether. At times the *Basochiens* and the *Enfants sans souci* (q.v.), with whom they were closely related, gave performances in common with the *Confrérie de la Passion* (q.v.). These consisted of sacred Mysteries followed by farces and *soties* (q.v.) and came to be termed *pois pilés.* From 1570 to 1580 the *Basochiens* produced many of **Larivey's**

comedies, and occasionally they performed tragedies. The dramatic performances of the *Basoches* came to an end *c.* 1590, though the *causes grasses* continued. The *Basoche* of the *Parlement* survived as a corporation until the Revolution.

Among the *Basoches* of the provinces were those of Aix, Angers, Avignon, Bordeaux, Lyon, and Rouen, but not all the provincial *basoches* made the same use of satire as their Parisian fellows, nor did all of them attempt dramatic representations.

Basselin, OLIVIER, a 15th-century fuller of Vire in Normandy, reputed author of drinking-songs, which were current in the *vau* or valley of the river Vire. They were known in consequence as *vaux-de-vire*, a name which was corrupted into *vaudeville*, and the type of song designated by it became caustic and satirical. For the later development of the *vaudeville* see under that word.

Olivier Basselin is the subject of a 15th-century dirge by an unknown Norman author, which suggests that he was killed in the English wars.

Bassompierre, FRANÇOIS DE (1579–1646), soldier and diplomat, born in Lorraine, became *maréchal de France* after serving in many campaigns. He was imprisoned by Richelieu in 1629, 'not for any wrong that he had done, but for fear that he might be led into mischief', and remained in the Bastille for twelve years. He has left interesting memoirs, which give a lively account of himself and his contemporaries and the manners of his day.

Bastard de Bouillon, Le, see *Baudoin de Sebourg.*

Bastiat, CLAUDE-FRÉDÉRIC (1801–50), born at Bayonne, political economist, was an early French advocate of Free Trade and wrote an account of the English movement (*Cobden et la ligue,* 1845). He met Cobden in England in 1845. His other works included the political tracts *Sophismes économiques,* issued at various dates: and he also, with Auguste Blanqui and others, edited *Le Libre Échange,* a journal published between November 1846 and April 1848. He died leaving his chief work, *Harmonies économiques,* unfinished.

Bastille, La, a fortress constructed (1370–82) under Charles V and Charles VI at the Porte Saint-Antoine in Paris. From the time of Richelieu (q.v.) it became the most redoubtable of the State prisons and many illustrious persons were confined there (Voltaire among others). To the people, the word 'Bastille' was synonymous with injustice and absolutism; and the first symbolic act of the Revolution was *la Prise de la Bastille* on 14 July 1789. At the time it was little more than a venerable scarecrow, containing some half-dozen convicted criminals and lunatics, and garrisoned by 95 Invalides and 30 Suisses. Its governor, the marquis de Launay, was murdered.

The anniversary of the taking of the Bastille was marked during the Revolutionary era by the *Fêtes de la Fédération.* Since 1880 it has been by law the foremost national holiday in France.

Bataille, a medieval form of literature, akin to the *débat* and *dispute* (see *Dit*), in which an armed combat is depicted between personifications, e.g. in the *Bataille des Sept Arts* by Henri d'Andeli, where the combatants are Literature and Dialectic.

Bataille, HENRI (1872–1922), author of psychological dramas which were a successful mixture of audacity and false sentiment: *Maman Colibri* (1904, the study of a middle-aged woman's passion for her son's friend), *La Marche nuptiale* (1905), *La Vierge folle* (1910), *L'Enfant de l'amour* (1911), *Le Phalène* (1913), *La Tendresse* (1921), &c. They appealed to a wide public.

Bataille d'Hernani, La, see *Hernani.*

Bateau ivre, Le, a poem by Rimbaud (q.v.), written in 1871, when he was sixteen. A boat's crew has been massacred: only the poet is left. Rudderless, the boat drifts through luminous seas, is tossed by hurricanes into birdless skies, and becomes the symbol of the poet's confused soul. The poem is packed with continually shifting images which have the fleeting clarity of hallucinations.

Baty, GASTON (1885–1952), a theatrical producer who, at his Théâtre Montparnasse, in Paris, brought forward many new dramatists and introduced many novelties of setting. He was known for his dramatizations of novels, e.g. *Crime and Punishment, Manon Lescaut, Madame Bovary.*

Baucent, the boar, in the *Roman de Renart* (q.v.).

Baucis, see *Philémon et Baucis.*

Baude, HENRI (*c.* 1430–*c.* 1496), poet and provincial official, born at Moulins in the Bourbonnais, an imitator of Villon. He was author of a satirical *moralité* (q.v.) containing reflections on the court, performed by the *Basoche* (q.v.) in 1486. For this and on other grounds he was repeatedly imprisoned, but maintained a cheerful attitude in his satirical poems, notably *Les Lamentations Bourrien* (directed against ecclesiastics) and *Le Testament de la mule Barbeau* (against the magistrature), and in his *Lettres à Mgr de Bourbon* pleading for release from prison.

Baudelaire, CHARLES (1821–67), poet and critic, was scantly appreciated in his lifetime but now counts among the great names of French literature. His place as a poet, and one of the main 19th-century influences on modern poetry, is firmly established. His value as a critic, of literature, painting, and music, has been increasingly emphasized in modern times (see *Critics and criticism,* para. 12).

(2) He was born in Paris, in comfortable circumstances. His father was sixty, his mother twenty-six. In 1827 his father died. In 1828 his mother, whom he adored, re-married and a new presence came (or intruded) into his life—his stepfather, Colonel (later General) Aupick. He was educated at Lyons, then Paris. His parents opposed his determination to become a poet and started him on a voyage to India (1841–2). At Mauritius he left the ship and returned to Paris where, being now twenty-one and in possession of an inheritance, he set up on his own. He contributed regularly to reviews, and discovered and also translated Edgar Allan Poe, whose aesthetic theories appealed to him. He was, too, it may be noted at this point, influenced by his reading of the mystic-philosopher Swedenborg. His life was one of excess, and with the years was to become desperate and sordid. The name of one of his mistresses, Jeanne Duval, a mulatto, remains because she was the *Vénus noire* of his poems. He treated her with extraordinary generosity and patience,

though their relations were agonizing, long after she had become a repulsive, besotted wreck. In 1857 his pride and consciousness of his genius, as well as his finances, received an overwhelming blow when, on publication of his poems *Les Fleurs du mal,* he was prosecuted and fined for offences to public morals (cf. *Flaubert* and *Madame Bovary*). Six of the poems were banned, and the edition could not be sold without their deletion. [They were omitted from the second edition (1861), and from the third, the posthumous edition of 1868, but they were printed in subsequent editions in France—illegally, and as an appendix, until May 1949 when the ban was raised—and they were also printed in *Épaves,* published in Belgium in 1866, see para. 5 below.] By 1864 his resources were exhausted and he went to Brussels with hopes, which foundered pitifully, of making money by lecturing. He lived there squalidly for two years, then his ruined constitution gave way. In 1866 he was brought back to Paris suffering from general paralysis. He lingered in a pitiable state for fifteen months and died on 31 August 1867.

(3) The poems of *Les Fleurs du mal* were written at various dates (the section entitled *Tableaux parisiens,* for instance, was not introduced till the second edition), but their grouping and the emotions they express give them intercoherence and unity. The theme is the antagonism between *spleen* and *idéal,* between evil and good, by which man is torn. The poet (§ I, *Spleen et Idéal*) discards his predecessors' criterion of idealized beauty. He will extract poetic magic from the hideous realities of life—'l'horreur et l'extase de la vie'. In the next three sections (*Tableaux parisiens, Le Vin, Les Fleurs du mal*) he finds inspiration in the streets and the mysterious, hidden life of Paris, or in evil itself, lingering over it with an almost mystical acuity of sensation. He analyses himself morbidly and is haunted by a sense of damnation which exasperates him to revolt and blasphemy. But these cannot prevail against God and he longs (*Révolte, La Mort,* the concluding sections) for death and the discovery of the Beyond: 'Nous voulons . . . Plonger au fond du gouffre, Enfer ou Ciel, qu'importe? Au fond de l'Inconnu pour trouver du *nouveau!*' (cf. *Rimbaud,* on whom his influence was strong).

(4) Baudelaire was said by Hugo to have

introduced a *frisson nouveau* into poetry, an essentially modern form of exacerbated sensibility which will quicken only to a beauty that contains the elements of corruption. His prosody was classical in its perfection, but he was a precursor of modern poetry by his perception of the symbolic correspondences of colours, scents, and sounds (cf. *Symbolisme*); by his exploration of the musical possibilities of the French language; and above all by his evocative power: with one phrase, or one word, he could suggest an infinity of passion, melancholy, or aspiration.

(5) His writings other than *Les Fleurs du mal* include: *Les Épaves* (1866, published in Belgium), a collection of twenty-three poem which contains the six banned from *Les Fleurs du mal*; *Petits poèmes en prose* (1869, posth.), influenced by the *Gaspard de la nuit* of Aloysius Bertrand (q.v.) and afterwards entitled, as Baudelaire himself had wanted, *Le Spleen de Paris*; *Les Paradis artificiels, opium et haschisch* (1860), essays which include a study of, and translated extracts from, De Quincey's *Opium-Eater*; *Histoires extraordinaires* and *Nouvelles histoires extraordinaires par Edgar Poë* (1856 and 1857), translations; *Salon de 1845, . . . de 1846, . . . de 1859, Richard Wagner et Tannhäuser* (1861), *Eugène Delacroix* (1863), all contained in *Curiosités esthétiques* (1868, posth.) and *L'Art romantique* (1868, posth.), criticism; also the interesting and often poignant jottings *Fusées* and *Mon cœur mis à nu*, first published *in extenso* in 1917 (and included in the Pléiade edition of his *Œuvres complètes*, 1931–2, 2 vols.; now in a single volume, 1951).

Baudoin d'Avesnes, see *History (Medieval period)*.

Baudouin, JEAN (1590–1650), a 17th-century translator of Tacitus, Suetonius, Tasso, Bacon, &c.

Baudouin de Condé, see *Trois morts et des trois vifs, Dit des*.

Baudouin de Sebourg, a romance in the form of a *chanson de geste* (q.v.) composed in the early 14th century and attached to the cycle of the Crusade (see *Antioche*). It relates the adventures, in the East and in Europe, of the hero, son of the king of Nimègue (Nijmegen in Holland) and educated by the lord of Sebourg. The episodes have to a large extent the burlesque character of *fabliaux* (q.v.), in which women and priests are the victims of the hero's enterprises. The complicated story is told with much liveliness and gives a realistic picture of contemporary manners. With its sequel, *Le Bastard de Bouillon*, it is among the last examples of the form of the *chanson de geste*.

Bayard, in the *chanson de geste* of *Renaud de Montauban* (q.v.), the wonderful horse belonging to that hero.

Bayard, PIERRE DU TERRAIL, CHEVALIER DE (*c.* 1473–1524), a famous French captain, who distinguished himself by his bravery in the Italian wars of Charles VIII, Louis XII, and François Ier. His exploits, especially the defence of the bridge of Garigliano against 200 Spaniards, caused him to be known as the 'chevalier sans peur et sans reproche'. They were recorded in the *Très joyeuse . . . histoire du gentil seigneur de Bayart* by Jacques de Maille, his 'loyal serviteur'.

Bayle, PIERRE (1647–1706), lexicographer, philosopher, and critic, born in the Comté de Foix, a man of erudition and intellectual probity, a Protestant who became a Catholic and reverted to Protestantism, finally a Pyrrhonian in religion, and a champion of toleration in opinion. For if religion, he held, is irrational, reason on the other hand leads to no certain conclusions. Forced to leave France, he taught philosophy at Sedan (1675), and in 1680 obtained for a time a chair of philosophy at Rotterdam. His condemnation of superstitions, his view that morality is independent of religion (for a man may be an atheist and yet have all the moral virtues), and his doctrine of toleration are set forth chiefly in his *Pensées sur la Comète* (1682, subsequently remodelled and enlarged) and in his *Commentaire philosophique sur les paroles de Jésus-Christ: 'Contrains-les d'entrer'* (1686), directed against the contention that these words justify persecution. He founded in 1684 and conducted until 1687 the *Nouvelles de la République des Lettres*, a critical literary review, published in Holland. His *Avis important aux réfugiés sur leur prochain retour en France* (published anonymously), purporting to be written from Paris by a Catholic, in which the doctrine of passive obedience is upheld and the refugees are condemned for their seditious attitude, was regarded as a betrayal of their cause. It brought Bayle into disgrace and he lost his professorship. His principal work remained to be written, his *Dictionnaire historique et critique* (1697, enlarged in 1702, and supplemented in 1704–6 by *Réponses aux questions d'un provincial*). This takes the form of, mainly, biographical articles on personages notable in ancient and modern history, with special reference to errors and omissions in the works of the author's predecessors (especially Moréri, and see *Dictionaries and Encyclopedias*), and with particular attention to philosophical and theological subjects, which are subjected to a free investigation. The text of the articles is substantially orthodox but is accompanied by voluminous footnotes, in which objections and criticisms are stated or insinuated. Eleven editions of the work appeared between 1697 and 1740 and an *Analyse* or abbreviation by the abbé de Marty was published in 1755. There were English editions from 1710. It was an armoury from which the *philosophes* drew many of their weapons. Bayle's attitude is expressed in these words: 'Il n'y a point de prescription contre la vérité; les erreurs pour être vieilles n'en sont pas meilleures.' Bayle's correspondence has also been published.

Bazard, ARMAND (1791–1832), born in Paris, a leader of the Saint-Simoniens (see *Saint-Simonisme*).

Bazin, RENÉ (1853–1932), novelist, born in Angers. His studies of provincial life, usually of families clinging to, or anxious to uproot themselves from, the soil, had a great sentimental and patriotic appeal for the novel-reading public of *c*. 1900. The most successful were: *La Terre qui meurt* (1899, Vendée); *Les Oberlé* (1901), about an Alsatian family after the Franco-Prussian war, faced with the choice between French and German nationality; *Donatienne* (1903, Brittany); *Le Blé qui lève* (1907), which describes, first, the struggles of foresters and poor farmers in the Morvan district of Burgundy and then life in the fat farming country of Picardy.

Béatrix, one of the 'scènes de la vie privée' in Balzac's *Comédie humaine* (q.v.).

Beauclair, HENRI (1860–1919), journalist and poet, part-author with G. Vicaire (q.v.) of *Les Déliquescences d'Adoré Floupette* (q.v.). He also—in *Les Horizontales* (1885)—parodied Hugo's *Les Orientales*.

Beauharnais, JOSÉPHINE TASCHER DE LA PAGERIE (1763–1814), born in Martinique, died at Malmaison (q.v.), married, first, the vicomte de Beauharnais (guillotined 1794) and second (1796), Napoléon Bonaparte. She became Empress Josephine in 1804. Her children by the first marriage were Eugène (1781–1824), whom Napoleon created Duke of Leuchtenberg, Prince of Eichstadt, and Viceroy of Italy as a reward for faithful service, and Hortense (1783–1837), who married Napoleon's brother Louis Bonaparte and became Queen of Holland (cf. *Napoléon III*). The Empress Josephine had no children by Napoleon, who divorced her in 1809 (see *Napoleon*).

Beauharnais, MARIE-ANNE-FRANÇOISE, *known as* FANNY, COMTESSE DE (1738–1813), *née* Mouchard, wife of Claude de Beauharnais, a naval officer. She was thus connected by marriage with the future Empress Josephine. She was the intimate and devoted friend of Dorat (q.v.) until his death and herself an authoress in a mild way. Her house was a literary centre, frequented by poets of whom Dorat was the chief, but also by Restif de la Bretonne, Mercier, &c.

Beaujeu, RENAUD DE, see *Guinglain*.

Beaumanoir, PHILIPPE DE REMI, SIRE DE (*c*. 1250–96), a jurist, author of a treatise on old French law, the *Coutumes du Beauvaisis*. He also wrote between 1270 and 1280 metrical romances of adventure entitled *Manekine* and *Jehan et Blonde* and a fabliau *La Fole Largece* (qq.v.). There are indications in the romances that he may have visited England.

Beaumarchais, PIERRE-AUGUSTIN CARON DE (1732–99), son of a Paris clock-maker of the name of Caron. The son took the title of Beaumarchais from a small property belonging to his first wife. He received little education, being intended for his father's trade, and became a capable artisan. In 1755 he obtained a minor post in the royal household, married the rich widow of his predecessor, but lost her fortune when she died shortly afterwards. His talent as a harpist soon caused him to be named music-master to the daughters of Louis XV. A service rendered to the famous financier, Paris-Duverney, brought him riches, enabling him to purchase a brevet of nobility and a more important office. He was henceforth occupied in a series of adventures, financial enterprises and speculations, political and other intrigues, and sensational litigation, and suffered more than one imprisonment. After the death of Paris-Duverney in 1770, a lawsuit relating to the accounts between the financier and Beaumarchais was the occasion for the latter's four brilliant *Mémoires* (1773-4) concerning the dealings he had had with the wife of the magistrate Goezman for the purpose of obtaining an audience of her husband. By their skilful combination of gaiety, comedy, and irony with reason and eloquence they won public opinion to the side of Beaumarchais and carried him to the height of popularity (though he lost his suit). He was subsequently sent on secret service missions to England and elsewhere by the Governments of Louis XV and Louis XVI. His multifarious activities included the organization of supplies for the insurgent American colonies and the equipping of ships in their support. He defended with success the financial rights of dramatic authors against the chicanery of the actors' companies. He undertook the difficult and, as it proved, unremunerative task of issuing at Kehl (in the duchy of Baden) a complete edition (1784-90) of the works of Voltaire which has become famous, purchasing for the purpose the type of the great English printer Baskerville. During the Revolution Beaumarchais, though an agent of the *Comité de salut public*, was in constant danger, coming under suspicion and being treated as an *émigré*. He however survived the Terror, with his fortune diminished, to continue his activities till 1799.

By way of diversion he wrote plays: *Eugénie* (1767), the story of a girl lured into a mock marriage by an English nobleman, who deserts her but finally repents of his misdeeds; *Les Deux Amis, ou le Négociant de Lyon* (1770), an unsuccessful romantic drama; then his two great comedies *Le Barbier de Séville* (1775) and *Le Mariage de Figaro* (1784), qq.v.; and finally a sentimental drama, *L'Autre Tartufe, ou la Mère coupable* (1792), a very inferior sequel to the two previous plays, in which Figaro reappears, but prosy

and morose. In the Tartufe of this play, by name Bégearss, the author pilloried the advocate Bergasse, his bitter enemy. His opera *Tavare* (1787), a philosophical allegory, hardly deserves mention in a literary connexion, though it had for a time some political importance.

Beaumarchais's varied activities made him renowned but not respected. He was kindly to his family, generous, of cheerful disposition and easy morals, something of an adventurer, with a mania for intrigue and speculation. He was always making a noise in the world (indeed he adopted as his device a drum with the motto 'Non sonat nisi percussus') and his very versatility brought him enemies. As a dramatist his importance lay not only in the audacity of his social satire, or in the fact that he revived, in his two great plays, the comedy of intrigue which had suffered eclipse since Molière: he had a further importance as the first dramatist to use fully the theories conceived by Diderot (q.v.) of stage-craft and acting.

Beaumont, CHRISTOPHE DE (1703-81), Archbishop of Paris, remembered for the active part he took in the repression of literary works in which the Catholic religion was attacked or criticized; his condemnation of Rousseau's *Émile* drew from the author of the latter a famous letter in reply.

Beaumont, MME DE, see *Leprince de Beaumont.*

Beaumont de la Bonninière, GUSTAVE-AUGUSTE DE (1802-66), man of letters and politician (Vice-President of the *Assemblée constituante* in 1848 and for some months during the same year French Ambassador in London). He was sent with Tocqueville (q.v.) to the U.S.A. in 1831 to study the penal system and collaborated with him in the ensuing *Traité du système pénitentiaire* (1833). From his observations of slave life and the American scene he wrote a novel, *Marie, ou l'Esclavage aux États-Unis* (1835).

Beau Ténébreux, see *Chimères, Les.*

Beauvoir, ROGER DE [the name adopted by Eugène-Auguste-Roger de Bully] (1806-66), minor writer, a 'dandy', of independent means (but he died gout-ridden and poor), one of the extreme Romantics (see *Romantisme*). His novel of medieval horrors

L'Écolier de Cluny ou le Sophisme (1832) is said to have given Dumas *père* the plot of *La Tour de Nesle* (q.v.). *Le Chevalier de Saint-Georges* (1840, 4 vols.) is usually accounted the best of his numerous works.

Beauvoir, SIMONE DE, contemporary novelist, see *Existentialisme*, para. 6.

Beaux-Arts, Académie des; École des, see *Académie royale de peinture et de sculpture*.

Beccaria, CESARE (1738–94), Italian author of a celebrated treatise (*Trattato dei delitti e delle pene*) on the reform of the penal system (1764), translated in 1766 by l'abbé Morellet (q.v.) under the title *Des délits et des peines* and the subject of a favourable commentary by Voltaire in the same year.

Béchellerie, La, the country property (Touraine) where Anatole France (q.v.) spent his last years.

Becket, Vie de Saint Thomas, see *Thomas Becket*.

Beckford, WILLIAM (1759–1844), author of *Vathek* (q.v.).

Becque, HENRI (1837–99), dramatist, whose *Les Corbeaux* (1882, q.v.) and *La Parisienne* (1885, q.v.) influenced the development of the French theatre. Plot was of minor importance, the object being to give a faithful picture of life. This was a new dramatic technique and helped to extend the naturalistic movement (see *Naturalisme*; *Théâtre libre*) to the stage. Becque's earlier plays were *La Navette* (1879) and *Les Honnêtes Femmes* (1880). His unfinished play *Les Polichinelles* (1910, posth.), a study of the financial world, was to have been his masterpiece.

Béda, NOËL (d. 1536), one of the principal opponents of the movement of religious reformation in France of the early 16th century known as *Évangélisme* (q.v.). He was head of the Collège de Montaigu from 1499. He questioned (not without reason) the orthodoxy of Marguerite of Navarre. François Iᵉʳ banished him for his officiousness to the Mont-Saint-Michel, where he died. Rabelais in his humorous catalogue of the library of Saint-Victor (see *Saint-Victor, Abbaye de*) attributes to him a work *de optimitate triparum* (Béda was an enormously fat man).

Bede or **Baeda** (673–735), historian and scholar, who spent most of his life at the monastery of Jarrow, author of *Historia Ecclesiastica Gentis Anglorum*, one of the sources on which Geoffrey of Monmouth (q.v.) drew for his *Historia Regum Britanniae*.

Bédier, JOSEPH (1864–1938), medievalist and literary historian. Modern theories of the origin of the *fabliaux* and the *chansons de geste* (qq.v.) are largely based on his two studies, *Les Fabliaux* (1893) and *Les Légendes épiques* (1908–13). A modernization of the primitive French version of the story of Tristan and Yseult (1900) and a critical edition of the *Chanson de Roland* (1921) are noteworthy among his numerous other publications. He was, with his one-time pupil Paul Hazard (q.v.), joint editor of the two-volume illustrated *Littérature française* (revised and augmented edition 1948–9), one of the most valuable of modern general histories of French literature (cf. *Appendix I*, § A (i)).

Béjart, MADELEINE and ARMANDE, see *Molière*.

Bel-Ami (1885), a novel by Guy de Maupassant (q.v.). Georges Duroy ('Bel-Ami') is a selfish, sensual, unscrupulous young man with an eye for the main chance and an unfailing attraction for women. His fortunes are at a low ebb when he accepts a chance offer of a post on a newspaper. He exploits his charms astutely, becomes editor of an important paper and marries the millionaire proprietor's daughter. It is clear that he will be no more faithful to her than to the women who were the other rungs of his career. There are many pictures of journalistic life and intrigue, and the tone of the book is brutally frank.

Belgiojoso, CRISTINA TRIVULZIO, PRINCESS (1808–71), a mid-19th-century Italian patriot and a figure in Parisian intellectual circles. She belonged by birth (Milan) to an old Italian family and was brought up by a Carbonarist step-father in an atmosphere of conspiracy. By sixteen she was married to Prince Belgiojoso. By twenty-three the marriage had ended. Thereafter she lived royally for a time in Paris. Her afternoon receptions, where historians, politicians, writers, and musicians met and talked, were celebrated, and she inspired admiration and several passions. She again became involved in Italian political conspiracies (these were the days of the *Risorgimento*, q.v.), and in 1848 she herself raised and equipped insurgent troops to deliver Lombardy from Austrian domination. (Deliverance came, not then, but before she died.) She lived in France again after 1853 but ended her days in Italy.

Belin, the ram, in the *Roman de Renart* (q.v.).

Bel Inconnu, Le, see *Guinglain.*

Bélisaire, an historical romance by Marmontel, published in 1766. It consists of conversations between the aged and blind Belisarius, the great military commander, on the one hand, and the emperor Justinian and his son on the other, on political and social systems. The 15th chapter, advocating freedom of opinion and toleration in religious matters, caused the work to be condemned by the Sorbonne and gave temporary importance to a dull book.

Bélise, a character in Molière's *Les Femmes savantes.*

Bella (1926), a novel by Jean Giraudoux (q.v.).

Belleau, REMI (1528?–77), born at Nogent-le-Rotrou, near Chartres, a member of the *Pléiade* (q.v.), author of a verse-translation (1566) of the pseudo-Anacreon which Henri Estienne had recently published, of some pleasant descriptions of the seasons (in his prose and verse *Bergerie,* including a famous *chanson* called *Avril*); of *Amours et nouveaux échanges des pierres précieuses* (1576), containing curious verse descriptions of precious stones, pearls, coral, &c., their physical properties and secret virtues; of *Petites inventions,* miscellaneous short poems; and of an unfinished comedy, *La Reconnue,* published after his death, largely on the theme of Plautus's *Casina.*

Belle au bois dormant, La, the story of Sleeping Beauty. It is one of Perrault's (q.v.) *contes.*

Belle Dame sans merci, La, see *Chartier, Alain.*

Belle et la Bête, La, the story of Beauty and the Beast. It is one of the *contes* of Mme Leprince de Beaumont (q.v.).

Belleforest, FRANÇOIS DE (1530–83), a failed poet and a superior literary hack, is remembered chiefly, with Pierre Boaistuau (q.v.), by the *Histoires tragiques* (from 1559 onwards), translations, mainly, from Bandello's (q.v.) *Novelle.*

Belle Hélène, La [i.e. Helen of Troy] (1864), a humorous operetta with music by Offenbach and libretto by Henri Meilhac and Ludovic Halévy (qq.v.). It was one of the brilliant successes of the Second Empire (cf. *Schneider, Hortense*).

Belle Poule, La, the frigate (under the command of the Prince de Joinville, third son of Louis-Philippe) in which Napoleon's ashes were brought from St. Helena to France. She docked at Cherbourg on 30 November 1840. (See *Légende napoléonienne.*)

Bellerophon, **H.M.S.** (Captain Maitland). After his abdication in 1815 Napoleon claimed protection from the British Government and boarded the *Bellerophon* at Rochefort (15 July).

Bellerose, PIERRE LE MESSIER, *known as* (17th century), an actor at the Hôtel de Bourgogne from about 1622, especially successful in serious comedy and tragedy, noted as the first to have introduced an element of grace and tenderness into French acting.

Belloy, PIERRE-LAURENT BUIRETTE, *known as* DE (1727–75), dramatist, author of the very successful patriotic tragedy, *Le Siège de Calais* (1764), and of others, mediocre and usually historical: *Gaston et Bayard, Gabrielle de Vergy, Pierre le Cruel,* &c.

Belphégor, one of the *Contes et Nouvelles* of La Fontaine, based on a story by Machiavelli.

Satan, having observed that most of the souls in hell attribute their damnation to their spouses, sends the devil Belphégor to the world of men to investigate the state of matrimony. Belphégor, in human guise, to complete his inquiries, himself takes a wife. She turns out a shrew, and leads Belphégor such a life that he is only too glad to escape from his human body and hasten back to hell. *Belphégor* is also the title of a collection of essays by the critic and essayist Julien Benda (see the following).

Benda, JULIEN (1867–1956), critic and essayist, was born in Paris, of Jewish parentage, and educated at the Lycée Charlemagne and the Sorbonne (classics, history, and philosophy). In one form or another his writings are the uncompromising expression of his conviction that human sentiment, judgement, and conduct should be dictated by reason and the intellect. They also express his unsparing contempt for any romantic, sentimental, mystical, or intuitional approach to life and literature, and for modern attempts to get behind words to the 'pure idea'. His views can be studied, developing or fully matured, in *La Jeunesse d'un clerc* (1936) and *Un Régulier dans le siècle* (1938), both autobiographical; *Dialogues à Byzance* (1900), philosophical commentaries on the Dreyfus (q.v.) case, first printed in a review; *Le Bergsonisme ou une Philosophie de la mobilité* (1912), an intellectual attack on Bergsonism (see *Bergson*), and in two challenging works, *Belphégor* (1918) and *La Trahison des clercs* (1927). The first, an *Essai sur l'esthétique de la présente société française*, discusses contemporary literature and asserts that neither the authors nor their readers understand the meaning of intellectual pleasure, literature for them being a matter of emotion and sensation, and no more. (This theme is elaborated, with much hard hitting, especially where such writers as Valéry or Gide are concerned, in *La France byzantine*, 1945.) In the second work Benda remarks on the way in which passions have been mobilized as political forces during the last century, e.g. class hatred, anti-Semitism, &c. Nor is this all. Formerly 'les clercs' (by whom he means writers, artists, and thinkers) were detached from politics. A Goethe, for instance, consecrated himself to intellectual pursuits, a Voltaire, a Kant, or a Renan urged that conduct should be guided by abstract principles, e.g. justice, truth, humanity. Nowadays intellectuals have betrayed their own kind; they have descended into the arena and allowed their convictions to be swayed by national, social, and political passions.

Other works by Benda are: *Dialogue d'Éleuthère* (1910), *Les Sentiments de Critias* (1917), *Le Bouquet de Glycère* (1918, 3 dialogues); *Délice d'Éleuthère* (1935), &c.; also *L'Ordination* (1911) and *Les Amorandes* (1922), novels of the conflict between sentiment and intelligence.

Benedictine order of monks. For their special connexion with literature see under *Maurists*. See also *Histoire littéraire de la France*.

Benoit, PIERRE (1886–), author of novels of adventure, notably *Koenigsmark* (1918) and *L'Atlantide* (1919).

Benoît de Sainte-Maure or **Sainte-More,** a 12th-century poet, probably of Sainte-Maure in Touraine, author of the *Roman de Troie* (q.v.). He also wrote, at the request of Henry II, in 43,000 octosyllabic lines, a history of the Norman dukes adapted from the Latin Chronicles. The work was not carried beyond the death of Henry I.

Benserade, ISAAC DE (1612–91), born in Normandy, poet, author of *Cléopâtre* (1635), *Méléagre* (1640), and other indifferent tragedies, devoted himself from 1651 to 1681 to the composition of *ballets* or masques, a favourite diversion at court during this period. His success in this sphere, due to the delicacy of his personal allusions, made him famous, wealthy, and a member of the *Académie française*. He translated Ovid's *Metamorphoses* and wrote a sonnet on Job which aroused such admiration that a keen dispute arose (in the midst of the *Fronde*) whether this or Voiture's sonnet on 'Uranie' was superior. Corneille had finally to intervene to appease the quarrel, which divided the literary world.

Béranger, PIERRE-JEAN [self-styled 'DE'] (1780–1857), author of *chansons* (light, popular verse, see *Chanson*), was in his lifetime accounted the national poet of France. Born in Paris, of humble parentage, he picked up an education in Péronne (Picardy), where he lived with an aunt, an innkeeper, then became a printer's apprentice. In 1804 his verses were seen by Lucien Bonaparte, brother of Napoleon, who procured him a small pension. Later, a minor clerical employment at the University afforded him freedom to write the *Chansons morales et autres*, collected in book form in 1815. This contained his already famous *Le Roi d'Yvetot* (q.v., and see *Caveau, Le*), a genial mockery of

Napoleon's despotism. *Chansons, 2ᵉ recueil* (1821), satirizing the abuses of the Restoration, earned him dismissal and a term in prison, where he began the *Chansons nouvelles* (published 1825). Nine months' imprisonment and a fine of 10,000 francs rewarded *Chansons inédites* (1828), this time because of his too freely expressed Bonapartist sympathies. But government persecution only increased his popularity, and his fine was paid by general subscription. After *Chansons nouvelles et dernières* (1833) he lived in retirement. Though many of his later songs were mordant political satires he owed his lifelong popularity to his light-hearted, witty facility for turning simple, at times ribald, jests and pleasures into verses which captivated by their lilt and gaiety.

Berchoux, JOSEPH (1765–1839), author of *La Gastronomie ou l'Homme des champs à table* (1801), a poem in six books.

Berçuire, PIERRE, see *Bersuire.*

Bérénice, a tragedy by Racine, produced in 1670. The theme is contained in the brief passage of Suetonius which tells how Titus, after promising marriage to Berenice, queen of Palestine, on his accession to the throne sent her away 'invitus invitam'. There is a story that Corneille and Racine adopted this theme simultaneously, each in ignorance that the other had done so, by the design of the duchesse d'Orléans, who had contrived a sort of poetic contest between them. Of the two tragedies produced, that of Racine was considered superior. (Cf. *Tite et Bérénice.*)

In Racine's play Titus, having just succeeded Vespasian on the throne, is about to marry Berenice. Antiochus, king of Commagene and friend of Titus, who has secretly loved Berenice for five years, decides to withdraw from Rome and takes leave of her. Titus learns that Roman opinion will not tolerate the marriage of the emperor with a foreigner, and resolves, in spite of his love for Berenice, to part with her. He charges Antiochus to inform the queen. She indignantly refuses to accept her dismissal from any other mouth than that of Titus. From him, with dignity and resignation, she accepts the sentence of Rome, and bids her lover an eternal farewell. Antiochus hopes to follow her, but she puts him aside, determined to love no one after Titus.

Bérésina, Berezina, see *Moscow, Retreat from.*

Bergerac, CYRANO DE, see *Cyrano.*

Bergeret, M. (LUCIEN), a provincial professor, a humanist, and a keen observer of life, figures in Anatole France's *Histoire contemporaine* (1896–1901). This keen satire of French life, politics, religion, monarchism, militarism, anti-Semitism—with the Dreyfus case in volume iv—is less a novel than a series of loosely-connected, character-revealing discussions. It is also an excellent picture of the various *coteries*, strata, and contending factions in a provincial town. There are four volumes—*L'Orme du mail* (1896; the *Mail* is the long, shady promenade where the townspeople walk and talk on summer evenings); *Le Mannequin d'osier* (1897; the tailor's dummy used by Mme Bergeret for home dress-making. It symbolizes the bullying to which M. Bergeret for long submits, till one day he destroys it); *L'Anneau d'améthyste* (1899; the amethyst ring worn by a bishop. Two local clerics are rival candidates for a vacant see); *M. Bergeret à Paris* (1901; M. Bergeret, with Riquet, his engaging dog, leaves the provinces for a chair at the Sorbonne).

Berger extravagant, Le, see *Sorel, Charles.*

Bergotte, in Proust's *A la recherche du temps perdu* (q.v.), a famous novelist, a hero to the young Marcel.

Bergson, HENRI-LOUIS (1859–1941), philosopher, born in Paris, the son of a Jewish father (a musician) and an English mother. He was a teacher by profession, and from 1900 a professor at the Collège de France. His principal works appeared as follows: *Essai sur les données immédiates de la conscience*, a thesis for the doctorate of the University of Paris (*Time and Free Will* is the English translation), in 1888; *Matière et mémoire* in 1896; *L'Évolution créatrice* in 1907; and *Les Deux Sources de la morale et de la religion* in 1932. His writings include many other monographs and lectures, some of them assembled in *L'Énergie spirituelle* (1919). *Le Rire, Essai sur la signification du comique*, appeared in 1900.

(2) His philosophy had a profound influence on modern thought and literature

(both creative and critical). Broadly speaking, he stated the problem of philosophy afresh and criticized the assumptions on which its task had previously been based. He sought (to use his own words) 'to rebuild the bridge (broken down since Kant) between metaphysics and science', a breach enlarged by the great development and specialization of the sciences since Kant's day. But whereas Kant thought of science as mathematica physics, and hence drew conclusions against metaphysics in general, Bergson examined the non-mathematical sciences (biology, physiology, and psychology) and sought in them a fresh approach to metaphysical problems. He observed that philosophers in describing change have taken time into account only in the sense of a conventional measure, spatial in character (as we measure time by the distance traversed by the hands of a clock), and have ignored real duration, *la durée*, 'what each of us apprehends when he reflects on his own conscious life, a process of change in which none of the parts are external to one another, but interpenetrating, where there is a perpetual creation of what is new' (A. D. Lindsay); and he perceived that organic change can only be studied by methods that recognize this duration as a reality. Psychical life he described as consisting in movement, but a movement which it is hard to express in words, because it is not in space, while we think habitually of the movement of material things and our language is adapted to this mode of thought.

(3) In studying psychical life he recognized in it, besides various causal elements, an element of spontaneity or freedom, a subject treated in his first work, *Les Données immédiates de la conscience*. This freedom, exercised only to a limited extent, is difficult to define and to demonstrate logically (except by showing that the contrary idea of necessary determination is inapplicable to psychic states), but can be observed empirically. It expresses itself in action, action which is in space, introducing something new and unpredictable amid the general laws of nature, deflecting the course of events. Mind thus acts on matter, and does so in a mysterious way, which Bergson examined in *Matière et mémoire*.

(4) The body, he contends, and particularly the brain, is solely an instrument of action. The brain, in perception, receives certain impulses from without and places these in relation with motor mechanisms selected with more or less freedom. *Presentations* are not produced in the brain; the function of the sense-organs is purely selective. Above all, memories are not stored in the brain. The orthodox theory which explains memory by 'physical traces' (a theory supposed to be confirmed by the study of such disorders as aphasia) owes its plausibility to an ambiguity. For the word 'memory' is used in two quite different senses. On the one hand there is habit-memory, as when we are said to remember how to play the piano or to repeat a poem learnt by rote. On the other, there is pure memory or memory proper, the awareness of past experiences. Habit-memory does depend upon the brain. Pure memory does not: it is a psychical, not a physiological, function. The past has not ceased to exist, and past psychical states have the same sort of independent survival as the material world. In relation to pure memory, the brain is rather the organ of forgetting than of remembering. It is the organ of 'attention to life', *l'attention à la vie*, and its function is to shut out from consciousness the greater part of our past, only letting through that small segment of it which is relevant to the practical activity of the moment. Pure memory itself is a spiritual manifestation, restricted to but not caused by the brain, and it is at this point of connexion between memory and perception that spirit influences matter. [Bergson's presidential address to the London Society for Psychical Research (1913, in the Society's *Proceedings*) throws valuable light upon the main doctrine of *Matière et mémoire*.]

(5) Proceeding from this, by a survey of the field of biology, Bergson was led to consider various theories, Darwinian and other, of evolution. This is the theme of *L'Évolution créatrice*. Bergson points out that more or less identical complex structures, such as the eye, are found in animals which have developed along very divergent lines, for example in molluscs on the one hand and vertebrates on the other. It is incredible that organs so similar should have developed in species so different if evolution were wholly due to the preservation and accumulation of chance variations, as the Darwinian theory maintains. Rejecting mechanical and teleological explanations, he finds in an original

impulse of life, *l'élan vital*, in a common effort on the part of individual organisms, that psychological factor in evolution which is the profound cause of the variations that are regularly transmitted and create new species. But evolution cannot be explained by the efforts of isolated individuals; it may be that the development of the species is effected by the effort of the species as a whole, and that the variations appear at the same time in all or most of its members, so that the whole is in some sense an individual, as a hive of bees is individual. In this connexion he shows, in a profound study of instinct and intelligence, that instinctive and intelligent life are divergent directions of development, not different stages in the same development. But intelligence, no less than instinct, has primarily a biological function. It does not reveal ultimate reality, but presents to us a simplified and above all a specialized picture of the world, adapted to meet the needs of action, especially of manipulative action. In so far as man is an intelligent animal, he should be described not as *homo sapiens* but as *homo faber*. Ultimate reality is revealed to us neither by instinct nor by intelligence, but by a third function which Bergson calls intuition. The essential feature of the Real, whether in external nature or in ourselves, is *la durée réelle*, and in it the hard and fast distinctions drawn by the spatializing intelligence have no place.

(6) Bergson's conception of the world as a whole, set out in the same work, is of the existence of two opposing currents: on the one hand inert matter pursuing its downward course; on the other, organic life striving upwards, overcoming the obstacles that matter places in its way, displaying a single original impulse, but following divergent lines of development. In a final chapter he examines two illusions: the one underlying the perturbing question, How came there originally to *be* anything at all, how, if we attribute the universe to some immanent or transcendent Principle, came that principle itself to exist, rather than nothing? And that second illusion by which, seizing only isolated states in the constant flux of reality, isolated moments in duration, we think we can interpret movement in terms of the immobile, with important consequences in the history of philosophy.

(7) In *Le Rire, Essai sur la signification du comique,* Bergson infers from an examination of many types of comic situations and characters that at the root of the comic element is a certain rigidity or inadaptability to circumstances or to the conventions of society, as a result of which a conscious being behaves like a mechanism, and that laughter is the means by which society tends to correct this defect.

(8) Bergson wrote in a brilliant, fluid style, marked (especially in *L'Évolution créatrice*) by the use of vivid metaphors and ingenious similes, and by the poetical quality of many passages. These, it may be thought, sometimes gain the reader's assent to propositions which would hardly carry conviction if expressed in plain and sober prose.

Berlioz, LOUIS-HECTOR (1803–69), musical composer, introduced the Romantic spirit into French music (see *Romantisme*). He was musical critic on the *Journal des Débats* (q.v.) from 1838 till 1863, and published several collections of essays: *Voyage musical en Allemagne et en Italie* (1844), *Soirées d'orchestre* (1852), *Les Grotesques de la musique* (1859), *A travers chants* (1862),&c., as well as *Mémoires* (1870) of great interest and a *Traité d'instrumentation et d'orchestration modernes* (1844).

Bernadette Soubirous, SAINT (1844–79), canonized 8 December 1933, a poor miller's daughter of Lourdes, in the Pyrenees, to whom the Virgin Mary is said to have appeared several times in February 1858 while she was guarding sheep on the mountain slopes. The happenings, and the tales of miraculous cures attendant on them, aroused both enthusiasm and scepticism, but after inquiry the Church (of Rome) pronounced that the apparitions had been authentic. A church was erected on the site and Lourdes has since become a great, and highly organized, place of pilgrimage. Saint Bernadette of Lourdes ended her days in a convent. The story inspired Zola's novel *Lourdes*.

Bernadotte, CHARLES-JEAN (later King Charles XIV of Sweden), one of Napoleon's marshals (see *Maréchal de l'Empire*).

Bernanos, GEORGES (1888–1948), novelist and polemical writer, born in Paris of partly Lorrain partly Spanish forebears, worked with an insurance company until in 1926 success enabled him to live solely by his pen. He was much in Majorca, but in 1938 he felt the Munich crisis so deeply that he settled with his family in Brazil. He returned to France in 1945 after the Liberation.

His novels, written with great force, sometimes with a violence that reflects the struggles described, all introduce the supernatural. In one sense they are pictures of the lives of country clergymen, but the souls of his humble village priests are battle-grounds for the warring forces of good and evil. *Sous le soleil de Satan* (1926) made his reputation. *Journal d'un curé de campagne* (1936) confirmed it and extended it beyond France. Other titles are: *La Joie* (1929); *Un Crime* (1935); *Nouvelle histoire de Mouchette* (1937), reintroducing a character from *Sous le soleil . . .*; *Monsieur Ouine* (published 1946, written much earlier).

Bernanos the polemist combated hypocrisy in all forms. His *Grande peur des bien pensants* (1931), an appreciation of Édouard Drumont (1844–1917), a notorious anti-Semitic writer of the Dreyfus (q.v.) period, expressed his own conception of Royalism and Catholicism and his disgust with the modern world. *Les Grands Cimetières sous la lune* (1937) sprang from his spiritual and political disillusionment after the Spanish civil war and is considered one of the finest modern examples of polemical writing. *Lettre aux Anglais* calls for mention among a number of his fine essays and broadcasts from Brazil during the 1939–45 war.

Bernard, Saint (1091–1153), born near Dijon, a great ecclesiastic, founder of the abbey of Clairvaux, one of the four 'Latin Fathers', the glory of the Cistercian Order. He was practically dictator of Christendom, securing in 1130 the recognition of Innocent II as pope against the claims of Anacletus. He preached the Second Crusade. He was a vigorous adversary and persecutor of Abélard (q.v.). He left some remarkable letters and theological treatises and was one of the founders of Latin hymnody. There is a French translation, made not earlier than the end of the 12th century, of eighty-four of his Latin sermons.

Bernard, Charles de, *pseud.* of CHARLES-BERNARD DU GRAIL DE LA VILLETTE (1805–50), journalist and novelist, best remembered by his novel *Gerfaut* (1838). *Le Nœud gordien* (1838) and *Paravent* (1839)

were collections of long-short stories. He was a friend of, and influenced by, Balzac.

Bernard, Claude (1813–78), experimental physiologist, born at Saint-Julien, near Lyons. His widely-read *Introduction à l'étude de la médecine expérimentale* (1865) had two main arguments : (*a*) that the art of medicine was a matter of observation and experiment, leading to the proof or demolition of hypotheses; and (*b*) that natural phenomena were explicable in the light of environment and precedent causes. The Naturalistic novelists applied his theories, imperfectly comprehended, to the art of the novel (see *Naturalisme*; *Zola*).

Bernard, Jean-Jacques (1888–), dramatist, son of Tristan Bernard (q.v.). His plays make skilful use of modern theories of the Unconscious, and he uses the silences rather than the words of his characters to reveal their thoughts—*Le Feu qui reprend mal* (1922), a study of retrospective jealousy), *Martine* (1922), *L'Invitation au voyage* (1924), *Le Printemps des autres* (1924), *L'Âme en peine* (1926), &c.

Bernard, Jean-Marc (1881–1915), *fantaisiste* (q.v.) poet, born at Valence-sur-Rhône, is remembered for the elegiac verses, love and nature poems, of *Sub tegmine fagi* (*Amours, bergeries et jeux*) (1913). He also founded *Les Guêpes*, a satirical and critical review which attracted attention. His moving poem *De profundis*, written shortly before his death in action, figures in many anthologies. His *Œuvres complètes* (poetry, essays, and criticism) were published in 1923 (2 vols.).

Bernard, Pierre-Joseph (1710–75), known as *Gentil-Bernard* from the epithet applied to him by Voltaire, poet, writer of *vers de société* and of an *Art d'aimer* on the Ovidian model. He was protected by Mme de Pompadour.

Bernard, Tristan (1866–1947), journalist, humorous writer, and playwright. His successful comedies, farcical comedies and vaudevilles, good-humoured satires and caricatures of middle-class life, include: *Le Fardeau de la liberté* (1897); *L'Anglais tel qu'on le parle* (1899); *Un Mari pacifique* (1901); *Le Petit Café* (1912). *Triplepatte* (1905, in collaboration with A. Godfernaux) studies character more closely than his other comedies. His novel *Les Mémoires d'un jeune homme rangé* (1899) was successful when published. He was a noted *raconteur* and wit.

Bernard de Morlaix (*Bernardus Morlacensis*), a Benedictine monk of Cluny of the 12th century, author of the Latin poem *De contemptu mundi*, of parts of which we have translations in John Mason Neale's *Jerusalem the golden* and other hymns.

Bernard de Naisil, see *Garin le Loherain*.

Bernard de Ventadour, see *Troubadour*.

Bernardin de Saint-Pierre, JACQUES-HENRI (1737–1814), born at Le Havre, of a family originally from Lorraine, naturalist and writer, was for a time a military engineer, but lost his position through his insubordinate temper. He now led a vagrant existence, travelling about Europe (including Russia and Poland) to promote a scheme for the regeneration of society, often without resources. In 1768 he was a member of an expedition to Madagascar but disembarked at the Île de France (Mauritius), and remained there for a time as an engineer. His *Voyage à l'Isle de France*, in the form of letters to a friend, published (1773) after his return to France, was only moderately successful, but his *Études de la Nature* (1784), depicting natural scenes and arguing from their order and harmony against atheism, a pioneer work in the literature of the picturesque, brought him fame and profit. *Paul et Virginie* (q.v.), by which he is chiefly remembered, appeared in vol. iv of the 1787 edition of the *Études*. His other works included Book I of *Arcadie* (an imaginary picture of primitive Gaul); *La Chaumière indienne* (1791, a learned traveller in search of truth and wisdom finds them only in the cottage of an Indian pariah); and *Les Harmonies de la Nature* (published in 1815), a poor repetition of the *Études*, marked by extravagant scientific notions. He was director of the Jardin des Plantes for a short time during the Revolution, and from 1795 a member of the Institut, where he constantly quarrelled with his colleagues. He was pensioned under the Empire.

Bernardin de Saint-Pierre, an adventurer, a malcontent, and a visionary, found consolation for his hatred of society in his love of nature, which he studied with the eye of an artist and depicted with careful accuracy, but which he endeavoured to explain in the light of sentiment, as a substitute for scientific knowledge and method. He was a friend of the later (1772–6) Rousseau, whose life he wrote (published in 1820), and developed his doctrines, religious and political, unintelligently and to exaggeration. He was a firm believer in final causes and saw in nature all sorts of providential arrangements, some of them of puerile absurdity, as that the ribs of the melon are designed for its apportionment at the family meal. But he wrote in a rich, supple, and attractive style, and some of his descriptions of natural scenes have great charm. In his feeling for the melancholy aspects of nature he was a precursor of Chateaubriand, and his pictures of the sea and tropical landscapes were a novelty in French literature.

Bernesque, Satire, see under *Satire*.

Bernhardt [Bernard], SARAH-HENRIETTE-ROSINE (1845–1923), French actress, one of the most famous, French or otherwise, of all time, was born in Paris and at thirteen was already training for the stage. Between 1862 (her first appearance) and 1880 she acted frequently at the *Comédie-Française* (q.v.) but she was never permanently associated with it. She acted much in other countries. In Paris, latterly, she was her own manager, with, in the end, her own *Théâtre Sarah Bernhardt*. She had a 'golden voice', of what is said to have been indescribable beauty. Her great parts included Phèdre, Doña Sol, Adrienne Lecouvreur (qq.v.), Sardou's La Tosca and Fédora, Marguerite in *La Dame aux camélias* (Dumas *fils*), and—one of her greatest triumphs—l'Aiglon in Rostand's play of that name about Napoleon's son, the *Roi de Rome* (q.v.). In 1872 she had played Cordelia in a production of *King Lear* in French at the Comédie-Française. In later life she played Hamlet. She published *Mémoires de ma vie* in 1907. She had a leg amputated in 1915 but returned to the stage occasionally even after that. She appeared last in *La Gloire* (produced October 1922), by Maurice Rostand (q.v.). The name part, written specially for her, permitted her to remain seated throughout the play.

Bernier, FRANÇOIS (*c.* 1625–88), physician and traveller, author of *Voyages* (1699), an account of his travels in the East. He visited India, where he was for a time physician to Aurung-zeb. He was prominent among the *libertins* or free-thinkers of the 17th century and wrote some philosophical works (*Abrégé de la philosophie de Gassendi*, 1678, *Traité du libre et du volontaire*, 1685).

Bernis (pron. as if *Berniss*), FRANÇOIS-JOACHIM DE (1715–94), abbé and later, thanks to the favour of Mme de Pompadour, cardinal and French ambassador at Venice, and in 1757 appointed minister of foreign affairs. In his earlier years he was a frequenter of the duchesse du Maine's court at Sceaux, and author of verses, mostly light and flowery, which earned for him from Voltaire the nickname of 'Babet la Bouquetière'. He was admitted to the *Académie* in 1744. As minister of foreign affairs he shared the responsibility for the French disasters of the Seven Years War.

When discharged in 1758 from a post to which he was unequal, he retired as archbishop of Albi. In 1769 he was sent as ambassador to Rome and there in a measure redeemed his previous failure. His memoirs show Mme de Pompadour in her political role.

Bernstein, HENRY (1876–1953), author of closely-constructed, 'powerful' dramas in which passions are usually violent and sometimes morbid, e.g. *La Rafale* (1905), *Le Voleur* (1907), *Samson* (1907), *L'Assaut* (1912), *Le Secret* (1913), *Judith* (1922), *La Galerie des glaces* (1925).

Berny, MME DE, see *Dilecta, La.*

Béroalde de Verville, FRANÇOIS (1558–1612), born in Paris, and from 1593 a canon of Tours, author of a romance *Les Aventures de Floride* (in two parts 1594 and 1601) and probably of the *Moyen de parvenir* (1610), the fantastic account of a symposium at which all sorts of grave personages of antiquity (such as Solon and Plutarch) and modern times (Commines, Budaeus) exchange anecdotes and jokes of a Rabelaisian obscenity interspersed with satires on the monks, the Church, the nobility, women, tax-collectors, &c. The tales are skilfully told, but the key to much of the satire is lost to the modern reader.

Béroul, see *Tristan.*

Berquin, ARNAUD (1749?–91), man of letters, remembered in particular as author of works for juveniles, *L'Ami des enfants* (24 vols., 1782–3), &c., known as *berquinades*. Some of these were translated into English and were very popular.

Berquin, LOUIS DE (d. 1529), one of the early leaders of the Reformation in France. He translated works of Luther into French and although protected by Marguerite de Navarre was executed in 1529.

Berry, CHARLES, DUC DE (1778–1820), second son of Charles X, was assassinated by Louvel, a saddler. In 1832 his widow tried to foment an insurrection in the Vendée against the government of Louis-Philippe (q.v.). It failed and she was imprisoned for some time. (Cf. *Bourbon*; *Chambord, comte de*).

Bersuire or **Berçuire** (d. 1362), remembered as author of a translation into French of Livy (1352–6), a work of wide influence. He made the acquaintance of Petrarch when the latter came to France in 1361.

Bertaut, JEAN (1552–1611), poet, born in the diocese of Bayeux, appointed reader to Henri III and later official court poet, a position which he obtained afresh under Henri IV; bishop of Séez (now Sées) in 1606. Judicious in his conduct he was the friend of everyone. As a poet he imitated Ronsard and Desportes with less talent, but with more propriety in his love poems. His verses are polished and pointed, sometimes tender and melancholy, but in general showing lack of vigour. As court poet and bishop he celebrated great events and wrote canticles on religious subjects and paraphrases of psalms. He confined himself in the main to quatrains and sixains of alexandrines. His serious poems were published in 1601, his love poems in the following year, anonymously. He is perhaps best remembered for a quatrain which had some fame:

Félicité passée
Qui ne peux revenir,
Tourment de ma pensée,
Que n'ay-je, en te perdant, perdu le souvenir!

It is quoted by Voltaire, in his *Dialogue de Mme de Maintenon et Mlle de l'Enclos*, and even by Le Maître de Saci (q.v.) in his commentary on Job (xvii. 11, 'Dies mei transierunt'). Mme de Motteville (q.v.) was Bertaut's niece.

Berthe aux grands pieds, wife of Pépin le Bref and mother of Charlemagne (qq.v.), is the subject of a *chanson de geste* (q.v.) of that name by Adenet le Roi (q.v.). It tells how on the night of the wedding another woman was successfully substituted by traitors for the true Berthe. The unfortunate princess, thus ousted from the throne, wandered in the forest, and suffered great hardships until the imposture was discovered (by her mother). This *chanson* is a rehandling of an earlier one; and the story is also the theme of one of the *Miracles de Notre Dame* (q.v.).

The adventures of Berthe's son Charlemagne, driven by the sons of the false Berthe to take refuge among the Saracens under the name of Mainet, are told in the *chanson Mainet,* of which fragments survive.

For historical facts concerning Berthe, see under *Charlemagne.*

Berthelot, MARCELIN (1827–1907), savant, celebrated for his work in organic chemistry, was born in Paris into a family of strong liberal and democratic traditions, and in circumstances sufficiently easy for him to pursue unremunerative scientific research. In 1860 he published *La Chimie organique fondée sur la synthèse,* on the results of his researches and their philosophic bearing. Soon afterwards he was appointed to a specially created chair of Organic Chemistry at the Collège de France (q.v.), which he held till his death. From 1870 he was also active in politics and held Ministerial office (National Defence and Education). His wide philosophical outlook and his view of philosophical systems as the expression of the contemporary state of scientific knowledge were apparent in *Les Origines de l'alchimie* (1885), an historical study, with translations, of Greco-Egyptian texts on alchemy, and *La Chimie au moyen âge* (1893), a study in three volumes of this ancient science and its transmission. He also left two volumes of collected essays and addresses, *Science et philosophie* (1886) and *Science et morale* (1897), which contain, among other items, an interesting picture of Paris and the part played by science during the siege of 1870–1 (see *Franco-Prussian War*), also a picture of the world as it might be, *c.* 2000, transformed by the progress of physical and chemical science. Natural energy would have been harnessed to provide heat and power, so that the need to dig for coal—and hence workers' strikes—would no longer exist; the earth would be one large garden, for man would subsist on chemical pills, and stock, crops, and even vineyards would be unnecessary; while aerial navigation would have abolished customs, trade barriers, wars, and bloodstained frontiers—provided that some spiritual alchemy could also be found to transform human nature.

Berthelot was a lifelong friend of Renan (q.v.) and influenced his thought. Their interesting *Correspondance* (1898) extends from 1847 to 1892.

Berthier, LOUIS-ALEXANDRE, one of Napoleon's marshals (see *Maréchal de l'Empire*).

Berthollet, CLAUDE-LOUIS, COMTE (1748–1822), French chemist, one of the founders of the École polytechnique (q.v.). He accompanied Napoleon to Egypt. The use of chlorine for bleaching was one of his discoveries.

Bertillon, ALPHONSE (1853–1914), born in Paris, and for many years head of the *Service d'identité judiciaire* at the *Préfecture de police,* did much by his research and initiative to improve police technique and the science of detection. He invented anthropometry, a system (known also as *Bertillonnage*) of identification based on the scientific measurement and classification of certain bony structures of the body, particularly the head. The system was for some time employed in France and other countries for the identification of criminals, but it had defects, and was superseded by the system of fingerprints.

Bertin, ANTOINE (1752–90), poet, born in the Île Bourbon in the Indian Ocean, friend of Parny (q.v.), wrote three books of graceful elegies (*Les Amours,* 1780) in which he tells the story of his life and loves.

Bertin, the name of a family famous in French journalism for its association with the *Journal des Débats* (q.v.), which Bertin aîné (Louis-François Bertin, 1766–1841) and his brother Louis-François Bertin de Vaux (1771–1842) bought in 1799. Bertin aîné was succeeded in the editorship by his second son Armand (1801–54). When Armand died, the eldest son François-Édouard (1797–1871), originally a landscape painter, took over.

Bertrand, HENRI-GRATIEN, COMTE DE (1773–1844), one of Napoleon's most faithful generals, was with him from the Egyptian campaign onwards. He followed him to Elba after the first abdication (1814) and, after the second (1815), to St. Helena where he remained until the end. At St. Helena he wrote, to Napoleon's dictation, a record of the *Campagne d'Égypte et de Syrie* (2 vols., 1847, posth.). He also, for his own purposes, kept a journal of life at St. Helena. This was published in 1948.

Bertrand, LOUIS (called Aloysius) (1807–41), poet, born at Ceva (Piedmont), of a French father and an Italian mother, was educated at Dijon. He came to Paris in 1829 and became known in the Romantic circles dominated by Nodier, Hugo, and Sainte-Beuve (qq.v.). Except for one period at Dijon editing a local paper he lived mainly in Paris. His life was a continual struggle with poverty and, latterly, ill health. He died of consumption. His name rests on one work, *Gaspard de la nuit*, written about 1830 but published posthumously (1842). This collection of 'fantaisies à la manière de Rembrandt et de Callot', an early example of the prose-poem, is written in ornate and rhythmical language and forms a succession of scintillating, often grotesque, images with touches of delicate naturalistic description. It was a sign of the Romantic revival of interest in the Middle Ages, but Bertrand has also been called a precursor of the *Symbolistes* and of the *Surréalistes* (see *Symbolisme*; *Surréalisme*). Baudelaire, in the preface to his *Petits Poèmes en prose*, recognized his influence.

Bertrand, LOUIS (1866–1941), novelist of French colonial life (Africa)—*Le Sang des races* (1899); *La Cina* (1901); *Pépète le bien-aimé* (1904), &c.

Bertrand de Bar-sur-Aube, a poet of the end of the 12th century, author of the *chanson de geste* of *Girard de Viane* and probably of *Aimeri de Narbonne*. He is said to have first suggested grouping the *chansons de geste*.

Bertrand de Born (*c.* 1140–*c.* 1215), a noted warrior and troubadour of Guyenne. Dante in the *Inferno* (xxviii. 134) places him among the 'sowers of schism' for having stirred up Prince Henry against his father Henry II of England.

Bertrand et Raton, names of the monkey and the cat respectively in La Fontaine's fable of *Le Singe et le chat*, in which the cat draws the chestnuts out of the fire and the monkey eats them. The names are sometimes used proverbially. One of Scribe's (q.v.) most successful historical comedies was entitled *Bertrand et Raton* (1833). The scene is Copenhagen in the year 1772. Bertrand von Rantzau is a statesman with the guile acquired from long years of experience. Raton, a rich silk merchant, popular with his fellow citizens, is a simple character, easily led, and anxious to rise in the world. Bertrand engineers a people's revolt on the pretext that Raton has been unjustly imprisoned by Struensee, the aged king's former physician, now the all-powerful First Minister. Struensee is overturned and Bertrand steps into his place. The play's interest, as usual with Scribe, depends mainly on a highly complicated plot, but the two chief characters are by no means lifeless.

Bérulle, CARDINAL PIERRE DE, see *Oratoire*.

Berwick, JAMES FITZJAMES, DUKE OF (1670–1734), Marshal of France, natural son of the Duke of York (James II) and Arabella Churchill. He was born and educated in France. He came to England after his father's accession and was created Duke of Berwick. He served with distinction, when only seventeen, against the Turks in Hungary; in 1689–90 he served against William III in Ireland; and in 1704 successfully commanded the French army in Spain. He was there again, in command of the Spanish army, in 1706–7, when he won the battle of Almanza. He was killed at the siege of Philippsburg in 1734. His *Mémoires*, written in a simple and natural style, are concerned mainly with military events. They contain a narrative of the battle of the Boyne and other matters of special interest to English readers.

Besançon, ALBÉRIC DE, see *Alexandre le Grand*.

Besant de Dieu, Le, a didactic religious poem in octosyllabic couplets by Guillaume le Clerc (12th–13th century), in which the author, taking as theme the *besant* or talent entrusted to each by God, reviews the failings of the various classes of the society of his day and urges amendment.

Bescherelle, Louis-Nicolas, see *Dictionaries and Encyclopedias*, under date 1843–6.

Besenval, Pierre-Victor, baron de (1722–91), a Swiss officer who served with distinction in the French army and spent much of his life at the French court. He left *Mémoires* which throw some interesting light on the persons who formed that court and on French society at the close of the *ancien régime*.

Bessières, Jean-Baptiste, one of Napoleon's marshals, see *Maréchal de l'Empire*.

Bestiaires, in medieval literature, collections of tales about animals (largely drawn from Greek and Latin sources), from which moral conclusions are drawn. They were common in France from the 12th century and popular also in England. The earliest surviving example is the *Bestiaire* of Philippe de Thaon, an Anglo-Norman writer, which dates from early in the 12th century. It was dedicated to Aélis (Adela) of Louvain, consort of Henry I, and written in six-syllabled couplets. It gives fantastic descriptions of animals, adding moral interpretations. The *Bestiaire d'amour* of Richard de Fournival (*c.* 1250) places a less pious interpretation on the traditional tales.

Bête humaine, La (1890), by Zola, one of his *Rougon-Macquart* (q.v.) novels. The chief characters are an engine-driver, his wife, and his wife's lover. The story is a melodramatic round of passion, crime, and homicidal mania, redeemed by Zola's forcible descriptive writing. His descriptions of trains are notable, and the strongest personality in the book is that of the engine, 'La Lison'.

Béthune, Anonyme de, see *History* (*Medieval period*).

Bettine, a comedy (one act, prose) by Alfred de Musset (q.v.), produced on 30 October 1851 (Théâtre du Gymnase) and published two days later in the *Revue des Deux Mondes*. It was included in the 1853 edition of *Comédies et Proverbes* (q.v.). A prima donna summons the notary to marry her to one man. There are delays, and the notary is set down to macaroons and muscatel wine. The morning passes. Bettine is still single, and disillusioned on the first lover's count, but more than half consenting to marry an old admirer. And the notary is still conveniently at hand.

Beuves (or **Boeve**) **de Haumtone.** The oldest extant version of this popular tale, preserved in many languages, appears to be a 12th-century Anglo-Norman text (3,850 lines in monorhyme stanzas). It was first translated into English as *Sir Beves of Hamtoun* (i.e. Southampton), probably in the 13th century, and several English versions have survived.

The mother of Beuves having procured the murder of her husband, Guion (Guy), earl of Southampton, by Doon de Mayence, she then marries the murderer and sells her son as a slave. After many adventures, including the defeat and conversion to Christianity of the giant Ascopart, Beuves is united with Josian, the king of Egypt's daughter whom he also converts to Christianity. Their son Miles marries the daughter of the English King Edgar.

Beuves's horse Arondel and his sword Morglay figure frequently in the story.

Beyle, Henri; **Beylisme,** see *Stendhal*.

Bèze [Latin form = Beza], Théodore de (1519–1605), Protestant and humanist, head of the Church of Geneva after the death of Calvin, author of an *Histoire ecclésiastique des Églises Réformées au royaume de France* (1580), of a religious drama, *Abraham sacrifiant* (1550), of translations in verse of some of the Psalms, and of a lively satire, *L'Épître de Benoît Passavant* (1553). He maintained relations with English Churchmen and presented the *Codex Bezae* of the four Gospels and Acts of the Apostles to Cambridge University. *Abraham sacrifiant*, in which Abraham is seen torn between temptation and his faith, is a landmark between the medieval Mystery and Renaissance drama.

Bible, a term sometimes used in the Middle Ages for verse treatises of a didactic or satirical character (see *Guiot de Provins*). The 'Bible' of Hugues II de Berzé (*c.* 1220), a former crusader, is a more serious work than that of Guiot; the author shows sincere contrition in his condemnation of the worldly life of the day.

Bible, French versions of the. The earliest known translations from the Scriptures into French are two Anglo-Norman versions of the Psalter of about the year 1100. There was a translation of the Apocalypse, also into Anglo-Norman, of the second half of the 12th century. To the same period belongs a version in prose of the four books of Kings written in pure French and elegant in style. About 1190 Herman de Valenciennes wrote a metrical version of the Old and New Testaments, as well as a number of lives of saints. In the South of France Valdus (see *Vaudois*) had a French version of parts of the Scriptures prepared and widely distributed among the Waldenses; it dated from the last quarter of the 12th century but the text is not extant. During the reign of Saint Louis (1226–70) the first translation of the Bible as a whole was prepared, accompanied in certain parts by glosses; the value of the translation of the various books was very unequal—that of Genesis clear, concise, accurate, and vigorous, and that of the Gospels also good, that of the Apocalypse, for instance, very bad. To about 1295 belongs the *Bible historiale*, the work of Guyart des Moulins, a free translation of the *Historia scolastica* of Pierre le Mangeur, itself an epitome of the Bible narrative with explanations in places; to this Guyart added translations of various scriptural passages. The work was very popular in the 14th century. In that century also, Jean de Vignay prepared, by order of Jeanne de Bourgogne, consort of Philippe VI, versions of the Epistles and Gospels in the offices of the day. After the Middle Ages the first complete translation of the Bible was that of Lefèvre d'Étaples (q.v., finished in 1528), shortly followed by that of Olivetan (q.v., 1535), which was the first Protestant version. This was published, as corrected by Calvin, at the expense of the Waldenses: it provided a model for another Catholic translation, published in 1550 (the Louvain Bible). In the same century the *Compagnie des pasteurs de Genève* entrusted the work of making a fresh (Protestant) translation to some of its members, including Bèze; this was published in 1588 and has kept its position as an authoritative version. It was in fact a revision of that of Olivetan. Various translations were made, of the whole or parts of the Scriptures, in the 17th and 18th centuries, notable among them that prepared by Le Maître de Saci and Antoine Arnauld, aided by other solitaries of Port-Royal. This version of the N.T. (known as the Nouveau

Testament de Mons because of its Mons imprint) was printed at Amsterdam in 1667 and had a wide circulation. Le Maître de Saci subsequently added a translation of the O.T. (1672–95). Richard Simon's translation of the N.T., published at Trévoux in 1702, was condemned by Bossuet, who himself translated certain portions of the Scriptures. A complete translation of the Bible by the Swiss theologian Jean-Frédéric Osterwald (1663–1747), published in 1744, is still the one most widely used in French Protestant churches. See also *Religious Writings*.

Bible de l'humanité, La (1864), by Michelet (q.v.), is a study of the origins and evolution of religious belief.

Humanity, the author says, has always had its *Bible*, based on ideas, at first elementary, of moral virtue, of justice, and respect for life, of toil, of education; and first and foremost of the family, out of which emerged its belief in deities and a Deity and in the sacred role of woman. These ideas have evolved with the ages, each great epoch making some fresh contribution, to be deduced from a study of its greatest or most characteristic works. Study and analysis of, for example, early Oriental literature, the literature and laws of ancient Greece and Rome and of Judaea, of the Pyramids of Egypt, show a fundamental similarity between the religious and cultural standards of the present century [i.e. the 19th, in which the author was writing] and those of the remote past, in spite of modifications due to scientific progress and discovery.

The book is written with fervour and a strong sense of discovery of the past, and of the present within the past. This can be appreciated when it is remembered that during the first half of the 19th century orientalists and archaeologists between them had suddenly revealed a hitherto unknown wealth of oriental literature and civilization.

Bible Guiot, see *Guiot de Provins*.

Bibliographical pointers to the study of French literature and its background, see *Appendix I*.

Bibliographie de la France, La, or *Journal de la Librairie et de l'Imprimerie*, an official weekly list (founded in 1811 by Imperial decree) of all the newly printed works delivered, by State requirement (the *Dépôt*

légal), to the *Bibliothèque nationale* (q.v., and cf. the analogous requirement in English law under which newly printed books are delivered to the British Museum and five other libraries (*see* Harvey, *Comp. to Eng. Lit.*, 3rd ed., 1946, App. ii)).

Bibliotheca Normannica, a German collection of writings in Anglo-Norman, edited 1879–99 at Halle by Hermann Suchier.

Bibliothèque bleue, collections of popular tales, legends, and romances of chivalry (e.g. *Les Quatre Fils Aymon, Robert le diable*), bound in blue, and due to the enterprise of Jean Oudot (*c.* 1665, a bookseller at Troyes). They were almost the sole reading-matter in country districts before 1789. (See *Children's reading*.)

Bibliothèque de l'Arsenal. This is the second of the great French libraries. (The *Bibliothèque nationale*, q.v., comes first.) It is in Paris, on the site of the ancient Arsenal in which munitions and armaments of the kings of France were housed and fabricated. It began in a small way as the private library of Antoine-René d'Argenson, marquis de Paulmy (1722–87), son of René-Louis and a nephew of Marc-Pierre (see *Argenson, D'*) and a great collector of books. In his capacity as Gouverneur du Bailliage de l'Arsenal he lived in the Hôtel de l'Arsenal (originally built for the King's Grand Master of Artillery) from 1757 onwards. In 1786 he sold his library to the comte d'Artois (later to become Charles X) but retained the use of it till he died. During the Revolution the comte d'Artois went into exile. His library was confiscated by the State, but preserved as a whole and thrown open to the public in 1797 as the *Bibliothèque de l'Arsenal*. At a later date large numbers of books and manuscripts confiscated from other sources were added. For a time during the reign of Charles X the library reverted to his possession, but readers were still admitted. At the present day it contains over a million printed books, *c.* 120,000 prints, and a fine collection of illuminated manuscripts. It is particularly rich in medieval and dramatic literature. One of its early curators was Charles Nodier (q.v.), whose Salon was famous as the first Romantic *cénacle* (see *Romantisme*). Another curator of literary renown was the poet Heredia (q.v.).

Bibliothèque de la Sorbonne, the name, from 1897 onwards, for a part of the *Bibliothèque de l'université de Paris* (see below) which has been housed since 1823 in the Sorbonne. A working library for the use of students in the faculties of Arts and Science, it comprises some 900,000 volumes, over 3,000 periodicals, and a complete set of university theses for Paris and the provinces, as well as a noteworthy collection of archives of the University of Paris from the 14th to the 18th centuries.

Bibliothèque de l'université de Paris. Under this general heading are included the various faculty libraries of the university, e.g. the *Bibliothèque de la Sorbonne* and the *Bibliothèque Sainte-Geneviève* (qq.v.), the *Bibliothèque de documentation internationale contemporaine* (books relating to the war of 1914–18, its causes and consequences); also certain private libraries bequeathed to the university, e.g. the collections of the philosopher Victor Cousin and of the medieval scholar Gaston Paris (qq.v.).

Bibliothèque de Saint-Victor, see *Saint-Victor, Abbaye de*.

Bibliothèque Mazarine, one of the famous libraries of Paris, had its nucleus in the splendid library of theological and historical works bequeathed to the nation by Cardinal Mazarin (q.v.) as part of the Collège des Quatre Nations, now the Institut de France (qq.v.). During the Revolution it secured a large share of the books and manuscripts confiscated by the State from ecclesiastical and private sources. It is now particularly rich in works dealing with the seventeenth century.

Bibliothèque nationale. This, the premier French library, had its origin in the libraries formed by the kings of France. Charles V possessed a collection of manuscripts which was sold under Charles VI to the Duke of Bedford. Later kings, e.g. Charles VIII, Louis XI, François Ier, themselves humanists and book-lovers, amassed the collections of books and manuscripts which form the nucleus of the present-day Library. François Ier assembled the various royal libraries in one place, the palace of Fontainebleau, and appointed the first Royal Librarian, the learned Guillaume Budé (q.v.). Foreign manuscripts were now also acquired.

For instance, the French ambassador at Venice (then principal mart for manuscripts of the classics) was instructed to secure such works as he could, and in 1541 he dispatched four cases of Greek manuscripts to France; and Guillaume Postel, an Oriental scholar, was sent to the East to gather manuscripts.

Under Louis XIV the Library, which had in the meantime been returned to Paris, was almost doubled in size by the efforts of Colbert, who installed it on its present site (rue Richelieu and rue Vivienne) in property belonging to himself. Under both Louis XV ('l'âge d'or de la Bibliothèque') and Louis XVI the collection was still further enriched, by donations and also, despite all the financial embarrassments of pre-Revolutionary France, by purchasing. With the Revolution it became national property and secured the largest share of the books and manuscripts confiscated from convents and châteaux. Its prosperity increased during the 19th century, and continues.

As early as 1692 the *Bibliothèque du Roi*, as it was then known, was thrown open to the public twice a week by the king's Librarian, the abbé de Louvois, who 'régala plusieurs sçavans d'un magnifique repas' to celebrate his act. After the Revolution, and renamed the *Bibliothèque nationale*, it was opened daily (in the mornings and since 1859 all day) to accredited readers. During the First and again during the Second Empire it was called *Bibliothèque impériale*.

The present-day *Bibliothèque nationale* is divided into eight departments: manuscripts; printed books (c. 6,000,000 volumes; under the terms of the *Dépôt légal*, which originated in the Ordonnance de Montpellier issued by François Ier in 1537, one copy of every book published in France is required by law to be deposited, as also of prints and of all photographs intended for sale); periodicals; maps; music; prints; medals, coins, and antiquities; new acquisitions.

Bibliothèque rose, a well-known series published by Hachette since the mid-19th century, of books—new or reprints—considered suitable for children's reading. They are bound in bright red (cf. *Children's reading*).

Bibliothèque Sainte-Geneviève. This, originally the library of the Abbaye de Sainte-Geneviève and now affiliated to the University of Paris, dates from c. 1624 and has been open to the public since 1759. It became national property in 1791 and was known for a time as *Bibliothèque du Panthéon*. It contains manuscripts, prints, and printed matter (including a number of rare works as well as most of the books required by university students). It is a favourite working library, always crowded.

Bicêtre [a corruption of 'Winchester]', on the outskirts of Paris, now a mental hospital and asylum for the aged, formerly a particularly sordid prison. From 1204 the site was occupied by a palace built for his own use by John, Bishop of Winchester, who lived at the court of Philippe-Auguste. Later the palace became a royal residence and then the home of a colony of Carthusian monks. In 1411, during the Bourgogne-Armagnac risings, it was burnt. The ruins remained for two centuries and became a place of evil repute. In 1632 the *Commanderie de Saint-Louis*, a hospital for disabled soldiers, was erected on the site. The *commanderie* moved into the newly-erected *Hôtel des Invalides* (q.v.) in 1675 and Bicêtre then became a prison, one of the most pestilential of the pre-Revolutionary era and so notorious that the word 'Bicêtre' connoted misfortune or a diabolically wicked person. Lunatics, or persons whom it was convenient to class as such, were confined there, together with cripples, paupers, thieves, vagrants, and youths of debauched habits (who were, by order of Louis XIV, 'fustigés à chaque pansement', if they were suffering from a venereal disease). Bicêtre was the last halt for prisoners on the way to penal servitude or execution, and there are references to this in Hugo's *Les Misérables* and *Le Dernier Jour d'un condamné*. The prison was the scene of some of the worst massacres of the Terror.

Bien-avisé et Mal-avisé, see *Moralité*.

Bien Bon, Le, the name by which Mme de Sévigné in her letters refers to her uncle, the abbé de Coulanges.

Bien public, see *Ligue du Bien public*.

Biens nationaux, Crown and Church or private (e.g. belonging to *émigrés* or suspects) lands and property confiscated by the State during the Revolution (cf. *Assignats*).

Bigorne, see *Chichevache, Dit de*.

Bijoux indiscrets, Les, see *Diderot*, para. 2.

Billaut, ADAM (1602–62), carpenter and poet of Nevers, known as *Maître Adam*, author of three collections of verses entitled (after instruments of his trade) *Chevilles*, *Vilebrequin*, and *Rabot*. Richelieu gave him a pension and he earned the respect of Corneille and Voltaire.

Biographie universelle ancienne et moderne, also known as the *Biographie Michaud*, first published 1811–28 (52 vols.) and 1834–54 (29 supplementary vols.), and later revised and augmented, is still one of the best-known French dictionaries of biography. It was due to the enterprise of a Paris bookseller, Louis-Gabriel Michaud (1772–1858). The articles were written by distinguished savants, historians, and critics. (See also *Michaud, Joseph*.)

Biron, ARMAND-LOUIS, DUC DE, see *Lauzun, Armand-Louis*.

Biron, CHARLES, DUC DE (1562–1602), a brave soldier, friend of Henri IV, who made him *maréchal de France, duc et pair*, and governor of Burgundy. But the ambition of Biron was not satisfied, and he conspired with Spain and Savoy for the dismemberment of France. He was arrested and beheaded.

Birotteau, CÉSAR, see *Histoire de la grandeur et de la décadence de César Birotteau*.

Bizet, ALEXANDRE - CÉSAR - LÉOPOLD [or GEORGES] (1838–75), born in Paris, composed operas and works for the piano. Works by which he is remembered include the music for *La Jolie Fille de Perth* (1867), the opera based on Scott's novel; *L'Arlésienne* (1872), based on Daudet's tale; and *Carmen* (1875), based on Mérimée's tale of Spanish gipsy life.

Blague, La, the term for a form of smart, cynical wit which flourished during the Second Empire, for example among the journalists, chroniclers, and *boulevardiers*. Marriage, the family, morals, and convention were all food for ridicule and caricature.

Blanc, LOUIS (1811–82), politician and historian, began as a journalist, writing on social and industrial questions. *L'Organisation du travail* (1839), a pamphlet advocating

State work for the unemployed, made him known. *L'Histoire de Dix Ans* (1841) followed, a retrospective survey, severely critical, of the July monarchy. It helped, like Lamartine's *Histoire des Girondins* (q.v.), to bring about the February Revolution (q.v., 1848). Blanc was a leader in this revolution but on the suppression of the *Ateliers nationaux* (q.v.), which were in fact not on the lines he had advocated, he fled to England. There he completed his *Histoire de la Révolution française* (1847–62), written with a socialistic bias and now largely superseded, but well documented and still a good guide to events. He also contributed articles on English political life to *Le Temps* (collected later in *Dix Années de l'histoire d'Angleterre*, 1879–81). In 1871 he returned to France and to political (extreme left-wing) life. His other writings include *Histoire de la Révolution de 1848* (1870).

Blancandin et l'orgueilleuse d'amour, a *roman d'aventure* of the latter half of the 13th century, telling how a knight wins the love of a proud lady by boldly kissing her, and later rescues her from her enemies.

Blanc et le Noir, Le, a philosophical tale by Voltaire, published in 1764.

The theme is the problem of destiny and the ridicule of Manichaeism. Rustan, a young Indian noble, whose wonderful adventures appear to have brought him to a premature death, finds that he has been attended during life by a good and an evil genius. He is puzzled to know how there can be at once such contrary principles in the universe, and what use they are, since their influence is over-ridden by destiny. Finally he wakes up to find that the whole series of adventures, as well as the geniuses, have been no more than a dream.

Blanche, JACQUES-ÉMILE (1861–1942), painter (well known in England as well as France for his portraits of contemporary writers), also art-critic (*Propos de peintre*, 1919–28; *Les Arts plastiques*, &c.). He published memoirs of some interest because of the *milieux*—literary, artistic, the *salons*—described (*Les Cahiers d'un artiste*, 1914–19; *Mes Modèles*, 1928). His father was the alienist Dr. Antoine-Émile Blanche who received more than one 19th-century author—e.g. Gérard de Nerval, Maupassant —for treatment in his private mental home at Passy (a district of Paris).

Blanche et Guiscard, a tragedy by Saurin, on the theme of James Thomson's *Tancred and Sigismunda* (itself based on a story in *Gil Blas*), produced in 1763.

The king of Sicily on his death-bed recognizes Guiscard as his successor on condition that he marries Constance, the king's sister. But Guiscard loves Blanche, the daughter of the chancellor Siffrédi, and she loves him. Siffrédi urges Guiscard to marry Constance in the interests of the State, and tries to force his hand by publishing, without Guiscard's authority, the intended marriage. Blanche, in despair at Guiscard's supposed abandonment of her, reluctantly consents to be married at once, as her father desires, to Osmont, the constable of Sicily. Too late she discovers Guiscard's fidelity. In a duel between Guiscard and Osmont the latter is slain, but not before he has turned his sword against Blanche and killed her.

Blanchefleur, in some of the *chansons de geste* (q.v.) relating to Charlemagne, the consort of the Emperor. She is traduced by the traitor Macaire; flees to Constantinople under the protection of the peasant Varocher; and her innocence is finally established. Another Blanchefleur, in the *Geste des Lorrains*, is the wife of Pépin, taken by him from Garin le Loherain (q.v.), and is a fomenter of strife between the parties. (See also *Floire et Blancheflor*.)

Blanqui, LOUIS-AUGUSTE (1805–81), revolutionary agitator, formed secret societies, was often imprisoned, and led the *Blanquiste* party which helped to bring about the downfall of the Second Empire after Sedan (q.v.). After the defeat of the *Commune* (q.v.) he was imprisoned for life, but released in 1879.

Blason, see *Rhétoriqueurs*.

Blémont, ÉMILE, the name taken by Léon-Émile Petitdidier (1839–1927), critic, dramatic author, and poet. His (usually one-act, verse) plays include: *Les Ciseaux* (1896), *Mariage pour rire* (1898), &c. *Théâtre moliéresque et cornélien* (1898) and *Théâtre légendaire* (1908) are criticism.

Bloch, a brilliant, vulgar, tactless, pushing young Jewish intellectual, in Proust's *A la recherche du temps perdu* (q.v.). By the last volume the passage of time has transformed him into a much-sought-after writer.

Bloch, JEAN-RICHARD (1884–1947), man of letters and novelist, born in Paris of Jewish parentage. He wrote three outstanding novels: *Lévy* (1912), a study of the Jewish character; ... *et Cie* (1913), the story of a Jewish family of cloth manufacturers who move from Alsace with all their employees after the Franco-Prussian war and starting again from scratch build up a flourishing business in the west of France; and *La Nuit kurde* (1925), an Oriental tale in which the beginnings of racialism are evoked with great imaginative force.

Bloch, MARC (1886–1944), one of the most distinguished of 20th-century French historians, who came of an old Jewish university family, died at the hands of the Germans during the 1939–45 war. His illuminating studies of feudal society and of rural conditions in medieval France include: *Rois et serfs, un chapitre d'histoire capétienne* (1920), his doctor's thesis; *Les Rois thaumaturges. Essai sur le caractère surnaturel attribué à la puissance royale* (1924); *Les Caractères originaux de l'histoire rurale française* (1931); *La Société féodale* (1939, 1940). His work and teaching (at the University of Strasbourg) went far to dispel the conception of historical study as a matter solely of scientific method and documentary scholarship. His unfinished but deeply interesting *Apologie pour l'histoire, ou Métier d'historien* was published posthumously (1949).

Bloch, OSCAR, see *Dictionaries and Encyclopedias*, under date 1932.

Blocus continental, Le. On 21 November 1806 Napoleon, from Berlin, declared a general economic blockade of the British Isles by the continental Powers. His decree reached the Senate with a message that he had been forced to resort to measures which went against his heart, 'car il lui en coûtait de ... revenir, après tant d'années de civilisation, aux principes qui caractérisent la barbarie des premiers actes des nations'. The blockade did not fully achieve its object, the destruction of British sea-power and sea-trade, and it returned, boomerang-like, on several of the continental Powers, whose economic existence was bound up with that of Britain. The resentment aroused was an ultimate factor in Napoleon's downfall.

Blondel, MAURICE (1861–1949), Neo-Catholic philosopher, a follower of Ollé-Laprune (q.v.) and one of the (French) school of 'Modernists' condemned in 1907 by a papal encyclical. The Modernist doctrines were a compromise between modern philosophical and scientific ideas and Roman Catholicism, and were less strictly based on theology than those of the Thomists (see *Thomisme* and cf. *Laberthonnière*; *Le Roy*). Blondel's chief work was his doctor's thesis, *L'Action: Essai d'une critique de la vie et d'une science de la pratique* (1893).

Blondel de Nesle in Picardy, a poet of the end of the 12th century, an early imitator in northern French of the songs of the troubadours (see *Lyric poetry*). Nothing is known of his life; but according to legend he was a follower of Richard Cœur de Lion. When the latter on his return from the Holy Land in 1192 was imprisoned in Germany, Blondel sought him and discovered him by singing under the window of Richard's prison a song which he and Richard had composed together. Half-way through it he paused, and Richard took up the other half and completed it. (Cf. *Sedaine*.)

Bloy, LÉON (1846–1917), born in Périgueux, turned author and became a Roman Catholic after a meeting with Barbey d'Aurevilly (q.v.). His writings of various kinds—essays and studies, religious, historical, and critical, also novels and tales—were violent ('Chacun de mes livres est un aveu arraché par la torture') and vituperative, embittered and immoderate in their judgements, but of an arresting visionary quality. His outstanding works include the two autobiographical novels, *Le Désespéré* (1886) and *La Femme pauvre* (1897); his journal, *Le Mendiant ingrat* (1898–1920, 8 vols.); *Le Pèlerin de l'absolu* (1914), &c.

Blum, LÉON (1872–1950), born in Paris, essayist, critic, and Socialist politician, of Jewish family. His later career, as politician and leader, is a matter for the historian of 20th-century France. But before circumstances or conviction drove him to devote his whole life to politics this Socialist intellectual had made his mark as a writer. Even the literary and dramatic criticism which he contributed as a young man to the *Revue blanche* (q.v.), much of it reprinted in *En lisant* (2 ser., 1906–9) and *Au théâtre* (4 ser., 1906–10), impresses by its clear-sighted maturity of judgement and its sureness of style. The *Nouvelles Conversations de Goethe avec Eckermann* (1901), discussions between a modern Goethe and a modern Eckermann on literature, aesthetics, political conceptions, &c., are still more impressive, as writing and as a progressive revelation of the author's intellectual, moral, and political ideals. These 'conversations' also appeared first in the *Revue blanche*. The masterly *Stendhal et le Beylisme* (1914 and 1930), the last of Blum's purely literary works, was a study of Stendhal as a writer and of his attitude to and impact on his own and succeeding ages. *Du mariage* (1907), on women and the marriage relationship, provoked discussion on its appearance. In later years he published *Souvenirs sur l'Affaire* (1935), of great interest as a picture of social, literary, and political circles during the Dreyfus (q.v.) crisis; also an inspiring portrait of the great Socialist leader Jaurès (*Jean Jaurès*, 1937), whose private secretary he had been.

The first volume of a collected edition of Blum's works was published in 1954.

Boaistuau or **Boistuau**, PIERRE (?–1566), compiler and translator. He was responsible, with Belleforest (q.v.), for the translations of Bandello's (q.v.) *Novelle* (*Histoires tragiques*).

Bocage, PIERRE-MARTINIEN TOUSEZ, *called* (1797–1863), one of the best and most popular actors of the Romantic era (see *Romantisme*), particularly successful in drama and melodrama (he made a fine, melancholy lover). He created the title-role in Dumas *père*'s *Antony*, played the chief part in the same author's *La Tour de Nesle*, *Angèle*, &c., and helped to make the success of plays by George Sand.

Bochetel, JEAN (16th century), author of a fine verse translation of the *Hecuba* of Euripides, printed by Estienne in 1544.

Bodel, JEAN, of Arras, who lived in the late 12th and early 13th century, but became a leper and retired to a lazar-house *c.* 1202, was author of a *chanson de geste*, the *Chanson des Saxons* (or *des Saisnes*), dealing with the war of

Charlemagne against Guiteclin (Witikind), king of the Saxons, the loves of Baudoin (brother of Roland) and Sebille, wife of Guiteclin, and the final suppression of the Saxons. Bodel was also author of a semi-religious, semi-profane dramatic piece called the *Jeu de Saint Nicolas* (in twelve- and eight-syllabled verse), relating a miracle worked by an image of the saint, found by Saracens in the camp of the Crusaders after a defeat of the latter. The intervention of the saint forces some rogues (represented as citizens of Arras) to restore the treasure of the Saracen king which they have stolen. The work contains a curious mixture of comic and epic elements. See also *Congé*.

In Bodel's *Chanson des Saxons* occur the often-quoted lines:

Ne sont que iij matières à nul homme atan-
dant,
De France et de Bretaigne et de Rome la
grant.

Bodin, JEAN (1530–96), political philo-sopher, an Angevin lawyer. He was professor of Roman Law at Toulouse, but in 1561 left his chair for the bar and in 1567 entered the service of the Crown and became *procureur du roi*, taking an important part in the *États Généraux* of 1576 (of which he wrote a journal). He visited England in 1581 in the suite of the duc d'Alençon, in connexion with the negotiations for the marriage of that prince with Queen Elizabeth. In 1576 he published his important work, *Six Livres de la République* (the title being taken from Plato's *Republic*). In this he opposed the doctrine of the sovereignty of the people put forward by Hotman (q.v.) in his *Franco-Gallia*, and opposed equally the monarchical absolutism commended by Machiavelli. Bodin is in favour of a powerful hereditary monarchy, restrained by certain checks, such as the control of the *États généraux* over taxation. This work, written in a spirit of moderation and realism, but diffuse and containing astrological and other rubbish, was the foundation of political science in France, an analysis of the State and of the political and economic relations of its consti-tuent parts. It condemns slavery and discusses the influence of climate on the character of peoples. The author prepared a Latin version of it in 1586 and it was translated into English (1606) and other languages. Bodin

also wrote a *Methodus ad facilem historiarum cognitionem* (in Latin, 1566) advancing many novel ideas on the study of history; a *Démonomanie des sorciers* (1580), representing sorcery as a serious danger to society (a be-lief generally held in his day) and intended as a manual for judges in trials of sorcerers; *Universae Naturae Theatrum* (1596), trans-lated as *Théâtre de la Nature entière* (1597), in which he arrives at a knowledge of the Deity from a survey of natural science; and a curious dialogue on religion, entitled *Hepta-plomeres*, in which seven different creeds are discussed and found, if sincerely held, equally worthy of respect, Bodin showing some preference for 'natural religion' with a tincture of Judaism. This work was not published until the 19th century. Bodin was a friend of Pibrac (q.v.).

Boèce [Boëthius] (*c.* 480–524), Roman philosopher and statesman, unjustly im-prisoned for treason by Theodoric and executed. During his imprisonment he wrote the most important and influential of his works, *De Consolatione Philosophiae* (see *Consolation de Philosophie*), widely translated and commented in the Middle Ages. His other works on theology, philosophy, and science helped to transmit the legacy of Greek thought to Western Europe.

Boétie, ÉTIENNE DE LA, see *La Boétie*.

Bœuf sur le toit, Le, a farcical ballet by Jean Cocteau (q.v.) with music by Darius Milhaud. The scene is a bar called 'Le Bœuf sur le toit or the Nothing doing Bar'. It was produced in Paris—with *décor* by the artist Raoul Dufy—on 21 February 1920. It can be found in the author's collected *Théâtre de poche* (1949).

Boïeldieu, FRANÇOIS-ADRIEN (1775–1834), French composer of light opera, came to Paris from Rouen, his birth-place, and was teaching (piano) at the Conservatoire when his opera *Le Calife de Bagdad* was performed with great success. He was Director of the Royal Opera in St. Petersburg, as it then was, between 1803 and 1811, then returned to Paris and was one of those (cf. *Méhul*) who made the fame of the *Opéra Comique*. Another of his operas, *La Dame blanche*, inspired by Scott's *Guy Mannering*, was so successful that it introduced a vogue for tartans.

Boileau, Étienne (d. *c.* 1269), provost of Paris, author of the interesting collection of trade guild regulations known as the *Livre des Métiers.*

Boileau, Gilles (1631–69), translator and poetaster, originally an advocate, then the holder of an office in the king's household. He was jealous of, and continually at odds with, his younger brother Boileau-Despréaux (see below).

Boileau, Jacques (1635–1716), brother of the preceding and of Boileau-Despréaux (see the following), a learned doctor of the Sorbonne. He studied obscure points of theology and ecclesiastical custom and wrote about them in Latin.

Boileau-Despréaux, Nicolas (1636–1711), generally referred to as 'Boileau', was born in Paris, where his father was a clerk to the *parlement.* He was educated at the university of Paris, studied law, and became an advocate, but the death of his father in 1657 left him well-to-do, and he thereafter devoted himself to literature. His first works were his *Satires* (q.v.), of which the first seven, after having become known among his friends, were published in 1666 together with a complimentary *Discours au Roi.* Two further satires appeared in 1668. About 1669 he was presented to Louis XIV, to whom he read his first *Épître* (q.v., likewise a complimentary piece), and received from him a pension. The edition of his works issued in 1674 contained, besides the above, four further epistles, the *Art poétique* (q.v.), four cantos of the *Lutrin* (q.v.), and a translation of *Longinus on the Sublime.* The rest of the *Lutrin* and Epistles VI–IX appeared in 1683. Meanwhile Boileau had been appointed, together with his friend Racine, historiographer to the king. His *Dialogue des héros de romans,* written *c.* 1665 to ridicule the heroic romances of the day, was not printed until 1713 to avoid offending Mlle de Scudéry.

Boileau's later years, owing to his ill health, were productive of comparatively few works. In 1684 he had been admitted to the *Académie,* at the king's instance. Three years later, at a special session of that body, the *Querelle des anciens et des modernes* (q.v.) flared up when he objected to Perrault's contention that the age of Louis XIV could be compared favourably with that of Augustus. To support his views Boileau wrote the *Ode sur la prise de Namur* (1693), a feeble attempt, burlesqued by Prior, to imitate Pindar; the *Réflexions sur Longin*; and the last three epistles and three satires. In 1701, however, he yielded some ground in his *Lettre à M. Perrault.*

Boileau was the warm friend and supporter of Racine, Molière, and La Fontaine. His Jansenist tendencies (he was devoted to Arnauld, on whom he wrote a fine epitaph) and certain writings such as his twelfth epistle and twelfth satire embroiled him with the Jesuits. Though a master of the art of writing in verse, he is less important as a poet than as a founder in France of literary criticism. A man of few but clear ideas, by his acute judgement, independence and sincerity, and brilliant power of vigorous expression, he made himself the arbiter of literary reputations, waged war on affectation, insipidity, pedantry, pomposity, dullness, and laid down the canons of good writing (deriving from Malherbe), as practised by the classical school and approved by the taste of his age. He was known as the *législateur du Parnasse.* He was a poet in his pursuit of perfection of form, but lacked inspiration, passion, and fancy. He was read and admired in England. Both the *Lutrin* and the *Art poétique* were translated more than once into English, and some of his satires also were translated or imitated. Dryden paid a high tribute to Boileau's merits.

Boisguillebert, Pierre de (1646–1714), political economist and advocate of reforms, author of *Détail de la France* (1695, 1707). He was a cousin of Vauban (q.v.).

Boisrobert, l'abbé François de (1592–1662), dramatist, a familiar of Richelieu and somewhat of a buffoon, who used his credit with the cardinal to benefit men of letters. He wrote many forgotten comedies and tragicomedies. His one good play was the comedy *La Belle Plaideuse* (1654), from which Molière borrowed a scene. It represented the *foire Saint-Germain* and the *rue des Orfèvres* and gives a picture of contemporary Parisian manners. Boisrobert was one of the *cinq auteurs* (q.v.) employed by Richelieu to write plays under his direction, and was an original member of the *Académie.*

Boissier, GASTON (1823–1908), was for long one of the best-known historians of Latin antiquity. His works include: *Cicéron et ses amis* (1865), *La Religion romaine d'Auguste aux Antonins* (1874), *Promenades* and *Nouvelles Promenades archéologiques* (1880 and 1886), *La Fin du paganisme en occident* (1891).

Boiste, PIERRE-CLAUDE-VICTOIRE, see *Dictionaries and Encyclopedias*, under date 1800.

Bollandistes, Belgian Jesuits who publish the *Acta Sanctorum*, legends of saints arranged according to the days of the calendar. The work was begun at Antwerp by Jean Bolland, a Flemish Jesuit (1596–1665), the first volume appearing in 1643, and the last volume of the original series in 1786 after the dispersal of the Jesuits. The Bollandistes were re-established in Brussels in 1837 and continued their hagiographical studies, but in a more historical spirit.

Bonald, VICOMTE LOUIS DE (1754–1840), political philosopher. He emigrated in 1790 and was a conservative politician under the Restoration. Like his contemporary, Joseph de Maistre, he was an ardent defender of the Altar and the Crown against the Revolution, holding the Catholic faith and the divine right of kings to be truths as incontrovertible as the laws of nature. He sought to establish these conclusions by rigorous deduction from a few fundamental propositions, such as that the type of society is the family, in which the father represents absolute power, as God does in the universe. He saw the ultimate proof of the existence of God in the gift of language to mankind. His chief works, containing lofty views, but written in a laborious, inelegant style, were his *Théorie du pouvoir politique et religieux dans la société civile* (1796), *Essai analytique sur les lois naturelles de l'ordre social* (1801); *La Législation primitive considérée . . . par les seules lumières de la raison* (1802).

Bonaparte, the French form of the Italian 'Buonaparte'. The young Corsican general in the Revolutionary armies, Napoleon Buonaparte, was appointed to the command of the Army of Italy in March 1796. Thereafter, until 1804 when he became Emperor (see *Napoleon*), he signed himself 'Bonaparte'. In allusions to events in which he figured before he became Emperor he is more usually called 'Bonaparte' than 'Napoleon'.

Bonaparte, PRINCE LOUIS-NAPOLÉON, see *Napoleon III*.

Bonaparte Family. Napoleon's father, CARLO MARIA BONAPARTE, was born at Ajaccio, 1746, and died at Montpellier, 1785, having gone there to consult specialists for a persistent disease of the stomach. He belonged to a family of Italian descent established in Corsica from the 16th century. He married MARIA LETIZIA RAMOLINO (b. Ajaccio 1750, d. Rome 1836), of Genoese origin. Of their several children only eight reached maturity, viz.

JOSEPH, b. Corte 1768, d. Florence 1844. Napoleon created him King of Naples in 1806 and then King of Spain (1808–13);

NAPOLÉON, b. Ajaccio 1769, d. St. Helena 1821, see *Napoleon*;

ÉLISA, b. Ajaccio, 1773(?4), d. 1820. She married a Corsican, Prince Bacciochi. Napoleon created her Grand Duchess of Tuscany in 1808;

LUCIEN, b. Ajaccio 1775, d. Viterbo 1840. He presided over the *Conseil des Cinq-Cents* in November 1799 at the time of the *coup d'état* (see *Dix-huit brumaire*), when his skilful handling of the proceedings helped to ensure success. He held various official posts during the Consulate and the Empire and patronized literature and the sciences. After a quarrel with Napoleon he set out for the U.S.A. He was captured by an English cruiser and spent three years as a prisoner in England. After the second Restoration he lived in Italy. His title *Prince de Canino* was a Papal honour (cf. *Wyse, Sir Thomas*);

LOUIS, b. Ajaccio 1778, d. Leghorn 1846, husband of Hortense Beauharnais, the Empress Josephine's daughter. Napoleon created him King of Holland (1806) but he abdicated in 1810. Napoleon III (q.v.) was his third, and last surviving, son;

PAULINE, b. Ajaccio 1781, d. Florence 1825. Her first husband was the General Leclerc sent by Napoleon to suppress San Domingo (see *Toussaint-Louverture*). Her second husband was Prince Camillo Borghese. She was a famous beauty;

CAROLINE, b. Ajaccio 1782, d. Florence 1839. She married Murat (see *Maréchal de l'Empire*) and thus became Queen of Naples in 1808;

JÉRÔME, b. Ajaccio 1784, d. Paris 1860, was King of Westphalia from 1807 to 1813. His first marriage, to Elizabeth Paterson of Baltimore, was dissolved. In 1807 he married Princess Catherine of Württemberg and had three children—Jérôme (1814–47), Mathilde (see *Mathilde, Princesse*, and Napoléon-Joseph-Charles-Paul (1821–91), the Prince Napoleon (nicknamed *Plon-plon*) who was for a time French Ambassador to Madrid and who, like his sister, was a patron of literature and the arts under the Second Empire. A grandson of Prince Napoleon is the present-day Bonapartist pretender to the French throne.

Bonheur (1891), a collection of poems by Verlaine (q.v.).

Bonnard, SYLVESTRE, see *Crime de Sylvestre Bonnard, Le.*

Bonne chanson, La (1872), by Verlaine (q.v.), a collection of lyrics.

Bonnes lettres, La Société des, one of a number of Societies (e.g. . . . *des bonnes œuvres,* . . . *des bonnes études*) founded after the Restoration by young men of religious and monarchical sympathies. Their interests were partly charitable, partly literary (they favoured such poets as Hugo, Lamartine, and Vigny, qq.v.), and their politics were anti-liberal. They maintained a contact with the *Congrégation* (q.v.) and came in for some of the popular suspicion with which that body was regarded.

Bonnet phrygien, see *Bonnet rouge.*

Bonnet rouge, the red cap, the emblem of the French Revolution. Its origin appears to lie partly in the *bonnet phrygien,* a name also given to it from its resemblance to the conical cap of liberty worn by the freed slaves of Greece and Rome, and the *bonnet rouge* customarily worn by *galériens* (i.e. convicts). As early as 1789 many French officers who had fought in the American War of Independence used seals on their letters which portrayed the cap of liberty surrounded by the thirteen stars of the U.S.A. Some of the earliest engravings and medals of the Revolution showed the image of Liberty with a Phrygian cap on her head or surmounting her pike. Voltaire's bust in the *Théâtre Français* was similarly adorned, and the usage of the Phrygian cap as a

symbol of liberty began to spread. The colour, however, was often grey. In August–September 1790, soldiers (mainly the Swiss from whom the French army at this time was largely recruited) in regiments garrisoned at Nancy were court-martialled for mutiny against unjust treatment by their officers. Their harsh sentence to thirty years convict labour (cf. *Galère*) at Brest provoked indignation, and after this date many of the *Jacobins,* the extreme Revolutionaries, took to wearing a *bonnet rouge,* though grey caps were still often seen. An amnesty brought about the release of the Nancy mutineers and in April 1792 a public welcome was organized for them in Paris. They arrived wearing the *bonnet rouge* of the *galériens,* after which time the red cap ousted the grey as the symbol of liberty. Two months later, when the mob broke into the royal apartments at the Tuileries on 20 June, the king consented to have a *bonnet rouge* placed on his head. On 14 July at the *Fête de la Fédération* the *fédérés* wore the *bonnet rouge;* and four days after the fall of the monarchy (10 Aug. 1792) the *bonnet rouge* was officially adopted as the emblem of the Revolution.

Bonneval, CLAUDE-ALEXANDRE, COMTE DE (1675–1747), a gallant officer but a man of unbalanced character, who in consequence of a dispute about his military accounts went over to Prince Eugène, and fought under him against the French and the Turks. He was rehabilitated by the Regent in 1717, but his hasty temper gave rise to fresh difficulties: he quarrelled with Prince Eugène, joined the Turks, and became a Moslem, receiving the rank of pasha from the Sultan. He died at Constantinople. There are references to him in Voltaire's writings and in the memoirs of Casanova. Bonneval repudiated the memoirs fabricated in his name.

Bonstetten, CHARLES-VICTOR DE (1745–1832), born at Berne and employed in the administrative service of his country, was a philosophical writer and a man of erudition and wide interests, an antiquarian and an economist, a traveller, and a friend of the Neckers and Mme de Staël. He wrote in French a pleasant *Voyage dans le Latium* (1804), *Recherches sur la nature et les lois de l'Imagination* (1807), *Études sur l'Homme, ou Recherches sur les facultés de sentir et de penser* (1821), *L'Homme du Midi et l'homme du Nord*

(1824), *La Scandinavie et les Alpes* (1826). Bonstetten spent some months at Cambridge in 1769, as the intimate friend of the poet Gray, who wrote some extant letters to him.

Bontemps, ROGER, whose name occurs continually in the popular poetry of the Middle Ages, is the embodiment of the hopes and fears, the regrets and illusions, of the people. When times are hard they say it is because *Bontemps* has disappeared, and they look forward to better days when *Bontemps* shall return.

Booz endormi, one of the famous *petites épopées* (the Old Testament story of Ruth), of Victor Hugo's *Légende des siècles*.

Borda, JEAN-CHARLES (1733–99), French savant, born at Dax, whose researches did much for the advancement of nautical science. He was one of the three scientists called upon by the *Assemblée constituante* to measure the arc of the meridian before the metric system (q.v.) was introduced. From 1852, when the State Naval College was transferred wholly to Brest, until 1913 the training vessel for naval cadets was called 'Le Borda'. Life at the College is described in Loti's (q.v.) *Prime Jeunesse*.

Bordeaux, HENRI (1870–), novelist of provincial life (usually his native province of Savoy). He writes often of homes in which neither family ties nor religious beliefs are strong enough to preserve unity. The following, among some fifty novels, widely read when they appeared, are usually mentioned: *La Peur de vivre* (1902), *Les Roquevillard* (1906), *La Robe de laine* (1910), *La Neige sur les pas* (1912). *Le Barrage* (1934) still has a topical interest in the light of hydroelectric development in France. A mountain village is submerged when a vast dam is constructed. The inhabitants are reinstalled in a model village but the advantages are not all on the side of scientific progress.

Borderie, BERTRAND DE LA, see under *Héroët*.

Borel, PETRUS (1809–59), poet and novelist, also a 19th-century translator of *Robinson Crusoe* (1836), called himself 'le Lycanthrope', apparently in reference to the saying 'Man is a wolf to man'. He was born at Lyons and after training as an architect in Paris turned to literature, and became leader of the group of exaggerated young Romantics known as *bousingos* (q.v. and see *Romantisme*). His most typical works were *Rhapsodies* (1832), poems; *Champavert, contes immoraux* (1833); and *Madame Putiphar* (1839), a novel. The two last are a mass of melodramatic horrors, intended to scandalize. The poems have a certain starkness and hard rhythm and give an unmistakable impression of a being whose attitude to the world is one of hate. The last years of this author's life were spent in Algeria in the Colonial Service, but he was dismissed for inefficiency some time before he died.

Borel, PIERRE, see *Dictionaries and Encyclopedias,* under date 1655.

Bornier, HENRI, VICOMTE DE (1825–1901), man of letters and author of poetic dramas, notably *La Fille de Roland* (1875), which is still played at the Comédie-Française on national occasions, and *Les Noces d'Attila* (1880).

Borodino, in Russia, between Smolensk and Moscow, where Napoleon defeated (7 Sept. 1812) but failed to destroy the Russians under Kutusov. At this 'bataille de la Moskova' (the French name) the slaughter on both sides was appalling.

Boron or **Borron,** ROBERT DE, see *Perceval*.

Bosco, HENRI (1889–), one of the most frequently mentioned among present-day regional novelists. His studies of a Provençal country life never very far removed from primitive mysteries include: *Pierre Lampédouse* (1924); *L'Âne culotte* (1936); *Le Mas Théotime* (1944); *Le Jardin d'Hyacinthe* (1946).

Bosse, ABRAHAM (1602–76), born at Tours, engraver, noted for his accurate representation of the *bourgeois* life of his day.

Bossuet, JACQUES-BÉNIGNE (1627–1704), born at Dijon, of a family of provincial magistrates, a cultivated humanist and ardent theologian, educated by the Jesuits at Dijon and at the Collège de Navarre. He entered the priesthood and after some years of active preaching at Metz (where there were many Protestants and Jews), settled in Paris in 1659, where during the next ten years his sermons made him famous. He was appointed Bishop of Condom in 1669, and in 1670 tutor to the Dauphin (the *Grand Dauphin*, q.v.), to which ungrateful task (for his pupil showed apathy and 'incuriosité') he devoted another ten years. In 1681 he was named Bishop of Meaux, and thenceforward devoted himself to the work of his see and of other important ecclesiastical offices, and to polemical writing.

Bossuet is famous for his sermons and funeral orations, for the educational works that he prepared for the Dauphin, and for his miscellaneous writings. Of his sermons he published only one, *Sur l'Unité de l'Église* (1682), a manifesto of the Gallican standpoint, preached at the opening of the council of the French clergy on the occasion of the conflict between Louis XIV and Innocent XI. Of his other sermons only drafts (many of them incomplete) survive. His principal funeral orations were preached on the deaths of: the Queen Mother, Anne of Austria (1666, this is lost); Henrietta Maria (wife of Charles I of England, 1669); Henrietta of England (daughter of Charles I, duchesse d'Orléans, 1670); Marie-Thérèse (wife of Louis XIV, 1683); Anne de Gonzague, Princesse Palatine (1685); Le Tellier (q.v., 1686); the Grand Condé (q.v., 1687). The last six were published by Bossuet himself; they combine the characters of a panegyric and a sermon, the preacher deriving religious instruction from events in the life, or traits in the character, of the person he is celebrating. They contain some of his most famous oratory, passages of greater pomp and solemnity than were usual in his sermons. His customary style of preaching was simple, touching, and persuasive. He courageously attacked the royal failings. He prepared his sermons with care, but never learnt them by heart, trusting to the inspiration of the moment for their final form.

As tutor to the Dauphin, Bossuet drew up a *Discours sur l'histoire universelle* (1681), a chronological abstract of the history of the world, followed by a commentary showing (a) the development of religion, and (b) the causes of the rise and fall of empires (a vindication of Providence). His *Politique tirée de l'écriture sainte* (several times remodelled and published posthumously, 1709) is an exposition of the doctrine of the divine right of kings and their duties to their subjects. The *Traité de la connaissance de Dieu et de soi-même* and the *Logique* are elementary philosophical treatises. His miscellaneous writings were for the most part polemical. The chief of them were: (1) the *Histoire des variations des églises protestantes* (1688), designed to show the lack of community and continuity of doctrine, and the subordination of authority to individual judgement, among the Protestant sects, incidentally attacking Burnet's 'History of the Reformation'. The work provoked replies to which Bossuet published rejoinders (Brunetière calls it 'le plus beau livre de la langue française'). (2) *Maximes et réflexions sur la Comédie* (1694), in which he showed himself hostile to the theatre. In this, as also in his *Traité de la concupiscence* (1731), in which he especially censured intellectual curiosity, he showed his sympathy with the Jansenists, although he condemned the five doctrinal propositions attributed to Jansenius. (3) He vigorously opposed Quietism (q.v.) and engaged in an acute controversy on this subject with Fénelon, winding up with his *Relation sur le Quiétisme* (1698). (4) His *Instructions sur la version du Nouveau Testament* and *Défense de la tradition et des saints Pères* (1702) were directed against some novelties of exegesis advanced by the Hebrew scholar Richard Simon (q.v.). He also opposed the philosophical doctrines of Malebranche and Spinoza. (5) In another category are his *Méditations sur l'Évangile* (1730–1) and *Élévations à Dieu sur les mystères*, works of religious edification, in which he reviews the great scenes of the Old and New Testaments.

Bossuet was eminent as a theologian, a moralist, and an orator. La Bruyère called him the 'last of the Fathers of the Church'. His polemical work was devoted to the defence of the traditional Catholic faith in its integrity, and was based on assiduous study of the Scriptures and of the Fathers, particularly St. Augustine and Tertullian. He was practical and moderate in exposition, luminous in discussion, conciliatory in polemics; he approved the revocation of the Edict of Nantes, but was opposed to the use of force against the Protestants. His style of writing was marked by a strong lyrical element (best seen in his *Méditations* and *Élévations*) and the use of concrete and picturesque terms. Lanson calls him 'le grand poète lyrique du 17e siècle'.

Bottin, Le, the shortened, familiar name for *Annuaire-Almanach du commerce et de* *l'industrie* (*Didot-Bottin*), the commercial directory to be found in French post offices and in cafés ('Ici on consulte le Bottin'). It is in several large, usually faded and well-thumbed volumes, for Paris and for the Departments. It also has a foreign section.

Sébastien Bottin (1764–1853), a priest whose interests were statistical, economic, and to some extent archaeological, was released from his vows in 1804 and became Secretary of the Préfecture du Nord (see *Préfet*). In 1819 he took over and developed the *Almanach du Commerce* founded in 1798 by one J. de Latynna, calling it *L'Almanach Bottin*. This, when Bottin died in 1853, was merged with the *Annuaire général du commerce* published by the house of Firmin-Didot, since when, under its present title, it has continued and expanded.

Boubouroche (1893), a comedy by Georges Courteline (q.v.).

Bouchardon, EDME (1698–1762), a distinguished sculptor, author of various works at Versailles, of the fountain in the rue de Grenelle in Paris, &c.

Bouchardy, JOSEPH (1810–70), born in Paris, was a writer of melodramas (*Gaspardo le pêcheur*, 1837; *Le Sonneur de Saint-Paul*, 1838; *Les Enfants trouvés*, 1843, &c.). He began as an etcher, and was for a time one of the *bousingos* (q.v.), the young extravagants of the Romantic Movement (see *Romantisme*).

Boucher, FRANÇOIS (1703–70), painter of graceful pastoral and mythological pictures, remarkable for their skilful grouping and decorative treatment, but showing a decline from the poetic spirit of Watteau.

Bouchet, GUILLAUME (*c.* 1513–93), a bookseller of Poitiers, author of three books of *Serées* (1584–98), conversations of citizens of Poitiers and their wives, meeting in the evenings to discuss all sorts of subjects, from marriage to fish, dogs, and wine, with anecdotes and maxims of antiquity, local scandal and mockery of lawyers and doctors; giving no doubt a fairly good idea of *bourgeois* society in a provincial city.

Bouchet, JEAN (1476–*c.* 1557), a successful attorney of Poitiers, and a very long-winded poet of the school of the *rhétoriqueurs* (q.v.); a friend of Rabelais, with whom he ex-changed epistles in mediocre verse. He styled himself 'Le Traverseur des voyes périlleuses'. His only work of some interest is to be found in his *Épîtres familières* by reason of the personages who figure in them, and the natural style in which they are written.

Bouciquaut, JEAN LE MAINGRE, *known as* (1365–1421), maréchal de France, fought and was taken prisoner at the battle of Nicopolis (1396), was governor of Genoa 1401–9, and was wounded and taken prisoner at Agincourt; he died in England. He was one of the originators of the *Cent Ballades* (q.v.). The *Livre des faits du bon messire Jean le Maingre, dit Bouciquaut*, written in the 15th century by an anonymous cleric, is a biography which is especially full and informative for the period of the governorship of Genoa; it represents Bouciquaut as a fine type of a disappearing class, the feudal noble.

Boudin, EUGÈNE-LOUIS (1825–98), painter. His small pictures are often of Normandy coast-scenes (he was born at Honfleur).

Bouffes-Parisiens, one of the famous homes of operetta and light comedy in Paris. It was opened by Offenbach (q.v.) in July 1855 in the small Salle Lacage (in the Champs-Élysées, so called from the name of the conjuror who had built it some years previously). Later, Offenbach transferred it to its present site in the Passage Choiseul, near the Opéra-Comique.

Boufflers (pron. as if *Boufflère*), STANISLAS-JEAN, CHEVALIER DE (1738–1815), cavalry officer and mediocre author of light verse, &c. He was admitted to the *Académie* in 1789. His mother, the marquise de Boufflers, a friend of Voltaire, is to be distinguished from the duchesse de Boufflers (maréchale de Luxembourg by her second marriage), a patroness of Rousseau; also from the comtesse de Boufflers-Rouveret (1725–post 1785), likewise a friend of Rousseau. Boswell (under the year 1775) relates an anecdote of a visit by the comtesse to Johnson in the Temple.

Bougainville, LOUIS-ANTOINE DE (1729–1814), circumnavigator. He was aide-de-camp to Montcalm at the battle of Quebec, and subsequently left the army for the navy. In 1766 he was sent to establish a French colony in the Falkland Islands, visited many

Pacific islands, and circumnavigated the globe, returning in 1769. His *Voyage autour du monde* was published in 1771. The tropical climbing plant *Bougainvillea* is named after him. (For the work entitled *Supplément au voyage de Bougainville* see *Diderot*, para. 2.)

Bougeant, L'ABBÉ GUILLAUME-HYACINTHE (1690–1743), taught in Jesuit colleges and wrote an *Amusement philosophique sur le langage des bêtes* (1739). It was translated into English and German but was frowned upon by his Order, so much so, indeed, that he was put in prison. He also wrote plays and historical works.

Bouhélier-Lepelletier, STÉPHANE [or SAINT]-GEORGES DE, see *Saint-Georges de Bouhélier.*

Bouhours, DOMINIQUE (1628–1702), known as *le père Bouhours*, a Jesuit and man of letters, the chief grammarian of his period (successor of Vaugelas). He was the author of *Entretiens d'Ariste et d'Eugène* (1671), dialogues on a variety of subjects (one on the French language), *Doutes sur la langue française* (1674), &c., showing him an advocate of the purification of the language pursued by the *Académie*. His Life of St. Francis Xavier was translated by Dryden (1686). He quarrelled with Ménage on grammatical questions.

Bouilhet, LOUIS-HYACINTHE (1822–69), minor poet and dramatist, schoolfellow and lifelong friend of Flaubert (q.v.), was born, and ended his days as town librarian, at Rouen. His historical dramas *Madame de Montary* (1856) and *La Conjuration d'Amboise* (1866) were moderately successful. His poetical works, on historical and scientific subjects, included *Melaenis* (1851, Rome in the days of the Emperor Commodus) and *Festons et Astragales* (1859, short poems describing the geological ages of the earth).

Bouillie de la comtesse Berthe, La (1845), a children's tale by Dumas *père* (q.v.).

Bouillon, GODEFROI DE, see *Godefroi de Bouillon.*

Boulainvilliers, HENRI, COMTE DE (1658–1722) historian, an advocate of political reforms, author of *État de la France* (1727),

Histoire de l'ancien gouvernement de France (1727), *Essai sur la noblesse de France* (1732), &c.

Boulanger, GÉNÉRAL GEORGES (1837–91), born at Rennes (Brittany), entered the army in 1856. By 1886 he was Minister for War, admired as a man of action, impatient of red tape. Energetic measures to reform army conditions, increase war material, and strengthen the Franco-German frontier gave him popular prestige as the 'général de la revanche', but his adversaries accused him of ambitious war-mongering and of being a tool for the anti-Republicans. His popularity became an embarrassment to his colleagues in the Government and in July 1887, to remove him from Paris, he was given command of an army corps at Clermont-Ferrand. He left Paris on the engine of his train to escape mobbing by enthusiastic crowds. A Boulangist movement, started at Clermont-Ferrand, soon became a national party, with 'Dissolution, Constituante [i.e. power to frame a new Constitution], Revision' as slogan, and with the General's favourite flower, a red carnation, as emblem. The party's objects were, roughly, the military rehabilitation of France and an end to the abuses of parliamentary government.

In January 1889 Boulanger, by an enormous majority, was elected Deputy for the Department of the Seine (i.e. Paris). By employing force promptly at this moment he might possibly have made himself master of France. But he temporized: and it was becoming evident that this popular hero enjoyed the limelight but, when it came to governing, had no clearly defined political conceptions. He seems also, at crucial moments, to have preferred the arms of his mistress, Mme de Bonnemains, to politics. On 1 April, believing his arrest imminent, he disconcerted his followers by taking flight to Brussels, and later to London. While there he was tried and condemned *in absentia* for treason and for mishandling public funds. He remained out of reach, in Jersey, and in France the Boulangist agitation subsided. He was finally discredited when he was discovered to have negotiated secretly, in 1888, with the Monarchists. In December 1891 he committed suicide in Brussels on the grave of his mistress. The movement was seen in retrospect as having revived French morale and 'redressé le pompon sur le képi du soldat français' [Maréchal Canrobert]. It is described in the novels *L'Appel au soldat*, by Maurice Barrès, and *Le Mystère des foules*, by Paul Adam.

Boulanger, LOUIS (1806–67), a painter prized by the Romantics (see *Romantisme*), a member of the second *cénacle* (q.v.), which met at Victor Hugo's home. Many of his drawings and water-colours were on subjects from Hugo's books.

Boulanger, NICOLAS-ANTOINE (1722–59), one of the *philosophes*, author of *L'Antiquité dévoilée* (1766), a work which in spite of the author's lack of talent exercised some influence. It attributes the origin of religion to the fear inspired in men by such calamities as the Deluge. The work was thought, though published under Boulanger's name, to be by d'Holbach, and it is uncertain what part the latter had in its preparation.

Boulangisme, Boulangistes, see *Boulanger, Général Georges*.

Boule or **Boulle,** ANDRÉ-CHARLES (1642–1732), a wood-carver of the reign of Louis XIV, who introduced the inlay of bronze or other material for the ornamentation of furniture.

Boule-de-suif, a masterly short story by Guy de Maupassant, first published, with tales by other naturalistic writers, in *Les Soirées de Médan* (1880, q.v.). It is an episode of the Franco-Prussian war. Among a small party of refugees leaving Rouen is 'Boule-de-suif', a well-known prostitute. Her companions are fulsomely attentive to her so long as the food she has brought, and her ample personal charms (the reason for her nickname), are of use in staving off their hunger or persuading a Prussian officer at a hotel *en route* to let them continue their journey. Once there is no more to fear their attitude reverts to one of contemptuous hostility.

Boulevard du Crime, in Paris, a section of the Boulevard du Temple (in the east, the busy commercial quarter), was so called in the early 19th century because the theatres playing melodrama were situated there. It was demolished, to make way for the present Place de la République, during the large-scale building operations of the Second Empire (see *Haussmann*; and see also *Theatres and theatre companies*, paras. 8, 9).

Boulogne, Camp de, see *Armée, La Grande*.

Bourbon, the name of a royal family of France, descended from a younger son of Louis IX, which first attained the throne in the person of Henri IV, the son of Antoine de Bourbon and Jeanne d'Albret, heiress of Navarre. The subsequent kings of France down to Louis-Philippe were direct descendants of Henri IV.

At the outbreak of the Revolution the chief members of the elder branch of the House of Bourbon were:

(i) the king, Louis XVI, with his queen (Marie-Antoinette) and their three children, Marie-Thérèse-Charlotte de France (1778–1851), 'Madame Royale' (see *Orpheline du Temple*); Louis-Joseph-François-Xavier, the first dauphin (1781–June 1789); and Louis-Charles, duc de Normandie, born 1785, who became dauphin on the death of his brother and died (1795) in the Temple (see *Orphelin du Temple*);

(ii) the comte de Provence ('Monsieur'), brother of the king, afterwards Louis XVIII (q.v.);

(iii) the comte d'Artois, second brother of the king, afterwards Charles X (q.v.), and his two sons, the duc d'Angoulême, who married 'Madame Royale' [see (i) above] in 1799, and the duc de Berry (q.v.; see also *Chambord, comte de*);

(iv) 'Mesdames', i.e. Madame Adélaïde (1732–1800) and Madame Victoire (1733–99), unmarried daughters of Louis XV. They emigrated in 1791 and died at Trieste;

(v) Madame Élisabeth (1764–94), sister of Louis XVI. She shared imprisonment in the Temple with the king and queen and their children and died on the scaffold.

A junior, collateral branch, the House of Orléans-Bourbon, was represented by Louis-Philippe-Joseph ('Philippe-Égalité'), the duc d'Orléans, and his son Louis-Philippe (q.v. and see *Orléans*), who became king in 1830, after the July Revolution.

Another collateral branch, the House of Condé, consisted at this time of Louis-Joseph de Bourbon, prince de Condé (1736–1818); his son Louis-Henri-Joseph, duc de Bourbon (1756–1830); and the latter's son Louis-Antoine-Henri de Bourbon, duc d'Enghien (1772–1804, q.v.). The prince de Condé was the first of the royal family to emigrate and was followed by his son and grandson. He was the leader of the *Armée de Condé* (see *Armée des émigrés*; *Condé, Le Grand*).

The Bourbons also furnished kings to Naples, and to Spain, through the duc d'Anjou, grandson of Louis XIV (see *Grand Dauphin*).

Bourdaloue, LOUIS (1632–1704), born at Bourges, a Jesuit priest and a famous preacher. His first sermons in Paris were delivered in 1669 (when Bossuet had almost ceased to preach) and were heard with admiration, and until his death he was regarded as the greatest preacher of his time. In strong contrast to Bossuet he appealed to the reason rather than the emotions; his exposition was simple and popular, without outstanding passages; his arguments were carefully marshalled and he analysed and subdivided his subject with dialectical thoroughness. He addressed himself principally to moral and practical themes, exposing with truth and appropriateness the vices of his time, without sparing any class of sinners, and with a profound knowledge of the human soul. His sermons are said to have had more fire and colour when delivered than is revealed in their edited form. He was a powerful adversary of the Jansenists.

Bourdet, ÉDOUARD (1887–1944), dramatist. For some years before his death he was Director of the Comédie-Française (q.v.). His plays—usually psychological analyses of modern problems—have been collected in four volumes of *Théâtre complet*, including: *Le Rubicon* (1920), *L'Homme enchaîné* (1924), *La Prisonnière* (1926), *Vient de paraître* (1927, a satirical comedy of literary life), *Les Temps difficiles* (1934), &c.

Bourdigné, CHARLES, see *Pierre Faifeu*.

Bourgeois de Molinchart, Les (1855), a novel of provincial life by Champfleury (q.v.).

Bourgeois de Paris, Journal d'un, for the years 1405–49, written by a priest of the University of Paris whose identity has not been discovered. It gives an extremely vivid account of the conditions prevailing in Paris during the period of English and Burgundian domination.

Bourgeois de Paris, Mémoires d'un (1853), see *Véron, Dr Louis-Désiré*.

Bourgeois Gentilhomme, Le, a *comédie-ballet* by Molière, produced in 1670.

M. Jourdain, a vain, ignorant *bourgeois*, hankers to figure as a man of quality. He takes lessons in dancing, fencing, and philosophy (and learns with surprise that he has been talking prose all his life without knowing it). His extravagant dress makes him a laughing-stock. He is cheated and fleeced by Dorante, a needy nobleman who flatters his conceit. He refuses his daughter to the worthy Cléonte because the young man is not of noble birth. Thereupon Cléonte masquerades as the son of the Grand Turk who has come to Paris as a suitor for the hand of Jourdain's daughter; he talks a ridiculous jargon which passes for Turkish, and confers on Jourdain the high dignity of *mamamouchi*. Such are the vanity and credulity of the foolish man that he swallows the absurd imposture, and gladly confers his daughter on this exalted suitor.

Bourges, ÉLÉMIR (1852–1925), author of long, grandiosely-imaginative novels—a mixture of myth, history, philosophy, and symbolism, and influenced by his admiration for Wagner and the Elizabethan dramatists. The best known are *Le Crépuscule des dieux* (1884) and *Les Oiseaux s'envolent et les feuilles tombent* (1893). *Sous la hache* (1885) is a stirring novel of the Chouannerie (q.v.). *La Nef* (1904–22) is a vast prose poem in two parts.

Bourget, PAUL (1852–1935), novelist and critic, born at Amiens, broke off studying medicine and philosophy for literature, which for some years meant tutoring by day and writing by night. After the early poetical collections *La Vie inquiète* (1875), *Edel* (1878, a long poem), and *Les Aveux* (1882), he made his name with *Cruelle Énigme* (1885) and *André Cornélis* (1887, q.v.), novels of psychological analysis. Thereafter he remained steadily in the front rank of late 19th- and early 20th-century novelists, with such solid, closely-constructed works as *Le Disciple* (1889, q.v.), *Cosmopolis* (1893), *L'Étape* (1903, q.v.). These almost invariably turned on a dilemma of conscience or (if not *and also*) some sociological problem; and like the works of his friend Henry James they described the life of the leisured classes.

As time passed, his moralistic attitude and his deepening Roman Catholic and Royalist sympathies were disproportionately evident in his writing (e.g. *Un Divorce*, 1904; *L'Émigré*, 1907; *Le Démon de midi*, 1914). Some of his shorter tales, e.g. *Le Justicier* (1919), *L'Échéance* (1921), have been praised as being more direct and less overweighted with ideology. Nowadays his criticism is held to be of more lasting value than any of his novels. It includes: *Essais* and *Nouveaux Essais de psychologie contemporaine* (1883 and 1886); *Pages* and *Nouvelles Pages de critique et de doctrine* (1912 and 1922).

Bourgmestre de Stilmonde, Le (1919), a drama by Maurice Maeterlinck (q.v.).

Bourgogne, Hôtel de, see *Hôtel de Bourgogne*.

Bourg régénéré, Le (1906), a 'conte de la vie unanime' by Jules Romains (q.v.).

Boursault, EDME (1638–1701), dramatist, author of the successful comedy, *Le Mercure galant* (1683, named from Donneau de Visé's periodical), a sort of *revue* of various ridiculous characters who seek to use the publicity of journalism for their own ends; also of *Ésope à la ville* (1690) and *Ésope à la cour*, somewhat ponderous satires on the manners of the day in the form of a framework for La Fontaine's fables; and of some indifferent tragedies. Boursault quarrelled with Molière (see *Impromptu de Versailles*), also with Boileau and Racine. Vanbrugh drew on him in some of his comedies.

Bourse, La, the Stock Exchange. In Paris, a Stock Exchange was established officially in 1724. Before that date various quarters of the city, e.g. the Pont au Change, the Palais de Justice, had served as meeting-places for merchants and bankers for purposes connected with the sale, purchase, and/or insurance of funds, foreign moneys, property and merchandise, and speculative dealings had been rife since Law's system (see *Law, John*). From 1826 *la Bourse de Paris* has functioned in the building (in the rue Vivienne, behind the *Bibliothèque nationale*) erected specially to the design of the architect Brongniard (1739–1813). The *Bourse* figures often in Zola's novels of the Second Empire (see *Rougon-Macquart, Les*; *Curée, La*), which was a period of feverish specula-

tion in France. The Paris *Bourse* was not the first to be established officially. It had been preceded by the Exchanges at, for example, Lyons and Toulouse.

Bousingo, bousingot, a name, after the July Revolution (q.v.), and especially *c.* 1831–2 in articles in *Le Figaro*, for a band of turbulent young Romantic writers and artists (see *Romantisme*). It is said to have stuck to them, together with a reputation for Republicanism, after a night when they patrolled the streets shouting 'Nous avons fait du bousingo' and ended in the lock-up. Petrus Borel (q.v.) was the *bousingo par excellence*. Other leaders were Théophile Gautier and Philothée O'Neddy (qq.v. and cf. *Jeunes-France*). The average age of the band was twenty. Among other eccentricities of costume they affected a wide-brimmed hat of the type worn by sailors. (This was often called a *bousingo*, a word which may be derived from the English word *booze*.) The young *bousingos* are described in G. Sand's novel *Horace* (1842). A collection of *Contes du bousingo, par une camaraderie*, which they are said to have planned, never saw daylight.

Bouteille à la mer, La, a poem by Alfred de Vigny (q.v.), first printed in the *Revue des Deux Mondes* (1 Feb. 1854), then included in his (posthumous) collection *Les Destinées*. The captain of a sinking ship seals his last records and chartings in a bottle and tosses it to the waves, trusting that one day it will be salvaged. So should the 'jeune homme inconnu', to whom the poem is addressed, entrust his work ('fruit tel que de l'âme il sort, Tout empreint du parfum des saintes solitudes') to posterity.

Boutroux, ÉMILE (1845–1921), was one of the outstanding French philosophers of the late 19th century. He believed that human evolution could not be reduced to a purely determinist process but, on the contrary, that it was governed ultimately by a creative principle which transcended theories of cause and effect, or of the possible and non-possible, and allowed room for spirituality and moral choice. Besides his chief work, *De la contingence des lois de la nature* (1874), his publications include: *Science et religion dans la philosophie contemporaine* (1908), *Questions de morale et d'éducation* (1895), and a number of important studies of the history of philosophy. *De l'idée de loi naturelle dans la science et la philosophie contemporaines* (1895), another important work, was the printed form of lectures he delivered at the Sorbonne in 1892–3.

Bouts rimés, verses composed on rhymes that are given. Competitions in this kind of exercise were fashionable in the 17th century.

Bouvard et Pécuchet (1881), an unfinished novel, published posthumously, by Gustave Flaubert.

Two copying clerks meet by accident and discover that they are twin souls. One inherits money, the other realizes his savings, they buy a farm and take to country life. They embark on a succession of experiments in agriculture, distilling, chemistry, &c., with a credulous and unflagging enthusiasm for scientific progress which is doomed to continual disappointment. After science they try philosophy, then religion, then they attempt an educational experiment, equally disastrous, with two orphans.

Flaubert worked on this book for over ten years, making of it a sort of monument to his disgust at human stupidity. The conclusion he had planned was that Bouvard and Pécuchet should decide to finish their days, as they had begun, as copyists. They were to transcribe passages from books consulted during their years of experiment— and incidentally and unwittingly to compile an anthology of the almost incredible lapses, errors, contradictions, and ineptitudes of which even the greatest minds are capable. This anthology would have formed a second volume, which would also have incorporated Flaubert's own collection of conversational platitudes or 'bromides' (see *Dictionnaire des idées reçues*).

Bouvines, near Lille, the scene of a battle in 1214 in which Philippe-Auguste (Philippe II of France) defeated the Emperor Otho IV.

Bovary, see *Madame Bovary*.

Boyer, ABEL (1667–1729), a French Huguenot who settled in England in 1689, author of an Anglo-French and Franco-English dictionary (1702) and of histories in English of William III and Queen Anne. He attacked Swift in a pamphlet, and Swift in his *Journal*

to *Stella* vowed vengeance on the 'French dog'. He also translated the *Mémoires de Gramont* and Racine's *Iphigénie* into English.

Boyer, L'ABBÉ CLAUDE (1618–98), author of numerous mediocre tragedies and tragi-comedies, beginning with *La Porcie romaine* (1646) and ending with *Judith* (1695).

Boylesve, RENÉ (1867–1926), novelist of small-town provincial life with its cliques, prejudices, rivalries, and care for appearances. His best-known works include: *Le Médecin des dames de Néans* (1896); *Mademoiselle Cloque* (1899), strife in clerical circles; *La Becquée* (1901) and its sequel *L'Enfant à la balustrade* (1903); *La Jeune Fille bien élevée* (1909) and its sequel *Madeleine, jeune femme* (1912).

Bradamante, the first French tragicomedy, by Robert Garnier, published in 1582, the subject drawn in part from the *Orlando Furioso* of Ariosto.

Bradamante, a warrior-maiden, and Roger, 'un simple chevalier', love one another; but her parents, Aymon and Béatrix, inspired by ambition and vanity, wish her to marry Léon, heir to the Emperor of Byzantium. Charlemagne, to whom the matter has been referred, decides that Bradamante shall marry whoever can defeat her in single combat. Meanwhile Léon has saved the life of an unknown knight (in fact, Roger in disguise) whom he begs, on learning of Charlemagne's pronouncement, to enter the lists against Bradamante on his behalf. There is thus a struggle in Roger's mind between love and honour, similar to that depicted by Corneille in *Le Cid*. Honour wins the day. Roger defeats Bradamante and rides off, 'saisi de merveilleuse tristesse'. But now Charlemagne decides that in fairness, since Bradamante had originally been promised to Roger, Léon should also fight and defeat Roger. This leads to the revelation that the latter is the unknown knight, and to Léon's surrender of Bradamante to him. There remains only the obstinacy of old Aymon (who provides the comic element) to be overcome, rather clumsily effected through the offer of the crown of Bulgaria to Roger, who is thus raised to a position of sufficient dignity.

Braille, LOUIS (1809–52), the inventor of the system, for the use of the blind, and named after him, of writing and printing in relief. Himself blind from the age of three, he was early admitted to the French Institution for the Blind at Coupvray-sur-Marne, where he spent the rest of his life and became a master. He was also an accomplished organist.

Brantôme, PIERRE DE BOURDEILLES, SEIGNEUR DE (*c.* 1540–1614), born in Périgord, spent his youth at the court of Marguerite de Navarre, accompanied Mary Stuart on her return to Scotland in 1561, was presented to Queen Elizabeth, saw military service in many countries (including Italy, Spain, Portugal), and fought in the civil wars on the side of the Guises. He received from Henri II the abbacy of Brantôme, from which he took his name. A fall from horseback (*c.* 1584) condemned him to inactivity for the rest of his life, which he spent in part in composing his *Recueil d'aucuns discours* on great captains, French and foreign (*Vies des grands capitaines français et étrangers*), and a second part, the *Recueil des dames*, dealing with certain great princesses, and also (in a section later known as the *Dames Galantes*) with scandalous anecdotes of the court. These memoirs, written in an easy lively style, with uncritical frivolity and absence of morality, but with evident sincerity when he has personal knowledge of what he relates, contain many details of interest, but depict only one side of the 16th century. They throw a vivid light on the externals of military and court life, and provide a document for the history of manners. They were published posthumously in 1665–6.

Bréal, MICHEL-JULES-ALFRED (1832–1915), was for over fifty years one of the foremost French philologists, an inspiration and guide to other scholars. His studies in semantics, in comparative grammar, and in the linguistic origins of mythology include *Mélanges de mythologie et de linguistique* (1877) and a notable *Essai de sémantique* (*science des significations*) (1897).

Brébeuf, GEORGES DE (1618–61), born in Normandy, poet, author of an epic (1654–5) adapted from Lucan's *Pharsalia*, at one time celebrated, but condemned by Boileau, who, however, conceded that it contained flashes of genius. His *Entretiens solitaires ou Prières et méditations pieuses* is his best work.

Brécourt, GUILLAUME MARCOUREAU, SIEUR DE (*c.* 1637–85), a comedian of Molière's company in the provinces and later in Paris. He also played minor parts in tragedy. He wrote comedies, quickly forgotten.

Bremond, L'ABBÉ HENRI (1865–1933), historian and critic, withdrew from the Jesuit Order and from teaching in Jesuit schools to devote himself to writing and research. His chief work, *Histoire littéraire du sentiment religieux en France* (1916–33, 11 vols., out of 14 contemplated), was a study of the religious element in French literature from the end of the Wars of Religion (1562–98) and, particularly, of the part played by mysticism: it did not get beyond the 17th century. He also wrote *L'Inquiétude religieuse* (1901 and 1909, essays); *Newman* (1905) and *Fénelon* (1910), studies in religious psychology; *Pour le romantisme* (1923), a plea for romanticism as the element of inspiration in literature; *Prière et poésie* (1925) and *La Poésie pure* (1927). Before his withdrawal (1904) from the Order he had spent several years in religious establishments in England and Wales.

Brendan, SAINT (484–577), an Irish saint, the subject of the medieval legend of the *Navigation of St. Brendan*. One version of this was an Anglo-Norman poem written by a monk Benedict and dedicated in 1121 to Adeliza of Louvain, consort of Henry I. In this the author describes the saint's odyssey in search of the earthly Paradise, among magic islands in the Western ocean, the *Île Rocheuse* (where invisible hands serve the repast), the *Île aux Oiseaux* (where birds sing the praise of God), and so forth. The legend had some influence on the later Breton romances. (Cf. *L'Île des pingouins*, by Anatole France.)

Breton, ANDRÉ (1896–), poet, founder, and theorist of the surrealist movement (see *Surréalisme*). His works include *Mont de piété* (1919), *Les Champs magnétiques* (1921, with Philippe Soupault), *Les Pas perdus* (1924), *Manifeste du surréalisme — Poisson soluble* (1924), *Nadja* (1928), a novel, to some extent autobiographical, and often praised, *L'Immaculée conception* (1930, with Paul Éluard), *Second manifeste du surréalisme* (1930), *L'Union libre* (1931), *Le Revolver à cheveux blancs* (1932), *Les Vases communicants* (1932), *Qu'est-ce que le surréalisme?* (1934),

Le Château étoilé (1937), collected *Poèmes* (1948), &c.

Breton lays, see *Romans bretons*.

Bretons, Geste des, see *Wace*.

Brichemer, the stag, in the *Roman de Renart* (q.v.).

Bridaine, JACQUES (1701–67), a preacher noted for his powerful but uncultured eloquence.

Brid'oison, a character in Beaumarchais's *Le Mariage de Figaro* (q.v.), the type of the foolish, ignorant, formalist magistrate.

Bridoye, a character, a judge, in Rabelais's (q.v.) *Gargantua et Pantagruel* (*Tiers Livre*).

Brieux, EUGÈNE (1858–1932), dramatist, had his first play produced at the *Théâtre-Libre* (q.v.). He is best remembered by *Blanchette* (1892), a study of a country girl whom too much education has stranded above her station in life, and *La Robe rouge* (1900), a study of legal circles. His other plays included *L'Engrenage* (1894), *Les Bienfaiteurs* (1897), *Les Trois Filles de M. Dupont* (1899), *Les Avariés* (1901), *La Femme seule* (1913). The dramatic balance of his work was frequently upset by his preoccupation with moral and social reform.

Brifaut, CHARLES (1781–1857), born at Dijon, is remembered as the author of *Ninus* (1813), a tragedy which underwent a last-minute transformation to suit the requirements of Napoleon's dramatic censors. The scene had been laid in Spain, the plot being based on an old Spanish fable. But Napoleon's army had just crossed the Pyrenees and allusions to military events were taboo. The author obligingly altered the scene of his tragedy to Assyria, making his hero king of that country.

Brillat-Savarin, ANTHELME (1755–1826), author of the famous *Physiologie du goût ou Méditations sur la gastronomie transcendante*, was born at Belley, in a part of France (the old province of Bresse) renowned for good food. He came of a family of magistrates and himself practised at the Bar. In 1789 he sat in the *Assemblée constituante* as a Deputy of the *Tiers État* (qq.v.) but had to flee the country during the Terror. He went to the U.S.A., returned to the France of the *Directoire*, and

eventually was attached to the *cour de cassation* (q.v.). He was a man of wit and culture, welcomed in literary *salons*, and very much a contrast to the eccentric gastronome Grimod de la Reynière (q.v.), his contemporary. His *Physiologie* is a sophisticated, amusing, eminently readable and eminently quotable collection of anecdotes, *pensées*, and aphorisms, inspired by an academic interest in food rather than any excessive devotion to the pleasures of the table. He also left writings on law and politics.

Brinvilliers, MARIE-MADELEINE, MARQUISE DE (1630–76), a famous criminal who murdered her father and attempted to kill her husband with poison (supposed to have been *aqua toffana*) from motives of cupidity. Her lover, Gaudin de Sainte-Croix, had learnt the art of poisoning in the Bastille from an Italian and had communicated it to her. Sainte-Croix perished from the accidental breaking of a mask while experimenting with poisons, and among his effects was found evidence incriminating Brinvilliers. She took refuge in England. An attempt to obtain her extradition failed, but she removed to Liège where she was lured into a trap, seized, and carried to France. She was executed in Paris. Mme de Sévigné in her letters recounts her death (17 July 1676).

Brioché, JEAN (*fl. c.* 1650), a famous mountebank, said to be the inventor of marionettes. His performances were well known in the fairs of Paris.

Brissot, JEAN-PIERRE (who took the name of Brissot de Warville) (1754–93), born in Chartres, son of a cookshop-proprietor, was educated for the Bar and became a journalist. He was a Deputy to the *Convention nationale* (q.v.) and a leader, first of the faction known as the *Brissotins*, later of the Girondins (q.v.). His paper *Le Patriote français* was the organ of the Girondins. He died on the scaffold.

Britannicus, a tragedy by Racine, produced in 1669, based on Tacitus. In this play Racine first met Corneille on his own ground, the drama of political intrigue.

The scene is Rome at the time when Nero after the moderation of the first years of his reign is shaking off the restraining influence of Burrhus and Seneca, and rebelling against the authority of his mother Agrippina.

The latter has favoured the proposed marriage of Britannicus (her son by the late Emperor Claudius) with Junia, a lady of the imperial house, a marriage not approved by Nero, who sees in his half-brother a possible rival for the throne. Nero causes Junia to be brought to the palace, and falls in love with her. Unable to win her from her devotion to Britannicus, he arrests the latter. Unmoved by the reproaches of Agrippina (though feigning contrition), then yielding to the expostulations of Burrhus, but finally spurred on to crime by Narcissus, the treacherous tutor of Britannicus, Nero, under pretence of a reconciliation, poisons his half-brother. The fierce invective which the crime draws from Agrippina is prophetic of his evil future. Junia escapes from the palace to become a vestal; Narcissus, who attempts to arrest her, is killed by the mob.

Brizeux, AUGUSTE (1803–58), poet, born at Lorient (Brittany), of Irish origin. His verse was conscientious, mainly about Brittany, and sometimes in the ancient Breton dialect. It includes *Marie* (1836), lyrics of childhood; *Les Ternaires* (1841), in a ternary measure uncommon in French versification; *Les Bretons* (1845); *Primel et Nola* (1852); *Histoires poétiques* (1855).

Brocéliande, a vast forest in Brittany, to-day the Forest of Paimpont, the scene of many medieval romances. In the Arthurian romances it was inhabited by Merlin the Enchanter.

Brodeau, VICTOR (*c.* 1502?–40), poet, son of a bourgeois of Tours and a favourite pupil of Clément Marot. He entered the service of Marguerite de Navarre and became her secretary and later her controller-general of finance. He was the author of two religious poems, *Louanges de Jesuchrist nostre sauveur* (1540), dedicated to Marguerite, and *Épître d'un pécheur à Jésus-Christ* (1543). He was also a court poet, writing rondeaux and epigrams on trivial subjects. The *Louanges* alone of his works is notable for passages of a vigorous simplicity.

Broglie (pron. *Bro-ye*), the name of a family —of Italian origin—distinguished in French history since the 17th century. The duchy of Broglie (in Normandy) was created in 1742.

When the Revolution broke out the then duc de Broglie was Minister of War. He left France after the fall of the Bastille, fought with the *Armée des émigrés* (q.v.), and died in 1804. His son at first favoured the Revolution but in the end was guillotined. His grandson, the duc Victor de Broglie (1785–1870), a prominent *doctrinaire* (q.v.) and leader of the Opposition, who later held Cabinet rank under Louis-Philippe, married (1814) Albertine, daughter of Mme de Staël. (Mme de Staël's son by her second marriage, Alphonse Rocca, was brought up in the Broglie household, with Doudan (q.v.) as his tutor.) This duke left four volumes of *Souvenirs* (1886) covering his early years to 1832. The 3rd and 4th volumes are political, and little more than lengthy quotations from his speeches, but the first two are interesting as a picture of Napoleonic and Restoration France and of a man of rigid principles, but modest and with a strong sense of duty, cast loose among the Romantics; and still more interesting for the many pen-portraits of his contemporaries (e.g. Benjamin Constant, Mme Récamier, Talleyrand). The statesman and historian Jacques-Victor-Albert (1821–1901), prince, later duc, de Broglie, was his son. The present duc (Maurice) de Broglie and his brother Louis (b. 1892), prince de Broglie, both physicists, are his grandsons. The latter was awarded the Nobel Prize for Physics in 1929.

Brossard, SÉBASTIEN DE, see *Dictionaries and Encyclopedias*, under date 1703.

Brosses, CHARLES DE (1709–77), *known as* the Président de Brosses, born at Dijon, a magistrate of the *parlement* of Burgundy, is remembered especially for his pleasant *Lettres familières écrites d'Italie en 1739 et 1740*; also for the quarrel that arose between him and Voltaire out of the purchase by the latter of a life-interest in the Président's château of Tourney near Ferney. An edition of Sallust by the Président appeared in 1777. He was one of the first to interest himself in the study of primitive man (*Histoire des navigations aux Terres Australes*, 1756; *Le Culte des dieux fétiches*, 1760).

Brou, Église de, at Bourg-en-Bresse, near Lyons, a beautiful church built (1511–36) by Marguerite d'Autriche (q.v.), wife of Philibert II, duke of Savoy. It contains exquisite tombs of Philibert, his wife, and his mother, Marguerite de Bourbon. It is celebrated in a poem by Matthew Arnold.

Broussel, PIERRE, see *Fronde*.

Brueys (pron. as if *Bruèss*), L'ABBÉ DAVID-AUGUSTIN DE (1640–1723), dramatist, born at Aix-en-Provence, a Protestant converted to Catholicism by Bossuet. He wrote some comedies and a tragedy *Gabinie*, a Christian drama of the time of Diocletian; but he is remembered especially for his collaboration with Palaprat (q.v.).

Bruges-la-Morte (1892), a novel by Georges Rodenbach (q.v.).

Bruianz, the bull, in the *Roman de Renart* (q.v.).

Brulard, HENRI, Stendhal's name for himself in his unfinished *Vie de Henri Brulard* (first published 1890), his 'Confessions, . . . comme Jean-Jacques Rousseau, avec plus de franchise'.

Brumaire, the second month of the Republican Calendar (q.v.). It ran from 22 (or 23) October to 20 (or 21) November (see also *Dix-huit brumaire*).

Brun, the bear [Bruin], in the *Roman de Renart* (q.v.).

Brun de la Montagne, a *roman d'aventure* of the second half of the 13th century. The scene is the Forest of Brocéliande (q.v.) in Brittany.

Brune, GUILLAUME-MARIE-ANNE, one of Napoleon's marshals (see *Maréchal de l'Empire*).

Bruneau, CHARLES, see *Brunot, Ferdinand*.

Bruneau, MATHURIN (1784–*c*. 1825), one of the many 'faux dauphins' (cf. *Orphelin du Temple*), was a Norman peasant, the son of a cobbler. He died in the prison on the Mont Saint-Michel.

Brunet, JACQUES-CHARLES (1780–1867), bibliographer, born and died in Paris. His *Manuel du libraire et de l'amateur des livres* (1810) and *Nouvelles recherches bibliographiques pour servir de supplément au 'Manuel'* (1834) are still authoritative works. (The 5th—1860–5—edition of the former should be used.) His first essay in bibliography was a *Supplément au Dictionnaire bibliographique de l'Abbé Duclos* (1802, see *Duclos*).

Brunet, JEAN, one of the original *félibres* (q.v.).

Brunet, PIERRE-GUSTAVE (1807–96), born and died in Bordeaux, man of letters and bibliographer. His works included a *Dictionnaire de bibliographie catholique* (1859); also *Les Fous littéraires* (1880) and *Livres perdus* (1882), two interesting books which he wrote under the pseudonym of 'Philomneste Junior'.

Brunetière, FERDINAND (1849–1906), literary historian and critic, born at Toulon, was professor of French Language and Literature at the École normale supérieure (q.v.) in Paris from 1886 and editor-in-chief of the *Revue des Deux Mondes* (q.v.) from 1893. He was a convinced admirer of the 17th century in French literature, an opponent of the 19th-century theories of *l'art pour l'art* or of *naturalisme* (qq.v.), which ran counter to his ideas of the necessity for a moral purpose in art; and he believed that the theories of evolution held good in literature as in science. These views were intensified by his reactionary religious and political beliefs, and at times lent an element of *parti pris* to his writing: but this can be discounted. His valuable studies of literature and history include: *Études critiques* (1880–1925, 9 series); *Le Roman naturaliste* (1883); *Histoire et littérature* (1884–6, 3 series); *L'Évolution des genres dans l'histoire de la littérature* (1890); *L'Évolution de la poésie lyrique au dix-neuvième siècle* (1894); *Manuel de l'histoire de la littérature française* (1897); *L'Art et la morale* (1898).

Brunetto Latini, see *Trésor, Livre du*.

Brunot, FERDINAND (1860–1938), philologist. His monumental *Histoire de la langue française des origines à 1900*, conceived from the point of view of literature and criticism as well as of philology, is concerned with the effect of political and social evolution on the evolution of French language and literature. The first ten volumes, published between 1905 and 1943, and the work of Brunot himself, carry the history down to 1815. The titles are:

　I. *De l'époque latine à la Renaissance*.
　II. *Le Seizième Siècle*.
　III. *La Formation de la langue classique (1600–1660)*.

This work is being continued, with the title *Histoire de la langue française des origines à nos jours*, by M. Charles Bruneau, who succeeded Ferdinand Brunot as Professor of the History of the French Language in the University of Paris and collaborated with him in other works. Vols. XI, XIV, and XV are still (1955) in preparation (*Le Français au dehors sous la Révolution, le Consulat et l'Empire; Le Symbolisme, 1885–1905 and 1905–1940*). Vol. XII, *L'Époque romantique (1815–1852)*, and pt. I (*Fin du romantisme et Parnasse*) of Vol. XIII, *Le Réalisme (1852–1886)*, were published in 1948 and 1953 respectively.

Brunschvicg, LÉON (1869–1944), born in Paris, was one of the leading 20th-century French philosophers. In the most important expressions of his highly intellectualist philosophy, *Les Étapes de la philosophie mathématique* (1913) and *Le Progrès de la conscience dans la philosophie occidentale* (1927), he studied the nature of thought, the high place to be accorded to intellectual judgement, and the close connexion between scientific and mathematical progress and the evolution of philosophical speculation. Other works on much the same lines include *L'Expérience humaine et la causalité physique* (1922), *De la connaissance de soi* (1931), *La Raison et la religion* (1939). He also wrote on Descartes and Pascal (and was a noted modern editor of the latter's works).

Bruscambille, the nickname of Des Lauriers, a 17th-century actor, famous for the prologues which, as was customary at that time, he used to deliver at the theatre of the Hôtel de Bourgogne, before the performance of a play, to induce patience in the audience while the house was filling. The prologues were burlesque satires, imitated from the Italian, describing characters and types and treating of all sorts of subjects (poltroonery, the gout, fleas, cabbage, &c.). They were very popular and were printed (1610).

Brut, see *Wace*.

Brutus, a tragedy by Voltaire, produced 1730, about the Lucius Junius Brutus who liberated Rome from the Tarquins.

In Act I Porsenna is attacking Rome in order to restore Tarquin. Rome, where Brutus and Valerius are consuls, has resisted successfully so far thanks to the brilliant leadership of Brutus's son Titus. The Senate repulse the Tuscan summons, made by Porsenna's ambassador Arons, to surrender, and even allow Tarquin's daughter Tullia, till now a captive in Rome, to return to him under Arons's escort. In the final acts Brutus, informed of a Tuscan plan to attack Rome at midnight, entrusts the defence to Titus and cannot understand Titus's anxiety to get out of this. Next he learns of a plot against Rome in which Titus's friend Messala seems strangely involved. Shortly afterwards he is told that the conspirators, among them Messala, Arons, and Tullia, have been seized and are now dead; and, moreover, to his shame and horror, that Tullia's last words had incriminated Titus. The Senate leave it to Brutus to decide his son's fate.

What had actually happened, as made clear by the intervening acts, was that the false Messala and the other conspirators, knowing Titus to be wildly in love with Tullia, had used Tullia as a snare to induce him to betray Rome and himself rule as king, with Tullia as his wife. Titus had held out desperately against Tullia's entreaties and reproaches but in the end had given way. Now, confronted with his father, he confesses his weakness. It had been momentary, but that moment had been too long and he insists on dying: it is his duty to his fellow Romans so as to harden their resistance. Father and son take leave of one another.

Brutus sends Titus to his death, then turns to defend Rome.

Voltaire dedicated this play to Lord Bolingbroke and prefaced it with a comparison of English and French tragedy.

Bubu de Montparnasse (1901), a novel by Charles-Louis Philippe (q.v.).

Buchanan, GEORGE (1506–82), born at Killearn in Stirlingshire, studied at St. Andrews and Paris, and became a professor at Bordeaux where he had Montaigne among his pupils. He had some influence on the history of the drama in France by his Latin translations of the *Alcestis* and *Medea* of Euripides (*c.* 1539) and his tragedies *Baptistes sive calumnia* (performed 1540) and *Jephthes sive votum* (performed *c.* 1542), also in Latin, written for his pupils. The last, a well-ordered dramatization of the story of the sacrifice of Jephthah's daughter, was more than once translated into French. Buchanan later returned to Scotland, professed himself a Protestant, became a bitter enemy of Mary in consequence of the murder of Darnley, and was tutor to James VI and I during 1570–8. Among his many writings was a Latin *Rerum Scoticarum Historia* (1582).

Buchez, PHILIPPE-JOSEPH-BENJAMIN (1796–1866), publicist and social reformer, studied medicine in Paris and was for a time associated with the Saint-Simoniens (q.v.). He parted company with them (1829) and developed a form of Christian socialism of his own (in his journal *L'Atelier*, 1840–50, which was known in England as well as France, and in lectures delivered at his own home). He had several disciples.

Budé, GUILLAUME (*c.* 1468–1540), often referred to under the Latin name *Budaeus*, of a Parisian family, a man of great erudition and one of the earliest of French humanists. He was sent by Louis XII as ambassador to the pope, and enjoyed the favour of François Ier, by whom he was appointed secretary and later librarian. It was at his instance that François Ier instituted the 'royal readers' in Hebrew, Greek, Latin, and mathematics, who formed the nucleus of the future Collège de France (q.v.). Budé's chief works were Latin translations from Plutarch, commentaries on the Pandects, a dialogue with the king *De philologia*, a treatise on ancient

coins (*De asse*, 1514), and *Commentarii Linguae Graecae* (1529). His *Institution du Prince* (published in 1747) was written in French. The chief French philological society of modern times, the 'Association Guillaume Budé', is named after him. We find Rabelais, during the period when he was at the Franciscan convent of Fontenay-le-Comte, in correspondence with Budé, and receiving from him encouragement in his humanistic studies.

Bueil, JEAN DE, see *Jouvencel*.

Buffon, GEORGES-LOUIS LECLERC, COMTE DE (1707–88), naturalist, born at the château de Montbard in Burgundy. His father was a magistrate, and he himself studied law and medicine. He wrote when a young man treatises on scientific subjects, including a translation (1735) of the *Vegetable Staticks* (1727) of Stephen Hales (1677–1761), and was admitted to the Académie des Sciences in 1734. From 1739 until his death he was curator of the Jardin du Roi (see *Jardin des Plantes*). He translated Newton's *Method of Fluxions* in 1740. The prospectus of his great *Histoire Naturelle* (1749–1804, 44 vols.) appeared in 1748, the first three volumes (*Théorie de la Terre* and general views on generation and man) in 1749; twelve on quadrupeds in 1755–67; nine on birds in 1770–83, and five on minerals in 1783–88; with a further seven in 1774–89 (one of these being the famous *Époques de la Nature*, 1779), on the geological periods of the earth. The final eight volumes, on reptiles, fishes, &c., were completed and published after Buffon's death by Lacépède (q.v.). Buffon's discourse (on *Style*) on his admission to the *Académie française* in 1753 contained the well-known dictum, 'Le style est l'homme même'.

Buffon spent the greater part of his life at the château de Montbard, leading with dignity the life of a *grand seigneur*, and dividing his time between the improvement of his estate and the composition of his great work. His annual visits to Paris were chiefly devoted to the affairs of the Jardin du Roi. He was a good husband, father, and landlord, and his humane nature is shown by his denunciation of slavery and his concern for the sad plight of the peasantry.

Buffon was the first of modern writers to translate the facts of nature into a history of nature, and his method was, at least in intention, scientific. He collected facts through correspondents all over the world and conducted experiments. But at the outset he was neither a botanist nor an entomologist, and his impatience with the slow methods of science led him to propound theories and systems which were criticized by the learned as unsupported by sufficient evidence and by the devout as contrary to Scripture, and which have in many cases been disproved. But his theories and hypotheses (e.g. his development of geographical zoology and of the idea of geological periods) were fertile, and he trod in paths subsequently followed by Lamarck and Darwin. Buffon had collaborators, notably Louis-Jean Daubenton (q.v.) in anatomical descriptions, and Guéneau de Montbéliard (1720–85) and the abbé Bexon (1748–84) in the study of birds.

He contributed one article (on Nature) to the *Encyclopédie*, but remained serenely aloof from the polemics of its supporters, though his spirit of inquiry into nature was also theirs. In general he showed a dignified disregard of personal criticism. The umbrage that his theory of the history of the earth gave to the theologians caused the Sorbonne to condemn in 1751 fourteen propositions drawn from the *Histoire Naturelle*. To avoid theological controversy Buffon thereupon signed a declaration abandoning anything in his work that might be contrary to the narrative of Moses, and later, when he published the *Époques de la Nature*, repeated his abjuration. He was not hostile to religion, but kept the spheres of faith and reason separate.

Buffon aimed at a clear, harmonious, majestic style, suited to the dignity of his subject. He is at his best, not in the descriptions of animals (though some of these are strikingly vivid), but in his great surveys of nature, e.g. in the *Théorie de la Terre* and the *Époques de la Nature*. The inscription on his statue, 'Maiestati naturae par ingenium', testifies to the estimation in which he was held by his contemporaries.

Bugeaud de la Piconnerie, THOMAS-ROBERT, MARÉCHAL DE FRANCE, DUC D'ISLY (1784–1849), a French officer remembered for his military and organizing genius, shown particularly during the conquest of Algeria (1836–40), and also because of the popular soldier's song, long a bugle-call:

> As-tu vu
> La casquette, la casquette,
> As-tu vu
> La casquette au Père Bugeaud?

Once during his African campaigns he turned out in answer to a night-alarm and, discovering that he was still wearing his nightcap, cried 'Ma casquette!' (i.e. *képi*, military cap). In 1848 Bugeaud was in command of the French troops who tried, unsuccessfully, to defend Paris and the Monarchy.

Bug-Jargal, a tale of the negro revolution in San Domingo in 1791, is one of Victor Hugo's early novels, written in 1818, revised, and published in 1826.

A noble savage, once a king in his own country, is the leader of the rebels. He saves the life of the narrator of the story, a young French soldier to whom he owed a debt of gratitude, but through a misunderstanding he is executed. The Frenchman's life thereafter is overshadowed by the remembrance of this injustice. The tale abounds in horrific and fantastic happenings, but contains descriptive passages which foreshadow the vivid pictorial writing of Hugo's later novels.

Bullant, JEAN (1510–78), a famous architect, who constructed the château of Écouen for the connétable Anne de Montmorency, was appointed by Henri II controller of royal buildings, and succeeded Delorme (q.v.) as architect of the palace of the Tuileries, of which he constructed a part. His total output was not great and he is best known by his books, which include a *Règle générale d'architecture* (1568).

Bulletin des lois, an official record of Laws of the French Government from the month of *Frimaire* (21 Nov. to 20 Dec.), An II de la République (1793, see *Republican Calendar*) to 1931.

Bulliard, PIERRE, see *Dictionaries and Encyclopedias* under date 1783.

Bullier, see *Bals populaires*.

Buloz, FRANÇOIS (1803–76), a leading figure in 19th-century French journalism, became editor of the *Revue des Deux Mondes* in 1831 and soon made it the most intellectually important of French reviews. He was also at one time editor of the *Revue de Paris* and Director of the Comédie-Française.

Buonarotti, MICHEL, see *Babeuf*.

Bureau d'adresse, see *Renaudot*.

Burgraves, Les (1843), an epic drama by Victor Hugo. (The 'burgraves' were medieval princes who inhabited the fortified castles of the Rhine and ranked second only to kings. They mostly led a lawless life, harrying the country and stopping at no crime.)

Through four generations of burgraves evil and corruption are shown driving out the rough ideas of honour which had hitherto existed side by side with ferocity. The great-grandfather Job, a centenarian, has spent his life in remorse for a crime committed in his youth; his son, though brave, is lawless and a tyrant; his grandson is corrupt and dissipated; and his great-grandson already betrays vicious and criminal instincts. Job is menaced with punishment for his crime through the hate of one of his victims, now an old woman, who plans to use the young lovers Regina and Otbert, the only creatures cherished by the old man, as innocent instruments of her revenge. Providence, in the shape of the Emperor Barbarossa, intervenes at the last moment to prevent yet another crime, and an old mystery of death and untimely disappearance is solved.

The complete failure of this play when produced at the Comédie-Française was the end of Hugo's career as a dramatist.

Buridan, JEAN (d. after 1358), born at Béthune, a nominalist philosopher, studied under Occam and in 1327 became Rector of the University of Paris. To him is attributed (without evidence in his writings) the sophism of the ass equally pressed by hunger and thirst and placed between a bundle of hay and a pail of water, who must die of hunger and thirst, having no determining motive to direct him to one or the other (*l'âne de Buridan*). Villon in the *Ballade des Dames du temps jadis* refers to a legend that Jeanne de Bourgogne, consort of Philippe le Long (Philippe V), caused him to be tied in a sack and drowned in the Seine.

Burlamaqui, JEAN-JACQUES (1694–1748), a Swiss (Genevan) publicist and philosopher, a professor of law whose works influenced Rousseau's *Discours sur l'inégalité*.

Burnouf, EUGÈNE (1801–52), a famous French orientalist and philologist, one of the founders (1830) of the *Société asiatique*; Professor of Sanskrit at the Collège de France. He was particularly renowned for his work on the origin and history of Buddhism and for his reconstitution and interpretation, following earlier work by Anquetil-Duperron (q.v.), of the ancient *Zend-Avesta*, the sacred writings attributed to Zoroaster.

Burrhus, a character in Racine's *Britannicus* (q.v.).

Bussy d'Amboise, LOUIS DE CLERMONT DE (second half of the 16th century), a favourite of the duc d'Alençon (brother of Henri III), prominent in the Massacre of St. Bartholomew and a noted duellist and marauder. He was assassinated by the comte de Montsoreau (q.v.), whose wife he had seduced. This is the theme of a romance (*La Dame de Monsoreau*) by Dumas *père*, and of a tragedy by Chapman.

Bussy-Rabutin, ROGER DE RABUTIN, COMTE DE BUSSY (1618–93), a Burgundian, cousin of Mme de Sévigné, a gallant soldier, but a man of disagreeable character, an unscrupulous libertine, arrogant, fatuously conceited, not without a certain wit and literary taste, caustic and slanderous. His career was ruined by the publication in 1665 of his *Histoire amoureuse des Gaules*, portraying, with scandalous anecdotes, various ladies of the court and including an ill-natured sketch of the virtuous Mme de Sévigné. For this he was sent to the Bastille and subsequently relegated to his estates. His exile lasted for seventeen years and although he was ultimately recalled he was not restored to favour. He was reconciled with Mme de Sévigné and there are many of his letters in the collection of her correspondence. He did not bear his exile with fortitude, and his letters, though written in a style of perfect urbanity and with an occasional show of high-minded resignation, nevertheless reveal him soured by disappointed ambition. Saint-Simon says of him merely 'qu'il est connu par son *Histoire amoureuse des Gaules*, et plus encore par la vanité de son esprit et la bassesse de son cœur'. Bussy's literary judgements are interesting. He was a member of the *Académie*. His *Histoire amoureuse* had a wide vogue: we find Pepys reading it, 1 May 1666.

C

Cabale (*Eng.* Cabbala; from the Hebrew qabbālāh, 'tradition'), esoteric—and traditional as opposed to written—doctrines concerning the mysteries of creation and the nature of God; largely the basis of occult and illuminist philosophies (see *Illuminisme*).

This mystical interpretation of the Bible is said to have been revealed in the first place to elect saints by the Holy Spirit, and afterwards preserved in hidden books which were to be delivered only to a privileged few, 'to such as be wise'. It was bound up with Jewish chronology and messianology, and based upon the belief that the twenty-two letters of the Hebrew alphabet, i.e. of the Biblical text, could be so decomposed and rearranged as to reveal hidden truths concerned with the infinite and the finite, and the abstractions or emanations by which the primal substances were gradually condensed into visible matter. These primal substances were inhabited by creatures purer than man, over whom the initiate could acquire power. Salamanders were the creatures of fire, sylphs of the air, nymphs of water, while gnomes inhabited the interior of the earth. Cabbalists and salamanders ornament Anatole France's *Rôtisserie de la Reine Pédauque* (q.v.), and before him were taken more seriously by, e.g., Gérard de Nerval and Rimbaud (qq.v.).

The following description of the Cabbala, given in 1633 by James Howell, the Historiographer Royal, may perhaps be recalled:

'They [the Jews] much glory of their mysterious Cabal, wherein they make the reality of things to depend upon letters and words: but they say that Hebrew only hath this privilege. This Cabal, which is nought else but a tradition, they say, being transmitted from one age to another, was in some measure a reparation of our knowledge lost in Adam, and they say it was revealed four times. First to Adam, who being thrust out of Paradise, and sitting one day very sad and sorrowing for the loss of the knowledge he had of that dependence the Creatures have with their Creator, the angel Raguel was sent to comfort him, and repair his knowledge herein. And this they call the Cabal, which was lost the second time by the Flood and Babel; then God discovered it to Moses in the bush, the third time to Solomon in a dream, whereby he came to know the beginning, mediocrity, and consummation of times, and so wrote divers books, which were lost in the grand captivity. The last time they hold that God restored the Cabal to Esdras (a book they value extraordinarily), who by God's command withdrew to the wilderness forty days with five scribes, who in that space wrote two hundred and four books. The first one hundred thirty and four were to be read by all; but the other seventy were to pass privately among the Levites, and these they pretend to be cabbalistic, and not yet all lost' [*Fam. Lett.* (1903)].

Cabale des dévots, see *Compagnie du Saint Sacrement.*

Cabanis (pron. as if —*niss*), GEORGES (1757–1808), a physician and materialist philosopher of the school of the 'idéologues' (q.v.), author of a *Traité du physique et du moral de l'homme* (1798–9), republished as *Rapports du physique et du moral de l'homme* in 1802. In this the author reduces the spiritual side of man to a function or faculty of his physical nature.

Cabaret, JEAN, author of the *Chronique du bon duc Louis de Bourbon,* see *History* (para. 3).

Cabarrus, THÉRÉSA, see *Tallien, Mme.*

Cabet, ÉTIENNE (born in Dijon, 1785, died in St. Louis, Missouri, 1856), social reformer. He took refuge in England in 1834, for political reasons, and came under the influence of Robert Owen. In *Voyage en Icarie,* a socialistic romance, published (1842) after his return to France, he depicted a sort of Utopia where fraternity was man's sole religion, where the economic system was based on equality of conditions and community of goods, where all were happy and where all did as they would be done by. He went to America and made three attempts, all failures, to establish the *Icarie* of his dreams (two in Texas, one in Illinois). His disciples turned against him and in the end he died of despair.

Cabinet des antiques, Le, one of the 'Scènes de la vie de province' in Balzac's *Comédie humaine* (q.v.).

Cabinet du roi, Le, a famous collection of commemorative prints formed by Louis XIV (see *Imprimerie nationale*).

Cabinet noir, a secret bureau, established by Louis XIV at the Hôtel des Postes, where letters were opened. It was abolished by the *Assemblée constituante* (q.v.) and again, finally, in 1830.

Cabinets de lecture, a feature of Parisian life during the 18th and 19th centuries. There are references to them in Sébastien Mercier's *Tableau de Paris* and in Balzac's *Illusions perdues* (qq.v.). They were small libraries or bookshops where, for a small daily, weekly, or monthly sum, people could read newspapers and periodicals, new novels, &c.

Cabrion, a character in Eugène Sue's (q.v.) *Mystères de Paris.*

Cacambo, a character in Voltaire's *Candide* (q.v.).

Cacouacs, Nouveau Mémoire pour servir à l'histoire des, an allegorical pamphlet caricaturing the Encyclopaedists, published anonymously in 1757, by Nicolas Moreau, later librarian and historiographer to Marie-Antoinette. A *Premier Mémoire sur les Cacouacs* had appeared in the *Mercure* earlier in the same year.

Cadet Buteux. The *chanson*-writer and vaudevillist Désaugiers (q.v.) was a happy parodist of operas, comedies, and tragedies in vogue during the First Empire. His pot-pourris, in couplets, and usually sung at *cafés-concerts*, often rivalled the success of the works they mocked. His hero and mouthpiece, Cadet Buteux, came to typify the rough, racy wit of the people. Cadet Buteux's habit was to roam the streets, pick up the gossip of the day, visit the theatre or the opera, and come home late at night to describe the piece scene by scene, with many comments, to his wife.

Cadet Roussel, see *Aude, Le Chevalier Joseph.*

Cadignan, La princesse de, the heroine of *Les Secrets de la princesse de Cadignan* (1839), one of the 'Scènes de la vie parisienne' of Balzac's *Comédie humaine* (q.v.). She figures also in *Illusions perdues* (q.v.) and *Le Député d'Arcis.*

Cadmus et Hermione (1673), a play by Quinault to music by Lulli (qq.v.).

Cadoudal, GEORGES ['GEORGES'] (1771–1804), sometime leader of Royalist insurrections in the Vendée (q.v.), was associated with Pichegru (q.v.) and others in 1804 in a plot to depose Bonaparte and restore the Monarchy. He was captured and executed. He appears as a character in Sainte-Beuve's novel *Volupté* (q.v.).

Café. Coffee is said to have been introduced in Marseilles in 1644, and in 1669 it was among the gifts brought to Louis XIV by the Turkish ambassador. A few years later the first *café*, or coffee-house, was established by 'un nommé Pascal', an Armenian, in the Foire Saint-Germain. The café speedily became an institution in the life of the nation, a place where one could sit and drink (little or much, coffee and other beverages), read the papers, write letters, meet one's friends, talk literature or politics, or play games. There were 300 cafés in Paris by 1715, and over 400 by the outbreak of the Revolution. Some, notably those in the Palais-Royal during the Revolution, were hotbeds of political intrigue—the Café de Foy, the Café de Chartres, the Café Chrétien; others are linked with the literary life of Paris as the places where great works received a first hearing, new movements were hatched, or new reviews founded. At the time of *l'esprit décadent* and *Symbolisme* (qq.v.), when little reviews pullulated, much of the editorial work was carried on in cafés: funds seldom ran to offices, and the circumstances of the editors' homes were rarely such as made for comfort in working: it was easier to adjourn to a café and revolutionize French poetry with the aid of a 'bock' (a glass of beer). The practice of associating particular cafés with particular movements still persists.

Cafés and café life are often mentioned in French novels and memoirs. There are early references in Montesquieu's *Lettres persanes* (1721) and in *La Valise retrouvée* by Le

Sage (1740, *Lett.* x, a description of a café and its frequenters).

The following were some of the more famous cafés:

CAFÉ ANGLAIS, founded at the beginning of the 19th century, and situated on the Boulevard des Italiens. After the Peace of Amiens (1802) it was patronized by the English who flooded Paris. When the Peace was broken and the English left, the café fell on bad days, but its prosperity reached new heights during the Second Empire. It became the greatest centre of luxury and extravagance of the time, the rendezvous of rich dandies, famous actresses, and demi-mondaines, as well as of the royalties of Europe. The fashion was to dine in its private room—le Grand Seize—on the first floor. It disappeared with the Second Empire.

CAFÉ CHRÉTIEN, in the Palais-Royal, a centre of Jacobin activity during the Revolution.

CAFÉ DE CHARTRES, in the Palais-Royal, a centre of Royalist intrigue during the Revolution.

CAFÉ DE FOY, a well-known café of pre-Revolution days, founded in the second half of the 18th century and frequented by politicians and *nouvellistes* (q.v.). From it Camille Desmoulins stepped into the garden of the Palais-Royal to harangue the people on 13 July 1789, the day before the taking of the Bastille. During the Restoration it was a resort of writers and artists. It closed in 1863.

CAFÉ DE LA RÉGENCE, founded early in the 18th century, a famous resort of chess-players. It was frequented by leading writers of the day, e.g. Chamfort, Diderot, who mentions it in *Le Neveu de Rameau*, Grimm, Marmontel, Rousseau, Voltaire. When Rousseau went there such crowds collected to see him that he had to be asked not to appear in public. Robespierre used to go there to play chess.

CAFÉ HARDY, one of the fashionable cafés of the early 19th century, situated on the Boulevard des Italiens. ('Au sortir de chez La Rive, we go at Hardy Coffee.' Stendhal, *Journal*, 20 Nov. 1804.) It was also a restaurant, hence a *mot* of the time: 'Il faut être bien *riche* pour dîner au café *Hardy*, et bien *hardi* pour dîner au café *Riche*'. It was

later transformed into the Maison dorée, a restaurant patronized by the gilded youth of the Second Empire.

CAFÉ MOMUS, remembered from Murger's (q.v.) *Scènes de la Vie de Bohème*. It was in the rue des Prêtres Saint-Germain l'Auxerrois in the old quarter of Paris, on the right bank of the Seine (near the Louvre).

CAFÉ PROCOPE, the most famous of the early cafés in Paris, opened well before 1700 by Francesco Procopio di Coltelli, a Sicilian living in Paris. It was situated on the left bank of the river, in the rue des Fossés Saint-Germain (afterwards rue de l'Ancienne Comédie), and as it was opposite the then home of the Comédie-Française its success was assured. It soon became the foremost literary and political café of the day. Voltaire frequented it, and the table at which he sat was long preserved as a memento. The idea of the *Encyclopédie* is said to have originated there in a conversation between Diderot and d'Alembert. Others who frequented it about this date were Buffon, Crébillon, Marmontel, and Rousseau. Before the Revolution it changed hands and became known as the Café Zoppi. Its clientèle, now revolutionary in complexion, included Danton, Fabre d'Églantine, Hébert, Marat, and Robespierre, and the *bonnet rouge* is said to have appeared there for the first time. In later years its habitués included Balzac, Théophile Gautier, Gambetta, Verlaine, J.-K. Huysmans, and Oscar Wilde.

CAFÉ RICHE, see *Café Hardy*.

CAFÉ TORTONI, situated at a corner of the Boulevard des Italiens, was founded at the end of the 18th century by Velloni, a Neapolitan, and became the most fashionable café of Paris during the Empire and the Restoration. It was frequented by politicians and men of letters, and by wealthy foreigners visiting Paris. It was a supper resort of the 'dandys' *c.* 1830; and in the afternoons the leaders of feminine society sat outside, in their carriages, eating ices.

CAFÉ VACHETTE, founded during the Empire as the Café des grands hommes, changed names under successive proprietors and from 1827 was known as the Café Vachette. The first shots of the revolution of 1848 are said to have been fired in front of it, and it was at all times a favourite meeting-place for students. Towards the end of the 19th century it became the haunt of writers, notably Moréas, Pierre Louÿs, Barrès.

Cagliostro, Giuseppe Balsamo, *known as* count (1743–95), a clever charlatan born at Bergamo, who acquired a great reputation in France as a wonder-worker. One of his principal dupes was the Cardinal de Rohan (see *Collier, L'Affaire du*). He was arrested in Rome in 1789 as a heretic and sentenced to death, but this was commuted to perpetual imprisonment. He is the chief character in the *Mémoires d'un médecin: Joseph Balsamo* of Dumas *père* (q.v.).

Cahiers d'André Walter, Les (1891), an early work by André Gide (q.v.).

Cahiers de la Quinzaine, Les (1900–14), a periodical publication founded by Charles Péguy, appeared irregularly and devoted each of its 238 numbers to one work or one author. It published essays, criticism, poetry, and novels by writers who later became celebrated, e.g. Benda, Romain Rolland (qq.v.), as well as Péguy's own writings (essays, poetry, and prefaces to work by other contributors); and in many ways it constitutes a guide to the opinions of a whole generation on morals, religion, politics, and education. Péguy's bookshop near the Sorbonne, from which the *Cahiers* were published, was for long a meeting-place for writers and intellectuals.

Cahiers du sud, Les, founded 1915, probably the best known of the present-day literary, critical, and philosophical reviews published outside Paris (at Marseilles). It appears every two months.

Caillavet, Gaston Arman de (1869–1915), the author, in collaboration with Robert de Flers (q.v.), of light, sophisticated, sometimes sharply satirical comedies, e.g. *Le Cœur a ses raisons* (1904); *L'Âne de Buridan* (1909); *Monsieur Bretonneau* (1914); *Le Roi* (1908); *Le Bois sacré* (1911), a satire of parliamentary life; *L'Habit vert* (1913), a satire of *Académie française* circles. (For mention of his mother, Mme Arman de Caillavet, and her salon see *France, Anatole*; *Salon*, para. 8.)

Caillé [Caillié], René (1799–1838), explorer. As a boy of sixteen he was fired by reading *Robinson Crusoe*, and set off for Africa. In 1824 he penetrated to Central Africa, finally reaching Timbuctoo in 1828, disguised as a Moslem. He was the first European to return from these parts, if not the first to reach them.

Ça ira, a famous Revolutionary song (three stanzas), rivalled *La Carmagnole* (q.v.) in popularity and, like it, was prohibited by Bonaparte when he became First Consul. It was first sung (to the tune of *Le Carillon national*, a country dance by Bécourt) by the work-people while Paris was preparing for the Fête de la Fédération of 14 July, 1790. A street-singer named Ladré claimed to have written the words. The original refrain was:

> Ah! ça ira, ça ira, ça ira!
> Le peuple, en ce jour, sans cesse répète:
> Ah! ça ira, ça ira, ça ira!
> Malgré les mutins, tout réussira.

This was altered during the Terror to:

> Ah! ça ira, ça ira, ça ira!
> Les aristocrates à la lanterne!

Calandre, see *History* (*Medieval period*).

Calas, Jean (1698–1762), a Protestant cloth merchant of Toulouse, was executed (broken on the wheel, exposed, and then strangled) in 1762 on the false charge that he had murdered his eldest son because the latter wished to become a Roman Catholic. The truth was that the son had committed suicide (on the family premises) and the father found the body. At this time suicide was a crime. The father tried at first to make out that his son had been assassinated. He could not substantiate this and almost immediately gave the true story, which was not accepted but from which he refused to depart throughout an interrogation and trial conducted by the Parlement of Toulouse with the utmost fanaticism and brutality. After the execution the Calas family removed to Geneva, where Voltaire heard of the case and took it up with such vigour that in 1765 the verdict was quashed and Calas's innocence established by the Conseil d'État. The case excited public sympathy at home and abroad. A subscription list opened in England for the family was headed by the King and the Archbishop of Canterbury.

Calendar, see *Republican Calendar; Year, Beginning of the.*

Calepino, AMBROGIO, see *Dictionaries and Encyclopedias,* under date 1502.

Caliban, one of Renan's *Drames philosophiques* (q.v.).

Calicot, a slang term for a counter-jumper in a shop selling cotton goods. It is said to have come from M. Calicot, a character in the vaudeville *Combat des montagnes ou la Folie Beaujon* (1817) by Scribe (q.v.) and his collaborator Dupin.

Callias, MME NINA DE, see *Salons,* para. 8.

Calligrammes (1918), collected poems by Guillaume Apollinaire (q.v.).

Callot, JACQUES (1592–1635), born at Nancy, an eminent engraver of his own drawings, a bold and fanciful artist, whose works are a vivid illustration of the France of his day. He was great-uncle of Mme de Graffigny (q.v.).

Calmet, DOM AUGUSTIN, see *Dictionaries and Encyclopedias,* under date 1720–1.

Calonne, CHARLES-ALEXANDRE DE (1734–1802), controller-general of finances 1783–7. His prodigalities and dishonesty completed the ruin of the French monarchy. He was disgraced and fled to England. He continued to play an unfortunate part among the French princes during the emigration.

Calonne, ERNEST DE (1822–87), an author who came into the public eye for a time in 1845 when he managed to pass off his comedy *Le Docteur amoureux* as a recently discovered work by Molière. As such it was produced at the Odéon theatre and at the same time, as additional evidence of authenticity, the manuscript itself, on old paper, in faded ink, was placed on view in the foyer of the theatre. For a time both public and critics were fooled, with the exception of Théophile Gautier, who had been suspicious from the beginning.

Calotte, a leaden cap with bells adopted in the 18th century as the badge of a company of satirical wits known as the *Régiment de la Calotte.* A comedy of that name by Fuzélier, Le Sage (qq.v.), and d'Orneval (died 1766, a collaborator rather than an independent author) was produced in 1721.

Calvin (from *Calvinus,* the latinized form of the family name *Cauvin*), JEAN (1509–64), was born at Noyon in Northern France of a well-to-do middle-class family. His father, a diocesan official at Noyon, destined him for the Church and sent him to Paris, where he was educated first at the Collège de la Marche, then at the Collège de Montaigu (q.v.). He subsequently studied canon law and civil law. In 1530 after the death of his father he abandoned these studies and attended lectures on Greek and Hebrew. In 1532 he published a commentary on Seneca's *De Clementia.* He had become interested in the doctrines of the Reformers, and in 1533 his friend Nicolas Cop, the rector of the University of Paris, pronounced a discourse, written by Calvin, showing Lutheran tendencies. As a consequence Calvin was obliged for a time to leave Paris. He left it once more in 1535, after the affair of the *placards* (q.v.), and in 1536 published at Basle the first edition (in Latin) of his famous *Institution de la religion chrétienne* (q.v.). In the same year he betook himself to Geneva, now a Protestant republic, where he taught theology. In 1538 he was banished by a faction and took refuge at Strasbourg, and there entered into relations with Luther, Melanchthon, Bucer, and other Reformers. There also he married. When the Protestant Clergy of Geneva in 1541 succeeded in establishing ecclesiastical government, this was organized by Calvin, who thereafter ruled the city, brooking no opposition. When the Spaniard Servet (or Servetus) published a book contesting some of his views, he caused him to be tried, condemned, and burnt (1553). In 1554 he published, in defence of his action, a *Déclaration où il est montré qu'il est licite de punir les hérétiques.* Calvin died exhausted by his labours (his health had always been delicate) in 1564, aged fifty-five. He remained poor to the end. Besides the French translation (1541–60) of the *Institution de la religion chrétienne,* his writings in French include controversial treatises, pamphlets, sermons, and a large number of letters of advice and admonition to princes and churches of the reformed faith. His style, without elegance, is marked by clarity and conciseness, sometimes by anger, irony, and contempt. The greater part of his works was in Latin. He was the first to write a theological treatise in the vernacular, and he helped to adapt the construction of the French sentence to the purposes of argument as distinct from narrative.

Camargo, MARIE-ANNE CUPPI, *known as* LA (1710–70), a celebrated dancer, born in Brussels, who obtained great success at the Paris Opera.

Cambacérès, JEAN-JACQUES RÉGIS DE (1755–1824), born at Montpellier, studied law and had already entered the magistracy when he became a Deputy to the *Convention nationale* (q.v.). His prudence and his legal knowledge were of great use to him in his career both during and still more after the Revolution. After the *coup d'état* of the *dix-huit brumaire* (q.v., 1799) he became Second Consul. He held high official posts under the Empire and was much trusted by Napoleon. In 1816 he was exiled, but he was allowed to return in 1818 and was reinstated in his rights and titles. He left interesting memoirs. (See also *Code civil.*)

Cambrai, Archevêque de, see *Fénelon.*

Cambronne, Le Mot de. During the battle of Waterloo Napoleon's Imperial Guard, led by General Cambronne (1770–1842), was hopelessly surrounded and was summoned by the English to surrender. The General's sublime but apparently apocryphal reply was: 'La garde meurt et ne se rend pas', words later engraved on the monument erected to him at Nantes. His actual *mot* is said to have been 'Merde!', a coarse but characteristic French exclamation of defiant disgust.

Camelots du roi, see *Action française.*

Camisards, Calvinists, inhabitants of the mountainous regions of the Cévennes, who rose up in rebellion (1703) as a consequence of the Revocation of the Edict of Nantes (q.v.). They were so called because they wore a sort of white canvas blouse or shirt (from the old Provençal word *camisa*, a shirt) over their other clothes. Their leader, Jean Cavalier (1680–1740), came to terms with the forces sent by Louis XIV to quell the insurrection, then, mistrustful of his followers, he escaped to England. He ended his life as Governor of Jersey.

Campagnes hallucinées, Les (1893), poems by Verhaeren (q.v.).

Campan, JEANNE - LOUISE - HENRIETTE GENEST, MME DE (1752–1822), the gifted and exceptionally well-educated daughter of the First Clerk in the Affaires Étrangères, was appointed Reader to the three daughters of Louis XV and then (1770) Lady of the Bedchamber to Marie-Antoinette. She served her mistress devotedly till 1792 and managed to survive the Terror. Penniless and in debt, with numerous relations to support, she opened a girls' boarding school which prospered and numbered Hortense de Beauharnais, Napoleon's step-daughter, among its pupils. Later, Napoleon appointed her head of the *pensionnat* founded by him for sisters and daughters of members of the *Légion d'honneur* (q.v.). Her pupils were taught manners and deportment, and also domestic economy, which pleased Napoleon, no advocate of higher education for women ('Il faut que les femmes tricotent'). The restored Bourbons showed her no favour and she died in retirement at Mantes. She left interesting *Mémoires sur la vie privée de Marie-Antoinette* (1823).

Camp du drap d'or, Le (the Field of the Cloth of Gold), near Calais, the scene of an unfruitful meeting, in 1520, between François Ier and Henry VIII. The name refers to the magnificence displayed by both monarchs (cf. *Fleurange*).

Campistron, JEAN-GALBERT DE (1656–1723), a brave soldier and author of several rather lifeless tragedies, marked by gentle melancholy, mostly on classical subjects (*Virginie*, 1683; *Arminius*, 1684; *Andronic*, 1685; *Tiridate*, 1691; &c.); also of two comedies, one of which, *Le Jaloux désabusé* (1709), was successful. He boasted himself a pupil of Racine, of whom he is essentially an imitator. His strongest play is perhaps *Tiridate*, a noble character carried away by a fatal passion; it had considerable success.

Campo Formio, a small town in northeast Italy from which was dated (17 Oct. 1797) Bonaparte's treaty with Austria. This marked the end of his first Italian campaign and broke up the First Coalition (q.v.). France obtained the upper hand in northern Italy and western Germany and extended her frontiers.

Camus, ALBERT (1913–   ), born in Algiers, contemporary novelist, essayist, and dramatist, with a high reputation due particularly to his two novels *L'Étranger* (1942) and *La Peste* (1947). The first is a study of a man whose even more than ordinarily uneventful life ends when, almost inexplicably, he commits murder and is condemned. His attitude towards all that happens to him is one of listless detachment. *La Peste*, on its surface value alone, is a remarkable description of life in a plague-ridden city. A deeper significance, as an account of life under the German occupation, can also be read into it; or, still more profoundly, it can be taken as an allegory of the human situation. It has been dramatized as *L'État de siège* (1948).

This author professes a form of *philosophie de l'absurde* which bears some resemblance to, but allows more room for hope than, *existentialisme* (q.v.). His ideas are stated (latterly with hint of change in his position) in the essays of *Le Mythe de Sisyphe* (1942) and *L'Homme révolté* (1951), and they are behind his plays *Caligula* (1938, produced 1946) and *Le Malentendu* (1945). He was awarded the Prix Nobel (q.v.) in 1957.

Camus, JEAN-PIERRE (1582–1653), Bishop of Belley, disciple and friend of Saint François de Sales (q.v.), wrote religious romances modelled on *L'Astrée* (q.v.). The best of them was *Palombe ou la femme honorable*.

Canada, see *French-Canadian literature*.

Canalis, poet, leader of the *École angélique*, a character who appears and reappears in Balzac's (q.v.) *Comédie humaine*, notably in *Illusions perdues* and *Modeste Mignon* (qq.v.). He is said to have been drawn (satirically) from Lamartine (q.v.).

Candide, a philosophical tale by Voltaire, published in 1759, suggested by the terrible earthquake at Lisbon of 1755. The work is a satire on the optimism of Leibniz and Rousseau (the latter of whom had defended Providence against Voltaire's poem on the earthquake), confronting them with the evils and calamities that befall mankind.

Candide is a gentle and sensible young man brought up in the household of a Westphalian baron, Thunder-ten-Tronckh, where he has been taught by the philosopher Pangloss, who believes that all is for the best in the best of possible worlds. A nascent love affair with Cunégonde, the baron's daughter, causes his violent expulsion from the house. He is forcibly enlisted in the Bulgarian army, is beaten nearly to death, and meets Pangloss, now in lamentable distress, but still an optimist. He learns from him that the baron and Cunégonde have been massacred by Bulgarian troops. Together, after a shipwreck, they reach Lisbon, and Candide nearly perishes in the earthquake. As the best means of averting further earthquakes, the inhabitants celebrate an *auto-da-fé*, in which Pangloss is hanged for his optimism, and Candide is beaten for listening to him. The latter is comforted by discovering Cunégonde, who has not been completely massacred, but sold into slavery. He kills her present lovers, a Jew and an Inquisitor, and Candide and Cunégonde escape to South America. Here, after having the misfortune to kill Cunégonde's brother, and meeting various perils, Candide, with his servant Cacambo, visits the blessed land of Eldorado, but pining for Cunégonde, from whom he has been separated, returns to Europe, in the company of the Manichaean philosopher Martin, whose misfortunes and observations have convinced him that God has handed over the world to some maleficent spirit. After suffering at the hands of various swindlers in France, he lands at Portsmouth, where Admiral Byng is being executed, because, he is told, 'dans ce pays-ci il est bon de tuer de temps en temps un amiral pour encourager les autres'. At Venice, where he is to meet Cunégonde, he finds six kings in exile, including Charles Edward the Young Pretender. He learns that Cunégonde, captured by pirates, is washing dishes on the shores of the Sea of Marmora. He hurries to Constantinople, ransoms Cunégonde (who has become very ugly), finds among the galley-slaves her brother whom he had not thoroughly killed, and Pangloss who had not been thoroughly hanged. They purchase a little farm and set to work, Pangloss expounding that all that has happened has been for the best. 'Cela est bien dit,' answers Candide, 'mais il faut cultiver notre jardin.'

None of the misfortunes that Voltaire narrates are in fact unexampled. We may see in the last words the moral either that work within his proper sphere is man's consolation for his unhappy lot; or that practical work is more profitable than vain philosophical speculation.

Canrobert, CERTAIN (1809–95), MARÉCHAL DE FRANCE, distinguished in French military history of the 19th century (Algeria, the Crimea, the Franco-Prussian war).

Cantilène, a name occasionally given in the Middle Ages to short poems intended to be sung or chanted, usually the story of a saint such as Ste Eulalie (see *Eulalie*). The term was also used in 19th-century French literary criticism to denote a supposed type of primitive historical poem, of which no trace has ever been found, nor any authentic reference to it, precursor of the *chansons de geste* (q.v., para. 3; and cf. *Moréas, Jean*).

Capétiens, the third dynasty of kings of France (preceded by the *Mérovingiens* and the *Carolingiens*, qq.v.). It began in 987 with Hugues Capet (q.v.) and extended in direct line to Charles IV, *le Bel* (d. 1328). The Valois (q.v.) branch of this dynasty extended from Philippe VI to Henri III, i.e. 1328–1589, and the Bourbon (q.v.) branch from Henri IV to Louis-Philippe, i.e. 1589–1848. 'Louis Capet' was the name by which the revolutionary extremists addressed Louis XVI after his deposition.

Capitaine Fracasse, Le (1863), a picaresque novel by Théophile Gautier (q.v.), is the story of the impoverished baron de Sigognac who, in the days of Louis XIII, falls in love with Isabelle, a young actress. Rather than lose her he joins the band of travelling comedians to which she belongs and is given the role of Capitaine Fracasse (a boisterous soldier of Italian comedy). He squires Isabelle through many adventures, thrilling and comic, protects her from an unwelcome admirer, and, when she turns out to be the daughter of the prince of Vallombrosa, is rewarded with her hand and the governorship of a province. The book's opening picture of the baron's dilapidated castle (the château de la Misère) and its half-starved inhabitants is one of Gautier's star passages of descriptive writing.

Caporal, le petit, a name given to the young military leader Napoléon Bonaparte by his soldiers. One version of its origin given, and possibly invented, by Dumas *père*

is as follows: When, aged twenty-seven, Bonaparte assumed command of the Italian campaign (1796) the soldiers were astonished at his youth and concluded that he must have jumped some promotions. They took it upon themselves, each time he returned victorious from a battle, to promote him to one of the ranks he had missed, e.g. corporal after Lodi (10 May 1796), sergeant after Castiglione (5 Aug. 1796). The name 'le petit Caporal' stuck to him.

Caprice, see *Un Caprice*.

Caprices de Marianne, Les, by Alfred de Musset, a prose comedy in two acts, first published in the *Revue des Deux Mondes* of 15 May 1833, then included in the second series (1834) of *Un Spectacle dans un fauteuil* (q.v.). It was produced at the Comédie-Française (then called 'Théâtre de la République') on 14 June 1851. The scene is Renaissance Naples.

Octave, a gay libertine, makes love to Marianne, Claudio's young wife, on behalf of the timid Célio. Marianne, uninterested in Célio, yields to a momentary caprice for Octave and gives him a rendezvous to which he sends Célio. The latter falls into a trap set by Claudio for his wife's lovers, and is killed. Octave, appalled by his friend's death, and with his eyes suddenly opened to his own worthlessness, takes a bitter leave of Marianne, though she would not be displeased if he stayed.

Captivité de Saint Malc, La, a religious poem by La Fontaine, composed at the request of the solitaries of Port-Royal, published in 1673. It is based on a story told by St. Jerome.

It relates the capture of the saintly Malc by Arab brigands; his life in captivity together with a virtuous lady whom the brigands have torn from her husband; their escape, pursuit, and miraculous delivery from their pursuers by a lioness.

Capus, ALFRED (1858–1922), journalist, novelist, and playwright whose amusing, superficial studies of Parisian life were highly successful at one time. They include: *Les Honnêtes Gens* (1878), short stories; *Années d'aventure* (1895), a novel; *La Bourse ou la vie* (1900), *La Veine* (1901), *Les Deux Écoles* (1902), *Les Maris de Léontine* (1903), *La Petite Fonctionnaire* (1904), comedies.

Carabas, MARQUIS DE, a character in the *Chat botté* ('Puss in boots') of Perrault. The miller's son is carried to fortune by the unscrupulous ruses of the cat, his sole inheritance, who represents him to the king as the wealthy Marquis of Carabas and secures for him the hand of the king's daughter. Béranger's (q.v.) popular *chanson Le Marquis de Carabas* was a satire on the arrogance of the returned nobles after the Restoration.

Carabosse, the bad fairy in the old tales, who can be counted on to turn up at christenings with a wand full of misfortunes.

Caractères de Théophraste, see *La Bruyère*.

Caran d'Ache [pseud.—from the Russian *Karandache* = pencil—of Emmanuel Poiré] (1858–1909). Born in Moscow, he came as a young man to Paris and contributed caricatures and other humorous illustrations to such papers as *La Vie parisienne*, *Caricature*, &c. He was celebrated for his silhouette (q.v.) drawings, and for a time his shadow play *L'Épopée*, on the victories of Napoleon's armies, attracted audiences to the *Chat noir* cabaret (q.v.).

Carbonari [plur. of *carbonaro*, an Italian word meaning *charbonnier*, or charcoal-burner], secret societies founded in Italy in the early 19th century and later extended to France. In Italy their object was to spread liberal ideas and struggle against the despotism of Napoleon. In France they became anti-monarchical and anti-Catholic. They grew rapidly about 1821, their members including Bonapartists, republicans, and constitutionalists. They were organized in lodges, or *ventes*, something after the manner of freemasons, with fantastic ceremonies and oath-takings. At first, in Italy, they met in charcoal-burners' huts in the forests, hence the name. (Cf. *Sergents de la Rochelle, Les Quatre*.)

Carco, FRANCIS [pseud. of François Carcopino] (1886–1958), born in New Caledonia. He lived in Paris from 1910. His verses and novels of artist life in Montmartre include: *La Bohème et mon cœur* (1912), short, *fantaisiste* (q.v.) poems, in which affinities with Corbière, Laforgue, Rimbaud, and Verlaine are readily seen; *Chansons aigres-douces* (1913); *Jésus-la-caille* (1914), *L'Équipe* (1919);

L'Homme traqué (1922), *Les Innocents* (1924); *L'Homme de minuit* (1938).

Carcopino, JÉRÔME (1881–   ), elder brother of the preceding, a distinguished historian of Latin antiquity and the social and political background of Latin literature. His works include *Virgile et les origines d'Ostie* (1919); *Le Mystère de la IVᵉ églogue* (1930); *L'Impérialisme romain* (1934); *La Vie quotidienne à Rome à l'apogée de l'Empire* (1939).

Carel de Sainte-Garde, JACQUES, see *Epic poetry*.

Carême [Lent]. Bourdaloue (q.v.) preached famous Lenten sermons (thirty-five in all) between 1672 and 1682. Massillon's (q.v.) were even more famous: the collections of forty, preached between 1699 and 1704, known as the *Grand Carême*, and ten, the *Petit Carême*, preached in 1718 before the young Louis XV.

Carême, MARIE-ANTOINE (ANTONIN) (1784–1833), the famous French cook who learnt his art in Napoleon's kitchens and afterwards served, and fed, various crowned heads of Europe. He left them for various reasons, e.g. Alexander I of Russia because Russia was too cold; the Prince Regent (George IV) because he did not appreciate cooking as a fine art; others because they were gluttonous or had stomach trouble. He was at the height of his powers as chef to the Baron Rothschild and as master of Talleyrand's kitchen, which he considered 'le sanctuaire de la cuisine française', during the Restoration years. He wrote *Le Pâtissier pittoresque* (1815); *Le Maître de l'hôtel français* (1822); *Le Cuisinier français ou L'Art de la cuisine au XIXᵉ siècle* (1833), &c.; and left memoirs (to be found in *Les Classiques de la table*, 1843).

Carillon. This name occurs frequently in French-Canadian patriotic literature of the early 19th century because it was at Fort Carillon, on 8 July 1758, that French-Canadian troops under Montcalm (q.v.) defeated a very much larger British force under Lt.-General Abercrombie. Fort Carillon (later called Fort Ticonderoga), built by the early French settlers in North America on a site dominating the present-day village of Ticonderoga (in the township of Ticonderoga, State of New York, U.S.A.), was a point of strategic importance because of its situation on the waterway between the British colonies and the French possessions in the valley of the St. Lawrence river.

Carloman (751–71), son of Pépin le Bref, reigned jointly as King of the Franks with his elder brother Charlemagne from their father's death in 768 till his own death in 771.

Carloman (865–84), second son of Louis II, *le Bègue*, was King of France jointly with his brother Louis III from their father's death in 879 till the death of Louis III in 882, then alone till his own death (an accident, when boar-hunting).

Carmagnole, La, perhaps originally a short-skirted coat with a large collar and rows of metal buttons, worn by Piedmontese labourers in the south of France. It was worn by the *fédérés* who came to Paris in 1792 and helped to storm the Tuileries (see *Revolutions*, I*a*). With the addition of black woollen trousers, scarlet or tricolour waist-coats, and red caps, it was adopted by the Jacobins (q.v.); and 'Carmagnole' signified the whole Revolutionary costume. Later, the name was given to a song composed in 1792 (author unknown) when Louis XVI was a prisoner in the Temple. Sung to an air said to have come from the neighbourhood of Marseilles, it became one of the most popular Revolutionary songs, a favourite marching-song of the troops and a usual accompaniment of executions. Like *Ça ira* (q.v.) it was prohibited by Bonaparte when he became First Consul. There were some eleven or twelve stanzas, to which additions and alterations were constantly made. The original first stanza was:

> Monsieur Véto [i.e. Louis XVI] avait
> D'être fidèle à son pays.   [promis
> Mais il y a manqué,
> Ne faisons plus quartié.
> Dansons la Carmagnole;
> Vive le son, vive le son,
> Dansons la Carmagnole,
> Vive le son du canon.

After the execution of Marie-Antoinette a new stanza was added:

> Madam' Véto avait promis
> De faire égorger tout Paris.
> Mais son coup a manqué,
> Grâce à nos canonniers!
> Dansons, &c.

Carmen (1847), a tale of Spanish gipsy life and love by Prosper Mérimée. Meilhac and Halévy (qq.v.) used it as a basis for their libretto for Bizet's opera *Carmen*.

Carmontelle, LOUIS CARROGIS, *known as* (1717–1806), painter and dramatic author, wrote amusing *Proverbes dramatiques* (1768–87), for private performance (see *Proverbes dramatiques*).

Carmosine, a *proverbe* (3 acts, prose) by Alfred de Musset (q.v.), first published as a *feuilleton* in *Le Constitutionnel* (24 Oct.–6 Nov. 1850), then included in the 1853 edition of *Comédies et Proverbes* (q.v.). It was produced at the Théâtre de l'Odéon (see *Luxembourg, Théâtre du*) in 1865. The theme is taken from one of the tales of the *Decameron*. The king learns that the young Carmosine is sick and nearly dying of love for him. He visits her and with his queen treats her with such sympathy and kindness that the young girl sees a happy future dawning, near him, but married to a husband whom he has chosen for her.

Carnavalet, see *Musée Carnavalet*.

Carolingiens (the Carolingians or Carlovingians), the second dynasty of French kings, which succeeded the *Mérovingiens* (q.v.) when the Maire du Palais (q.v.), Pépin le Bref, in 751 deposed Childeric III and mounted the throne. His son was Charlemagne (q.v.). The dynasty lasted until the death of Louis V, *le Fainéant*, in 987. But the kingdom which had been kept together by the strong hand of Charlemagne fell to pieces under his successors, and a period of internal strife and growing disorder followed, aggravated by invasions of Normans, Hungarians, and Saracens.

Carolus-Duran, the name taken by Charles Durand (1837–1917), French portrait-painter, particularly of women and children. He was for several years director of the French Academy at Rome. One of his best-known portraits is *La Dame au gant*—of his wife, painted in 1869.

Caron, PIERRE (1875–1952), archivist (Director of the *Archives nationaux*, q.v., 1937–41) and bibliographer. His compilations include: *Répertoire méthodique d'histoire moderne et contemporaine de la France* (covering the period 1898–1913); *Répertoire des périodiques de* *langue française* (1935, with supplements in 1937 and 1939); and the indispensable *Manuel pratique pour l'étude de la Révolution française* (first published 1912). He also published collections of documents on Revolutionary history and a study (1936) of *Les Massacres de septembre*.

Carrel, ARMAND (1800–36), a well-known figure in 19th-century French journalism. In 1830 with Thiers and Mignet (qq.v.) he founded *Le National*, the daily paper which helped to provoke the July Revolution (q.v., and see *Press, Development of,* para. 10). He was killed in a duel with Émile de Girardin (q.v.), another journalist, with whom he had been carrying on a passionate political dispute.

Carrière, EUGÈNE (1849–1906), painter and lithographer, known for his scenes of family life and his portraits of contemporary authors and artists, e.g. Verlaine, Daudet, Rodin (qq.v.).

Carrosse du Saint-Sacrement, Le, a one-act comedy by Prosper Mérimée, included in his *Théâtre de Clara Gazul* (q.v.). It is now in the permanent repertory of the Comédie-Française.

Carte de Tendre, an allegorical map of the region of the tender sentiments, composed by Mlle de Scudéry with the frequenters of her *salon*, and introduced by her in *Clélie* (q.v.). It is often referred to as 'Carte *du* Tendre', but the first edition (Première partie, Livre I, p. 406) reads: '. . . elle [cette Carte] fit pourtant un si grand bruit par le monde, qu'on ne parlait que de la Carte de Tendre'.

The main features of the map are three cities of *Tendre*, on three rivers, *Tendre sur Estime, Tendre sur Reconnaissance,* and *Tendre sur Inclination.* Three roads, all starting from *Nouvelle Amitié,* lead to the several cities, passing through stages appropriate to the respective goals, such as *Sincérité, Probité,* or *Petits soins, Empressement.* But wrong turnings take the traveller to the *Lac d'Indifférence* or the *Mer d'Inimitié.*

Cartesianism, the philosophical system and method of Descartes (q.v.).

Cartier, JACQUES (1491–1557), the famous French navigator and explorer. He was born and died at Saint-Malo, was sent by François Ier in 1534 and later years on voyages of discovery to North America. On the second of these he sailed up the St. Lawrence river to an Indian village called Hochelaga, where Montreal now stands, and took possession of 'la Nouvelle France'. (Montreal began as a religious settlement, established in 1642 by Paul de Chomedy de Maisonneuve, who had been sent from France for the purpose by the abbé Jean-Jacques Olier, 1608–57, the founder of the Seminary, and the Order, of Saint-Sulpice.) His *Voyages* have been published more than once, notably the edition of 1924 (Ottawa, Historical Archives of Canada).

Cartouche, LOUIS-DOMINIQUE BOURGUIGNON, *known as* (1693–1721), born in Paris, the son of a wine-merchant, said to have been stolen as a child by gipsies. He became the leader of a famous band of robbers, and was finally broken on the wheel. His skill and daring made him a legendary figure, and he figured in more than one play of the period, e.g. *Arlequin-Cartouche* and *Cartouche ou les Voleurs.*

Casanova de Seingalt, GIACOMO (1725–98), an Italian born at Venice, author of memoirs written in an imperfect but lively French, which give an account of his rogueries, adventures, and disreputable amours in most countries of Europe, and incidentally a highly entertaining account of 18th-century European society.

Casaubon, ISAAC (1559–1614), born at Geneva of French Huguenot refugees, a famous Hellenist. He was appointed, through the agency of the président de Thou, to a chair of classical literature at Montpellier; he went thence to Paris on the invitation of Henri IV, and subsequently to England on that of James I. He left a Latin journal of his life from 1597. He married the daughter of Henri Estienne (q.v.). A life of Casaubon was written by Mark Pattison (1875).

Cassandre (1644–50), a novel by La Calprenède (q.v.).

Castel, JEAN (d. 1476), historiographer and poet, grandson of Christine de Pisan (q.v.), author of *Le Spécule des pécheurs,* a moralizing poem in Latin and French.

Castellio, Castellion, or **Châteillon,** SÉBASTIEN (1515–63), Protestant theologian, a professor of Greek at Basle, was the author of a Latin translation of the Bible (1551, dedicated to Edward VI), a *Traité des Hérétiques* (1554), &c.

Castelnau, MICHEL DE (1520–92), diplomatist, author of important political memoirs.

Castoiement d'un père à son fils, the title of two French versions, in verse, of the Latin *Disciplina clericalis,* one of the late 12th, the other of the 13th century. The Latin work was composed in Spain early in the 12th century and consists of a number of short tales related by a father for the edification of his son. The poem set the example for other *castoiements* or cautionary poems.

Catalauniques, Les Champs, the scene, between Troyes and Châlons-sur-Marne, of the great battle in 451 in which the Roman General Aëtius defeated the Huns under Attila, one of the decisive events of European history.

Cateau-Cambrésis, Treaty of, in 1559, the treaty between Henri II and Philip II of Spain which brought to an end the long conflict between France on the one hand and the emperor Charles V and his son Philip II on the other. By it France definitely renounced her claims on Naples and Milan, and abandoned in effect Savoy and Piedmont. The frontier between France and the Netherlands was settled.

Cathédrale, La (1898), a novel by J.-K. Huysmans (q.v.).

Catherine II (1729–96), Empress of Russia from 1762. She had intellectual tastes and corresponded with Voltaire, Grimm, and Diderot (qq.v.). Of the last she was a liberal benefactress, as she was, also, of Sénac de Meilhan (q.v.). She left curious *Mémoires* in French.

Catherine de Médicis (1519–89), daughter of Lorenzo de' Medici, duke of Urbino (grandson of Lorenzo the Magnificent). She was consort of Henri II and mother of François II, Charles IX, and Henri III. She was regent during the minority of Charles IX.

Cathos, one of the pedantic women in Molière's *Les Précieuses ridicules* (q.v.).

Catinat, NICOLAS DE (1637–1712), MARÉCHAL DE FRANCE, one of Louis XIV's most able captains, originally an advocate, who abandoned the law for a military career and rose solely through merit; prudent and careful of his men's lives. He won Nice and Savoy from Prince Victor Amadeus (1690–1). He left *Mémoires.*

Caton, Distiques de, see *Distiques.*

Caturce, JEAN DE (d. 1532), born at Limoux, licentiate of laws, an early disciple of Luther's doctrines, burnt at the stake at Toulouse.

Caulaincourt, ARMAND-AUGUSTIN-LOUIS, MARQUIS DE (1773–1827), after serving with distinction in the Republican armies became aide-de-camp to Bonaparte (then First Consul) in 1802. In 1804 he was promoted general, with the office of *Grand Écuyer* (Master of the Horse) and the title of duc de Vicence (Vicenza). He was one of Napoleon's most trusted advisers, all the more so because he was a man of upright character, not afraid of speaking his mind. He was charged with many diplomatic missions, went (unwillingly) as Ambassador to Russia in 1807, was beside Napoleon throughout the disastrous Russian campaign of 1812, the retreat from Moscow, and the return to Paris; and it was he who, in 1814, was sent by Napoleon to the Allied Powers to offer the Emperor's abdication. (He gives a detailed account of these periods in his interesting, and reliable, memoirs, published in 1933, 3 vols.) In 1815, during the Hundred Days, he was Minister of Foreign Affairs, but he resigned all his offices after Napoleon's second abdication and lived in retirement during the Restoration. In 1804 he had been accused, unjustly, of having been a party to the kidnapping of the duc d'Enghien (q.v.).

Causeries du lundi, Les, so called because they appeared on Mondays, the famous weekly essays, critical and biographical, which Sainte-Beuve (q.v.) contributed between 1849 and 1869 to *Le Constitutionnel* (Oct. 1849–Nov. 1852 and Sept. 1861–Jan. 1867), *Le Moniteur* (Dec. 1852–Aug. 1861 and Sept. 1867–Nov. 1868), and *Le Temps* (1869). In book form they were published as *Causeries du lundi* (1851–62, 15 vols.), comprising the articles of 1849–61, and

Nouveaux lundis (1863–70, 13 vols.), the articles of 1861–9.

In 1874–5 Sainte-Beuve's last secretary, J. Troubat, edited three volumes of *Premiers lundis* selected mainly from Sainte-Beuve's earlier writings in *Le Globe*, *La Revue de Paris*, and *La Revue des Deux Mondes* (cf. *Critiques et Portraits littéraires*).

Causes grasses, in the Middle Ages, burlesque caricatures of legal proceedings, performed by the *Basoche* (q.v.) on the *jours gras* of carnival. For examples see under *Coquillart*.

Cavalier, JEAN, see *Camisards*.

Cavalier Misérey, Le (1887), a realistic novel of army life in peacetime, by Abel Hermant (q.v.), and a severe indictment of army conditions at the time it was written. It is the story of a young recruit, a raw, far from keen-witted, but good-natured country lad who goes to pieces under a brutalizing environment. The book provoked so much indignation and scandal when it first appeared that the colonel of one regiment is said to have ordered all the copies in his barracks to be brought out and burnt. Much of it can still be read with interest, e.g. the descriptions of days out on manœuvres, or of the way in which even the most stolid recruits develop a sense of 'the regiment' and a spirit of loyalty and devotion to their officers.

Caveau, Le, a literary and convivial club founded (1729) by Piron, the elder Crébillon, and others. It came to an end in 1739 but was revived in 1759 by Pelletier, with Suard, Marmontel, &c. After a lapse during the Revolution it was again revived (1796–1802) as Les Dîners du Vaudeville and, from 1805, as Le Caveau moderne. About this time the company included Béranger and Désaugiers, the *chanson*-writers, also Méhul, the composer, and Brillat-Savarin, the *gastronome*. Béranger's *Le Roi d'Yvetot* was sung there for the first time.

Le Caveau continued, irregularly, and with some changes of name, well into the middle of the 19th century.

Caves du Vatican, Les (1914), a *sotie* by André Gide (q.v. and cf. *Acte gratuit*).

Cayet, PIERRE VICTOR PALMA-, see *Palma-Cayet*.

Caylus (pron. as if *-luss*), CLAUDE-PHILIPPE DE TUBIÈRES, COMTE DE (1692–1765), son of the marquise de Caylus (see below), a distinguished archaeologist and traveller, author of *Tableaux d'Homère et de Virgile* (1757), &c.; the 'antiquaire acariâtre et brusque' of an epitaph by Diderot.

Caylus (pron. as if *-luss*), MARIE-MARGUERITE, MARQUISE DE (1673–1729), *née* de Villette-Murçay, a great-grand-daughter of Agrippa d'Aubigné (q.v.) and a cousin of Mme de Maintenon (by whom she was converted to catholicism). She dictated to her son, shortly before her death, her *Souvenirs* of the court of Louis XIV, told with simplicity, good taste, and independence of judgement and containing interesting details and vivid portraits of some of the chief personages, such as Mme de Maintenon and Mme de Montespan. The *Souvenirs* were published by Voltaire with a preface and notes in 1770. Mme de Caylus was noted for her beauty, grace, and wit, and acted with great success at Saint-Cyr the part of Esther in Racine's drama of that name. Her letters (chiefly to Mme de Maintenon) have been published.

Cayrol, JEAN (1911–   ), contemporary poet. Since the early, surrealistic poems of *Le Hollandais volant* (1936) his verse has shown a religious tendency: *Les Phénomènes célestes* (1939); *Miroir de la Rédemption* (1944); *Poèmes de la nuit et du brouillard* (1945), &c.

Cazalis, HENRI, see *Lahor, Jean*.

Cazamian, LOUIS (1877–   ), literary historian and English scholar, author of a *History of English Literature* (1924) written in collaboration with Émile Legouis (q.v.) which has become a standard work; of the chapter on Richardson in the *Cambridge History of English Literature* (vol. x), &c. In 1955 he broke new ground with a *History of French Literature* intended primarily for English readers. His interesting *Retour d'un anglicisant à la poésie française*, delivered originally in Oxford in 1938 as the Zaharoff Lecture, should also be mentioned.

Cazotte, JACQUES (1719–92), man of letters, with a taste for the occult sciences, of whose writings *Le Diable amoureux* is alone remembered. This is an original and well-written tale in which the Devil, evoked by a Spanish gentleman, assumes the form of a young woman, wins his love by submissiveness and devotion in this guise, and then reveals himself. Cazotte became suspect in the Revolution and was guillotined.

Céard, HENRY (1851–1924), novelist, born in Paris, a naturalistic writer who contributed the tale entitled *La Saignée* to the *Soirées de Médan* (q.v. and see *Naturalisme*). He was also an original member of the *Académie Goncourt* (q.v.). He wrote two novels—*Une Belle Journée* (1881, q.v.), a triumph of naturalistic dullness, and *Terrains à vendre au bord de la mer* (1906).

Ceci n'est pas un conte, see *Diderot.*

Cécile, fragment of a novel by Benjamin Constant de Rebecque (q.v.).

Céladon, a character in Honoré d'Urfé's *L'Astrée* (q.v.). The name became proverbial for a constant timid lover.

Celestina or The Tragi-Comedy of Calisto and Melibea, a dialogue in twenty-one acts by Fernando de Rojas, first printed *c.* 1500; a work of importance in the literary history of Spain and France on account of its vivid realism. It was translated into French in 1527, 1578, and 1633.

The principal interlocutors are these: Calisto, a young gentleman; Melibea, a young lady of high birth; Celestina, a crafty old bawd; Parmeno and Sempronio, rascally braggart servants of Calisto. Calisto casually meeting Melibea falls violently in love with her, but, from her modesty, is repulsed. On the advice of one of the servants he calls in the aid of Celestina, who interposing in the affair deflects Melibea from the path of virtue and brings about a general catastrophe. Celestina is murdered by Parmeno and Sempronio for a share in the reward that she has received, and these are punished with death for their crime. Calisto is killed in one of his secret meetings with Melibea, and she in despair takes her own life.

Célibataires, Les, the inclusive title of three of Balzac's 'Scènes de la vie de province' (see *Comédie humaine*), namely, *Pierrette*; *Le Curé de Tours*; *La Rabouilleuse*; also (1934), a novel by Henri de Montherlant (q.v.).

Célimène, a character in Molière's *Le Misanthrope* (q.v.).

Céline, LOUIS-FERDINAND [pseud. of L.-F. Destouches] (1894–), a doctor turned novelist whose *Voyage au bout de la nuit*, a truculent, disgusted satire, aroused considerable and often hostile attention when published in 1932. The narrator, Bardamu, who in the course of the work becomes a slum medical practitioner of dubious ethics, pours out a slangy, profane, obscene, occasionally tough-but-tender record of the French scene and his experiences during and after the 1914–18 war.

Cellamare, ANTOINE DE (1657–1733), an Italian by birth, Spanish ambassador in Paris, who in 1718 at the instigation of the Spanish minister Alberoni, intrigued with the duchesse du Maine for the overthrow of the Regent. The plot was discovered and Cellamare expelled.

Cellini, BENVENUTO (1500–71), a great Florentine metal-worker and sculptor, who spent the years 1540–4 in France at the invitation of François Ier (as vividly recorded in Cellini's autobiography). His workshop was at the Petit Nesle (see *Nesle*), and there he produced the *Nymph of Fontainebleau*, one of his principal pieces of sculpture, now in the Louvre.

Cénacles, coteries or groups which formed round the early leaders of the Romantic Movement (see *Romantisme*). The first originated in the *salon* of Charles Nodier (q.v.) at the Bibliothèque de l'Arsenal. The second, and most famous, met at the home of Victor Hugo (q.v.). A later 'cénacle de Joseph Delorme' centred on Sainte-Beuve; and 'le petit cénacle', the group formed by the more violent young Romantics, was led by Petrus Borel (q.v.).

Cendrars, BLAISE (1887–), novelist and poet of Swiss origin, associated with the early Cubist movement (see *Cubisme* and cf. *Apollinaire, Guillaume*). His publications include: *Le Panama ou les Aventures de mes sept oncles* (1918), *Du Monde entier* (1919), verse; *L'Or* (1925), *Les Confessions de Dan Yack* (1929), *Rhum* (1930), &c., novels which seize the world of travel and marvellous adventure with the speed, and at the unusual angles, of a cinema camera. Of another kind, the *Petits contes nègres pour les enfants blancs* (1928) deserve mention.

Cendrillon [Cinderella], the heroine of Perrault's (q.v.) fairy-tale.

Censorship, Dramatic. Dramatic censorship, in the sense of a system designed to prevent, by the requirement of previous licensing, the performance of plays that were politically obnoxious or contrary to public morality, can hardly be said to have been effectively organized in France until 1706, in the reign of Louis XIV. Before this, control of the liberty of the drama had been in the main repressive: that is to say, the production of plays considered undesirable on account of political allusions, attacks on individuals, or indecency had been followed by their suppression and the punishment of those concerned. In this connexion the *parlement* had shown itself an active guardian of the public conscience. An attempt in 1442 to exercise a preventive censorship of the plays performed by the *Basoche* (q.v.) appears to have been abortive, for in 1476 the performances of that society were altogether prohibited. The University in the 15th century imitated the *parlement* in endeavouring to restrain the satirical vein of its students. Liberty was restored to the stage by Louis XII, an enlightened monarch, who saw in this liberty an aid to his own policy. Under François Ier preventive censorship by the *parlement* was re-established, but a conflict arose between that body and the king in regard to the performance of Mysteries. Instances are recorded of a preventive censorship of these religious plays in the 15th and 16th centuries by the clergy, and they were now viewed with disfavour by the *parlement* for reasons of public order, though their performance was repeatedly authorized by the king. From 1548 the *parlement* succeeded in prohibiting them entirely in Paris.

(2) Conflicts of authority again arose in the reign of Henri III, whose pleasure-loving tastes had little regard for public morality and who favoured the loose comedies of the Italian company of the *Gelosi* (see *Theatres and theatre companies*). In 1609, at the end of Henri IV's reign, a magistrate, the *procureur du roi*, was constituted dramatic censor and no play was to be produced without his authority: a measure provoked by the growing licence of the players. But under Louis XIII a large measure of liberty was accorded, and the censorship was rather one of inti-midation, exercised through fear of the displeasure of the king, of Richelieu, and of the *parlement*. Richelieu in 1641 issued a declaration enjoining on actors, under threat of severe penalties, to refrain from anything indecent in their performances. *Tartuffe* was prohibited from 1664 to 1667 (and in its original form to 1669). In 1697, under Louis XIV, the Italian actors were banished for ridiculing Mme de Maintenon. Finally, in 1706, the king ordered all plays to be submitted to censorship before production, the lieutenant-general of police being given absolute control over the theatres. This officer gave or refused authority for performance of a play on the report of the dramatic censor, an official chosen for this function from among the royal censors charged with the examination of books (see *Librairie*), or of a censor selected specially to deal with a particular play. But the lieutenant of police, who sometimes disregarded the opinion of the censor, was subject to various influences, such as that of the court, the ecclesiastical authorities (notably in the 18th century the archbishop of Paris, Christophe de Beaumont), the *parlement*, or some minister or ambassador; whence lack of consistency in the working of the censorship.

(3) In the 18th century the development of the *philosophe* movement provoked from time to time an increased severity of dramatic censorship, and many plays were prohibited or suffered to appear only with more or less considerable alterations. Voltaire's *Samson*, for instance, was prohibited; *L'Enfant prodigue* was altered; *Mahomet* was withdrawn at the instance of the *parlement*. There was a good deal of intrigue for or against the production of certain plays. The position of dramatic censor, held successively by the abbé Chérier (a *bon vivant*), the elder Crébillon, Marin (a dramatist and intriguer involved in the affair of Beaumarchais and Mme Goezman), Crébillon *fils*, Sauvigny (for a brief period), and Suard, was not an easy one. An error of judgement might lead to the Bastille, as it did in the case of Marin, who in licensing Dorat's *Théagène et Chariclée* had overlooked a passage condemnatory of royalty which an audience hostile to the authorities applauded.

(4) Under Louis XVI there was some relaxation of severity. For instance Collé's *Partie de chasse de Henri IV*, which the

susceptibility of the Government had banned during the reign of Louis XV, was now performed. A curious situation arose when Palissot's *Les Courtisanes*, a violent satire against a class of women at that time very prominent in the life of Paris, was refused by the Comédie-Française as contrary to public morals, though authorized by the censorship with the approval of the archbishop. This relaxation of severity came to an end about 1783, when political excitement led to the adoption of rigorous measures for the exclusion from the drama of anything capable of being construed as an allusion to current events. Permission for the performance of Beaumarchais's *Mariage de Figaro*, at first vehemently refused by the king, was obtained only in 1784 after a hard struggle in which the author had the support of the king's brother, the comte d'Artois. But the Revolution was now at hand and there was little left for the censorship to do. Of the dramatic censors named above, the elder Crébillon and Suard had been the most distinguished. The former had the difficult task of meeting the first onset of the new philosophical ideas; the latter was the last defender, in that capacity, of the monarchical institution. Both carried out their duties conscientiously.

(5) For the first eighteen months of the Revolution the office of dramatic censor in Paris was attached to the Municipality. The spirit of the time made strict censorship impossible and in 1791 we find Bailly (Mayor of Paris) refusing to license M.-J. Chénier's *Charles IX* and being over-ruled by the *Assemblée nationale*. Thereupon the play was produced with rousing success. Unofficial censorship was for some time also exercised by the Comédie-Française, which refused to produce plays of revolutionary tendencies. Dramatic censorship was abolished by law in January 1791. New theatres, for which preliminary authorization was no longer required, were made subject to inspection by officers of the municipalities, who had power to prohibit or suspend performances. The extent of this power was debatable, and municipal decisions to suspend performances were frequently revoked by the *Convention nationale*. In August 1793, however, the *Convention* itself forbade the production of plays of a subversive (i.e. Royalist) tendency, or having titled persons among

their characters. In 1794 dramatic censorship, both preventive and repressive, was officially re-established. It was severe, all the more so as plays even when authorized were often denounced by individuals or parties, and their suppression demanded. In Paris, censorship was exercised by the *Commission de l'instruction publique*; in the provinces by the police or by municipal officers. The system continued during the *Directoire*. With the Consulate, and still more during the Empire, it became rigorous. New plays had to be authorized ministerially (at first by the *Ministre de l'intérieur* and later, after 1804, confirmed by Imperial decree of 1806, by the *Ministre de la Police*, namely Fouché, q.v.). Authorization depended on moral and political suitability, as reported by an examining body of five dramatic censors, themselves attached to the *Ministère de l'instruction publique*. The Emperor's sanction was required for new theatres; the repertories of the Opéra, the Comédie-Française, and the Opéra comique were decided ministerially; and dramatic censorship in the provinces was brought under the central authority.

(6) The Charter (v. *Charte, La*) granted by Louis XVIII in 1814 guaranteed freedom to the Press, but not to the stage; and between 1815 and 1830 the censorship continued with little change. With the advent of Louis-Philippe in 1830, after the July Revolution, censorship as such was totally abolished, but whether this implied dramatic as well as Press censorship was not clear. In 1832 Victor Hugo's *Le Roi s'amuse* was suppressed after the first performance because Royalty had been portrayed in an undignified fashion. Hugo brought a lawsuit but lost, and had to pay costs, the judgement being that the censorship abolished had referred only to printed matter. The position was clarified by a law of 1835 which re-introduced preliminary authorization and empowered the Government to suspend performances and close theatres.

(7) If the 1848 Revolution brought a short spell of freedom, the Second Empire re-established the censorship more strictly than ever. Authorization to produce plays became subject to withdrawal at any time, and in any case was not confirmed till after the dress rehearsal, which had to be attended by special inspectors. The censorship was

operated, through examining and inspecting committees, by the Minister attached to the Emperor's Household. (After 1864 the requirement of preliminary sanction for new theatres was dropped). The laws covered plays, sketches, cantatas, songs, in fact practically every form of stage spectacle.

A few years of liberty after the fall of the Second Empire were again followed (1874) by a revival of the censorship. The responsible Minister (de l'instruction publique) delegated his duties of examination and inspection to the Division des Beaux-Arts. Otherwise the legislation of the Second Empire was confirmed and remained in force under the Third Republic.

(8) From 1789 onwards the spirit in which the censorship was exercised had altered with successive forms of government. During the Revolution, and under the Directoire, plays new and old were suppressed or freely altered in the interests of Republicanism. Characters could not be called 'Monsieur' or 'Madame'; they became 'Citoyen' and 'Citoyenne'. M.-J. Chénier's tragedy Timoléon was withdrawn because it wounded Robespierre's susceptibilities; Voltaire's Zaïre was suspected of clericalism and banned. Racine and Molière were edited; and when Phèdre was performed the unhappy queen's bosom was covered with a large tricolour cockade as she declared her love for Hippolyte.

(9) Under Napoleon even such plays as were authorized were mutilated and bowdlerized, often with comical effects; and the imperial wrath fell heavily on any censor who allowed crowned heads to be discredited or the philosophes to be glorified, or who missed passages that even by a stretch of imagination could be construed as allusions to religion or politics. A similar policy of suppression and alteration continued between 1815 and 1830. Now the word 'liberté' was suspect and replaced by 'indépendance'; kings must be of perfect character; ministers intelligent and of flawless virtue; religion (particularly Roman Catholicism) and the ancienne noblesse must be treated with special tenderness, the clergy rarely if at all allowed to appear on the stage. Morals were also guarded but on the whole the censors were mainly preoccupied with politics. During the July Monarchy, even after the Act of 1835, the censorship was more liberal, though political allusions were still disliked (the growth of the Napoleonic legend caused uneasiness). As moral judges, the censors of this eminently bourgeois reign had their wives and daughters in mind. The Second Empire returned to a nervous severity; allusions to high finance were unwelcome (Balzac's Mercadet, for example, was prohibited); ministerial susceptibilities were more tender than ever; religion was too dangerous a subject; the remotest allusions to home or external politics were excised, historical subjects or allusions frowned upon. Morals and manners were less of a stumbling-block and La Dame aux Camélias and La Belle Hélène were passed without difficulty.

(10) After the law of 1874, and increasingly with the years, more liberal views prevailed. The 20th-century censors are unlikely to intervene unless a play appears likely to provoke crime or embarrass diplomatic relations, or unless it presents public characters in an objectionable light.

Censorship, Literary, see Librairie.

Centaure, Le. (1) A prose poem by Maurice de Guérin (q.v.). (2) A literary and artistic quarterly de luxe, founded 1896 by Pierre Louÿs, H. de Régnier, André Gide, and others of what is sometimes called the second generation of Symbolists (see Symbolisme). It published work by these and other writers, including Valéry (q.v.).

Cent Ballades, Les, a collection of ballades (q.v.) of the end of the 14th century written by fourteen princes and nobles of the court of Charles VI, for a sort of poetical competition, on the theme whether fidelity or inconstancy in love is to be approved; one of the most agreeable products of the artificial poetry of that period. The competition was organized by four nobles, who had been prisoners of war together in Cairo in 1388–9 during a crusade: Jean le Sénéchal, the comte d'Eu, Jean de Crésecque, and Bouciquaut (q.v.).

Cent Jours, Les ['The Hundred Days']. The period of Napoleon's temporary return to power in 1815 lasted from his arrival in Paris (20 March), after his escape from Elba, till 6 July, when Louis XVIII returned for the second time.

Cent Nouvelles Nouvelles, a collection of prose tales, most of them licentious, presented by its author to Philippe duc de Bourgogne in 1462. Who this author was is unknown. He probably belonged to the court of Burgundy. The work has frequently been attributed to A. de la Sale (q.v.), but it is inferior in merit to that author's *Petit Jehan de Saintré* (q.v.).

The tales, on the model of Boccaccio's *Decameron*, purport to be told by various members of the Burgundian court, including the duke himself. Some of the tales are derived from the *Facetiae* of Poggio. The work shows as a whole a great advance in comic and dramatic quality on the *fabliaux*, but the comical element consists solely in burlesque; there is little humour or wit.

Cercle, Le, the title of comedies by Poinsinet and by Palissot (qq.v.).

César Birotteau, see *Histoire de la grandeur et de la décadence de César Birotteau.*

Cézanne, PAUL (1839–1906), French painter, was born and educated at Aix-en-Provence. There, and for many years afterwards, he was a close friend of Émile Zola (q.v.), whom he followed to Paris in 1861 when he was allowed to give up law for art. (The break with Zola came after the publication of Zola's novel *L'Œuvre* in which he spoke slightingly of the Impressionists; see *Impressionnisme*.) Cézanne was one of the first Impressionists, but his development took him away from the strictly impressionistic interest in effects of light to the massive effects of form and volume which characterize his later work. He painted landscapes, mostly of Provence, also still-lifes and portraits. Fame was coming to him only when he died.

Chabrier, EMMANUEL (1841–94), a French composer of light music, was a Civil Servant in Paris to begin with but gave this up after his first success, a comic opera. His opera *Le Roi malgré lui* and his orchestral rhapsody *España* are still frequently performed. He had many friends among the first symbolists and impressionists and was one of the early devotees of Wagner in France.

Chactas, an aged Indian, the narrator in Chateaubriand's *Atala* (q.v.).

Cham [pseud. of AMÉDÉE DE NOË, son of the marquis de Noë—hence *Cham fils de Noë*] (1819–79), humorous illustrator, particularly of small happenings of street life. He flourished during the Second Empire.

Chambord, the first château in France built by François Ier. The plan of the central portion (a square with large towers at the angles) is that of a feudal castle, such as may previously have existed on the site.

Chambord, COMTE DE (1820–83), posthumous son of the duc de Berry (q.v.) and grandson of Charles X (see *Bourbon*), was Legitimist claimant to the throne of France after the death of his grandfather, and known to his supporters as 'Henri V'. He lived in exile—for a time at Holyrood, mainly in Austria—from 1830 until his death. In 1873 *Légitimistes* and *Orléanistes* (qq.v.) sank their differences in a plot to place him on the throne. It augured well but failed at the last moment because 'Henri V' refused to accept the tricolour flag introduced at the Revolution and adopted later by Louis-Philippe and the Orleanists. He declared that 'Henri V ne pouvait abandonner le drapeau de Henri IV', i.e. the traditional royal white flag of the Bourbons. He died without issue.

Chambre ardente, a special court instituted in the 16th century in the *parlement* of Paris to try cases of heresy and other exceptional crimes such as poisoning. It was draped in black and lit with torches even during the day-time. A *chambre ardente*, known also as *Chambre de l'Arsenal*, was charged in 1677 with the investigation of the *affaire des poisons*, an alleged plot to poison the king and the dauphin. A woman named La Voisin was implicated and was burnt alive for selling poisons and charms. Charges were brought by her accomplices against some of the highest personages in the land, without foundation, as having been parties to the supposed plot.

The term *chambre ardente* was also applied to the special tribunal set up under the Regency (1716) to force the rapacious tax-farmers who had robbed the state and the tax-payer to disgorge their illicit gains.

Chambre des comptes, under the Monarchy, an administrative court comprising ten presidents and sixty-two *maîtres de comptes* which revised the public accounts of the kingdom, exercising jurisdiction over the accountants and even some measure of control over the king himself. It was restored in an improved form by Napoleon as the *Cour des Comptes*.

Chambre des Députés, see *Assemblée nationale*; *Député*.

Chambre des Pairs, see under *Pairs, Les Douze*.

Chambre étoilée, La, the French name for the Star-chamber of English history.

Chambre introuvable. Very thorough, at times terrorist, measures were taken to prevent the return of any anti-Royalist Deputies to the Chamber elected in 1815 after the second Restoration. The results were so surprisingly satisfactory that Louis XVIII called the new Chamber the 'Chambre introuvable'.

Chamfort, NICOLAS-SÉBASTIEN ROCH, *known as* DE (1741–94), of illegitimate birth, miscellaneous writer, author of some mediocre dramatic works (*La Jeune Indienne*, a successful sentimental comedy, 1764; *Le Marchand de Smyrne*, comedy, 1770; *Mustapha et Zéangir*, a successful tragedy, 1776), and of two good critical works, *Éloge de Molière* (1766) and *Éloge de La Fontaine* (1774). Thanks to these and to his wit, he met with considerable social success, was granted a pension, and in 1781 was admitted to the *Académie*. A certain bitterness and disillusionment, engendered by disease and directed especially against the high society on which he felt himself dependent, together with penetration and a gift for succinct ironical expression, are seen in his *Maximes, caractères et anecdotes*, published after his death, and alone of his works now read. He was an ardent supporter of the Revolution and a close friend and inspirer of Mirabeau. In spite of this he became suspect under the Terror, attempted to take his own life, and died soon after. He was the author of the revolutionary slogan, 'Guerre aux châteaux, paix aux chaumières'. His interpretation of 'Fraternité' as 'Sois mon frère, ou je te tue' is also well known.

Chamisso, ADELBERT VON (1781–1838), German poet, novelist, and botanist, born in France of a family which emigrated to Germany during the Revolution. He was a

friend of Mme de Staël and became known in France to the later generation of Romantics, when his romances and ballads (half melancholy, half ironical, usually on traditional themes) and his novel *Peter Schlemihl* (the story of a man who sold his shadow to the devil) were translated (see *Foreign Influences on French literature*, para. 20).

Champagne or **Champaigne,** PHILIPPE DE (1602–74), portrait painter, born in Brussels, spent his life in France. He left a number of remarkable portraits, including those of many notable members of the Port-Royal community.

Champavert, contes immoraux (1833), tales by Petrus Borel (q.v.).

Champ de mai, the name for the political consultative assemblies held under the Carolingian dynasty (see *Carolingiens*), always in the month of May. The name was also applied to the general representative assembly convoked by Napoleon for 26 May 1815. In fact, this was held on 1 June, on the Champ-de-Mars (see the following article). Napoleon signed the *acte additionnel* (q.v.) intended to inaugurate a more liberal form of government, swore to defend the independence of the French people, and conferred many new honours.

Champ-de-Mars, Le, a large open space on the left (south) bank of the Seine in Paris, originally (from 1770) the parade-ground of the École Militaire, from which it extends to the river.

Here the first of the Revolutionary *Fêtes de la Fédération* was held, on 14 July 1790, the first anniversary of the fall of the Bastille, and Talleyrand said the Solemn Mass. Here Sylvain Bailly (q.v.), the last Mayor of Paris, was executed in 1793; and on 8 June 1794 the *Fête de l'Être Suprême* was celebrated, with Robespierre heading the procession. Here Napoleon, Emperor but not yet crowned, held the first investiture of the *Légion d'honneur*, on 14 July 1804, and eleven years later, between Elba and Waterloo, proclaimed (1 June 1815) the *acte additionnel aux constitutions de l'Empire* which Benjamin Constant (q.v.) had drafted for him. Here, too, after the Restoration, Paris watched horse-racing. (Flaubert's Frédéric Moreau, in *L'Éducation sentimentale*, took Rosannette to the races at the Champ-de-Mars in 1848.)

After the racing moved to Longchamp the site was used for successive World Fairs, beginning with the *Exposition Universelle* of 1867, until it became a public open space in 1908.

Champ d'oliviers, Le, a short story, one of his finest, by Guy de Maupassant (q.v.).

Champfleury (1529), see *Tory, Geoffroy.*

Champfleury [*nom de plume* of Jules Husson or Fleury] (1821–89), born at Laon in northern France, novelist (whose *Le Réalisme,* 1857, was one of the first studies of the movement, see *Réalisme*), art historian, and in later life Director of the State porcelain factory at Sèvres. His chief works of fiction were *Chien-Caillou* (1847), a tale about an engraver; *Les Aventures de Mademoiselle Mariette* (1853), scenes from a much less sentimentalized *vie de Bohème* than that of Murger (q.v.); *Les Souffrances du professeur Delteil* (1853); and *Les Bourgeois de Molinchart* (1855), a study of provincial life. The first chapter of this has a spirited description of a hunted deer landing in the toy-merchant's shop and wrecking it. Besides other works which fall into the domain of art, Champfleury is remembered, perhaps even more than by his novels, by *L'Histoire de la caricature* (1865–90) and some interesting studies of books and personalities of the Romantic Movement, e.g. *Les Excentriques* (1852), *Les Vignettes romantiques* (1883).

Champier, SYMPHORIEN (1472–1539), remembered as a man of letters and poet of the Lyons school (see under *Scève*), author of *La Nef des Dames vertueuses* (1503), mingled prose and verse, &c. He also practised, and wrote about, medicine, and founded a medical school at Lyons.

Champion des Dames, Le, see *Le Franc, Martin.*

Champlain, SAMUEL (1567–1635), French navigator and explorer, born at the small port of Brouage on the Bay of Biscay, one of the great names in the early development of Canada. He founded Quebec (1608) and discovered and explored Lakes Champlain and Ontario. Louis XIII sent him to govern Canada in 1620. In 1628–9 he was besieged by the British in Quebec and finally had to capitulate, but he returned as Governor when Quebec was restored to the French in 1632, and died there.

Champmeslé, MARIE DESMARES (1642–98), wife of an actor of the name of Champmeslé, a tragic actress, mistress, in his youth, of Racine and famous in the parts of his heroines, Bérénice, Roxane, Monime, Phèdre, &c.

Under the name of her husband were produced three comedies in the composition of which La Fontaine is thought to have had some part (see under *La Fontaine*).

Champollion, JEAN-FRANÇOIS (1790–1832), now recognized as the founder of Egyptology, though his claim to be the first to decipher hieroglyphics was disputed for some years after his death. He came from Grenoble to Paris in 1807. The chair of Egyptian Antiquities at the Collège de France (q.v.) was specially created for him.

Champs-Élysées, Les, a district in the west of Paris, on the right (north) bank of the river, once marshy and insalubrious, in parts given over to market gardens, but progressively laid out and architecturally embellished from the seventeenth century onwards. It reached heights of splendour and elegance under Napoleon and again during the Second Empire. Its central features are the gardens and traffic ways which form a prolongation of the Tuileries from the Place de la Concorde (q.v.) to the Rond-Point des Champs-Élysées, and the broad, glittering Avenue des Champs-Élysées which from there sweeps up to the Arc de Triomphe (q.v., in the Place de l'Étoile) and remains magnificent in spite of all present-day commercialization. Foreigners make their way here, some welcomed or tolerated as tourists, others, unwelcome armies, resented but sullenly endured—the Cossack encampment in 1814, the Prussians in 1871, Hitler's troops in 1940. But here, too, on great national occasions the processions begin or end and the people rejoice or mourn—mourn for the death of a hero, or a poet, or rejoice that after long years of occupation their country has been liberated.

Champs-Élysées, Comédie des, see *Avant-garde, Théâtre d'*.

Champs magnétiques, Les (1921), a surrealist work by André Breton and

Philippe Soupault (qq.v., and see *Sur-réalisme*).

Chamson, André (1900–), novelist, born at Nîmes, a Protestant, and at his best in his studies of life in the Cévennes, with its hardships, austerities, and Protestant traditions, e.g. *Roux le bandit* (1925); *Les Hommes de la route* (1927); *Le Crime des justes* (1928).

Chandelier, Le, by Alfred de Musset, a prose comedy in three acts, first published in the *Revue des Deux Mondes* of 1 November 1835, then included in the first (1840) edition of *Comédies et Proverbes* (q.v.). It was played for the first time in 1848.

Jacqueline, the young wife of Maître André, diverts her husband's suspicions from her intrigue with Clavaroche, an officer of dragoons, by encouraging the adoration of the young clerk Fortunio. Fortunio is so gentle and loving, so selflessly devoted even when he discovers that he is being made use of, that Jacqueline falls in love with him in good earnest, to the discomfiture of Clavaroche.

Chanson. The medieval French *chansons* were originally any poems composed to be sung, such as the *chansons à danser, à personnages, de toile* (qq.v.); or as the *chansons de geste* (q.v.), which narrated heroic exploits and were the early form of epic poetry. In the 12th and 13th centuries the word *chanson* was also used in the specific sense of a lyric love poem of the Provençal type in 5, 6, or 7 stanzas in three groups (2+2+1, 2+2+2, or 2+2+3). Each group was marked (usually) by the repetition of the same rhymes, and the rhymes in each stanza were similarly divided into three groups, of which the first and second were identical. Subject to this the *chanson* showed infinite variety of detailed arrangement. Thus the majority of the *chansons* of Gace Brulé (q.v.) have six stanzas (some five), and in the majority the stanzas are of eight lines (in others ten, nine, or seven). The number of syllables in each line may be ten, eight, seven, rarely six or less. Frequently a refrain or *envoi* is introduced. An example of the scheme of rhymes and syllables in a ten-lined stanza is:

      rhyme a b a b a b a b c c
    syllables 7 6 7 6 7 6 7 6 4 5

From the days of Clément Marot, Ron-sard, and later writers the word has been used for poems of a great variety of metrical forms, hardly distinguishable from the *ode* of the light, gay, amorous, bacchic, political, or satirical type. *Chansons* of recent years are the love and patriotic poems by Louis Aragon (q.v.).

Chanson d'Antioche, see *Antioche*.

Chanson de Roland, La, the earliest extant and the most celebrated *chanson de geste*, probably composed, in the form in which we have it, very early in the 12th century. It is in decasyllabic verse. The oldest manuscript (now in the Bodleian) was written in England about the middle of the 12th century. The last line mentions a certain Turoldus, who may be the author of the poem or of the poem's source, or (less probably) a scribe. It was perhaps an earlier version of this poem which, as recorded by Wace (q.v.) in the *Roman de Rou*, developing a statement by William of Malmesbury, Taillefer sang before Duke William at the Battle of Hastings:

> De Karlemainne et de Rollant,
> Et d'Ollivier et des vassals
> Qui morurent en Raincesvals.

Charlemagne has been seven years in Spain and has conquered the whole country except Saragossa, which is still held by Marsile, the Saracen king. Marsile makes perfidious overtures, in order to induce Charlemagne to leave Spain. The members of Charlemagne's council are divided; Roland (q.v.) is for rejecting the proposals, Ganelon for accepting them. The latter's opinion prevails. Roland, angered by Ganelon's taunts, proposes that Ganelon shall be selected to carry the acceptance to Marsile, a dangerous mission, for Marsile has executed the previous envoys of the French. In spite of the anger of Ganelon the proposal is adopted. Ganelon accepts rich presents from Marsile and decides to betray Roland and the rearguard of the army, as it withdraws from Spain, to the enemy. Roland, on the advice of Ganelon, is appointed to command the rearguard of 20,000 men, and the army crosses the Pyrenees. The rearguard is surrounded in the pass of Roncevaux by 400,000 Saracens. Roland is urged by Olivier (q.v.) to sound his horn and recall the main body to his support, but refuses.

In spite of the heroic deeds of the Twelve Peers (see *Pairs, Les Douze*), who have gathered round Roland, the force is gradually annihilated. In the last stages of the fight only sixty French remain alive, and Roland at last sounds his horn; but it is too late. Before Charlemagne can approach the field, the survivors are reduced to four, desperately wounded. We have the farewell of Roland and Olivier, the last blessing of Turpin (q.v.), and, as the trumpets of the French army are heard, Roland lays his body face to the enemy and delivers his spirit to St. Gabriel:

Morz est Rollant, Deus en a l'anme es cels.

Charlemagne and his army arrive and avenge their dead; they rout the Saracens and enter Saragossa. Aude, the sister of Olivier and Roland's betrothed, falls dead when she is told of the disaster. Ganelon, after a trial by single combat, is quartered.

The historical facts behind the legend are these. In 778 Charlemagne, at the invitation of two Moslem emirs hostile to the Emir of Cordova, entered Spain with an army of French, Germans, and Lombards. He captured Pampeluna and perhaps Saragossa, but was then recalled by a revolt in Saxony. His rearguard, while crossing the Pyrenees, was surprised by Basques in the pass of Roncevaux and entirely destroyed.

Hatred of the infidel and self-sacrifice in the cause of loyalty to the Emperor are the poem's dominating motives. The poet's narrative is simple, direct, and vivid. He can create live and convincing characters, and he has a sense of dramatic effect and epic breadth; there is grandeur and restrained pathos in the long account of the deaths of Olivier and Roland.

Chanson des Gueux, La (1878), collected poems by Jean Richepin (q.v.).

Chanson des Saisnes or ***des Saxons,*** see *Bodel, Jean.*

Chansons à danser, medieval songs, of which the oldest that survive date from the middle of the 13th century, in a variety of metres, composed as a musical accompaniment to dances. It is not possible to define their metrical forms with precision because these *chansons* were not a genre; moreover the art of the courtly poets of this period required that each song should differ in form from all its predecessors.

The principal dance was the *carole*, a sort of round dance, in which one of the dancers led the accompanying song and the others replied in a refrain. This gave rise to the general form of poem known as the *rondet* or *rondet de carole*, roughly equivalent to the modern *triolet* (q.v.). The *ballette*, another dance song, consisted of three stanzas, with a refrain repeated at the end of each (rhyming, for instance, a b a b b c C C, where the capitals indicate the refrain). The *virelai*, sometimes classed as a *chanson à danser*, might take the form A B c c a b A B. Other dances more elaborate than the *carole*, in which some simple scene, involving two or even three parts, was enacted, might be accompanied by song.

Chansons à personnages, or *chansons dramatiques*, medieval songs in dialogue form, representing a quarrel between husband and wife, or lovers regretting the dawn that obliges them to part (*aube*), or a love passage between knight and shepherdess (*pastourelle*), or a song of spring (*reverdie*) in which the birds take part. Cf. *Romances.*

Chansons de Bilitis (1894), see *Louÿs, P.*

Chansons de geste (from L. *gesta*, deeds, in the sense of a historical narrative), poems of heroic and often legendary exploits situated, loosely, in the age of Charlemagne and his immediate predecessors and successors. They are the beginnings of the epic in French literature (see *Epic poetry*). Some 80–100 of them survive, in manuscript versions of the 12th–15th centuries which in some cases are said by the medievalists to be remodellings of much earlier originals. The dates of actual composition assigned to the poems range from the 11th to the 12th–13th centuries (when the genre was at its height) and into the early 14th century. Since the early 19th-century revival of interest in medieval life and literature (see, for example, *History*, para. 4; *Romantisme*, para. 2) nearly all the extant *chansons de geste* have been edited by scholars. Many of them have been printed in a modernized form so as to bring them within reach of the general reader (cf., in English, the modernized versions of Chaucer).

(2) In length the *chansons* might be anything from 1,000 lines, or fewer, to 20,000 lines or more. An average for the greater number is 8,000 to 10,000 lines. In form they were in monorhyme stanzas (*laisses*) of varying length, with lines generally of ten syllables, sometimes eight or, latterly, twelve syllables. They rhymed by assonance, later by consonance (qq.v.).

(3) The origin of these epic poems has been much debated. The 19th-century view, held by the medievalist Gaston Paris (q.v.) and long accepted, was that they had been preceded by epic chants, the so-called *cantilènes* (q.v.), more or less contemporary with the events described, and influenced in their turn by Germanic traditions and folklore. Thus the *chansons de geste* represented popular or family traditions containing, some of them, a historical nucleus, and developed and added to by the imagination of poets in order to meet the public demand for the heroic and the marvellous. Another view was advanced by Joseph Bédier (q.v.) in the early 20th century and still holds the field, though recent scholars have questioned its reduction to a minimum of the historical and traditional element. It rebuts the possibility of Germanic origin and sees in the poems little beyond the inventions of *trouvères* and *jongleurs* (see below) working on stories told by monks to the pilgrims who visited shrines connected with the memory of heroes, e.g. Roland, Ogier, Girard de Roussillon, and Guillaume d'Orange. The shrines frequently lay on pilgrimage routes, and in the first instance the monks' stories would be drawn from Latin chronicles, lives of saints, or perhaps merely their own imagination.

(4) The chansons were composed—by *trouvères* (q.v.), the early poets—to be chanted to musical accompaniment (on the *vielle*, a primitive stringed instrument of the viol family), and were sung by professional minstrels (*jongleurs*, q.v.) or by the *trouvères* themselves for the diversion of lords in their halls or of public audiences as the minstrels wandered about France. Thus variant versions came into being; or whole new tales or episodes sprang from the parent stock; some forming connecting links between those already existing, some carrying the matter of the most popular tales farther back, to the *enfances* or early deeds of the heroes, or forward to the exploits of the heroes' descendants. This led to the poems being grouped by the *trouvères* of the 13th century in three main cycles or *gestes*, each inspired by a central idea, loyalty to a feudal chief, for instance, or to the Christian faith (the two predominant motives of heroic action in the earlier poems). The leaders after whom the *gestes* were named—Charlemagne, Garin de Monglane, Doon de Mayence—were credited with a sort of mystical kinship due to the circumstances of their birth.

(5) The first cycle, the *Geste du roi* (Charlemagne), contains the oldest and finest of all the known *chansons de geste*, the *Chanson de Roland* (q.v.), as well as a score of other poems connected with the legendary history of Charlemagne and his divine mission as defender of Christianity. The cycle of Garin de Monglane (also known as the *Geste de Guillaume* or *des Aimerides*) contains twenty-four *chansons* dealing with the exploits of Garin de Monglane (q.v.) and successive generations of his descendants, each of which is driven from home by its father to seek fiefs and glory at the expense of the pagans. The third cycle, of Doon de Mayence (q.v.), assembles the tales relating to the 'traitors' or rebels against royal authority, whose revolt ends in each case in repentance and humility. There was also a subordinate cycle known as the *Geste des Lorrains* (see *Garin le Loherain*).

(6) The *trouvères* very rarely invented new characters, and a small number of types, the valiant hero, the traitor (brave or cowardly), the Saracen giant, and so forth, are repeated with monotonous uniformity. Variety was obtained in other ways, especially as time went on and the original themes were rehandled. Into the simple presentation of a heroic, if legendary, past (as in the *Chanson de Roland*) were introduced fabulous or extravagant features, such as the fairy Oberon (in *Huon de Bordeaux*, q.v.) or the marvellous horse Bayard (in *Renaud de Montauban*, q.v.). The taste of popular audiences was studied (a comic element is already prominent in the *Pèlerinage de Charlemagne*). The heroic element tended to give place to the grotesque; even the great figure of Charlemagne was debased and ridiculed, while yeomen and peasants were exalted. The role assigned to women is frequently an ignoble one, though there are remarkable exceptions.

(7) During the 14th century the subject-matter of the great *chansons de geste* of the earliest age continued to be rehandled. There was also some revival of epic poetry, inspired by contemporary events such as the Hundred Years War (e.g. the *Chanson de Bertrand du Guesclin* by Cuvelier, *c.* 1384). It produced little of merit, and with the *Geste des Bourguignons* early in the 15th century poems in monorhyme stanzas came to an end. Prose adaptations of several of the chansons, such as *Fierabras* and *Huon de Bordeaux*, were issued in the early decades of the age of printing (late 15th and early 16th centuries).

(8) Without historical value as regards the events they relate, the *chansons de geste* throw a light on the customs, sentiments, dress, and arms of their period. Their influence on the literature of other countries is seen in the translations and imitations to which they gave rise in English, German, and other languages (particularly in Italian, in the works of Pulci, Boiardo, and Ariosto). Translations or imitations in English are noted in this book under the headings of the several poems.

For the principal *chansons*, see *Aimeri de Narbonne, Aliscans, Anseïs de Carthage, Aspremont, Berthe aux grands pieds, Bodel* (*Jean*, for the *Chanson des Saxons*), *Doon de Mayence, Fierabras, Garin de Monglane, Garin le Loherain, Girard de Viane, Girard de Roussillon, Gui de Bourgogne, Guillaume, Huon de Bordeaux, Ogier de Danemarcke, Pèlerinage de Charlemagne, Raoul de Cambrai, Renaud de Montauban, Roland.*

(9) Certain poems unconnected with the legendary history of France and its families also took the form (monorhyme stanzas) of the *chansons de geste*: see *Alexandre le Grand, Ami et Amile, Baudouin de Sebourg, Beuves de Haumtone, Chevalier au Cygne, Horn.*

Chansons des rues et des bois (1865), a collection of lyrics by Victor Hugo (q.v., para. 9).

Chansons de toile or sewing-songs, little medieval poems, so named from early times, because they frequently present women spinning or plying the needle, or perhaps were sung at the spinning-wheel. They take the form of monorhyme stanzas with a refrain, and relate some love episode.

In style they are remarkably simple, vivid, and graceful. Some are obviously very old, the latest probably not later than 1200.

Chant du départ, Le, a famous Revolutionary song (sometimes called 'the second Marseillaise'), with words by M.-J. Chénier and music by Méhul (qq.v.). It was probably first heard at the *Fête de la Fédération* (q.v.) of 14 July 1794. It received a second hearing the following September when Marat's remains were transported to the Panthéon, and subsequently it became the official song at national festivals. The first of several stanzas (intended to be sung by choirs of old men, mothers, children, &c.) runs:

La Victoire en chantant nous ouvre la
    barrière,
La Liberté guide nos pas,
Et du Nord au Midi la trompette guerrière
A sonné l'heure des combats.
Tremblez, ennemis de la France,
Rois ivres de sang et d'orgueil!
Le peuple souverain s'avance;
Tyrans, descendez au cercueil!

ref. La République nous appelle,
    Sachons vaincre ou sachons périr:
    Un Français doit vivre pour elle,
    Pour elle un Français doit mourir.

Chantecler, the cock, in the *Roman de Renart* (q.v.).

Chantecler (1910), a drama in four acts (verse) by Edmond Rostand (q.v.). It is allegorical, symbolical, and satirical. The characters, the day-to-day creatures of farmyard and forest, are animated by the same sentiments of egotism, jealousy, and emulation as human beings. They are sometimes tender, frequently fickle, often ruthless. Chantecler the cock imagines that it is his beautiful song that makes the sun rise. His pride has a fall, but he masters his disillusionment and returns with a good heart to the more humble role of wakening his farmyard.

Chantefable, a narrative work in alternating passages of prose and verse. This name was given by the author of *Aucassin et Nicolette* (q.v.) to his work, but disappeared from later use.

Chantilly, the name of a town, forest, and château in the department of the Oise, twenty-three miles north-east of Paris. The little town is the famous French training centre for race-horses. The château, on a site originally occupied by a Gallo-Roman fortress, dates from the Middle Ages. It was reconstructed, in two parts, in pure Renaissance style, by its 16th-century owner, the Connétable Anne de Montmorency, and repeatedly embellished by later owners, notably the Condé family. It suffered greatly at the time of the Revolution but was restored by the duc d'Aumale (1822–97) (4th son of Louis-Philippe), heir of the last Condé, and himself a distinguished historian, a member of the *Académie française*. He bequeathed it with its magnificent library and art collections—now the Musée Condé —to the *Institut de France*.

Chant royal, a type of poem composed of five stanzas of eleven decasyllabic lines and an *envoi* of five lines. Each stanza rhymes as follows:

a b a b c c d d e d e

and the *envoi* as follows:

d d e d e.

The last line of the first stanza forms a refrain, being repeated as the last line of each of the succeeding stanzas and of the *envoi*. According to the strict rule the whole poem should be a single allegory, of which the full explanation is furnished only in the *envoi*. The finest examples of this form of poem are by Clément Marot (q.v.).

Chants du crépuscule, Les (1835), lyrics and other poems by Victor Hugo, many of them reflecting the poet's growing republican sympathies, in contrast to the royalism of his earlier days (e.g. *À la Colonne, Napoléon II*).

Chants du soldat (1872), a collection of patriotic verse by Paul Déroulède (q.v.).

Chapeau, see *Un Chapeau de paille d'Italie.*

Chapelain, JEAN (1595–1674), man of letters and critic, a member of the original *Académie française*, author of a preface to the *Adone* of Marino, of *Odes*, and of an unsuccessful epic, *La Pucelle*, of which the first twelve cantos appeared in 1656 after twenty years' labour. The remaining twelve cantos were not published until 1882. Chapelain was a strong advocate of the classical form in literature (in particular of the unities in drama), and exerted, in the interval between Ronsard and Boileau, considerable influence in this direction. He was much esteemed by

Richelieu. It was he who drafted the *Académie*'s censure on Corneille's *Le Cid* (q.v.) and he who conceived the idea of the *Académie*'s dictionary. He was an *habitué* of the Hôtel de Rambouillet (q.v.), and his reputation in his day rested rather on his conversation than on his writings.

Chapelle, CLAUDE-EMMANUEL LUILLIER, *known as* (1626–86), poet, friend of Boileau, Molière, Racine, and La Fontaine, a jovial bohemian, author (with Bachaumont) of the lively *Voyage en Provence et Languedoc* (1656), in verse and prose, a medley of burlesque descriptions of scenery, much eating, and literary satire. Chapelle was an ardent disciple of Gassendi (q.v.).

Char, RENÉ (1907–), contemporary author (poet, particularly), born in Provence, where he still lives. He wrote some surrealist verse, collected in *Arsenal* (1929), *Artine* (1930), *Le Marteau sans maître* (1934), but broke with the movement (see *Surréalisme*) in 1937. His reputation was more firmly established after the 1939–45 war with the poems, often prose poems, in *Seuls demeurent* (1945); *Feuillets d'Hypnos* (1946), a poetical journal; *Fureur et Mystère* (1948), poems written between 1938 and 1947; *Les Matinaux* (1950), &c.

Charbonnerie, see *Carbonari.*

Chardin, JEAN (1643–1713), author of *Voyage en Perse et aux Indes Orientales* (Amsterdam 1711, 3 vols., the first complete edition), containing a valuable record of his travels. See also *Tavernier.*

Chardin, JEAN-BAPTISTE-SIMÉON (1699–1779), painter of still life and of genre pictures of bourgeois life.

Chardri, see *Barlaam et Josaphat.*

Charenton, a well-known mental hospital near Paris. Anyone who commits a rash or senseless act risks being called a 'pensionnaire de Charenton' or 'digne d'aller à Charenton' (cf. *Bicêtre*).

Charité and ***Miserere,*** the titles of two religious poems in octosyllabic stanzas, composed early in the 13th century, and so named from the first word of each, by an author who calls himself the Reclus de Molliens. They are elaborate exhortations to a godly life.

Charivari, Le, the prototype of *Punch*, was founded by Charles Philipon (q.v.) in 1832 as a daily satirical pamphlet. The many caricaturists on its staff (Cham, Daumier, Gavarni, &c., qq.v.) made its cartoons celebrated, particularly those attacking the July monarchy, Louis-Philippe himself, and the bourgeoisie. It flourished again during the Second Empire, when its scope was extended to include politics, literature, and the drama. It continued into the 20th century.

Charlemagne [Charles I] (742–814), one of the greatest figures of the Middle Ages, son of Pépin le Bref, succeeded his father as King of the Franks (jointly with his brother Carloman) in 768 and became sole king in 771. In 800 he was crowned Emperor of the West by Pope Leo III. His empire, which he established by continuous wars, chiefly against the Saxons, extended from the North Sea to the Pyrenees and the Ebro, and in Italy to the Garigliano, and from the Elbe to the Atlantic. In this Empire he endeavoured to establish order and justice and protected learning. He entertained friendly relations with the Empire of the East and with the Caliph Haroun-al-Raschid. His mother, Berthe, daughter of Caribert, Count of Laon, was a woman of much character and moral worth, who helped to guide her son's policy until her death in 783.

Many legends relating to him, almost entirely imaginary, are embodied in the Charlemagne and other cycles of *chansons de geste* (q.v.). Of these there are examples in *Berthe aux grands pieds, Aspremont, Pèlerinage de Charlemagne, Chanson de Roland, Fierabras, Chanson des Saisnes, Girard de Viane,* and in the *chansons* of the cycle of *Doon de Mayence* (qq.v.). Charlemagne's consort is Blanchefleur or Sébile (q.v.); his famous sword is called Joyeuse. For his Twelve Peers see *Pairs, les Douze* (cf. also *Carolingiens*).

Faire Charlemagne, in the language of the gaming table, is to retire from the game after winning, without allowing a revenge.

Charles II *le Chauve,* born 823, fourth son of Louis I, *le Débonnaire,* succeeded his father as King of the Franks in 840 and reigned till his own death in 877. He belonged to the *Carolingien* (q.v.) dynasty (cf. also *Serments de Strasbourg, Verdun*).

Charles III *le Simple,* born 879, posth. son of Louis II *le Bègue,* reigned in opposition to Eudes (q.v.) from 893 till the latter's death in 898, then reigned alone. He was deposed in favour of Robert I in 922. A year later he killed his rival in battle though he lost the battle itself, and another rival king (Raoul, q.v.) was elected. Charles escaped but was later imprisoned and died (929) in captivity. He belonged to the *Carolingien* (q.v.) dynasty.

In 911 he had given his daughter and part of his territory to the Norman pirate Rollo who thus became the first Duke of Normandy.

Charles IV *le Bel* (1294–1328), son of Philippe IV *le Bel,* succeeded his brother Philippe V *le Long* as King of France in 1322 and reigned till his own death in 1328. The direct line of the *Capétien* (q.v.) dynasty ended with him.

Charles V *le Sage,* b. 1337, King of France from the death of his father, Jean II, in 1364 till his own death in 1380. He belonged to the Valois branch of the *Capétien* (q.v.) dynasty. His second son, Louis d'Orléans (assassinated in 1407), was the grandfather of Louis XII by one son and the great-grandfather of François Iᵉʳ by another.

Charles VI *le Bien-aimé,* born 1368, succeeded his father Charles V in 1380 and reigned till his own death in 1422. During the last twenty years of his reign he was mad and the country was a prey to anarchy and faction (cf. *Armagnacs*). He belonged to the Valois branch of the *Capétien* (q.v.) dynasty.

Charles VII *le Victorieux,* born 1403, son of Charles VI, acted as Regent when his father was mentally incapacitated and succeeded him as King in 1422, reigning till his own death in 1461. His reign saw the episode of Jeanne d'Arc and the end of the Hundred Years War. He belonged to the Valois branch of the *Capétien* (q.v.) dynasty.

Charles VIII *l'Affable,* born 1470, succeeded his father Louis XI in 1483 as King of France and reigned till his own death in 1498. His reign was notable for the invasion of Italy to assert the rights of the French crown to the kingdom of Naples. He belonged to the Valois branch of the *Capétien* (q.v.) dynasty.

Charles IX, born 1550, 2nd son of Henri II and Catherine de Médicis, became King of

France in 1560 on the death of his brother François II. His reign lasted till his own death in 1574 (two years after the Massacre of Saint Bartholomew), but though he had attained his legal majority in 1564 his mother was for long the real ruler of the country. He was a patron of letters and a friend of Ronsard. He belonged to the Valois branch (Valois-Orléans line) of the *Capétien* (q.v.) dynasty. (See *Kings of France*; *Orléans*; also *Chronique du règne de Charles IX*.)

Charles IX (1789), a tragedy in verse by M.-J. Chénier (q.v.), set in Paris before the massacre of St. Bartholomew. This has been planned by Catherine de Médicis and her Guise relations, but a pretended reconciliation with the Protestants has been staged to disarm suspicion. The order to begin must be given by the young king Charles IX, who is portrayed as weak and cowardly, always influenced by the last speaker. Finally his mother rushes him into a decision and the massacre takes place.

This tragedy delighted Revolutionary audiences, who took the allusions to the intrigues and feebleness of Royalty as veiled analogies with events of their own day.

Charles X (1757–1836), who at first bore the title of comte d'Artois, was a younger brother of both Louis XVI and Louis XVIII, and a grandson of Louis XV. An *émigré* in 1789, he conspired against the Revolution, and spent several years in England. He returned at the Restoration and led the *Ultras* (q.v.), the extreme Royalist party. He succeeded to the throne in 1824 on the death of Louis XVIII. Hostility aroused by his anti-liberal, pro-Catholic policy culminated in the July Revolution (1830) which brought the rule of the elder branch of the Bourbons to an end (see *Bourbon*; *Louis-Philippe Ier*). Thereafter he spent his life in exile, partly in Edinburgh (at Holyrood), partly in Prague. He died at Gorizia. His coronation at Rheims (29 May 1825) was an occasion of great pomp, with a religious emphasis which shocked many. (See also *Chambord, comte de*.)

Charles XII, Histoire de, see *Histoire de Charles XII*.

Charles Blanchard (1913) (unfinished), a novel by Charles-Louis Philippe (q.v.).

Charles Demailly (1860), a novel of literary life by Edmond and Jules de Goncourt (qq.v.).

Charles d'Orléans (1391–1465), poet, born in Paris, son of Louis d'Orléans (brother of Charles VI, assassinated in 1407) and Valentine Visconti; thus half Italian by birth.

He was taken prisoner at Agincourt and carried to England, where he remained in captivity for twenty-five years. He spent the latter part of his life at Blois, where he devoted himself to poetry, and his court was a literary centre.

His first poems, graceful and tender *ballades* (q.v.), celebrating (probably) his wife and forming what is known as the 'Livre de la Prison', were composed in England. The *rondeaux* and *ballades* of his later years are similarly graceful trifles showing great technical skill, style, and measure, but without depth of feeling. He was the last and perhaps the best of the 15th-century *poètes courtois*. (See also *Orléans*.)

Charles le Gros, born 839, succeeded his father Louis *le Germanique* (q.v.) in 876 as King, and in 882 became Emperor, of Germany. On the death of Carloman (884) he also became King of France. He was deposed in 887 and died in 888. Eudes (q.v.), to whom in 886 he had mainly left the defence of Paris against the Norman pirates, was elected king in his place. He belonged to the *Carolingien* (q.v.) dynasty.

Charles le Téméraire [Charles the Bold], one of the last of the powerful feudal vassals of the kings of France, was born at Dijon in 1433 and succeeded to the Dukedom of Burgundy in 1467. He married (his third wife) Margaret of York, sister of Edward IV, in 1468, thus forming an alliance with England. He was rashly courageous, cruel, arrogant, and devouringly ambitious, a continual threat to the crown and the developing national unity of France. Besides the Duchy of Burgundy his vast territorial possessions included a great part of the Low Countries. He hankered after Alsace-Lorraine, to make his territory continuous and enable him to create a new realm, a Middle Kingdom, with Nancy as capital. He besieged Nancy in January 1477 and was killed in battle. He figures in Scott's *Anne of*

Geierstein and is also—miraculously resurrected—*le Solitaire* of the enormously successful Gothic novel of this name (1821) by the vicomte d'Arlincourt (q.v.).

Charles Martel, see *Maire du Palais.*

Charlus, PALAMÈDE DE GUERMANTES, BARON DE ('Mémé' for his intimates), in Proust's *A la recherche du temps perdu* (q.v.), is the chief vehicle for the author's lengthy, excessively detailed, but serious and compassionate treatment of the theme of inversion. He comes into prominence at the beginning of *Sodome et Gomorrhe* when Marcel, watching an encounter between him and the tailor Jupien, becomes alive to his true character, as yet successfully hidden from his friends. Thereafter he dominates the novel. He is highly cultured, and can manifest a charm, at times even a sweetness, surpassed only by his overpowering insolence and occasionally burlesque aggressiveness. With age, and as his affair with the violinist Morel progresses and finally ends (in a dramatic episode in the Verdurin salon, see *La Prisonnière*). he yields more and more unashamedly to his instincts and touches the lowest depths of vice. His personality disintegrates: and a last glimpse of 'le vieux prince déchu' shows him fallen from arrogance to an abject, palsied affability.

Charmes (1922), a collection of poems by Paul Valéry (q.v.).

Charmettes, Les, a country house near Chambéry, the residence from 1738 to 1740 of Mme de Warens and Rousseau.

Charpentier, FRANÇOIS (1620–1702), scholar and man of letters, perpetual secretary of the *Académie*, author of a work on *L'Excellence de la langue française* (1683).

Charpentier, GUSTAVE (1860–1956), composer of, notably, *Louise* (produced 1900), an opera about life and love in Paris. The heroine, a seamstress (there is one scene in the dressmaker's workroom where she is employed), forsakes home and parents to live with her artist lover Julien in a little house in a garden in Montmartre (the setting for a love-duet). Charpentier was his own librettist in this work.

Charrette, Chevalier à la, see *Chevalier à la Charrette.*

Charrière, MME DE, *by birth* Isabella van Tuyll van Serooskerken, *also known as* Belle de Zuylen (1740–1805), a Dutchwoman of good family, great intelligence and originality, and considerable beauty. She numbered among her many suitors James Boswell, who quickly reconciled himself to her rejection of his hand. Declining more brilliant matches she married her brother's Swiss tutor, the dull but worthy M. de Charrière. Her unhappy married life was brightened by an ardent intellectual friendship with Benjamin Constant, until she was ousted by Mme de Staël. There is an interesting account of her life in Geoffrey Scott's *Portrait of Zélide*, 'Zélide' being the name that she gave to herself in an early self-portrait. Her novels (in French) include *Lettres neuchâteloises* (1784), *Mistress Henley* (1784), *Lettres écrites de Lausanne* (1785) and its sequel *Caliste* (1787), *Trois femmes* (1797). The second, third, and fourth are largely autobiographical and reveal the disappointments of the writer's married life, *Mistress Henley* in particular presenting the theme that a woman may be made utterly miserable by the very excess of a dull husband's virtues. It was part of the irony of the situation that M. de Charrière used to make fair copies of his wife's works for the publisher.

Charroi de Nîmes, Le, a *chanson de geste* (q.v.), one of the *Garin de Monglane* (q.v.) cycle.

Charron, PIERRE (1541–1603), religious and philosophical writer, a Parisian lawyer who became a priest and a successful preacher, a friend of Montaigne, to whose daughter he bequeathed his property. He published in 1593 *Les Trois Vérités*, these being: the truth of the existence of God (against the atheists), that of Christianity (against the infidels), and of the Catholic faith (against the Protestants). His *Discours Chrétiens* appeared in 1600. Later, in 1601, he published *De la Sagesse*, a work of stoic philosophy after the manner of Montaigne, designed to bring philosophy to the support of religion, but containing chapters which taken apart from his earlier work exposed him to the charge of scepticism, as suggesting that the study of man can produce a code of morality independent of religious dogma. Charron set about preparing a revised edition but was unable to appease the theologians before his death.

'Did you ever read Charron on Wisdom?' Charles Lamb asks Wordsworth (9 Aug. 1815), adding that, if not, he has a great pleasure before him.

Charte, La. On 4 June 1814, at the bidding of the Allied Powers, the newly restored monarch, Louis XVIII, granted a charter (*La Charte constitutionnelle*) which upheld the social and administrative order resulting from the Revolution and the Napoleonic era. It provided, further, for government by a constitutional monarchy, with a largely hereditary House of Peers nominated by the king, and an elected House of Deputies. The franchise did not extend below a certain income. Roman Catholicism became the official state religion. The Press was nominally free but could be, and in fact was, restricted by law. Ministerial responsibility was not clearly defined, a fact which led to an abuse of power by Charles X and thus to the July Revolution (see *Revolutions*, II).

Chartier, Alain (*c.* 1390–*c.* 1440), poet and prose writer, born at Bayeux in Normandy, was employed in the service of Charles VI and Charles VII, and was sent on diplomatic missions to Germany, Venice, and Scotland. There was a story that Margaret of Scotland kissed him on his lips while he slept, for the beautiful words and thoughts, she explained, that issued from them. He was made a canon of Paris. His first poem, the *Livre des quatre dames*, written immediately after Agincourt, in which four ladies lament the loss of their lovers on that same day, expresses the bitterness and sorrow that followed the defeat of the French chivalry. His *La Belle Dame sans merci* (1424), a short poem on a lover who dies of despair in consequence of his lady's cruelty, met with remarkable success. His best-known prose work is the *Quadrilogue invectif* (1422), written when France was in the depth of confusion and humiliation from internal strife and the conquest of her territory by Henry V. Its object is described as 'ad morum Gallicorum correctionem' and it takes the form of a dialogue between four characters, France, the nobility, the people, the clergy. France reproves her citizens for their defection and exhorts them to courage. The people bring a formidable accusation of selfishness and in-

competence against the nobility. The nobility blame the people for their sedition, ingratitude, and lack of faith. The clergy urge discipline and loyalty on both. France demands from them union and co-operation. The work contains passages of admirable vigour. Chartier also wrote a *Traité de l'espérance*, *Bréviaire des nobles*, and *Débat du Réveille-matin*. His prose, written in a style modelled on the Latin orators, is the outcome of an early revival of humanist letters. He wrote in Latin a satire on court life, *De vita curiali*; the translation of this, entitled *Le Curial*, is not by him.

Chartier, ÉMILE-AUGUSTE (1868–1951), philosopher, famous as teacher and—over the pen-name 'Alain'—essayist, was a veterinary surgeon's son from Normandy, born at Mortagne (Orne). He was educated at the lycée of Vanves (later Lycée Michelet), on the outskirts of Paris, and the École normale supérieure (q.v.). After taking his degree (see *agrégation*) in arts he entered upon a teaching career which lasted till 1933, with a break during the 1914–18 war when, aged forty-seven, he joined up and served in the ranks. He taught philosophy: in provincial lycées, notably Rouen, until 1900, then in Paris, beginning with the Lycée Condorcet. From 1909 onwards, as teacher of philosophy at the Lycée Henri IV, he filled the highest post in the French system of State secondary education. He also lectured at the Collège Sévigné, a girls' school of high standing. He was thus a formative influence on French thought, second only, it has been said, to Bergson (q.v.), for some forty years.

In 1906, in the *Dépêche de Rouen*, he began a series of daily *Propos d'un Normand*, which soon made him known far beyond the world of his pupils. They were short essays, or improvisations, on divers subjects (*Propos sur... le bonheur, le Christianisme, l'esthétique, la littérature, l'éducation, la politique*, &c.). In manuscript, they never exceeded two sheets of letter paper, and the author allowed himself no erasures. They continued over many years and fill several volumes in book form. It was now for the first time that Chartier used the pen-name 'Alain', after the poet Alain Chartier (cf. above) whom, sleeping, Margaret of Scotland kissed.

Alain invented no new system of philosophy. His force lay in his study and understanding of the best of the old systems, from Aristotle and Plato down through Descartes (perhaps especially, but he remarked that no one system ever captivated him), Spinoza, Kant, Hegel, Rousseau, and Auguste Comte. It lay, too, in his own, independent and wonderfully clear-sighted, consideration, derived from such study, of the problems of life, religion, art, literature, and politics. It was due, lastly, to his gift for communicating knowledge by encouraging his pupils to think, re-think, and re-define for themselves, to strip inherited values and beliefs, and the words themselves in which these are expressed, of the great mass of associations and commonplaces which distort judgement.

The evolution of his thought can be studied in the absorbing *Histoire de mes pensées* (1936), a book which he himself treated only as a long preface to a later work *Les Dieux* (1934), in *Souvenirs de guerre* (1937), and in the volumes of *Propos* already mentioned. His *Propos de littérature* (1933) are particularly interesting as criticism. They are complemented by the separate studies *Stendhal* (1935), *Avec Balzac* (1937), *En lisant Dickens* (1945), also by *Commentaires* (1936) on the poetry of Paul Valéry (q.v.), notably on *Charmes* and *La Jeune Parque*. His *Système des Beaux-Arts* (1920), a guide, with flashes of revelation, to the understanding and appreciation of painting, sculpture, architecture, music, literature, &c., was written during his Army years. Much of it is amplified, particularly as regards poetry, in *Vingt leçons sur les beaux-arts* (1931). He had come to poetry only after his war years, but once this happened, and he had seen the gods 'courir avec les hommes', it provoked some of his finest, most stimulating, and in themselves fundamentally poetical writings on language, philosophy, and the creative process.

Other volumes of a corpus which richly repays study are the philosophical essays *Les Idées et les âges* (1927), *Entretiens au bord de la mer* (1931), and also the short *Visite au musicien* (1927). The musician is Beethoven, whose happiness lay in his will to happiness.

The *Mémoires* of André Maurois (vol. i), the same author's *Alain* (1950), and the *Hommage à Alain* (1952) published by the *Nouvelle Revue Française*, contain interesting studies of this great thinker, teacher, and personality.

Chartreuse de Parme, La (1839), a novel by Stendhal, a picture of life and intrigues at a small Italian court between 1815 and 1830. It is based on the chronicles of the Farnese family, sovereigns of Parma in the 16th century, especially Alexander Farnese, later Pope Paul III, whose son was Duke of Parma.

The sixteen-year-old Fabrice del Dongo joins Napoleon's armies in France. After many adventures, culminating in the battle of Waterloo (of which he sees little), he returns to Italy, somewhat suspect because of his French escapades. His aunt, the Duchess de Sanseverina ('la Sanseverina', a vital, beautiful young woman, of infinite resource, who dominates the book), is mistress of Count Mosca, chief minister at the Court of Parma. Through her influence he finds himself on the threshold of a successful ecclesiastical career. Count Mosca's enemies, aware—perhaps even more than she is herself—that la Sanseverina loves Fabrice, plot the young man's removal from the capital, for the duchess would certainly follow him and the count would not stay behind her. The plot succeeds, thanks to Fabrice's imprudent amours with a young actress. He is imprisoned, but with the aid of the duchess and Count Mosca, and helped by the prison governor's daughter Clélia Conti, he escapes. Meanwhile the duchess has contrived to have the reigning Prince of Parma poisoned. Through her influence, again, the new prince pardons Fabrice, who becomes a prominent cleric and a popular preacher, and renews his liaison with Clélia Conti, now married. Their son, Sandrino, is born and, two years later, kidnapped by Fabrice, who wishes to have his child to himself. The boy dies and Clélia does not long survive him. Fabrice retires to the Carthusian monastery of Parma ('la Chartreuse de Parme'). His death a year later is followed by that of la Sanseverina.

Balzac, one of the earliest admirers of *La Chartreuse de Parme*, hailed it as the novel that Machiavelli would have written if he had been banished from Italy in the 19th century (cf. *Revue parisienne, La*).

Chasles, PHILARÈTE (1798–1873), man of letters and critic, did much by his writings, based on a wide knowledge of European literature and civilization, to familiarize readers of his day with the literature of foreign countries. In early life he spent seven years in England, employed by a firm of publishers on the supervision of editions of Greek and Latin works. In later life he held the chair of Modern European Languages and Literature at the Collège de France (q.v.) and was on the editorial staff of the *Journal des Débats* (q.v.). His works included: *Le Dix-huitième siècle en Angleterre* (1846); *Études sur l'antiquité* (1847); *Études sur l'Espagne et sur les influences de la littérature espagnole en France et en Italie* (1847); *Études sur la littérature et les mœurs de l'Angleterre au XIXᵉ siècle* (1850); *Voyages d'un critique à travers la vie et les livres* (1865–8); also two volumes of (occasionally ill-natured) *Mémoires* (1876–7) which contain many portraits of his contemporaries.

Chasse au Chastre, La (1853, first published 1837 in the *Revue de Paris* as *La Chasse d'un artiste*), by Joseph Méry (q.v.), an amusing tale about a Provençal musician who takes a day off to go shooting. He puts up a *chastre* (a rare bird), misses it several times, but stalks it with such ardour that some weeks later he finds himself at Rome. Here he is arrested as a suspicious character who carries a gun, can produce no papers, and speaks an unknown language (the Provençal dialect). Dumas *père's La Chasse au chastre* (1841 as a tale, 1850 as a play) relates the same episode, which was told him in the first place by Méry.

Chasse spirituelle, La. A long prose poem with this title was published by the publishing house of the *Mercure de France* in May 1949 as a lost work by Rimbaud (q.v.), one referred to by Verlaine but never brought to light. The day after publication the real authors came forward in the persons of Mme Akakia-Viala (Marie-Antoinette-Émilie Allevy) and Nicolas Bataille, members of an experimental theatre company. They said—and for a good while many critics refused to believe their story— that they had concocted this pastiche to prove, in the face of adverse criticism of some of their productions, that they did understand Rimbaud. They had handed their typed manuscript, they said, without their names, to a bookseller and thereafter

it had come by devious ways, as an apparently genuine work, to the *Mercure de France*. This, unintentionally on the part of the authors, was one of the most celebrated literary hoaxes of modern times. (Some weeks later Mme Akakia-Viala and her collaborator made over their authors' rights to the Musée Rimbaud at Charleville.)

Chasseur vert, Le, see *Lucien Leuwen*.

Chastelard, Pierre de Boscosel de (1540–64), a gentleman of Dauphiné, grandson of Bayard, a man of poetical and musical gifts. He conceived a violent passion for Mary Stuart, whom he followed to Scotland after the death of François II (her first husband); he was discovered in her room, and executed. He is the subject of Swinburne's tragedy of this name (1865).

Chastellain or **Chastelain,** Georges (*c.* 1405 or *c.* 1415–75), a Fleming, who became councillor of the Duke of Burgundy and historiographer of his house; author of a 'Chronique des choses de ce temps' (viz. 1419–75) preserved in fragmentary form, in which he judges with a high independence the princes of his day, in a style based on Latin models. This chronicle was continued by Jean Molinet (q.v.). Chastellain was also a poet, of the school of the *rhétoriqueurs* (q.v.), and author of various moral and political pieces including *Les Princes*, a political poem presenting twenty-four types of bad rulers. Charles the Bold did 'le grand Georges' the signal honour of dubbing him with his own hand a knight of the Golden Fleece.

Chastellux (pron. as if *Châtelu*), François-Jean, marquis de (1734–88), military commander and man of letters, author of *De la félicité publique* (1772).

Chastiement des dames, a medieval collection of precepts of good manners for ladies, by Robert de Blois (13th century).

Chat botté, Le, Puss in Boots of the fairy-tale (one of Perrault's, q.v., *Contes*).

Chateaubriand, vicomte François-René de (1768–1848), born in Saint-Malo, 10th child of an old Breton family, was the outstanding literary genius of the early 19th century. His schooling (at Dol, Rennes, and Dinan) was intermittent, his childhood being spent mainly at the parental château of Combourg (q.v.). In his *Mémoires d'outre-tombe* (see below) he recalls days of wandering through the deserted forests and marshes of the Combourg countryside, alone or with his much-loved sister Lucile (1764–1804), and long, silent evenings with his parents, in a gloomy drawing-room.

In 1788, aged twenty, he went to Paris with an army commission, was presented at court, and made literary friends (notably Fontanes, q.v.). The Revolution interrupted his career and in 1791 he set out for America, bent, so he said, on discovering the North-West passage. His American travels were fruitful, though in fact not extensive. They ended in 1792 when he heard by chance of the fall of the monarchy and returned to France. He fought with the *Armée des émigrés* (q.v.), was wounded during the siege of Thionville, and escaped to England (1793). During his exile (in London mainly, with an interlude at Bungay in Suffolk) he supported himself meagrely by translations, wrote *Les Natchez* (q.v.), a long prose epic not published till 1826, also an *Essai historique, politique et moral sur les révolutions anciennes et modernes dans leurs rapports avec la révolution française* (1797, published in London), and began writing a work of Christian apologetics.

He returned to France in 1800. In 1801 he made a reputation suddenly with the short tale *Atala* (q.v.). In 1802 he won resounding fame with *Le Génie du christianisme*, the work begun in London, now finished and published opportunely at the moment when Roman Catholicism was once more to become the official religion of France. The work also earned him Napoleon's favour and an appointment to the Embassy at Rome. (This he resigned in 1804, disgusted by the execution of the duc d'Enghien, q.v.) Between 1806 and 1807 he travelled in Greece, the Near East, and Spain. On his return—to La Vallée-aux-Loups, a small property near Paris which he had bought and later was obliged to sell—he devoted himself to literature and journalism. He was a regular contributor to the *Mercure de France* (q.v.) between 1800 and 1814. He became increasingly hostile to the Empire and fell foul of Napoleon more than once, but he was not exiled. On his election to the *Académie française* (q.v.) in 1811 his *discours*

de réception was so openly provocative that he was not allowed to read it.

His political career began with Napoleon's downfall. He was one of Louis XVIII's ministers at Ghent; and later, as French Ambassador in London, he lived with a pomp that contrasted gloriously with his previous sojourn. During the July Monarchy he lived in Paris in retirement, editing his autobiography (*Mémoires d'outre-tombe*, 1849–50, q.v.). To the end of his life he was a constant, and the most welcome, frequenter of Mme Récamier's (q.v.) *salon*. With the years he became increasingly a grand old man of literature, accepting the homage of a few distinguished friends, superbly remote from the fever of daily life. He died in Paris but was buried by his special desire in an island tomb (*le rocher du Grand-bé*, q.v.) off Saint-Malo. Flaubert's *Par les champs et par les grèves* has a magnificent description of the tomb.

Chateaubriand was, by all accounts, a sublime *poseur*, a sublime egotist, and a sublime day-dreamer, seeing the world in and through himself. When his grandiose visions were not realized he could persuade himself that he had not desired the reality actively enough, and substitute others. Hence came the spirit of imaginative melancholy, the continually frustrated yearning for the infinite, the 'volupté mélancolique des horizons', that infused his creative writing (e.g. his famous tale *René*, q.v., first included in *Le Génie du christianisme* but published separately in 1805). By his emotional appeal he was, as Mme de Staël (q.v.) was by her ideas, one of the great precursors of *le Romantisme* (q.v.) and a lasting influence on French literature. His style, too, was of great influence, rhythmic and flowing, evocative of the poetry, colour, and harmonies of the scenes he described.

His works, besides those already mentioned, include the short tale *Les Aventures du dernier Abencérage* (1826, q.v.); *La Vie de Rancé* (1844), a highly subjective biography of the famous Trappist (see *Rancé*; *Trappe, Abbaye de la*); *Les Martyrs* (1809, q.v.), a prose epic of early Christianity; the travel sketches of *Itinéraire de Paris à Jérusalem* (1811, q.v.) and of *Voyage en Amérique* (1827), *Voyage en Italie* (1826), and *Voyage au Mont Blanc* (1806), describing journeys undertaken in 1791, 1803–4, and 1805 respectively; and a number of miscellaneous political pamphlets and critical writings, including the pamphlet *De Buonaparte et des Bourbons* (1814), a piece of invective said by Louis XVIII to have been worth an army to him in propaganda value.

Chateaubriand et son groupe littéraire sous l'Empire (1861), see *Sainte-Beuve*.

Château de la misère, the poverty-striken, ancestral castle of Gautier's *Capitaine Fracasse* (q.v.).

Châteaux en Espagne, see *Espagne*.

Châtel, FERDINAND - FRANÇOIS [l'abbé Châtel], 1795–1857, born in Gannat (Allier), began life as a tailor's apprentice but was later ordained and was for a time an army chaplain. In Paris he got into trouble over his unorthodox views and was forbidden to preach in church. After the 1830 Revolution, with a following of discontented priests, he founded the *Église catholique française*, with services in French, names of great men (e.g. Parmentier, who brought the potato to France) on the walls, no confessional, and a married priesthood; and with himself as *Primat des Gaules*. It was suppressed by the police in 1842. 'L'Abbé Châtel' made a reappearance during the 1848 Revolution, as an advocate of women's rights and of easy divorce. In 1850 he was convicted of offences against morality and religion. He is said to have ended by keeping a grocer's shop. His works included a *Code de l'humanité ou l'humanité ramenée à la connaissance du vrai Dieu et au véritable socialisme* (1838).

Châtelain de Coucy, see *Coucy*.

Châtelaine de Vergi, La, a metrical romance of the second half of the 13th century, which has perhaps some historical foundation.

A knight loves the Châtelaine de Vergi, niece of the duke of Burgundy. Her little dog, which has been trained for the purpose, brings him the summons to their meetings. She has warned her lover that he will lose her if he reveals their secret. The duchess of Burgundy falls in love with the knight; but he, faithful to his lady, repulses her advances. The duchess, from mortification, denounces him to the duke as having attempted her honour. The duke, who esteems the knight, gives him an opportunity to exculpate himself. To do this the knight, under pledge of strictest confidence, reveals his secret. But the duchess worms this out of her husband and nurses her revenge. On an occasion when her ladies are assembled she alludes to the châtelaine's lover and their little dog. The châtelaine, convinced of her lover's infidelity to her, dies of a broken heart. The knight, finding her dead, kills himself upon her body; and the duke, incensed with his wife, slays her with the sword drawn from the knight's body. The story is told with much charm and delicacy. It forms in substance the seventieth tale of the *Heptaméron* of Marguerite de Navarre.

Châtelet or **Grand Châtelet**, in Paris, originally constructed on the north bank of the Seine for the defence of the Pont au Change, a tribunal and prison where the *prévost*, assisted by a *lieutenant criminel* and a *lieutenant civil*, exercised the royal jurisdiction over the city. Clément Marot who was acquainted with it as a prison satirized it in his *Enfer*. In the 18th century the tribunal of the Châtelet showed activity in repressing subversive publications: for instance it caused Delisle de Sales's *Philosophie de la nature* to be burnt and sentenced the author to banishment. The building was demolished in 1802.

The *Petit Châtelet* was a quadrangular castle on the south bank of the Seine for the defence of the Petit Pont. It was the official residence of the *prévost* of Paris and part of it was used as a prison. It was demolished in 1782.

Châtelet, MARQUISE DU, see *Du Châtelet*.

Châtiments, Les (1853), poems written by Victor Hugo during his first year of exile. The volume contains some of the finest satirical and denunciatory verse in the French language. It opens with a sinister picture of the night before the *coup d'état* of 2 December 1851. Nothing can dull the memory of the horrors which, the poet cries, have filled with hate a heart that had been overflowing with love. A hundred poems follow, divided into seven books with such ironical titles as *L'Ordre est rétabli* (because the innocent people in the streets have been massacred), or *La Société est sauvée* (because corruption has triumphed and the defenders of liberty have been deported). The poet, who some time earlier had taken no small share in fostering *la légende napoléonienne* (q.v.), denounces Napoleon III ('Napoléon le petit') as the betrayer of his country. *Expiation* has descriptions of the retreat from Moscow and the battle of Waterloo (the latter was described again by Hugo in *Les Misérables*, q.v.). *Lux*, the last poem, proclaims the poet's faith in the restoration of liberty and the establishment of a universal republic.

Chat-Noir, Le, a café and cabaret in Montmartre (one of the artists' quarters of Paris), became celebrated *c.* 1880. Its sign was a black cat (Art) with tail erect, holding a terrified goose (the *Bourgeoisie*) under its paw. Over the door was the legend 'Passant, sois moderne'. At first it was frequented by local poets and painters who got up entertainments for their own pleasure. In time, outsiders were attracted, many paying high prices to find themselves in 'Bohemia'. Its proprietor, Rodolphe Salis, retired with a fortune, and many authors who had written sketches for his cabaret had their works produced later at the *Théâtre Libre* (q.v.).

Chatrian, ALEXANDRE, see *Erckmann-Chatrian.*

Chats-fourrez, see *Pantagruel (Cinquième livre).*

Chatterton (1835), a drama (prose) by Alfred de Vigny (q.v.), deals with an imaginary episode in the life of the English poet Thomas Chatterton (1752–70). It has been called the history of a man who writes a letter in the morning and commits suicide in the evening on receiving the reply.

The young poet hopes, if he can be free to write, to make enough money to pay his debts. He takes lodgings under an assumed name with John Bell, a prosperous, materialistic business man. A sympathy which both hesitate to acknowledge grows between him and Kitty Bell, his landlord's young wife, a tender, compassionate creature who has so far known no emotion stronger than maternal love. Chatterton writes to the Lord Mayor of London, an old friend of his father, to ask for help and employment. While he awaits a reply some former friends

appear by chance and reveal his identity. The Lord Mayor answers his letter in person, jeers at him, offers him a valet's post, and hands him a newspaper in which he reads that he is accused of plagiarism. The poet, all hope dashed, goes to his room, burns his manuscripts, and takes poison. Kitty Bell has followed, meaning to tell him of her love and her belief in him. She arrives too late and dies of grief. (See also *Stello.*)

Chaudon, DOM LOUIS-MAYEUL, see *Dictionaries and Encyclopedias*, under date 1766.

Chaulieu, GUILLAUME AMFRYE, ABBÉ DE (1639–1720), poet, born at Fontenay in Normandy, accompanied M. de Béthune on a mission to John Sobieski, King of Poland, and later attached himself to the two sons of the duc de Vendôme (the younger duke and the prior of the *Temple*), becoming manager of their affairs and receiving benefices as his reward. He frequented the corrupt society that underlay the superficial rigorism of the later years of Louis XIV, and was the Anacreon of the *Temple* (q.v.), an easygoing genius, enjoying pleasures with refinement. His later poems show a melancholy disillusionment, and contain some of his most delicate work. He was a constant friend of the marquis de la Fare (q.v.), to whom he addressed some pleasant verses; these and his *Fontenay, La Retraite*, and lines on death are perhaps best worth reading of his poems. In old age he was a friend of Mlle Delaunay (q.v.).

Chaumeix, ABRAHAM-JOSEPH DE (*c.* 1730–90), an opponent of the *philosophes*, author of *Préjugés légitimes contre l'Encyclopédie* (1758–9). Voltaire called him 'barbouilleur de papier'.

Chaumière indienne, La (1761), a philosophical romance by Bernardin de Saint-Pierre (q.v.).

Chauvin, NICOLAS, a soldier in the wars of the Revolution and the Empire. He was wounded seventeen times and became celebrated for his patriotism and his devotion to Napoleon. Songs were written about him and the word *Chauvinisme* was coined to denote the sentimental, almost fanatical, patriotism of the soldiers of that time.

Chef-d'œuvre inconnu, Le, one of the 'Études philosophiques' of Balzac's *Comédie humaine* (q.v.).

Chemin de paradis, Le (1894), by Charles Maurras (q.v.), philosophical tales.

Chemin de velours, Le (1902), by Remy de Gourmont (q.v.), essays.

Chêne de Vincennes, the oak under which, it is said, Saint Louis administered justice to his subjects and protected the widow and the orphan. It is sometimes referred to as symbolical of the king's ancient status as head of the judicature.

Chênedollé, CHARLES - JULIEN DE (1769–1833), born at Vire (Normandy), author of *Le Génie de l'homme* (1807), a didactic poem, and *Études poétiques* (1820), odes. He is better remembered as a lover of literature and the admirer and friend of his more famous contemporaries, e.g. Chateaubriand, Mme de Staël, Rivarol, Joubert, &c. (qq.v.). As an *émigré* in Hamburg (q.v.) he came under the spell of Rivarol and for two years played a devoted, at times critical, Boswell to the great wit's Johnson (*L'Esprit de Rivarol*, 1808). Later he was one of Mme de Staël's circle at Coppet (q.v.). He was allowed to return to France in 1799. From 1810 he filled an educational post at Rouen and Caen and lived contentedly among his flowers and orchards. The strong love of nature shown in some of his *Études poétiques* brought him into sympathy with the young romantic poets (see *Romantisme*), to whose reviews (e.g. *La Muse française*) he occasionally contributed. He has thus a certain importance as a link between two contrasting generations of writers.

Chénier, ANDRÉ (1762–94), generally regarded as the greatest French poet of the 18th century, was born at Constantinople, where his father was French consul. His mother, a Greek, settled in Paris when he was five, his father having been moved to Morocco. After a year in the army he travelled in Switzerland and Italy, and was for three years (1787–90) attached to the French Embassy in London, a distasteful sojourn. He was active in the early revolutionary movement but protested against its later excesses. He was imprisoned for four months during the Terror, and tried, condemned, and executed two days before the fall of Robespierre. It is said that before being guillotined he touched his head and said: 'Pourtant, il y avait quelque chose là.'

Only two of his poems (*Le Serment du Jeu de Paume* and the *Hymne sur l'entrée triomphale des Suisses révoltés du régiment de Châteauvieux*) were published in his lifetime. Chateaubriand included extracts from his work in *Le Génie du Christianisme* (q.v.) and an edition of his poems (by Henri de Latouche, q.v.) appeared in 1819. The first edition to approach completeness was that of 1874. A definitive edition (Dimoff), from the manuscripts bequeathed to the Bibliothèque nationale, was published between 1908 and 1919 (3 vols.).

Chénier conceived some great philosophical poems (*Hermès, L'Amérique*), tracing through the ages the history of man and the course of science and discovery, but he died too soon to complete them. His most characteristic work, which won him the name of 'the French Theocritus', is in his shorter eclogues, idylls, odes, and elegies (*La Jeune Tarentine, La Jeune Captive, Clytie,* &c.) and a few longer poems, e.g. *L'Aveugle* (Homer welcomed on Scyros) and *Le Mendiant*. They show his intense devotion to ancient classical literature, especially the Greek elegiac poets with whom his mind was pervaded. He carried into his poems their delicate grace and melody, giving expression in the old pagan spirit to his love of nature, youth, and beauty. His *Iambes*, lyrical satires written during his imprisonment (and smuggled out of prison), reveal his disgust and despair at the atrocities of the Terror.

Chénier has been called the last of the Classics and the first of the Romantics because, while purely classical in spirit, he prepared the way for the Romantics (see *Romantisme*) by his metrical innovations: he departed from the convention that rhythmical and grammatical pauses should coincide, and by his free use of *enjambement* (q.v.) he restored to French versification a harmony and suppleness which had disappeared during the 18th century. His literary doctrine is set forth in the poem *L'Invention*, 400 lines on the literary art.

Chénier, MARIE-JOSEPH (1764–1811), brother of the preceding, author of tragedies, many on subjects from French national history (notably *Charles IX*, q.v., 1789, which fanned the flames of the Revolution); also of odes, of satires and epistles in a sober and vigorous style, and of many patriotic songs and hymns. These, often composed to order, were usually heard for the first time at the *Fêtes de la Fédération* (q.v.). They include the famous *Chant du départ* (1794, q.v.), the *Chant du 14 juillet*, the *Hymne à la liberté*, and the *Hymne à l'Être Suprême*. His *Épître sur la calomnie* (1797) was an eloquent reply to accusations of complicity in the death of his brother André. He also wrote a *Tableau historique de l'état et des progrès de la littérature française depuis 1789* (1808).

Chennevière, GEORGES (1884–1929), *unanimiste* (q.v.) poet, author of *Le Printemps* (1910), *Appel au monde* (1919), *Le Chant du verger* (1923), *Pamir* (1926), *La Légende du roi d'un jour* (1927), &c., and of collected *Œuvres poétiques* (1929). He collaborated with Jules Romains (q.v.) in a *Petit traité de versification* (1923) defining the aims of *l'unanimisme*.

Cherbuliez, VICTOR (1829–99), of Swiss origin, wrote successful novels of manners in which sensational happenings were often placed against an historical or archaeological background, e.g. *Le Comte Kostia* (1863), *Un Cheval de Phidias* (1864), *Le Prince Vitale* (1864), *Le Roman d'une honnête femme* (1866), &c.

Chéri (1920) and ***La Fin de Chéri*** (1926), novels by Colette (q.v.).

Chérie (1884), a novel by Edmond de Goncourt (q.v.).

Chérubin, a character in Beaumarchais's *Mariage de Figaro* (q.v.).

Cherubini, SALVATORE (1760–1842), composer, Florentine by birth, later naturalized French, lived in Paris from 1788. He composed much of the official music of the Revolution, and from 1821 was Director of the Paris *Conservatoire de musique*. (See also *Méhul*.)

Chevalier à la Charrette, Le, or ***Lancelot,*** a *roman breton* (q.v.) by Chrétien de Troyes (q.v.), composed about 1172, but left unfinished and completed by Godefroy de Lagny. The subject of the poem had been indicated to him by Marie de Champagne

(daughter of Eleanor of Aquitaine). This subject is the love of Lancelot for Queen Guinevere, conceived as 'amour courtois' (q.v.), the absolute subjection of the lover to the caprices of his mistress. Meleagant, son of Bademagne king of Logres, a land 'dont nus estranges ne retorne', has carried off Queen Guinevere, having defeated Keu the seneschal, to whom, in reply to Meleagant's challenge, she had been entrusted. Lancelot and Gauvain (Gawain) set out in pursuit. They meet a cart driven by a dwarf, and Lancelot asks the dwarf whether he has seen the queen. The dwarf replies that if Lancelot will get into the cart he will learn what has become of her. Lancelot hesitates for a moment before consenting to what is utter degradation for a knight, then mounts the cart. After braving danger and temptation, Lancelot reaches Logres, defeats Meleagant, and rescues the queen, only to be received by her with contemptuous coldness, because of his momentary hesitation before mounting the cart. However, after Lancelot has been treacherously seized by Meleagant's men and a report of his death has reached Guinevere, she repents of her harshness, greets Lancelot kindly, and finally admits him at night to her chamber. This occasions a second successful combat with Meleagant and a second treacherous imprisonment, and it is Gauvain who conducts the queen back to Arthur's court. Here, at a tourney, Lancelot is further tested by his lady, for on the first two days, appearing as an unknown knight, he is ordered to play the coward, and only on the third day is allowed to show his prowess.

In this poem a very special sense is given to 'amour courtois': it is not only unlawful and clandestine; its commands override those of every duty. The character of Guinevere is in striking contrast to those of Chrétien's earlier heroines, Énide and Fénice.

Chevalier à la mode, Le, a comedy in prose by Dancourt, produced in 1687, generally considered his best work; a good comedy of manners, illustrating by many touches the society of the day.

The principal characters are the Chevalier, an adventurer in search of a rich marriage, but also susceptible to the charms of a pretty face; Mme Patin, the foolish purse-proud widow of a tax-farmer, a typical *parvenue*;

the Baronne, another wealthy widow; and Mme Patin's niece, a pretty but gullible damsel. The chevalier is paying court to all three, undecided which of the widows he shall marry, while he has won the niece's heart by masquerading as a marquis. Trouble arises when the three ladies find that each has received from her admirer an identical set of verses composed expressly for her; but from this difficulty the Chevalier ingeniously extricates himself. Finally an injudicious attempt simultaneously to marry Mme Patin and to carry off her niece leads to the confrontation of the Chevalier with both his intended victims at the same time, and to his consequent frustration; but he remains imperturbable in his impudence.

Chevalier à l'épée, Le, a 13th-century metrical romance of the Round Table cycle, relating an episode in the life of Gauvain (Gawain), who escaping the attack of a magical sword in the castle of a treacherous knight, wins his daughter; but she presently deserts him for a rival.

Chevalier au barisel, Le, a medieval verse tale of an impious knight who confessing himself, in a spirit of defiance, of his misdeeds to a hermit, is ordered for sole penance to fill a little barrel at a neighbouring stream. This he light-heartedly undertakes to do, and is infuriated to find that the water invariably runs away. For a year he strives, but without success. He returns to the hermit, who implores the mercy of God on him. Moved by the hermit's prayer, the knight lets drop a single tear of humility, which immediately fills the barrel. Then the knight dies, in a state of perfect repentance.

Chevalier au Cygne, Le, with the **Roman de Godefroi de Bouillon** and **Elioxe** (or *Naissance du Chevalier au Cygne*), forms a group of 13th-century poems in monorhyme stanzas embodying legends connected with the house of Godefroi de Bouillon and therefore attached to the cycle of the Crusade (see *Antioche*). The history of the house and of Godefroi himself form the subject-matter of the first two poems. According to the first, Elias, the ancestor of the house, gained the name of 'chevalier au cygne' by coming forward as champion of the countess de Bouillon in a skiff drawn by a swan. He married the daughter of the countess, and

their grandson was Godefroi de Bouillon (cf. the legend of Lohengrin). In *Elioxe*, a poem of somewhat later date, the ancestor above mentioned is one of six brothers metamorphosed by enchantment into swans, of whom he alone recovers human shape.

There is a 14th-century English version of the legend called *Chevalere Assigne*.

Chevalier au lion, Le, see *Yvain*.

Chevalier aux deux épées, Le, an Arthurian metrical romance of the early 13th century containing more than 12,000 lines, relating the adventures of Meriadeuc, known as the knight of the two swords (because he alone succeeds in unloosing a certain sword from its fastening and girds it by the side of his own). Many adventures of Gauvain (Gawain) are interwoven with the story.

Chevalier de Maison Rouge, Le (1846), an historical novel of the Revolution, by Dumas *père*. (See *Maison Rouge*.)

Chevalier des Touches, Le (1864), by J. Barbey d'Aurevilly (q.v.), is a stirring tale, set in the immediately post-Revolutionary period, of the adventures, imprisonment, and amazing rescue of a Chouan leader (see *Chouannerie, La*). It has a notable opening picture of decayed provincial aristocrats exchanging reminiscences at their evening gathering.

Chevaliers de la Table Ronde, the Arthurian Knights of the Round Table (see *Romans bretons*). They are burlesqued in *Les Chevaliers de la Table Ronde* (1937), a play by Cocteau (q.v.).

Chevaux de Diomède, Les (1897), a novel by Remy de Gourmont (q.v.).

Chèvrefeuille, see *Marie de France*.

Chevreuse, MARIE DE ROHAN, DUCHESSE DE (1600–79), daughter of Hercule de Rohan, a faithful supporter of Henri IV, married first the duc de Luynes, constable of France, and secondly Claude de Lorraine, duc de Chevreuse. A woman of beauty and restless energy, she is famous for the plots and intrigues in which she took a leading part against Richelieu and later against Mazarin, down to the time of the Fronde. Her conspiracies were foiled and she suffered repeated exile (she was in England for some years from 1648). She finally accepted her defeat, was reconciled with Mazarin, and died in retirement.

Chevrillon, ANDRÉ (1864–1957), man of letters and critic, author of *Études . . .* and *Nouvelles études anglaises* (1901 and 1910), *Kipling* (1903), &c., studies which did much to deepen French understanding and appreciation of contemporary English writers, e.g. Galsworthy, Kipling, Meredith, Wells. His output also included a critical study of Taine, who was his uncle (*Taine, formation de sa pensée*, 1932), and several volumes of travel sketches, interesting, and poetically written: *Sanctuaires et paysages d'Asie* (1905), *Un Crépuscule d'Islam: Maroc* (1907), *Marrakech dans les palmes* (1920). His evocation of *La Bretagne d'hier* (1925) was highly praised.

Chichevache, Dit de, a medieval satire in which Chichevache (for *Chiche face*, thin-face) is a fabulous monster said to feed only on patient wives, and is fearfully thin in consequence, while Bigorne, who feeds on patient husbands, fattens on his abundant diet. Chaucer, in the *Clerk's Tale*, ll. 1132 et seq., has:

O noble wyves, ful of heigh prudence,
Let noon humilitie your tongues nayle . . .
Lest Chichevache you swolwe in her
    entrayle.

Chicot, the king's gentleman jester, a character in historical romances by Dumas *père*, e.g. *La Dame de Monsoreau, Les Quarante-cinq*, &c. His prototype was a Gascon country nobleman, Antoine d'Anglerays (killed, 1592, at the siege of Rouen), who came to court and became the friend and unofficial adviser of Henri III.

Chien-Caillou (1847), a tale by Champfleury (q.v.).

Chien de Montargis. Aubry de Montdidier, a gentleman of the court of Charles V, was assassinated in 1371 by a man named Richard de Macaire, in a forest near Montargis. Aubry's dog, by its behaviour, roused suspicion against Macaire. The king ordered a judicial combat between dog and man. Macaire was overcome by the dog, confessed his crime, and was executed (cf. *Macaire*).

Children's reading. For long after the invention of printing French children had no special reading matter of their own. They read sacred books, or shortened versions of the books read by their elders. Or they had catechisms and grammars. The 17th century enlarged their field with the legends and romances of the *Bibliothèque bleue* (q.v.), though these, like La Fontaine's *Fables,* also of the 17th century, were not intended specially for children. In 1689 Fénelon, in his *Traité de l'éducation des filles,* suggested that something more was required. Fénelon himself wrote fables, and *Télémaque* (q.v.), with the idea of entertaining and at the same time instructing his young pupil the duc de Bourgogne, grandson of Louis XIV; and the something more he had in mind came with Perrault's *Contes de ma mère l'oye* (1697), traditional tales remembered from childhood and collected and set down for other children. *Le Petit Chaperon rouge, Le Petit-Poucet, La Belle au bois dormant,* &c., were in this. A year later (1698) Mme d'Aulnoy's *Contes des fées* were published, containing such well-known tales as *Gracieuse et Percinet.*

Eighteenth-century children were steered carefully out of fairyland by Mme Leprince de Beaumont and Mme de Genlis. Both had been governesses in royal families, and both held that every hour of a child's time should be made to instruct and edify. Mme Leprince de Beaumont made one happy slip: her *Magasin des enfants, contes moraux* (1757) contained the story of Beauty and the Beast. But Mme de Genlis never wavered. Her theories can be found in *Adèle et Théodore, ou Lettres sur l'éducation* (1782): no fairy-tales, no make-believe; marvels must always be capable of a rational explanation. On those lines she wrote the *Veillées du château* (1784), the priggish, moral, and instructive tales which—so the plan of the book goes—were read aloud in the evenings to three children aged ten or so as a reward for good behaviour during the day. (The poor wretches were sometimes basely ungrateful and preferred to hide in a corner with a fairy story.)

In 1782 Berquin (q.v.), the publisher, issued the first small volume of his *Ami des enfants,* dialogues, tales, and sketches about children who spent their lives doing good to the (always servile) poor; who were transformed by wise guardians from insufferable little bullies into considerate little playmates; and who, if seldom convinced, were certainly crushed by their parents' common-sense replies to their questions. During the Revolution Berquin was denounced as a Girondin. Everyone turned against him and he lived out a neglected old age. Perhaps the immense popularity of his tales consoled him.

Bouilly, another Revolutionary politician, forgot *Liberté, Égalité, Fraternité* every morning while he taught his daughter to spell. He dictated the beginnings of tales, but insisted on their being correctly copied before he would supply the ends. The method must have succeeded, for his *Contes à ma fille* (1809) and *Contes aux enfants de France* (1824–5) disputed childish preferences with Berquin's tales. The child Anatole France read both authors, and in old age paid loving tribute to them (in *Le Petit Pierre*).

Some of Bouilly's tales appeared in the *Dimanche des enfants*. By the mid-19th century children had a choice of periodicals, e.g. *Le Journal des enfants* (founded 1833), and *La Semaine des enfants* (founded 1857). *Le Magasin d'éducation et de récréation* (founded 1864) was of the *Boys' Own Paper* type. It serialized many tales by Jules Verne (q.v.) for older children; and it contained pictures and stories for very young children. These last, from 1863, had *La Poupée modèle* of their own. The *Comic Cuts* type of paper, with stories told chiefly by picture, began about 1890, e.g. *Le Petit Français illustré* (1890–6). Already from about 1850 special children's sets of *Images d'Épinal* (q.v.) were being produced, sheets of coloured pictures (cf. our own *scraps*) illustrating legend, history, and contemporary events. They sold at something like two for one *sou*.

During the 19th century children's books were produced in increasing number. The pattern was still very much that set by Berquin and Bouilly. A naturally lively, impetuous child learns through many painful experiences—watched with a sadistically stoic eye by the parents—that things are not what they seem. The description 'ouvrage qui intéresse toutes les mères en jetant dans les jeunes cœurs les germes de la morale, les semences de la vertu' fitted all of them. But morals and virtues apart, the tales were for children, about children; and they had the detailed fidelity to daily life which children demand even in a fairy-tale. Bound in the bright red of the *Bibliothèque rose*, a series guaranteed safe for childish reading, they sold

in their thousands. Far and away the most popular were the 'Sophie' books, the stories which, to begin with, the invalid Mme de Ségur told to her own children because she could not play with them (*Les Petites Filles modèles*, 1858; *Les Vacances*, 1859; *Les Malheurs de Sophie*, 1864; *Un Bon Petit Diable*, 1865, &c.). Sophie was a French younger sister of Miss Edgeworth's Rosamund. Rosamund, given the choice between having her shoes repaired or buying the purple jar in a chemist's window, preferred to hop about, protesting comfort, in a shoe with a flapping sole: Sophie cut off her eyebrows to make them grow thick.

There were, too, highly popular tales, perhaps not for the youngest children, by writers associated usually with an adult public: *La Fée aux miettes* and other tales of gentle fantasy by Nodier; *Histoire d'un casse-noisette*, *La Bouillie de la comtesse Berthe*, by Dumas *père*; the *Contes d'une grand-mère* of George Sand; Paul de Musset's *Monsieur le Vent et Madame la Pluie*. Animal stories were written, and read: the hardworking, astute Cadichon of Mme de Ségur's *Mémoires d'un âne* (1860) and the bears of Genin's *La Famille Martin* (1868) were favourites.

The much younger children seem to have had no nursery rhymes, no literature of sheer inconsequence, but they had the old French songs—*Sur le pont d'Avignon*, *Au clair de la lune*—and, in the 19th century, adaptations of La Fontaine's *Fables*. They and their older brothers and sisters also had the fairy tales of Grimm and Hans Andersen (translated *c.* 1840) to add to their own Perrault. When they reached adventure-story age they had over sixty books by Jules Verne (1828–1905, q.v.), or the popular historical tales by Erckmann-Chatrian (q.v.); and in translation they had Fenimore Cooper and Mayne Reid.

It was, in fact, on translations that the older French children of the 19th century were chiefly brought up. They read and loved, as not only French children have done, many books that were not always written in the first place for children: *Robinson Crusoe*, the reading chosen by Rousseau for his *Émile* (there were many *Nouveaux Robinson*); *Gulliver's Travels*; *Don Quixote*; *The Baron von Münchhausen*; the *Arabian Nights*; Dickens, especially

Dickens. A later, and to this day still a great, favourite was Kipling. His *Just So Stories* and the Jungle Books were to become minor classics in French as well as in their native tongue.

Each 20th-century Christmas peoples the children's bookshops with new characters. Some young people were fortunate enough to read Max Jacob's *Histoire du Roi Kaboul Ier et du Marmiton Gauwain* and *Le Géant du soleil* (both 1904) before these two tales became unobtainable. Marcel Aymé's *Contes du chat perché* (1934) and Saint-Exupéry's *Le Petit Prince* (1943) are rightly loved. But Perrault is still read, with Sophie a good second.

Chimène, the heroine of Corneille's *Le Cid.*

Chimères, Les, twelve sonnets by Gérard de Nerval (q.v.), published in 1854 as an appendix to *Les Filles du feu.* Their beauty and magic of language triumph over an obscurity due to mythological and occult allusions and also—a surprisingly modern note—to the elliptical quality of the poet's writing. The best known are: *El Desdichado* (' Je suis le ténébreux, le veuf, l'inconsolé'), *Artémis,* and *Le Christ aux oliviers,* a sequence of five which had already been published, in 1853, in the author's *Petits châteaux de Bohême.* The title *El Desdichado* is said to be taken from the disguised champion in *Ivanhoe* (I. ix), whose shield bore the device of a young oak tree pulled up by the roots, with the Spanish word 'Desdichado', signifying disinherited.

Choderlos de Laclos, PIERRE, see *Laclos.*

Choisy, FRANÇOIS-TIMOLÉON, ABBÉ DE (1644–1724), descended through his mother from the Chancelier de l'Hôpital (q.v.), an eccentric and effeminate character, who after receiving the education of a courtier and spending many years in frivolity and dissipation (he had a mania for masquerading as a woman) became a missionary and made in 1685 a voyage to Siam (of which he has left an agreeable *Journal*). He wrote some second-rate historical works, and left interesting *Mémoires pour servir à l'histoire de Louis XIV*, published in 1727. They are scattered fragments, written in a familiar attractive style, and contain some striking portraits, e.g. of Colbert. He was admitted to the *Académie* in 1687.

Choix des élues (1939), a novel by Jean Giraudoux (q.v.).

Cholières, NICOLAS, SIEUR DE (second half of the 16th century), an advocate of Grenoble and prose writer, author of *Neuf Matinées* (1585) and *Après-Dinées* (1587), conversations between friends giving occasion for tales, after the style of, but inferior in interest to, the *Propos rustiques* of Noël du Fail and the *Serées* of Guillaume Bouchet (qq.v.).

Chopin, FRÉDÉRIC-FRANÇOIS (1810–49), composer, born near Warsaw of half Polish, half French parentage. He left Poland under the Russian oppression in 1831 and thereafter lived mainly in Paris. His place in the present *Companion* is due to his connexion with the novelist George Sand (q.v.). He died, aged thirty-nine, of consumption, from which he was already suffering when he made the unhappy expedition described in *Un Hiver à Majorque* (1841, q.v.). There are many interesting references to him in Delacroix's (q.v.) *Journal.*

Chouannerie, La, the Royalist insurrections in Brittany and Normandy during the Revolution (cf. *Vendée*). 'Chouan', a Breton dialect word for 'owl', is said to have been applied to the insurgents because of the long, fluttering cry with which they signalled to one another during the night. Historical novels of the *Chouannerie* are: Balzac's *Les Chouans;* Hugo's *Quatre-vingt-treize;* Barbey d'Aurevilly's *Le Chevalier des Touches; Sous la hache* by Élémir Bourges (qq.v.).

Chouans, Les (1829), an historical novel of the *Chouannerie* (see above), was Balzac's first successful novel and the first written under his own name. It became one of the 'Scènes de la vie militaire' of his *Comédie humaine* (q.v.). Mlle de Verneuil, a beautiful dancer at the Opera, and the illegitimate daughter of a noble, comes to Brittany on a Government mission. She is to make the acquaintance of the leader of the Royalist insurgents, win his affection, and induce him to betray his forces. She falls genuinely in love with her victim and dies in an unsuccessful attempt to save his life.

Chourineur, Le, a character in Eugène Sue's (q.v.) *Les Mystères de Paris.*

Chrestien, Florent, see *Satire Ménippée.*

Chrétien de Troyes, who flourished in the second half of the 12th century, was the author of the earliest *romans bretons* (q.v.) that have reached us. He frequented the court of Marie of Champagne (daughter of Eleanor of Aquitaine) and probably visited England. His earliest works, with the exception of *Philomena* (on the story of Procne and Philomela as told by Ovid), are lost; they included a poem, composed *c.* 1165, on Mark and Iseult. He wrote *c.* 1168 *Erec* (q.v. on an Arthurian knight of that name) and (*c.* 1170) *Cligès* (q.v., containing episodes taken from Oriental tradition, but adapted to the purposes of the Breton cycle); a little later (*c.* 1172) the *Chevalier à la Charrette* (q.v.) or *Lancelot* (finished by another hand); later again *Yvain* (q.v.) or the *Chevalier au Lion*; and finally (*c.* 1175) *Perceval* (q.v.) or the *Conte del Graal.*

Chrétien was one of the great literary figures of his time, and his works were widely translated and imitated. His fame and influence rested on his skill as a narrator, interweaving love and adventure, and on his imagination and his use of the mysterious and supernatural. He is also remarkable for his subtle delineation of character, his elegance of expression and easy and varied handling of the octosyllabic couplet. His studies of moral and psychological questions connected with love also interested his contemporaries. He wrote for a cultivated and aristocratic society, largely dominated by women, where the ideal of courtly love (*amour courtois*, q.v.) was fostered, and it is courtly love which is chiefly analysed in his poems. With the deeper emotions he is not concerned.

Christ aux oliviers, Le, by Gérard de Nerval; see *Chimères, Les.*

Christine de Pisan (*c.* 1364–*c.* 1430), born in Venice, the daughter of an Italian physician in the service of Charles V, and brought up in Paris. She was left a widow at twenty-five, and, afflicted by private and public misfortunes, ended her life in a convent. She was a woman of intelligence and education (a 'blue-stocking' in the opinion of some), and wrote both in prose and verse. Her prose works include *La Cité des dames* (largely a translation of the *De claris mulieribus* of

Boccaccio) and *Le Livre des Trois Vertus* (a treatise on women's education). In her *Épître au dieu d'amour* (1399) and *Dit de la Rose* (1400) she ardently took up the defence of her sex against the strictures of Jean de Meung. She also wrote a *Livre des faicts et bonnes meurs du roi Charles* (i.e. Charles V). Her poetry comprised *ballades* (q.v.) and longer poems on themes of love, also a *Ditié en l'honneur de Jeanne d'Arc* (whose early successes she witnessed), showing her devotion to the country of her adoption. Of this and her other patriotic tales an English translation was printed by Caxton (*The Fayttes of Arms*, 1489). Another translation, *The City of Ladies*, was probably printed originally by Wynkyn de Worde.

Chronicles [Chroniques]. For those relating to the Crusades, see *Croisades.* For those relating to French and general history, see *Grandes Chroniques*; *Froissart*; and under *History* (Medieval period), where there is reference to the chronicles of Philippe Mousket, Geoffroy de Paris, Guillaume Guiart, the Ménestrel de Reims, the *Chroniques de Hainaut* (or of Baudouin d'Avesnes), the Anonyme de Béthune, Bouciquaut, Juvénal des Ursins, the Bourgeois de Paris, &c.

Chronique des Pasquier (1933–45), the covering title of ten novels by Georges Duhamel (q.v.) about a family (in many ways resembling the author's) who grow up in the late 19th and early 20th centuries. The early volumes are dominated by the vigorously drawn character of the father, the amoral but immortal—by his own testimony —Raymond Pasquier, who is continually embarking on new ventures. He trails his family around in the process but remains magnificently unrepentant in face of their haphazard growth and the embarrassments in which he lands them. The worlds of music and science are portrayed; and vol. 5, *Le Désert de Bièvres*, is a thinly disguised account of Duhamel's own experiences (*c.* 1907) as one of the *Abbaye* (q.v.) community.

The titles of the separate volumes are:

(1) *Le Notaire du Havre*; (2) *Le Jardin des bêtes sauvages*; (3) *Vue de la terre promise*; (4) *La Nuit de la Saint-Jean*; (5) *Le Désert de Bièvres*; (6) *Les Maîtres*; (7) *Cécile parmi nous*; (8) *Combat contre les ombres*; (9) *Suzanne et*

les jeunes hommes; (10) *La Passion de Joseph Pasquier.*

Chronique du règne de Charles IX, (1829), an historical novel by Prosper Mérimée. The principal episode is the massacre of Saint Bartholomew. Georges de Mergy has renounced his Protestant faith and joined the king's bodyguard. His brother Bernard joins the Protestant troops raised by Coligny. In Paris Bernard falls in love with Diane de Turgis (a Catholic) and during the massacre of Saint Bartholomew his life is saved by the mere chance that he has been spending the night with his mistress. He escapes to La Rochelle disguised as a monk. During the siege of La Rochelle he strikes down one of the besiegers and discovers that he has killed his own brother.

In one of the early chapters Bernard de Mergy, on his way to Paris, spends a night at an inn filled with Huguenot soldiers. He joins them for dinner and listens to the legend of the Pied Piper of Hamelin told by a camp follower.

This work has neither the dramatic nor the poetic quality of its famous contemporaries *Notre-Dame de Paris* and *Cinq-Mars* (qq.v.), but is sometimes preferred to either for its fidelity to history and the effective sobriety of its telling.

Chronique scandaleuse, a name given (without good grounds) to the *Journal de Jean de Roye*, a chronicle covering the reign of Louis XI.

Chrysale, a character in Molière's *Les Femmes savantes* (q.v.).

Chute des feuilles, La, one of the elegies by which the poet Millevoye (q.v.) is remembered.

Chute d'un ange, La (1838), by Lamartine, the opening fragment of an uncompleted epic intended to depict the gradual purification of the human soul (cf. *Jocelyn*, another fragment). The work was coldly received. Plan and themes required more vigorous powers of dramatic narrative than Lamartine possessed.

In the early days of the creation the angel Cédar becomes enamoured of Daidha, a daughter of Eve. He defies Divine wrath and assumes man's shape to win her love. The two experience a series of disastrous adventures which at one point take them to the city of the tyrant Nemphed, on the banks of the Euphrates, and which are the occasion for long, strained descriptions of vice, profligacy, and horror. Finally their children perish of thirst in the desert and Daidha succumbs to her miseries. Cédar makes a funeral pyre of the bodies, and afterwards leaps into the flames himself. A spirit scatters the ashes and prophesies that the fallen angel must expiate his sin throughout nine incarnations. The poem ends with the first rains of the Deluge.

Cid, Le, a tragedy by Corneille (described in the earlier editions of his works as a tragicomedy), produced in 1637, his most famous drama. It is based on *Las Mocedades del Cid* (1621), a play by Guilhem de Castro, dealing with the youth of Rodrigo Ruy Diaz de Bivar, el Cid Campeador, the partly historical partly mythical hero of Spain.

The scene is Seville. Rodrigue, a young Castilian noble, and Chimène, a lady of high birth, are in love with one another, and their marriage is in contemplation. But a quarrel breaks out between his father, Don Diègue, and the count, her father, in which the former receives the unforgivable affront of a slap in the face. He draws his sword, but his age makes him no match for his younger adversary. He calls upon his son to avenge the insult, and Rodrigue, after a brief conflict between his love for Chimène and his sense of honour, calls out the count and kills him. Chimène rushes to the king, demanding Rodrigue's life as the penalty. The king temporizes. Rodrigue presents himself to Chimène, offers her his sword, and begs her to kill him, preferring death at her hand to death by the executioner. A fine scene follows, in which Chimène is torn between her passion for Rodrigue and her duty to her dead father; and the two lovers, each recognizing the noble motives of the other, lament their hard destiny. She refuses to kill Rodrigue, but will pursue her demand for vengeance, yet hoping that it may not be granted. The approach is announced of a Moorish fleet threatening Seville. At once Rodrigue sets off with five hundred retainers of his father to meet it. By prodigies of valour he destroys the Moors and captures their two kings, who hail him as 'le Cid' ('El Seyd', the lord). This feat wins for him the king's pardon, but Chimène again demands vengeance. The king consents to a single combat between Rodrigue and a champion of Chimène; her hand is to be given to the victor. Rodrigue again presents himself to Chimène: he will not defend himself in the duel, and accepts death. But Chimène's love for him will not allow this. She urges him to fight and win, if only to save her from marriage with his rival. He fights and disarms his adversary, but spares his life. Chimène's emotion when, seeing the latter return alive from the combat, she infers that Rodrigue is dead, convinces the king that she still loves Rodrigue. This she confesses, but even now she cannot reconcile her sense of duty with marriage to her father's slayer. The king sends Rodrigue to command his armies against the Moors, trusting that time and his achievements will solve the conflict. The issue is left uncertain.

The production of this great play, very different in character from any that had preceded it, marked an epoch in the history of French drama. For the conflict of opinion to which it gave rise, see under *Corneille* and *Richelieu*. An English version by Joseph Rutter was performed in England within about a year of the appearance of the original.

Ci-devant, a name during the Revolution for the aristocrats or for persons attached by title or office to the *ancien régime*.

Cigogne, Contes de la, traditional fairy-tales, also known as *Contes de ma Mère l'Oye* (see *Perrault*); or any fanciful tales.

Cimetière marin, Le (1922), Valéry's (q.v.) famous poem on the theme of death.

Cinna, a tragedy by Corneille, produced in late 1640 or early 1641, based on a passage in Seneca's *De clementia* (i. 9), which Montaigne had reproduced in his *Essais* (i. 24). The character of Aemilie was invented by the poet.

Cinna, a grandson of Pompey, although he enjoys the favour and confidence of Augustus, is leader of a conspiracy to assassinate him and restore the liberty of Rome. The magnanimity of the emperor shakes him in his resolve, but he loves Aemilie, daughter of C. Toranius, a victim of the proscriptions of the Triumvirate, and she, though she has been nourished in the emperor's house, spurs Cinna on, making the avenging of her father the price of her hand. Maxime, another prominent conspirator though also in the Emperor's confidence, causes the plot to be revealed to Augustus, under pretence of repentance, but in reality because he secretly loves Aemilie and hopes to induce her, after the arrest of Cinna, to escape with him from Italy. But Aemilie proudly rejects the proposal. The emperor, horrified at Cinna's treachery, but weary of bloodshed, hesitates what course to follow. In a final sequence of scenes we have Cinna and Aemilie admitting their ingratitude and begging to die together; and Maxime, whom the Emperor believes to have revealed the plot from remorse, confessing his base betrayal of his friend, of his love, and of his master. Augustus, overwhelmed by this avowal, decides to triumph over his anger, pardons all three, and restores them to favour, thereby winning their repentance and future allegiance.

The play is an example of Corneille's interest in political themes, of which his later dramas afford other examples.

Cinq auteurs, Les. Cardinal Richelieu (q.v.), who had literary ambitions and decided views about the drama, employed five authors to write plays under his direction. Sometimes he chose the subject himself, as in the case of *La Comédie des Tuileries* (in which Corneille had a large share), performed before the king in 1635. The five authors were Corneille, Boisrobert, Colletet, L'Estoile, and Rotrou (qq.v.). Other titles remembered are *La Grande Pastorale*, *L'Aveugle de Smyrne*, &c.

Cinq grandes odes (1910), by Claudel (q.v.).

Cinq-Mars, ou Une Conjuration sous Louis XIII (1826), an historical novel by Alfred de Vigny, based on the conspiracy against Cardinal Richelieu headed by the king's favourite, the young Henri Coiffier de Ruzé, marquis de Cinq-Mars (1620–42), and his friend De Thou (q.v.). The plot failed, a secret treaty enlisting Spanish support was discovered, and the two leaders perished on the scaffold. The book is slow-moving, but poetical in conception. Much of its interest lies in its background, painted with lavish, if not unfailingly accurate, detail. Noteworthy incidents are the trial of Urbain Grandier, a priest whom Richelieu has reasons for putting out of the way; the evening in the *salon* of the courtesan Marion Delorme, at which the conspiracy comes to a head, while the young Descartes (q.v.) and the poet Milton are among the unwitting guests; and the stately progress of Cardinal Richelieu's barge up the Rhône, towing another barge on which are the prisoners, Cinq-Mars and De Thou.

Cisterciens, see *Cîteaux.*

Cité, Île de la, the island in the Seine on which stands the cathedral of Notre-Dame de Paris. It was the centre of the city in Roman times, a holy place where Roman and Gallic gods were worshipped, the 'beloved Lutetia' of the emperor Julian. It was connected by two bridges with the left and right banks of the river, known later as the Petit Pont and the Grand Pont respectively.

Cité antique, La: Étude sur le culte, le droit, les institutions de la Grèce et de Rome (1864), by Fustel de Coulanges (q.v.), a study—out of date in the light of later knowledge but still eminently readable—of the manner in which the theory of the state in ancient Greece and Rome developed from the primitive belief that each family was protected by its exclusive god. As the families formed groups, then cities, and the cities were eventually incorporated in the state, the family gods were retained, but other gods arose who were common to the groups and cities and finally became more important. To begin with, the laws of the city were framed for the benefit of the families who formed the framework of society and to control religious observance, then religion became a matter of rites by which political and religious government were regulated. With the advent of Christianity the relationship between belief and law weakened, and the fabric of the state was undermined.

Cîteaux [Lat. Cistercium], in Burgundy, south of Dijon, where in 1098 Robert, Abbot of Molesme, founded a monastic order, an offshoot of the Benedictines, known as Cistercians. Saint Bernard was a member of this order.

Cité des Dames, La, see *Christine de Pisan.*

Cité des eaux, La (1902), a collection of poems by Henri de Régnier (q.v.).

Cladel, LÉON (1835–92), born at Montauban, author of realistic tales and novels describing peasant or vagrant life in the district known formerly as Le Quercy (chief town Cahors). They included *Le Bouscassié* (1869), *Les Va-nu-pieds* (1873), *N'a-qu'un œil* (1882), &c.

Claire Lenoir (1867), a tale of mystery and horror by Villiers de l'Isle-Adam (q.v.).

Clairi, ROBERT DE, see *Crusades.*

Clairières dans le ciel (1906), collected poems by Francis Jammes (q.v.).

Clairon, CLAIRE LEGRIS DE LATUDE, *known as* MLLE (1723–1803), a distinguished tragic actress, noted for her acting in Voltaire's tragedies. She died in poverty. Her *Mémoires* were published in 1799.

Claque, a band of people engaged, in fulfilment of a contract ('entreprise de succès dramatique') between a theatre manager and a 'chef de claque', to applaud at theatres. The manager agrees to deliver a certain number of tickets nightly to the *chef de claque* in return for a small sum and an undertaking to produce applause at specified passages. In his *Souvenirs sur le Théâtre Libre* Antoine (q.v.) contrasts his youthful theatre-going as one of a *claque* with his later, director's, stall at the Odéon (q.v.). The origin of the *claque* is said to be in Roman antiquity, when the Emperor Nero played before the people and applause was organized.

Clara d'Ellébeuse, the heroine who has stepped out of a *keepsake* into the tale of this name by Francis Jammes (1899, and included with other tales in *Le Roman du lièvre*, 1903). Brought up by adoring, indulgent parents and adoring, indulgent nuns, amidst all the taboos which were the birthright of a gently born young miss of the eighteen-forties, she was still, at seventeen, romantically, ludicrously ignorant of the facts of life. This led her to fancy that a shy kiss given to a schoolfellow's brother had engendered the 'sad fruit of a lover's embraces'. Shame and terror so tortured her that she wasted in decline before her parents' eyes. And one day she remembered the phial of laudanum in her mother's medicine-chest, and drank it. Bathos would be easy, but the tale is so poetically written, so gracefully and delicately handled, that it is avoided.

Claretie, ARSÈNE-ARNAUD (called *Jules*), (1840–1913), a prolific, versatile, glib but not profound journalist, man of letters, critic, and chronicler whose 20 volumes of *La Vie à Paris* cover the years from 1881 to 1911. His *Portraits contemporains* (1873–5) are popular biography. His dramatic criticism is collected in *Profils de théâtre* (1904).

Clarke, MARY (Mme Jules Mohl) (1793–1883), an Englishwoman, born in London, lived mainly in Paris after 1814 with her widowed mother and became a well-known figure in intellectual circles, the friend of many distinguished men, e.g. Ampère, Cousin, Thierry, and Fauriel (qq.v.), especially the last-named whom at one time she had hoped to marry. Between 1831 and 1838, when she and her mother had rooms at l'Abbaye-aux-Bois (q.v.), where Mme Récamier was living, she was often to be found dispensing tea in Mme Récamier's *salon* (cf. *Récamier*; *Salon*, paras. 6, 7). She was herself a highly gifted woman, a good conversationalist, and her own *salon* before and still more after her marriage in 1847 to the orientalist Jules Mohl (1800–76) was a meeting-place for writers, politicians, and savants, French, English, and German. Dean Stanley and Thackeray were among her English visitors; and so, too, was Mrs. Gaskell.

Classicisme. From the 19th century onwards this word has been employed frequently, in a limited sense, when French literature of the 17th century is discussed, in opposition to *Romantisme* (q.v.). It is with this limited sense that the present, necessarily over-simplified, article is concerned. (The word itself, it may be noted, was still treated as an inadmissible neologism by the 1933 edition of the *Dictionnaire de l'Académie française*.)

(2) 'Classicisme', then, in the present connexion denotes *l'esprit classique*, or *les doctrines classiques*, that is to say, the predominant intellectual attitude of the French 17th and early 18th centuries—the classical era—and, more particularly, the conventions which governed French literature (mainly poetry and poetic drama) at the height of that period, i.e. *c.* 1660–*c.* 1690. The *romantisme* of the 19th century was largely a revolt against these conventions or perhaps, more exactly, against their excessive and exclusive observance as taught and practised at the end of the 18th century by, e.g., La Harpe and Delille (qq.v.).

(3) The whole classical era, from *c.* 1590 to *c.* 1715, is usually considered as falling into three distinguishable periods. There was, first, a so-called formative period (*c.* 1590–*c.* 1660) of reaction against the literary and grammatical precepts of the *Pléiade* and the extravagance and *préciosité* that had crept into literature as a result of Italian and Spanish influence. During these years the language was being purified, in other words freed from archaisms, neologisms, Latinisms, dialect words, &c., and transformed into a clear, intelligible (but less lyrically rich) instrument of literature. At the same time the technique of versification was being elaborated, tragedy as a dramatic form— with the unities an important feature—was evolving, and the potentialities of a prose literature were being realized. Various influences, too, were combining to provoke discussion and formulation of the aesthetic and philosophical bases of literature, for instance the increasing availability of translations from the literature—both creative and critical—of Greece and Rome; and also contemporary social, political, and religious circumstances; for now order and rule, and a revival of religious (i.e. orthodox Roman Catholic) faith, after years of upheaval, encouraged a similar desire for stability and discipline in the arts. (See *Malherbe*; *Balzac, Guez de*; *Bossuet*; *Chapelain*; *Corneille*; *D'Aubignac*; *Pascal*; *Rambouillet, Hôtel de*; *Saint François de Sales*; *Scudéry*; *Vaugelas*.)

(4) These formative years were succeeded by a 'peak' period, *l'âge de raison* (*c.* 1660–*c.* 1690), when technical, aesthetic, and philosophical principles still largely in accord with the doctrines of revealed religion were further, and it seemed for a time finally, evolved (see paras. 6–8 below).

(5) The third period (*c.* 1690 to the death of Louis XIV in 1715) was one of transition to the age of Voltaire and the *philosophes* (qq.v.), to ideas of progress and, with the spread of Cartesianism and the Cartesian

principles of philosophic doubt (see *Descartes*), to religious scepticism: these were ultimately to undermine aesthetic dogmatism.

(6) The conventions which reached their full elaboration during the period *c.* 1660–*c.* 1690 were based on the conviction that the absolute of beauty in literature had already been achieved by *les anciens*, the great writers of Greek and Latin antiquity. These, therefore, were the compulsory, and only admissible, models; and the general and more technical principles of the literary craft could be deduced from their works (notably from Aristotle and Horace). For instance, the object of literature—which itself signified, as it were, the discursive representation of life—was not only to please, but to preserve fidelity to nature. Genius, imagination, and inspiration were undoubtedly prerequisite qualities for the production of the true literary masterpiece, but it was necessary for these to be disciplined by, perhaps almost subordinated to, reason, and to care for artistic perfection.

(7) Reason (in the sense of 'the guiding principle of the human mind in the process of thinking', *O.E.D.*) implied intelligence, judgement, and the care and search for truth—religious, philosophic, and psychological (hence examination of character and motives; hence method and the exercise of common sense; hence also a check on spontaneity, and distaste for any personal element). It implied, further, care for probability, because man, a rational being, is interested in, and thus pleased by, what is generally rather than exceptionally true: 'Le vrai peut quelquefois n'être pas vraisemblable'; 'L'esprit n'est point ému de ce qu'il ne croit pas' (BOILEAU, *Art poét.*). And it implied a comprehension of one's subject so full that one could convey it to the reader with complete clarity: 'Avant donc que d'écrire apprenez à penser' (again Boileau).

(8) The way to artistic perfection was by observance of *les règles des bienséances et des genres.* 'Les bienséances' regulated choice and treatment of subject. They exacted from the writer a sense of fitness (grandeur of subject, with diction and versification in keeping; avoidance of coarseness and triviality; avoid monotony, but *never* attempt to secure a pleasing variety by mixing the sublime and the ridiculous); a sense, too, of proportion (the parts harmonizing with the whole, the avoidance of detail and excess). 'Les règles des genres' concerned the different (at first mainly poetic and dramatic) kinds, and the language, style, and prosodic forms appropriate to them.

(9) *La raison, les bienséances, les genres* were expounded many times by, notably, Boileau (in his *Art poétique*, q.v., also in the *Satires* and *Épîtres*; and cf., too, his *Dialogue des héros de roman*). Great creative and critical writers also associated with this peak period of classicism are La Fontaine, Molière, and Racine.

(10). Taste (*le goût*) at this time became an increasingly important quality—the innate discernment, equilibrium, and technical artistry which enabled an author to observe conventions of subject and treatment drawn from the literature of antiquity and at the same time please and capture the spirit of his 17th-century public. (His public, it is to be noted, consisted mainly of the leisured, aristocratic, and critical circles of the court, 'a small, vital, passionate world … clothed … in ordered beauty': STRACHEY, *Landmarks in Fr. Lit.*) For a time, indeed, during the third, transitional, period (see para. 5 above) *le goût* was all-important. Nevertheless the decline of classicism had set in when *les modernes* threw doubts upon the supremacy of *les anciens* (see *Perrault*; *Querelle des anciens et des modernes*; *Fontenelle*). A new conception, of the *relativité du goût*—that standards of beauty and of artistic perfection must change with the changing spirit of an age—was to develop as time passed. It became one factor in the Romantics' claim that literature should be untrammelled by fixed conventions, and it provided matter for controversy long after the romantic battles had been won. (Cf. *Staël, Mme de*; *Cromwell*; *Racine et Shakespeare*; *Critics and Criticism*.)

Classiques français du Moyen Age, a 'collection de textes français et provençaux antérieurs à 1500' started in 1910 by the publisher Champion under the general supervision of the Directeur-adjoint de l'École des Hautes Études.

Claude (1499–1524), daughter of Louis XII and consort of François Ier, now remembered chiefly as the *Reine Claude* who gave her name to a kind of plum (the greengage).

Claude, JEAN (1619–87), a learned theologian and Protestant pastor, remembered for his controversies with Bossuet. He was much respected by all parties and when, at the Revocation of the Edict of Nantes (1685), he was banished from France the king himself provided him with an escort to the frontier. He spent his remaining years in Holland.

Claude de Pontoux, a 16th-century physician and poet of Chalon, author of a sonnet-sequence entitled *L'Idée*, one of the sources of inspiration of Drayton's *Idea*.

Claude Gueux (1845), by Victor Hugo, a tale written as an indictment of the social system (and first published in 1834, in the *Revue de Paris*). It contains the germ of *Les Misérables* (q.v.). Claude Gueux, an uneducated but intelligent worker, a victim of unemployment, steals a loaf of bread to feed his starving family and is sentenced to five years' hard labour. In prison he is persecuted by a malicious warder. His conduct is exemplary till the warder deliberately removes the fellow prisoner whose sympathy has made his life bearable to another building. In cold despair at this final injustice he murders his persecutor, then tries unsuccessfully to kill himself. For four months he is nursed back to health, then tried and executed.

Claude le Lorrain, Claude Gelée *or* **Gellée,** *known as* (1600–82), born in the Vosges, a famous French landscape painter, who spent his life in Italy.

Claudel, PAUL - LOUIS - CHARLES - MARIE (1868–1955), diplomat, poet, and dramatist, born at Villeneuve-sur-Fère, in the Champagne country, was educated mainly in Paris. About 1890 he frequented Symbolist circles (see *Symbolisme*) and Mallarmé's (q.v.) 'Tuesdays', but he had already entered the Ministère des affaires étrangères and after 1893 he spent some forty years on consular and diplomatic service, much of it in the U.S.A., South America, and the Far East, but also in Europe. His last post was Brussels, in 1933.

Claudel wrote with lyric fervour, bold imagery, and a sensuously religious emotion (he was converted to the Roman Catholic faith after a sudden mystical experience in 1886). His poetic development was also, by his own testimony, influenced by Aeschylus, whom he frequently translated, and by Rimbaud's (q.v.) *Illuminations*. He almost invariably employed the *verset claudélien*, a verse-poem of his own invention, possibly inspired by the Bible, half-way between verse and prose, with neither rhyme nor metre, and limited as it were by the in and out take of a breath. ('L'homme absorbe la vie et restitue, dans l'acte suprême de l'expiration, Une parole intelligible': *La Ville*.)

His early poetic dramas were Symbolist in tendency, and literary rather than dramatic, e.g. *Tête d'or* (1890) and *La Ville* (1893), both included—in revised versions—in the collection *L'Arbre* (1901) which also contains *La Jeune Fille Violaine*. Another play, *Partage de midi*, was published at this time (1906) in a limited edition but only became known when it was produced, and created considerable interest, in 1948. The two works which definitely established his reputation were *L'Otage* (1911, q.v.) and *L'Annonce faite à Marie* (1912, q.v., a later version of *La Jeune Fille Violaine*). These were followed by *Le Pain dur* (1918) and *Le Père humilié* (1920), which complete the trilogy begun by *L'Otage*, and then by the very long drama *Le Soulier de satin* (1925–8, produced in an acting version 1943), described as an 'action espagnole en quatre jours' and set in Spain, Bohemia, and at sea off the Balearic Isles at the end of the 16th century. It is one of Claudel's most elaborate and passionate treatments of his recurrent theme—man, clinging to his earthly, carnal desires and defying the love of God, but experiencing, ultimately, the exquisite joy of surrender.

Claudel's poetical works include, notably, *Cinq grandes odes suivies d'un Processional pour saluer le siècle nouveau* (1910) and *Corona benignitatis anni Dei* (1914); also *Le Chemin de la Croix* (1911), *Deux poèmes d'été* (1914), *Poèmes de guerre 1914–1916* (1922), *Feuilles de saints* (1925). Of his prose, the following may also be mentioned: *Connaissance de l'est* (1900), with some fine descriptive writing; *Art poétique* (1907), reflections on poetic form (his own) and the poetic understanding; and, towards the end of his life, several collections of essays on divers subjects, including much Biblical commentary, e.g. *Accompagnements* (1949), *Une Voix sur Israël* (1950).

Claudine, the heroine, first encountered in *Claudine à l'école*, of a series of novels by 'Colette Willy', see *Colette*.

Claveret, JEAN (1590–1666), dramatist, author of *L'Esprit fort* (1630), the earliest example of the French comedy of manners, presenting the type of man who makes a pretence of strength of character and independence of public opinion; *La Place Royale* (1633), from which Corneille borrowed the title for one of his plays; and other plays of minor importance. He was an adversary of Corneille in the dispute to which *Le Cid* gave rise. He also wrote a *Traité du poëme dramatique*, in which he protested against the rule restricting the period of a drama to twenty-four hours.

Clélie, a romance by Madeleine de Scudéry, in ten volumes, published 1654–60. It is based on the Roman legend of the Cloelia who, having been given as a hostage to the Etruscan king Porsenna, escaped, and swimming the Tiber returned to Rome. In the romance Aronce, son of Porsenna, is in love with Clélie, daughter of a Roman exile. His rival Horace, a young Roman patrician, carries her off to Rome. The Tarquins are expelled from Rome and with Porsenna and Aronce besiege the city. A truce is concluded and Clélie is given by the Romans as a hostage, but to escape the attentions of Sextus Tarquinius swims the Tiber and returns to Rome. Sent back once more as a hostage, she is carried off by Sextus. Aronce pursues and slays him and is united with Clélie. As in the *Grand Cyrus* (q.v.) this principal thread of story is interrupted by a great number of episodes, digressions, and discussions of points of gallantry; and various contemporaries of the author, such as Louis XIV, Fouquet, Ninon de Lenclos, are depicted under ancient names. At the end of the first part Mlle de Scudéry introduced the famous *Carte de Tendre* (q.v.).

Clément, JACQUES, a Dominican friar, who assassinated Henri III in 1589.

Cléomadès or **Le Cheval de Fust,** a fantastic metrical romance of the late 13th century, by Adenet le Roi (q.v.), in which a wooden horse, flying through the air, carries those who ride it to various adventures. The romance is of special interest for the picture it gives of the mode of life of Pinçonnet, a *ménestrel* (q.v.).

Cléopâtre captive, the first French tragedy, by Jodelle (q.v.); it was performed in 1553 (New Style), 1552 (Old Style), at the house of the archbishops of Rheims in Paris, in the presence of the king. It is based on Plutarch's narrative and is written, except the choruses, partly in alexandrines, partly in decasyllables. The play is constructed on ancient models, as will be seen from the following summary.

In Act I the shade of Antony announces that it has bidden Cleopatra kill herself so that she may not figure in the triumph of Octavian; Cleopatra appears, blames herself for the death of Antony, and states her intention to die; the chorus moralizes. In Act II Octavian debates with his council: he wishes to preserve Cleopatra to grace his triumph. In Act III Octavian and Cleopatra are confronted; she seeks to obtain liberty by the surrender of her treasure; her steward denounces her for concealing part of it (an incident taken from Plutarch). Act IV is occupied with Cleopatra's preparations for death. Act V announces her death, which has taken place between the two acts, and the lamentations of the chorus end the play.

Clermont, see *Collège de Clermont*.

Clermont, ÉMILE (1880–1916), novelist, died in action during the 1914–18 war. He had published two novels of promise: *Amour promis* (1910) and, particularly, *Laure* (1913).

Cleveland, the abbreviated title of the romance *Le Philosophe anglais ou les mémoires de Cleveland* by the abbé Prévost (q.v.).

Cligès, a metrical romance written by Chrétien de Troyes (q.v.) about 1170, containing episodes based on Oriental tradition, but otherwise forming part of the Breton cycle.

Alexandre, son of the Emperor of Constantinople, goes to the court of King Arthur, and after proving his prowess marries the king's niece, Soredamors. This is a sort of prologue in which the author, relating the progress of the sentiments of the two lovers, reveals his power of psychological analysis. Their son Cligès is the hero of the second part of the story. The principal theme of this is the devotion of Fénice, daughter of the emperor of Germany, to her lover Cligès. The uncle of Cligès, who holds the throne of Constantinople (to which Cligès is heir) on condition that he shall never marry, nevertheless marries Fénice against her will. She, expressly rejecting the example of Iseult, on the one hand, by the help of a magic potion administered to her husband, keeps herself intact; on the other refuses herself to her lover while she is nominally the wife of his uncle. Then by a simulated death and after a terrible ordeal she succeeds in escaping from the palace and liberating herself, as she conceives, from her duty as empress, and is reunited with her lover. In this part of the poem, again, there is acute analysis of sentiment and of moral problems.

Clitandre, (1) a tragi-comedy by Pierre Corneille (q.v.); (2) a character in Molière's *Les Femmes savantes.*

Cloots, JEAN-BAPTISTE DU VAL DE GRÂCE, BARON DE (1755–94), self-styled 'Anacharsis' Cloots, politician of Prussian origin, nephew of the philosopher and diplomat Cornelius de Pauw (1739–99). He came to France, joined the Encyclopédistes (q.v.) and adopted revolutionary principles, which for him included the establishment of a 'universal family of nations' and the replacement of religious beliefs by the cult of reason. He called himself the 'Orateur du genre humain' and 'citoyen de l'humanité'. In August 1792 the *Assemblée législative* conferred French citizenship on him. He was a member of the *club des Jacobins* (q.v.)—until Robespierre had him expelled—and of the *Convention nationale* (q.v.). Later, he was condemned and executed with the Hébertistes (see *Hébert*).

His many writings included *Adresse d'un Prussien à un Anglais* (1790), the Englishman in question being Edmund Burke; *L'Orateur du genre humain ou Dépêches du Prussien Cloots au Prussien Hertzberg* (1791); *La République universelle* (1792).

Clotilde de Surville, see *Surville.*

Clovis (pron. as if Cloviss) I or **Chlodovech** (c. 466–511), the first king of the Franks and founder of the *Mérovingien* (q.v.) dynasty, succeeded his father in 481 at the age of sixteen, as chief of the tribe of the Salian Franks. Bold yet prudent, an unscrupulous bandit and assassin, he defeated the Roman governor Syagrius in 486, and subsequently the Alamanni, the Burgundians, and the Visigoths, thus establishing his authority over the greater part of Gaul. He was recognized by Anastasius, Roman emperor of the East, as his lieutenant. He married Clotilda, a Christian princess, and was baptized a Christian (probably in 496 and perhaps in consequence of a vow made at the time of his battle with the Alamanni) at Rheims, it is said, by Saint Remi. The choice of Paris as capital was due to him. The name Clovis is a contraction of Chlodovech, and is equivalent to the later form 'Louis'.

Clovis is the title of an epic by Desmarets de Saint-Sorlin (q.v.).

Club breton, see *Jacobins.*

Club de l'Entresol, a club whose members met in the *entresol* of the abbé Alary in the house of the président Hénault, Place Vendôme, Paris, during the period 1724–31, for the discussion of public affairs, in particular economic reforms. It gave umbrage to Cardinal Fleury and had to dissolve. Among its frequenters were the abbé de Saint-Pierre, Montesquieu, and d'Argenson (qq.v.).

Cluny, Abbaye de, a famous Benedictine abbey founded in 910 at Cluny, near Mâcon in Saône-et-Loire. It was the centre of the Cluniac order of monks, which separated from the Benedictines in the 11th century. The abbey church was one of the largest churches in Europe, only a little smaller than St. Peter's in Rome. It was wrecked in the Revolution and only part of it survives. The rest of the abbey buildings have been applied to other purposes.

Cluny, Musée de, a museum of national antiquities and industrial art, mainly of the 14th, 15th, and 16th centuries, housed in the former Hôtel de Cluny, in Paris. This Hôtel was constructed *c.* 1490 (on a plot adjacent to ancient Roman remains known as 'les Thermes') as a town residence for the abbots of Cluny. It was confiscated and sold by the state in 1790, and occupied later by the famous collector M. du Sommerard. When he died, his collection was bought by the state and thrown open (1844) to the public together with the ruins and gardens of *les Thermes*.

Clytemnestre, a character in Racine's *Iphigénie* (q.v.).

Coalitions, military alliances formed against France by other European Powers, first of all in the reign of Louis XIV, then during the Revolution and the Napoleonic era. There were seven of the last, namely (1) 1791: Austria and Prussia, joined later by Britain, Spain, Sardinia, Sicily, &c. This was dissolved, some months after the decisive defeat of the Austrians at Rivoli (q.v.), by the Treaty of Campo Formio (q.v.); (2) 1799: Austria, Britain, Russia, Turkey, Sicily. Ended by Austrian defeats at Marengo and Hohenlinden (qq.v.), followed by the Treaties of Lunéville and Amiens (qq.v.); (3) 1805: Austria, Britain, Russia and, later, Prussia, broken by the Austro-Russian defeat at Austerlitz (q.v.), followed by the Treaty of Pressburg (q.v.); (4) 1806: Britain, Prussia, Russia, Sweden, broken by the Prussian defeat at Jena (q.v.) and the Russian defeat at Friedland (q.v.), followed by the Treaty of Tilsit (q.v.); (5) 1809: Britain and Austria, broken by the Austrian defeat at Wagram (q.v.), followed by the Treaty of Vienna; (6) 1813: Austria, Britain, Prussia, Russia, Spain, Sweden, and most of the other European Powers. Ended with the capitulation of Paris (q.v.) and Napoleon's first abdication; (7) 1815: the same Powers. Ended by the decisive defeat of Napoleon at Waterloo.

Coblenz. During the Revolution one of the largest colonies of *émigrés* (often called 'les gens de Coblentz') had its centre in this town. It was the rallying-point for the *Armée des émigrés* (q.v.).

Cocagne, Dit de, a facetious medieval poem or *fabliau* representing a fabulous country of luxury and idleness, where roast pigs walk about the streets ready to be carved and the gutters run with wine, and where 'qui plus y dort, plus y gagne'. There are references to the land of Cockayne in early English literature.

Cocagne, Le Roi de, a comedy by Legrand (1718), a light piece of comic fantasy.

Coconas, ANNIBAL, COMTE DE (died 1574), an Italian adventurer who came to France under the regency of Catherine de Médicis, was noted for cruel deeds in the massacre of St. Bartholomew, became a favourite of the duc d'Alençon, and plotted with La Mole and others to place that prince on the throne in preference to Henri III. Catherine de Médicis had the two chief conspirators arrested and executed. Coconas is a leading figure in *La Dame de Monsoreau* by Dumas *père*.

Cocteau, JEAN (1892–   ), a versatile writer whose acute intelligence and sensitivity made him an advance guard (and at times *accoucheur*) to literary and artistic movements between the 1914–18 and 1939–45 wars. His numerous publications include: (*a*) COLLECTED POETRY, e.g. *Le Cap de Bonne Espérance* (1919), *Vocabulaire* (1922), *Plainchant* (1923, poems modelled on 16th-century authors rather than the more *fantaisiste* or *cubiste* verse of the earlier volumes), all united in *Poésies 1916–23* (1924); *Opéra 1925–1927* (1927, containing the frequently mentioned *Ange Heurtebise* of 1925); *Poésies* (1947); (*b*) POÉSIE DE THÉÂTRE, e.g. [the dates are those of publication] *Orphée* (1927), a 'tragédie en un acte et un intervalle'; *Antigone* (1928), after Sophocles, modernized; *La Voix humaine* (1930, one act), a woman talks on the telephone to the lover who has abandoned her; *La Machine infernale* (1934), a tragedy on the Oedipus theme; *Les Chevaliers de la Table Ronde* (1937), Arthurian legend treated flippantly; *Les Parents terribles* (1938), modern psychological drama; *L'Aigle à deux têtes* (1946), romantic drama in the Ruritanian tradition; also ballets, sketches, and monologues, often written for Diaghilev's Russian ballet, with music by *Les Six* (q.v.) and *décor* by Picasso, Braque, Dufy, and other modern painters, e.g. *Parade* (1919); *Le Bœuf sur le toit* (1920); *Les Mariés de la Tour Eiffel* (1924); *Les Biches* (1924), &c.; (*c*) POÉSIE DE ROMAN, e.g. *Le Potomak* (1913); *Thomas l'Imposteur* (1923); *Le Grand Écart* (1923), and *Les Enfants terribles* (1929), a study of four young people who live and for a time flourish, innocent yet sinister plants, in an unreal, hot-house world of their own making which inevitably collapses; (*d*) POÉSIE CRITIQUE (i.e. essays and criticism), e.g. *Le Rappel à l'ordre* (1926), a collection in which 'Le Secret professionnel' may be singled out; *Opium* (1930), a form of journal written during treatment for drug-addiction.

This author's work for the cinema, in more recent years, should also be noted; and also, on his election to the *Académie française* (q.v.) in 1955, his brilliant *Discours de réception* (with the elegant reply of M. André Maurois).

Code civil. The idea of codifying the French law is said to have originated with Louis XI, but few steps were taken to effect this until the reigns of Louis XIV and Louis XV. Codification was promised in the constitution of 1791, but drafts presented by Cambacérès (q.v.) to the *Convention nationale* and again during the *Directoire* were rejected. During the Consulate and the Empire, thanks to Napoleon's energy, five codes (dealing with civil law, civil procedure, commercial, criminal, and penal law) were drawn up. The first, the *Code civil*, was voted by the *Corps législatif* in 1804. The others followed between that date and 1810. Napoleon himself presided over the Commission which drafted the *Code civil* (also, in 1807, called *Code Napoléon*) and took a vigorous share in the discussions. This code took only four years to complete and though since modified it is still largely operative. Its three books contain well over 2,000 articles. Book I deals with the law in regard to individuals. Books II and III concern the law of property. The style has no object except to express every intricacy of the law with the utmost lucidity. There are no unnecessary words, but no repetition is feared if by that means ambiguity can be avoided. Stendhal, in a letter to Balzac shortly after the publication of *La Chartreuse de Parme* (q.v.), said that while he was writing this novel he read two pages of the *Code civil* every morning so as to give himself the correct tone.

Code de la Nature, see *Morelly*.

Coëffeteau, NICOLAS (1574–1623), a Dominican friar, preacher to Henri IV, whose funeral ovation he pronounced, Bishop of Marseilles in 1621, author of a *Tableau des passions humaines* (1620) and of an *Histoire romaine* (1621).

Coffret de santal, Le (1873), a collection of poems by Charles Cros (q.v.).

Coignard, l'ABBÉ JÉRÔME, see *Rôtisserie de la Reine Pédauque*.

Colardeau, CHARLES-PIERRE (1732–76), poet, author of *Héroïdes* (after the manner of Ovid, including a famous *Lettre d'Héloïse à Abélard*), of a tragedy *Caliste* (1760), of an *Épître à M. Duhamel*, &c. He was elected to the *Académie* in the year of his death.

Colas, see *Vache à Colas*.

Colbert, JEAN-BAPTISTE (1619–83), the great finance minister of Louis XIV. He started his career in the ministry of war under Le Tellier (q.v.), but first made his mark as assistant to Mazarin, who enriched him and in his will recommended him to the king. Colbert helped to overthrow Fouquet (q.v.) and took his place as *intendant des finances* from 1661 and *contrôleur général* from 1665. He was also minister of marine and created a powerful French navy. He introduced great reforms in the financial system; though sometimes high-handed in his procedure (as in the arbitrary reduction of the charge for the national debt) and inclined to excessive protection and regulation of industry, his aim in general was to make France great through the prosperity of her people and by lightening the burden of taxation and the remedy of abuses. But his policy was thwarted by the king's inclination to costly wars (encouraged by Louvois) and the prodigal expenditure of the court. One of the most useful economic measures of his administration was the creation of the *canal du Languedoc* (or *du Midi*) connecting the Mediterranean with the Atlantic, designed and constructed by Pierre-Paul Riquet and inaugurated in 1681. Colbert showed himself an enlightened minister in other ways: he founded the academies of science, of architecture, and of inscriptions, and the French academy at Rome; he encouraged the establishment of the *Journal des Savants*; he collected pictures and statues for the Louvre; he extended and reorganized the royal library besides forming a great library of his own; and he protected men of erudition, such as Mabillon and Baluze.

Colet, LOUISE, *née* Revoil (1808–76), authoress, born at Aix-en-Provence, lived in Paris after her marriage to Hippolyte Colet (1808–51), a professor at the Conservatoire. She won some renown with her poetry (*Fleurs du midi*, 1836; *Poésies*, 1844; *Ce qui est dans le cœur des femmes*, 1852, &c.) and much notoriety on account of her violent behaviour and her liaisons with famous men, notably Flaubert and Alfred de Musset. She describes these in detail in an autobiographical novel *Lui, roman contemporain* (1851). The early volumes of Flaubert's *Correspondance* contain many interesting letters addressed to her.

Colette, SIDONIE-GABRIELLE (1873–1954), the outstanding French woman writer of modern times, and the first woman to be President of the *Académie Goncourt* (q.v.), was born and brought up at Saint-Sauveur-en-Puisaye (Burgundy). She was brought to Paris by her first husband, the novelist and music-critic Henri Gauthier-Villars, with whom she collaborated in a series of novels—*Claudine à l'école* (1900), *Claudine à Paris* (1901), *Claudine en ménage* (1902), *Claudine s'en va* (1903)—first published under his pen-name of 'Willy'. Their mixture of engaging freshness and flippantly perverse sensuality aroused interest and some scandal. The collaboration ended in 1904 and the first marriage (there were two later marriages) in 1906. Between 1904 and 1916 Mme Colette wrote under the name of 'Colette Willy' and thenceforward she used the name 'Colette' alone. The first work to be signed 'Colette Willy' was *Dialogues de bêtes* [between the dog Toby-chien and the cat Kiki-la-doucette] (1904). Others were *La Retraite sentimentale* (1907), *Les Vrilles de la vigne* (1908), lyrical impressions of country life with a note of autobiography; *L'Envers du music-hall* (1913), based on personal experiences of music-hall life between 1906 and 1914; the novels *L'Ingénue libertine* (1909), a reworking of two earlier novels written in collaboration, *La Vagabonde* (1910) and its sequel *L'Entrave* (1913), both about music-hall life; and *La Paix chez les bêtes* (1916), a continuation of the *Dialogues*. Outstanding among her later works are the novels *Chéri* (1920), *Le Blé en herbe* (1923), *La Fin de Chéri* (1926), and the subtle study of jealousy *La Chatte* (1933), in which the characters are a wife, her husband, and the husband's cat; also the reminiscences of childhood and the author's mother, and of literary beginnings, *La Maison de Claudine* (1923), *La Naissance du jour* (1928), *Sido*

(1929), *Mes Apprentissages* (1936). The reminiscences of early years are among the best examples of Colette's writing—a supple, musical prose admirably fitted to her sensuous feeling for Nature and her intuitive sympathy with the unexplored or perverse sides of human nature.

Colette Baudoche (1909), a patriotic novel by Maurice Barrès (q.v.).

Coligny, GASPARD DE, AMIRAL (1519–72), leader of the Huguenots under Charles IX, a man of high character and merit, a victim of the massacre of Saint Bartholomew. He wrote a good account of the siege of Saint-Quentin (1557) by the Imperialists.

Colin Muset, a 13th-century lyric poet of Lorraine, a *jongleur* and an epicurean who wrote songs in praise of good cheer; also of love, sometimes facetiously or by way of parody of the courtly poets.

Collé, CHARLES (1709–83), dramatist, son of a Paris magistrate, and reader and secretary to the duc d'Orléans, to whom his gaiety and good humour mingled with subtlety and originality recommended him. After a phase in which he wrote highly popular *chansons* on every sort of event of the day, he turned to the stage with *La Vérité dans le vin*, a comedy of contemporary manners, in which shameless wives and credulous husbands are depicted with the coarse realism of the old *fabliaux*. The public performance of the play was prohibited at the instance of the Archbishop of Paris. This was followed by a sentimental comedy in irregular verse, *Dupuis et Desronais* (q.v., 1763, and see *Vers libres*), and a historical comedy in prose, *La Partie de chasse de Henri IV* (q.v., performed in 1774), in which he popularized the legend of Henri IV as 'le bon roi', living familiarly with his subjects, in contrast to the grandeur of Louis XIV. Both the latter plays were successful, though the production of the *Partie de chasse* was not permitted until Louis XVI came to the throne.

Collège, see *Lycées and Collèges*; *Universities*, paras. 1, 3.

Collège de Boncourt, founded 1353, one of the early colleges of the University of Paris (see *Universities*, *A*). Étienne Jodelle's

Cléopâtre captive (q.v.) had its second performance here.

Collège de Clermont, the first teaching establishment founded by the Jesuits (1562) in Paris. From 1682 it was called Collège Louis-le-Grand (see *Lycées and Collèges; Prytanée*). Molière was a pupil.

Collège de Coqueret, founded 1463, one of the former colleges of the University of Paris (see *Universities, A*). Jean Dorat (q.v.), when Principal, numbered Ronsard, Baïf, Belleau, du Bellay, and Jodelle (qq.v.) among his pupils.

Collège de France, a famous institution in Paris, independent of the University, for the disinterested pursuit of higher studies. Students are not prepared for examinations; and its lecture courses are public, and free. Its nucleus dates from 1530 when François Ier, on the advice of his librarian Guillaume Budé, instituted royal readers in Greek, Hebrew, Latin, and mathematics with the object of supplementing the conservative teaching of the Sorbonne. The *lecteurs royaux* resisted opposition from the Sorbonne and in time became a corporate body (*collegium regium Galliarum*) with, by the reign of Louis XIII, their own institution. Their scope, too, was widened by the creation of new chairs.

This College was rare among educational foundations in surviving the Revolution, being, indeed, protected by the *Ministère de l'Intérieur*. Its fame continued, and its scope was still further extended, during the 19th century. It is maintained by the state, but the professorial staff, since a decree of 1873, enjoy a high measure of autonomy in their administration, selection, and appointment, and in the choice of subjects to be taught. Famous philosophers, scholars, and poets associated with its teaching within the past century include Bergson, Michelet, Gaston Paris, Renan, Valéry (qq.v.).

Collège de Montaigu, founded 1314 by Gilles Aycelin de Montaigu (died 1318), an ancient college in the University of Paris, frequently referred to in the literature of the 16th century. It had been rebuilt and revived under the care of John Standouck of Malines who was appointed its head in 1483. Its some 200 poor students (who included Erasmus, Calvin, and Ignatius Loyola) were brought up in extreme asceticism. Erasmus in one of his *Colloquies* refers to its verminous condition in the following passage: 'Unde prodis? — E collegio Montis acuti — Ergo ades nobis onustus literis — Imo pediculis.' Rabelais (I. xxxvii) makes allusion to the same. The college was suppressed at the Revolution. (See also *Hôtel des haricots*.)

Collège de Navarre, founded in 1304 by Jeanne de Navarre, queen of Philippe le Bel, as a hostel for poor students of the University of Paris; twenty students in grammar were to receive an allowance of four *solidi* (see *Money*) a week, thirty in arts six *solidi*, and twenty in theology eight *solidi*. Each class of students was presided over by a master, the master of the theologians being rector or 'Grand-maître' of the college. There were chaplains; and each class also had its own hall, kitchen, and dormitory. Fee-paying students, sons of the great nobles, were admitted at a later date. The college revenues were confiscated at the Revolution and it closed in 1792. It was replaced on its site on the Montagne Sainte-Geneviève, behind the Sorbonne, by the École polytechnique (q.v. and cf. *Villon*).

Collège des Quatre-Nations, the name frequently given to the Collège Mazarin founded under the will of Cardinal Mazarin (q.v.) and opened in 1688 for sixty young men, preferably of noble birth, coming from the four provinces (hence 'quatre nations') made part of France under the Treaty of the Pyrenees (q.v., 1659). It occupied the site of the Hôtel de Nesle (q.v.) on the left bank of the Seine. During the Revolution the College was put to various uses. For a time it was a prison; and it also housed the École des Beaux-arts. In 1806 it became, and has since remained, the home of the Institut de France (q.v.).

Collège Sainte-Barbe. This famous boys' school in Paris had its origin in 1460 when Geoffroi Lenormant, a teacher of philosophy in the University of Paris, founded a college (see *Lycées and Collèges; Universities, A*) intended to serve both as a hostel and as an educational institution for paying pupils. It flourished at first but later endured periods of difficulty and lost its independence. It was finally suppressed during the Revolution but this had barely happened when a new Collège Sainte-Barbe was opened to continue the old traditions. It is now run as a company by an association of former pupils. The history of its origins was written by Quicherat (q.v.), who gives interesting details of life in the early colleges. The 'Sainte-Barbe' of modern times is described in *Notre cher Péguy* by the contemporary historian and critic Daniel Halévy.

Collège Stanislas, a well-known Roman Catholic boys' school in Paris. It was founded in 1804 and accorded full status as an educational establishment in 1822 by Louis XVIII, who gave it the name of Collège Stanislas after the King of Poland whose daughter Marie Leszczinska had married his grandfather Louis XV. Anatole France was one of its many famous pupils.

Collerye, ROGER DE (*c.* 1470–*c.* 1538), born in Paris, one of the last of the *rhétoriqueurs* (q.v.), became secretary to the Bishop of Auxerre, but remained to the end of his life poor and miserable. Nevertheless he was author of some amusing monologues and dialogues for the *Enfants sans souci* (q.v.). The best of his shorter poems, the *rondeaux* in which he laments his poverty and his lost youth, have a quality of genuine feeling which recalls Villon.

Colletet, FRANÇOIS (1628–*c.* 1680), a minor poet whose works have been described as 'tombées dans un juste oubli'. He is not to be confused with his better-remembered father (see the following).

Colletet, GUILLAUME (1598–1659), poet, author of indifferent plays (he was one of the *cinq auteurs* (q.v.) who collaborated under Richelieu's direction) and somewhat better poems, *Divertissements* (1631–3), *Banquet des Poètes* (1646), *Épigrammes* (1653). He was a member of the first *Académie*. He was also a good critic and left in manuscript 'Lives of the French poets', of which Sainte-Beuve made frequent use, but which perished when the library of the Louvre was burnt during the Commune (1871); about one-half of the work had been copied or published by students before this.

Collier, L'Affaire du, the name given to the plot, successfully carried out in 1783–4, of Jeanne de Valois, comtesse de la Motte, a clever adventuress, to get possession of a diamond necklace from the jeweller who had

made it, on the pretence that Marie-Antoinette had consented to purchase it. The comtesse de la Motte had persuaded the cardinal de Rohan, her dupe, who was desirous of dispelling the disfavour in which he was held at court, that she was in favour with the queen; she had even effected an interview between the cardinal and a woman who impersonated the queen. The cardinal was next led to believe that the queen wished to purchase the necklace and to employ him as intermediary. By this means and a forged document purporting to signify the queen's acceptance of the terms of purchase, the comtesse got possession of the necklace. It was broken up and the jewels sold. The cardinal and the comtesse were arrested; the former was acquitted, the latter was branded and imprisoned. She escaped to England and wrote her memoirs before her death. Though the innocence of the queen is now established, much suspicion and discredit attached to her for a time. The episode forms the plot of *Le Collier de la Reine* (1849–50), a well-known historical novel by Dumas *père* (see also *Archives nationales*).

Collin d'Harleville, JEAN-FRANÇOIS (1755–1806), author of successful comedies in verse, notably *Le Vieux Célibataire* (5 acts), which was produced during the Revolution (1792) and is not yet forgotten. (A rich old bachelor is gradually being inveigled into marriage by his housekeeper, but a nephew and his wife turn up in disguise and eventually outwit the housekeeper and capture the old man's favours.) Among his other comedies were: *L'Inconstant* (1786); *L'Optimiste* (1788); *Les Châteaux en Espagne* (1789), all 5 acts; and *Malice pour malice* (1803), 3 acts. M. de Crac, from the one-act farce *M. de Crac dans son petit castel* (1791), has remained the type of the boastful country gentleman—from Gascony—hero of innumerable fantastic, and imaginary, adventures.

Collin d'Harleville's *Théâtre et poésies fugitives* were first collected and published (1805) by his friend (also a playwright) François Andrieux (q.v.).

Colline inspirée, La (1913), a novel by Maurice Barrès (q.v.), sometimes considered his finest work. It has some foundation in fact.

Vaudémont and Sion, two ruined pilgrim

sites in Lorraine, were, like many such places, so ancient that the mysterious religious emotion pervading them seemed to extend far back to the pagan origins of humanity and to make them a prey for superstition and perverted religious ecstasy. For a time in the 19th century they were restored to their former glory and affluence by the priest Léopold Baillard, but once his work was accomplished he fell into heresy, became a disciple of Vintras (q.v., a mid-19th-century religious reformer accused of sorcery), and allowed the holy places, and the convent which had been established, to be profaned by sacrilegious orgies. Then persecution followed, and the wrath of the Church, and return to desolation.

Collot d'Herbois, JEAN-MARIE (*c.* 1750–96), an actor and theatre manager (often producing his own plays) who became a Revolutionary politician, a *Jacobin*, a member of the *Comité de salut public* in 1793, and a Terrorist. He was President of the *Convention nationale* on the day of his enemy Robespierre's fall (le 9 Thermidor, An II, i.e. 27 July 1794). Eight months later he was deported to Cayenne, where he died. In 1791 he published *L'Almanach du père Gérard*, a highly successful piece of Revolutionary propaganda.

Colomba, by Prosper Mérimée, a long short story of a Corsican vendetta, and perhaps his finest work, was first printed in the *Revue des Deux Mondes* in 1840: the first French edition in book form appeared in 1841. Orso, the hero, returns to Corsica completely Europeanized after many years' army service. In the interval his father has been murdered by ancient enemies of the family, and his sister Colomba looks to him to avenge the family honour. At first Orso refuses, but gradually his native instincts are reawakened. He is on his way to meet his English fiancée and her father when the sons of his father's assassin ambush him. He kills them and takes to the Corsican *maquis*. Colonel Nevill and his daughter had heard the shooting and save him from being outlawed by testifying that he fired in self-defence.

The remarkable character of the story is Colomba, a young girl of great beauty and innocent savagery, and single-minded in her thirst for revenge.

Colombe, MICHEL (1430–1512), born in Brittany, an eminent sculptor, one of the principal artists of the French Renaissance. Little of his work survives: allegorical figures on the tomb of François II of Brittany at Nantes and a figure of St. George for the Château de Gaillon are the best-known examples. He made designs for the tombs in the church of Brou (q.v.) but these were, it appears, only in part followed.

Colombine (Columbine), the Colombina of the Italian Commedia dell'arte, a stock character of the *Comédie italienne* in Paris (see *Italiens*). She was originally a serving-maid, a ward of Pantalon. Later she was one of the lovers, paired with Harlequin, usually eloping with him.

Colon, JENNY [Marguerite] (1808–42), an actress, gay, captivating, and capricious, at the Opéra-Comique and at other Paris theatres. She was loved in life, in substance, and still, after her death, in the fantasies he wove around her, by Gérard de Nerval (q.v.).

Colonel Chabert, Le, one of the 'Scènes de la vie privée' of Balzac's *Comédie humaine* (q.v.). It appeared originally (1832), entitled *La Transaction,* in a review. Colonel Hyacinthe Chabert, of Napoleon's Imperial Guard, a Grand Officier of the Légion d'honneur, a Count of Napoleon's Empire, supposed to have died gloriously at Eylau in 1807, had in fact been buried alive on the battlefield. He had managed to escape and, after twelve terrible years of hardship, to reach Paris. His 'widow' in the meantime had flourished socially and financially (on his fortune) and had remarried. He confronted her, but she played on his feelings and tricked him so successfully that he sacrificed himself and disappeared again. Many years later he was still alive in a pauper institution, as No. 124, Ward Seven, whose days were spent in senile preoccupation with tobacco and liquor.

Colonne [originally **Juda**], JULES-ÉDOUARD (1838–1910), born in Bordeaux, a violinist and conductor who in 1873 founded his own orchestra and the *Concerts Colonne*, the regular symphony concerts which are still an institution of Paris Sunday afternoons. He introduced many young or imperfectly appreciated French composers, as well as much foreign music, to French audiences (cf. *Lamoureux*; *Pasdeloup*).

Combat avec l'ange (1927), by Jean Giraudoux (q.v.), a novel.

Combat des Trente, see *Trente*.

Combourg, a small country town in Brittany, near Saint-Malo. The Château de Combourg was the parental home of Chateaubriand, where he spent much of his youth. Arthur Young visited Combourg— 'one of the most brutal filthy places that can be seen'—in 1788 and said of the château: 'Who is this Mons. de Chateaubriant, the owner, that has nerves strung for a residence amidst such filth and poverty?'

Combray, the small country town where Marcel, in Proust's *A la recherche du temps perdu* (q.v.), spent childhood holidays at his grandparents' home (as Proust himself had spent holidays at Illiers, a small town near Chartres). Here his daily walks followed either of two directions — *le côté de chez Swann* or *le côté de Guermantes* — which all through life bore a symbolical meaning for him. The former represented the world of the rich, cultured middle class (his own milieu); the latter an aristocratic world which scorned (but was ultimately engulfed by) the bourgeoisie.

Comédie-ballet, a dramatic form developed by Molière from the *ballet* (q.v.), by introducing the latter in the intervals between the acts of a comedy, and giving it a satirical or farcical character connected with the theme of the comedy. His first example of the *comédie-ballet* was *Les Fâcheux* (1661), composed for an entertainment given at Vaux by Fouquet for Louis XIV. It proved successful, and Molière wrote in all fourteen such plays.

Comédie de la mort, La (1838), a narrative poem by Théophile Gautier (q.v.).

Comédie-Française, La, the first State theatre of France, officially entitled *Le Théâtre Français*, and also known as *La Maison de Molière*. Its nucleus was the company of actors established by Molière in 1658 at the Théâtre du Petit-Bourbon (see *Theatres and theatre companies*, para. 3). After the death of Molière the company was merged with the company of the Théâtre du Marais and, having moved to new quarters in the rue Guénégaud, became known as the Théâtre Guénégaud. In 1680 the Théâtre Guénégaud and the players from the Hôtel de Bourgogne (see *Theatres and theatre companies*, paras. 1–3) were combined to form the company which has survived as the *Comédie-Française*. It received a subvention from the king.

From 1689 to 1770 the company's theatre was in the rue des Fossés-Saint-Germain-des-Prés (on the left bank of the Seine, the street now called rue de l'Ancienne Comédie). This was succeeded by temporary quarters in the *Salle des machines* at the Tuileries. On 9 April 1782 the *Comédie-Française* played for the first time in a new theatre specially built for them near the Palais du Luxembourg, the Théâtre de l'Odéon, nowadays the *Théâtre Français (Salle Luxembourg)*. See *Luxembourg, Théâtre du.*

During the Revolution the company split into two factions. One, the pro-Revolutionary, became the Théâtre de la République but failed by 1799. The other was imprisoned in 1793 for Royalist tendencies, and though released after the Terror it failed to re-establish itself on a permanent footing. In the end the government reconstituted the original company, with its official home in the rue de Richelieu, in the theatre known (from May 1799) as the *Théâtre Français* and which the company still occupies. Its official title today is *Théâtre Français (Salle Richelieu)*.

Originally, the constitution of the *Comédie-Française* was regulated by royal command. When the company was re-formed after the Revolution Napoleon himself redrafted its constitution, in minute detail and on a basis which has remained fundamentally the same, in a decree issued from Moscow in 1812. Members of the company are known as *pensionnaires* while still on probation, and thereafter as *sociétaires*, i.e. full members, with a right to pension on retirement.

Comédie humaine, La (1842–8), by Honoré de Balzac. Between 1842 and 1848 Balzac published a collected edition (17 vols.) of his novels and tales, grouping them from the outset (1842, preface to vol. i), under the generic title *La Comédie humaine*, into a pattern of French society from the Consulate to the July monarchy. (For a more detailed description of the general theme and characteristics of the *Comédie humaine* see under *Balzac*.)

It was not always easy to fit into a pattern works which had originally been written without thought of their place in a larger whole, but design had already been apparent in previous collections—*Scènes de la vie privée* (1830, 2 vols.; 1832, 4 vols.); *Études de mœurs au XIXe siècle* (1834–7, 12 vols., comprising *Scènes de la vie de province* and *Scènes de la vie parisienne* as well as the *Scènes de la vie privée*); *Études philosophiques* (1835–40). These became the basis of the groups and subsections of the *Comédie humaine* of 1842–8, with new tales inserted and a third group, *Études analytiques*, added. In 1845 Balzac drew up a prospectus for a second edition in which he proposed to re-group, in some cases, and to insert further tales (projected or already written). But he did not live to fulfil his purpose. After his death the *Comédie humaine* was re-edited at various dates, either alone or as part of his *Œuvres complètes*. In recent years it has been edited with notes by Marcel Bouteron and Henri Longnon (vols. 1–33 inclusive of the *Œuvres complètes*, 1912–) and in the Bibliothèque de la Pléiade series (1935–7, 10 vols.). This last edition is based on Balzac's prospectus of 1845 as modified by him in subsequent notes, and its order of contents is followed in the list given below of the novels and tales which constitute the *Comédie humaine*. The dates in brackets after the several titles are the printed publication dates. In addition, works not included in the first (1842–8) edition are starred(*); and the sign † denotes works summarized under their own titles in the present *Companion*.

La Comédie Humaine

ÉTUDES DE MŒURS:

SCÈNES DE LA VIE PRIVÉE: *La Maison du chat qui pelote* (1830); *Le Bal de Sceaux* (1830); *Mémoires de deux jeunes mariées* (1841–2); *La Bourse* (1832); *Modeste Mignon* (1844)†; *Un Début dans la vie* (1842); *Albert Savarus* (1842); *La Vendetta* (1830); *Une Double Famille* (1830); *La Paix du ménage* (1830); *Madame Firmiani* (1832); *Étude de femme* (1830); *La Fausse Maîtresse* (1841); *Une Fille d'Ève* (1838–9); *Le Message* (1832); *La Grenadière* (1832); *La Femme abandonnée* (1832); *Honorine* (1843); *Béatrix* (1839); *Gobseck* (1830)†; *La Femme de trente ans* (1831–4); *Le Père Goriot* (1834–5)†; *Le Colonel Chabert* (1832)†; *La Messe de l'athée*

(1836); *L'Interdiction* (1836); *Le Contrat de mariage* (1835); *Autre étude de femme* (1842).

SCÈNES DE LA VIE DE PROVINCE: *Ursule Mirouët* (1841)†; *Eugénie Grandet* (1833)†; *Les Célibataires* — (i) *Pierrette*, (ii) *Le Curé de Tours*†, (iii) *La Rabouilleuse*† (1840, 1832, 1841–2); *Les Parisiens en province* — (i) *L'Illustre Gaudissart*†, (ii) *La Muse du Département* (1833, 1843); *Les Rivalités* — (i) *La Vieille Fille*, (ii) *Le Cabinet des antiques* (1836, 1836–8, 1839); *Illusions perdues*† — (i) *Les Deux Poètes*, (ii) *Un Grand Homme de province à Paris*, (iii) *Les Souffrances de l'inventeur* (1837, 1839, 1843).

SCÈNES DE LA VIE PARISIENNE: *Histoire des Treize* — (i) *Ferragus*, (ii) *La Duchesse de Langeais*†, (iii) *La Fille aux yeux d'or* (1833, 1833–4, 1834–5); *Histoire de la grandeur et de la décadence de César Birotteau* (1837)†; *La Maison Nucingen* (1838); *Splendeurs et misères des courtisanes* — (i) *Comment aiment les filles*, (ii) *À combien l'amour revient aux vieillards*, (iii) *Où mènent les mauvais chemins*, (iv) *La Dernière Incarnation de Vautrin*★ (1838–47)†; *Les Secrets de la Princesse de Cadignan* (1839); *Facino Cane* (1836); *Sarrasine* (1830); *Pierre Grassou* (1840); *Les Parents pauvres* — (i) *La Cousine Bette*†, (ii) *Le Cousin Pons*† (1846, 1847); *Un Homme d'affaires* (1845); *Un Prince de la Bohème* (1840); *Gaudissart II* (1844); *Les Employés* (1837); *Les Comédiens sans le savoir* (1846); *Les Petits Bourgeois* (posth.)★; *L'Envers de l'histoire contemporaine* — (i) *Madame de la Chanterie*, (ii) *L'Initié*★ (1842, 1848).

SCÈNES DE LA VIE POLITIQUE: *Un Épisode sous la Terreur* (1830); *Une Ténébreuse Affaire* (1841)†; *Le Député d'Arcis* (1847, finished in 1854 by Ch. Rabou); *Z. Marcas* (1840).

SCÈNES DE LA VIE MILITAIRE: *Les Chouans* (1829)†; *Une Passion dans le désert* (1830).

SCÈNES DE LA VIE DE CAMPAGNE: *Les Paysans* (1844)★; *Le Médecin de campagne* (1833)†; *Le Curé de village*† (1839); *Le Lys dans la vallée* (1835)†.

ÉTUDES PHILOSOPHIQUES:

La Peau de chagrin (1830–1)†; *Jésus-Christ en Flandre* (1831); *Melmoth réconcilié* (1835)†; *Massimilla Doni* (1839)†; *Le Chef-d'œuvre inconnu* (1831); *Gambara* (1837)★; *La Recherche de l'Absolu* (1834)†; *L'Enfant maudit* (1831–6); *Adieu*(1830); *Les Marana*(1832–3); *Le Réquisitionnaire* (1831); *El Verdugo* (1830); *Un Drame au bord de la mer* (1835); *Maître Cornélius* (1831); *L'Auberge rouge* (1831);

Sur Catherine de Médicis (1841); *L'Élixir de longue vie* (1830); *Les Proscrits* (1831); *Louis Lambert* (1832)†; *Séraphita* (1834–5).

ÉTUDES ANALYTIQUES:

Physiologie du mariage (1829)†; *Petites misères de la vie conjugale* (1830, 1840, 1845)*. [The *Répertoire de la Comédie humaine* (1893), by A. Cerfberr and J. Christophe, and the recent *Dictionnaire biographique des personnages fictifs de la Comédie humaine* (1952), by F. Lotte, are guides to Balzac's personages.]

Comédie larmoyante, see *La Chaussée*; *Comedy*; *Drame*.

Comédies et Proverbes, collected dramatic works by Alfred de Musset (q.v.). The first edition (1840) contained the works already published (1834) in the second series of *Un Spectacle dans un fauteuil* (q.v.) plus *La Quenouille de Barberine* (see *Barberine*), *Le Chandelier, Il ne faut jurer de rien,* and *Un Caprice* (qq.v.), all prose. A new, revised, and corrected edition published in 1853 contained five further works, viz. *Il faut qu'une porte soit ouverte ou fermée, Louison, On ne saurait penser à tout, Carmosine,* and *Bettine* (qq.v.), again all, except *Louison,* in prose.

Comedy
[NOTE. Fuller mention of authors, works, dramatic forms, &c. referred to below is given under separate headings.]

(1) The origins of French comedy have been much discussed and remain in part obscure. It appears that although there is no connexion, on the literary side, between the Latin classical comedy and the medieval comedy in the vernacular, on the personal side the *jongleurs* of the Middle Ages may well have been the lineal descendants of the actors (*histriones, joculatores*) of the period of the Roman decadence, and may have inherited part of their oral *répertoire*. We are on surer ground when we trace the origin of French comedy, at least in part, to the comic element introduced at an early date in the liturgical drama, especially† in the passages in the vernacular with which the Latin text was 'farci' to serve as explanations for the ignorant audience. From the liturgical drama the comic element passed into the general vernacular drama, religious or profane, monologues and dialogues, Miracles and Mysteries. Early examples of this are

Bodel's *Jeu de saint Nicolas* and *Courtois d'Arras*, a late 12th- or early 13th-century adaptation of the story of the Prodigal Son. The little dialogue (270 lines) *Le Garçon et l'Aveugle, c.* 1270, in which a lad tricks and robs a blind man whom he leads about, is a relic of what may have been an extensive form of literature. Early types of a more developed comic drama survive in the remarkable *Jeu de la Feuillée* and *Jeu de Robin et de Marion* by Adam de la Halle (13th c.).

(2) The evolution of comic drama in the 14th and 15th centuries is somewhat obscure, for surviving texts are rare, and comic performances, though no doubt numerous, were not thought of sufficient importance to be recorded. They were given by confraternities of which the *Basochiens* and the *Enfants sans souci* were the best known; also by professional actors and by students. The plays performed were *moralités, soties,* and *farces,* three dramatic types not always easily distinguishable, except that from the last may be excluded any piece inculcating a moral and whose characters are allegorical. Some of the best-known examples of the first two are mentioned in the articles herein on *Moralités, Soties. Pathelin* (1464) is the pre-eminent example of the 15th-century farces. The *Franc-Archer de Bagnolet* is the masterpiece of a number of farcical monologues.

(3) The literary renaissance of the 16th century brought with it true comedy, at first seeking its models in the drama of antiquity or in Italian adaptations thereof. Jean Meschinot, Octavien de Saint-Gelais, Charles Estienne, Antoine de Baïf, and others translated or adapted comedies of Plautus and Terence, and Ronsard translated the *Plutus* of Aristophanes. The earliest original French comedy is the *Eugène* (1552) of Jodelle, which is Terentian in character, followed by *Les Esbahis* (1561) of Grévin. In all these comedies the pseudo-classical element is artificial and foreign; such life as they have is derived from the element of native farce which enters into the best of them, with its sharp sense of realism and the ridiculous, and its *esprit gaulois*. A little later (1579) we have Larivey's comedies from the Italian (the beginning of a phase of Italian influence on the French comic stage); about 1580 Odet de Turnèbe (q.v.) wrote *Les Contens,* one of the best of the early comedies, showing the author's acquaintance with

Celestina, which had been more than once translated from the Spanish during the century. Early comedies (before Molière's day) were as a rule written in octosyllabic verse; Jean de la Taille, Larivey, and Odet de Turnèbe wrote comedies in prose, but their example was little followed.

(4) For a time, in the early 17th century, comedy is rare, and the stage is largely occupied with *pastoral* (q.v.) drama. In 1629 appeared Corneille's *Mélite*, followed by his other plays of love intrigue, and about 1630 we have the beginning of the comedy of manners. The *Vendanges de Suresne* (1635) by du Ryer, in form a pastoral, is in essence a comedy of that kind, and other early examples are *L'Esprit fort* (1630) by Claveret, *Le Railleur* (1636) by Mareschal, and *Les Visionnaires* (1637) by Desmarets. From about 1640 comedy turned frequently to Spanish models; of such early imitations the most notable instance is Corneille's *Le Menteur* (1644), which is at the same time an excellent example of the comedy of character. Scarron now introduced the element of burlesque in comedy, in his *Jodelet* (1645) and *Don Japhet* (1652). Then came Molière, whose best work, broadening the domain of comedy, extended from 1659 to 1673. Among comic authors contemporary with him may be mentioned: Racine (*Les Plaideurs*), Quinault (*La Mère coquette*), Montfleury (*L'École des jaloux*), Cyrano de Bergerac (*Le Pédant joué*).

(5) A number of successors revived various aspects of Molière's genius, chief among them Dancourt and Le Sage, who imitated his realism; Regnard, his gay, farcical fancy. Others of less importance also wrote comedies of manners—Dufresny, d'Allainval, Poinsinet. But as the 18th century proceeded, the vein of comedy of manners and character showed signs of exhaustion. Marivaux, a disciple of Racine rather than Molière, made love the essential, instead of an episodic, element in his plays. Destouches was the first of a group of authors whose comedies of character and manners show a tendency to moralizing, as seen in his *Le Glorieux*, followed by Piron's *Métromanie* and Gresset's *Le Méchant*. We come thus to the *comédie larmoyante* or sentimental comedy of La Chaussée, in which the pathetic element dominates the comic, and situations play a larger part than character. Other examples of the sentimental comedy, of about the same period, were Voltaire's *L'Enfant prodigue* and *Nanine*. This form was later developed by Diderot in his *drames* (*Le Fils naturel*, *Le Père de famille*), by Sedaine in his *drame bourgeois*, *Le Philosophe sans le savoir*, and by Mercier in his domestic dramas. Meanwhile, at the *Théâtre de la foire*, farcical comedy had been developed by Le Sage and his successors in the direction of comic opera, first in the form of *comédies en vaudeville* (with lyrics sung to popular tunes), then of *comédies à ariettes* (with music specially composed for the songs), the most successful work in the latter kind being *Les Trois Sultanes* of Favart (1761). Other forms of comedy of which the 18th century furnishes examples are the satirical, such as *L'Écossaise*, of Voltaire, and *Les Philosophes*, of Palissot; the historical, such as Collé's *La Partie de chasse de Henri IV*; and finally the brilliant plays of Beaumarchais, which envelop audacious social and political satire in gaiety and wit.

(6) Comedy did not thrive on a Revolutionary stage invaded by politics and propaganda, though its popularity revived under the Directoire. The most notable authors—Fabre d'Églantine (*Le Philinte de Molière*) and Collin d'Harleville (*Le Vieux Célibataire*, 1792)—still copied Molière, as did also Andrieux (*Le Vieux Fat*, 1810), who had most official recognition under Napoleon. During the Empire and the Restoration, when on the whole the dramatic censorship weighed less heavily on comedy than on tragedy, Étienne (*Les Deux Gendres*), Picard (*Les Marionnettes*, *Les Deux Philibert*), and Duval (*Le Tyran domestique*, *La Fille d'honneur*) developed the comedy of manners, with lively sketches, often satirical, of daily and provincial life. Casimir Delavigne's *L'École des vieillards* (1823) departed from the conventional treatment of the elderly infatuated husband as a subject for ridicule and made him a sympathetic character; and N. Lemercier's *Pinto* introduced a genre of historical comedy, or drama, in which historical events were shown arising from petty causes. This was imitated at intervals throughout the century, e.g. by Scribe (see para. 7 below), Dumas *père* (e.g. *Mademoiselle de Belle-Isle*, 1839; *Les Demoiselles de Saint-Cyr*, 1843), Ponsard (*Le Lion amoureux*, 1866), Sardou (*Madame Sans-Gêne*, 1893).

(7) The outstanding innovator of the first half of the 19th century was Scribe (1791–1861), in whose comedies, vaudevilles, and historical comedies (*Bataille de dames, Une Chaîne, Le Solliciteur, Le Verre d'eau, Bertrand et Raton*) movement, intrigue, plot, and subplot were everything, and character was of no importance. In time the public reacted against the lifelessness of his plays, and his reputation faded rapidly. His dramatic technique, however, had made him one of the main influences on the theatre which came after him.

For the development of comedy during the later 19th and early 20th centuries see *Theatre of the 19th and 20th centuries*.

Comité de salut public, an emergency executive body constituted in March 1793 by decree of the *Convention nationale* (q.v.) to frame and administer internal and external political and defence measures. Its members (originally nine, afterwards increased to twelve) included Danton (soon excluded), Robespierre, Saint-Just, Carnot, Collot d'Herbois, Couthon, &c. It was largely responsible for the Terror. On the other hand it organized the Revolutionary armies. It was suppressed on the establishment of the *Directoire* (q.v.) in 1795.

Comité de sûreté générale, a body constituted by the *Convention nationale* (q.v.) in October 1792. It controlled the police and the prisons and was responsible for arrests.

Commedia dell'arte, the primitive improvised comedy, with stock characters, of the Italian actors (see *Italiens*) whose performances in France began in the sixteenth century and continued into the eighteenth.

Commines or **Commynes,** PHILIPPE DE (*c.* 1446–*c.* 1511), born in Flanders, was in the service of Charles, comte de Charolais, afterwards Duke of Burgundy, first as squire, later as councillor and chamberlain, from 1464 to 1472. In the latter year he transferred his services from Charles the Bold to Louis XI, whose political acumen he had had an opportunity of comparing with that of the duke, notably when Louis XI paid his famous visit to Péronne in 1468. He became one of the most influential advisers of the French king, and by his favour, supplemented by his own active pursuit of wealth, became very rich (though

the title to the estates conferred on him by the king was contested). By his marriage he acquired the domain of Argenton in Poitou, and thereafter is constantly referred to in contemporary documents as *M. d'Argenton*. In the troubles that followed the accession of Charles VIII (1483) Commines was imprisoned first at Loches (in an iron cage), then at Paris, and thereafter was sent into retirement and obliged to surrender a large part of his wealth. He was restored to favour about 1491 and accompanied Charles VIII on his Italian expedition (1494–5), an enterprise to which he was opposed. After the king's death he left the court, but returned in 1505 and took part in the Genoa campaign of 1507. Of the remainder of his life we know nothing of interest.

Of the eight books of his Memoirs (the division into books is by his editors) the first six deal with the reign of Louis XI and were composed probably in 1489–90; the last two deal with the Italian expedition of Charles VIII and were composed in 1497–8. The former are an exposition of the political, diplomatic, and military transactions of the reign, tracing events to their causes, estimating characters, laying bare the elements of the various situations; the work is written for the instruction of princes and statesmen. The last part includes a vivid account of the battle of Fornovo (1495), where the retreating French, now only 10,000 in number, fought their way through 40,000 of the enemy.

Commines was a man of lucid intelligence, deeply interested in the art and science of politics, and he found in Louis XI a kindred spirit whom he could admire. He shows himself a statesman of almost modern quality. He has a poor opinion of the old feudal chivalry and regards war as a great evil, not from sentimentality, but because it doesn't pay. He wishes to see just and orderly, not arbitrary, government, and a prosperous people. In particular he thinks that there should be no taxation without the consent of the taxpayers, and that the power of a king depends, not on the degree of his despotic power, but on the affection of his subjects. He regards England as the best-administered State of the day, because violence is not done there to the people. With all his admiration for foresight and sagacity in the conduct of affairs, he repeatedly refers to divine intervention in the course of events. He is himself religious and regards the decline of religious faith as the source of war and other political evils (chapters 18–20 of Bk. V contain an interesting exposition of his views on these subjects). His grave and somewhat melancholy outlook is shown in Bk. VI, ch. 12, where he discourses on the miserable life of men in general and of the great in particular. He judges the princes of the day, including Louis XI and Charles of Burgundy, with impartiality and penetration, and is measured in censure and in praise. His memoirs consequently, by their seriousness and total lack of picturesque quality, are very different in character from those of his predecessors Joinville and Froissart; they resemble rather those of Villehardouin, but show a far more vigorous intelligence than any other French work of the Middle Ages. The style of Commines is hardly equal to his subject-matter; it is somewhat flat and his sentences are often long and involved. The Memoirs were translated into many languages (into English by Thomas Danett, 1596). They inspired Scott's *Quentin Durward*, in which Commines himself figures.

Commune

(1) LA COMMUNE DE PARIS and LA COMMUNE INSURRECTIONNELLE (1789–94). The *Commune de Paris* was an improvised assembly which came into being in July 1789 after the fall of the Bastille and assumed responsibility for the government of Paris. Among its first acts were the appointment of a mayor (Bailly, q.v., was the first) and the creation of the *Garde nationale* (q.v.). It was composed to begin with of appointed delegates of the districts into which Paris had been divided in the spring of 1789 for the purpose of electing representatives to the *États Généraux* (q.v.). It worked at first through a Permanent Committee but it was more than once reorganized in an increasingly unsuccessful attempt to combat and isolate the extremist elements in its ranks. Matters came to a head on 10 August 1792 when the extremists formed themselves into a *Commune insurrectionnelle*, which expelled the earlier body and forced the *Assemblée législative* to declare the monarchy at an end. Thereafter the *Commune insurrectionnelle* exerted pressure on the *Assemblée législative*, and on the *Convention nationale* which suc-

ceeded it, and was the power behind the worst excesses of the Terror. It collapsed after the fall of Robespierre (10 July 1794). Since that time there has never been a mayor of Paris; and since Napoleon's administrative reforms of 1800 the system of local government in Paris has been exceptionally designed so as to make it impossible for a municipality to usurp the functions of the central government. (See also *Police*, para. 2.)

(2) LA COMMUNE (March–May 1871), the council established by the insurrectionists who seized power in Paris in March 1871. The Government of National Defence established after the *Révolution du 4 septembre* (q.v.) had been concerned with the conduct of the Franco-Prussian War (q.v.). In February 1871, while peace was being negotiated, an *Assemblée nationale*, strongly monarchist in character, was elected and decided to sit at Versailles. Paris, where the revolutionary element predominated, had suffered badly during a winter of siege. Living-conditions were dislocated; the people, undermined by hunger, bitterly resented the thought of a Royalist Assembly at Versailles; they were infuriated by the clause of the peace terms which permitted the German occupation of Paris; and they were still armed, from having served in the *Garde nationale* (q.v.). On the day of the German entry Republican bands removed the cannon from the Champs-Élysées, destined as German quarters, to the poorer districts of the city, and there formed a *Fédération républicaine de la garde nationale*. Insurrection followed. The city was in the hands of the insurgents, who established a *Conseil communal* or *Commune* (26 March), intended to exercise power and legislate for the whole country. (But the country did not follow the lead of Paris.) Meanwhile the Government, at Versailles, formed an army of regulars under General MacMahon to combat the army of *communards*. The ensuing civil war lasted two months and was in effect a second siege of Paris. The worst period (21 to 28 May, after the Army of Versailles entered Paris) was known as 'la semaine sanglante', from the violent street fighting and massacres which characterized it. By the end of May the *Commune* was suppressed. Reprisals and punitive measures followed and lasted till 1875.

[NOTE: The substantive 'commune'

signifies the smallest unit of administration in the French system of local government, see *Département*.]

Compagnie de Jésus, see *Jésuites*.

Compagnie des Quinze, an experimental theatre company, founded in France *c*. 1930 (disbanded *c*. 1936) by the actor and producer Michel Saint-Denis (1897–   ), a nephew of Jacques Copeau (q.v.), with whom he had been associated at the Théâtre du Vieux-Colombier and afterwards at Copeau's theatrical school in Burgundy, out of which the Company grew. The *Compagnie des Quinze* was more than once seen in England, in plays by André Obey, Jean Giono (qq.v.), and others. [Saint-Denis founded a school of acting in London at a later date and was also at one time producer and director of the Old Vic Theatre.]

Compagnie du Saint Sacrement (or **du Très Saint Sacrement de l'autel**), **La,** a powerful secret society or *congrégation* (q.v.) for faith and good works which existed from 1627 till some time after 1665 and whose members, secular and clerical, included several important figures of 17th-century—counter-Reformationary—France. It had headquarters in Paris, affiliations all over the country, and a network of agents, spies, and informers planted in all walks of life. It never acted as a body, but always through the members as individuals, and these religious enthusiasts—or busybodies—shrank from no means, however dubious, that might further their ends. The ends, of positive well-doing or often, and more dangerously, of seeking out evil in order to remedy it, included such things as helping the poor and the oppressed; improving the lot of convicts in the galleys (see *Galère*); propagating the (Roman Catholic) faith in France and, through missions, in foreign countries; suppressing blasphemers; chasing Protestants from the land and prostitutes from the streets; writing anonymously to inform husbands of their wives' adultery; securing the prohibition of duels, and keeping unsuitable plays from the boards. It was thanks to the influence at court of this 'cabale des dévots' that the King, in 1664, prohibited the public performance in Paris of Molière's *Tartuffe* (q.v.), which contained veiled attacks upon them. This, however,

was one of the *Compagnie*'s dying flickers, for its existence had become known, Mazarin was hostile to it, and it was soon to disperse.

Compagnon du Tour de France, Le (1840), a novel by George Sand (q.v.). The scene is a French village, the time some years after the Restoration (1815), when liberalism and discontent with the Monarchy were rife and secret societies (cf. *Carbonari*) flourished. Two young carpenters lose their hearts to the granddaughter and niece respectively of the comte de Villepreux, who has commissioned them to restore the carvings in his château. The count pays lip-service to social equality until it impinges upon his daily life. The young men, who take their ideals more seriously, have been *compagnons du Tour de France*, i.e., their apprenticeship ended, they had travelled across France, perfecting their craft and becoming affiliated to one of the trades guilds which at this time still existed. The slender plot supports a rehash of information about the origin and customs of these *compagnonnages*. It also affords scope for the author's humanitarian fervour.

Complaintes, Les (1885), poems by Jules Laforgue (q.v.).

Comput, in medieval literature, a chronological treatise or ecclesiastical calendar, giving scope for moralization. Didactic works of this kind were in favour in the 12th and 13th centuries. See *Philippe de Thaon*.

Comtat Venaissin, see *Vaucluse*.

Comte, see *Duc*.

Comte, AUGUSTE (1798–1857), one of the great influences on 19th-century philosophy, the founder of Positivism, a system of philosophy which recognizes only positive facts and observable phenomena. After passing out of the École polytechnique (q.v.) he taught mathematics and became a disciple of Saint-Simon (q.v.) but quarrelled with him in 1824. He delivered lectures in his own rooms which attracted many great thinkers of the day and in which—as also in the journal *Le Producteur* (1825 and 1826)—he first outlined his philosophical doctrines. A mental breakdown unfitted him for work till 1828, when he resumed lecturing, became external entrance examiner for the École polytechnique, engaged in various public-spirited activities, and began publication of his *Cours de philosophie positive* (1830–42). The most brilliant period of his intellectual career ended in 1842. So did his appointment at the École polytechnique, largely because of his arrogant and intolerant behaviour. A number of English admirers, headed by John Stuart Mill, came to his financial aid, but their generosity faded before his assumption that his friends had a duty to support him. From 1849 until his death he was enabled to devote himself to writing and lecturing, thanks to a fund collected on his behalf by Littré (q.v.).

Comte's positivist philosophy applied to society the laws, based upon observation and deduction, used in what he classified as the six abstract sciences—mathematics, astronomy, physics, chemistry, biology, and sociology (a science of which he was in effect the founder). He confined himself to the recognition of facts and their objective relations, waiving any attempt to explain ultimate causes because, he considered, such questions belonged to earlier, theological or metaphysical, stages in the history of thought. The two exceptionally brilliant sections of the *Philosophie positive* are his classification of the sciences and his history of social evolution. After 1842 he attempted to transform his philosophy into a religion, substituting the worship of Humanity for the worship of a Deity. After 1845 this religion (defined by T. H. Huxley as 'Catholicism without God') was complicated by the introduction of a mystical element, a result of his romantic passion for Mme Clotilde de Vaux (q.v.) whom he constituted the patron saint of Humanity. He defined the tenets of this religion in his *Catéchisme positiviste* (1852), a series of questions and answers between a female believer and the *Grand-Prêtre de l'Humanité* (himself). In a preface he listed the books essential for the library of a devout Positivist: thirty volumes of poetry and fiction ranging from the *Odyssey* by way of Racine, Shakespeare, and the *Arabian Nights* to Byron (minus *Don Juan*); thirty volumes of science; sixty volumes of history; and thirty volumes of 'synthesis', i.e. religion and philosophy. Before he had completed his *Cours de philosophie positive* he had decided that he himself had read enough to serve for the remainder of his life. Thenceforward, except for some poetry and the *Imitatio Christi*,

reading (including even newspapers and scientific journals) was banished from his scheme of life.

Comte's habit when writing was to put no word on paper until he had composed the whole work, even to the form of his sentences, in his head. He then, by an extraordinary feat of memory, wrote the whole book straight off and sent it to the printer, making no changes and allowing himself only one proof.

Other works by Comte include: *Système de politique positive* (1851–4, 4 vols.), also a *Calendrier positiviste* (1849) which substitutes the names of great men for the names of saints.

Comte de Comminges, Le, see *Arnaud, Baculard d'*.

Comte de Monte-Cristo, Le (1844–5), by Dumas *père*, one of the great thrillers of all literature.

When the tale opens Napoleon is in exile on Elba. Edmond Dantès, a young sea-captain and an alleged Bonapartist conspirator, is imprisoned in the Château d'If, a fortified prison near Marseilles. He is the innocent victim of Villefort, a magistrate, Fernand, a fisherman, and Danglars, a ship-broker's agent, three villains who would profit by his disappearance. He is befriended by a fellow prisoner, the abbé Faria, from whose vast learning he benefits, and who tells him about a fabulous treasure hidden in the Island of Monte Cristo. The abbé dies. Dantès substitutes himself for the corpse, is flung into the sea from the battlements of the Château d'If, but escapes miraculously. He finds the Island and the treasure and, as comte de Monte-Cristo, comes to Paris. Here he finds Villefort (now Procureur du Roi), Fernand (now a general, comte de Morcerf, and a *Pair de France*), and Danglars (now a wealthy banker, a baron). Monte-Cristo's riches, and the mystery surrounding him, give him the entry into the highest circles, and without disclosing his true identity he sets to work to avenge his wrongs. He stalks through the book like a mysterious, avenging Providence, come down to earth via the *Arabian Nights*. He adopts many personalities, smooths his path with Arab steeds, emeralds, and millions, with assassinations, poisons, and suicides, rakes up lurid pasts, and visits the sins of the fathers upon the children. Finally, his vengeance completed, he revisits the scene of his captivity and then, with his beautiful Greek slave Haydée, sets sail for unknown waters.

This long tale of vengeance seldom flags. The intricate plot and sub-plots are skilfully manœuvred, and the characters are by no means puppets.

Comte de Paris, see *Henri, comte de Paris.*

Comtesse de Charny, La (1852–5), an historical novel of the Revolution, by Dumas *père.*

Comtesse de Rudolstadt, La (1843–5), by George Sand, the sequel to *Consuelo* (q.v.).

Comtesse d'Escarbagnas, La, a one-act comedy in prose by Molière, produced in 1671.

The scene is Angoulême. It is a slight sketch of the affectations, insipid gallantries, and other absurdities of provincial society. The plot is trivial. The comtesse is an old coquette, who apes the elegances of Paris (where she has spent two months) and lords it over her admirers, the local magistrate and tax-collector. Under pretence of paying court to her, a country gentleman uses her house as a place of assignation with his lady-love.

Conciergerie, La, a celebrated prison in Paris, said to be the oldest in Europe, forms part of the Palais de Justice. In medieval times it was the portion of the building inhabited by the *concierge,* later called *bailli, du palais,* a royal office (dating from the 10th century, suppressed 1416, whose holder had jurisdiction over a large surrounding district as well as many chances to acquire power and wealth). Famous prisoners of the Conciergerie include: Ravaillac, assassin of Henri IV, the marquise de Brinvilliers, the famous poisoner, Damiens, would-be assassin of Louis XV, and Marie-Antoinette (after the execution of Louis XVI). It was crowded during the Revolution. Charlotte Corday, Danton, Desmoulins, and Robespierre, among others, were there, the last for the one night before his execution. It is now used for prisoners waiting to appear before the assizes or the Court of Appeal. [One memorable description of the Conciergerie is in Balzac's *Splendeurs et misères des courtisanes,* q.v.]

Concile féerique, Le (1886), by Jules Laforgue (q.v.), a poem in dialogue form.

Concini or **Concino,** an Italian adventurer, favourite of Marie de Médicis, whom he accompanied when she came to France to marry Henri IV. With his wife, Leonora Galigai, he dominated the queen. He became minister under Louis XIII, being known as the maréchal d'Ancre. His greed and insolence caused deep resentment, not least to the young king, by whose order he was assassinated in 1617.

Concordat, an agreement between the Roman See and a secular government on matters that concern both.

(1) By the *concordat* of 1516, between Leo X and François Ier, the king took power to appoint bishops and abbots in France, while the Pope was to have restored to him the annates of which he had been deprived by a pragmatic sanction of Charles VII.

(2) The *concordat* of 1801, ratified by law in 1802, between Pius VII and the First Consul Bonaparte, re-established Roman Catholicism and its free practice as the religion of the majority of Frenchmen; defined the relations between France and the Holy See; and demarcated the temporal and spiritual powers of the Church (e.g. as regarded the nomination, institution, and payment of the clergy, and claims to Church property). The settlement between Church and state lasted till 1905, when the Church was disestablished and disendowed.

[For two ineffective *concordats,* of historic interest—(a) the *concordat de Fontainebleau* (1813), forced by Napoleon on the Pope when he was imprisoned at Fontainebleau but denounced by the latter as soon as he regained freedom; and (b) a *concordat* of 1817 agreed between Louis XVIII and the Pope but never ratified by law—see Lavisse, *Histoire de la France contemporaine,* iii. 313 and iv. 130.]

Concorde, see *Place de la Concorde.*

Condamnation de Banquet, La, see *Moralité.*

Condé, L'Armée de, see *Armée des émigrés.*

Condé, Le Grand (Louis II, prince de Condé, 1621–86), a member of a collateral branch of the royal house of Bourbon (q.v.), a great captain in the wars of Louis XIV. He first distinguished himself when still very young by the victories of Rocroy, Nordlingen, and Lens. In the troubles of the *Fronde* he joined the enemies of the court, even entering into alliance with Spain against it. He was subsequently pardoned and restored to high command. He fought the drawn battle of Seneffe with the Prince of Orange in 1674. His funeral oration was delivered by Bossuet. His youthful inclination to free thought may be noted, and his later position as a patron of literature. We have his letters, which are the work of a skilled writer.

Condillac, ÉTIENNE DE (1715–80), generally known as *l'abbé de Condillac,* philosopher, born at Grenoble, 'le philosophe des philosophes' (Lanson) and a close friend of some of the leaders among these, such as Diderot and Helvétius. He was author of an *Essai sur l'origine des connaissances humaines* (1746), *Traité des systèmes* (1749), *Traité des sensations* (1754), *Traité des animaux* (1754, in the main a polemical work directed against Buffon), *Cours d'études du prince de Parme* (1769–73), and of some articles in the *Encyclopédie.* He was a man of lucid intelligence, who took little part in the violent controversies of his time. A student of Locke, he went beyond him in tracing the development of the various human faculties— memory, imagination, reflection, &c.—to their origin in sensations, and held that it was possible to apply logical reasoning in metaphysics and morals with the same precision as in geometry, and proceed by this method from accurate ideas of the external world to social and political science, and even to the idea of God and the immortality of the soul. His French Grammar (1775) treats of language as the instrument of reasoning.

Condition humaine, La (1933), by André Malraux, one of the outstanding French novels of the 20th century (see *Grand Prix des meilleurs romans du demi-siècle*). It is primarily a novel of action, concerned with abortive revolutionary activities in Peking in the early days of Chinese communism; and it is difficult, because the reader, like a participant in history, must piece together his own fragmentary impressions of events. But, more profoundly, from the conversations of the characters, it is also a study of conspiracy and the psychology of conspirators, their motives and ideals, or lack of ideals, their fundamental loneliness, yet their recognition of a fraternity which unites men in the face of betrayal and failure.

Condom (pron. as if *Condon*), ÉVÊQUE DE, a term sometimes used to designate Bossuet, who was bishop of the see 1669–72. Condom is a small town in south-west France, in the department of Gers.

Condorcet, ANTOINE-NICOLAS DE (1743– 94), born in Picardy of a noble family, mathematician and philosopher, and later politician. He was perpetual secretary of the *Académie des Sciences* (for which he wrote *Éloges* of the academicians who had died from 1666 to 1790) and later a member of the *Académie française.* He was a friend of d'Alembert, Turgot, and Voltaire; of the two last he wrote lives (1786 and 1787), sharing Voltaire's antipathy to the Church and Turgot's ardour for the improvement of the human lot. He also edited (1776) Pascal's *Pensées,* with notes in which he demurred to the author's estimate of man's vileness. His reputation is chiefly based on his *Tableau historique des progrès de l'esprit humain* (q.v.). This was written (1793–4) during the period when, although an ardent partisan of the French Revolution and a member of the Legislative Assembly and the Convention, he was under proscription as a Girondin. He took poison to avoid the guillotine. He also wrote a number of dissertations on political subjects during the Revolution.

It is related that this eminent mathematician lost his life through not knowing how many eggs are required for an omelet. Fleeing from proscription he came to an inn and demanded an omelet. 'How many eggs, citizen?' asked the hostess. 'Oh, a dozen, I suppose', replied the innocent Condorcet. The hostess, suspecting that such ignorance betokened an aristocratic past, denounced him to the authorities.

Confédération du Rhin, La, a league of certain southern and south-western German States formed by Napoleon after he abolished the Holy Roman Empire (1806). It pledged military support to the French Empire in return for protection. It lasted till 1813.

Confession de Claude, La (1865), by Zola, his first novel. After this he depended on his writing for a living.

Confession de minuit (1920), one of Duhamel's *Salavin* (q.v.) novels.

Confession d'un enfant du siècle, La (1836), a novel by Alfred de Musset, is to some extent autobiographical because the spark for the author's creative impulse was his unhappy liaison with the novelist George Sand (q.v.). It is also autobiographical in its (frequently quoted) testimony to the disillusionment felt by the youth of the early 19th century. Moreover, it is a remarkable early novel of psychological analysis (at times almost an anticipation of Proust, q.v.). The hero, deceived by a mistress, takes to debauchery, then falls in love with an honest woman, a widow. He is jealous, and jealous of her past. There are quarrels and reconciliations. He torments her, and takes pleasure in destroying today all the good in the love of yesterday. His love is killed by possession and revivified by jealousy. He watches his beloved asleep, and soliloquizes. In the end he effaces himself so that Brigitte can be happy with the man she really loves.

Confessions, Les, an autobiography by J.-J. Rousseau, written between 1764 and 1770 and published posthumously, Books I–VI in 1781, VII–XII in 1788. They cover the period from his early life to 1766, when he left the island of Saint-Pierre and before he came to England. In them Rousseau claims to present a man 'in all the truth of nature', and this he does with a vivid minuteness, setting forth all the incidents of an agitated life, his reactions to them, and his spiritual development, while concealing nothing to his discredit, even his meanest actions and his sexual abnormalities. Though written under the influence of persecutions, real and imaginary, and consequently in some degree an apologia, and in spite of some distortions of fact, they appear to be on the whole a work of sincere self-revelation. They depict a man who, with many admirable qualities, paid little regard to accepted morality and social conventions, and was the victim not so much of the hostility of others as of his own revolt and morbid sensibility. They contain many passages of exquisite description of scenery and homely life.

Confidences (1849) and **Nouvelles Confidences** (1851), Lamartine's nostalgic, poetically-written reminiscences of early years with his parents and sisters at Milly (q.v.) and at Mâcon, of first travel, and of first love. His short autobiographical novels *Graziella* (q.v.) and *Raphaël* (about his love for Julie, i.e. the invalid Mme Charles, the 'Elvire' (q.v.) of his poems) are largely lifted from the 1849 volume.

Confrérie de la Passion, La, was the most famous of the *confréries sérieuses*, societies or confraternities of players formed by the tradesmen and other citizens of Paris and some of the provincial towns to perform the cycles of the Mysteries (see *Mystères*) when the representation of these passed from the clerics to laymen. The earliest known *confrérie* is that of Nantes (1371). The *Confrérie de la Passion* was licensed at Paris in 1402 by Charles VI, and gave performances of Mysteries, particularly the Mystery of the Passion, either at its headquarters in the hospital adjacent to the Église de la Trinité (outside the Porte Saint-Denis) or on the steps before the church, or, at times, such as royal entries, in processions through the city. On occasion they joined forces with the *confréries joyeuses*, the *Basoche* and the *Enfants sans souci* (qq.v.), to add a comic element to their repertory, and at such times the performance of a Mystery might be followed by a farce or *sotie* (q.v.). The *Confrérie de la Passion* moved in 1539 to the Hôtel de Flandre, where in the year 1540 they performed the long and elaborate Mystery of the *Actes des Apôtres* (written by Simon Greban in the 15th c.). After this their prestige began to decline. It was objected that their processions through the streets were the cause of public disturbance; that the players, being ignorant artisans, turned what should have been matter for edification into ridicule; and that the performance of the Mysteries, with their mingling of the sacred and the burlesque, of truth and legend, had become contrary to religious decency. In the end the *Confrérie de la Passion*, who had been forced to leave the Hôtel de Flandre, were forbidden to perform sacred dramas in the new quarters they had procured in 1548 on the site of the ancient Hôtel de Bourgogne (q.v.), while retaining the monopoly in Paris of other theatrical performances. For over a hundred years afterwards the record is one of struggle for the retention of their rights. From 1578 the *Confrérie* let their premises from time to time to companies of professional actors, who in turn sometimes tried to oust the proprietors. The *Confrérie*, however, continued itself to give occasional performances, but these appear to have ceased from 1588. Finally, by an edict of 1676, the confraternity was dissolved.

Congé, a form of medieval lyric of which Jean Bodel (q.v.) provides the first known example. When he contracted leprosy and was about to retire from the world he took leave of his friends in a poem of forty-two stanzas, addressing a stanza to each. This was imitated by Adam de la Halle (q.v.) when he left Arras in consequence of political troubles, in a poem which was in fact a satire on his fellow citizens. It was imitated again by a poet named Baude Fastoul, who like Bodel became a leper.

Congrégation de Saint-Maur, see *Maurists*.

Congrégations. In the Roman Catholic Church this word denotes 'a community or order bound together by a common rule, either without vows (as the Oratorians) or without solemn vows (as the Passionists, Redemptorists)' [*O.E.D.*]. It was also used in an extended sense in France for the lay, or mingled lay and clerical, associations for prayer and good works which originated in the 16th century among the pupils in Jesuit colleges. These were suppressed during the Revolution, but revived more or less clandestinely during the Empire and more openly after the Restoration, with a lay and clerical membership drawn from the aristocracy and the *haute bourgeoisie*. About 1820 popular opinion credited them with an underground share in plots to restore religious and monarchical ascendancy. Such appears to have been the object of a central, secret *Congrégation* of which the comte d'Artois, later Charles X, was for some time at the head. The *Sociétés des bonnes lettres, des bonnes œuvres,* and *des bonnes études* were said to be offshoots of this central body. The *Société des bonnes études* provided lectures, classes, cheap meals, and moral supervision for young men, usually office workers of some sort.

Connaissance de l'est (1900), essays and prose poems by Claudel (q.v.).

Connards, see *Sociétés joyeuses*.

Connétable des lettres, Le, see *Barbey d'Aurevilly*.

Conon (or Quesnes) **de Béthune** (d. 1224), poet, a native of Picardy and a man of high birth (an ancestor of Sully), who took part in the Crusades of the end of the 12th century (in connexion with which he is well spoken of by Villehardouin), and was at one time (1219) regent of the Empire. He was one of the principal imitators in northern French of the courtly poetry of the troubadours (see *Lyric poetry*), in a vivacious, occasionally ironical style. He was much nettled when the Queen of France mocked the provincialism of his language, and retorted in a poem in the course of which he says:

Encor ne soit ma parole françoise
Si la puet on bien entendre en françois.
Ne cil ne sont bien apris ne cortois
S'il m'ont repris, se j'ai dit mot d'Artois
Car je ne fui pas norris a Pontoise [in the Île-de-France].

Conque, La (1891, 11 numbers), an exclusive literary review, founded by Pierre Louÿs (q.v.), published original work by young poets, and was issued in a limited edition. The frontispiece was always a work by a poet of accepted standing, e.g. Leconte de Lisle, Heredia, Mallarmé, Swinburne. Most of Valéry's early poems appeared in this. Other contributors were Gide, Henri de Régnier, &c.

Conquérants, Les (1928), a novel by André Malraux (q.v.).

Conquête de Jérusalem, La, see *Antioche*.

Conquête de Plassans, La (1874), one of Zola's *Rougon-Macquart* (q.v.) novels. In the early days of the Second Empire the ambitious and domineering abbé Faujas arrives in Plassans, the Provençal town where the history of the Rougon-Macquart families began. Gradually, despite his uncouth exterior and dubious past, he manœuvres himself into a position of supreme importance in the little town, transforming it from a Legitimist stronghold to support of the Empire, and engineering ecclesiastical promotions to suit his own purposes. He lodges, and spreads himself, with his mother and other objectionable relations, with M. and Mme Mouret (the one a Macquart, the other a Rougon), and so effectively upsets their tranquil household that the mental instability latent in the pair comes to the surface. The simple, home-loving Marthe Mouret develops religious mania; her husband becomes a homicidal maniac and sets his house, with its undesirable occupants, on fire. This novel is not subordinated to Zola's theories of heredity. Political and ecclesiastical intrigues provide the main plot, and the descriptions of these, and of provincial society, are excellent. The final tragedy is enlivened when the local worthies ensconce themselves comfortably in armchairs, at a safe distance, to gossip and to watch the conflagration. Their horror at the manner of the Abbé's death mingles with relief at deliverance from his domination.

Conrart, VALENTIN (1603–75), man of letters, a Huguenot, an authority on grammar and style, remembered especially for the part he played in the foundation of the *Académie française* (q.v.), of which he was appointed perpetual secretary. He wrote little and Boileau ridiculed him in the line 'J'imite de Conrart le silence prudent'. He left *Mémoires,* of which only a part has been preserved (published in 1824; the account of the *Fronde* in 1652 is of high interest), followed by detached pieces, anecdotes, and fragments. Conrart was an intimate friend of Guez de Balzac.

Conscience, La, one of the poems of *La Légende des siècles* (q.v.), by Hugo.

Conseil de la République, the upper chamber of the French parliament which under the constitution of 27 October 1946 (see *Republics,* para. 11) replaced the former *Sénat* (q.v.) and consisted of indirectly elected members, still known as *Sénateurs,* with its seat still, as formerly, in the Palais du Luxembourg (q.v.).

Conseil des anciens, see *Directoire.*

Conseil des cinq cents, see *Directoire.*

Conseil d'état.

(*a*) UNDER THE ANCIEN RÉGIME the royal council, after a long period of evolution, took definite shape under Louis XIV. The term then covered four councils, distinct in functions, though composed to some extent of the same members:

(1) The *Conseil d'état* proper, often called the *Conseil d'en haut,* in which were treated high matters of State, such as foreign affairs, or important litigious questions. It was presided over by the king and was composed of a few selected ministers, such as Louvois, Pomponne, Colbert, besides the chancellor.

(2) The *Conseil privé* or *des parties,* the supreme judicial body of the realm, judging cases reserved for it or evoked from inferior courts, presided over nominally by the king, in practice by the chancellor. The Council included *ex-officio* members, viz. the *ducs et pairs* (who rarely attended the meetings), the ministers and secretaries of state, and certain financial officials; and in addition specially appointed members, whose number was restricted after 1673 to thirty, twenty-four of whom were lawyers. The position of *conseiller d'état* was a dignity, not an office, and was retained for life.

(3) The *Conseil des dépêches,* dealing with questions of internal administration, and composed of the members of (1) together with the chancellor and such secretaries of state as were not members of (1); the king presided, and members of the royal family attended the meetings.

(4) The *Conseil des finances.* The reorganization of this was one of the first of Colbert's tasks. By the regulation of 1661 it dealt with the assessment of the direct taxes, contracts for the farming of the indirect taxes, the royal domains, the currency, and the state accounts; it also had jurisdiction in litigious financial questions. It was presided over by the king and comprised the chancellor, a *chef du conseil,* and three *conseillers,* of whom Colbert as *intendant des finances* and later *contrôleur général* was one. In this form it endured substantially unaltered until the end of the monarchy, although under the despotic financial control of Colbert its importance was rather apparent than real.

(*b*) THE PRESENT-DAY CONSEIL D'ÉTAT, which has its origin in the *conseil d'état* created, or reintroduced, during the Consulate (13 Dec. 1799), is a supreme judicial body in the nature of both an advisory council and a tribunal. Its concern is with the interpretation and execution of laws and decrees, or cases arising out of them, in so far as they affect government departments or, it may be, private citizens in their dealings with government departments. The president is the President of the Republic and the effective head is the Vice-President of the Republic, who is always automatically a high-ranking magistrate and an authority on administrative and constitutional law.

Conservateur, Le, an ultra-Royalist journal, or miscellany, published irregularly so as to evade censorship, was founded in 1818 in opposition to *La Minerve française* (q.v.) and lasted till 1820. Contributors included Chateaubriand and Lamennais (qq.v.).

Conservateur littéraire, Le (1819–21), a literary review founded by Victor Hugo (aged seventeen) and his brother Abel (aged barely twenty-one). The former was the life and soul of the venture, the latter did the hack work. Although orthodox and unprogressive to begin with, it became one of the principal organs of the Romantics (see *Romantisme*).

Considérant, VICTOR (1809–93), gave up an army career to become one of the most active disciples of the social reformer Fourier (q.v.).

Considérations sur les causes de la grandeur des Romains et de leur décadence, a work of history and political philosophy by Montesquieu, published in 1734, republished with corrections and additions in 1748.

Repudiating the idea that chance dominates the destiny of nations (ch. xviii), the author deduces from a summary history of Rome, extending from the foundation of the Republic to the destruction of the Empire, the underlying causes of its rise and decline. He sees in the early Roman State certain qualities—homogeneity, frugality, devotion to liberty, and concentration on foreign conquest—which were well adapted to its aggrandizement. But when internal dissension developed into civil war, when the principles by which the world had been conquered gave place to luxury, when alien nations were incorporated in the State, and a series of bad emperors controlled its fortunes, the decline of Rome began. Barbarian invasions brought the Western Empire to an end and the Eastern Empire

entered on its slow agony. 'Tolluntur in altum, ut lapso graviore ruant' is the author's theme. The work contains an interesting study of the Roman spirit and of the Republican Senate; but the author is quite uncritical with regard to his sources, nor does he include economic factors in his survey, or any reference to Roman religion; and he is inclined to hasty generalizations, and shows lack of practical knowledge of the limited extent to which human prudence helps to shape the destiny of a people. But the work is an interesting example of early scientific non-religious history, in which events are traced to their natural causes, without reference to a guiding Providence.

Consolation de Philosophie, La, translations of the *De consolatione philosophiae* of Boëthius (q.v.). Among these was one made in the 12th century by Simon de Freine, and another by Jean de Meung (q.v.) *c.* 1285 for Philippe le Bel.

Consolations, Les (1830), poems by Sainte-Beuve (q.v.).

Consonance, agreement in the terminal sounds of two or more metrical lines, such that the last stressed vowel and any sounds following it are the same, while the sounds preceding it are different [*O.E.D.*]. This is modern rhyme, as distinguished from *Assonance* (q.v.).

Consonne d'appui, see *Rime riche*.

Constant, see *Wairy, Louis-Constant*.

Constant, L'ABBÉ ALPHONSE-LOUIS [ÉLIPHAS LÉVI] (1810–75), after an early education for the priesthood became interested in *Fouriérisme* (q.v.) and various other, more fantastic, forms of semi-mystical socialism which flourished *c.* 1840–50. Later still he took to occultism and under the name of 'Éliphas Lévi' published *Histoire de la magie* (1860), a book well known in its own sphere. Works of his earlier phase (when he was for a time associated with H.-A. Esquiros, q.v.) include *La Bible de la liberté* (1840), *Doctrines religieuses et sociales* (1841), *La Mère de Dieu* (1844),&c. He ended life as a fruit-farmer.

Constant de Rebecque, HENRI-BENJAMIN [BENJAMIN CONSTANT] (1767–1830), a celebrated politician and polemist while alive, endures for posterity as the author of one short novel *Adolphe* (q.v.). Born at Lausanne, of Protestant stock, he was educated privately and at the universities of Erlangen and Edinburgh. The first half of his career was marked by liaisons with women older than himself, among them Mme de Charrière and, notably, Mme de Staël (qq.v.). He met the latter in 1794 and for seventeen years she maintained a hold over him which no effort, not even the disclosure of his secret marriage with another woman (Charlotte de Hardenberg, in 1808), could break. He was at her beck and call in Paris, at Coppet (q.v.), or on her travels, and—for his political phase had now begun—when his politics displeased Napoleon (1803) he shared her exile. The final rupture came at Lausanne in 1811, although he saw and corresponded with her in later years. He retired to live in Germany and in 1813, from Hanover, published *De l'esprit de conquête et de l'usurpation*, a famous pamphlet attacking Napoleon. This did not, however, prevent him from taking office under Napoleon in Paris during the Hundred Days. He left France for Brussels, then London, after the second Restoration—and published *Adolphe* in London in 1816—but returned two years later. Thenceforward until his death he had a brilliant political career, both within the Chamber, as a leader of the Liberal opposition, and without, as a journalist.

Other works published in his lifetime include *De la religion considérée dans sa source, ses formes et ses développements* (1824–31), political and religious treatises which he had been writing intermittently since his youth, and *Mélanges de littérature et de politique* (1829). He kept, for his own use and with no thought of publication, a *Journal intime* of the greatest interest. Some of it was published for the first time in 1895. A much more complete edition, making use of further manuscripts, is the *Journaux intimes de Benjamin Constant* (1952, édit. intégrale ... avec un index et des notes par Alfred Roulin et Charles Roth). His *Cahier rouge* (1907), another posthumous publication of great literary interest, contains reminiscences of childhood and youth ending with his 20th year. The exact title is *Ma vie, 1767–1787*, but it is called the *Cahier rouge* because the notebook in which it was written had a red cover. In 1951 yet another fragmen-

tary work—*Cécile*—was published from a recently discovered manuscript. It is, again, autobiographical, but, like *Adolphe*, in the form of a tale.

Constantinople, La Conquête de, see *Villehardouin*.

Constituante, La; Constituants, the *Assemblée constituante* (q.v.) and its members.

Constitution civile du clergé, La, a law of 1790 by which the *Concordat* (q.v.) of 1516 was repudiated. The Church was subordinated to the government, reorganized, and freed from Papal control. Provision was made for local election of bishops and clergy. A decree of the same year (26 Dec.), which became effective in January 1791 and was condemned by the Pope (Pius VI) two months later, directed every practising clergyman to swear acceptance of this *Constitution civile*. Those who accepted were known as *prêtres assermentés* or *jureurs*. Those, a large number, who refused were the *insermentés* or *réfractaires*. Their refusal counted as resignation of office and they were often persecuted and driven into hiding (cf. Lamartine's poem *Jocelyn*).

Constitutionnel, Le (first called *L'Indépendant*), was founded by former revolutionaries in 1815, during the Hundred Days, as a liberal, anti-clerical paper. It was suppressed for a time after the second Restoration because of its Bonapartist sympathies, but reappeared and became one of the most popular Opposition journals, noted also for its literary *feuilleton* and its disapproval of the Romantic movement. It fell on evil times during the July Monarchy but was restored—by Dr. Véron (q.v.), who bought it in 1844—to a prosperity for which the *romans-feuilletons* of George Sand, Eugène Sue (notably his *Juif errant*), and Dumas *père* were largely responsible. Some years later, inspired from Bonapartist headquarters, it did much to prepare public opinion for the *coup d'état* of December 1851. It supported the Second Empire and flourished on the literary side. It was in this paper that Sainte-Beuve (q.v.) began his famous *Causeries du lundi*.

Constitutions [in the sense of 'the system or body of fundamental principles according to which a nation, state, or body politic is constituted and governed', O.E.D.]. France had her first written constitution in 1791 and has had others at various stages of her history since then. The first, voted by the *Assemblée nationale constituante* (q.v.), was an attempt to apply the principles of the *Déclaration des droits de l'homme et du citoyen* (q.v.), those two especially which have remained fundamental (though at times weakened), namely, the sovereignty of the people and the separation of powers (i.e. the distinction, in the organization of government, between legislative, executive, and judicial responsibilities). The notable dates are:

(*a*) 1791; 1793; 1795; 1799; 1802 (see *Revolutions*, Ia; *Directoire*; *Consulat*);

(*b*) 1804 (see *Empire, le Premier*, and cf. *Acte additionnel aux Constitutions de l'Empire*; *Charte, La*; *Revolutions*, IIa);

(*c*) 1848; 1852; 1870 (see *Republics*, para. 3; *Empire, le Second*);

(*d*) 1875 (see *Republics*, para. 4);

(*e*) 1946 (see *Republics*, para. 11).

Consuelo (1842–3), by George Sand (q.v.), a novel of 18th-century musical life and adventure, begins in Venice but soon moves to Austria and Bohemia. History and memoirs of the courts of Maria Theresa, of Frederick the Great, and of the small Principalities of the time have provided background material for the early career of Consuelo, a young singer of gipsy extraction. Her genius, innocence, and sincerity melt the most villainous hearts and bring her unscathed through adventures which culminate in her marriage with the mysterious Count Albert de Rudolstadt a few moments before he dies. Her wanderings, in peasant-lad disguise, with the young Joseph Haydn, when the two sing and play their way to Vienna, are among the most readable chapters of a long, formless work said by the author herself to contain material for three or four novels. *La Comtesse de Rudolstadt* (1843–5) was a sequel.

Consulat, Le, the form of Government by three Consuls which was introduced in France after Bonaparte's *coup d'état* (q.v.) of 9 November 1799 (*le dix-huit Brumaire, An VIII*) by the Constitution of 13 December 1799 (*le 22 Frimaire, An VIII*), see *Revolutions*, Ia. It lasted until the proclamation of the Empire in 1804 (see *Empire, le Premier*).

Bonaparte was First Consul, the two others being Sieyès (1748–1836, q.v.) and Roger Ducos (1754–1816) to begin with, succeeded by Cambacérès (1753–1824) and Lebrun (1739–1824). The functions of the Second and Third Consuls, as of the various State bodies (*le Conseil d'état, le Tribunat, le Corps législatif, le Sénat conservateur*), were nominal. Bonaparte exercised a form of dictatorship, still more so after he secured a modification of the Constitution by the *Senatus-consultum* of 4 August 1802 (*le 16 Thermidor, An X*) which made him Consul for life, with power to nominate his successor and the sole power of initiation or veto in regard to legislation, administration, war, or peace. Some of his most famous administrative measures date from these years.

Conte, a term sometimes used in a special sense to designate a class of fictitious narratives (distinct from *romans* and, though hardly so in modern times, from *nouvelles*) which do not purport to represent real life, and with the characters of which the reader does not, in imagination, identify himself. They interest by their drollery or wit or charm, by the allegory that they offer, or the moral that they inculcate. Such as La Fontaine's *Amours de Psyché et de Cupidon* (1669), Perrault's *Contes de ma Mère l'Oye*, and Voltaire's *Candide* and other philosophical tales. Writers of *contes*, which were often well spiced with licentiousness, were numerous in the 18th century and include, besides the two latter authors, Hamilton (*Fleur d'Épine*, &c.), Crébillon *fils* (*Le Sopha*), Duclos (*Acajou et Zirphile*), Voisenon (*Le Sultan Misapouf et la princesse Grisemine*). In the 19th century Flaubert's *Trois Contes* might equally well be described as *nouvelles* (q.v.). Maupassant also called his short stories *contes*.

Conte de la Charrette, Le, see *Chevalier à la Charrette*.

Contemplations, Les (1856), a famous collection (2 vols.) of lyrics by Victor Hugo. Most of them were written after the poet had retired to Jersey, but he dated them according to the events to which they referred and himself called them the *Mémoires d'une âme*. Vol. I, *Autrefois* (books 1–3: *Aurore, L'Ame en fleur, Les Luttes et les rêves*), contains reminiscences of early life, its dawn and flowering, of childhood, love, and the battles of the Romantic Movement (see *Romantisme*). Vol. II, *Aujourd'hui* (books 4–6, *Pauca meae*, *En marche*, *Au bord de l'Infini*), is on a deeper note. Sorrows, both personal and patriotic, had overtaken the poet and his thoughts dwelt increasingly on God, life, death, and the infinite. The moving elegies of the 4th book and the semi-philosophical poems of the 6th book (notably *Ce que dit la bouche d'ombre*) call specially for mention.

Contemporains, Les (1885–99; 1918), collected literary criticism by Jules Lemaître (q.v.).

Contens, Les, see *Turnèbe*.

Contes à Ninon (1864), a collection of short stories by Zola, his first published work. They give little indication of his later, naturalistic, novels. Some are fairy tales.

Contes cruels (1883), see *Villiers de l'Isle-Adam*.

Contes de la bécasse (1883), a collection of short stories by Maupassant (q.v.).

Contes des fées, see *Aulnoy*; *Leprince de Beaumont*; *Perrault*.

Contes d'Espagne et d'Italie (1830), poems—and one short play, *Les Marrons du feu*, in verse—by Alfred de Musset (q.v.).

Contes drolatiques, tales written by Balzac (q.v.) for recreation, in which he imitated Rabelais and, generally, the licentious tales of the 16th century. They were published in three sets of ten each (1832, 1833, 1837).

Contes du jour et de la nuit (1885), collected short stories by Maupassant (q.v.).

Contes du lundi, Les (1873), short stories by Alphonse Daudet (q.v.), mostly sketches of life during the Franco-Prussian War (1870–1, q.v.).

Contes et Nouvelles en vers, by LA FONTAINE, published in successive collections in 1664, 1665, 1666, 1671, and 1674. These are verse tales drawn from Ariosto, Boccaccio, Machiavelli, and other sources, mostly light licentious tales (of the type of *Joconde*, q.v.), devoid of serious thought, told with grace and charm. They have been gravely censured on the score of immorality, but they did not offend contemporary readers. They

were approved by Boileau and Mme de Sévigné. Some of them, such as *Le Faucon* (q.v.), *Belphégor* (q.v.), *La Matrone d'Éphèse* (from the *Satyricon* of Petronius Arbiter), are not open to the above censure. La Fontaine, when converted in his old age, made a public disavowal of the *Contes*.

Conti, name of a younger branch of the house of Bourbon-Condé. Armand, prince de Conti (1629–68), brother of the grand Condé (q.v.), figured in the *Fronde* and married a niece of Mazarin. For a time he befriended Molière, and offered him a post as his secretary. Later he turned against the theatre and wrote a *Traité de la comédie et des spectacles* (1666), of some interest. He and his son appear in Mme de Sévigné's letters. For Louis-François (1717–76), who played a considerable part under Louis XV, see *Temple, Le*.

Conti, CLÉLIA, a character in *La Chartreuse de Parme* (q.v.), a novel by Stendhal.

Contrat de mariage, Le, one of the 'Scènes de la vie privée' of Balzac's *Comédie humaine* (q.v.).

Contrat social, see *Du Contrat social*.

Contrerimes, Les (1921), poems by Paul-Jean Toulet (q.v.).

Contr'un, see *La Boétie*.

Convention, or **Convention nationale, La,** an elected body, the most memorable of the Revolutionary Assemblies, which succeeded the *Assemblée législative* (q.v.) on 20 September 1792, and gave way to the *Directoire* (q.v.) on 26 October 1795. At its first session it decreed the abolition of the monarchy. It sentenced Louis XVI (1793) and a few months later fulfilled the purpose for which it had been elected by voting a new Constitution (suppressed immediately in favour of the continuance of Revolutionary government). It created the *Tribunal révolutionnaire*, the *Comité de salut public*, and the *Comité de sûreté générale* (qq.v.), defeated the first European coalition against France (see *Coalitions*), introduced the Republican Calendar, and legislated for social and educational reform. (See also *Commune* (1); *Girondins*; *Marais* (2); *Montagnards*; *Plaine*; *Revolutions*, Ia.) Thomas Paine, author of *The Rights of Man*, was an elected member.

Coolus, Romain (1868–1952), playwright. His light, sentimental comedies include: *Les Amants de Suzy* (1901), *Petite Peste* (1905), *L'Enfant chérie* (1906), *Les Vacances de Pâques* (1928). The characters are usually *femmes entretenues*, their lovers, their lovers' friends, and children who provide humorous embarrassment.

Copains, Les (1913) a tale of *la vie unanime* by Jules Romains (q.v.).

Copeau, JACQUES (1879–1949), actor and producer, the famous director of the experimental *Théâtre du Vieux-Colombier* (q.v.) in Paris. He had previously been associated with the group of the *Nouvelle Revue Française* (q.v.). After his Vieux-Colombier years he went to Burgundy and from 1924 devoted himself to training a band of young actors who later became the *Compagnie des Quinze* (q.v.). From 1936 to 1941 he was one of the producers at the *Comédie-Française* (q.v.). He published interesting *Souvenirs du Vieux-Colombier* (1931), wrote many books on the theatre, and translated some of Shakespeare's plays.

Coppée, FRANÇOIS (1842–1908), poet and dramatist, born in Paris, was called the 'poète des humbles' because he wrote about humble people whose drab exteriors might conceal pitiful romances or tragedies. His work has been accused of banality but it had great popular appeal. The poems of his first collection *Le Reliquaire* (1866) were Parnassian in manner. His most typical works were *Intimités* (1868), *Les Humbles* (1872), *Le Cahier rouge* (1874), *Promenades et Intérieurs* (1875), *Les Récits et les Élégies* (1878), also the successful short comedies *Le Passant* (1869) and *Le Luthier de Crémone* (1876). *Severo Torelli* (1883), *Les Jacobites* (1885), *Pour la couronne* (1895), &c., were romantic verse-dramas. In later life Coppée became a fervent Roman Catholic and wrote a novel of religious experience *La Bonne Souffrance* (1898). During the Dreyfus (q.v.) case he was prominent in connexion with the notoriously die-hard and anti-Semitic *Ligue de la patrie française*.

Coppet, a château on Lake Geneva, was bought in 1784 by the father of Mme de Staël (q.v. and see *Necker*). In medieval times the lands of Coppet had belonged to Humbert, seigneur d'Aubonne et de Coppet, whose daughter married (1365) Oton de Granson (q.v.), Chaucer's 'prince of poets'. The château became Mme de Staël's headquarters after her exile from France, and took the place of her *salon* in Paris. Life at Coppet was one long conversation, philosophical, literary, elevated, witty, varied by excursions into the country, or performances of plays written by Mme de Staël or her guests (among them Benjamin Constant, Schlegel, Sismondi, Mme Récamier, qq.v., and, on more passing visits, the whole world of European culture).

Coq-à-l'âne, a term applied to a class of nonsense verses which concealed a satirical intention under a veil of incoherence. The fashion was set by Clément Marot and they were for a time very popular. Marot's *coq-à-l'âne* addressed to Lyon Jamet from his exile at Ferrara contains, besides satirical shafts directed at the papacy and the magistrature, some slight personal notes.

Coq gaulois, Le. A cock appeared as the French national emblem on flags, standards, &c., for the first time during the French Revolution. Its origin is uncertain. The Gauls did not display the emblem of a cock on their standards. Confusion may have been caused by the Latin word *gallus*, which means both *coq* and *Gaulois*.

Coquelin, CONSTANT-BENOÎT (1841–1909), French actor, called Coquelin *aîné* to distinguish him from Coquelin *cadet*, his younger brother Ernest-Alexandre-Honoré (1848–1909), who was also an actor. Both were for long associated with the Comédie-Française, though Coquelin *aîné* was the more famous of the two and he was also well known in London. Coquelin *aîné* created the name part in Rostand's (q.v.) *Cyrano de Bergerac* and played with Bernhardt in the same author's *L'Aiglon*.

Coquillards (from *coquille*, shell, the pilgrim's emblem), members of a band of discharged soldiers, vagabonds, and malefactors, who about the middle of the 15th century, after the close of the Hundred Years War, infested the roads of France, particularly of Burgundy. They had a 'king', statutes, and a secret language (called 'jargon'). Villon (q.v.) had relations with some of them, and wrote for them his *Ballades en jargon*. (The *Coquillards* are not to be confused with the *Suppôts du Seigneur de la Coquille* at Lyons, see *Sociétés Joyeuses*).

Coquillart, GUILLAUME (*c.* 1450–1510), poet, born in Champagne, in later life a jurist and canon of Rheims, wrote in his student days between 1477 and 1480 for the *Basoche* (q.v.) of Paris two *causes grasses* (q.v.), the *Plaidoyer d'entre la simple et la rusée* and the *Enquête d'entre la simple et la rusée*, caricatures of the legal proceedings supposed to arise out of the struggle of two women for the possession of one man. A third piece, in octosyllabic verse, by the same author, entitled *Droits Nouveaux*, is a caricature of works of civil and canon law and at the same time a political and social satire. Coquillart also wrote a *Blason des armes et des dames*, enumerating the rival merits of each, and an amusing monologue, *La Botte de foin* (a lover who hides himself in a hay-loft to escape the husband).

Coran, CHARLES (1814–83), a minor poet of the tail end of the Romantic period, was the author of *Onyx* (1840), *Rimes galantes* (1847), *Dernières Élégances* (1868), &c.

Corbeaux, Les (1882), by Henri Becque (q.v.), one of the first naturalistic dramas. When the rich M. Vigneron dies, leaving his affairs unsettled, his widow and her three daughters are at the mercy of the 'vultures'— the lawyers, tradespeople, and others who gather round and fight to secure the dead man's fortune for themselves. The most unscrupulous is Teissier, an old man, who had been M. Vigneron's partner. He takes a fancy to Marie, one of the daughters, and in the end she consents to marry him as the only means of securing the future of her mother and sisters and shaking off the other would-be beneficiaries.

Corbière, ÉDOUARD-JOACHIM, self-styled TRISTAN (1845–75), poet, was born and spent most of his life at Coat-Congar (Brittany). He was little known until Verlaine included him in his gallery of *Poètes maudits* (q.v.). Since then his reputation has increased. His poems about sailors and seafaring life, *Gens de mer* (in *Les Amours jaunes*, 1873), are forcible, elliptic, at times slangily expressed, but remarkable for their irony and realism.

Corday d'Armont, CHARLOTTE (1768–93), born in Champeaux (Normandy), descended from a sister of Corneille, came to Paris in the summer of 1793 fired with the idea of avenging the downfall of the Girondins (q.v.). On 13 July she penetrated to the apartment of Marat (q.v.) and assassinated him (by stabbing) in his bath. She was guillotined on 17 July. There is a fine chapter about her in Lamartine's *Histoire des Girondins*.

Cordeliers, Le Club des, or **Société des amis des droits de l'homme et du citoyen,** an extremist Revolutionary club founded in 1790 by Danton and Marat, with Camille Desmoulins (qq.v.). It met in the former convent of the Cordeliers (Franciscans) and had Marat's *Ami du peuple* (q.v.) as its printed organ. Its power was greatest during the struggle with the Girondins (1792). Later, it became the headquarters of the Hébertistes and disowned both Danton and Desmoulins for their moderate views. After the fall of Hébert (q.v.) and his followers it gradually dissolved.

Cordière, La Belle, see *Labé, Louise*.

Cordon bleu. This originally signified the broad sky-blue sash of the *Ordre du Saint Esprit* (q.v.). It then came to mean a mark or a person of special eminence in one profession or another, and later, facetiously, of special eminence in cooking. Louis XV is said to have so much appreciated a dinner offered to him by Mme du Barry that he wanted to engage her cook for the Royal Household, whereupon he was informed that the cook was a woman—a woman who ought to have a reward worthy of her, nothing less than the *cordon bleu* (*Larousse du XIXᵉ siècle*).

Corinne (1807), a novel by Mme de Staël (q.v.). Lord Oswald Nelvil, a melancholy, reserved Englishman, visits Italy after his father's death and in Rome meets Corinne, a poetess of genius and beauty, who has been crowned at the Capitol. The two fall in love, but the English noble shrinks from marriage, from the mystery surrounding Corinne, and from her unrestrained, artistic temperament. Also, his father's dying wish has half bound him to Lucile Edgermond, a young English girl.

Corinne tells Oswald that she is herself

a daughter of Lord Edgermond by his first wife, an Italian, and thus half-sister to Lucile. At one time she had lived with her father and his second wife and suffered the boredom of English country life (an entertaining part of the book). Indeed, Oswald's father, a family friend, had at this period considered her as a possible wife for his son, but had mistrusted her vivacity. She had quarrelled with her stepmother when her father died, and left England.

Oswald returns to England firmly resolved to marry Corinne, but once there he yields to convention and family pressure and marries Lucile. Corinne dies of grief.

Descriptions of Italian landscape, literature, and art fill many chapters of this long book; and a minor character, the young comte d'Erfeuil, an *émigré*, typifies the French qualities of witty, self-sufficient, superficial charm which Mme de Staël described later in *De l'Allemagne* (q.v.) when she contrasted the French and German characters.

Corisande, La belle, a name frequently given to Diane d'Ando[u]ins, comtesse de Guiche, mistress of Henri IV for some years from 1581. She was grandmother of the Philibert de Gramont of the *Memoirs* (q.v.). She was on friendly terms with Montaigne, who dedicated Essay I. 29 to her.

Cormenin, LOUIS-MARIE DE LA HAYE, VICOMTE DE (1788–1868), jurist (author of a standard work on administrative law) and politician; a poet in youth and a philanthropist in age; and in between times the 'Timon le misanthrope' who consistently attacked the July monarchy in pamphlets (*Très humbles remontrances de Timon* . . ., 1838; *Questions scandaleuses d'un jacobin* . . ., 1840); in *Études sur les orateurs parlementaires* (1836 and later, augmented editions), a gallery of witty, malicious, often cruel portraits of contemporary politicians; and in *Entretiens de village* (1846). He was widely read but never, as a polemist, reached the excellence of Paul-Louis Courier (q.v.).

Corneille, PIERRE (1606–84), dramatist, born at Rouen of a family of magistrates. His brother Thomas (q.v.), twenty years younger and a lesser talent, was like him a dramatist. His sister was mother of Fontenelle (q.v.). Pierre Corneille was educated at a Jesuit school, studied law, and purchased

two minor offices in the magistrature at Rouen, which he held until 1650. He was simple, candid, and devout, a churchwarden in his parish; at the same time proud and sensitive; needy all his life (in spite of a pension, irregularly paid, during his later years), for his plays brought him more fame than money. He appears to have been happy in his home life. Intellectually he was timid and self-tormenting, minutely scrutinizing and endlessly correcting every verse. A love affair of his own, which he dramatized in *Mélite* (q.v., composed not later than 1629), revealed his poetical gift. The play was successfully performed in Paris by Mondory's company at the Théâtre du Marais (see *Theatres and theatre companies*), where it is probable that all Corneille's earlier dramas were produced. *Mélite* was followed, probably in 1632, by the tragi-comedy *Clitandre*, the complicated story of the love of Rosidor for Caliste, crossed by the latter's unfounded jealousy and the machinations of Pymante, who vainly loves Dorise (sister of Caliste), who in her turn loves Rosidor. Then came (1633–5) a series of comedies, *La Veuve*, *La Galerie du Palais*, *La Suivante*, *La Place Royale*, plays of sentiment and romantic adventure of only secondary interest. *La Galerie du Palais* owed its attraction in part to its realistic representation of that locality, with its booksellers', drapers', and milliners' stalls. It is a singular piece also in that the character of the hero plays a greater part than in the other comedies, for in his mania for independence he throws over the woman he loves and drives her into a convent, because he is afraid of becoming a slave to his passion. In all Corneille's comedies love is governed by reason, unlike the love in Racine's plays.

About this time Corneille was one of the *cinq auteurs* (q.v.) employed by Richelieu to write plays under his direction; *La Comédie des Tuileries*, of which Corneille probably wrote the third act, was performed in 1635. His first tragedy *Médée* (q.v.), performed in late 1634 or early 1635, was followed in 1635 or 1636 by the comedy *L'Illusion comique* (q.v.). *Le Cid* (q.v.), whose appearance was an event of capital importance in the history of French drama, was produced early in January 1637. It introduced the new theme, which Corneille frequently resumed, of the conflict in a human soul between duty or honour on the one hand and passion on the other. It gave rise to acute controversy. It was highly approved by the public, while Corneille's rivals such as Scudéry, supported by Richelieu (q.v.), attacked it and procured a judgement on it by the *Académie* (*Sentiments de l'Académie sur le Cid*, 1638), drafted by Chapelain, criticizing the work on points of style and grammar. Though the play triumphed, the author was discouraged and produced nothing further for three years. In 1640 appeared his great tragedies of *Horace*, *Cinna*, and perhaps *Polyeucte* (but more probably late 1641 or winter 1642) (qq.v.). *La Mort de Pompée* (q.v.), probably produced in late 1642 or early 1643, was followed by the comedy *Le Menteur* (q.v., spring 1643), the success of which led to the addition of a sequel, *La Suite du Menteur*. *Rodogune* (q.v.), regarded by some as the greatest of his dramas, appeared in late 1644 or early 1645. The fine but unsuccessful tragedy *Théodore* (q.v., 1645), on the theme of the ordeal of a Christian virgin martyr, was followed by *Héraclius* (q.v., 1646 or 1647), a tragedy which in spite of its complication was greatly applauded. The spectacle play *Andromède* (1649, q.v.) was of little literary importance, but *Don Sanche d'Aragon* (q.v.) possibly earlier in the same year was a remarkable though unsuccessful tragi-comedy (or as the author described it 'heroic comedy'). *Nicomède* (q.v., late 1650 or early 1651), the last of Corneille's great tragedies, was a success. The tragedy *Pertharite* (q.v.) in, probably, late 1651 was a failure and for seven years Corneille wrote no more. He withdrew from the theatre to his home at Rouen (later, in 1662, transferred to Paris). He received a pension in 1663. The works of his decline, *Œdipe* (1659), *La Toison d'or* (1660, lyrical tragedy, a spectacle, or machine, play written in honour of Louis XIV's marriage with the Infanta Maria Theresa), *Sertorius* (1662), *Sophonisbe* (1663), *Othon* (1664), *Agésilas* (1666), *Attila* (1667), and *Suréna* (1674), all tragedies; *Tite et Bérénice* (1670) and *Pulchérie* (1672), heroic comedies, all (with the exception of *La Toison d'or*) briefly summarized herein under their titles, are unequal and on the whole of less interest than his earlier works, though they contain, in the vivid figures of statesmen and of women concerned in state

affairs, some notable features, and much of the verse is fine. They deal mostly with historical and political themes from which passion is eliminated. They were produced variously at the Hôtel de Bourgogne, the Théâtre du Marais, or by Molière's company. In 1670 Corneille contributed to *Psyché* (q.v.) the charming verses of the greater part of Acts II–V. During his retirement from the drama he wrote a singular verse adaptation of the *Imitation of Christ* and other devotional pieces.

Corneille is remarkable, so far as his best plays are concerned, for the great tragic personages that he presents, for the grandeur of his style, and for the high ethical quality of his drama. His principal tragic heroes and heroines are depicted, it has been said, as more than life size: they display strength of will, pride, and reason to an almost superhuman degree; and they are placed in situations where these qualities are brought into conflict with instinct, or sentiment, or outward circumstance, and sometimes lead them to sublime self-sacrifice. Instead of lamenting the impotence of man in the face of destiny (the Greek tragic notion), Corneille exalts man's freedom and strength of will, whereby he fashions his own destiny or rises superior to it. Corneille's tragedies present some definite problem for solution; external incident is excluded where it does not contribute to the spiritual movement of the drama. His style is distinguished by the force and clearness, the dialectical brilliancy, sometimes rising to passionate ardour, with which his characters argue out their destiny, rather than by warmth and colour. As regards the unities, it may be said that in general, at any rate after he wrote the *Cid*, Corneille observed them, not meticulously, but reasonably, in the interests of realism and concentration. Much information regarding Corneille's view of the dramatic art is to be derived from the *Discours* which he prefixed to the three volumes of the 1660 edition of his plays and from the *Examens* or criticisms which he attached to each drama. Voltaire wrote a *Commentaire sur Corneille* (1764). For a comparison of Corneille and Racine see under the name of the latter.

Seventeenth-century English translations of Corneille include those (the best) by Mrs. Katherine Philips, *The Matchless Orinda*. Some were performed.

Corneille, THOMAS, *known also as* Corneille de l'Isle (1625–1709), brother (twenty years younger) of Pierre Corneille, author of numerous tragedies, tragi-comedies, and comedies. His most successful play was *Timocrate* (1656), a romantic tragedy (based on an episode in the *Cléopâtre* of La Calprenède), in which he reintroduced into tragedy the element of romantic intrigue. Timocrate besieges the queen of Argos in her capital, penetrates into the city under a false name, wins the queen's love, and defends the city against his own army. *Ariane* (1672), again, on the story of the betrayal and desertion of Ariadne by Theseus, suggests the rising influence of Racine. Other important tragedies by this author were: *Stilicon* (1660), *Camma* (1661), *Maximien* (1662), *Laodice* (1668), *La Mort d'Hannibal* (1669), *Le Comte d'Essex* (1678). His *Festin de pierre* (1677) is a verse adaptation of Molière's *Don Juan*. His best comedy was *Le Geôlier de soi-même* (1655).

Thomas Corneille was also a grammarian and compiled a dictionary of arts and sciences for the *Académie Française* (see *Dictionaries and encyclopedias*, under date 1694). He collaborated with Donneau de Visé in the editorship of the *Mercure galant* (q.v.). He lacked his brother's genius and was rather a skilful playwright and imitator (some of his plays are close reflections of those of his brother) than an original dramatist. He wrote with great facility—his *Ariane* was composed in seventeen days. With Quinault (q.v.) he filled the interval in the history of French drama between the zenith of Pierre Corneille and the advent of Racine.

Corneille des boulevards, Le. See *Pixerécourt, Guilbert de.*

Cornuel, ANNE-MARIE BIGOT, MME (1605–94), a *bourgeoise* famous for her mordant wit, whose *salon* was much frequented by men of letters in the second half of the 17th century.

Corot, JEAN-BAPTISTE-CAMILLE (1796–1875), famous landscape painter, born in Paris, a forerunner, by his poetical treatment of light, of the Impressionist school.

Correspondances, a famous sonnet by Baudelaire, first published in *Les Fleurs du mal* ('Spleen et Idéal' section) in 1857 (cf. *Symbolisme*).

Correspondances littéraires. Epistolary literature reached its highest excellence in France in the 17th century. Literary correspondences of interest for their literary and stylistic merit, or as a guide to the intellectual climate of an age, or as human documents, were left both then and in the succeeding centuries by the following, all of whom receive mention under separate headings:

SEVENTEENTH CENTURY:

Balzac, Guez de; Boileau; Bossuet; Bussy-Rabutin; Chapelain; Condé; Corneille; Descartes; Fénelon; François de Sales, Saint; Henri IV; La Bruyère; La Fayette, Mme de; La Fontaine; La Rochefoucauld; Marianna Alcaforado (see *Lettres portugaises*); Louis XIV; Maintenon, Mme de; Malherbe; Palatine, la Princesse; Pascal; Patin, Gui; Racine; Retz; Richelieu, Cardinal de; Saint-Évremond; Saint-Simon; Sévigné, Mme de; Vincent de Paul, Saint; Voiture.

EIGHTEENTH CENTURY:

Aïssé, Mlle; Desmoulins; Diderot; Du Deffand, Mme; Graffigny, Mme de; Grimm; La Harpe; Launay, Mlle de; Lespinasse, Mlle de; Métra; Mirabeau; Roland, Mme; Rousseau, J.-J.; Voltaire.

NINETEENTH AND TWENTIETH CENTURIES:

Ampère, A.-M. and J.-J.; Balzac; Baudelaire; Claudel; Delacroix; Doudan; Fiévée; Flaubert; Gide; Guérin, Eugénie and M. de; Jacob, Max; Jacquemont; Maistre, J. de; Mérimée; Napoléon I; Proust; Récamier, Mme; Renan; Rivière; Sainte-Beuve; Sand, George; Sismondi; Taine; Tocqueville; Valéry.

Corsaire, Le (founded 1823), later *Le Corsaire-Satan*, a small review, mainly literary, sometimes political. It often printed new writing, notably poems by Baudelaire. It petered out during the Second Empire.

Corydon (1924), by André Gide (q.v.).

Cosette, one of the main characters in *Les Misérables* (q.v.), by Hugo.

Cosi-Sancta, a philosophical tale by Voltaire published in the Kehl edition of 1784, probably written about 1747. The story is founded on a passage in St. Augustine, *De sermone Domini in monte* (*Patrologia Latina*, xxxiv. 1254), the theme being that it is permissible to do a small wrong if a greater good results. Cosi-Sancta by her virtue causes the death of her lover and endangers the life of her husband; but by three successive infidelities to the latter saves his life and those of her brother and her son, and is canonized in consequence.

Cosroès, a tragedy by Rotrou, produced in 1649. The scene is the court of the aged Persian king Cosroès, and the drama centres in the sanguinary struggle for power between his son Siroès supported by his father-in-law Palmiras, and Sira, the king's second wife, who hates Siroès and desires to see him supplanted by her own son Mardesane.

Costar, PIERRE (1603–60), man of letters, belonging to the society of the Hôtel de Rambouillet; author of *Défense des ouvrages de M. Voiture* (1653), *Entretiens de M. Voiture et de M. Costar* (1654), *Suite de la défense des œuvres de M. Voiture* (1655), *Apologie de M. Costar,* and letters (1658); a somewhat pedantic writer.

Cotart, JEHAN, an official of the ecclesiastical court of Paris, for the repose of whose soul Villon (q.v.) composed a famous *ballade* (*Testament,* ll. 1238–65).

Côté de Guermantes, Le, the third section of Proust's long novel *A la recherche du temps perdu* (q.v.).

Cotgrave, RANDLE, see *Dictionaries and Encyclopedias,* under date 1611.

Cotin, CHARLES (1604–82), known as l'abbé Cotin, a man of considerable learning and a preacher and writer of some reputation in his day, an *habitué* of the Hôtel de Rambouillet. He was ridiculed by Molière as Trissotin in *Les Femmes savantes* and by Boileau in his *Satires.* His *Recueil de Rondeaux* and *Poésies chrétiennes* show little poetic talent.

Cottin, MADAME 'SOPHIE', *née* MARIE RISTAUD (1770–1807), novelist, born at Tonneins, on the Garonne, and brought up at Bordeaux. She was married young to a rich banker, widowed at twenty, and thereafter lived in the country near Paris. She published five novels, popular in their day, which combined a moral strain with sensation and sentimentality: *Claire d'Albe* (1799); *Malvina* (1801); *Amélie Mansfield* (1803); *Mathilde* (1805), a tale of the Crusades, so successful

that it influenced women's fashions; and *Élisabeth, ou les exilés de Sibérie* (1806, q.v.). Mme Sophie Cottin is said to have committed suicide—a melancholy end to a life which at times reflected the romantic passions of her books.

Couard, the hare, in the *Roman de Renart* (q.v.).

Coucy, GUI, CHÂTELAIN DE, a lyric poet of the end of the 12th century, author of songs of love of a noble and melancholy character. Under the name of his successor Renaut, he was made the hero of a legend which related that his heart, sent home from the Holy Land, where he died, to the lady whom he loved, and intercepted by her jealous husband, the Seigneur de Faiel, was served to her by the latter in a dish. This tale was made the subject of a metrical romance by Jakemon le Vinier, a poet of the end of the 13th century.

Coulanges, CHRISTOPHE DE, ABBÉ DE LIVRY (d. 1687 aged about eighty), was the uncle and (in her youth) the guardian of Mme de Sévigné, the 'bien bon' of her letters, and her devoted friend till his death.

Coulanges, PHILIPPE-EMMANUEL, MARQUIS DE (1633–1716), cousin and friend of Mme de Sévigné, with whom he corresponded. He also wrote light poetry and left memoirs. His wife, Marie-Angélique du Gué Bagnoles (1641–1723), was also an intimate friend of Mme de Sévigné.

Coup d'état, a violent and unconstitutional stroke of policy by which one form of government is substituted for another. In French history the *coups d'état* of le dix-huit brumaire, An VIII (9 Nov. 1799) and 2 December 1851 were notable. By the first, the *Directoire* was overthrown and a provisional government (see *Consulat*) set up which undertook to frame a new Constitution within a given period. By the second, Prince Louis Napoleon, nephew of Napoleon I, and at that date President of the Republic, used military force and dissolved the *Assemblée nationale législative* elected (1849) in accordance with the Constitution of 1848 (see *Republics*, para. 3; *Napoleon III*).

Coupée, Dame, a hen, in the *Roman de Renart* (q.v.).

Coupe et les lèvres, La (1833), by Alfred de Musset, see *Un Spectacle dans un fauteuil.*

Couperin, FRANÇOIS (1668–1733), 'Couperin le Grand', composer of harpsichord music and in his day a celebrated organist. There were five generations of well-known musicians in the Couperin family.

Courbet, GUSTAVE (1819–77), French landscape painter, born at Ornans (Doubs), came to Paris in 1839 to study law but turned at once to painting. Like many of his artist and writer friends, Baudelaire (on whose portrait he was working in February 1848) and Champfleury among them, he shared the Revolutionary ideas and ideals of the years leading up to 1848 (see *Revolutions,* III; and cf. the description of this period in Flaubert's *L'Éducation sentimentale*). He exhibited at the Salons, e.g. *L'Après-midi d'Ornans* (1848), *L'Enterrement à Ornans* (1850); and at a one-man show (1855) of forty paintings which included the celebrated *Atelier du peintre,* where Baudelaire can be seen in one corner bent over a book. He also practised and preached doctrines of *l'art réaliste* which were developed and transformed (notably by Champfleury) into *le réalisme* (q.v.) in literature. Courbet was an active revolutionary during and after the Commune of 1871 and eventually had to take refuge in Switzerland, ending his days there in exile.

Cour d'amour, an association of ladies and gentlemen said to have existed in Provence about the end of the 11th century, which discussed and decided questions of gallantry.

Cour de cassation (a creation of the *Assemblée législative* in 1790 and first called the *Tribunal de cassation*), the supreme legal body, at the summit of the French system of civil and criminal law, which has power to nullify a judgement, thus rendering a new trial, before a new court, necessary. Its sole concern is to determine whether the law has been properly interpreted and whether the technicalities of legal procedure have been properly observed.

Cour des aides, under the French monarchy, a court of law, including two presidents and two benches, each of twenty-six judges, which tried suits arising out of the collection, farming, &c., of the taxes. It also had executive functions in connexion with public works, payment and rationing of troops, &c.

Cour des comptes, see *Chambre des comptes.*

Cour des Miracles, a quarter of medieval Paris, north of the river, inhabited by beggars and vagabonds, the cripples, paralytics, and blind of the daytime streets, whose ailments disappeared miraculously when they returned home at nights. It is well described in Hugo's *Notre-Dame de Paris* (q.v.).

Cour des monnaies, under the French monarchy, a court of law which tried suits in connexion with the coinage and with transactions in the precious metals.

Courier, PAUL-LOUIS (1772–1825), pamphleteer and scholar, son of a landed proprietor in Touraine, joined the army in 1792 to please his father, served in Italy, and found that in the great Italian libraries he could indulge his passion for classical study. He retired from the army in 1809 but remained for another three years of study in Italy.

He came into prominence with the *Lettre à M. Renouard sur une tache faite à un manuscrit de Florence* (1810). M. Renouard was a French scholar. The manuscript was an unknown fragment of Longus which Courier (and M. Renouard) had discovered. After the passage had been transcribed Courier spilt ink on the manuscript, either by accident or to conceal misreadings. The *Lettre,* which turned the affair into ridicule, was his reply to the scandal caused by the damage. His translation of the *Daphnis and Chloe* of Longus was published in 1810.

After his return to France in 1812 Courier managed his property in Touraine. He became interested in the people, and wrote a series of pamphlets (signed 'Paul-Louis, Vigneron') and letters to newspapers in which he upheld the rights of the peasants against oppression by the clergy and local government officials. He met a violent death at the hands of a farm labourer whom he had dismissed. Four years later his *Œuvres complètes* were published (1829–30), including his interesting correspondence of the years 1787 to 1812, the *Lettres écrites de France et d'Italie* (q.v.). His most famous pamphlets rank, after the *Provinciales* of Pascal, among the masterpieces of French polemical writing. They include: *Pétition aux deux Chambres* (1816); *Pétition pour des villageois qu'on empêche de danser* (1820); *Le Simple Discours de Paul-Louis, Vigneron de la Chavonnière* (1821).

Cournot, ANTOINE-AUGUSTIN (1801-77), French mathematician, economist, and the philosopher of *probabilisme* (a doctrine of which the main tenet is that in matters of knowledge it is not possible to arrive at absolute truth; one can only distinguish between what is more or less probable). Apart from purely mathematical treatises his works include: *Exposition de la théorie des chances et des probabilités* (1843); *Essai sur les fondements de nos connaissances et sur les caractères de la critique philosophique* (1851); *Traité de l'enchaînement des idées fondamentales dans les sciences et dans l'histoire* (1861).

Couronnement de Renart, see *Roman de Renart.*

Courrier de Provence, Le (1789-91), a journal founded by Mirabeau, was devoted mainly to reports and commentaries of proceedings in the *Assemblée nationale*, but had columns open to correspondents. It appeared three times weekly and replaced the *Lettres du comte de Mirabeau à ses commettants*, which in their turn had succeeded Mirabeau's *États Généraux* (published—in four quarto pages of two columns—the day after the *États Généraux* opened). It continued for six months after Mirabeau's death.

Courrier des départements, Le, see *Courrier de Versailles à Paris . . . .*

Courrier de Versailles à Paris et de Paris à Versailles, Le (known after 1792 as *Le Courrier des départements*), a journal founded in July 1789 by Antoine-Joseph Gorsas (1751-93), a schoolmaster at Versailles who became a publicist and a deputy to the *Convention nationale*. It was one of the chief organs of the Girondins and waged violent war against Marat's *Ami du peuple*. The last number appeared on 31 May 1793, the day of the fall of the Girondins. Gorsas was guillotined.

Courteline, GEORGES [pseud. of Georges Moineaux] (1861-1929), probably the greatest humorous writer of modern French

literature, was born in Tours, the son of a Paris journalist. He failed to obtain a degree, then tried various careers, all distasteful. When ministerial influence secured him a post in a government department he made a happy arrangement by which he himself never went to the office, his work being done by a colleague who drew, and kept half, his salary. After two years the colleague asked for a holiday, so Courteline resigned. He took to regular humorous journalism in 1883, and in 1890 began his long years of collaboration with the daily paper *L'Écho de Paris* in which most of his work first appeared. His prolific output (until 1912, when he stopped writing) included tales, sketches, comedies, and reminiscences. It was based upon experience and caustic observation of the small happenings of daily life, and ranged from farce to profound satire. His masterpieces were *Boubouroche* (1893, a comedy on the eternal theme of the gullible cuckold); *Les Gaîtés de l'escadron* (1886), *Le Train de 8h. 47* (1888), *Lidoire et la biscotte* (1892), a series of short, farcical sketches of military life; *Messieurs les ronds-de-cuir* (1893, satirical sketches of bureaucrats at work). Other well-known titles are *Le Droit aux étrennes* (1896), *Un Client sérieux* (1897), *Les Boulingrin* (1898), *La Paix chez soi* (1903), *Les Linottes* (1912, a novel). *La Conversion d'Alceste* (1905) was an attempt at a sequel to Molière's *Le Misanthrope.*

Courtilz de Sandras, GATIEN DE (1644-1712), soldier and literary adventurer, author of libellous pamphlets, of works having historical pretensions (*Vie de Turenne, Histoire de la guerre de Hollande*), and of fabricated memoirs (notably the *Mémoires de M. d'Artagnan*, 1700, the source of Dumas père's *Les Trois Mousquetaires*, q.v.; also the *Mémoires de M. le marquis de Montbrun*).

Courtois d'Arras, see *Comedy.*

Cousin, VICTOR (1792-1867), philosopher, son of a watchmaker, was born and educated in Paris. In 1815 he was appointed Professor of Modern Philosophy at the Sorbonne, but university appointments were in the control of the Government, and between 1820 and 1827 his courses were suspended because of his *doctrinaire* (q.v.) sympathies. Between 1830 and the *coup d'état* of 1851, when he was Director of the École normale supérieure (q.v.), also a member of the Royal Council (and then Minister) of Public Instruction, he did much to organize education in France, and exercised great influence on philosophic thought.

He was a brilliant and inspiring lecturer and, with Guizot and Villemain (qq.v.), made the academic renown of the Sorbonne about the year 1830. Two of his lecture-courses were particularly famous, the first delivered in 1818 (published in 1836 as *Cours de philosophie* and republished in 1853 as *Du vrai, du beau, et du bien*), and the second delivered between 1828 and 1830 and largely devoted to the philosophy of Hegel, then a new name in France. His other publications included: *Fragments philosophiques* (1826), *Cours d'histoire de la philosophie* (1826), *De la métaphysique d'Aristote* (1835), *Cours d'histoire de la philosophie moderne* (1841–46), *Fragments pour servir à l'histoire de la philosophie* (1865), and some writings of a more purely literary and historical character (*La Jeunesse de Mme de Longueville*, 1853, *La Société française au XVIIe siècle*, 1856, &c.); also the first and for long the major edition (1824–26) of the *Œuvres complètes* of Descartes, the first edition of the *Discours de la méthode* since 1724. (See also *Art pour l'art, L'*.)

Cousin is said to have founded the school of *eclectic* philosophy because he produced no novel system, but applied psychological method to the history of philosophy, making a synthesis of what he considered the integral part of former systems (sensationalism, idealism, scepticism, and mysticism) and discarding what he thought false or incomplete. His teachings gave a new impetus to the study of the history of philosophy.

Cousin Pons, Le (1847), a novel, one of the best known 'scènes de la vie parisienne' in Balzac's *Comédie humaine* (q.v.), is a study of a poor relation (cf. *La Cousine Bette*, with which it forms *Les Parents pauvres*). Sylvain Pons, a seedy musician, has two passions —collecting and good food. All his patrimony has gone on the first: he gratifies the second by making the round of his wealthy relations, submitting to insults in return for rich meals. He lives with his devoted German friend Schmucke, also a music master. Pons tries to engineer a marriage between a young cousin and the rich Frédéric Brunner. Negotiations fail, his

relations accuse Pons of plotting to humiliate them, and this family quarrel worries him into a serious illness. Mme Cibot, the concierge, discovers that his collection of pictures, bibelots, &c., is worth a fortune; and the dying musician and his naïve friend now become victims of cupidity and of the blackest side of human nature. Mme Cibot, the doctor, a second-hand dealer on the ground floor, a shady solicitor, the relations—all scheme and intrigue over the death-bed. Pons dies, having willed his property, despite opposition, to Schmucke. But Schmucke, broken-hearted, and helpless against intriguers, signs away his inheritance for a minute income. He soon dies; and the relations, having triumphantly scooped the pool, speak always of their '*dear* Cousin Pons'.

Cousine Bette, La (1847), by Balzac, one of the 'scènes de la vie parisienne' (and one of the key-novels) of his *Comédie humaine*. With *Le Cousin Pons* (q.v.) it forms the single whole entitled *Les Parents pauvres*. Lisbeth Fischer ('la cousine Bette') is a peasant from the Vosges, greedy, jealous, and unable to forgive her cousin Adeline for being beautiful and saintly, and for having made a splendid marriage with Baron Hulot. When the book opens (in the reign of Louis-Philippe) we learn that Baron Hulot, a respected Government official, has become the depraved victim of his sexual passions; la cousine Bette, for her part, has for some time been sheltering a young Polish artist, Count Wenceslas Steinbock, on whom she lavishes a bullying tenderness. Her niece Hortense Hulot and the count meet by chance, fall in love, and their marriage is arranged. When this comes to la cousine Bette's knowledge she betrays no fury, but she plots secretly to ruin her relations. She allies herself with Baron Hulot's latest passion, Mme Marneffe, an avaricious, heartless siren who, aided by a complacent pimp of a husband, appears respectable but is more harmful, more costly, than the most flaunting of courtesans. While accepting the baron's protection and ruining him financially she also carries on an intrigue with the wealthy ex-merchant Crevel (father-in-law of Hulot's son); throws dust in the eyes of a rich Brazilian lover; and schemes, only too successfully, to seduce Count Wenceslas from his young wife. She is helped at every turn by la cousine Bette, now her *chère amie*, who manœuvres so cleverly that her relations consider her their one salvation and believe her story that she only feigns friendship with Mme Marneffe to guard their interests. The plot is crowded with incident. La cousine Bette, ambitious as well as vengeful, nearly succeeds in marrying the Maréchal Hulot, the Baron's elder brother, but the Maréchal dies of shock on learning that his brother has embezzled Government funds. Baron Hulot, forced to resign his post, now follows his vice beyond all limits of decency and disappears. La cousine Bette sends him money clandestinely to facilitate his degradation. Meantime the widowed Mme Marneffe has married Crevel for his money, but her Brazilian lover discovers her treachery and procures her own and her new husband's death by poison. Crevel's daughter and her husband, young Hulot, inherit his fortune. Thus la cousine Bette sees wealth restored to the family she had hoped to ruin. She succumbs to disappointment and a chill, and dies. The next to die is Mme Hulot, stricken by overhearing her husband, who had returned home apparently a reformed character, anticipating her death and proposing marriage to the kitchenmaid. The marriage of the now decrepit baron to the Norman servant-girl ends this powerful study of the havoc wrought by jealousy and uncontrollable libertinism.

Couthon, GEORGES (1755–94), Revolutionary politician, practised at the Bar at Clermont, was elected to the *Assemblée législative*, and became a member of the *Convention nationale*. He was a fanatical revolutionary, and formed with Robespierre and Saint-Just (qq.v.) what was sometimes called 'le triumvirat de la Terreur'. He was guillotined the day after *le 9 Thermidor* (q.v.), i.e. on 28 July 1794.

Coutumes du Beauvaisis, see *Beaumanoir, Philippe de.*

Crac, Monsieur de, see *Collin d'Harleville, Jean-François.*

Crainquebille, the title piece in a volume of tales (1904) by Anatole France. Crainquebille is a costermonger who is imprisoned on a false charge of having said 'Mort aux vaches' ('Down with the coppers') to a policeman. After his release he finds it impossible to make a living. He decides that he would be better off in prison, and accosting a policeman he does in fact say 'Mort aux vaches'. But his plan miscarries, for the policeman is kindhearted and only moves him on.

Cramer, PHILIBERT and GABRIEL (18th c.), publishers at Geneva, who printed most of Voltaire's works from 1755.

Crébillon, CLAUDE-PROSPER JOLYOT DE (1707–77), known as Crébillon *fils*, son of the following, author of tales and dialogues (*Les Égarements du cœur et de l'esprit*, 1736; *Le Sopha*, 1745, &c.) reflecting the moral depravity of the day, and containing elements of social satire and literary criticism. He was imprisoned in 1734 on account of one of these. Like his father, Crébillon *fils* was dramatic censor (see *Censorship, Dramatic*). He married an English lady and is said to have been a devoted husband.

Crébillon, PROSPER JOLYOT, SIEUR DE (1674–1762), born at Dijon of a family of magistrates, tragic dramatist, whose literary activity extended over some fifty years. His principal plays, *Idoménée* (1705), *Atrée et Thyeste* (1707), *Électre* (1708), *Rhadamiste et Zénobie* (q.v., his masterpiece, 1711), *Xerxès* (1714), *Sémiramis* (1717), *Catilina* (1748), show a partiality for violent episodes and romantic complications, rather than development of character and truth to life. His plays are in fact melodramas of a highly tragic character; he seeks, as he says, to evoke pity by terror. His *Électre*, for instance, had little resemblance to that of Sophocles. He began a play on Cromwell, but the Government showed umbrage and the work was left unfinished. He was greatly esteemed in his day, a member of the *Académie* and dramatic censor (see *Censorship, Dramatic*). Marmontel relates (in Bk. IV of his memoirs) how Crébillon was used by the enemies of Voltaire to oust the latter from favour at court.

Crécy, ODETTE DE, see *Odette.*

Crenne, HÉLISENNE DE (16th c.), authoress, of whom little is known except that she was probably a native of Picardy, and was still alive in 1550 after publishing in 1538 *Les Angoysses douloureuses qui procèdent d'amours,* the first work in French literature that may be distinctly classed as a sentimental romance. It is written under Italian influence (resembling Boccaccio's *Fiammetta*), and purports to be the confession of a girl married when very young, living for several years happily and faithfully with her husband, then suddenly struck with an overwhelming passion for a young stranger. The mental anguish and domestic troubles that ensue are detailed with skill, and the subsequent events and ultimate unhappy issue are related in Parts II and III of the work by her lover Guénélic.

Créqui, RENÉE-CAROLINE DE FROULLAY, MARQUISE DE (1714–1803), a friend of d'Alembert and J.-J. Rousseau and in her old age of Sénac de Meilhan. The memoirs attributed to her were fabricated by a certain M. de Courchamps and contain gross inaccuracies of biographical fact, besides anachronisms and misrepresentations, but they are entertaining. Some authentic letters of Mme de Créqui have been published.

Crétin, GUILLAUME (d. 1525), born in Paris, one of the *rhétoriqueurs* (q.v.), author of patriotic allegorical poems on current events, and of an unfinished epic *La Chronique française* (which was continued after his death by a monk René Macé), an uncritical versification of ancient chronicles. Crétin, in spite of his insipidity, enjoyed a surprising reputation in his day and was praised by Clément Marot as 'souverain poète'. The *rondeau* quoted by Rabelais in his *Tiers Livre* (ch. xxi) is by Crétin.

Crève-Cœur, Le (1940), collected poems by Aragon (q.v.).

Crime de Sylvestre Bonnard, Le (1881), the novel (in diary form) which won fame for Anatole France (q.v.). An elderly scholar abducts the daughter (in later editions *granddaughter*) of the woman he had once loved and hoped to marry from the boarding-school where she is ill-treated. He sells his precious library to provide a dowry for her.

Crispin rival de son maître, a one-act comedy in prose by Le Sage, produced in 1707, his first success.

Valère is in love with Angélique, daughter of the rich Oronte, and she returns his love.

But she has been promised to Damis, son of Orgon, an old provincial friend of Oronte. Damis himself is unknown to her and her family. Meanwhile Damis has secretly married another girl, and Orgon sends his servant to Paris to explain matters to Oronte and break off the proposed match with Angélique. Orgon's servant falls in with Crispin, the servant of Valère. The two valets, tempted by Angélique's dowry, devise a plan by which the news of Damis's marriage shall be suppressed, and Crispin shall pose as Damis, marry Angélique, and bolt with the dowry. The plot progresses favourably at first, for Oronte is gullible and his wife is susceptible to flattery, and the rascally valets ingeniously extricate themselves from difficulties which threaten their exposure; but they are finally shown up and Angélique is given to Valère. However, thanks to their smooth tongues, they win not only the pardon of Oronte, but good places.

Critics and criticism

[NOTE. The authors, movements, &c. referred to in this article receive fuller mention under separate headings.]

INTRODUCTORY

(1) The abundantly productive literature of medieval France included treatises on Rhetoric (signifying both Oratory and Poetics) which dealt mainly with the technicalities of the *ballade*, *rondel* and other verse-forms then employed. Eustache Deschamps's *Art de dictier* (c. 1500), Molinet's *Art et science de rhétorique* (1493) are examples. The period between the Renaissance and the 19th century is marked by the evolution of criticism in the sense of defining what makes for good or bad literature and so forming criteria of judgement on which criticism in a second, more modern, sense of appraisal then comes to be based. But until the 19th century this criticism of appraisal is seldom anything but illustrative, serving for guidance and lending force to theory; and dogmatic, tied to *les règles* (see *Classicisme*). In general, the critics are the essayists, letter-writers, and men of taste of the 17th and 18th centuries, writing for the comparatively small world of their fellows. With the growth of the Press and the reading public during the 19th century the professional critic comes into being. Criticism at its best now becomes a separate form of literature. Its fundamental

principles receive increasing attention. It becomes much less dogmatic, and as the 19th century merges into the 20th it takes on a new sense, of aesthetic interpretation rather than appraisal.

RENAISSANCE TO NINETEENTH CENTURY

(2) The world of the Renaissance, thirsty for knowledge, was ready for a reaction against the *rhétoriqueurs*. The introduction of printing (1470) made the great body of Greek, Latin, and Italian literature, and of classical criticism, suddenly available on a large scale. The Reformation intensified the growing cleavage between purely theological and philological studies and a conception—of language as an instrument of literature—which was to dominate the 16th century and with which criticism in France may be said to begin. The conception owes its development largely to the Pléiade group of poets, notably to Du Bellay's *Défense et illustration de la langue française* (1549); and in these early stages the criticism was verbal, concerned with language and form (mainly the form of poetry). Du Bellay's treatise led to the adoption of French instead of Latin as the language of French literature and to the gradual acceptance of new themes and forms, based on Greek, Latin, and Italian models (e.g. epic poetry, the Pindaric or Horatian ode, or the Petrarchan sonnet, the Aristotelian unities). There were, naturally, some abuses; and towards the end of the (16th) century the vernacular threatened to become clogged by the neologisms and borrowings—the *auréations*—recommended by the Pléiade. This danger was largely averted by Malherbe, who worked to make the language grammatically clear and supple, and who also laid down rules of versification (alexandrine, ode, sonnet) which lasted for some two hundred years.

(3) By the 17th and 18th centuries, the practitioners of literature, the *honnêtes gens*, the theorists, and the savants, had moved on to discuss and develop conceptions of literature as one of the arts. Oral discussion proceeded in the *salons* (e.g. the Hôtel de Rambouillet) and literary coteries, and in the *Académie Française*. Richelieu had conferred official status upon this body and in 1638 he invited it to deliver judgement upon the merits of Corneille's *le Cid*—in fact, to

criticize it. The *Académie Française* was also the scene, some years later, of the opening passages of the famous *Querelle des anciens et des modernes* (q.v.; cf. also *Perrault, Fontenelle, La Fontaine*) concerning the relative virtues of classical and modern literature. In print, discussion took the form of essays, prefaces, letters, and *arts poétiques*. The many writers whose theories made a contribution, temporary or lasting, to the evolution of criticism included Chapelain, who largely wrote the *Académie's Sentiments sur* [Corneille's] *Le Cid*; Corneille himself; Guez de Balzac; Descartes (whose *Discours de la méthode* shaped a course far wider than that of purely philosophic thought); Vaugelas; Boileau; Molière; Racine; Saint-Évremond; Houdar de la Motte; l'abbé Du Bos; Bayle; Voltaire, and Diderot.

(4) The general objects of discussion were to determine: what made for good or bad literature; what models should be followed (from the Renaissance to the 19th century the classical conventions prevailed, with few exceptions); whether pleasure, a necessary factor, could be produced by conforming to *les règles*, i.e. to general principles and rules of composition and diction, or to rules (e.g. the dramatic unities) more precisely adapted to the evolving literary genres; how best to represent nature and truth, and the need to avoid confusing art with nature; the importance of logic, systematized thinking, and reason *vis-à-vis* inspiration; the welcome to be extended to ideas of progress; and the doubts, inspired by such ideas, as to whether the sole models to be adopted should be those of classical antiquity. (A further question—the place of the individual in literature—arising largely out of the writings of Rousseau, received more attention in the 19th century.)

(5) Thus, by the late 18th century, as a result of this interplay of theory and practice various literary dogmas had been formulated, which served as a basis for the development of criticism in its second sense of appraisal. By this time, too, in such literary reviews as existed (see *Press, Development of*) space was devoted to criticism, and the critic as a type of independent professional journalist was beginning to appear. The criticism practised, however, remained, with rare exceptions, dogmatic, a matter of assessing the merits of a work by

its conformity to rules. Typical examples of the dogmatic criticism of the period are La Harpe's *Cours de littérature* (1799–1805), or the critical writings of Suard; or the book reviews and dramatic criticism of the *Journal des Débats* in its Empire and Restoration days (see *Feletz, Geoffroy, Hoffman*).

NINETEENTH CENTURY

(6) The 19th-century spread of education, with the rapid expansion of the Press and of a reading public in need of information and guidance, and interested in its social, historical, and cultural background, fostered the growth of the new class of professional critics, a recognizable phenomenon from the Restoration onwards. They were of two kinds: those who made literature and literary journalism their career and whose numbers and importance increased as the century wore on, and the academic critics, university professors whose official standing for long lent additional weight to their judgements. They delivered public lectures which were eagerly attended or read later in book form, and they also acted as critics on the staff of newspapers and reviews, at times even holding the position of editor.

(7) From the early years of the century, too, the fundamental principles of criticism itself were changing. Ideas were gaining ground (largely owing to Mme de Staël and Chateaubriand) that literature was the reflection, therefore constantly changing, of social history, and that standards of beauty and taste must vary according to the formative influences of race, religion, and civilization. Together with the revolutionary distinction between *classical* and *romantic* literature they led to the victory of *le romantisme* (q.v.) and the undermining of the classical conventions. The *liberté dans l'art* thus won introduced a new sense of relativity into criticism, and the conception that a work of art should be judged on its own merits, independently of standards of subject and treatment. Important writings in this connexion are Mme de Staël's *De la littérature* and *De l'Allemagne*; Chateaubriand's *Le Génie du christianisme*; Hugo's prefaces to *Cromwell* and *Les Orientales* and, later, his *William Shakespeare*.

(8) Villemain, in his *Tableau de la littérature française* (1828), was one of the first critics to consider new writing in its relation to general and literary history, to see in literature the expression of the ideas of an era, and to intersperse his work with biographical and historical notes. Other outstanding critics of the Restoration and the July Monarchy periods included Saint-Marc Girardin, Nisard, Fauriel, Magnin, Marmier, &c. Some, e.g. Nisard, were less liberal in their outlook than others. Some, like Villemain, combined the critic's with an academic (at times also a political) career. Some, e.g. Fauriel, Marmier, by their studies of foreign literature were forerunners of comparative criticism. (Later in the century Renan added considerations of anthropology, philology, and orientalism to the comparative field.)

(9) During the middle years of the century the scientific spirit of the age and the new trends in criticism were all clearly evident in one man, Sainte-Beuve, the dominating figure of 19th-century literary journalism, for instance in his objective approach (with rare exceptions) to literature and his belief in documentation, as also the insight and imaginative sympathy which he brought to his *Portraits* and *Causeries*. His appreciations of the great and lesser figures of French literature were in effect so many psychological reconstructions of the men, the women, and their epochs. When he died (1869) he left literary criticism firmly established as a genre in itself with at its best a value second only to that of the highest creative writing.

(10) Two distinguished contemporaries of Sainte-Beuve, who both outlived him, were Schérer and Montégut, men widely read in their own and foreign literatures and solidly informative and explicative in their criticism. His successor Taine made the application of scientific methods to criticism nearly if not quite the *raison d'être* of the critic's function, with results that could be brilliant, inspiring, or frankly astonishing. A somewhat younger critic, Brunetière (1849–1906), who was also a literary historian (a growing class, represented later notably by Lanson), a professor at the Sorbonne, and editor of the *Revue des Deux Mondes*, was also strongly influenced by the scientific ideas of the age and sought to apply the doctrines of evolution to literary history. As time went on he became intensely dogmatic and assessed literary value in terms of moral influence. He has been much decried in modern times,

but the earlier, more objective chapters of his *Évolution des genres* repay study.

(11) 'Impressionistic' criticism developed considerably in the late 19th century and has persisted to the present day. It is not concerned with the general pattern into which a writer can be fitted but with his personality or his ideas as revealed by his performance, e.g. the highly subjective and frequently brilliant criticism of Barbey d'Aurevilly, a militant Catholic and Royalist, or Faguet's psychological appreciations of politicians and moralists. Alternatively, what interests this type of critic is his own personal reaction to the work he is discussing, and the result is, for example, the various series of *Impressions de . . .* of Jules Lemaître or the explorations among books of Anatole France's *Vie littéraire*.

TWENTIETH CENTURY

(12) Intellectual judgement is still considered a necessary factor in much of the more academic criticism of the 20th century, though it has become increasingly analytic, reasoned, and relative and is now rarely tied to literary or scientific doctrines. But a new conception has also become apparent in modern times, of a criticism which is anti-intellectual, less a matter of assessing merit than of intuitive understanding and imaginative re-experience (thus showing itself a translation of the Bergsonian intuitionism into terms of critical theory). It is also a conception of criticism as interpretation, hence, at times, of the creative artist as the most if not the only satisfactory critic. This latter conception is already to be found in Baudelaire, whose criticism and reflections upon critical theory waited many years after his death (1867) to be appreciated.

(13) One of the first and most important of the anti-intellectualist critics was Remy de Gourmont, who largely introduced the psychology of linguistics and the 'dissociation des idées' into criticism. His understanding of the changing spirit of the literature of his day did much to set the note for his 20th-century successors, e.g. the critics associated with the early *Nouvelle Revue Française*, or Alain, above all for Valéry. The last-named is the supreme example of a modern type of criticism (see, for instance, his *Variétés*) which attempts to get behind language itself and to fathom the mysteries

of the creative process. (For 20th-century critics see also *Benda*; *Gide*; *Jaloux*; *Lasserre*; *Proust*; *Suarès*; *Thibaudet*.)

Critique de l'École des Femmes, La, a one-act prose comedy by Molière produced in 1663.

L'École des femmes having aroused criticism, notably in respect of the alleged indecency and irreverence of certain passages, Molière in this comedy ridiculed his adversaries. He stages a conversation in which *L'École des femmes* is attacked and defended, among its critics being the envious fellow dramatist Lysidas, a stupid marquis, and the prudish *précieuse* Climène. Molière's main defence is that the play is good because it has given pleasure; if it infringes the rules, the rules must be bad. See also *Impromptu de Versailles*.

Critique philosophique, La, a weekly (later monthly) periodical founded in 1872 by Renouvier (q.v.).

Critiques et Portraits littéraires (1832, 1 vol., 1836–9, 5 vols.), by Sainte-Beuve (q.v.), collections in book form of critical and biographical studies published originally, for the most part, in *Le Globe*, *La Revue de Paris*, *La Revue des Deux Mondes*, *Le National*, *Le Journal des Débats* (qq.v.), &c., that is to say, during the first part of his career as a professional critic, before the period of the *Lundis* (see *Causeries du Lundi*). He revised and augmented these essays more than once, and added new ones. He also, beginning in 1844, divided them into the three well-known groups of *Portraits littéraires* (3 vols. in later editions, published first as *Portraits littéraires*, 2 vols., 1844, and *Derniers Portraits littéraires*, 1 vol., 1852); *Portraits de femmes* (1844 and subsequently); *Portraits contemporains* (3 vols. to begin with, 1846; 5 vols. by the edition of 1869–71). The first two groups excluded studies of living persons. The *Portraits de femmes* made room, exceptionally, for a study of La Rochefoucauld (q.v.) as a necessary complement to a study of Mme de La Fayette (q.v.).

Criton, the pseudonym with which Charles Maurras (q.v.) signed many of his polemical articles in the paper *L'Action française* (q.v.).

Croche, MONSIEUR, see *Debussy*.

Croisades, see *Crusades*.

Croiset, MARIE-JOSEPH-ALFRED (1845–1923) and MAURICE (1846–1935), his brother, Hellenists whose *Histoire de la littérature grecque* (1887–99) remains a standard work.

Croisset, on the Seine near Rouen, Flaubert's home for the greater part of his life. The house was sold after his death, and demolished, a factory being later erected on its site. All that survives is a small *pavillon* by the river where Flaubert used occasionally to entertain his friends.

Croisset, FRANCIS DE [pseud. of Frantz Wiener] (1877–1937), of Belgian origin, author of successful comedies and travel sketches, e.g. *Le Bonheur, Mesdames* (1906), *Les Vignes du Seigneur* and *Les Nouveaux Messieurs* (1923 and 1926, in collaboration with R. de Flers, q.v.); *La Féerie cinghalaise* (1926), *Nous avons fait un beau voyage* (1930).

Croix de feu, an association of ex-soldiers (serving soldiers were included later), under the leadership of an ex-army officer, Colonel de la Rocque (1886–1946), which came into prominence during a time of acute political crisis in 1934 and was often involved in street disturbances. At first it was professedly non-party, prepared to support any government which had the national welfare at heart. Later, it agitated for social reform, adopted a 'mystique patriotique', and became progressively military in organization. It was officially dissolved in 1936.

Cromedeyre-le-vieil (1920), a play by Jules Romains (q.v.).

Cromwell (1827), a long historical drama (in verse) by Victor Hugo, based on the life of the Protector. It was not produced in Hugo's lifetime, but the author's preface, a plea for 'la liberté de l'art contre le despotisme des systèmes des codes et des règles', became the prime manifesto of the Romantic Movement (see *Romantisme*).

The evolution of poetry, he maintained, corresponded to three stages in the history of mankind. Lyric poetry, the eternal, spontaneous expression of emotion (typified by the Bible) dated from primitive times. Epic poetry (typified by Homer) had developed with ancient civilization as the world progressed and history was sung. The drama of more modern times reflected life after Christianity had awakened men's con-

sciousness to the continual struggle between a lower and a higher nature (here Shakespeare was the example). But hitherto the aesthetic conventions governing choice and treatment of subject had prevented the drama from being a faithful representation of life. They should be discarded. Beauty could exist only if there were ugliness to throw it into relief; the sublime entailed the grotesque; and true art must be free to take account of life's contrasts, to choose not necessarily the beautiful, but the characteristic. Language should be freed from the shackles of poetic diction; the conventional unities of time and place should be abolished; action should take place upon the stage instead of being narrated. And to emphasize the importance of this last innovation, historical truth should be respected.

The preface ended with a plea for more objectivity in criticism.

Croque-mitaine, a legendary monster or ogre with which nurses frighten children.

Cros, CHARLES (1842–88), was known in youthful Symbolist circles for his monologues, a form he is said to have created (*Le Hareng saur, Le Bilboquet, &c.*). His lyrics, prose-poems, and *rondes*—collected in *Le Coffret de Santal*, 1873; *Le Fleuve*, 1875 —are still mentioned. He was also a pioneer in colour-photography, and his invention of a form of phonograph is said to have preceded Edison's.

Crusades. The Crusades were the subject of a number of medieval French works, both in verse and prose. The following are some of the most important.

1st Crusade (1095). Graindor de Douay's poems, the *Chanson d'Antioche* and the *Conquête de Jérusalem* (see *Antioche*), purport to deal with the historical events of the Crusade; but other poems were composed on the same subject containing all manner of fantastic inventions, many of them centring in Godefroi de Bouillon, whose grandfather in these poems is the fabulous *Chevalier au Cygne* (q.v.). The whole group of poems is known as the Cycle of the Crusade.

3rd Crusade (1182–92). See *Ambroise*.

4th Crusade (from 1202). See *Villehardouin*. Robert de Clary, a native of Picardy, also wrote a prose narrative of the expedition (in which he had taken a humble part), containing vivid and interesting passages.

The *Chronique d'Ernoul* is a history of the kingdom of Jerusalem from its foundation to the year 1229, briefly told as regards the earlier part, more fully from 1183 when the author relates events of which he was a witness. It is written from the standpoint of the Christians established in Syria who saw the successive Crusades with a critical eye. The author was probably Seigneur de Giblet (the ancient Byblos).

7th Crusade (1248–50). See *Joinville*. An interesting letter on the commencement of the expedition was written by a certain Jean Sarrazin; it is followed by an anonymous continuation, which gives a clearer account than Joinville does of the incidents of the Crusade.

See also *Albigeois, Terre Sainte, Livre de la,* and *Henri de Valenciennes.*

Cry, a solemn proclamation made throughout the town, at crossroads and in public places, to announce the forthcoming performance of a Mystery by the *Confrérie de la Passion* (q.v.) of Paris. A *cry* took place in December 1540 to announce the performance some months later of the *Actes des apôtres* and, in view of the large cast required, to recruit actors.

Cubisme. Literary Cubism (the sole concern of this article) seeks to apply to literature the aims of Cubism in art, to give several aspects of an object at once, as well as every image associated with that object at the moment of writing, and to seize the disordered, often distorted, cinematographic effect of perceptions imprinting themselves on the brain. Surprise, an essential element, is emphasized by making the word-associations those of sound and suggestion, rather than sense. Some extreme Cubist poems combine the use of words as intellectual symbols with pictorial, emblematic typography, e.g. Apollinaire's *Il pleut* (in *Calligrammes*, 1918), in straggling, vertical lines, or Max Jacob's *Poème en forme de demi-lune* (in *Le Cornet à dés*, 1917). The six poets most representative of *Cubisme* in its heyday were: Guillaume Apollinaire, Blaise Cendrars, Léon-Paul Fargue, Max Jacob, Pierre Reverdy, André Salmon (qq.v.). In some cases their poetry transcended their theories.

Cujas (pron. as if *Cujass*), JACQUES (1522–90), born at Toulouse, a celebrated French jurisconsult. He wrote commentaries on the *Corpus Iuris* of Justinian. There was a prolonged quarrel between him and Bodin (q.v.).

Culture des idées, La (1901), by Remy de Gourmont (q.v.), critical studies.

Cunégonde, a character in Voltaire's *Candide* (q.v.).

Curé de Tours, Le (1832), a study of clerical life by Balzac, one of the 'Scènes de la vie de province' of his *Comédie humaine* (q.v.). The scene is Tours, in 1826. The genial but tactless abbé Birotteau offends his landlady and is envied by his fellow lodger the abbé Troubert. He becomes the object of their hatred and of a persecution so malevolently organized that his career and his health are wrecked.

Curé de village, Le (1838–9), one of the 'Scènes le la vie de campagne' of Balzac's *Comédie humaine* (q.v.). The period is the July Monarchy. The curé is the abbé Bonnet, who has reformed his poverty-stricken and once lawless flock at Montégnac, near Limoges. But this is only one feature of a book which nearly approaches crime fiction (with at times some excellent discussion of possible clues and accomplices), for the plot turns on two murders and a theft committed at Limoges by Jean Tascheron, an artisan of good character and a Montégnac man. He is quickly caught and executed but makes no confession, and his motive remains a mystery. The explanation comes some years later with the death-bed confession of the owner and revered benefactress of Montégnac, the wealthy Mme Graslin, widow of a Limoges banker, who, with the abbé Bonnet's guidance, has called upon modern engineering science to bring irrigation to her stony, arid lands and prosperity to her villagers.

In addition, this work is a first-rate example of Balzac's grasp of, and his capacity for keeping his readers interested in, technical and financial detail.

Curée, La (1830), by Auguste Barbier (q.v.), a satire in verse.

Curée, La (1872), a key novel in Zola's *Rougon-Macquart* (q.v.) cycle. Aristide Rougon, known as Aristide Saccard, follows his brother Eugène (see *Son Excellence Eugène Rougon*) to Paris and at the time of the Second Empire schemes of building development makes a fortune by shady speculation. His wife dies leaving a young son and daughter (Maxime and Clotilde) who are sent for their upbringing to relatives in Plassans. Meanwhile Aristide remarries for money and position.

From now on the novel follows a complicated course, heavily descriptive of seductions, vice, and the frenzied luxury and pleasure-seeking typical of some sections of Second Empire society. The bored, dissipated young wife Renée flirts with the vicious, precocious Maxime, who has joined the household, and eventually seduces him—no difficult matter. Maxime makes a marriage arranged by Aristide, who is aware of the whole situation but turns a blind eye so as to preserve his social position and bolster up his precarious finances. In the end the distraught Renée dies.

Curel, FRANÇOIS DE (1854–1928), dramatist, born at Metz, became known with two plays produced at the *Théâtre Libre* (q.v.) in 1892—*L'Envers d'une sainte* (an embittered woman imperils the happiness of those around her and finally takes refuge from herself in a convent), and *Les Fossiles* (a family of decayed nobility are so imbued with pride of race that they cover up an unsavoury scandal rather than let their name die out). His other plays, all of the problemplay type, or heavy treatment of current ideas, included *L'Invitée* (1893), *Le Repas du lion* (1897), *La Nouvelle Idole* (1899), *La Fille sauvage* (1902), *La Danse devant le miroir* (1914), *L'Âme en folie* (1920).

Curie, PIERRE (1859–1906), born in Paris, the famous French physicist who discovered radium. His wife, Marie Sklodowska (1867–1934), born in Warsaw and educated there and at the Sorbonne, was associated with him in all his researches from their marriage in 1895. After his death she succeeded him in the chair of Physics at the Sorbonne. She was the first woman to hold a post of such high academic rank.

Curieux impertinent, Le, a comedy by Destouches, produced in 1709, his first play.

Léandre and Julie love one another, but Léandre distrusts the constancy of Julie's affection. To test it, he induces his friend Damon, against the latter's wish, to pay court to Julie. Damon's wooing is at first a pretence, but he falls in love, and his wooing becomes real and successful. Léandre learns to his cost that true love implies confidence.

Curiosités esthétiques (1868, posth.), collected (largely art) criticism by Baudelaire (q.v.).

Cuvier, Farce du, see *Farce*.

Cuvier, GEORGES (1769–1832), a famous zoologist and palaeontologist, investigated the structure of living and fossil animals, and largely founded the sciences of comparative anatomy and palaeontology. He was an opponent of Lamarck's evolutionary theories and became involved in a difference of opinion with Geoffroy Saint-Hilaire (q.v.) over the fundamental laws of zoology. His famous *Leçons d'anatomie comparée* (1800–5) were first delivered as lectures at the *Muséum d'histoire naturelle* (see *Jardin des plantes*). His other publications include: *Discours sur les révolutions du globe*, the famous preface to his collected *Recherches sur les ossements fossiles* (1821–4), and an important work of zoological classification *Le Règne animal distribué d'après son organisation* (1816). His Saturday evening receptions in his home at the Jardin des Plantes were a favourite meeting-place for scientists and writers *c.* 1820–30.

Cycle, a group of narrative poems connected with a central heroic figure, recounting his exploits or boyhood or the story of his forebears, descendants, or companions. The *jongleurs* gathered material for three cycles of *chansons de geste* centred in Charlemagne, Garin de Monglane, and Doon de Mayence (see *Chansons de geste*). Other cycles are those of *Alexandre le Grand* (q.v.) and the *Saint Graal* (see *Perceval*). Poems on the adventures of the Crusaders formed the *Cycle de la Croisade* (see *Antioche*).

The term is also used in a broader sense of a mass of poems of this sort on more diverse subjects, but akin in background and tradition, e.g. the Arthurian legends and the *Romans de l'Antiquité* (q.v.). See also *Roman-cycle*.

Cymbalum Mundi, see *Des Périers*.

Cyrano de Bergerac, SAVINIEN (1619–55),

a writer of fantastic and burlesque romances, a Parisian, educated in Paris at the collège de Beauvais. (Bergerac was the name of a family estate near Paris, in the Chevreuse Valley.) He was a free-thinker, a soldier, and a duellist, of grotesque appearance (his long nose was celebrated), and at the same time studious, original, and with a tincture of poetry. Author of a comedy *Le Pédant joué* (1654), from which Molière drew the 'Que diable allait-il faire dans cette galère?' of the *Fourberies de Scapin*; of a tragedy, *La Mort d'Agrippine* (1653), in which he expressed the free-thinking tendencies of the day; and of the fantastic *Histoire comique des états et empires de la Lune* and *Histoire comique des états et empires du Soleil* (published after his death in 1656 and 1661 respectively). In these the author visits the moon and the sun and describes their inhabitants and institutions, which provide occasion for social and political satire.

Cyrano de Bergerac (1897), by Edmond Rostand (q.v.), a poetic, cape-and-sword drama, notable with other lastingly successful qualities as a vivid picture of life in seventeenth-century Paris. The first act is specially effective—a noisy, bustling representation of an evening at one of the three theatres of the time, the Hôtel de Bourgogne.

The chivalrous Cyrano de Bergerac (a Gascon knight in the play) has the noble heart beneath a comical exterior of his prototype (see above). On learning that Roxane, the object of his passion, loves Christian de Neuvillette, he aids his rival with heroic self-sacrifice, writes his love-letters, and is at hand beneath the balcony to prompt him when he woos his lady. De Neuvillette is killed in battle and for fifteen years Cyrano helps Roxane to keep his memory green. He reveals his own love, and how he had helped his rival, only when he is on the point of death.

D

Dabit, EUGÈNE (1898–1936), novelist, originally a Parisian locksmith, author of *Hôtel du Nord* (1929), a successful novel (and later, film, with Jouvet, q.v., in the chief part) of life in a small hotel in a poor district of Paris, the picturesque old quarter of the Canal Saint-Martin. It was hailed as an excellent example of the *roman populiste*, a type of novel much spoken of at this period, which sets out to describe lives that are humble but not necessarily only drab and sordid. Dabit published other, less successful, novels and left a *Journal intime* (*1928–36*).

Dacier, ANDRÉ (1651–1722), an editor and translator of the classics, notably of Horace. With his wife (see below) he took part in the quarrel of the Ancients and the Moderns (see *Querelle*) on the side of the Ancients. His work on Horace is mentioned in Congreve's *The Double Dealer*.

Dacier, MME (c. 1654–1720), *née* Anne Lefebvre, wife of the preceding, a learned Hellenist and Latinist who was employed on the preparation of classical texts *ad usum Delphini*, published editions of Florus,

Callimachus, Anacreon, &c., and translations of comedies of Aristophanes, Plautus, and Terence, and (her principal works) of the *Iliad* (1711) and the *Odyssey* (1716). It was on her translation that La Motte (q.v.) based his travestied *Iliad*, thereby provoking her to defend the ancient text. The long controversy between Ancients and Moderns was thus revived, and others participated in it. Mme Dacier and La Motte were reconciled in 1716.

Dacquin, JEANNE-FRANÇOISE [Jenny] (1811–95), daughter of a *notaire* at Boulogne, was the *Inconnue* with whom Mérimée (q.v.) corresponded regularly from 1831 till a few hours before his death in 1870 (*Lettres à une inconnue*, 1873). Their meetings were infrequent. The correspondence began when, after reading his *Chronique du règne de Charles IX* (q.v.), Mlle Dacquin wrote to Mérimée in English (she was for a long time a companion in an English family) calling herself 'Lady Algernon Seymour' and asking for an autograph. Some time afterwards Mérimée met her and learnt her true identity. She inherited money and lived comfortably in Paris, read a lot, studied foreign languages, and had a fondness for sweet cakes about which Mérimée often teased her.

Dadaïsme, a short-lived movement—largely but not wholly French—in literature and art. It preceded *Surréalisme* (q.v.) and was characterized by incoherence and a destructive spirit ('Dada détruit et se borne à cela'), and it asserted the importance of instinctive expression, independent of control by the intelligence. Words could have a purely fortuitous significance, i.e. could mean anything or nothing. It originated during the 1914–18 war (*c.* 1916) among refugee writers and artists who had drifted to Zurich, notably Tristan Tzara (q.v.), a Rumanian, Hans Arp, an Alsatian, Hugo Ball, a German. Between 1916 and 1919 a similar group from New York (leaders Marcel Duchamp and the artist Francis Picabia, a Spaniard) joined the Zurich group. In 1920 the movement made Paris its headquarters and the review *Littérature* (1st ser., 1919–21) its organ. A few *dadaïste* matinées and festivals were held, usually ending in disorder and free fights. By the middle of 1922 the movement was spent, though some of its ideas were to be given further expression by the *Surréalistes. Dadaïste* reviews and anthologies which appeared between 1916 and 1919 included *Cabaret Voltaire* and *Dada.* [The name '*Dada*' is said to have been chosen at random. Its dictionary definition is 'cheval d'enfant' (hobby-horse), but for the *dadaïstes* its fortuitous significance was 'nothing at all'.]

Dagobert, see *Mérovingiens.*

Daguerre, LOUIS-JACQUES-MANDÉ (1787–1851), gave his name to the *daguerréotype,* one of the earliest photographic processes (by which images were fixed on silver-plated copper by use of light). The initial experiments were conducted independently, then after 1829 with Daguerre, by Joseph-Nicéphore Niepce (1765–1833), the actual inventor of photography, but Niepce died in 1833. Previously, Daguerre had invented the *diorama,* which produced effects of nature by a clever combination of lighting, scenic painting, and transparent screens. He had begun life as an interior decorator, much admired for his work in Paris theatres.

Daguesseau [or, but wrongly, **d'Aguesseau**], HENRI-FRANÇOIS (1668–1751), orator and moralist, born at Limoges, a magistrate of high character, erudition, and moderate views, who became Chancellor of France in 1717, but proved unsuccessful as a politician and was twice relegated to his estates (1718–20 and 1722–7). He wrote *Méditations sur les vraies ou les fausses idées de justice* (a fine work, showing belief in a natural idea of justice based neither on interest nor on utility), *Instructions* for the education of his son, an impressive biography of his father, &c. He was famous for his *mercuriales,* discourses pronounced at judicial assemblies on Wednesdays (*dies Mercurii*), by the presiding magistrate, on the administration of justice.

Though out of sympathy with the philosophical movement of his day, he granted, in his official capacity, the *privilège* for the publication of the *Encyclopédie.*

D'Alembert, see *Alembert.*

Damas, Chemin de, the 'road to Damascus', used proverbially to signify a sudden spiritual or intellectual illumination, with reference to Acts ix.

Dame aux camélias, La (1848), a novel, dramatized in 1852 with great success, by Alexandre Dumas *fils* (q.v.; and cf. *Traviata, La*).

Marguerite Gautier, a courtesan, called 'la dame aux camélias' from her passion for this flower, falls deeply in love with Armand Duval and the two live in quiet happiness in the country. Armand's father visits Marguerite. He refuses to believe her love for his son sincere, and when bribes fail implores her to give Armand up. She gives way and returns to Paris, letting Armand believe she has left him for a rich nobleman. But the sacrifice has been too great and her already consumptive condition grows rapidly worse. Armand learns of his mistake and hastens to Paris in time for Marguerite to die in his arms.

Marguerite had a prototype in real life (see *Duplessis, Marie*).

Dame de Monsoreau, La (1846), an historical romance (*c.* 1578, in the days of Henri III), by Dumas *père.* It is known in English as *Chicot the Jester.* (Cf. *Bussy d'Amboise; Coconas.*)

Damiens, ROBERT-FRANÇOIS (1714–57), a fanatic who in 1757 attempted the life of Louis XV. He was tortured and executed.

Dancourt, FLORENT CARTON, SIEUR D'ANCOURT (1661–1725), *known as,* born at Fontainebleau of a good family of magistrates and financiers, was educated by Jesuits and studied the law, but fell in love with an actress, whom he married, and became an actor and playwright. His comedies, written in prose, are realistic pictures, witty and free from bitterness, of the life and society he saw about him—a bourgeoisie corrupted by its wealth, decayed aristocrats, and seedy adventurers. His style is loose and careless, but he had a strong sense of a comical situation and he knew how to take advantage of some passing topic or event of the moment: a fraudulent lottery in Paris suggests *La Loterie* (1697), the popularity of a restaurant suggests *Le Moulin de Javelle* (1696), the refusal of the law-courts to acquit a woman of murdering her husband though that husband is still alive suggests *Le Mari retrouvé* (1698). The best known of his comedies is *Le Chevalier à la mode* (q.v., 1687); others are *Le Notaire obligeant* (1685), *Les Bourgeoises à la mode* (1692), *Les Bourgeoises de qualité* (1700; like the preceding on the theme of women of the middle class aping ladies of quality), *Les Agioteurs* (1710, on the frenzy of speculation then prevalent). Dancourt retired from the stage in 1718 and devoted himself to good works. Vanbrugh's *The Confederacy* is adapted from Dancourt's *Les Bourgeoises à la mode.*

Dandin, George, see *George Dandin.*

Dandin, Perrin, the judge in Racine's *Les Plaideurs* (q.v.). It is he also who decides in an amusing manner the dispute in La Fontaine's fable *L'Huître et les plaideurs.* The name is taken from Rabelais's Perrin Dendin (*Le Tiers Livre,* ch. xli), a peasant of Poitou who was a successful arbitrator.

Dangeau, PHILIPPE, MARQUIS DE (1638–1720), an assiduous courtier who for thirty years from 1684 recorded in his *Journal,* daily and with exactitude, the minute incidents of the court of Louis XIV, also literary events so far as they interested the court, and political events as seen from its standpoint. The work, though of no literary merit, is of considerable chronological value, and Saint-Simon, though he attributed to him 'une fadeur à faire vomir', made extensive use of the *Journal* in the composition of his *Mémoires.* Dangeau, in an age when gambling at cards was fashionable, made a fortune in this way.

Danican, FRANÇOIS-ANDRÉ, *known as* Philidor (1727–95), composer and famous chess-player; composed many comic operas and a few operas. During the Revolution he retired to London and died there.

Danse macabre [or **macabré**], or Dance of the Dead, of which many representations were made in the 15th and 16th centuries, had its germ much earlier. The idea of the ubiquity of Death the leveller is seen in such works as the *Vers de la Mort* of Hélinand (*c.* 1195) and the *Dit des trois morts et des trois vifs* (latter part of 13th century). In the 14th century, perhaps under the influence of the visitations of the plague and of the preaching of the mendicant friars, the notion of a parade of all classes of society on their way to death took more precise shape. There is reason to think that it first took the form of a mimed sermon or liturgical drama, in which various characters representing pope, emperor, soldier, peasant, &c., stepped forward in turn and were each seized by the hand and hurried away by a figure representing a corpse. The first known painting in Europe of this *danse macabre* was made in 1425 in the cemetery of the Innocents in Paris. This was destroyed in the 17th century, but it can be reconstructed in essentials from various documents, notably the *Danse Macabre* of Guyot Marchant, published in 1485. The fine wood-engravings of this work, accompanied by verses forming dialogues between the dead and the living, appear to be a free imitation of the fresco of the cemetery. They represent thirty couples, each consisting of a member of some order of society, from pope to ploughman, and a corpse; but the latter is not, as in later developments of the Dance, a personification of Death in the abstract, but the corpse of the living figure, what he will hereafter be. This corpse seizes and hales off its living counterpart. Marchant's work was so successful that in 1486 he published a second edition and also a volume including a *Danse macabre des femmes,* of less merit. Representations of the Dance were made in various churches and cloisters of France, and the idea underwent some development in literature and illustration; the German artists (including Holbein) who depicted it appear to have drawn inspiration from French sources.

The name appears to be more correctly *Macabré*, and is of doubtful origin. A Latin form *Macchabæorum chorea* has been taken to indicate an obscure connexion with the tragic history of the Maccabees.

A more recent view [see R. Eisler in *Traditio* (1948), vi. 187 ff.] is that *macabre* corresponds to the Biblical Hebrew for 'grave-digger'; that the dance itself derives from the lugubrious funeral pantomime of Jewish and Syrian grave-diggers, members of Jewish and Syrian burial confraternities known to have existed in medieval France; and, further, that this would provide an explanation for various extended uses of the word *macabre* and for the occurrence of *Macabré* as a proper name both in medieval French literature (e.g. in the *Chansons de geste*) and in early French records.

Danton, GEORGES-JACQUES (1759–94), famous Revolutionary statesman and orator, born at Arcis-sur-Aube, near Troyes. He was president of the Club des Cordeliers (q.v.), Minister of Justice, and head of the Revolutionary Government formed after the downfall of the monarchy (1792) and, later, a Deputy to the *Convention nationale*. He was responsible for the initiation of the Revolutionary Tribunal in March 1793 and was himself condemned by it the following year because his attitude was too moderate for the extremists of the Terror. He was executed on 5 April 1794 together with Camille Desmoulins and Fabre d'Églantine (qq.v.).

Danton was a man of violent energy. There seems to be little doubt that he made money out of the Revolution, but he was none the less a passionate patriot, active in organizing resistance to foreign attack. His rousing speech in the *Assemblée législative* after the battle of Longwy (Sept. 1792) urged attack (on the Prussian armies besieging Verdun) as the best means of defence and contained the famous words: 'Pour les vaincre il nous faut de l'audace, encore de l'audace, toujours de l'audace, et la France est sauvée.'

Darmesteter, ARSÈNE, see *Dictionaries and Encyclopedias*, under date 1890–3.

Darmesteter, JAMES (1849–94), orientalist and philologist, author of numerous studies of Persian language and literature; also of *Les Prophètes d'Israël* (1892), collected essays on Jewish ideals and dogmas.

Daru, COMTE PIERRE-ANTOINE-NOËL BRUNO (1767–1829). He was responsible, as Intendant général de la grande armée, for keeping Napoleon's forces supplied on several campaigns, notably in Russia. He was also a man of letters whose many publications included a didactic poem in six cantos on Astronomy (1820) and a solid—and his most noted—work: *L'Histoire de la République de Venise* (1819). Stendhal (q.v.), a cousin, has many references to him and his family, e.g. in his *Journal* and the *Vie de Henry Brulard*.

Dash, COMTESSE, the pseudonym adopted by the vicomtesse de Poilloüe de Saint-Mars (1804–72), who suffered reverses of fortune *c.* 1840 and thereafter became an indefatigable writer of sentimental novels, popular guides to life in high society. She left gossipy reminiscences, *Mémoires des autres* (1896–7).

Dates, see *Year, Beginning of the.*

Daubenton, LOUIS-JEAN-MARIE (1716–99), naturalist and anatomist, belonged to Montbard, in the Côte d'Or, as did Buffon (q.v.) for whose *Histoire naturelle* he supplied a large number of the anatomical descriptions and whom he also helped considerably with the replanning of the Jardin du Roi (see *Jardin des Plantes*) in Paris. He gave his name to a form of medicinal lozenge made of ipecacuanha—the *pastilles de Daubenton*.

Daudet, ALPHONSE (1840–97), novelist, born at Nîmes (Provence), spent a youth very like that of the boy Daniel in his semi-autobiographical tale *Le Petit Chose* (1868, q.v.)—childhood games round the family warehouse; school at Lyons, where his parents started afresh after his father (a silk-merchant) lost his money; an unhappy period (1855–6) as pupil-teacher, bullied alike by masters and boys; then migration to Paris (1857) to join his brother Ernest, already in employment, and try fortune as a writer. After his first published work, *Les*

Amoureuses (1858, verse), he wrote tales and short theatrical sketches, and by 1861 was contributing to *Le Figaro* (q.v.). From 1861 he was private secretary to the duc de Morny (d. 1865), an influential Minister, half-brother to Napoleon III. He had financial security, and leisure to write, and made his name as a novelist.

(2) Today Daudet is remembered chiefly by the *Lettres de mon moulin*, delicately sentimental, humorous sketches of Provençal life which appeared first in *Le Figaro* (1866) and in book form in 1868; by *Le Petit Chose* (already mentioned) and by the unforgettable *Tartarin* burlesques (*Tartarin de Tarascon*, 1872, q.v., *Tartarin sur les Alpes*, 1885, *La Défense de Tarascon*, 1886, *Port-Tarascon*, 1890). His novels, which made his fame in his lifetime, have been somewhat unjustly forgotten. For a time he was a leading *naturaliste* (see *Naturalisme*), writing with the care for documentation typical of the movement, but his work comes alive by his gift for vivid, impressionistic description and because his naturalism never excluded the warm, poetic, fantasy-loving side of his character. He depicted the business, political, or social world in *Fromont jeune et Risler aîné* (1874, q.v.); *Jack* (1876); *Le Nabab* (1877, q.v.); *Les Rois en exil* (1879, q.v.); *Numa Roumestan* (1881, q.v.). Psychology played more part in *L'Évangéliste* (1883), a painful study of religious mania, and *Sapho* (1884), the history of two lovers whose relationship is continually broken off and renewed. *L'Immortel* (1888), a novel of the world of the *Académie française*, which satirized the victim of the Vrain-Lucas (q.v.) forgeries, roused much indignation.

(3) Daudet's other writings included plays, notably *L'Arlésienne* (1872, with incidental music by Bizet, q.v.) and *La Dernière Idole* (1889); *Les Contes du lundi* (1873) and *Contes et récits* (1873), short, patriotic tales, perhaps inspired by his period of service in the *Garde nationale* (q.v.) during the Franco-Prussian war; also *Souvenirs d'un homme de lettres* (1888), *Trente ans de Paris* (1888), and *Notes sur la vie* (1899, posth.). He was one of the authors of *Le Parnassiculet contemporain* (1867; see *Pastiche*).

(4) His death, sudden in the end, followed thirteen years of painful illness. The old mill of the *Lettres*, at Fontvieille, near Arles, was restored and is now a Daudet museum.

Daudet, LÉON (1868–1942), son of the preceding, journalist, publicist, and novelist, abandoned medicine for political journalism in 1894, identifying himself with Rightwing publications and, after 1908, with the advanced Royalist and Roman Catholic paper *L'Action française*, which he helped to found. His articles were amusing, often brilliant, but violent, biased, and at times scurrilous. His critical essays, *Le Stupide XIXe Siècle* (1922), are a French equivalent of the anti-Victorian reaction in England. He also published some more or less erotic novels, and *Souvenirs des milieux littéraires, politiques, artistiques et médicaux de 1890 à 1905* (1914–21).

Dauguet, MME MARIE [*née* Aubert] (1865–   ), author of the nature poems included in *A travers le voile* (1902), *Par l'amour* (1904), *Les Pastorales* (1908), *L'Essor victorieux* (1911).

Daumier, HONORÉ (1808–79), born in Marseilles, one of the most famous lithographers and caricaturists of the 19th century, flourished during the July Monarchy and the Second Empire. His caustic satires of political and legal circles, and his scenes from low-class life, above all his cartoons of the legendary cad and booster *Robert Macaire* (q.v.), helped to make the reputation of *Charivari*, *Caricature*, and *Le Figaro* (qq.v.). *Gargantua*, one of his first drawings, which appeared in *Caricature* in 1832, was a caricature of a king swallowing enormous budgets. It cost him six months in prison. His eyesight failed after 1875 and he was awarded a state pension.

Daunou, PIERRE-CLAUDE-FRANÇOIS (1761–1840), born at Boulogne, was ordained priest in 1787. He welcomed the Revolution, adhered to the *Constitution civile du clergé* (q.v.), and was prominent in Revolutionary politics until the fall of the Girondins (q.v.), when he was arrested. He returned to public life after the fall of Robespierre (see *Thermidor, le 9*) and for many years took a leading share in organizing important legislative, scholarly, and scientific reforms and innovations. A historian and savant, he was appointed Keeper of the National Archives in 1804. From 1816 to 1838 he was editor-in-chief of the *Journal des savants* (q.v.), and from 1819 to 1830, at the Collège de France, he lectured on the study and writing of history, attaching an importance by no means generally recognized at that date to method and to thorough documentation from the sources (*Cours d'études historiques*, 1842–6, 20 vols.).

Dauphin, the title of the eldest son of the King of France from 1349 to 1830; originally a title attached to certain seigneuries. According to Littré the title *Dauphin*, borne by the seigneurs of the Viennois, was a proper name *Delphinus* (the same word as the name of the fish, dolphin); at any rate the ruling house bore a dolphin on its arms; whence the province subject to them was called the Dauphiné. When Humbert III, the last lord of the Dauphiné, ceded the province to Philippe de Valois in 1349, he made it a condition that the title should be perpetuated by being borne by the eldest son of the French king.

The edition of the classics *ad usum Delphini* was prepared for the son of Louis XIV (see *Grand Dauphin*).

Daurat, JEAN, see *Dorat, Jean*.

David, JACQUES-LOUIS (1748–1825), famous French historical painter, came of a family of drapers long established in Paris. He was awarded the Prix de Rome in 1774 and on returning to France became court painter to Louis XVI. He was from the outset an ardent Revolutionary, a member, and for a short time President, of the *Convention nationale*. He voted for the death of the king and organized several of the Revolutionary *fêtes*, notably the elaborate *Fête de l'Être Suprême* (q.v.) of 8 June 1794. Both at this time and later, under Napoleon, he exercised a quasi-dictatorship over French art, insisting on a return to the formal severity of classical standards. The work of his later years, however, heralded the romantic spirit soon to characterize French art, so much so that Delacroix (q.v.) called him 'le père de la peinture moderne'. Among his famous paintings of Greek and Roman antiquity are *Le Serment des Horaces* (commissioned for Louis XVI), *L'Enlèvement des Sabines*, &c. His paintings and drawings of contemporary events and personages, which constitute a magnificent pictorial record of two eras, include *Le Serment du Jeu de Paume*, *Marat assassiné*, *Marie-Antoinette allant à l'échafaud* (a bitter sketch, from a window on the route), *Le Sacre de*

l'Empereur Napoléon Ier, *La Distribution des aigles*, and the well-known portrait of Mme Récamier. Most of his work can be seen at the Louvre or at Versailles.

David d'Angers, PIERRE-JEAN (1783–1856), sculptor, born in Angers (Anjou), lived mainly in Paris. His statues and medallions of celebrated contemporaries were his finest work. He was a supporter of the Romantic Movement (see *Romantisme*).

Davout, LOUIS-NICOLAS, one of Napoleon's marshals (see *Maréchal de l'Empire*).

De arte honeste amandi, see *Amour courtois*.

Débâcle, La (1892) by Émile Zola, the penultimate volume of his *Rougon-Macquart* (q.v.) novels. The characters are merely figures in a vast historical fresco. The work is a detailed, realistic, and impressive study of the Franco-Prussian war, particularly of the days before, during, and after the disaster of Sedan (q.v.) in August 1870. (By the close the scene has shifted to Paris during the Commune.) Various human relationships are formed or shattered as events sweep on. Two friends, Maurice Levasseur, an educated man defeated by circumstances, and Jean Macquart, a peasant, unquestioningly resigned to his duty as a soldier, represent the worn-out Second Empire and the vigorous, hopeful France of the future.

Débat, see *Dit*.

Débat du corps et de l'âme, see *Religious Writings* (medieval period).

Deburau, JEAN (1796–1846), born in Bohemia, spent a miserable childhood with small travelling circuses, but ended in Paris as the most famous mime of the day. The modern conception of Pierrot as a lovelorn, ludicrous yet pathetic figure, eternally disappointed yet eternally hopeful, is due to his rendering of the part. For years Paris flocked to the *Théâtre des Funambules* (q.v.) to see him. He fell during a performance and died of his injuries—an incident which may have suggested the end of Edmond de Goncourt's fine novel of circus life *Les Frères Zemganno*.

Debussy, CLAUDE-ACHILLE (1862–1918), born at Saint-Germain-en-Laye, near Paris, one of the musical composers most closely associated with the Symbolist Movement (see *Symbolisme*). His *Prélude à l'après-midi d'un faune* was the musical counterpart of Mallarmé's (q.v.) poem; Maeterlinck's (q.v.) *Pelléas et Mélisande* provided the libretto for his one opera; and he set to music poems by, amongst others, Verlaine, H. de Régnier, P. Louÿs (qq.v.). He created the personage of 'Monsieur Croche, anti-dilettante' as a mouthpiece for some of his interesting, often witty, musical criticism (collected in volume form and published under this title, posthumously, in 1921).

Décadent, Le, a literary review (1886–9, weekly, later fortnightly) founded by Anatole Baju (1861–1903). Contributors included Jean Lorrain, Jules Renard, Laurent Tailhade, and Verlaine. When contributions were lacking the editors filled the gaps with *décadent* manifestoes (see *L'Esprit décadent*), abusive criticism, or verse purporting to be written by Rimbaud, at that date still a legendary figure supposed to be emblazing a trail of orgiastic splendour across the Orient.

Décade philosophique, littéraire et politique, La (1794–1807), one of the most notable periodicals of its era, particularly in matters religious (the question of separation of Church and State was being agitated at the time) and literary (see *Ginguené*).

Décades, see *Pontigny*.

Déclaration des droits de l'homme et du citoyen, La, voted by the *Assemblée constituante* on 27 August 1789, and modelled on the American Declaration of Independence, set forth the guiding principles of the French Revolution. It consisted of a preamble and seventeen articles, from which the following extracts are taken: 'Les représentants du Peuple Français . . . considérant que l'ignorance, l'oubli ou le mépris des droits de l'homme sont les seules causes des malheurs publics et de la corruption des gouvernements, ont résolu d'exposer dans une Déclaration solennelle, les droits naturels, inaliénables et sacrés de l'homme. . . .

i. Les hommes naissent et demeurent libres et égaux en droits; les distinctions sociales ne peuvent être fondées que sur l'utilité commune. . . .

ii. [Les] droits [naturels et imprescrip-

tibles de l'homme] sont la liberté, la propriété, la sûreté et la résistance à l'oppression. . . .

iii. Le principe de toute souveraineté réside essentiellement dans la nation. . . .

iv. La liberté consiste à pouvoir faire tout ce qui ne nuit pas à autrui. . . .

vi. La loi est l'expression de la volonté générale. . . .

xi. La libre communication des pensées et des opinions est un des droits les plus précieux de l'homme. . . .

Défense et illustration de la langue française, La, a manifesto in prose of the doctrines of the school of the *Pléiade* (q.v.), by Joachim du Bellay, published in 1549.

It maintains the fundamental equality of all languages and the capacity of the French language for the treatment of the noblest themes, if its poetry is perfected by the study and assimilation of classical models (mere translation from classical authors is insufficient). It recommends the invention, within discreet limits, of new words, the recovery of ancient words, the adoption of terms used by various craftsmen, &c. It approves the intermixture of masculine and feminine rhymes, but not as rigorously binding. Above all it asserts that the natural facility of the poet is not enough, but must be supplemented by labour and art. The *Défense* was unfair in its condemnation of poets such as Clément Marot and Mellin de Saint-Gelais, who already applied much of what it advocated.

Défense nationale, Gouvernement de la (1870), see *Republics,* para. 4.

Défenseur de la Constitution, Le, a journal, or news-letter, founded by Robespierre in June 1792 to express his theories of the Revolution and to defend himself against his adversaries. Two months later it was renamed *Lettres de Maximilien Robespierre, membre de la Constitution nationale de France, à ses commettants.* It lasted till March 1793.

Deffand, MARQUISE DU, see *Du Deffand.*

Deffoux, LÉON, see *Pastiche.*

Degas (pron. as if *Degass*, EDGAR (1834–1917), French painter, associated for a time with the Impressionists (see *Impressionnisme*). His most famous works include studies of horses and horse-racing, and pastels of ballet-dancers, all characterized by his genius for capturing movement. In his last years, although he could still work, he was partially blind.

Deimier, Pierre de (1570–1618), a mediocre poet at the court of Marguerite de Valois, is remembered by his treatise *L'Académie de l'art poétique* (1610), which contains theories of poetry and poetic diction very similar to those of his contemporary Malherbe (q.v.).

Delacroix, Eugène (1798–1863), son of the Revolutionary politician Charles Delacroix, and founder of the Romantic school of French painting, was born at Charenton-Saint-Maurice on the outskirts of Paris. He left school (the Lycée Louis-le-Grand) to study painting, and exhibited his first picture *Dante et Virgile* at the Salon of 1822. The protest and discussion it created—because of a dash and roughness of technique opposed to the smooth finish then conventional (cf. *Ingres*)—were renewed by subsequent works, though eventually he won ample recognition. He lived mainly in Paris except for a trip to Morocco and Algeria in 1831. His *Journal* (first published posthumously, 3 vols., 1893–5) is one of the most interesting and valuable of 19th-century diaries, not only as a revelation of personality and a picture of the circles in which he moved, but also from the point of view of painting (aesthetics and technique) and, hardly less, from that of literature and music. His *Correspondance* (1936–8, 5 vols.) is also of great interest.

De la littérature considérée dans ses rapports avec les institutions sociales (1800), a work of literary criticism by Mme de Staël (q.v.) which had a profound influence upon French thought of the early 19th century (cf. *De l'Allemagne*). The author reviews (chaps. xi–xvii) the literature of preceding ages and other countries, namely, Greece, Rome, Italy, Spain, and the countries of Northern Europe, from the standpoint (then new) that all literature reflects the society and thought of its day, while through its masterpieces it influences the progress of humanity. Turning to the France of her own day, she then shows its literature torn between formal traditions, with their bases in the pagan antiquity of Greece and Rome, and the philosophical,

more imaginative spirit that dates from the rise of Christianity and the influence of the Northern races. In the closing chapters the author attempts to forecast the literature that will spring from the contemporary French ideals of liberty and equality, and she ends with an enthusiastic profession of faith in human 'perfectibility'.

Mme de Staël incurred Napoleon's severest displeasure because in the second section of the book she compared her own age with the decadent Roman Empire before the Christian invasion.

De l'Allemagne (1810), a work of literary criticism by Mme de Staël (q.v.), had its first publication in 1813, in England. The original (1810) edition, of 10,000 copies, was seized on the very eve of publication in France because of Mme de Staël's emphasis on the contrast between the two nations, France and Germany, and her plea that the French should no longer surround themselves with a spiritual Great Wall of China. All but four copies (of which one is in the Bibliothèque nationale in Paris) were destroyed, the type was broken up, and the author was ordered to leave the country within twenty-four hours.

The work is in four parts: (1) 'De l'Allemagne et des mœurs des Allemands'; (2) 'De la littérature et des arts'; (3) 'La philosophie et la morale'; (4) 'La religion et l'enthousiasme'. To begin with, and again in a famous chapter in Pt. 2, 'De la poésie classique et de la poésie romantique', the author returns to a familiar theme (see *De la littérature*) and derives European literature from two main sources, Paganism and Christianity. The Paganism of antiquity is responsible for the 'classical' literature of the Southern—Latin—races, with its insistence upon clarity and form. Christianity and medieval chivalry in their turn have produced the 'romantic' literature of the Northern—Germanic—races; and it is into this that enthusiasm, Nature, and the soul have found their way. It will live, and grow, because rooted in the soil. Form is less important than sentiment. The chapter 'De l'esprit de conversation' contrasts the French and German minds, and in 'De la religion et de l'enthousiasme' the author maintains that without these two qualities no subject can be thoroughly understood and appreciated.

The studies of German poets (Goethe, Schiller, &c.) and philosophers (Kant, Fichte) contained in the work did much to make these figures known to the French.

De l'amour (1822), by Stendhal, a study which 'décrit froidement les diverses phases de la maladie de l'âme nommée *amour*' (author's preface). Love, he says, may be *l'amour-passion* (e.g. that of Héloïse and Abelard); *l'amour-goût* (a drawing-room amusement played according to rules, in which no one ever loses control of himself); *l'amour de vanité* (it is as important to run a love-affair as to go to a good tailor), and *l'amour physique* (rough-and-tumble pleasure). The initial process, described in a famous passage in Bk. I, is much the same owing to the lover's faculty for finding something to worship in everything pertaining to his beloved. It resembles the process of crystallization in the salt mines of Salzburg. The bare branch of a tree, if thrown into the mine, would be found three months later encrusted to the tip of the smallest twig with an infinitude of minute salt deposits, glittering like diamonds. 'Ce que j'appelle crystallisation, c'est l'opération de l'esprit, qui tire de tout ce qui se présente la découverte que l'objet aimé a de nouvelles perfections.' In Bk. II Stendhal outlined views, advanced for his day, on marriage and the position of women. The two books also contain observations on politics, morals and literature, and anecdotes of Italian society.

Delandine, Antoine-Joseph, see *Dictionaries and Encyclopedias*, under date 1766 (*Dict. historique portatif . . .*).

Delaroche, Hippolyte, *called* Paul (1797–1856), a famous historical painter, born in Paris (cf. *Géricault* and *Delacroix*). Although his finest work includes several small pictures of incidents from the Passion he usually depicted subjects from English and French history, e.g. *Les Enfants d'Édouard* (the Princes in the Tower); *La Mort de Jane Gray*; *Richelieu remontant le Rhône* (cf. A. de Vigny's description in his novel *Cinq-Mars* of Richelieu's barge towing the boat containing Cinq-Mars and De Thou on their way to execution). Delaroche used the smooth, solid technique from which Delacroix was the first to depart.

Delarue–Mardrus, Lucie, *née* Delarue (1880–1945), born at Honfleur, French poetess and prose-writer, wife of Dr. J.-C. Mardrus, the celebrated translator of the *Mille et une nuits* (1899–1904, 16 vols.). Her best poems are evocative of Normandy land- and sea-scapes (*Par vents et marées*, 1911; *Souffles de tempête*, 1918). Earlier collections (*Occidents*, 1901; *Ferveur*, 1902; *Horizons*, 1904; *La Figure de proue*, 1908) were more often inspired by eastern themes or scenes. Her novels of rural life and of childhood and adolescence should also be mentioned, e.g. *Marie fille-mère* (1908), *Le Roman des six petites filles* (1909), *Comme tout le monde* (1910), *Un Cancre* (1914).

'De l'audace . . .', see *Danton*.

De Launay, Mlle, see *Launay*.

Delavigne, Casimir (1793–1843), dramatist and poet, born at Le Havre, brought up in Paris, was highly popular in his day with the general public and with the critics of the classical school. His successful, conventional verse, of no marked poetic quality, celebrated events of national interest, e.g. *Les Messéniennes* (1818), elegiac verse inspired by the sufferings of Greece and the trials of France after Waterloo. His tragedies have a literary interest as transition pieces which relaxed some of the classical conventions without wholly embracing the liberty claimed by the dramatists of the Romantic school. *Le Paria* (1819), *Les Vêpres siciliennes* (1821), *Marino Faliero* (1829), *Louis XI* (1832), *Les Enfants d'Édouard* (i.e. the princes in the Tower, 1833), were the most successful. He is best remembered by his comedies, particularly *L'École des vieillards* (1823), one of the great successes of the period.

Delavigne is said to have found the labour of writing so distasteful that he composed his works by reciting them to himself, and in the end wore out both his voice and his health. His reputation declined quickly after his death.

De l' Esprit, an ethical treatise by Helvétius (q.v.), published in 1758 and condemned by the *parlement* after having been authorized by the censorship.

The author, holding that religion has failed as the basis of morality, and that the true basis of this and of legislation is the public interest, that is, the interest of the greatest number (the doctrine in fact of Utilitarianism), proceeds to the opinion that the interest of the individual is solely his pleasure and pain and that he is actuated only by egoistic impulses. He further advances the view that the human mind, at birth, varies little in different individuals, and that progress and general happiness therefore depend entirely on education, institutions, and laws. Helvétius was one of the first to conceive the idea of a moral science, for he held, like Condillac, that the effect of moral forces may be calculated in the same way as that of physical forces.

Bentham recognized Helvétius's book as one of the sources of his inspiration.

Delibes, LÉO (1836–91), composer of operas (e.g. *Lakmé*), operettas, and ballets (notably *Coppélia*, 1870). Many well-known writers furnished him with libretti, e.g. Labiche; Ludovic Halévy; Méry (qq.v.).

Délices, Les, the house just outside Geneva where Voltaire spent the summer months between 1754 and 1760, when he settled at Ferney.

Délie. Object de plus haulte vertu (1544), by Maurice Scève (q.v.), a series of 449 *dizains* (ten-line stanzas) which treat of the poet's attitude to life and to love (an unsatisfied but gradually purified sentiment). They are often obscurely symbolical and occultistic, or metaphysical, but often, equally, of a beauty that anticipates the 'pure' poetry of Mallarmé and Valéry (qq.v.). Modern editors consider that by 'Délie' the poet had in mind the young poetess Pernette du Guillet (q.v.) whom he had long loved (she died in 1545), and not merely the anagram for *l'idée*.

Delille, JACQUES, ABBÉ (1738–1813), a mediocre poet and an agreeable and lively talker, popular in his day, author of descriptive and didactic poems, *Les Jardins* (1782), *L'Imagination* (1788), *L'Homme des Champs* (1800), *Les Trois Règnes* (1809), and of translations of Virgil's *Georgics* (1770) and *Aeneid* (1804), which, though elegant, fail to render the spirit of the original; also of Milton's *Paradise Lost* (1805). He was ridiculed by Rivarol in the latter's *Le Chou et le navet*. He was elected to the *Académie* in 1772, but his admission was deferred until 1774 by the king, who suspected him of

being an 'encyclopédiste'. Charles Lamb, sending his verses on *Hester* to Thos. Manning in Paris (March 1803), remarks, 'If you have interest with the Abbé de Lisle, you may get 'em translated: he has done as much for the Georgics.'

De l'intelligence (1870), a famous work, containing the sum of his philosophical thinking, by Hippolyte Taine (q.v., paras. 3, 4).

Déliquescences d'Adoré Floupette, Les (1885), by Gabriel Vicaire and Henri Beauclair, an amusing collection of 'poèmes décadents' parodying the *Symbolistes* and the *Décadents* (qq.v.). It was taken seriously by some critics when it appeared, and in fact helped to draw attention to the poems of Verlaine and Mallarmé.

Delisle, LÉOPOLD-VICTOR (1826–1910), medievalist, a man of great erudition who was for many years head of the *Bibliothèque nationale* (q.v.) in Paris. He compiled an invaluable inventory and history of the acquisition and provenance of the manuscripts in this library (*Le Cabinet des manuscrits de la Bibliothèque nationale*, 1868–81, 3 vols.). He also published many studies of medieval times and society, and of medieval acts and cartularies.

Delisle de Sales, JEAN-CLAUDE IZOUARD, *known as* (1741–1816), a member of the group of the *philosophes*, a man of mediocre talent. He was author of *Philosophie de la Nature* (1770), a work condemned by the Châtelet in 1775 and its author imprisoned. The Châtelet after lengthy proceedings sentenced Delisle to perpetual banishment on absurdly inadequate grounds, but the sentence was quashed by the *parlement*. The work itself was an indifferent reproduction of the philosophical commonplaces of the day.

Delorme, Joseph, see *Vie, Poésies et Pensées de Joseph Delorme*.

Delorme, MARION (c. 1611–50), a famous courtesan of the time of Louis XIII. She was the mistress of Cinq-Mars (q.v.) and had considerable vogue in Paris society, numbering distinguished men such as Richelieu, Saint-Évremond, the comte de Gramont, &c., among her admirers; also, in a different social circle, Des Barreaux. Hugo made her the heroine of his poetic drama *Marion de*

Lorme (q.v.). She also figures in Vigny's historical novel *Cinq-Mars* (q.v.) and in Bulwer Lytton's *Richelieu* (1839), an historical drama.

Delorme, PHILIBERT (*c.* 1515–70), a celebrated architect, who built the château of Saint-Maur for the Cardinal du Bellay, and that of Anet for Diane de Poitiers, and was taken into favour and enriched by Henri II. He prepared plans, at the request of Catherine de Médicis, for the palace that bore the name of the Tuileries. But his plans were only in small part carried out. He published a *Traité d'architecture* and another technical work.

Delphin Classics: *ad usum Delphini*, see *Grand Dauphin*.

Delphine (1802), a novel in letter-form by Mme de Staël (q.v.). Many mishaps and misunderstandings prevent the loves of Delphine d'Abbémar, a young widow, and Léonce de Mondoville from running smoothly. The main obstacle is the character of Delphine herself, perhaps the first 'modern woman' in French fiction, whose ideas of how women behave are not those of her conventionally-minded lover. Léonce marries another woman, Delphine takes the veil; Léonce's wife dies; and the Revolution frees Delphine from her vows. Once more the two are free to marry, but once again the spiritual barriers between them are too strong. Léonce becomes an *émigré* and in the end is shot. Delphine poisons herself.

Demi-Monde, Le (1855), a play by Alexandre Dumas *fils* (q.v.). He coined the word to describe the world of *les déclassées* portrayed in the play—a world which begins 'où l'épouse légale finit' and finishes 'où l'épouse vénale commence'. The word was recognized by the *Académie française* and defined as 'la société des femmes de mœurs légères' (*Dict. de l'Acad. Franç.*, 1932).

Démocratie en Amérique, La (1835 and 1840), see *Tocqueville*.

Démocrite, a comedy in verse by Regnard, produced in 1700.

The author represents Démocrite, the 'laughing philosopher' (though scarcely resembling the sage of Abdera), summoned from retirement in the desert to the court

of the king of Athens. The play, otherwise of little interest, has one amusing scene. Strabon, the servant of Démocrite, has not seen his wife for twenty years, mutual hatred having caused them to part. They meet at the court without knowing one another and fall in love; but an exchange of reminiscences brings recognition, recognition revives their violent aversion, and they hurl insults at one another.

Demolder EUGÈNE (1862–1919), born at Brussels, one of the numerous Belgian writers associated actively or by sympathy with the Symbolist Movement (see *Symbolisme*). He abandoned the law for literature and wrote novels (*La Route d'émeraude*, 1899; *Le Jardinier de la Pompadour*, 1904; *Les Patins de la Reine de Hollande*, 1901) and criticism.

Denier, MAURICE, 19th-century dramatist, author (in collaboration with A. Guinon, q.v.) of *Les Jobards* (1892) and of *Gens de bien* (1893; M. and Mme Dubreuil, who are given to good works, learn that the happiness of both parties is not always assured by making the seducer marry his victim).

Denis, LOUISE, MME (*c.* 1710–90), *née* Mignot, niece and companion of Voltaire (q.v.).

Denis, SAINT, according to Gregory of Tours, a bishop sent under the reign of Decius (249–51) to preach to the Parisians, who after divers torments suffered martyrdom. According to tradition he, with two companions, was decapitated on the hill of Montmartre (q.v.). But his tomb was at Saint-Denis a few miles north of Paris (see *Saint-Denis, Abbaye de*), whither legend says he carried his own head after execution.

Département. By a decree of 15 January 1790 the *Assemblée constituante* (q.v.) divided France into *départements* intended to serve administrative purposes (civil, religious, and military) and as electoral divisions. They were named after their geographical features, e.g. Hautes-Pyrénées, Basses-Pyrénées, Seine-et-Marne, &c. In size they were calculated to make the *chef-lieu* (= county town) accessible from any part within one day; and care was taken, in general, that the new territorial divisions should respect the boundaries, and so preserve the historical and racial associations, of the former provinces. To begin with there were eighty-three departments. In December 1955 there were ninety (including Corsica and three departments in Algeria) in Metropolitan France; see Appendix II, Map 1, and cf. *Provinces, Les Anciennes*. There were also at this date four oversea departments, the *départements d'outremer*—Guadeloupe, Guyane, Martinique, and Réunion).

The subdivisions of a department are the *arrondissements*, the *cantons*, and the *communes*. Of these the *communes*, which may be large or small, densely or sparsely populated, rural or urban, are the basic territorial subdivisions for local government purposes. *Arrondissements* and *cantons* are, roughly speaking, administrative or electoral rather than territorial subdivisions.

The chief official in a department is the *Préfet* (q.v.), who is directly appointed by, and responsible to, the central government. He has an elected body, the *conseil général*, to assist him. In the *communes* there is a Mayor who is elected by, and (though not as regards all his functions) responsible to, a *conseil municipal*. Paris is an exception (see *Commune* (1); *Police*, para. 2).

D'Épinay, MME, see *Épinay*.

Dépit Amoureux, Le, an early comedy by Molière, produced in 1656.

Éraste is in love with Lucile, and has received a favourable letter from her, which he shows to his rival, Valère. But Valère only laughs at him, for he believes that he has himself been secretly wedded to Lucile the previous night. In fact it is her sister Ascagne who has inveigled him. Ascagne has from childhood been disguised and passed off as a boy, in order to retain in the family an inheritance which, if her father had no son, would pass to the family of Valère. Her marriage to Valère, to which the latter is readily reconciled, puts an end to the deception and resolves the difficulty between the families. But meanwhile the misunderstanding has estranged Lucile and Éraste, and there is a charming scene where they renounce their vows and return their mutual gifts, and then find they are still in love with one another. There are amusing scenes in which the young men's valets, Lucile's maid, and a pedant, Métaphraste, are involved. (The play consists of two distinct elements. The scenes relating to the quarrel and reconciliation of the lovers, which are of Molière's own invention, are generally separated from the rest and alone acted. The remainder is a somewhat laboured imbroglio imitated from the Italian of Nicolò Secchi.)

Dépôt légal, see *Bibliothèque nationale*.

Député, a member, directly elected by universal suffrage, of the Assemblée nationale (q.v.), the lower chamber of the French legislature (cf. *Conseil de la République*; *Palais-Bourbon*).

Député d'Arcis, Le, one of the 'Scènes de la vie politique' in Balzac's *Comédie humaine* (q.v.). It was left unfinished by Balzac and completed (1854) by Charles Rabou (1803–71).

Déracinés, Les (1897), a novel by Maurice Barrès (q.v.), forms Pt. I of his trilogy *Le Roman de l'énergie nationale* (q.v.). Seven young Lorrainers, during their last school-year at Nancy, fall strongly under the influence of their professor, M. Bouteiller, and his teaching of the Kantian philosophy of pure reason. They come to Paris, where alone careers are to be made. But in Paris they find themselves adrift, lacking the cultural or spiritual roots to aid their development. Disillusionment follows, to which they react in divers ways. The book is ideological at the expense of story and character, and difficult to follow without some knowledge of the politics of the Third Republic, but it is an interesting study of the intellectual climate of the generation described. It contains passages often referred to, e.g. the imaginary conversation between Roemerspacher, one of the *déracinés*, and Taine (q.v.); the reunion of the seven at the tomb of Napoleon; and the description of the funeral of Victor Hugo.

Derème, TRISTAN [pseud. of Philippe Huc] (1889–1942), *fantaisiste* (q.v.) poet, author of *La Flûte fleurie* (1913), *La Verdure dorée* (1922), *L'Enlèvement au clair de la lune* (1925), *Poèmes des colombes* (1929), &c. He experimented freely with rhyme and metre.

Dernier Jour d'un condamné, Le (1829), a tale by Victor Hugo, an indictment of capital punishment and the publicity with which, at the time he was writing, the death sentence was carried out.

On a hot summer's morning a prisoner hears himself condemned to death. He spends the next few weeks in the condemned cell at the notorious prison of Bicêtre (q.v.) and we get his experiences and his reflections. He watches a convict gang setting off, chained together, for the prison at Toulon; and when his own time comes he is conducted across Paris in an open cart to execution.

Déroulède, PAUL (1846–1914), author and politician, born in Paris, served in the army during the Franco-Prussian war. In 1882 he founded the *Ligue des Patriotes* (q.v.) and later was sentenced to ten years' exile because of his subversive political activities. His patriotic verse was very popular: *Chants du soldat* (1872), *L'Hetman* (1877, a verse-drama), *Le Livre de la Ligue des Patriotes* (1887), *Refrains militaires* (1889), &c. He died at Nice.

Des Adrets, FRANÇOIS DE BEAUMANOIR, BARON (1513–87), born in the Dauphiné, noted for his cruelty. In the Civil Wars he joined the Protestants from pique and led their forces in the Dauphiné, showing great ferocity. He later turned Catholic.

Désaugiers, MARC-ANTOINE (1772–1827), born at Fréjus (Provence), wrote popular comedies and vaudevilles (*Le Mari intrigué*, 1806; *Le Valet d'emprunt*, 1807; *Les Petites Danaïdes*, 1817), also songs and light verse of the type, though by no means the quality, of those written by Béranger (q.v.). These included *Chansons et Poésies diverses* (1808–16, 3 vols.).

Des Autels, GUILLAUME (1529–81), at first a poet on the fringes of the *Pléiade* (*Le Repos de plus grand travail*, 1550; *La Suite du repos*, 1551; *L'Amoureux Repos*, 1553); later a defender of Catholicism, a man of law, and writer of court and official poems.

Des Barreaux, JACQUES VALLÉE, SIEUR (1599–1673), poet, friend and disciple of Théophile de Viau (q.v.), free-thinker and epicurean, whose materialism and licentiousness are reflected in much of his poetry (some of his amatory pieces celebrate Marion Delorme, q.v.). He is remembered especially

for a fine sonnet of repentance, *Recours du pécheur à la bonté de Dieu*.

Desbordes-Valmore, MARCELINE (1786–1859), poetess, was born at Douai and brought up in struggling circumstances. She went on the stage, but had to leave it for a time—when she began to write poetry —because an illness threatened her with loss of voice. On her recovery, she returned to the stage, married an actor (1817), and for twenty years toured the country with him. She continued to write, some prose, but mostly poems of love and childhood which were gentle and unsophisticated but genuinely lyrical (*Élégies, Marie* [a prose tale] *et romances*, 1819; *Élégies et Poésies nouvelles*, 1825; *Les Pleurs*, 1833; *Pauvres Fleurs*, 1839; *Bouquets et Prières*, 1843). She had three children, and after 1839, in Paris, she struggled to support the whole family by doing hack work for publishers. Sainte-Beuve (q.v.) edited a collection of her poems in 1842, prefacing them with a friendly, appreciative essay; and in 1884 Verlaine included her in his gallery of *Poètes maudits* (q.v.).

Descartes, RENÉ (1596–1650), philosopher and mathematician, was born in Touraine; his ancestors were gentry of Poitou, and his father was a magistrate. He was educated by the Jesuits, saw military service for a short time under Maurice of Nassau and the Duke of Bavaria, and travelled widely. Thereafter he went into studious retirement, first in Paris, then (in 1629) in Holland, where he spent twenty years in the tranquillity of Leiden, Amsterdam, Utrecht, and other towns. But his philosophical views exposed him to persecution by the theologians, and in 1649 he accepted the invitation of Queen Christina to visit Sweden, where he died in the following year. His principal works were published as follows: the *Discours de la Méthode* and *Traité des passions de l'âme*, in French, in 1637 and 1649 respectively; the *Meditationes de prima philosophia* (together with the *Objectiones* of various philosophers, and replies by Hobbes and Descartes) and the *Principia philosophiae*, in Latin, in 1641 and 1644. The Latin works were subsequently translated into French. The *Discours de la Méthode* was written for a wide public and provides a sketch not only of the method of philosophical inquiry adopted by Descartes, but also of his general philosophical system, metaphysical, physical, physiological, and moral. These are more fully developed in the other works named above, which are, moreover, supplemented by Descartes's published letters.

As regards Descartes's *method* to which he attached supreme importance, all the sciences, he held, must be studied together (for they are interconnected) and by a single process designed to distinguish what is clear and certain from what is probable. He rejects the syllogistic method as sterile (since the conclusion can contain no more than the premisses) and substitutes a progression by deduction from the most simple and absolute truths, known by intuition, to the more remote. Intuition is a 'firm conception arising in a healthy mind attending only to the light of reason', not to the deceptive appearances of the senses; this intuition may be of a simple notion or of a relation or connexion. Descartes's point of departure is the famous 'cogito, ergo sum' ('I think, therefore I am'). From this and the notion that the mind possesses of infinity and hence of perfection, he passes by deduction to the affirmation that God exists, and, since God must be trusted in the interpretation (corrected by reason) of the evidence of the senses, to the existence of the material world. Intuition and deduction are supplemented by the analysis of the complex into the simple, a contrary process of ascent from the simple to the complex, and a general review to secure that no difficulty has been overlooked. Descartes's *Discours de la Méthode* may thus be contrasted with Bacon's *Novum Organum*, which had appeared seventeen years earlier.

Descartes reached the conclusion that the essence and sole primary quality of material objects is their extension, and this conclusion is the basis of his physics. Extension or space being capable of quantitative mathematical expression, he arrived at a purely mathematical conception of the universe. He sought to explain its mechanical arrangement by his famous hypothesis of *tourbillons* or vortices, innumerable whirlpools of material particles, varying in size and rotating with different velocities, and affording in his view the only possible basis for motion in a closely packed universe. The animal body he regarded as a piece of mechanism capable of physical analysis. But the human body is in relation with a spiritual soul, capable of thought and will, and of this relation of the spiritual to the material he advanced no satisfactory explanation. The doctrine of free will, which Descartes upheld, coupled with the intuitive knowledge of God and of the immortality of the soul, forms the basis of his remarkable *Traité des passions* (1649), in which he shows how the passions, which are not evil in themselves but only in their excess, can be disciplined and their effects regulated by reason. He advanced mathematics by his development of analytical geometry, and optics by his discovery of the law of refraction; but his theory of vortices was ousted by the work of Newton. Gassendi was his principal contemporary critic.

Cartesianism, as the doctrine of Descartes is called, was widely applauded in his own day for the rational process that it inculcated. Descartes was careful to distinguish between the realms of science and of faith, and moreover was led by his method to certain conclusions, indicated above, consonant with the Christian religion. He had supporters for instance at Port-Royal in Arnauld and Nicole, and at the Oratoire, which produced his disciple Malebranche. Thus for a time the fundamental lack of harmony between his system and the Catholic faith escaped general observation. But it was perceived by Pascal and Bossuet. Descartes had in fact erected reason into a universal instrument. Applied to politics, its product is seen in the *Esprit des lois*; applied to religion, in the *Encyclopédie* (qq.v.). In the literary sphere it exalted scientific truth and encouraged order and logic, thus harmonizing with the spirit of the classical literature of the 17th century. In the quarrel of the ancients and moderns, it favoured the latter, as seen notably in Perrault and Fontenelle. Descartes exerted a powerful general influence on the philosophic thought of Europe: this is seen in England, for instance, in the works of the Cambridge Platonists and of Locke, even when they differed from his conclusions. His style has been variously judged; though not free from defects, it shows vigour and precision, and he may be regarded as a pioneer in the formation of scientific and philosophic language.

Descaves, LUCIEN (1861–1949), born in Paris, novelist, dramatist, and critic, one of five authors who broke away from their master, Zola (q.v.), and issued a manifesto (1887) against *le naturalisme* (q.v.). His best novels, written after this time, have a background of social history, e.g. *Les Emmurés* (1894), *La Colonne* (1901), *Philémon, vieux de la vieille* (1913), depicting small suburban life in Paris during the *Commune* (q.v.) of 1871; *L'Imagier d'Épinal* (1919; cf. *Images d'Épinal*), the life of small tradespeople, Bonapartists, still harking back to the Napoleonic legend (see *Légende napoléonienne*). *Sous-offs* (1889) was a study, provocative in its day and much criticized, of the deadliness and horrors of army life in peacetime.

Deschamps (Deschamps de Saint-Amand), ANTOINE-FRANÇOIS-MARIE, *called* ANTONY *or* ANTONI (1800–69), a minor poet of the Romantic Movement (see *Romantisme*) and a translator (1829) of Dante; a brother of Émile Deschamps (q.v.) but of a more feverishly romantic temperament. His mental health failed in 1834.

Deschamps (Deschamps de Saint-Amand), ÉMILE (1791–1871), elder brother of Antony Deschamps (see above), a minor poet of the Romantic Movement (see *Romantisme*), one of the founders of *La Muse française* (1823, q.v.), and a good friend to younger authors, notably Hugo and Vigny. His writings, mainly translations and imitations, stimulated interest in German, Spanish, and English literature and included *Études françaises et étrangères* (1828), poems prefaced by an essay on the Romantic doctrines; also translations of *Romeo and Juliet* (1839), *Macbeth* (1844), &c.

Deschamps, EUSTACHE (*c.* 1346–*c.* 1406), also called MOREL, born in Champagne, perhaps a nephew of Guillaume de Machaut (q.v.), by whom he was educated. He held various offices at the court of Charles V and in the provinces. He was author of a large number of *ballades* and *rondeaux* (qq.v.), not of the conventional order, but on a variety of themes, patriotic, moral, or satirical. He also wrote a long unfinished poem, a satire on women called the *Miroir de mariage*, and a prose *Art de dictier et de faire ballades et chants royaux*, a treatise on

versification. His verses are frequently vigorous, but he lacked poetic inspiration. He addressed a complimentary *ballade* to Chaucer, whom he styled 'grant translateur'. Deschamps wrote some dramatic pieces: the *Farce de Maître Trubert et d'Antroignart* and the *Dit des quatre offices de l'Ostel du Roy*, the former a farce in which a crafty lawyer finds his match in the client he intends to dupe, the latter a *moralité* with gastronomy for its subject.

Desdichado, El, see *Chimères, Les.*

Désert de l'amour, Le (1925), by François Mauriac (q.v.), a novel.

Désespéré, Le (1886), by Léon Bloy (q.v.), an autobiographical novel.

Des Essarts, see *Herberay des Essarts.*

Des Esseintes, the hero of J.-K. Huysmans's novel *A rebours* (q.v.).

Desfontaines, PIERRE-FRANÇOIS GUYOT, ABBÉ (1685–1745), left the Jesuit Order and lived by his pen. He wrote in the *Journal des savants* (q.v.) during the period 1724–7, and subsequently conducted the *Nouvelliste du Parnasse* (1730–2), the *Observations sur les écrits modernes* (1735–43), and the *Jugements sur quelques ouvrages nouveaux* (1743–5). His *Dictionnaire néologique* (1726), sometimes mentioned, made fun of the language and works of some of his contemporaries and was preceded by an *Éloge historique de Pantalon-Phœbus*, a composite personage made up of the authors satirized. But Desfontaines is chiefly remembered for his controversies with Voltaire. He also translated *Gulliver's Travels* (1727). (See also *Argenson, comte de.*)

Des Grieux, CHEVALIER, see *Manon Lescaut.*

Deshoulières, ANTOINETTE LIGIER DE LA GARDE, MME (1638–94), poetess, wife of Guillaume de Boisguérin, seigneur des Houlières. Her husband, an adherent of Condé, was involved in the political troubles of the time, and she joined him in the Spanish Netherlands. She was ultimately ruined and for the last twelve years of her life suffered from cancer. She is best known by the somewhat insipid pastoral idylls and eclogues preserved in anthologies, but her best verses are those which were inspired by her misfortunes and the approach of death. She inherited the *samedis* of Mlle de Scudéry and received in her *salon* Corneille, Ménage, Conrart, Benserade, Fléchier, Mascaron, Quinault, &c. She was the centre of the clique that attacked Racine's *Phèdre*.

Desjardins, PAUL (1859–1940), philosopher and critic, founder and director of the *décades* at Pontigny (q.v.).

Des Lauriers, see *Bruscambille*.

Desmasures, LOYS (*c.* 1515–74?), secretary to the cardinal of Lorraine and a man of erudition, was converted secretly, *c.* 1550, to Protestantism in Geneva on his way back to France from Rome. He settled in Lorraine but in 1562 fled the country to escape arrest for heresy. His trilogy of religious dramas on the history of David, an endeavour to reconcile the classical model of tragedy with the medieval tradition of the mystery, was printed in 1566. He also translated the *Aeneid* and many of the Psalms into French verse, and wrote a morality entitled *Bergerie spirituelle*.

Desmarets de Saint-Sorlin, JEAN (1596–1676), poet, a familiar of Richelieu and holder of high administrative office, an original member of the *Académie*. He was an adversary of Boileau in the literary disputes, and of Port-Royal in the religious conflicts, of the time. He was author of the epics, *Clovis ou la France chrestienne* (1657), in twenty-six cantos, and *Esther* (1673) in seven books; and in various writings (including the *Délices de l'esprit humain*, 1658, which provoked the *Visionnaires* of Nicole (q.v.)), defended the adoption of national and Christian themes as the subjects of epic poems, a doctrine condemned by Boileau in his *Art poétique*. He also wrote a romance, *Ariane* (1632), of which the scene is Rome under Nero, and comedies, of which the best known is *Les Visionnaires* (1637), a study of characters, in which various extravagant types in polished society are ridiculed, with possible allusions to Mme de Rambouillet and other women famous at that time. Molière drew on the play in *Les Femmes savantes*.

Desmoulins, CAMILLE (1760–94), born at Guise, in Northern France, one of the outstanding figures of the Revolution, was originally a lawyer, then became a journal-ist. He was a popular hero for a time after his appeal of 12 July 1789 to the people of Paris to rise and defy the king's armies. Later, he was secretary to Danton and, in the *Convention nationale*, an enthusiastic *Montagnard* (q.v.). From November 1789 to December 1791 he conducted the newspaper *Les Révolutions de France et de Brabant* and from 1793 to 1794 *Le Vieux Cordelier* (q.v.). His *Histoire des Brissotins ou Brissot dévoilé* (1793) contributed largely to the downfall of the Girondins (q.v. and see *Brissot*), but his protest against the excessive bloodshed of the Terror (printed in *Le Vieux Cordelier*) cost him his life. He was executed on 5 April 1794 together with Danton and Fabre d'Églantine. His wife Lucile followed him to the scaffold shortly afterwards.

Desorgues, JOSEPH-THÉODORE (1763–1808), born at Aix-en-Provence, author of Revolutionary songs and hymns. The best known—*Hymne à l'Être Suprême*—was sung in 1794 at the *Fête de la Fédération* (q.v.) In later life he wrote against Napoleon and was confined at Charenton (q.v.), where he died.

Des Périers, BONAVENTURE (d. *c.* 1544), a Burgundian learned in the classics, who was *valet de chambre* at the court of Marguerite de Navarre and a friend of Clément Marot. He collaborated in the preparation of Olivetan's Bible (1535) and of Dolet's *Commentaires de la langue latine*. He published in 1538 *Cymbalum Mundi*, a prose work purporting to be translated from the Latin. It consists of four satirical dialogues in the style of those of Lucian (e.g. Mercury comes to earth to have the Book of Destiny rebound, but it is stolen from him by some rogues, who use it for their own purposes). The work is directed against the Christian faith, liturgy, and discipline; its suppression was ordered by the *parlement* and only one copy survived.

Another work, entitled *Nouvelles Récréations et joyeux devis*, is attributed to Des Périers and is probably in the main by him, though enlarged by his editor (1558) after his death. It is a collection of short facetious tales (some from Italian sources) admirably related and containing occasional vivid pictures of contemporary manners. Des Périers also wrote some graceful verses, and translated Plato's *Lysis*, the *Andria* of Terence, and the first satire of Horace. He died by his own hand.

Desportes, PHILIPPE (1546–1606), poet, born at Chartres, visited Italy, obtained favour at court, and wrote verses celebrating not only his own loves but those of his patrons, Charles IX and the duc d'Anjou (whom he accompanied to Poland). His importance and prosperity increased when the latter came to the throne as Henri III; from him he received rich benefices, including the abbacy of Tiron (after which he is frequently referred to as the 'abbé de Tiron'). He made generous use of his wealth and influence, which consequently aroused no enmity (except that of d'Aubigné and Malherbe). His benefices were for a time confiscated by Henri IV, but were restored, and Desportes ended his life in peaceful luxury. He was uncle of Régnier (q.v.). His *Premières Œuvres* appeared in 1573, and were added to in subsequent editions. His *Psaumes*, versifications of the Psalms of David, were published in 1592 and 1595. A disciple of the *Pléiade*, but with some developments under the influence of the contemporary Italian school, a lucid though subtle poet, Desportes introduced a new delicacy in his melodious and polished love poems. He was vigorously condemned by Malherbe. He wrote sonnets, quatrains and sixains in alexandrines, and a number of charming *chansons* (including the famous *O nuit! Jalouse nuit!*, a translation from Ariosto, in which he is perhaps at his best). His *Psaumes*, in a great variety of metres, show more gravity and nobility of diction than those of Marot. With Ronsard, Desportes exerted a considerable influence on the English poets of the end of the 16th century, including Spenser, Lodge, and Daniel. 'Few men', wrote Lodge in his *Margarite of America* (1596), 'are able to second the sweet conceits of Philippe Desportes, whose poetical writings ... are ordinarily in everybody's hand.'

Despréaux, see *Boileau-Despréaux*.

Desqueyroux, Thérèse, the chief character in François Mauriac's novels *Thérèse Desqueyroux* (1927, q.v.) and *La Fin de la nuit* (1935).

Des Roches, MADELEINE, and her daughter CATHERINE (16th c.), patronesses of literature and poetesses, remembered for the hospitality that they offered in their house at Poitiers, then a literary centre, to all men of letters. See *Puce*.

Destinées, Les, a posthumously published collection (1864) of *poèmes philosophiques* by Alfred de Vigny (q.v., para. 3).

Destouches, PHILIPPE NÉRICAULT, *known as* (1680–1754), dramatist. He was for a time an actor in his youth, and his subsequent career as a dramatist was interrupted by his employment from 1717 to 1723 as the Regent's diplomatic agent in England. On his return he was admitted to the *Académie*. The principal comedies (in verse) of his earlier period were *Le Curieux impertinent* (q.v. 1709), *L'Ingrat* (1712), *Le Médisant* (1715), and of his later period, *Le Philosophe marié* (1727, in which the author dramatized an incident of his own life, a secret marriage contracted in England and revealed by the indiscretion of his young sister-in-law) and *Le Glorieux* (q.v., his masterpiece, 1732). *Le Dissipateur* (1753, recalling in parts Shakespeare's *Timon of Athens*) and *Le Tambour nocturne* (adapted from Addison's *The Drummer*, 1733) also deserve mention. His posthumous comedy *La Fausse Agnès* (1759) contains some amusing scenes. Of a strongly religious character, Destouches aimed at making comedy moral and edifying and thereby worthy of esteem. But in fact his comedies are somewhat lacking both in comic and pathetic qualities, though they include a few lively scenes. It was Destouches who wrote (in *L'Obstacle imprévu*), 'Les absents ont toujours tort'.

Destutt de Tracy, ANTOINE-LOUIS-CLAUDE (1754–1836), see *Idéologues*.

Des Ursins, MARIE-ANNE DE LA TRÉMOILLE, PRINCESSE (c. 1642–1722), wife by her second marriage of the Italian Prince Orsini (whence her name), and again widowed. A woman of strong political sense and ambition, she was chosen by Louis XIV in 1701 as companion for the young consort of his grandson Philip V, king of Spain. As superintendent of the queen's household, having acquired a strong influence over the king and queen, she played for thirteen years (with a short interruption in 1704–5) an important part in Spanish politics and the intrigues of the court. She was summarily deported when the new queen, Elizabeth of Parma, came to the throne. Her correspondence with Mme de Maintenon during the period of her ascendancy throws an interesting light on the characters of the two women, as well as on the events of the time.

Des Yveteaux, see *Vauquelin des Yveteaux.*

Deux décembre, Le, i.e. the Prince-President Louis Napoleon's *coup d'état* (q.v.) of 2 December 1851 (see also *Napoleon III*; *Republics*).

Deux Héritages, Les, by Prosper Mérimée, a comedy in one act, published in book form with two other short pieces in 1853. It had already been printed (1850) in the *Revue des Deux Mondes* as *Les Deux Héritages ou Don Quichotte*, Moralité à plusieurs personnages.

Devéria, ACHILLE (1800–57), engraver and lithographer, frequented the Romantic *cénacles* (q.v.). He was a noted book-illustrator, particularly of books by Romantic authors.

Devéria, EUGÈNE (1805–65), painter and lithographer, brother of the preceding, a friend of Victor Hugo and a frequenter of the *cénacles* (q.v.). His *Naissance de Henri IV* (1827), said to be his finest work, is in the Louvre.

Devin du Village, Le, a light opera by Jean-Jacques Rousseau. It had a first and very successful performance at Fontainebleau in October 1752 before Louis XV. At a later performance Mme de Pompadour played one of the parts.

Dezobry, CHARLES-LOUIS, and **Bachelet,** THÉODORE, see *Dictionaries and Encyclopedias*, under dates 1857 and 1862.

Diable, Île du, in French Guiana, one of a small archipelago to the north of Cayenne, the Îles du Salut, used by the French Government since 1854 as a convict settlement (cf. *Galère*). A law hurriedly passed in 1895 enabled the settlement to be used for political prisoners, after which Dreyfus (q.v.) was sent there.

Diable amoureux, Le, see *Cazotte.*

Diable au corps, Le (1923), a novel by Raymond Radiguet (q.v.).

Diable boiteux, Le, a novel by Lesage, published in 1707, imitated in framework and title from the *Diablo cojuelo* of Guevara (1641).

Asmodée, known as the 'diable boiteux', is released by Don Cléophas Zambullo from a bottle in which he has been imprisoned by an astrologer. To divert his benefactor, Asmodée lifts the roofs off the houses of Madrid and shows him what is passing within. This provides the author with an opportunity for a satirical picture of the Parisian society of the day in all its perversity. There is a slender thread of romance, for the devil assists Don Cléophas in various adventures and effects his union with the beautiful Seraphina.

Diaboliques, Les (1874), by J. Barbey d'Aurevilly (q.v.), a collection of tales which includes *Le Dessous des cartes d'une partie de whist, Le Bonheur dans le crime, Le Rideau cramoisi, Un Dîner d'athées*, &c. They recall the 'satanisme' of the last Romantics (see *Romantisme*) but have a certain interest as period (*c.* 1820) pieces.

Diafoirus, two characters, father and son, doctors, in Molière's *Le Malade imaginaire* (q.v.).

Dialogue des héros de roman (1713), a Lucianesque dialogue by Boileau (q.v.), a lively, amusing, and telling satire of the type of precious, pseudo-historical, pseudo-heroic novel (by La Calprenède, Mlle de Scudéry, &c.) in vogue in the early 17th century. Though he composed it about 1665 Boileau did not publish it, or indeed commit it to print, till after Mlle de Scudéry's death.

Pluto is complaining to Minos the Lawgiver that the dead are no longer what they used to be. They have no common sense. They all speak an affected jargon called *galanterie*, and despise those who are shocked by it as *bourgeois*. But he cannot believe this to be true of the great heroes and conquerors such as Cyrus and Alexander, and to ascertain the facts for himself he has summoned a number of the illustrious dead to appear before him. They come, to his increasing wrath and the ironical amusement of Minos, a succession of precious, languishing shepherds and shepherdesses, concerned now only with *tendresse, galanterie, amitié,* and *amour.* All ends well, however, when Mercury arrives and tells Pluto that a joke has been played upon him : he has been entertaining a troop of 'fantômes chimériques, qui . . . ont eu pourtant l'audace de prendre le nom des plus grands héros de l'antiquité . . . Ne voyez-vous pas que ces gens-là n'ont nul caractère des héros? Tout ce qui les soutient aux yeux des hommes, c'est un certain oripeau et un faux clinquant de paroles. . . .'

Dialogue de Sylla et d'Eucrate, a short dialogue by Montesquieu, published in 1722, in which Sulla after his surrender of the dictatorship defends his past tyranny and proscriptions.

Dialogues des morts (1683), see *Fontenelle*.

Dialogues des morts, composés pour l'éducation d'un prince (1712), see *Fénelon*.

Diane de Poitiers (1499–1566), DUCHESSE DE VALENTINOIS, mistress of Henri II. The splendid *château* of Anet in Eure-et-Loir was built for her by Philibert Delorme (q.v.).

Diaries, see *Memoirs*.

Diatribe du docteur Akakia, médecin du pape, a prose satire by Voltaire, published at Potsdam in 1752. The first two editions were destroyed by order of Frederick II. In this work the author ridicules the scientific views of Maupertuis (q.v.), president of the Berlin Academy. (Akakia was the actual name of two 16th-century French physicians, a father and son; the elder, who had changed his name Sans-Malice to its Greek equivalent, attended Clément Marot when ill. It was also the name of a respectable man of business of the nuns of Port-Royal.)

Dictionaries and encyclopedias. Dictionary-making in France as in other countries goes back to the glosses, glossaries, and word-lists (Latin into French) to be found in the Latin manuscripts of medieval times. Out of these glossaries grew dictionaries, which were at first, broadly speaking, of two kinds. There were, for instance, the bilingual (i.e. Latin–French) dictionaries, which in time became polyglot dictionaries (i.e. Latin, French, and other languages). These latter, in the 15th century, were often called *catholicon*, because they aimed at being universal, e.g. the *Catho-*

licon parvum, a Latin–French dictionary issued at Geneva in 1487 (and cf. also the *Dictionarium* of Ambrosius Calepinus under date 1502 in the list below which, after beginning as a Latin dictionary alone, added French, Italian, and Spanish, and finally seven other languages). Secondly, there were the dictionaries of the French language alone, with derivations, definitions, and equivalents of words, i.e. the beginnings of the study of etymology and synonyms, as well as, in time, examples of literary and proverbial usage and of changing sense, i.e. the beginnings of the philosophy of grammar. At the outset, the Latin–French dictionaries were, naturally, in the majority. But by the beginning of the 17th century French was well established as the language of official usage (see *Villers-Cotterets*) and of literature, and the number of French–French dictionaries grew rapidly.

It is indeed with the 17th century that dictionaries acquire their fascination from the point of view of literature and become treasure-houses for the writer striving to bring thought to utterance. 'De beaux mots bien propres & bien assis sans affectation, croyez-moi qu'ils ont la meilleure grâce du monde.' The quotation is from the 17th-century Jesuit Binet, whose collection of lexicographical studies *Essay des merveilles de la nature* was intended for 'tous ceux qui font profession d'éloquence' and who 'faute de sçauoir le propre mot de quelquechose... vont tournoyant tout autour du pot'. Such a man has an undeniable spiritual kinship with Zola, labouring over the vocabulary of *L'Assommoir* (q.v.), or with Proust, not only the Proust whose linguistic curiosity is so often evident, but the young Proust, the Marcel driving home from Martinville who gazes enthralled at the landscape and has no peace until he can capture its beauty in words. In the 17th century, too, the word 'dictionary' takes on its modern sense of 'a book of information or reference on any subject or branch of knowledge; an alphabetical encyclopedia' [*O.E.D.*]. The word 'encyclopédie' seems to have formed part of a title for the first time in 1657 (see the list below); and it is in the 17th century that the encyclopedic spirit comes to the fore, though the 'fièvre encyclopédique' (l'abbé Bremond's words) is not at its height till the 18th century.

Thus, by the end of the 17th century, according to Bayle (q.v.) in his preface to Furetière's *Dictionnaire universel*, the public was 'assez convaincu qu'il n'y a point de livres qui rendent de plus grands services ni plus promptement ni à plus de gens que les dictionnaires'. Moreover, a glance at the works listed below will show that by the same time the lines of future dictionary-making are already clear. Encyclopedic on the one hand, with the field continually expanding from words to persons and things, to biography, and to the sciences and the arts and the various branches of knowledge. Specialized on the other, concerned with words *qua* words, their grammatical, cultural, and ideological origin and morphology.

Progress is again remarkable in the 19th century, when methods and methodology are improved and elaborated. Lexicography becomes a science; encyclopedia-making almost an industry. The great dictionaries and encyclopedias of the 19th century transform, extend, and perfect the earlier works but are none the less based upon them.

The following list of dictionaries and encyclopedias is confined, with rare exceptions, marked by an asterisk, to works compiled by Frenchmen and, in the case of dictionaries, to dictionaries concerned solely or in part with the French language. Titles (of first editions unless otherwise stated, and verified so far as possible from the printed catalogue of the *Bibliothèque nationale*) are given in full so as to present the best idea of the contents and purpose of the works mentioned. For the most part brief descriptive remarks are added, and subsequent editions may be mentioned of items which, as perhaps inevitably happens with works of reference, only reached their full usefulness at a later editing. In most cases, too, dates and brief biographical notes of the compilers have been supplied. It must, however, be emphasized that the list sets out to be neither a bibliographical guide nor a student's guide to the best French dictionaries. It is at most an attempt to give a bird's-eye view of the evolution of dictionary- and encyclopedia-making in France, of the gradual building-up of the daily companions and arsenals of literature, criticism, and thought itself.

1502 **Dictionarium ex optimis quibusquam authoribus studiose collectum . . .* Reggio. By one of the first of the great European lexicographers, the Augustinian monk Ambrosius Calepinus (Ambrogio Calepino, 1435–1511), an Italian who spent his whole life on his dictionary and went blind in old age. This was the dictionary most frequently used during the 16th century and constantly reprinted, revised, and augmented. From being originally a Latin, it became a polyglot dictionary, of eleven languages. The first edition to be printed in Paris was that of 1514. From this dictionary the French language derives the word *calepin* which, as the bibliographer Brunet (Jacques-Charles) said, 'est resté pour désigner un gros volume, un recueil d'extraits et de notes, et ce mot de *calepin* est employé par des gens qui probablement ne savent pas toujours si c'est le nom d'un homme, d'un livre, ou d'un agenda'.

1539 *Dictionaire françois–latin, autrement dict les mots françois, avec les manières d'user d'iceulx, tournez en latin.* Paris. With many subsequent, revised and augmented editions. By Robert Estienne, one of the famous family of scholars and printers (see *Estienne*). This was the first dictionary of the French, or of French and another, language to be printed. It was a precursor of later etymological dictionaries, for the words were grouped by family, according to the root-words, the latter themselves being in alphabetical order. Estienne's Latin *Dictionariolum puerorum* (1542, Paris) was substantially the same work.

c. **1550** *Les Mots propres de marine, venerie et faulconnerie,* compiled by Aimar de Ranconnet [printed in *Nicot* 1606, see below]. Ranconnet (1498–1559), scholar, and counsellor successively at the *Parlements* of Bordeaux and Paris, had a chequered career both domestically and in public life and died in the Bastille.

1553 *Dictionarium historicum ac poeticum, omnia gentium, hominum, locorum, fluminum ac montium antiqua recentioraque, ad sacras ac prophanas historias poetarumque fabulas intelligendas necessaria, vocabula . . .*

complectens. Paris. By Charles Estienne, younger brother of Robert. Although said to have been a mediocre work it was continually read and augmented and it was the basis of later biographical, historical, and geographical dictionaries.

1572 *Dictionnaire des rymes françoises de feu M. Jehan Le Fèvre* [Jean Lefèvre, Chanoine de Langres]. Paris. This work is better known in the edition of 1587, see the following.

1587 [also 1588] *Dictionnaire des rymes françoises premièrement composé par J. Le Fèvre . . ., depuis augmenté, corrigé et mis en bon ordre par le seigneur des Accords* [i.e. Étienne Tabourot, q.v., nephew of Jean Lefèvre]. Paris. The order was now alphabetical instead of, as in 1572, by vowels.

1596 *Le Dictionnaire des rimes françoises selon l'ordre des lettres de l'alphabeth, auquel deux traitez sont ajoutez: l'un, des conjugaisons françoises, l'autre, de l'orthographe françoise, plus un amas d'épithètes recueilli des œuvres de Guillaume de Salluste, seigneur Du Bartas.* Paris. By Odet de La Noue (d. 1618), the eldest son of François de La Noue (q.v.).

1606 *Thrésor de la langue françoyse tant ancienne que moderne; auquel entre autres choses, sont les mots propres de marine, vénerie et faulconnerie, cy devant ramassez par Aimar de Ranconnet, suivi d'une grammaire françoise et latine . . . et d'un Recueil des vieux proverbes de la France.* Paris. By Jean Nicot. This, described by the modern scholar M. Ch. Beaulieux as 'véritablement le premier dictionnaire français', was one of the main sources of subsequent dictionaries, not only its immediate successors, but those of much later date.

Nicot (1530–1600), diplomat and scholar, the son of a lawyer at Nîmes, became known at the court in Paris. He was sent on missions and was at one time Ambassador to Portugal. He has another title to fame as the man after whom tobacco was named (*Nicotiana*). He is said to have

been given some by a Flemish merchant returned from America and to have presented a share of this to Catherine de Médicis.

1611 *★A Dictionarie of the French and English Tongues.* London. By Randle Cotgrave, a scholar of St. John's College, Cambridge, who died in (?) 1634. This, the work of an Englishman, is included because it was by far the best French–English dictionary that had so far appeared. It gave genders, grammatical rules, illustrative phrases, and explanations of the origins of expressions; and it is still of value for the light it throws on contemporary French and English usage.

1635 *Invantaire des deus langues françoise et latine assorti des plus utiles curiositez de l'un et de l'autre idiome.* Lyon. By le Père Philibert Monet (1566–1643), a Jesuit scholar, grammarian and antiquarian. A feature of this work was that the words were *defined* in the first place in French, and sometimes at length, before the Latin equivalents were given.

1640 *Curiositez françoises pour supplément aux dictionnaires, ou Recueil de plusieurs belles propriétez, avec une infinité de proverbes et quolibets pour l'explication de toutes sortes de livres.* Paris. By Antoine Oudin (d. 1653), a court interpreter, like his father César Oudin before him, and Italian master to Louis XIV. He also compiled grammar books and a Spanish–French dictionary or *Trésor.* His *Curiositez* probably count as the earliest slang dictionary.

1643 *Dictionnaire théologique, historique, poétique, cosmographique et chronologique.* Paris. By Juigné Broissinière, sieur de Mollières. Like Charles Estienne (see above, 1553), whose work he largely used, he was a very popular step on the way to Moreri, 1674.

1650 *Les Origines de la langue française.* Paris. Called *Dictionnaire étymologique ou Les Origines . . .* from the 2nd edition (1694, posth.). By Gilles Ménage (q.v.). This was one of the outstanding works of the 17th century, the first properly etymological dictionary, and in spite of many errors a basis for future similar dictionaries. The study of comparative philology may be said to date from it. The 1750 edition included, together with numerous additions and corrections, the *Dictionnaire des termes du vieux françois, ou Trésor des recherches . . .* of Pierre Borel (see the next item).

1655 Trésor des recherches et antiquitez gauloises et françoises. Paris. By Pierre Borel (c. 1620–89), a learned physician and antiquarian who made a study of patois. He came from the Midi to Paris and became Physician-in-Ordinary to the king. His *Dictionnaire des termes du vieux françois, ou Trésor . . .*, a dictionary of Old French words no longer current, with illustrative quotations, and a preface on the development of the French language, was included in the 1750 edition of Ménage (see the foregoing item).

1657 L'Encyclopédie des beaux esprits, contenant les moyens de parvenir à la connaissance des belles sciences. Paris. By le sieur Saunier. Apparently the first work to have the word *encyclopédie* in the title.

1660 Le Grand Dictionnaire des Prétieuses, ou La Clef de la langue des ruelles. Paris. By Antoine Baudeau de Somaize (q.v.). It enumerates 700 of the Précieuses (see *Rambouillet*) under their pseudonyms, and gives their principal maxims, also examples of their writings and locutions.

1674 Le Grand Dictionnaire historique, ou Le Mélange curieux de l'histoire sainte [in later editions **sacrée**] **et profane.** Lyon. By the cleric and lexicographer Louis Moreri (1643–80), who devoted his life to the work. It was the most noteworthy of the early encyclopedic dictionaries (cf. Charles Estienne, 1553, and Juigné Broissinière, 1643, above). Bayle (q.v.) undertook to remedy its faults in his Dictionary of 1697 (see below). It was vastly corrected and augmented by later editors. From being one volume in 1674 it had become ten by 1759 (the 20th edition) and is still of value.

1678 Glossarium ad scriptores mediae et infimae latinitatis. Paris,

3 vols. By Charles Du Fresne, seigneur Du Cange (see *Du Cange*). This is still the great dictionary of medieval Latin, called by Brunot (q.v.) a 'monument gigantesque', and it is of high importance for the study of Old French. It was constantly re-edited and augmented. The edition published by the Benedictines in 1733 (6 vols., with a supplement by Dom Carpentier in 1766, 4 vols.) remained the basis for later editions. A glossary of Old French was added to the 1840–50 (7 vols.) edition.

1680 Dictionnaire françois, contenant les mots et les choses, plusieurs nouvelles remarques sur la langue françoise; ses expressions propres, figurées et burlesques; la prononciation des mots les plus difficiles; le genre des noms; le régime des verbes; avec les termes les plus connus des arts et des sciences; le tout tiré de l'usage et des bons auteurs de la langue françoise. Genève. By César-Pierre Richelet. This is one of the great 17th-century French dictionaries and is said to be the first compiled on philosophical principles. It was reprinted, re-edited, revised, and variously augmented or abridged well into the 19th century. It is also one of the most entertaining dictionaries to read, for Richelet, like Johnson, did not fear to be subjective. Of the word *bain* he says: 'Quand les médecins ne savent plus où ils en sont ils ordonnent le bain à leurs malades'; of *chat*: 'Sa cervelle trouble l'esprit.' His remark on '*Doüane*' is a criticism of 20th-century civilization: 'De toutes les marchandises qu'on décharge à la Doüane il n'y a que les livres qui ne païent rien.' Richelet (1631–98) gave up practising at the Bar in Paris to devote himself to his linguistic, grammatical, and lexicographical studies. He moved in literary circles, to which he had been introduced by Perrot d'Ablancourt (q.v.).

1685 Dictionaire général et curieux, contenant les principaux mots et les plus usitez en la langue françoise, leurs définitions, divisions et étymologies, enrichies d'éloquens discours, soutenus de quelques

histoires, des passages des Pères de l'église, des autheurs et des poètes, les plus anciens et modernes, avec des démonstrations catholiques sur tous les points qui sont contestez entre ceux de l'Église romaine et les gens de la religion prétendue réformée . . . Lyon. By César de Rochefort (d. *c.* 1690), jurist and lexicographer.

1690 *Dictionnaire universel, contenant généralement tous les mots françois, tant vieux que modernes, et les termes de toutes les sciences et des arts, par feu Messire Antoine Furetière.* Rotterdam, 3 vols. It was because he was working on a dictionary of his own, and presumably profiting by the material amassed for the compilation of the *Académie*'s dictionary (see 1694 below), that Furetière (q.v.) was turned out of the *Académie française.* He sued the *Académie* and died (in 1688) while the case was proceeding. In 1684 he had published a sort of prospectus of his work entitled *Essais d'un dictionnaire universel* . . . The dictionary itself when published had a preface by Bayle (q.v.). It was the best dictionary that had yet appeared and a much more complete work than that of the *Académie.* The second edition (1701, 3 vols. La Haye), revised and augmented by Henri Basnage de Beauval (q.v.), was almost completely the basis of the *Dictionnaire de Trévoux* (see 1704 below).

1694 *Dictionnaire de l'Académie française.* Paris, 2 vols. For the inception of this work see *Académie française,* para. 2. It was intended as, and remains, a *dictionnaire d'usage,* not a philological dictionary: its chief concern is to give words acceptable from a literary point of view and as such it undergoes periodical revision. There have been eight editions to date—1694; 1718; 1740; 1762; 1798; 1835; 1877 and 1932-5, and work is proceeding on the ninth edition. In the first edition the words were grouped by families. From the second onwards the order was alphabetical. The fifth edition was practically ready for press when the Revolution broke out and the *Académie*

was suppressed. The manuscripts were preserved, thanks largely to the abbé Morellet (q.v.), and publication was eventually undertaken, following a decree (17 Sept. 1795) of the *Convention nationale,* by the *Comité de l'instruction publique.* The preface to this edition upholds the principles of the Revolution. A *Dictionnaire de l'Académie française,* the so-called *Moutardier edition* of 1802 (see this date below), also published while the *Académie* was suppressed, was condemned. The preface to the sixth (1835) edition was by Villemain (q.v.). The seventh (1878) edition reprinted the prefaces to the six preceding editions.

In 1858 publication was begun of a *Dictionnaire historique de la langue française comprenant l'origine, les formes diverses, les acceptions successives des mots, avec un choix d'exemples tirés des écrivains les plus autorisés,* but this never got beyond the letter 'A'. In 1842 a *Complément du Dictionnaire de l'Académie française* was published, containing over 100,000 special and technical terms not admitted by the *Académie.*

1694 *Dictionnaire des arts et des sciences.* Paris, 2 vols. By Thomas Corneille (q.v.), brother of Pierre Corneille. One advantage of Furetière's dictionary over that of the *Académie française* had been that it included the language of science and the arts. The *Académie* commissioned and sponsored Corneille's work as a manner of supplement to their own. The edition of 1731 was revised by Fontenelle (q.v.).

1697 *Dictionnaire historique et critique.* Rotterdam, 2 vols. By Pierre Bayle. This 'véritable ancêtre de l'Encyclopédie, tant au point de vue des idées que de la forme' is described in the article on Bayle himself (q.v.).

1697 *Bibliothèque orientale, ou Dictionnaire universel, contenant généralement tout ce qui regarde la connaissance des peuples de l'Orient.* Paris. By Barthélemy d'Herbelot (1625-95), French orientalist. This erudite, discursive, and vastly entertaining work is said to have been written first in Arabic and translated into French for printing. It was much enlarged in subsequent editions, notably that of 1777–9 (La Haye, 4 vols.).

1703 *Dictionnaire de musique, contenant une explication des termes grecs, latins, italiens et françois les plus usitez dans la musique.* Paris. By Sébastien de Brossard (1660–1730), cleric and musician. This, the first dictionary of music to be published in France, was much used by Rousseau (see 1768 below). It was translated into English in 1740.

1704 *Dictionnaire de Trévoux,* the name given to the *Dictionnaire universel françois et latin contenant la signification et la définition tant des mots de l'une et de l'autre langue . . . que des termes propres de chaque état et de chaque profession . . . l'explication de tout ce que renferment les sciences et les arts* compiled by the Jesuits and first published (3 vols.) at Trévoux (q.v.). In its first edition it appears to have been little more than a reprint of Furetière (see 1690 above), but in later editions it became an entirely independent work which the Jesuits accused the *Encyclopédistes* of using without acknowledgement. The fifth (1743, 6 vols.) and seventh (1771, 8 vols.) editions were notable.

1708 *Dictionnaire universel géographique et historique.* Paris, 3 vols. Another compilation by Thomas Corneille (see 1694 above).

1709 *Dictionnaire œconomique, contenant divers moïens d'augmenter son bien et de conserver sa santé.* Lyon. By l'abbé Noël Chomel (c. 1623–1712), a rural economist. Later editions added 'l'art de faire valoir les terres'.

1718 *Dictionnaire comique, satyrique, critique, burlesque, libre et proverbial, avec une explication très fidelle de toutes les manières de parler burlesques . . . qui peuvent se rencontrer dans les meilleurs auteurs, tant anciens que modernes.* Amsterdam. By Philibert-Joseph Le Roux, of whose life little is known except that he died at Amsterdam. His dictionary, of which the edition of

1786, in two volumes, is said by the bibliographer Brunet to be the best, included the *Dictionnaire des proverbes français avec leur explication et leur origine* (1710) of the Belgian printer and bookseller George de Backer.

1720–1 *Dictionnaire historique, critique, chronologique, géographique et littéral de la Bible.* Paris, 4 vols. By Dom Augustin Calmet (1672–1757), an erudite Benedictine whose works also included a commentary on the Old and New Testaments. (See also below under date 1845 *Encyclopédie théologique.*)

1726 *Dictionnaire néologique à l'usage des beaux esprits du siècle,* see *Desfontaines, l'abbé Pierre-François Guyot.*

1726–39 *Le Grand dictionnaire géographique et critique et historique.* La Haye, 10 vols. By Antoine-Auguste Bruzen de la Martinière (1683–1749), geographer and antiquarian, who was sent on a mission to Holland, remained there, and died at the Hague. He was a relation of the scholar Richard Simon (q.v.). His dictionary was much prized and often re-edited during the next hundred years.

1736 *Synonymes françois, leurs significations, et le choix qu'il en faut faire pour parler avec justesse.* Paris. By l'abbé Gabriel Girard (c. 1677–1748), grammarian and linguist, a Court secretary and interpreter. In an early form his work was entitled *La Justesse de la langue française* (1718). It was highly praised by Voltaire, and was several times re-edited and augmented (notably by some of the Encyclopedists, including Diderot). Morin incorporated it in his dictionary of 1802, as did also Guizot in 1829. (See below under these dates.)

1748 *Dictionnaire des proverbes françois et des façons de parler comiques, burlesques et familières.* Paris. By André-Joseph Panckoucke (see *Panckoucke*).

1750 *Dictionnaire de l'art de vérifier les dates des faits historiques, des chartes, des chroniques et autres anciens monuments depuis la naissance de Notre-Seigneur jusqu'à l'année 1750, par le moyen d'une table chronologique . . . avec deux calendriers perpétuels* . . . This vast work of erudition, far more than a dictionary of dates, was compiled by Dom Maur Dantine and several of his fellow Benedictines of the Congrégation de Saint-Maur (see *Maurists*). It was first published in one volume, and revised and augmented editions followed before 1800. It was issued in 1854 as one of the volumes of the abbé Migne's *Encyclopédie théologique* (see 1845–63 below). [The *Dictionnaire de statistique religieuse et de l'art de vérifier les dates* specially compiled for the *Encyclopédie théologique* and published in 1851 was concerned with dates in religious history.]

1750 *Manuel lexique ou Dictionnaire portatif des mots françois dont la signification n'est pas familière à tout le monde.* Paris, 2 vols. By l'abbé Prévost (q.v.). [There was still a long way to go from a '*dictionnaire portatif*' of 1750 (in two volumes) to the pocket-size dictionary of modern times.]

1751–80 *L'Encyclopédie ou Dictionnaire raisonné des sciences, des arts et des métiers, par une société de gens de lettres. Mis en ordre et publié par M. Diderot, et, quant à la partie mathématique, par M. d'Alembert.* Paris, 35 vols. See *Encyclopédie*.

1752 *Dictionnaire portatif des beaux-arts ou Abrégé de ce qui concerne l'architecture, la sculpture, la peinture, la gravure, la poésie et la musique, avec la définition de ces arts, l'explication des termes et des choses qui leur appartiennent.* Paris. By Jacques Lacombe (1724–1801), an advocate and bookseller, said to have been the father-in-law of the composer Grétry (q.v.). This work, as the full title indicates, was a true ancestor of present-day 'Companions'. It had subsequent editions and was translated into Italian (1758). Lacombe was responsible for some of the volumes of the *Encyclopédie méthodique* (see 1781–1832 below), e.g. on sports, recreations, gardening.

1752 *Dictionnaire historique portatif, contenant l'histoire des patri-*

arches, des princes hébreux, des empereurs, des rois et des grands capitaines, des dieux, . . . des Papes, des SS. Pères, des évêques, . . . des historiens, poètes . . . et mathématiciens, etc., avec leurs principaux ouvrages et leurs meilleures éditions; des femmes savantes, . . . et . . . de toutes les personnes illustres de toutes les nations du monde. Paris, 2 vols. By l'abbé Jean-Baptiste Ladvocat. This was an immensely popular abridgement of Moreri (see 1674 above), though said to be full of faults. During the next seventy years it was alternately revised, expanded, and again abridged. Ladvocat (1709–65), a Hebrew scholar, was first librarian, then a professor, at the Sorbonne.

1754 *Dictionnaire portatif historique et littéraire des théâtres contenant l'origine des différents théâtres de Paris.* Paris. By Antoine de Léris (1723–95), a man of letters who was also an official of the *Chambre des comptes*.

1756 *Projet d'un glossaire de l'ancienne langue française.* Paris. By Jean-Baptiste de la Curne de Sainte-Palaye. Sainte-Palaye (1697–1781), born at Auxerre, gave up a diplomatic career for scholarly pursuits. He studied early French history and went on to compile a dictionary of French antiquities with a complete glossary of the variations of the language. Only this specimen, of 30 pages, was printed in his lifetime. The remainder was deposited—61 vols. of manuscript—at the *Bibliothèque nationale* and was a valuable source for subsequent lexicographers, e.g. Littré. The whole work was printed at Niort in 1875–82: *Dictionnaire historique de l'ancien langage françois ou Glossaire de la langue françoise depuis son origine jusqu'au siècle de Louis XIV* (10 vols. The 10th volume contains a biography of La Curne de Sainte-Palaye). See also 1829 below.

1759–65 *Dictionnaire universel dogmatique, canonique, historique, géographique et chronologique des sciences ecclésiastiques.* Paris, 5 vols. By the Dominican Father Charles-Louis Richard (1711–94). He had collaborators, notably l'abbé Giraud, and there were later, corrected and much enlarged editions, notably that of 1822–7 (29 vols.). Le Père Richard took refuge in the Low Countries during the Revolution but was discovered at Mons in 1794 and shot, because, it is said, in one of his works he compared the execution of Louis XVI by the Revolutionaries to the execution of Christ by the Jews.

1762–70 Dictionnaire géographique, historique et politique des Gaules et de la France. Paris, 6 vols. By l'abbé Jean-Joseph d'Expilly (1719–93), a traveller and geographer who was also at times sent on court missions. This was his most popular work but it stops at the letter 'S'. He also wrote a *Description historique et géographique des Isles Britanniques ou des royaumes d'Angleterre, d'Écosse et d'Irlande* (1759).

1764 Dictionnaire philosophique portatif. London. By Voltaire. This was a collection of short articles, in alphabetical order, on such subjects as *Âme, Ange, Athée, Christianisme, Dieu.* The idea of it was conceived at Potsdam in 1752 at the king's supper-table; the work was begun at once, soon suspended, and resumed in 1760. It consists largely of attacks on religious dogma; at the same time it shows the author's abhorrence of falsehood, obscurity, and oppression, and is written with simplicity and lucidity coupled with lively malice and sarcasm. It was at once ordered to be burnt at Geneva, and was subsequently (1765) condemned by the *parlement* and by Rome. Voltaire found himself obliged to disavow it though he prepared further editions (the later ones under the title *La Raison par alphabet*) with additional articles. In the Kehl edition (see under *Voltaire*) the work printed under the title of *Dictionnaire philosophique* is swollen by much additional material, including the *Lettres philosophiques* (q.v.), which originally had no connexion with it.

1764 Dictionnaire raisonné universel d'histoire naturelle. Paris, 5 vols. (with supplement in 1768 and then many later editions). By Jacques-Christophe Valmont de Bomare (1731–1807), a naturalist who went on many scientific expeditions and was later a distinguished lecturer and

teacher. During the Terror he destroyed the narrations of his voyages, also his correspondence with Linnaeus and Rousseau.

1766 Dictionnaire historique portatif ou Histoire abrégée de tous les hommes qui se sont fait un nom. Amsterdam (Avignon). This first edition, 'par une société de gens de lettres', was largely the work of Dom Louis-Mayeul Chaudon (1737–1817), a Benedictine monk of Cluny (who also compiled a *Dictionnaire anti-philosophique* (1767–9) and a dictionary of ecclesiastical authors). There were several editions, notably the eighth (1804) which contained many biographies of Revolutionary figures. The name of Antoine-Joseph Delandine (1756–1820) appears on the title-page of the later editions. He sat for the Forez Department in the *États Généraux* of 1789, was later arrested as a suspect, and ended as Town Librarian at Lyons.

1766 Dictionnaire du vieux langage françois. Paris. By François Lacombe. This was the first dictionary of Old French to be printed (but cf. 1756 above). It was called *Dictionnaire de la langue romane* in a 1768 edition. Lacombe (1733–95) was born at Avignon and was a Commissary of Police at Montpellier when he died. His literary activities were various—this Dictionary; a fabricated secret correspondence from Queen Christina of Sweden to eminent contemporaries; *Observations sur Londres et ses environs* (1780); and translations from English.

1766 Dictionnaire portatif des arts et métiers, contenant en abrégé l'histoire, la description et la police des arts et métiers, des fabriques et des manufactures de France et des pays étrangers. Paris, 2 vols. This is said to have been compiled by Philippe Macquer (1720–70), a minor man of letters. It was the basis of a much fuller work by l'abbé Jaubert, see date 1773.

1766–1815 Dictionnaire pour l'intelligence des auteurs classiques grecs et latins, tant sacrés que profanes. Paris, 37 vols. By François Sabbathier (1732–1807), a learned compiler whose work was largely drawn upon by Lemprière.

1767 *Dictionnaire historique des mœurs, usages et coutumes des François.* Paris, 3 vols. By François-Alexandre Aubert de La Chesnaye des Bois (1699–1784), an indefatigable compiler of dictionaries, e.g., as well as the above, of agriculture and gardening, genealogy and heraldry, the nobility, a military dictionary, a *Dictionnaire domestique portatif*, and possibly also one of food and drink.

1768 *Dictionnaire typographique, historique et critique des livres rares, singuliers, estimés et recherchés.* Paris, 2 vols. By Jean-Baptiste-Louis Osmont (*c.* 1700–73), bibliographer, of a family of printers and booksellers. This was the first bibliographical manual to list works in alphabetical order.

1768 *Dictionnaire de musique.* Paris. By Jean-Jacques Rousseau (q.v.). In this Rousseau collected and elaborated some of the musical articles he had written for *L'Encyclopédie* (q.v.; and cf. 1703 above).

1773 *Dictionnaire raisonné universel des arts et métiers . . .* Paris, 4 vols. By l'abbé Pierre Jaubert (*c.* 1715–*c.* 1780). This was an expansion and elaboration of Macquer's similar dictionary of 1766 (see above). It had the same detailed title. A 1793–1801 edition in 5 volumes contained a technical vocabulary (vol. v).

1777–83 *Dictionnaire universel des sciences morale, économique, politique et diplomatique, ou Bibliothèque de l'homme d'état et du citoyen.* London, 30 vols. By Jean-Baptiste-René Robinet (1735–1820), a one-time Jesuit who became one of the *philosophes*. He was poor but erudite, published philosophical and grammatical treatises, an English–French dictionary, and this work.

1781–1832 *Encyclopédie méthodique, ou par ordre de matières, par une société de gens de lettres, de savans et artistes . . .* Paris, 201 vols. This was a rearrangement of *L'Encyclopédie* (q.v.) by subject. There were volumes on, e.g., *Agriculture, Architecture, Beauxarts, Geography, Jurisprudence*, &c., with the articles in alphabetical order within each volume. The idea originated with Panckoucke (Charles-Joseph, q.v.), who began publication and acted as editor. His widowed daughter Mme Thérèse-Charlotte Agasse carried on after his death.

1783 *Dictionnaire élémentaire de botanique.* Paris. By Pierre Bulliard. An early work of its kind, revised and improved by later editors. The botanist Bulliard (*c.* 1742–93), remembered also for the botanical plates which he executed himself, was at work on a large illustrated *Herbier de France* when he died (13 vols. published 1780–95).

1787–8 *Dictionnaire critique de la langue française.* Marseille, 3 vols. The author, l'abbé Jean-François Féraud (or Ferraud) (1725–1807) gave up the Church for the study of philology. He compiled three dictionaries: a *Nouveau Dictionnaire des sciences et des arts* (1753), sometimes considered a supplement to the *Dictionnaire de l'Académie* (and cf. Thomas Corneille's dictionary under date 1694 above); a *Dictionnaire général de la langue française* (1761), which had several editions; and this work, which is still of value. Féraud emigrated during the Revolution, then returned to his native Marseilles and died in great poverty.

1788–1825 *Dictionnaire d'architecture.* Paris, 3 vols. By Antoine-Chrysostome Quatremère de Quincy (1755–1849), an antiquarian of high repute in his day. He was caught up in politics during the Revolution but returned to his original pursuits during the Empire. This first edition formed the 'Architecture' volumes of Panckoucke's *Encyclopédie méthodique* (see 1781–1832 above). In 1832 he published a new edition (2 vols.) entitled *Dictionnaire historique d'architecture*.

1789 *Dictionnaire de grammaire et de littérature.* Liège, 6 vols. By Jean-François Marmontel (q.v.) and Nicolas Beauzée (1717–89), the grammarian. It consisted of articles from *L'Encyclopédie* (q.v.), among them those which Marmontel reworked for his *Éléments de littérature*.

1792 *Dictionnaire des arts de peinture, sculpture et gravure.* Paris, 5 vols. By Claude-Henri Watelet and Lévêque. Watelet (1718–86), man of letters and book-illustrator, spent his wealth on travel and civilized pursuits and at his home 'Le Moulin joli', near Paris, introduced one of the first *jardins anglais* into France. He wrote on gardens for *L'Encyclopédie* (q.v.). His dictionary was completed and published by Lévêque.

1800 *Dictionnaire universel de la langue française.* Paris. By Pierre-Claude Victoire Boiste (1765–1824). A work highly appreciated in its day and often revised and augmented, once (1834) by Nodier (q.v.), who called it a *pan-lexique*. It gave examples from the best authors and contained a treatise on grammar and spelling and a manual of Old French.

1801 *Néologie ou vocabulaire des mots nouveaux, à renouveler ou pris dans des acceptions nouvelles.* Paris, 2 vols. By Louis-Sébastien Mercier (q.v.).

1802 *Dictionnaire de l'Académie française. Nouvelle édition, augmentée de plus de vingt mille articles.* Paris, 2 vols. This was, so to speak, an unofficial edition, produced by the Paris publisher Moutardier during the period of the *Académie*'s suppression (i.e. 1793–1803, see *Académie française*, para. 3; and see also above under date 1694). It led to disputes and legal proceedings and was in the event condemned. Moutardier had entrusted the work of editing and recompilation to Laveaux (see below under date 1818).

1802 *Dictionnaire universel des synonymes de la langue française publiées jusqu'à ce jour.* Paris, 3 vols. This, said to be the work of Benoît Morin (1746–1817), a learned Paris publisher and bookseller, was apparently a collection and tidying up of similar previous works. It was used by the *émigré* Lévizac, working in London, and superseded by Guizot (see below 1807 and 1809).

1806–9 *Dictionnaire des ouvrages anonymes et pseudonymes composés, traduits ou publiés en français, avec les noms des auteurs, traducteurs et éditeurs.* Paris, 4 vols. This work, still constantly used, was compiled by the learned bibliographer and librarian Antoine-Alexandre

Barbier, who was official librarian to Napoleon and created libraries for him at Saint-Cloud, Compiègne, and Fontainebleau.

1807 *Dictionnaire universel des synonymes de la langue française.* London. By l'abbé Jean-Pont-Victor Lacoutz de Lévizac (d. 1813). This was a work compiled from previous similar dictionaries by a grammarian who fled from the Revolution and ended up teaching grammar, editing French classics, &c., in England. He died in London.

1808 *Dictionnaire du bas-langage ou des manières de parler usitées parmi le peuple.* Paris, 2 vols. By d'Hautel, a Paris publisher and bookseller of whose life little is known.

1808 *Dictionnaire raisonné des onomatopées françaises.* Paris. By Charles Nodier (q.v.). This dictionary of imitative words (compiled when Nodier was twenty-three) was intended to show that speech had originated with imitation of the sounds of nature. Nodier, an erudite dilettante, was always interested in philology. In 1828 he published an *Examen critique des dictionnaires de la langue française ou Recherches grammaticales et littéraires sur l'orthographe . . . et l'étymologie des mots.*

1809 *Nouveau dictionnaire universel des synonymes de la langue française.* Paris, 2 vols. By the historian François-Pierre-Guillaume Guizot (q.v.). It was a hack compilation of his early years in Paris, but the most comprehensive work of its kind then to be found and one which held the field well into the middle of the century.

1818 *Dictionnaire raisonné des difficultés grammaticales et littéraires de la langue française.* Paris; and

1820 *Nouveau Dictionnaire de la langue française, où l'on trouve tous les mots de la langue usuelle, les étymologies, l'explication détaillée des synonymes,* &c. Paris, 2 vols. These, and also a Dictionary of Synonyms in 1826, were the work of the lexicographer Jean-Charles-Thibault de Laveaux (1749–1827). He was Professor of French language and literature at

Berlin University, whither Frederick the Great had summoned him, and was back in Paris during the Revolution, where he edited a Revolutionary journal and was in and out of prison. After Thermidor he returned to the safer pursuit of lexicography and was responsible for the 'Moutardier edition' of the *Dictionnaire de l'Académie française* (see 1802 above). When that was condemned he produced dictionaries of his own—works of labour and learning which were prized and went into several editions. As a lexicographer he may have found profit in his employment in later life as Inspector of prisons and hospitals.

1819 *Trésor des origines et dictionnaire grammatical raisonné de la langue française.* Paris. By Marie-Charles-Joseph de Pougens (1755–1833). This was only a specimen of a projected work. The compiler's notes for it (100 folio vols.) are in the library of the Institut de France and were much used by Littré. Pougens, who was said to be a natural son of the Prince de Conti, went blind at twenty-four. He had begun by studying painting in Rome, was in England on a mission (and married an Englishwoman), and when ruined by the Revolution turned printer and bookseller. The *Trésor des origines* was his life's work. The posthumously published *Archéologie française, ou vocabulaire de mots anciens tombés en désuétude* (Paris, 1821–5, 2 vols.) was compiled from his manuscript notes. His *Mémoires et souvenirs* (1834) are said to be interesting.

1819–22 *Dictionnaire françois de la langue oratoire et poétique, suivi d'un vocabulaire de tous les mots qui appartiennent au langage vulgaire.* Paris, 2 vols. By Joseph Planche (1762–1853), a Greek scholar and lexicographer, sometime librarian at the Sorbonne. The main part of this dictionary gives illustrative quotations.

1821 *Dictionnaire des proverbes français.* Paris. By Pierre de La Mésangère (1761–1831). This was the most complete collection of French proverbs until *Le Livre des proverbes français* of Leroux de Lincy (q.v.) in 1842. La Mésangère had a varied career. He took orders, taught

philosophy in the Jesuit college of La Flèche (cf. *Prytanée nationale de la Flèche*), and at a later date wrote books on women's clothing, owned and edited an *Almanach des Modes*, and compiled this work.

1829 *Dictionnaire étymologique de la langue française.* Paris, 2 vols. By Jean-Baptiste Bonaventure de Roquefort (1777–1834). It was preceded by a Dissertation on Etymology (by another author) and seems to have been an etymological dictionary only in so far as the words were arranged by groups, in families. Roquefort had fought in the Revolutionary wars and taught music in Paris before turning to scholarly activities, and he had already, in 1808, published a *Glossaire de la langue romane* largely based on La Curne de Sainte-Palaye (see 1756 above).

1835 *Dictionnaire général et grammatical des dictionnaires français.* Paris, 2 vols. By Napoléon Landais (1803–52), grammarian and, at times, novelist. This *dictionnaire universel et progressif*, though superseded by the Larousse encyclopedic dictionaries (see 1865–76 below) contains much miscellaneous information and can still be useful, especially the 1853 edition, which was revised by a body of specialists and included a complementary section with biographical and rhyming dictionaries, also dictionaries of homonyms, paronyms, and antonyms.

1838–44 *Lexique roman, ou Dictionnaire de la langue des troubadours, comparée avec les autres langues de l'Europe latine . . .* Paris, 6 vols. By François Raynouard (q.v.). This work also contains historical and philological articles, a summary of *grammaire romane*, and an anthology of Provençal poetry.

1838–49 *Encyclopédie catholique.* Paris, 18 vols., with supplement, 3 vols., in 1859. This was a *Répertoire universel et raisonné des sciences, des lettres, des arts et des métiers, avec la biographie des hommes célèbres*. It was an early example of the big encyclopedic undertakings of the 19th century.

1841–9 *Dictionnaire universel d'histoire naturelle.* Paris, 13 vols., with 3 volumes of plates. By Charles Dessalines d'Orbigny (1806–76), one of a distinguished family of naturalists. He had a team of collaborators.

1843–6 *Dictionnaire national ou Grand dictionnaire critique de la langue française, contenant pour la première fois, outre tous les mots mis en circulation par la presse et qui sont devenus une des propriétés de la parole, les noms de tous les peuples anciens et modernes,* &c. Paris, 2 vols.; with many subsequent editions. By Louis-Nicholas Bescherelle (1802–83), with some help from his brother Albert Bescherelle (Bescherelle *jeune*). Both were indefatigable compilers of popular dictionaries, grammars, guides to conjugating verbs, correspondence manuals, &c. Bescherelle *aîné*, in addition, was librarian of the Louvre from the age of twenty-four.

1845–63 *Encyclopédie théologique, ou série de dictionnaires sur toutes les parties de la science religieuse.* Paris, 50 vols. This was published under the general editorship of the abbé Migne (q.v.). A second series (53 vols.) was published from 1851 to 1859 and a *Troisième et dernière Encyclopédie théologique* (66 vols.) from 1855 to 1866. Various earlier works, such as Dom Calmet's Dictionary of the Bible, or *L'Art de vérifier les dates* (see 1720–1 and 1750 above), were among the volumes.

1857 *Dictionnaire général de biographie et d'histoire, de mythologie, de géographie ancienne et moderne* . . . Paris, 2 vols. By Charles-Louis Dezobry (1798–1871) and Théodore Bachelet (1820–79) and 'une société de littérateurs, de professeurs et de savants'. Between first publication and the end of the century this dictionary was often re-edited and supplements were added. It is a good example of a number of similar French 19th-century productions—a full, competently-compiled biographical and historical dictionary which takes the marrow from earlier works and adds new meat of its own. It can still be consulted with profit. Dezobry was a man of letters

and historian who also ran a bookshop and produced classical texts. Bachelet was a professor at the lycée of Rouen.

1857 *Dictionnaire des synonymes de la langue française.* Paris. With subsequent editions, and a supplement in 1865. By Pierre-Benjamin Lafaye (1809–67), a professor of philosophy and Dean of the Faculty of Letters at Aix-en-Provence. This work had an introductory essay on the theory of synonyms.

1862 *Dictionnaire général des lettres, des beaux-arts et des sciences morales et politiques.* Paris, 2 vols. This was produced under the general editorship of Dezobry and Bachelet (see 1857 above) but it was much less popular.

1863–73 *Dictionnaire de la langue française, contenant la nomenclature la plus étendue . . . la signification des mots depuis les premiers temps* [the 12th c.] *de la langue française jusqu'au XVIᵉ siècle, et l'étymologie comparée.* Paris, 4 vols. By Émile Littré (q.v.). A supplement was published in 1877 and the whole work was reprinted in 1950. This is the great French dictionary of the 19th century and still the finest work of its kind for the study of the changing use and meanings of words. There are illustrative quotations for the post-16th-century period.

1864 *Dictionnaire critique de biographie et d'histoire.* Paris. By Auguste Jal (1795–1873), who after first training for the Navy became a journalist, art critic, naval historian, and compiler. His *Glossaire nautique, répertoire polyglotte de termes de marine anciens et modernes* (1848) has also retained its value.

1865–76 *Grand dictionnaire universel du XIXᵉ siècle, français, historique, géographique, mythologique, bibliographique, littéraire, scientifique,* &c. Paris, 15 vols.; with two supplementary vols. 1877–90. This was edited and partly compiled by Pierre Larousse (1817–75), the founder of the publishing firm of Larousse. It was the first of the famous Larousse series of dictionaries, encyclopedias, compendia, universal histories, &c., which are invaluable sources of information on French history, literature, art, customs, &c.

It was followed (1897–1904, 8 vols., with a supplement in 1907) by the *Nouveau Larousse illustré*, and again (1927–33, 6 vols., with a supplement in 1954) by the *Larousse du XXe siècle*, edited by Claude (1854–1924) and by Paul Augé respectively. The eternally popular one-volume *Nouveau Petit Larousse illustré* was first published in 1924.

1866 **Dictionnaire de la langue verte. Argots parisiens comparés.** Paris. By Alfred Delvau (1825–67), a popular journalist and man of letters who wrote much about the by-ways of Parisian life.

1881–1902 **Dictionnaire de l'ancienne langue française et de tous ses dialectes du IX^eau XVe siècle.** Paris, 11 vols. including three volumes of *complément*. By Frédéric-Eugène Godefroy (1826–97). The object of this, still the standard dictionary of Old French, was to give the words, and their various forms, with examples of use, that had been current in the Middle Ages but had since disappeared from the language.

1885–1903 **La Grande Encyclopédie. Inventaire raisonné des sciences, des lettres et des arts.** Paris, 31 vols. By a body of savants and men of letters. Edited by a committee which included some of the most distinguished names of the day. This valuable 'œuvre de haute vulgarisation', impartial and factual, is on the lines of the *Encyclopaedia Britannica* or the German *Brockhaus*. The first volume has an interesting preface on the manner of compiling an encyclopedia.

1887 **Nouveau dictionnaire classique illustré.** Paris. By Louis-Augustin-Léon Gazier (1844–1922), at one time Professor of French Language and Literature at the Sorbonne and author of works on religious history, notably a history of Jansenism (see *Jansenius*; *Port-Royal*, para. 5). This is said to have been the first illustrated dictionary.

1890–1900 **Dictionnaire général de la langue française du commencement du XVIIe siècle jusqu'à nos jours.** Paris, 2 vols. By Adolphe Hatzfeld (1824–1900) and Arsène Darmesteter (1846–88), a brother of the orientalist James Darmesteter (q.v.). After Darmesteter died

he was succeeded by André-Antoine Thomas (1857–1935). The three were among the leading philologists and etymologists of the later 19th century. This is one of the most comprehensive and competently-produced modern French dictionaries, a standard work for pronunciation, for examples of first and subsequent use of words, and for its etymological notes. It is preceded by an important treatise on the formation of the French language.

1894 **La Langue verte. Dictionnaire d'argot et des principales locutions populaires, précédé d'une histoire d'argot par Clément Casciani.** Paris. By Jean La Rue.

1897–1904 **Le Nouveau Larousse illustré,** see 1865–76 above.

1925– **Dictionnaire de la langue française du XVIe siècle.** Paris. By Edmond-Eugène-Auguste Huguet (1863–?1947). This specialized dictionary of one period reached the letter 'M' with the 42nd fascicule (1952).

1927–33 **Larousse du XXe siècle,** see 1865–76 above.

1932 **Dictionnaire étymologique de la langue française.** Paris. By Oscar Bloch (1877–1937).

1935– **Encyclopédie française.** Paris. By a body of specialists under the general editorship of Lucien Febvre (q.v.). This is intended to present a summary or conspectus of human knowledge in the 20th century. The volumes are planned according to an organic, or ideological, division of subject-matter; and the arrangement of the articles, short treatises, and illustrations within the volumes is no longer alphabetical, on the lines of a *dictionnaire raisonné*, but methodic, in the Baconian sense. The conception thus goes back beyond the *Encyclopédie* of Diderot or the *Encyclopédie méthodique* of Panckoucke (see 1751–80 and 1781–1832 above) to the *summa* of medieval times. The eleven volumes published by 1950 (out of twenty-one projected, including index volumes) include those on *Arts et littérature* (xvi and xvii, 1935–6) and *La Civilisation écrite* (xviii, 1936).

1936–8 **Recueil général des lexiques français du moyen âge (XIIe–XVe** *siècle*). I. *Lexique alphabétique*. Paris, 2 vols. By Mario Roques. Publication of these collected reprints, from manuscripts, of medieval word-lists and glossaries is planned in sections, as follows:

I. alphabetically-arranged word-lists and glossaries, mainly bilingual [the only section published down to 1955];

II. word-lists compiled in subject-order;

III. general and specialized lexicons;

IV. an index of textual glosses.

Publication of Anglo-Norman and Provençal lexicons is also contemplated.

1938 *Dictionnaire étymologique de la langue française.* Paris. By Albert Dauzat (1877–1955).

1946 *Dictionnaire des synonymes de la langue française.* Paris. By René Bailly.

1947 *Dictionnaire d'ancien français, moyen âge et renaissance.* Paris. By Robert Grandsaignes d'Hauterive.

1951– *Dictionnaire alphabétique et analogique de la langue française.* Paris. By Paul Robert. This work, of which the first of three volumes contemplated was published in 1951, combines two types of dictionary which have hitherto been treated separately—the alphabetical, with derivations and definitions of words, and the analogical, concerned with the association of ideas. There are grammatical notes and numerous illustrations of usage, literary and proverbial. The description 'nouveau Littré' has more than once been applied to it.

Dictionnaire des girouettes (1815), a satirical guide, by comte César de Proisy d'Eppes (man of letters, 1788–1836), to the many persons who, within his own lifetime, were known to have trimmed their convictions to the political winds. Against each name stood as many small symbols of weathercocks as the times the person in question had changed his politics.

Dictionnaire des idées reçues, a collection of 'bromides', or trite remarks, which Flaubert took pleasure in compiling all through his life. There are frequent references to it in his correspondence and he

had planned to incorporate it in the second volume of the unfinished *Bouvard et Pécuchet* (q.v.). Among papers found after his death were folders containing about 1,000 entries. These, or some of them, were printed as an appendix to *Bouvard et Pécuchet*. They have also been published separately (e.g. *Dictionnaire des idées reçues*, 1951), and translated.

Dictionnaire de Trévoux, see *Dictionaries and Encyclopedias,* under date 1704.

Dictionnaire philosophique portatif, by Voltaire, see *Dictionaries and Encyclopedias,* under date 1764.

Diderot, DENIS (1713–84), the son of a cutler of Langres, philosopher, encyclopedist, novelist, dramatist, art critic, and an ardent disseminator of the philosophical ideas of his time. He was a man of striking personality, not fully revealed by his writings, affable, generous, a faithful friend, free-spoken, bubbling over in his conversation with ideas, enthusiasm, and coarse gaiety (his talk has been likened to a display of fireworks); at the same time violent and unbalanced.

(2) After an education by the Jesuits, he rejected the more regular professions in order to devote himself to literature, supporting himself at first by giving lessons and by other modest expedients. He also studied natural science, in which he was deeply interested and which he made the basis of his philosophy. One of his first published works was a free translation (1745) of Shaftesbury's *Inquiry concerning Virtue or Merit.* The direction of the *Encyclopédie* (q.v.), which he undertook in 1745, was the most notable of his contributions to the advancement of knowledge, and a vast burden, of which, with great courage and perseverance, he bore the main share. It made him well known, and he began to visit the *salons* of the day, those of Mme Geoffrin, Mme d'Épinay, &c. (though he was never a constant member of any of these circles), and to frequent the house of d'Holbach (q.v.). His *Pensées philosophiques* (1746, condemned by the *parlement*) showing an attitude of scepticism towards religion, but not yet the atheism that he was to reach later, were designed as an answer to the *Pensées* of Pascal, of whom they contain (§ 14) an

interesting appreciation. *Les Bijoux indiscrets* (1748) was a licentious romance, containing some serious criticism notably of the French drama. His *Lettre sur les aveugles* (q.v.), published in 1749, led to his temporary imprisonment (though the real motive is said to have been an offence which Diderot gave to the mistress of d'Argenson, the minister). It was about this time that he encouraged Rousseau to write his memorable discourse against civilization. His other principal philosophical publications were the *Suite de l'apologie de l'abbé de Prades* (1752; see under *Prades*), the *Lettre sur les sourds et les muets* (1759, dealing with the development of language and questions of aesthetics), the *Pensées sur l'interprétation de la nature* (1754), the *Entretien d'un philosophe avec Mme la duchesse de ★ ★ ★* (1776), and the *Essai sur la vie de Sénèque le philosophe* (1779). A number of other minor philosophical works, notably the *Rêve de d'Alembert* (a dialogue on materialistic philosophy, dealing unsparingly with details of human physiology, and not intended for publication) and the *Supplément au Voyage de Bougainville* (a dialogue on monogamy based on the customs of the Tahitians), appeared only after his death. *Les Deux Amis de Bourbonne*, a simple moral tale, was published in 1773, but his other tales, *La Religieuse, Jacques le fataliste*, and *Le Neveu de Rameau* (qq.v.), and various shorter ones (e.g. *Ceci n'est pas un conte*, which develops in the form of a dialogue between the narrator and his listener) were published posthumously, as were also his letters, of which the most remarkable are those to Mlle Sophie Volland, a woman of intelligence and culture, whom he loved with ardour and made the confidant of his thoughts.

(3) Diderot has been called the founder of art criticism in France, by the accounts that he wrote for Grimm (q.v., for his *Correspondance littéraire*) from 1759 to 1781 of the biennial *salons* of the Louvre, where contemporary works of art were exhibited. The author in a lively conversational style combines descriptions of individual pictures, anecdotes, and digressions with vigorous judgements. By their variety of approach, their freshness, and their sincerity, Diderot's *Salons* form good examples of the literary criticism of art, though his underlying principles are full of fallacies and the works

he was dealing with were as a whole of a poor order of merit (cf. *Salon*).

(4) Diderot wrote two prose *drames* (q.v.) or serious comedies, *Le Fils naturel* and *Le Père de famille*, published in 1757 and 1758 and performed respectively in 1771 and 1761. These were illustrations of his dramatic theory (expounded in *Entretiens* appended to *Le Fils naturel* and *Dissertation sur le poème dramatique*, 1758) that between tragedy and comedy there is an interval to be filled by plays that are neither tragic nor comic, but serious discussions of the problems of middle-class life. The plays themselves are mediocre sentimental dramas, moral and edifying, totally devoid of humour, written in prose in an unnatural inflated style, with a good deal of sermonizing; for Diderot held the mistaken view that he could make the drama a moral influence by putting moral exhortations in the mouths of his characters. His views on the drama are further contained in his *Réflexions sur Térence* and *Paradoxe sur le comédien* (a dialogue in which the discussion turns, more particularly, upon actors and what constitutes good acting). Among his other attempts at domestic comedy, which were not acted, may be mentioned *Est-il bon? Est-il méchant?* and an adaptation of Moore's *The Gamester*.

(5) Diderot published an enthusiastic *Éloge de Richardson* (1761), in which he praised the novelist's penetration and truth, his compassion for the unfortunate, and the soundness of his moral teaching, which he said had an elevating influence on himself. He had an admirer and supporter in Catherine II of Russia, who purchased his library from him, while leaving it in his hands and paying him as her librarian. He visited Russia in 1773–4. He was a close friend of Grimm.

(6) Diderot was in philosophy a determinist and an experimental materialist; that is to say, he advocated a materialism based on the ascertained facts of natural science, arguing from the imperceptible transition from inert to living matter, and from sentient to thinking matter, and anticipating in some respects later evolutionary ideas. He was an ardent moralist, although opposed to the traditional morality. He held that man is naturally inclined to virtue (which he reduced to beneficence), and that he is, moreover, incited to virtue by self-interest, but that his innocent nature has been perverted by

society. The basis of morality is to be found accordingly in conscience, experience, and interest, which are thwarted by bad example, bad education, and bad laws. In politics Diderot was a moderate and practical reformer, no violent revolutionary.

(7) Diderot's chief importance lies in the wide span of his constructive conceptions, in his scientific approach to philosophical problems (herein showing superiority to Voltaire and Rousseau), and in the ardour and success with which he disseminated and popularized scientific knowledge and philosophic doctrines, principally through the medium of the *Encyclopédie*. He wrote, as he talked, with ease and animation, often with coarseness and lack of taste, without order or composition, setting down ideas as they poured from his fervid brain, and constantly digressing from the main course of his argument or story. He had not the patience and method required to produce any single great work.

Didier, the hero of Victor Hugo's poetic drama *Marion de Lorme* (q.v.).

Dierx, LÉON (1838–1912), Parnassian poet (see *Parnassiens*), was born in Reunion Island (cf. *Leconte de Lisle*, by whom, especially in his frequently very pessimistic verse, and also by Baudelaire, Dierx was strongly influenced). He came young to France and became a civil servant in Paris. His various poetical collections (*Les Lèvres closes*, 1867, was the best, containing the fine poem *Lazare* and other evocations of Biblical scenes) were united in his *Œuvres complètes* (1872 and, augm. edit., 1888). In 1898, as the result of an inquiry conducted by the review *La Plume* and the newspaper *Le Temps*, he was chosen to succeed Mallarmé as 'prince des poètes'.

Dieu, see *Légende des siècles*.

Dieux ont soif, Les, the concluding words of the last number of Camille Desmoulins's paper *Le Vieux Cordelier* (q.v.), and the title of a fine novel (1912) of the French Revolution by Anatole France.

Dilecta, La, the name given by Balzac (q.v.) to his Egeria, Mme de Berny, a woman some twenty years older than himself. He mourned her bitterly when she died in 1836. She was said to have inspired

the character of Mme de Mortsauf in *Le Lys dans la vallée* (q.v.).

Dimanche, MONSIEUR, a character in Molière's *Dom Juan*, the typical timid creditor who allows himself to be fobbed off with fine words by his debtor.

Dimanches d'un bourgeois de Paris, Les (a civil servant's Sunday outings), sketches by Guy de Maupassant, contributed weekly in the first place (1882) to *Le Gaulois.*

Dîme de pénitence, La, a moral poem of the same character as the *Besant de Dieu* (q.v.), composed at the end of the 13th century by Jean de Journi, a knight of Picardy who had settled in Cyprus.

Dîme royale, La, a single tax, a form of combined poll-tax and income-tax, suggested by Vauban (q.v.) in 1707 in his book of this title as being more fair than existing methods of taxation. His egalitarian tendencies lost him the king's favour and his book was seized.

Dindenault, see *Pantagruel* (*Quart Livre*).

Dîners Magny. These were fortnightly dinners at the restaurant Magny, in the Latin quarter of Paris, at which men of letters and painters met between 1862 and *c.* 1875. The idea originated, as an attempt to distract Gavarni (who died in 1866), with Dr. François-Auguste Veyne (1813–75), physician and friend of many 19th-century writers, artists, and politicians. Regular *convives* were Flaubert, Théophile Gautier, Renan, Sainte-Beuve, Taine (qq.v.), the Russian novelist Turgenev, and the brothers Edmond and Jules de Goncourt (qq.v.). The *Journal* of the last-named contains many interesting descriptions of the company and conversation.

Dipsodes, see *Pantagruel.*

Directoire, Le, the form of government which existed in France from 27 October 1795 to 9 November 1799 (5 brumaire, An IV–18 brumaire, An VIII). In accordance with the Constitution of 22 August 1795 (5 fructidor, An III) it replaced the *Convention nationale* (see *Constitutions; Coup d'état; Revolutions,* I, Ia). Two chambers shared the legislative power—the *Conseil des Cinq Cents,* who framed the laws, and the *Conseil des Anciens,* who passed or rejected them. The executive power was exercised by a *Directoire exécutif de* *la République française* of five members elected by the *Anciens* from a list of ten candidates supplied by the *Cinq Cents*. The first five Directors to function, all former *conventionnels*, were: Paul Barras (q.v.); Jean-François Rewbell (1747–1807); Lazare Carnot (1753–1823); Louis-Marie Larevellière-Lépeaux (1753–1824); and Charles Letourneur (1751–1817). The Directors were theatrically costumed in sweeping cloaks and plumed hats.

Disciple, Le (1889), a novel by Paul Bourget (q.v.). The positivist philosopher, Adrien Sixte, himself leads a life of monastic regularity but believes that human sensibility is of animal origin and that actions which are the inevitable outcome of natural laws cannot be classed as morally good or bad. His 'disciple', Robert Greslou, had become a tutor in the family of the marquis de Jussat, and is now in prison awaiting trial for the murder of Charlotte de Jussat. He sends Sixte a memorandum establishing his innocence, but prohibits its use. He had formed a dislike for André, the eldest son of the house, a very moderately intelligent, country-loving young army officer in whom he yet sensed a certain nobility lacking in himself. To compensate his sense of inferiority he determined to seduce André's sister Charlotte. She yielded when he threatened suicide, but only on condition that after one night together they should kill themselves. When the time came Greslou recanted, but Charlotte committed suicide after warning him that she had sent a confession to her brother. Greslou, arrested on circumstantial evidence of murder, knows that if he remains silent, and André will not establish his innocence, he must be condemned to death. Still, he refuses to speak, wishing to prove that he too can act like a 'gentilhomme'. His memorandum demonstrates that Sixte's philosophy had provided him with authority at every stage, but he begs for intellectual comfort and support from his Master, for, he says, he is now overwhelmed with remorse. Sixte is appalled at being held ultimately responsible, and attends the trial. At the last moment André reveals Greslou's innocence and procures his discharge, after which he shoots him. Adrien Sixte watches Mme Greslou praying over her son's dead body and asks himself

whether people in trouble would pray instinctively to 'Our Father which art in heaven' if no heavenly Father existed. Sixte is supposed to be drawn from the philosopher Taine (q.v.) and the long, heavy novel itself is an indictment of positivist philosophy.

Disciplina clericalis, see *Castoiement*.

Discours by J.-J. Rousseau on two themes proposed by the *Académie* of Dijon: *Si le rétablissement des sciences et des arts a contribué à épurer les mœurs* and *Sur l'Origine et les fondements de l'inégalité parmi les hommes*; the first published in 1750, the second in 1754 (cf. *Vincennes*).

In the first, Rousseau expounds the doctrine that man, originally simple and natural, has been corrupted by the advance of art and science, which has bred mutual suspicion, treachery, conquest, inequality, and luxury (bringing in its train cowardice and other vices). While ignoring the advantages, he insists on the evils that the discoveries of science have brought to mankind.

A large part of the second *Discours* is occupied with a description of primitive man as Rousseau imagined him to have been: living in isolation in the forests, self-sufficient, equal to his fellows because independent of them; then gradually forming primitive societies based on the family and carrying with them a sense of mutual obligation. Thus far primitive man, he holds, had remained free and happy. But with the advent of the idea of property (arising from the cultivation and enclosure of land), the natural differences between men in point of strength and intelligence had for the first time their consequence in the enrichment of some, the poverty of others, violent disorders, the precarious tyranny of the strong, with a stifling of the instinct of pity which at first prevailed among men. The final stage in the process of evolution is that, in order to remedy these disorders, a constitution is set up which, on the pretence of establishing peace and justice, perpetuates the inequalities between men. The author states his belief that all government is founded on a contract between the people and their rulers, a doctrine which he developed in his *Contrat social*. Rousseau's account of the state of nature and of the evolution of society is quite unscientific; the importance of the discourse lay in its forcible denunciation of social conditions as they were in his day.

Discours de la lanterne, a pamphlet by Camille Desmoulins (q.v.), sometimes mentioned as a piece of typical inflammatory writing of the Revolutionary period. In fact, though it begins with a few provocative sentences, it continues as an appeal for moderation.

Discours de la méthode, see *Descartes.*

Discours sur les révolutions du globe, see *Cuvier.*

Discours sur les sciences et les arts, see *Discours* (by J.-J. Rousseau) above.

Discours sur l'histoire universelle, see *Bossuet.*

Discours sur l'inégalité, see *Discours* (by J.-J. Rousseau) above.

Discours sur l'universalité de la langue française, see *Rivarol.*

Dispute, see *Dit.*

Distiques de Caton, gnomic verses containing advice on conduct, translated from a Latin collection, in the 12th century in an Anglo-Norman version, in the 13th by Adam de Suel and other poets. There are several ME. versions. The work was very popular and was used as a school-book in the Middle Ages.

Dit, in medieval literature, a somewhat vague and wide term for a metrical composition, sometimes restricted to a description of an object and its qualities, or giving an account of a profession (such as that of baker) or of the streets or cries of Paris; sometimes of a more didactic or moralizing turn; sometimes used as equivalent to *fabliau* (q.v.). See also *Cocagne* (*Dit de*).

The *débat* or *dispute* is a variety in dialogue form of the didactic *dit,* the dialogue being usually between personifications (e.g. the *Débat de l'hiver et de l'été*). Some deal with religious themes (e.g. the remarkable *Débat du corps et de l'âme,* see *Religious Writings*).

Both *dits* and *débats* are to be found among the poems of Rutebeuf, e.g. *Débat du croisé et du non-croisé,* which gives arguments for and against taking part in the

Crusades. Villon wrote a *Débat du cœur et du corps.*

Ditié d'Urbain, a medieval collection of precepts of good manners.

Divagations (1897), critical writings and some prose poems by Mallarmé (q.v.).

Dive Bouteille, L'Oracle de la, see *Pantagruel.*

Divoire, FERNAND (1883–), poet of Belgian origin whose collections of *simultanéiste* verse include: *La Malédiction des enfants* (1910); *Orphée* (1922); *L'Homme du monde* (1926). (See *Simultanéisme.*)

Dix, Les, the ten members of the *Académie Goncourt* (q.v.).

Dix-huit brumaire, Le, An VIII (9 Nov. 1799), the day of the fall of the *Directoire* and of Bonaparte's accession to power, see *Consulat.*

XIXᵉ Siècle, Le, founded 1871, was one of the most widely read conservative dailies during the early years of the Third Republic. From 1872 it was edited by Edmond About (q.v.) with a staff of writers who were, like himself, ex-Normaliens (see *École normale supérieure*) and anti-clerical in their opinions.

Dizain, in French prosody, a stanza of ten lines, usually decasyllabic (rarely octosyllabic), rhyming as follows:
a b a b b c c d c d.

Djinns, Les, see *Orientales, Les.*

Docteur amoureux, Le, see *Calonne, Ernest de.*

Docteur Pascal, Le (1893), the final novel in Zola's *Rougon-Macquart* (q.v.) cycle.

Doctrinaires, Les, a small but powerful political party led by Royer-Collard and Guizot (qq.v.) after the restoration of Louis XVIII, and composed of moderate and constitutional royalists. Their policy, the translation into action of a clearly reasoned and expressed political philosophy, was to steer a middle course ('le juste milieu') between rabid monarchism and the sovereignty of the people. The king, according to their conception, was a monarch who reigned but did not govern, while the people, the electoral mass whose voice should influence the government, meant the middle classes, the bourgeois ranks of merchants, manufacturers, tradesmen, &c. The *doctrinaires* were strongest under Louis XVIII. Their influence waned during the ultra-royalist reign of Charles X, and had disappeared by the revolution of 1848.

Doctrinal, see *Rhétoriqueurs.*

Dolet, ÉTIENNE (1509–46), born at Orleans, a humanist and ardent Ciceronian, a printer of learned books, suspected of being a materialist if not an atheist (he was probably indifferent to religious dogma), a friend of Clément Marot and Rabelais. He was devoted to literature, but vain, quarrelsome, unruly, and given to intemperate language in controversy, a character which brought him many enemies and repeated imprisonments, and contributed to his ultimate fate. His principal writings were *Dialogus de imitatione Ciceroniana* (1535), a Latin dialogue in defence, against Erasmus, of the Ciceronian cult; *Commentarii linguae Latinae* (1536–8), discussions of individual Latin words, classed according to the ideas they expressed, a valuable contribution to Latin scholarship; and various translations from Cicero, Plato, &c. He commenced business as printer at Lyons in 1538, issuing in the course of the next five years works by Clément Marot and Rabelais among others. In 1536 he had killed a man, apparently in self-defence, and had obtained the royal pardon, an occasion celebrated by a famous banquet at which were present some of the chief figures of the French Renaissance, Budé, Clément Marot, and Rabelais. In 1542 he was tried before the Inquisitor-General, Mathieu Ory ('nostre maistre Doribus' of Rabelais), at the instance of the master printers of Lyons, whom he had antagonized, on the charge of publishing heretical books (e.g. translations of the Scriptures). He was sentenced to death, but once more pardoned by the king; but was again arrested, convicted of blasphemy and other offences, and hanged and burnt in the Place Maubert in Paris, where a statue commemorates him.

Dolopathos, the title of a French metrical version made *c.* 1222–5 by a certain Herbers from a Latin text by a monk of the abbey of Haute-Seille (in the diocese of Metz), of a collection of tales resembling (with certain marked differences) the collection known as the *Roman des Sept Sages* (q.v.). Lucinien,

son of Dolopathos, king of Sicily, is condemned to death on the accusation of his stepmother; but his execution is adjourned by the successive arrival of seven sages who relate tales, three of them identical with the tales in the *Roman des sept sages.* Finally Virgil appears, denounces the queen, and effects the liberation of Lucinien.

Domaine public, i.e. public property preserved, administered, or exploited by or on behalf of the State or a local authority in the common interest. Roads, for instance, rivers, museums, art galleries, &c., fall into this class. In a literary connexion a work is spoken of as 'tombée dans le domaine public' when the copyright expires. (Under French law the copyright of works published during an author's lifetime lasts for fifty years beginning with the year after the year of the author's death.)

Domat, JEAN (1625–96), jurist, author of *Les Lois civiles dans leur ordre naturel* (1694); a friend of Pascal.

Dom Garcie de Navarre, ou Le Prince jaloux, a comedy by Molière, produced without success in 1661. (Until the 18th century *Dom* is often found in French for the Spanish *Don.*)

Don Garcie is in love with Elvire, princess of Léon, and she returns his love; but he suffers from incurable jealousy, thereby giving ground for her resentment. He finds the half of a torn letter in her writing, evidently to a lover; it turns out to have been addressed to himself. He sees her embracing a man, but the man is in fact her friend Doña Ignès in disguise. He finds her in the arms of a supposed rival, but this rival is discovered to be her brother. There is a good situation in the fourth act where Elvire offers to justify herself, but adds that if Don Garcie accepts, she will never be his. Jealousy is stronger than love, and he accepts. The play ends, rather weakly, in reconciliation and marriage. Molière used many of the lines in later comedies, e.g. *Le Misanthrope.*

Dom Juan ou Le Festin de Pierre, a comedy by Molière in prose, produced in 1665.

Don Juan Tenorio, an insolent and unscrupulous libertine (typifying some of the noblemen of the day), has carried off Elvire from a convent and married her, and being soon tired of her has deserted her to pursue other amorous intrigues. The appeal of his wife leaves him unmoved and he mocks at the expostulations to which his conduct moves even his valet, Sganarelle. The brothers of the injured Elvire demand satisfaction, but a service which he has rendered to one of them enables him to postpone the issue. He arrives by chance at the tomb of the Commander, a gentleman whom he has killed. In mockery he bids Sganarelle invite the statue of the Commander to supper; the statue bows its head in assent. Don Juan recovers from his momentary dismay, and resumes his arrogant attitude. As he sits at supper, the statue arrives, and he receives it with unshaken effrontery. The statue invites him to sup with it the next night. Don Juan now makes himself even more odious by assuming a hypocritical devoutness. The statue arrives to lead him to supper. As it takes his hand, Don Juan cries out in agony; a burning chasm opens and swallows him up.

The grim drama of Don Juan's depravation is relieved by one or two pleasant scenes: the picture of a village coquette, and the interview between Don Juan and his creditor, M. Dimanche, whom he so overwhelms with civilities that the poor man dares not speak of the money that is due to him.

The play was very successful, but it also evoked violent disapproval; within a month from its first performance it was suppressed. After Molière's death it was versified by Thomas Corneille.

Dominique (1863), by Eugène Fromentin (q.v.), one of the comparatively few novels of psychological analysis in French literature before about 1880. It is a study, partly autobiographical, presented with a sobriety that borders upon flatness, of a character who has missed supreme happiness in love and in work, but has learnt to content himself with the second best. Dominique de Bray, the narrator, while still an adolescent, had developed a passion for Madeleine d'Orsel, cousin of a school friend. She discovered this after she was a married woman, elected to cure him, and herself fell in love. An accident forced her to betray her feelings, but Dominique so pitied her state of moral distress that he agreed never to see her again. He left Paris and abandoned a literary career which,

though promising, would only have been second-rate. In the country he leads a full, useful life, managing his property and, in time, marrying.

Doña Sol, heroine of *Hernani* (q.v.), a drama by Victor Hugo.

Donat, a name used, especially in the Middle Ages, to signify the *Ars Grammatica* of Aelius Donatus (a 4th-c. Latin grammarian), the standard Latin grammar of those times. It was one of the books in which Thubal Holoferne instructed the young Gargantua (Rabelais, I. xiv).

Don Bernard de Cabrère, a tragicomedy by Rotrou performed in 1647, regarded as his most successful attempt at this form of drama. The main theme is the perverse ill luck with which a gallant soldier, Don Lope, is unremittingly pursued, to the point of comicality. Whenever his brave deeds are related to the king, the latter is either preoccupied, or crossed in love, or falls asleep; the poor soldier meets with no reward, nor is he more happy in love. With him is contrasted the fortunate Don Bernard, the king's favourite, for whose hand noble ladies contend. However, at the end the tide of Don Lope's ill luck begins to turn.

Don César de Bazan, the impoverished noble who becomes a bandit and who is impersonated at Court by a lackey, in Victor Hugo's drama *Ruy Blas* (q.v.).

Dondey, THÉOPHILE, see O'Neddy, Philothée.

Dongo, FABRICE DEL, hero of *La Chartreuse de Parme* (q.v.), a novel by Stendhal.

Don Japhet d'Arménie, a comedy by Scarron, produced with great success in 1652.

Don Japhet is a crazy countryman whose follies have for a time diverted the emperor Charles V, and who has in consequence acquired an exaggerated idea of his dignity. His self-importance and grandiloquent language, and the grotesque humiliations to which he is exposed, provide an element of buffoonery. A thin thread of romance is added in the adventure of Don Alphonse, a young cavalier, who takes service with Don Japhet in order to pursue a courtship.

Donnay, MAURICE (1859–1945), playwright, began by writing humorous sketches for the cabaret *Le Chat-Noir* (q.v.). *Lysistrata*

(1893), an adaptation and modernization of the play by Aristophanes, was well received, but his success came with elegant, never very profound comedies of Parisian life. The best-remembered is *Amants* (1895), which turns on a demi-mondaine's struggle between love for one man and affection for her protector, the father of her child. Absence works a cure. *La Douloureuse* (1897), *L'Affranchie* (1898), *L'Autre Danger* (1902), and *Les Éclaireuses* (1913) are other titles.

Donneau de Visé, see *Visé, Jean Donneau de.*

Don Ruy Gomez de Silva, a Spanish grandee, guardian of Doña Sol, in Victor Hugo's drama *Hernani* (q.v.).

Don Sanche d'Aragon, a drama by Corneille (described by him as a 'Comédie héroïque'), produced in 1649, one of the best of the French tragicomedies.

Fernand, king of Aragon, has sent away, by the hands of Don Raymond, his confidant, his infant son, Don Sanche, that he may not fall into the hands of the rebels menacing his kingdom, which in fact presently passes into their power. The child has been left with the wife of a poor fisherman, together with a casket which, when he grows up, is to reveal his identity. The boy, who is known as Carlos and believes himself the fisherman's son, runs away when sixteen, joins the army of Castile, and performs such feats of valour that he wins the high esteem of the king of Castile and his sister, Isabelle. This king dying, Isabelle ascends the throne. She is unmarried, and, in default of a royal suitor, three grandees of Castile are proposed to her from whom she is to choose a husband. About the same time the usurpers of the throne of Aragon are overthrown, Don Raymond is released from a long imprisonment and at once sets out in search of Don Sanche. He is discovered in the person of the gallant Carlos, who by general consent marries Isabelle.

Doon de Mayence, a *chanson de geste* (q.v.) of some 11,500 alexandrines, dating in the form in which we have it probably from the 13th century. The first half, which perhaps formed a separate poem, deals with the youth of Doon. His father, the count Gui, having become a hermit, his wicked seneschal Herchembaut sets about the

destruction of the count's wife and children. Doon escapes the fate designed for him, rescues his mother, and hangs the traitor.

In the second half, Doon, having been spoken of contemptuously by Charlemagne, beards the monarch and exacts from him the city of Vauclère in Saxony, then in the hands of the Saracen king Aubigant, who is being besieged by Danes. The city is won thanks to prodigies of valour by the French, and Doon marries Flandrine, Aubigant's daughter.

Doon de Mayence, Geste de, the name given to a group of *chansons de geste* (q.v.) dealing with the exploits of various rebels against royal authority, who are, as a rule, finally brought to repentance. The oldest of these is the tale of *Gormond et Isembard* (of which a fragment only survives), dating from about 1130. Isembard, a young French knight resentful of unjust treatment by King Louis, has joined the pagan King Gormond and induced him to invade France. In a great battle, in which Isembard fights with his own father, the invaders are defeated, and Isembard, mortally wounded, is reconciled with the Church.

Other *chansons* of the same group are entitled *Doon de Mayence, Ogier, Renaud de Montauban, Raoul de Cambrai, Girard de Roussillon* (qq.v.).

Dorante, a frequent name for characters in 17th-century comedy, e.g. in Corneille's *Le Menteur* (hero); in Molière's *Le Bourgeois Gentilhomme* (the sycophantic nobleman), *Les Fâcheux* (minor character), and *La Critique de l'École des femmes* (important).

Dorat, CLAUDE-JOSEPH, CHEVALIER (1734–80), poet and for a time *mousquetaire*, author of indifferent tragedies and comedies, and of lively and graceful miscellaneous verse (Epistles, including *Avis aux sages du siècle* which annoyed Voltaire, *Héroïdes* after the manner of Ovid, *Les Baisers, Le Mois de mai*, fables, &c.), and a descriptive poem *La Déclamation*. The best of his comedies is *Le Célibataire* (1775). Another, *Les Prôneurs* (1777), ridiculed the intellectual *salons* or *bureaux d'esprit*. He made repeated but unsuccessful attempts to obtain election to the *Académie*. He was regarded as the head of a school of the light poets of the period.

Dorat or **Daurat**, JEAN (1508–88), born at Limoges, principal of the Collège de Coqueret and a professor at the Collège de France, sometimes included among the members of the *Pléiade*, less on account of his poetry than as the humanist who inspired Ronsard, Du Bellay, and Baïf with a love of classical literature. He wrote remarkable Latin poems, some in imitation of the Odes of Pindar.

Doré, GUSTAVE (1832–83), book-illustrator and caricaturist, born at Strasbourg, was established in Paris from 1847, partly for his education and largely because his talent had already been discovered by the caricaturist Philipon (q.v.), who gave him work on his papers, e.g. *Le Charivari* (q.v.). He soon added book-illustration to his work as a caricaturist, and between 1860 and 1870 produced some of his best work, notably the illustrations for Rabelais, Dante, Perrault's *Contes*, Balzac's *Contes drolatiques*, *Don Quixote*, the Bible, &c. He was famous in England, where his drawings and paintings of London life and characters were almost more appreciated than in France. A Doré Gallery, where his works were on permanent exhibition, was opened in London in 1867 and existed for many years.

Dorgelès, ROLAND [pseud. of R. Lécavelé] (1886–), novelist, born at Amiens, author of *Les Croix de bois* (1919), a successful novel of the 1914–18 war. His later works include *Le Cabaret de la belle femme* (1919, short stories), *Saint Magloire* (1921, a novel), also travel literature and reminiscences.

Dorine, a character in Molière's *Le Tartuffe*, a servant proverbial for her free-spoken and clear-sighted advocacy of the interests of her employers.

Dormi secure (Lat., 'sleep in peace'), a collection of sermons, ready for delivery, for the use of the clergy, produced about 1395. There is a reference to it in Rabelais (I. xiv).

Dorval, MARIE (1798–1849), an actress who came to Paris from the provinces. She was a success in melodrama at the *Théâtre de la Porte Saint-Martin* and, at the same theatre, in Dumas *père*'s *Antony* (q.v.). Through Alfred de Vigny's (q.v.) influence she was taken into the company of the Comédie-Française and there had her greatest triumph, as Kitty Bell, in *Chatterton* (q.v.).

Double Ballade, see *Ballade.*

Double inconstance, La, a comedy by Marivaux, produced in 1723, his own favourite among his plays.

Silvia and Arlequin are simple country folk and faithful lovers. But the prince, in the character of a gentleman of the court, has fallen in love with Silvia (whom he has seen when out hunting) and has had her brought to the palace. She is heart-broken at her enforced separation from Arlequin. On the advice of Flaminia, a lady of the court, Arlequin is also brought to the palace, both are kindly treated, and the minds of the lovers are set at rest. Little by little they take a fancy to their new friends, till they unconsciously forget each other and fall in love with the new partners designed for them, Arlequin with Flaminia, and Silvia with the prince, still retaining his character of a gentleman of the court until Silvia's affection is secured.

Double Méprise, La (1833), a long short story by Prosper Mérimée, first published as by the author of the *Théâtre de Clara Gazul* (q.v.).

Double Veuvage, Le, a comedy by Dufresny, in prose and verse, produced in 1702.

The theme is the hypocritical pretence of a husband and wife that they love each other. This is exposed when each is induced to believe that the other is dead. The supposed widow promptly proposes to marry her husband's nephew in memory of the defunct; the supposed widower to marry his wife's niece with the same pious purpose. Widow and widower are confronted, ostensibly to their joy. Each, to annoy the other, now supports the idea that the nephew shall marry the niece.

Doudan, XIMÉNÈS (1800–72), critic and *pensée*-writer, born at Douai (Flanders), studied in Paris, then (1825) entered the family of the duc de Broglie as tutor to the young Alphonse Rocca, son of Mme de Staël (q.v.) by her second marriage. He became the cherished friend and counsellor of the family, spending the remainder of his life with them at Broglie, at Coppet (q.v.), or in Paris. In spite of real or imaginary poor health he lived a tranquil, contented life, reading extensively, delighting some friends with his letters, others with his conversation, and contributing to reviews, notably the *Journal des Débats*. His *Mélanges et lettres* (1876-7) and *Lettres* (1879), among the most enjoyable 19th-century collections of correspondence and a good source for the study of the period, range from 1823 to 1872, the year of his death. They contain lively criticism and discussion of books, people, and events, varied by pictures of life in the country, herb-collecting, walks with a favourite dog, or occasional expeditions to Geneva; and the reader is left with a real fondness for their gentle, witty, good-natured writer. Another posthumously-published work, *Pensées et fragments, suivis des Révolutions du goût* (1881), contains a long essay on the continually changing standard of the Beautiful, a theme already treated by Stendhal.

Dragonnade, the practice of billeting dragoons or other soldiers on communities or individuals whom it was desired to punish; extensively applied against the Huguenots from 1680 to 1685.

Drama. For the primitive forms of the drama in France see under *Mystères, Moralités, Sotties, Farces*. The period of these came to an end in the 16th century and was succeeded by a phase in which Greek and Latin dramatic forms were introduced into France, under the influence of the humanist revival, either in the shape of Latin or French translations of Greek originals, or of dramas on Greek or Senecan models (see *Baïf, Lazare de; Buchanan; Saint-Gelais; La Péruse; Jodelle; Grévin; Garnier*). There were also a few plays on biblical themes, such as Buchanan's Latin *Baptistes* and *Jephthes*, La Taille's *Saül le furieux*, and Garnier's *Les Juives*. There followed a transitional period in which Hardy (q.v.) is the principal figure, when complete freedom from dramatic rules prevailed, when pastoral plays and tragi-comedies shared the stage with the older forms, and Italian and Spanish influences made themselves felt. True French classical drma began in the 17th century with the *Sophonisbe* of Mairet and the *Cid* of Corneille (1634 and 1637, qq.v.). For its further developments, see under *Tragedy, Comedy, Tragi-comedy, Drame*, and *Opéra-comique*.

For the evolution of the French theatrical companies see under *Theatres and Theatre Companies*.

Drame, in a specialized sense, the name given to a class of dramatic works intermediate between tragedy and comedy of which the theory was developed by Diderot in the discourses which he attached to his plays, *Le Fils naturel* and *Le Père de famille*, but of which earlier examples may be found in Voltaire's *L'Enfant prodigue* and *Nanine* and in the 'comédies larmoyantes' of Nivelle de la Chaussée. According to Diderot's conception they were to be serious dramas treating of the domestic problems of middle-class life. Among the chief authors of early *drames*, besides those mentioned above, were Sedaine and L.-S. Mercier, distant precursors of Augier and Dumas *fils*. (See also *Theatre of the 19th and 20th centuries; Romantisme; Hugo, &c.*)

Drames philosophiques (1878-86), by Ernest Renan (q.v.), four short philosophical dramas typical of the indulgently sceptical view of the universe adopted by this author in later life. In *Caliban* (1878) Shakespeare's Prospero, once more Duke of Milan, is dethroned by Caliban, who represents the ignorant masses, unresponsive to science and thought. Caliban discovers that it pays him to protect Prospero and exploit his brains. Prospero, with his leisure safeguarded, finds himself more free to pursue his researches. In *L'Eau de Jouvence* (1881), a sequel, Prospero discovers the elixir of life. In *Le Prêtre de Némi* (1885) the priest Antistius struggles to abolish the traditional rites and bloodshed attached to his office and to introduce a religion of love and good works. He meets with opposition inspired by ignorance, convention, and political motives, and falls a victim to mass hatred. *L'Abbesse de Jouarre* (1886), an episode of the Revolutionary era, is based on the idea that if the end of the world were known to be imminent no moral or social considerations would hold the passion of love in check. The opening scenes are laid in the notorious Prison du Plessis, where suspects spent their last night on the way to the Revolutionary Tribunal or the guillotine.

Dreyfus, L'Affaire. In the summer of 1894 the French Ministry of War came into possession of an unsigned letter held by the German Embassy, with an appended memorandum ('le bordereau') in which were enumerated details of French military secrets to be sent to the German Military Attaché, Colonel Schwartzkoppen. The handwriting resembled that of Captain Alfred Dreyfus, a Jewish officer of blameless record, employed at the War Office. Dreyfus protested his innocence, but he was court-martialled in December 1894, convicted, degraded, cashiered, and sent to solitary confinement for life on Devil's Island (see *Diable, Île du*). Shortly afterwards it was rumoured that he had been convicted on the strength of secret and doubtfully authentic documents produced by the Minister of War but not communicated to Dreyfus or his counsel.

In March 1896 Colonel Picquart, newly appointed head of the Information Branch of the Secret Service, discovered convincing evidence that a Major Esterhazy, an officer of dubious character, was in German pay, and that his handwriting was that of the *bordereau*. This was suppressed by the War Office. About the same time Colonel Henry, Colonel Picquart's deputy, produced a letter alleged to be from the Italian Military Attaché, Colonel Panizzardi, referring to Dreyfus by name and making his guilt clear. In March 1897 Matthieu Dreyfus (brother) also discovered evidence which incriminated Esterhazy, and accused him. The resulting agitation ended in a court martial at which Esterhazy was acquitted. Thereupon *L'Aurore*, one of the pro-Dreyfus (*Dreyfusard*) newspapers, published the famous open letter by Émile Zola, *J'accuse* (q.v.), to the President of the French Republic, accusing the War Office of hushing up material evidence and concealing a grave miscarriage of justice. Zola was prosecuted for libel and sentenced to a year's imprisonment (he escaped to England), but his trial gained Dreyfus many supporters. By this time the feelings aroused by *l'Affaire* had split France into two camps. Against Dreyfus were the whole military caste and the traditional forces of law and order. Also, he was a Jew, and anti-Semitic feeling ran high. But for him there was an enthusiastic band, at first small and recruited largely from the intelligentsia, who believed that if an error of justice had been committed it should be set right at no matter what loss of prestige.

For nearly four years emotion swept the country. Families were divided, friendships broken, and Dreyfus became alternatively an object of execration or a symbolic figure of truth and justice. A public petition for a retrial was signed by many people hitherto uninterested in public affairs, and eventually the *revisionniste* party became so strong that in July 1898 Cavaignac, the Minister for War, read the alleged Panizzardi letter—the main proof of Dreyfus's guilt—aloud in the Chamber. A month later Colonel Henry admitted to having forged this letter himself. He was arrested and imprisoned in the fortress of Mont Valérien, where he committed suicide. This decided the Government to press for a reversal of the Dreyfus sentence and a new trial by court martial was held at Rennes in September 1899. Contrary to all expectation the verdict was still 'Guilty' (but with extenuating circumstances, and with the sentence reduced to ten years). A fortnight later the Government pardoned Dreyfus; and in 1906 the *Cour de Cassation* finally reversed the sentence of 1894. Dreyfus was then reinstated in the army with the rank of major. He resigned two years later but rejoined during the 1914–18 war, was promoted lieutenant-colonel and awarded the *Légion d'honneur* (q.v.).

The spiritual and political crisis engendered by *l'Affaire* was strongly reflected in French literature. In Zola's *Vérité* it is transformed into fiction. It is described by Anatole France in *M. Bergeret à Paris* and (ironically) in *L'Île des pingouins*; and by Roger Martin du Gard (fervently) in *Jean Barois*. Novels by Gyp and plays by Lavedan or Donnay give the anti-Semitic point of view. In the early volumes of *A la recherche du temps perdu* Proust shows ancient friendships destroyed by party feeling, while his recently discovered youthful work *Jean Santeuil* contains a description of the trial itself. Léon Blum, in *Souvenirs sur l'Affaire*, Charles Péguy in *Notre jeunesse*, and Jaurès in *Preuves*, recall the effect of the crisis upon the generation just reaching manhood.

In 1930 Esterhazy's guilt was again confirmed in extracts which appeared from the papers of Colonel Schwartzkoppen.

Drieu La Rochelle, PIERRE-EUGÈNE (1893–1945), a well-known writer of the period between the 1914–18 and 1939–45 wars. He published novels (*L'Homme couvert de femmes*, 1926; *Gilles*, 1939, &c.) and also essays of a political (and especially Fascist) tendency. He was direct or of the *Nouvelle Revue Française* (q.v.) during the period of its publication under the German occupation of France, and guided its policy. He died by his own hand.

Droits de l'homme, Déclaration des, see *Déclaration*.

Drouet, JULIETTE (1806–83), actress, met Victor Hugo when she acted in his drama *Lucrèce Borgia* (q.v.). The friendship ripened into a liaison which lasted, with the utmost devotion on her side, for the remainder of their lives. She followed Hugo into exile, and during these years she acted as his amanuensis, recopying all his manuscripts. The famous *Tristesse d'Olympio* (q.v.) is one of the many poems Hugo wrote for her.

Droz, ANTOINE-GUSTAVE (1832–95), novelist and journalist, born in Paris, helped to ensure the success of *La Vie parisienne* (q.v.) with *Monsieur, Madame et Bébé* (published in book form in 1866), light, sentimental sketches of the intimacies of family life that at times left little to the imagination. A similar series, *Entre nous*, followed in 1867. His novels, *Autour d'une source* (1869) and *Un Paquet de lettres* (1870), were more ambitious.

Druidisme, see *Literary isms*.

Drumont, ÉDOUARD (1844–1917), polemical and violently anti-Semitic journalist, became known first with *La France juive* (1886, 2 vols.), an attack on Jews and Jewish financiers. In 1892 he founded and edited *La Libre Parole*, an anti-Dreyfus (q.v.) paper.

Du Barry, JEANNE BÉCU, COMTESSE (1743–93), mistress of Louis XV after the death of Mme de Pompadour. She was executed under the Terror.

Du Bartas (pron. as if *Bartass*), GUILLAUME DE SALLUSTE, SIEUR (1544–90), a Gascon gentleman who in 1566, after a studious youth, took up arms in the service of Henri de Navarre. He was sent on embassies and appeared in 1587 at the court of James VI of Scotland, where he was received with distinction. He was a very simple country squire in his home life, and at the same time an important Protestant poet, who in *La*

Semaine or *La Création du monde* (1578), an epic in alexandrine couplets, assembled all the scientific knowledge of his day in the guise of a description of the seven days of the Creation. In his *Seconde Semaine*, of which only four 'days' were completed (1584–1603), Du Bartas contemplated an encyclopaedic history of mankind. The execution of these poems was not equal to the splendour of their design. There are passages of a certain grandeur, such as the opening of the 7th canto of the *Semaine* (much admired by Goethe); but the whole is marred by lapses into bathos, pedantry, and bad taste; and the poet carried to excess Ronsard's ideas on the formation of new words. The work (especially the *Semaine*) was for a time extremely successful and was translated into other languages, including English (by Joshua Sylvester, as *Divine Weekes and Workes* (1605), a poem which appears to have influenced Milton). It earned praise from English poets such as Daniel, Drayton, Lodge, and Marston, but Dryden thought some of it 'abominable fustian'. Du Bartas's other poems include earlier epics, *Judit*, *Uranie*, and *Le Triomphe de la Foi* (published 1574), and some lyrics.

Du Bellay, GUILLAUME (1491–1543), a distinguished general in the service of François Ier, author of *Mémoires*. Rabelais formed part of his suite when he was governor of Turin in 1540.

Du Bellay, JEAN (1492–1560), brother of the preceding, bishop successively of various sees, cardinal (1535), and diplomatic agent of François Ier on many occasions, notably in England and Italy; patron of men of letters, in particular of Rabelais, and of Étienne Dolet, Michel de l'Hôpital, &c.

Du Bellay, JOACHIM (1522–60), poet, of a noble family of Anjou (cousin of the preceding), next to Ronsard the most famous member of the *Pléiade* (q.v.), studied law at Poitiers, and literature in Paris. It is related that, when a young man, he met Ronsard at an inn, that their conversation revealed their common passion for poetry, and that du Bellay was led by it to join Ronsard's 'Brigade' in Paris, and under the guidance of the humanist Dorat (q.v.) to pursue the task of reforming French poetry. His first collections of sonnets and other lyrics appeared in 1549 and 1550; of these L'Olive was a sequence of 115 sonnets inspired by his cousin, Olive de Sévigné. In 1549 he also published, under the ambitious title of Défense et illustration de la langue française (q.v.), the manifesto of the new school of poetry (see Pléiade). In 1553 he accompanied his cousin, the cardinal Jean du Bellay (q.v.), on a mission to Rome and there spent four years in the cardinal's service. The impressions made on him by Rome and his regret for the 'douceur angevine' of his own country evoked the two collections of poems entitled Antiquités de Rome and Regrets (1558), which contain some of his finest work; they show dignity and sentiment, and liberation from the influence of Petrarch under which his earlier poems had been written. In 1558 appeared also his Latin poems, and Divers jeux rustiques. Du Bellay, unlike Ronsard, was a Latinist, familiar with Horace, Ovid, and Virgil, rather than a Hellenist; he was less pagan in spirit than his great contemporary. He was a master of the sonnet (which he first acclimatized if he did not introduce in France), whether he employed it to satirize the life of Rome, to call up the melancholy of its ruins, or to lament his own exile. He also wrote pleasant chansons (some, e.g. the Vanneur de blés aux vents, imitated from the Latin of the Italian Naugerius or Navagero), and other lyrics, and handled with ease the alexandrine, as in the satirical Poëte courtisan and several epistles. He translated the 4th and 6th books of the Aeneid.

In 1569 Spenser, then a young man, contributed translations of a number of du Bellay's sonnets, as Visions of Bellay, to a tract entitled A Theatre for Worldlings; these translations were subsequently republished, with some changes, in the collection of his minor works called Complaints. Spenser also translated du Bellay's Antiquités under the title Ruins of Rome.

Dubois, GUILLAUME, CARDINAL (1656–1723), son of a doctor of Brive-la-Gaillarde, a man of unscrupulous character but an able diplomatist, rose under the Regency of the duc d'Orléans (whose preceptor he had been) to be archbishop of Cambrai, cardinal, and minister. He negotiated the triple alliance of 1717 between France, England, and Holland.

Dubois, PAUL-FRANÇOIS (1793–1784), journalist, part-founder (1824) of Le Globe (q.v.).

Du Boisgobey, FORTUNÉ-HIPPOLYTE-AUGUSTE, see Lecoq, Monsieur.

Du Bos (pron. as if Boss), CHARLES (1882–1939), born in Paris of partly American ancestry, man of letters and a critic exceptionally well qualified by birth, education, travel, and sympathies to interpret foreign thought and literature to his own countrymen. His influence was also exercised through his many friendships, which had repercussions on contemporary literary history, and to no small extent by his remarkable powers as a conversationalist. He suffered from chronic ill health, which limited his output, and in 1927 he became a convert to Roman Catholicism. His interest in philosophy and religion can be deduced from some of the titles of his works, e.g. Byron et le besoin de la fatalité (1929), Du spirituel dans l'ordre littéraire (articles printed in Vigile, 1930), François Mauriac et le problème du romancier catholique (1933). He is at his most typical in his Journal (6 vols. published by 1955), of particular interest because of his remarks on English literature and English authors; in the short essays, on religion and the arts, collected in Approximations (1922–37, 7 vols.), and also in Qu'est-ce que la littérature? (1940, posth.), lectures delivered in English in 1938 at an American university.

Dubos or **Du Bos,** JEAN-BAPTISTE, ABBÉ (1670–1742), a man of letters and historian, author of an Histoire critique de la monarchie française (1734) and of Réflexions critiques sur la poésie et la peinture (1719, completed in 1733). The latter work is interesting for the doctrine it advances that poetry cannot be judged by rules and principles but only by the emotion it produces. In the dispute between the Ancients and the Moderns Du Bos is on the whole in favour of the former, holding with Boileau that tradition is valuable as indicating the coincidence of many opinions on the merit of certain authors.

Duc, comte, marquis. The empire of Charlemagne was divided for administrative purposes into comtés or counties, the comté being the territory assigned to a comte (Lat. comes, a 'companion' of the emperor) for him to govern. This territory might vary at the emperor's pleasure. A *marquis* was a *comte* entrusted with a territory on the *marches* or frontiers of the empire; his duties were consequently of a more specially military character. A *duc* (Lat. *dux*, leader) was appointed, according to the needs of the moment, to have authority over several *comtes*. The appointments of *duc*, *marquis*, and *comte* were temporary, not hereditary. The persons appointed to them were officials, selected for their fitness for the particular post, from the members of the emperor's court. The principal duty of a *comte* was the administration of justice, in which he was assisted by a council of notables of his district. He had to see to the provision by the district of the military contingent required of it; and to appear in person annually before the emperor to report. He received no regular salary but was entitled to a third of the produce of the fines he inflicted, and sometimes to other revenues.

Towards the end of the 9th century, with the weakening of the monarchy, the holders of these various appointments tended to become irremovable, and the appointments themselves hereditary. The heredity of such offices is recognized in an edict of Charles le Chauve, 877. (See also *Noblesse*; *Napoleonic aristocracy*.)

Du Camp, MAXIME (1822–94), journalist and novelist, born and educated in Paris, is remembered largely for his association with Flaubert (q.v.), whom he accompanied on a trip to the Near East, and by his *Souvenirs littéraires* (1882–3). He also edited the *Revue des Deux Mondes* and wrote books of travel, history, art criticism, &c., and some novels—*Souvenirs et paysages d'Orient* (1848), *Les Convulsions de Paris* (1878–9, a narrative of the insurrections of 1871), *Les Six Aventures* (1857), *Les Buveurs de cendres* (1866), &c.

Du Cange, CHARLES DU FRESNE, SIEUR (1610–88), a man of great erudition, author of a celebrated *Glossarium ad scriptores mediae et infimae Latinitatis* (1678), and editor of the chronicles of Joinville (an incorrect text) and Villehardouin.

Ducasse, ISIDORE, the rightful name of the author who called himself, and is usually remembered as, the comte de Lautréamont (q.v.).

Du Cerceau, JACQUES ANDROUET (?1510–?), the first of a dynasty of architects who flourished in the second half of the 16th century and in the 17th century, and who were attached to the court. One of his two sons, Baptiste (*c.* 1540–90) and Jacques (? – 1614), began the construction of the Pont-Neuf for Henri III in 1578. A grandson began the Pont au Change in 1639.

Duchâtel, PIERRE (1480–1552), a humanist of wide erudition, who enjoyed the favour of François Ier and taught Greek to the latter's sister Marguerite. He was the king's librarian at Fontainebleau.

Du Châtelet, GABRIELLE-ÉMILIE, MARQUISE (1706–49), by birth de Breteuil, known for her long liaison with Voltaire, whom she received and protected at her *château* at Cirey-sur-Blaise, near the frontier of Lorraine. She was a woman of virile intellect, devoted to mathematics (though the soundness of her mathematical knowledge has been questioned), science, and philosophy, knowing Latin, Italian, and English; at the same time an honest, trustworthy, and devoted friend. She translated Newton's *Principia* into French, adding a commentary. She was unpopular in the worldly society of the day and was bitterly satirized by Mme du Deffand in a famous page.

Duchesne, MONSEIGNEUR LOUIS (1843–1922), prelate and scholar, one of the most distinguished religious historians of the 19th century, also a renowned archaeologist. He was for many years Professor of Archaeology and Ecclesiastical History at the *Institut catholique* in Paris, and in 1895 he became Director of the *École française de Rome*. His chief works include an edition (1886–92) of the *Liber pontificalis*, *Les Origines du culte chrétien* (1889), a study of the Latin Liturgy before Charlemagne, and *Histoire ancienne de l'Église* (1906–8).

Duchesse de Langeais, La (1833–4), one of the 'Scènes de la vie parisienne' of Balzac's *Comédie humaine* (q.v.), the second episode of the trilogy entitled *Histoire des Treize*, is the story of a passion. In the early years of the Restoration the beautiful and witty duchesse de Langeais is a leader of Paris society. She plays fast and loose with the marquis de Montriveau, but is brokenhearted when he seemes to tire of her. She compromises herself in trying to recapture him, then disappears from Paris. After long years of searching Montriveau runs her to earth in a Carmelite convent on an island in the Mediterranean. He speaks to her in the presence of the Mother Superior and later, with a band of friends (*Les Treize*), plots to kidnap her. But when the kidnappers reach her cell they find her dead. They bear her corpse away and bury it at sea.

Ducis (pron. as if *Duciss*), JEAN-FRANÇOIS (1733–1816), dramatist, wrote two very mediocre tragedies—*Œdipe chez Admète* (1778), combining themes from Sophocles and Euripides, and *Abufar* (1795), a tragedy of Arabian pastoral life. He did something to introduce Shakespeare to the French stage by his verse adaptations, feeble though they were, of *Hamlet* (1769), *Roméo et Juliette* (1772), *Le Roi Léar* (1783), *Macbeth* (1784), and *Othello* (1792). To suit French taste he introduced confidants in the classical manner, and provided *Othello* with an alternative ending in which Othello discovers his mistake in time and does not murder Desdemona. Ducis, whom Sainte-Beuve called a 'profanateur innocent', did not know English but worked on the translations of Laplace and Letourneur. He was, though a poor poet, a man of independent spirit who refused honours offered him by Napoleon.

Duclos, CHARLES PINOT or PINEAU (1704–72), born in Brittany, historian, moralist, and novelist, noted also for his witty conversation, a man of energy and practical sense rather than of much talent. He left fragmentary memoirs of his dissipated youth, which are of some literary interest. His chief works were a full but colourless *Histoire de Louis XI* (1745), *Considérations sur les mœurs de ce siècle* (1750) showing penetration and containing sound observations but discreet in its censures, and *Mémoires secrets sur les règnes de Louis XIV et de Louis XV* (for which he was in great part indebted to the manuscript of Saint-Simon); these were published posthumously in 1790. They extend to the negotiations for the alliance of France and Austria and the beginning of the Seven Years War, but (although the author as historiographer had access to State documents) are concerned rather with the characters and intrigues of those who took part in the great

events of the period than with the events themselves; there are a good many references to the financier, Law. Duclos also wrote some romances, *Histoire de Mme de Luz* (1741), a tale of gallantry of the period of Henri IV; *Confessions du comte de ★ ★ ★* (1742), which throws light on the dissolute morals of contemporary society and had considerable success in its day, partly for the portraits of real persons that it contained; the modern reader will find little to recommend these works. Duclos was a friend of Voltaire and Rousseau and a supporter of the *philosophes* and of the *Encyclopédie*, but retained his independence. He was historiographer from 1750 and perpetual secretary of the *Académie* from 1754. He writes in a concise and somewhat dry and abrupt, occasionally caustic and epigrammatic, style. He shows sincerity but little heart.

Du Contrat Social, a treatise of political philosophy by J.-J. Rousseau, published in 1762, expounding a theory of the social state which the author supposes to have followed the state of nature.

The central doctrine propounded is that since man is born free, and force cannot be the source of right, the subjection of man to the authority of government must be based on a compact. Primitive man, to overcome the obstacles that threatened his safety in a state of nature, sought a form of association with his fellows such that each, uniting with all the rest, yet obeyed only himself and remained free as heretofore. By this association he created a moral collective personality called the *sovereign* when active, the *State* when passive. Each person is a member of the sovereign, and as such a *citizen*, and at the same time a subject of the State (a subversion of the feudal theory). From this association arises moral duty, justice now replaces instinct, man gains civil liberty and right of property (subject to limitations), and his force is increased. Sovereignty is inalienable and indivisible; it cannot be transferred to representatives (the English are much mistaken in thinking themselves a free people: they are so only at the moment of their elections). Law is the definition of rights and duties, and the principal objects of legislation are liberty and equality (to the extent that the exercise of power shall be in conformity with the law, and the enjoyment of wealth shall preclude the servitude of the poor). *Government* is an intermediate body (prince or magistrates) between the sovereign people and the individual citizens, an agent of the sovereign, charged with the execution of the law and the maintenance of liberty. The government may be democratic, aristocratic, monarchic, or mixed, according to the number composing the governing body. The establishment of a government is not a compact, but a legislative and executive act of the sovereign. As regards religion, the citizens should be required to profess a civil faith of which the articles are determined by the sovereign. These must be few and simple: belief in an intelligent beneficent God and in a future life and retribution, acceptance of the sanctity of the social compact and the law; intolerance of other creeds is precluded, so long as these contain nothing contrary to the duties of the citizen.

The treatise is written with a somewhat misleading air of dry precision and simplicity, which disguises the assumptions on which it is based and its disregard of the actual facts of history and the complexity of human affairs. Its occasional historical illustrations are drawn from the small states of ancient Greece and there are references to such questionable sources as the Laws of Minos and the constitution of Lycurgus, though it is only fair to remark that Rousseau's polity was drawn up from the standpoint of a small community such as Geneva and Corsica. In consequence of the difficulty of obtaining copies of the work, for its introduction into France was strictly prohibited, and of the relatively small circle to which it appealed, its influence was not at first great. It made itself felt especially after 1789. But it contributed, not in France alone, to the growth of new ideas, for it enforced the principle of the sovereignty of the people, not of a single order or ruler. The opening words of Chapter I, 'L'homme est né libre, et partout il est dans les fers', struck a note which resounded far.

Du côté de chez Swann (1913), the first section of Proust's novel *A la recherche du temps perdu* (q.v.).

Ducray-Duminil, FRANÇOIS-GUILLAUME (1761–1819), author of highly popular sensational novels with a moral strain—

Alexis ou la Maisonnette dans les bois (1788), *Victor ou l'Enfant de la forêt* (1796), *Caelina ou l'Enfant du mystère* (1798), *Les Petits Orphelins du hameau* (1800), &c. They were dramatized with almost equal success.

Du Deffand, MARIE, MARQUISE (1697–1780), one of the most celebrated Frenchwomen of her century, whose *salon* was frequented, not only by the highest society, but also by Turgot, the président Hénault, d'Alembert, and other *philosophes* (though she was hostile to the *encyclopédistes* as a sect). She had a somewhat stormy youth and in later life became blind. At the age of sixty-eight she made the acquaintance of Horace Walpole (see his letter to Gray of 25 Jan. 1766), conceived for him a deep affection, and ultimately left him all her papers. Her correspondence with him, with her intimate friend the président Hénault, and with others, written in admirable prose, reveals the sureness and independence of her judgement and displays the social and intellectual characteristics of her period. When she became blind she employed as reader Mlle de Lespinasse (q.v.), whose charm drew away from Mme du Deffand's *salon* many of its frequenters, a defection which led to a quarrel between the ladies and caused much perturbation in the literary world.

Du Fail, NOËL (1520–91), a Breton who held high judicial appointments in his province, relaxing from his official duties in the life of a country gentleman. He published in 1547, when probably still a student of law, and under the anagrammatic pseudonym Leon Ladulfi, *Propos rustiques*, purporting to be conversations of old villagers under an oak, in which they compare old customs with new, describe a broil between two villages, or relate some other village incident. The dominating theme is the happiness of the simple rural life. The purpose is in part didactic, but the pictures of village life and the portraits of rural types are of extraordinary vividness, the outcome of the author's profound sympathy with his subject. This work was followed in 1548 by *Baliverneries d'Eutrapel*, more mixed in subject-matter and of less merit; and much later, in 1585, by the *Contes et discours d'Eutrapel*, a miscellany of anecdotes and conversations, to some extent autobiographical, in which the didactic and satirical

element is more pronounced. The three inter-
locutors are Eutrapel (the author himself;
from εὐτράπελος, witty, lively), his brother
Polygame, and the shifty lawyer Lupolde.
Du Fail also wrote on professional matters
(*Notables et solennels arrêts du Parlement de
Bretagne*, 1579).

Du Faur de Pibrac, GUY, see *Pibrac*.

Dufay, PIERRE, see *Pastiche*.

Dufrénoy, ADÉLAÏDE-GILBERTE BILLET, MME
(1765–1825), a minor writer whose two
poetic collections, *Élégies* (1807) and *Poésies
diverses* (1821), won some notice. She also
wrote instructional works and *vaudevilles*
(q.v.) and translated English novels. She had
married young and been ruined by the
Revolution. Napoleon gave her a pension.

Dufresnoy, CHARLES-ALPHONSE (1611–55),
painter and poet, remembered by his Latin
poem *De arte graphica Liber* (1668). An English
translation by William Mason was published
in 1783 with annotations by Sir Joshua
Reynolds.

Dufresny, CHARLES RIVIÈRE (1648–1724),
dramatist and novelist. He wrote *Le Chevalier joueur* (1697), a prose counterpart of
Regnard's *Le Joueur*, depicting the passion of
gambling with more force and depth than
his rival. His *L'Esprit de contradiction* (q.v.,
1700) and *Le Double veuvage* (q.v., 1702),
comedies of conjugal life, were very successful. He also wrote *Amusements sérieux et
comiques d'un Siamois* (1699), depicting the
impressions of a Siamese visitor to Paris, a
prototype of the *Lettres Persanes*. Dufresny
was a man of originality and varied apti-
tudes but desultory and a spendthrift. He
was for a time controller of the royal gardens,
in the designing of which he showed novel
ideas. He was editor of the *Mercure* (q.v.)
after the death of Donneau de Visé (1710),
but soon sold the appointment.

Duguay-Trouin, RENÉ (1673–1736), born
at Saint-Malo, a privateer who ended
an adventurous and glorious career as
lieutenant-général des armées navales. His
achievements included the capture of an
English convoy (1707) and of Rio de
Janeiro (1711). His *Mémoires* (1740, posth.)
contain interesting descriptions of naval
encounters with the Dutch and English.

Du Guesclin (now pron. as if *Ghéclin*),
BERTRAND (*c.* 1320–80), a great captain, born
near Dinan, thickset, sturdy, noted for his
ugliness, illiterate, but famous for courage
and wisdom. When only seventeen, he
successfully defended Rennes against the
Duke of Lancaster. He was then named
captain of Mont-Saint-Michel (q.v.). He
ridded France of the brigand bands known
as the *Grandes Compagnies* by leading them
into Spain to fight in the war for the crown
of Spain between Pedro the Cruel (supported
by the English) and his brother Henry of
Trastamare. Here he was captured by the
English at the battle of Navarette (1367) and
was ransomed (himself fixing the price at a
high figure in accordance with his estimate
of his own value). At Montiel in 1369 he
defeated and captured Pedro the Cruel.
He was made Constable of France and
successfully carried on the war against the
English.

Du Guillet, PERNETTE (*c.* 1520–45), born at
Lyons, a poetess of the school of Maurice
Scève (q.v., and cf. *Délie*), who died young,
leaving a number of short poems of some
merit.

Du Haillan, BERNARD PIRARD, SEIGNEUR
(1535–1610), born at Bordeaux, author of
an *Histoire générale des rois de France* (1576)
which in the main reproduces the *grandes
chroniques* (q.v.), amplifying them with
imaginary speeches and debates; a pioneer
work in the transition from chronicles to
history, seeking to present events in their
regular and logical development, though the
author lacked sympathetic understanding of
ancient times. The work was very popular
in its day.

Duhamel, GEORGES (1884–   ), poet,
novelist, dramatist, and essayist, was born in
Paris and had no very settled education.
After some years' wandering on foot across
Europe he studied medicine in Paris, at cost
of considerable hardship, and qualified in
1909. He was already writing. He had joined
forces with the *Abbaye* (q.v.) community
(and was for some time also associated with
the *unanimistes*, q.v.). His publications of
these years include poetry: *Des légendes, des
batailles* (1907, printed on the *Abbaye* press),
L'Homme en tête (1909, verse and prose),
Selon ma loi (1910), *Compagnons* (1912); and

plays: *La Lumière* (1911), *Le Combat* (1913). He was an army surgeon during the 1914–18 war and wrote two collections of sketches from his experiences: *Vie des martyrs* (1917) and the ironically-entitled *Civilisation 1914–17* (1918). The latter was awarded the Prix Goncourt. Both are unsparing descriptions of the hideous scenes in the hospitals behind the lines, but a tribute, also, to the heroism and amazing good fellowship of the wounded. They are full of the compassion for the suffering which is one of this author's strongest characteristics.

After 1920 Duhamel's career was mainly literary. His large output includes: the five *Salavin* (q.v.) novels (*Vie et Aventures de Salavin*, 1920–32), an absorbing study of an eccentric, over-sensitive character who sets out to become a saint; the *Chronique des Pasquier* (q.v., 1933–45), another cycle of novels; literary criticism (*Propos critiques*, 1912, *Paul Claudel*, 1913, *Essai sur le roman*, 1925); essays on various aspects of modern civilization (*La Possession du monde*, 1919, *Entretiens dans le tumulte*, 1919, *Entretien sur l'esprit européen*, 1928, *Scènes de la vie future*, 1930, *Au chevet de la civilisation*, 1938, &c.); 4 volumes of reminiscences (*Lumières sur ma vie*, 1950); some delightful nature studies, e.g. *Fables de mon jardin*, 1936; and some later poetry (*Élégies*, 1920, *Voix du vieux monde*, 1925) and plays (*L'Œuvre des athlètes*, 1920, *La Journée des aveux*, 1924, *Quand vous voudrez*, 1924).

Du Hausset, MME, *femme de chambre* to Mme de Pompadour and author of memoirs (published in 1809) throwing light on the latter's period of power.

Dujardin, ÉDOUARD (1861–1949), born near Blois, educated in Paris, was associated from the beginning with the Symbolist Movement (see *Symbolisme*). He founded the *Revue wagnérienne* (1885) and the *Revue indépendante* (1886), published verse, notably *Poésies* (1913) and *Mari Magno* (1922), and also two volumes of *Théâtre* (1920–4) containing some plays which, when produced, had been landmarks in the Symbolist drama. His novel, *Les Lauriers sont coupés* (1888), an early instance of the use of the *monologue intérieur* (stream of consciousness), is said to have given James Joyce the idea for the form of *Ulysses*.

Dujardin was also a distinguished writer

and lecturer on the history of religious belief.

Dukas, PAUL-ABRAHAM (1865–   ), French composer. His works include the music for Maeterlinck's *Ariane et Barbe-bleue* (prod. 1907) and the symphonic poem *L'Apprenti Sorcier*.

Dullin, CHARLES (1885–1949), actor and producer, founder of the *Théâtre de l'Atelier* (q.v.).

Du Maine, DUCHESSE, see *Maine*.

Dumarsais, CÉSAR CHESNEAU (1676–1750), a grammarian who lived and died in poverty, a hack contributor to *L'Encyclopédie* (q.v.). His *Traité des tropes* (1730) is also mentioned.

Dumas, ALEXANDRE [Dumas *père*] (1802–70), novelist and dramatist, was born at Villers-Cotterêts (q.v.) near Soissons, the grandson of the marquis Antoine-Alexandre Davy de la Pailleterie and a negress, Marie Dumas, with whom the grandfather had lived during twelve years spent in San Domingo. His father was Thomas-Alexandre Davy de la Pailleterie, who took the name of Dumas, fought in the Revolutionary armies and became a general, but later fell on bad times and died in poor circumstances in 1806. The young Alexandre Dumas's education was scanty. In 1822, thanks to his beautiful handwriting, he found employment in Paris in the household of the duc d'Orléans (afterwards Louis-Philippe, q.v.). He read voraciously, discovered Shakespeare, Scott, and Schiller, found his way into the *cénacles* (q.v.), and began to write. In 1829 his historical drama *Henri III et sa cour* (q.v.) was produced at the Théâtre Français with a success that was hailed as a triumph for the Romantics (see *Romantisme*) as well as for its author. It flung the dramatic conventions to the winds, took no account of the unities, and was written in prose. Also, more important from the box-office point of view, it was good, exciting drama. Dumas soon bettered its success with *Antony* (1831, q.v.), a society drama, and then with *La Tour de Nesle* (1832, q.v.), another historical drama; and for the next twenty years he was one of the most popular dramatists. Outstanding examples of his works in this genre are: *Charles VII chez ses grands vassaux* (1831, a tragedy), *Don Juan de Marana* (1836) and *Kean* (1836), dramas, if not melodramas; *Mademoiselle de Belle-Isle* (1839), *Un Mariage sous Louis XV* (1841), and *Les Demoiselles de Saint-Cyr* (1843), comedies.

About 1839 he turned to novel-writing, mainly historical novels, with even greater success. He frequently used collaborators, of whom Auguste Maquet (q.v.) was the best known, and digs were made at the 'Fabrique de romans Alexandre Dumas et Cⁱᵉ'; but the collaborators' share was confined to supplying plots or historical frameworks which depended on Dumas himself for life and development. He had great gifts of narrative and dialogue, and a powerful imagination, together with small critical sense, small care for historical accuracy, but an immense faculty for seizing the situations and characters that would best render historical atmosphere. He wrote with unflagging gusto and an instinctive conviction, uncomplicated by hankerings after psychology or analysis, that 'l'action et l'amour' were the two essential things in life, hence in fiction. His novels usually appeared first in the newspapers (see *Roman-feuilleton*), and throughout many years he kept his public palpitating from one day to the next while he 'elevated history to the dignity of the novel' (his own words), by means of romantic love-affairs, intrigues, imprisonments, hairbreadth escapes, and innumerable duels. His best work can still be read with effortless enjoyment.

His most brilliantly successful novel was non-historical—*Le Comte de Monte-Cristo* (1844–5, q.v.). His three series of historical novels are also famous: (*a*) *Les Trois Mousquetaires* (1844, q.v.), period *c.* 1625–8, the time of Louis XIII and Cardinal Richelieu; *Vingt ans après* (1845), period 1648–9, the time of the *Fronde* and the execution of Charles I; *Le Vicomte de Bragelonne* (1848–50), period 1660–73, a picture of the court of Louis XIV: (*b*) *La Reine Margot* (1845), period 1572–5, with a fine description of the massacre of Saint Bartholomew (cf. Mérimée's *Chronique du règne de Charles IX*) and the closing years of the reign of Charles IX; *La Dame de Monsoreau* (1846), period 1578–9, which introduces the well-known character of Chicot, the king's gentleman-jester, and has a sequel, *Les Quarante-Cinq* (1848), period 1584–5, dealing with the Guise intrigues: (*c*) *Mémoires d'un médecin:*

Joseph Balsamo (1846–8), a picture of court life and intrigues in the years between Marie-Antoinette's arrival in France and the death of Louis XV (the charlatan Balsamo, better known as Cagliostro, q.v., is one of the chief characters); *Le Collier de la Reine* (1849–50), period 1784–5, the story of the diamond necklace (see *Collier, L'Affaire du*); *Ange Pitou* (1851), period 1789 during the weeks before and after the fall of the Bastille, and *La Comtesse de Charny* (1852–5), period 1789–94. Another stirring historical novel *Le Chevalier de Maison-Rouge* (1845), not in this series, relates the conspiracy of the Chevalier de Rougeville to rescue Marie-Antoinette from the prison of the Temple. Three tales of country life, among his other works of fiction, call specially for mention: *Conscience l'innocent* (1852), *Catherine Blum* (1854), and *Le Meneur de loups* (1857). (Cf. also *La Chasse au chastre*.)

Dumas also wrote lively travel literature—*Impressions de voyage* to various places, beginning with reminiscences of a trip to Cadiz in 1846 (1847–8). In 22 volumes of *Mes Mémoires* (1852–5) the story of his life, told with verve, wit, enjoyment and perhaps inventiveness, becomes another novel of adventures: the volumes dealing with his early years, the beginnings of the Romantic Movement and the Revolution of 1830, are of special interest. His numerous other works include: a biographical study of Napoleon; amusing reminiscences of his menagerie of monkeys, parrots, fowls, cats, and almost legendary dogs (*Histoire de mes bêtes*, 1868); many popular children's stories (e.g. *Histoire d'un casse-noisette*, 1845, *La Bouillie de la comtesse Berthe*, 1845), and a *Grand Dictionnaire de cuisine*, by one who was himself an inspired cook (1873, posth.). His *Œuvres complètes* fill 103 volumes in the Calmann-Lévy edition. By his output, his exuberance, his popularity, the amount of money he made and his fantastic ease in spending it, he remains one of the prodigies of 19th-century French literature.

Dumas, ALEXANDRE [Dumas *fils*] (1824–95), novelist and dramatist, natural son of the above, born in Paris, took to literature to pay his debts. His novel *La Dame aux camélias* (1848, q.v.) made him famous immediately and when dramatized (1852) was said to have brought the heart back to the stage. He became one of the most successful dramatists of the Second Empire. His plays were well constructed, showed good theatre-sense, and contained some excellent dialogue, but they were marred by an increasing tendency to preach reform of evils (which they depicted freely). Among the most notable were *Le Demi-Monde* (1855), *La Question d'argent* (1857), *Le Fils naturel* (1858), *L'Ami des femmes* (1864), *Les Idées de Mme Aubray* (1867), *La Femme de Claude* (1873), *La Princesse de Bagdad* (1881), *Denise* (1885), *Francillon* (1887). The collected edition of his plays (*Théâtre complet*, 1868–92, 7 vols.) includes a series of interesting prefaces. His semi-autobiographical novel *L'Affaire Clemenceau* (1886) is still remembered.

Duméril, ÉDELESTAND PONTUS (1801–71), literary historian, philologist, and palaeographer, known for his studies and editions of the popular poetry of the Middle Ages: *Histoire de la poésie scandinave* (1839); *Essai philosophique sur le principe et la formation de la versification* (1841); *Essai sur l'origine des runes* (1844); *Poésies populaires latines du moyen âge* (1847); *Poésies inédites du moyen âge* (1854).

Dumouriez, CHARLES-FRANÇOIS (1739–1823), born at Cambrai, Commander-in-Chief of the Revolutionary armies, had the victories of Valmy and Jemmapes (qq.v.) to his credit but in 1793 went over to the enemy and was relieved of his command. He died in obscurity in England.

Dunois, JEAN (1402–68), also known as the *Bâtard d'Orléans*, natural son of Louis d'Orléans, brother of Charles VI, celebrated for his prowess in the Hundred Years War, in which he fought by the side of Jeanne d'Arc.

Dupanloup, MONSEIGNEUR FÉLIX-ANTOINE-PHILIBERT (1802–78), theologian and educationalist, a noted preacher and polemist, later canon of Notre-Dame and Bishop of Orleans. His published works (chiefly educational treatises of a reactionary character) included: *De l'éducation* (1851), *De la haute éducation intellectuelle* (1866), &c. His *Lettres sur l'éducation des filles* (1867–8), however, advocated greater freedom of education for girls.

Dupérier, FRANÇOIS, remembered as the friend to whom Malherbe (q.v.) addressed a famous ode on the death of his daughter Rose in 1599.

Du Perron, JACQUES DAVY (1556–1618), Archbishop of Sens, cardinal in 1604, an orator and a formidable religious controversialist; remembered, for instance, as the victor in the *Conférence de Fontainebleau*, a debate on Catholicism *v.* Protestantism organized by Henri IV. (Duplessis-Mornay, q.v., was an opponent.) He was also esteemed as a writer of light poetry (disciple of Ronsard) and of some official heroic poems, and a witty critic. He introduced Malherbe to Henri IV.

Dupes, Journée des, 11 November 1630, the day on which the Queen Mother and Anne of Austria, having previously during the illness of Louis XIII obtained his promise that he would dismiss Richelieu, thought that they had finally secured his downfall. But Richelieu defeated their scheme and retained the king's confidence.

Dupin, AURORE, see *Sand, George.*

Dupin, JEAN-HENRI (1787–1887), author of over 200 vaudevilles and light comedies. He usually wrote in collaboration, very often with Scribe (q.v.), to whom, he said, he had taught his craft in the first place, or with Dumersan (1780–1849).

Dupin, LOUIS-ELLIES (1657–1719), religious historian. His lengthy *Nouvelle Bibliothèque des auteurs ecclésiastiques*, in fifty-eight volumes, was too strong in some of its criticisms, notably of the Pope's authority, and was suppressed by the *Parlement* in 1696. Later, Dupin was removed from his chair of philosophy at the Collège de France because of his Jansenist tendencies.

Dupleix (pron. as if *Dupleks*), JOSEPH-FRANÇOIS (1697–1763), governor of the French possessions in India, an able administrator and gallant soldier. The rivalry of La Bourdonnais defeated his efforts to extend the French rule in that country; he was recalled and his merits were left unrecognized.

Duplessis, MARIE (1824–47), a well-known courtesan in the Paris of the eighteen-forties, the prototype of Marguerite Gautier in *La Dame aux camélias* (q.v.) by Dumas *fils*. She came originally from a poverty-stricken home in a Normandy village. Her real name was Alphonsine Plessis.

Duplessis-Mornay, PHILIPPE DE MORNAY, SEIGNEUR DU PLESSIS (1549–1623), political philosopher, theologian, and Huguenot leader, author of a famous Latin work, *Vindiciae contra tyrannos* (1578), in which the theory of popular sovereignty and consequent limitation of the rights of monarchy is carried to its ultimate consequence, the right of rebellion; and of a *Traité de la vérité de la religion chrestienne* (1581), in which, from the standpoint of a broad-minded and cultured Protestant, he urges religious appeasement; also of a *Traité de l'Eucharistie* (1598). (Cf. also *Du Perron*.)

Du Plessys, MAURICE (1864–1924), poet, one of the *École romane* (q.v.), author of *Dédicace à Appolodore* (1891), *Études lyriques* (1896), *Odes olympiques* (1912), &c.

Dupont, PIERRE (1821–70), writer of *chansons*, son of a Lyons blacksmith, came to Paris as a young man and soon became a popular author of patriotic songs which at their best rivalled those of Béranger (q.v.). He wrote most successfully of peasant life — *Les Bœufs* (1846, *J'ai deux grands bœufs dans mon étable*), *Le Chant des ouvriers* (1848), *Le Chant des paysans* (1849), *Le Chant du pain* (1849), &c.

The 1851–4 edition of his *Chants et chansons*, with music by Ernest Reyer (1828–1909), has a laudatory preface by Baudelaire (q.v.).

Dupont de Nemours, PIERRE-SAMUEL (1739–1817), political economist and politician. In the former capacity he belonged to the school of the physiocrats or *économistes* (q.v.) and popularized their doctrines by his writings. He was a friend of Turgot and supported him during his brief tenure of power; later he was a deputy to the *États généraux* in 1789 and (after a period of proscription) a member of the *Conseil des Anciens* in 1795. His hostility to the *Directoire* led to his voluntary emigration to America.

Dupuis et Cotonet, see *Lettres de Dupuis et Cotonet*.

Dupuis et Desronais, a comedy in *vers libres* (q.v.) by Collé, produced in 1763, combining the gay and the touching.

The play has little action, showing two lovers, Desronais and Marianne, in conflict with the obstinacy of the latter's father, Dupuis, who loves them both, but refuses to allow them to marry so as the better to retain their affection for himself.

Durandal or **Durendal,** in the *chansons de geste* (q.v.), the name of the sword of Roland (q.v.).

Durant, ESTIENNE (1585–1618), a poet at the court of Marie de Médicis. He had some share in spreading defamatory libels against the king, was convicted of *lèse-majesté*, broken on the wheel and burnt. His few works included a novel, *Les Épines d'amour* (1604), and a collection of love-poems—*Méditations*—sonnets and elegies expressing genuine feeling. Only a very few copies of these were published, clandestinely, in 1611.

Durant, GILLES (1550–1615), jurist and poet, author of the *Trespas de l'asne ligueur*, a witty piece of mockery appended to the *Satire Ménippée* (q.v.), and of various lyrics of some merit, marked here and there by a melancholy, meditative spirit.

Duranty, PHILIPPE (1833–80), novelist, born in Paris, was a leader of the *réalistes* (see *Réalisme* and cf. *Champfleury*) but later joined the *naturalistes* (see *Naturalisme*). His best and most typical novel, *Le Malheur d'Henriette Gérard* (1860, q.v.), is a study of provincial life.

Duras, CLAIRE LECHAT DE KERSAINT, MME DE (1778–1828), born at Brest (Brittany), was the wife of the duc de Duras, a returned *émigré* who received many honours from Louis XVIII. Her literary *salon* was among the most brilliant of the Restoration period, and she herself wrote two remarkably successful short novels, *Ourika* (1824) and *Édouard* (1825). Her characters are consumed by passions that for reasons of social inequality cannot be satisfied. A young negress, brought up from childhood in a rich, cultivated French household, burns with hopeless love for a noble young Frenchman; her race is the barrier to her happiness (*Ourika*). A young man, son of an ironmaster, is adopted by a nobleman and falls in love with his adopted sister. He realizes that his love cannot be told (*Édouard*). Ourika retires to a nunnery and dies. Édouard goes to a soldier's death. The tales are told with great simplicity.

Durkheim, ÉMILE (1858–1917), sometimes called the father of modern sociology, was one of the best known of a number of French sociologists (cf. *Tarde, G.*; *Lévy-Bruhl, L.*) prominent about 1900. He founded (1898) *L'Année sociologique*, the first sociological review. His most important work was *Les Règles de la méthode sociologique* (1895). After this come: *De la division du travail social* (1893); *Le Suicide* (1897), which he considers a social phenomenon rather than a matter of individual impulse; and *Les Formes élémentaires de la vie religieuse: le système totémique en Australie* (1912), a study of moral systems as products of social evolution.

Durtain, LUC [pseud. of André Nepveu] (1881–), born in Paris, and a doctor by profession, was associated with the *Abbaye* and *Unanimiste* (qq.v.) groups of writers. His works include: poetry: *L'Étape nécessaire* (1907), *Pégase* (1908), *Kong Harald* (1914, a sea-trip round the Norwegian coast), *Le Retour des hommes* (1920, an army doctor's poems of trench warfare), *Perspectives* (1924), *Quatre continents* (1935), &c.; essays: *Face à face, ou Le Poète et toi* (1921); plays: *Le Donneur de sang* (1929), *Le Mari singulier* (1937); novels: *Douze cent mille* (1922), *La Source rouge* (1924), *Le Globe sous le bras* (1936), *La Femme en sandales* (1937), &c. Each novel is complete in itself but a generic title, *Les Conquêtes du monde*, signifies a common theme, namely, man's discovery of his true self, hidden by successive layers of convention and conformism.

Durtal, the character whose spiritual progress is recorded in a number of novels by J.-K. Huysmans (q.v.), beginning with *Là-bas*.

Duruy, VICTOR (1811–94), ancient historian. His chief works include: *Histoire des Romains* (1843–5 and later, augmented editions) and *Histoire des Grecs* (1887–9). Duruy held office for a time at the *Ministère de l'instruction publique*, where he did much to modernize and improve the teaching of history in universities.

Du Ryer, PIERRE (c. 1600–58), dramatist, a contemporary of Corneille and Rotrou. He succeeded his father as 'secrétaire de la chambre du roi' and later became secretary to the duc de Vendôme. After 1640 he appears to have supported himself by his dramas and by translations from the classics. His early dramatic work (1630–4) consisted of tragi-comedies, *Argénis et Poliarque*, *Lisandre et Caliste*, *Cléomédon*, *Alcimédon*, romantic or heroic plays crowded with incident and devoid of study of character or manners. His *Clarigène* (published 1639) shows an advance, presenting a conflict of generosity between two friends. A play of some interest is the author's pastoral, *Les Vendanges de Suresne* (q.v., 1635). His later tragi-comedies include *Bérénice* (in prose, 1645), *Nitocris* (1650), *Anaxandre* (published 1655). But Du Ryer's most important work is to be found in his tragedies: *Lucrèce* (published in 1638, on the story of Tarquin and Lucretia), *Alcionée* (q.v., a successful romantic tragedy, published in 1640), *Saül* (published in 1642, Saul struggling with the divine power against the punishment called down by his sin); *Esther* (probably produced in 1642, published in 1644); *Scévole* (q.v.), regarded as his masterpiece, probably produced in 1644, published in 1647. His last tragedy *Thémistocle* (1646 or 1647) deals with the residence of the exiled Themistocles at the court of Persia. Du Ryer was at his best in his two Roman plays.

Dussault, FRANÇOIS-JOSEPH (1769–1824), man of letters and critic on the *Journal des Débats* (q.v.) in its early days. His articles in this paper were collected in book-form—*Annales littéraires* (1824). Mme d'Abrantès (q.v.) calls him a very just critic who read books before he wrote about them.

Du Vair, GUILLAUME (1556–1621), statesman and moral philosopher, born in Paris of a noble family of Auvergne. As deputy of the city of Paris at the *États généraux* of the Ligue (q.v.) in 1593, he strongly supported the candidature of Henri de Navarre to the French crown. He was sent on a mission to Queen Elizabeth I in 1596. In his last years, under Henri IV, he was Chancellor of France, also Bishop of Lisieux. A creator of French prose in his political discourses (notably his *Exhortation à la paix*), Du Vair was also important as a Christian moralist, by his paraphrases of the *Psaumes de la Pénitence* and the *Psaumes de la Consolation* (c. 1580), also later of Job, Jeremiah, and Isaiah, by his treatises *De la Sainte Philosophie* (*c.* 1580), *De la Philosophie morale des Stoïques*, and by his translation of the *Manual* of Epictetus (*c.* 1585). In the latter works he called ancient philosophy to the support of the Christian faith. His *Traité de la constance et consolation ès calamités publiques* is a remarkable Ciceronian dialogue, composed during the civil war, in which three of his friends, men distinguished for character and learning, discourse on constancy in misfortunes, on the role of Providence, and on faith in a future life. Du Vair also wrote a *Traité de l'éloquence française* in which he attributed its poverty to the excess of erudition that it sought to display. Malherbe received guidance and advice from him.

Duval, ALEXANDRE (1767–1842), author of numerous dramas and comedies, had a varied career at sea, in the army, as an engineer, architect, painter, and actor. He ended up as librarian of the *Bibliothèque de l'Arsenal* (q.v.) and a member of the *Académie française*. Performances of *Édouard en Écosse ou la Nuit d'un proscrit* (1802), an historical drama, and his best-remembered work, were prohibited by Bonaparte's police as likely to arouse monarchist sympathies.

Duval, JEANNE, a mulatto, the *Vénus noire* of many of Baudelaire's (q.v.) poems.

Duval, PAUL, see *Lorrain, Jean.*

Du Verdier, ANTOINE (1544–1600), remembered as an early bibliographer, compiler of *La Bibliothèque d'Antoine Duverdier*

contenant le catalogue de tous les auteurs qui ont écrit ou traduit en français, 1580 (see also *La Croix du Maine*).

Du Vergier de Hauranne, JEAN (1581–1643), ABBÉ DE SAINT-CYRAN, born at Bayonne, theologian and mystic, a man of ardent and contagious piety and great austerity, director from 1635 of Port-Royal (q.v.). He introduced there the religious conceptions of his friend Jansenius (q.v.), with whom for some years from about 1611 he had studied the Fathers, and especially St. Augustine, at Bayonne. He was imprisoned by order of Richelieu from 1638 to 1643, for what precise reason is unknown, but generally, no doubt, from suspicion of his great spiritual power. He was author of religious and controversial works, and his correspondence with Jansenius and other letters have been published. His *Petrus Aurelius*, a collection of Latin pamphlets in defence of the rights of the bishops against the Jesuits and monks, appeared in 1632–3 and met with great success. (Du Vergier de Hauranne was the name of three prominent 19th-century liberal politicians who belonged to the same family as the abbé de Saint-Cyran.)

Duvernois, HENRI (1875–1937), author of numerous tales in which everyday people and their foibles were described with a mixture of irony and indulgence (*Crapotte*, 1908, *Edgar*, 1919). Some were dramatized.

Dynamisme, see *Literary isms.*

E

Eau de Jouvence, L', one of Renan's *Drames philosophiques* (q.v.).

Eaux et Forêts, a branch of the French Government service which deals with the conservation of national waterways and forests. It has been under the *Ministère des Finances* since the Revolution, but it originated well back in the *ancien régime*. La Fontaine (q.v.) succeeded his father in 1647 as *Maître des Eaux et Forêts*. The *École nationale des eaux et forêts*, or *forestière*, at Nancy, provides the two years' specialized training required.

École alsacienne, a well-known Protestant boys' school in Paris, founded 1873, and privately run. Gide (q.v.) was an early pupil.

École de Rome (the *Villa Médicis*, at Rome), originally an offshoot of Mazarin's *Académie de peinture et sculpture* (q.v.). Painters, sculptors, musicians, &c. who win the *Grand Prix de Rome* are entitled to three years' residence here.

École des bourgeois, L', a comedy of manners by d'Allainval, produced in 1728, one of the best of the period between Lesage and Beaumarchais.

The marquis de Moncade proposes to restore his fortunes by marrying Benjamine, the daughter of a rich *bourgeois* widow, Mme Abraham. He sinks his pride and flatters the family; but an imprudent letter to a noble friend inviting him to the wedding and revealing his sentiments of contempt for the family with which he is allying himself falls into the wrong hands and defeats the project.

École des femmes, L', a comedy by Molière in five acts in verse, produced in 1662.

Arnolphe has been accustomed to scoff at husbands who suffer by the infidelity of their wives. In order to avoid a similar fate himself, he has caused Agnès, supposed to be a peasant's daughter, to be so brought up that she shall remain in the most unsophisticated innocence, and designs to marry her. But during his absence, Horace, a young man, makes her acquaintance, falls in love with her, and thanks to her very artlessness is enabled to gain access to her and win her heart. The situation is made more comic by the fact that the young man confides the successive steps of his amour to Arnolphe, in ignorance of the latter's relation to the girl. Agnès runs away with Horace, is entrusted by him unsuspectingly to Arnolphe, and is about to be hurried off by the latter to a convent, when it is discovered that she is the daughter of the wealthy Enrique, who has arranged with the father of Horace to marry her to the young man.

The play was severely criticized from a literary and a moral point of view. Molière replied to his adversaries in the *Critique de l'École des Femmes* and (attacking more especially his dramatic rivals) in *L'Impromptu de Versailles* (qq.v.).

École des jaloux, L', a comedy by Montfleury (q.v.), produced in 1664.

Santillane so worries his wife Léonor with his jealous suspicion that his brother-in-law, the Governor of Cadiz, to cure him of his mania, contrives to have him and his wife carried off by pretended Turkish corsairs. The Grand Turk, it appears, proposes to make Léonor his favourite. Léonor resists, wishing to remain faithful to her husband. To overcome this obstacle and give Léonor

her freedom, the Turk proposes to hang Santillane. Santillane now begs Léonor to put aside her scruples, accept the Turk's proposal, and so save his life.

École des langues orientales vivantes, in Paris, founded 1869, an *école spéciale* (q.v.) for the training of consuls and interpreters, with an approach to the subjects studied that is more practical than profoundly academic.

École des maris, L', a comedy in three acts in verse by Molière, produced in 1661.

The play borrows from the *Adelphi* of Terence the contrast of two educations, one indulgent, the other severe, but applied not to boys but to girls. The harsh guardian Sganarelle has brought up Isabelle with the utmost austerity and destines her to be his wife. Ariste has brought up her sister Léonor on the opposite method and places no restraint on her inclinations. Isabelle detests Sganarelle and pays him out, when he signifies his intention of marrying her in a week, by making him the unwitting means of conveying to Valère, whom she loves, the state of her affections, and finally fools him into assenting to her marriage with her lover in the belief that it is not herself but her sister Léonor (so laxly brought up by his brother) who has taken refuge in the young man's house and is to be married to him.

École libre des sciences politiques, see *Institut d'études politiques.*

École militaire. This, the first military college in France, was founded by Louis XV in 1751, at the instance of Mme de Pompadour, for 500 'fils de gentilshommes nés sans biens ou morts à la guerre'. Construction to the plans of the architect Gabriel (q.v.) began in 1752, the college itself opened in 1760, and the chapel (in which the *cadet gentilhomme* Napoléon Bonaparte was confirmed) in 1769. One façade of the building extends along the north-west end of the Champ-de-Mars (q.v.), which was originally its *champ-de-manœuvres*. In 1792 the École militaire was transformed into barracks. In 1803 an École militaire was again founded, by the First Consul Bonaparte, at Fontainebleau (see *Saint-Cyr*).

École nationale des Chartes, in Paris, founded 1821, the State *école spéciale* (q.v.) for archivists and librarians. The subjects studied are palaeography, methods of documentary and bibliographical research, the handling of ancient records (the *chartes* or archives of the history of France) and, generally, the science of diplomatic. A thesis must be presented for the diploma of *Archiviste-paléographe*.

École normale, École normale supérieure. An *école normale*, or *école normale primaire*, is a State training college for primary school teachers. The idea was projected by Napoleon but only put into force in 1831 under the July Monarchy (q.v.). There are two *écoles normales* in every *département* (q.v.), one for men and one for women. The biographical description, however, of *normalien* or 'educated at the *École normale*' signifies that the subject of the biography spent his three or four university years at the famous *école spéciale* (q.v.) known as the *École normale supérieure*, in Paris. This in its original form dates from 1794 and the vast schemes of the *Convention nationale* for a comprehensive State system of secondary education. It was again established in 1808, by a decree of Napoleon, as an autonomous body, to ensure a continual supply of teaching staff for the *université impériale* created by the same decree. It underwent occasional periods of closure in the first half of the 19th century, but since 1843 it has existed without interruption in its own premises in the rue d'Ulm, not far from the Sorbonne. Since 1903 it has been affiliated to the Sorbonne and its students, of whom some are boarders, follow the recognized university courses and sit for the usual university degrees in science and the humanities. Lectures on some subjects, also specialized training in teaching, are still organized by the *École* itself. Students who have passed their university examinations, and especially those students who wish to go on to teach in the State-controlled *lycées* (q.v.), usually follow this up by sitting the very severe competitive examination known as the *concours d'agrégation* (q.v.), though this is not obligatory. Students of the *École normale supérieure* are usually the carefully sifted pick of the whole country's *lycées* and *collèges*. They form a close corporation, with their own customs and a special *École normale* jargon which can be studied in, for instance, the conversations of Jerphanion and Jallez, the two *normaliens* in *Les Hommes de bonne volonté* (q.v.). They are said to carry with them through life the *esprit normalien*, a

mental attitude characterized by intellectual arrogance, a sceptical outlook, a cynical wit, a taste for paradox, and in literature a distaste for innovations. There has seldom been a period when the staff of the *École normale* did not include some of the greatest of French savants. Equally, many of the greatest French thinkers, writers, and public figures have been *normaliens*. Nor do by any means all students of the *École normale* make teaching their career. A fact long recognized is that its glory is 'autant ou plus de donner au pays des savants et des écrivains que de pourvoir les classes de professeurs'.

An *École normale secondaire de jeunes filles*, from which teachers in girls' secondary schools are similarly recruited, was founded in 1881, at first at Sèvres.

École palatine, an academy for the promotion of learning and literature founded *c.* 782 by Charlemagne. He attached it to his palace household (hence *palatine*, from Lat. 'palatium', a palace) and placed Alcuin (q.v.), whom he had met in Italy, at its head. Women as well as men attended. Theology, grammar, and rhetoric were subjects of discussion. Poems were read, and riddles propounded. A practice was for members of the academy to go by names taken from antiquity. Charlemagne himself was David. Alcuin was Albinus Flaccus.

École polytechnique, L', in Paris, one of the most famous of the State-run *écoles spéciales*. It is of military status and of very high standard. After a two years' training its pupils are commissioned in the artillery or the engineers, or appointed to the engineering branches of the public services, or take up other careers requiring a highly developed knowledge of the mathematical, physical, and chemical sciences. Founded in 1794, it owes its existence, like many other French educational institutions, to the *Convention nationale*. Its status at first was civilian, its pupils were day pupils. Napoleon transformed it into a military college for boarders.

A distinctive feature of the uniform worn by the Polytechniciens is the *bicorne*, a cocked hat.

École pratique des hautes études, founded in 1868, in Paris, a graduate school for advanced research in history, philology, mathematics, physics, and natural science and, since 1886, in the historical and comparative study of religion. Work is conducted on the seminar system, by critical and laboratory rather than by theoretic methods. No degrees are conferred (cf. *Collège de France*) but on presentation of a thesis students may obtain a diploma which carries with it high academic distinction. This institution is united to the Sorbonne.

École romane, the name adopted about 1891 by a group of young poets (Jean Moréas, Charles Maurras, Ernest Raynaud, Maurice du Plessys, Raymond de la Tailhède, qq.v., &c.). They hoped, in opposition to the Symbolists (see *Symbolisme*), to revive the Greco-Latin traditions which had influenced French poetry of the 16th and 17th centuries. Archaic words and expressions characterized their writing.

Écoles françaises d'Archéologie, institutions, founded 1846 (one at Athens and one at Rome), for post-graduate study in the language, history, and archaeology of ancient Greece and Rome. (Cf. the similar British Schools.)

Écoles libres, privately-run schools, generally denominational and for the most part Roman Catholic. In Paris, the Collège Sainte-Barbe and the Collège Stanislas, and also the École alsacienne (qq.v.), are *écoles libres*, the first two Roman Catholic, the third Protestant.

Écoles spéciales, State-run institutes of higher education, intended for the training of students for specialized careers, e.g. learned, academic, diplomatic, &c. Admission is by competitive examination, the *concours général*.

Écolier limousin, see *Pantagruel*.

Économie politique, Traité de l', see *Montchrétien, Antoine de.*

Économies royales, the short title under which Sully's *Mémoires* are known. The full title, which occupies three paragraphs, runs: 'Mémoires des sages et royales économies d'état... de Henri le grand l'exemplaire des rois . . . et des servitudes utiles . . . et administrations loyales de Maximilien de Béthune . . . dédiés à la France, à tous les bons soldats et tous peuples françois'.

Économistes, a name given in the latter part of the 18th century to the physiocrats or school of Quesnay and Gournay (qq.v.), who held that land was the only source of wealth (to which manufacture and commerce added nothing), and increase of the products of the soil the only means to prosperity. Property in land for them was the basis of the social order. Hence follow the idea of a single tax, to be levied on the land; the limitation of authority by laws defending the rights and liberties of agriculture; the doctrine of *laisser faire* (in effect unrestricted competition among individuals working on an equal footing). The views of the school, of which Turgot was the most eminent disciple, are clearly set out in the writings of Dupont de Nemours (q.v.), *Origine et progrès d'une science nouvelle* (1768), *Abrégé des principes* (1773), &c. However defective its views may have been, the school may be said to have founded the science of political economy in France. The *économistes* and the *philosophes* had some principles in common and there was considerable sympathy between them. Quesnay was a collaborator in the *Encyclopédie*.

Écossaise, L', (1) a tragedy by Montchrétien (q.v.), published in 1601, on the death of Mary Queen of Scots (the correct title is *La Reine d'Écosse*); (2) a sentimental comedy with a satirical purpose, in one act in prose, by Voltaire, produced in 1760, directed against Fréron (q.v.), the critic of the *Encyclopédie* and of Voltaire himself. In it Fréron under the name of 'Frélon' (altered to 'Wasp' when the play was acted) is depicted as a rascally journalist and political spy, who plays a part in a quarrel between two Scottish families. The comedy is of no literary merit, and has importance only as an incident in the conflict between the *philosophes* and their opponents.

Écriture artiste, the term used by Edmond and Jules de Goncourt (qq.v.) to describe their nervous, mannered, impressionistic style. ('Écrire, selon l'exemple des Goncourt, c'est forger des métaphores nouvelles, c'est n'ouvrir sa phrase qu'à des images inédites ou retravaillées, déformées par le passage forcé au laminoir du cerveau. . . . C'est avoir un don particulier et une sensibilité spéciale.' Remy de Gourmont, *Masques.*)

Écriture automatique. Automatic writing was the form of literary composition favoured by the *surréalistes* in the early days of the movement (see *Surréalisme*). They sat prepared with pencil and blank paper and wrote down whatever words and phrases entered their heads. There was no preconceived subject, and no mental censorship was supposed to operate; and the effect was often one of nightmarish incoherence. *Les Champs magnétiques* (1921), by A. Breton and P. Soupault, is said to have been written in this way.

Édit de Nantes, an edict of Henri IV dated 13 April 1598, by which the Protestants were granted liberty of conscience, the right of public worship according to their tenets in certain localities, and admissibility to all offices, together with some safeguards: certain towns, for instance, such as La Rochelle, Montauban, Cognac, were constituted *places de sûreté*. The Edict was revoked by Louis XIV in 1685.

Édition. In a bibliographical sense this word has the same meaning in French and in English, viz. the total number of copies of a book, pamphlet, &c., printed from one setting-up of type ('composition'). In referring to first editions, i.e. the total number of copies printed from the original setting-up of type, the terms *édition princeps*, *première édition*, and *édition originale* are all found. *Édition princeps* is usually confined to the first printed edition—i.e. in the early days of printing—of a work originally known and circulated in manuscript form. *Première édition* and *édition originale* are used of modern works.

The total number of copies of which an edition consists is not necessarily determined in advance or all printed at one time. If the first run, or printing (*tirage*, *impression*), is not sufficiently large to meet demands it may, if all that is needed is a reprint pure and simple, be succeeeded by further printings (*nouveaux tirages*; *nouvelles impressions*; *réimpressions*), but these still form part of the one edition. On the other hand, if modifications, suppressions, or additions which have become necessary, or loss or dispersal of type due to lapse of time, involve partial or complete resetting of type, the copies then printed belong to a *deuxième*, or *nouvelle*, *édition*. And so on.

The term *édition originale* rather than *première édition* is usually employed in the case of modern and contemporary works (particularly modern novels, or works issued in *éditions de luxe*) likely to be of interest to collectors (and a complication may be noted here in the use, especially by booksellers, of *deuxième édition originale*, *troisième*, &c., for works like Montaigne's *Essais* or Baudelaire's *Fleurs du mal*, where considerable new material is added in later editions). If, again, the work is illustrated the word used may be *tirage* rather than *édition*. In such a case the copies are usually numbered serially, since it may happen that the printing of the illustrations is less clear in the later than the earlier numbers.

The following description of the *édition originale*, made up of sets of copies printed on various types of paper, is taken from the reverse of the title-page of a novel (*L'Imposteur*) by the contemporary author Marcel Jouhandeau:

'Il a été tiré de cet ouvrage, . . . trois mille trois cent trente-neuf exemplaires, à savoir: trente-deux exemplaires sur vergé de Montval satiné, numérotés Montval 1 à 20 et i à xii; cent sept exemplaires sur vélin pur fil . . . numérotés vélin pur fil 1 à 95 et i à xii; deux mille huit cent cinquante exemplaires sur Alfa Mousse . . .; et trois cent cinquante exemplaires de presse sur vélin Édita [a trade mark] des Papeteries Prioux, numérotés vélin Édita s.p. 1 à s.p. CCCL. le tout constituant l'édition originale.'

Éducation des filles, L', see *Traité de l'éducation des filles.*

Éducation sentimentale, L' (1869), a novel by Gustave Flaubert, preferrred by some critics to his *Madame Bovary*. (A first version, which was abandoned for the time being, was written between 1843 and 1845.) It belongs to the type of realistic fiction which depicts uneventful lives in detail upon a consistently low note, and in this case with consummate artistry. The political and social background are painted with such fidelity, the ideals and enthusiasms against which the characters are seen, in which at times they share, that the book has been called Flaubert's *Atelier du peintre*, and its value as the picture of an era is generally recognized.

It begins during the reign of Louis-

Philippe. Frédéric Moreau, the hero, is in Paris to study law. He has various dreams and ambitions, no driving enthusiasm. He inherits money, which allows him to lead a life of pleasure without working. He is in love with Mme Arnoux, the wife of an amiable sensualist and waster. This devotion dates from the day when, as an eighteen-year-old student returning home for the vacation, he had first encountered Mme Arnoux. [Cf. Flaubert himself who, at sixteen, fell in love with Mme Maurice Schlésinger, the wife of a Paris editor, whom he met equally by chance and to whom he was devoted for most of his life.] But it remains idealistic, partly owing to circumstances but more because in its nature it is a sort of prolonged, timid, tender calf-love. He does have one or two half-hearted though less Platonic love-affairs (one of them at its height during the spring of 1848), and he is nearly drawn into marriage. Arnoux and his family disappear from Paris after a financial crash. Frédéric travels, aimlessly, then returns to Paris. Once, after nearly twenty years of a monotonous, unthinking existence, he is surprised by a visit from Mme Arnoux. They talk of the past and of what might have been, for she had guessed his love and returned it. Then she goes, leaving him a lock of her hair, now white. 'Et ce fut tout.' Sometimes, in the evenings, Frédéric and his friend Dussardier sit by the fire recalling the companions, the ambitions, and escapades of their youth.

Effarés, Les, an early poem by Rimbaud (q.v.), one of twenty-two written in 1870, when he was sixteen, and entrusted to a friend for safe keeping. It is about five urchins, crouched in the cold against the grid of a bakehouse, lost to everything but the sight of the baker at work and the fine, hot smell of the new bread.

Effrénéisme, see *Literary Isms.*

Eginhard or **Einhard** (*c.* 770–840), a Frankish scholar, educated at the monastery of Fulda, who was distinguished for his learning at the court of Charlemagne. He assisted in promoting the revival of letters associated with the emperor's name and wrote a Latin life of him which is important as a probable source of the *Chanson de Roland* (q.v.).

Eichendorff, JOSEPH FREIHERR VON (1788–1857), German romantic writer, born in Upper Silesia, one of the foreign precursors of the romantic movement in France. He was pre-eminently a lyric poet, but he also wrote short romantic tales (e.g. the well-known *Aus dem Leben eines Taugenichts,* 1826) and dramas. He was in Paris in 1808, and fought in the Prussian army in 1814–15.

Eiffel Tower, see *Tour Eiffel.*

Élan vital, see *Bergson.*

Elba, the small (now Italian) island in the Mediterranean over which Napoleon was allowed to retain sovereignty and to which he retired when he abdicated in 1814. He escaped after ten months.

El Desdichado, see *Chimères, Les.*

Élections, see *Fiscal system.*

Éliacin, the name by which the child Joas, in Racine's *Athalie* (q.v.), was known while he was kept secretly in the Temple.

Éliante, in Molière's *Le Misanthrope* (q.v.), cousin of *Célimène.*

Elioxe, see *Chevalier au Cygne.*

Élision, in French prosody, the suppression, in pronunciation, of the final mute *e* of a word when followed in the same line by a word beginning with a vowel or a mute *h.* For instance, in the line,
    Assise auprès du feu, dévidant et filant,
the last vowel of 'assise' is elided. (Cf. *Hiatus.*)

Élisabeth, ou Les Exilés de Sibérie (1806), a novel by Mme Sophie Cottin (q.v.). A young girl undertakes the difficult journey from Siberia to St. Petersburg with no equipment but a passionate longing to procure the Tsar's pardon for her exiled father. The tale was retold some years later, with less highly coloured detail, in *La Jeune Sibérienne* by Xavier de Maistre (q.v.).

Élixir de longue vie, L', one of the 'Études philosophiques' in Balzac's *Comédie humaine* (q.v.).

Ellénore, heroine of *Adolphe* (q.v.), by Benjamin Constant.

Elle et lui (1859), by George Sand, her version of her liaison with Alfred de Musset (qq.v.).

Elmire, the wife of Orgon in Molière's *Le Tartuffe* (q.v.).

Éloa, a narrative poem in three cantos, called by the author, Alfred de Vigny, a *mystère*. It was written in 1823, first published in 1824, then included in the 'livre mystique' of *Poèmes antiques et modernes* (1826, q.v.). Éloa, an angel of pity born of one of Christ's tears, leaves Paradise to find and save the banished Lucifer. On the confines of Hell she meets him, 'l'Ange ténébreux', 'jeune, triste et charmant', 'exilé' and 'réprouvé'; and she listens. For a moment her innocence fills him with nostalgia for his lost purity, but when he sees her half-sensing danger and about to take wing again he once more becomes 'l'ennemi séducteur' and swears that her love and her voluntary exile from Paradise alone can save him. She turns back:

> Je t'aime et je descends. Mais . . .
> Où me conduisez-vous, bel Ange? . . .
> . . . Qui donc es-tu? — Satan.

Éloge de Richardson, see *Diderot*, para. 5.

Éloi, Saint (*Saint Eligius*) (588–659), a skilful goldsmith who gained the favour of the Merovingian kings Clotaire II and Dagobert, and became the latter's treasurer and bishop of Noyon. A life of him was written in verse at Noyon in the 13th century.

Elstir, in Proust's *A la recherche du temps perdu* (q.v.), a famous painter whose life touches Marcel's (q.v.) at many points, e.g. through his former connexion with the Verdurin *salon* where he was known as 'Monsieur Biche'. Marcel gets to know him, and through him Albertine, whom he will one day love, on a first holiday at Balbec. Their many talks quicken Marcel's interest in the Impressionist painters.

Éluard, PAUL (1895–1952), one of the finest of modern French poets, a love-poet, was a leader of the *surréalistes* (see *Surréalisme*) during the early years of the movement. His works include: *Le Devoir et l'Inquiétude* (1917); *Mourir de ne pas mourir* (1924); *Capitale de la douleur* (1926); *L'Amour de la poésie* (1929); *L'Immaculée Conception* (1930, in collaboration with another surrealist leader, André Breton); *La Vie immédiate* (1932); *La Rose publique* (1934); *Les Yeux fertiles* (1936); *Les Mains libres* (1937); *Cours naturel* (1938), &c. Good selections of his poems, made by himself, are: *Poésie et vérité* (1942), *Choix de poèmes* (1946), *Le Livre ouvert* (1947).

El Verdugo, one of the 'Études philosophiques' in Balzac's *Comédie humaine* (q.v.).

Élus, see *Fiscal system*.

Elvire. (1) Don Juan's wife in Molière's play (see *Dom Juan*); (2) the name by which the poet Lamartine idealized Mme (Julie) Charles, the invalid wife of a Paris physician, with whom he was at one time deeply in love. The two met at Aix-les-Bains in 1816 and 'Elvire' died in 1817. She inspired several of the poems of the *Méditations poétiques* (q.v.), notably *Le Lac*; (3) Lamartine also, especially in *Nouvelles Méditations*, used the name for a composite character inspired by Mme Charles, his own wife, and the Italian girl *Graziella* (q.v.).

Élysée, Palais de l', the official residence (since 1873) of the President of the French Republic, originally constructed for the comte d'Évreux (1718). It became national property during the Revolution and was used later as a royal residence or to house royal guests (e.g. Queen Victoria on her visit to Paris during the Second Empire). Napoleon signed his second deed of abdication here.

Émaux et Camées (1852 and subsequent, enlarged, editions), by Théophile Gautier (q.v.), short poems (often in octosyllabic quatrains) which perpetuate moments, seasons, and landscapes. Their serene loveliness, and absence of uneasy emotion, class the author with the poets of the Parnassian school (see *Parnassiens*) rather than with the Romantics. Well-known poems of this collection are the graceful *Premier Sourire du Printemps*; the *Symphonie en blanc majeur*, a description of a woman whose pale, statuesque beauty causes the poet to ask,

> 'Oh! qui pourra mettre un ton rose
> Dans cette implacable blancheur?'

Another, *L'Art*, which contains the Parnassian doctrines in essence, advises the poet to model himself on the sculptor and immortalize his inspiration in the *bloc résistant* of form.

Émigré, L' (1797), by Sénac de Meilhan (q.v.), a novel in letter-form, slight, but sensitively written. The marquis de Saint-Alban, an émigré fighting with the Prussian forces (see *Armée des émigrés*), is wounded and takes refuge in a castle on the Rhine. He falls in love with the châtelaine, who becomes a widow during his stay. Before they can marry honour compels him to rejoin Condé's army. He is taken prisoner and dies on the scaffold.

Émigrés, see *Armée des émigrés*.

Émile, a treatise on education by J.-J. Rousseau, in five books, published in 1762. It was condemned by the *parlement* and the author was obliged to leave France to avoid arrest.

As in his other writings, the author bases his doctrine on the return to nature: he advises that the infant should be born and brought up in the country, suckled by his mother, and be kept free of swaddling clothes. His early education should be directed to the development of the heart and the intelligence by sympathy and example, and by allowing acts to be followed by their natural consequences, with an avoidance of verbal lessons, reasoning, books, and authority, so as to produce spontaneity in good conduct, also to the development of a healthy body by exercise, cold baths, the avoidance of feather beds, and similar details. Instruction, as his age increases, is to come from the observation of natural phenomena, and presently of the mutual dependence of the members of a society. From this arises the necessity that each boy should learn a handicraft, so that he may have his assured place in the social scheme. He will thus acquire respect for the humbler members (the vast majority) of society. His moral education (which rests ultimately on self-love and self-respect) is further developed at a rather late age by a study of ancient history and particularly of the biographies of the great men of old, and ultimately by travel. Religion and philosophy enter very late into the scheme, and Émile (the author's ideal pupil) has not even heard mention of God until his reason is mature. The nature of the religious teaching recommended by Rousseau is indicated in the famous excursus interposed in the middle of the treatise and entitled the 'Profession de foi du vicaire savoyard'.

In this the author exposes his belief, through a process of deduction from elementary consciousness, in a benevolent Deity regulating the universe, in an immortal soul, and in an innate principle of justice and virtue (the conscience). This is the natural religion and the author repudiates revealed religion, while speaking of it with reverence.

The last book is devoted to the education of women and is in surprising contrast to what has preceded. Women should be so trained as to be a help and consolation to men, but to remain in a state of mental inferiority and docility, submissive in opinion to their husbands. Sophie (the ideal female pupil), brought up on these principles, is brought into contact with Émile, and the description of his courtship forms a charming but unconvincing idyll. (In a singular sequel, *Émile et Sophie*, the author relates the breakdown of their happy conjugal life and the infidelity of Sophie.)

In spite of obvious errors and deficiencies, the influence of the educational treatise was good, for it threw a flood of light on a subject hitherto governed by prejudice and obscurantism, and stimulated reflection and discussion not only in France but in England and Germany. It was at once translated into English. The religious doctrine audaciously set out in the 'Profession de foi' led to the author's prolonged persecution by the authorities.

Éminence grise, L', nickname of Joseph le Clerc du Tremblay (1577–1638), a Capuchin friar, known also as le Père Joseph, the trusted adviser and diplomatic agent of Richelieu. The expression is used proverbially of an unobtrusive influential adviser.

Emmanuel, PIERRE (1916–), contemporary poet. His shorter works can be found in *Élégies* (1940), *Tombeau d'Orphée* (1941), *Le Poète et son Christ* (1942), *Combats avec tes défenseurs* (1942), *Le Poète fou* (1944), *La Liberté guide nos pas* (1945); also in *Cantos* (1943) and *Chansons du dé à coudre* (1947), lighter poems. *Babel* (1951) is a long rhetorical mixture of poetic prose (the narrative by 'le Récitant') and poetry, notable apart from its intrinsic merit as one of the rare 20th-century revivals of the epic (see *Epic poetry*). The theme is the creation, rise, and downfall of mankind. *Qui est cet homme?* (1947), prose, is a form of spiritual autobiography.

Empire, Le Premier (1804–14). The Empire was proclaimed on 18 May 1804, and on 2 December of the same year the coronation of Napoleon I took place in the Cathedral of Notre-Dame. The Pope (Pius VII) had come specially from Rome for the ceremony. This Empire ended with Napoleon's abdication in April 1814 but was resuscitated in 1815 for the interregnum known as 'les cent jours', between Napoleon's return from Elba in March and his second and final abdication in June. (See also *Napoleon I.*)

Empire, Le Second, came into being after the *coup d'état* of 2 December 1852, and the Prince-President Louis Napoleon Bonaparte became Emperor Napoleon III (q.v.). It was confirmed by plebiscite the following February, and lasted till September 1870.

For the first half of this period political freedom, whether of action or comment, was suppressed. The Press was muzzled, and many persons hostile to the Government were in compulsory or self-imposed exile. A slightly more liberal attitude obtained after 1860 but no fundamental reforms were introduced till about 1868; and by this time the 'Empire libéral' was overshadowed by external political complications.

During the Second Empire France was several times involved in war. From 1854 to 1856 she fought, with Great Britain, in the Crimea; from 1857 to 1860 in China. In 1859 she helped Italy in her war of independence against Austria. She conquered Cochin-China in 1859 to 1862; and in 1862 she intervened with unhappy results in Mexico. In August 1870, war with Prussia, which had threatened for some years, finally broke out. The reverses of the first month, culminating in the defeat at Sedan (q.v.), brought general discontent to a head. On 4 September the Empire was overthrown without opposition and a Republic was proclaimed (see *Révolution du 4 septembre*).

Materially, the period of the Second Empire was one of progress and of financial and industrial expansion. Banks were founded, means of communication increased (telegraphs, railways, the Suez canal), and Paris and other cities undertook schemes of urban development. To some extent, also, indus-

trial conditions improved, but socialistic ideas and a new Republican movement were making silent headway. The positivist and materialistic spirit of the time showed itself in the pursuit of money and pleasure, and in brilliant social life, the example being set by the Imperial Court, the most resplendent in Europe: the Exhibitions held in 1855 and 1867 attracted millions of visitors from near and far. (Life under the Second Empire is described time and again in novels by Alphonse Daudet and by Zola.)

Encyclopedias, see *Dictionaries and encyclopedias.*

Encyclopédie, L', one of the great literary monuments of the 18th century, an encyclopedic dictionary of the knowledge of the day, including the arts, sciences, and trades. It was originally suggested by the *Cyclopaedia* of Ephraim Chambers (1728), which two publishers, Le Breton and Briasson, proposed to have translated. But Diderot, to whom they applied, persuaded them to give the work an ampler scope, the systematic classification of knowledge on Baconian lines. The *privilège* or licence for publication was granted in 1746, the Prospectus appeared in 1750, and seventeen volumes of text, supplemented by eleven volumes of admirable plates, were published between 1751 and 1772. Seven additional volumes in which Diderot had no hand, and comprising four of text, one of plates, and two index volumes, appeared in 1776–80.

The *Encyclopédie* embodied the philosophic spirit of the 18th century, and its attempt to given a rational explanation of the universe is marked by love of truth and contempt of superstition. Its sceptical tendency in regard to religion brought upon it the hostility of the clergy and (with some notable exceptions, such as the comte d'Argenson, Malesherbes, Mme de Pompadour) of the official classes. Its publication was twice prohibited, in 1752 through Jesuit influence, and in 1759 after the appearance of the article on *Genève* and the publication in 1758 of the book *De l'esprit* (q.v.) by Helvétius. The issue of the *Encyclopédie* nevertheless continued, the government being half-hearted in its condemnation and Malesherbes (q.v.), *directeur de la librairie* and responsible for the censorship, being in fact in its favour. The articles in volumes viii–xvii, however, which were issued simultaneously, were mutilated without the knowledge of the editors by the printer Le Breton, who erased everything likely to lead to a conflict with the authorities.

The principal director of the enterprise was Diderot, with d'Alembert as his chief assistant (until 1758, after which Diderot bore the burden alone), and with Jaucourt, Marmontel, and Voltaire in different degrees as lieutenants. Among some fifty other contributors the most famous names are those of Montesquieu, Turgot, Rousseau, and Buffon. The house of the baron d'Holbach was the principal meeting-place of the *encyclopédistes*. Diderot's short prospectus appeared in 1750. The *Discours préliminaire* by d'Alembert (1751) sets forth the objects of the enterprise: to expound the order and connexion of human knowledge, the general principles of the arts and sciences, and the essential details thereof. The sciences and arts are then traced back to their origin in sensation and are classified according to the faculties on which they depend (memory, reason, imagination). There follows an historical exposition of the growth of science from the time of the Renaissance under the names of the most eminent thinkers, Bacon and Descartes, Newton and Locke, down to the author's contemporaries, Buffon, Montesquieu, and Voltaire. The *Discours* has, in a less degree, the same sort of dignity as some of Bacon's philosophical writings: it sees the universe as one great single fact, and all the sciences that explain it as branches of a single truth.

In the articles of the *Encyclopédie* itself little survives of value, owing to the progress of knowledge, but it propagated the scientific spirit and thereby combated superstition and (with Bacon) assigned to science its practical purpose. On the other hand the system it taught was purely rationalistic: there was no room in it for anything that reason could not explain. Its doctrines were founded on the three main principles of nature, reason, and humanity: under the first it combated the supernatural and the fabulous in history; under the second it combated authority as the source of the religious doctrines and the political institutions that the encyclopedists regarded as irrational (e.g. the doctrine of eternal damnation); under the third it attacked intolerance and persecution. It

attempted to found morality on reason, rendering it independent of religion. The articles on religious subjects are outwardly orthodox and even full of unction; but the show of piety is hypocritical (a hypocrisy no doubt imposed by the conditions under which the work was produced): religious dogmas are asserted, then criticized, or their incredible character insinuated; religious scepticism is thus encouraged. The political articles are more straightforward: with increasing boldness as the work progressed the authors censured the unequal distribution of wealth, fiscal privileges, and other abuses, especially those connected with the administration of justice. The *Encyclopédie* did not attack the monarchical system, but held that the king should be good and just and that there should be civil equality before the law. War should be resorted to only when unavoidable, and should be rendered more humane; the industries of peace are exalted, and the protection of infant life and reforms in education are advocated.

Among the articles by famous authors are those on *Goût* by Montesquieu, on *Étymologie, Existence, Foires*, and *Fondations* by Turgot, on *Éloquence, Esprit, Grâce*, &c., by Voltaire, on *Économie politique* by Rousseau. Buffon furnished an article on 'Nature', but this appears not to have been printed. In general, however, these eminent persons gave little but their names and support or countenance to the enterprise; the bulk of the work was done by hack-writers under the direction of the chevalier de Jaucourt. Diderot wrote the technical descriptions of the mechanical arts. For others who wrote for, or influenced, the *Encyclopédie* see *Condillac, Duclos, Helvétius, Holbach, Marmontel, Morellet, Raynal.*

The work suffered from considerable faults of execution. The length of some of the articles was disproportionate to their importance. There were contradictions, incoherences, and errors of fact. A few articles were absurd; and there was much unacknowledged copying from earlier dictionaries (such as those of Bayle and Moreri). Among the chief critics and adversaries of the *Encyclopédie* were Fréron, Nonnotte, Palissot, Barruel, Le Franc de Pompignan (bishop of Le Puy) and his brother, and the Jesuit authors of the *Journal de Trévoux* (qq.v., and see also *Cacouacs*).

As a commercial undertaking the *En-*

cyclopédie was highly successful. The outlay is said to have amounted to about one million francs, and the profit to have been nearly 300 per cent.

Encyclopédistes, a word used to designate, without great precision, the group of *philosophes* (q.v.) and others who, in greater or less degree, promoted or supported the *Encyclopédie* (q.v.). These, though only loosely bound together by community of doctrine and purpose, did on the whole, in spite of some feuds, form a sort of brotherhood, and the idea of brotherhood was fostered by Diderot and d'Alembert. Chief among them, besides these two, were Voltaire, Condillac, Helvétius, d'Holbach, Jaucourt, Morellet, Raynal, Duclos, Marmontel, and Turgot (qq.v.).

Eneas, see *Romans d'antiquité.*

Enfances Ogier, see *Ogier.*

Enfantin, BARTHÉLEMY-PROSPER ['Le Père Enfantin'] (1796–1864), born in Paris, was one of the *pères suprêmes* of the Saint-Simoniens (see *Saint-Simonisme*). After the dissolution of the Community he went to Egypt. Some years later he settled in Paris. A persuasive speaker, he was considered by some a charlatan, by others a prophet. He wrote *Économie politique* (1831), *Morale* (1832), &c.

Enfant prodigue, L', a sentimental comedy in ten-syllabled verse by Voltaire, produced in 1736, interesting as an early example of this type of drama, otherwise of little merit. The prodigal son returns to be forgiven and just in time to save the girl to whom he had formerly been betrothed from being married against her will to his pompous avaricious brother. The play met with some success in spite of the poverty of the comic element and the unreality of many of the characters.

Enfants sans souci, Les. This was the best known of the medieval *confréries* or *sociétés joyeuses* (q.v.). It existed in Paris, and its members, like those of other *sociétés joyeuses* in France, called themselves *sots* (fools), or *compagnons du Prince des Sots*, their chief, their second dignitary being the *Mère Sotte*. This appellation of *sots* appears to go back to the expulsion of the *Fête des Fous*

(q.v.) from the cathedrals, and the secularizing of the profane drama. They did not, like the *Basochiens*, belong to any defined profession, but may have included *Basochiens* in their number. The *Enfants sans souci* acted always in fool's costume with cap and bells, and mainly, though not always, performed *soties* (q.v.). Like the *Basochiens*, they flourished during the reign of Louis XII, who found the undisguised satire of the *soties* both enlightening and politically useful. One of the most famous members of the *Enfants sans souci* was Gringore (q.v.), who both wrote and acted in *soties*, and was at one time *Mère Sotte*. Another member for a time was Clément Marot (q.v.); and possibly the most popular of all in his day was Jean de l'Espine (q.v.), known as 'Jean du Pont-Alais' or 'Songe-Creux'. The *Enfants sans souci* had ceased to exist by the first quarter of the 17th century.

Enfants terribles, Les (1929), a novel by Jean Cocteau (q.v.).

Enfer de la Bibliothèque nationale, L', the section of the Bibliothèque nationale (q.v.) reserved for books that for various reasons (obscenity, blasphemy, &c.) are *enfermés* (and shelf-marked '*enfer.*') and cannot be issued generally. A book with this title by Guillaume Apollinaire was published in 1913.

Enghien (pron. as if *Anghin*), DUC D', the title habitually borne by the eldest son of the Prince de Condé (see *Bourbon*).

Enghien, LOUIS-ANTOINE-HENRI DE BOURBON, DUC D' (1772–1804), the last of the House of Condé to bear this title, born at Chantilly, left France early in the Revolution with his father and grandfather and fought in the *Armée des émigrés* (q.v.). After 1801 he lived in Germany at Ettenheim, near Baden. In March 1804 he was kidnapped and brought to Vincennes (q.v.). On 21 March, after a perfunctory court martial on the charge of plotting to overthrow Napoleon, he was shot and buried at midnight in a grave already dug to receive him. There was little doubt that Napoleon, in his determination to remove possible Royalist rivals from his path, was directly responsible. The incident provoked fierce indignation.

English Influence on French literature, see *Foreign Influences* ....

English literature, French influence on.
[NOTE: Only some of the more prominent features of this vast subject can be mentioned here.]

13TH–15TH CENTURIES

(1) French literature, which became dominant in Europe from about 1200, was introduced into England largely by the Norman Conquest and the establishment of a French-speaking aristocracy in the conquered country. Its influence on English writings may be seen in the metrical romances of the 14th and 15th centuries, especially those relating to the *matière de Bretagne*, though its precise extent is debatable. Stories and adventures were borrowed from the *chansons de geste* (e.g. *Sir Ferumbras*) or from the *lais* of Marie de France (*Sir Launfal*), or from Benoît de Sainte-More's *Roman de Troie*. Chaucer, 'the founder of the art of English poetry' (Courthope), adopted from France the method of writing in rhyme. In him the influence of the French courtly writers can also be seen, such as Guillaume de Lorris (*Romaunt of the Rose, Boke of the Duchess*) and of writers of *ballades* and *rondeaux*, such as Guillaume de Machaut and Deschamps.

16TH CENTURY

(2) A fresh wave of influence may be observed in the 16th century. Wyatt and Surrey studied the metrical forms of Clément Marot and Saint-Gelais. Daniel's debt to Desportes has been recognized. Spenser translated some of the poems of du Bellay and admired Marot. Sylvester's translation of the *Semaine* of du Bartas was much read between 1590 and 1606. Translations from French prose—a French that was itself frequently translated from another tongue—included works familiar to the Elizabethan dramatists, such as North's *Plutarch* (1579), from Amyot (and cf. also *Bandello*). They culminated towards the end of this period in Danett's *Commines* (1596) and Florio's *Montaigne* (1603). Bacon took the title of his *Essays* from Montaigne, but not the spirit or the style. Shakespeare's familiarity with Montaigne is evident in his later plays. There was no translation of Rabelais till Urquhart's day (1653), but he was certainly read in England in the 16th century.

17TH AND 18TH CENTURIES

(3) The exile of the English court and many English men of letters to France favoured French influence, noticeable especially after the Restoration, on the English stage. Even before the Restoration English heroic tragedy was feeling the influence of the romances of La Calprenède and Mlle de Scudéry, translated from 1652 onwards, and imitated, and for long the reading of thousands (to the contemptuous astonishment of Lord Chesterfield, writing in 1752). The paramount French influence on Restoration drama (comedy), largely introduced by Etherege and Sedley, was Molière, from whom plots and characters were borrowed by d'Avenant, Dryden, Wycherley, Vanbrugh, and others. Corneille and Racine were translated, imitated (e.g. the *Cato* of Addison, himself well steeped in French literature and criticism), and adapted (e.g. Ambrose Phillips's *Distrest Mother*, 1712, from Racine's *Andromaque*); and there was much discussion of the rules, and the comparative merits, of French classical drama (cf. Dryden's *Essay of Dramatic Poesy*).

(4) The influence of French literary criticism during these two centuries was ultimately stronger than that of the drama. Dryden recognized Boileau (whose *Lutrin* and *Art poétique* were translated in 1682 and 1683 respectively) as one of the foremost authorities of the time. The *Traité du poème épique* by Le Bossu and the critical works of Rapin and Dacier on Aristotle and Horace were also studied and there is a reference to them in Congreve's *The Double Dealer*. Bouhours is frequently mentioned. A revived interest in Montaigne can be seen in the essays of Cowley and Temple and led to a new translation (1685) by Cotton. Other (17th-century) translations of note include the *Lettres* of Guez de Balzac (1638, the year in which a translation of Corneille's *Le Cid* was performed); the *Lettres* of Voiture, some of Scarron's works (an influence on Burlesque), Pascal's *Lettres Provinciales* and Descartes's *Traité des passions*, all about the middle of the century; Pascal's *Pensées* in 1688; La Rochefoucauld's *Maximes* (favourite reading of Lord Chesterfield) in 1694; the *Caractères* of La Bruyère in 1699. French residents in, or visitors to, England at this time must also be taken into account (cf., for instance, the many displaced Huguenot men of letters circulating in London). Saint-Évremond lived and died (1703) in

England and was regarded as an oracle on literary matters. On the other hand, though Voltaire and Montesquieu both made long stays and had many literary contacts in England between 1726 and 1731, their influence is more recognizable later, after their greatest works had been written (see next para.). Conversely, the influence can be noted of French literary and philosophical *salons* on English visitors to France.

(5) English writers of the Augustan age still adhered to the French classical principles of rule and restraint, but this dominance weakened gradually as the intellectual horizon extended beyond a polished circle of wits. For now (*c.* 1730) the English country gentleman is beginning to visit the Continent, and the middle class 'is beginning to read, and will read, what it really likes, without bothering about Aristotle or M. Bossu'. But French influence on the developing genre of the novel was considerable (cf. Smollett's debt to *Gil Blas*); and by the mid-18th century, beyond the more closely defined bounds of creative literature, it was profound via Voltaire and Montesquieu on political and economic thought and on the general philosophic and synthetic conception of history (cf. Hume, Gibbon, Robertson, whose works were published between 1754 and 1788). The ideals of Rousseau and the early, abstract enthusiasms of the Revolution can be found reflected in, for example, Godwin's *Political Justice* or in the passionate belief in progress, freedom, humanity, and equality which inspires the early Coleridge, Wordsworth and Southey, or Burns, or Shelley, Godwin's disciple.

1800–c. 1850

(6) The English attitude towards France, hostile during the later Revolution and the Napoleonic era, was in general politically, spiritually, and aesthetically unreceptive for some fifty years after the Restoration. New developments in French literature were not, however, unremarked. In poetry, Hugo's genius and powerful imagination were recognized, and his romantic drama *Hernani* won some favour for its Shakespearian quality. Balzac and George Sand were admittedly the foremost contemporary French novelists (with Paul de Kock and Eugène Sue surprisingly close behind); but they were seldom recommended or imitated.

Perhaps the chief sign that French literature exercised any influence between 1830 and 1850 is that the critics, voicing public opinion, frequently deplored its cynicism, indecency, audacious passion, lack of high moral purpose, and subversive effect on morals.

POST-1850

(7) Appreciation of the French classical tradition and of newer aspects of the French genius was revived and stimulated after 1850, thanks at first to G. H. Lewes, to Matthew Arnold (whose admiration for Sainte-Beuve is seen in his view of the need for 'curiosity' in criticism), and to Meredith (cf. his *Odes in Contribution to the Song of French History*). The Positivist philosophy of Auguste Comte—a more real influence on George Eliot than her early reading of George Sand, and a basis for the philosophy of Herbert Spencer—became known through the writings of J. S. Mill and G. H. Lewes and the translations of Harriet Martineau. Medieval and Renaissance writers were increasingly studied and translated.

(8) In the second half of the century, too, contacts developed, with stimulating effect, between the younger artistic and literary groups and their French fellows. The Swinburne of *Poems and Ballads* was a disciple of Hugo, Gautier, and Baudelaire. Through him, Gautier's defiant creed of *l'art pour l'art* (q.v.)—the dissociation of aesthetic beauty from moral or didactic purpose—developed later by Baudelaire, Flaubert, and the Parnassiens, influenced the pre-Raphaelite revolt and, still more strongly, between 1870 and 1900, the aesthetic movement associated with Pater. (The latter's debt to Baudelaire and Flaubert is evident in his 'beauty, into which the soul with all its maladies has passed' and his insistence on form, the 'absolute accordance of expression to idea'.) Towards the end of the century *l'art pour l'art* was mocked by Gilbert and Sullivan (*Patience*) and over-exploited by Wilde, but it had helped to bring a more objective spirit into both the creative and the critical function.

(9) In the novel, the interest aroused by *réalisme* and *naturalisme* (qq.v.), and the influence of Flaubert, the brothers Goncourt, Maupassant, Zola, Huysmans, &c.,

is apparent in the late 19th and early 20th centuries in George Moore (*The Mummer's Wife, Esther Waters,* and cf. his *Confessions of a Young Man*), Gissing (his novels of drab North London life), Bennett, Conrad, &c. (and cf. also the interpretative criticism of, for example, Henry James, Edmund Gosse).

(10) In poetry, impressionism and the symbolist (see *Symbolisme*) doctrines—evocation and imagery rather than precise description, the 'correspondances' between literature and music, or literature and the plastic arts—were a strong influence on Yeats, Synge, and their group. Visits to Paris reinforced the influence, and talk (e.g. at Mallarmé's 'Tuesdays') with those they regarded as masters. In more modern times T. S. Eliot (attracted to the Symbolists by A. Symons's *Symbolist Movement in Literature*) has spoken of Laforgue's influence on his poetic development.

(11) About the mid-20th century the chief point for remark is that play and interplay of ideas is more immediate than ever before in the literary evolution of the two countries. Proust became a landmark in the English as quickly as in the French novel; and the *surréaliste* movement set young English poets to work, like their French fellows, to discover new significance in Baudelaire and Rimbaud.

Enjambement, in French prosody and particularly in the *alexandrin* (q.v.), or twelve-syllabled line—the carrying on of a phrase or sentence beyond the end of one line into the first words of the next. Boileau, in his *Art poétique,* laid it down that breaks in the sense should coincide with metrical divisions. Though this rule was based on no good authority and was not observed by great poets such as Corneille, Racine, Molière, and La Fontaine, Boileau's dictum exerted a great restrictive force on the minor poets of the following period.

(In English prosody 'enjambment' is the carrying on, in couplet metres, of a sentence beyond the end of a couplet into the next.)

Enlèvement de la redoute, L', a famous short tale of military glory, by Prosper Mérimée (q.v.), first published in the collection *Mosaïque* (1833). It is said to have been founded on an incident of Napoleon's Russian campaign of 1812, when the attack on the redoubt of Schwardino began

at four o'clock in the afternoon and ended in victory exactly one hour later.

Ennemi du genre humain, L', i.e. William Pitt, the younger, so proclaimed by the *Convention nationale* (q.v.), 7 August 1793.

Ennery, ADOLPHE-PHILIPPE D' (1811–99), author of popular melodramas, including *Cartouche* (1859), *Les Mystères du vieux Paris* (1865), *Les Deux Orphelines* (1875), &c. (See also *Mercadet.*)

Enquête sur la monarchie, L', an inquiry conducted about 1900 by Charles Maurras (q.v.) by means of interviews and correspondence with (exiled) officials of the Royalist Party and with prominent authors and public personages. The object was to determine whether French opinion would welcome a return to monarchical government and, if so, in what form. The doctrines of the *Action française* (q.v.) were based on the results of this inquiry (first published in the *Gazette de France,* a paper which soon afterwards ceased to exist).

Enragés, Les, an extremist popular movement in Paris during the Revolution, without representation in the *Convention nationale* (q.v.). Many of their slogans were taken up by the *Hébertistes* (q.v.), who contributed to their fall in September 1793. Their leader, l'abbé Jacques Roux, committed suicide.

En route (1895), the second of four novels of spiritual pilgrimage by J.-K. Huysmans, see *Là-bas.*

Ensorcelée, L' (1854), a novel, set in Normandy, by J. Barbey d'Aurevilly (q.v.).

After a dissolute youth in the monastery of Blanchelande during the last years of the *ancien régime* the abbé de la Croix-Jurgan took part in the Chouan risings (see *Chouannerie*) and crowned his acts of sacrilege by attempting to commit suicide when the insurrectionists were defeated. When the story opens he has returned to clerical life as parish priest in a village not far from the monastery of his youth, now a ruin. Everything about him is monstrous—his hideously-scarred face (the result of torture at the hands of the Republican troops), his stature, and his pride. One of his parishioners, a rich farmer's wife, bewitched by vengeful nomad shepherds, falls passionately in love with him and kills herself. The *abbé* himself can be convicted of no sin except inordinate pride and after a period of penance he is permitted to resume his functions. During High Mass on Easter Sunday, his first Office, he is shot at the altar by the dead woman's husband. In after years travellers crossing the deserted heath of Lessay can hear the bell of the derelict abbey of Blanchelande. The windows are strangely lit, and within the building a phantom priest celebrates a phantom Mass which he must always recommence but never finish.

The wild country and the old Normandy customs are excellently described.

Entresol, Club de l', see *Club de l'entresol.*

Entretiens d'Ariste et d'Eugène, see *Bouhours.*

Entretiens sur la pluralité des mondes, see *Fontenelle.*

Envers de l'histoire contemporaine, L'. Two of the 'Scènes de la vie parisienne' of Balzac's *Comédie humaine* (q.v.)—*Madame de la Chanterie* and *L'Initié*—are united under this title.

Envoi, 'sending on the way', the final stanza in certain types of poem. Examples of *envois* are seen especially in *ballades* (q.v.). Traditionally, but with many exceptions, the *envoi* begins with such words as 'Prince', 'Princesse', 'Roi', 'Reine', 'Sire'. See also *Jeux partis.*

Éon de Beaumont, CHARLES D', generally known as the *Chevalier d'Éon* (1728–1810), political adventurer, employed as a secret agent by Louis XV at the court of Elizabeth of Russia and later in London. He assumed at the Russian court the character and dress of a woman. He died in London.

Épervier, Lai de l', a typical *fabliau* (q.v.). A knight loves a lady. One day, when her husband is absent, the knight sends his squire to ask if he may see her. The squire makes love to the lady. The knight arrives and the lady hides the squire. While she is talking to the knight, she sees her husband returning. By her instruction the knight assumes an appearance of great anger, and goes off uttering threats as the husband enters. She reassures the latter by explaining that the knight was pursuing his squire who, having lost his master's hawk and dreading his anger, had taken refuge in her house; and she brings the squire out from his hiding-place.

Épices, a term used, until the 16th century, to signify the presents of sweetmeats which it was customary for litigants to make to the judge; subsequently these presents became a fixed and obligatory honorarium payable to the judge in advance.

Epic poetry, one of the earliest forms of French literary activity, of which the principal examples are found in the *chansons de geste* (q.v.). The best of these narrate heroic deeds in a style of grandeur combined with *naïveté*. There is an epic element in the medieval poems on the Crusades, such as the *Chanson d'Antioche*, and in the *Romans d'antiquité*, such as the *Roman de Thèbes* (qq.v.). But the romantic element soon prevailed over the epic. The epic metre of the earlier *chansons de geste*, as seen in the *Chanson de Roland*, was pre-eminently the ten-syllabled line.

(2) There was no considerable revival of epic in France until the Renaissance. In the 16th century we have Ronsard's unsuccessful *Franciade* in ten-syllabled verse, d'Aubigné's *Les Tragiques* (the last books of which have an epic quality), and *La Semaine* (the religious epic of Du Bartas), both in the twelve-syllabled *alexandrin* (q.v.), the form which now prevailed. In the middle of the 17th century there was an outburst of epic poetry: *La Pucelle* by Chapelain (1656), *Moyse sauvé* by Saint-Amant (1653), *Saint Paul* by Antoine Godeau (1654), *Clovis* by Desmarets (1657), *Charlemagne* by Louis le Laboureur (1664), *Childebrand* by Carel de Sainte-Garde (1666), &c. None of these has escaped oblivion, though the *Saint Paul* of Godeau, Bishop of Vence, contains passages of Christian eloquence. Voltaire's *La Henriade* (1728), an epic on the career of Henri IV, was one of his earliest and not most successful works. André Chénier planned two great epics, on the subject of human perfectibility, but did not live to write more than the briefest fragments.

(3) Early in the 19th century Alfred de Vigny published *Héléna* (1822), an epic of Greek antiquity (which he suppressed from later editions of his works). He also wrote *Le Déluge* (1823) and *Éloa* (1824) which, like Lamartine's *Jocelyn* (1836) and *La Chute d'un ange* (1838), are hardly epics so

much as long narrative poems. Other long, and sometimes less than mediocre, epics of the early and mid-19th century were of divers types. Some were historical and patriotic, e.g. Edgar Quinet's *Napoléon* (1835), Soumet's *Jeanne d'Arc* (1845), or the *Franciade* (1863) of Viennet which recounted, on the Virgilian model, the legend of the French race through the exploits of a hero. Others were religious, mythological, or mystical, reflecting occasionally the romantic humanitarianism of the years before the 1848 Revolution (see *Revolutions*, III and IIIa), e.g. Soumet's *Divine Épopée* (1840), in which all-redeeming love triumphs over evil; Leconte de Lisle's *Quaïn* (written 1845, published 1869 in the second *Parnasse contemporain*, q.v.) and *La Passion* (1858); and Louis Ménard's *Prométhée délivré* (1843) or his pessimistic *Euphorion* (1855) in which a symbolic figure, the offspring, born in Hades, of Helen and Achilles, rises to earth and is condemned eventually to an eternal voyage across time. Others, again, were semi-scientific, or philosophical, e.g. the *Atlantide ou la Théogonie newtonienne* (1812) of Lemercier (better remembered by his *Panhypocrisiade*, a historico-satirical poem); Louis Bouilhet's *Les Fossiles* (1854), on the emergence of mankind from a prehistoric past; or Sully Prudhomme's *Le Bonheur*, on the pursuit of happiness and its final realization through self-sacrifice. A forgotten poet, Amédée Pommier (1804–77), wrote a semi-burlesque epic in which the punishment meted out to adulterers was an eternal tête-à-tête; and Victor de Laprade, almost equally forgotten, called his *Pernette* (1868) an epic of rural life. Two works of the first half of the 19th century, perhaps more genuinely epic in character than any of the others mentioned, but which are written in prose, are Chateaubriand's *Les Martyrs*, narrating the conflict between Christianity and paganism and the final triumph of Christianity, and Quinet's semi-mystical drama *Ahasuérus* (1833), on the theme of the Wandering Jew's reappearances in the successive ages of humanity.

(4) In 1859 Victor Hugo, now in the second phase of his career, stepped easily into place with the first series of *La Légende des siècles* as the supreme epic poet of the century. He introduced a new form of short epic, the *petite épopée* (his own name for it), in which

some legend or fable, briefly told, evokes the whole history and spirit of an age, while a series of such poems, linked together, presents successive phases of a ruling theme. The theme in this case was the spiritual and historical progress of the human race across the centuries. The type of *petite épopée* had been foreshadowed much earlier by Vigny's *Le Cor* in *Poèmes antiques et modernes* (1826); and in forsaking the older conventions of the epic Hugo may have been influenced by Leconte de Lisle, whose aim (*c.* 1850–60) in many poems on Biblical, Greek, Nordic, and Celtic themes was the reconstitution of past epochs rather than straightforward narration.

(5) The move away from straightforward narration was itself a sign that the epic was a dying genre. There have been some 20th-century attempts to revive or transform it (for instance by Pierre Emmanuel and Saint-John Perse) but they do little to discount what Baudelaire wrote in 1862:

'Excepté à l'aurore de la vie des nations, où la poésie est à la fois l'expression de leur âme et le répertoire de leurs connaissances, l'histoire mise en vers est une dérogation aux lois qui gouvernent les deux genres, l'histoire et la poésie; c'est un outrage aux deux Muses. Dans les périodes extrêmement cultivées . . . celui qui tente de créer le poème épique tel que le comprenaient les nations plus jeunes, risque de diminuer l'effet magique de la poésie . . . et en même temps d'enlever à l'histoire une partie de la sagesse et de la sévérité qu'exigent d'elle les nations âgées.'

Épinay, Louise-Florence, Mme d' (1726–83), née d'Esclavelles, wife of a farmer-general of taxes, a distinguished member of the intellectual society of her day, a protectress of J.-J. Rousseau, a friend of Diderot, for twenty-seven years on intimate terms with Grimm, and after 1769 the correspondent of Galiani (qq.v). Besides her letters, she left an autobiographical romance (published as *Mémoires* in 1818), giving a vivid picture of the circle in which she moved, and throwing light on a phase of Rousseau's career; also *Conversations d'Émilie* on educational subjects.

Épîtres (65 in all), by Clément Marot (q.v.), written on various occasions and often closely connected with events of his life.

Épîtres, by Boileau, twelve dissertations in verse, on the model of Horace's *Epistles*, addressed to the king and other persons of distinction, published at various dates from 1674 onwards. They deal with divers subjects, the most interesting being those in which the author expounds his views on literary matters, notably Epistle VII to Racine, Epistle IX, and Epistle X. His twelfth Epistle *sur l'Amour de Dieu* was one of the writings that brought him into conflict with the Jesuits.

Époques de la Nature, see *Buffon*.

Eracle, a metrical romance composed about 1165 by Gautier d'Arras.

Eracle, the son of a noble Roman, has a miraculous gift of discerning the merits of precious stones, horses, and women. His mother, after his father's death, sells him and all her goods for the benefit of the poor. He is bought by the seneschal of the emperor, and shows in his employ his gifts as a diviner (a part of the story told with considerable charm and humour). Later Eracle is elected emperor of Constantinople and recovers the Cross, which had been removed from Jerusalem by the king of Persia, and restores it to the Holy Sepulchre.

Eracles, Livre d', see *Terre Sainte, Livre de la*.

Erasmus, DESIDERIUS (1466–1536). After renouncing his monastic vows, this Dutchman (born at Rotterdam) who was to become the master of European humanism settled in Paris for a period of study before embarking upon further travels. He supported himself by giving private lessons, learnt Greek, and was (aged thirty and already a scholar of repute) a boarder at the Collège Montaigu (q.v.). His *Adagia*, a small compilation, but from which 'toute la lumière de l'antiquité se répand à flots sur le monde', was first published in Paris in 1500. Within the next thirty years it had as offspring the translations, dictionaries, and grammars of antiquity which were alike the inspiration and the *apparatus criticus* of early Renaissance literature and scholarship.

Erckmann–Chatrian [ÉMILE ERCKMANN, 1822–99 and ALEXANDRE CHATRIAN, 1826–90]. These two Alsatians collaborated for many years in writing historical novels ('romans nationaux et populaires', popular school-prize literature) of the Revolution and the Napoleonic wars, e.g. *L'Illustre Docteur Mathéus* (1859), *Mme Thérèse ou les Volontaires de 1792* (1863), *L'Ami Fritz* (1864, q.v.), *Histoire d'un conscrit de 1813* (1864), *Waterloo* (1865), *Histoire d'un paysan* (1868–74, 4 vols., q.v.), and many others.

A quarrel and litigation ended this long collaboration.

Erec, a *roman breton* by Chrétien de Troyes, written about 1168, the story of a knight of Arthur's court who gains his wife Enid by his prowess. After marrying her, he is mortified to discover that she believes that love has made him neglect his knightly duties. Hence he sets out with her in search of chivalrous adventure, enjoining her to keep absolute silence on the way, an order which she cannot refrain from disobeying each time that she perceives a new danger threatening her husband, until, in a dramatic scene, her fidelity brings reconciliation.

The same theme has been treated by Tennyson in his *Geraint and Enid*.

Ermenonville, a village about 35 miles to the north-west of Paris, where Rousseau died (q.v. and see *Girardin, René-Louis, marquis de*).

Ermitage, L', a small house in the Forêt de Montmorency, about 10 miles north of Paris, where Rousseau was installed (April 1756) by Mme d'Épinay and where he lived till December 1757. Later, it was bought, and lived in till his death, by the composer Grétry (q.v.).

Ermitage, L' (1890–5 and 1897–1906), one of the most active of the Symbolist reviews (see *Symbolisme*), with articles on literature, history, philosophy, music, painting, and the theatre. Its early contributors included Pierre Louÿs, Henri de Régnier, Francis Vielé-Griffin. After them came Paul Claudel, Jacques Copeau, André Gide, Remy de Gourmont, Francis Jammes, &c. (qq.v.).

Ernoul, Chronique d', see *Crusades*.

Esbahis, Les, a comedy by Jacques Grévin (q.v.), produced in 1561, one of the earliest original French comedies.

Josse, a grey-beard widower, wishes to marry Madelon, daughter of his friend Gerard. But Madelon returns the love of a young advocate. The latter's valet procures some of Josse's clothes, and the lover, disguised in these, visits Madelon. He is seen with her by Gerard and mistaken for Josse, which leads to a quarrel between Gerard and Josse. Finally Josse's wife, a termagant whom he supposed to be dead, appears on the scene, and he is left discomfited. Among the characters is Panthaleone, a caricature of the braggart Italian adventurer, who is made a fool of and beaten.

Escobar y Mendoza, ANTONIO (1589–1669), a Spanish Jesuit, noted as a casuist, who sustained the maxim that purity of intention justifies actions that are otherwise immoral or criminal. His doctrine was attacked by Pascal in the *Provinciales*.

Escoufle, L', a metrical *roman d'aventure* of about 1200, unsigned but almost certainly by Jean Renart (q.v.).

Guillaume, son of a gallant Norman count who has distinguished himself as a Crusader and won the affection of the emperor of Rome, is affianced to the emperor's daughter Aelis. But after his father's death the betrothal is cancelled through the influence of the emperor's evil counsellors. The young couple, who are in love, elope to Normandy; but on the way, when Guillaume goes in pursuit of a kite (*escoufle*) which has carried off the lady's purse, they get separated and lose one another. Their search for each other lasts for many years, during which they meet with many adventures. An incident in which a kite again figures brings them at last together. They are married, and Guillaume becomes in the end emperor of Rome. The story is agreeably told and some passages throw an interesting light on medieval manners.

Esménard, JOSEPH-ÉTIENNE (1769–1811), author and publicist, came to Paris in 1790 to represent the Department of the Bouches-du-Rhône at the Fête de la Fédération (q.v.). He left France after the fall of the Monarchy (1792) and travelled on land and sea (and utilized his experiences in a didactic poem *La Navigation*, 1805). During the Empire he was successively Dramatic Censor, Directeur de l'Imprimerie, and special censor of the *Journal des Débats*, then called *Journal de l'Empire*, but he incurred Napoleon's displeasure, was exiled, and died in Italy.

Esméralda, a gipsy dancer, heroine of Victor Hugo's historical novel *Notre-Dame de Paris* (q.v.).

Ésotérisme, see *Literary Isms.*

Espagne, Faire des châteaux en, an expression found as early as the 13th century, varied with *châteaux en Asie, en Albanie,* and probably meaning only to build castles in a foreign country where one has no standing-ground; Spain being finally chosen as the nearest Moorish country to Christendom [*O.E.D.*].

Mme de Sévigné quotes Mme de Villars as saying: 'Il n'y a qu'à être en Espagne pour n'avoir plus envie d'y bâtir des châteaux.'

Esparbès, GEORGE-THOMAS D' (1864–), author of patriotic and historical novels, usually of the Revolutionary and Napoleonic eras, e.g. *La Légende de l'Aigle* (1893).

Espion du Grand Seigneur, L', by Giovanni Paolo Marana, a Genoese residing in Paris, published 1684–6; letters purporting to be written from Paris by a Turkish spy, discussing the political and social affairs of France. The work was the prototype of Montesquieu's *Lettres persanes.*

Esplandian, in the romance of *Amadis de Gaule,* the son of Amadis and Oriane; his exploits are related in the continuation of the original story (Bk. V).

Esprit, JACQUES (1611–78), a man of letters whose gifts of conversation admitted him to society, notably to the *salons* of Mme de Rambouillet and Mme de Sablé. He was author of *Fausseté des vertus humaines,* on the same theme as La Rochefoucauld's *Maximes.*

Esprit décadent, L', the term used—perhaps by the poet Jules Laforgue for the first time—to describe the state of mind prevalent between 1880 and 1890 in the small literary societies known as *Les Hirsutes, Les Hydropathes, Les Zutistes,* &c., where politics, philosophy, and poetry were discussed, and which were to some extent the cradle of the Symbolist movement (see *Symbolisme*). The spirit was one of overwhelming *langueur,* futility, distaste for any moral or religious restraint, a horror of banality, and a seeking after any novelty of sensation, however unnatural. The name may have come from Verlaine's sonnet

Je suis l'Empire à la fin de la décadence, and it was of the word *décadence* itself that Verlaine said: 'Ce mot suppose . . . des pensées raffinées d'extrême civilisation, une haute culture littéraire, une âme capable d'intensives voluptés. . . . Il est fait d'un mélange d'esprit charnel et de chair triste et de toutes les splendeurs violentes du Bas-Empire . . . .'

The spirit was reflected in verses, criticism, and manifestoes published in little reviews, e.g. *La Nouvelle Rive gauche*, *La Revue indépendante*, *La Revue wagnérienne*, *Le Décadent*, *La Vogue* (qq.v.). Many of 'les décadents' found the resources of the language inadequate to express their complex sensations, and coined new words or disintegrated old ones with great inventiveness. A *Petit Glossaire pour servir à l'intelligence des auteurs décadents et symbolistes* appeared in 1888 (see *Adam, P.*; also *Arène, P.*; *Déliquescences*).

Esprit de contradiction, L', a one-act prose comedy by Dufresny, produced in 1700.

Oronte's wife is a termagant with a spirit of contradiction; to obtain her support in his design to marry their daughter to a rich suitor, he pretends to support the latter's rival, favoured by the daughter. But the daughter warns her mother, who from the same spirit of contradiction, unexpectedly falls in with her husband's pretended view.

Esprit des lois, De l', a treatise on the general principles and historical origins of law, in thirty-one books, by Montesquieu, published in 1748, in the first instance anonymously. Some twenty further editions were issued within eighteen months. Its subject had interested the author, he tells us, since he first studied law, and its composition had occupied twenty years.

The theme of the work may be gathered from the full title of the first edition: *De l'Esprit des lois, ou du rapport que les lois doivent avoir avec la constitution de chaque gouvernement, les mœurs, la religion, le commerce*, &c. Laws the author defines as necessary relations resulting from the nature of things. Law (*le droit*) being human reason applied to the government of men, the various laws (*les lois*) are applications of this reason to particular circumstances, such as the particular type of government (despotism, constitutional monarchy, or republic), or the physical and moral conditions of the people (climate, occupation, degree of liberty, wealth, religion). It is this relation between law and circumstances which Montesquieu understands by *Esprit des lois*, and which he proceeds to examine in the light of innumerable instances drawn from ancient and contemporary constitutions and from the commentaries of political writers, classical, French, English, and Italian.

Among the three types of government the author recognizes the ideal superiority of the republic, of which the underlying principles are virtue (respect for the law and patriotism) and frugality. But a republican government lacks stability, and Montesquieu shows his preference for constitutional monarchy, in which equilibrium is maintained by certain intermediate bodies between prince and people. He especially commends (xi. 6) the English constitution, where the independence of the three bodies, executive, legislative, judiciary, secures a high degree of liberty. He abhors despotism, of which the underlying principle is fear. His enlightened and humane attitude is shown, for exmple, in his disapproval of slavery and of agressive war, in his censure of religious intolerance (see in particular the remonstrance addressed by a Jew to the Inquisition, xxv. 13) and of the cruelties of the penal code, and in his scepticism in regard to accusations of witchcraft. In an interesting chapter (x. 14) on the career of Alexander he commends that conqueror's liberal policy. The last five books differ in character from the rest, forming a technical treatise on the origins, Roman and Germanic, of French law.

The composition of the treatise is defective, and it is somewhat difficult to trace in it a coherent plan. It has also been criticized for its excess of epigram and brilliancy of style (which led Mme du Deffand to remark that it was 'de l'esprit sur les lois') and for the tendency to generalization from insufficient premisses. But it was none the less the first example of the application of the comparative method to the study of social institutions, a great manifesto of reason and humanity, a grave indictment of the abuses of the French monarchy and of the defects of contemporary civilization. Its doctrine, of which it has been said that it changed the thought of the world, was prominent in France in the political experiments of the Revolution and in the parliamentary constitutions that followed 1815. Its influence on the framing of the American Constitution is notable, in the idea of federation and the extreme application of the principle of separation of powers.

Esprit du boulevard, L', a form of wit which flourished in Paris during the Second Empire (1852–70) in the cafés, restaurants, and theatres situated within a short radius of the present Place de l'Opéra and frequented by *le Tout-Paris* (q.v.). It was a wit of *bon mots* and *à peu près* (slight distortions of words or phrases, such as the name 'Madame Réclamier' for a lady given to self-advertisement), a blend of gaiety, gossip, irony, malice, and of veiled comment on events at a time when the Press was muzzled. Though mainly a wit of the spoken word it was reflected in, for instance, the chronicles by Aurélien Scholl in *Le Figaro* (q.v.).

Esprit gaulois, a term used to signify the talent for giving an amusing and good-humoured turn to indecency that is characteristic of certain branches of French literature, such as the *fabliaux* (q.v.). 'Le besoin de rire', says Taine on this subject, 'est le trait national.'

Esprit pur, L', by Alfred de Vigny (q.v.), written in 1863, the concluding poem of the posthumous collection *Les Destinées*. The poet meditates on his noble ancestors, all men of action. Their name will remain for posterity, not because of their exploits but because he, the last of the race, has inscribed it 'sur le pur tableau des livres de L'ESPRIT'.

Esprits, Les, a comedy by Larivey (q.v.), published in 1579. It is an adaptation (in prose) of the *Aridosio* of Lorenzino dei Medici, itself a combination of the *Aulularia* and *Mostellaria* of Plautus with the *Adelphi* of Terence. Like the last it presents two brothers brought up on contrasted systems of education, respectively harsh (by the father) and lenient (by an uncle). It is the son who has been severely brought up who profits by his father's absence to entertain his mistress in his father's house. The consequences of the latter's unexpected return are averted, as in the *Mostellaria*, by the pretence that the house is haunted by ghosts. And, as in the *Aulularia*, a purse which the avaricious father had buried is abstracted and returned

to him only on his consent to the lovers' marriage.

Molière's *L'Avare* and *L'École des maris* contain resemblances to this play.

Esquiros, HENRI-ALPHONSE (1814–76), born in Paris, was in his beginnings one of the 'frenetic' romantics of the eighteen-thirties (cf. *Borel, P.*; *Romantisme*), when he published verse and two novels (*Les Hirondelles*, 1834; *Le Magicien*, 1837, *Charlotte Corday*, 1840). He was interested in occultism, and a familiar of l'abbé Constant (q.v.); and he wrote, and at times got into trouble over, works of idealistic social republicanism, e.g. *L'Évangile du peuple* (1840). He took part in the 1848 revolution, and spent the years of the Second Empire (q.v.) in exile in England. He returned, later, to France and to active political life.

Esquisse d'un tableau historique des progrès de l'esprit humain (1795), by Condorcet, see *Tableau historique*.

Essai sur le goût (1748), see Montesquieu.

Essai sur les données immédiates de la conscience, see *Bergson, Henri* (esp. para. 3).

Essai sur les Fables de la Fontaine (1853), see *Taine, Hippolyte*.

Essai sur les mœurs et l'esprit des nations, an historical work by Voltaire published in its definitive form in 1769. In 1740 he had set about an abstract of general history for Mme du Châtelet, from the time of Charlemagne to that of Louis XIV. Fragments of it were published by the *Mercure* in 1745–6 and 1750–1, and in 1753 an *Abrégé de l'Histoire universelle* in two volumes was published at The Hague, which Voltaire repudiated. A complete text was published at Geneva in 1756 under the title of *Essai sur l'histoire générale et sur les mœurs et l'esprit des nations depuis Charlemagne jusqu'à nos jours*. This was modified in various ways in the final edition of 1769, including a preamble on *La Philosophie de l'histoire*.

The work is a compilation, but drawn on the whole from good sources. Its purpose is to relate the history, not only of kings and wars, but of the human mind, and of the development of civilization, commerce, manners, and the arts; and to extend the narrative not only to Europe but to the whole world. Voltaire strives to indicate how people lived at various epochs with such illustrations as the prices of bread and meat, the dates of various inventions, and other characteristic details. He shows the progress of humanity under the pressure of its needs and circumstances. He points out the obstacles that man himself has placed in the way of his progress, notably war and religious fanaticism; not omitting to blame the writers, whether primitive chroniclers or later historians, who by their adulation of force and fraud have contributed to maintain mankind in its errors. The treatise thus contributes to support the Voltairean doctrines, and does inadequate justice to the good work done in certain directions by the papacy and the monks. It was very successful and was reprinted at least sixteen times between 1753 and 1784.

Essai sur l'indifférence en matière de religion, (1817–23), see *Lamennais.*

Essais de critique et d'histoire (1858), see *Taine, Hippolyte.*

Essais de morale (1671), see *Nicole.*

Estang, LUC (1911–), a contemporary poet, of religious inspiration, whose published collections include: *Transhumances* (1939), *Puissance du matin* (1941), *Invitation à la poésie* (1944), *Les Béatitudes* (1945). He has also written some novels.

Estaunié, ÉDOUARD (1862–1942), novelist, born at Dijon (originally a civil engineer). Subdued, somewhat etiolated melancholy and a Roman Catholic bias characterize his studies of superficially placid lives which conceal emotional stress, spiritual suffering, occasionally even crime—*Les Choses voient* (1913), *L'Ascension de Monsieur Baslèvre* (1921), *L'Appel de la route* (1921), *L'Infirme aux mains de lumière* (1924, short stories), *Le Silence dans la campagne* (1925), &c.

Esther, a tragedy in three acts by Racine, interspersed with songs by a chorus of young Israelite girls. It was composed at the request of Mme de Maintenon for performance by the young ladies receiving education at Saint-Cyr and was produced in 1689.

The play sets forth the story of Ahasuerus (Assuérus), Esther, Mordecai (Mardochée), and Haman (Aman), as related in the Book of Esther.

Esthétique de la langue française, L' (1899), essays by Remy de Gourmont (q.v.).

Estienne (pron. *ès-tienne*; in Latin form STEPHANUS), the name of a famous family of printers and scholars, including (1) *Henri Estienne* (d. 1520), who came to Paris from Provence in 1502 and founded a printing-house; (2) *Robert Estienne* (1503–59), his son, printer to François Ier and, after being exiled for his Protestant religion, to Calvin at Geneva; author of a famous *Thesaurus Linguae Latinae* (1532), the best Latin dictionary of the time (and cf. *Dictionaries and Encyclopedias,* under date 1539); (3) *Henri Estienne* (c. 1531–98), the son of Robert. He spent most of his life at Geneva, where he printed for the Republic, but visited France, Italy, Flanders, and England. He was father-in-law of Isaac Casaubon (q.v.). He was an ardent Hellenist and author of an admirable *Thesaurus Graecae Linguae* (1572). Of his works in French, his *Apologie pour Hérodote* is a satire on his age and particularly on the Catholics of his day: the credulity of Herodotus is humorously justified by a comparison of his tales with the Biblical and other marvellous stories believed in Estienne's time; anecdotes are added of the crimes and vices of the age. His *Dialogues du nouveau françois italianisé* (1578) is a satire, in the form of a dialogue between two courtiers, directed at the corruption of the French language by Italian influences. His *Précellence du langage françois* (1579) is a more profound work on a similar theme, the aptness of the French language for all purposes of expression. It was Henri Estienne who wrote, 'Si jeunesse savait; si vieillesse pouvait.' (4) *Charles Estienne* (1504–64), brother of Robert, a physician by profession and a man of learning. He accompanied Lazare de Baïf to Italy as tutor to his son Antoine. He took over the family printing business, but failed and died in prison for debt. He wrote some miscellaneous works, including a prose translation of the *Andria* of Terence (1540).

Est-il bon, est-il méchant? see *Diderot,* para 4.

Estoire d'outre-mer, see *Terre Sainte.*

Estrées, GABRIELLE D' (1573–99), mistress of Henri IV from about 1591. The ducs de Vendôme were her descendants.

Her brother, François-Annibal, maréchal d'Estrées (1573–1670), left *Mémoires* relating to the public affairs of his time.

Étape, L' (1902), a novel by Paul Bourget (q.v.), in which plot and character serve to demonstrate the theories that no stability can be found outside the Roman Catholic church and that it is impossible to rise in one move from the peasant to the professional (in this case professorial) class.

États généraux, the assembly, summoned from time to time (by the king only, and at his discretion), of representatives of the three Estates of the realm, i.e. the clergy, the nobility, and the *tiers état* (in practice the burghers of the towns of France). They were instituted by Philippe le Bel (the first recorded meeting, 1302, was held in Paris, in Notre-Dame), without powers of initiative or free discussion, to give support or ratification to the king's proposals. The representatives of the towns were elected by universal or restricted suffrage in towns possessing a municipal organization, and by the general assembly of the people in towns dependent on the power of the king or feudal lord, or they might be nominated by the lord in agreement with the assembly.

The *états généraux* were summoned fairly regularly, though on the whole at lengthening intervals, until 1614, a turbulent session in Paris on the occasion of Louis XIII's majority. Thereafter they were not summoned till 1789 when their opening session, on 5 May, at Versailles, marked the outbreak of the French Revolution.

États généraux, Les, see *Courrier de Provence.*

Étienne, CHARLES-GUILLAUME (1777–1845), journalist and dramatist, was appointed editor-in-chief of the *Journal des Débats* (then called *Journal de l'Empire*) when Napoleon placed that paper under government control. In later life he edited *Le Constitutionnel*. He was also one of the founders of *La Minerve française* (q.v.). He wrote successful comedies, notably *Brueys et Palaprat* (1807) and *Les Deux Gendres* (1810). In the latter, a comic treatment of the same theme as *King Lear*, he was said to have

plagiarized an early 18th-century play by a Jesuit (*Conaxa*, 1710) and his popularity suffered.

Étienne de Fougères, see *Livre des Manières.*

Étienne Mayran, by Hippolyte Taine (q.v.), a fragment of a novel of intellectual awakening. It was begun and abandoned about 1860 and published posthumously in 1910. It opens some time during the July Monarchy in a small provincial town. The fourteen-year-old Étienne Mayran, after an upbringing in cultured surroundings, is orphaned and left practically penniless. There is talk of apprenticing him to a trade, but he sees a chance of remaining in the world to which he feels he belongs, and with a cold logic astonishing for his age he drives a bargain with the head of a boys' pensionnat in Paris (such as the one in which Taine himself was educated) that in return for his board and tuition he will succeed so well in examinations, e.g. by winning competitive prizes, passing first into the *École normale* (q.v.) and so on, as to be a profitable advertisement for the school. Should he fail the headmaster will have a right to his tiny patrimony. The other chapters depict the solitary boy's life and hardships, his schoolmates, his tutors, his dogged application and the sacrifices he makes so that he can live up to his side of the bargain; and finally, after a period of doubt and depression, his sudden awakening to the world of ideas which lies beyond mechanical study. Henceforward he will be possessed by the passion for knowledge.

Étourdi, L', Molière's first comedy, produced at Lyons in 1655, imitated from the *Inavvertito* of Nicolò Barbieri (better known under the pseudonym 'Baltrame').

The scene is Messina. Lélie, the *étourdi*, a hare-brained fellow, has fallen in love with Célie, a slave-girl, but has no money to purchase her. Moreover, his father has a marriage in view for him, and there are rival aspirants for Célie's favours. Lélie's servant, Mascarille, an ingenious knave (after the manner of Plautus's slaves), contrives a succession of simple ruses for getting possession of the girl, and the comedy consists in the perversity with which Lélie, a perfect bungler, manages to defeat by his interference Mascarille's efforts on his behalf.

However, in spite of this, matters are finally arranged to everyone's satisfaction.

The play was adapted, as *Sir Martin Mar-All*, by Dryden from a translation by the Duke of Newcastle. Pepys saw this acted in August 1667 and 'never laughed so' in all his life.

Être Suprême, L'. A decree of 18 floréal, An II (7 May 1794) of the *Convention nationale* began with the words: 'Le peuple français reconnaît l'Être Suprême et l'immortalité de l'âme.' This instituted the cult of the Supreme Being, which Robespierre hoped would replace both the Christianity formerly practised and the orgies celebrated more recently in the name of Reason. A festival, hurriedly organized by David the painter (q.v.), took place on 20 prairial (8 June) in the Jardin des Tuileries. Robespierre, in the leading part, set fire to an effigy of Atheism, while the people sang the *Hymne à l'Être Suprême* written specially for the occasion (by Desorgues, with music by Gossec, qq.v.). The crowd then marched to the Champ-de-Mars to plant a tree of Liberty. The festival was only held once: the *culte de l'Être Suprême* perished with Robespierre.

Études analytiques, see *Comédie humaine, La.*

Études de la nature (1784), see *Bernardin de Saint-Pierre.*

Études de mœurs, see *Comédie humaine, La.*

Études historiques, (1831, 4 vols.), by Chateaubriand. These were originally designed to form part of a history of France, which he never wrote. There is an introduction on history and historians. Other essays, some unfinished, are on Christianity and the progress of civilization.

Études philosophiques, see *Comédie humaine, La.*

Étui de nacre, L' (1892), collected short stories by Anatole France (q.v.).

Eudes [Odo], born 858, duc de France and comte de Paris, was King of France from 888, after Charles le Gros (q.v.) was deposed, until his death in 898. From 893 he had reigned jointly with Charles III, le Simple (q.v.). The *Capétien* (q.v.) dynasty stemmed

remotely from his father Robert le Fort, died 866, whose youngest son Robert I was the grandfather of Hugues Capet (q.v.).

Eudore, the young Greek convert to Christianity in Chateaubriand's *Les Martyrs* (q.v.).

Eugène, a comedy by Jodelle, the first French dramatic work of its class, in octosyllabic verse, acted in 1552.

It is a lively piece concerned with the rivalry of a rich and licentious abbot (Eugène) and a soldier (Florimond), the rejected suitor of the abbot's sister, for the favours of a certain Alix, whom the abbot has married for his own purposes to an imbecile Guillaume. The soldier, an old lover of Alix, returning from the wars and furious at discovering her relations with the abbot and Guillaume, terrifies the abbot, and the arrival of a creditor adds to the latter's perplexity. The abbot gets out of his difficulties by handing over his sister to the soldier, and a benefice to satisfy the creditor. The play, like so many of the old farces, is in large part a satire on the higher clergy.

Eugénie (1767), a play by Beaumarchais (q.v.).

Eugénie, Empress. Maria Eugenia de Guzman, comtesse de Teba (1826–1920), who became Impératrice Eugénie des Français in 1853 upon her marriage with Napoleon III, was the daughter of a Spanish grandee, the comte de Montijo, and his wife (see *Montijo, comtesse de*). She was a woman of great beauty, animated and pleasure-loving, under whose influence the court of the Second Empire (at the Tuileries and at Compiègne) became the most splendid in Europe. She did harm when she tried to extend her influence to politics. After the fall of the Second Empire she lived mainly in retirement in England, a widow from 1873 and still further bereaved when her only son, the Prince Imperial, was killed fighting in Africa in 1879.

From a literary point of view mention may be made of Mérimée's affectionate and respectful devotion to her. He had known her since she was a child of four, and after she married it was at her instance that he was made a Senator and became a familiar of the Court. He sent her the manuscript of one of his last *nouvelles*—*La Chambre bleue* (1866)—on which he had written 'composé et écrit par P. Mérimée fou de S. M. l'Impératrice'.

Eugénie Grandet (1833), a novel by Balzac (q.v.), one of the most famous 'Scènes de la vie de province' of his *Comédie humaine*. In 1819, in the small town of Saumur, M. Grandet, a rich miser, lives in penurious simplicity with his wife, their daughter Eugénie, and their devoted servant Nanon. His nephew Charles, a spendthrift young dandy, arrives unexpectedly from Paris, followed immediately by news that the Paris house of Grandet has failed and that Charles's father has committed suicide. Charles, now penniless, embarks for India to seek his fortune, taking with him Eugénie's heart and her 'treasure', a store of gold pieces given her each birthday by her father. The latter's fury on learning of this so distresses his wife that she falls ill and dies. Eugénie remains alone with her father, now besotted with avarice and a helpless invalid. On his death she inherits his fortune and waits faithfully for her cousin to return and marry her. But Charles, once more rich and in Paris, tells Eugénie in a letter of his forthcoming marriage with Mlle d'Aubrion. At the same time Eugénie learns indirectly that he has refused to settle honourably with his father's creditors and that the marquis d'Aubrion will not let his daughter marry a bankrupt's son. She pays the creditors in full, then writes to wish Charles happiness and encloses receipts in full for his debts. She lives on very simply in Saumur, cared for by Nanon and devoting herself to charity.

Eulalie, Séquence de sainte, a church song (*cantilène*) in fourteen couplets in praise of the saint, one of the earliest extant writings in French, of about the year 880.

Eupalinos ou l'architecte (1923), a Socratic dialogue by Paul Valéry (q.v.).

Eutrapel, Contes et discours d', see *Du Fail*.

Évadisme, see *Mapah*.

Évangélisme, L', the name given to that early phase of the Reformation in France which sought religious truth in direct recourse to the text of the Scriptures. This movement was stimulated by the new interest in ancient languages, and the appointment by François Ier of 'royal readers' in Hebrew, Greek, and Latin. It was bitterly opposed by the Sorbonne or theological faculty of the University of Paris. The principal leader of the movement was Lefèvre d'Étaples (q.v.), and its principal opponent was Noël Béda (q.v.), syndic of the Sorbonne. *Évangélisme* later developed into Calvinism, whose rigid doctrines alienated the humanists, such as Rabelais.

Évangéliste, L' (1883), by Alphonse Daudet (q.v.), a novel.

Évangile des femmes, L', a 12th-century satire in quatrains; the first three lines of each of these contain eulogies on women, the effect of which is cancelled by the fourth line.

Ève, ANTOINE-FRANÇOIS, called Maillot *or* Demaillot, see *Angot, Mme*.

Événement, L', a daily paper founded, and dominated, by Victor Hugo, with his son Charles-Victor Hugo (q.v.) as co-editor, in 1848. It stood for a poetical and socialist approach to political controversies. Balzac, Champfleury, Gautier, and Alphonse Karr (qq.v.) and the publicist Alexandre Erdan (1826–78), all wrote for it. Publication ceased after the *coup d'état* of December 1851.

Éviradnus (1859), one of the poems of Victor Hugo's *La Légende des Siècles* (q.v., first series), set in a medieval Germany which resembles that of *Les Burgraves* (q.v.) in its misty, crenellated savagery and grandeur. A knight-errant, Éviradnus, whose 'grande épée était le contrepoids de Dieu', arrives opportunely and slays two royal but murderous villains who had plotted to murder the Margravine Mahaud and divide her lands between them. He symbolizes the central idea of the *Légende*—the gradual triumph of Justice in the world.

Évolution créatrice, L', see *Bergson, Henri* (esp. paras. 5 and 6).

Exemples (*exempla*), short tales of an edifying character, or of the nature of parables, introduced into their Latin sermons by medieval preachers. Many of these have survived either in sermons or in collections of them made for the use of preachers.

Existentialisme. The philosophy known as Existentialism, or Existenz-Philosophie, is concerned with existence (specifically human existence) in an active sense rather than with the abstract nature of existence or of the universe. It derives ultimately from concepts expressed by the Danish writer Sören Kierkegaard (1813–55) in, for example, *The Concept of Dread*, *The Sickness unto Death*, &c. These concepts were later elaborated and systematized by, notably, two German philosophers, Martin Heidegger (1889–) and Karl Jaspers (1883–). The *existentialisme* of the contemporary French writer and philosopher Jean-Paul Sartre is the pessimistic form in which, since about 1945, existentialist doctrines have penetrated far beyond the philosophic world to a wide public of novel-readers and playgoers.

(2) It should be noted at this point that in the language of philosophy the words 'exist', 'existence' do not imply, as they do in daily speech, *passive continuance in being*. On the contrary, they have the sense of their Latin root (*ex* out+*sistere*, from *stare* to stand) and imply something active, an emergence, so to speak, from the passive state.

(3) A feature of previous philosophical systems has been the conception that since man, the individual, forms a part (explicable or inexplicable according to the system) of the general purpose, or essential nature, of the universe this purpose, or *essence*, common to all men, must precede the actual fact of individual existence. The postulate common to the various forms of existentialism is that *existence* precedes *essence*, for man only exists in so far as he shapes his own existence and thus confers an essence upon it by his own conscious choice. This, roughly, is what is called the doctrine of the 'liberty of man'; and this, perhaps, may be taken as the starting-point for a brief and necessarily over-simplified summary of the ideas, and the vocabulary, made familiar by the Sartrean form of *existentialisme*.

(4) The complex of circumstances into which man is born is his *situation*. It is a void, or *néant*, a sort of primeval mud (*le visqueux*), in which it is quite possible for him to continue, until he dies and passes from one *néant* to another, in a state of passive, barely conscious, awareness of himself. But occasionally he does become aware of himself as a reflective (and intrinsically lonely, because

reflective here implies *subjective*) being, and he suffers moral anguish (*angoisse*) and a sense of *absurdité* and consequent despair, which may lead to the violence of senseless revolt, at the realization that he can emerge from the void, i.e. exist, if he chooses; but that existence can only signify what he chooses to make it; that he, by his own gratuitous choice, can give a shape to human existence and confer meaning and purpose upon the universe; and that thus, in the sense that choice means shaping his existence according to subjective values, he can, ultimately, confer upon truth the essential quality of being true. He is overawed by his own liberty. What values is he to choose and what justification has he for making any choice? What are systems of philosophy, religious faiths, the conception of an ordered, bourgeois morality, but so many inducements to *mauvaise foi*, so many excuses for backsliding, for evading one's liberty to determine values for oneself?

(5) According to Sartre's *L'Existentialisme est un humanisme* (1946) it seems that man can succeed, and some individuals in fact do succeed, in emerging from this miserable state of indetermination by becoming *engagés*, that is to say, by a supreme act of will (*engagement*) they commit themselves to a positive part in social and political affairs (which can be equated with a kind of advanced left-wing near-communism), and thus to an awareness of others as well as of themselves. And by the fact of their commitment they provide a definite shape for their existence and a common, integrating purpose for humanity.

(6) The Sartrean *existentialisme* was probably the most marked influence on thought and literature, not French alone, for some years after 1945, but it is conceivable that in years to come it may be regarded less as a system of philosophy than as the metaphysical expression of the spiritual dishevelment of a post-war age. More, even, than by purely philosophical treatises it was disseminated by novels and plays (for those by Sartre himself see under the author's name), but these have been more taken up with describing the existentialist *néant* and the despair with which existentialist man contemplates his 'freedom', than with suggesting a solution for his dilemma (see, however, para. 5 above). A review, *Les Temps modernes*,

founded in 1946 by Sartre, is devoted to the work of existentialist writers including, for example, Simone de Beauvoir (1908–), novelist and essayist (*L'Invitée*, 1943; *Le Sang des autres*, 1944; *Le Deuxième Sexe*, 1949; *Les Mandarins*, 1954), and Maurice Merleau-Ponty (1906–), essayist and philosopher. M. Jean Wahl, Professor of Philosophy at the Sorbonne, has written and lectured much about existentialism in general, including the *existentialisme* of Jean-Paul Sartre. The word *existentialisme* is said to have been given currency in the vocabulary of French

philosophy by the philosopher and dramatist Gabriel Marcel (q.v.), who himself professes a form of *existentialisme chrétien*, in an article on *Existence et Objectivité* in the *Revue de métaphysique et de morale* (1925).

Expiation, L', see *Châtiments, Les*.

Expilly, l'abbé Jean-Joseph d', see *Dictionaries and Encyclopedias* under date 1762–70.

Exposition du système du monde (1796), a treatise on the planetary system, by the marquis de Laplace (q.v.).

F

Faber Stapulensis, see *Lefèvre d'Étaples*.

Fables choisies, mises en vers, by La Fontaine, published, the first six books in 1668, five further books in 1678–9, the twelfth book in 1694.

The fables are drawn from many sources, ancient (Aesop, Phaedrus, Horace, Bidpai) as well as modern, but the originals are only the skeleton which La Fontaine has filled out and vivified with details drawn from his own observation of nature and society. They are little pictures of life, universal in their quality, in which, often under the symbols of animals and by means of lively dialogues and sudden vicissitudes, men of all classes of society are depicted and their failings held up to gentle ridicule. The author enters into his characters, knows their lives and affairs, and talks and argues as they would. The quaint expressions (e.g. 'la gent trotte-menu' for mice) and somewhat archaic language, the ingenious use of free versification (see *Vers libres*), the mingling of human and animal traits (e.g. the rat dragged under water by the frog 'contre le droit des gens, contre la foi jurée') contribute to the charm of the stories. The moral is indicated at the end or the beginning of the fable, or is left to be inferred; but the moral in this traditional form, somewhat utilitarian and unheroic as a rule, a counsel of prudence and moderation, is not perhaps of prime importance. La Fontaine was no moralist but an Epicurean, kindly, indulgent, and easy-going, and the fables

express his attitude. Though, owing to their variety, it is impossible to classify the Fables rigidly, those of the second collection (Bks. vii–xi) have as a whole less Aesopic simplicity, are more serious and philosophical, and are most of them longer, than those of the first collection. The last book, though it contains some admirable fables, shows in the main some decline. We find in the whole work many lines and phrases that have become proverbial, such as 'promettre monts et merveils', 'contenter tout le monde et son père', 'un Tiens vaut mieux que deux Tu l'auras'. La Fontaine, it may be noticed, combated the Cartesian doctrine of *bêtes-machines*: that animals are merely automata, acting mechanically without volition or reasoning powers.

Fables, see also *Florian*; *Houdar de la Motte*; *Marie de France*.

Fabliaux (the usual form of the more correct French word *fableaux*), verse tales, generally in octosyllabic couplets, composed for reading as well as recitation, which were produced during the latter part of the 12th century, the 13th century, and the beginning of the 14th century. The view that these tales had an oriental origin is now discredited. A few of them, as appears from internal evidence, can have been invented only in France; but the subjects of most of them are not peculiar to any region or period and are so simple as to be adaptable to the conditions of any country. The *fabliaux* are short narratives, generally of about 300–400 lines, of some episode, usually of a burlesque character. They are without literary pretension, marked by simplicity, realism, and conciseness, composed in a mocking spirit, and designed solely to amuse. They range in character from light, ironical presentations of everyday life to the extreme of coarseness. Many of them display an acute contempt of women, as creatures of incorrigible perversity (in strong contrast to the doctrines of *amour courtois*, q.v., simultaneously prevailing), others show a hatred of priests. Some deal not very reverently with religious subjects, e.g. *Le Vilain qui conquit le paradis* by telling home truths to the saints who opposed his entry, and *Saint Pierre et le Jongleur*, where Saint Peter wins at dice the souls in hell entrusted by the Devil during his absence to the custody of the *Jongleur*. Their authors included amateur poets such as Philippe de Beaumanoir (q.v., a distinguished jurisconsult); Rutebeuf (q.v.), the *jongleur* and poet; wandering clerks, and minstrels attached to the courts of the nobility. About 150 *fabliaux* have survived; a collection of them by Montaiglon and Raynaud in six volumes was published in 1872–90. Some account of the best-known *fabliaux* is given herein under the headings *Auberée, Aveugles de Compiègne, Housse partie, Lai d'Aristote, Épervier, Richeut, Vilain Mire, Vilain qui conquist le paradis*. There is an echo of the *fabliau Gombert et les deux clers* in Chaucer's *Reeve's Tale*; in fact, the *Canterbury Tales* as a whole are in some ways the English equivalent of *fabliaux*, written by a great artist and poet.

Fabre, ÉMILE (1870–   ), author of solidly constructed dramas of domestic and public life, e.g. *La Vie politique* (1901, the intrigues and upheavals caused by an election in a provincial town), *Les Ventres dorés* (1905, a satire of financial circles), *La Maison d'argile* (1907, the problem of divorce).

Fabre, FERDINAND (1827–98), novelist, born at Bédarieux (Languedoc), took to literature after being educated for the priesthood. His novels of life in the Cévennes were distinguished for their portraits of country clerics, notably the priest in *L'Abbé Tigrane* (1873, q.v.), considered his best work. *Les Courbezon* (1862), *Mon Oncle Célestin* (1881), and *L'Abbé Roitelet* (1890) are also well known. His work has been likened to that of both Anthony Trollope and Thomas Hardy.

Fabre, JEAN-HENRI (1823–1915), naturalist, spent many years as a school-teacher in or near Avignon. After his retirement he lived at Selignan, near Orange, where he set up a small laboratory (bought by the nation after his death and converted into a museum). His studies of insect life (*Souvenirs entomologiques*, 10 vols., 1919–24) have both literary and scientific value.

Fabre d'Églantine, PHILIPPE (1755–94), dramatist and poet, assumed the name of 'Églantine' after winning, in his youth, the *prix de l'Églantine* or wild rose at the *Jeux floraux* (q.v.) of Toulouse. He was a prominent Revolutionary journalist, a member of the *club des Cordeliers* (q.v.) and a Deputy to the *Convention nationale* (q.v.). The renaming of the months in the Republican Calendar (q.v.) was his work. He ended on the scaffold with his friends Camille Desmoulins and Danton (qq.v.). The first line of his *chanson* 'Il pleut, il pleut, bergère' (q.v.) is still quoted. His comedy *Le Philinte de Molière ou la Suite du Misanthrope* (1790) is sometimes mentioned.

Fabre d'Olivet, ANTOINE (1767–1825), born at Ganges (Hérault), near Montpellier, began a career in Paris as apprentice to an uncle in the silk trade but had literary ambitions. He wrote some unsuccessful plays and lived in wedded poverty. He is sometimes remembered by *Le Troubadour, poésies occitaniques* (1803), a collection, with translations appended, of what purported to be and in some cases apparently was authentic medieval verse in Provençal and other dialects derived from the ancient *langue d'oc*. To some extent it was a literary hoax, but it antedated the revival of interest in Provençal literature (see *Félibrige*). It had no more success than his other works, and thereafter the author turned to occultism and was at work on a philosophical history of mankind when he died.

Fabrice del Dongo, the hero of *La Chartreuse de Parme* (q.v.), by Stendhal.

Fâcheux, Les, a *comédie-ballet* by Molière, in three acts in verse, produced in 1661. The play was hurriedly composed for an entertainment given by Fouquet to Louis XIV.

The theme is an expansion of that of Horace, *Satires* I. ix, and of Régnier's eighth satire. The author depicts a variety of bores, who by their untimely importunity interrupt the course of the hero's courtship: such as the man who stops him to recount at length the incidents of a stag-hunt, another who must tell him of a wonderful hand at piquet, and so forth.

Fagotin, a name, derived facetiously from *fagoter,* to dress badly, given by the celebrated mountebank Brioché (17th c.) to his monkey; whence used generically for a dressed-up monkey, or a merry andrew. Fagotin is referred to by Molière and La Fontaine.

Facino Cane, one of the 'Scènes de la vie parisienne' of Balzac's *Comédie humaine* (q.v.).

Fæneste, Aventures du baron de, a satirical pamphlet by Agrippa d'Aubigné published in 1617, consisting of a series of dialogues in which the principal interlocutors are Fæneste (from φαίνεσθαι to appear), a young papist, and Enay (from εἶναι to be), a virtuous old Huguenot. Within this framework, by theological discussions, scandalous tales of monks, bitter irony and invective, the author conducts a spirited attack on the papacy and all the enemies of the Reformation.

Faguet, ÉMILE (1847–1916), literary historian and critic, an indefatigable writer, with widely-ranging interests, though his favourite period was the 17th century. His criticism, though seldom profound, and inclined to generalize, was stimulating by reason of his interest in men and ideas and his lively manner of treatment. His works of literary history included—*Le XVIIᵉ Siècle* (1885), *Le XIXᵉ Siècle* (1887), *Le XVIIIᵉ Siècle* (1890), *Le XVIᵉ Siècle* (1894). His critical studies included—*Les Grands Maîtres du XVIIᵉ siècle* (1885), *Politiques et moralistes du XIXᵉ siècle* (1891–1900), *Politique comparée de Montesquieu, de Rousseau et de Voltaire* (1902). For twenty years he was dramatic critic on the *Journal des Débats* (q.v.), his articles being later collected: *Notes sur le théâtre contemporain* (1889–91), *Questions de théâtre* (1890–8), *Propos de théâtre* (1903–7).

Fagus, pseud. of Georges Faillet (1872–1933), a poet whose affinity with Villon and Verlaine can be remarked in, for instance, *Fière tranquille* (1918), *La Danse macabre* (1920), *La Guirlande à l'épousée* (1921); or in the shorter poems, often *chansons*, in *Pas perdus* (1926) and *Le Clavecin* (1926).

Faiel, Seigneur and dame de, see *Coucy.*

Faillet, GEORGES, see *Fagus* above.

Faiseur, Le, by Balzac, see *Mercadet.*

Falloux, La Loi, a law of 1850 regulating primary and secondary education, and named after its most active supporter the Catholic Deputy Falloux.

Famine ou les Gabaonites, La, see *Saül le furieux.*

Fanfan la tulipe, a 19th-century nickname for the French soldier proverbially fond of wine, women, and glory. It originated (in 1819) with a song of this name, written to a well-known melody, by Émile Debraux (1796–1831), a *chanson*-writer of something the same type as Béranger (q.v.) though on a lower level. The song became very popular and engendered a number of vaudevilles and comedies. The one most often remembered is *Fanfan la tulipe* (1858) by Paul Meurice (1820–1905), a romantic comedy of a rough but chivalrous soldier in the bodyguard of Mme de Pompadour.

Fanny (1858), a realistic novel by Ernest Feydeau (q.v. and see *Réalisme*). It had a *succès de scandale.*

Fantaisiste, Le Groupe, the name adopted about 1911 by a group of young poets (including Tristan Klingsor, Jean-Marc Bernard, Tristan Derème, qq.v., &c.) who thought the time had come to introduce a gayer strain into French poetry. At times an overtone of irony in their verses recalls the *Complaintes* of Jules Laforgue (q.v.).

Fantasio, by Alfred de Musset, a prose comedy in two acts, first published in the *Revue des Deux Mondes* (Jan. 1834), then included in the second series (1834) of *Un Spectacle dans un fauteuil* (q.v.). It was produced at the Comédie-Française in August 1866.

Fantasio, a young gentleman of Munich, disguises himself as the king of Bavaria's jester to escape from his creditors and secure a free lodging at court. One of his tricks of buffoonery so upsets the dignity of the prince of Mantua, a visitor at the court, that plans for a royal marriage between the prince and the king's daughter all come to grief. War may now be unavoidable between Mantua and Bavaria, but at least the gentle young Princess Elsbeth will not have been sacrificed to a pompous fool.

Fantine, the mother of Cosette, in Hugo's *Les Misérables* (q.v.).

Fantin-Latour, IGNACE-HENRI-JEAN-THÉO-DORE (1836–1904), French painter and lithographer. He painted many portrait-groups of his writer and artist contemporaries, among them *Hommage à Delacroix* (1865), also the well-known group of writers *Coin de Table* (1872) in the Louvre, from which the seated figures of Verlaine and Rimbaud (qq.v.), who were soon to leave Paris together, are a detail frequently reproduced. Several of his lithographs, which are more poetical and imaginative in style, were inspired by Wagner.

Fantomas, the character, probably as well known in the 20th century as Rocambole or Rouletabille (qq.v.) in the 19th, who gives his name to a long succession of popular thrillers by Marcel Allain (1885–   ), alone or in collaboration. The works abound in murders, mysterious appearances and disappearances, escapes and other sensational adventures. The equivalent in English would be somewhere between the Sexton Blake stories and Edgar Wallace. Another familiar character in the series is the mute, stubborn Detective Inspector Juve.

Fantosme, JORDAN, an Anglo-Norman cleric and writer of the 12th century, chancellor of the diocese of Winchester, who wrote in monorhyme stanzas an account of the war waged by Henry II with William the Lion, king of the Scots, in 1173–4, containing some interesting historical material.

Farce [from the L.L. past part. 'farsa', from *farcire*, 'to stuff', in the sense, at first, of introducing passages in the vernacular into Latin religious texts], a form of dramatic representation popular in France in the later Middle Ages, and said to date back to the expulsion from the churches of the *Fête des*

Fous (q.v.), the farcical element introduced into the form of the liturgy at certain times of the year. It was usually written in octosyllabic couplets, and made frequent use of triolets. Its average length was about 500 lines. By choice and treatment of incident (strongly resembling the incidents of the *fabliau* (q.v.) of an earlier period) the vices and foibles of everyday domestic, and occasionally political, life were burlesqued and caricatured, and its object was good-natured fun (cf. *sotie*). In the later history of the French theatre the *farce* developed into the one-act comedy or farce, and was in fact the ancestor of French comedy in its most successful and characteristic form. Some 150 medieval farces have survived out of what must have been a much greater number. The most famous of these is *Pathelin* (q.v.). Others popular in their day were *La Farce du Pâté et de la Tarte*, in which two famished rascals plan to steal an eel-pie and a tart from a pastry-cook's wife, but are discovered before they have completely succeeded, and soundly belaboured by the pastry-cook; *Le Chaudronnier*, a wager between a husband and his wife as to which one of them will remain motionless the longer (the husband loses, for he spring out of his immobility to assault a waggish tinsmith for kissing his wife); *Le Poulier*, in which a miller takes appropriate revenge on two gentlemen who are courting his wife; *Le Cuvier*, in which a hen-pecked husband is made by his wife to write down a list of all the tasks he must perform for her. One day his wife falls into the washtub; but when she cries to her husband to rescue her he consults his *rollet*, or list of tasks, and finds that pulling his wife out of the washtub is not one of them.

Among the lost texts, mention may be made of the amusing little farce of which Rabelais attributes to himself the authorship (Bk. III, ch. xxxiv), of the man who had married a dumb wife. He gets her cured of her infirmity, whereupon the torrent of her talk sends him back to the physician to get her made dumb again. This being impossible, the husband gets himself made deaf instead, which in turn drives the disappointed wife stark mad. The husband's deafness serves as a plea for not understanding the physician's demand for his fee, and the leech thereupon sends him crazy with a powder. The farce ends in a general mêlée.

Farel, Guillaume (1489–1565), a Roman Catholic who was converted to Protestantism largely under the influence of Lefèvre d'Étaples. He became a follower of Calvin, an at times almost excessively zealous preacher and Reformer.

Faret, Nicolas (c. 1600–46), man of letters, an early member of the *Académie française*. His *Honnête Homme ou l'art de plaire à la cour* (1633), still remembered, was modelled on Castiglione's *Il Cortegiano*.

Fargue, Léon-Paul (1876–1947), poet, born in Paris, traversed various literary movements, influenced younger writers, and was already high among modern poets when he died. He was, about 1894, one of the Symbolist circle of *Le Mercure de France* (q.v.) and wrote *Tancrède*, a sequence of short poems (published 1895 in the review *Pan* and separately in 1911) and *Poèmes* (1912, and again, with *Pour la musique* added, in 1918). Later collections, e.g. *Espaces* and *Sous la lampe* (both 1929), contain verse of his Cubist phase, sophisticated and ironical, making play at times with dislocation and deformation of words. His memoirs of life and literary circles in Paris (*Le Piéton de Paris*, 1939) are interesting and have much poetica lcharm.

Farrère, Claude [pseud. of Édouard Bargone] (1876–   ), born at Lyons, a naval officer, followed in the wake of Pierre Loti (q.v.) and wrote novels (much more vigorous, often merely melodramatic) with exotic settings. After *Fumée d'opium* (1904) he had three big popular successes, *Les Civilisés* (1905, Saigon), *L'Homme qui assassina* (1907, Constantinople), *La Bataille* (1911, Japan). *Mademoiselle Dax, jeune fille* (1907), unlike the others, is a satirical picture of middle-class life in Lyons.

Fatrasie, in medieval literature, rhymed nonsense designed to produce a comical effect; often of a satirical tendency. A precursor of the *coq-à-l'âne* (q.v.).

Faublas, see *Amours du Chevalier de Faublas, Les.*

Faubourg Saint-Germain, a quarter of Paris, on the left bank of the Seine, formerly outside the city's fortifications, a centre of aristocratic society in the 17th–18th centuries, and again in the 19th century when the *émigrés* returned. There is a very good description of it at this latter period in Balzac's *Duchesse de Langeais* (q.v.). 'Faubourg Saint-Germain' survives as a figurative expression for aristocratic society without specific reference to locality. Proust, for instance, employs it in this sense.

Fauchet, Claude (1529–1601), magistrate, historian, and critic, author of *Antiquités gauloises et françoises* (1579–99) and *Recueil de l'origine de la langue et poésie françoise, rime et romans* (1581), a compilation of value for the purposes of literary history.

Faucon, Le, one of the *Contes et Nouvelles* of La Fontaine, perhaps the pleasantest of these tales. It is drawn from Boccaccio.

Fédéric, a rich Florentine, has wasted all his substance in the vain hope of winning the heart of a lady, but the lady, faithful to her husband, is inexorable. He now lives in poverty, still cherishing his love, on the single farm that remains to him. He has one falcon and takes pleasure in hawking. The lady's husband dies, and their child is very ill. The child has taken a longing for Fédéric's hawk and is likely to die if his fancy is thwarted. The devoted mother decides to humiliate herself by visiting Fédéric and asking him to give up his hawk. Fédéric, overwhelmed by the favour of her visit, searches out the scanty materials for a meal to offer her. After the meal she humbly states the object of her visit, and Fédéric has to confess that having nothing better to offer her, he has killed the hawk and served it to her. The child dies; but the lady has at last been touched by this supreme mark of her lover's devotion, and marries him.

Faugère, Prosper (1810–87), man of letters and scholar, responsible for the first critical edition of Pascal's *Pensées* (1844). Evidence supplied by him at the time of the Vrain-Lucas (q.v.) case proved conclusively that supposedly genuine autograph letters of Pascal's were a forgery.

Faujas de Saint-Fond, Barthélemy (1741–1819), geologist, author of a *Voyage* [in 1784] *en Angleterre, en Écosse et aux Îles Hébrides* (1797) of which an English translation (anon.) was published in 1799 and again, edited and annotated by Sir Archibald Geikie, in 1907. It is an interesting, often lively and amusing work, which 'may be recommended to every lover of the Highlands; it makes a third with Johnson's *Journey to the Western Isles* and Boswell's *Tour in the Hebrides'*. (W. P. Ker, *Collected Essays*, ix.)

Fauquembergue, Journal de Clément de, see *History* (medieval period).

Fauré, GABRIEL-URBAIN (1845–1924), a celebrated French composer of, particularly, songs and chamber music. He was one of the composers associated with the Symbolists (see *Symbolisme*).

Fauriel, CLAUDE (1772–1844), critic and historian, translator of the *Parthénéide* of the Danish poet Baggesen (1810, with a preface supporting the literary views of the 'idéologues', q.v.), and (1823) of the tragedies of Manzoni. He also wrote histories of Provençal and Italian literature.

Fausses confidences, Les (1737), a comedy by Marivaux (q.v.).

Faustin, La (1882), a novel by Edmond de Goncourt (q.v.), a study of an actress who sacrifices a brilliant career to please her aristocratic English lover. In time she finds her nostalgia for the stage almost uncontrollable. Her lover falls ill. La Faustin, by his death-bed, suddenly forgets her anguish and, unconsciously yielding to her dramatic instinct, begins to imitate his last agonies.

Faute de l'abbé Mouret, La (1875), a novel by Émile Zola, one of his *Rougon-Macquart* cycle. The abbé Mouret's sin is his lapse from chastity. This book is often mentioned as typical of Zola's most lyrically descriptive writing; typical also of the pains he took to acquire the information and vocabulary (in this case botanical) required for filling in his background.

Fauteuils académiques. In the early days of the *Académie française* only the Directeur was privileged to sit in an armchair. The story goes that another member, the Cardinal d'Estrées, who was in failing health, begged permission to bring his own chair. This came to the ears of Louis XIV who realized that such a concession might lead to invidious distinctions and tactfully presented the *Académie* with forty armchairs from the royal store.

Fauves, Les, a group of French post-Impressionist painters (see *Impressionnisme*) prominent about 1906. Matisse (Henri Matisse, 1869–1954) was their leader. Others were Georges Rouault (1871–1958), Maurice de Vlaminck (1876–   ), and Raoul Dufy (1877–1953).

Faux Démétrius, Les (1852), by Prosper Mérimée, a study based on an episode of 16th-century Russian history.

Faux-Monnayeurs, Les (1926), by André Gide, his only novel, in his own sense of the word, as opposed to his *récits*, or *soties* (see *Gide*, para. 3).

The many characters, who are treated objectively, fall into groups of divers ages—small, and vividly unpleasant, schoolboys, who attend the Pension Azaïs and whose attempts to circulate counterfeit coins provide the title for the book; undergraduates; young men and women, the children's parents; and the grandparents, whose age has only accentuated their unpleasant characteristics. A focal point is provided by Édouard, a novelist, whose journal forms a large part of the book and who is himself writing a novel to be called *Les Faux-Monnayeurs*. Édouard is the uncle of Olivier, a student at the École normale supérieure, and has a secretary Bernard, Olivier's friend, who has left home to 'live dangerously'. He surprises Georges, one of the leaders of the schoolboy criminals, in the act of stealing a book in a bookshop, and discovers that he is Olivier's youngest brother and his own nephew. He goes to Switzerland with Laura, a daughter of the Pension Azaïs, who had once been in love with him but had married Professor Douviers and later taken a lover, who deserted her. From Switzerland he returns with Boris, the young grandson of a music-master at the Pension Azaïs.

In the end Édouard's nephew Olivier has been corrupted, first by Passavant, a novelist of Satanic character, and then by Édouard himself; Laura has returned to live unhappily with her husband, who agrees to accept her child; Boris, dared by his schoolfellows, one of whom is Georges, has committed suicide in class; and Bernard has returned to his father. The book deals with vitiated people and unpleasant situations from beginning to end, but the characters take on life, especially the nasty little boys and their older brothers, with their perplexities and un-happinesses. From the point of view of technique, its lack of construction and its apparently spasmodic and disconnected happenings are intended, the author claim-ing that a preliminary framework would have deprived the portrayal of his characters of all the uncertainty of real life. Édouard's journal within the book, recording the pro-gress of his own novel, has its counterpart in Gide's *Journal des Faux-Monnayeurs* (1926), kept while his work was in progress.

Favart, CHARLES-SIMON (1710–92), drama-tist, son of a Paris pastry-cook and rhymer. He married a clever actress and became director of the Opéra-Comique. He wrote numerous light comic operas which show the transition from the *comédie à vaudevilles* (popular airs) to the *comédie en ariettes* (tunes specially composed). The best known of his plays are *La Chercheuse d'esprit* (1741, a trifling comedy of the awakening of innocence to love), *Les Amours de Bastien et Bastienne* (1752, a parody of Rousseau's *Devin du village*), and *Les Trois Sultanes* (1761), in which the lively and self-asserting Roxelane triumphs over her rivals for the sultan's favour, and brings the prospect of liberal reforms to the sultan's court. Favart combined wit and gaiety with sentiment and an easy flowing style.

Favier, JEAN-LOUIS (*c.* 1720–84), born at Toulouse, publicist, a spendthrift who turned his political acumen and considerable understanding of diplomacy and diplomatic history to account and was employed on State and secret missions. He was often in danger, at one time took refuge in Holland, then in England, and at another was a prisoner in the Bastille. He left some political writings and reminiscences, a translation, *Mémoires secrets de Bolingbroke* (1754), and is remembered as a wit.

February Revolution (24 Feb. 1848), see *Revolutions*, III.

Febvre, LUCIEN (1878–   ), one of the best-known contemporary historians of 16th-century Europe from the standpoint of social and economic conditions, and the head of an important modern school of historiography of which Marc Bloch (q.v.) was another distinguished representative. His works include: *La Terre et l'évolution*

humaine (1922 and 1949), *Civilisations, le mot et la chose* (1930), *Le Problème de l'incroyance au XVIe siècle; la religion de Rabelais* (1942); also a study of Martin Luther (*Un destin: Martin Luther*, 1928).

Fédération, Fédérés. Growing enthu-siasm and a sense of national unity were manifested throughout France during the early months of the Revolution by the formation of *fédérations*, or unions of patriots. Delegates (*fédérés*)—often from local detachments of the newly-instituted *Garde nationale*—met and proclaimed them-selves citizens of one empire, bound to uphold the laws passed by the *Assemblée constituante*. National festivals instituted to celebrate important anniversaries were called *Fêtes de la Fédération*. The first (14 July 1790, the anniversary of the taking of the Bastille) was attended by delegates—60,000 in all—of the eighty-three *départements* (q.v.) into which the country had recently been divided. It was half religious, half political in character. On an altar erected in the middle of the Champ-de-Mars a solemn mass was celebrated by the Bishop of Autun (Talleyrand, q.v.). After this the king, followed by the delegates, swore fidelity to the new Constitution amid general enthusiasm. A hymn was sung, *Dieu du peuple et des rois*, written for the occasion by M.-J. Chénier (q.v.).

Feletz, CHARLES-DORIMOND DE (1767–1850), critic and man of letters, born at Grimont, near Brive (Corrèze), was educated for the priesthood but refused, when the Revolution came, to accept the Civil Con-stitution of the clergy. In 1794 he was arrested and condemned to deportation but saved at the last moment by the fall of Robespierre. He turned journalist and in 1801 joined the *Journal des Débats*, becoming one of its leading critics (with Dussault, Geoffroy, Hoffmann, qq.v.). His sound—strongly classical—literary taste, and his conversa-tional powers, were celebrated. *Mélanges de philosophie, d'histoire et de littérature* (1828) and *Jugements historiques et littéraires* (1840) are selections from his writings for the *Journal des Débats* and other papers.

Féli, Monsieur, the abbreviation used by his friends for Félicité-Robert de Lamennais (q.v.).

Félibien, name of a 17th-century family of architects and historians, best remembered by André (1619–95) and his son Jean-François (c. 1658–1733), both architects, the father also a historian of art and architecture; Jacques (1636–1716), brother of André, a theologian, author of works on religious history and doctrine; and Michel (1666–1719), also a son of André and also a religious historian. He became a Benedictine monk.

Félibres, Félibrige. The movement, known as le Félibrige, for the restoration of Provençal as a living language and for the renaissance of a Provençal literature began (1854) when seven Provençal poets met to consider how best this could be effected. They decided first to revive interest in the Provençal spirit, customs, and history, and next to restore the spelling and grammar of the Provençal tongue and agitate to have it taught in schools. They called themselves *félibres*, in reference to an old Provençal tale in which the infant Jesus is found disputing in the temple among 'li sét felibre de la léi' (which Mistral, q.v., took as meaning 'the seven Doctors of the Law'). In 1855 the *félibres* founded an annual which still exists, *L'Armana* [i.e. Almanach] *prouvençau*, a repertory of Provençal literature and information. These founders of the Movement, whose own works were written in Provençal, were: Frédéric Mistral, Joseph Roumanille, Théodore Aubanel (qq.v.), Jean Brunet (1823–94), Paul Giéra (1816–61), Remy Marcellin (1832–1908), and Anselme Mathieu (1828–1925). They were soon joined by Alphonse Tavan (1833–1905).

The *Félibrige* led the way for similar movements, and it stimulated the development of 'regional' literature.

Feminine lines and rhymes, see *Masculine.*

Femme, La (1859), by Michelet (q.v.), a treatise on the place of women in the home and in society, a fond picture of family life, with the husband explaining Virgil to his wife, and quiet, well-behaved children reading edifying books on Sunday afternoons.

Femme abandonnée, La, one of the 'Scènes de la vie privée' of Balzac's *Comédie humaine* (q.v.).

Femme de trente ans, La, one of the 'Scènes de la vie privée' of Balzac's *Comédie humaine* (q.v.).

Femme et le pantin, La (1898), by Pierre Louÿs (q.v.), a novel.

Femme juge et partie, La, a comedy by Montfleury, produced in 1669.

Bernadille, unjustly suspicious of his wife, abandons her on a small island in the Mediterranean, and believing her dead, meditates remarriage. But the wife returns, disguised in gentleman's dress, and proceeds to take vengeance on her husband, finally getting herself named provost of the town, summoning him before her tribunal, extorting a confession, sentencing him to the gallows, enjoying his terror for a while, and then revealing herself.

Femmes savantes, Les, a comedy by Molière, produced in 1672.

The fashion had changed in the thirteen years since Molière wrote *Les Précieuses ridicules* (q.v.): it was now the vogue in elegant circles to affect the cult of grammar (as prescribed by Vaugelas), of philosophy (after Descartes), and of astronomy. Molière here ridicules the extravagances of this new fashion, in the persons of Philaminte, wife of the bourgeois Chrysale, his daughter Armande, and his sister Bélise, all three devotees of the new cult and admirers of the ridiculous Trissotin, a sorry wit and poetaster, and of the pedant Vadius (reported to know Greek). In contrast to them we have the simple charming Henriette, Armande's younger sister, whose hand is sought by Clitandre, an agreeable courtier. Chrysale is a timid hen-pecked husband, who makes an occasional show of feeble resistance; he favours Clitandre's suit, but his wife is determined that Henriette shall marry Trissotin. Shamed by the reproofs of his sensible brother, Ariste, Chrysale takes courage to resist her, and insists that Henriette shall marry Clitandre. The notary is summoned and receives contradictory instructions from the pair. Even now Chrysale wavers; but, on a false report that the family fortune is lost, Trissotin reveals his interested motives by withdrawing his suit, and Clitandre triumphs.

In Trissotin Molière ridiculed the abbé Cotin, in Vadius he is thought to have depicted Ménage, though Ménage states that Molière denied this.

Fénelon, FRANÇOIS DE SALIGNAC (or SALAGNAC) DE LA MOTHE- (1651–1715), theologian, of an old Gascon family, received a good classical education, became a priest and a disciple of Bossuet (q.v.). He was appointed in 1678 Superior of certain convents in Paris, and after the revocation of the Edict of Nantes (1685) was employed in the conversion of Huguenots in the west of France, 'to perfect the work done by the Dragoons', as Mme de Sévigné with mild irony put it. He became the spiritual leader of a devout group at court which included the duc de Beauvilliers (tutor of the duc de Bourgogne, the king's grandson) and was favoured by Mme de Maintenon. It was about this time that he wrote his Platonic *Dialogues sur l'éloquence* (not published till 1718) and his *Traité de l'éducation des filles* (1687, q.v.), a work showing both good sense and insight into the feminine mind, and not devoid of charm. In 1689 Fénelon was charged with the education of the duc de Bourgogne, a refractory pupil whom he successfully transformed, and this important appointment brought other honours in its train: he was admitted to the *Académie* in 1693 and named Archbishop of Cambrai in 1695. But his successful career was checked before long. He had come under the influence of Mme Guyon and had been captivated by the doctrine of Quietism (q.v.). This brought him into conflict with Bossuet, and alienated from him Mme de Maintenon and the king, especially when Fénelon appealed to Rome on the point of doctrine. His *Explication des Maximes des saints* (1697) in defence of Mme Guyon was condemned by the Pope in 1699. The surreptitious publication in the same year (1699) of his *Télémaque* (q.v.), written for the education of his pupil and containing passages reflecting on the government of Louis XIV, completed his disgrace. Fénelon was now deprived of his preceptorate and relegated to his diocese. He however maintained relations with his devout followers at court and with his pupil, and his hope of return to favour revived when that pupil by his father's death became the direct heir to the throne. But the death of the young man cut short these hopes, and Fénelon himself

died unpardoned, remaining for fifteen years in his diocese, where he discharged his episcopal duties in an admirable manner. His numerous literary works, other than those mentioned above, include the *Dialogues des Morts* (1700–18), presenting for the edification of his pupil heroes and statesmen of antiquity and modern times. The *Traité de l'existence de Dieu* (1713, second part posthumous) seeks proof of the existence of the deity in the wonders of nature, in the structure of the human body and human mind, and in certain of our ideas. The *Lettre à M. Dacier sur les occupations de l'Académie française* (1714, published 1716) is an interesting work. The *Académie* was considering to what it should address itself when its dictionary was completed. Fénelon suggests the preparation of a grammar and of treatises on rhetoric, &c., discussing with great fertility of ideas a multitude of literary questions. The *Lettre à Louis XIV* or *Lettre secrète*, written about 1694, contains criticisms of the prevailing political system; it may have been no more than a rhetorical exercise. The *Tables de Chaulnes* is the name given to a scheme of political reforms drawn up by Fénelon and the duc de Beauvilliers in 1711 to be submitted to a future king, involving the restriction of the royal power by a popular element in the constitution. His *Lettres spirituelles*, letters of religious instruction to various persons (published in 1718), show him as a priest and a Christian.

Fénelon was a man of curiously complex character: affectionate and possessing a seductive charm, humane and philanthropic, an aristocrat in tastes and ideas, supple and elusive in controversy, obstinate and ambitious with an ironical assumption of humility, a mystic in religion, lacking the male vigour of Bossuet, a blend of the politician and the Christian priest. His character, his rapid rise to influence, followed by vicissitudes and disgrace, are admirably depicted in the pages of Saint-Simon. He wrote in an easy, simple, harmonious style, and his *Télémaque* has been described as the first prose poem in French. This and other works show his affection for certain of the Greek and Latin classics, as well as a fertile imagination, and a resemblance to Lamartine as artist and poet.

Fénéon, Félix (1861–1944), a critic closely

associated by taste, influence, and friendships with the Symbolist, Impressionist, and Neo-Impressionist movements in literature and art, and one of the first to appreciate their importance. He wrote mostly in reviews, and for a time edited the *Revue indépendante* (q.v.). He also, for two years (1905–6), conducted a News in Brief column ('Nouvelles en trois lignes') in the daily paper *Le Matin* which shows him a master of the art of compression (e.g. '"Mourir à la Jeanne d'Arc!" disait Terbaud, du haut d'un bûcher fait de ses meubles. Les pompiers de Saint-Ouen l'en empêchèrent'). Selections from his writings—*Œuvres*, ed. J. Paulhan—were published in 1950.

Féraud or **Ferraud**, L'ABBÉ JEAN-FRANÇOIS, see *Dictionaries and Encyclopedias*, under date 1787–8.

Fermat, PIERRE DE (*c.* 1595–1665), a counsellor to the *Parlement* of Toulouse, and a mathematician of standing (but he kept his papers badly and published little). Pascal, his friend and correspondent, called him 'le premier homme du monde'. He had some lively differences of opinion with Descartes.

Fermiers généraux. Under the *ancien régime* the office of collecting certain indirect taxes (see *Gabelle* and cf. *Fiscal system*), which implied also the right to exploit them, was farmed out, or leased for fixed periods, to private persons. These *fermiers généraux* paid highly in the first instance for the privilege, which was frequently auctioned to the highest bidder, but they made such a good rake-off that they were able to amass very large fortunes (which some of them used to encourage literature and the arts). The system dated from the 13th century and was so much abused that it became a powerful factor in the economic discontent of the pre-Revolutionary era.

Ferney (now generally called **Ferney-Voltaire**), a village a few miles north-west of Geneva but within the French frontier, where Voltaire resided from 1758 to 1778.

Ferragus, in the *Entrée en Espagne*, a *chanson de geste* (q.v.) of the Charlemagne cycle, is a Saracen giant who defeats in single combat and captures eleven of the twelve peers of Charlemagne. He is finally killed by Roland.

Ferragus, by Balzac (see *Comédie humaine*), the first of the three 'Scènes de la vie parisienne' which form the trilogy *Histoire des Treize.*

Ferronnière, La Belle, a bourgeoise of Paris, a favourite of François Ier. She is said to have been so called either because her husband's name was Ferron or because he was a *ferronnier*, an iron-worker or iron-merchant. She was not the original of Leonardo da Vinci's portrait (in the Louvre), called *La Belle Ferronnière*, in which the woman is wearing round her forehead a *ferronnière*, a type of chain secured in front with a single jewel or cameo.

Fersen, HANS AXEL, COMTE DE (1755–1810), born and died in Stockholm, Swedish statesman. He was for a time a French army officer, serving in America, then becoming *colonel-propriétaire* of the *royal-suédois* regiment. He was a favourite at the French court and a worshipper of Marie-Antoinette. It was he, disguised as a coachman, who drove the royal fugitives' coach on the first stage of the flight to Varennes (1791). When Louis XVI was arrested he fled to Belgium. His later activities, after his return to Sweden, belong to Swedish history. He became very unpopular and was eventually murdered during a people's rising.

Festin de pierre, Le, see *Dom Juan.*

Fête des fous (*festum stultorum* or *follorum*), the Feast of Fools, the farcical element introduced by the lesser clergy into the liturgy of the medieval cathedrals, especially in France, during the special celebrations which took place between Christmas and the Octave of Epiphany (13 Jan.). Into the ordinary form of the Mass and Ceremonial Office were interpolated such revels as 'a drinking-bout, the bringing of an ass into the church . . . and the ending of certain liturgical pieces with a bray' (K. Young, *The Drama of the Medieval Church*), the object being to parody the ecclesiastical hierarchy. By the middle of the 15th century these revels had mostly been abolished; they were succeeded in the history of the drama by the profane plays (farces, moralities, *soties*, &c.) performed by lay confraternities (*confréries* or *sociétés joyeuses*, q.v.).

Fêtes galantes (1869), early poems by Verlaine (q.v.).

Feu, Le (1916), a novel of the 1914–18 war, by Henri Barbusse (q.v.).

Feuillantisme, a contemptuous term for the doctrines of the *Club des Feuillants* (see the following).

Feuillants, Le Club des, was founded in 1791 by constitutional royalists and moderate democrats who seceded from the *Jacobins* (q.v.). They met in a building near the Tuileries formerly occupied by the Feuillants (a reformed order of Cistercian monks), hence their name; and the subscription was high. From the ultra-democratic point of view it became as much of a sin to be a *Feuillant* as to be an *aristocrat*.

Feuilles d'automne, Les (1831), lyrics, by Victor Hugo, more peaceful and intimate in character than the earlier ones of *Les Orientales* (q.v.). The themes are family affection, reminiscences of childhood (e.g. the meditative autobiography *Ce siècle avait deux ans*), and regrets for the passing of time.

Feuillet, OCTAVE (1821–90), one of the most popular of 19th-century French novelists, is remembered particularly by his romantic, sentimental *Roman d'un jeune homme pauvre* (1858), the tale of a chivalrous, impecunious young man who refuses to marry the rich young heroine. He destroys the proof that he is the rightful owner of her fortune, but by a miraculous coincidence he inherits even greater wealth, so the marriage does, after all, take place. Other novels by Feuillet include *Monsieur de Camors* (1867), feebly reminiscent of *Les Liaisons dangereuses* (see *Laclos, Choderlos de*), and *Julia de Trécœur* (1872). His plays, almost equally successful, include *Le Pour et le contre* (1853), *La Belle au bois dormant* (1867), *La Partie de dames* (1883).

Feuilleton, a supplement issued with a newspaper. The most famous of early feuilletons was the one created about 1800 by Geoffroy, the dramatic critic of the *Journal des Débats* (q.v.). It formed an appendix to the rest of the paper, being printed across the lower part of the page and detachable at will. The innovation was so successful that other journals quickly followed suit, printing literary and dramatic feuilletons and, later, *romans-feuilletons* (q.v.).

Féval, PAUL (1817–87), a prolific author of sensational novels. A number of them were early examples of the *roman-feuilleton* (q.v.), e.g. *Les Mystères de Londres* (1844), *Les Amours de Paris* (1845), *Le Fils du Diable* (1846), *Le Bossu* (1858), &c.

Feydeau, ERNEST (1821–73), novelist, born in Paris, began as a stockbroker and also studied archaeology (when he wrote *Histoire des usages funèbres et des sépultures des peuples anciens*, 1856). He frequented Flaubert (a distant relative) and Gautier (qq.v.), and in 1858 published *Fanny*, a novel which ranked as one of the triumphs of *le Réalisme* (q.v.). Its theme was adultery and jealousy (the hero retires to a hut on a desolate sea-shore to try and overcome his jealousy of his mistress's husband), and its success—one of scandal only—for a time surpassed even that of Flaubert's *Madame Bovary* (1857). Feydeau's later works (e.g. *Daniel*, 1859, *Sylvie*, 1861, *La Comtesse de Chalis*, 1867) made little stir.

Feydeau, GEORGES (1862–1921), son of the foregoing, author of highly successful, uproarious, but often witty and ingeniously constructed vaudevilles and farcical comedies, e.g. *Tailleur pour dames* (1888), *La Dame de chez Maxim's*, *Feu la mère de Madame*, *Occupe-toi d'Amélie*, all contained in his *Théâtre complet* (1948–50).

Fiammetta, a novel by Boccaccio, remarkable for its delicate psychological observation. It was translated into French in 1532 (see *Novel*, para. 5).

Fichet, GUILLAUME (later 15th c.), humanist, rector of the university of Paris. He procured the establishment (1470) in the college of the Sorbonne of the first printing-press that worked in Paris. He inculcated the study of the ancient Latin authors and was one of the pioneers of the Renaissance of French literature.

Fierabras, a *chanson de geste* (q.v.) of the Charlemagne cycle, of the late 12th or early 13th century. Fierabras is a giant, son of the Saracen king Balant; he has captured Rome and removed the holy relics, is defied by the emperor and his knights, is defeated by Olivier in single combat, and baptized. His sister Floripas falls in love with the knight Gui de Bourgogne, and when Gui, as well as

Olivier, Roland, and other knights chance to fall into the hands of Balant, she sets about their liberation, bringing them together so that they can offer united resistance to their jailers. Charlemagne comes to their rescue, Balant is captured and, refusing baptism, is executed. Floripas is baptized and marries Gui, and the holy relics are recovered.

The English metrical romance *Sir Firumbras* and the latter part of the *Sowdone of Babylon* (both late 14th century) are taken from this or from other versions of the same story.

Fière, the lioness, in the *Roman de Renart* (q.v.).

Fieschi, JOSEPH, an habitual delinquent of Corsican birth (1790), was executed in Paris (16 Feb. 1836) with two accomplices for having attempted the life of Louis-Philippe on 28 July 1835. They had set off a *machine infernale* (q.v.), erected in the window of a house in the Boulevard du Temple, while a royal procession was passing in the street below. The king and the princes were unhurt, but eighteen people were killed and many injured.

Fiévée, JOSEPH (1767–1839), publicist and journalist, born in Paris, at one time editor of the *Gazette de France* and a contributor to *Le Mercure* (qq.v.). As one of Napoleon's special counsellors he had the duty of supplying confidential surveys of public opinion. He was for a time editor-in-chief of the *Journal des Débats* (q.v.) while that paper was under Government control. His correspondence (*Correspondance politique et administrative*, 1814–15–19, and *Correspondance et relations avec Bonaparte*, 1837) contains a good picture of events and of the movement of ideas in the early 19th century. His short novel of 'sensibility', *La Dot de Suzette* (1798), was praised by Sainte-Beuve.

Figaro, the hero of Beaumarchais's *Le Barbier de Séville* and *Le Mariage de Figaro* (qq.v.). He figures also in the author's *L'Autre Tartufe ou la Mère coupable* (see under *Beaumarchais*).

Figaro, Le, still one of the leading French dailies, had existed in a small way as a weekly for many years when it was acquired in 1854 and transformed by H. de Villemessant (1812–79). He collected the wittiest journa-

lists of the day on his staff, e.g. Edmond About, Théodore de Banville, Charles Monselet, Aurélien Scholl, Barbey d'Aurevilly, and published his paper twice weekly till 1867, then daily. It was typical of the spirit of the Second Empire, and at a time when politics were banned it featured successful dramatic and literary columns and satirical, often scandalous, society chronicles. It was called 'un journal où l'on ne s'occupe guère que des littérateurs, des boursiers, et des comédiennes. Les articles sur les boursiers y sont faits par les littérateurs, les articles sur les littérateurs y sont faits par les comédiennes.' The *Figaro* of later years has maintained a high standard of literary and dramatic criticism.

Fille aux yeux d'or, La, by Balzac (see *Comédie humaine*), the third of the 'Scènes de la vie parisienne' which form the trilogy *Histoire des Treize*.

Fille de Mme Angot, La, see *Angot, Mme*.

Fille de Roland, La (1875), a poetic, patriotic drama, see *Bornier, Henri de*.

Fille Élisa, La (1877), a typical naturalistic novel, by Edmond de Goncourt (q.v.), is the gloomy history of a girl who becomes a prostitute, first in the provinces, then in a poor quarter of Paris near the École Militaire. She falls in love with a soldier and murders him one day in an hysterical rage. She gets a life-sentence, and from this point the book becomes a protest against the conditions of penal servitude. It depicts the imprisoned woman's rebellion, resignation to compulsory silence, and final lapse into complete imbecility.

Filles de la Charité, see *Vincent de Paul, Saint*.

Filles du feu, Les (1854), a collection of prose tales and of poetry by Gérard de Nerval (q.v.).

Filleul, Nicolas, see *Pastoral*.

Filocopo, a prose romance by Boccaccio, a version of the story told in the 13th-century metrical romances *Floire et Blanchefleur* (q.v., French) and *Flores and Blancheflour* (English). The *Thirteen Questions*, or love problems, of the fifth book were translated into French in 1531 and are often mentioned in studies of foreign influences on the evolution of the French novel.

Fils de Giboyer, Le (1862), a drama by Émile Augier (q.v.).

Fils naturel, Le (1757), see *Diderot*, para. 4. This is also the title of a play (1858) by Dumas *fils* (q.v.).

Fin, La, the last of the 'Gens de mer' poems in Tristan Corbière's (q.v.) *Les Amours jaunes* (1873). It is frequently contrasted with Hugo's *Oceano nox* (q.v.).

Fin de Satan, La, see *Légende des siècles*.

Fiscal system under the Monarchy. The kingdom of France was divided for fiscal purposes into twenty-one *généralités*, and the *généralités* into *élections* (a name originating from the time when the distributors of taxes were elected by the taxpayers); under the *élections* were the parishes. About the year 1600 there were 149 *élections* and 23,159 parishes. In each *généralité* was a *bureau général* or board composed of about ten *trésoriers de France*, which drew up annual estimates of receipts and expenditure. Basing itself on these estimates, the king's council each year settled the schedule of the amount of taxes payable by each *généralité*. The board of the *généralité* distributed this amount among the *élections*. In each *élection* a *bureau*, composed of about ten *élus* (from the time of Louis XI appointed by the king), distributed the sum payable among the parishes. In each parish the parishioners elected two or four *collecteurs* (according to the importance of the sum to be levied) who assessed the individual taxpayers according to their presumed income and were held responsible for collecting the amount due. In five of the *généralités*, however, known as *pays d'États* in contrast to the *pays d'élections*, the provincial *états* or assemblies discussed with the king the amount that the *généralité* should pay, and then distributed that amount among its parishes on the basis of a cadastre of real property.

The tax levied by the above machinery was the *taille*, the principal source of revenue of the State, a direct tax either on real or personal property. The nobility and clergy and a number of judicial, fiscal, and municipal officials were exempt from it, and its inequitable incidence contributed to bring about the Revolution. In 1657 its yield was 53,400,000 livres and Colbert reduced it to 35,000,000 livres; the far greater part of it was drawn from the *pays d'élections*.

In addition there were a number of indirect taxes: the *gabelle* (q.v.), customs (at the frontiers of the provinces as well as of the State), excise, tolls, &c., which were farmed out (see *Fermiers généraux*), a system which also gave rise to grave abuses. In spite of the reduction of the *taille*, the yield of the total revenue increased under Colbert from 84 to 116 million livres. The national budget rose to some 200 million livres before the Revolution.

Flamberge, in the *chansons de geste*, the name of the sword of Renaud de Montauban (q.v.).

Flaubert, GUSTAVE (1821–80), the famous French novelist, was born and educated at Rouen, where his father was chief surgeon at the hospital. From 1840–3 he studied law in Paris but failed to pass his examinations and was then allowed to devote himself to literature, at home. (This was partly because for some years about this time he was subject to something very like epileptic seizures.) After his father's death (1846) he remained with his mother (d. 1872) in their country home at Croisset, near Rouen. With them, until her marriage, lived his niece Caroline (later Mme Commanville), over whose education Flaubert took great pains. He led a hermit-like existence, subordinating everything to his writing. This advanced slowly because of his high, self-imposed standards; and his first published novel *Madame Bovary* (q.v.) did not appear till 1857. Occasionally he made brief visits to Paris to see his friends (Gautier, the Goncourts, George Sand, Renan, Taine, Turgenev, &c.) or his publishers; and twice he was absent for longer periods when he travelled in the Near East and Tunisia (in 1849–51, a trip with his friend Maxime du Camp, and in 1857, when he went to collect material for *Salammbô*).

The man and his life can best be studied in his *Correspondance* (first published 1887–93; the definitive edition is that of Conard, 1925–8, with a supplement, 4 vols., in 1954). These letters, among the most interesting in French literature, show Flaubert first as schoolboy and student, already writing tales and short plays, and with a robust sense of fun that he will keep throughout life. He is an extravagant Romantic (see *Romantisme, Le*), and he detests, and will go through life detesting, all that is *bourgeois*, petty-respectable, platitudinous, and self-satisfied. He becomes the lover of Mme Louise Colet (q.v.), at first impassioned, then growing impatient, finally throwing off a yoke that threatens his work (1846–55: but Flaubert's lasting devotion, for all that it was Platonic, was for a Mme Schlésinger whom he first met when he was fourteen and whom he never forgot, cf. *Éducation sentimentale, L'*; *Mémoires d'un fou*). He is a devoted son and uncle; a generous friend and critic, finding no pains too great if he can help other writers, bestowing all possible praise. He is an enthusiastic traveller, his fundamentally romantic temperament revelling in all that is gorgeous, luxurious, and unrestrained in the East; but from travel he returns to the years of toil involved by the documentation as well as by the actual writing of his works. *Madame Bovary* (1857, q.v.), for instance, his famous novel of provincial life, was based on close personal observation; *Salammbô* (1862, q.v.), a novel of ancient Carthage, required painstaking research in books. This care for accurate documentation won him a reputation as a master of the *réalistes*, but he was not fundamentally a realistic novelist and he objected to being classed as one. The spadework of documentation was indeed, for Flaubert, essential for the absolute verity of the background of his novels but it was not, as with the *réalistes pur sang* (see *Réalisme*), an object in itself. His aim was to achieve a rigidly objective and impersonal work of art, presented in the most perfect form. To this end he imposed the severest restraint on the romantic, exuberant side of his nature, and his letters are a day-to-day record of the tortures his writing entailed. He would work seven hours a day, long days on end, over one page, writing, rewriting, reading aloud, recasting, trying to attune his style to his ideal of balanced, harmonious perfection.

His letters, especially those of later years to George Sand, abound in valuable literary criticism; and those written during the Franco-Prussian war (1870) are a good picture of an intellectual forced by circumstances to remember the outside world. In 1875 he sacrificed his modest fortune to help

his niece's husband, and as a result his last years were overshadowed by money worries. He died, suddenly, in May 1880.

Besides those already mentioned his works include : *L'Éducation sentimentale* (1869, q.v.); *La Tentation de Saint Antoine* (1874, q.v.); *Trois Contes: Un Cœur simple, La Légende de Saint Julien l'Hospitalier, Hérodias* (1877, q.v.; the first is the moving tale, told with the perfection of simplicity, of the drab, self-sacrificing life of a faithful servant); *Bouvard et Pécuchet* (1881, q.v., posth. and unfinished), *Par les champs et par les grèves* (1885, posth.), the record of a walking-tour in Brittany undertaken by Flaubert and Maxime du Camp (q.v.) in 1847 and written by the two of them, chapter about; also other early works—notably *Mémoires d'un fou* (q.v.) and the tale *Novembre*—collected and published in 1914–20 under the title *Premières Œuvres*.

Fléchier, ESPRIT (1632–1710), born at Pernes near Avignon, Bishop of Nîmes, a frequenter of the society of the Hôtel de Rambouillet (in its decline), a preacher famous for the elegance of his sermons. He delivered funeral orations on Turenne (1676) and other men and women of distinction, including Julie d'Angennes (see *Rambouillet, Hôtel de*). His eloquence was much admired by Mme de Sévigné. He also wrote *Mémoires sur les Grands-Jours d'Auvergne* of 1665 (published 1844), special assizes held at Clermont for the repression of crime in that province. Fléchier accompanied M. de Caumartin, one of the magistrates employed at the assizes, and wrote for the entertainment of the Rambouillet circle a narrative of the voyage and the proceedings, with descriptions of provincial society, anecdotes and digressions, an interesting document on contemporary life in the provinces. Fléchier also wrote a history of Theodosius, letters, and light verse. He was a member of the *Académie*.

Flers, ROBERT DE (1872–1927), dramatic author, collaborated successfully with G.-A. de Caillavet and, later, with Francis de Croisset (qq.v.).

Fleurange, ROBERT DE LA MARCK, SEIGNEUR DE (d. 1537), maréchal de France, left interesting memoirs of the period 1499–1521, including an account of the field of the Cloth of Gold and of the battle of Marignan.

Fleurs du mal, Les (1857), a collection of poems by Baudelaire (q.v.).

Fleurus, a small town in Belgium where, on 25 June 1794, the French Revolutionary Army of Sambre-et-Meuse under Jourdan defeated the united Austrian and Netherlands armies.

Fleury, ANDRÉ-HERCULE, CARDINAL DE (1653–1743), Bishop of Fréjus, cardinal from 1726, tutor and subsequently chief minister of Louis XV; a careful administrator who, in conjunction with Walpole, pursued a policy of peace for many years. He allowed France, however, to be drawn into the wars of the Polish and the Austrian Successions.

Fleury, CLAUDE (1640–1723), author of an important *Histoire ecclésiastique* (1691–1720).

Fleury, JULES, see *Champfleury*.

Flicoteau, a cheap restaurant, named after its proprietor, in the Latin Quarter (it was in the rue de la Sorbonne) in the early 19th century and frequented by students and seedy journalists. Balzac describes it in *Illusions perdues* (q.v., *Un Grand Homme de province à Paris*). It was typical of such establishments for at least a century to follow: a *prix fixe* meal (well seasoned with garlic to disguise more suspicious flavours), *vin compris*, *pain à discrétion* (that is to say, a very large quantity), and one's table napkin, mysteriously knotted, kept in a pigeon-hole from one day to another.

Floire et Blancheflor, an early 13th-century metrical *roman d'aventure*, of which there are two versions in French; also an English version of about 1250. The story was also treated by Boccaccio (*Filocopo*, q.v.).
   It is the tale of a boy and a girl who are brought up together and fall in love. The girl is carried off to Babylon, but Floire succeeds (by concealing himself in a basket of roses) in joining her in the emir's seraglio where she has been placed. They are ordered to execution, but their beauty and their devotion to each other win their pardon. The poem contains a charming picture of the visionary wonders of the East.

Floovent, a *chanson de geste* (q.v.) of the 12th century recounting the story of the Merovingian Floovent, son of Clovis. It is based on earlier poems which have not survived.

Floral games of Toulouse, see *Jeux floraux*.

Floréal, the eighth month of the Republican Calendar (q.v.). It ran from 20 (or 21) April to 19 (or 20) May.

Florian, JEAN-PIERRE CLARIS DE (1755–94), novelist and fabulist, born in the Cévennes, a connexion of Voltaire (whose niece married Florian's uncle) and a favourite of the old man, though his works show him rather a disciple of Rousseau. He was attached to the service of the philanthropic duc de Penthièvre (grandson of Louis XIV). Florian was author of a series of mild comedies of bourgeois life (*Le Bon Ménage, Le Bon Père,* &c.) in which Arlequin (q.v.) figures as a sentimental character, and of insipid romances, domestic, pastoral, or pseudo-historical (*Galatée,* 1783, adapted from Cervantes; *Numa Pompilius,* 1786, a moralizing imitation of Fénelon's *Télémaque* and Marmontel's *Bélisaire*; *Estelle et Némorin,* 1787, a pastoral; *Gonzalve de Cordoue,* 1791, the capture of Granada in 1492 with romantic episodes). He also wrote agreeable *Fables* (1792), which, however, were overshadowed by La Fontaine's greater genius and acuter understanding of animals. He recounted his early life, disguising the names of persons and places, in the *Mémoires d'un jeune Espagnol*. He was admitted to the *Académie* in 1788.

Floupette, Adoré, see *Déliquescences d'Adoré Floupette, Les.*

Foch, FERDINAND (1851–1929), maréchal de France, the famous French army leader who in the last year of the 1914–18 war became General-in-Chief of the Allied Armies.

Focillon, HENRI, (1881–1943), author of, notably, *Vie des formes* (1934), as well as other studies ranging from romanesque sculpture to 20th-century painting.

Fogg, PHILEAS, and his valet Passepartout, the chief characters in *Le Tour du monde en quatre-vingts jours* by Jules Verne (q.v.).

Foire, Théâtre de la. From the end of the 16th century it was customary for strolling players to erect their booths at the fairs held in Paris in winter (the *foire Saint-Germain* in the Saint-Germain quarter) and in summer (the *foire Saint-Laurent*, where the Gare de l'Est now stands). Here they presented comic dialogues, which gradually developed into dramatic scenes after the Italian players had been expelled in 1697 (see *Theatres and theatre companies*). To this invasion of its monopoly the Comédie-Française offered opposition; but the *théâtre de la foire* gradually established itself. It combined with the Italian players when these returned in 1716, and specialized in *opéra-comique* (romantic comedy interspersed with song and dance), besides producing various other forms of comedy suited to popular audiences. Among the chief dramatic authors who wrote for it were Lesage, Favart, and Piron.

Foire sur la place, La (1908), the fifth volume, often mentioned for its picture of literary and artistic Paris about 1912, of Romain Rolland's long novel of musical life, *Jean-Christophe* (q.v.).

Folantin, Monsieur, the chief character in *A vau l'eau* (q.v.) by J.-K. Huysmans.

Fole Largece, La, a *fabliau* by Philippe de Beaumanoir (q.v.). A salt-merchant has to go four leagues to the sea to fetch his salt. He tells his wife to be careful to sell, during his absence, the salt that remains in stock. Instead of this she foolishly gives it away to her gossips. To cure her of her folly the merchant takes her with him on his next expedition and makes her carry a share of the salt; by the time they reach home the cure is effected.

Folengo, TEOFILO (1496–1544), born at Mantua, a Benedictine monk in early and again in later life; author during the period of his return to the world, and under the pseudonym Merlin Cocai, of a long macaronic poem *Baldus* (the name of the hero) which influenced Rabelais by its mixture of parody and realism. It was translated into French in 1606 (*Histoire maccaronique de Merlin Coccaie, prototype de Rabelais*).

Folies amoureuses, Les, a comedy in verse by Regnard, produced in 1704.

This charming trifle illustrates the well-worn theme of young love defeating the jealousy of old age. Albert, the aged guardian of Agathe, wishes to marry her, and tries by bars and bolts to prevent the access of younger suitors. But love finds out a way. Agathe feigns madness—the result of Albert's harsh restraint. Crispin, her young lover's valet, posing as a physician, undertakes to cure her. Albert, distracted by the sight of her disorder, eagerly accepts the offer. The pretended cure provides an opportunity for the elopement of the young couple.

Folie Tristan, La, two episodic poems of the Tristan legend, see *Tristan*.

Folle de Chaillot, La (1945), a play by Jean Giraudoux (q.v.), a bitter satire of a 20th century in which money is the god, and only madwomen still believe in love and honour.

Folle Journée, La, see *Mariage de Figaro*.

Fontainas, André (1865–1948), poet and critic, of Belgian birth, who studied and later lived mostly in Paris. He was in the thick of the Symbolist movement (see *Symbolisme*), a disciple of Mallarmé, and a contributor to the *Mercure de France* and other symbolist reviews. His works include: *Les Vergers illusoires* (1892), *Les Estuaires d'ombre* (1896), *Le Jardin des îles claires* (1901), *La Nef désemparée* (1908), *Récifs au soleil* (1922, showing the influence of Valéry); also translations of Keats and Meredith, and reminiscences of Symbolist days.

Fontaine, CHARLES (1513–87), poet, a prominent supporter of Clément Marot (q.v.) in his quarrel with Sagon, and later a defender of the style of Marot against the innovations of the Pléiade. He called his poems *Ruisseaux de la Fontaine*.

Fontaine, NICOLAS (1625–1709), secretary and companion in his imprisonment of Le Maître de Saci (q.v.), a humble member of the society of Port-Royal, of which in his *Memoirs* he has left a naïve and vivid picture.

Fontainebleau, Palais de [from *fons Blaudi*, fontaine de Blaud], a fortress before the 12th century, was a favourite palace of the kings of France. François Iᵉ and Henri IV, in particular, took pleasure in rebuilding and beautifying it. The library established there in 1363 by Charles V was later moved to Paris and formed the nucleus of the *Bibliothèque nationale* (q.v.). The palace was abandoned during the Revolution but became a prison during the Terror. Napoleon restored it at great cost. In 1812–13 he kept Pope Pius VII there in semi-captivity (cf. *Servitude et Grandeur militaires*, by Alfred de Vigny); and there, on 6 April 1814, he signed his first abdication. The Palace is today an historical monument, open to the public except for certain parts reserved for army and educational purposes.

Fontaine de jouvence, La, a mythical fountain possessing the gift of restoring youth, belief in the existence of which was widespread in the Middle Ages. It is first met with in French literature in Alexandre de Bernay's metrical romance on Alexander the Great (see *Alexandre le Grand*). There it is a stream in which Alexander and his army bathe and are restored to the prime of youth.

Fontaines, MARIE-LOUISE-CHARLOTTE DE GIVRY, MME DE (d. 1730), novelist, an imitator of Mme de La Fayette, author of an *Histoire de la comtesse de Savoie*, a romance of the 11th century.

Fontanes, LOUIS DE (1757–1821), statesman and man of letters, *Grand-Maître* of the University under the Empire, was brought up among the didactic poets of the 18th century and maintained their traditions well into the nineteenth. He is remembered for his encouragement of Chateaubriand (q.v.) in the latter's young days. His works include *Fragment d'un poème sur la nature et sur l'homme* (1777), *Essai sur l'astronomie* (1788, poem), and a translation of Pope's *Essay on Man*.

Fontaney, ANTOINE-ÉTIENNE (1803–37), minor poet, a frequenter of the Romantic *cénacles* (q.v.), and at one time attached to the French Embassy in Spain. He wrote *Ballades, mélodies et poésies diverses* (1829) and *Scènes de la vie castillane et andalouse* (1835).

Fontanges, MARIE-ANGÉLIQUE, DUCHESSE DE (1661–81), the successor of Mme de Montespan as favourite of Louis XIV. The word *fontange*, signifying a certain mode of dressing the hair, was derived from her name.

Fontenay-Mareuil, FRANÇOIS DU VAL, MARQUIS DE (c. 1594–1665), soldier and diplomatist under Richelieu and Mazarin. He was ambassador in England 1630–3. He left interesting memoirs, chiefly of the period 1609–24, giving also a faithful picture of Henri IV.

Fontenelle, BERNARD LE BOVIER, SIEUR DE (1657–1757), miscellaneous writer, born at Rouen, nephew of Corneille. He was a man of wide curiosity and learning, and of a cool and unemotional intelligence. He began, under the guidance of his uncle Thomas Corneille, by writing dramas and other verse of no literary importance. His more notable works include *Dialogues des Morts* (1683), on the Lucianic model, and his famous *Entretiens sur la pluralité des mondes* (1686). The latter treatise, by its lucidity and the charm and grace of its method (dialogues, between the author and a lady of his acquaintance), awakened general interest in astronomy and popularized the scientific system of inquiry; it also emphasized the small place occupied by man and this planet relatively to the rest of the universe. The work was ridiculed by Voltaire, though it suggested his *Micromégas*. In the *Histoire des Oracles* (1687), based on an erudite work by the Dutchman van Dale, Fontenelle disproved their supernatural origin and analysed the causes of the credulity which accepts the marvellous; and in his *Digression sur les Anciens et les Modernes* (1688) he took part in the celebrated dispute on this subject on the side of the moderns. In general he was a precursor of the attack which before long science was to make on religion, unostentatiously encouraging freedom of thought by substituting the play of mechanical forces for Providence in explanations of natural phenomena. His *Réflexions sur la poétique* (written c. 1695, printed 1742) also deserves mention: he classifies tragic interest according to the misfortune that is its source, giving the lowest position to misfortune the outcome of fate (the source of Greek tragedy). He also points out that, the object of dramatic rules being the pleasure of the spectator, an irregular drama which pleases conforms to rules that have not yet been discovered. Fontenelle was a member of the *Académie française* and of the *Académie des inscriptions*, and perpetual secretary (from 1697) of the *Académie des Sciences*. He wrote a history of the last of these with an analysis of its proceedings, and remarkable *éloges* of its members. He was a member of the Royal Society of London.

Fontenoy, near Tournai in Belgium, the scene of a battle in 1745 in which after a stout defence the English and Dutch under the Duke of Cumberland were defeated by the French under the maréchal de Saxe.

Forain, JEAN-LOUIS (1852–1931), artist, book-illustrator, and caricaturist. His humour was caustic.

Forbin, CLAUDE, COMTE DE (1656–1733), naval officer, wrote somewhat vainglorious memoirs, whose accuracy has been questioned. They were published in 1729 and provoked a dispute between him and Duguay-Trouin (q.v.), whom Forbin disparaged. They contain an account of the abortive attempt of James III to land in Scotland in 1708.

Force, Prison de la, originally a mansion built in the 13th century for Charles d'Anjou, King of Naples and Sicily. The street in which it stood is still called rue du Roi de Sicile. It was bought by the Government in the mid-18th century from its then owner the duc de la Force, and converted (1782) into a prison, one part for men, the other (till *c.* 1830) for prostitutes. During the Revolution it was used for political prisoners. It was demolished in 1850.

Forces tumultueuses, Les (1902), poems by Verhaeren (q.v.).

Foreign Influences on French Literature. [Note: Authors and movements referred to below receive fuller mention under separate headings.]

1100–1700

(1) Oriental and Byzantine influence, largely the result of the Crusades, can be seen in the fantasy and lavish colouring of the medieval romances. Arabic influence left traces (via Provençal) on courtly poetry and is found in scientific and didactic literature. But the most considerable foreign influences during these centuries (excluding those of classical antiquity) on French literature were Italian, Spanish, English, and German. The first two were manifest principally during the 16th and 17th centuries (see paras. 2–5). As regards the second two, the connexion between France and Anglo-Norman England left some traces; the existence of some hundreds of Germanic words is the chief witness to the conquest of Gaul by the Franks (the theory of the Germanic origin of the *chansons de geste* has now been abandoned); in the 16th

century Louis de Berquin translated some of the works of Luther, whose initiative and doctrine had a resounding effect; and in the 17th century the principle of religious liberty and freedom of thought, so prominent from Bayle (1647–1706) onwards, owes more to Luther than to Calvin. On the whole, however, English and German influence was slight before the 18th century.

(2) Italian influence, notably Petrarch's, on poetry first becomes marked in the early 16th century, especially at Lyons, a centre of Italian connexions. (Maurice Scève discovered the tomb of Petrarch's Laura there in 1535.) It is evident in Clément Marot (*fl.* 1532–44), who spent some time at the court of the Duchess of Ferrara, and in Mellin de Saint-Gelais. Castiglione's *Cortegiano* (tr. 1537) introduced the Platonic conception of love and the ideal of the court lady, which inspired Heroët's *Parfaicte Amye* (1542). Du Bellay plainly mentions Italian poetry among the inspirations of the *Pléiade* (1556); and the sonnet-form (q.v.), also introduced from Italy, was much employed by him, by Ronsard, Pontus de Tyard, and Louise Labé. (Dante, first tr. 1596–7, was little appreciated before the 19th century.)

(3) From the mid-16th century translations and imitations of Italian plays were common. (Those of Larivey appeared in 1579 and 1611.) Seventeenth-century dramatists frequently borrowed plots from Italian, and from Spanish, sources (e.g. Corneille's *Le Cid* and several of Molière's comedies); and an Italian company of actors, the Gelosi, in Paris in 1576, was established there throughout the 17th century (cf. *Theatres and theatre companies*). The Italian and Spanish influences were stronger on comedy than on tragedy. Pastorals, such as the *Aminta* (1573) and *Il Pastor fido* (1590) of the Italians Tasso and Guarini, or the *Diana* (1578) of the Spaniard Montemayor, inspired a vogue in France which may be seen in the pastoral plays of Hardy (early 17th century). Italian influence also contributed to the development of tragi-comedy (q.v.) as a genre, and in the 17th century imitations of Spanish burlesque were common.

(4) In prose fiction Boccaccio is a definite early influence (and the possibility of earlier Italian influence on the development of the *nouvelle*, q.v., has been discussed). The *Decameron* (tr. 1485 and again, a better

version, 1545; both several times reprinted) was a model as early as 1462 for the *Cent Nouvelles nouvelles* and again in 1558 for Marguerite de Navarre's *Heptaméron*. Two of the tales—of Griselda and of Guiscard and Gismonde, qq.v.—were especially popular and were published separately. The same author's *Filocopo* was partially translated in 1531, his *Fiammetta* in 1532. The *Histoire d'Eurialus et Lucrèce* by Aeneas Sylvius (Pope Pius II) was translated three or four times, and material for collections of tales was also drawn from Poggio's *Facetiae* (1510) and Bandello's *Novelle* (tr. 1580). Interest in Spain is attested as early as the 15th century by translations of the *Amadis* and of many Spanish romances, later by translations of the writings of Baltazar Gracián (1584–1658), by the popularity of *Don Quixote*, and by Honoré d'Urfé's pastoral novel *Astrée* (1607–27) inspired largely, again, by Montemayor's *Diana*. It continues in the 17th century with Scarron, and extends well into the 18th with Lesage. (Their picaresque novels have a recognizable prototype in *Lazarillo de Tormes*.) Scarron's *Nouvelles tragi-comiques* (1655–7), notable early examples of the *nouvelle* (q.v.), were largely imitated from the Spanish. (Cf. also *Novel*.)

(5) In the *salons* of the 17th century, too, the taste for preciosity (i.e. elegance, refinement, subtlety and paradox) was reinforced by examples of the artificial writings of the Italians Guarini and Marino (e.g. the latter's *Adone*, 1623, published in France), which abounded in *concetti*, hyperbole, and metaphors. (*Cultismo*, a kindred movement in Spain, which exaggerated mannerism to the point of obscurity—and which was also called *Gongorism*, from Góngora, 1561–1627, its principal exponent—had small influence, if any.)

1700–*c*. 1800

(6) In the 18th century French interest turned increasingly to English and German literature, especially after 1750, when it coincided with the pre-Romantic movement of ideas. (Mention must also be made, in passing, of the 18th-century 'orientalism' in French literature, for which one responsible factor was Galland's translation of the *Arabian Nights*, 1704–17.)

(7) Between 1700 and 1750 the German philosopher Leibniz (1646–1716) wrote his *Essais de Théodicée* in French. He was at first more esteemed in France than in his own country, though Voltaire ridiculed some of his ideas in *Candide*. Works by his disciple Christian von Wolff (1679–1754) were also translated. From England, political and philosophical ideas reached France before 1750, partly through Voltaire's *Lettres philosophiques*. Montesquieu, like Voltaire, had commended the English political system; and Bacon, Hobbes, Halifax, Shaftesbury, Newton, and Locke were widely appreciated.

(8) English essayists, playwrights, and novelists were also becoming known. Temple, Addison, and Steele were translated or imitated, as also were Wycherley and Vanbrugh, De Foe and Swift. *Le Pour et Contre* (1733), by Prévost, gave information about English literature in general.

(9) English influence, again, is apparent in the novel. Fielding and Richardson were translated between 1740 and 1763, Goldsmith's *Vicar of Wakefield* was translated in 1767, Sterne in 1760–87. Diderot imitated Sterne in *Jacques le fataliste*. He also wrote an enthusiastic *Éloge de Richardson* (1761), and the method of romantic narrative by means of letters was adopted by, for example, Rousseau (*La Nouvelle Héloïse*) and Choderlos de Laclos (*Les Liaisons dangereuses*). The novels of Horace Walpole, Mrs. Radcliffe, and 'Monk' Lewis were much admired; and tombs, sensibility, and delirious passion appealed to some minor authors (e.g. Baculard d'Arnaud, L.-S. Mercier, Léonard), though the real vogue for the Gothic novel came at the end of the century.

(10) From Germany, Wieland's (1733–1813) *Agathon* (1766–7), an early psychological novel, may have given Barthélemy the form of his *Voyage du jeune Anacharsis*. Goethe's novel of romantic love, *Werther* (translated fifteen times between 1776 and 1797), had an overwhelming influence, not so much on the novel as on the mental outlook of a whole generation (see para. 20).

(11) In poetry, the sombre qualities of Young's *Night Thoughts* (tr. 1768), Gray's *Elegy* (tr. 1769), and Ossian (first translated by Letourneur, 1762–77) were much appreciated; while English and German influences coalesce (the former supplied by Thomson's *Seasons*, tr. 1769, and the latter by Haller's *Die Alpen*, tr. 1750) in strengthening the descriptive element which becomes

marked about this time in French didactic verse (cf. Saint-Lambert's *Les Saisons*, 1769; Roucher's *Les Mois*, 1779, and, later, J.-J. Rousseau).

(12) The *Choix de poésies allemandes* (1766, 4 vols.), with a history of German literature and notes on authors, published by Huber (1727–1804, a German living in Paris), also helped to make German poetry known, as did letters by Grimm in the *Mercure de France* (q.v.). The idyllic poems of the German-Swiss Gessner (1730–88) were particularly admired (e.g. the *Death of Abel*, tr. 1759; the *Idylls*, tr. 1762), and contributed to the Back-to-nature movement. They had imitators (e.g. Berquin and Léonard), and their influence can be traced in André Chénier and Florian. Klopstock's *Messiah* (first tr. 1769) had admirers (e.g. Chênedollé). Wieland's poems, though read, were more fully appreciated in the following century (see para. 19).

(13) In the drama, Shakespeare, at first praised and imitated, and later censured, by Voltaire, was more argued about than appreciated. Translations of his plays filled four of the eight volumes of the *Théâtre anglais* (1745–8) of P.-A. de Laplace, and subsequent 18th-century translations and adaptations were by Letourneur and Ducis (qq.v.). Other English dramatists made known by Laplace included Otway and Lillo (whose domestic tragedy was praised by Voltaire, imitated in Saurin's *Beverley*, 1768, and an influence on Diderot). Moore's *The Gamester* was more than once adapted.

(14) Interest in German drama developed more slowly. Lessing's (1729–81) plays, though occasionally imitated, were in general coldly received. His *Dramaturgie* (tr. 1785), on the other hand, and later his *Laocoon* (essays on the limitations of poetry and the plastic arts, not translated till 1802) were to contribute, with the repercussions of the *Sturm und Drang* movement, to the reaction against the classical form of tragedy as well as to the evolution of dramatic criticism.

c. 1800–c. 1830

(15) In the early 19th century foreign influences, weakened during the Revolution, gathered impetus. This was accentuated after 1814 by political happenings, by the development of literary journalism, and not least by the information about the thought, customs, and culture of other countries which was spread by returning *émigrés* and travellers.

(16) Several reviews, miscellanies, and anthologies were devoted to translation and criticism of English, German, and also Italian and Spanish, literature—e.g. the *Archives littéraires de l'Europe* (1804–7), the *Bibliothèque germanique* (1805), the *Mélanges de littérature étrangère* (1808), the *Collection des chefs-d'œuvre des théâtres étrangers* (1821–2), the *Revue britannique* (founded 1825).

(17) Chateaubriand's *Génie du Christianisme* (1802) revivified interest in English literature. Mme de Staël's *De l'Allemagne* (1810), a laudatory study of German literature, drama, and art, contained in germ the doctrines of *le romantisme* (q.v.) and inspired an enthusiasm which for many years coloured French appreciation of German thought. Italy, dear to the Romantics because of Dante and for its association with medieval art and Christianity, was put more clearly on the map by Mme de Staël's novel *Corinne* (1806), Ginguené's *Histoire littéraire d'Italie* (1811–19), Sismondi's *Histoire des littératures du midi de l'Europe* (1812), Stendhal's *Rome, Naples et Florence* (1817). The Spanish *romanceros* (short poems on themes from national history and legend), translated by Creuzé de Lesser (*Romances du Cid*, 1814; 1823), were a fruitful source for the Romantic poets and dramatists (cf. Mérimée's *Théâtre de Clara Gazul*, 1825; Hugo's *Hernani*, 1830, *Ruy Blas*, 1838; Émile Deschamps's *Études françaises et étrangères*, 1828). *Don Quixote* was translated several times.

(18) Individual foreign influences can also be noted on the Romantics' fight for freedom in the drama, e.g. (*a*) German: Schiller (*Wallenstein* was translated in 1809 by Benjamin Constant, who appended *Réflexions sur . . . le théâtre allemand*; his other dramatic works were translated from 1816 onwards); A. W. Schlegel, from whom Mme de Staël took many ideas on literature, and whose Vienna lectures on the drama were translated by Mme Necker de Saussure (*Cours de littérature dramatique*, 1814); Goethe, whose dramatic works were translated from 1821 and in whose Faust, driven by a despairing, Satanic energy, the Romantics found a fitting companion to the Byronic hero; (*b*) Italian: Manzoni (whose

Lettre à M. Chauvet sur les deux unités classiques prefaced Fauriel's translation of his *Tragédies*, 1823); (c) English: Shakespeare (the overwhelming foreign influence) was translated by Guizot (1821), by Bruguière de Sorsum (1826), by A. de Vigny (1827, 1829), and performed in English in Paris in 1822 and—to enthusiastic audiences—1827. He was continually quoted in defence and illustration of the Romantic doctrines (cf. Stendhal's *Racine et Shakspeare*, 1823–5; Hugo's Preface to *Cromwell*, 1827).

(19) On the poetry of the Romantic Movement English—as personified by Byron—was undoubtedly the strongest foreign influence (cf. the works of Lamartine, A. de Musset, &c.). He was translated (1822–5) by Amédée Pichot (1795–1877), whose own *Voyage historique et littéraire en Angleterre et Écosse* (1825) included studies of Byron, Shelley, and the Lake Poets (the latter a noticeable influence on Sainte-Beuve). A collection of *Ballades, Légendes et Chants populaires de l'Angleterre et de l'Écosse* (1825) was also much read. German poetry, e.g. Goethe's *Erlkönig*, Schiller's *Lied von der Glocke*, Bürger's *Lenore* (tr. by G. de Nerval in *Poésies allemandes*, 1830), fostered the vogue for the macabre; and Wieland's *Oberon* (translated by Loeve-Weimars, 1825) was now appreciated. Enthusiasm for Greece and Greek antiquity, also noticeable during these years, was stimulated by Chateaubriand's *Itinéraire de Paris à Jérusalem* (1811), by Latouche's collected edition (1819) of André Chénier, by the Greek war of independence, and by Fauriel's *Chants populaires de la Grèce moderne* (1824–5), with an appended *Discours . . . sur la poésie naturelle et populaire*.

(20) In the novel, romantic love, introspection, and the personal element found in, for example, Senancour's *Obermann*, Chateaubriand's *René*, Musset's *Confession d'un enfant du siècle*, Nodier's *Le Peintre de Salzbourg* owe much to Goethe's *Werther*. Other German influences were, for example, Hoffmann (1776–1822, q.v.), Novalis (1772–1808), La Motte Fouqué (1777–1843), Eichendorff (1788–1857), &c. Their fantastic and mystical tales—often inspired by medieval legend—were translated or imitated by, for example, Nodier and Gérard de Nerval, also by Gautier and Petrus Borel (and see *Romantisme*). Another powerful influence

was English. The sense of the historical past and the case for atmosphere evident in, for example, Vigny's *Cinq-Mars*, Mérimée's *Chronique du règne de Charles IX*, Hugo's *Notre-Dame de Paris*, derive largely from Scott (translated by Defauconpret, 1822). The English Gothic novels were also much read and imitated.

c. 1830–*c.* 1880

(21) Foreign influence during the July Monarchy (1830–48) and the Second Empire (1852–70) shows most clearly in the work of essayists, historians, and critics. The main source was German idealist philosophy. Fichte (1762–1814), Hegel (1770–1831), Schelling (1775–1854), &c., became known between 1815 and 1830 largely through Victor Cousin's Sorbonne lectures. They were translated for the most part before 1850. Interest in Hegel was further stimulated by the critic Schérer's *Introduction à la philosophie de Hégel* (1864). A debt to Herder is apparent in the historical mysticism and philosophical symbolism of Edgar Quinet (who in 1827 had translated Herder's *Idées sur la philosophie de l'humanité*) and in the historian Michelet's theories of the evolution of humanity as a continual struggle between Nature and the Spirit.

(22) The influence of German philosophy is above all marked in Taine and Renan, the two critics revered by young writers *c.* 1875. Hegel, Goethe, Herder, and Kant (leavened by study of English philosophers) were behind the determinism and scientific philosophy elaborated in Taine's Introduction to his *Histoire de la littérature anglaise* (1864–9; see also para. 24). They were still more solidly behind Renan's theories of the all-importance of science in philosophical thought (cf. his *Avenir de la science*, 1857) and of the evolution of the myth of Christianity (cf. his *Origines du christianisme*, 1861–81).

(23) German philosophy can also be seen as an influence on mid-19th-century poetry, in the vague pantheism and the pessimistic outlook of the Parnassiens (e.g. Leconte de Lisle, Sully Prudhomme, Léon Dierx). But it was not the sole foreign influence. Parnassian verse also reflects the interest aroused by the 19th-century development of oriental and archaeological studies (e.g. Leconte de Lisle's *Poèmes antiques*, 1852; *Poèmes bar-*

bares, 1862). Heine's mixture of lyricism and irony had an effect on, for example, Gautier, Banville (*Odes funambulesques*, 1857), and Baudelaire; and the last-named was among the first French writers to be influenced by the American Edgar Allan Poe (whom he translated).

(24) Foreign influence on the novel, on the other hand, such as it was during this period (mainly after the mid-19th century), was almost wholly English. English fiction was reviewed and discussed by the critics Villemain, Schérer and, notably, Montégut. The humour, realism, and solid humanitarianism of Dickens, Thackeray, and George Eliot were much appreciated. (Resemblances to Dickens are sometimes remarked in Daudet's sympathetic depictions of humble life.) The importance attached by Flaubert, the brothers Goncourt, or, later, by Zola and Maupassant, to objective description and to the collection and significant grouping of small facts has some connexion with the English philosophical ideas (Darwin's, for instance) that filtered into French literature through the Positivism of Comte and through Taine, the theoretician of *naturalisme* (q.v. and cf. *réalisme*). *The Origin of Species* was translated in 1866 by Clémence Royer.

c. 1880–1900

(25) German influence on French thought did not end with the Franco-Prussian war (1870). *Les Déracinés* (1897), a novel by Barrès, deplores the place of Kantian doctrines in French teaching. In poetry, the spiritual nihilism of Hartmann (tr. 1877, *La Philosophie de l'inconscient*) and of Schopenhauer (tr. 1880–1, *Le Monde considéré comme volonté et représentation*) is reflected in the Symbolists' retreat from external reality to a more subjective universe; while the Symbolists' debt to Wagner is apparent in their love of the vague, their mingling of music, poetry, and the other arts, and their attempts at *orchestrated verse*. (Enthusiasm for Wagner was at its height in France *c.* 1885. The *Revue wagnérienne* was founded in 1883.)

(26) There were, however, other influences at work. Symbolist poetry was written (in French) by Belgians and Americans as well as by Frenchmen. Symbolist drama, and the French theatre generally, owes much to the Scandinavians (e.g. Ibsen, Bjoernsen, Strindberg), whose works were played in Paris *c.* 1890 (see *Théâtre Libre*; *Théâtre de l'Œuvre*).

(27) In the novel after 1880 an enthusiasm for Russian writers coincided with a reaction against *naturalisme* and was largely inspired by Melchior de Vogüé's *Le Roman russe*, 1884. (Mérimée had already translated or written on Gogol, Turgeniev, &c., and Turgeniev himself, moving freely in Parisian literary circles, constituted a link with Russian literature.) Between 1880 and 1900 Tolstoy and Dostoievsky were frequently translated. The novel of ideas (social reform, religion, &c.) has a debt to the former (e.g. Romain Rolland's *Jean-Christophe* cycle). Dostoievsky waited for the spiritual insecurity of the inter-war years (1919–39) for his full effect.

THE 20TH CENTURY

(28) There are signs in 20th-century French literature, e.g. in André Gide (himself author of a study of Dostoievsky), of the interest aroused in Nietzsche's Superman by H. Lichtenberger's *Philosophie de Nietzsche* (1898) and by subsequent translations. The philosophy of the unconscious, and modern psycho-analytical theories originating largely in Austria and Germany, are factors in the evolution of psychological fiction and drama in France as in other countries. Any study of the contemporary French novel must also take account of the Irishman James Joyce and of American writers (e.g. Faulkner). Sympathy with Russian communism between the two wars influenced the development of the Surrealist movement and encouraged a tendency both in poetry and the novel to fetter the creative impulse to political theory.

(29) But in modern times the study of foreign influences can, more than ever, acquire an undue significance. With the development of education, of international relations (and of the international book-trade), new works are introduced to other countries almost immediately by review or translation even if they are not read in their original language. They have their share, often with the foreign element introduced by contemporaneous movements in music, painting, and sculpture, in forming the intellectual climate of a country. It should suffice to end the present article by noting that some of the most penetrating studies of

foreign literature in general, as well as of foreign influences on French literature, are due to French scholarship (cf. the *History of English Literature* by É. Legouis and L. Cazamian, 1921, and articles, &c., contributed to the *Revue de littérature comparée*, founded in 1921 by P. Hazard and F. Baldensperger).

Forgeries, see *Hoaxes and forgeries*.

For-l'Évêque (*forum episcopi*), in the rue Saint-Germain-l'Auxerrois in Paris, originally an episcopal court of justice and a prison belonging to the Archbishop of Paris. After 1674 it was a royal prison for debtors and, especially, delinquent actors. The latter did not fare too badly; they were usually able to leave prison in the evenings to play their parts at the theatre. The prison was demolished in 1780.

Fort, PAUL (1872–   ), poet, born at Rheims, whose *Ballades françaises*, since he first—*c.* 1895—began publishing them in reviews or as small pamphlets, have filled over thirty volumes. They are poems and *chansons*, at times of high quality, of the town and country scene, or of the legends and history of France. Rhyme and verseforms are employed, or experimented with, but the poems are printed as prose so as to emphasize the all-importance of rhythm, cadence, and assonance.

Paul Fort founded (1905), and for several years edited, *Vers et Prose*, a literary review associated with the poet Valéry; and it was he, aged eighteen, who founded the *Théâtre d'Art* (q.v.) to encourage the production of Symbolist drama. In 1912, as the result of a referendum organized by the newspaper *Gil Blas* (q.v.), more than 400 of his contemporaries elected him 'Prince des poètes'.

Fort comme la mort (1889), a novel by Guy de Maupassant (q.v.).

Fortune des Rougon, La (1871), by Émile Zola, the opening volume of his *Rougon-Macquart* (q.v.) cycle.

Fouché, JOSEPH (1759–1820), politician, famous Minister of Police under Napoleon (who created him duc d'Otranto in 1810), was teaching in a Jesuit college when the Revolution began. He came to Paris in 1792 and as a member of the *Convention nationale* was noted for his anti-clericalism. He was one of the instigators of mass-shootings at Lyons in 1793 when an anti-Jacobin rising was suppressed. Later, when President of the *club des Jacobins* (q.v.), he was an enemy of Robespierre. His talent for intrigue manifested itself under the *Directoire* when, his record notwithstanding, he was appointed Minister of Police. He organized a powerful system of espionage which he was to develop still further under Napoleon. He had a share in the *coup d'état* of 18 Brumaire which brought Napoleon to power, and retained office, first as Minister of Police, then as *Ministre de l'Intérieur*, till 1810 (with an interval of two years from 1802 till 1804). Though dismissed in 1810 he was too useful to Napoleon to be disgraced. After Waterloo he transferred his allegiance openly to Louis XVIII (having intrigued with him clandestinely for some years previously). He again became Minister of Police but soon resigned and eventually retired to Prague. In 1818 he became an Austrian subject. He died at Trieste.

Fouché was largely responsible for the repressive censorship of books, plays, and newspapers which characterized Napoleon's Empire (see *Censorship, Dramatic*; *Librairie*).

Foucher, ADÈLE (1803–68), whom Victor Hugo knew from childhood, became his wife in 1822. She wrote—largely, it is said, to his dictation—*Victor Hugo raconté par un témoin de sa vie* (1863, 2 vols.). See also *Sainte-Beuve*.

Fouillée, ALFRED (1838–1912), a philosopher whose system of *idées-forces* was an attempt at a compromise between an idealistic philosophy and materialism His numerous works include, notably: *La Liberté et le Déterminisme* (1872), his doctor's thesis, *L'Évolutionnisme des idées-forces* (1890), *La Psychologie des idées-forces* (1892), *Le Mouvement idéaliste et la réaction contre la science positive* (1896), *Morale des idées-forces* (1907).

Fouquet or **Foucquet,** JEAN (*c.* 1416–80), painter and miniaturist, who worked for Charles VII, Louis XI, and Étienne Chevalier, the Treasurer. Some of his beautifully illuminated manuscripts have been preserved in the Louvre and the Bibliothèque nationale in Paris and in the Musée Condé at Chantilly.

Fouquet or **Foucquet,** NICOLAS (1615–80), an able and unscrupulous financier, became *surintendant des finances* under Mazarin in 1653, and acquired, in part by peculation, enormous wealth, which he spent generously, protecting men of letters (Corneille, Gombault, La Fontaine, Molière, Perrault, Scarron) and building the splendid Château de Vaux-le-Vicomte (q.v.). But he made an enemy of Colbert, and his lack of tact offended the young Louis XIV. He was arrested (1661), condemned for malversation in spite of the discourses in his defence addressed to the king by his secretary Pellisson (q.v.), and spent the last nineteen years of his life imprisoned at Pignerol. Mme de Sévigné was his devoted friend. See under *La Fontaine* for that poet's *Élégie aux nymphes de Vaux* on the occasion of the minister's disgrace.

Fouquier-Tinville, ANTOINE-QUENTIN (1746–95), the Public Accuser attached to the *Tribunal révolutionnaire*, was one of the men most dreaded during the Terror (see *Terreur*). He was himself executed during the *réaction thermidorienne* (q.v.).

Fourberies de Scapin, Les, a farcical comedy by Molière, produced in 1671, based on the *Phormio* of Terence.

The scene is Naples. Octave and Léandre, two young men, have got entangled in love-affairs while their fathers are absent on a voyage. Octave, having found a young lady (Hyacinthe) in destitution, weeping for a dying mother, has married her, but has no means of supporting her. Léandre has fallen in love with an Egyptian girl (Zerbinette) and wishes to purchase her from her owners and marry her, but likewise has no money. The fathers return unexpectedly, and Octave's father (Argante) is furious at the news of the marriage of his son, for he intended to marry him to the daughter of Géronte, the father of Léandre. This daughter has been brought up at Tarentum and is now expected at Naples with her mother. Scapin, a resourceful valet, extricates the young men from their difficulties. On pretence that he has arranged with a fictitious brother of Hyacinthe to annul the marriage of Octave in consideration of a money payment, he extracts from Argante the sum that Octave requires. He bamboozles Géronte with a story that his son has gone on board a Turkish galley and been carried off to sea and held to ransom, thereby procuring from Géronte the money required for the purchase of Zerbinette (the famous repeated exclamation of Géronte 'Que diable allait-il faire dans cette galère?', and the accompanying scene, were developed by Molière from the *Pédant joué* of Cyrano de Bergerac). Scapin's knavery is brought to light, but all ends well, for it is discovered that Hyacinthe is the very daughter of Géronte whom Octave was intended to marry, and that Zerbinette is the lost daughter of Argante.

Fourest, GEORGES, see *Pastiche.*

Fourier, CHARLES (1772–1837), social reformer, founder of the economic doctrine called *Fouriérisme* (see the following). He was born at Besançon (Franche-Comté), spent many years in business in Lyons, and eventually settled in Paris. His writings are listed under *Fouriérisme.*

Fouriérisme, a doctrine of social reform, named after its founder Charles Fourier (see above). It was contained in germ in his first work, the *Théorie des quatre mouvements* (1808), i.e. the four categories into which the universe is divided—society, animal life, organic life, and the material universe. The book was a mixture of social philosophy, projects for economic and agricultural reform, and a riotously imaginative picture of a universe destined to last 80,000 years and follow a curve from chaos to the apogee of happiness and down again to chaos. During the era of complete Harmony (to last 8,000 years) the North Pole would be milder than the Riviera, the sea (no longer salt) would become like lemonade, and the world would contain 37 million poets equal to Homer, 37 million geometricians equal to Newton, 37 million dramatic authors equal to Molière ('Ce sont là des estimations approximatives'), and no woman would have fewer than four husbands or lovers simultaneously. A *Traité de l'association domestique et agricole* (1822) and *Le Nouveau Monde industriel* (1829–30) were rather more practical elaborations of these ideas.

In 1838 the first of a series of *phalanstères* was established at Condé-sur-Vesgre, near Rambouillet. In principle these were social communities composed of co-operative, mainly agricultural, groups of 100 families each, called *phalanges*. The members (some 1,700 in all) were to live, in complete physical and moral harmony, in a building or set of buildings called a *phalanstère*, a word said to have been coined by Fourier from *phalange* and the termination of *monastère* (Bloch et Wartburg, *Dict. étym. de la langue franç.*). Profits were to be shared, the largest share going to labour. For women, the co-operative system implied emancipation and free love. The experiment ended in failure.

The chief work of Fourierist literature was Victor Considérant's (q.v.) *Destinée sociale* (1834). The Fourierist ideas (which for a time, it may be noted, influenced the poet Leconte de Lisle) are reflected in fiction in novels by George Sand (e.g. *Le Compagnon du Tour de France*, *Le Meunier d'Angibault*) and, to some extent, in Zola's *Les Quatre Évangiles*.

Fournier, HENRI-ALBAN, better known now by his pseudonym Alain-Fournier (1886–1914), wrote *Le Grand Meaulnes* (q.v.), one of the outstanding French novels of the 20th century, first published in the *Nouvelle Revue Française* in the autumn of 1913. A schoolmaster's son, he spent his childhood at Épineuil, the small town in the Department of the Cher from which the Sainte-Agathe of his novel is partly drawn. His later school and university years were spent in Paris and he also took a clerical post for a time in England. He failed to pass his *agrégation* (q.v.) at the École normale supérieure and had turned to journalism when he was killed in action. (Cf. *Rivière*.)

Fracasse, see *Capitaine Fracasse*.

Fragonard, JEAN-HONORÉ (1732–1806), born at Grasse, a charming painter of scenes of gallantry.

Franc-Archer de Bagnolet, Le, a lively dramatic monologue in octosyllabic verse by an unknown author, composed in 1468, a caricature of the militia created by Charles VII in 1448, an unpopular force, suppressed by Louis XI in 1480. The *Franc-archer* of this piece is a boastful warrior who is terrified by a scarecrow.

France, ANATOLE [pseud. of Jacques-Anatole-François Thibault] (1844–1924), novelist, critic, and man of letters, born in Paris (quai Malaquais), the only son of a book-dealer. His childhood, schooldays at the Collège Stanislas (q.v.), and his more profitable education, self-acquired through voracious reading, are described with tenderness, humour, and some admixture of fiction (e.g. he makes his father a doctor) in *Le Livre de mon ami* (1885), *Pierre Nozière* (1899), *Le Petit Pierre* (1918), *La Vie en fleur* (1922). Soon after leaving school he obtained employment with Lemerre, the publisher. During the next twenty years, besides bibliographical and cataloguing work, his work as publisher's reader, and the writing of prefaces for editions of the classics (collected, 1913, in *Le Génie latin*), he contributed to reviews and published a study of Alfred de Vigny (1868), also *Poèmes dorés* (1873) and *Les Noces corinthiennes* (1876, a poetic drama), both influenced by the Parnassiens (Lemerre was publisher of *Le Parnasse contemporain*, q.v.). From 1876 to 1890 he was an assistant librarian at the Senate, with ample free time. He now wrote regularly for *Le Globe* and *L'Univers illustré*. He also published tales (*Jocaste et le Chat maigre*, 1879) and one highly successful novel, *Le Crime de Sylvestre Bonnard* (1881, q.v.). In 1888 he became literary editor of *Le Temps* (q.v.), a leading daily. About this time his association began with Mme Arman de Caillavet, whose *salon* was a centre of French literary life. She encouraged and inspired him for many years after his first marriage ended (1892). He entered actively into the world of contemporary letters and had come to dominate it by 1897, a year after his election to the *Académie française* (q.v.). The Dreyfus (q.v.) case aroused his strong sympathies and in later years he developed socialist leanings, at times taking part in public meetings. His last years were spent in retirement in his Touraine property, La Béchellerie. He was awarded the Nobel Prize for Literature in 1921.

La Vie littéraire (1888–92, 4 vols.; 1950, 1 vol.), a collection, far from complete, of his fortnightly literary *causeries* in *Le Temps*, shows Anatole France as a subjective critic ('qui raconte les aventures de son âme au milieu des chefs-d'œuvre'). It also illustrates his particular charm as a writer, which lies in his graceful, perhaps too richly allusive, erudition; his love of beauty, of pagan antiquity, and of 18th-century French classicism; his scepticism and *douce mélancolie*; his delicate, subtle, and biting irony;

his dislike of extremes and extremists; his clarity of thought; and his elegant, melodious style. These qualities are still more apparent after 1890 in (a) his novels and (b) his tales, e.g. (a) *Thaïs* (1890, q.v.); *La Rôtisserie de la Reine Pédauque* (1893, q.v.); *Le Lys rouge* (1894), his one novel of contemporary society, a study of love and jealousy, mainly in a Florentine setting; *L'Histoire contemporaine* (1896–1901), four satirical volumes which put 'M. Bergeret' (q.v.) in the gallery of celebrated literary characters; *L'Île des pingouins* (1908, q.v.); *Les Dieux ont soif* (1912), one of the finest novels of the French Revolution and typical of the author's outlook, e.g. in the contrast between the tolerant humanist Brotteaux and the fanatical revolutionary Gamelin; *La Révolte des anges* (1914, q.v.): (b) *L'Étui de nacre* (1892), which includes the two well-known tales *Le Jongleur de Notre-Dame* and *Le Procurateur de Judée* (q.v.); *Le Jardin d'Épicure* (1894), a miscellany; *Crainquebille* (1901, q.v.); *Sur la pierre blanche* (1905), in which four Frenchmen in Rome meet for discussion and reading. One of them reads *Gallion*, a tale of the Proconsul Gallio mentioned in Acts xviii. 12–17.

One of Anatole France's least successful works was his *Vie de Jeanne d'Arc* (1908, 2 vols.). It romanticized history and is said to lack accuracy in places.

France, Kings of, see the table under *Kings of France*. See also under separate headings, e.g. *Louis Ier, II*, &c.; *Henri Ier, II*, &c.; *Mérovingiens*; *Carolingiens*; *Bourbon*, &c.

France littéraire, La, see *Quérard*.

Franc Gontier, Les Contredits, see *Villon*. Gontier is the honest countryman who lives by labour in the fields. He, with his wife Hélène, had been celebrated in *Les Ditz de Franc Gontier* by a certain Philippe de Vitry (d. 1351). To his praise of the simple rural life Villon opposes his 'contredits', in praise of the easy sensual life, with the refrain 'Il n'est tresor que de vivre à son aise'.

Franciade, La, see *Ronsard*.

Francien, a term in use by philologists to signify the standard language of Old French, a standardized form of the dialect of the Île-de-France, hence also called Central French.

Francion, La Vraie Histoire Comique de (1623), see *Sorel (Charles)*.

Franck, ADOLPHE (1809–93), author of a *Dictionnaire des sciences philosophiques* (1843–9) and of several works on oriental philosophy, Jewish learning, occultism, &c.

Franck, CÉSAR-AUGUSTE (1822–90), a composer of Belgian birth who received his musical education in Paris, lived there afterwards, and died there. For a long time he was organist in the church of Ste-Clotilde. In later years he taught the organ at the *Conservatoire de musique*. Fame came to him late in life. His works, romantic and often religious in character, include a symphony, a string quartet, and various works for piano and orchestra, violin and orchestra, violin and piano, and piano alone.

François Ier (1494–1547) was the son of Charles, comte d'Angoulême, and Louise de Savoie and the great-great-grandson of Charles V. He married (1514) Claude de France, daughter of Louis XII, became King of France in 1515 when the latter died without male issue, and reigned till his own death. He was notable in a literary connexion for the part he played in the development of the Renaissance in France. Much influenced by his intelligent and open-minded sister Marguerite de Navarre (q.v.), and himself a man of wide interests, an admirer of Erasmus, Leonardo, and Petrarch, he protected and encouraged authors such as Clément Marot and Rabelais, and men of erudition such as Budé, Lefèvre d'Étaples, and Robert Estienne (whom he used to visit in his printing-house). He founded (at Budé's instigation) chairs of Latin, Greek, and Hebrew, the nucleus of the *Collège de France* (q.v.), and a royal library (see *Bibliothèque nationale*). He was also an eager patron of art, a great builder of châteaux (notably Chambord and Fontainebleau), and a rhymer of indifferent verses. At the same time he was imperious and violent, weak and inconstant, and showed callous cruelty in the persecution of the Vaudois. He belonged to the Valois branch of the *Capétien* (q.v.) dynasty. (See also *Kings of France*; *Orléans*.)

François II (1544–60), eldest son of Henri II and Catherine de Médicis, and married while still dauphin to Mary Queen of Scots, succeeded his father as King of France in 1559 and died the following year. He belonged to the Valois branch of the *Capétien* (q.v.) dynasty.

François de Sales, SAINT (1567–1622), religious moralist, born in Savoy, a man of an amiable, benign character. He was employed as an evangelist among the Protestants of Savoy, became Bishop of Geneva (1602), and was a friend of Mme de Chantal, with whom he founded the Order of the Visitation in 1610, as an asylum for souls seeking retreat from the world. He preached in Paris in 1602 and 1619, and became the centre of religious life for France by his sermons, correspondence, and more considerable writings. The chief of these was his *Introduction à la vie dévote* (1609, definitive edit. 1619), marked by psychological penetration, a free and graceful style, and the abundant use of similes; its purpose was to reconcile the Christian life with the life of the world. The work was immensely successful and was translated into seventeen languages. It served as the model of Jeremy Taylor's *Holy Living*. Saint François also wrote a mystical *Traité de l'amour de Dieu* (1616). His letters inculcate a rational system of morality, free from excessive austerity and independent of its mystical basis, in contrast with the spirit of Jansenism (see *Jansenius*) which followed.

François le Champi (1850), a romance of country life by George Sand (q.v.). A foundling boy (*champi* means a child who has been abandoned in the fields) has been adopted by a miller's wife, herself little more than a girl, and grows up to be in his turn his adopted mother's protector when she is left a widow, ill, and struggling with the debts accumulated by a worthless husband. The bond of gratitude and affection between them insensibly becomes something closer, and the two confess their love on the spot where the young woman had discovered the *champi*. (See also *A la recherche du temps perdu*, para. 7.)

Françoise, the devoted and tyrannical family servant in Proust's *A la recherche du temps perdu* (q.v.).

Franco–Prussian war (1870–1). This had been threatening for several years before it broke out, and it had an immediate cause in the summer of 1870 when the Prussian prince Leopold of Hohenzollern-Sigmaringen offered himself as a candidate for the throne of Spain, then vacant. This threat to the southern frontier of France aroused such a storm of protest that the prince withdrew. France still demanded assurances that the King of Prussia would oppose any similar attempt in the future. When these were not forthcoming she declared war (19 July 1870). Hostilities lasted until 1 February 1871. During the first month the Imperial forces suffered a number of reverses which culminated at Sedan (q.v., 1 Sept. 1870), when the Emperor Napoleon III surrendered at the head of the army before Châlons (MacMahon's army). The main army, at this time besieged in Metz, capitulated on 27 October. Meantime the Second Empire (q.v., and see *Révolution du 4 septembre*) had been overthrown and the German invasion and the siege of Paris were being resisted by hastily-levied and untrained armies. Paris capitulated on 28 January 1871 (after a siege of over four months), forced by famine and internal discontent. Three days later the army which, organized largely by Gambetta (q.v.), had been attempting to cut the German communications from the East narrowly escaped capture by taking refuge in Switzerland.

The German Empire, proclaimed at Versailles on 18 January 1871, imposed heavy peace terms on the French. The main points were—a heavy war indemnity (paid off with surprising rapidity), severe occupation terms (but by Sept. 1873 the last occupation troops had gone), and the surrender of Alsace and Lorraine. (From this time until the two provinces were recovered in 1918 the statue of Strasbourg in the Place de la Concorde in Paris was shrouded in crape.) The terms were ratified on 1 March and concluded, by the Treaty of Frankfort, on 10 May 1871.

(Zola's *La Débâcle*, 1892, is a fine novel of the Franco-Prussian War; and cf. also *Les Soirées de Médan*.)

Frayssinous, L'ABBÉ DENIS DE (1765–1841), a noted French preacher and lecturer on religious subjects. In 1803, with addresses at the church of Saint-Sulpice on the *Défense du christianisme et des libertés gallicanes* (published 1825), he initiated the custom of giving series of lectures on religion and theology in churches. He held posts of high ecclesiastical and official, and at one moment political, dignity and was chaplain to Louis XVIII.

Frederick the Great, Friedrich II of Prussia (1712–86), ascended the throne in 1740. He was educated by a worthy Frenchman of the name of Duhan and developed a strong love of the French language and French literature. In the latter he achieved a certain eminence, writing good prose but bad verse: his *Mémoires de la maison de Brandebourg* (the history of Prussia prior to his reign), his narratives of the Seven Years War and other events of his reign, and his correspondence, are written in excellent French. He patronized French men of letters, notably Voltaire and d'Alembert. For his relations with the former see under his name. Frederick's correspondence with him began as early as 1736 and testifies to his admiration for Voltaire's brilliant intellect. For d'Alembert he shows esteem and friendship.

French-Canadian literature. In 1763, under the Treaty of Paris which ended the Seven Years War, some 60,000 French settlers in the Valley of the St. Lawrence River became British subjects. From 1791 they had a parliament of their own, and this separate political organization lasted till the British and the former French-Canadian provinces were joined by the Act of Union of 1840. The Dominion of Canada was constituted by the Act of 1 July 1867. About 30 per cent. of its present-day population is of French origin.

(2) French traditions, French culture, and the French language persisted after 1763 in the one-time French provinces. Folk-lore and songs were handed down; a *Gazette du Commerce et Littéraire* was founded in 1778; and in Quebec and Montreal there were attempts at *salons* and literary societies. Some of the *Relations* of Jesuit missionaries in Canada make interesting, at times picturesque, reading.

(3) A distinctly French-Canadian literature only begins after 1840, after orators, pamphleteers, and journalists (e.g. Hippolyte Lafontaine, 1807–64; Étienne Parent, 1802–74), and still more after historians, had made the people conscious of their early glories and vicissitudes. Much the most influential historian was François-

Xavier Garneau (1809–66), of whose eloquent *Histoire du Canada* a modern French-Canadian writer (Berthelot Brunet) says: 'Son Histoire, ce sont nos *sagas* et notre *Chanson de Roland*.' Garneau was a boy clerk in a solicitor's office when he decided to write this work. He spent most of his life educating himself for his task, at cost of struggle and sacrifice. In its first form (1845–8, 3 vols.) it stopped with the constitution of 1791. Later editions continued it to the Act of Union of 1840.

(4) Other historians who fostered a sense of the past include the abbé Henri-Raymond Casgrain (1831–1904), with the semiromantic *Biographies canadiennes* (1846); *Pèlerinages aux pays d'Évangéline* (1885); *Les Pionniers canadiens* (1885); *Une Seconde Acadie* (1894, see *Acadie*), and l'abbé Jean-Baptiste Ferland (1805–65), whose *Cours d'histoire du Canada* (1861; 1865, 2 vols.), more religious than political, gives interesting pictures of the early missionaries and religious settlements. The political evolution of the French in Canada under the British régime between 1760 and 1867 and, more recently, the position and continuance of the French race in North America have been studied by Senator Thomas Chapais (1858–1946) in *Cours d'histoire du Canada* (1919–34, 8 vols.) and the cleric (and professor at the University of Montreal) Lionel Groulx (1878–   ) in *La Naissance d'une race* (1919), *La Confédération canadienne; ses origines* (1918), &c.

(5) The poetry of this developing literature was at first (*c.* 1850—*c.* 1895), as might be expected, patriotic and heroic in character, rhetorical and on the whole unadventurous in form, and only subsequently touched by French romanticism (see *Romantisme*). Octave Crémazie (1827–79), who has been compared to Béranger (q.v.), exemplifies it, for example, in *Le Vieux Soldat canadien* and *Le Drapeau de Carillon* (see *Carillon*), the former written in 1855 when the corvette *La Capricieuse* sent by Napoleon III anchored in the St. Lawrence River and hoisted the French flag. Crémazie (*Œuvres complètes*, 1882) was a bookseller in Quebec who fell on evil days and had to leave Canada (he died in poverty at Le Havre), but before the end came his book-shop was the meeting-place for writers of the group known as the *École de Québec*. Louis-Honoré Fréchette

(1839–1908) was equally typical of the period with the short epics of *La Légende d'un peuple* (1887; here Hugo was a model), and other collections, e.g. *Les Fleurs boréales, les Oiseaux de neige* (1879).

(6) About 1895, with the founding of *l'École littéraire de Montréal*, and at a time when the literature of other countries was becoming more readily accessible, e.g. the work of the *Parnassiens* and the *Symbolistes* (qq.v.) from France, French-Canadian poetry became more lyrical and intimate, e.g. the nature poems of Albert Ferland (1872–1943), collected in four volumes, *Le Canada chanté* (1908–10); the nature and love poems (*L'Âme solitaire*) of Albert Lozeau (1878–1924), an invalid who watched life but could take no active part in it; and the more robust verse of Jean Charbonneau (1875–   ). Poets who eventually dominated this phase, experimenting with verse-forms, introducing a new suppleness, a sophisticated, epigrammatic quality, a note of travel and the exotic, and a sense, at times, of bitterness and disillusionment, were René Chopin (1885–   ), author of *Le Cœur en exil* (1913) and later collections; Paul Morin (1889–   ), with *Le Paon d'émail* (1911), *Poèmes de cendre et d'or* (1922); Guy Delahaye (1888–   ), with *Phases* (1910), *Allons voir si la rose* (1912), &c.; and, above all, though only briefly, Émile Nelligan (1879–1941). Nelligan's feverish, bitter (or perhaps sometimes only peevish) verse, with sudden flashes of imagery, has reminded critics variously of Rollinat (rather than Baudelaire) and of Rimbaud (qq.v.). His *Poésies complètes* (1896–9) contain two works frequently mentioned, *Romance du vin* and *Le Vaisseau d'or*.

(7) For several years the Montreal poets met to read and discuss their works at the Château de Ramesay, originally (built 1704) the residence of the chevalier de Ramesay, Governor of Montreal. They issued anthologies of their work, e.g. *Les Soirées du château de Ramesay* (1900), *Les Soirées de l'école littéraire de Montréal* (1924).

(8) French-Canadian poetry of still more recent times is chiefly remarkable for its absence of any specifically national characteristic. Names often mentioned are those of Alain Grandbois (1900–   ), author of *Les Îles de la nuit* (1944) and *Rivages de l'homme* (1948); Saint-Denys Garneau (1912–

43), author of *Regards et Jeux dans l'espace* (1937) and *Poésies complètes* (1949); and Anne Hébert (1916–   ), with *Les Songes en équilibres* (1942) and *Le Tombeau des rois* (1953).

(9) French-Canadian novelists, for the most part, have found inspiration in history, or the soil. *Les Anciens Canadiens* (1863), by Philippe Aubert de Gaspé (1786–1871), is still remembered as a particularly successful picture of the life of the early settlers and their conflicts with the British. (This author also left interesting *Mémoires*, 1866.) Settlers and trappers, their hardships and exploits, again provided material for, for example, the poetical, semi-idyllic *Jacques et Marie* (1866), by Napoléon Bourassa (1827–1916), and *Forestiers et Voyageurs* (1863), by Joseph-Charles Taché (1821–94), who was both journalist and chronicler. (The outstanding journalist of the 19th century was Arthur Buies, 1840–1901, who modelled himself on the French journalist and polemical writer Henri Rochefort, q.v.) *Jean-Rivard le défricheur* (1862) and *Jean-Rivard économiste* (1864) are two solidly ideological novels of the back-to-the-land type by Antoine Gérin-Lajoie (1824–82). *Angéline de Montbrun* (1884), on the other hand, is a novel of psychological analysis by Laure Conan (pseud. of Félicité Angers, 1845–1922), an author noticeably and self-confessedly influenced by Eugénie de Guérin (q.v.). The young heroine, whose letters and diaries tell the tale, is schooled by bereavement and her own disfigurement to acceptance of a loveless life. Finally she encases herself in religion.

(10) For long, however, the rural and backwoods, or the historical, novel held the field, especially after *Maria Chapdelaine* (1916), which for many people counts as the epic *par excellence* of French-Canadian life— and which was written by a Frenchman born (see *Hémon, Louis*). Thus lumbermen and log-rolling on the St. Lawrence River are the background of the much-praised *Menaud, maître draveur* (1937), by l'abbé Antoine Savard (1896–   ). *Nord–Sud* (1931) and *Les Engagés du grand portage* (1938), by Léo-Paul Desrosiers (1896–   ), are about rural Quebec (the province) in the early 19th century and fur-trapping in the North-West respectively. *Les Habits rouges* (1923) and *D'un océan à l'autre* (1924), by Robert de Roquebrune (1889–   ), are his-

torical. Reaction came with, for example, *Un homme et son péché* (1933), by Claude-Henri Grignon (1894–), and *Trente arpents* (1938), by Ringuet (pseud. of Philippe Panneton, 1895–), which depict peasant life in its more gloomy, or vicious, aspects, but more recently one of the outstanding younger women novelists, Germaine Guèvremont (1900–), has returned to the genial rustic tradition (*En pleine terre*, 1942; *Le Survenant*, 1946). Another woman writer, Gabrielle Roy (1909–), came to the front with *Bonheur d'occasion* (1945), a sensitive but in no way sentimental or laboured novel of humble life in Montreal during the 1939–45 war years. Three other novelists of the post-1945 period have already established themselves, namely André Langevin (1927–), with *Évadé de la nuit* (1951) and *Poussière sur la ville* (1953); Jean Filiatrault (1919–), with *Terres stériles* (1953); and, notably, Roger Lemelin (1919–), author of *Au pied de la pente* (1944), *Fantaisies sur les péchés capitaux* (1945), *Les Plouffe* (1948), *Pierre le magnifique* (1952), &c.

French influence on English literature, see *English Literature, French influence on.*

French Language, The, is essentially the product of the conquest and occupation of Gaul by the Romans. These brought with them not only classical Latin, which was taught in the schools and adopted in the literature of Roman Gaul, but the popular Latin of soldiers and merchants. It was the latter which, with further modifications, established itself in the mass of the inhabitants, driving out the original Celtic, of which however it retained a few words, such as *chemin* and *lieue*, and by which it was probably influenced in some degree. This popular Latin gradually evolved, losing many of its flexional endings, and out of it developed the Romance vernacular, that is to say French (see para. 3). The transition from standard Latin to French included some notable features, such as the adoption of *habere* 'to have', followed by a passive participle, to express the meaning of the perfect as distinct from the aorist or preterite; the extension of the verb *esse* with the past participle to the whole of the passive; the disappearance of the system of case-inflexions (except for a partial survival of a two-case system into Old French) and its

replacement by the use of prepositions; the development of the definite and indefinite articles, derived from *ille* and *unus*. In the course of the same process the Latin vocabulary underwent many changes, including some striking changes of meaning: for instance *testa*, 'a pot', came to mean 'a head' (*tête*); *minari*, 'to threaten', became *minare*, 'to drive (cattle)', and thence *mener*, 'to lead'; *pacare*, 'to pacify', came to signify 'to pay (a creditor)' and gave the verb *payer*.

(2) The Frankish invasion did not modify the Gallo-Roman character of the language, but it added a considerable number of words of Germanic origin, of which many have since become obsolete but a majority subsist, such as *fauteuil*, *guerre*, *riche*. The first written record of Romance words is found in the 8th century, and in the *Serments de Strasbourg* (842) we have the first extant document in the French language, followed by the first literary work, *La Séquence de sainte Eulalie* (*c.* 880). This popular speech, composed of simple and concrete terms, was supplemented, as the need arose, through the agency of learned clerks, with fresh words derived from Latin chiefly to express abstract and general ideas, such as *créature*, *esprit*, *justice*. Such learned words were of course multiplied in Middle French and later (see *Pléiade*).

(3) But it was not a single language that was thus developed in France. South of a line drawn roughly from the mouth of the Gironde eastwards to the Alps the language was the *langue d'oc* (q.v.), a group of dialects which found its literary expression in the Provençal of the troubadours. The crusade against the Albigenses (q.v.) and the subjection of the southern provinces which followed it (13th c.) carried the French of the north to the Mediterranean; Provençal remained the popular speech in those provinces, but Provençal literature perished, to be revived only centuries later (see *Félibrige*). North of the line above indicated, a multitude of different dialects were spoken, those of the Île-de France, Normandy, Picardy, Champagne, Lorraine, Burgundy, Franche-Comté, Anjou, and Poitou. Yet, from an early time (12th c.), a common language, that in the main of the Île-de France, Paris, and the court, acquired pre-eminence; its correct use became an object of aspiration to literary writers and a common literature was formed, no doubt with local peculiarities

here and there, but showing substantial unity.

(4) This common language was enriched from time to time from various sources, of which the principal are these. From the moment of the subjection, already referred to, of the southern provinces, the solidarity of north and south led to the introduction into French of a number of Provençal words, a tendency favoured in the 16th century by the accession to the crown of Henri IV, a southerner, and by the credit of such southern writers as Marot, Monluc, Du Bartas, and Montaigne. Italian words of various kinds were introduced between the 14th and 17th centuries but particularly so during the great movement of the Renaissance, which followed the expeditions into Italy of Charles VIII and Louis XII, and which led to their adoption in large numbers, notably in the spheres of literature, art, and war. Many importations from the Spanish took place at the end of the 16th and in the 17th centuries. There have been additions from many other languages, such as English, Dutch, Arabic and other oriental tongues, &c. To the vocabulary of the modern period of French, English has been the chief contributor.

(5) The French language has been carried far beyond the territory of France. The Norman Conquest carried it to England, where it had important consequences in the formation of English; it was for a time the exclusive language of the courtly and wealthy classes, it enriched English literature from its vocabulary and methods of expression, and it favoured the intercourse of English and continental scholarship (see *Anglo-Norman*). Though it was ousted by English in everyday speech, it survived as 'Law French' until the 17th century, and was replaced in the courts by English only when the latter had absorbed from it scores of law terms. Its influence on many other foreign vocabularies has been considerable, e.g. German, Dutch, Italian, Greek, Russian. It had also a temporary vogue in the Middle Ages in particular places, such as Naples, Greece, and Cyprus. It permanently established itself in parts of Switzerland and Belgium, where it produced distinct literatures, and of Canada, as well as in the French Colonial Empire. Its inherent qualities, together with political circum-

stances, have made it pre-eminently the language of diplomacy, and in some countries during certain periods (Germany, Russia) the polite language of society—at times, too, the preferred language of writers (cf. *Frederick the Great*). It should be noticed that it has been subjected to self-appointed dictators (grammarians such as Vaugelas) and to official interference; it has a *dictionnaire d'usage*, produced and periodically revised by the *Académie française* (q.v.).

French literature and its background, Bibliographical pointers to, see Appendix I.

French literature, Foreign influences on, see *Foreign influences* . . . .

French Revolution, see *Revolutions, I.*

Frêne, see *Marie de France.*

Fréquente Communion, La, see *Arnauld, Antoine.*

Frères ennemis, La Thébaïde ou les, see *Thébaïde.*

Frères mineurs [fr. med. Latin *Fratres minores*], the Friars Minor, the order founded by St. Francis of Assisi in 1209. From early days in France they were called 'cordeliers' from the rope girdle which formed part of their habit.

Frères prêcheurs, Dominican friars, members of the order of preaching friars founded by St. Dominic in 1215.

Frères Provençaux, Les, a well-known restaurant in 19th-century Paris (in the Palais-Royal, q.v.). From modest beginnings (1786) it became celebrated, and a favourite dining-place of literary men, e.g. Stendhal, Mérimée.

Frères Zemganno, Les (1877), a novel of circus life by Edmond de Goncourt (q.v.).

Fréret, NICOLAS (1688–1749), a distinguished historian and archaeologist, perpetual secretary of the *Académie des Inscriptions*. He was the author of, among other works, a *Mémoire sur la certitude historique*.

Fréron, ÉLIE (1718–76), an eminent critic, a disciple of Desfontaines (q.v.). He conducted two of the earliest periodicals, *Lettres sur quelques écrits de ce temps* (from 1749) and (from 1754) the more famous *Année littéraire* (q.v.), giving space in both to his attacks on Voltaire, the *philosophes*, and the *Encyclopédie*, which he carried on with moderation, irony, and good sense. Voltaire ridiculed and abused him in *Le Pauvre Diable*, in *La Pucelle*, and, under the name of 'Frélon', in his comedy *L'Écossaise* (1760). Fréron in his review of this play retorted with effect. Dr. Johnson records visiting Fréron during his stay in Paris (Boswell, 14 Oct. 1775).

Friedland, in East Prussia, where Napoleon defeated the Russians (14 June 1807) during his campaign against the Fourth Coalition (q.v.). The capture of Königsberg followed.

Frimaire, the third month of the Republican Calendar (q.v.). It ran from 21 November to 20 December.

Froissart, JEAN (*c.* 1337–*c.* 1410), historian and poet, born at Valenciennes in Hainault of a bourgeois family. He came to England in 1361, where he obtained the protection of Queen Philippa, his compatriot, and visited Scotland, collecting materials for his future chronicles. He accompanied the Black Prince to Bordeaux (1366) and the Duke of Clarence to Milan (1368). After the death of Queen Philippa in 1369 he retired to Valenciennes and completed the first version of the first book of his *Chroniques* dealing with events from 1325. He now obtained the favour of new protectors, in particular of the comte de Blois, and received ecclesiastical appointments. He travelled in Flanders and France, paying a notable visit to Gaston-Phébus, comte de Foix, and in 1394–5 revisited England. He carried his chronicle to the year 1400. The date of his death is unknown (*post* 1404).

Of the first book of the *Chroniques* Froissart issued three versions, relying in the first of these, for the earlier years, on the narrative of Jean le Bel (q.v.), but in the later texts substituting to a large extent his own account of events and showing himself more favourable to the French cause. The second book was completed in 1387, the third in 1390, the fourth was written in the last years of the century. The original part of the narrative begins with the battle of Poitiers (1356).

Froissart's work is in the main a record (to adopt the words of his translator, Lord Berners) of 'the honourable adventures of feats of arms, done and achieved by the wars of France and England', diligently gathered by personal inquiry from participants in the events whom he met in the course of his continual travels. That is to say it is a narrative of the principal occurrences of the period of the Hundred Years War, including many particulars relating to affairs of Italy, Spain, Germany, &c., but chiefly of the battles and sieges, repressions of popular risings, massacres and pillage, seen as exploits of the feudal chivalry of France and England. These the author recounts with admiration, while scantily recognizing the sufferings of the innocent victims (see Scott's comment on Froissart in *Old Mortality* (c. xxxv) put into the mouth of Claverhouse). He is concerned mainly with the externals of history, the pageant of adventures; he relates the atrocities of the *Jacquerie*, for instance, without discussion of its origin, and deals perfunctorily with the causes of Wat Tyler's revolt, though he is conscious of its importance. He writes with impartiality and candour, quite unaware of the formidable indictment of feudal chivalry which his narrative constitutes. The result is a work of extraordinary vividness and (in spite of errors of chronology and topography) of high historical value for the picture it presents of the conditions and sentiments prevailing in this period. Among passages of interest as illustrating Froissart's method of collecting information and his high sense of the importance of his task are the accounts of his visit to the comte de Foix in the third book, and of his second visit to England and introduction to Richard II in the fourth book. The *Chroniques* were admirably translated into English by Lord Berners (1523–5). A continuation to them was written by Monstrelet (q.v.). Gray calls Froissart 'the Herodotus of a barbarous age'.

Froissart was likewise a considerable poet judged by the standard of his times. He wrote for one of his patrons, Wenceslas of Brabant, a long verse romance, *Méliador*, in which the choice of the best knight in the world to be the husband of a king's daughter gives occasion for a great many chivalrous adventures. Some of the lyrics of the author's patron, Wenceslas, are interspersed in the romance. Froissart also composed other long poems as well as *lais* and *ballades*, some of which contain personal reminiscences.

Among the best of these are the *Dit du Florin* and the *Dialogue du cheval et du levrier*.

Frollo, Claude, archdeacon of Notre-Dame, a character in Victor Hugo's historical novel *Notre-Dame de Paris* (q.v.).

Fromentin, EUGÈNE (1820–76), novelist, artist, and art-critic, gave up the law for art, then literature, and won most success with his writings. The earliest, *Un Été dans le Sahara* (1857) and *Une Année dans le Sahel* (1859), fragments from a journal of wanderings in North Africa between 1846 and 1853, are partly travel-literature and partly the reflectively-descriptive notes of an artist considering how best to transfer what he sees to canvas. After *Dominique* (1863, q.v.), a novel of psychological analysis, and his chief work, he felt unable to satisfy his high literary standards and returned to painting. Shortly before his death he published *Les Maîtres d'autrefois* (1876), essays on the Dutch and Flemish painters, of high and continuing value both as art-criticism and as literature.

Fromont jeune et Risler aîné (1874), a novel, set in Paris, by Alphonse Daudet.

The Alsatian Risler, designer for Fromont's, wall-paper manufacturers, lodges with his younger brother Franz in a tenement overlooking the factory. Fellow occupants are the family Chèbe, a man and wife with one daughter Sidonie, a pretty, greedy, selfish shop-girl. The Fromonts had made her a companion for their daughter Claire, and although half engaged to Franz, her ambition is to marry Georges Fromont, Claire's cousin and presumably heir to the family business. Old Fromont dies. By his will Georges becomes head of the firm if he marries Claire, and Risler aîné's long services are rewarded with a partnership. Thereupon Sidonie breaks with Franz, declares she has always loved Risler aîné, and marries him. Franz, in despair, goes to the colonies. Risler and his wife, and Georges Fromont and his wife, share the factory house. Sidonie, daily more envious of Claire, sets to work to attract Georges and succeeds so well that soon everyone is aware of their liaison except Risler (devoted, unsuspecting, and absorbed in an invention destined to revolutionize the business) and Claire (happy in her son and too sweet-natured to be suspicious). Franz returns and

discovers what is afoot, but his sister-in-law talks him round and soon has him in her toils again. Risler *aîné* suddenly awakens to Georges's intrigue with Sidonie and to the fact that the firm is nearly bankrupt. He becomes implacable, turns his wife out, and sets to work to restore the firm's stability. His only hope for the future is that Franz may one day return to live with him. This is shattered when a letter comes his way revealing that a few months earlier Franz had tried to persuade Sidonie to abscond with him. Confronted with this last piece of treachery he commits suicide.

The book's mixture of realism, humour, and sentimentality has sometimes caused Daudet to be compared to Dickens. It contains many excellent descriptive passages, e.g. the sketches of the other inhabitants of Risler's tenement, the broken-down actor Delobelle, his invalid daughter Désirée who worships Franz in secret, and Chèbe, Sidonie's work-shy father.

Fronde, La, the name (taken from a boys' game in which slings, *frondes*, were used) given to two revolts against the absolutism of the crown, the First and the Second Fronde, caused by the unpopularity of Mazarin and the fiscal measures adopted to finance the German and Spanish wars. But the *frondeurs* had no united programme and the great leaders were divided by rivalries. The First Fronde (1648), in effect an alliance between the *bourgeoisie* and some of the nobility, was led by the *parlement* of Paris. When Broussel (the venerable champion of the *parlement*) was arrested (August 1648), the mob of Paris, led by Paul de Gondi (see *Retz*), rose and erected barricades. A little later the court left Paris, which was besieged by royal forces. Peace was restored in 1649. The Second Fronde began in 1651, after Mazarin had imprisoned Condé, the famous but arrogant victor of Rocroy. The intrigues of Gondi, the activities of great ladies such as the duchesse de Longueville, the military intervention of Turenne, caused Mazarin's flight from Paris and the liberation of Condé. But Condé and the mutinous nobles who supported him soon lost popularity; Gondi was won over by a cardinal's hat, and the movement came to an end in 1652 in Paris, though it continued at Bordeaux and elsewhere in the provinces until 1653.

Frontin, a frequent name for the valet in French comedy, for instance, notably, in Lesage's *Turcaret* (q.v.).

Front populaire, Le, a left-wing political combination of Socialists, Radicals, and Communists which won the French elections of 1936 after which M. Léon Blum (q.v.), as Prime Minister, formed the first Socialist Government in France. During the short life of this Government various measures were introduced, destined to improve the lot of the worker, e.g. the forty-hour week, holidays with pay, the principle of collective bargaining for employers and employed.

Fructidor, the twelfth month of the Republican Calendar (q.v.). It ran from 18 or 19 August to 16 or 17 September. *Le 18 fructidor An V* (4 Sept. 1797) was the date of the military *coup d'état* by which Royalist plots to undermine the *Directoire* (q.v.) were frustrated. The support of General, later Marshal, Augereau, then in command of the Paris troops, had been enlisted and success was largely due to his impressive show of force. (Cf. *Maréchal de l'Empire*; *Press, Development of,* para. 7.)

Fugitive, La, see *Albertine disparue.*

Funambules, Théâtre des, a well-known Paris theatre (founded 1816, situated on the Boulevard du Temple) where pantomimes, vaudevilles, and melodrama were played. After 1830 it was especially famous, when the clown Deburau (q.v.) was associated with it. It disappeared in 1862 during the reconstruction of Paris (cf. *Boulevard du Crime*).

Funck-Brentano, FRANTZ (1862–1947), historian, a native of Luxembourg, was known to a wide public by his many studies of scenes and personages of, particularly, the pre-Revolutionary era, e.g. *Légendes et archives de la Bastille* (1898); *Le Drame des poisons* (1900); *L'Affaire du collier* (1901), &c. He was general editor of *L'Histoire de France racontée à tous* (1909–33, 11 vols.), a work of popular appeal.

Furetière, ANTOINE (1619–88), lexicographer and novelist, a man of erudition who became a member of the *Académie française* (q.v.) in 1662, and finding that body tardy in the preparation of its dictionary, compiled and published his own *Dictionnaire universel* (see *Dictionaries and Encyclopedias* under date 1690) and was in consequence excluded from the *Académie*. He was also author of the *Roman bourgeois*, one of the remarkable realistic novels of the 17th century (1666, q.v.); of the *Histoire des derniers troubles arrivés au royaume de l'Éloquence* (1658), of satirical *Poésies* (1666), and of *Le Voyage de Mercure*, a satire directed against literary and learned humbugs. He was a friend of Racine, Boileau, Molière, and La Fontaine.

Fusionisme, one of the many fantastic gospels, partly religion, partly social reform, of the mid 19th century. It was propounded about 1850 by one Louis de Tourreil after a vision in the Bois de Vincennes. His *Doctrine fusionienne* (1846, 2 vols.) spoke of a fusion of spirit and matter, of universal emanations and absorptions, and of universal love and fecundity.

Fustel de Coulanges, NUMA-DENIS (1830–89), the outstanding historian of the second half of the 19th century, born in Paris, was Professor of History at Strasbourg University for a time, then returned to Paris (1870), and in 1878 became Professor of Medieval History at the Sorbonne. His chief work, *La Cité antique* (1864, q.v.), viewed history from the anthropological standpoint, then new; it also introduced the modern practice of presenting history as a collection of solidly documented information with no attempt at romantic colouring. His other works included: *Histoire des institutions politiques de l'ancienne France* (1875–89, re-ed. 1900–7 by Camille Jullian from notes left by the author); *Recherches et nouvelles recherches sur quelques problèmes d'histoire* (1885 and 1891), &c. The unfinished *Leçons à l'Impératrice* (1930, posth.) are little masterpieces of simplified history delivered in the first place as lectures to the Empress Eugénie and her ladies-in-waiting. They consist of studies of Gaul (prehistoric and under Roman and Merovingian rule), of the feudal system, of the emergence of France as a kingdom under St. Louis and the development of the monarchic system under Louis XI: all demonstrating the development of governmental institutions and the formative influences on modern French civilization.

Futurisme, a movement, in art and literature, launched by the Italian poet F. P. Marinetti (q.v.) in his 'Manifeste du futurisme' printed in *Le Figaro* of 20 February 1909. For a time it had enthusiastic supporters in advanced French and Italian circles. In literature, sound and fury were its main features: futurist poets tried to reproduce the disorderly, confused, and tumultuous noises of the machine age, and they glorified danger, war, and destruction.

Fuzélier, LOUIS (1672–1752), man of letters (one-time editor of the *Mercure de France*, q.v.) and a mediocre comic dramatist. He sometimes collaborated with Lesage.

G

Gabaonites, Les, see *La Taille, Jean de.*

Gabelle, the salt-tax. In most parts of France there was, under the *ancien régime*, a government monopoly of salt, which was sold at an exorbitant price and of which each inhabitant was required to purchase a minimum quantity (the *sel du devoir*). But the price varied in different provinces; some provinces moreover had redeemed their liability to the tax, and others were exempt by the terms of their inclusion in the monarchy. Certain individuals also enjoyed exemption. The *gabelle*, though frequently condemned by reformers from Vauban onwards, was not abolished until 1790. Under Colbert its yield was reduced from 24 to 19 million livres a year, by lowering the price of salt (cf., under *Fiscal system*, the yield of the *taille*).

Gaboriau, ÉMILE (1832–73), born at Saujon (Charente-Maritime), father of the *roman policier*, or detective novel, in France, sometimes called the Edgar Allan Poe of French literature. His best-known novels, which nearly all appeared first as *feuilletons* (see *Roman-feuilleton*), were: *Le Crime d'Orcival* (1867); *Le Dossier nº 113* (1867); *Les Esclaves de Paris* (1868); *L'Affaire Lerouge* (1868); *Monsieur Lecoq* (1869); *La Corde au cou* (1873). His famous detective Monsieur Lecoq (q.v.) is the precursor of Sherlock Holmes. (See also *Tabaret, Le Père.*)

Gace Brulé (d. *c.* 1220), a knight, native of Champagne, an early imitator in northern French of the poetry of the troubadours (see *Lyric poetry*).

Gaguin, ROBERT (1433–1501), chronicler, humanist, and diplomatist. He wrote (1497) a Latin *Compendium supra Francorum gestis,* chronicles of French history from Pharamond to 1491, and was a professor of rhetoric at the University of Paris, publishing a treatise on Latin versification and urging conscientious study of the ancient writers. He was one of the pioneers of the literary Renaissance. Among his works were two poems of some merit: a *Débat du laboureur, du prestre, et du gendarme,* in which each points out the defects of the others; and *Le Passetemps d'oysiveté,* a plea for peace on the one hand and a defence of war on the other.

Gaimar, GEFFREI, an Anglo-Norman poet of the 12th century who lived in the north of England. He composed between 1147 and 1151 an *Estoire des Engleis,* in octosyllabic verse, from mythical origins (the story of the Argonauts, the Trojan War, and the arrival of the Trojan Brutus in Britain) down to the death of William Rufus. He incorporated in it a translation of Geoffrey of Monmouth's *Historia Regum Britanniae.* Only a portion of the poem has survived. See also under *Haveloc.*

Gai saber (i.e. *savoir*), the gay science, the poetry of the troubadours, a Provençal term given currency, it is said, by the poets of the school of Toulouse in the 14th century.

Gaîtés de l'escadon, Les (1886), farcical sketches (some are grim) of military life by Georges Courteline (q.v.).

Galaad, son of Lancelot, see *Perceval.*

'Galère, Que diable allait-il faire dans cette——?'—a proverbial phrase since Molière's *Fourberies de Scapin* (q.v.). The question is repeated ten times by the miserly

Géronte (act II ,sc. xi) when he is duped into believing that his son is a prisoner, awaiting ransom, on a Turkish galley.

Galères, Galériens. From the reign of Charles VI (1380–1422), if not earlier, the French kings possessed fleets of galleys, manned by oarsmen, which they used in the Mediterranean. Some of the oarsmen (only a very few) were recruited voluntarily, others were Turkish slaves. By far the greatest number were convicts condemned for various offences (crime, vagabondage, petty offences, religious beliefs) to row in the king's galleys, a form of penal servitude in force by law from the reign of François Ier (1515–47). Conditions in these floating prisons were appalling. After 1748 galleys manned by oarsmen were no longer employed. From then until changes introduced during the Revolution the convicts—still called *galériens* —were set to labour in the large naval dock-yards and arsenals, and were kept in specially constructed convict prisons, called *bagnes*. The *bagnes* in their turn were gradually suppressed after the establishment *c.* 1854 of a penal colony in French Guiana. (See also *Bonnet rouge*; *Diable, Île du.*)

Galiani, FERDINAND, ABBÉ (1728–87), a Neapolitan, of diminutive size, secretary at the embassy in Paris from 1759, a witty and amusing talker, of considerable learning and originality of views ,somewhat of a buffoon, much appreciated in the literary and philosophical society of the day and a friend in particular of Diderot and Grimm. His *Dialogues sur les blés*, a work remarkable for lively wit as well as force of argument, combating the doctrines of the more extreme physiocrats, appeared in 1770, after his departure from Paris in 1769. From that time he carried on a correspondence with Mme d'Épinay until her death in 1783; his letters to her, to Mme Geoffrin, and to Mme Necker have been published.

Galilée, Empire de, see *Basoche*.

Gall, FRANZ JOSEPH (1758–1828), founder of phrenology, a system of psychology and character-reading, was born at Tiefenbrunn, near Pforzheim, Baden, and studied medicine at Strasbourg and Vienna. After qualifying he practised in Vienna but spent more time investigating a possible connexion between the external appearance of the skull and the

faculties of the human mind. He lectured on his theories in Vienna (till the government stopped him), then in German university towns, exciting both interest and indignation. In 1807 he arrived in Paris with his collection of human and animal skulls (eventually bequeathed to the *Jardin des Plantes*). His lectures were again crowded, and despite ridicule in the Press and disapproval in august quarters he made many influential converts. He adopted French nationality in 1819, visited England, exciting little attention, in 1823, and died in Paris in 1828—of apoplexy. (Cf. *Lavater, Mesmer,* and see also *Balzac.*)

Galland, ANTOINE (1646–1715), orientalist; he translated the *Arabian Nights* (1704–17).

Gallicanism, the principles and practice of the school of French Roman Catholics which maintains the claim of the French Church to be in certain respects self-governing and free from papal control. Its doctrines were authoritatively set out in the declaration of the clergy of France in 1682 (at the time of the conflict between Louis XIV and Innocent XI), drawn up by Bossuet and known as the *Déclaration des quatre articles.* The opposite view, which asserts absolute papal supremacy, is known as *Ultramontanism.*

Gambara, one of the 'Études philosophiques' of Balzac's *Comédie humaine* (q.v.).

Gambetta, LÉON (1838–82), born at Cahors of a Genoese father (a grocer) and a French mother, had his schooling at Montauban and Cahors, then studied law in Paris and became a barrister (1860) as the first step to a political career. He was soon known as a brilliant orator and an opponent of the Second Empire. Deputy in 1869 for Paris and Marseilles, he became leader of the advanced opposition party. In 1870, after Sedan (q.v.), when a Republic was proclaimed (4 Sept.), he was the most energetic member of the Government of National Defence. When Paris was surrounded by the Prussians (Oct. 1870) he left the city in a balloon, and from Tours carried on the Government of National Defence, organized resistance, and restored the country's morale. But when Paris was starved into surrender (January 1871) the Government there signed an armistice with the Prussians without consulting Gambetta, who soon resigned office. During the *Commune*, a period of violence of which he strongly disapproved, he was in the South of France. Back in Paris in July 1871 as Deputy to the National Assembly for the Departments of the Var and the Bouches-du-Rhône, he was a leader of the Republican Party and instrumental, with Thiers (q.v.), in forming the Third Republic (1875). He became President of the Chamber of Deputies in 1879 but thereafter his influence declined: he was accused of war-mongering, and his projects for parliamentary and electoral reform were unpopular. He retired from parliamentary life in January 1882. In the following December his death, the result of an accident, was mourned by the whole nation.

Gamon, CHRISTOFLE DE (1575–1621), Protestant poet, wrote *La Semaine ou Création du Monde* (1609), a refutation of the better-known epic of the same name by du Bartas (q.v.); as well as other poems on biblical subjects (e.g. the Plagues of Egypt) contained in *Le Verger poétique* (1597).

Ganelon, the traitor, see *Chanson de Roland.*

Gannau or **Ganneau,** see *Mapah.*

Garamond, CLAUDE (d. 1561), the famous 16th-century type-founder remembered especially by his 'Grecs du roi' (so called because commissioned by François Ier), the Greek type which he cut in 1541 for the King's Printer Robert Estienne (q.v.) to use in his editions of Greek classics. The type was imitated from the beautifully executed manuscripts of Ange Vergèce (d. 1569), a Greek copyist and cataloguer employed in the Royal Library at Fontainebleau.

Garasse, FRANÇOIS (1585–1631), known as *le Père Garasse,* a Jesuit who in his *Doctrine curieuse des beaux esprits du temps* (1623) vehemently attacked the *libertins* (q.v.) of his day, notably Théophile de Viau (q.v.). His *Somme théologique* (1625) is largely an attack on Charron (q.v.), whose treatise *De la Sagesse* was regarded as giving support to the views of the *libertins.*

Garat, DOMINIQUE-JOSEPH (*c.* 1750–1832), man of letters and journalist, born near Bayonne, was a deputy to the *États Généraux* in 1789, prominently associated with the Revolutionary newspaper *Le Journal de Paris*

(q.v.), Minister of Justice under the *Convention nationale* in 1792, and a Senator during the First Empire. His *Mémoires historiques sur la vie de M. Suard* throw a light on the 18th-century *idéologues* (q.v.).

Garçon, le, a grotesque personage invented by Flaubert and his friends (see the earlier volumes of Flaubert's *Correspondence*) as a type of bourgeois respectability and complacency; an ancestor of M. Homais in *Madame Bovary* (q.v.).

Garçon et de l'Aveugle, Jeu du, see *Comedy.*

Garde nationale, in the first instance a form of citizen militia established by the Commune de Paris (see *Commune*) in July 1789 to maintain order. It was voluntary at first, but between 1790 (when provincial battalions were also organized) and 1793 it was transformed into a compulsory armed force, employed under the direction of the civil or municipal authorities. It was recruited largely from the taxable middle and lower-middle classes (and later open to all) and included able-bodied men from sixteen to sixty. Many of its officers, who were paid, had held commissions or been N.C.O.s in the pre-Revolutionary army and were later to serve in the Army of the Republic (which was an amalgamation, in 1793–4, of the old army and various forces recruited either voluntarily or compulsorily since 1789).

The *Garde nationale* counted for little and was at times in abeyance during the Consulate and the First Empire. It was revived at the Restoration, suppressed in 1827 by Charles X, but again revived in 1830 after the July Revolution. Allusions to it are frequent at this period in novels (e.g. Balzac's), vaudevilles (e.g. Scribe's), and caricatures. In 1831 it was reorganized as a force for the defence of the constitutional monarchy, to uphold the law and preserve peace, and with a greater proportion of members from the *haute bourgeoisie.* Feelings ran high about it during the February Revolution (1848) and in the months following, when some companies sided with the *Assemblée nationale* against the people and others, recruited from the working classes, either did not turn up for service or (notably during the June insurrections) fought against the Government at the *barricades* (q.v. and cf. the references to it in Flaubert's *L'Éducation sentimentale*). It was under much stricter official control during the Second Empire. For a time in 1870 it took part in defensive fighting against the Prussians (see *Commune*). It ceased to exist after 1871.

Garde républicaine, special divisions—both mounted and foot—of the *Gendarmerie nationale* (see *Gendarmerie*), a familiar sight in Paris. They guard official buildings, are a highly decorative presence on all state occasions, and have a famous band.

Gargamelle, the mother of Gargantua (q.v.).

Gargantua, La vie très horrificque du grand, by Rabelais (q.v.), published under the pseudonym 'Alcofribas Nasier' (an anagram of his own name) in 1534. The author was led by the success of *Pantagruel* (q.v.) to produce the story of Pantagruel's father, on the same general plan—the birth and childhood of the giant, his education, the war with his neighbour Picrochole. Some features in the story—the names of Gargantua and his parents (Grandgousier and Gargamelle), his gigantic mare, the theft of the bells of Notre-Dame, are taken from the *Grandes et inestimables cronicques* (the chap-book referred to under *Pantagruel*). The fantastic elements are more restricted than in *Pantagruel* and there are numerous allusions to localities near Rabelais's birthplace and to incidents connected therewith. The war with Picrochole, for instance, is a comical development of a local quarrel with a landed proprietor, Gaucher de Sainte-Marthe (see *Sainte-Marthe, Charles* and *Scévole de*), who was usurping certain water-rights.

After the description of Gargantua's birth and early years, we are told how, having profited little by the instruction he receives at home from old-fashioned pedagogues and schoolbooks, he is finally sent to Paris. There he takes the bells of Notre-Dame to hang round his mare's neck; a deputation from the University under maître Janotus de Bragmardo, sent to ask for their return, gives occasion for a caricature of the Sorbonne and its eloquence. The special type of education to which Gargantua is now subjected, in contrast to the traditional course, is a development of Rabelais's ideas on this subject as expressed in *Pantagruel*. Gargantua is then recalled to help defend his father's territory against Picrochole's invasion. The theatre of war (of Lilliputian dimensions) is around La Devinière, Rabelais's birthplace. Gargantua directs the operations, but the chief exploits are performed by Frère Jean des Entommeures (i.e. 'of the mincemeat'), a remarkable figure of a vigorous, active, and courageous monk, who drives the enemy from the abbey close, while his sluggish brethren have taken refuge in prayer in the chapel. Gargantua's final victory is celebrated by the erection of the Abbey of Thélème (whose architectural design follows that of the great *châteaux* of the period), where, in contrast with the ordinary monastic institutions, the code of rules contains only one clause: 'Fay ce que vouldras' ('Do what thou wilt') 'because men and women that are free, well born, well instructed, and conversant in honest Companies, have naturally an instinct and spur that prompteth them ever to virtuous actions, and withdraws them from vice, the which is called honour' (Urquhart).

Garibaldi, GIUSEPPE (1807–82), Italian general and patriot, born at Nice, played an outstanding part, during the middle years of the 19th century, in the Italian *Risorgimento* (q.v.). He made his mark on French history in 1870 when he left his retirement in the small island of Caprera, off Sardinia, and offered his aid, with his famous 'red-shirt' legion of volunteers, to France, at that time invaded by the Prussians. His offer was accepted (by Gambetta, q.v.) but he was defeated near Dijon. He was elected Deputy to the National Assembly (1871) in gratitude but his part had been played. He soon retired and returned to Italy. He died at Caprera.

Garin de Monglane, Geste de, also known as the cycle of the 'Aimerides' or of 'Guillaume', a group of some score of *chansons de geste* (q.v.) dealing with the exploits, chiefly against the Saracens in southern France, of the descendants in several generations of Garin de Monglane, who are sent out to conquer fiefs for themselves with their swords. The principal *chansons* of this cycle are *Girard de Viane*, *Aimeri de Narbonne*, and the *Chanson de Guillaume* (rehandled in *Aliscans*) (qq.v.).

Garin le Loherain, a *chanson de geste* (q.v.) which, with other *chansons* of the same cycle, sometimes referred to as the 'Geste des Lorrains', relates the long war between two families, of Lorraine and Bordeaux respectively, originating in a dispute between Hérois of Metz and Hardré de Bordeaux, and pursued from generation to generation with battle and pillage, siege and massacre, till the posterity of Hardré are exterminated. A notable figure in this *geste* is Bernard de Naisil, the perfidious sower of discord. He is represented as making the famous boast:

> Si je tenoie l'ung pié en paradis
> Et l'autre avoie au chastel de Naisil,
> Je retrairoie celui de paradis
> Et le mettroie arrier dedans Naisil.
>
> (Text P. Paris)

Garnier, ROBERT (1534–90), born at La Ferté-Bernard in the Perche, and a magistrate by profession, was the most important of the early tragedians of the French Renaissance, a disciple of the Pléiade. His first tragedy *Porcie*, on the Senecan model, dealing with the death of Brutus and the suicide of Portia, appeared in 1568 and was followed by other tragedies, *Cornélie* (the wife of Pompey), *Hippolyte* (an early French treatment of the *Phèdre* theme), *Marc-Antoine*, *La Troade*, *Antigone*, *Les Juives*. The last, on the cruel treatment of Zedekiah and his children by Nebuchadnezzar after the capture of Jerusalem (2 Kings xxv. 7), shows force and pathos, and is the best of these works. In one particularly interesting play, however, *Bradamante* (q.v.), Garnier inaugurated tragicomedy (q.v.) as a dramatic form.

Garnier was a considerable poet; he had style, eloquence, imagination, and lyric power (displayed in the songs of the chorus, which he retained in his tragedies). His *Marc-Antoine* was translated into English by the Countess of Pembroke (1590), and his *Cornélie* by Thomas Kyd.

Garnier de Pont-Sainte-Maxence, see *Thomas Becket.*

Garo, the hero of La Fontaine's fable *Le Gland et la citrouille*, prototype of the pretentious ignoramus.

Garonne, LA, one of the four chief rivers of France. It rises on the Spanish side of the Pyrenees, enters France by way of the gorge known as the Pont du Roi, and flows roughly north-east to Toulouse, then north-west to Bordeaux. Shortly after Bordeaux it is joined by the Dordogne and becomes the estuary known as the Gironde, opening finally on to the Atlantic at Cape Grave on the left and Cape Royan on the right. Its chief tributaries before it reaches Bordeaux are the Ariège, the Tarn, the Lot, and the Gers, all of which give their name to departments (see Appendix II).

Gaspard de la nuit, a collection of prose-poems by Louis, called Aloÿsius, Bertrand (q.v.).

Gassendi, PIERRE (1592–1655), born in Provence, philosopher and mathematician, an adversary of the Aristotelian philosophy, a critic of his contemporary Descartes, and a supporter of the philosophy of Epicurus, whose atomic theory he sought to revive. Besides treatises on these subjects, he wrote lives of Tycho Brahe, Copernicus, and Regiomontanus, and many mathematical, philosophical, and other works. He wrote in Latin. He was professor of mathematics at the Collège de France (q.v.) from 1645. Chapelle and Molière, among literary men, are said to have been his disciples.

Gaster, MESSER [fr. Gk. $\gamma\alpha\sigma\tau\acute{\eta}\rho$], a character in Rabelais's *Pantagruel*; also in La Fontaine's fable *Les Membres et l'estomac.*

Gastrolatres, see *Pantagruel* (*Quart livre*).

Gaudissart, see *Illustre Gaudissart, L'.*

Gauguin, PAUL (1848–1903), painter, a grandson of Flora Tristan (q.v.), gave up the Stock Exchange (1883), and his wife and children too, for his art. For a time, although he broke with them later, he was one of the Impressionists (see *Impressionnisme*), one of those most closely associated with *Symbolisme* (q.v.) in literature. After 1891, with only one return to France (in 1893–5), he lived in Tahiti, sharing the life of the natives, finding inspiration in them and the landscape. He was so desperately poor that he was often unable to buy paints and canvases. His correspondence and diaries have been published and translated, also *Noa-Noa*, a record of his experiences written in collaboration with the symbolist Charles Morice (q.v.).

Gaulois, Le, founded in 1867, became a leading Monarchist daily during the Third Republic, with a high standard of writing. This was the paper read by Proust's Guermantes (q.v.) world.

Gaultier-Garguille, see *Gros-Guillaume.*

Gautier, JUDITH, daughter of Théophile Gautier and at one time wife of the poet Catulle Mendès (q.v.), author of *Le Livre de Jade* (1867), poems from the Chinese, also of essays and novels which reflected her interest in orientalism and music. She was the first woman member of the Académie Goncourt (elected 1910).

Gautier, MARGUERITE, heroine of *La Dame aux camélias* (q.v.) by Dumas *fils.*

Gautier, THÉOPHILE (1811–72), poet, novelist, and journalist, born at Tarbes (Gascony), lived in Paris from early childhood and died there. On leaving school (Collège Charlemagne) he entered the studio of the artist Louis-Édouard Rioult (1780–1855) to study painting. Like his friends Gérard de Nerval and Petrus Borel (qq.v.) he plunged into *le romantisme* (q.v.), especially the frenetic variety, characterized by a taste for vampirism and Hoffmannesque horrors. He was a hero-worshipper of Victor Hugo, and on the first night of *Hernani* (q.v.) he led the faction that clapped, argued, shouted, at times fought, the play to success. (He used to say that the scarlet doublet he wore on this occasion had remained on his back ever since.) By now (1830) he had given up painting in order to write.

During the next ten years—his extreme Romantic period—he produced: *Poésies* (1830); *Albertus ou l'Âme et le Péché* (1832, q.v.), a racily-macabre poem; *Les Jeunes-France, romans goguenards* (1833), bantering sketches, often autobiographical, of life among the young Romantics; *Les Grotesques* (1835), studies of 15th, 16th, and 17th-century authors (including Villon, Théophile de Viau, Scarron, qq.v.); *Mademoiselle de Maupin* (1835, q.v.), a novel written partly to scandalize the despised, respectable, middle classes and partly as a testimony to his theories of *l'art pour l'art* (q.v.); *La Morte amoureuse,* one of the most famous of vampire stories, and *Fortunio,* an Arabian Nights-like tale set in Paris (1836 and 1837, both first published in book-form in *Nouvelles,*

1845); *La Comédie de la mort* (1838), another fantastic narrative poem.

From 1835, when Balzac helped him to a post on the *Chronique de Paris,* Gautier the exuberant Romantic was gradually replaced by Gautier the busy, successful journalist of *La Presse, Le Moniteur, La Revue de Paris* (qq.v.), &c. He became an important, well-liked, literary personality of the Second Empire ('le bon Théo'). For nearly forty years he wrote weekly literary, dramatic and—perhaps particularly—art criticism of a very high order, collected at intervals in book-form, e.g. *Rapport sur le progrès des lettres depuis vingt-cinq ans* (1868); *Portraits et Souvenirs littéraires* (1875); *Histoire de l'art dramatique depuis vingt-cinq ans* (1858, 6 vols.); *Les Beaux-Arts en Europe* (1855, 2 vols.); *L'Art moderne* (1855). He also, after a trip to Spain in 1840, began the many series of travel-sketches which contain some of his finest descriptive writing, e.g.—dates refer to publication in book-form—*Voyage en Espagne* (1845); *Caprices et Zig-zags* (1845, mostly English life); *Voyage en Italie* (1852); *Constantinople* (1853); *Voyage en Russie* (1866). He found time, too, for creative writing.

In 1835 (*Mademoiselle de Maupin*) Gautier had said 'Ce qui est beau physiquement est bien, tout ce qui est laid est mal'. *Beauty* meant 'éclat, solidité, couleur . . . Jamais ni brouillard ni vapeur, jamais rien d'incertain et de flottant'. His romantic frenzies cooled, but these, his aesthetic convictions, strengthened; and they were shared by his friends, e.g. Flaubert, Baudelaire, Théodore de Banville. The love of visual, palpable beauty became the chief feature of his work. It is apparent time and again, intensified by his painter's eye and his feeling for, and command of, language, so that many passages both of his prose and poetry read like transpositions from canvas to paper (and lend a certain lifelessness to his writing). It is especially noticeable in the short poems of *Émaux et Camées* (1852, q.v.) on which his poetic fame largely rests. Their serene, impersonal quality shows the one-time Romantic leader turning to the concentration on perfect form and expression which was to characterize the poetry of the Parnassiens (q.v.).

Although Gautier disdained politics and reserved himself for his art he was greatly affected by the events of 1870 (Franco-

Prussian War, q.v.). Whether coincidence or not, the heart disease from which he eventually died dates from this time.

Besides the works already mentioned his abundant output included—TALES: *La Peau de tigre* (1852), *Nouvelles* (1858); NOVELS: *Le Roman de la momie* (1856), *Le Capitaine Fracasse* (1863, q.v.); BALLETS AND DRAMATIC SKETCHES: *Théâtre* (1872); and the interesting, but unfinished, *Histoire du romantisme* (1874).

Gautier d'Arras, a 12th-century poet of considerable talent, author of *Eracle* (q.v.) and a *roman breton, Ille et Galeron.*

Gautier de Coincy, see *Religious writings* (Medieval period).

Gautier de Metz, see *Image du monde.*

Gautier d'Épinal (*fl.* 1180–1200), one of the poets who first imitated in Northern France the lyric poetry of the troubadours, a skilful manipulator of varied metres.

Gauvain (Engl. *Gawain*), the nephew of King Arthur, and one of the most famous knights of the Round Table. He figures as the perfect knight in the poems of Chrétien de Troyes; as a prominent champion in Arthur's wars and in other episodes in the early prose romances relating to the history of the Grail (where he finally meets his death at the hand of Lancelot); and also as the hero of several episodic poems of the 13th century, such as *Le Chevalier à l'épée, La Mule sans frein* (qq.v.).

Gavarni [pseud.—from the Cirque de Gavarnie, a beauty-spot in the Pyrenees—of SULPICE-GUILLAUME CHEVALIER] (1804–66), a famous lithographer and caricaturist of the mid-nineteenth century. After early years in a land-surveyor's office at Tarbes, his birthplace, he came to Paris and quickly became known by sketches of Parisian life (students, grisettes, carnival costumes, and women's clothes) contributed to illustrated journals. From 1837 onwards he contributed two notable series—*Fourberies de femme en matière de sentiment* and *Les Lorettes*—to *Charivari* (q.v., and see *Lorette*). In later life, especially after a stay in London where he observed the misery and vices of the poor, his work was more bitter in tone. This later period is represented by the collections *Masques et Visages* (1857) and *Les Douze Mois* (1869). Pithy captions written by him-

self were an integral feature of his work. The brothers Goncourt, his intimate friends, wrote his life (*Gavarni, l'Homme et l'Œuvre*, 1873).

Gavroche, a guttersnipe, and a typical *gamin* of Paris, a character in Victor Hugo's social novel *Les Misérables* (q.v.).

Gaxotte, PIERRE (1895–), contemporary historian and journalist, editor of the weekly paper *Candide* and author of several historical works of interest to the general reader, e.g. *La Révolution française* (1928), *Histoire des Français* (1951).

Gay, DELPHINE, see *Girardin, Mme Émile de.*

Gay, MADAME SOPHIE (1776–1852), mother of the foregoing, wrote novels of French society under the Directoire and the Empire (*Laure d'Estelle*, 1802; *Un Mariage sous l'Empire*, 1832, &c.).

Gaymar, GEFFREI, see *Gaimar.*

Gazette, a word derived probably from *gazzetta*, the Italian name of a small Venetian coin which, it appears, was paid at Venice in the 16th century for a copy of a news-sheet or for permission to read it. (Cf. *Gazette, La,* below; also *Nouvellistes.*)

Gazette, La, later known as ***Gazette de France,*** the first French newspaper, founded in 1631 by Théophraste Renaudot (q.v.), who edited it under Richelieu's and later Mazarin's patronage. It began as a weekly (four, later eight, quarto pages), appearing on Saturdays, costing one sol parisis (see *Money*), and giving, with an honest attempt at truth, news foreign and domestic without comment. Its scope was gradually extended to include official and historical documents, and Richelieu used it as an instrument of policy. In 1762 it became the *Gazette de France*, bore the royal arms, appeared twice weekly, and assumed an official in lieu of a semi-official character, being placed under the direction of the Minister for Foreign Affairs. It expired temporarily after the execution of Louis XVI but was resurrected and during the Empire (by now a daily, and read by the clergy) was one of the few political papers tolerated by Napoleon. It was the leading Royalist paper during the Restoration, when it acquired a literary feuilleton. Under the July monarchy it was fierily legitimist. It continued through-out the 19th century and still manifested Royalist sympathies.

Gazette nationale, see *Moniteur universel.*

Gazul, Clara, see *Théâtre de Clara Gazul.*

Geffroy, GUSTAVE (1856–1926), journalist, novelist (interested in social questions), and, perhaps chiefly, art critic. His articles on artists, exhibitions, Impressionism and the Impressionists, &c., are collected in *La Vie artistique* (1892–1903, 8 series) and *Les Musées d'Europe* (1902–13, 12 vols.).

Gelée or **Gellée,** CLAUDE, see *Claude le Lorrain.*

Gelée, JACQUEMART, see *Roman de Renart* (para. 4).

Gelosi, see *Italiens*; *Theatres and Theatre companies* (para. 4).

Gendarme, Gendarmerie nationale. The word 'gendarme' (at first employed only in the plural 'gens d'armes') dates from the days of chivalry, when bodies of troops in France were composed of men-at-arms (*gens d'armes*), mounted and armed *cap-à-pie*, with attendant, more lightly armed, soldiers of their own. At a later date the *gendarmerie du roi* signified *corps*, or *compagnies*, *d'ordonnance*, composed of fully armed *gendarmes*, which preserved order and maintained the king's authority. The organization developed under Louis XIV but was swept away by the Revolution and replaced by the *gendarmerie nationale*, in effect a national constabulary for the maintenance of public security. This was modified and reorganized during the 19th and the present centuries. It is now a military force counting as part of the French army though not solely under the aegis of the Ministry of Defence. It is employed on varying duties, among them being police duties in country districts (cf. *Police*, para. 5). In towns, too, the *gendarme* performs certain duties, e.g. in a town the offender against the law is arrested by the *agent* (the municipal policeman), in the country by the *gendarme*, but in the police court in either case the accused sits in the box between two *gendarmes*. (See also *Garde républicaine.*)

Gendre de Monsieur Poirier, Le (1855), a comedy by Émile Augier in col-laboration with Jules Sandeau (qq.v.), a genial satire of the conflict between bourgeoisie and nobility which was characteristic of French life in the mid-19th century.

M. Poirier, a retired merchant in search of influence to help him to a title, manages to marry his daughter Antoinette to the ruined and dissolute marquis de Presle. The marquis, though now surrounded with luxury and with all his debts paid, makes no change in his former habits. He discovers his father-in-law's ambitions and makes game of him while pretending to further them. M. Poirier determines to humble his arrogant son-in-law, cuts off supplies, and insists on a legal separation between him and Antoinette. There is much intrigue, and a threatened duel, but by Act IV the marquis has fallen in love with his wife and is prepared to reform; and M. Poirier, professedly cured of his ambition, is calculating in an aside how soon he can hope to become 'un pair de France'.

Généralités, see *Fiscal system.*

Geneviève, SAINTE, a semi-legendary young woman of Nanterre, who at the time when the Huns under Attila were menacing Paris (451), calmed and reassured the inhabitants of the city, who were about to fly in panic. She was later regarded as the patron saint of Paris.

For the *École de Sainte-Geneviève* see *Sainte-Geneviève.*

Geneviève de Brabant, a legendary heroine, wife of Siegfried, count palatine of Treves. His seneschal, according to the legend, makes dishonourable advances to the lady and meets with a rebuff. To avenge himself, he accuses himself to the count of adultery with her. This and her consequent persecution have been made the subject of divers romances and plays. Her story is included in the *Legenda aurea* (*c.* 1260), a collection of lives of saints, with legendary elements.

Génie du christianisme, ou les Beautés poétiques et morales de la religion chrétienne, Le (1802), a work of Christian apologetics by Chateaubriand, appeared at a moment sensationally conducive to its success on the eve of the Easter Sunday Service at Notre-Dame which the First Consul Bonaparte attended in state to mark the restoration of Roman Catholicism as the official religion of France. The author's purpose was to revive Christianity as a moral force and to emphasize its appeal as the most poetical, the most human, the most favourable to all liberty, he claimed, of all the religions that had ever existed.

The work is in four parts. Pt. I, *Le Dogme et la doctrine*, is mainly theological, except for the 5th Book, a purely descriptive chapter in which the wonders of Nature are shown as the work of a Divine Providence. Pt. 2, *Poétique*, maintains the superiority of Christianity by reason of its poetic force. Great works of literature, such as the Bible and the *Divine Comedy*, are products of the Christian faith and have influenced man's thought and his feeling for Nature. Pts. 3 and 4, *Beaux-Arts et littérature* and *Culte*, are concerned with the superiority of Christian art. The author evokes the monuments and ceremonies of the Christian religion, dwells on the beauties of Gothic church architecture (at that time imperfectly appreciated), and re-creates the glories of the past.

As a whole the work—of which *Atala* and *René* (qq.v.) originally formed part—survives by its poetical qualities rather than as a reasoned argument in favour of Christianity. (See also *Ballanche*.)

Genlis (pron. as if *liss*), FÉLICITÉ DUCREST DE SAINT-AUBIN, MME DE (1746–1830), born near Autun, a woman of encyclopaedic information (though her early education had consisted of 'a little catechism and many ghost stories') and with a mania for instructing others. She lived in Paris from 1758, captivated society, and in 1762 married the comte de Genlis (who, in 1793, was the first of the Girondins to be beheaded). After 1770 she was lady-in-waiting to the duchesse de Chartres, to whose children (among them Louis-Philippe) she became governess, teaching them on novel, practical-cum-theoretical lines and writing and producing plays for their benefit (*Le Théâtre de l'éducation*, 1779). She emigrated in 1793 and until her return to France in 1802 lived by her pen in England and Switzerland. Napoleon paid her to furnish him with letters on literature, politics, &c. She lived on through the Restoration, a decayed, not wholly unrespected survivor of the great ladies of the 18th century. She was an inexhaustible writer

of popular romances which combined sentiment and sensation, morals and history, but lacked simplicity or humour—*Mademoiselle de Clermont* (1802, her most noted work), *La Duchesse de la Vallière* (1804), *Mademoiselle de La Fayette* (1813). An early collection of tales, *Les Veillées du château* (1784), was also popular. Her *Mémoires inédits sur le XVIIIᵉ siècle et la Révolution française* (1825) give a fairly scandalous picture of the society of her day.

Gentil-Bernard, see *Bernard, Pierre-Joseph.*

Gentillet, INNOCENT (d. *c.* 1595), jurist, a Huguenot who settled in Geneva; author of a *Discours sur les moyens de bien gouverner et maintenir en bonne paix un royaume . . . contre N. Machiavel le Florentin* (1576), translated into English by Simon Patericke (1602).

Geoffrey (Gaufrei) of Monmouth (1100?–54), probably a Benedictine monk of Monmouth, Bishop of St. Asaph from 1152, author of the Latin *Historia Regum Britanniae* in which he purported to give an account of the kings of Britain before the Christian era, and especially of King Arthur and his successors. He drew on Bede and Nennius (qq.v.), on British traditions, perhaps on Welsh documents now lost, and probably on his imagination. 'A most ancient book in the British tongue' which he claimed was one of his sources is probably in the main a mystification. He gave consistency and an appearance of truth to the Arthurian legends, thereby increasing their vogue. His work was translated into French by Geoffrei Gaimar and by Wace (qq.v.), and two other French translations were made in the 12th century. It appears to have been in large measure the source of inspiration of the French Breton romances.

Geoffrey also wrote a Latin version of the prophecies of Merlin, and a life of the latter in Latin hexameters is also doubtfully attributed to him.

Geoffrin, MME MARIE-THÉRÈSE RODET (1699–1777), born in Paris of a *bourgeois* family, was famous for the *salon* where, after the death of Mme de Tencin (q.v.), and in succession to her, she used to receive on Mondays artists (such as Boucher, La Tour, &c.), and on Wednesdays men of letters (Fontenelle, Marivaux, Marmontel,

Helvétius, d'Holbach), 'one of the institutions of the 18th century' (Sainte-Beuve). She was intelligent, had little learning but much penetration of character and knowledge of the world, and ruled her *salon* by a mixture of severity (prohibiting politics and religious topics) and good offices; for she was kindly and generous. Horace Walpole, who frequented her *salon* before he became devoted to Mme du Deffand, had a high opinion of her good sense (see his letter to Gray of 25 January 1766). One of her maxims, 'Il ne faut pas laisser croître l'herbe sur le chemin de l'amitié', is characteristic. The empress Catherine of Russia kept up a correspondence with her. Only a few of her letters survive. Her *salon* was caricatured in a satire, *Le Bureau d'esprit*, by the chevalier de Rutlige. In 1766 she travelled to Poland to visit King Stanislas Poniatowsky, whom she had known young.

Geoffroy, JULIEN-LOUIS (1743–1814), journalist, born at Rennes, spent the period of the Terror schoolmastering in the country, then returned to newspaper life in Paris, on the *Journal des Débats*. His dramatic criticism, to which a separate section—a *feuilleton*—was devoted, was largely responsible for the success of the paper. His collected articles were published in 1819–20 (*Cours de littérature dramatique*).

Geoffroy de Paris, see *History* (Medieval Period).

Geoffroy Saint-Hilaire, ÉTIENNE (1772–1844), a celebrated French scientist whose theories of evolution, contained in his *Philosophie anatomique* (1818–22), led to a famous dispute in 1830 with Cuvier over the fundamental laws of zoology. He was largely responsible for the remarkable progress, in late 18th- and early 19th-century France, of the study of natural science. In 1793 he was appointed to the staff of the newly reorganized *Muséum d'histoire naturelle* (q.v.). The menagerie here, for the furtherance of zoological studies, was his creation, enriched with many specimens collected in the course of scientific expeditions. (His influence on 19th-century French literature can be remarked in the work of Balzac, q.v.)

George Dandin, a comedy in prose by Molière produced in 1668. It formed part of the 'Grand Divertissement royal de Versailles' of that year.

George Dandin, a rich peasant, wishing from vanity to raise himself in the social scale, has married Angélique, the daughter of a country gentleman. Without consulting the lady he has addressed himself to her parents, who have arranged the match for the money it will bring. Dandin finds his punishment in the contempt of his wife, a worthless woman, and the arrogance of her parents, M. and Mme de Sotenville. He discovers an intrigue between his wife and a young gallant, complains to her parents, but they readily accept the denial of the couple, and seize the opportunity to humiliate Dandin. His wife leaves the house one night to meet her lover; Dandin, perceiving this, shuts her out and sends for her parents, intent on convincing them of her misconduct. The wife, alarmed, entreats forgiveness, and when Dandin is obdurate, pretends to kill herself. Though incredulous, Dandin decides to see for himself what has happened. As he goes out of the house, she slips in and locks the door upon him. When the parents arrive Dandin is once more confuted and humiliated. 'Vous l'avez voulu, George Dandin' is his melancholy comment on his misfortunes, and he concludes that his best course is to go and drown himself.

'George, Mlle', the stage-name of Marguerite-Joséphine Weimer (1787–1867), whose acting, beauty, and temper were alike celebrated. She played in classical tragedy at the Comédie-Française during the Empire and the Restoration period. Later, at the Odéon (q.v.) and the Théâtre Saint-Martin, she created the principal rôle in several of the Romantic dramas, e.g. Hugo's *Lucrèce Borgia*, Vigny's *La Maréchale d'Ancre*, Dumas *père*'s *La Tour de Nesle*.

Georges, see *Cadoudal*.

Gérard de Montréal, see under *Philippe de Novare*.

Gérard de Nerval, see *Nerval*.

Gerbert d'Aurillac (or *Gerbert of Aquitaine*), Pope Sylvester II (999–1003), born at Aurillac in Auvergne, reckoned a magician for his knowledge, inventor, mathematician, astronomer, scholar. He gave the names *ut, re, mi, fa, sol, la* (from the initial syllables of a hymn to St. John), to the musical notes. He was archbishop successively of Rheims and Ravenna before his election to the papal see, and was the teacher of King Robert II.

Gerbet, MONSEIGNEUR PHILIPPE (1798–1864), who was Bishop of Perpignan when he died, and a writer on ecclesiastical subjects, is also remembered as the abbé Gerbet of some thirty years earlier, when he was a disciple of Lamennais (q.v.) and one of his circle at La Chesnaie.

Géricault, THÉODORE (1791–1824), French painter, born at Rouen, was one of the earliest Romantics of 19th-century French art, noted for his bold, often violent imagination and his dramatic use of light and shade. These are exemplified in his famous picture *Le Radeau de la Méduse* (1819, now in the Louvre). A riding accident cut short his life. He was an early influence on, and much admired by, Delacroix (q.v.). He was in England in 1820–2 and made many sketches of English sporting (horse-racing) and daily life.

German Influence on French Literature, see *Foreign Influences* . . . .

Germinal, the seventh month of the Republican Calendar (q.v.). It ran from 21 (or 22) March to 19 (or 20) April.

A reference to 'Germinal' signifies the fall of the two factions the *Hébertistes* (q.v.) and the *Indulgents* (3 germinal An II, i.e. 23 March 1794).

Germinal (1885), by Émile Zola, one of his *Rougon-Macquart* (q.v.) novels. Étienne Lantier, a machinist (son of Gervaise, the laundress in *L'Assommoir*, q.v.), has been dismissed from his employment at Lille. He walks the country looking for work and comes to a mining district where the miners struggle to exist on starvation wages. He gets a job in the pits and soon acquires an ascendancy over his mates. His developing socialist sympathies are fed by the misery around him, by ill-digested reading, and by his friendship with Souvarine, an exiled Russian nihilist. He incites the miners to strike, but is helpless when hunger, sabotage, and fighting result. Finally the men resume work with no alleviation of their lot. Souvarine engineers an explosion which brings disaster; the pits are flooded and many die, among them Catherine, a young girl with whom Lantier had fallen in love. Lantier himself is rescued after twelve days, and on leaving hospital he is dismissed from his employment. It is springtime, and as he sets out once more in search of work he dreams of a *Germinal*, or seed-time, to be followed one day by the right to life and happiness for all men. The book is very long, and powerfully written, if at times almost painstakingly revolting.

Germinie Lacerteux (1864), a novel by Edmond and Jules de Goncourt (qq.v.).

Géronte (from Gk. γέρων, old man), the name given to the stock character of the old man in early French comedy. His ridiculous side developed with time until he became the foolish, credulous, opinionated, and finally avaricious personage of Molière's *Médecin malgré lui* and still more of *Les Fourberies de Scapin* (qq.v.).

Gerson, JEAN CHARLIER DE (1363–1429), of Gerson in the Ardennes, a learned doctor and later chancellor of the University of Paris, and its representative at the Council of Constance (1414). He was an eloquent preacher and writer of discourses on various questions of the day, addressed to the king or the people. In these he shows his devotion to the Church, to the university, and to France, and his faith and charity; also his humanistic tastes. He supported Christine de Pisan (q.v.) in her defence of women against the strictures of Jean de Meung (q.v.). The authorship of *De Imitatione Christi* has been (improbably) attributed to him.

Géruzez, EUGÈNE (1799–1865), born at Rheims, critic and man of letters, author of *Cours de philosophie* (1833, frequently re-edited), *Essais d'histoire littéraire* (1839), *Nouveaux Essais* . . . (1845), &c.

Gessner, SALOMON (1730–88), a Swiss of Zürich, landscape painter and author of rustic and narrative idylls in verse and prose, which were translated into French (by Turgot, among others, in 1760–1), were much admired, and exerted an influence on some of the French writers of the latter part of the 18th century, such as Bernardin de Saint-Pierre, Berquin, Léonard, and even André Chénier.

Gesta Dei per Francos, a collection (published 1611) of Latin chronicles and historical documents on the Crusades, mainly the work of monks.

Gesta Francorum, the first three (and the only) volumes, for the years 254 to 752, of a history of France begun by the 17th-century historian Adrien de Valois, seigneur de La Mare (1607–92).

Gesta Romanorum, a collection of tales in Latin chiefly of oriental origin, with a moral to each, compiled on the Continent in the 14th century. They were translated into French in the same century.

Geste, see *Chansons de Geste.*

Geste du roi, de Garin de Monglane, de Doon de Mayence, the three principal cycles of *chansons de geste* (q.v.).

Gestes des Chiprois, see under *Philippe de Novare.*

Ghéon, HENRI [pseud. of Henri Vanglon] (1875–1944), dramatist, critic, and essayist, also medical practitioner. His association with the early *Nouvelle Revue française* (q.v.) occasioned the interesting essays *Nos Directions: réalisme et poésie* (1911). He was converted to Roman Catholicism during the 1914–18 war (see his *L'Homme né de la guerre. Témoignage d'un converti,* 1919) and thereafter wrote many religious dramas, e.g. *Jeux et miracles pour le peuple fidèle* (1922, 2 vols.).

Ghil, RENÉ (1862–1925), poet, born at Tourcoing, in Northern France, was one of the theorists of the Symbolist movement (see *Symbolisme*). In the critical essays *Le Traité du verbe* (1886) and *De la poésie scientifique* (1909) he expounded the doctrine of 'l'instrumentation verbale', i.e. that the musical quality of a poem could be intensified and the theme, as it were, orchestrated, by the conscious use of certain groups of vowels and consonants as if they were parts of an orchestra. His poetry, obscure, and much influenced by Mallarmé, is in *Légendes d'âmes et du sang* (1885), and *Œuvres* (1887–97 and 1898–1920), 13 volumes of verse and prose.

Gide, ANDRÉ (1869–1951), essayist, critic, novelist, and dramatist (Nobel Prize for Literature, 1947), was born in Paris, of Cévenol Protestant stock on his father's side. His mother, a Protestant of Roman Catholic origin, came from Normandy, where much of his own childhood and later life was spent. He was educated, intermittently owing to ill health, at the Protestant *École alsacienne* in Paris, where school contacts introduced him to Symbolist circles; and comfortable family circumstances enabled him to devote himself to literature, music, and travel.

(2) His writings can be divided into three groups. First come the youthful works, influenced by *Symbolisme* (q.v.), e.g. *Les Cahiers d'André Walter* (1891, published anon.), a study of adolescent unrest, and an early example of the journal form which he frequently employed; *Traité du Narcisse* (1891); *Les Poésies d'André Walter* (1892); *La Tentative amoureuse* (1893), and *Le Voyage d'Urien* (1893), partly narrative, partly dialogue.

(3) A second group includes works written between *c.* 1896, following three years in Algeria, and 1914. This Algerian visit, the first of many, had had a profound effect on his character, causing him to react against restraints and inhibitions imposed by a narrowly Protestant upbringing (described in *Si le grain ne meurt,* see below) and to find himself, when once he returned to it, stifled by the atmosphere of literary Paris. He now became interested in Nietzsche and Dostoievsky (his first study of the latter was published in 1911), the two authors whose influence, with Montaigne's and Goethe's, is most frequently remarked in his work; and it may also be noted at this point that Gide was soaked in the Bible to an extent less often encountered in French than in English writers.

(4) The two first works of this second group, *Paludes* (1896) and *Les Nourritures terrestres* (1897, q.v.), went almost unnoticed when they first appeared but found a wide public twenty years later. The one (from Lat. *palus,* a swamp, plur. *paludes*) is a satire of literary conventionalism. The other consists of seductively lyrical exhortations, addressed to a non-existent youth Nathanaël, to follow impulse and abandon himself to sensation. They were followed by *Philoctète* (1897), again, like the earlier *Narcisse,* a *traité* or symbolical treatment of a moral question; *Le Prométhée mal enchaîné* (1899),

termed by the author a *sotie* (q.v.) because, although the intention is satirical, the treatment is farcical; two dramas (published together in 1904), *Le Roi Candaule* (3 acts in rhythmic prose, produced 1901), and *Saül* (written *c.* 1895, produced 1922), the latter, in contradistinction to the counsels of *Les Nourritures terrestres*, showing King Saul as a broken-down old man, worn out through having yielded to all his desires; *L'Immoraliste* (1902), a novel (later termed a *récit*, see below) in which the chief character follows every impulse (a swing back to *Les Nourritures*) regardless of morals or humanity; *Prétextes* (1903), a collection—like *Nouveaux Prétextes* (1911)—of lectures and critical writings; *Amyntas* (published 1906, written earlier), Algerian travel impressions from which the intoxicating effect of a first contact with the East can well be gauged; *Le Retour de l'enfant prodigue* (1907), on an eating-one's-cake-and-having-it theme: the prodigal son returns, but helps his younger brother to run away; *La Porte étroite* (1909, q.v.), with which the author initiated his practice of giving the name *récit* to a type of studiedly simple but intrinsically ironic tale told by, and from the point of view of, one character (reserving the term *roman*, the novel proper, for works of complicated structure such as his own *Les Faux-Monnayeurs*, q.v.); *Isabelle* (1911), another *récit*, about a family secret and its discovery, a conscious little masterpiece of restrained style and subdued background; and, finally, *Les Caves du Vatican* (1914), a *sotie*, a succession of complicated adventures in which the chief character, Lafcadio, lives dangerously and performs a motiveless murder (an *acte gratuit*, q.v.).

(5) During the greater part of these years Gide, though known to a small circle and, as a founder in 1908 of the *Nouvelle Revue Française*, an influence on the *littérature d'avant-garde*, had made little impression on the general public. He had his first bookshop success with *La Porte étroite* and between then (1909) and the outbreak of the 1914–18 war his reputation grew considerably, all the more, perhaps, because some critics found, and denounced, a subversive tendency in his writing.

(6) The third group contains works first published after 1918. Gide was now to become one of the foremost representatives of the modern literature of introspection (with sexual abnormality as a recurrent theme, cf. *Proust*), self-confession, and moral and religious—at times also social and political—uneasiness; and he stood high among critics. He was widely read and even more widely discussed, with an influence upon the aesthetic and moral values of a whole inter-war generation. The chief works of this group are: *La Symphonie pastorale* (1919), *L'École des femmes* (1929), *Robert* (1930), *Geneviève* (1937), *Thésée* (1946), all *récits*; *Les Faux-Monnayeurs* (1926, q.v.), his one novel in his own sense of the word, with an added interest as an innovation in technique; *Œdipe* (a drama, 3 acts, prose, published 1931, produced 1932) on the moral problem by which Gide was continually exercised—'la lutte entre l'individualisme et la soumission à l'autorité religieuse'; *Voyage au Congo* (1927) and *Le Retour du Tchad* (1928), two works in which French colonization in Africa is studied and severely criticized; *Pages de journal* (1934) and *Retour de l'U.R.S.S.* (1936), marked alternately by sympathy with Communism and by disillusionment; *Les Nouvelles Nourritures* (1935), new counsels, addressed this time (before disillusionment had set in) to 'Camarade'; *Dostoïevsky, articles et causeries* (1923), *Incidences* (1924), *Essai sur Montaigne* (1929), criticism; a number of translations, notably of Shakespeare (*Antony and Cleopatra*, *Hamlet*) and Conrad; and, finally, *Corydon* (1924), Socratic discussions on the theme of homosexuality, *Si le grain ne meurt* (1926), very self-revealing autobiography, and his long, interesting *Journal, 1885–1939* (1939), completed later for the years *1939–42* (1946) and *1942–9* (1950), followed by two fragments *Et nunc manet in te* and *Ainsi soit-il, ou Les jeux sont faits* (1951, posth.). Reminiscences, and some essays, are also to be found in *Feuillets d'automne* (1949); and the Correspondence of Gide and Claudel (published 1949), largely the record of a religious flirtation on the part of the former, throws interesting light on two very different characters.

Gide, CHARLES (1847–1932), political economist, uncle of the foregoing. His publications include: *Études sur la philosophie morale au XIXe siècle* (1904); *Cours d'économie politique* (1930, 2 vols.), &c.

Giéra, PAUL, one of the original *félibres* (q.v.).

Gigogne, MÈRE, a character of marionette drama, represented as the mother of a numerous progeny.

Gigonnet, the nickname by which the moneylender Bidault, in Balzac's *Comédie humaine* (q.v.), was universally known in Paris. (He had come there from Auvergne.) He figures notably in *Histoire de la grandeur et de la décadence de César Birotteau* (q.v.) but appears also in several other volumes.

Gilbert, GABRIEL (*c.* 1620-80), a mediocre dramatist, also poet, probably a Protestant, of interest for the use later dramatists made of his themes and ideas: e.g. his *Rodogune* (1644) was a precursor of Corneille's; his *Hippolyte* (1646) of Racine's *Phèdre*. He was for a time resident secretary at Queen Christina of Sweden's court in France.

Gilbert, [NICOLAS-JOSEPH-] LAURENT (1751-80), a poet of promise who died young and poor; an adversary of the 'philosophes' whom he attacked in his satires with bitter shafts occasionally recalling Tacitus and Juvenal; author of *Le Dix-huitième Siècle* (1775), *Mon Apologie* (1778). His *Adieux à la vie* was his last and best work.

Gilberte, the daughter of Charles Swann, a key character in Proust's *A la recherche du temps perdu* (q.v.). Marcel first sees her in childhood at Combray. Later, in Paris, their boy-and-girl affair is his first experience of the continually-renewed hopes and disappointments of, and the deadening effect of absence on, love.

Time as a transforming agent—one of the main themes in the novel—can be seen at work in Gilberte. Her paternal grandfather was an Alsatian Jew, her mother (Odette, q.v.) an ex-courtesan whom Swann's friends in the aristocratic, 'Guermantes', world had refused to know. She herself becomes a Guermantes by her marriage with Marcel's friend Robert de Saint-Loup. Her sixteen-year-old daughter will one day (in *Le Temps retrouvé*, pt. II) represent for Marcel the point at which the *Swann* and *Guermantes* paths of his life coalesced.

Gil Blas (pron. as if *Blass*) **de Santillane,** a picaresque romance by Lesage, in four volumes, published, the first two in 1715, the third in 1724, the fourth in 1735.

Gil Blas, the son of humble Spanish parents, is a young man of ordinary character, with nothing heroic about him, sane, intelligent, easy-going, adaptable, in fact a favourable sample of the average man. At seventeen he is sent off on a mule, with a few ducats in his pocket and little in the way of scruples or morality, to the University of Salamanca. He never reaches it, but falls in with robbers, by whom he is detained. This is the beginning of a long series of adventures, in the course of which he takes service with Dr. Sangrado (a quack physician) and becomes a physician himself, with the archbishop of Granada (who after inviting Gil Blas's criticisms on his sermons, resents it when given), and with a variety of other persons. A happy chance introduces him to the duke of Lerma, prime minister of Spain, who makes him his secretary and confidant. Thereby Gil Blas acquires great wealth. But prosperity corrupts him and he becomes proud and heartless, a disposition which is checked when he falls into disgrace and is imprisoned. After an interval he returns to court, where Olivares is now prime minister, and is once more employed. He has now acquired worldly wisdom and even some tincture of benevolence and morality from his experiences. On the death of the minister he retires to a peaceful country life. By the ingenuous avowal of his faults he has retained the reader's liking, if not his esteem.

Lesage's presentation of life with its vicissitudes and recoveries, the total absence of bitterness from his satire, give the work, as Sainte-Beuve says, a remarkable consolatory character. Scott said of it that it leaves the reader pleased with himself and with mankind. Pitt considered it, we are told, the best of all novels. But it has been censured for its levity, e.g. by Joubert. Its moral is that life is not so bad after all, provided we make the best of it and profit by experience; and moreover that life as a rule makes man better. *Gil Blas* was translated into English (or the translation was revised) by Smollett.

Gil Blas, a political and literary daily, founded in 1880. It was brilliant, witty, and frequently scurrilous and made a feature of interviews. It did not outlive the 1914-18 war.

Gill, ANDRÉ [pseud. of Louis-Alexandre

Gosset de Guines] (1840–85), humorous artist. His series of political caricatures, *Nos députés*, was much appreciated.

Gilles, a typical character in French pantomime, a silly timid creature; the subject of a remarkable painting by Watteau in the Louvre.

Gilles de Retz (or Rais), see *Retz*.

Gillet de la Tessonnerie (1620–60?), dramatist, author of the comedies *Le Déniaisé* (1647) and *Le Campagnard* (1657), which show originality and comic power.

Gilliatt, the hero of *Les Travailleurs de la mer* (q.v.), by Hugo.

Gilliéron, JULES (1854–1926), philologist, Swiss by birth, French by naturalization. He was for the greater part of his life a Professor at the *École des hautes études* in Paris, where he had first come to study in 1876. He was particularly learned in the morphology of the French language and the dialectal variants of words and constructions. Between 1902 and 1910, in collaboration with E. Edmond, he published an *Atlas linguistique de la France*, a collection, in portfolio fascicules, of maps of France, each one of a total of 1,920 maps recording, department by department, the various local transformations of one particular word or phrase (e.g. *abeille*). A supplementary volume was published in 1920. The necessary information was collected locally by M. Edmond, in 639 districts, by means of a carefully framed questionnaire.

Gillot, JACQUES, see *Satire Ménippée*.

Gilson, ÉTIENNE (1884–   ), born in Paris, one of the foremost contemporary exponents of medieval philosophy, especially of Thomism, and the influence of Christianity on the development of modern civilization. He has held the chair of History of Medieval Philosophy at the Collège de France (q.v.) since 1932 and is also founder and director of the Institute of Medieval Studies at the University of Toronto. His works include: *La Liberté chez Descartes et la théologie* (1913); *La Philosophie au moyen âge* (published in 1922 and again, amplified, in 1944), a study of early systems of philosophy and of the transmission of Greek and Latin culture and the dawn of humanism; *Le Thomisme: Intro*

duction à la philosophie de saint Thomas d'Aquin (1922); *L'Esprit de la philosophie médiévale* (1931–2), Gifford lectures delivered at the University of Aberdeen; *Les Idées et les lettres* (1932) with a particularly interesting preface on the value to be attached by literary historians to the study of sources.

Ginguené, PIERRE-LOUIS (1748–1816), a critic of the older, dogmatic, school which prevailed before, and in some cases outlasted, the Revolution (cf. *La Harpe*). He wrote for reviews of the *Directoire* and Empire periods, notably the *Décade philosophique* (q.v.). His *Histoire littéraire d'Italie* (1811–19, 9 vols., the final ones by another hand) was widely read. (See also *Gluck, Gluckistes*.)

Giono, JEAN (1895–   ), novelist, of partly Italian ancestry, was born at Manosque (Basses-Alpes). He describes a pastoral life in the lower mountain-slopes of Provence that is close to primitive Nature and not only simple, beautiful, and poetic. *Colline* (1929), *Un de Baumugnes* (1929), and *Regain* (1930) make up the early trilogy *Pan*. *Le Grand Troupeau* (1931), a novel of the 1914–18 war, has some grimly descriptive passages. *Jean le bleu* (1933) is semi-autobiographical, based on the author's childhood. Other titles include: *Que ma joie demeure* (1935), *Les Vraies Richesses* (1936), *Batailles dans la montagne* (1939); the short stories *Solitude de la pitié* (1932) and *La Femme du boulanger* (1935); also some more recent novels (termed 'chroniques' by the author) in which distaste for so-called civilization and its horrors is more evident than a sense of kinship with nature (e.g. *Le Hussard sur le toit*, 1951, about the cholera epidemic of 1848). *Le Lanceur de graine* (1932) is a pastoral play.

Girard, L'ABBÉ GABRIEL, see *Dictionaries and encyclopedias* under date 1736.

Girard de Viane (i.e. Vienne in the S. of France), a *chanson de geste* (q.v.) by Bertrand de Bar-sur-Aube (q.v.), one of the *Garin de Monglane* (q.v.) cycle. It relates the conflict of the sons of Garin with Charlemagne (arising out of a gross affront put by the empress on Girard, one of the sons) and includes the capture of the emperor in the forest of Vienne. (See also *Olivier*.)

Girardin, ÉMILE DE (1806–81), publicist and journalist, born in Paris, founded *La Presse*, the paper which, in 1836, initiated the cheap press in France (see *Press, Development of*, para. 14), also a number of low-priced instructive journals. Duels, and skirmishes with the authorities, characterized his political and journalistic career. His works included: *De la presse périodique au xix*^e *siècle* (1837); *De la liberté de la presse et du journalisme* (1842); *Questions de mon temps, 1836 à 1856* (1858, 12 vols., political articles), collected newspaper articles, &c.

Girardin, MME ÉMILE DE [*née* Delphine Gay] (1804–55), wife of the foregoing and daughter of Mme Sophie Gay (q.v.). As a young girl she contributed to *La Muse française* (q.v.), the organ of the Romantics, and wrote verse (*Essais poétiques*, 1824; *Nouveaux Essais poétiques*, 1825). Her poetic talent—even more, perhaps, her spirit and beauty—made her the adored queen of the Romantic *cénacles*. In 1827, during a visit to Italy, she was crowned in the Capitol in emulation of Mme de Staël's *Corinne* (q.v.). In later life, under the pseudonym 'Charles de Launay', she was the highly successful innovator of a weekly gossip column (1836–9, published in 1843 as *Lettres parisiennes*) in her husband's paper *La Presse*. Her other works included short novels and some comedies in verse and prose: *Le Lorgnon* (1831), *Le Marquis de Pontanges* (1835), *La Canne de Monsieur de Balzac* (1836), *Il ne faut pas jouer avec la douleur* (1853), *C'est la faute du mari* (1851), *Lady Tartufe* (1853), *La Joie fait peur* (1854), &c.

Girardin, RENÉ-LOUIS, MARQUIS DE (1735–1808), born in Paris, of Italian ancestry, is remembered as the friend and protector of J.-J. Rousseau, who tutored his son, and who lived for some weeks, and died suddenly, in a pavilion in the grounds of his château at Ermenonville, near Paris. He was the author of a much admired book on landscape-gardening, *De la composition des paysages, ou des moyens d'embellir la nature* (1777), and put his theories into practice by laying out the grounds of his château in the 'English' manner, with wooded clumps and groves, ornamental rivers, waterfalls and lakes, an island (*l'Île des peupliers*, where Rousseau was at first buried), and rocks engraved with moral exhortations.

Girardin, see *Saint-Marc Girardin*.

Girardon, FRANÇOIS (1628–1715), an eminent sculptor of the period of Louis XIV, known for his monumental and decorative statuary. His masterpiece is the tomb of Richelieu.

Girart de Roussillon, a *chanson de geste* (q.v.) of the late 12th or early 13th century, one of the *Doon de Mayence* (q.v.) cycle. Girard, having been robbed by Charles Martel (see *Maire du Palais*) of the woman whom he was to wed, takes up arms against him. Chastened by the trials to which God subjects him, he helps with his own hands to erect the shrine of the Madeleine at Vézelay. The poem was rendered into prose in the 15th century by the compiler Jean Wauquelin or Vauquelin (q.v.).

Giraudoux, JEAN (1882–1944), born at Bellac (Limousin), a diplomat by career, was also among the most distinguished and original modern French authors. He made his name first with novels, written in a highly personal and impressionistic style (and often containing charming portraits of young girls who combine extreme sophistication with disarming innocence), e.g. *Provinciales* (1909); *Simon le pathétique* (1918); *Suzanne et le Pacifique* (1921, a happy parody of the desert-island type of novel); *Siegfried et le Limousin* (q.v., 1922, a study of the German and the French mentalities); *Juliette au pays des hommes* (q.v., 1924); *Bella* (1926. Two young members of rival families play Romeo and Juliet in a satire of contemporary political life); *Églantine* (1926); *Combat avec l'ange* (1927. Tragedy nearly enters into a gay love-affair when one partner, a rich, beautiful young South American, develops a social conscience); *Les Aventures de Jérôme Bardini* (1930); *Choix des élues* (1939).

In 1928 Giraudoux turned to play-writing, with even greater success. His irony, amused sympathy, poetical fancy, and constant use of paradox and imagery (fatiguing at times in the novels) lent themselves to the discipline of dramatic form and stylized dialogue. His dramatic personages belong to a world of fairy-tale and classical myth, but their inconsistencies are human and they symbolize the conflicts which agitate humanity. His dramatic output included:

Siegfried (1928, after the novel); *Amphitryon 38* (1929; a modern treatment of a myth dramatized, so he said, 37 times before Giraudoux—by Molière, for instance, and Dryden. Jupiter comes to Alcmena at night in the shape of her husband Amphitryon. Alcmena, one of Giraudoux's most endearing female characters, teaches Jupiter that human friendship may triumph over a god's desire); *Judith* (1931, a psychological tragedy, from the Apocryphal story); *Intermezzo* (1933); *La Guerre de Troie n'aura pas lieu* (q.v., 1935); *Électre* (1937); *L'Impromptu de Paris* (q.v., 1937); *Cantique des cantiques* (1938); *Ondine* (1939, based on the tale by La Motte Fouqué); and two plays produced during the 1939–45 war, *Sodome et Gomorrhe* and *La Folle de Chaillot* (qq.v., 1943 and 1945).

Giraudoux's occasional collections of essays, critical and patriotic, include *Lectures pour une ombre* (1917); *Adorable Clio* (1920); *Les Cinq Tentations de La Fontaine* (1938); *Pleins pouvoirs* (1939), on the position of France in the world, and *Littérature* (1941).

Girondins, Les, a political party during the Revolution (so called because many of them were deputies from the department of the Gironde), the guiding body of the *Assemblée législative* and, later, the right, or moderate, group in the *Convention nationale*. They were republicans in theory, and advocated the overthrow of the monarchy, extreme measures against the clergy and the *émigrés*, and an aggressive foreign policy: but once the Republic was established they found themselves helpless in face of the fanatical revolutionary spirit let loose. Their attempts to maintain law and order, their protestations against the violent measures adopted by Danton, Marat, and Robespierre, and their opposition to the Revolutionary Commune, only succeeded in rousing the hostility of the people and in June 1793 they were overthrown. Twenty-one of their leaders were imprisoned, and executed some months later after a mere pretence of a trial. Prominent Girondins were: Brissot (their leader, after whom they were also known as *Brissotins*), Condorcet, Pétion, Roland, and Vergniaud (qq.v., and cf. *Montagnards*). They met frequently in the *salon* of Mme Roland (q.v. See also *Histoire des Girondins*).

Giry, ARTHUR (1848–99), scholar, distinguished as an editor of texts and for his critical studies of ancient documents. He compiled a *Manuel de diplomatique* (1894), and *Nouveau Traité de diplomatique*, works of capital importance for students engaged in documentary research.

Gismonde, see GUISCARD.

Glatigny, ALBERT (1839–73), minor poet, born at Lillebonne (near Le Havre), frequented Parnassian circles when in Paris but for the most part led a hand-to-mouth existence touring the provinces as prompter, and at need play-writer, to a company of actors. He had begun life as a printer's apprentice. His verse, strongly influenced by Théodore de Banville (notably by the *Odes funambulesques*) and Leconte de Lisle, included *Les Vignes folles* (1860), *Les Flèches d'or* (1864), *Gilles et Pasquins* (1872). His comedy of stage life, *L'Illustre Brizacier* (1873), is sometimes mentioned.

Globe, Le, a daily founded in 1824 by Pierre Leroux (q.v.) and Paul-François Dubois (1793–1874). It is remembered as the paper in which Sainte-Beuve (q.v.) began his career as a literary critic and, thanks to him, for its sympathetic attitude towards the young Romantic writers. In politics it reflected the ideas of the *doctrinaires* (q.v.), and Thiers (q.v.) was among its chief contributors. In 1831 it came into the limelight for a brief spell as the organ of the Saint-Simoniens (see *Saint-Simonisme*). It failed in 1832 for lack of funds.

Glorieux, Le, a comedy by Destouches, generally considered his masterpiece, produced in 1732.

The comte de Tufière is insufferably arrogant and proud of his high birth. He conceals the fact that his family is impoverished, and he hopes to marry Isabelle, the daughter of the rich *parvenu* Lisimon, who is equally proud of his money-bags. The comedy illustrates the conflict between the ruined nobility and the newly enriched *bourgeoisie*. The comte's vainglory is finally humiliated when his poverty-stricken father appears on the scene, and Isabelle's maid is found to be his own sister. Reconciliation and marriage follow. Destouches had intended to show the comte incorrigible and punished by the rejection of his suit; but it is said that the actors insisted on a happy ending.

Gluck, Gluckistes. The German composer Christoph Willibald von Gluck (1714–87), whose revolt against the Italian conventions of opera was largely due to Rameau's (q.v.) influence, had a large following in Paris between 1770 and 1780. The Italian composer Nicola Piccini (1728–1800), also in Paris from 1776, was likewise at the height of his popularity and the musical public was divided between *Gluckistes*, led by l'abbé Arnaud and Suard (qq.v.), and *Piccinistes*, led by Marmontel, La Harpe, and Ginguené (qq.v.). The quarrel is mentioned in memoirs of the period, and satirized in *Polymnie* (1819), a posthumously published poem by Marmontel (cf. *Grimm*; *Musical controversies*).

Gobelins, Manufacture des, a State factory of tapestry in Paris, named after Jean Gobelin (d. 1476), head of a family of dyers who settled in Paris about 1450, and made a great reputation by the discovery of a scarlet dye. In the 16th century the works were purchased for Louis XIV and since then (with a short break during the Revolution) have been run as a State concern for the manufacture of upholstery, furniture, and carpets.

Gobineau, JOSEPH-ARTHUR, COMTE DE (1816–82), diplomat, novelist, and historian, born at Ville d'Avray, near Paris, educated in France and Switzerland, entered the diplomatic service and was for a time secretary to Tocqueville (q.v.). For some years from 1855 an appointment as First Secretary at Teheran suited his interest in oriental languages and history. Later in his career he returned to Persia as Ambassador. He travelled after retirement, and ended his days in Italy.

Gobineau's name was for long associated chiefly with his *Essai sur l'inégalité des races humaines* (1853–5), a work from which pan-Germanic propagandists of the 20th century extracted a doctrine known as *le Gobinisme*. His own philosophy of racial aristocracy—by no means necessarily coincident with *le Gobinisme*—can also be studied in the *Correspondance entre Tocqueville et Gobineau* (1843–59) (1908).

His much more lasting fame—as a *conteur*—rests on his four oriental tales, *Nouvelles asiatiques* (1876), and on such small masterpieces (often published only in newspapers or reviews during his lifetime) as

L'Abbaye de Typhaine (1867), *Adélaïde* (1913), *Mademoiselle Irnois* (1920), *Le Prisonnier chanceux* (1925). A long novel, *Les Pléiades* (1874), shows the influence of Stendhal (whom Gobineau, like Balzac, appreciated when few other critics did). His other works included *Trois ans en Asie* (1859); *Les Religions et les philosophies dans l'Asie centrale* (1865); *Souvenirs de voyage* (1872), and *La Renaissance* (1877), a series of dramatic scenes from the lives of, for example, Savonarola, Caesar Borgia, Michael Angelo.

Gobseck (1830), a tale in Balzac's *Comédie humaine*, one of the 'Scènes de la vie privée', is an episode in the career of Gobseck, a miserly Jewish moneylender, who appears more than once in the whole work.

Goddam, a nickname, derived from the English oath, currently given to the English by the French during the Hundred Years War. Figaro in the *Mariage de Figaro* was of opinion that with this word he knew 'le fond de la langue anglaise'.

Godeau, ANTOINE (1605–72), born at Dreux, an *habitué* of the Hôtel de Rambouillet (q.v.), where owing to his small stature he was known as the 'nain de Julie' (Mme de Rambouillet's daughter). He was made Bishop of Grasse and Vence by Richelieu. He wrote, besides profane poems and better sacred odes, a good preface to the works of Malherbe, *Épîtres morales* containing interesting literary allusions, an *Histoire de l'Église* (1653–78), and an epic on *Saint Paul*. He was a member of the first *Académie*.

Godefroi de Bouillon (1058–1100), one of the leaders of the first Crusade, and first king of Jerusalem. (See *Chevalier au cygne* and *Assises de Jérusalem*.)

Godefroy, FRÉDÉRIC-EUGÈNE, see *Dictionaries and Encyclopedias*, under date 1881–1902.

Goethe, JOHANN WOLFGANG VON (1749–1832), famous German poet, dramatist and philosopher, born Frankfort-on-Main, died Weimar. For his influence on French literature see *Foreign Influences on French literature*, paras. 10, 18, 20; also *Werthers, Die Leiden des jungen*.

Golias, a fictitious personage, of uncertain origin, patron of wandering scholars, and reputed author of scores of satirical Latin (Goliardic) poems; he was dignified with the titles of *Episcopus* and *Archipoeta* in the 12th and 13th centuries. He came into prominence in France about the time of the conflict between Abélard (q.v.) and Bernard of Clairvaux. He is the type of the jovial railer, greedy, drunken, licentious, witty, original, and insubordinate.

Gombauld or **Gombault** or **Gombaud**, JEAN OGIER DE (1570–1666), poet, an *habitué* of the Hôtel de Rambouillet, who though a Huguenot obtained a place at court. He wrote, besides elegies and sonnets and some forgotten tragedies, a pastoral (verse) drama, *Amaranthe* (printed in 1631), and a (prose) romance, *Endymion* (1624), in which, under a transparent allegory, he expressed his love for the queen-mother, Marie de Médicis. He was an original member of the *Académie française* (q.v.).

Gomberville, MARIN LE ROY, SIEUR DE (1600–74), novelist, member of the original *Académie*, and later in life an ardent Jansenist. He was author of romances of heroic adventure and gallantry in a pseudo-historical setting, *La Caritie* (1621), *Polexandre* (q.v., his principal work, 1629–37), *La Cythérée* (1640), in which he conveys the reader to distant countries (never seen by the author)— Egypt, Mexico, Senegal, the West Indies. In 1651, after his conversion to Jansenism, he wrote *La Jeune Alcidiane*, a sort of Christian romance and sequel to *Polexandre*, in remorse for the demoralizing effect he attributed to the latter. He is remembered in the annals of the *Académie* as having desired to abolish the conjunction *car*.

Goncourt, EDMOND (1822–96, born at Nancy) and JULES (1830–70, born in Paris) DE [*Les Frères Goncourt*], novelists and men of letters, lived and died in Paris. They wrote in such sensitive collaboration that although death ended the partnership early they are seldom mentioned apart. They were highly artistic, nervous creatures, with two overwhelming interests—literature and collecting *objets d'art*—and ample means to indulge them. At first they wrote monographs on art and history—social history of a type then novel, based on study of contemporary customs, periodicals, and correspondence (e.g. *Histoire de la société française pendant la*

Révolution, 1854; . . . *pendant le Directoire*, 1855; *L'Art du dix-huitième siècle*, 1859–75; *La Femme au XVIII⁵ siècle*, 1862, &c., all still read and quoted). In 1851 they published their first novel, *En 1851* . . . , and also began the famous *Journal des Goncourt* (q.v.).

Their novels, though little read nowadays and often unsuccessful when first published, helped to make literary history. They originated the *roman documentaire* and are among the most frequently mentioned examples of *réalisme* and *naturalisme* (qq.v.) in 19th-century French fiction. The novelist's function, for these authors, was to write 'history which might have happened', to base an absolutely faithful picture of life on authentic observation and record of existing conditions, just as history was based on research into past conditions. ['Le roman actuel se fait avec des *documents* racontés, ou relevés d'après nature, comme l'histoire se fait avec des documents écrits.' *Journal*, 24 Oct. 1864; and cf. *Préfaces et manifestes littéraires*, 1888.] Thus their best-known novel, *Germinie Lacerteux* (1864), is the history of a domestic of their own who served them faithfully for years and was, they learnt later, all the time leading a life of vice and debauchery which ended miserably with her death in a workhouse. The principal character of *Madame Gervaisais* (1869), a study of religious mania, was drawn from a relative, and they spent many months in Rome, where she had lived, documenting themselves on actual scenes and happenings. For *Sœur Philomène* (1861) they made many expeditions to study hospital life from the inside, painful experiences which resulted in prostration for these 'historiens des nerfs'.

These three novels dealt with abnormal types; and *Les Hommes de lettres* (1860, first entitled *Charles Demailly*) had described a world of over-wrought, over-sensitive men of letters. *Renée Mauperin* (1864, q.v.) and *Manette Salomon* (1867, q.v.) were more in the nature of novels of manners. In all of them the authors adopted a form peculiarly their own: short, impressionistic, almost disconnected tableaux, written in a mannered, precious style (*l'écriture artiste*, q.v.) with many words borrowed from the language of painting and many coined by themselves.

Les Frères Goncourt thought themselves pursued by animosity. Their first novel had appeared the morning after the *coup d'état* of 1851, thus being doomed to failure. It was quickly withdrawn. Not long after, they were prosecuted (but acquitted) for having quoted some licentious verses of the 16th century in an article. Their play *Henriette Maréchal,* when produced at the Comédie-Française in 1865, occasioned an anti-Government demonstration. They took each mishap personally; and when less sensational ill-success greeted their other works they suffered just as acutely. When Jules de Goncourt died in 1870 his survivor called him a martyr to literature.

Recognition came to Edmond de Goncourt with the years. He was one of the convives at the *dîners Magny* (q.v.). His literary *salon* in the *Grenier des Goncourt* (q.v.) was a meeting-place for young, and older, writers. When he died he left a sum of money to found the *Académie Goncourt* (q.v.). He had returned to novel-writing in 1877 with *La Fille Élisa* (q.v.) followed by *La Faustin* (1882, q.v.), *Chérie* (1884, said to be a portrait of Marie Bashkirtseff, q.v.), and *Les Frères Zemganno* (1879). This last, a fine novel of circus life, is written with real feeling (the chief characters are two devoted brothers), and the impressionistic method suits the scenes described. (Some of the above-mentioned novels were dramatized.)

Edmond de Goncourt also did much to awaken interest in Japanese art (cf. his *Art japonais du XVIIIᵉ siècle: Outamaro,* 1891; and *Hokusaï,* 1896).

Gondi, PAUL DE, see *Retz.*

Gondinet, EDMOND (1829–88), was the author of popular light comedies—*La Cravate blanche* (1867), *Le Panache* (1875), *Le Chef de division* (1874), *Les Braves Gens* (1881), &c.

Gongorisme, MARINISME, terms derived from the names of the Spanish author Luis de Góngora (1561–1627) and the Italian Giovanni Battista Marino (q.v., 1561–1625) to signify the highly artificial style that they developed, akin to what is known in English literary history as Euphuism. This affectation of style was somewhat widely prevalent among French authors in the early 17th century and was vigorously condemned by Boileau. To what extent it was in fact due to foreign influences is doubtful.

Gorgibus, a character, (1) in Molière's *Les Précieuses ridicules,* (2) in his *Sganarelle.*

Gormond et Isembard, see *Doon de Mayence, Geste de.*

Gossec, FRANÇOIS-JOSEPH (1734–1829), composer, a figure in the history of French music. He wrote much official music during the Revolution, e.g. for Mirabeau's funeral, for M.-J. Chénier's *Hymne à l'Être Suprême* (q.v.), &c.

Goujon, JEAN (*fl.* 1540–60), a sculptor, of whose biography little is known, famous for the grace and delicacy of his work. He collaborated in the decoration of many of the important constructions of his day, notably of part of the Louvre, making much use of antique or mythological subjects, Tritons and Naiads, fauns, nymphs, and caryatids.

Gounod, CHARLES (1818–93), born in Paris, the composer of *Faust,* one of the world's most popular operas, produced first in 1859.

Gourgaud, GASPARD, BARON (1783–1852), one of Napoleon's generals, followed Napoleon to St. Helena and spent two years there. His *Sainte Hélène, Journal inédit de 1815 à 1818* (1889, posth., 2 vols.) is a good record of life at Napoleon's villa of Longwood. He also collaborated with Montholon (q.v.) in the *Mémoires pour servir à l'histoire de France sous Napoléon* (1823).

Gourmont, REMY DE (1858–1915), essayist, critic, and novelist, came by birth (Bazoches-en-Houlme) and long descent from Normandy. He was educated at Coutances and the University of Caen. From 1883 he lived in Paris. His interests were predominantly literary and scholarly: he edited and modernized old texts, held a post at the *Bibliothèque nationale* (q.v.) from 1884 to 1891, and in 1889 helped to found the *Mercure de France* (q.v., chief among Symbolist reviews), contributing to it regularly till he died. After 1891 a painfully disfiguring skin disease intensified his naturally recluse-like habits.

He was one of the finest critics associated with the Symbolist movement, e.g. in the impressionistic sketches of Symbolist writers in *Le Livre des masques* (1896) and *Le Deuxième Livre des masques* (1898), or the more serious criticism of *Promenades littéraires* (7 series, 1904–27).

Eclectic rather than profound scholarship, intellectual (and erotic) curiosity, a keen analytical mind, irony, and a distaste for lazy, conventional thinking are features of his essays, e.g. *Le Latin mystique* (1890, studies and translations of medieval Latin religious and mystical verse); *Esthétique de la langue française* (1899, linguistics); *La Culture des idées* (1901. This contains an essay, frequently mentioned, on the *Dissociation des idées*, in which he asserts the need to get away from the unquestioning acceptance of ideas and associations of ideas which have become commonplaces, and for thought to proceed by imagery rather than by ideas); *Le Problème du style* (1902); *Le Chemin de velours* (1902); *Physique de l'amour: essai sur l'instinct sexuel* (1904); *Promenades philosophiques* (3 series, 1905–9).

A tendency to regard human behaviour in terms of biological urge, and a lack of any real generosity of feeling, are the chief characteristics of his novels, which include *Sixtine: roman de la vie cérébrale* (1890. Life, for Hubert d'Entraves, only becomes real when he has analysed it and turned it into literature. His abortive love-affair with Sixtine Magne ends when she revolts against his deliberate wooing and takes a lover with less brain and more feeling); *Les Chevaux de Diomède* (1897); *Une Nuit au Luxembourg* (1906, a philosophical fantasy); *Un Cœur virginal* (1907), &c. His other works included collections of 'precious' short stories, e.g. *Histoires magiques* (1895), *Le Pèlerin du silence* (1896), *D'un pays lointain* (1898), *Couleurs* (1908); *Oraisons mauvaises* and *Simone*, the early—at times would-be Baudelairean—poems collected in *Divertissements* (1912); two dramatic prose poems, *Lilith* (1892, the Paradise Lost theme, introducing Lilith the demon-woman of Rabbinical literature, Eve's predecessor) and *Théodat* (1893); *Épilogues* (1903–7, contemporary commentaries); and the *Lettres à l'Amazone* (1921), written to an American woman whose friendship brightened his last years.

Remy de Gourmont and Marcel Schwob (q.v.) are often mentioned together as the two scholar-essayists produced by the Symbolist movement who were also imaginative writers.

Gournay, MARIE DE JARS, DEMOISELLE DE (1566–1645), adopted daughter of Mon-

taigne. After his death she issued an edition of his *Essais* and defended with vigour, and often with reason on her side, both Montaigne and Ronsard against the grammatical censures of the school of Malherbe, in pamphlets collected in *L'Ombre* (1626), and again in *Les Advis ou les Présens* (1634). She was an early blue-stocking, a prolific writer on moral themes, on the defence of the female sex, on the French language, &c. She figures in Saint-Évremond's *Comédie des Académistes*.

Gournay, VINCENT DE (1712–59), economist and *intendant du commerce* in the Government service, one of the founders (with Quesnay) of the school of the physiocrats or *économistes* (q.v.). The maxim 'Laissez faire, laissez passer' (q.v.) is generally attributed to him, but he left no writings.

Gourville, JEAN HÉRAULT DE (1625–1703), memoir-writer and something of an adventurer, whom Sainte-Beuve aptly compares to Gil Blas. He began life as *valet de chambre* in the La Rochefoucauld family, followed his master (the author of the *Maximes*) to the wars, and rose by adroitness and resource, wit and good humour, to a position of importance as a negotiator acceptable both to Mazarin and the princes in the troubles of the middle of the 17th century. Gourville, whose aptitude as a man of business had won the favour of Fouquet (q.v.), was involved in the latter's disgrace. After a period of exile, spent principally in the Netherlands but including a visit to England, he regained the favour of those in power, and attached himself especially to the house of Condé. He became financial agent of the family and in this capacity showed skill and fidelity. Colbert, though for many years he sought to recover from Gourville sums the latter had misappropriated, showed respect for his abilities. Gourville's memoirs are written with simplicity and sincerity and make in parts agreeable reading. They contain interesting references to William III.

Gouvion-Saint-Cyr, LAURENT, one of Napoleon's marshals (see *Maréchal de l'Empire*).

Gozlan, LÉON (1803–66), author of a novel, *Le Notaire de Chantilly* (1836), which owed something to Balzac; of sensational dramas, and of somewhat heavy comedies, e.g. *Le Gâteau des reines* (1855), *Il faut que jeunesse* *se paye* (1858). His one-act *proverbes* (q.v.) had more merit, e.g. *Le Lion empaillé* (1948), *Une Tempête dans un verre d'eau* (1849), *La Pluie et le beau temps* (1861). He was on friendly terms with Balzac and wrote useful and interesting reminiscences of him (*Balzac en pantoufles*, 1856).

Graal, Le saint, the Holy Grail, see *Perceval.*

Gracchus Babeuf, see *Babeuf.*

Graffigny, MME FRANÇOISE DE (1695–1758), author of *Lettres d'une Péruvienne* (q.v., 1747); also of a sentimental comedy *Cénie* (1750) which had a great momentary popularity. Among her letters are some describing the mode of life of Voltaire and Mme du Châtelet at Cirey, where Mme de Graffigny had taken refuge from ill-treatment by her husband.

Graindor de Douai, see *Antioche.*

Graindorge, M. FRÉDÉRIC-THOMAS, see *Notes sur Paris.*

Grammaire de l'Académie française, Towards the end of the 19th century the idea of an Academy's Grammar was revived, see *Académie française*, para. 2. In 1932 a *Grammaire de l'Académie française*, said to be largely the work of Abel Hermant (q.v.), was published. It provoked hostile criticism, notably the *Observations sur la Grammaire de l'Académie française* (1932) by the grammarian Ferdinand Brunot (q.v.), printed in double columns with quotations on one side and caustic remarks on the other, but after this died down it seems never to have been taken seriously. In fact the compilation was not a work of philology but a guide to grammatical usage (its self-avowed object).

Gramont, or **Grammont,** ANTOINE, DUC DE (1604–78), maréchal de France, whose *Mémoires* were composed from his papers by his second son.

Gramont or **Grammont, Mémoires du comte de,** written by his brother-in-law Anthony Hamilton (q.v.) and published in 1713. Philibert, comte de Gramont (1621–1707), brother of Antoine de Gramont (q.v.) and grandson of la belle Corisande (q.v.), was a man of illustrious family, a gambler and a libertine, whose lack of scruple as shown in the memoirs was judged lightly in his day. He lived for a time at the court of Louis XIV, from which he was banished in consequence of his attentions to a royal favourite; then at the court of Charles II of England, where he married Elizabeth Hamilton. The first part of the memoirs, down to Gramont's exile, appears to have been dictated by Gramont to Hamilton. The remainder was probably composed by Hamilton. The memoirs are written in admirable French, in a light, easy, slightly ironic style. The first portion, relating to the adventures of Gramont's early life, is the most entertaining. The rest is largely concerned with scandals of the court of Charles II, on which it throws a vivid light, though the historical trustworthiness of the work is questionable.

Grand-Bé, see *Rocher du Grand-Bé.*

Grand Cyrus, Artamène ou le, a romance by Madeleine de Scudéry, published under the name of her brother Georges in ten volumes (1649–53). It relates the endless adventures, amid Eastern wars, of characters whose names are taken from the ancient history of Persia, but in whom the author sought to depict distinguished personages of her day, Artamène, for instance, representing Condé, and Mandane Mme de Longueville.

The main element in the plot is the attempt of the mysterious hero Artamène, commander of the army of the Medes, to rescue Mandane, princess of Media, whom he loves and who has been carried off by the prince of Assyria. He forces his way into the burning city of Sinope, where she is held captive, only to find that she has been borne off on a ship by another rival, and apparently, but not really, drowned. Artamène, the reader is now informed, is in fact Cyrus (grandson of Astyages), whom the hostility of his uncle Cyaxares (father of Mandane) has obliged to conceal his identity and to attempt to win Mandane by his brave exploits in the service of her father. This he finally does, but only after many volumes of battles, assaults, and incredible feats, in which Artamène is always on the point of recovering his beloved and always disappointed. With this main thread of the story are intertwined the adventures of scores of other characters facing similar obstacles with equal fortitude. The action is delayed and the tedium increased by long biographies and monologues. The prudery of the female characters, it may be noted, is much more pronounced than in *L'Astrée*. The work was, however, immensely successful and very profitable to the publisher. It was translated into English and much read, among others by Dorothy Osborne and Mrs. Pepys; and episodes in it were adopted by English dramatists, such as Dryden and Killigrew.

Grand Dauphin, Le, i.e. Louis de France (1661–1711), the Dauphin, only son of Louis XIV and Maria Theresa, called the *Grand Dauphin* after his death to distinguish him from his eldest son Louis duc de Bourgogne (1682–1712) who succeeded him as Dauphin but died ten months later (see also *Monseigneur*; *Fénelon*). His second son, Philippe duc d'Anjou (1683–1746), who became Philip V of Spain in 1700, was the first Bourbon king of Spain (see *Bourbon*). The edition of the classics *ad usum Delphini* was prepared for the *Grand Dauphin*.

Grande Mademoiselle, La, see *Montpensier*.

Grandes Chroniques de France, a translation in French of the Latin chronicles of the early kings of France carried out by Primat, a monk of Saint-Denis, and presented to Philippe le Hardi about the year 1274, the first important historical work in the French language. The work of Primat was continued from time to time by the chronicles of later reigns (those of Louis IX and Philippe II by Guillaume de Nangis, another monk of Saint-Denis); from the 14th century they were written in French from the outset. The first French book printed in France was an edition of these *Chroniques* (Jan. 1476 o.s.).

Grandet, Le Père, a miser, a character in Balzac's novel *Eugénie Grandet* (q.v.).

Grandgousier, the father of Gargantua (q.v.).

Grand Meaulnes, Le (1913), a novel by Alain-Fournier (q.v.), a landmark in modern French fiction by its treatment, in terms of a childlike dream world, of happenings which all the time have a rational explanation.

Augustin Meaulnes, an uncouth but dynamic seventeen-year-old, galvanizes the small country school to which he comes as a boarder. The schoolmaster's son, François Sorel, becomes his worshipping companion.

At Christmas M. Sorel's parents are due for their annual visit. They are to be met, as usual, at the nearest railway station, but le Grand Meaulnes, on his own, sets out with a hired pony and trap to meet them at the junction, more distant. The grandparents arrive, having been fetched from the customary station. Next day, the pony and trap are brought back, and a few days later an exhausted, silent Meaulnes turns up. In time he tells his adventures to François.

He had lost his way in the dark, tethered the pony while he sought a night's lodging, and returned from his search to find pony and trap gone. The next day, after sleeping in a barn, he had wandered still farther astray, and at nightfall had come upon an old house in a wood, all lit up. Within, he found himself as it were in an enchanted world where a gay company, many of them children in bygone dress, were holding revels to celebrate the engagement of Frantz de Galais, the owner's son. Meaulnes, for whom a beautiful costume with a scarlet silk waistcoat was conveniently to hand, was accepted without question as one of a troupe of travelling actors engaged for the occasion. A sympathy sprang up between him and Yvonne de Galais, daughter of the house, when the two met, and talked, and took part in the strange, unreal festivities. Back in his room, he found a distraught young man, Frantz de Galais himself, home in secret only to go off again leaving word that rejoicings could cease for his fiancée had disappeared. On all sides the stricken company seemed to vanish. Le Grand Meaulnes was escorted to a crossroads and set on the road leading to his school in the village of Sainte-Agathe. As day was breaking he reached home, to dream now of Yvonne and of the fairytale world he had known for a few days—a lost world, for he had come upon it, and left it again, in the dark. His one tangible souvenir, carefully hidden, was the scarlet waistcoat.

One day among some gipsies in the village he recognized Frantz de Galais, who had taken in despair to a vagabond life. They talked, and Meaulnes pledged himself, at whatever cost, to help Frantz to recover his lost love. The quest took him to Paris and a life different from, yet uneasily intermingled with, the past. He interrupted it to marry Yvonne, for she, her father, and the lost domain, had been discovered by François Sorel. But Yvonne could not hold le Grand Meaulnes, driven back to Paris by conscience and the thought of his unfulfilled pledge. One day, however, his promise performed, he came home, and found that Yvonne had died when their daughter was born. The child had been cared for by François, now the local schoolmaster. It is he who tells the tale and in the telling keeps it firmly yet sensitively anchored to reality even when it seems to stray farthest into fantasy.

Grand Prix des meilleurs romans du demi-siècle. In 1950 a special selection jury decided that the twelve best novels of the first half of the 20th century were: *La Colline inspirée* (M. Barrès), *Journal d'un curé de campagne* (G. Bernanos), *Confession de minuit* (G. Duhamel), *Les Dieux ont soif* (A. France), *Les Faux-Monnayeurs* (A. Gide), *Silbermann* (J. de Lacretelle), *Fermina Marquez* (V. Larbaud), *La Condition humaine* (A. Malraux), *Thérèse Desqueyroux* (F. Mauriac), *Un Amour de Swann* (M. Proust), *La Douceur de la vie* (J. Romains), *La Nausée* (J.-P. Sartre). Another novel, *La Vagabonde* by Colette, who formed one of the jury, was specially added to this list. (See under these authors; and cf. also *Prix littéraires*.)

Grands Cimetières sous la lune, Les (1937), see *Bernanos, Georges*.

Grands-jours, extraordinary assizes formerly held by delegations of the *parlement* in provinces where crime and brigandage, including the misdeeds of tyrannical nobles, were especially rife. Fléchier (q.v.) has left a curious account of such special assizes in Auvergne in 1665.

Grand Siècle, Le, the age of Louis XIV (1643–1715).

Grand Testament, Le, see *Villon*.

Grandville [pseud. of Jean-Ignace-Isidore Gérard] (1803–47), born at Nancy, caricaturist and illustrator, became known when he contributed to Philipon's (q.v.) satirical journal *Charivari*. His satire usually took the form of portraying people as animals, e.g. in his series *Les Métamorphoses du jour* (1828). His illustrations for La Fontaine's *Fables* were celebrated.

Grasse, FRANÇOIS-JOSEPH-PAUL, COMTE DE (1722–88), naval commander distinguished in the American War of Independence, finally defeated by Rodney in 1782.

Graziella, by Lamartine, a tale (founded on an episode of the poet's early life) of a young Frenchman who travels in Italy and lives for some months in the household of a Neapolitan fisherman. A friendship with the daughter of the house ripens into love, more genuine on her side than on his. When he is called back to France she falls ill and dies. It was published in book form in 1852 but had already been told in Lamartine's *Confidences* (q.v.) in 1849.

Greban, ARNOUL and SIMON, see *Mystères*.

Green, JULIEN (1900–), a novelist of American parentage, born in Paris, writes in French and has lived in France except for 1919–22 (at the University of Virginia) and 1940–45 (again in the U.S.A.). After *Mont-Cinère* (1926, avarice and puritanism in an American (southern state) setting), his novels include: *Adrienne Mesurat* (1927), *Léviathan* (1928), *Épaves* (1932), *Le Visionnaire* (1934), *Minuit* (1936), *Varouna* (1940)— Zolaesque studies, the first three especially, of narrow, thwarted lives which conceal passion, vice, crime, and at times hallucination. The hallucinatory quality grows stronger in his later novels. His *Journal*, of which the first volume appeared in 1938, and *Memories of Happy Days* (1942), reminiscences, in English, should be mentioned.

Gregh, FERNAND (1873–), born in Paris, man of letters, critic and poet, author of *La Maison de l'enfance* (1897), *La Beauté de vivre* (1900), *Les Clartés humaines* (1904), *L'Or des minutes* (1905), *La Chaîne éternelle* (1910), *La Gloire du cœur* (1932), &c., poetry; and *La Fenêtre ouverte* (1901), *Étude sur Victor Hugo* (1904), &c., critical and biographical studies. He founded (1902) a short-lived poetical movement known as *Humanisme* (q.v. and cf. *Literary Isms*).

Grégoire de Tours (*c.* 538–594), a man of good family, who became Bishop of Tours in 573 and defended the rights of the church against royal inroads. He was author of a history which is an essential source for the Merovingian period.

Grenier des Goncourt, Le, two rooms, filled with books and collector's pieces, at the top of the house at Auteuil (Paris) where *les frères Goncourt* (q.v.) lived and where Edmond de Goncourt in later life held his literary *salon*. In the *Journal des Goncourt* for 14 December 1894, two years before his death, Edmond describes the Grenier as it then appeared.

Gresset, JEAN-BAPTISTE-LOUIS (1709–77), born at Amiens, poet and dramatist, for a time attached to the order of the Jesuits, and a teacher in their colleges. His poem *Vertvert* (q.v., 1734), a charming trifle in lively decasyllabic verse on the adventures of a parrot, gained him celebrity; but a further poem, *La Chartreuse* (1735), disquieted his superiors and his connexion with the order was severed. In 1745 he produced the successful satirical comedy *Le Méchant* (q.v.). He was admitted to the *Académie* in 1748, and ended his days in religious devotion. Frederick II had tried in vain to attract him to Berlin.

Grétry, ANDRÉ-ERNEST-MODESTE (1741–1813), musical composer, born at Liège in Belgium, lived most of his life in Paris. He was famous for his comic operas, in which he happily adapted the music to the sentiment of the scene. Marmontel relates in his *Mémoires* how he supplied Grétry, then a young musician on the verge of despair, with his first libretto, *Le Huron* (1768). (See also *Ermitage, L'.*)

Greuze, JEAN-BAPTISTE (1725–1805), genre and portrait painter, whose works are marked by a charming, sentimental *naïveté*.

Grève, PLACE DE, nowadays, much enlarged, the Place de l'Hôtel-de-Ville (q.v.), in Paris. In the Middle Ages the *Grève*, a sandy stretch by the Seine, became a centre of the water trade and thus of the municipal life of Paris (because the 'marchands par eau' were the nucleus of the municipality). Grain and wine were unloaded at the Port de Grève and the Place itself was a market which came to be bordered by houses built over a pillared arcade. After 1357, when one of these houses became the Hôtel de Ville, the Place de Grève became a public open space, the site till about 1830 (when it was renamed Place de l'Hôtel-de-Ville) of most of the notorious executions in

French history. It was the scene, in July 1789, of the creation of the Municipal Government of Paris and the *Garde nationale* (q.v.), and for long a gathering-place for insurrectionists or for dissatisfied or unemployed workers. The latter were said to 'faire grève', which by extension came to mean 'go on strike'.

Grévin, ALFRED, see *Musée Grévin*.

Grévin, JACQUES (1538–70), born at Clermont near Beauvais, a versatile man of letters, physician, and poet of the school of Ronsard, author of lyrics of merit, but known especially as a dramatist. He produced in 1559 *La Trésorière* (a satirical comedy against women and financiers), and in 1561 *La Mort de César* (q.v., a Senecan tragedy) and *Les Esbahis* (q.v., a comedy). He also wrote a treatise on the virtues of antimony, and translations from the classics. He became a Protestant and twice took refuge in England. He died at Turin in the service of the Duchess of Savoy.

Gribouille, a proper name probably adapted from the verb *gribouiller* to indicate a type of simpleton who runs into the difficulties he seeks to avoid, 'qui se jette à l'eau crainte de pluie'.

Grignan, MME DE, daughter of Mme de Sévigné (q.v.).

Grimarest, JEAN-LÉONOR LE GALLOIS, SIEUR DE (1659–*c.* 1715), man of letters and language master, remembered as the first biographer of Molière (*Vie de M. de Molière*, 1705, and *Additions à la vie de M. de Molière*, 1706).

Grimbert, the badger, in the *Roman de Renart* (q.v.).

Grimm, FRÉDÉRIC-MELCHIOR, BARON DE (1723–1807), a German, born at Ratisbon, employed in Paris at first in tutorial and secretarial posts, who entered literary society partly through friendship with J.-J. Rousseau, and with the help of Diderot developed into a good literary critic. He became from 1753, in succession to Raynal, the Paris correspondent of various German sovereigns on literary and artistic subjects. His letters, which were in effect a sort of private newspaper circulated in manuscript to privileged persons, extend to 1773 (after 1768 Diderot and Mme d'Épinay frequently replace him). They were imperfectly published as *Correspondance littéraire, philosophique et critique* in 1812, and edited afresh in 1877–82 by M. Tourneux. They contain much sound and interesting criticism (e.g. his comparison of Shakespeare and the French dramatists) and valuable appreciations of such prominent writers as Voltaire, Buffon, Rousseau, Helvétius, and Duclos. (The *Correspondance* was continued from 1773 to 1790 by J. H. Meister, q.v.) Grimm also corresponded from 1774 till 1796 with the Empress Catherine and was highly esteemed by her. He was an honest, able, and helpful man in spite of a brusque manner, firm and clear-headed, sceptical and pessimistic in philosophy and politics; an intimate friend of Mme d'Épinay. His friendship with Rousseau was interrupted by a resounding quarrel, in which it would seem that Rousseau was in the wrong. Grimm held various official posts indicative of the confidence that he inspired. In 1753 he had taken, on the Italian side, an active part in the dispute then raging with regard to the relative merits of French and Italian music, in his pamphlet *Le Petit Prophète de Boehmischbroda* (see *Gluck, Gluckistes; Musical controversies*).

Grimod de la Reynière, BALTHAZAR (1758–1838), a noted gourmand and eccentric, came of a line of gourmands. His grandfather died at table of a surfeit of *pâté de foie gras*. His father inherited both the grandfather's office of *fermier général* and his appetite.

After an education in Paris the young Balthazar made the grand tour of Europe and when, as yet unaware of what life had in store for him, he saw the Grande Chartreuse he was tempted to become a monk. But he returned to Paris, aged eighteen, was called to the Bar, where he practised without fees or ambitions for eight years, and developed a passion for the theatre which remained with him through life. He was later to write dramatic criticism for *Le Censeur dramatique* (1797–8) and acquire a set of waistcoats embroidered with portraits of the principal members of the Comédie-Française (q.v.). Disappointed love sent him to food for consolation, which he sought so voraciously that he was discovered to have a tapeworm. This was removed but the

appetite—the family inheritance—remained. His interest in matters gastronomic developed and he began to entertain in lavish and eccentric fashion. Guests who came to his twice-weekly *déjeuners philosophiques* had to remain, once they arrived, and to observe rules written in gold letters on the wall. The president at each déjeuner was the guest who first swallowed twenty-two cups of coffee. The talk, inspired by large quantities of coffee, bread and butter, and roast beef (three helpings obligatory), was of literature. The guests at one of the more elaborately-contrived banquets sat each with a coffin behind him.

The banquets stopped when, with a regrettable lack of fellow feeling, M. de la Reynière *père* determined to curb his son's appetite and his hospitable instincts by having him imprisoned by means of a *lettre de cachet* for two years. Shortly after his release Balthazar, now in the Midi, was overtaken by the Revolution. Hard put to it to fill either his purse or his stomach he became a travelling salesman.

On his return to the Paris of the *Directoire* (q.v.) he combined literary journalism with a renewed interest in good living. The former brought him neither profit nor glory, but he turned the latter to good account and founded, and for the most part wrote, with knowledge and wit, the *Almanach des Gourmands, servant de guide dans les moyens de faire grande chère* (1803–12, 8 vols.). This was so successful that he received an embarrassing number of presents in kind. He also wrote a *Manuel des Amphitryons* (1808), an elaborate guide to table etiquette and 'les éléments de la politesse gourmande', and a *Journal des gourmands et des belle,* (1806–7), containing a history of cooking, in dialogue, from earliest times.

After 1815, no longer hampered by financial cares, he lived in the country, in a château fitted with numerous mechanical devices to make banqueting, and practical jokes at the expense of his guests, more easy. Various unsuccessful attempts were made to have him confined as a madman but he managed to continue his career to the end in freedom. He still entertained lavishly, and was at all times secured from loneliness by the company of a pig, with its seat of honour at table, its mattress to sleep on at night, and a servant specially detailed to attend to its toilet.

His many eccentricities and the streak of cruelty in this 'cynique méchant et atra-bilaire' may have had a psychological explanation in the fact that he was hideously web-handed and had to wear special gloves to hide the disfigurement.

Gringoire. Pierre Gringore (see the following) figures, in a travestied character and with his period antedated, as 'Gringoire' in Victor Hugo's *Notre-Dame de Paris* (q.v.); and he is also the half-starved poet, hero of Théodore de Banville's *Gringoire* (1866), a sentimental comedy (one act, prose) in which Louis XI plays matchmaker.

Gringore, PIERRE (*c.* 1475–1538), a Norman by birth and a man of varied talents, whose motto was 'Raison par tout, Tout par Raison, Partout Raison'; he was Mère-Sotte in the society of the *Enfants Sans souci* (q.v.) and an organizer of mysteries and farces. He wrote a long mystery *La Vie monseigneur Saint-Louis*, not without dramatic interest in its pictures of feudal life, though of little historical value as a record of events; a paraphrase of the Penitential Psalms; and a number of political and moral poems in the allegorical style characteristic of the school of the *rhétoriqueurs* (q.v.). Among these poems may be mentioned *La Chasse du cerf des cerfs* (Pope Julius II) and the *Blazon des hérétiques* (an enumeration and condemnation of all the enemies of orthodoxy down to Martin Luther); also a remarkable work, *Les Folles Entreprises* (1505), partly reminiscent of the *Narrenschiff* of Sebastian Brandt, but consisting in the main of disquisitions on the political, moral, and theological questions of the day. Gringore's most famous composition, however, was the *Jeu du Prince des Sots* (1512), a complete tetralogy, comprising a *cry* (or advertisement of the performance), a *sotie*, a *moralité*, and a *farce*, in the second and third of which pieces he supported the policy of Louis XII by vigorous satire of Julius II. In the *sotie* Mother Church (*Mère-Sotte* wearing ecclesiastical garments over her own) plots with her prelates to increase her temporal power, wages war with princes, and is finally exposed and shown not to be the true Church but only *Mère-Sotte* disguised. The *moralité* was entitled *L'Homme obstiné*; it presented personifications such as *Simonie* and *Hypocrisie*,

which are converted by *Punition divine*, only *l'homme obstiné* (the Pope) remaining impenitent. After the accession of François Ier Gringore entered the service of the duc de Lorraine as herald.

Grippeminaud, see *Pantagruel* (*Cinquième livre*).

Griseldis, Griselidis, i.e. the humble, patient Griselda of the last tale in Boccaccio's *Decameron* (1353). Two French prose versions of the tale, made before 1400, were translated from Petrarch's Latin translation (which was used also by Chaucer in the *Clerk's Tale*). Petrarch called the heroine Griselidis. One of the prose versions, by an unknown author, was called *Le Livre Griseldis*. The other, made between 1384 and 1389 by Philippe de Mézières (*c.* 1326–1405), and surviving only in manuscript collections, is said to be the source of the *Histoire de Griseldis* (*c.* 1395; in octosyllabic couplets), apparently the first serious secular French play, and probably also by Philippe de Mézières.

Grisette, the name, in the first half of the 19th century, for the young sempstresses, milliners' assistants, laundresses, &c., of the *Quartier Latin* (q.v.). The popular idea of them as hard-working, underfed, of easy virtue, but always cheerful, always ready for love and gaiety, and loyal to their lovers of the moment, was that given by, for example, Alfred de Musset's *Mimi Pinson* or Murger's *Vie de Bohème*.

Grisi, CARLOTTA (1819–99), Italian dancer, cousin of the following, became one of the ballerinas of the Paris Opera. She married, and lived in Switzerland after 1850. Gautier wrote the ballet *Giselle* for her and corresponded with her for over twenty years. Her sister Ernesta, a singer, for long shared Gautier's life.

Grisi, GIULIA (1811–69), Italian opera-singer (mezzo-soprano) and a fine *tragédienne*, born in Milan. She was a triumphant success for several seasons (1832 onwards) at the *Théâtre-Italien* in Paris.

Grognards (fr. *grogner*, to grumble). The veterans of Napoleon's *Garde impériale* were commonly known by this name. He treated them with confidence and intimacy and they grumbled at the hardships they had to endure but served him with an almost fanatical devotion.

Gros, BARON ANTOINE-JEAN (1771–1835), French historical painter, born in Paris, died at Meudon, near Paris, a pupil of David (q.v.), particularly noted for his scenes of battle, and an early Romantic painter by his sense of life and colour. His famous *Pestiférés de Jaffa* and *Champ de bataille d'Eylau* are in the Louvre. Neglected and discouraged in his later years, he fell a prey to melancholy and drowned himself.

Gros-Guillaume, Gaultier-Garguille, and **Turlupin,** a trio of actors at the theatre of the *Hôtel de Bourgogne* early in the 17th century, who delighted the public by their performance of coarse popular farces. They also played in tragedy under different names (La Fleur, Fléchelles, Belleville). Their real names were respectively Robert Guérin (d. 1634), Hugues Guéru (d. 1633), and Henri Legrand (d. 1637).

Gros-René, Éraste's valet in Molière's *Le Dépit amoureux* (q.v.), who constitutes himself the friend rather than the servant of his master.

Grotesques, Les (1835), critical essays by Théophile Gautier (q.v.).

Guèbres, Les, a tragedy by Voltaire, produced in 1769, directed against religious persecution. Its performance was prohibited.

The scene is Apamea in Syria; the Guèbres are a Parsee sect persecuted by the Roman rulers and their priests. A Parsee maiden Arzame is discovered by the latter engaged in sun-worship and they demand her death from Iradan, the Roman governor of the place, and Césène, his brother and lieutenant. These men, who abhor the cruelty of the Roman persecution, try to save Arzame. But Arzémon, her supposed brother, from a mistaken belief that Iradan intends treachery, attempts to assassinate him. It is now revealed that Arzame and Arzémon are the children respectively of Césène and Iradan who had married Persian wives; these children were thought to have perished in a siege. Meanwhile the priests have accused the Roman officers of disloyalty, and they and their children appear doomed to destruction, when the arrival of the emperor himself and his announcement

of a general measure of clemency and toleration save the situation.

Guénée, ANTOINE, ABBÉ (1717–1803), remembered as the author of *Lettres de quelques Juifs . . . à M. de Voltaire* (1769), exposing Voltaire's errors, contradictions, and perversions in his treatment of the Scriptures.

Guêpes, Les, see *Karr, Alphonse.*

Guérin, CHARLES (1873–1907), born in Lunéville, minor poet of the post-Symbolist period, wrote musical, reflective, at times somewhat morbidly religious verse, e.g. *Le Cœur solitaire* (1899), *Le Semeur de cendres, 1899–1900* (1901), *L'Homme intérieur, 1901–1905* (1905), &c.

Guérin, EUGÉNIE DE (1805–48), born at the Château du Cayla, near Albi, a lonely, melancholy, intensely emotional and religious woman whose possessive love for her younger brother (see the following), whom she brought up after their mother died, absorbed her life. She was a natural poet, but conscience made her feel that time spent in writing was mis-spent. Her repressed emotions and creative gifts, and her rare feeling for nature, found an outlet in a remarkable *Journal intime* written for her brother from 1834 and continued, after his death, till 1842. It was edited in 1862 (*Journal et Fragments d'Eugénie de Guérin*) by G.-S. Trébutien, with whom, as also with Barbey d'Aurevilly (q.v.), she was in contact during the nine years she survived her brother, when she agitated for publication of his works. Trébutien had already (1855) published *Reliquiae d'Eugénie de Guérin* for private circulation. She never married; and rarely left her father's home, where domestic duties, good works, correspondence, and her journal filled her days. Sainte-Beuve considered her her brother's equal, if not his superior, in talent; Ximénès Doudan (q.v.) speaks of her tenderly as 'un rossignol . . . qui se tait par un jour de froid'.

Guérin, MAURICE DE (1810–39) is remembered by his prose poem *Le Centaure,* written c. 1835, published posthumously. (Melampus, a young mortal, seeks out the aged centaur Chiron, now alone on his mountaintop, and hears the story of his early days. The work, marked by a sensuous perfection of form, rhythm, and language, is a rare evocation of pagan Nature.) Born at the

Château du Cayla, near Albi, Maurice de Guérin spent a solitary childhood, brought up after his mother's death by his possessively devoted sister Eugénie (see the preceding) in an atmosphere austere with religion and his father's mourning. He was destined for the Church and educated first at Toulouse, then in Paris at the Collège Stanislas, where he met Barbey d'Aurevilly (q.v.), his close friend in later years. In 1832 he entered Lamennais's (q.v.) community at La Chesnaie in Brittany, and there realized that his love of nature and poetry was stronger than his religious vocation. He returned to a secular life after the community was dissolved in 1833. In Paris he tried unsuccessfully to live by his pen, then took to schoolmastering and private tuition—a hard life which, added to emotional stress and social distractions, finally undermined his health. Marriage (1837) with the sister of one of his pupils brought financial security but no great happiness; and in any case came too late. The following year he was taken home to Le Cayla to die of tuberculosis.

He had published nothing during his lifetime. In May 1840 the *Revue des Deux Mondes* printed *Le Centaure,* with a memoir by George Sand (q.v.) and some extracts from his letters. His works, *Maurice de Guérin. Reliquiae* (2 vols., ed. G.-S. Trébutien, with a preface by Sainte-Beuve), were published in 1861 and again, with additions which include another prose-poem *La Bacchante,* in 1862 (*Journal, lettres et poèmes*). A recent edition is of 1930. The *Journal intime,* also called *Le Cahier vert,* begun in July 1832 shortly before he went to La Chesnaie, ends in Paris in 1835 at a time when he was weighed down by the need to wear his spirit out for the sake of the body's subsistence. But besides its introspective interest it is full of a feeling for nature which at times, though much more subjective, recalls the *Notebooks* of G. M. Hopkins in its detailed awareness of sights and sounds.

Matthew Arnold's sensitive appreciations (in *Essays in Criticism,* 1865) are among the first English studies of Maurice and Eugénie de Guérin.

Guermantes, the name of the historic family to which several characters in Proust's *A la recherche du temps perdu* (q.v.) belong.

The chief representatives are the duc et duchesse de Guermantes ('Basin' and 'Oriane'), the duke's brother the baron de Charlus (q.v.), and the prince and princesse de Guermantes. Others include Mme de Villeparisis, the marquis (Robert) de Saint-Loup (qq.v.), &c., &c.

For Marcel, day-dreaming in childhood among the effigies in the church at Combray (q.v.), the name 'Guermantes' signified French history and legend. It also symbolized those remote fastnesses of Parisian society to which the bourgeoisie (his own milieu) could never penetrate. When, later, thanks to Saint-Loup, this world was thrown open to him he studied it, as we do through his eyes, on many occasions—at the theatre, in Mme de Villeparisis's *salon,* at dinner-parties and receptions given by the duchesse or the princesse de Guermantes. He was alternately flattered to be made free of it, disillusioned by its fundamental banality, and intrigued by its mannerisms or by the passions and vices hidden beneath its surface.

At the reception described in the concluding volume (*Le Temps retrouvé,* pt. II) the middle-aged Marcel observes the havoc wrought by time in this magic world of his early fancies, however much for a newcomer it may still spell glamour and history. His host, the prince de Guermantes, ruined by war, has remarried. His hostess, the new princesse de Guermantes, is none other than the one-time Mme Verdurin (q.v.) whose *salon* had once seemed poles apart from the *monde élégant.* Charlus, now sunk in vice, no longer figures in the society he once dominated, but his one-time violinist protégé, Morel, the valet's son, is a war-time hero, welcomed everywhere. The aged duc de Guermantes is madly in love with the equally aged Odette, once Mme Swann (q.v.) and before that a *demi-mondaine.* Time's transformations are above all noticeable in the person of the young Mlle de Saint-Loup—in her features even, for they partake both of her Alsatian Jew grandfather (through her mother Gilberte Swann) and her Guermantes father.

Guernes de Pont-Sainte-Maxence, see *Thomas Becket.*

Guerre, MARTIN, a Gascon gentleman of the 16th century, who after ten years of married life disappeared from the country. Subsequently a certain Arnaud du Thil, bearing a close resemblance to Guerre, presented himself as the missing man, of whose circumstances he had made a close study. He was recognized by Guerre's wife as her husband, and lived with her until a soldier published the fact that the true Martin Guerre was living in Flanders. After a long trial, which excited great interest, and the final reappearance of Guerre himself, du Thil was convicted and executed in 1560.

Guerre de Troie n'aura pas lieu, La (1935), a drama by Giraudoux (q.v.), a fine example of his gift for tragic irony and his use of wit and paradox to emphasize the conflict of human values. Hector returns to Troy victorious, but sickened of war, and finds a new war already threatening, for Helen, kidnapped by Paris, is in Troy and the Greeks demand her return. The play's two acts are taken up with the struggle between those who, like Hector, are convinced that war is evil and wish to return Helen to Menelaus, and those, the warmongers, who back their refusal with talk of patriotism, heroism, manly virtues, and so on. Finally Hector prevails. The great gates of Troy, open only in time of war, are closed and Helen will return to Greece in the charge of Menelaus's envoy Ulysses. (A moving argument between Hector and Ulysses has led up to this.) At this moment a drunken man and a drunken killing serve to mark the inevitable course of destiny. As the curtain falls the gates of war are seen slowly opening—and behind them Helen, infinitely variable, infinitely obliging, is seen embracing Troilus.

Guesde, JULES [Mathieu Basile] (1845–1922), born in Paris, one of the chief French followers of Karl Marx, one of whose daughters he married. He was at first a government office clerk and then a socialist agitator. He edited *L'Égalité*, a socialist weekly, and was leader of the *Guesdistes*, a Labour party which worked for an international Labour movement. He was Deputy for Lille for many years, and held Ministerial office during the 1914–18 war.

Gui, châtelain de Coucy, see *Coucy*.

Gui de Bourgogne, the title of a *chanson de geste* (q.v.) of the Charlemagne cycle. The warriors have for twenty-seven years

been absent from their homes at the war in Spain. Their sons join them, and help them to win the victory.

Gui de Warewic, an Anglo-Norman metrical romance, probably dating from the first half of the 13th century. The earliest extant English version (*Guy of Warwick*) dates from the 14th century.

Gui is the son of Siward, steward of the Earl of Warwick. The poem recounts his exploits undertaken to win the hand of Felice, the Earl's daughter. After his marriage and many adventures, he fights for King Athelstan before Winchester against the giant Colbrand, champion of the invading Danish king Anlaf. He slays the giant and retires to a hermitage. Finally he makes his presence known to Felice, but dies as she reaches the hermitage.

Guiart, GUILLAUME, see *History* (medieval period).

Guibert, COMTE DE, see *Lespinasse*.

Guiche, ARMAND DE GRAMONT, COMTE DE (1638–73), son of the maréchal de Gramont (q.v.), a military commander who wrote a spirited *Relation du Passage du Rhin* of 1667, in which he had taken a prominent part.

Guignol, a marionette who seems originally to have been introduced into the outdoor puppet shows established at Lyons about 1815 by the puppet-master Laurent Mourquet (1745–1844), who also, later, started a café where he installed a *Théâtre de Guignol*. (Mourquet died in Vienna, aged ninety-nine.) In Lyons Guignol became an even greater favourite than Polichinelle. He was, like the Lyons silk-worker or the Dauphiné peasant, good-natured, easily duped, but cunning, and never finally worsted.

The children's puppet theatres in Paris (e.g. in the Champs-Élysées and the Jardin du Luxembourg) are called *théâtres de Guignol*; and 'by some twist of nomenclature', says the *Oxford Companion to the Theatre* [possibly from affinity with *guignon*= evil fortune?] the *Théâtre du Grand Guignol* of modern times, in Paris, specializes in crude plays of horror and violence.

Guilbert de Pixerécourt, see *Pixerécourt*.

Guillaume, Chanson de, a *chanson de geste* probably of the first half of the 12th century, the finest of these epics after the *Chanson de Roland*, forming part of the cycle of *Garin de Monglane* (q.v.). It celebrates the life and exploits of Garin's great-grandson, Guillaume d'Orange or Guillaume 'au court nez' (from the shape of his nose damaged by a Saracen sword). His historical prototype lived in the 8th century, was named comte de Toulouse by Charlemagne, fought repeatedly with the Saracens, and ended his life as a monk at Aniane, near Montpellier, having built near by and endowed a monastery known later as Saint-Guilhem-le-Désert.

This *chanson*, of which that entitled *Aliscans* is a rehandling, begins with the grievous defeat of a small Christian force under Vivien, nephew of Guillaume, by Saracens, in the plain of Larchamp or Aliscans (from *Elysii campi*, the name given to the Roman cemetery near Arles). Overcome by numbers Vivien sends a messenger to summon Guillaume to the rescue. Guillaume comes in haste, but is defeated. His wife, Guibourc, has raised another army, but this and all Guillaume's followers are destroyed. He arrives, pursued by the enemy and half-dead, at the gate of Orange. Guibourc, who commands the place in his absence, at first refuses to recognize her husband in the fugitive who asks admission. At last she has the gate opened and questions him as to the fate of his various followers. He tells the tale of the disaster, and the pair in silent sorrow go to the great hall, where all is prepared for the expected banquet, but which will now be for ever deserted. On the morrow, encouraged by Guibourc, Guillaume sets out again, and with reinforcements from the king, defeats the Saracens. The exceptional role played by the woman here is noteworthy.

Guillaume, Geste de, see *Garin de Monglane.*

Guillaume d'Aquitaine (1071–1127), the 7th comte de Poitiers and the 9th duc d'Aquitaine, the earliest known troubadour. He led a stormy life, incurred the wrath of the Church, and was finally excommunicated. Only a very small number of his *chansons* is extant. They were probably composed between 1087 and 1127 and are of two kinds: some diffident, mannered lyrics of *l'amour courtois* (q.v.), others licentious in the extreme.

Guillaume de Champeaux (*c.* 1070–1121), a French realist philosopher, under whom Abélard studied at Paris.

Guillaume de Digulleville, or **de Deguileville,** or **de Guileville,** author (*c.* 1320) of a poem entitled *Pèlerinage de la vie humaine,* a sort of *Pilgrim's Progress,* which was translated into English by John Lydgate as *The Pilgrimage of Man.*

Guillaume de Dole, a metrical *roman d'aventure* of the early 13th century by Jean Renart (q.v.).

The Emperor Conrad of Germany falls in love with Liénor, the beautiful and virtuous sister of Guillaume de Dole, on the strength of the report given of her by the Emperor's minstrel. He summons Guillaume to his court, is delighted with his knightly prowess, and tells him that he wishes to marry his sister. But a wicked seneschal traduces her, to the despair of Conrad and Guillaume. Liénor comes to the court and is able to confound the seneschal. The romance is interspersed with songs borrowed from famous *trouvères.*

Guillaume de Lorris (pron. as if *Lorriss*), author of the first part of the *Roman de la Rose* (q.v.), probably flourished in the first half of the 13th century. His name appears to be derived from the little town of Lorris between Orleans and Montargis. Nothing certain is known about him.

Guillaume de Machaut or **Machault** (*c.* 1300–77), whose name is taken from a village in the Ardennes, was a poet and musical composer, for many years in the service of John of Luxembourg, king of Bohemia (who was killed at Crécy), and subsequently attached to the houses of Charles, King of Navarre, and the princes of France. From 1337 he was a canon of Rheims. Machaut enjoyed renown among his contemporaries as the chief of a school, and he certainly occupied a considerable place in the transition period which preceded the Renaissance. His poetic activity took two forms, (*a*) long narrative and didactic poems, and (*b*) lyrics. Of the former, the following may be mentioned: the *Dit dou vergier,* probably his earliest work, a feeble imitation of the allegory of the *Roman de la rose*; the *Jugement du roy de Behaingne* (Bohemia), written before 1342, a debate between a lady who has lost her lover and a knight who has been betrayed by his mistress as to which is more to be pitied, decided by the king in favour of the knight; this decision, which appears to have been criticized, was reversed by the poet in his *Jugement du roy de Navarre* (*c.* 1349) in an analogous debate (preceded by an account of the terrible events of 1348-9, the year of the Black Death); the *Livre de la fontaine amoureuse*, an allegorical poem from which Chaucer borrowed in his *Boke of the Duchesse*; the *Confort d'Ami*, written to his patron Charles of Navarre in captivity; the *Prise d'Alexandrie*, narrating the deeds of Pierre Ier of Lusignan, king of Cyprus. These poems are generally in octosyllabic couplets; exceptionally the *Jugement du roi de Behaingne* is in stanzas of three lines rhyming together and a fourth line rhyming with the first three lines of the following stanza. Elements of originality in them are the development, from the old *jeux-partis* (q.v.), of the 'debate' on some theme of love; and the introduction by the author of his own person as participating in the action, giving a more realistic character to the poem.

As regards his lyric work, Machaut was one of the first authors of *ballades* and *rondeaux* (qq.v.) in their rigid forms, and helped to give popularity to this type of poetry. His pieces are generally the artificial treatment of some theme of *amour courtois* (q.v.), but in one instance (the *Voir dit* or *True Tale*) he presents himself as loved in his old age, for his literary reputation, by a young lady of high rank. Machaut appears to have been a composer of merit, and his musical settings probably contributed to the fame of his lyrics. The extent of his influence on Chaucer has been variously estimated.

Guillaume de Nangis, see *Grandes Chroniques*.

Guillaume de Palerne, an early-13th-century French metrical romance of which there is an English 14th-century version, *William of Palerne*.

Guillaume is the prince of Apulia. He is carried off and saved from poisoning in childhood by a werewolf, who is in reality heir to the kingdom of Spain, but has been enchanted by his stepmother, the queen of Spain. Brought up by peasants, and later taken to the court of the Emperor of Rome, Guillaume falls in love with Melior the emperor's daughter, and during his flight with her is once more protected by the werewolf. He then fights with the king of Spain, captures him, and forces the stepmother to undo her magic. The werewolf, restored to human form, reveals the identity of Guillaume.

The poem was composed for Ioland, daughter of the count of Hainault, and is probably derived from a Latin source.

Guillaume de Saint-Amour, see under *Rutebeuf*.

Guillaume le Clerc, see *Besant de Dieu*.

Guillaume le Maréchal, Histoire de, a historical poem on the life of William the Marshal, Earl of Pembroke, regent of England during the minority of Henry III, written soon after the death of the earl in 1219, by some continental subject of the King of England. It is an interesting and well-written work, throwing light not only on the characters it deals with but on the social life of the times.

Guillaumin, ÉMILE (1873–   ), one of the better-known French regional novelists. His works, descriptive of life in Central France, the ancient province of Bourbonnais, include: *Tableaux champêtres* (1901), *La Vie d'un simple* (1904), *Baptiste et sa femme* (1911).

Guillemette, a character in *Pathelin* (q.v.).

Guilleragues, GABRIEL-JOSEPH DE LA VERGNE, VICOMTE DE (d. 1685), was most probably the translator, and has also been claimed as the author, of the *Lettres portugaises* (q.v.). A magistrate's son, himself an advocate, he spent some years in Bordeaux as Premier Président of the *Cour des aides* (q.v.) but returned in 1666 to Paris and life at the court of Louis XIV. In 1679, through the good offices of Mme de Maintenon, his friend in earlier days, he was sent as French Ambassador to Constantinople. He was a friend of Boileau and Racine.

Guillet, Pernette du, see *Du Guillet*.

Guillotine, La, the instrument by means of which capital punishment is effected in

France, is wrongly supposed to have been invented by Joseph-Ignace Guillotin (1738–1814), a professor of anatomy of the Faculty of Paris, a Deputy to the *États Généraux* in 1789, and then a member of the *Assemblée constituante*. He proposed that beheading, hitherto reserved for the nobility, should be the sole method of capital punishment, and that if possible a machine should be found to do the work. The proposal was adopted by the *Assemblée* and a German mechanic named Schmidt built a machine to the specifications of Dr. Louis, then secretary of the French College of Surgeons. It was brought into use on 25 April 1792, and for a time went by the name of 'Louisette'. Among Revolutionary terms for the guillotine, or to be guillotined, were: 'la sainte guillotine', 'le rasoir national', 'mettre la tête à la fenêtre', 'faire la bascule', 'essayer la cravate à Capet', 'demander l'heure au vasistas', &c.

Guillotine sèche, La, a name for the practice of deportation frequently adopted under the *Directoire* in place of capital punishment.

Guinglain or **Le Bel Inconnu,** a metrical romance of the Arthurian cycle composed early in the 13th century by Renaud de Beaujeu.

A young knight of unknown name and parentage comes to the court of Arthur and is granted the adventure of the 'Fier baiser'. In his quest of this he displays his prowess in numerous encounters and, coming to the Île d'Or, he slays the defender of the bridge leading to the castle of the 'Damoiselle aux blanches mains', who announces her intention of marrying him. But he pursues his enterprise and reaches a mysterious castle where he undergoes the ordeal of the 'Fier baiser', the kiss of a monstrous serpent. The monster disappears and Blonde Esmerée, queen of Wales, thus released from the enchantment which had transformed her into a serpent, takes its place. The knight learns that he is Guinglain, son of Gawain, and (although distracted for a time by the charms of the Damoiselle) finally marries Blonde Esmerée. The author interposes here and there references to his own love affairs: he seeks by his tale to win the favour of his mistress.

There is a 14th-century English metrical version of the tale.

Guinon, ALBERT (1863–1923), dramatist, author (in collaboration with Maurice Denier) of *Les Jobards* (1898, produced 1891), the study of a man who is the victim of his own honesty; also of *Le Partage* (1898), *Le Joug* (1902), &c.

Guiot de Provins (12th–13th c.), a *jongleur* in early life and a *trouvère* who, after retirement to a monastic life, composed between 1205 and 1218 a 'Bible' (q.v.), known as the *Bible Guiot*, and one of the most important of its kind, in which he reviews in verse the various classes of contemporary society, knights, theologians, monks, lawyers, doctors, criticizing them on grounds of a worldly rather than a moral order, and showing a survival of the jester in the monk.

Guiraud, ALEXANDRE (1788–1847), minor poet. His *Le Petit Savoyard*, in *Poèmes et chants élégiaques* (1823–4), was much praised. He also wrote conventional tragedies (*Les Macchabées*, 1822, &c.) and helped to found *La Muse française* (q.v.).

Guirlande de Julie, a vellum book, decorated with flowers by the miniaturist and flower-painter Nicolas Robert (1614–85), and inscribed by the calligrapher Nicolas Jarry (c. 1630–c. 1670) with ninety-one poems (eighty-seven madrigals, two sonnets, two epigrams) by nineteen *habitués* of the Hôtel de Rambouillet (q.v.), among them Chapelain, Conrart, Desmarets de Saint-Sorlin, Gombaud, Georges de Scudéry, Tallemant des Réaux. It was presented on 22 May 1641 (her saint's day) by the marquis de Montausier to Julie d'Angennes (Mme de Rambouillet's daughter), whom he subsequently married.

Guiscard et Gismonde, characters in a tale in Boccaccio's *Decameron* (IV. i). The story was made popular in France by three verse translations of the end of the 15th and the 16th centuries.

Gismonde is the daughter of Tancred, prince of Salerno. Her father, having discovered her love for his squire Guiscard, slays the latter and sends his heart in a golden cup to Gismonde, who takes poison and dies. The father, repenting his cruelty, causes the pair to be buried in the same tomb.

Guise, the name of a branch of the princely house of Lorraine. René II, duc de Lorraine, having come to France, fought on the French side at Marignan and in 1527 was created duc de Guise by François Ier. The importance of the family rapidly increased. The eldest son, François, who succeeded his father in 1550, was an eminent captain and councillor under Henri II. The second son, Charles, became Cardinal of Lorraine. The eldest daughter married James V of Scotland and was mother of Mary Stuart, who married François II of France. During the reign (1559–60) of the latter (a boy of fifteen), the Guises, as uncles of the queen, secured control of the government and led the campaign of repression against the Protestants. The early death of François II, the accession of a minor (Charles IX, 1560), and the regency of Catherine de Médicis, put an abrupt end to their power. François de Guise was assassinated in 1563. For the revival of the influence of the family under Henri, third duc de Guise, see Ligue.

Guitry, LUCIEN (1860–1925), actor, born in Paris, also theatre manager and playwright. He was for long one of the leading actors on the French stage and he also made extensive continental tours, his son Sacha (see below) being born on one of these, in the then St. Petersburg. At one time he partnered Bernhardt (q.v.).

Guitry, SACHA (1885–1957), son of the foregoing, actor, producer, and playwright. His numerous productions include vaudevilles, e.g. Le Veilleur de nuit (1911), La Prise de Berg-op-Zoom (1912); slight, dramatized biographies, e.g. Deburau (1918), Pasteur (1919), Béranger (1924), Jean de La Fontaine (1934); and light comedies. These, e.g. Faisons un rêve (1916), have all been much alike, with three characters—wife, husband, and lover—and the principal part played by the author.

Guizot, FRANÇOIS (1787–1874), historian and statesman, born at Nîmes of a Protestant family, was brought up in Geneva by his mother. His father had been a victim of the Terror. In 1805 he came to Paris and studied history, paying his way by teaching and journalism. From 1812 to 1830 he was Professor of Modern History at the Sorbonne. His publications of this period include: Histoire des origines du gouvernement représentatif en Europe (1821–2); Essais (six, on the

development of political institutions down to the 10th century) sur l'histoire de France, first published (1823) as a supplement to an annotated text of Mably's (q.v.), Observations sur l'histoire de France; Collection des mémoires relatifs à l'histoire de France from the origins to the 13th century (1823–35) and Mémoires relatifs à la révolution d'Angleterre (1823–5), two monumental series of source-collections; Histoire de la révolution d'Angleterre, a work in three parts, published at wide intervals, tracing the development of the constitutional monarchy in England [Histoire de Charles Ier, 1826–7; Histoire de la république d'Angleterre et de Cromwell (1649–1658), 1854; Histoire du protectorat de Richard Cromwell et du rétablissement des Stuarts (1658–1660), 1856]; and, lastly, Histoire générale de la civilisation en Europe (1828) and Histoire de la civilisation en France (1829–32). These two books, famous examples of Guizot's methodical, solidly-documented work and lucid historical narrative, were the published form of Cours d'histoire moderne, the lectures he delivered at the Sorbonne between 1828 and 1830. They are studies, for Europe until the Revolution, for France until the 14th century (political happenings had cut short his lectures), of the evolution of social, political, and religious institutions; of the progress of philosophy and literature, the influence of individuals upon the course of history, the gradual emergence of the middle classes (for Guizot the most active and the most decisive element in French history) and the importance of their role in maintaining equilibrium between monarchical absolutism and democratic ideals of liberty.

Guizot's political career began after the Restoration, when he became a leader of the doctrinaires (q.v.), the party which favoured a constitutional monarchy. These sympathies led to his Sorbonne lectures being officially suspended between 1822 and 1828. Under the July Monarchy (1830–48) his career was wholly political. As Minister of Education (1832–7) he introduced important educational reforms. He was French Ambassador in London for a few months in 1840, and then became Foreign Minister and Prime Minister. His downfall came with the February (1848) Revolution, for which his policy was held largely responsible. After a year in England he returned to live in retirement in Normandy, devoting himself once more to history, e.g. *Discours sur l'histoire de la révolution d'Angleterre* (1850); *Histoire parlementaire de France* (1863); *Histoire de France racontée à mes petits-enfants* (1870–5). Other writings of these years included: *Méditations et études morales* (1851); *Méditations sur l'essence de la religion* (1864); *Méditations biographiques et littéraires* (1868), and *Mémoires pour servir à l'histoire de mon temps* (9 vols., 1858–68).

Guttinguer, ULRIC (1785–1866), minor poet and man of letters associated with *le romantisme* (q.v.), when he contributed to *La Muse française* (q.v.) and published *Nadir* (1822, critical essays), *Mélanges poétiques* (1826), *Recueil d'élégies* (1829). His later writings included *Arthur* (1837), an autobiographical novel which includes the *philosophe inconnu* L. de Saint-Martin among its characters (an earlier version—*Arthur, ou Religion et solitude*—had been published anonymously in 1834); *Fables et Méditations* (1837); *Deux âges du poète* (1844), &c.

Guyart des Moulins, see *Bible* (*French versions of the*).

Guyau, JEAN-MARIE (1854–98), a philosopher who died young but whose belief in an instinctive force which underlies human activity, and the need for the voluntary subordination of the individual to the general good of society, had a considerable influence on French thought about 1880. He was a stepson of, and had early been influenced by, Fouillée (q.v.). His outstanding work was *L'Irréligion de l'avenir* (1887), a study of what he considered to be the sociological basis of religion and an attack, not on religion itself but on religious dogmas. His other works included: *Esquisse d'une morale sans obligation ni sanction* (1885) and *L'Art au point de vue sociologique* (1889, posth.). His *Vers d'un philosophe* (1881) should also be mentioned.

Guyon, MADAME, see *Quietism*.

Guys, CONSTANTIN (1805–92), black-and-white artist and draughtsman, made a reputation, which has steadily increased, with his sketches of the Parisian life of pleasure, in all walks, under the Second Empire (q.v., 1852–70). He was born in Holland, of French parents, and had a varied career before settling in Paris about 1865. He was in London (*c.* 1842) as tutor to the grandchildren of Thomas Girtin the artist, while 1852 found him in the Crimea following the war as artist-correspondent for the *Illustrated London News*. Baudelaire's *L'Art romantique* (collected art-criticism, 1868, posth.) has an appreciation of him ('Le Peintre de la vie moderne').

Gwynplaine, the hero of *L'Homme qui rit* (1869, q.v.), a novel by Victor Hugo.

Gyp [pseud. of MARIE-ANTOINETTE DE RIQUETTI DE MIRABEAU, comtesse de Martel de Janville] (1850–1932), wrote light, entertaining, sometimes wittily satirical, novels and sketches of society life. They were much read in their day and are still perhaps of some interest as period pieces (*Petit Bob*, 1868; *Autour du mariage*, 1883; *Mademoiselle Loulou*, 1888; *Le Mariage de Chiffon*, 1894, &c.).

H

Habert, GERMAIN (*c.* 1615–54), abbé de Cérisy, younger brother of the following; an original, and active, member of the *Académie française* and a frequenter of the Hôtel de Rambouillet. He contributed to the *Guirlande de Julie* (q.v.).

Habert, PHILIPPE (*c.* 1605–37), friend of Conrart (q.v.) and an original member of the *Académie française* (like his brother, see the preceding); a soldier, also, whose *Le Temple de la mort* (1637) was an elegy on the death of Mme de la Meilleraye, wife of his friend and protector the maréchal de la Meilleraye.

Hachette, LOUIS (1800–64), founder (1826) of the publishing firm of Hachette, which has long been noted for its series of classical texts and of dictionaries. It began by publishing school textbooks.

Hagiography, see *Saints, Lives of*

Hahn, Reynaldo (1874–1947), born in Venezuela, was sent to Paris at eleven for his musical education. In time he became the leading dramatic composer in France, and was for many years director of music at the Casino of Monte Carlo. He also composed operas and some chamber music, but was most widely known by his songs, particularly the *Chansons grises*, settings of lyrics by Verlaine, and the *Chansons latines* and *espagnoles*. He wrote the musical settings for *Les Plaisirs et les Jours* by Proust, his friend and correspondent.

Halévy, Daniel (1872–), son of Ludovic and brother of Élie Halévy (qq.v.), essayist, critic, and social historian. He was associated with Péguy in the conduct of *Les Cahiers de la quinzaine* (q.v.) and described the venture in *Charles Péguy et les Cahiers de la quinzaine* (1919). His other works include: *La Fin des notables*, *La République des comités*, *La République des ducs* (1930–37), studies of the Third Republic; *Pays parisien* (1929), reminiscences of late 19th-century Paris, &c.

Halévy, Élie (1870–1937), historian, son of Ludovic Halévy (q.v.) and elder brother of the foregoing, made English social and political history of the 19th century his particular province. His great work was the *Histoire du peuple anglais au XIXᵉ siècle* (1912–23 and 1926–32), a study of political, economic and religious evolution—particularly of the rise of non-conformity—in England after 1815, and an attempt to account for the spirit of voluntary obedience which, he considered, underlies the English conception of liberty. The volumes published in his lifetime consisted of three for the period 1815–41 [*L'Angleterre en 1815*, 1912; *Du lendemain de Waterloo à la veille du Reform Bill* (*1815–1830*), 1923; *De la crise du Reform Bill à l'avènement de Sir Robert Peel* (*1830–1841*), 1923] and two volumes of *Épilogue* covering the period 1895–1914: *Les Impérialistes au pouvoir* (*1895–1905*); *Vers la démocratie sociale et vers la guerre* (*1905–1914*). Three further volumes were contemplated for the period 1841–95 but never finished, though another volume, *Le Milieu du siècle* (*1841–1852*), was prepared from notes left by the author and published posthumously (1948).

Halévy, Ludovic (1834–1908) is remembered as librettist, with Henri Meilhac (q.v.), for Offenbach's (q.v.) *La Belle Hélène* (1865), *La Vie parisienne* (1867), *La Grande Duchesse de Gérolstein* (1867), &c., operettas which were the rage of Paris in the last years of the Second Empire. Their drawing-room comedies, e.g. *Froufrou* (1869) and *La Petite Marquise* (1874), were a divertingly impertinent mixture of farce, irony, and (in the former) a certain pathos. This literary partnership lasted some twenty years.

Halévy on his own was also a successful writer of fiction, e.g. *La Famille Cardinal* (1883), the entertaining scenes from the life of a low-class Parisian family during the early years of the Third Republic, *Un Mariage d'amour* (1881), and the sentimental but entertaining *Abbé Constantin* (1882), still remembered, and in its day an immediate best-seller with a public beginning to weary of Zola's gallery of criminals and alcoholics (cf. *Naturalisme*; *Rougon-Macquart, Les*). His *Carnets*, of which two volumes, covering the years 1862–70, have been edited and published posthumously (1935), are interesting, almost daily, jottings about people and politics, and a good picture of the agitated period before the outbreak (1870) of the Franco-Prussian war.

Halphen, Louis (1880–1950), medieval historian, notably of the Carolingian epoch. He was general editor, with Philippe Sagnac, of the series of historical monographs entitled *Peuples et civilisations*, see Appendix I, § H (ii).

Halte-clere, Olivier's sword, in the *Chanson de Roland* (q.v.).

Hamburg. During the Revolution a colony of some 40,000 *émigrés* settled in Hamburg. They had their own theatre, newspapers, and reviews, and a café in which they met. Among them were Rivarol, Beaumarchais, and Mme de Genlis (qq.v., and cf. *Coblenz*).

Hamelin, Octave (1856–1907), a philosopher of considerable importance whose career was unfortunately cut short when he was drowned trying to save two swimmers who had got into difficulties. For a time he taught the history of philosophy at the University of Bordeaux, then came to Paris and the Sorbonne. He was at first a disciple of Renouvier (q.v.), but he developed a philosophy of his own, which regarded the human personality as a synthesis of opposites, and in which the notion of relativity played

a fundamental part. ('La pensée est ce pro-
cessus bilatéral lui-même, le développement
d'une réalité qui est à la fois sujet et objet,
ou conscience.') It was expounded in his
doctor's thesis (presented in 1907, the year
of his death), *Essai sur les éléments principaux
de la représentation*, from which the above
quotation is taken.

Hamelin's system is a form of dialectical
idealism in which intuition plays no part and
is thus, in its rationalism, basically opposed
to the anti-intellectualism of Bergsonisme.
But his influence was decided, if less clearly
remarked than that of Bergson (q.v.), upon
the intellectual climate of the late 19th and
early 20th centuries.

Mention should also be made of his
Système d'Aristote, a collection of studies in
the history of philosophy (1920, posth.).

Hamilton, ANTHONY (ANTOINE) (1646?–
1720), grandson of the first Earl of Abercorn,
and a Jacobite officer who fought at the
Boyne; author or part author of the *Mémoires
du comte de Gramont* (see *Gramont*). He came
to France during the first exile of the Stuarts
(1649–60) and settled there after 1688. He
had become the intimate friend of Gramont
when the latter came to England, and in
1663 Gramont married Hamilton's sister
Elizabeth. Hamilton's French writings include verses and some witty fairy-tales, of
which the best is the *Histoire de Fleur d'épine*.
Anthony Hamilton's brother Richard,
having been sent by William III with proposals to the Irish Catholics in 1689, deserted
to Tyrconnel, commanded at the siege of
Londonderry, and was captured at the
Boyne.

Hamon, JEAN (1618–87), a physician of
the faculty of Paris and from 1650 a solitary
of Port-Royal (q.v.), where he tended the
nuns and the poor. He was something of
a mystic and author of devotional treatises,
including *La Pratique de la prière continuelle*,
praised by Mme de Sévigné, and of some
remarkable letters. He was greatly esteemed
by Racine.

Hamp, PIERRE [pseud. of Pierre Bourillon]
(1876–   ), novelist, began as a pastry-
cook's apprentice, was later a railway employee, and became known as a writer when
some of his work appeared in *Les Cahiers de
la quinzaine* (q.v.). His many long novels

usually follow the processes of industry from
raw material to final product, e.g. *La Peine
des hommes*: *Marée fraîche* (1908–fish), *Vin de
Champagne* (1909—wine, from vineyard to
London club), *Le Rail*: *Vieille histoire* (1912),
L'Enquête (1914), *Le Cantique des cantiques*
(1922), &c. *Mes Métiers* (1931) describes his
early life.

Han d'Islande (1823), a romance by
Victor Hugo. The scene is 17th-century
Norway. Two young lovers are united after
the hero has gone through many adventures,
taken part in conspiracies, fought single-
handed with the 'killer' Han d'Islande, a
demonic bandit, and rescued the heroine and
her father from unjust captivity.

Hanotaux, GABRIEL (1853–1944), diplomat
and historian of the 17th century (*Histoire
du cardinal de Richelieu*, 1893–1903) and the
Third Republic, and general editor and part
author (the political history) of an *Histoire de
la nation française*; see Appendix I, § C (i).

Hanska, COMTESSE ÉVELINE, *née* Rzewuska
(1801–82), Balzac's (q.v.) *Étrangère*, whom
he married shortly before his death in 1850,
after a correspondence lasting eighteen years.
She was of Polish nationality.

Haraucourt, EDMOND (1856–1941), whose
poetry belonged to the Parnassian aftermath,
was the author of *L'Âme nue* (1885) and
L'Espoir du monde (1899), collections of verse,
also of *La Passion* (1890), a *mystère*.

Hardy, ALEXANDRE (*c.* 1569–75—1632), a
Parisian, a prolific playwright, purveyor of
plays to a company of professional actors,
at first in the provinces, later performing at
the Hôtel de Bourgogne, where they were
known as the 'Comédiens du Roi'. In the
course of some thirty years he composed or
arranged several hundred plays. Of these he
published (1623–8) thirty-four, tragedies,
tragicomedies, pastoral and mythological
plays. He was an innovator, and sustained
serious drama in a period of its decadence.
He was without genius, taste, or style, but he
had dramatic instinct (as contrasted with his
predecessors, whose works were lyrical or
declamatory), and his rough popular dramas
show progress in their animation and
rapidity, and in the life which he gave to
some at least of his characters, particularly
in the tragicomedies. He soon dropped the

chorus, shortened monologues and recitals, confronted his principal characters with one another, placed scenes of violence on the stage, and in general got rid of the Senecan influence. The tragedies dealt with classical themes such as the death of Dido or that of Achilles (based on Dictys Cretensis and Dares Phrygius). The best of them is perhaps *Mariamne*, in which Herod, torn between love and jealousy, puts Mariamne to death and then repents. For his tragicomedies he sought subjects in Lucian, Cervantes, Montemayor, &c. He wrote half a dozen pastoral plays (q.v.), conforming to a fashion that had spread from Italy to Spain. One of his early works is an adaptation of Heliodorus's tale of Theagenes and Chariclea in eight successive tragicomedies. In general it may be said that he aided the transition from the medieval drama and the cold tragedies of the Renaissance to the classical drama of the following period.

Haricots, see *Hôtel des Haricots*.

Harlequin, see *Arlequin*.

Harmonie du soir, one of the finest poems of Baudelaire's (q.v.) *Les Fleurs du mal*; one in which he appears clearly as a precursor of the Symbolists.

Harmonies poétiques et religieuses, Les (1830), by Lamartine, a collection of odes and lyrics, mainly religious (at times vaguely pantheistic) in sentiment. The omnipresence of God in the universe is the theme of *Jéhovah, Le Chêne, L'Humanité,* and *L'Idée de Dieu,* a sequence of four *harmonies. Milly, ou la terre natale* is a tenderly nostalgic description of the poet's early home.

Harpagon, the miser in Molière's *L'Avare*.

Harpignies, HENRI (1819–1916), French landscape painter, of the Barbizon school, but he also exhibited in 1874 with the first group of Impressionists (see *Impressionnisme*).

Hatteras, CAPITAINE, see *Verne, Jules*.

Hatzfeld, ADOLPHE, see *Dictionaries and Encyclopedias*, under date 1890–3.

Haussmann, EUGÈNE-GEORGES, BARON (1809–91), born in Paris, was *Préfet de la Seine* (q.v.) during the Second Empire. The large-scale urban development of Paris undertaken at this time was due to his initiative.

Haussonville, GABRIEL-OTHENIN, COMTE D' (1843–1924), man of letters, a nephew of the duc Léonce-Victor de Broglie (q.v.), was the author of *Le Salon de Madame Necker* (1882) and of biographical studies in English and French. He also edited the correspondence of Doudan (q.v.).

Hauteroche, NOËL LE BRETON, SIEUR DE (1617–1707), actor and comic dramatist, imitator of Molière, author of a successful comedy *Crispin médecin* (1674) ridiculing the medical profession; *Le Souper mal apprêté* (1669); *Le Deuil* (1672); *Les Nobles de province* (1678); *La Dame invisible* (1684).

Hauteville House, Guernsey (now owned by the Municipality of Paris). Victor Hugo lived here in exile for fourteen years.

Hautpoul, ANNE-MARIE DE MONTGEROULT DE COUTANCES, COMTESSE D' (1760–1837), woman of letters, wrote verse, some novels and pastoral romances (e.g. *Zilia*, 1796, partly in verse, partly in prose), and a number of instructional tales for youthful readers.

Hauts-Ponts, Les (1932–5), a novel (trilogy) by Jacques de Lacretelle (q.v.).

Haveloc, Lai d', an Anglo-Norman 12th-century romance (1112 ll.) in rhyming couplets. The story also forms an episode in the *Estoire des Engleis* of Geffrei Gaimar; and an English version of it survives in the 14th-century *Lay of Havelok*.

Haveloc is the son of Gunter, king of Denmark. A mystic flame issuing from his mouth when he sleeps marks his royal birth. Gunter has been treacherously killed by Odulf, who obtains the kingdom; but the king before his death has entrusted Haveloc to one of his men named Grim. Grim carries the boy in a boat to England, landing at the future Grimsby, where the boy is brought up. Achebrit, king in that part of England, has entrusted his daughter Argentille to her uncle Edelsi, until she shall come of age, when she is to be married to the strongest man in the land. Haveloc, now called Cuaran, takes service as scullion with Edelsi, and distinguishing himself by his great strength is chosen by Edelsi as husband for Argentille, whom Edelsi in his own interest seeks to degrade. A dream and the mystic flame lead Argentille to discover the royal

lineage of her husband. Haveloc returns to
Denmark, is there recognized, slays Odulf,
and recovers his kingdom and afterwards the
English kingdom of Argentille.

In the English version Achebrit is called
Aethelwold, Argentille Goldborough, Odulf
Godard, and Edelsi Godrich. The romance
of Haveloc Cuaran appears to be founded
on the romantic career in the 10th century
of Aulaf Cuaran, son of a Viking chief. Aulaf
married the daughter of Constantine III of
Scotland, was with him defeated at Brunan-
burh, and won and lost a succession of kingdoms.

Hazard, PAUL (1878–1944), scholar and
literary historian, especially distinguished in
the field of comparative literature. He
taught—in lycées, then as Professor of French
Literature at the Sorbonne, and at the
Collège de France (q.v.); and he was, with
Joseph Bédier (q.v.), joint editor of the
Histoire illustrée de la littérature française
(1923–4; revised and augmented edition
1948–9). He made two notable contributions to the history of European thought in
La Crise de la conscience européenne, 1680–1715
(1935) and the posthumously published
*La Pensée européenne au XVIIIème siècle de
Montesquieu à Lessing* (1946, 3 vols.). His
graceful, scholarly study of children's books,
Les Livres, les enfants, et les hommes (1937),
should also be mentioned.

Heaulmière, Les Regrets de la Belle,
see *Villon*. 'La belle heaulmière' (a seller of
armour) was a real person, a well-known
courtesan, who had been mistress of a
certain Nicolas d'Orgemont, lame and
wealthy, *maître de la Chambre des Comptes*
and a canon of Notre-Dame. Her lament for
her lost beauty and her *ballade* addressed to
the prostitutes of Paris are among the
most striking passages of Villon's *Testament*
(ll. 453–560).

Héautontimorouménos, L' [the self-
tormentor], one of the 'Spleen et idéal'
poems of Baudelaire's (q.v.) *Les Fleurs du mal.*

Hébert, JACQUES-RENÉ (1755–94), born at
Alençon (Orne), died on the scaffold, an
extreme and violent Revolutionary and a
leader of the *Commune insurrectionnelle de
Paris* (v. *Commune*). His newspaper, *Le Père
Duchesne* (q.v.), was notorious.

Hébertistes. After the fall of the *Girondins*,
the *Montagnards* split into two factions : the
Hébertistes, led by the most violent atheists
and revolutionaries such as Hébert and Anacharsis Cloots (qq.v.), and the *Indulgents*, who
were less extreme and included Danton,
Camille Desmoulins, and Fabre d'Églantine
(qq.v.). Above both factions were Robespierre and the *Comité de salut public* (q.v.).
Robespierre, who attacked Hébert's atheistic
views and through him the ascendancy of
the *Commune insurrectionnelle*, waited until
the *Indulgents* had destroyed the *Hébertistes*,
then brought about the fall of the *Indulgents*
(see *Revolution* , I; Ia).

Heine, HEINRICH (1800–56), German lyric
poet and man of letters, born at Düsseldorf
of Jewish parentage, died in Paris. Heine had
a considerable influence upon French literature (see *Foreign influences on French literature*,
para. 23). His early years had been coloured
by his enthusiasm for Napoleon. Later on,
when the July Revolution aroused his lively
democratic sympathies to an extent which
brought him into disfavour in his own country, he left Germany for good and lived
thenceforward in Paris. There he moved
freely in literary circles, especially those of
the later Romantics, and he also, from 1836
to 1848, drew a pension as a 'political refugee'
from French Government funds. His works
were translated separately and in a complete
edition (*Œuvres complètes*, 1852–68, 14 vols.).
Of these, *État de France* and *Lutèce* are translations of his *Französische Zustände* and
Lutezia, the short amusing chronicles of life
and letters in Paris which he contributed
in the first place to the *Augsburg Gazette*;
in the *Nuits florentines* he is seen as a lover
and interpreter of Paris; his *Salon* (of 1833–
9) consists of essays on French art and the
French stage; and the first volume of *Impressions de Voyage* (his *Reisebilder*) opens
with an interesting essay on him by Théophile Gautier.

Hélinand, see *Religious Writings* (medieval
period).

Hellequin, probably associated with the
German *Erlkönig*, a fierce demon of medieval
legend who rode through the night carrying
destruction. See *Arlequin.*

Hello, ERNEST (1828–85), born at Lorient
(Brittany), author of critical and philo-

sophical essays, Roman Catholic and often strongly mystical in tendency. He was an influence on the Roman Catholic revival of the late 19th century and still has admirers. (*M. Renan, l'Allemagne et l'Athéisme au XIXᵉ siècle*, 1858; *L'Homme*, 1872; *Physionomie des Saints*, 1875; *Les Paroles de Dieu*, 1878; *Les Plateaux de la balance*, 1880; *Le Siècle, les hommes et les idées*, 1895, posth.; &c.)

Héloïse, see *Abélard*.

Helvétius, CLAUDE-ADRIEN (1715–71), philosopher, a rich farmer-general of revenues (an office which he threw up in 1751), and one of the 'encyclopédistes', a man of somewhat narrow and superficial talent, author of *De l'esprit* (q.v., 1758), a work condemned by the *parlement* and burnt. After his death his amplification of the above, entitled *De l'homme*, was published in 1772; also a poem on *Le Bonheur*. Marmontel in Bk. VI of his memoirs states that Helvétius, in contrast with the philosophical views that he advanced, was generous and charitable from kindness of heart.

His wife, Mme Helvétius, without high intellectual claims, but a woman of charm and devoted to her friends, presided over a *salon* frequented by d'Alembert, d'Holbach, Duclos, Turgot, Condorcet, &c.

Hémon, LOUIS (1880–1913), novelist, born at Brest, wrote a novel of sporting life (*Battling Malone*, 1925), spent some time in England, then, about 1910, went to Canada. Life among French Canadian settlers provided material for *Maria Chapdelaine* (1916), the novel which brought him posthumous fame (he died in a railway accident three years before it appeared).

It is a simple tale—poetically rather than brutally realistic—of a French-Canadian family in an isolated settlement. Existence is governed by the rigours of the seasons: and love, illness, even death itself fall into perspective before the indomitable pioneering spirit of the colonist.

Hénault, CHARLES-JEAN-FRANÇOIS (1685–1770), known generally as the président Hénault, a magistrate of the Paris *parlement*, a man of letters who frequented the best society, an intimate friend of Mme du Deffand, author of a *Nouvel Abrégé chronologique de l'Histoire de France* (1744), a somewhat dry work, showing a bias in favour

of absolute monarchy, and of *Mémoires* containing some interesting historical passages and portraits, besides some light verse and forgotten tragedies. He was admitted to the *Académie* in 1723.

Hennique, LÉON (1851–1935), novelist and dramatist, associated with the Naturalist movement, came early to France from his birthplace, Guadeloupe. He wrote *L'Affaire du grand 7* for *Les Soirées de Médan* (q.v. and see *Naturalisme*); also *La Dévouée* (1878), *Élisabeth Couronneau* (1879), *L'Accident de Monsieur Hébert* (1883), *Un Caractère* (1889), *Minnie Brandon* (1899), &c., novels, and *Jacques Damour* (1887), *La Mort du duc d'Enghien* (1888), &c., dramas.

Henri Iᵉʳ, born 1005, King of France from the death of his father Robert II in 1031 until his own death in 1060. He belonged to the *Capétien* (q.v.) dynasty.

Henri II, born 1519, succeeded his father François Iᵉʳ as King of France in 1547 and reigned till 1559, when he died (an accident) while taking part in a tournament held to celebrate the treaty of Cateau-Cambrésis (q.v.). His death was said to have been predicted by Nostradamus (q.v.). It was he who came to the aid of the Scots against Edward VI, then brought the young Mary Stuart to France and married her (1558) to the Dauphin. He belonged to the Valois branch of the *Capétien* (q.v.) dynasty.

Henri III, born 1551, 3rd son of Henri II, succeeded his brother Charles IX as King of France in 1574 and was assassinated in 1589 by a Dominican friar, Jacques Clément. He was Italianate, and dubious, in his manners, given to favourites (called *mignons* by the people) on whom he showered wealth and offices, but he was also a considerable patron of literature (cf. *Desportes*). The Valois branch of the *Capétien* (q.v.) dynasty ended with his death.

Henri III et sa cour (1829), a historical drama by Dumas *père*.

The duc de Guise learns that the courtier Saint-Mégrim is in love with his wife. He forces her, by crushing her wrist in his iron gauntlet until she consents, to give Saint-Mégrim a rendezvous at her palace. When her young lover arrives the terrified duchess tells him of the trick. He tries to escape but is seized in the courtyard by the Duke's men. From a window the Duke throws the assassins a scarf, to strangle Saint-Mégrim: 'La mort lui sera plus douce; il est aux armes de la duchesse de Guise.'

Henri IV, HENRI DE BOURBON, ROI DE NAVARRE, born at Pau in 1553, the son of Antoine de Bourbon and Jeanne d'Albret, was King of France, the first of the Bourbon (q.v.) branch of the *Capétien* (q.v.) dynasty, from 1589 till he died, assassinated by Ravaillac (q.v.), in 1610. He married Marguerite de Valois, daughter of Henri II, in 1572, and in 1600, after his divorce from her, Marie de Médicis (qq.v.). As a descendant of Louis IX through that king's sixth son Robert de Clermont, this Protestant prince became heir to the crown of France when the duc d'Anjou, last brother of the childless Henri III, died in 1584. His claim was rejected by the *Ligue* (q.v.) and war broke out in consequence. Henri III was assassinated in 1589, the *Ligue* under the duc de Mayenne was defeated at Ivry in 1590, and Henri IV abjured the Protestant faith in 1593. After this he obtained general recognition as king, though the *Ligue* in alliance with Spain continued the war. A man of great and supple intelligence, Henri IV proved an excellent ruler; he was aided in the pacification and administration of the realm by an admirable minister, Sully (q.v.). The Edict of Nantes, granting toleration to the Protestants, was issued in 1598. The famous scheme for a sort of federation of Europe, with which Henri IV is credited by Sully, remained a dream, any attempt to give effect to it being forestalled by the king's assassination. His letters, both official and private, have been published and contain much that is of high interest, illuminating his character both as a brave military commander and intelligent ruler, and also (less creditably) as a lover. They are agreeably written in a simple, natural style, with occasional vivid, racy expressions. They include several letters to Queen Elizabeth I, of whom, moreover, on her death, he writes a warm eulogy in a letter to Sully of 10 April 1603. Among his favourite books were the *Théâtre d'agriculture* of Olivier de Serres and the *Commentaires* of Monluc. (See also *Henriade*.)

'Henri V', see *Chambord, comte de.*

Henri, COMTE DE PARIS, the present Pretender, see *Louis-Philippe Ier* (last para.).

Henriade, La, an epic poem in ten cantos by Voltaire, published in 1723 under the title of *La Ligue*, republished in 1728 (with alterations) under the present title and dedicated to Queen Caroline, consort of George II.

The hero of the epic is Henri of Navarre, later Henri IV of France. It deals at length with the siege of Paris (which the duc de Mayenne holds for the *Ligue*, q.v.) by Henri III assisted by Henri of Navarre, in 1589. It also recounts the assassination of Henri III, the defeat of the Ligue at the battle of Ivry, and the entry of Henri IV into Paris. The poem opens with the narrative of an imaginary mission of Henri of Navarre to Queen Elizabeth I, to whom he relates the history of the troubles in France (including the massacre of St. Bartholomew, perhaps the finest part of the poem), and is amplified by a vision in which St. Louis reveals to Henri IV the destinies of his country. The characters of Mornay (Henri's counsellor) and Guise are well depicted. But the abjuration of Henri makes an indifferent culmination to the epic. The poem incidentally expresses the author's condemnation of civil discord and religious fanaticism.

Henri d'Andeli, a witty author of the 13th century, who wrote a *fabliau* entitled *Lai d'Aristote* (q.v.), a *Bataille des vins blancs*, and a *Bataille des sept arts* (the struggle between Literature and Dialectic).

Henri de Valenciennes (*fl.* 13th. c.), author of a chronicle of the war waged against the Bulgarians by Henri, the second Latin emperor of the East (1207–16). It is a vivid and eloquent work, written in prose (in the form in which we have it), but perhaps originally in verse. The author was probably a minstrel attached to the emperor's court.

Henriette, the heroine of Molière's *Les Femmes savantes* (q.v.).

Henriette d'Angleterre (1644–70), daughter of Charles I of England and his French queen Henrietta Maria (daughter of Henri IV and Marie de Médicis), wife of Philippe duc d'Orléans (the brother of Louis XIV). Her early death was lamented in a famous funeral oration by Bossuet, who a year earlier had pronounced an equally famous oration on the death of her mother. Her friend Mme de La Fayette wrote a history of her life.

Heptaméron, L', the name given by their editor in 1558 to a collection of tales by Marguerite de Navarre (q.v.), of which the form is modelled on the *Decameron* of Boccaccio. The tales purport to be told on successive days by ten travellers (five men and five women) detained by bad weather at an abbey in the Pyrenees. Of the hundred contemplated, Marguerite completed only seventy-two tales before her death in 1549. The travellers are real persons, under fictitious names, all part of the authoress's circle. The authoress claims, too, that the incidents related are true and of contemporary or recent occurrence; the date and locality are sometimes given.

The subject of the majority of the stories is love, depicted, not, or only infrequently, as in the licentious tales of the *Cent Nouvelles Nouvelles* in the form of vulgar gallantry, but as a serious and sometimes a tragic passion. Each tale is followed by a discussion in which views commonly current at the time, e.g. on the nature of love and its manifestations, are advanced, and opposed by the more moral and religious opinions of Marguerite herself (in the character of Parlamente), who finds ground for grave censure in the laxity which had provided amusement to readers of the earlier tales and *fabliaux*. In spite of its coarseness of expression, which was in accordance with the tone of the times, there is no doubt that the *Heptaméron* was designed to have an elevating and civilizing influence. The tales throw light on details of life and custom among the upper classes of the day.

Montaigne thought this work 'un gentil livre pour son étoffe', but regarded questions of morals and theology as outside the province of women.

Heptaplomeres, see *Bodin, Jean.*

Héraclius, a tragedy by Corneille produced in 1647, developed from a passage in the *Annales* of Baronius (q.v.). The scene is Constantinople.

The plot turns on the fact that the usurper Phocas had not, as he imagined, put to death

both sons of Maurice, emperor of the East (also murdered). One son, Héraclius, had been preserved by his nurse Léontine, who substituted him, first for her own son Léonce (sacrificed to make this possible) and then, to make imposture doubly sure, a second time for her foster-child, Phocas's son Martian. Thus Héraclius grows up as Martian, and the true Martian grows up as Léonce.

This mass of complications becomes still worse when Phocas decides that Pulchérie, daughter of the emperor Maurice (and preserved by him when he killed the father), shall marry—as he thinks—his son Martian, in fact her brother Héraclius. There are generous confessions, which are not believed; the irate and mystified Phocas nearly murders both young men and marries Pulchérie himself; but a timely conspiracy ends his life and clarifies the situation, and Héraclius ascends the throne.

Herbelot [or **Herbelot de Molainville**], BARTHÉLEMY, see *Dictionaries and Encyclopedias*, under date 1697.

Herberay des Essarts, NICOLAS (died *c.* 1552), author of a prose translation or adaptation of eight books of the Spanish romance of *Amadis* (q.v.); these were published in 1540–8 (the remaining books were translated by others).

Heredia, JOSÉ-MARIA DE (1842–1905), poet, born in Cuba (his father was Spanish, his mother French), was educated in France (1851–9) and from 1861 lived in Paris. He studied law, and attended the *École des Chartes* (q.v.), but soon devoted himself wholly to poetry and was one of the first *Parnassiens* (q.v.). From 1901 he was Keeper of the *Bibliothèque de l'Arsenal* (q.v.). His fame rests on the 118 sonnets, among the most beautiful in French literature, of *Les Trophées*, published in book-form in 1893 (a year before his election to the *Académie française*, q.v.). There are five groups: *La Grèce et la Sicile, Rome et les Barbares, Le Moyen Âge et la Renaissance, L'Orient et les Tropiques, La Nature et le Rêve.* The poet, inspired, it may be, by a line of an ancient text or an ornate Renaissance binding, transfixes some fleeting image of beauty from antiquity or a less remote past. The effect is one of sculptural perfection, suddenly transcended by the great evocative power of the last lines; and the sonnets stand as the perfect expression of the Parnassian ideals.

Héritage, L', by Guy de Maupassant (in the collection *Miss Harriet*), a cruel story of a couple who stand to inherit a fortune if they have a child within a stipulated period. It was first published in *La vie militaire* in 1884.

Herman de Valenciennes, see *Bible, French versions of the.*

Hermant, ABEL (1862–1950), born in Paris, novelist, also an essayist and critic whose studies on grammar and style, written under the pseudonym 'Lancelot', were for several years a feature of the newspaper *Le Temps* (q.v., and cf. *Grammaire de l'Académie*). His earliest novels were naturalistic, e.g. *Monsieur Rabosson* (1884), a satirical picture of university life, or his much-talked-of attack on the army conditions of its day, *Le Cavalier Miserey* (q.v., 1887), still often mentioned. After these, until about 1938, he produced an almost uninterrupted succession of novels of sentimental analysis, light, satirical, often libertine pictures of rich Parisian life. Many were grouped into a series entitled *Mémoires pour servir à l'histoire de la Société*. They were entertainingly, often elegantly, written.

Hermeline, the vixen, wife of Renart, in the *Roman de Renart* (q.v.).

Hermione, a leading character in Racine's *Andromaque* (q.v.).

Hermite de la Chaussée d'Antin, L', see *Jouy, J. E.*

Hermonyme, GEORGES, of Sparta, a teacher of Greek who came from Italy to France in the latter part of the 15th century and was one of the propagators there of Greek culture. He taught Greek to Lefèvre d'Étaples and Guillaume Budé (qq.v.).

Hernani (1830), a poetic drama by Victor Hugo.

Don Ruy Gomez de Silva, a Spanish grandee, proposes to marry his ward Doña Sol, who is preparing to elope with the bandit Hernani. Don Carlos, king of Spain, appears in Doña Sol's room and attempts to seduce her, but is interrupted by the arrival of Hernani. Hernani, too chivalrous to kill the defenceless king, helps him to escape. The king rewards him with outlawry. Don Ruy Gomez shelters Hernani (disguised), then discovers that he is Doña Sol's lover. The king arrives suddenly, and in spite of their rivalry Don Ruy Gomez refuses to betray his refugee guest. The king departs in wrath, with Doña Sol as hostage. Hernani obtains permission from Don Ruy Gomez to help in rescuing Doña Sol on condition that he will kill himself whenever Don Ruy Gomez, by sounding a golden horn that Hernani gives him, so ordains. Don Carlos, now Holy Roman Emperor, frustrates a conspiracy to murder him. He learns that Hernani, one of the conspirators, had acted from motives of vengeance, his father having been murdered by the father of Don Carlos. Don Carlos restores Hernani's ancestral titles and gives him Doña Sol in marriage. The two are on their balcony on the wedding night when Hernani hears the distant sound of a horn. Don Ruy Gomez appears, to hold him to his pledge. Doña Sol snatches the phial of poison meant for Hernani and drinks half. Hernani finishes it; the two die in each other's arms; and Don Ruy Gomez falls on his sword.

The first two performances of *Hernani* (at the Comédie-Française, 25 and 27 Feb. 1830) count among the great battles of the Romantics (see *Romantisme*). News had spread that the piece was in every way— subject, treatment, and versification—a break with the dramatic conventions, and the theatre was packed with partisans. Below, in the expensive seats, were the traditionalists, determined to crush the play and with it the dangerous innovations of the new School. Above were the hordes of Hugo's admirers—young writers, artists, and musicians—led by Théophile Gautier (wearing a cherry-coloured satin doublet which became legendary) and Petrus Borel (qq.v.), and all equally determined to win the day. At both performances they outclapped, outshouted, and generally outdid the occupants of the stalls and boxes, with such effect that the success of the play—and of the Romantic Movement—was thenceforth assured. [A lively account of the first performance is contained in Gautier's *Histoire du romantisme*, 1874. The second is described by Hugo's wife in *Victor Hugo raconté par un témoin de sa vie*, 1863.]

Hérodiade, see *Mallarmé.*

Hérodias, one of Flaubert's *Trois Contes* (q.v.).

Héroët, ANTOINE (1492–1568), a poet of the circle of Marguerite de Navarre (q.v.), author of the *Parfaicte Amye* (1542), a poem written in reply to the *Amye de Court,* in which Bertrand de la Borderie (a friend of Clément Marot) had depicted a cynical court lady who cares only for gallantry. The *Parfaicte Amye* is a subtle mystical mono-logue in which pure love is exalted as the supreme happiness, and the Platonic doctrine of love is set out (an early example of the influence of Platonism in the French Renais-sance). Héroët also translated Ovid's *Ars amatoria* and wrote a poem (*Androgyne*) on the myth told by Aristophanes in Plato's *Symposium* to explain the origin of the mystery of love.

Herr, LUCIEN (1864–1926), a brilliant pupil, then from 1888 until his death Librarian, of the École normale supérieure (q.v.). He was an ardent socialist, an influence on Jaurès, Léon Blum, and (for a time) Péguy (qq.v.), a force behind the convictions of the generations of *Normaliens* whose reading he guided. He was a keen supporter of Dreyfus (q.v.) at the time of the *Affaire* and, in 1904, one of the founders of the then socialist daily paper *L'Humanité.* Léon Blum called him 'le confesseur, le convertisseur, le guide . . . le directeur de conscience et de pensée. . . . La vérité était conçue par lui avec une puissance si complète . . . qu'elle se commu-niquait sans effort. . . . On ne savait plus s'il vous avait persuadé ou s'il vous avait révélé à vous-même.'

Hersent, Dame, the she-wolf, in the *Roman de Renart* (q.v.).

Hervieu, PAUL (1857–1915), dramatist and novelist. His dramas turned on family problems, e.g. the relations between hus-bands and wives or parents and children: *Les Tenailles* (1896), *La Loi de l'homme* (1897), *La Course du flambeau* (1900). *Théroigne de Méricourt* (1902), his successful drama of the Revolution, was written expressly for Sarah Bernhardt. His best-known novels were *Flirt* (1890) and *Peints par eux-mêmes* (1893).

Hiatus, the coming together without elision of two vowel sounds, of which one ends a word and the other (or the other preceded by a mute *h*) begins the following word, e.g.

Le front si beau, et la bouche et les yeux
(Ronsard).

Until the time of Ronsard poets allowed hiatus to occur in their lines. Later, hiatus was regarded as a fault and the interdiction was extended to the placing before a word beginning with a vowel of a word ending in a syllable, such as *on, an, et,* in which the final consonant is not sounded, e.g.

Raison aura sur vous maistrie
(Charles d'Orléans).

Hippolyte, the hero of Racine's tragedy *Phèdre* (q.v.).

Hirsutes, Les, a short-lived literary society remembered for its association with *les décadents* and the beginnings of the Sym-bolist movement (see *Hydropathes*; *Sym-bolisme*).

Histoire amoureuse des Gaules, see *Bussy-Rabutin.*

Histoire contemporaine, L', see *Ber-geret, M.*

Histoire de Charles XII, an historical work by Voltaire, published in 1731, in which he traces lightly and clearly and with substantial accuracy the adventurous and dramatic life of Charles XII of Sweden and the vicissitudes of his struggle with Peter the Great of Russia. Its philosophic conclusion is that a career of conquest is inferior to that of a pacific and beneficent monarch.

Histoire de Jenni, see *Jenni.*

Histoire de la grandeur et de la déca-dence de César Birotteau (1838), a novel by Balzac, one of his 'Scènes de la vie privée' (see *Comédie humaine*). César Birotteau, an honest scent-merchant, is un-businesslike but flourishes thanks to good luck and his wife's restraining influence. He is awarded the Legion of Honour for services to his municipality while Deputy Mayor, and gets carried away by dreams of wealth and grandeur. He launches a new hair oil (*Huile céphalique*), speculates, and falls prey to unscrupulous financiers. To crown all, he gives a grand ball which necessitates re-building his house entirely. His dreams end in bankruptcy, after which he, his wife, and their daughter Césarine slave to earn enough to pay his creditors. Aided by a few faithful friends, among them Anselme Popinot, his former employee, in love with Césarine, he pays his debts in full, to the admiration of the business world. But his efforts have worn him out. He returns to his old home and dies that evening.

Histoire de la langue française des origines à 1900, see *Brunot, Ferdinand.*

Histoire de la littérature anglaise, see *Taine,* para. 5.

Histoire des Girondins (1847), by Lamar-tine, a work of romanticized history, written with extreme revolutionary fervour. Well-remembered passages are the sketches of Robespierre, of Charlotte Corday, and of Mme Roland, the description of the Sep-tember massacres and the trial of Louis XVI, also the fall of the Girondins. The work made a profound impression on its first appearance.

Histoire des Treize, by Balzac, a trilogy comprising three 'Scènes de la vie pari-sienne' of his *Comédie humaine* (q.v.), namely *Ferragus*; *La Duchesse de Langeais* (q.v.); *La Fille aux yeux d'or.*

Histoire d'un crime (1877), one of Victor Hugo's best-known pieces of polemical writing (prose), a savage description of the *coup d'état* (q.v.) of 2 December 1851. It is divided into four sections, i.e. four days: *Le Guet-apens, La Lutte, Le Massacre, La Victoire.* Though not published till 1877 it was written in 1852 immediately after Hugo arrived in Brussels (see under *Hugo, V.,* para. 5).

Histoire d'une fille de ferme, a tale of farm life in Normandy, by Guy de Maupassant, first published in his collection *La Maison Tellier* (1881).

Histoire d'un paysan (1868–74), one of the best known of many 'romans nationaux et populaires' by the collaborators Erck-mann–Chatrian (q.v.), has no pretensions to be anything but simplified history. It gives a homely, day-to-day picture of events before, during, and immediately after the Revolution as they affected the life of an Alsatian village community and, more closely, of the narrator, an aged man but once a fervent Revolutionary and a soldier with the Revolutionary armies.

Histoire littéraire de la France, a vast series of historical and critical studies of the principal authors and works of medieval French literature, initiated in the 18th century by the Benedictines of the *Congréga-tion de Saint-Maur* (see *Maurists*), under the superintendence of Dom Rivet. The first volume appeared in 1733. By 1749, when Dom Rivet died, eight volumes had been published. Thereafter publication lagged. Vol. XII (to the middle of the 12th century) was published in 1763. After a complete hiatus due to the Revolution and the dis-persal of the Benedictines the work was resumed in 1807 under the aegis of the *Académie des inscriptions et belles-lettres,* and with the publication of vol. XXXVIII in 1951 had reached the middle of the 14th century. (The year 1500 is contemplated as the end of the period to be covered.) The studies in the later volumes contain very full bibliographies.

Many similar large-scale works of erudi-tion were initiated in the 17th and 18th centuries by the religious orders—Bene-dictines, Dominicans, Jesuits, and Ora-torians.

Histoire naturelle (1749–88), see *Buffon.*

Histoire naturelle des animaux sans vertèbres (1815–22), by Lamarck (q.v.).

Histoire philosophique et politique des . . . deux Indes (1770), see *Raynal.*

Histoire universelle (1616–20), see *Aubigné.*

Histoire universelle, Discours sur l' (1681), see *Bossuet.*

Historiettes, see *Tallemant des Réaux.*

History

MEDIEVAL PERIOD

(1) The earliest narratives of French his-tory were written in Latin and therefore could not be read by the lay public, who had nothing better to replace them than the *chansons de geste* (q.v.). The first true his-torical narratives in French date from the

Crusades; the chief works relating to these (including the narratives of Villehardouin and Joinville) will be found enumerated under that heading. See also *Henri de Valenciennes* and under *Gaimar, Wace, Benoît de Sainte-Maure, Fantosme (Jordan)*, and *Pierre de Langtoft* for some early rhymed chronicles in French or Anglo-Norman.

(2) In the 13th and early 14th centuries a number of works on French and general history, some of them translations from the Latin, were written in prose or in verse; notable among them were: the *Grandes Chroniques* (q.v.); the rhymed chronicles of Philippe Mousket, a Fleming, bishop of Tournai (written *c.* 1240–50; starting from the siege of Troy and including other fabulous elements); of Geoffroy de Paris (to 1304) and Guillaume Guiart (1300–16); the anecdotes of the Ménestrel de Reims (written *c.* 1260–70, also known as the *Chronique de Rains*, relating events from the time of the Second Crusade); the *Chroniques de Hainaut*, also known as the *Chroniques de Baudoin d'Avesnes* from the name of the noble who caused them to be composed, about 1278. There are also two prose narratives of the early 13th century, probably by the same anonymous author (a native of Artois, known as the 'Anonyme de Béthune'), one dealing with the struggle between John and the English barons, and the other a valuable account of the reign of Philippe II, preceded respectively by summary histories of the Norman kings of England and of the kings of France. It is a curious fact that the 13th century saw the production of several histories of Greece and Rome, one in the form of a rhymed abstract of Orosius by a certain Calandre.

(3) Next for mention are the important works of Jean le Bel and Froissart (qq.v.), followed by the *Livre des faits du bon messire Jean le Maingre, dit Bouciquaut* (see *Bouciquaut*), a work in parts well written and of considerable interest. The chronicle by Juvénal des Ursins of the reign of Charles VI is a notable addition to the *Grandes Chroniques*. The *Chronique du bon duc Louis de Bourbon* written in 1429 by a certain Jean Cabaret to the order of the comte de Clermont on the life of a great feudal noble of the 14th century, and the *Chronique* of Perceval de Cagny (containing interesting information on Jeanne d'Arc), also of the

first half of the 15th century, are of some historical importance. The *Journal d'un bourgeois de Paris* (q.v.) and the *Journal de Clément de Fauquembergue*, who was clerk to the *parlement* of Paris (1417–36), throw light on the conditions of life in the capital during the same period. The remarkable memoirs of Philippe de Commines deal with the reign of Louis XI and part of that of his successor, and though not purporting to be a history, provide historical material of the highest value. With them may be mentioned the *Journal de Jean de Roye* (sometimes called without good grounds the *Chronique scandaleuse*), covering the reign of Louis XI. Jean d'Auton, historiographer to Louis XII, left chronicles of some value. The 15th-century Burgundian chronicles of Chastellain and Olivier de la Marche (qq.v.) also deserve notice.

THE RENAISSANCE

(4) The most important historical work of this period is the *Historiae sui temporis libri CXXXVIII* of Jacques-Auguste de Thou (q.v.), written in Latin and later translated into French. Du Haillan wrote an *Histoire générale des rois de France* (1576), the first attempt at a connected history, as distinct from chronicles, of France. Étienne Pasquier (1529–1615) and Claude Fauchet (1529–1601) wrote on the ancient history of the country. Besides a number of minor histories, memoirs, and journals, there are the anecdotal works of Brantôme and the *Commentaires* of Blaise de Monluc (qq.v.).

17TH AND 18TH CENTURIES

(5) The principal historical work of the 17th century was the great *Histoire de France* of Mézeray (q.v.). Péréfixe wrote a history of Henri IV, and Maimbourg a history of the *Ligue*. Fleury and Tillemont (qq.v.) were important ecclesiastical historians, and Rapin de Thoyras (q.v.) is of interest for his history of England. There was a tendency under Louis XIV for history to lose the high character it had previously shown, to be hampered by political circumspection, and to become official and untrustworthy. (The learned Fréret was imprisoned for the views he published on the origins of the French.) But the sceptical and critical spirit (in which Bayle was a leading influence) on the one hand, and erudition on the other (cf., for instance, *Mabillon*; *Maurists*), ultimately prevailed.

Posthumous memoirs enjoyed a great liberty, and those of the Cardinal de Retz (q.v.) are, for the 17th century, the most striking example of a form of literature of which many others are to be found in the historical memoirs of the duc de Rohan, La Rochefoucauld, Louis XIV, La Fare, Mme de Caylus, Mme de La Fayette (qq.v.), &c. The comte de Guiche's *Relation du passage du Rhin* and the *Conspiration de Fiesque*, by Retz, are examples of historical essays. The *Discours sur l'histoire universelle* was written by Bossuet for his pupil, the Dauphin. The great memoirs of Saint-Simon (q.v.), which form a sort of bridge between the 17th and 18th centuries, were not published *in extenso* till the 19th century. The historical works of chief literary merit in the 18th century are Montesquieu's *Considérations sur les causes de la grandeur des Romains et de leur décadence*, and Voltaire's *Histoire de Charles XII* and *Siècle de Louis XIV* (qq.v.), and to a great extent also the latter's *Histoire de la Russie sous Pierre le Grand*. Voltaire's treatises, by their method and style, combine to give a readable and substantially accurate narrative of definite periods of history, while his *Essai sur les mœurs* is an interesting account (marred by the author's prejudices) of the progress of the human mind over the centuries. Mention may also be made of the Président Hénault's *Abrégé de l'histoire de France* and of Duclos's somewhat frigid history of Louis XI.

19TH AND 20TH CENTURIES

(6) During the 19th century history became a subject of live general interest and of increasingly specialized study. The historians can at first, till about 1850, be classified roughly as *narrative* and *philosophical*. The former reconstituted and often dramatized the past with a wide sweep of historical imagination. They were outstandingly represented by three historians of early and medieval France: Barante (*Histoire des ducs de Bourgogne*, 1824-6), Augustin Thierry (*Récits des temps mérovingiens*, 1840), and, above all, Michelet, in the 'Origins to Renaissance' cycle (1833-43) of his vast *Histoire de France*, with its famous evocation of medieval France in vol. ii (see also para. 10 below). They were stimulating reading for generations brought up on Chateaubriand's *Génie du christianisme* (q.v.), Scott's novels (tr.

1822), and the romantic manifestoes (see *Romantisme*). They fed patriotic sentiment, and illumined a past for long barely visible across the abyss of the Napoleonic era and the Revolution. (See also *Michel, F.-X.*, and *Sismondi*.)

(7) The philosophical historians, appreciated by more politically conscious readers, were concerned primarily with political and sociological causes and effects; with the evolution of peoples and institutions; with the future as well as the past. Guizot's *Histoire générale de la civilisation en Europe* and *. . . en France* traced the rise of the middle classes. Tocqueville's *Démocratie en Amérique* (1835-40) attempted to draw a lesson for the Old World from an analysis of the workings of democracy in the New. His *Ancien Régime* (1856, an early example of history based upon administrative records) treated the Revolution as one phase in a continuing process of governmental evolution. Quinet's historical thinking was influenced by the German philosopher Herder, whose *Philosophie der Geschichte* he translated and published in 1834. (See also *Mignet*.)

(8) From the early years of the century, opportunities for historical research were continually multiplying. Interest in foreign history and its relation to French history, in ancient and in oriental civilizations, was stimulated by, for example, narrations of travel, the Greek War of Independence, the rapid progress of archaeological and oriental studies. A selection of dates from the first half of the century alone is revealing: the *Société asiatique* was founded in 1821, as was also the *École des chartes* (see *École nationale des chartes*), the *Société française d'archéologie* in 1830, the *Revue archéologique* in 1844, the *Société de l'histoire de France* in 1833, and the *École française d'Athènes* (q.v.) in 1846. Government-sponsored archaeological expeditions enriched the national collections with their finds. Historical and fine arts commissions were set up about 1837. Publication began about 1830 of many series of documents, source-collections of the highest importance for the study of history. Memoirs were published and widely read (e.g. those of Saint-Simon, first published 1829-30); and the creation of special chairs both in Paris and in provincial Faculties gave history a new, much higher status as a university subject.

(9) As the century wore on, written history, reflecting the positivist spirit of the age, became more and more scrupulously objective, the fruit of systematic research and documentation. Fustel de Coulanges was the initiator of modern historical method (see the 'Monarchie franque' section of his *Histoire des institutions politiques de l'ancienne France*, 1875–92). But Fustel de Coulanges, like his famous contemporaries Renan and Taine (see below), presented facts with such skill and artistry that his works retained great narrative value even when, as happened with his masterpiece *La Cité antique* (q.v.), the theories on which they rested became outmoded. Renan's various works of religious history helped largely to inaugurate, in France, the study of comparative religion. Modern historians in the direct line of descent from Fustel de Coulanges include (besides some of the historians of the Revolution, mentioned below): Camille Jullian, Ch.-V. Langlois, E. Lavisse, A. Rambaud, Ch. Seignobos (qq.v.). All were authorities on particular aspects or periods of history, e.g. Jullian on Gaul, Langlois on medieval France, Lavisse on the 17th century and also on German history.

(10) The Revolution attracted historians of every type beginning with J.-C.-D. de Lacretelle (*Lacretelle jeune*), an eyewitness who later became Professor of History at the Sorbonne. Mignet and Thiers (whose *Histoire du consulat et de l'empire*, 1845–62, was also notable) wrote clear, factual narrative. Michelet's seven 'Revolutionary' volumes (1847–53, forming part of his *Histoire de France*) and Lamartine's *Histoire des Girondins* (1847) were vivid, impassioned narrative, full of democratic fervour, less reliable as fact. The Revolutionary and post-Revolutionary volumes of Taine's *Origines de la France contemporaine* contain an analysis, brilliant and persuasive, of the excesses, strife, and disorders of the period, but too subjective and too uncritical in documentation to be acceptable as history. Historians who viewed the period from the socialist standpoint were Louis Blanc, the revolutionary of 1848 (*Histoire de la Révolution française*, 1847–62) and, half a century later, the great socialist leader and orator Jean Jaurès, in vols. i–iv (1902–3) which he wrote for the complete *Histoire socialiste* (*1789–1900*). Modern systematic study of the causes and different phases of

the Revolution is based on research into vast and often still unpublished collections of manuscript material in national and provincial archives. It began with Aulard, the first Professor (1886) of the History of the Revolution. His almost equally famous pupil Albert Mathiez is usually mentioned after him because he held views of the economic institutions of the Terror utterly opposed to those of his former master. Henri Sée (1864–) also devoted his attention solely to the economic causes. Albert Sorel studied the Revolution in relation to general European history. Georges Lefebvre (q.v.) is the first historian to study the impact of the Revolution on the peasant classes. No mention of the importance attached by the late 19th- and early 20th-century historians to this type of documentary study would be complete without reference to the important work of Pierre Caron (q.v.). Less severely scientific historians of the Revolution, with a wider appeal for the general reader, include Louis Madelin and two writers of Royalist and Catholic sympathies, Funck-Brentano and Pierre Gaxotte (qq.v.).

(11) Omnibus histories, or series of historical monographs, compiled by specialists (usually with one scholar as general editor) are a feature of modern publishing. Descriptions of some of these will be found in Appendix I, §§ C (i); H (ii).

Hoaxes and forgeries, see *Calonne, E. de*; *Chasse spirituelle, La*; *Courtilz de Sandras*; *Fabre d'Olivet*; *Louÿs, P.*; *Mémoires*; *Mérimée, P.*; *Surville, Clotilde de*; *Vrain-Lucas*; and cf. also *Libri*; *Maugérard*.

Hoche, LOUIS-LAZARE (1768–97), a famous general of the Republican armies, said to have been a man of great nobility and generosity of character. He began life as a stable-boy, son of one of Louis XVI's kennel-men at Versailles, and owed his glory to his own merits and his education to his own determination. At sixteen he enlisted in the *Gardes françaises* (the King's Household Guard). He was a sergeant when the Revolution broke out and became a (paid) sergeant in the *Garde nationale* (q.v.) after the fall of the Bastille. His brilliant career began in 1792 when he was commissioned in an infantry regiment. By 1793 he was General in command of the Army of the Moselle. Later in that year, and until his release after the fall of Robespierre, he profited by a spell of imprisonment (due to Saint-Just's hatred of him) to read and study. In 1794 he married the daughter of an army store-keeper. In 1795–6 he commanded the Army of the West which finally pacified the insurrectionist Vendée (and cf. *Quiberon*), after which he led an unsuccessful expedition intended to seize and hold Ireland against the English. In 1797 he was in command of the Army of Germany when he died suddenly in his headquarters, possibly poisoned.

Hoffmann, ERNST THEODOR AMADEUS (1776–1822), German musician, artist, and writer, was the author of *Phantasiestücke in Callots Manier* (1814) and other tales and novels of great imaginative force and usually of a gruesome or grotesque character. They were famous throughout Europe, and had a strong influence in France upon the later— 'frenetic'—writers of the Romantic movement (see *Foreign influences on French literature*, para. 20; *Romantisme*; cf. also *Offenbach*). The *Phantasiestücke* were translated into French as *Contes fantastiques*. His *Œuvres complètes* were translated in 1830 by Loève-Weimars (q.v.).

Hoffmann, FRANÇOIS-BENOÎT (1760–1828), journalist and dramatic poet, born at Nancy, a leading critic on the *Journal des Débats* during the First Empire (cf. *Dussault, Feletz, Geoffroy*). He wrote much for the theatre and was particularly successful as a librettist for opera and light opera. His *Œuvres complètes* were published (10 vols.) in 1828–9.

Hohenlinden, a village in Bavaria, where the French Army of the Rhine, under General Moreau (q.v.), routed the Austrians (3 Dec. 1800) during the campaign of 1800–1 against the Second Coalition (q.v.).

Holbach, PAUL THIRY, BARON D' (1723–89), born at Hildesheim in Baden, a materialist and atheist philosopher, a man of wide erudition, modest, rich, generous, cheerful, and simple, who spent most of his life in France. His hospitable houses, in Paris and in the country at Grand-Val, were the chief centres of the *encyclopédistes* (q.v.); there is much about d'Holbach's circle in Diderot's letters to Mlle Volland. About 1767–8 d'Holbach, with his associate Naigeon, issued a large number of tracts and pamphlets directed to the discredit of religion. His most

famous work is *Système de la Nature* (q.v., 1770), conveniently abbreviated in *Le Bon Sens, ou Idées naturelles opposées aux idées surnaturelles* (1772). His other writings include *Le Christianisme dévoilé* (1761 and 1766), *Politique naturelle* (1773), and *Le Système social* (1773). He is supposed to be depicted in Rousseau's Wolmar (see *Nouvelle Héloïse, La*).

Holger Danske, see *Ogier de Danemarcke*.

Holy Alliance, see *Alliance, la Sainte*.

Homais, Monsieur, the apothecary, a typical local worthy, a character in Flaubert's novel *Madame Bovary* (q.v.).

Homme approximatif, L' (1930), by Tristan Tzara (q.v.), an early Surréaliste work, often mentioned (see *Surréalisme*).

Homme au Masque de fer, see *Masque*.

Homme aux quarante écus, L', a satire on French fiscal legislation by Voltaire, published in 1768, in which various economic questions are treated mainly in the form of dialogues between an agriculturist, owner of a piece of land yielding an income of forty *écus*, and a 'géomètre philosophe'. They discuss such questions as the agricultural production of France, the national income, the proposed 'single tax' on land, the growth of the population, the institution of monasticism, and other matters of more general character, such as the iniquities of the judicial procedure. The work was condemned by the *Parlement*.

Homme obstiné, L', see *Gringore*.

Homme qui rit, L' (1869), a novel by Victor Hugo. The narrative is frequently powerful, but obscured by absurdities and the lengthy expression of the author's views upon divers subjects. It gives an unintentionally amusing picture of English society and hereditary customs at the end of the 17th century.

Ursus, a vagabond quack and philosopher, lives in a caravan with Homo, a trained wolf, for company. He succours two children, a boy and a baby girl. The boy, Gwynplaine, fighting his way through a blizzard after being abandoned on a lonely seashore, had found the girl, Dea, in the snow beside a dead woman. Dea is blind, while Gwynplaine's face has been so mutilated that it bears a perpetual, grotesque grin which drives all beholders to helpless laughter.

In London we meet Lord David Dirry-Moir, destined to succeed the Earl of Clancharlie if no legitimate son turns up, and the Duchess Josiane of Clancharlie, a bastard daughter of the king. The former, described with ironic gusto as a typical athletic English aristocrat, delights in going among the people disguised as 'Tom Jim-Jack': and Josiane is a magnificent lump of flesh with pretensions to culture. Josiane and Lord David have an enemy in Barkilphedro, Receiver of Jetsam at the Admiralty.

Ursus establishes himself in Southwark with his caravan ('the Green Box'), Homo the wolf, Gwynplaine, and Dea. The two young people are in love and the blind Dea imagines her lover to be as beautiful as a god. Gwynplaine is known as 'l'homme qui rit', and the fame of his performance spreads to the court. Suddenly mysterious officials (among them the 'Wapentake') appear, and take Gwynplaine away. The reason is that among other jetsam Barkilphedro has received a sealed bottle containing proof that Gwynplaine is the long-lost legitimate son of the late Lord Clancharlie. (He had been stolen, then abandoned, by *comprachios*—vagrants whose custom was to procure children, deform or mutilate them, and sell them again for use as exhibits.) This is Barkilphedro's chance to injure Lord David Dirry-Moir and the Duchess Josiane. He causes Ursus to be informed officially that Gwynplaine is dead and that he himself must leave the country at once with Homo and Dea. Meantime Gwynplaine, now a peer, is introduced to the House of Lords. His fellow peers are so overcome with mirth at the sight of him that he has to leave the Chamber. He makes for Southwark and the 'Green Box', but finds the site deserted. Suddenly Homo the wolf appears. Gwynplaine follows him to the waterside and finds a Dutch vessel about to sail with Ursus and Dea on board.

The end is sorrow. Gwynplaine makes himself known, but the shock of joy kills Dea. Thereupon Gwynplaine throws himself into the water and is drowned.

Hommes de bonne volonté, Les (1932–47), the collective title of twenty-seven

novels by Jules Romains (q.v.) which, together, constitute a survey of French life and thought, and to some extent of modern civilization, between 1908 and 1933. The work as a whole, however, differs from, for example, Balzac's *Comédie humaine*, Zola's *Les Rougon-Macquart*, or R. Rolland's *Jean-Christophe* (qq.v.) in refusing to create any artificial link between the volumes for the sake of plot or unity, in having no scientific theory to demonstrate, and no central figure in whose life-history all the other characters are involved. Individuals and groups, clerical and lay, in high and low life, in Paris and the provinces, are taken up and studied for a while then dropped, perhaps never to reappear, while others come to the fore. Thus the author's now panoramic now detailed technique gives the reader a window-seat view of life, with all the sense of the haphazard and the incomplete that this entails. Even when most strongly delineated the characters emerge only temporarily from a background of action or ideas. The impression finally intended and on the whole achieved is of the forces of good-will struggling to make headway against the inert and destructive forces of ignorance and greed.

The several volumes are as follows:

1. *Le 6 octobre* (1932). The work opens with a picture of Paris on a crisp, golden morning in October 1908. On all sides the Parisians are setting out to work. Their interests and anxieties are domestic or local. A very few see the menace of European war already on the horizon. Some leading characters are introduced out of more than a thousand who will appear.

2. *Crime de Quinette* (1932). The underworld of crime. A respectable bookbinder takes to murder as a hobby. Glimpses of his later history and his contacts with other characters in the book are given in vols. 17, 18, 24 (when he dies), and 27. Two young men of good-will, Pierre Jallez and Jean Jerphanion, destined to reappear frequently, make friends on entering the *École normale supérieure* (q.v.). The one, a Parisian, already sophisticated, will become a novelist and journalist as the work proceeds. The other, from the mountainous district of central France, and still raw and uncouth, will be a successful, and honest, politician. Their walks across Paris, and their many

conversations about life, form the greater part of vols. 3 and 4, *Les Amours enfantines* (1932) and *Éros de Paris* (1932). Some fresh characters, also some personages from real life, are introduced. These first four volumes in themselves form a picture of Paris in the last quarter of 1908.

5. *Les Superbes* (1933); 6. *Les Humbles* (1933). The first of these two contrasting volumes deals with the world of the rich, sometimes the shady, company-promoting rich. The second depicts the very seamy side of life. The Parisian scene and the French social hierarchy are viewed through the eyes of an English journalist, Bartlett.

7. *Recherche d'une église* (1934); 8. *Province* (1934); 9. *Montée des périls* (1935); 10. *Les Pouvoirs* (1936). These volumes range over ecclesiastical, political, diplomatic, and industrial milieux. Jallez and Jerphanion graduate from the *École normale* and pause before the world and their future.

11. *Recours à l'abîme* (1936). This volume plods through filth, then turns to the world of literature and science, elaborated in vol. 12, *Les Créateurs* (1936), with glimpses of *Académie française* (q.v.) circles and of 'abstract' poets at work.

13. *Mission à Rome* (1937); and 14. *Le Drapeau noir* (1937) are largely taken up with international politics. Mionnet, a young cleric, destined to high preferment, is sent on a secret mission to Rome to obtain information about Vatican activities. There is a fine picture of Paris on the eve of the 1914–18 war.

15. *Prélude à Verdun* (1937); 16. *Verdun* (1938). These two volumes, the high-spots of the whole work, are an absorbing, emotional, but restrained picture of the French nation fighting for its existence. Profiteers are the reverse side of the picture.

17. *Vorge contre Quinette* (1939). *See* under vol. 2 above. We are now in the post-war world. 18. *La Douceur de la vie* (1939). An interlude in the life of Jallez, who is a mixture of an intellectual and *un homme* more than *moyen sensuel*.

19. *Cette grande lueur à l'est* (1941). Paris in 1922, when all eyes are turned to Russia. Problems of the inter-war world.

20. *Le Monde est ton aventure* (1941). Jallez and Jerphanion are in Russia. The volume is interesting for an almost documentary description of their adventures and impressions, what they see, how much they do not see.

21. *Journées dans la montagne* (1942). Jerphanion conducts a successful election campaign in his native mountain country. In the course of hard days out he comes across a household in which crime and drama are apparently being enacted. The puzzle will, tantalizingly, remain as fragmentary and unsolved for the reader as for Jerphanion.

22. *Les Travaux et les Joies* (1943). The successes of Jerphanion, in politics, and of Haverkamp, a profiteer who is not all bad. (He crashes in vol. 25 and in vol. 26 is seen living anonymously and contentedly in Yugoslavia.)

23. *Naissance de la bande* (1944). A group of young people take to political gangsterism.

24. *Comparutions* (1944). Several characters encountered in the course of the work take stock of themselves and of world affairs.

25. *Le Tapis magique* (1946). Jallez seeks amorous distraction in various capitals of Europe. Back in Paris, in the midst of growing international unrest, he falls seriously in love with a girl of his own world whose virtues as a listener, while he walks her about Paris (vol. 26. *Françoise*), are unquestionable.

27. *Le 7 octobre* (1947). In early spring 1933 the Parisians are struggling as they had not needed to struggle twenty-five years ago with the mechanics of existence. Political and social problems invade every conscience and the world is rushing helplessly into a new war. There is, after all, some tying up of ends, for the work finishes, as it began, with a picture of Paris; and Jerphanion and Jallez are among the last characters we meet, as they were among the first.

Honorine, one of the 'Scènes de la vie privée' of Balzac's *Comédie humaine* (q.v.).

Horace, a tragedy by Corneille, produced in 1640, based on the story of the Horatii and the Curiatii in Livy (1. 23 et seq.), but the character of Sabine was invented by the poet.

Rome and Alba are at war; it has been agreed that the struggle shall be decided by the combat of three champions on each side. Horace and his brothers are chosen by Rome,

Curiace and his brothers by Alba. Now, these two families are bound by close ties. Horace is married to Sabine, sister of Curiace; and Curiace is betrothed to Camille, sister of Horace. Horace welcomes this opportunity of sacrificing all other interests to patriotism. The more sensitive and humane Curiace is horrified by this blow of fate, but accepts it with fortitude. When, as the combat progresses, news is brought that Horace, his two brothers having been killed, is fleeing from his three adversaries, his old father laments his disgrace and vows to wipe it out in his son's blood that very night. A revulsion of feeling comes when it is learnt that the flight of Horace was a feint, to enable him to deal separately with his foes, and kill them all. As Horace returns victorious, his sister Camille meets him. She bewails the death of her betrothed; her fierce imprecations on Rome infuriate Horace, who kills her. Brought before the king for this crime, Horace hardly deigns to defend himself. Sabine, bound to a man who has killed her three brothers, appalled at her fate, asks that her life may be taken in place of his. The father of Horace pleads for his son, and the king decides that his glorious deed effaces his crime.

Horla, Le (1886), a tale of hallucination and horror, by Maupassant (q.v.).

Horn, Roman de, a 12th-century French metrical romance, cast in the form of a *chanson de geste* (monorhyme stanzas), of which the general plot is the same as that of the English *King Horn*.

The Saracens under Rodmund have occupied the kingdom of Suddene, killed Aaluf its king, and found the boy Horn his son with fifteen companions hidden in a garden. The children are turned adrift in a boat on the sea and carried to Brittany, where they are kindly received by king Hunlaf. Horn, educated by the seneschal Herland, excels, as he grows up, in all knightly qualities, and Ri(g)mel, Hunlaf's daughter, falls in love with him. By his prowess he defeats a Saracen invasion, and thereafter he and Rimel plight their troth. But Wikes (or Wikele), a cousin of Horn, traduces them to Hunlaf, and Horn is banished, after receiving a magic ring from Rimel. Horn goes to Ireland in the quality of a poor adventurer, assuming the name

Gudmod. He is well received by Gudereche the king, and here again he defeats a Saracen invasion. But in this the king's sons are killed, and the king offers Horn his realm and his daughter. Horn declines, remaining faithful to Rimel. He now learns that under pressure from Hunlaf and Wikes, Rimel is to be married to Modin, king of Fenoie. He returns to Brittany with a party of followers and arrives at the marriage feast in the guise of a pilgrim, is recognized by Rimel by means of the ring, defeats Modin, and threatens the city of Hunlaf. The latter makes peace with Horn and cedes him Rimel. Horn pardons Wikes. He now reconquers his kingdom of Suddene from the Saracens. His mother Samburc, who had survived there in hiding, is recognized by him. He defeats a treacherous plot by which Wikes attempts to get possession of Rimel (who has remained in Brittany), and slays the traitor. He thereafter lives with Rimel happily in Suddene.

Hôtel Carnavalet, see *Sévigné*. It is now the Musée Carnavalet.

Hôtel d'argent, L', in the neighbourhood of Les Halles, in Paris, was leased as a theatre in the 16th and 17th centuries to companies from the provinces, notably to Mondory's (q.v.) company which moved later to the Théâtre du Marais (see *Theatres and theatre companies*).

Hôtel de Bourgogne, an ancient residence in Paris of the dukes of Burgundy in the neighbourhood of Les Halles. All that remains of it is the fine *tour* (or *donjon*) *de Jean sans Peur* (1371–1419, Duke of Burgundy from 1404 to 1419). For its connexion with the French theatre, see *Confrérie de la Passion; Theatres and theatre companies*.

Hôtel de Rambouillet, see *Rambouillet*.

Hôtel des Haricots. The first place used when members of the *Garde Nationale* had to be imprisoned for dereliction of duty was the former Collège Montaigu (q.v.), where the students were said to have been fed mainly on beans, hence 'hôtel des haricots'. The name stuck, though the prison several times changed quarters. During the July Monarchy—the prison was then at 92 rue de la Gare, behind the Jardin des Plantes— certain *cellules des artistes* were reserved for artists and writers, who often spent most of their by no means uncomfortable stay in writing or drawing upon the walls. Later, when the building was demolished, these cells were removed to the Musée Carnavalet (q.v.).

Hôtel des Invalides, see *Invalides.*

Hôtel des Tournelles, in the Marais (q.v.) quarter of Paris, a royal residence standing in a wood (the Parc des Tournelles) used by Louis XI, Charles VIII, Louis XII, and François Ier. Louis XII died there, and so did Henri II after being wounded in a tourney. Catherine de Médicis, the widow of the latter, caused it to be in part demolished, and in Henri IV's reign its site was utilized for the creation of the new Place Royale.

Hôtel de Ville, the town- or guild-hall in French towns. The present-day Hôtel de Ville in Paris stands on the site of a house in the Place de Grève (q.v.) bought in 1357 by Étienne Marcel (q.v.), the *Prévôt de la Hanse des marchands par eau* (the Hanseatic Guild of Paris, which controlled the commerce of the city and out of which the municipality developed). This *Maison des piliers* took the place of the former so-called *Parloir aux bourgeois* (situated in the near-by Place du Châtelet) and by 1359 was already known as the Ostel de Ville. It was the residence of the Prévôt, was altered, enlarged, and rebuilt at various dates, and was for long the centre of the political as well as municipal life and events of Paris. At the Revolution it became the headquarters of the Municipal Government (formed in July 1789), and between 1792 and 1794 the place of assembly for the Commune de Paris (q.v.). During the First Empire it became (as it is today) the seat of the Préfecture de la Seine (see *Préfet de la Seine*). At the July Revolution (1830) it was besieged but not captured by the insurgents. After the proclamation of the Second Republic (1848) it was the seat of the Provisional Government. From 18 March till 24 May 1871 it was occupied by the Commune, then destroyed by fire to prevent its being surrendered to the troops from Versailles. The new Hôtel de Ville, erected on the old site, was opened in 1880. When Paris, the city, entertains guests she receives them at the Hôtel de Ville.

Hôtel-Dieu, L', the oldest hospital in Paris, today a modern Public Assistance hospital. It goes back to a Hospice founded by saint Landri, a 7th-century Bishop of Paris, beside the church of Notre-Dame. (It is still beside Notre-Dame but no longer on the original site.) Here, until it was secularized in the 16th century, the aged and sick poor were maintained by the clergy with aid from royal and private benefactors, of whom Louis IX was the most famous. It experienced various changes of name before it became the Hôtel-Dieu (and for a time during the Revolution it was called *la Maison de l'humanité*).

Hôtel Drouot, the usual name for the Hôtel des Ventes Mobilières situated in the rue Drouot (so called after one of Napoleon's generals), in Paris, off the Boulevard Montmartre. These well-known sale-rooms occupy much the same place in the life of Paris as Sotheby's or Christie's in London.

Hotman, FRANÇOIS (1524–90), born in Paris of a family of Silesian origin, a Huguenot and a jurist, author of *Franco-Gallia* (1573, French translation 1574), a Latin work of political theory professing to show with the aid of history that monarchy should be elective and constitutional. The work was combated by Jean Bodin (q.v.) in his *De la République.* He was also author of a pamphlet attacking the Cardinal de Lorraine, entitled *Épître envoyée au Tigre de la France*; and of a translation of Plato's *Apology.*

Houdar de la Motte, ANTOINE (1672–1731), son of a hatter, a talented poet and critic. He suffered most of his life from paralysis and partial blindness, but frequented the salons of the day and the court of the duchesse du Maine. He was the author of *Odes* (in fact dissertations in verse on such themes as 'Bienfaisance', 'Émulation') accompanied by a discourse on poetry in general (1709), *Fables* (1719), dramas (*Les Originaux*, 1693, comedy; *Les Macchabées*, 1722, a lyrical tragedy; and *Inès de Castro* (q.v.), 1723, which was very successful), and of various discourses on tragedy (1730, to which Voltaire replied in an introduction to his *Œdipe*). He took up the position of an advocate of modernism in the *Querelle des Anciens et des Modernes* (q.v.), and wrote in 1714 an adaptation in verse of the *Iliad* designed to suit the manners of a polite age (see *Dacier*). He was influenced in his literary views by his friend Fontenelle, and in spite of his own efforts in verse advanced the theory that poetry (as distinct from verse) is independent of conventional form (measure and rhyme) and can be expressed in prose, a partial truth which ignores one side of poetry. He also condemned slavish adherence to the unities and in general the dramatic conventions established by Corneille and Racine, making the pleasure of the spectator the supreme criterion. But in his dramas he as a rule abandoned his revolutionary opinions and conformed to the routine of the day.

Houdetot, ÉLISABETH-SOPHIE, COMTESSE D' (1730–1813), sister-in-law of Mme d'Épinay, a woman of sprightly and amiable character rather than of much physical beauty, with whom J.-J. Rousseau fell passionately in love when at Montmorency. But Mme d'Houdetot remained faithful to a previous lover, Saint-Lambert. Rousseau's passion influenced the composition of his *Nouvelle Héloïse*.

Houdon, JEAN-ANTOINE (*c.* 1741–1828), a noted sculptor, who made busts and statues of distinguished personages of his day, including Voltaire, Buffon, Diderot, Rousseau, Washington, and Franklin.

Houssaye, ARSÈNE (1815–96), man of letters and one-time Director of the Théâtre Français, was prominent in the literary life of the July Monarchy and Second Empire. He published interesting *Confessions: souvenirs d'un demi-siècle (1830–1880)* (4 vols. 1885, with another 2 vols., 1891, extending the period to 1890). He also wrote a large number of novels, now forgotten, and (1855) an amusing *Histoire du 41ᵉ fauteuil de l'Académie française*. [The number of members of the *Académie française* (q.v.) is limited to forty.]

Housse partie, La, a *fabliau* (q.v.). There are many European versions of the story. It tells how an ungrateful son, about to drive his aged father from his house, is shamed into changing his mind by the action of his own son. Just as he is turning the old man out of doors, he consents to give him a horse-cloth for a cloak, and sends the child to fetch it. The child cuts it in two and brings only one half to his grandfather. 'Why?' asks the father. 'Because', replies the child, 'I have kept the other half for you, when you are old in your turn.'

Houville, Gérard d' [pseud. of Mme Henri de Régnier, q.v.] (1875–   ), poetess and prose writer, born in Paris. Her poems, conventional in form, treat themes of love, nature, and death or, like those of her father, the poet J.-M. de Heredia (q.v.), subjects from classical antiquity—*Le Diadème de Flores: poèmes en prose* (1925), *Poésies* (1930). Her novels include *L'Inconstante* (1903), *L'Esclave* (1905), *Le Temps d'aimer* (1915).

Hozier, PIERRE DE LA GARDE D' (1592–1660) and his son RENÉ (1640–1732), genealogists, whose name has been adopted as a generic designation for works of genealogical research.

Hubert, SAINT (d. 727), Bishop of Liège and Maestricht, traditionally the patron saint of hunters. His festival is on 3 November.

Huc, PHILIPPE, see *Derême, Tristan*.

Huet, PIERRE-DANIEL (1630–1721), a learned scholar, who took holy orders when forty-six and became Bishop of Avranches. He began the preparation, under Bossuet, of the edition of the classics *ad usum Delphini*. La Fontaine addressed to him his *Épître à Huet*, and Ménage corresponded with him. His letters have been published, besides a number of learned works: *De Interpretatione* (a dialogue on translation, 1661), *Origenis Commentaria* (1668), *Traité de l'origine des romans* (1670, first published as an introduction to Mme de La Fayette's *Zaïde*), *Demonstratio evangelica* (1679), *Censura philosophiae Cartesianae* (1689), *Histoire du commerce et de la navigation des anciens* (1716), *Traité philosophique de la faiblesse de l'esprit humain* (1723).

Hugo, ABEL (1798–1855), elder brother of Victor Hugo, with whom in 1819 he founded the *Conservateur littéraire* (q.v.). He devoted much of his later career as a man of letters to Spanish literature and history.

Hugo, CHARLES-VICTOR (1826–71), elder son of Victor Hugo. From 1848–51 he was co-editor of *L'Événement* (q.v.) and for a time (1848) Lamartine's secretary at the *Ministère des Affaires Étrangères*. He followed his father into exile in 1851 and on his return to Paris helped to found *Le Rappel* (q.v.).

Hugo, EUGÈNE (1800–37), brother of Victor Hugo, had himself begun to write, but in

1822, the day after his brother's wedding to Adèle Foucher, with whom he too was in love, he had a severe mental collapse from which he never recovered.

Hugo, JEAN-FRANÇOIS-VICTOR (1828–73), younger son of Victor Hugo and himself a man of letters, followed his father into exile in 1851 and spent much of his time studying English. He published translations and studies of Shakespeare's plays (1859–65) and was also the first translator of the *Sonnets* (1857).

Hugo, VICTOR-MARIE (1802–85), the greatest poet of 19th-century France, perhaps of all French literature, also novelist and dramatist, and the grand figure of the Romantic Movement (see *Romantisme*).

(1) He was born at Besançon, where his father (Sigisbert, comte, 1774–1828), a general of Napoleon's armies, was stationed. His first ten years were spent mainly in Corsica, Italy, and Spain : military duties took the father to these places, and the family followed. Then the parents separated, and from 1812 Mme Hugo lived in Paris with her three sons Abel, Eugène, and Victor. The house and its large garden are described in *Ce qui se passait aux Feuillantines*, one of the poems of *Les Rayons et les Ombres* (1840, q.v.).

(2) His decision to be a writer (a Chateaubriand or nothing) was taken early. A poem written while he was still at school was noticed by the *Académie française* (q.v.), and he had also carried off a prize from the *Jeux Floraux* of Toulouse (q.v.). In 1819, with his brother Abel, their respective ages being seventeen and twenty, he founded the *Conservateur littéraire* (q.v.), one of the famous literary reviews associated with the Romantic Movement. In 1822—the year of his marriage to Adèle Foucher (q.v.)—his first collection of poems (*Odes et poésies diverses*) came by chance to the notice of Louis XVIII, who awarded him a small pension from his privy purse. Another pension rewarded his novel *Han d'Islande* (1823, q.v.). This work also gained him the friendship of Charles Nodier (q.v.), whose *salon* at the Arsenal Library was the first Romantic *cénacle* (q.v.). The second *cénacle* was Hugo's own house, its leader Hugo himself; and the dominant friendship here, which ended unfortunately but had fruitful literary consequences, was that of Sainte-Beuve (q.v.).

(3) The first *Odes et poésies diverses* were followed by *Nouvelles Odes*. A third collection, *Odes et Ballades* (1826), introduced a period of amazing literary productivity—novels, essays, travel literature, another five collections of poems (*Les Orientales*, 1829; *Feuilles d'automne*, 1831; *Les Chants du crépuscule*, 1835; *Les Voix intérieures*, 1837; *Les Rayons et les Ombres*, 1840), and the major part of his dramatic output. This ended suddenly in 1843. The failure of his poetic drama *Les Burgraves* had disheartened him and he was prostrated for a time by the death of his eldest, and idolized, daughter Léopoldine in a boating accident with her husband: he had also, with success and the years, developed political ambitions.

(4) These now occupied him. After his youthful ultra-Royalism he had accepted the constitutional monarchy of Louis-Philippe. He was created a *pair de France* (q.v.) in 1846 as a reward for his support; but by 1848, when the monarchy was overturned, he was a firm Republican, and was elected a people's representative to the *Assemblée législative* (q.v.). He was active in support of measures for free education, universal male suffrage, &c. What was more, his articles in *L'Événement*, a newspaper founded by himself at this time, did much to facilitate Louis Napoleon's entry upon the scene (see *Légende napoléonienne*). His republicanism was mingled with political ambition; and disappointment followed when he received no offer of high office in the government formed by Louis Napoleon on becoming Prince-President.

(5) Anger at what he considered Louis Napoleon's treachery to himself soon gave place to a more generous fury aroused by the *coup d'état* (q.v.) of 2 December 1851, by which the Second Empire (q.v.) was founded. Preferring exile to the Empire he left Paris, disguised as a workman. After some months in Brussels he went to Jersey (1853). In 1855 he settled in Guernsey (see *Hauteville House*). He refused to return to France some years later when an amnesty would have made this possible, declaring that he would wait until Liberty returned. His exile was shared by his family and a few faithful friends, including his devoted mistress, the actress Juliette Drouet (q.v.). Friends from the mainland visited him at intervals, and at one period he went through

a spiritualist phase when he believed himself to be in communication with spirits from the other world, who even dictated poems to him. But his life was essentially solitary, his writing his absorbing occupation, his most real companion the sea.

(6) At the fall of the Second Empire (1870) he returned to Paris to find that in his absence a *légende Victor Hugo* had arisen, and after the siege of Paris he was elected to the *Assemblée nationale* by 214,000 votes. But his influence waned: with the Assembly, because he preached a gospel of a universal republic which no one was prepared to take seriously; with the *Communards* (see *Commune*), because they doubted his readiness to translate his republican enthusiasms into action. The publication of *L'Année terrible* (poems inspired by the events of 1870-1) restored his prestige and he was elected a Senator of the Third Republic. He had no political influence, but his genius, his age (he was now seventy-three), and his battles for liberty of the people and the arts alike, had made him a national figure. After 1878 his health failed and he died on 22 May 1885. His lying in state and his funeral have been many times described, e.g. in the novel *Les Déracinés* (q.v.) by Maurice Barrès, and in Léon Daudet's *Souvenirs* (q.v.). His body lay in state under the *Arc de Triomphe* (q.v.), guarded by cuirassiers with lighted torches. The next day it was placed, as he himself had wished, on a pauper's hearse and borne across Paris to be buried in the Panthéon (q.v.).

(7) When politics are omitted, Hugo's literary career can be seen falling into two parts. During the first he was, even if not always the prime innovator, the leader, the shining light, and also the champion and theorist, of *le romantisme*, attempting all genres—drama, the novel, poetry—and revolutionizing them all. As a dramatist, he waged war against the old conventions governing the French stage (see *Cromwell*), and with *Hernani* (q.v.) established the right to liberty both of subject and of treatment. His novel of medieval Paris, *Notre-Dame de Paris* (q.v.), was a revelation of what the historical novel could be. To poetry he brought a new sense of the beauty of words and the effects of sonority, light and shade, colour, that the French language could yield. He also allowed himself hitherto rarely attempted liberties of versification,

e.g. new rhythms, and a daring freedom in the manipulation of the traditional alexandrine verse (see *Alexandrin*), aided by protracted *enjambement* (q.v.), unusual placing of the caesura, and a skilful use of the French silent *e*. These, together with his disregard for the periphrases of poetic diction, aroused storms of protest from the critics, though later poets were to adopt them as a matter of course. Generally, as opposed to technically, his great service to French poetry was that he established the personal note, the *moi*, or continual laying bare of the Self, of the Romantics. But as his genius developed the *moi* that he had to communicate became the Self in its relation to life and life's happenings, and it was on this wider conception of the poet's function that the first phase of his literary career ended, in 1843.

(8) The second phase opened with the publication of *Napoléon le petit* (1852), a lampoon written in Brussels (see para. 5.) Within a year of his arrival in Jersey came a collection of satirical and invective verse, *Les Châtiments* (q.v.). A quieter period followed, with Paris, politics, the literary and social world behind him. Now, in his undisturbed leisure he elaborated his theory of the Poet (i.e. himself) as a man of ideas, a torch-bearer, who should lead the people and interpret for them the events of history and civilization. To this, as time passed, he joined a vast, phantasmagoric conception of a universe that had come into being through man's imperfection: in which original sin had been transmuted into matter; and all forms of life, animal, vegetable, or mineral, the repulsive toad by the wayside or the stones of the condemned cell, imprisoned some haunted soul being punished for the sins of a previous existence. The philosophy is negligible, though Hugo, whose vanity was as colossal as his genius, insisted upon its value. Its importance is that it released a torrent of words, symbols, and imagery, and some visionary writing of the highest order, for instance in the 6th book of *Les Contemplations* (1856) and the last volume of *La Légende des siècles* (1883). But such ideas by no means dominated Hugo's output in this second phase. His varied inspiration is sufficiently indicated by the earlier epics of the *Légende des siècles*, the elegiac verse of the 4th book of *Les Contemplations*, and the lighter, more pastoral

lyrics of the *Chansons des rues et des bois* (1865); while the novels *Les Misérables* (1862, q.v.) and *Les Travailleurs de la mer* (1866, q.v.) reveal his interest in sociological problems and his gift for vivid, pictorial writing.

(9) The list below is a far from complete enumeration of Hugo's vast output. Titles already mentioned are repeated for the sake of chronology, and an asterisk marks any work described separately.

(*a*) POETRY: *Odes et Poésies diverses* (1822), *Nouvelles Odes* (1824), *Odes et Ballades* (1826)★, *Les Orientales* (1829)★, *Les Feuilles d'automne* (1831)★, *Les Chants du crépuscule* (1835)★, *Les Voix intérieures* (1837)★, *Les Rayons et les Ombres* (1840)★, *Les Châtiments* (1853)★, *Les Contemplations* (1856)★, *La Légende des siècles* (1859–83)★, *Les Chansons des rues et des bois* (1865), *L'Année terrible* (1872)★, *L'Art d'être grand-père* (1877)★, *Le Pape* (1878), *La Pitié suprême* (1879), *L'Âne* (1880), *Religions et Religion* (1880), *Les Quatre Vents de l'Esprit* (1881)★; also the posthumous *La Fin de Satan* (1886, unfinished), *Toute la lyre* (1888–93)★, *Dieu* (1891, unfinished), *Années funestes* (1898), *Dernière gerbe* (1902). (For the first and third of these last see under *Légende des siècles, La.*)

(*b*) NOVELS: *Han d'Islande* (1823)★, *Bug-Jargal* (1826)★, *Le Dernier Jour d'un condamné* (1829)★, *Notre-Dame de Paris* (1831)★, *Claude Gueux* (1834)★, *Les Misérables* (1862)★, *Les Travailleurs de la mer* (1866)★, *L'Homme qui rit* (1869)★, *Quatre-vingt-treize* (1873)★.

(*c*) DRAMA: *Cromwell* (1827, verse)★, *Amy Robsart* (1828, prose), *Hernani* (1830, verse)★, *Marion de Lorme* (1831, verse)★, *Le Roi s'amuse* (1832, verse)★, *Lucrèce Borgia* (1833, prose)★, *Marie Tudor* (1833, prose)★, *Angelo* (1835, prose)★, *Ruy Blas* (1838, verse)★, *Les Burgraves* (1843, verse)★, *Torquemada* (1882, verse), and a posthumous collection of short plays, *Le Théâtre en liberté* (1886);

(*d*) POLITICAL, CRITICAL, AND MISCELLANEOUS WRITINGS: *Étude sur Mirabeau* (1834), *Littérature et philosophie mêlées* (1834), *Le Rhin* (1842)★, *Napoléon le petit* (1852)★, *Histoire d'un crime* (1852–77)★, *William Shakespeare* (1864)★, *Actes et Paroles*: I. *Avant l'exil* (1841–51), II. *Pendant l'exil* (1852–70), III, IV. *Depuis l'exil* (1870–85), and, finally, *Choses vues* (1887–1900, posth.), the poet's journal.

Huguenots. The citizens of Geneva in the Middle Ages resisted the claim of the dukes of Savoy over their city, maintained its independence, and sought external support in a federation with the cantons of Fribourg and Berne. Hence they were called *Eidgenossen* or confederates; and this word is said to be the origin of 'huguenot', a name of opprobrium subsequently given in France to the Calvinists, whose stronghold was Geneva.

Hugues Capet, born *c.* 938, son of Hugues le Grand (d. 956) and grandson of Robert Ier, was King of France from 987 until his death in 996. He was the first of the *Capétien* (q.v.) dynasty, having been placed on the throne by the nobles in preference to the Carolingian Charles de France or de Lorraine, 2nd son of Louis IV d'Outre-Mer (q.v.). Various derivations have been suggested for the surname Capet, e.g. *capito*, a large head, *chappatus*, a man wearing a cape, &c.

Huitain, in French prosody, a stanza of eight lines, either of ten or of eight syllables, usually rhyming as follows:

a b a b b c b c.

Villon's *Lais* and *Testament* are written in octosyllabic *huitains*.

Hulot, or **Hulot d'Ervy,** BARON HECTOR. A character in Balzac's novel *La Cousine Bette* (q.v.).

Humanism, see *Renaissance*.

Humanisme, a poetic movement launched in 1902 by Fernand Gregh (q.v.). It had little existence beyond the first manifesto in *Le Figaro*, but the name is still mentioned at times. It stood for a reaction against the Symbolist love of vagueness and medieval legend, as well as against the Parnassian impersonality, and demanded a return to the humanistic spirit of antiquity.

Humilis, pseudonym of *Germain Nouveau* (q.v.).

Huon de Bordeaux, a 13th-century *chanson de geste* (q.v.) of the Charlemagne cycle, typical of the degradation of the older form of *chanson de geste* into an amusing story of marvellous adventures and fairy intervention. Charlemagne is now in his old age. Huon, treacherously attacked by Charlot, the emperor's son, kills the latter, not knowing who his assailant is. After an ordeal by battle in which Huon is successful, he is nevertheless condemned to death by the emperor, but is reprieved on condition that he will go to the court of Gaudisse, emir of Babylon, bring back his beard and four of his teeth, and kiss Esclarmonde his daughter. By the help of the fairy king Oberon Huon performs all these tasks. The work was translated into English by Lord Berners and printed by Wynkyn de Worde in 1534. Huon's adventure is the theme of Gluck's opera *Oberon*; and it provided Shakespeare with the fairy king of *A Midsummer Night's Dream*.

Huon de Rotelande, a 12th-century Anglo-Norman poet, author of *Ipomedon* (q.v.), also of *Protesilaus*, another metrical romance, whose subject is derived ultimately from Greek sources.

Huon le Roi (13th c.), author of the verse tale *Le Vair Palefroi* (q.v.). The same or another Huon le Roi also wrote poems on religious themes (lives of saints, and miracles).

Huret, JULES (1864–1915), a journalist who is remembered by *L'Évolution littéraire*, an *Enquête sur le déclin du naturalisme et l'avenir du symbolisme naissant* (see *Naturalisme*; *Symbolisme*) which he conducted in 1890 by means of interviews and correspondence with representative authors. The results, published in 1891 in *L'Écho de Paris*, a daily paper, and afterwards in book form, are an interesting reflection of change in the contemporary literary scene.

Huron, Le. The early French settlers in Canada gave the name 'Huron' (a derivative from *huré* = rough-headed, bristled, uncouth) to tribes of Iroquois Indians found in the regions round Toronto (the *Wyandot* Indians, in American and English parlance, who later settled in Ohio). In 18th-century France 'le Huron' became a typical expression for 'le bon sauvage'—the uncouth but innately noble being who comes to Europe from the wilds and is amazed by the paradoxes of so-called civilization (cf. Voltaire's *L'Ingénu*, and see also *Lahontan*).

Husson, JULES, see *Champfleury.*

Huysmans, JORIS-KARL (1848–1907), novel-

ist, of Dutch descent, was born, educated, lived mainly, and died in Paris (from cancer, after months of suffering). For thirty years, till 1898, he combined his writing with employment in the Direction de la Sûreté Générale (see *Sûreté*). His first publication was *Le Drageoir aux épices* (1874), prose poems and short sketches. For some years thereafter his output, more usually tales than full-length novels, was typical of *le naturalisme* (q.v.) at its dingiest. It included *Marthe, histoire d'une fille* (1876), *Les Sœurs Vatard* (1879, drawn from two sisters employed in a book-binding business which he inherited), *Croquis parisiens* (1880), *En ménage* (1881), *A vau l'eau* (1882, q.v.), *En rade* (1887); also *Sac au dos*, the tale he wrote for *Les Soirées de Médan* (1880, q.v.), and a novel *A rebours* (1884, q.v.), frequently cited as the supreme expression of *l'esprit décadent* (q.v.).

A later series of novels, largely autobiographical, follows the spiritual progress of a personage Durtal (very much Huysmans himself), who arrives at Roman Catholicism by the perverse route of Satanism (*Là-bas*, 1891). After a retreat in a Trappist monastery (*En route*, 1895) he goes to live at Chartres (*La Cathédrale*, 1898. This is in effect an elaborate guide to the cathedral of Chartres, with excursions into ecclesiastical symbolism, church architecture in France, and hagiography). In the last volume (*L'Oblat*, 1903) Durtal is an oblate in a monastery. (Huysmans was himself an oblate in the Benedictine Abbey of Ligugé, near Poitiers, from 1899 to 1901.)

Huysmans also wrote art criticism, e.g. *L'Art moderne* (1883), *Certains* (1889)—some of the earliest appreciations of the Impressionists—and *Trois primitifs* (1904), essays on the work of the painter Matthias Grünewald.

His books, whether novels or criticism, were written in an elaborate, mannered style, full of neologisms and syntactical contortions.

Hydropathes, Les, one of three literary societies frequently mentioned in descriptions of the beginnings of the Symbolist Movement (see *Symbolisme*). The other two were *les Hirsutes* and *les Zutistes*. They flourished about 1880 and consisted of young authors and artists who met in cafés to read their works and discuss new aims in literature, especially poetry, and art. Paul Bourget, Moréas, Maupassant, the not-so-young François Coppée (qq.v.) could be seen among the *Hydropathes*. Fewer well-known names were associated with the other two. Charles Cros (q.v.) presided over the *Zutistes*, the most short-lived of the three.

Hylas, the champion of inconstancy in Honoré d'Urfé's *L'Astrée* (q.v.).

Hymne à l'Être Suprême, a famous Revolutionary hymn, with words by M.-J. Chénier and music by Gossec (qq.v. and see *Être Suprême, L'*).

I

Iambes. André Chénier and Auguste Barbier (qq.v.) both called their satirical verse *Iambes* (though it was not in iambics) in allusion to the classical Latin satirists who always used this measure.

Ibrahim ou l'illustre Bassa (1641), a long novel (set in Constantinople) by Mlle de Scudéry (q.v.), of interest nowadays for the preface by her brother Georges de Scudéry. This early instance of Reflections on the Art of the Novel emphasizes, among other points, the importance of framework, a main plot with strictly subsidiary episodes; of confining the action within definite temporal limits, beyond which the method of indirect narration should be preferred; of being sparing with coincidences and marvels ('My Heros', says the 17th-century translator, 'is not oppressed with such a prodigious quantity of accidents'); and of considering deeds in terms of motives.

Idéologues, the term for a group of thinkers and men of letters, disciples of Condillac, such as Condorcet, Volney, Cabanis, during the revolutionary and subsequent period, who professed to establish a science of psychology (even seeking its basis in physiology) and who held the doctrine of the perfectibility of the human race. They incidentally judged literary works by the impression that these produced on the reason, sensibility, or imagination, regardless of whether they conformed to the classical rules. The philosophy of the *idéologues* was fully set forth by Destutt de Tracy (1754-1836) in his *Éléments d'Idéologie* (1801-5).

The doctrines of the 18th-century thinkers were to some extent continued, under the Restoration, by a group of Republicans, political and philosophical theorists who believed that civil liberty and individual happiness must rest on political liberty.

Igitur ou la Folie d'Elbehnon, an unfinished prose tale (published 1925) by Mallarmé (q.v.).

Iéna (Jena), in central Germany, near Weimar, scene (14 October 1806) of one of Napoleon's signal victories over the Prussians during his campaign against the Fourth Coalition (q.v.).

Île Bourbon, the name of Reunion Island (Île de la réunion) until the Revolution and again between 1815 and 1848.

Île-de-France, one of the most ancient provinces of France, so named from the 14th century onwards, apparently because in shape it resembled an island formed by the rivers Seine, Marne, Ourcq, Aisne, and Oise. Except for a brief period at the end of the 10th century, it was always owned by the crown; and Paris was its centre. When, in 1790, France was divided into *départements* (q.v.) the following were carved out of the Île-de-France: the whole department of the Seine, the greater part of the departments of Seine-et-Oise, Seine-et-Marne, Oise, and Aisne, and a part of Somme. The name Île-de-France is still constantly used (cf. 'Home Counties' for the region round London): there are poets of the Île-de-France, or novelists of the Île-de-France; pictorial maps of the Île-de-France are issued for sightseers; and so on. (See also *French Language*, para. 3.)

Île de France, the name for Mauritius until this became a British possession in 1810. It was the setting of Bernardin de Saint-Pierre's *Paul et Virginie*.

Île des pingouins, L' (1908), a satirical novel by Anatole France. Through the agency of an early Christian missionary an Arctic-island colony of penguins, metamorphosed into human beings, is transported, still in a state of primeval innocence, to the coast of Brittany. The centuries pass, and the penguin-humans evolve into a modern, progressive people, who accept revolutions, war, racial and industrial hatred, in the name of civilization. The book contains an ironic description of the Dreyfus (q.v.) case.

Il faut qu'une porte soit ouverte ou fermée, a *proverbe* (prose) by Alfred de Musset, first published (1845) in the *Revue des Deux Mondes* and produced at the Comédie-Française in April 1848. It was included in *Comédies et proverbes* (q.v., the 1853 edition).

This is a witty, fencing dialogue, between a *comte* and a *marquise*, in which, as usual in Musset's comedies, deep emotion is seldom expressed, though easy to sense. At intervals one or other of the speakers opens the door to leave the room in disgust. In the end the two admit their love for each other and leave together.

Illuminations, Les (first published, incomplete, 1886), a collection of prose poems by Rimbaud (q.v.).

Illuminés, Les (1852), by Gérard de Nerval (q.v.).

Illuminisme, an occult philosophy based on the Cabale (q.v.) and akin to theosophy and the mystical doctrines of Swedenborg (q.v.). It became known in France in the late 18th century, largely through the writings of Louis-Claude de Saint-Martin (q.v.), and influenced such later writers as Joseph de Maistre, Ballanche, and Balzac (qq.v.). The *illuministes* considered that man, himself an embodiment of God's thought, had been placed by God in a dark world of symbols. When he had learnt to interpret these by developing his latent faculties, or by occult means, he would become an *illuministe*, one with God's radiance and the universal soul. He would then understand, and himself be able to practise, the mysteries of divine creation.

Illusion comique, L', a comedy by Corneille, produced in 1636.

In this singular play the author presents a father who having, years before, by harsh treatment driven his son, Clindor, from home, is now filled with remorse and, anxious to discover the son's fate, consults a magician. The latter shows him a vision of his son employed as the agent of Matamore (a ridiculous cowardly braggart) and engaged in a love intrigue in which he wins Isabelle from Matamore and another rival; then a second vision in which Clindor and Isabelle, in another adventure, both lose their lives. The father is filled with despair, until the vision proceeds to reveal that Clindor and Isabelle are now members of a company of actors, who are seen dividing up the takings after performing the tragedy in which the pair are supposed to have met their death. The play ends with an eloquent defence of the actor's profession, and is of interest to students of French drama as immediately preceding the appearance of *Le Cid*.

Illusions perdues (1837–43), a novel (in three closely-connected tales) by Balzac. It is in the 'Scènes de la vie de province' of his *Comédie humaine* (q.v.). Lucien Chardon, a young poet of beauty, charm, and intelligence, takes his mother's name of de Rubempré and leaves Angoulême to conquer fame in Paris. He finds a corrupt literary world, where advancement depends on money and a journalist must be prepared to deride genius one day, puff filth the next, and climb to success over the reputation of his best friend. (The descriptions of literary circles are good.) Lucien succumbs to the city's evil influence and brings destitution on his family. On the point of suicide he encounters the abbé Carlos Herrera (the criminal Vautrin in disguise) who promises him wealth and success. His further adventures are told in *Splendeurs et misères des courtisanes* (q.v. and see *Vautrin*).

Illustrations de Gaule, see *Lemaire de Belges.*

Illustre Gaudissart, L' (1834), one of the 'Scènes de la vie de province' in Balzac's *Comédie humaine* (q.v.). Gaudissart, the hero, is the archetypal commercial traveller, vulgar, bouncing, astute, good-natured, able to exercise all his talents for the profit of whatever line of goods he is running. He reappears in *Splendeurs et misères des courtisanes*, *Le Cousin Pons*, *César Birotteau* (qq.v.), &c.

Illustre Théâtre, L', the dramatic company founded by Molière (q.v.) in conjunction with the Béjart family in 1643.

Il ne faut jurer de rien, a *proverbe* by Alfred de Musset, first published (1836) in the *Revue des Deux Mondes*, then included in the first (1840) edition of *Comédies et proverbes* (q.v.). It was produced at the Comédie-Française in June 1848.

The hero, Valentin, swears that women are faithless. He wagers that he can prove his words and that Cécile, whom his uncle wishes him to marry, will be a coquette like the rest. His experiment fails, for her innocence is incorruptible.

Il pleut, il pleut, bergère (1780), a *chanson* by Fabre d'Églantine (q.v.), very popular in its day. Its first line is still quoted frequently. The first stanza runs—

> Il pleut, il pleut, bergère,
> Presse tes blancs moutons:
> Allons sous ma chaumière,
> Bergère, vite, allons.
> J'entends sur le feuillage
> L'eau qui tombe à grand bruit:
> Voici, voici l'orage
> Voici l'éclair qui luit.

Image du Monde, an encyclopaedic verse treatise written in 1247 by a cleric of Metz probably named Gossouin (often referred to as Gautier de Metz).

Images d'Épinal. Épinal, a town in the Vosges, was famous from the mid-18th century for *images*, sheets of little coloured pictures, a development from the woodcuts in almanacs and the early volumes of the *Bibliothèque bleue* (q.v.). They illustrated legends, Bible stories, historical and contemporary events, or life in foreign lands. They were hawked and sold throughout the country (and are now collectors' rarities). The best were made by the family of Pellerin (who figure in the novel *L'Imagier d'Épinal* by Lucien Descaves, q.v.). From about 1850 sets were issued specially for children.

Imitation de Jésus-Christ. The most famous of the many 17th-century prose

translations of Thomas à Kempis's *Imitation of Christ* was that of Le Maître de Saci (q.v.) in 1662. It is still well known. There were also verse renderings, the best known being Corneille's, in 1651, and one by Desmarets de Saint-Sorlin (qq.v.) in 1654.

Imitation de Notre-Dame la Lune, L' (1881), by Jules Laforgue (q.v.).

Immoraliste, L' (1902), a *récit* by André Gide (q.v.).

Immortels, Les, a term often applied to the members of the *Académie française* (q.v.), possibly from the fact that a crown of laurel with the words 'A l'immortalité' was engraved on the seal originally used for countersigning the *Académie*'s documents. Alphonse Daudet's novel *Les Immortels* was a bitter satire on Academic circles.

Importants, Les, the name given to a group of eminent personages including the duc de Beaufort, Mme de Chevreuse, &c., who at the beginning of the reign of Louis XIV conspired against Mazarin.

Imposteur, L', see *Tartuffe*.

Impressionnisme, a movement in art which was more or less contemporary and had many affinities with *Symbolisme* (q.v.) in literature.

At the *Salon des refusés* of 1863 (so called because the works exhibited had been refused for the *Salon* proper) one of the pictures which provoked most sensation and derision was Manet's *Déjeuner sur l'herbe*. With Manet (q.v.), a number of painters who sympathized with his ideas formed a new school, and in 1874 they held a show of their own in the rooms of the photographer Nadar (q.v.). Those exhibiting included the two older painters Eugène Boudin and Henri Harpignies (qq.v.); Berthe Morisot (1831–93), Camille Pissarro (1830–1903); Cézanne, Degas, and Renoir (qq.v.); also Claude-Oscar Monet (1840–1926), whose one picture, of the sun rising over water, was called *Impression, soleil levant*. The weekly paper *Le Charivari* (q.v.) ridiculed the exhibition, calling the artists 'Impressionnistes' and their technique 'Impressionnisme'; and the names stuck.

Apart from the important differences of technique which separated their work from that of the traditional school, the Impressionists had a wholly different conception of what a painting should represent. Manet summed it up thus: 'On ne fait pas un paysage, une marine, une figure: on fait l'impression d'une heure de la journée dans un paysage, dans une marine, sur une figure' (in *Manet raconté par lui-même*, 1945).

Just as, in literature, the Symbolists were followed by various smaller groups (see *Literary Isms*), so the Impressionists were succeeded by the groups to whom in 1910, at an exhibition of their work organized by him in London, the art-critic Roger Fry gave the all-embracing title of *Post-Impressionists*. They included *Neo-Impressionists, Expressionists, Les Fauves, Les Nabis, Cubists*, &c. All expressed some form of reaction against Impressionism, possibly mainly against the Impressionist technique but often, more fundamentally, reasserting old values or proposing entirely new ones.

A feature of the sympathy between writers and artists which has developed increasingly in the 20th century is that most of these small movements were the counterpart of similar movements in literature, or vice versa (e.g. *Cubisme, Surréalisme*). Indeed, the theories underlying such movements were so often the same that at times the medium of expression—whether words (usually poetry), painting, sculpture, or even music—seemed almost to be a matter of individual choice and capacity. This atmosphere of close creative affinity is apparent time and again in the reminiscences and correspondence of 20th-century writers and artists, e.g. Apollinaire, Breton, Carco, Cocteau, Jacob, Salmon.

Zola's novel of artist life, *L'Œuvre* (q.v.), depicts the first Impressionists and their doctrines. Félix Fénéon (q.v.) was one of the earliest critics to understand and appreciate them (and he is said, also, to have been the first to use the term *Néo-Impressionnisme*). Huysmans (q.v.) was another. Both are still read and quoted. Mallarmé (q.v.) also wrote about them and had friends among them, notably Manet.

Impressions de théâtre (1888–98; 1920), collected dramatic criticism by Jules Lemaître (q.v.).

Imprimerie nationale, L', the French State Printing Office, founded 1640. It is responsible for all official government printing (cf. *H.M. Stationery Office*). But it is much more than this. From its earliest days this institution has printed editions, plain and illustrated, of French, classical, and oriental texts which are recognized masterpieces of the art of book production. Sometimes they represent State enterprise, as regards both editing and production, in the interests of learning and of art; or again the State's concern is solely with the technical side of fine book production, on behalf of private publishers. The types used are also famous, e.g. the *Grecs du roi*, for Greek work, designed and cut by the engraver Garamond (q.v.), or those designed specially to the order of Louis XIV and still used and recognizable by certain distinctive signs, or the thousands of very beautiful punches and matrices, also specially designed and cut, used in printing oriental works.

The origins of the *Imprimerie nationale* go back beyond its actual foundation. The young art of printing (introduced in Paris in 1470) was protected from early days by the French kings. François Ier, especially, when he founded the Collège de France (1530, q.v.) also encouraged the production of fine types for the setting up of Greek and Latin manuscripts, and in 1538 (1539) he created the office of Royal Printer attached to the king's household. The holders, men of great erudition such as the famous humanist Robert Estienne (q.v.), set themselves to ensure that royally sponsored printing should reach the highest possible standards of beauty as well as of scholarly accuracy. In the 17th century, again, Louis XIII, largely at Richelieu's instigation, granted privileges and exemptions which brought both printing and publishing under royal protection (cf. *Librairie*); and in 1640 he founded a State printing office to which were entrusted the printing of official acts and proceedings, the private printing for the king's household, and the printing of the great monuments of religion and literature. The royal printing house—at that date called *Imprimerie royale*—had its first quarters in the king's own palace of the Louvre. The course of history brought changes both in name and in locale, and the *Imprimerie nationale*—so called during the Revolution and again since 1870—is now situated in the rue de la Convention, in the modern industrial quarter of Javel (on the left bank of the Seine, beyond the Champ-de-Mars and the École Militaire).

Notable early productions of the *Imprimerie royale* include: *De Imitatione Christi* (1640, the first book printed there); the great collections of oriental texts now preserved at the *Bibliothèque nationale* (q.v.); the collections, known as *Le Cabinet du roi* (i.e. Louis XIV), of large engraved plates commemorating court festivals, royal triumphs, &c., and intended for presentation to foreign royalties or ambassadors. Buffon's *Histoire naturelle* (1749) was an outstanding production of the 18th century.

Impromptu de Paris, L' (1937), a one-act prose comedy by Giraudoux (q.v.) modelled on Molière's *L'Impromptu de Versailles* (see the following). The scene is the stage of the actor-producer Jouvet's (q.v.) theatre l'Athénée. The company are preparing to rehearse when an intruder is spotted who explains that he is a government representative seeking worthy objects for the disposal of surplus funds. A lively, much-interrupted series of questions and answers serves as a vehicle for the expression of Giraudoux's views on the art and objects of the drama.

Impromptu de Versailles, L', a one-act prose comedy by Molière, produced in 1663, soon withdrawn, and not published until after Molière's death.

A dramatist named Boursault (q.v.), believing himself to have been ridiculed by Molière in the character of Lysidas in the *Critique de l'École des femmes* (q.v.), had retorted in a play, *Le Portrait du peintre*. The king allowed Molière to defend himself in a comedy to be performed at court. Molière here presents himself and his company rehearsing a play for performance before the king; in the course of this he ridicules Boursault, mimics the acting of various players of the Hôtel de Bourgogne, and scoffs at pedants, prudes, and the *précieuses* of the Hôtel de Rambouillet; and the mock rehearsal is of interest and importance in itself as showing Molière's methods behind the scenes.

L'Impromptu de Versailles provoked various rejoinders, by Donneau de Visé (see *Mercure Galant*) and by a son of Montfleury (q.v.).

Impulsionnisme, see *Literary Isms*.

Incipit des poèmes français antérieurs au XVIᵉ siècle, Les, a bibliography of pre-16th-century French poems (other than *chansons de geste* and lyrics) arranged in the alphabetical order of their opening lines, by A. Långfors (1917; only vol. i published).

Inconstant, L', the brig in which Napoleon escaped from Elba to the mainland in 1815. He left Elba on 26 February and landed near Antibes on 1 March.

Incorruptible, L', see *Robespierre*.

Incroyables, a name, *c.* 1796, for the young elegants (usually reactionaries) of *Directoire* society. Their clothes and their style of hairdressing were exaggerated; and their particular affectation in speaking was to avoid pronouncing the 'r'. A favourite exclamation was 'En véité, c'est incoyable!' (cf. *Merveilleuses*; *Muscadins*.)

Indes galantes, Les (1735), an opera-ballet by Rameau (q.v.).

Indiana (1831), the first novel written by George Sand (q.v.) without a collaborator. The heroine, Indiana, a beautiful Creole, escapes from the Île Bourbon (Reunion Island) and a sadistic elderly husband to join Raymon de Ramière in France, but finds that this accomplished seducer has no further use for her. She is rescued *in extremis* by 'Sir' Brown, her cold, misunderstood, silently adoring English cousin, who suggests that they should return to the Île Bourbon to commit suicide in a picturesque spot designed by Nature for this romantic purpose. The two arrive at the island vastly improved in health and spirits after a voyage spent mainly in discussing the virtues of suicide. At the last moment 'Sir' Brown unburdens his heart to Indiana, who realizes that she loves him alone. He gathers her in his arms for the death-leap but—plans miscarry. Years afterwards the two are found living in idyllic seclusion in their log cabin, far removed from inhibiting conventions.

This farrago of romantic passion punctuated by fainting-fits, typical of the early George Sand, is written with spontaneity and complete conviction. It has racy moments and some fine descriptive passages.

Indifférence en matière de religion, Essai sur l', see *Lamennais*.

Indulgents, see *Hébertistes.*

Indy, PAUL-MARIE-THÉODORE-VINCENT D' (1851–1931), French composer of symphonies, chamber music, &c., a pupil and disciple of César Franck, and associated with the Symbolist movement (see *Symbolisme*). He did much to make Wagner known in France. He also founded the Schola Cantorum, a school of (mainly) religious music.

Inès de Castro, the daughter of a Castilian nobleman attached to the court of Alphonso IV of Portugal. Prince Pedro married her secretly and lived with her in happy seclusion. When the marriage was discovered, the king authorized the murder of Inès. Pedro on his accession (1357) took vengeance on the murderers. The story is the subject of a tragedy by Houdar de la Motte (q.v.) and, in modern times, of Montherlant's (q.v.) *La Reine morte.* It has been treated also by poets of other nationalities such as Camoens and Landor.

Infâme, L', see *Voltaire*, para. 5.

Ingénu, L', a philosophical tale by Voltaire, published in 1767.

L'Ingénu is a young man born in Canada of French parents, but brought up for twenty years among the Huron (Wyandot) tribe of Indians. He then comes to France, and is recognized as the lost nephew of an old French prior and his sister. Confronted with the conventions of society and the doctrines of the Catholic religion, his simplicity, frankness, and natural good sense produce some comical situations. By his bravery he averts an English landing in Brittany; and he falls in love with a young Breton lady, Mlle de Saint-Yves. But he is secretly denounced on account of the sympathy he shows for the Huguenots (suffering under the recent revocation of the Edict of Nantes), and is imprisoned in the Bastille, where he has for companion a kindly Jansenist priest. His searching observations on religious sectarianism end by shaking the confidence of the good old man. Mlle de Saint-Yves, who returns his love, courageously goes in person to Versailles to secure his release, and finds she can only obtain it by sacrificing her honour to a powerful minister. She is advised to comply by her confessor and her confidant, and after a cruel mental struggle does so. Her lover and the Jansenist are released, but she has been mortally stricken, and dies of grief and remorse.

The story, which contains thinly veiled allusions to several high officials of the reign of Louis XV, is both a protest against abuses of power (such as *lettres de cachet*) and an exposure of some of the absurdities of our conventions.

Ingres, JEAN-AUGUSTE-DOMINIQUE (1780–1867), a famous French historical and portrait painter, noted for the classical purity of his work and for the firm yet delicate lines which make his drawing particularly beautiful. The Louvre in Paris has a fine selection of his works and there is an interesting small collection at Montauban, his birthplace. There was much rivalry between Ingres and Delacroix (q.v.), whose conception of art was far more romantic.

Ingres is said to have fancied himself as a performer on the violin and to have set great store by compliments on his playing, hence the expression *violon d'Ingres* for a secondary occupation, or hobby.

Institut catholique de Paris, the most widely known among the Roman Catholic universities established in France after freedom of education was restored by a law of 1875. (Students at these independent institutions sit the State exams.)

Institut de France, a learned society, originally called *L'Institut national*, created by art. 298 of the 'Constitution de l'an III' (1795, the work of the *Convention nationale*). Its objects were defined as the collection of discoveries and the improvement of the arts and sciences. It replaced former literary and scientific societies (including the *Académie française* and the *Académie des inscriptions*, qq.v.) which had held Letters Patent but had been suppressed in 1793. At first this 'création grande et monstrueuse' comprised three classes—Mathematical and Physical Sciences, Moral and Political Sciences, Literature and the Fine Arts. In 1803 it was reorganized into four classes—Physical and Mathematical Sciences, French Language and Literature, Ancient History and Literature, and Fine Arts. Moral and Political Sciences were dropped. In 1805 it moved to its present quarters in the Palais Mazarin and from 1806 it was called *L'Institut de France.* It was again reorganized in 1816, the title of *académie* was restored to each class, and priority of rank followed original priority of creation as royal institutions, i.e. *Académie française* (q.v., founded 1635, the 'second class' of 1803); *Académie des inscriptions et belles-lettres* (q.v., founded 1663, the 'third class' of 1803); *Académie des sciences* (q.v., founded 1666, the 'first class' of 1803); *Académie des beaux-arts* (q.v., various sections founded by Colbert and Mazarin and amalgamated in 1795, the 'fourth class' of 1803). In 1832 the 'Sciences morales et politiques' were restored as a fifth *académie*. The five *académies* meet regularly as separate bodies and the *Institut* as a corporate body also holds joint sessions.

Institut d'études politiques, so called since 1945, when it was attached to the University of Paris; formerly the *École libre des sciences politiques*. It prepares students for the public services and the liberal professions.

Institution de la religion chrétienne, the French translation of Calvin's *Christianae religionis institutio*. The Latin text was first issued in 1536 at Basle, and a revised and enlarged edition at Strasbourg in 1539, and there were two further editions of this text. A first French translation, made by Calvin himself, appeared in 1541; a second version, containing additions dictated by Calvin, was issued in 1560.

The work was intended as a reply to writings defamatory of the new religion and as an introduction and guide to the Scriptures. In its original form it dealt with the subject-matter under six heads: (1) the Law (according to Moses), (2) the Faith (according to the New Testament), (3) Prayer, (4) the sacraments of Baptism and Communion, (5) the sacraments added by the Church, (6) Christian liberty and church discipline. Rejecting the old scholastic methods of theological argument, the author bases himself for the defence of morality and the reform of religion on the text of the Scriptures and on the character of man as a moral being. His dominant doctrine, which he derived from the writings of St. Paul, was that of predestination, by which some are ordained to eternal life, others to eternal damnation. The work refutes the contrary opinions of various Fathers, anticipates objections based on human ideas of justice, and criticizes the doctrines of the Catholic Church. It shows a passionate earnestness, and is popular in tone and free from pedantry.

Instrumentisme (*or* Instrumentation verbale), see *Literary Isms*.

Intégralisme, see *Literary Isms*.

Intendants, under the monarchy, direct representatives of the king in the provinces, instituted by Richelieu. Their importance was increased under Louis XIV. They controlled the judicial, fiscal, police, and even military administration.

Intermédiaire des chercheurs et curieux, L', a periodical (founded 1864), the French equivalent of the English *Notes and Queries* (founded 1849), devoted to the interchange of correspondence and information about matters of antiquarian interest and obscure points of scholarship (literary, historical, &c.). It finally ceased publication in 1939.

Intermezzo (1933), a comedy (3 acts, prose) by Jean Giraudoux (q.v.); a fantasy of youth in love with melancholy but finally awakening to life.

Intimé, L', a character in Racine's comedy *Les Plaideurs* (q.v.).

Intimisme, see *Literary Isms*.

Introduction à la vie dévote (1608), a famous work of devotion by St. François de Sales (q.v.).

Inutile beauté, L', the name tale of one of Maupassant's finest collections of short stories (1890).

Invalides, Hôtel des, situated in Paris, in the Faubourg Saint-Germain (left bank of the Seine), was built to the order of Louis XIV between 1670 and 1674 (for the most part) as a hospice for old and disabled soldiers. It was designed, as was also the chapel, except for the dome, by the architect Libéral Bruant (d. 1697) and is one of the finest examples of the architecture of its period. At one time its *invalides* inmates numbered about 7,000: today there are barely 200 and the building is the seat of the Military Governor of Paris. The Army Museum is also housed here. The golden dome of the chapel, visible from all parts of

Paris, is the work of Mansart (q.v.), chief architect of the Palace of Versailles. It was to this chapel that the ashes of Napoleon were brought from St. Helena in 1840 (see *Légende napoléonienne*). The tomb and a memorial chamber containing Napoleonic relics are in the crypt under the dome. During the Revolution the Hôtel des Invalides was called, variously, *Temple de l'humanité* and *Temple de Mars*.

Invitation au voyage, L', one of the best-known poems of Baudelaire's *Les Fleurs du mal* (in the 'Spleen et idéal' Section).

Iphigénie en Aulide, a tragedy by Racine, produced in 1674, based, with important alterations, on the play of Euripides.

The Greek fleet collected at Aulis for the expedition against Troy is detained by contrary winds, and an oracle has demanded as the price of its release the sacrifice of Iphigenia. The priest Calchas and Ulysses have insisted that Agamemnon shall sacrifice his daughter, and Agamemnon has reluctantly sent to Argos for her on the pretext that Achilles, to whom she is betrothed, wishes their marriage to be celebrated before the departure for Troy. But Agamemnon vacillates, torn between his love for his daughter and obedience to the gods. At one moment he tries to revoke his summons, but fails, and Iphigenia and her mother Clytemnestra arrive. Iphigenia is to be led to the altar in the belief that she is to be married there; but the true intention is revealed. Clytemnestra and Achilles are infuriated, but the gentle Iphigenia is prepared to accept her fate, and tries to deter Achilles from resisting her father's command. Agamemnon is shaken by the fierce imprecations of Clytemnestra, and although his pride is incensed by the interference of Achilles, he finally yields to his natural feelings and bids Clytemnestra and Iphigenia depart secretly from the camp. But their purpose is disclosed to Calchas by Ériphile (a character invented by Racine), a young captive of Achilles, of unknown birth, who loves him, is bitterly jealous of Iphigenia, and hopes to win Achilles through the death of his betrothed. Iphigenia is led to the altar and a struggle breaks out between Achilles with his supporters and the rest of the army. At this moment Calchas interposes and declares that the gods have now explained their

oracle to him. The victim they require is Ériphile, who is a daughter of Theseus and Helen, named at her birth Iphigenia. Ériphile rushes to the altar and takes her own life.

Ipomedon, a metrical romance of the 12th century by the Anglo-Norman poet Huon de Rotelande (q.v.). There are two English versions of the poem.

The theme is that of a young prince enamoured of a princess who will wed only the best knight in the world. Ipomedon performs the greatest knightly feats, but always conceals his identity, except to the lady herself, while ostensibly he behaves as a coward and a fool, to the lady's confusion. Ultimately his true character is revealed to all, and the lovers are united. The scene is laid in southern Italy and Sicily.

Irène (1778), by Voltaire, a tragedy (5 acts, verse) of little intrinsic merit—though the heroine's final hair-splitting with her conscience is of some interest—but memorable as the occasion of what has been called Voltaire's 'apotheosis' (see *Voltaire*, para. 4). The plot turns on the love between Irène, married against her will to Nicéphore, the tyrant Emperor of Constantinople, and Prince Alexis Comnenius of Greece, with whom Irène has grown up and whose throne Nicéphore has usurped. Alexis engineers a revolt in which Nicéphore is killed. Irène would now be free to marry Alexis, but her very joy makes her feel that her love for him had been guilty and she kills herself.

Iron Crown, The, of the Lombard kings, with which Charlemagne was crowned after his conquest of the Lombards (774), was a golden crown in which was set an iron circlet, said to have been made from nails of the Cross. The Iron Crown is now preserved at Monza.

Iron mask, Man with the, see *Masque de fer*.

Irrésolu, L' (1713), a play by Destouches (q.v.).

Isabella, the heroine of Racine's *Les Plaideurs* (q.v.).

Isabelle (1911), a *récit* by André Gide.

Isabey, JEAN-BAPTISTE (1767–1855), miniaturist and caricaturist, born at Nancy, came to Paris in 1786 and at first made his living by painting snuff-boxes and coat-buttons. His most flourishing period was during the First Empire, when he not only painted royalties and notabilities but was called upon to design official ceremonies and decorations, e.g. Napoleon's coronation and the *Légion d'honneur* (q.v.).

Isengrin, the wolf, in the *Roman de Renart* (q.v.).

Isle Sonnante, L', see *Pantagruel* (*Cinquième livre*).

Ismène, confidante of Aricie, in Racine's *Phèdre* (q.v.).

Isolement, L', by Lamartine, see *Méditations poétiques*.

Isopet, see *Marie de France*.

Italian influence on French literature, see *Foreign Influences* . . . .

Italiens, Les, the name given to a company of Italian actors (the *Gelosi*) who in the 17th century were authorized to play Italian impromptus (*commedia dell' arte*) in Paris. They gradually introduced scenes in French, parodied tragedies, and in general exceeded the limits that had been assigned to their performances. Regnard and Dufresny wrote for them. They were expelled in 1697, ostensibly for indecency, in reality for ridiculing Mme de Maintenon in a piece called *La Fausse Prude*, but returned in 1716

and were welcomed by the public. Marivaux composed for them some of his best comedies. Later in the century they were fused with the company of the Opéra-Comique (see *Foire, Théâtre de la*; and *Opéra-Comique*).

Itinéraire de Paris à Jérusalem et de Jérusalem à Paris, L' (1811, 3 vols.), by Chateaubriand (q.v.), describes his journey of 1806-7 to collect material for the setting of *Les Martyrs* (q.v.). It is in seven parts, the 'Voyages de' (1) la Grèce, (2) l'Archipel, l'Anatolie et Constantinople, (3) Rhodes, Jafa, Bethléem et la Mer morte, (4 and 5) Jérusalem, (6) l'Égypte, (7) Tunis et retour en France. Much of it is a historical reconstruction of the places visited, aided by lengthy passages of quotation from the Bible, early histories, voyages, &c., but the books devoted to Greece and the Near East contain some of Chateaubriand's finest descriptive writing. The reading he took with him was *Racine, Tasso, Virgil,* and *Homer*: he found libraries to utilize *en route*.

Itinéraire de Paris à Jérusalem par Julien, domestique de Chateaubriand, see *Julien*.

Ivain, see *Yvain*.

Ivry, near Évreux, on the Eure (Normandy), the scene of the battle in which, in 1590, Henri IV defeated the *Ligueurs* under the duc de Mayenne. It is the subject of a lay by T. B. Macaulay.

J

J'accuse, a famous open letter in defence of Dreyfus (q.v.) from the novelist Émile Zola to the President of the French Republic (published in *L'Aurore*, 13 Jan. 1898). It ended with several paragraphs denouncing the Army, each one beginning with the words 'J'accuse'.

Jacob le bibliophile, see *Lacroix, Paul*.

Jacob, MAX (1876-1944), Cubist poet (see *Cubisme* and cf. *Apollinaire, G.*), of Jewish birth, came to Paris from Quimper (Brittany) and lived for many years—with

little to live upon—among writers and artists. He was converted, dramatically, to Roman Catholicism towards 1914, and after 1921 he settled, with long absences in Paris or in foreign countries, at Saint-Benoît-sur-Loire in the shadow of the famous old Benedictine abbey. Writing, and the fervent practice of religion, occupied his time. During the 1939-45 war the Germans put him in the concentration camp at Drancy, where he died.

His works include: *Le Cornet à dés* (1918), prose poems, partly autobiographical, written between 1904 and 1918; *La Défense de Tartufe. Extase, remords visions prières poèmes et méditations d'un Juif converti* (1919); *Le Laboratoire central* (1921); *L'Homme de chair et l'homme reflet* (1924, a novel). His poetry was usually racy, punning, conversational, and ironic, shying determinedly away from deep emotion. Some of his short poems mingle the everyday and the macabre in authentic ballad fashion, e.g. 'Pour demain soir' in *Rivage* (1931); and he also wrote some delightful children's tales and verses.

Jacobins, Le Club des, the most famous political club during the Revolution, was founded at Versailles in 1789, mainly as a debating club, by a group of Deputies of the left. It was then known as the *Club Breton*, because most of its members came from Brittany. It moved to Paris with the *Assemblée constituante* (Oct. 1789) and met in the ancient convent of the Jacobin friars in the rue Saint-Honoré. [The Dominican friars in France were called 'Jacobins' because their first house in Paris was in the rue Saint-Jacques.] In 1791 the club was called *Société des amis de la constitution, séante aux Jacobins à Paris*. After the fall of the monarchy it became *Société des Jacobins, amis de la liberté et de l'égalité*.

From a body whose views were only mildly democratic in the beginning, the Jacobins became a powerful and highly organized revolutionary force. They instituted affiliated clubs throughout the country, opened their ranks to radical politicians and journalists, and admitted the public to their sittings. Robespierre became their dominating figure, and after his fall they led a harassed existence and were finally suppressed.

Jacquemart Gelée, see *Roman de Renart* (para. 4).

Jacquemont, VICTOR (1801–32), naturalist, born in Paris, spent three and a half years between 1828 and 1832 in (what was then) India on a one-man scientific expedition for the *Muséum d'histoire naturelle* (q.v.). He arrived at Pondicherry, spent some months learning Persian and Hindustani, then from Calcutta proceeded up through Kashmir and the Punjab and along the Tibetan border. He had the minimum of servants, bearers, and equipment and lived a most arduous

life, enduring—perhaps too often fighting —privations and climatic conditions which finally got the better of him. At Bombay, a few months before he was due to return home, he fell dangerously ill and died a month later of an abscess on the liver. The record of his expedition is contained in the posthumous *Voyage dans l'Inde* (3 vols., 1841, with 3 vols. of maps and plates, 1844). His letters of this period to his family and friends (2 vols. 1833, posth., and see below) give a lively, keenly-observed, critical, often humorous but never censorious picture of the English in India. (He had been in England in 1825, he spoke and wrote English, had many introductions from scientific circles in England, and was well received and made friends wherever he went.) They are, too, interesting as a revelation of the writer's charm, his gay and affectionate disposition combined with a certain thoughtful remoteness, solid common sense, and stoicism— notably in the sad last letter to his brother.

As a young man in Paris, frequenting scientific and literary society, his friends included Mérimée and Stendhal (qq.v.). Mérimée said that whenever he found himself in a tight place he asked himself what advice Jacquemont would give (Introduction to *Correspondance inédite de Victor Jacquemont . . .* , 1867). Jacquemont's *Lettres à Stendhal* and *Lettres à Jean Charpentier* (a Swiss scientist, 1786–1855) were published in 1933.

Jacquerie, the name given to a rising of the peasantry of the Île-de-France in 1358, occasioned by their sufferings in consequence of the English invasion. See *Jacques Bonhomme,* whence *Jacquerie* is derived.

Jacques Bonhomme, a name given, especially in the 14th century, to the peasantry, in a humiliating sense, suggesting serfdom.

Jacques de Lalaing, Le Livre des faits de, a prose work of the latter part of the 15th century, of unknown authorship (sometimes attributed to Chastellain or Antoine de la Sale), incorporating passages from contemporary chronicles. It is a romantic account of the feats of chivalry of an accomplished knight (according to a conception already moribund) who goes about Europe seeking adventures at tourneys.

Jacques de Lalaing was a real person, who died in the middle of the 15th century.

Jacques de Vitry (d. 1240), Bishop of Acre. Collections have been published of the edifying tales (in Latin) which he employed as *exempla* in his sermons.

Jacques le fataliste, a novel by Diderot, published posthumously in 1796. Like *Le Neveu de Rameau* it had first appeared in a German version (1792).

The work was suggested to Diderot by Sterne's *Tristram Shandy,* which it resembles in its incoherence and in the subordination of narrative to digressions. Jacques, like the author, is a fatalist, also an indefatigable talker. His conversations with his master in the course of their random travels and adventures are vividly recounted. The main but disconnected thread is the story of Jacques's disreputable love affairs, but many other anecdotes are interspersed, the most substantial of which is that of the cruel vengeance taken by Mme de la Pommeraye on her lover, the marquis des Arcis, for his infidelity. The work, so far as it has a discernible purpose, is an exposition of the doctrine of fatalism, but, for lack of the finer qualities of its model, makes as a whole rather heavy reading.

Jacques Vingtras, by Jules Vallès (q.v.), an autobiographical trilogy—*L'Enfant,* 1879; *Le Bachelier,* 1881; *L'Insurgé,* 1886.

Jadis et naguère (1885), a collection of poems by Verlaine (q.v.). His famous *Art poétique* is in this.

Jal, AUGUSTE (1795–1873), see *Dictionaries and encyclopedias,* under date 1864.

Jallez, a character in *Les Hommes de bonne volonté* (q.v.) by Jules Romains.

Jaloux, EDMOND (1878–1949), born in Marseilles, novelist, and a critic of wide reading and sympathies. His novels were usually nostalgic but sensitive recollections of a happy or an unhappy past. They include: *Le Reste est silence* (1909), an unhappy ménage observed by a child, *L'Éventail de crêpe* (1911), *Fumées dans la campagne* (1918), *La Fin d'un beau jour* (1920), set in Versailles, *La Balance faussée* (1932), &c. His criticism includes studies of English and German writers. Those of Jane Austen, Meredith, George Moore, Henry James, James Joyce, and Virginia Woolf in the collected essays *Figures étrangères* (1926) and *Au Pays du roman* (1931) are of interest. *L'Esprit des livres* (1923–31) contains essays and book reviews which he contributed weekly for many years to *Les Nouvelles littéraires.* He lived in Switzerland after 1940 and died there, unfortunately before he could complete his fine *Introduction à l'histoire de la littérature française.* Only two volumes have been published: *Des origines à la fin du moyen âge* and *Le XVIe Siècle* (both 1946).

Jammes, FRANCIS (1868–1938), poet and novelist, born at Tournay (Hautes-Pyrénées), was educated at Pau and at Bordeaux where for a short time he worked in a lawyer's office. Afterwards he lived mostly in or near Orthez, not far from Pau, but made many literary friends in Paris after the *Mercure de France* published his poems *De l'angélus de l'aube à l'angélus du soir, 1888–1897* (1898). He wrote with *naïveté* (at times, perhaps, studied) about nature, animals, and the daily encounters and events of rustic life; and for a time, *c.* 1895, he was one of the poetic group known as *Naturistes* (see *Naturisme,* which was also occasionally called *Jammisme*; and cf. *Literary Isms*). Beginning with *Clairières dans le ciel, 1902–1906* (1906) his later verse became increasingly religious in tone. He was one of a number of early 20th-century French writers whose conversion (or whose refusal to be converted) to Roman Catholicism took on the aspect of a literary event (cf. *Claudel, Gide*). He dwells on it in *Les Caprices du poète,* the 3rd volume of his interesting *Mémoires* (1922–3).

His other collections of verse include: *Le Deuil des primevères 1898–1900* (1901, very personal lyrics of love and piety); *Jean de Noarrieu* (1901, a long, pastoral epic); *Les Géorgiques chrétiennes* (1911–12, 3 series); *Le 1er et le 2e Livre des quatrains* (1923). His novel of clerical life, *Monsieur le curé d'Ozéron,* appeared in 1918, but he is more often remembered by *Le Roman du lièvre* (1903), the tale of the hare who, in heaven, sighed for the risks and excitements of his former existence; or by his tales of *jeunes filles* and their romantic agonies—*Clara d'Ellébeuse* (1899, q.v.); *Almaïde d'Étremont* (1901), *Pomme d'Anis* (1904).

Jamyn, AMADIS (1538?–85), poet of the
school of Ronsard, born at Chaource near
Troyes. He translated the last twelve books
of the Iliad, thus completing the work of
Salel (q.v.), and wrote much miscellaneous
poetry.

Janet, PAUL (1823–99), philosopher, a
disciple of Cousin and also influenced by
Maine de Biran (qq.v.). *Principes de métaphysique et de psychologie* (1897, 2 vols.) was
one of his most important works. He also
wrote a life of Cousin (*Cousin et son œuvre*,
1885).

Janin, JULES-GABRIEL (1804–74), born at
Saint-Étienne (Loire), educated at Lyons and
Paris, abandoned law studies for journalism.
He became a noted literary and (especially)
dramatic critic, a personality of mid-19th-
century literary life, solely responsible after
1835 for the weekly dramatic *feuilleton* of the
Journal des Débats. His criticism was more
often around than to the point, possibly so as
to avoid writing seriously about worthless
plays, but it was spirited, amusing, and gracefully discursive; and the selections loosely
strung together and published (1858, 6 vols.)
as *Histoire de la littérature dramatique* form
a guide to some thirty years of French
theatrical production.

Janin also published several novels, including one success, *L'Âne mort et la femme
guillotinée* (1829), in which he may have been
satirizing, or parodying, the more horrifi-
cally romantic fiction; the *Contes fantastiques
et contes littéraires* (1832), &c., and essays
(historical, travel, and miscellaneous).

He wrote a witty *Discours de réception à la
porte de l'Académie française* (1865) when his
first bid for election failed. Five years later
he was elected to Sainte-Beuve's (q.v.) chair
(see *Académie française*).

Jannequin, CLÉMENT, a famous musical
composer of the first half of the 16th century,
one of the first French composers to show
genius and originality in his work.

Janot, a character invented by the 18th-
century playwright and actor Dorvigny
(1742–1812); a grotesque ninny whose way
of getting his words muddled was called
janotisme. (Cf. *Jocrisse*.)

Janotus de Bragmardo, see *Gargantua*.

Jansénisme, see *Jansenius*.

Jansenius (CORNELIUS **Jansen**) (1585–1638),
Bishop of Ypres in Flanders (where he was
buried), the originator of the doctrine of
Jansénisme, which he drew from the works
of St. Augustine and developed in his
Augustinus (published posth. in 1640). This
doctrine approximated to Calvinism, repudiating the efficacy of the human will and
asserting predestination and the sole virtue of
divine grace as against the Pelagian doctrine
of salvation by works. It was introduced at
Port-Royal (q.v.) by du Vergier de Hauranne
(q.v.), director of the abbey from 1634. Its
strength lay in its moral austerity, which
influenced many who did not accept its
doctrines. By the end of the 17th century
this influence permeated the court, the
society, and the literature of France.
Brunetière states that of the great writers of
the period, only Molière and La Fontaine
had escaped it. Jansenism was strongly opposed by the Jesuits and condemned by
several popes, notably Innocent X in 1653
(by whom five propositions drawn from the
Augustinus were censured) and Clement XI
in his Bull *Unigenitus* (1713). Its most famous
exponent was Pascal (q.v.). Its views were defended in the *Nouvelles ecclésiastiques*, periodical pamphlets published from 1728 to 1803
and at first circulated clandestinely.

Jardin de Bérénice, Le (1891), an early
novel by Maurice Barrès (q.v.).

Jardin d'Épicure, Le (1894), dialogues
and sketches by Anatole France (q.v.).

Jardin des Plantes, the popular name for
the *Muséum d'histoire naturelle*, in Paris. In
1625 Guy de la Brosse (d. 1641), physician-
in-ordinary to Louis XIII, founded at the
king's expense a garden for the cultivation
of medicinal herbs and where lectures in
botany, natural history, pharmacy, &c.,
were given—a sign of the developing
interest of the 17th century in experimental
scientific study. From 1640 this *Jardin royal
des herbes médicinales*, later known as the
Jardin du Roi, was open to the public and
in time it became a well-loved haunt of
Parisians. During the 18th century, notably
under the curatorship of Buffon (q.v.) from
1739–88, its teaching facilities were extended
and its physical layout was both extended
and embellished (with a mound, a maze, a
miniature Swiss valley, and long, tree-lined

avenues). During the Revolution it became national property (see *Lakanal*) and received (1794) its present official title. It was still further developed, and has continued to the present day, as a centre for scientific study, with professorial chairs and with specialized museums, laboratories, and departments for observation and experiment; and at the instigation of Bernardin de Saint-Pierre (q.v.), curator from 1792, a menagerie was added (many of whose inhabitants had to be killed in 1870-1, during the Franco-Prussian war, to feed besieged Paris).

Famous scientists associated with the *Jardin des Plantes* include Cuvier, Daubenton, Geoffroy Saint-Hilaire, Jussieu, Lamarck, Lacépède (qq.v.).

Jardin des racines grecques, see *Lancelot, Claude.*

Jardin du Roi, see *Jardin des Plantes.*

Jardin sur l'Oronte, Un (1922), by Maurice Barrès (q.v.), his last novel.

Jargon, Ballades en, see *Villon.*

Jarnac, Coup de. In a duel fought in 1547 before Henri II and the French court by two young nobles, Jarnac and La Châtaigneraie, Jarnac by an unexpected blow hamstrung his opponent. The *coup de Jarnac* became proverbial for an unforeseen and decisive blow.

Jarry, ALFRED (1873–1907) is remembered chiefly by his satirical farce *Ubu Roi* (1896), in which the principal character, 'Le Père Ubu', is a repulsively grotesque creature, the embodiment of ugliness, cowardice, and avarice. It was originally conceived as a caricature of a master at the Lycée of Rennes, where Jarry and his fellow pupils played it as a puppet-show, called *Les Polonais*. Later, when Jarry was in Paris, trying to make a name with exaggerated Symbolist verse in reviews, he reworked and renamed it, and it was performed at the *Théâtre de l'Œuvre* (q.v.). Its success was one of scandal only, helped by eccentricities of production, but 'le père Ubu' nevertheless became something of a legendary character. So did Jarry. By degrees he adopted all Ubu's absurdities, a shrill squeaky voice, strange oaths and Rabelaisian distortions of words, puppet-like manners, and fantastic dress, until finally

he appears to have lost his own identity in that of the creature of his imagination.

Jarry's other works, e.g. *Les Minutes de sable, Mémorial* (1894), *César-Antéchrist* (1895), *L'Amour en visites* (1898), *L'Amour absolu* (1899), *Le Surmâle* (1902), *Ubu enchaîné* (1911), are verse and tales at times livened by arresting imagery and a dialectical wit, but more often only blasphemous and scatological. His professed desire to leave the mind more open to hallucination by emptying it of intelligence, and his 'pataphysique', or science of 'solutions imaginaires', have given him a place among the precursors of *Surréalisme* (q.v.). He lived a life of excess and dissipation and died of alcoholism.

Jaubert, L'ABBÉ PIERRE, see *Dictionaries and Encyclopedias,* under date 1773.

Jaucourt, LOUIS, CHEVALIER DE (1704–79), one of Diderot's most assiduous lieutenants in the preparation of the *Encyclopédie* (q.v.), an industrious compiler, who actually wrote a large part of the work and supervised the labours of the hack-writers employed on it. He was a Protestant, a man of wide knowledge and decent life.

Jaurès, JEAN-LÉON (1859–1914), born at Castres, near Albi (Tarn), of an ancestry more seafaring than scholarly, was educated at Castres and at the École normale supérieure (q.v.) in Paris, graduating in philosophy and passing the *concours d'agrégation* (q.v.). He then taught in the provinces, but soon gave up teaching for journalism and active political life, though he took his doctor's degree in 1891 with an important thesis *La Réalité du monde sensible.* He was elected Deputy for Albi in 1885 and thereafter was seldom out of Parliament. He was known for his fearlessness, e.g. when he agitated for a revision of the verdict in the Dreyfus (q.v.) case; also for his fervent democratic principles, which combined with his amazing oratorical gift, his honesty, charm, and faculty of inspiring confidence, to make him one of the greatest personal forces for democracy in the Europe of his day. He was assassinated in a Paris café a few days before the outbreak of the 1914–18 war. References to his influence and to the shock caused by his death can be found in *Les Hommes de bonne volonté,* by Jules Romains, *Les Thibault,* by Roger Martin du Gard, *Les Beaux Quartiers*, by Louis Aragon (see these titles), and in writings by Léon Blum and Charles Péguy (qq.v.).

Jaurès founded and edited the (at that time socialist) daily paper *L'Humanité*. He was also general editor and in great part author of the *Histoire socialiste (1789–1900)*. The four volumes on the French Revolution are solely his work (*La Constituante*, 1902; *La Législative*, 1903; *La Convention*, 1903, 2 vols.). His high conception of what socialism can mean can be gathered from a lecture he delivered in 1894 on *L'Idéalisme de l'histoire* (to be found in *Pages choisies* (1922)).

Javert, in Victor Hugo's novel *Les Misérables* (q.v.), is a police officer in whom devotion to duty has crushed all human sentiment.

Jean [Ier] le Posthume, born 1316, the posthumous son of Louis X *le Hutin*, was proclaimed king of France at birth but died five days later.

Jean II le Bon, born 1319, king of France (in succession to his father Philippe VI) from 1350 till his death in 1364. He was defeated at Poitiers in 1356 by the Black Prince and taken captive to England. He spent most of the remainder of his life, and died, in captivity. He belonged to the Valois branch of the *Capétien* (q.v.) dynasty. (See also *Marcel, Étienne*.)

Jean Barois (1913), an early novel by Roger Martin du Gard (q.v.). It brings in the Dreyfus (q.v.) case.

Jean-Christophe (1906–12), a novel—a *roman-fleuve*, q.v.—in ten vols., by Romain Rolland (q.v.). It follows the career from birth to death, in the later 19th and early 20th centuries, of Jean-Christophe Krafft, a musical genius of German birth who comes in early manhood to Paris and makes France his second country. The scene of the early volumes is his birth-place, a small Rhineland town where the local prince still holds court and patronizes the arts. Vols. 1, 2, 3—*L'Aube, Le Matin, L'Adolescent*—describe his childhood and adolescence and his emergence as a musical prodigy. He experiences the usual enthusiasms, difficulties, and growing-pains of youth, all intensified by his own turbulent nature and by a family

background of poverty and drunkenness. In vol. 4, *La Révolte*, he is on the threshold of manhood. At his widowed mother's entreaty he remains with her but chafes at the tie. He is already composing furiously but has not yet formulated his musical ideas except in so far as he begins to revolt against accepted conventions and the German mentality in music. [Passages of this volume are interesting as musical criticism.] A fracas which renders him liable to arrest is his liberation. He crosses the frontier and makes for Paris. Vols. 5, 6, 7, and part of 8, all set in Paris, follow his cultural (especially musical), emotional, and spiritual development. In vol. 5, *La Foire sur la place* (a volume frequently mentioned for its heavy indictment of the circles it describes), he makes contact with the much-vaunted cultural world of Paris. He observes life in musical, literary, artistic, and dramatic circles and is disgusted at every turn with its speciousness and corruption. The fashionable musical world accepts neither his personality nor his musical idiom, and he scorns to win success or even a living by flattery or complaisance. He retires into himself and his composition, but nearly starves to death in a bitter struggle for existence. A new, absorbing interest comes into his life in the person of Olivier Jeannin, a charming, delicate young intellectual whose sister Antoinette, now dead, he had once encountered in Germany. (Vol. 6 —*Antoinette*—tells the early life of this pair.) In vol. 7, *Dans la maison*, the close friends Jean-Christophe and Olivier have set up house together. Jean-Christophe now learns to know the true France, for Olivier shows him not only the good and bad sides of French life and thought ('les sommets de la pensée française où rêvent les esprits qui sont toute lumière') but also teaches him to understand and sympathize with the vast, struggling, kindly and uncultured mass of the people. In vol. 8, *Les Amies*, Jean-Christophe and Olivier drift apart, separated by Olivier's marriage. Fame comes at last to Jean-Christophe. He makes new emotional ties and renews old ones, perhaps to the profit of his music. In vol. 9, *Le Buisson ardent*, he experiences a period of intense emotional and spiritual stress. He is once again united to Olivier, whose marriage has come to grief. He mixes with revolutionaries and becomes involved in May Day riots, during which Olivier is wounded and he himself kills a policeman. Friends manœuvre him out of the country to Switzerland, where he learns that Olivier had died of his wounds. Dazed and half mad with grief he finds refuge with an old friend, now a doctor in a small Swiss town. His creative genius seems to have deserted him and he remains for some months more dead than alive. A fresh emotional crisis brings him agonizingly back to life. Now all his pent-up passion and unhappiness find expression in a marvellous outburst of creative energy, when his music reaches strange new heights of beauty. He realizes as never before that the creative fire is like a burning bush, now smouldering and apparently dead, but ready to leap into flame at any moment.

Vol. 10, *La Nouvelle Journée*, finds the aged genius once more in Paris. Success, friendship, and affection surround him. Though new sorrows befall him even these are bearable, for he can now look back on his long, turbulent existence and see the pattern gradually working to its close.

This novel was for long widely read and translated. It still comes up for quotation and discussion as an outstanding work of the earlier 20th century. The style is impressionistic, each of the short volumes being little more than a series of sketches strung together.

Jean d'Arras, see *Mélusine.*

Jean d'Auton (*c.* 1465–1528), of Poitou or Saintonge, historiographer to Louis XII. As a writer of verse he displays the worst faults of the *rhétoriqueurs* (q.v.). His prose *Chroniques* are comparatively meritorious; the author relates clearly what he has seen or has conscientiously inquired into, and gives many interesting details.

Jean de Bueil, see *Jouvencel.*

Jean de Journi, see *Dîme de pénitence.*

Jean de l'Espine or **du Pont-Alletz** or **Pont-Allais** (from the *pont des Halles* in Paris, near which he set up his stage), also nicknamed *Songe-creux*, a famous member of the *Enfants sans souci* (q.v.), and a very popular actor in *soties* and *moralités* in the early part of the 16th century (he played before François Ier); probably also an author (perhaps of the satirical *Contredits de Songe-*

creux). He was imprisoned in 1516 for satirizing the queen-mother in the guise of Mère-sotte. Bonaventure des Périers (q.v.) has various anecdotes about him, and Rabelais refers to him twice (as Songe-creux, I, ch. xx, and II, ch. vii).

Jean de Meung or **Meun,** JEAN CHOPINEL or CLOPINEL of Meung on the Loire (died *c.* 1305), author of the second part of the *Roman de la Rose* (q.v.). He translated into French the *De re militari* of Vegetius (under the title of *L'Art de Chevalerie*) and the *De Consolatione Philosophiae* of Boethius (the latter for King Philippe le Bel); also the Life and Letters of Abélard and Héloïse. He was also perhaps author of two poems, the *Testament maistre Jehan de Meun* and the *Codicile maistre Jehan de Meun,* in which the various classes of society are criticized. But his fame rests on his continuation of the *Roman de la Rose* (q.v.).

Jean de Paris, see *Jehan de Paris.*

Jean de Roye, see *History* (medieval period).

Jean de Vignai (14th c.), a Hospitaller of the order of St. Jacques du Haut Pas and a translator into French of many Latin works, including the *Speculum* of Vincent de Beauvais (q.v.), Vegetius's *De re militari,* itineraries of the Holy Land, the *Legenda aurea,* chronicles, &c.

Jean des Entommeures, see *Gargantua.*

Jean du Pont-Alais or **Pont-Allais,** see *Jean de l'Espine.*

Jean le Bel see *Le Bel, Jean.*

Jean le Maingre, dit Bouciquaut, Livre des faits de, a prose chronicle in four books by an unknown cleric in the first half of the 15th century, relating the story of the maréchal de France who was taken prisoner at Agincourt. The two books on the hero's governorship of Genoa (1401–9) are the most interesting and well-informed part of the work. (Cf. *History,* Medieval period.)

Jean sans Peur, born 1371, duke of Burgundy from 1404 to 1419, the period when the dissension between Burgundians and Armagnacs (q.v.) was at its height.

Jean Sbogar (1818), a novel by Charles Nodier (q.v.). From the fastnesses of his

Illyrian castle a mysterious, high-souled bandit defies cramping laws and conventions. The work was typical, on a high level, of the romantic novels of its day.

Jeanne d'Arc or **Darc,** *Joan of Arc* (1412–31), daughter of Jacques Darc, a peasant proprietor of Domremy in the Meuse valley, an illiterate girl who contributed powerfully to the liberation of France from the English in the reign of Charles VII. Early in 1429, at the age of seventeen, she heard mystic voices summoning her. Having convinced those about her of her divine mission, she joined the king and led his army to the relief of Orleans, then besieged by the English. Having driven these off, she conducted the king to his coronation at Rheims. Here her mission should have ended, but she continued with the army, showing independence of the royal commands, was captured at Compiègne by the Burgundians, and was handed over to the English. She was condemned by a French court of ecclesiastics as a heretic, and burnt by the English (30 May 1431). She was canonized in 1920. In French literature, she is the subject of Chapelain's and of Voltaire's *La Pucelle*; Michelet's *Histoire de France* has a famous study of her; Anatole France wrote her life; and in the 20th century she has inspired Péguy's *Le Mystère de la charité de Jeanne d'Arc* (a dramatic poem), Claudel's *Jeanne au bûcher* (a dramatic poem, music by Honegger), and Anouilh's *L'Alouette* (a play).

Jeanne d'Arc, Ditié en l'honneur de, see *Christine de Pisan.*

Jeannin, Pierre (1540–1623), a magistrate and diplomatist, and later controller-general of Finances, in the service of Henri IV. He wrote *Négociations*, a record of his diplomatic transactions with the Netherlands.

Jeannot et Colin, a short story by Voltaire, published in 1764.

Jeannot and Colin, village boys, are devoted friends, till Jeannot's father moves to Paris, and by speculation becomes rich; Jeannot now despises Colin. But presently ruin overtakes Jeannot's family. At the moment of their despair, Colin, who has won his way by steady industry and has remained faithful to his old friend, arrives in Paris and rescues them.

Jehan, see also *Jean.*

Jehan de Paris, a prose romance written in the last years of the 15th century by an unknown author. It purports to be translated from the Spanish, a literary fiction.

The princess of Spain is about to marry the king of England, an elderly widower, her parents having forgotten a promise given by them to the late king of France that she shall marry his son. The young king of France decides to go to Spain incognito but with imposing pomp to see the princess for himself before pressing his suit. He travels in the character of a wealthy bourgeois of Paris and falls in with the king of England who is on his way to his wedding. The magnificence of his suite and equipment and his charm and dignified bearing astonish the Spaniards, and when Jehan de Paris, as he has called himself, reveals that he is king of France, he has no difficulty in ousting his rival, who cuts throughout rather a sorry figure.

The story is told with much art, especially the growing admiration and excitement of the Spaniards as the splendour of Jehan's retinue is gradually unfolded. The theme was perhaps suggested by the historical events attending the marriage of Charles VIII to Anne of Brittany; while some features (notably certain riddles propounded on the way by Jehan to the king of England) are derived from the metrical romance *Jehan et Blonde* (q.v.).

Jehan et Blonde, a metrical *roman d'aventure* by Philippe de Beaumanoir (q.v.), written between 1270 and 1280.

Jehan is the son of a French knight. When twenty he sets out for England to seek his fortune. There he meets the comte d'Osenefort, accepts service with him, and falls in love with his daughter Blonde and she with him. Two years of innocent happiness together are interrupted by the arrival of a messenger announcing that his father is dying and summoning Jehan to France to do homage for his fief. Blonde promises to wait for him one year, and when her father grants her hand to the rich Earl of Gloucester, she obtains the postponement of the marriage to a date four months distant. The fatal day approaches and Jehan returns to England. He falls in with the Earl of Gloucester and his retinue on their way to the wedding. Blonde awaits him anxiously in the orchard.

He arrives and carries her off. They are pursued and there is an affray at Dover, in which Jehan succeeds in placing Blonde on a boat and escaping to France. Jehan marries Blonde, is made a count by the king of France, and is reconciled to Blonde's father.

There are two independent English translations of the tale: one written about 1440, the other printed by Wynkyn de Worde about 1510–15.

Jemmapes (or **Jemappes**), in Belgium, where the Revolutionary army under Dumouriez defeated the Austrians in November 1792.

Jena, see *Iéna.*

Jenni, Histoire de, ou l'Athée et le Sage, a philosophical tale by Voltaire published in 1775, of especial interest as indicating the author's later views on religion.

Jenni, a young Englishman, captured by the Spaniards at Montjuich in 1705 and in imminent danger of being burnt by the Inquisition (because the Inquisitor's mistress has fallen in love with him), is saved by Lord Peterborough's opportune capture of Barcelona. After a lively dialogue in which Jenni's father, the wise Mr. Freind, doctor of theology, convinces a bachelor of the university of Salamanca of the superiority of the Protestant over the Roman Catholic faith, we have an account of Jenni's dissipated life in London, his flight to America, and his rescue from Indians by his father. Finally comes the main element in the work, an eloquent defence of the existence of God, in the form of a dialogue between Freind and one of Jenni's atheistical companions.

Jérôme Paturot à la recherche d'une position sociale (1842), by Louis Reybaud (q.v.), a successful satire of life under the July Monarchy, is still often referred to if seldom read. The young hero returns to the prosperous but unexciting family business of selling cotton nightcaps after unsatisfactory experiences as a Romantic poet, a Saint-Simonien, a company-promoter, a journalist, &c. *Jérôme Paturot à la recherche de la meilleure des républiques* (1848), a sequel, was less successful.

Jerphanion, a character in *Les Hommes de bonne volonté* (q.v.) by Jules Romains.

Jérusalem, Conquête de, see *Antioche.*

Jésuites [JESUITS], members of the *Compagnie de Jésus*, a religious society founded by the Spaniard St. Ignatius Loyola (1491–1556) in 1534, authorized by papal bull in 1540, and bound by vows of chastity, poverty, obedience, and submission to the Holy See. Their principal activities were preaching, instruction, and hearing confessions. The original objects of the Society in the 16th century were to combat the views of the Reformation and to spread Christianity among the heathen. It became extremely powerful in France and other Catholic countries, but its political and other intrigues provoked bad feeling. In the 17th century its violent campaign against the Jansenists brought about the fall of Port-Royal (q.v.) and aroused an implacable enemy. About 1755 the bankruptcy of Père la Vallette, Superior of the Jesuits at Martinique, where he carried on a large industrial undertaking, involved his creditors in heavy losses. The suit brought by them against the Society gave the Jansenist *parlement* its opportunity. It condemned the doctrines of Loyola in 1761, closed the Society's schools in 1762, and dissolved the Society in 1764. Finally Clement XIV pronounced its suppression in 1773 and it was not re-established until 1814.

Jésus-Christ en Flandre, one of the 'Études philosophiques' of Balzac's *Comédie humaine* (q.v.).

Jeu Adam, see *Jeu de la Feuillée.*

Jeu d'Adam, see *Religious writings* (medieval period).

Jeu de la Feuillée (so named perhaps from the leafy bower under which it was performed) or *Jeu Adam*, a dramatic work by Adam de la Halle (q.v.), first performed *c.* 1262. It is a curious Aristophanic medley, in which fairies are introduced in the middle of a personal satirical realistic comedy. The author tells of his marriage, of his decision to leave his wife and return to Paris, and of his father's avarice. His friends and neighbours of Arras are presented and their defects made fun of. A physician, a monk with relics, and a lunatic are vehicles for the author's satire. Then three fairies arrive and bestow gifts, but one has been neglected and is vindictive. A Wheel of Fortune is displayed by them, with images of high personages of

Arras attached to it. The play ends in a tavern scene, where the monk is made to pay the bill.

Jeu de l'amour et du hasard, Le, a comedy by Marivaux, produced in 1730, considered by many his masterpiece.

Dorante and Silvia, who do not know one another, are, by arrangement of their parents, to be married, provided that they like each other on acquaintance. Silvia, the better to judge her destined husband, changes places with her maid. But the young man has had the same idea and has changed places with his valet. Under this double disguise, love springs up between Silvia and Dorante, and places each in an embarrassing position. At last Dorante confesses his identity to Silvia; but Silvia for her part, to test the depth of her lover's affection, maintains the imposture until Dorante, braving social prejudice and his father's expected anger, proposes marriage to the pretended servant-girl. Meanwhile a parallel complication, similarly resolved, has arisen from the falling in love of the valet and the maid in their assumed characters.

Jeu de mail, see *Mail*.

Jeu de paume, see *Paume*.

Jeu de Robin et de Marion, a dramatic pastoral by Adam de la Halle (q.v.), produced probably at Naples *c.* 1283 and subsequently at Arras. The theme is simple: a knight makes love to Marion, a shepherdess, but she is faithful to her shepherd lover Robin; an attempt to carry her off fails owing to her firmness, and the approaching marriage of the shepherd pair is celebrated in a rustic feast. The play includes a number of songs and is in fact an early form of comic opera. The characters are represented with much spirit and the play is moreover interesting for the light it throws on the peasant life of the 13th century. It is intended for a more refined audience than the *Jeu de la Feuillée* (q.v.).

Jeu de Saint Nicolas, see *Bodel*.

Jeu du garçon et de l'aveugle, see *Comedy*.

Jeu du Prince des Sots, see *Gringore*.

Jeune Captive, La, see *Chénier, André*.

Jeune Fille Violaine, La (1893), see *Claudel*.

Jeune Parque, La, a long poem by Paul Valéry (q.v.), one of his most difficult and most beautiful.

Jeunes-France, Les, the name of a group of exaggerated young Romantics of the second generation (see *Romantisme* and cf. *Bousingos*). One of their leaders for a time was Théophile Gautier (q.v.). He satirized them light-heartedly in *Les Jeunes-France, romans goguenards* (1833).

Jeune Tarentine, La, see *Chénier, André*.

Jeux floraux de Toulouse, said to have been founded in 1323 by seven troubadours of that city, who constituted themselves into a college 'du gai sçavoir' and invited all troubadours to meet in 1324 and compete, with poems on the Virgin, for the prize of a golden violet. The festival became an annual occurrence, two other prizes being added (of a silver marigold and a silver eglantine for certain categories of poems), and the institution won wide celebrity and was imitated elsewhere. A century and a half later the college and the games, which had lost some of their importance, were revived by Dame Clémence Isaure, who endowed the college with the property which it still enjoys. Du Bellay attacked this institution in the *Défense et illustration de la langue française* (q.v.). Remembered names among prizewinners include Du Bartas, Fabre d'Églantine, and Victor Hugo (qq.v.).

Jeux partis, a popular form of medieval lyric, invented by the troubadours and imitated in Northern France, in which one poet challenges another to a debate, leaving it to his adversary which side he will support. The decision was sometimes submitted to an arbitrator in an *envoi*. The subject was generally connected with courtly love (see *Amour courtois*).

A similar form, but rarer in French, was the *Tençon*, in which two poets or a poet and a fictitious character support opposite views on some subject in alternate stanzas.

Jeux rustiques et divins (1897), a collection of poems by Henri de Régnier (q.v.).

Jézabel, i.e. Jezebel the infamous wife of Ahab king of Israel, mother of Athaliah

(Racine's *Athalie*, q.v.), see 1 Kings xvi, xix; 2 Kings ix; 2 Chronicles xxii, xxiii.

Joad, the High Priest, in Racine's *Athalie* (q.v.).

Joan of Arc, see *Jeanne d'Arc.*

Joas, the child king of Judah, in Racine's *Athalie* (q.v.).

Jocaste et le chat maigre (1879), a tale by Anatole France (q.v.).

Joceaume, a character in *Pathelin* (q.v.).

Jocelyn (1835), a narrative poem by Lamartine, a later episode in the uncompleted epic begun by the fragment *La Chute d'un ange* (q.v.). It purports to be the diary of a young seminarist who flees from the Revolution to a hiding-place in the mountains. He shelters the 'boy' Laurence but trouble brews when Laurence turns out to be a girl and the two fall in love. The bishop, Jocelyn's former spiritual director at the seminary, is in prison awaiting execution. He wishes to ordain Jocelyn so that he may receive the last sacrament at his hands. Jocelyn pleads his love for Laurence but is overruled and becomes a priest. The Terror ends and with the restoration of religious liberty Jocelyn is appointed to a lonely parish. He tries to forget Laurence who has turned from her agony at being forsaken to a brilliant life of dissipation in Paris. One day Jocelyn, summoned to a death-bed at the village inn, finds Laurence. He gives her absolution and reveals his identity before she dies. Some months later he dies in an epidemic. His parishioners, who have learnt his story, bury him beside Laurence.

Certain passages of familiar narrative in this poem (e.g. descriptions of peasant life and of the country round the remote parish of Valneige) have caused Lamartine to be compared to Wordsworth.

Jockey Club, Le. This was founded in 1833, very much on the English model, as a society for the improvement of bloodstock and for organizing horse-races and regulating matters pertaining to the turf. The *Prix du Jockey Club*, founded 1836 and run yearly at Chantilly, the principal racing centre of France, is the French equivalent of the Derby. But *le Jockey Club* is also a social club, the most exclusive in France. Admission to membership is jealously safeguarded and still counts as a very high social asset. In Proust's *A la recherche du temps perdu* (q.v.) it was a sign of Swann's brilliant social position that he was a member.

Joconde, the first of the *Contes et Nouvelles* (1664) of La Fontaine, based on Ariosto. It was the occasion of a dissertation by Boileau on the talent of the author.

It is a gay licentious tale of a prince of Lombardy and his friend, who, although they are the two most handsome men on earth, have the mortification of discovering that their wives are unfaithful. They seek compensation elsewhere and are presently reconciled to their lot.

Jocrisse, syn. for a typical credulous simpleton. He was a stock character in old comedy, farces, and vaudevilles, e.g. in Molière's *Sganarelle* and *Le Désespoir de Jocrisse* by Dorvigny (1734–1812, actor and comic author; cf. *Janot*). Veuillot (q.v.) dismissed Victor Hugo contemptuously as 'Jocrisse à Patmos'.

Jodelet, JULIEN LESPY, *known as* (*c.* 1590–1660), a famous comic actor who entered Mondory's company at the Marais in 1610, and subsequently the company of the Hôtel de Bourgogne. He acted the part of Jodelet in Scarron's *Jodelet ou le maître valet* (1645) and in Molière's *Les Précieuses ridicules* (q.v.), the ancestors of a long line of comic valets. In the former comedy Jodelet is the valet of Don Juan d'Alvarade. The latter has been offered the hand of Isabelle by her father, in consequence of the latter's friendship with Don Juan's father, though Don Juan himself is not known to father or daughter. Don Juan, coming to claim his bride, sees a young man escape from Isabelle's balcony. To clear up the mystery before declaring himself, Don Juan arranges that Jodelet shall impersonate him, while he assumes the part of valet. Jodelet dismays Isabelle and her father by his ugliness, coarse manners, and (when a duel is forced on him) his poltroonery, till the situation is cleared up to everyone's satisfaction. The name Jodelet came to signify a person who provokes laughter by his absurdities.

Jodelle, ÉTIENNE (1532–73), SIEUR DE LYMODIN, born in Paris, a member of the *Pléiade* (q.v.), and a man of great and varied talents. He died in extreme poverty. He was the author of lyrics of a somewhat serious tone, but he is chiefly remembered as a pioneer of the drama. He composed as a young man a tragedy *Cléopâtre captive* (q.v.) and a comedy *Eugène* (q.v.), which were acted in 1552/3 and created a great sensation as the first French dramas of their kind. He subsequently wrote another tragedy, *Didon*, in alexandrines (*Cléopâtre* had been written, except for the choruses, partly in alexandrines partly in decasyllables); the play is based on the story as told by Virgil.

Joffre, JOSEPH-JACQUES-CÉSAIRE (1852–1931), one of the famous French generals of the 1914–18 war. In 1916 he was promoted maréchal de France (q.v.), a dignity in abeyance since 1870 and revived in his honour.

Johannot, ALFRED (1800–37), painter, engraver and book-illustrator, brother of the following.

Johannot, TONY (1803–52), painter and etcher, brother of the preceding, was noted for his delicate book-illustrations. He was born in Germany but lived and died in Paris. He frequented the Romantic *cénacles* (q.v.) and illustrated works by Romantic writers.

Joie de vivre, La (1884), one of Zola's *Rougon-Macquart* (q.v.) novels.

Joinville, JEAN, SIRE DE (1224–1317), a native of Champagne, of which province he became seneschal (an office hereditary in his family). He took part in the first crusade of Louis IX (1248–52), became an intimate friend of the saintly king, fought in the disastrous battle of Mansourah, and shared the king's captivity. After their ransom he accompanied the king to Palestine and in 1254, after an absence of six years, returned to his home. In 1270, in spite of the king's entreaty, he refused to take part in his second crusade, for the good reason that his first duty was to his children and vassals and that his absence overseas was grievously detrimental to them. He lived to see four of the successors of Louis IX on the throne. His memoirs, which he entitled *Histoire de saint Louis*, were composed and dictated by him at the request of Jeanne de Navarre, the consort of Philippe le Bel, but were not finished until

1309, four years after the death of that princess, and were dedicated to Louis le Hutin (q.v.), her son. They are principally occupied with a narrative of the king's first crusade, vivid and detailed (though the account of the military operations is not very clear) and told with an engaging simplicity and sincerity. His own brave exploits are narrated with modesty (he received five wounds and his horse fifteen at the battle of Mansourah) and he does not hesitate to say that he was often extremely frightened. There are many other human and vivid touches, and the spirit of the crusaders is well shown by the exclamation of the comte de Soissons to the author as they stood together hard pressed at the battle of Mansourah, 'Seneschaus, lessons huer cette chenaille, que, par la Coiffe Dieu! (ensi comme il juroit), encore en parlerons nous de cele journée es chambres des dames.' It is Joinville who has preserved the legend of the terror inspired by Richard Cœur de Lion, that Saracen mothers, to stop their children crying, would say 'Hush, or I'll fetch King Richard!' Among the most entertaining features of the work are the conversations Joinville relates between himself and the king, in which the king's devout exaltation contrasts with Joinville's more human piety and good sense. The memoirs also contain some interesting observations on the physical features and inhabitants of Egypt, the Nile flood, the Bedouin, the Mamelukes, &c., about which the author displays a curiosity which recalls Herodotus.

Less dry than his predecessor and compatriot Villehardouin, more moving by his qualities of heart than Froissart, Joinville is one of the pleasantest of medieval French authors.

Joly, GUY (17th c.), a magistrate, like his father, of the Paris *parlement*, attached himself to Cardinal de Retz (q.v.), and took a somewhat prominent part in the troubles of the Fronde (q.v.). He followed Retz in his exile, but later entered the service of the court. He wrote memoirs of the Fronde period and the subsequent career of Retz (q.v.) down to 1665, which are more methodical and accurate, if less well written, than those of the latter, for whose character and conduct the author shows a mixture of admiration and contempt.

Jongleurs, from L. *joculatores*, were in the Middle Ages amusers of the public, descendants of the *mimi* and *histriones* who wandered about the Roman world; the term included musicians, acrobats, jugglers, exhibitors of animals, as well as reciters of literary works. Among the poems that they recited or sang were lives of saints, *chansons de geste*, *fabliaux*, Breton lays, and other metrical romances; and they found audiences both in the halls of the nobles and in public places, especially at the shrines and churches that lay on the pilgrim routes. They also sometimes accompanied the leader of a military expedition; there is notably the case of the *jongleur* Taillefer who sang of Charlemagne and Roland at Hastings. They were sometimes retained in the permanent employment of a prince or noble, in which case they were generally known as *ménestrels* (q.v.). The *jongleur* was not always distinguished from the *trouvère* (q.v.): a *trouvère* might sing his own poems, a *jongleur* might have composed the verses that he sang; the poet Rutebeuf (q.v.), for instance, was a *jongleur*. The *jongleurs* were responsible for the traditional arrangement of the various *chansons de geste* in cycles such as that of *Garin de Monglane*.

The *jongleurs* reached the zenith of their importance in the 13th century and were much favoured by Louis IX. Their decline began in the 14th century. Their complex functions were now distributed among separate classes of artists and performers, and poets, musicians, singers, actors, acrobats, &c., came to be distinguished according to the quality of their respective talents. Authors and musicians rose in social standing, the other categories fell. See also *Puy*.

Josabeth, wife of the high priest Joad in Racine's *Athalie* (q.v.).

Josse, MONSIEUR, a character in Molière's *L'Amour médecin* (q.v.), a goldsmith, who recommends a jewelled trinket as a cure for Lucinde's melancholy. 'Vous êtes orfèvre, Monsieur Josse' is Sganarelle's reply, which has become proverbial in respect of a person suspected of giving interested counsel.

Joubert, JOSEPH (1754–1824), *pensée*-writer, noted for his devotion to literature and the fineness of his judgement. A doctor's son, born at the small town of Montignac

(Périgord), he was educated mainly at Toulouse in a Jesuit college. He had a small income and after 1778 he led an uneventful life, mainly in Paris or the country. He read, meditated, amassed a library, married late, frequented the literary *salons* when his health permitted, and was surrounded by friends who came to him for inspiration and advice. Notable among these were Chateaubriand, Fontanes (at whose urgent recommendation Napoleon appointed him a member of the Governing Body of the University in 1809; see *Université de France*, para. 2), Mme de Beaumont, and Mme Récamier (qq.v.). In 1838 Chateaubriand edited a selection from his notebooks (*Recueil des pensées*, re-edited and augmented in 1842 by Pierre de Raynal—*Pensées, Maximes, Essais et Correspondance*). Joubert is said to have cared more for perfection than for fame. He produced no sustained piece of writing but his meditations on life, literature, philosophy, ethics, education, &c., place him in the front rank of *pensée*-writers. They contain abstract criticism of the highest value, expressed in a concentrated but invariably lucid form which recalls his own complaint that he was a man tormented by 'la maudite ambition de mettre tout un livre dans une page, toute une page dans une phrase, et cette phrase dans un mot'.

Joueur, Le, a comedy in verse by Regnard, produced in 1696.

Valère is an inveterate gambler and borrows money right and left to satisfy his dominating passion. When he loses and is out of funds he is in love with Angélique, but his love gives place to indifference when he wins. Hence some amusing changes of situation. Angélique, who returns his love against her better judgement, finally revolts when she finds that he has pawned the jewelled portrait she has given him, and gives her hand to his steady-going uncle.

The light and limited treatment of this dangerous vice is characteristic of Regnard as contrasted with Molière. See also *Dufresny* and *Saurin* for other presentments of the gambler.

Jouffroy, SIMON-THÉODORE (1796–1843), spiritualist philosopher, an elevated thinker and moralist, one of the distinguished French teachers and lecturers of the first half of the 19th century. He was born in a village in the Jura, and educated first at Pontarlier and Dijon. He then proceeded to Paris, to the École normale supérieure (q.v.), where he studied philosophy and was for a time (1817–22) a pupil-teacher, and where, some years later, by which time he was also on the Faculty of the Sorbonne, he returned as *Maître des conférences*.

He attached great importance to the observation and analysis of human conduct, and held that the inadequacy of man's earthly existence was in itself a proof of the immortality of the soul. Among his most important writings are the Preface to his translation of the Scottish philosopher Dugald Stewart (*Esquisses de philosophie morale*, 1826) and his *Mélanges* and *Nouveaux Mélanges philosophiques* (1833 and 1842). He contributed to various periodicals, notably, in its early days, to *Le Globe* (q.v.).

Joufroi, a *roman d'aventure* of the first half of the 13th century, by an unknown author, recounting the knightly and amorous adventures in England and France of the comte de Poitiers at the time of Henry I of England. The story, apart from the Don Juan episodes, is based on a certain amount of historical fact, and differs from the usual type of these *romans* in that the author introduces a personal note, saying that the tale was written to please his lady. The story is straightforward, without fantastic or miraculous elements.

Jouhandeau, MARCEL (1888–   ), contemporary novelist and essayist. His novels, *récits*, and tales usually depict the inhabitants of 'Chaminadour', a country town near Limoges in which his birthplace Guéret (where his father was the butcher) is recognizable. Three main figures recur: Théophile, Juste Binche, and Monsieur Godeau—who are all (and notably the last) projections of the author himself. Other familiar characters are the Pincengrain family, especially the sisters Véronique and Éliane; and Élise is the author's wife, originally a dancer by profession (she belongs to his life in Paris where she eventually became a schoolmaster). His first novel was *La Jeunesse de Théophile* (1921). Other titles among very many are: *Les Pincengrain* (1925); *Les Térébinthes* (1926); *Monsieur Godeau intime* (1926); *Le Parricide imaginaire* (1930, about

the character Juste Binche); *Monsieur Godeau marié* (1932); *Chaminadour I* and *II* (1934; 1936); *Chroniques maritales* (1938), &c. *Essai sur moi-même* (1946), *Éloge de la volupté* (1952), *Confidences* (1954), essays, throw some light on what has been called this author's *mystique de l'enfer*, an approach to the Christian faith which finds a vivid apprehension of evil as necessary as a belief in immortality.

Jourdain, MONSIEUR, the chief character in Molière's *Le Bourgeois Gentilhomme* (q.v.).

Jourdain de Blaivies (i.e. Blaye), a medieval French romance in the form of a *chanson de geste*, of some interest because the second part of it is an imitation of the Greek romance of *Apollonius of Tyre*, which forms the basis of Shakespeare's *Pericles*.

Jourdan, JEAN-BAPTISTE, one of Napoleon's marshals (see *Maréchal de l'Empire*).

Journal de la librairie, see *Bibliographie de la France*.

Journal de Paris or *Poste du Soir, Le,* the first French daily newspaper, founded on the model of the *London Evening Post* in 1777. It recorded, besides official edicts and notices, the minor events of the capital and of society, the publication of new books, the proceedings of the law courts and of the Academies, the weather, and current prices of commodities, besides publishing anecdotes, *bons mots*, and short pieces of verse. In the early days of the Revolution its politics, though guardedly expressed, were liberal and counter-Revolutionary. It was forced to suspend publication between August and October 1792 and became moderately Republican on its reappearance, reporting the sessions of the *Assemblée* and the *Convention*. At this time Garat (q.v.) was its editor and its contributors included André Chénier and Condorcet (qq.v.). Throughout the Consulate it was the organ of the philosophers and the Jacobins, but it also reported accidents, suicides, gossip, &c. It was among the few political papers tolerated by Napoleon. Under the Restoration it remained one of the leading journals, constitutional-Royalist in complexion, but its influence was lessening. Publication ceased in 1840.

Journal de Perlet, Le, a political and literary journal founded in August 1789 (and called *Versailles et Paris* for the first few numbers) by Charles Perlet (1765–1828), a bookseller with political interests. It reported the proceedings of the *Assemblée nationale* and the *Commune de Paris* (qq.v.) and was moderate in tone and popular with the middle classes. It was suppressed by the *Directoire* in 1797.

Journal des Débats, Le, a famous daily paper founded August 1789 as *Journal des Débats et Décrets*. Its main contents were reports of discussions in the *Assemblée nationale* and the *Commune de Paris* (qq.v.), fearlessly and ironically written. In 1799 it was bought for the then large sum of 20,000 francs by the brothers Bertin (q.v.), who made it a leading journal, with the large circulation of 32,000. Its articles on literature and the drama were celebrated. It also had Stock Exchange and correspondence columns and was one of the first papers to print a daily feuilleton with reviews of new books and plays, fashion notes, advertisements, &c. At this time its regular contributors included Bonald, Chateaubriand, Geoffroy, Dussault, Feletz, Hoffmann, Nodier, Royer-Collard (qq.v.). Napoleon placed it under special censorship, appointed new editors (1807), changed its name to *Journal de l'Empire*, and finally (1811) confiscated its property, making it over to shareholders nominated by himself.

In 1814 the brothers Bertin regained possession and hastily issued a news-sheet (headed *Journal des Débats*) filled with the events of the day, the entry of the Allied Armies into Paris, the Royalist demonstrations in the streets, &c. It was then ultra-Royalist, but its politics soon became more liberal, favouring a constitutional monarchy, and in 1830 it played a leading part in the struggle for freedom of the Press which led to the July Revolution (see *Press, Development of*, para. 10). Under the July Monarchy, when it was widely read by the bourgeoisie, it was somewhat unprogressive, though its interest in new ideas was always lively. This was one of its brilliant periods. Leading historians and critics were on its staff. Jules Janin wrote the literary feuilletons as well as the dramatic criticism, while Berlioz was responsible for the music criticism. Under the Second Empire it withdrew from active political journalism. It made its policy the good of the country, irrespective of the régime, and became the most literary newspaper of its day. Practically all the great names of journalism were on its staff, among them Silvestre de Sacy, Saint-Marc Girardin, Prévost-Paradol, J.-J. Weiss (qq.v.): and as time went on Taine and Renan also wrote for it. Occasionally it published translations of English novels, by Wilkie Collins, Ouida, and Trollope amongst others. It was suppressed during the *Commune* (q.v., 1871) but soon revived and continued at a steady level of excellence until 1939. It did not reappear after the 1939–45 war.

Journal des États Généraux, see *Courrier de Provence.*

Journal des Faux-Monnayeurs, see *Faux-Monnayeurs, Les.*

Journal des Goncourt, Le, one of the famous diaries of French literature, begun in 1851 by *les frères Goncourt* (qq.v.) and continued after 1870 by Edmond, the survivor of the two. It is a mine of valuable, surprisingly modern, literary criticism, and also of literary (and artistic) information and gossip, for the authors habitually transcribed any conversation in which they had taken part. Most of the leading writers of the period 1851–95 figure in it, at times less than kindly treated. The entries (winter 1870–1) describing life in Paris during the Franco-Prussian war and the *Commune* are of particular interest, also the many thumb-nail sketches of people and events. Some parts were published before Edmond de Goncourt died in 1896. The whole, under the terms of his will, should have been published eighteen years after his death. A so-called 'definitive' edition (1935–6) in nine volumes (the first three covering the Second Empire period) was still incomplete, but publication of the work in its entirety began in 1956.

Journal des savants, Le, the first literary and scientific periodical in France, and in Europe, was founded in January 1665 by Denis de Sallo, an erudite magistrate of Paris. (The *Philosophical Transactions* of the Royal Society first appeared in London in March 1665.) It appeared weekly, recording new publications in Europe, with analyses and brief appreciations of their contents, and noting scientific discoveries and occurrences of literary interest. It was favoured by Colbert, and prospered. In 1702, having been purchased by the government, it was placed under an editorial committee of persons eminent in various branches of learning. From 1724 it was issued monthly. In 1792 its publication was interrupted and not successfully revived until 1816, substantially on its original basis. It still exists, and since 1903 has been sponsored by the *Institut de France* (q.v.).

Journal de Trévoux, originally entitled *Mémoires pour servir à l'histoire des sciences et des beaux-arts,* a literary and critical monthly, founded in 1701 by the Jesuits at Trévoux (q.v.). It was well written and well informed and it was especially directed to the defence of religion and the discredit of the doctrines of the *philosophes.* In spite of attacks by Voltaire, J.-B. Rousseau, and others, it continued (after having in 1731 been transferred to Paris) until the expulsion of the Jesuits in 1762. Thereafter it struggled on for a few years, under new direction, but its great days were over.

Journal d'un curé de campagne, Le (1936), a novel by Georges Bernanos (q.v.).

Journal d'un poète (1867), see *Vigny, Alfred de.*

Journalism. For the beginnings of journalism in France see in particular *Gazette, La*; *Journal de Paris*; *Loret*; *Nouvellistes*, and see also *Press, Development of the.*

Journal officiel, Le, founded in 1868 and still existing, replaced the *Moniteur universel* (q.v.) as the official daily medium for the publication of full proceedings in both Chambers, as well as the text of government decrees, official appointments, lists of honours, &c. (Cf. the *London Gazette.*)

Journal universel, Le, better known as *Le Moniteur de Gand,* was founded at Ghent in 1815, during the Hundred Days, by one of the brothers Bertin (cf. *Journal des Débats*). It was intended primarily as a medium for disseminating information about the government of Louis XVIII and was edited by four of his Ministers (Chateaubriand being one). The first number (14 April 1815) announced the arrival at Ghent of the Ministers of England, the Low Countries, and Russia, and published a manifesto signed by the official representatives of the Coalition (q.v.) Powers declaring Napoleon an enemy and disturber of the peace of the world. The last number appeared on 21 June, two days after Waterloo.

Journaux intimes, see *Memoirs.*

Journée du guichet, La, a memorable day (25 Sept. 1609), when la Mère Angélique de sainte Madeleine, the young abbess who reformed the convent of Port-Royal-deschamps (see *Port-Royal*), insisted that her parents, who were visiting her, should observe the rules of the cloister and remain in the convent parlour, speaking to her only through the *guichet* (a hatch, like the clerk's desk in a booking-office, with the aperture obscured by a grating and a curtain). There is a dramatic description of the occasion in vol. i of Sainte-Beuve's *Port-Royal.*

Journée du 9 thermidor, An II (27 July 1794), the day of the fall of Robespierre and the end of the Terror. (See also *Republican Calendar.*)

Journées de juin, Les, see *Republics* (B); *Ateliers nationaux.*

Journées des barricades, Les, see *Fronde*; *Ligue.*

Jouve, PIERRE-JEAN (1887–   ), born at Arras, poet and novelist, was at one time associated with the Abbaye (q.v.) Group. An interest in Freudian psychology and his conversion to Roman Catholicism (*c.* 1924) were later, much stronger influences, to be seen in the mixture of eroticism and mysticism which characterizes the bulk of his writing. The poems of *Heures* (1919) and *Tragiques* (1923) are of the earlier period. Thereafter, *Les Mystérieuses Noces* (1925), *Les Noces* (1928), *Sueur de sang*, prefaced by an essay on poetry and the unconscious (1935), and *Matière céleste* (1937) contain some of his best work. *Témoins* (1943) is a good representative collection. His poems of the war years and the Resistance (1940–4), such as *Vers majeurs* (1942), are all included in the collection *La Vierge de Paris* (1945). His novels, of less value, were all written before 1939, e.g. *Paulina 1880* (1925), *Le Monde désert* (1927).

Jouvencel, Le, a military romance written between 1461 and 1468 by Jean de Bueil (died *c.* 1478), a capable officer of Charles VII's army. It relates, disguising the names of the participants, some of the principal episodes of the last part of the Hundred Years War, describing with much interesting detail both the pitiful state of the devastated country and the conduct of military operations according to the practice of the day. The hero is no longer a feudal knight but a true professional military officer, in spite of the retention of some of the ancient terms of chivalry.

Jouvet, LOUIS (1887–1951), actor and producer, was with Copeau and his *Vieux Colombier* (q.v.) company from 1913 to 1922. He then left to set up on his own as an actor-manager, and from 1934 until he died was established at the *Théâtre de l'Athénée*. It was he who introduced Giraudoux (q.v.) to the public, and indeed largely helped to form him, as a dramatist. He also produced, with much success, the farcical comedy *Knock* (q.v.) by Jules Romains. He was particularly interesting as a producer and actor of Molière.

Jouy, JOSEPH-ÉTIENNE, self-styled DE JOUY (1764–1846), author of vaudevilles, comic operas, and a tragedy—*Tippo-Saïb*, 1813—which was set in India and made some attempt at local colouring. Part of his early life, more exciting than his recollections of it, was spent on army service in India. He also wrote popular satirical sketches of Paris and the provinces under the Empire and the Restoration—*L'Hermite de la Chaussée d'Antin* (1812–14) and *L'Hermite en province* (1824).

Joyeuse, the name given in the *chansons de geste* (q.v.) to the sword of Charlemagne.

Judicial system under the Monarchy, see *Parlement, Bailli.*

Judith (1931), a tragedy by Giraudoux (q.v.).

Juif errant, Le (1844–5), one of the best-remembered of many popular sensational novels by Eugène Sue (q.v.).

Juives, Les, see *Garnier, Robert.*

Julie, ou la Nouvelle Héloïse, see *Nouvelle Héloïse.*

Julien, the 'domestique de Chateaubriand' about whom little is known (Chateaubriand

in the *Mémoires d'outre-tombe* says that he took to drink in later life and had to be pensioned off), accompanied his master on the *Itinéraire* (q.v.) of 1806–7. He kept a *Note du voyage que j'ai fait de Paris à Jérusalem* which was of some service to Chateaubriand when he came to edit his own work. It was edited (by Édouard Champion) from the ill-spelt, ill-written manuscript and published in 1904 (*Itinéraire de Paris à Jérusalem par Julien, domestique de Chateaubriand*).

Juliette au pays des hommes (1924), a novel by Giraudoux (q.v.). The young heroine consults her diary then sets out for Paris a month before her wedding to find the other men she might have fallen in love with. She returns to her native Auvergne rid of phantoms and newly awake to the beauty of reality in the person of her patient lover. In one remembered chapter of this slight work Juliette visits the Narrator himself ('Juliette vint me voir aussi'). It is May Day. From the top of the Eiffel Tower he has been looking down upon 'les cinq mille hectares du monde où il a été le plus pensé, le plus parlé, le plus écrit', and like Renan after seeing the Acropolis (cf. *Souvenirs d'enfance et de jeunesse*) he has come home to write a *Prière* (*sur la Tour Eiffel*). He reads it to her.

Jullian, CAMILLE (1859–1933), historian of Gaul (*Histoire de la Gaule*, 1907–27; *De la Gaule à la France*, 1921, &c.). He prefaced his *Extraits des historiens français du XIXᵉ siècle* (1896) with a short but still very useful survey of the development of historical studies in France between 1800 and *c.* 1870.

Jullien, JEAN (1854–1919), a dramatist associated with the early days of the *Théâtre Libre* (q.v.), author of *L'Échéance* (1889), *Le Maître* (1890, a realistic study of avaricious peasants), *La Mer* (1891), *La Poigne* (1902).

July Revolution (29 July 1830), see *Revolutions,* IIa.

Junie, heroine of Racine's *Britannicus* (q.v.).

Junot, see *Abrantès, duc d'.*

Jurieu, PIERRE (1637–1713), Protestant pastor and theologian, famous as an adversary of Bossuet, author of *Lettres pastorales adressées aux fidèles de France* (1686–9) written from Holland after the revocation of the Edict of Nantes.

Jussieu, ANTOINE DE (1686–1758), born at Lyons, physician and naturalist. He settled in Paris after studying at Montpellier and became Professor of Botany at the *Jardin du Roi* (see *Jardin des Plantes*).

Jussieu, BERNARD DE (1699–1777), brother of the above and a still more celebrated naturalist. He made several botanical expeditions and did much to enrich and classify the collections at the *Jardin des Plantes* (q.v.) to which he was attached. He was twice in England, and the great cedar of Lebanon in the *Jardin des Plantes* is said to have been planted by him and to have sprung from a seed (or seedling) given him by Sherrard, founder of the chair of Botany in Oxford.

Jussieu, JOSEPH DE (1704–79), brother of the above, was also a botanist. He spent thirty-six years exploring in South America and discovered the *Heliotropium peruvianum*, the common heliotrope, or 'cherry-pie'.

Justine ou les malheurs de la vertu (1791), a novel by the marquis de Sade (q.v.).

Juvénal des Ursins, JEAN (1388–1473), historian, a magistrate, author of a chronicle of the reign of Charles VI, a continuation of the *Grandes Chroniques* (q.v.).

K

Kahn, GUSTAVE (1859–1936), Symbolist poet, born at Metz, contributed to, and occasionally founded, reviews and was one (but not the sole) inaugurator of the prosodic form known as *vers libre* (q.v., and see *Symbolisme*). He wrote much about *vers libre*, notably an essay which forms the preface to his collected *Premiers poèmes* (1897, comprising *Palais nomades*, 1887, *Chansons d'amant*, 1891, *Le Livre d'images*, 1897).

Karr, ALPHONSE (1808–90), novelist and journalist, wrote *Sous les tilleuls* (1822), *Le Chemin le plus court* (1836), *Geneviève* (1838), *Clotilde* (1839), &c., novels which owed their popularity to a mixture of wit and sentimentality. He had a biting wit, which he exercised in monthly pamphlets on current events (*Les Guêpes*, 1839–47, later continued as contributions to *Le Figaro* and other journals). One of the best known of his many epigrams is 'Plus ça change plus c'est la même chose' (written in Jan. 1849 apropos of revolutions). In 1855 he went to live at Nice and took to flower-farming.

Kellermann, FRANÇOIS-CHRISTOPHE, one of Napoleon's marshals (see *Maréchal de l'Empire*).

Kings of France, see p. 380.

Kléber, JEAN-BAPTISTE (1753–1800), born at Strasbourg, a stone-mason's son who was given a first-class military education by the good offices of patrons and eventually became one of the famous generals of the Revolutionary armies. Between 1792 and 1795 he covered himself with glory in the Vendée (q.v.), at Fleurus (q.v.), and with the Army of the Rhine. Later, he was with Bonaparte in Egypt, taking over command of the army when Bonaparte returned to France. He fought against the Turks in Lower Egypt, and at Heliopolis defeated their army of 80,000 men with an army only 10,000 strong. Shortly after this he was assassinated in Cairo by a fanatic Moslem.

Klingsor, TRISTAN [pseud. of Léon Leclerc] (1874–), born at La Chapelle (Oise), *Fantaisiste* poet, also art critic. His poetical works, often in a very musical *vers libre*, include: *Schéhérazade* (1903), songs and lyrics later set to music by Ravel; *Le Valet de cœur* (1908), *Humoresques* (1920), *L'Escarbille d'or* (1922), &c.

Knock, ou le Triomphe de la médecine (1923), a robustly satirical farce by Jules Romains (q.v.) which established the author's reputation as a comic dramatist. It was produced originally, and played, by Louis Jouvet (q.v.).

Dr. Knock arrives at Saint-Maurice, the small centre of a backward mountain district, to take over the practice of Dr. Parpalaid. But, he finds, there are no patients. The inhabitants are too healthy, or too ignorant, to call upon the services of a doctor. He sets to work to change the

KINGS OF FRANCE FROM THE CAROLINGIAN DYNASTY ONWARDS

[For particulars of each king see under separate headings. See also *Bourbon*; *Capétiens*; *Carolingiens*; *Orléans*; *Valois*. For earlier rulers see *Clovis I*^{er}; *Maire du Palais*; *Mérovingiens*; *Pharamond*.]

THE CAROLINGIAN DYNASTY	Born	Reigned	Died
Pépin le Bref	714	751–768	768
Charlemagne	742		814
[At first he shared the throne with his brother			
Carloman (b. 751, d. 771)		768–771	
then he ruled alone]		771–814	
Louis I, *le Débonnaire*	778	814–840	840
Charles II, *le Chauve*	823	840–877	877
Louis II, *le Bègue*	846	877–879	879
Louis III [with his brother Carloman]	860	879–882	882
Carloman alone	865	882–884	884
Charles *le Gros*	839	884–887	888
Eudes [an ancestor of the Capetian dynasty]	858	887–898	898
Charles III, *le Simple*	879		929
[At first he reigned in opposition to Eudes		893–898	
After the death of Eudes he reigned alone		898–922	
From 922 he was opposed by			
Robert I (brother of Eudes)	c. 865	922–923	923
in whose favour he was deposed. He killed Robert I almost immediately in battle but was again deposed, this time in favour of			
Raoul (duc de Bourgogne, son-in-law of Robert I)]	?	923–936	936
Louis IV, *d'Outre-Mer*	c. 921	936–954	954
Lothaire	941	954–986	986
Louis V, *le Fainéant*	966	986–987	987
THE CAPETIAN DYNASTY			
A. *Direct line*			
Hugues Capet	c. 938	987–996	996
Robert II, *le Pieux*	c. 970	996–1031	1031
Henri I	1005	1031–1060	1060
Philippe I	1053	1060–1108	1108
Louis VI, *le Gros*	1081	1108–1137	1137
Louis VII, *le Jeune*	1120	1137–1180	1180
Philippe II (Philippe-Auguste)	1165	1180–1223	1223
Louis VIII, *le Lion*	1187	1223–1226	1226
Louis IX (Saint Louis)	1215	1226–1270	1270
Philippe III, *le Hardi*	1245	1270–1285	1285
Philippe IV, *le Bel*	1268	1285–1314	1314
Louis X, *le Hutin*	c. 1290	1314–1316	1316
Jean I [was proclaimed king, but died, at birth]	1316		1316
Philippe V, *le Long*	1293	1316–1322	1322
Charles IV, *le Bel*	1294	1322–1328	1328
B. *Valois Branch*			
(i) *Direct Valois line*			
Philippe VI	1293	1328–1350	1350
Jean II, *le Bon*	1319	1350–1364	1364
Charles V, *le Sage*	1337	1364–1380	1380
Charles VI, *le Bien-Aimé*	1368	1380–1422	1422
Charles VII, *le Victorieux*	1403	1422–1461	1461
Louis XI	1423	1461–1483	1483
Charles VIII, *l'Affable*	1470	1483–1498	1498
(ii) *Valois-Orléans line*			
Louis XII, *le Père du peuple*	1462	1498–1515	1515
François I	1494	1515–1547	1547
Henri II	1519	1547–1559	1559
François II	1544	1559–1560	1560
Charles IX	1550	1560–1574	1574
Henri III	1551	1574–1589	1589
C. *Bourbon Branch*			
(i) *Direct Bourbon line*			
Henri IV, *le Grand*	1553	1589–1610	1610
Louis XIII, *le Juste*	1601	1610–1643	1643
Louis XIV, *le Grand*	1638	1643–1715	1715
Louis XV, *le Bien-Aimé*	1710	1715–1774	1774
Louis XVI	1754	1774–1792	1793
[The Monarchy fell on 10 Aug. 1792 and was abolished by decree of the Convention on 21 Sept., and the Republic was proclaimed, but until his death Louis was still Louis XVI for the *émigrés* and the Foreign Powers.]			
Louis XVII [never reigned, but was known as Louis XVII by the *émigrés* and the Foreign Powers]	1785	——	1795
Louis XVIII [known as Louis XVIII by his royalist supporters from 1795]	1755	1814–1824	1824
Charles X	1757	1824–1830	1836
(ii) *Bourbon-Orléans line*			
Louis-Philippe I	1773	1830–1848	1850

situation, organizes his publicity and an astute system of free consultations, and so successfully exploits the superstitious peasant mentality that he soon has the whole countryside in the throes of temperatures, colics, or nervous prostration, and only too anxious to pay to be cured.

Kock, CHARLES-PAUL DE (1794–1871), born in Paris, the prolific and immensely popular author of rollicking, risky, or more often frankly coarse, frequently sentimental, and fundamentally good-natured novels. Written with an untiring comic vigour which made up for their complete lack of style, they were also good pictures of the life and amusements of the people in Paris and the country *c.* 1825–45. They were read and enjoyed in England (by Macaulay and Elizabeth Barrett Browning among others); and at a time when Balzac and G. Sand were exciting interest in France they were more representative of contemporary French fiction for the average English reader than the works of these authors. *Georgette* (1820), *Gustave ou le mauvais sujet* (1821), *Mon voisin Raymond* (1822), *L'Amant de la lune* (1847), were favourites among numerous titles.

Kostrowitzky, WILHELM APOLLINARIS, see *Apollinaire, Guillaume.*

Kotzebue, AUGUST FRIEDRICH FERDINAND VON (1761–1819), German dramatist, born at Weimar, a disciple of Lessing, was a particularly successful author of *drames bourgeois* (q.v.). He wrote over 200 pieces— dramas, tragicomedies, and farces. Several were translated into French in 1799 in the *Collection des théâtres étrangers* and at least two were produced and played often in Paris (*Misanthropie et repentir*, 1799, and *Les Deux Frères*, 1801).

Krüdener, BARBARA JULIANA VON VIETINGHOFF, BARONESS VON (1764–1824), religious mystic, born at Riga, sometime wife of Baron von Krüdener, Russian ambassador in Berlin. In her youth she was a somewhat dissipated, inordinately vain woman, with literary pretensions. She was known in the Paris *salons*, was one of the Coppet (q.v.) circle for a time, and in 1803 published a sentimental, semi-autobiographical romance *Valérie*, which had some vogue. She became a religious mystic, welcome, with her great wealth, in various sects, and for a time acquired an influence over the Emperor Alexander I of Russia whom she accompanied to Paris in 1815. (Her claim to have inspired the Holy Alliance—see *Alliance, La Sainte*—may have had some foundation.) In later years she wandered about Germany and Russia, preaching and prophesying, often being asked to move on when her religious enthusiasms embarrassed the authorities. She died in the Crimea when about to set up a colony for repentant sinners.

Krysinska, MARIE (d. *c.* 1922), a poetess of the early Symbolist period. In the introductions to *Rythmes pittoresques* (1890) and *Intermèdes* (1904) she claimed to have been the innovator of *le vers libre* (q.v.) with verses printed in little reviews: in 1881 in *La Chronique parisienne* and in 1882 in *Le Chat noir* (e.g. 'Symphonie en gris') and *La Vie moderne.*

L

La Balue, JEAN, CARDINAL DE (1421–91), a minister of Louis XI, who was imprisoned in an iron cage from 1469 to 1480 for conspiring with Charles the Bold.

Là-bas (1891), the first of four novels by J.-K. Huysmans (q.v.) dealing with the progress from unbelief to Roman Catholicism of the chief character, Durtal. In this, probably the best known of the four, deep anxiety for faith of some sort leads Durtal to experiment with occultism and black magic.

Labé, LOUISE (*c.* 1525–65), born at Lyons, said to have gone to the wars accoutred as a soldier when sixteen, the wife of a wealthy rope-maker and sometimes in consequence referred to as 'la belle cordière', was a poetess of the school of Maurice Scève (q.v.). Her lyrics (three elegies and twenty-three sonnets) express the joys and sufferings of love with the passion and sincerity of an ode of Sappho, and a slight tincture of antiquity. Saintsbury notes their similarity in many places to the ring of Shakespeare's sonnets. She wrote also a prose *Dialogue d'Amour et de Folie.*

La Beaumelle, LAURENT ANGLIVIEL DE (1726–73), man of letters, remembered for his controversies with Voltaire.

Laberthonnière, L'ABBÉ LUCIEN (1860–1932), neo-Catholic (anti-Thomist) philosopher, a follower of Blondel (q.v.). His publications include: *Le Dogmatisme moral* (1898), *Essais de philosophie religieuse* (1903), *Le Réalisme chrétien et l'idéalisme grec* (1904). The last two were placed on the Index.

Labiche, EUGÈNE (1815–88), born in Paris, wrote non-stop farcical comedies and burlesques which were the great successes of his own day and which still entertain when revived. *Un Chapeau de paille d'Italie* and *Le Voyage de Monsieur Perrichon* (qq.v., 1851 and 1860), also *Le Misanthrope et l'Auvergnat* (1852), *L'Affaire de la rue Lourcine* (1857), *La Poudre aux yeux* (1862) are well-known titles. His *Théâtre complet* (1878–9) fills ten volumes.

La Boderie, see *Le Fèvre de la Boderie, Guy.*

La Boétie, ÉTIENNE DE (1530–63), born at Sarlat in the Dordogne, a colleague of Montaigne in the *parlement* of Bordeaux. Montaigne had a deep affection and admiration for him. La Boétie was imbued with classical literature and translated the *Oeconomicus* of Xenophon, but is chiefly remembered for his *Contr'un* or *Discours de la servitude volontaire,* an ardent youthful declamation, supported by passages from Plutarch, Xenophon, and Tacitus, against the tyranny of princes. The work was not published till 1576, after the author's death. La Boétie also wrote a *Mémoire sur l'édit de janvier,* which shows his loyalty to existing political institutions, and some sonnets, preserved by Montaigne (*Essais,* I. xxix).

La Borderie, BERTRAND DE, see under *Héroët.*

Labrunie, GÉRARD, see *Nerval, Gérard de.*

La Bruyère, JEAN DE (1645–96), born in Paris and educated for the law, was admitted

at the instance of Bossuet to the household of the prince de Condé and was charged with the education of his grandson, the duc de Bourbon. He published in 1688 his famous work, the *Caractères de Théophraste traduits du grec, avec les Caractères ou les Mœurs de ce siècle* (subsequently enlarged; final edition 1694). He was admitted to the *Académie* in 1693, a triumph for the party of the Ancients (of which his book had shown him a supporter) in the quarrel of the Ancients and the Moderns. In his later years of retirement he wrote *Dialogues sur le Quiétisme,* taking the side of Bossuet in this controversy.

His *Caractères* show him a pessimist, without much depth or originality in his philosophy, but a man of independence, sensibility, and penetration, passing judgement with sober scorn on the vanities of the men and the frivolity of the women whom he saw about him, criticizing faulty institutions, and viewing with sympathy the sufferings of the poor. The work (apart from the translation of Theophrastus) consists substantially of a series of observations on character and conduct, mingled with portraits, many of them of living people under disguised names, exemplifying the failings which he describes. These observations are grouped under headings, such as *De la cour, Des biens de fortune.* Under the heading *Des ouvrages de l'esprit* are given his opinions on literary matters, together with some appreciations of individual authors. The work is written with great art, in a terse rapid style, with the resources of a rich vocabulary, and with realistic picturesque touches which lend vividness to his portraits in their outward physical aspect. La Bruyère was a master of irony. The work was translated into English in 1699, and probably influenced the English essayists of the reign of Queen Anne.

Lac, Le, by Lamartine, see *Méditations poétiques.*

La Calprenède, GAUTHIER DE COSTES DE (1614–63), a Gascon by birth, author of tragedies and tragicomedies of some merit, *La Mort de Mithridate* (1635), *Bradamante, Jeanne d'Angleterre, Le Comte d'Essex* (later remodelled by Thomas Corneille), *La Mort des enfants d'Hérode,* &c. But he is better known for his very long pseudo-historical romances which were much admired, imitated, dramatized, and translated into English and other languages, though found intolerably tedious today. These were: *Cassandre* (10 vols., 1644–50), which has for its heroine the daughter of Darius whom Alexander the Great married; *Cléopâtre* (12 vols., 1647–56), of which the heroine is not Antony's Cleopatra, but a supposed daughter of their marriage, and one of the characters is a certain Artaban, who became proverbial for pride; *Pharamond* (12 vols., 1661–70, the last 5 vols. by a continuator), which deals with the early legendary history of France.

Lacépède, ÉTIENNE DE (1756–1825), naturalist and author who at first had some idea of devoting himself to music and composed an opera (*Omphale*). His scientific writings were to some extent modelled upon Buffon (q.v.), who got him a post at the *Jardin du Roi* and whose *Histoire naturelle* he continued. After the Revolution he held a Chair at the *Muséum d'histoire naturelle*, as the *Jardin du Roi* had become (see *Jardin des Plantes*). He turned historian late in life and also held various high official posts. One biographer says of him: 'Il ne fut jamais riche, car il pratiquait largement la bienfaisance.'

La Ceppède, JEAN DE (c. 1550–1622), man of law and poet. His *Théorèmes sur les mystères de la Rédemption* and *Seconde Partie des théorèmes spirituels sur les mystères de la descente de Jésus-Christ aux enfers* (1613–21, 2 vols.) are an interesting mixture of symbolism and a crude but vivid realism.

La Chaise, PÈRE FRANÇOIS DE (1624–1709), Jesuit priest, confessor of Louis XIV. His name survives as that of the famous cemetery (*cimetière du Père-Lachaise*) which covers a hill in the eastern part of Paris, once the site of an estate owned by the Jesuits and used as a place of rest by the order. Père de la Chaise frequently resided on the estate and interested himself (c. 1680) in its development. It was bought and converted into a municipal cemetery in 1803–4. From the heights of this cemetery Balzac's Rastignac (q.v.) surveyed the magnificent view and determined at all costs to win his fight with Paris ('A nous deux maintenant!').

La Châtre, EDME, COMTE DE (d. 1645), a courtier who took a prominent part in the political intrigues of the last years of Louis XIII and the beginning of the regency of Anne of Austria, and left memoirs with regard to these. He is, however, principally remembered for the *mot* referring to him of Ninon de Lenclos (q.v.).

La Chaussée, PIERRE-CLAUDE NIVELLE DE (1692–1754), born in Paris, dramatist. Well-to-do, gay, and dissipated, he attracted attention at the age of forty by a verse *Épître à Clio* (1731) directed against the anti-poetic doctrines of Houdar de la Motte. He was the originator in France of sentimental comedy, *comédie larmoyante* as it was called, in which the pathetic element, drawn from the realistic presentation of the difficulties and sufferings of everyday domestic life, outweighs or entirely obliterates the comic. La Chaussée's plays, written in a somewhat colourless verse, are skilfully contrived to arouse the interest of his audience, and besides appealing to the sensibilities generally have some slight edifying purpose. The author is fond of moralizing (see *Raison raisonnante*) and Piron mockingly addressed him as 'révérend père La Chaussée'. He was admitted to the *Académie* in 1736. His principal plays were: *La Fausse Antipathie* (1733), *Le Préjugé à la mode* (1735), both of them pleas in favour of conjugal love, *Mélanide* (q.v., his masterpiece, 1741), *Paméla* (an adaptation from Richardson), *L'École des mères* (1744), *La Gouvernante* (1747).

Lachelier, JULES (1832–1918), an idealist philosopher whose work continued and clarified the doctrines of Ravaisson (q.v.). His great influence on modern French philosophy was exercised more through his teaching (lectures, from 1864 to 1875, at the *École normale supérieure*, q.v.) than by written works. Of the latter, the two most important, both very short, were *Du fondement de l'induction* (1871) and *Psychologie et métaphysique* (1885, in the *Revue de métaphysique et de morale*). He left instructions that no edition of his lectures was to be published after his death.

La Chesnaie, near Dinan (Brittany) the family home of Lamennais (q.v.) where for a time (c. 1820) he formed a Christian community.

Laclos, PIERRE CHODERLOS DE (1741–1803), born at Amiens, an artillery officer, remembered as the author of the novel in letter form *Les Liaisons dangereuses* (1782). He was an affectionate husband and brother and a good officer; he aspired, it is said, to be a moralist, and pursued this end by the questionable method of depicting, with a gift for psychological analysis and vivid, dry, vigorous description, the professional seducer and his victims in the higher grades of society. The seducer, Valmont, is a well-born, cynical, and unscrupulous blackguard, whose delight in the corruption and seduction of women is proportionate to the difficulties he encounters. Many of the letters pass between himself and his accomplice Mme de Merteuil, who touches even blacker depths of villainy than he does, and relate the artifices by which he debauches two of his victims, driving one through shame and remorse to death, and the other into a nunnery. Valmont is killed in a duel with a rival. Mme de Merteuil's machinations are then discovered. She is publicly ostracized, and before long so hideously disfigured by small-pox that she would be better dead.

Lacombe, FRANÇOIS, see *Dictionaries and Encyclopedias*, under date 1766 (*Dict. du vieux langage françois*).

La Condamine, CHARLES-MARIE DE (1701–74), scientist. He was one of a mission dispatched in 1735 to measure a degree of the meridian in Ecuador, at the equator, at about the same time that Maupertuis (q.v.) was making a similar observation in Lapland. On his return in 1744 La Condamine descended the Amazon. He published a *Relation abrégée d'un voyage fait dans l'intérieur de l'Amérique méridionale* (1745).

Lacordaire, JEAN-BAPTISTE-HENRI ['Le Père Lacordaire'] (1802–61), Roman Catholic priest, was a disciple of Lamennais in his early days and helped, with Montalembert, to found *L'Avenir* (q.v.). He remained in the Church when Lamennais (q.v.) broke away. Later, he entered the Dominican Order (preaching friars) and became a brilliant orator. In his last years he was head of a famous educational college at Sorèze, near Carcassonne. His published works included collections of the funeral orations for which he was celebrated.

Lacretelle, JACQUES DE (1888–   ), novelist, born at Cormatin near Mâcon, a grandson of Lacretelle *jeune* (see the following), educated Paris and Cambridge, published his first novel *La Vie inquiète de Jean Hermelin* in

1920. It was followed by *Silbermann* (1922), a study of a young Jew whose racial precociousness is at odds with the spirit of French culture. *Les Hauts-Ponts* (1932–5), a long novel of provincial life, definitely established his reputation. It is in four parts: *Sabine* (1932), *Les Fiançailles* (1933), *Années d'espérance* (1934), *La Monnaie de plomb* (1935). The theme is the tenacious love of property. The chief character, the lonely, ambitious, avaricious Lise, half peasant, half aristocrat by birth, has one aim in life, to regain possession of the home in which she was born, the Château des Hauts-Ponts. Her father's shiftlessness had lost it, and by the end of the book she has won it back, then seen it sold again to pay her son's debts. Her life is spent almost wholly in a cottage on the estate; and her passion for the land and for nature, and the book's many scenes of country life, are described with fine poetic sensitiveness.

Other novels by this author are: *La Bonifas* (1925); *Amour nuptial* (1929) and *Le Retour de Silbermann* (1930), originally intended as one book and continuing the *Silbermann* theme, and the more recent *Le Pour et le contre* (1946). This contains pictures of literary life in Paris between 1918 and 1939.

Lacretelle, JEAN-CHARLES-DOMINIQUE DE (1766–1855), *known as* Lacretelle *jeune*, historian and publicist, younger brother of Pierre-Louis de Lacretelle (below), born at Metz, was educated at Nancy. In Paris from 1789 he reported the proceedings of the *Assemblée nationale* for the *Journal des Débats* (q.v.). After the Terror he devoted himself to literature and history and from 1812 was Professor of History at the Sorbonne. His works, straightforward, clearly presented, seldom profound, included: *Histoire de France pendant le XVIIIe siècle* (1808); *Histoire de France pendant les guerres de religion* (1814–16); also—some of the first studies of this era—*Précis historique de la Révolution française* (1801–6) and *Histoire de la Révolution française* (1821–7). His memoirs (*Testament politique et littéraire*) appeared in 1840.

Lacretelle, PIERRE-LOUIS DE (1751–1824), 'Lacretelle aîné', politician and publicist, born at Metz, elder brother of the preceding. In Paris before the Revolution he was one of a circle that included Condorcet, d'Alembert,

Buffon (qq.v.). He returned to public life under the *Directoire*. He left writings on politics, also *Mélanges de philosophie et de littérature* (1802–7). At one time, with Benjamin Constant (q.v.), he edited *La Minerve française* (q.v.).

Lacroix, PAUL ['le bibliophile Jacob'] (1807–84), remembered as bibliographer, cataloguer, and editor of (not only) scholarly texts; also as the author, in his earlier days, of wildly romantic novels and of shorter tales, e.g. *La Dame macabre, histoire fantastique du XVe siècle* (1832), *Contes du bibliophile Jacob à ses petits-enfants* (1831).

La Croix du Maine, FRANÇOIS GRUDÉ, SIEUR DE (1552–92), bibliographer, born at Le Mans, author of *La Bibliothèque française* (1584; the 1776 edition included the *Bibliothèque* of Du Verdier, q.v.) and other works. He was assassinated at Tours.

La Curne de Sainte-Palaye, JEAN-BAPTISTE DE, see *Dictionaries and encyclopedias*, under date 1756.

La Devinière, near Chinon, the small farm where Rabelais was born and spent his early years. It is now State-owned.

Ladvocat, L'ABBÉ JEAN-BAPTISTE, see *Dictionaries and encyclopedias*, under date 1752.

La Fare, CHARLES-AUGUSTE, MARQUIS DE (1644–1712), born in Languedoc, author of light epicurean verse and of memoirs. After distinguished military service and a period of fervent admiration for Mme de la Sablière, he left the army (having made an enemy of Louvois and been refused promotion) and wasted the last thirty years of his life in idleness and dissipation. He was a close friend of Chaulieu and a member of the epicurean society of the Temple (q.v.). His poems include translations from Virgil, Horace, Catullus, Tibullus, and Lucretius, and a lyrical tragedy *Penthée* on the story of Pentheus and Dionysus; they are of little importance. His well-written *Mémoires* contain some interesting portraits and criticism of his age, notably a severe judgement of Louis XIV.

La Fayette, MARIE-MADELEINE, COMTESSE DE (1634–93), *née* Pioche de la Vergne, novelist. After living in the country till 1659, she settled in Paris, having separated from her husband, and enjoyed the friendship of Madame Henriette (d. 1670), sister of Charles II of England and wife of the duc d'Orléans, brother of Louis XIV; also of Ménage, Huet, Segrais, and Mme de Sévigné. La Rochefoucauld was her intimate friend in the later years of his life (1665–80) and may have influenced her masterpiece, *La Princesse de Clèves* (q.v.). Her principal works were the short romance *La Princesse de Montpensier* (1662), the longer romances *Zaÿde* (1670 published under the name of Segrais) and *La Princesse de Clèves* (1678), and *La Comtesse de Tende* (again a short work, published posthumously in 1724). *Zaÿde*, a collection of loosely connected tales on the model of the *Grand Cyrus* but in a Spanish setting, is in the main a study of love in its less happy aspects, for instance in the ruin of the happiness of Ximenès and Bélasire by his morbid incurable jealousy of her former lover, now dead. The other three romances are studies of married life, a field hitherto unexplored by the novelist. Mlle de Mézière marries the prince de Montpensier, a political marriage; Mlle de Strozzi marries the comte de Tende, a marriage of ambition. In neither marriage is love present; both are supremely unhappy and end in tragedy. In the more famous *Princesse de Clèves* (q.v.) we have, as in Corneille's tragedies, the triumph of will and duty over passion. But the moral is melancholy, that to do one's duty does not necessarily bring happiness. With these works the authoress may be said to have inaugurated the French novel of character. She replaced the grandiloquence and incredible adventures of Mlle de Scudéry's interminable romances by proportion, simplicity, and sincerity; her style is easy and sober, without affectation or sentimentality.

Mme de La Fayette also wrote an *Histoire de Madame Henriette d'Angleterre*, her friend, published posthumously in 1720; and *Mémoires de la Cour de France* for 1688 and 1689, published in 1731. These include an account of the arrival of James II at the French court and his departure for Ireland.

La Fayette, MARIE-JOSEPH, MARQUIS DE (1757–1834), general and politician, born in Auvergne, was from early years an enthusiast for the doctrines of the *philosophes* (q.v.), for Liberty, and the rights of man. He fought in the American War of Independence, returned to France, and in 1789 was elected a Deputy to the *États Généraux*. He was prominent at the beginning of the Revolution, Commandant of the newly-created *Garde nationale* (q.v.), and the prime mover of the *Déclaration des droits de l'homme* (q.v.). As time elapsed he became a sort of buffer between the people and the royal family, yet powerless either to prevent the latter's flight or to save them from the people's vengeance. His own prestige was lost and in the end he had to flee the country. He reappeared in political life after the Restoration, but except for a period during the July Revolution (q.v.) when, once more Commandant of the *Garde nationale*, he helped to put Louis-Philippe on the throne, he was never again an important figure.

Lafcadio, the hero of André Gide's (q.v.) *Les Caves du Vatican* (cf. *Acte gratuit*).

Lafenestre, GEORGES (1837–1919), minor Parnassian poet, also art-historian and critic. His poetical collections include: *Les Espérances* (1863), *Idylles et chansons* (1873), and a later volume, on a note of reminiscent melancholy, *Images fuyantes* (1902).

Laffitte, PIERRE (1823–1903), philosopher and savant, was, like Littré, a follower of Auguste Comte (qq.v.), but more completely so, for he accepted all Comte's doctrines, even his *religion de l'humanité*. His best-known work was *Les Grands Types de l'humanité* (1875–6, 2 vols.). The Chair of 'Histoire générale des sciences' was specially created for him at the Collège de France (q.v.) in 1892.

La Flèche, see *Prytanée national de La Flèche*.

La Fontaine, JEAN DE (1621–95), poet and fabulist, was born at Château-Thierry in Champagne, where his father held a post in the administration of the *Eaux et forêts*. He received part of his education at the Maison de l'Oratoire, an Oratorian college in Paris, and contemplated entering the Church. Then he studied law, but showed a disinclination for steady work and was content to spend ten years in idleness in his native town and most of the remainder of his life as the pensioner of wealthy patrons. He appears to have been a man of weak and inconstant character, feckless and absent-minded, but

sincere, affectionate, loyal, highly impressionable, a lover of nature, of keen intelligence, power of observation, and poetic genius. Saint-Simon says he was 'pesant en conversation'. He married in 1647 and had a son, but later separated from his family. He succeeded to his father's appointment but relinquished it. He had ardent literary tastes, his admiration extending to Plato, Plutarch, the Latin poets, Marot, Voiture, Malherbe, Racan, the Italians, *Don Quixote*, and *L'Astrée*; he aptly described himself in the *Discours* in verse which he delivered when admitted to the *Académie* as 'papillon de Parnasse' (see also *Baruch*). He started as a disciple of Voiture and the society poets of the day; but in his *Fables* (q.v.), his most characteristic work, his individuality effaced all outer influences. In 1654 he published an imitation of the *Eunuchus* of Terence. In 1656 he became a pensioner of Fouquet, the wealthy minister of Louis XIV; he wrote light verses for him, the more considerable poem *Adonis*, and the pleasant comedy *Clymène*. After the minister's disgrace in 1661 he wrote his famous *Élégie aux Nymphes de Vaux*, in which he invites them to implore the king's clemency for his patron. Later he obtained other protectors, such as the duchesse de Bouillon, and from about 1672 for some twenty years enjoyed the hospitality of Mme de la Sablière, and finally of M. d'Hervart. In 1663 he wrote to his wife a series of six letters (in prose and verse) describing a journey to Limoges; this charming little work (*Le Voyage en Limousin*) was published after his death. At intervals from 1664 onwards (when he was over forty) appeared successive collections of his *Contes et nouvelles* (q.v.), imitated from, among others, Boccaccio and Ariosto. The first collection of his *Fables* (q.v.) appeared in 1668 (when he was forty-seven) and the second ten years later; the last book a year before his death. In 1669 he published the *Amours de Psyché et de Cupidon*, imitated from the fable of Cupid and Psyche in Apuleius (see *Psyché*), set in the pleasant framework of a Platonic conversation in the park of Versailles between Polyphile, Acante, Ariste, and Gélaste (who are no longer, as once, supposed to have stood for La Fontaine, Racine, Boileau, and Molière or Chapelle). In 1673 appeared his religious poem on *La Captivité de saint Malc*, a task set him by the solitaries of Port-Royal, and in 1682 a poem entitled *Quinquina* (qq.v.). His miscellaneous poems include the *Épître à Huet* (q.v., at that time Bishop of Soissons, later Bishop of Avranches) and the *Discours à Mme de La Sablière* (1687 and 1684), interesting for the light they throw on his literary art, his advocacy of the side of the Ancients in the dispute of the Ancients and the Moderns (see *Querelle des Anciens*), and (the latter) his attitude to the Cartesian view of animals. Three comedies, in the composition of which La Fontaine appears to have had some part, are included by editors in his works: *Ragotin* (1684, from an episode in Scarron's *Roman comique*), *Le Florentin* (1685), and *La Coupe enchantée* (1688). La Fontaine was admitted to the *Académie française* in 1684, after some opposition by the king. In 1692 a serious illness occasioned his religious conversion and his public disavowal of his *Contes*, the licentious character of some of which had been a matter of reproach.

La Fontaine's fame rests on his *Fables*, which, while they have been criticized from a strict ethical standpoint, are told in a familiar persuasive style and with an inimitable *naïveté* and a semi-pagan sentiment for nature which make them delightful to all readers. But the easy style is deceptive, for La Fontaine wrote very laboriously. The *Fables* were much read in England (but not translated into English until the next century), and La Fontaine was invited to London, where his admirers 'engaged to find him an honourable sustenance'.

La Fontaine et ses Fables, title of the revised form (1860) of Taine's (q.v.) doctoral thesis of 1853.

Laforgue, JULES (1860–87), one of the Symbolist poets (see *Symbolisme*), was born in Montevideo, where his father taught French. He was educated at Tarbes, in the Pyrenees, and came to Paris in 1876 to live on scanty means. In 1881 friendly influence secured for him the post of reader to the German Empress Augusta, grandmother of the Emperor Wilhelm II. For the next five years his life, mainly in Berlin, was comfortable but dull. In 1886 he married an English governess (Leah Lee) and the young couple returned to Paris to a life of poverty. Seven months later he died of tuberculosis.

Laforgue's poetic idiom heralds the Fantaisistes (q.v.) of the 20th century. He was an inaugurator of *vers libre* (q.v.), conversational, even slangy, in his choice of language. He deflated fantasy with irony, and rose abruptly (and self-consciously) from the commonplace to the poetic or philosophical. His chief works (all contained in *Œuvres complètes*, 1901–3; 1922–30) were *Les Complaintes* (1885), *L'Imitation de Notre-Dame la Lune* (1886), *Le Concile féerique* (1886); and, in prose, the *Moralités légendaires* (1887, posth.), six elaborately written, satirical versions of, or embroideries upon, old tales, e.g. *Salomé*, dialogues which parody Flaubert's *Hérodias*; also the posthumous collections *Derniers Vers* (1886–7) and *Les Fleurs de bonne volonté* (1890).

La Fosse, ANTOINE DE (*c.* 1653–1708), author of a few tragedies, of which the only one of note is *Manlius Capitolinus* (1698), based on Livy's narrative and modelled on Otway's *Venice Preserv'd* (1682).

La Fresnaye, VAUQUELIN DE, see *Vauquelin de la Fresnaye*.

Lagneau, JULES (1851–1894), a man who, like his pupil and disciple Alain (see *Chartier, É.-A.*), is remembered as a great teacher of philosophy. For the greater part of his career he taught philosophy at the Lycée Michelet, in Paris, and the works published during his lifetime were mainly reprints of addresses delivered on official occasions. *L'Existence de Dieu*, published posthumously (1925), is a version, from notes taken at the time by his pupils, of lectures he delivered in 1892–3.

La Grange, CHARLES DE (1639–92), born at Amiens, actor, a member of Molière's company from 1659. He kept a register of the plays produced, takings, &c., an invaluable document for the study of Molière and the early days of the *Théâtre Français*.

Lagrange, JOSEPH-LOUIS (1736–1813), born at Turin of French parents, mathematician and astronomer, to whom are owed important advances in the sciences that he studied. He was appointed director of the Academy of Berlin in 1766, his work having been favourably noticed by Euler. He settled in Paris from 1787, receiving a pension from Louis XVI. His principal work, *Mécanique analytique,* was published in 1788 (revised 1811).

Lagrange-Chancel, FRANÇOIS-JOSEPH DE (1677–1758), author of tragedies on Greek themes but without a shred of the Greek spirit: *Oreste et Pylade* (1697), *Méléagre* (1699), *Amasis* (1701), *Alceste* (1703), *Ino et Mélicerte* (1713), &c. He is remembered rather for his *Philippiques*, virulent satires against the regent, the duc d'Orléans.

La Halle, ADAM DE, see *Adam de la Halle.*

La Harpe, JEAN-FRANÇOIS DE (1739–1803), dramatist, journalist, and a typical critic of the dogmatic school which prevailed at the end of the 18th century; a disciple and friend of Voltaire (whom nevertheless he criticized); author of *Warwick* (1763), *Philoclète* (1783), and other indifferent tragedies, including *Mélanie* (1778), attacking the system of the cloister, based on the true incident of a girl hanging herself to avoid being forced to become a nun, a play which was never acted. La Harpe was also author of a more valuable work of literary criticism, *Lycée, ou Cours de littérature ancienne et moderne* (1799–1805), a collection of lectures given as professor of literature at the *Lycée* (q.v.). His literary correspondence, of the years 1774–91, with the Grand Duke of Russia (Paul I), published in 1804–7, has many interesting comments on literature, people, and events and is in a much livelier style than his other works.

Lahontan, LOUIS-ARMAND, BARON DE (1666–*c.* 1715), an early French traveller in Canada (he went there first as a soldier) whose *Voyages* (1703) influenced both French and English literature: for instance, in French, Chateaubriand's *Les Natchez.* They contained a *Dialogue curieux entre l'auteur et un sauvage* [a *Huron* (q.v.), or Wyandot, Indian] *de bon sens qui a voyagé*, which may have helped to make 'le Huron' an 18th-century synonym for 'le bon' or 'le noble sauvage'.

Lahor, JEAN, the name taken later by Henri Cazalis (1840–1909), a minor Parnassian poet and a friend of Mallarmé: he was also a doctor. His interests, reflected in his verse (*L'Illusion*, 1875 and 1888), lay also with oriental studies and occultism. It was he who gave the Hebrew cabbalistic name *Nabis* (prophets) to a group of young Post-Impressionist painters formed about 1888 (see *Impressionnisme*; *Nabis*).

Lai, in medieval literature a short narrative poem in octosyllabic verse, or a lyric, often on the subject of love and with a supernatural element. They may be of Breton origin, but the point is obscure. There are a dozen such *lais* by Marie de France (q.v.). Of others the author is unknown. The name is sometimes applied also to *fabliaux* (q.v.) of a more refined character, such as the *Lai d'Aristote* (q.v.). [*Lai* in the above sense must be distinguished from *Lais*, i.e. *legs*, legacy, the title of Villon's poem.]

Lai d'Aristote, Le, one of the most agreeable of the *fabliaux* (q.v.), composed by Henri d'Andeli (q.v.). The story is also found in oriental collections of tales.

Alexander the Great has conquered India but has fallen victim to the charms of an Indian maiden and wastes his days in dalliance. Aristotle reproves him and the king promises amendment. But he cannot forget the beauty of the charmer, who learns from him the cause of his melancholy and vows prompt vengeance on the crusty old grammarian. Let the king be watching at dawn on the morrow from a tower that overlooks the garden. Next day at dawn the philosopher is distracted from his books by the song of the maiden, and gradually so allured and bewitched by her skilful coquetry that he puts himself body and soul at her command. She asks only that he shall satisfy her whim and let her ride a little on his back as he crawls on all fours about the orchard. In this ridiculous posture, saddled and bridled, with the girl singing on his back, he is discovered by the king. But the philosopher wittily turns his discomfiture to account: 'Sire, see how right I was to warn you against the dangers of love. I have added example to precept.'

Lai de l'ombre, Le, a poem of the early 13th century by Jean Renart (q.v.).

A knight visits his lady and presses his suit upon her, but she repels him. During their dispute he succeeds in passing his ring on her finger. As they sit by a well-head in the court of the castle she bids him take his ring back. He says he shall then give it to her whom he loves next best. He leans over the well where the lady's image is reflected and drops the ring. 'See,' he says, 'she has taken it.' The delicate compliment wins the lady's heart.

Lais, Le (i.e. 'legs', legacy), of Villon, see *Villon*.

Laissez faire. 'Laissez faire et laissez passer' was the maxim of the *économistes* (q.v.) or physiocrats of the 18th century; it is usually attributed to Gournay (q.v.). (The phrase 'laissez faire' also occurs in a collection of *Maximes du Docteur Quesnay* published by Dupont de Nemours in the *Revue philosophique, politique et littéraire*.) It expresses the physiocrats' disapproval of interference with the liberty of industry, and of obstacles to the free movement of goods whether from province to province or from state to state.

Lakanal, JOSEPH (1762–1845) was, when the Revolution broke out, a member of the religious order of the *Doctrinaires*, or *Prêtres de la doctrine chrétienne*. When this was suppressed he voted for the *constitution civile du clergé* (q.v.), was elected a deputy to the *convention nationale* (q.v.), and in 1792 voted for the death of Louis XVI. A man passionately interested in education, he was responsible for many of the educational projects of the Revolutionary era. It was thanks largely to his recognition of its scientific importance that the *Jardin du roi* was made national property and reorganized as the *Muséum d'histoire naturelle* (more generally known as the *Jardin des plantes*, q.v.).

Lakanal's former anti-monarchical activities brought about his exile in 1816. He went to the U.S.A. and was for a time a planter in Alabama. In 1832 he returned to France.

Lakistes, Les. The English lake poets met with a deep response in France and had a strong influence on *le romantisme* (q.v. and see *Foreign Influences on French Literature*, para. 19). A. Pichot's *Voyage historique et littéraire en Angleterre et en Écosse* (1825) referred to them in detail, and Sainte-Beuve had a sympathetic study of them in his review of this book [in his *Œuvres complètes* (Pléiade edit.), i. 122].

Lalaing, Le Livre des faits de Jacques de, see *Jacques de Lalaing*.

Lally, THOMAS-ARTHUR, BARON DE TOL-[L]ENDAL, COMTE DE (1702–66), French general, born in France of Irish Jacobite descent, ended his life unjustly on the scaffold. A brilliant soldier, he had been promoted brigadier on the field of Fontenoy (1745) by Louis XV, the next year was in Scotland as aide-de-camp to the Young Pretender at the battle of Falkirk, and again distinguished himself in battle in the Low Countries in 1748. When war broke out between France and England in 1755 he was sent to India in command of an expedition against the English. At first things went well but difficulties arose, of his own and other people's making, he met with reverses, and in the end surrendered to the English at Pondicherry in 1761. He was taken as a prisoner of war to London and there learnt that accusations of treachery were being made against him in Paris. He returned to France on parole and constituted himself a prisoner in the Bastille. When his trial did begin, after two years, it was conducted with great unfairness and dragged on till 1766. All efforts to interest the king (Louis XV) on his behalf failed, he was sentenced to death and beheaded three days later. His legitimated son the marquis de Lally-Tol[l]endal (1751–1830) spent many years trying to get his father's innocence judicially established. He had the support of Voltaire and of Louis XVI but he never wholly succeeded.

La Marche, OLIVIER DE (c. 1425–1502), poet and chronicler, a native of la Bresse who entered the service of the dukes of Burgundy and wrote *Mémoires* of the period 1435–67 celebrating especially their house. He was also author of poems, chiefly of a courtly character. In these he makes abundant use of allegory, after the manner of the *rhétoriqueurs* (q.v.), to which school he belongs. In his *Parement et triumphe des dames*, a moral allegory, a lover provides his mistress with a complete outfit of virtues, from the slippers of humility to the head-covering of hopefulness. His *Le Chevalier délibéré* is another allegorical work, in which the author goes forth in the autumn of his life, accompanied by Thought, to fight with Accident and Weakness in the forest of Fate (Atropos); he sees Philip of Burgundy conquered by the latter, and Charles the Bold by the former.

Lamarck, JEAN-BAPTISTE DE (1744–1829), a celebrated French naturalist, one of the originators of the doctrine of biological evolution. His several works on botany and zoology included: *Flore française* (1778); *Philosophie zoologique* (1809), in which his theories of *transformism* are outlined, i.e. the persistence of types, modified by and adapted to environment and always improving; *Histoire naturelle des animaux sans vertèbres* (1815–22). He was blind during the latter part of his life.

Lamartine, ALPHONSE-MARIE-LOUIS DE PRAT DE (1790–1869), born at Mâcon (Saône-et-Loire), one of the four great poets of the Romantic Movement (cf. *Romantisme*; *Hugo*; *Musset*; *Vigny*). He was a man of action as well as a creative writer— a statesman and a great orator. He came of an old family of Franc-Comtois landowners, whose traditional careers had been arms and agriculture. His father, a Royalist, imprisoned during the Revolution, settled after July 1794 at Milly (q.v.), a small family property in pleasant country near Mâcon. The poet grew up in a tranquil family atmosphere, went to school at Lyons (but ran away after two years) and then to the Jesuit college at Belley (1803–7). At home thereafter he learnt Greek and led a perhaps irksomely quiet existence. His only distractions until 1816 were a journey to Italy, where his senses revelled in the colour, light, and warmth, and a short term of service in the royal bodyguard after the Restoration.

In 1816, at Aix-les-Bains for his health, he met the 'Elvire' (q.v.) of many of his poems, the invalid wife of a Paris doctor. The two fell in love, and when she returned to Paris he followed her. The next spring he was again at Aix, awaiting her coming, but she was too ill to travel. By the autumn she was dead. This emotional experience awakened the poet's inspiration and he set to work seriously on the *Méditations poétiques* (1820, q.v., his first published work). The melodious, plaintive verses met with instant success. They reintroduced into French poetry a lyricism that had been lost for some centuries; expressed the poet's appreciation of Nature as a reflection of his own moods; put into terms of poetry the *mal du siècle* of *Obermann* and *René* (qq.v.); and to the French who had recently discovered Byron they gave a Byron of their own—one whose melancholy was gentle but never terrifying, whose gloom never turned to revolt, who

called from his unhappiness on God and not on Satan.

Meanwhile, at Naples, Lamartine had begun his diplomatic career, which lasted till about 1830. In 1825 he went to Florence as Embassy Secretary. He had also married (1820) Anna Eliza Birch, a young Englishwoman of means. His poetic output continued. The *Nouvelles Méditations* (1823), a poorer repetition, coldly received, of the earlier collection, contained two well-known poems, *Ischia* and *Le Crucifix*. *La Mort de Socrate* (1823) was a philosophico-religious poem in which (following Plato's account in the *Phaedo*) Socrates talks to his friends before going to his death. *Le Dernier Chant du pèlerinage d'Harold* (1825) was a compliment to Byron. *Harmonies poétiques et religieuses* (1830, q.v.) was a collection of lyrical and elegiac verse.

Lamartine abandoned diplomacy after the July Revolution (1830, q.v.). His Royalist sympathies had weakened and he began to see himself as a sort of poet-cum-prophet-cum-leader of the people (cf. *Hugo*). He stood for the Chamber of Deputies but was not elected. He then postponed his political ambitions and, like his predecessor in Romanticism, Chateaubriand (q.v.), travelled— *en grand seigneur* and with a numerous retinue —in Greece, Syria (where he visited Lady Hester Stanhope), and Palestine. The tour is described in *Souvenirs, Impressions, Pensées et Paysages pendant un voyage en Orient* (1835). During his absence he was elected to the Chamber.

When, in 1833, he took his seat as a deputy he allied himself to no particular party, and made no striking impression. Soon, however, by his forceful oratory and his lofty, if none too practical, conception of a human society free from base self-interest, striving to realize ideals of liberty and justice, he captured popular opinion throughout the country. Among his great speeches were those on 'la peine de mort', 'la liberté de la presse', 'la translation des cendres' (Napoleon's), 'l'abolition de l'esclavage'.

In 1836 and 1838 respectively he published the narrative poems *Jocelyn* and *La Chute d'un ange* (qq.v.). In 1839 the collected *Recueillements poétiques* marked the end of his poetical career except for some occasional verse. In 1847 he published *Histoire des Girondins* (q.v.), a work of little historical value, which bathed the worst excesses of the Terror in a flood of revolutionary fervour. It was immensely successful and committed him to advanced Republicanism. During the 1848 Revolution his courage, rousing speeches, and determined action made him a people's idol and for a short time he exercised a power almost amounting to dictatorship. But this did not last. At the 1849 elections no department would accept him as a candidate and he retired into private life.

He had always lived far beyond his means, spending and giving lavishly and indulging what was almost a mania for speculation in land. He now set himself to pay five million francs of debts, sold his family estate and became a literary hack. His wife's death (1863) left him in growing poverty, with failing powers. After 1867 he ended his days more smoothly with a government pension.

Lamartine's other prose works include— NOVELS AND TALES: *Raphaël* (1849), *Le Tailleur de pierres de Saint-Point* (1851), *Graziella* (1852, q.v.); AUTOBIOGRAPHY: *Les Confidences* (1849), *Nouvelles confidences* (1851); POLITICAL WRITINGS AND COLLECTED SPEECHES: *Œuvres oratoires et écrits politiques* (1864–5), &c.; also numerous volumes of history and biography.

Lambert, ANNE-THÉRÈSE, MARQUISE DE (1647–1733), author of works of moral instruction (*Avis d'une mère à son fils* (1726) and *Avis à sa fille* (1728), containing much sage counsel; and of *Réflexions sur les femmes* and *Traité de l'Amitié* and *de la Vieillesse*; famous for the *salon* where twice a week from 1710 until her death she received members of the aristocracy and of the literary world. She was noted for her high principles and refined judgement, and her *salon* was said to be potent in the selection of members of the *Académie*. She was a pupil of Bachaumont, who had married her widowed mother.

Lambin, DENIS (1516–72), a learned humanist and philologist, from whose name the verb *lambiner* 'to work slowly, to dawdle', is perhaps derived.

Lamennais, or **La Mennais**, FÉLICITÉ-ROBERT DE ['Monsieur Féli' to his intimates] (1782–1854), religious writer and Christian democrat, was born at Saint-Malo, a shipowner's son. At thirty-four, with the doubtful equipment of an irregular education, ardent religiosity, and a difficult temperament, he became a priest. In 1817 he came to the front as a Catholic writer with the first volume of an *Essai sur l'indifférence en matière de religion*, which sought to establish the verities of the Catholic faith as well as a return to the active practice of religion. He was hailed as a new Bossuet (q.v.) and several enthusiasts (notably Lacordaire, Montalembert, and the young Maurice de Guérin, qq.v.) became his disciples, forming a Christian community at La Chesnaie, near Dinan, his old home.

Three further volumes of the *Essai* (1821–3) and a new work *De la Religion considérée dans ses rapports avec l'ordre politique et civil* (1824) caused uneasiness to Church and State by their—subversively ultramontane (q.v.)—contention that subordination to religion and hence to the supreme authority of the Pope was the only salvation for society. He developed this, on less traditional lines, into a conception of a liberal democracy in which the people, discarding outworn monarchical theories, would unite for Liberty, taking matters temporal into their own hands but leaving spiritual authority with the Church. About this time his influence was felt by the Romantic writers, e.g. Hugo, Lamartine, and perhaps especially Sainte-Beuve. (In his later phase it was strong on George Sand.) In his newspaper *L'Avenir* (q.v., f. 1830) he elaborated his beliefs. He incurred censure, went to Rome to defend his attitude before the Pope (Gregory XVI), and on his way back to Paris was overtaken by the Encyclical *Mirari vos* (15 Aug. 1832) signifying the Church's profound disapproval. A time of spiritual stress followed, when he wrote his famous apologia *Paroles d'un croyant* (q.v., 1834). Book and author were promptly condemned in another Encyclical, *Singulari nos* (15 July 1834), whereupon Lamennais broke with the Church and with his former disciples. He took himself and his pen over to the advanced Republicans and was more than once in trouble, if not in prison, for his writings. After the February Revolution (q.v., 1848), though elected to the *Assemblée Constituante* (q.v.), he showed no talent for constructive politics. He retired into private life, embittered by events, after the *coup d'état* (q.v.) of 1851. He died unreconciled with the Church and at his own wish was given a pauper burial.

His other writings include *Le Livre du peuple* (1837), *De l'esclavage moderne* (1840), *Esquisse d'une philosophie* (1841–6, 4 vols.), &c.

Lamentations, see *Mathieu.*

La Mésangère, PIERRE DE, see *Dictionaries and Encyclopedias,* under date 1821.

La Mesnardière, HIPPOLYTE-JULES PILET DE (1610–63), author of a *Poétique* (1639; only the first volume was published) in which Aristotle and the Italian classical poets were his guide. He was at one time physician to the duc (Gaston) d'Orléans (q.v.).

La Mettrie, JULIEN OFFROY DE (1709–51), physician and materialist philosopher; author of *Histoire naturelle de l'âme* (1745), a work which excited violent hostility as being subversive of religious belief. The following year he took refuge in Holland but had to flee that country after expressing even more dangerously materialistic views in *L'Homme machine* (1748). Frederick II considered him a victim of intolerance and invited him to Berlin, where he died. His works of this period include *L'Homme plante* (1749) and *Sur l'origine des animaux* (1750).

Lamiel, the novel on which Stendhal was working during his last years. It was published in 1889.

La Mole, BONIFACE DE (d. 1574), a Provençal, executed with Coconas (q.v.) for his share in the plot to place the duc d'Alençon on the throne. He figures prominently in *La Dame de Monsoreau* by A. Dumas *père.*

La Môle, MATHILDE DE, a character in *Le Rouge et le noir* (q.v.), by Stendhal.

La Monnoye, BERNARD DE (1641–1728), man of letters, born at Dijon, remembered as the author of *Noëls bourguignons,* humorous familiar scenes in the Burgundian *patois,* in the framework of the old Mysteries of the Nativity, such as were still current. La Monnoye was also author of the song on M. de La Palice (q.v.) which perpetuated the legend of his simplicity.

La Mothe le Vayer, FRANÇOIS DE (1588–1672), a magistrate and a man of letters and erudition, a *libertin* or sceptic in his philo-

sophic views. He wrote on a multitude of subjects, under the pseudonym of 'Orasius Tubero', *Dialogues à l'imitation des anciens* (1630), *Discours chrétiens de l'immortalité de l'âme* (1637) *Considérations sur l'éloquence française* (1638), *Traité de la vertu des payens* (1642), *Hexaméron rustique* (1670). He was admitted to the *Académie* and appointed preceptor to the duc d'Orléans, brother of Louis XIV.

La Motte, HOUDAR DE LA, see *Houdar de la Motte.*

La Motte, JEANNE DE VALOIS, COMTESSE DE (1756–91), see *Collier, L'Affaire du.*

La Motte Fouqué, FRIEDRICH, BARON DE (1777–1843), German poet and novelist, one-time army officer, who used the legends and traditions of the Middle Ages rather than those of Greek and Roman antiquity for his themes, and had thus an appeal for the French romantic writers (see *Foreign Influences on French literature,* para. 20). He is remembered particularly by his fairy romances *Sintram* and *Undine.* Giraudoux (q.v.) turned to the latter for his play *Ondine,* the nymph who married a mortal and realized her ambition to possess a soul. But she also learnt what it was to be unhappy.

Lamourette, ADRIEN (1742–94), Bishop of Lyons and, in the Revolution, member of the *Assemblée législative,* where on 7 July 1792, by a moving speech, he brought about a momentary reconciliation between the parties. But within a few hours the strife was as bitter as ever. Whence a *baiser Lamourette* signifies an ephemeral reconciliation. Lamourette was executed in 1794.

Lamoureux, CHARLES (1834–99), orchestral conductor, did much to make Wagner, and some Russian composers, known in France. He conducted the first performance of *Lohengrin* in Paris in 1887. The Sunday *Concerts Lamoureux,* which he founded in 1881, are a feature of Parisian musical life.

Lancelot, one of the later figures among the heroes connected with the legend of King Arthur, apparently first mentioned in the *Erec* of Chrétien de Troyes (q.v.), later in his *Cligès* (q.v.) and in his *Chevalier à la Charrette* (q.v.), of which Lancelot is the hero and where he appears as the lover of Guinevere.

The legend of Lancelot, an illustrious

knight of Arthur's court and lover of the queen, was included as the central element in the great 13th-century prose cycle (see *Perceval*) whose other branches dealt with the story of the Holy Grail and of Arthur's legendary kingdom. In the *Lancelot* branch, amid a multitude of tangled episodes, we have the boy Lancelot, after the death of his father King Ban, carried off and brought up by the Lady of the Lake; he is sent to the court of Arthur, where he falls in love with Guinevere; in the course of his adventures he takes the castle of Dolorous Gard, later named Joyous Gard after he has rid it of enchantments. Here he is visited by Arthur and his queen, and the story of his passion for Guinevere is continued, with the hostile intervention of Morgain la Fée. Among many adventures Lancelot visits the Grail castle, where under magic influence he takes the daughter of its king for Guinevere, and becomes father of Galahad. The story is resumed in the last two branches of the cycle: Lancelot is debarred by his sins from the quest of the Grail and is smitten with remorse, but in the *Mort Artu* he is once more the queen's lover, is taken in the queen's chamber, rescues her from death at the stake, and carries her to Joyous Gard. He makes an enemy of Gawain by unwittingly killing his brother, and in single combat mortally wounds him. Finally he restores Guinevere to Arthur; he ends his life in a hermitage, Guinevere in a nunnery.

In medieval English romances, except *Le Morte Arthure* (late 14th c.), which tells the story of the Maid of Astolat and of the tragic end of the loves of Lancelot and the queen, Lancelot plays no important part, until Malory gave him prominence in his *Morte Darthur*.

Lancelot, CLAUDE (1615–95), one of the solitaries of Port-Royal (q.v.), for twenty-five years an instructor of the young there and in the family of the princesse de Conti, was author of *Jardin des racines grecques* and of two volumes of admirable memoirs of Saint-Cyran.

Lancret, NICOLAS (1690–1743), a distinguished painter in the style of Watteau (q.v.).

Lanfrey, PIERRE (1828–77), born at Chambéry, a historian whose vigorous style lent

emphasis to his anti-clerical and, even more, anti-Napoleonic views. His publications include: *L'Église et les philosophes au XVIIIe siècle* (1855); *Essai sur la Révolution française* (1858); *Histoire politique des papes* (1860); *Histoire de Napoléon Ier* (1867–75, his chief work, interrupted by his death); also a sociological novel in letter-form, *Les Lettres d'Éverard* (1860). He was active in reconstructive politics after the Franco-Prussian war.

Långfors, A., see *Incipit*.

Langtoft, PIERRE DE, see *Pierre de Langtoft*.

Languedoc, Canal du, see *Colbert*.

Langue d'oc and **langue d'oïl.** The Latin language spoken in Roman Gaul was transformed in the mouths of the population of various regions into a number of dialects, each of which had something in common with those of the neighbouring regions. These dialects formed two language-groups, the *langue d'oc* and the *langue d'oïl*, so called after the words used in them respectively to signify affirmation (*oui*), namely 'oc', from the Latin *hoc*, and 'oïl', a contraction of *hoc ille*. The *langue d'oc*—the Provençal language —was spoken south of a line running roughly from the mouth of the Gironde eastward to the Alps. The *langue d'oïl*, which prevailed and became the French language, was spoken north of this line (see *French language*). Present-day Provençal retains, more than French, the character of Latin in respect of its vowel sounds, also to a greater degree its inflexions; it is softer and more harmonious than the northern language.

Langue farcie, language in which French and Latin words are mixed, sometimes used in medieval works.

Languet, HUBERT (1518–81), a French Protestant who settled in Germany, author of *Vindiciae contra tyrannos* (1579), treating of the relations of peoples in general with their rulers; a pioneer work in political science, in which the idea of contract first emerges, and hence the right of insurrection.

Lannes, JEAN, one of Napoleon's marshals, (see *Maréchal de l'Empire*).

La Noue, FRANÇOIS DE (1531–91), a Breton Protestant soldier, defender of La Rochelle, who wrote in captivity *Discours politiques et* *militaires* (1587), showing a patriotic tolerant spirit which was recognized even by his adversaries. They include his own memoirs.

Lanson, GUSTAVE (1857–1934), born at Orleans, professor and literary historian, and a critic whose interest lay perhaps chiefly in ideas and their philosophical implications. This bent is noticeable in his *Histoire de la littérature française* (1894 and subsequent editions), one of the most useful manuals of its kind. Among his many other works were: *Principes de composition et de style* (1887); studies of Bossuet (1890) and Boileau (1892); *Hommes et livres. Études morales et littéraires* (1895); *L'Idéal français dans la littérature de la Renaissance à la Révolution* (1928), also a *Manuel bibliographique de la littérature française moderne, depuis 1500 jusqu'à nos jours* (1909–12, 4 vols.), an indispensable tool for those engaged in research into French literature.

Lanterne, La, a weekly paper in the form of small, bright red pamphlets, founded in 1868 by the journalist Henri Rochefort (q.v.). It attacked the existing régime and in particular Napoleon III with a savage wit that caused it to be widely read, and helped considerably to undermine the Second Empire. The opening sentence of the first number (23 May 1868) was: 'La France contient, dit *l'Almanach impérial*, trente-six millions de sujets, sans compter les sujets de mécontentement.' Rochefort was soon prosecuted, but he escaped to Belgium and from there continued his paper. The first series ran from May to October 1868. Another series was published, also in Brussels, from 1874 to 1875.

Lantier, AUGUSTE, in Zola's novel *L'Assommoir* (q.v. and see *Rougon-Macquart*), the lover of the laundress Gervaise Macquart. Their eldest son Claude becomes an artist and is the chief character of *L'Œuvre* (q.v.). Another son, Étienne, is the chief character in the novel of mining life *Germinal* (q.v.). A third son, Jacques, a homicidal maniac, is the engine-driver in *La Bête humaine* (q.v.).

Lantier, ÉTIENNE-FRANÇOIS DE (1734–1826), born in Marseilles, was a cavalry officer who came to Paris and took to writing. He was called 'l'Anacharsis des boudoirs' after his pseudo-antique romance *Les Voyages d'Anténor en Grèce et en Asie* (1798), a gay,

very superficial imitation of Barthélemy's (q.v.) *Voyage du jeune Anacharsis*. Though now forgotten it was remarkably successful when published, and was translated into most European languages. Lantier also wrote *L'Impatient* (1778), a one-act comedy in verse, *Contes en prose et en vers* (1801), &c.

Lanval, see *Marie de France.*

La Palice, JACQUES DE CHABANNES, SEIGNEUR DE (c. 1470–1525), maréchal de France, who distinguished himself in the Italian wars of Charles VIII, Louis XII, and François Ier, and was killed at the battle of Pavia. A song by La Monnoye (q.v.) ridiculing his simplicity has given rise to the expression 'vérité de La Palice' for a self-evident truth.

La Pérouse, JEAN-FRANÇOIS DE (1741–88), a famous navigator. On a voyage of discovery ordered by Louis XVI he was killed by the natives of Vanikoro, one of the Polynesian islands.

La Péruse, JEAN BASLIER DE (1529–56), a poet of the school of Ronsard, born in the Vendômois, who died young, leaving a tragedy *Médée*, imitated from Seneca; also some minor poems of promise.

Lapidaires, medieval works in which the curative and talismanic properties of precious stones were set forth, sometimes with allegorical interpretations. Of this description was a Latin poem by Marbode, Bishop of Rennes (d. 1123), which was translated into French verse early in the 12th and again more than once in the 13th centuries. Philippe de Thaon (q.v.) was the author of another *lapidaire*.

Laplace, PIERRE-ANTOINE DE (1707–93), author of a *Théâtre anglais* in eight volumes, published 1745–8, of which four volumes contain the first French translations, partly in verse partly in prose, of ten of Shakespeare's plays (in most of which, however, some of the scenes are merely summarized) and the plots of twenty-six others, together with a critical introduction showing sympathy with Shakespearian drama. The work aroused great interest in France and caused much annoyance to Voltaire.

Laplace, PIERRE-SIMON, MARQUIS DE (1749–1827), mathematician and astronomer, the son of a peasant farmer in Normandy, came to the notice of d'Alembert (q.v.), whose recommendation helped him in the initial stages of his scientific career. He was one of the savants prominent in public affairs after the Revolution, becoming Minister of the Interior for a time during the Consulate, and a Senator during the Empire (when a report by him led to the abandonment of the Republican Calendar, q.v.). He was ennobled by Louis XVIII. His famous treatises include: *Exposition du système du monde* (1796); *La Mécanique céleste* (1799–1825); *Théorie analytique des probabilités* (1812), and *Essai philosophique sur les probabilités* (1814).

La Pommeraye, Mme de, and **le marquis des Arcis,** see *Jacques le fataliste.*

La Porte, PIERRE DE (1603–80), in the service of Anne of Austria and subsequently *valet de chambre* to the young Louis XIV, author of memoirs covering the years 1624–66 (Louis XIII, Anne of Austria and Mazarin, Louis XIV). They are occupied mainly with court intrigues and the author's justification of his own conduct, and hardly touch on the important events of the period.

Laprade, VICTOR-RICHARD DE (1812–87), poet, born at Montbrison (Loire), was educated and lived at Lyons where he was Professor of French Literature from 1847 to 1861. His large poetical output (collected in *Œuvres poétiques,* 1878–81, 6 vols.) was mainly classical and biblical in inspiration, with a strong feeling for nature, e.g. *Odes et Poèmes* (1844) which contains the well-known elegy *La Mort d'un chêne*; *Poèmes évangéliques* (1852); *Les Symphonies* (1855), showing the influence of Lamartine; *Les Idylles héroïques* (1858). *Psyché* (1841) was the narrative poem that made his name. *Pernette* (1868), another, is also remembered.

La Ramée (in Latin form, RAMUS), PIERRE DE (1515–72), philosopher and grammarian, holder of a royal professorship, famous as an adversary of Aristotle and scholasticism, author of a *Dialectique* (1555) in which he opposed the Aristotelian logic; it was one of the first works of its kind to be written in French. He became a Protestant and was a victim of the massacre of St. Bartholomew.

Larbaud, VALÉRY (1881–1957), born at Vichy, a widely read and much travelled novelist and man of letters. He created a personality of 20th-century French literature in the character of Archibaldo Olson Barnabooth, a blasé young South American millionaire with an unsatisfied soul, who wanders about Europe (for the most part in a *wagon-lit*) in search of distraction and the Absolute (*A. O. Barnabooth: ses œuvres complètes; c'est-à-dire un conte, ses poésies et son journal intime,* 1913). The earlier *Fermina Marquez* (1911) was a picture of boys'-school life and the ferment caused by the presence in the neighbourhood of two Spanish-American girls, sisters of a new pupil. *Enfantines* (1918) contains tales of childhood. In *Beauté mon beau souci* (in the collection *Amants, heureux amants,* 1920) the scene is England, which the author knew well. The sketches of French provincial life in *Allen* (1927, imaginary conversations) should be mentioned, also the essays and critical studies, frequently of English literature, in the two collections *Ce vice impuni, la lecture* (1925: a title taken from Logan Pearsall Smith's description—in *Trivia*—of reading as 'this polite and unpunished vice') and *Jaune, bleu, blanc* (1927).

Largillière, NICOLAS DE (1656–1746), a distinguished portrait painter under Louis XIV.

Larguier, LÉO (1878–1950), poet, literary journalist, and novelist. His collected poetical works include: *La Maison du poète* (1903), *Les Isolements* (1906), *Jacques* (1907, a narrative poem), *Orchestres* (1914), *Les Ombres* (1935), *Mes vingt ans et moi* (1944).

Larivey, PIERRE DE (*c.* 1540–1612), dramatist, son of an Italian settled at Troyes (his name is a punning adaptation of that of his family, Giunti (*Les arrivés*), who were famous printers in Florence). He published in 1579 six comedies, and three more in 1611, lively adaptations from the Italian to French conditions. They are in prose, a form of comedy of which we find no further example before Molière. The best known of them is *Les Esprits* (q.v.). He translated many other Italian works, including the *Nights* of Straparola, and thus helped to establish Italian literary influence in France.

La Rochefoucauld, FRANÇOIS, DUC DE (1613–80), moralist, known as *prince de Marsillac* (or *Marcillac*) until the death of his father. He showed during the earlier years of his life a feverish activity, taking part in the intrigues against Richelieu (in conspiracy with Mme de Chevreuse, q.v.), and later in the *Fronde* (from hatred of Mazarin and under the influence of his love for Mme de Longueville, q.v.). He was severely wounded in the fighting in Paris (1652), and his political activities ended in discomfiture. His susceptibility to female influence, a certain gentleness and meditative tendency and consequent irresolution, in fact unsuited him for a life of intrigue and turmoil. Thereafter he lived in retirement, amid a small highly intellectual society, which included Mme de Sablé, Mme de Sévigné, and in particular Mme de La Fayette, to whom in his later years (after 1665) he was united by a devoted friendship. His *Mémoires* appeared at first (1662) in an unauthorized and incorrect form, and the authentic text was not published until recent times. They are clear and elegant in style and remarkable for the penetration and subtlety of the portraits of persons with whom he was associated in his intrigues. The first (Paris) edition of the *Réflexions ou sentences et maximes morales* (generally known as the *Maximes*), his famous work, was published in 1665 (it followed a clandestine edition published anonymously at The Hague in 1664); modifications and additions were made in later editions. His *Réflexions diverses* did not appear until long after his death. The high degree of polish in the phrasing of the *Maximes*, which excel in conciseness, precision, and appropriateness of expression, is to some extent due to discussions of the text among his friends (in which Mme de Sablé took a prominent part). The work is a collection of some 500 gnomic sentences in which the author analyses the motives of human conduct with merciless penetration. While he recognizes in rare cases the existence of pure virtue and disinterested sentiments, he finds them tainted, almost universally, with some element of self-love or interested motive. Man, in pretending to virtue, generally deceives himself as well as others, for egoism is his dominating sentiment, and the moment that virtue becomes conscious it loses its purity. The *Maximes* thus provide a valuable check on complacency. But it may be doubted, having regard to the author's character and conduct, whether many of the maxims were sincerely held by him. He attenuated the doctrine in successive editions;

we should perhaps regard the *Maximes* as to some extent a literary *tour de force*, the maintenance of a paradox, rather than as the deliberate conviction of a moralist. Many of them, it may be added, and of the *Réflexions diverses*, deal not so much with the motives of ethical conduct as with social relations in general: see, for instance, the sound remarks 'De la Conversation' in the latter work. The bitter and pessimistic philosophy that La Rochefoucauld professed had a wide influence; it was approved by the Jansenists, who saw in it a confirmation of their doctrine of the vileness of fallen man. Voltaire's *Candide* and the writings of Chamfort derive in part from it. Vauvenargues displays the inevitable reaction against it. Voltaire said that La Rochefoucauld contributed greatly to form the taste of the nation: 'il accoutuma à penser et à renfermer ses pensées dans un tour vif, précis et délicat'. There is an admirable portrait of the author in the memoirs of the Cardinal de Retz. The *Maximes* were translated into English by Mrs. Aphra Behn, and another version appeared in 1694.

Laromiguière, PIERRE (1756–1837), philosopher, born at Lévignac (in the Midi, near Rodez), came to Paris (1795) after teaching philosophy in the provinces. For a time he devoted himself to politics, but with Napoleon's rise to supreme power he returned to his first interests and in 1811 was appointed Professor of Philosophy, and also Librarian, at the Sorbonne. In a celebrated course of lectures (published 1815–18 as *Les Principes de l'intelligence, ou sur les causes et sur les origines des idées*) he established a form of compromise between sensationalism (e.g. that of Condillac and the *idéologues*), in that he recognized the senses as a passive source of knowledge, and spiritualism, because, he held, man's intelligence, his moral consciousness, and his will depend for their exercise on a more elevated faculty of awareness, or 'sentiment', which once admitted leads to a belief in a First Cause, and in God.

Larousse, PIERRE, see *Dictionaries and Encyclopedias* under date 1865–76.

La Sablière, MARGUERITE, MME DE (1636–93), one of the famous literary ladies of her period, especially remembered for the hospitality which for twenty years she gave to La Fontaine.

La Sale or **Salle,** ANTOINE DE (b. 1388, d. *post* 1469), romance writer, served the house of Anjou in his earlier years as squire and soldier, visiting various countries. Later he was tutor to the son of René d'Anjou (q.v.), and to the sons of the Burgundian comte de Saint-Pol. His most famous work is the *Petit Jehan de Saintré* (q.v., *c.* 1456). He had previously written a treatise on the art of government (*La Salade, c.* 1440) which includes lively chapters on the author's visit to the Lipari islands and to the 'Paradis de la Sibylle', with which the legend of Tannhäuser is connected; also an ethical treatise named *La Salle* (*c.* 1451). He has often been thought, probably erroneously, to be the author of the *Quinze joyes de mariage* and the *Cent nouvelles nouvelles* (qq.v.). His *Réconfort de Madame de Fresne* (1458) deals with an episode of the Hundred Years War. The theme is the struggle in the heart of a mother between two alternatives: whether to save her son, a hostage in enemy hands, who will be executed if his father does not surrender the place which he commands, or to sacrifice her son and save her husband's honour as a warrior.

Lascaris, ANDREAS JOANNES or JANUS (*c.* 1445–1535), a learned Greek grammarian, brought to Italy in childhood after the fall of Constantinople, eventually found refuge in Florence at the court of Lorenzo de' Medici. Later, in France, he encouraged the study of Greek letters. He was the teacher of Guillaume Budé (q.v.) and was employed with him by François Ier on the formation of the royal library at Fontainebleau.

Las Cases, EMMANUEL-AUGUSTIN-DIEU-DONNÉ-MARTIN-JOSEPH, COMTE DE (1766–1842), emigrated during the Revolution but returned during the Consulate and held public office under Napoleon. After Waterloo he followed Napoleon to St. Helena but was expelled from the island in November 1816. He returned to France after Napoleon's death and published the much-read *Mémorial de Sainte-Hélène* (1822–3), a record of Napoleon's life in exile, with notes of conversations in which Napoleon expressed his views on politics, history, &c.

La Serre, JEAN PUGET DE (1600–65), born at Toulouse, a mediocre dramatist, author, among other plays, of a successful prose tragedy *Thomas Morus, ou le triomphe de la foi et de la constance* (1641).

Lassailly, CHARLES (1806–43), a minor figure of the later, so-called 'frenetic' romantics (see *Romantisme*). He founded small reviews and published a fantastic novel, *Les Roueries de Trialph* (1833), which abounds in murders and ends in suicide. Loss of reason, followed by suicide, ended his own life.

Lasserre, PIERRE (1867–1930), a literary critic (for some years on the staff of the *Action française*, q.v.) whose *Le Romantisme français, essai sur la révolution dans les sentiments et dans les idées au XIXe siècle* (1907) was a highly provocative championship of Classicism *v.* Romanticism. Another work, *Les Chapelles littéraires*, i.e. literary cliques (1920), consisted of studies of Claudel, Jammes, and Péguy.

La Suze, COMTESSE DE, *née* HENRIETTE DE COLIGNY (1618–73), was the author, with Pellisson (q.v.) and some others, of a *Recueil de pièces galantes* (1663), also called *Recueil La Suze-Pellisson*, one of the most popular 17th-century verse and prose miscellanies. She was born a Protestant, grand-daughter of Gaspard de Coligny (q.v.), but turned Roman Catholic, after which her marriage to the drunken, jealous comte de La Suze was dissolved. (A first marriage had ended within a year with the death of her husband Thomas Hamilton, Earl of Haddington.) She is said to have been worldly, and a beauty, a *précieuse* who corresponded with Guez de Balzac and Saint-Évremond (qq.v.), and whose *salon* was a sort of annexe of the Hôtel de Rambouillet.

La Tailhède, RAYMOND DE (1867–1938), born at Moissac (Tarn-et-Garonne), poet, one of the founders of the *École Romane* (q.v.), was educated in Paris and lived there after 1888. His published collections of verse include *De la métamorphose des fontaines, poème suivi des Odes, des Sonnets, et des Hymnes* (1895), *Hymne pour la France* (1917), *Le Deuxième Livre des odes* (1920), *Le Poème d'Orphée* (1926).

La Taille, JEAN DE (1540–1608), an early writer of tragedies, whose *Saül le furieux* (q.v.) appeared in 1572, preceded by a dedicatory epistle in which he treats of the nature of tragedy, and insists on the unities of place and time. His other Biblical tragedy, *La Famine, ou les Gabaonites*, appeared in 1573. He also wrote a satiric poem, *Le Courtisan retiré* (1574). His comedy *Les Corrivaux* (1574) was the first French comedy to be written in prose.

JACQUES DE LA TAILLE was his younger brother. He died in 1562 when only twenty, having already composed two tragedies, *Daire* and *Alexandre*, of little merit.

Latouche, HENRI DE (pseud. of Hyacinthe Thabaud) (1785–1851), born at La Châtre (Indre), a well-known man of letters of the Romantic period. He—the first to do so—edited (1819) the works of André Chénier (q.v.), then translated (1820) Schiller's *Maria Stuart*, and from 1825 edited *Le Mercure de France au XIXᵉ siècle*, a literary review of romantic tendencies. His published writings include *Olivier* (1826), *Fragoletta* (1829), novels; and *La Vallée-aux-Loups* (1833), *Les Agrestes* (1845), verse.

La Tour, MAURICE QUENTIN DE (1704–88), celebrated painter of portraits in pastel, including portraits of Mme de Pompadour, of Marie Leczinska (wife of Louis XV), &c.

La Tour du Pin, PATRICE DE (1911–   ), contemporary poet, born in Paris, became known shortly before the 1939–45 war (during which he was wounded on active service and taken prisoner). His *La Quête de joie* (1933), which aroused great hopes, was the first of several collections of poems and prose-poems of spiritual adventure. In 1946 these collections were all included as component parts of Part I of a work in progress, a vast, unequal *Somme de poésie*. This author's poetry is religious in tone and consciously un-modernist in style and approach.

La Tour Landry, Livre du Chevalier de, an educational work written *c.* 1372 for the benefit of the author's young daughters, embodying instructive tales from the Scriptures and the ancient writers, and examples of conduct from contemporary life. The author was a member of the provincial nobility and the work throws light on the society to which he belonged. Cf. *Ménagier de Paris*.

La Trappe, see *Trappe*.

Latude, JEAN-HENRI MASERS DE (1725–1805), an adventurer who sought to advance his fortunes by revealing a pretended plot (of his own concoction) against Mme de Pompadour. In consequence he was imprisoned in the Bastille and other places for thirty-five years (1749–84). He left memoirs.

Launay, BERNARD-RENÉ-JORDAN, MARQUIS DE (1740–89), was Governor of the Bastille when it was taken on 14 July 1789. He was foully murdered by the mob.

Launay, MARGUERITE CORDIER DE, MME DE STAAL (1684–1750), a woman of learning and intelligence, and friend of Fontenelle, Chaulieu, and Mme du Deffand. Her father's name was Cordier, but she called herself de Launay, the name of her mother's family. She was early left penniless and obliged to accept a humble post in the service of the duchesse du Maine (q.v.). Her abilities secured her promotion to the post of reader to the duchesse and she was her confidant to some extent in the conspiracy which was fomented at Sceaux against the Regent. In consequence she suffered a long imprisonment in the Bastille. After her release, weary of her life of servitude, she tried to obtain an independent position, but the tyrannical selfishness of the duchesse frustrated her attempts. She was married against her will in 1735 to the baron de Staal, an elderly Swiss widower, but remained in the duchesse's service. She left, besides letters to Mme du Deffand and others, *Mémoires* written with elegant simplicity and an occasional epigrammatic turn. These contain a pleasant narrative of her earlier years, depict the unhappy conditions under which she lived at Sceaux, and relate with interesting detail her imprisonment in the Bastille. Of this she says, 'c'est le seul temps heureux que j'ai passé en ma vie. . . . Il est vrai qu'en prison on ne fait pas sa volonté; mais aussi on ne fait point celle des autres'. Her letters to Mme du Deffand relate a visit of Voltaire and Mme du Châtelet to the duchesse du Maine.

Launay, VICOMTE DE, see *Girardin, Mme Émile de*.

Laure persécutée, a tragicomedy by Rotrou, performed in 1637.

Orantée, son of the king of Hungary, is in love with Laure, a lady of unknown birth.

The king intends him to marry an Infanta and is furious at his projected misalliance. He arrests Orantée and seeks Laure to put her to death. He endeavours to convince Orantée of Laure's infidelity by an artifice similar to Borachio's in Shakespeare's *Much Ado*. This, at first successful, is presently revealed, and Laure is discovered to be a sister of the Infanta.

Lauriers sont coupés, Les (1888), a novel by Édouard Dujardin (q.v.).

Lautréamont, COMTE DE, the pseudonym of Isidore Ducasse (1846–70) and the name by which he is remembered. He is said to have taken it from the hero of Eugène Sue's (q.v.) historical novel *Latréaumont* whose superhuman arrogance drives him to revolt and blasphemy. Little is known of Lautréamont's life except that he was born of French parents in Montevideo and in 1867 came, an exceptionally gifted youth, to Paris where he intended to take the examinations of the École polytechnique (q.v.), but where he seems to have spent most of his time writing or declaiming what he wrote, and where, three years later, he died.

In 1868 he published the first of his lyrical fragments in prose, *Les Chants de Maldoror*. It was republished in 1890, twenty years after his death, with an additional five fragments. Maldoror, a demonic figure, expresses his hatred of mankind and the Deity, and his adoration of the Ocean (this is one of the famous passages), blood, octopuses, toads, &c. There are nightmarish episodes with vampires or with mysterious beings encountered on the seashore. The work is an astonishing profusion of apostrophe and imagery—delirious, erotic, blasphemous, grandiose, and horrifying by turns or all together, but its style and language are also so remarkable that it stands as an example of 'les hallucinations servies par la volonté' [R. de Gourmont]. Because of this hallucinatory quality the surréalistes (see *Surréalisme*) claim Lautréamont as one of their precursors.

Lautréamont published *Poésies* in 1870, with an interesting, but incomplete, preface which was an ironical attack on the type of literature represented by *Maldoror*. Modern editions of his works include one by the *surréaliste* poet Philippe Soupault (q.v.).

Lauzun, ANTONIN NOMPAR DE CAUMONT, later duc de (1632–1723), a Gascon gentleman and a member of the court of Louis XIV, a strange combination of courage, wit, insolence, and servility ('le plus insolent petit homme qu'on eût vu depuis un siècle', says La Fare), by some condemned as a crafty adventurer. He had a chequered career. He won, then lost, the affection of the king. The Grande Mademoiselle (q.v.) fell in love with him, and obtained the king's sanction to their marriage; but this was withdrawn three days later (1670), and Lauzun was imprisoned for ten years at Pignerol. Then he was restored to favour. It is said that he was secretly married to Mademoiselle. But he was ungrateful for the benefits she had heaped upon him and they quarrelled and separated. When James II in 1688, in preparation for his own flight from England, secretly sent the queen and the infant Prince of Wales to France, it was Lauzun who escorted them. He commanded the French troops at the Boyne.

Lauzun, ARMAND-LOUIS DE GONTAUT-BIRON, DUC DE, later DUC DE BIRON (1747–93), brought up in the household of Mme de Pompadour, a brave soldier and noted Don Juan, left memoirs (to the year 1783) of his military and amorous adventures, including a not wholly trustworthy picture of the circle of Queen Marie-Antoinette. Ruined by continual extravagance, he turned to more serious occupations and held high military command against the English on the west coast of Africa in 1779 and in America in 1780–3. Having lost favour at court, he joined the party of the duc d'Orléans, became during the Revolution a general in the Republican army, and was executed on the last day of 1793 or the first of 1794 on a charge of having favoured by his inactivity the rebellion in the Vendée. His memoirs were published in 1821, giving rise to a good deal of scandal. A romantic but not heroic figure, he married Mlle de Boufflers, and treated her with gross contumely; she was executed in 1794.

La Vallière, LOUISE DE LA BAUME LE BLANC, DUCHESSE DE (1644–1700), mistress of Louis XIV in the early part of his reign, a woman of a 'touching rather than triumphant beauty' (Sainte-Beuve), and of a modest, disinterested, and tender character. She was supplanted in the king's affections by Mme de Montespan, and in 1674 retired to a Carmelite convent. Mme de Sévigné refers to her as 'cette petite violette qui se cachait sous l'herbe'. She was mother of Mlle de Blois, who married the prince de Conti.

Lavater, JOHANN-KASPAR (1741–1801), a pastor in his native town of Zürich, is perhaps best remembered as a physiognomist, author of *Physiognomische Fragmente* (1775–8) as well as some 130 other philosophical, theological, poetic, and dramatic works. It contained theories, of small scientific value, about the art of divining character, and past and future fortunes, from facial conformation. When translated into French (*Fragments philosophiques*, 1783) it excited great interest. He was a man of enthusiasms and contradictions: a Protestant pastor with leanings to Roman Catholicism and mysticism, a believer in the Scriptures and in black magic. He died believing he was the Apostle John. He had shown great patriotism during the Swiss risings against the French occupation of Zürich (1799) and his death was a consequence of a shot received at this time. (See also *Gall, Mesmer*.)

Laveaux, JEAN-CHARLES THIBAULT DE, see *Dictionaries and Encyclopedias*, under dates 1818 and 1820.

Lavedan, HENRI (1859–1940), dramatist, author of comedies of manners which portrayed Parisian life in its worldly, frivolous aspects. They tended occasionally to introduce social themes or a moral. The most successful were *Le Prince d'Aurec* (1894, a study of impoverished aristocrats) and *Le Marquis de Priola* (1902). Others included *Le Duel* (1905), *Le Nouveau Jeu* (1907), *Le Vieux Marcheur* (1909).

La Vigne, ANDRÉ or ANDRIEU DE (d. *c.* 1515), poet and dramatist, born at La Rochelle, secretary to the duc de Savoie, and later to Anne of Brittany. He accompanied Charles VIII on his expedition to Italy, and wrote a verse journal thereof, forming part of a work entitled *Le Vergier d'honneur*. In 1496 a Mystery of Saint Martin written by him was performed at Seurre in Burgundy. He wrote one or two other dramatic works (*soties* and *moralités*, see *Aveugle et le Boiteux*), polemical poems supporting the policy of Louis XII against the papacy, and

rondeaux on the death of his patroness the queen.

Lavisse, ERNEST (1842–1922), historian, the general editor (with collaborators), and also part author, of large-scale histories of France from the earliest times until the Armistice of 1919 (published between 1891 and 1922). These have become standard works (see Appendix I, § C).

Lavoisier, ANTOINE-LAURENT (1743–94), famous French chemist, one of the creators of modern chemistry, discoverer (simultaneously with Priestley) of oxygen and of the composition of air. Having obtained a post of *fermier général* of taxes to meet the cost of his experiments, he was condemned under the Revolution and executed. Arthur Young recounts a visit to his laboratory (16 Oct. 1787).

Law, JOHN (1671–1729), son of an Edinburgh goldsmith, escaped from prison after being sentenced to death for killing his adversary in a duel, fled to the Continent, and obtained the favour of the Regent of France. He persuaded the French government to adopt the use of paper money, convertible into coin through the medium of the *Banque Générale*, which he founded in 1716 in the rue Quincampoix in Paris. The bank-notes proved a great success, and Law extended his operations, creating the Mississippi Company, a vast enterprise which exploited colonial commerce. Law, moreover, undertook the farming of the French taxes. The *Banque Générale* became the *Banque Royale* in 1718, and Law was named controller general of finance early in 1720. The frenzied speculation to which his operations gave rise collapsed later in the same year, causing widespread ruin. He had introduced some wise fiscal reforms, but had to fly the country and died at Venice. Law's 'système' and the rue Quincampoix are frequently referred to in contemporary literature.

Lazarillo de Tormes, a Spanish picaresque romance, the first of its kind, of uncertain authorship and date (about the middle of the 16th c.), the prototype of *Gil Blas*, &c.

Léautaud, PAUL (1872–1956), essayist and man of letters, was for years associated with the *Mercure de France* (q.v.), for a time as dramatic critic (*Théâtre de Maurice Boissard* [his pseudonym] *1907–1923*, 1927). He was co-editor, with Adolphe van Bever, of *Poètes d'aujourd'hui*, a well-known anthology of Symbolist poetry. His *Journal* (1954–) is at times cynical and rancorous reading, embittered by remembrance of an unhappy childhood, but it is interesting as a record of literary life and encounters. The three volumes published between 1954 and 1956 cover the years 1893–1921. Léautaud loved dogs and cats and wrote much about them. *Le Petit Ami*, 1903, is autobiography.

Le Bel, JEAN (*c.* 1290–*c.* 1370), a wealthy and well-born canon of Liège, author of a chronicle of the period 1329–61, written in a clear and vigorous style, and with an evident desire for truth and impartiality. A substantial part of this was incorporated by Froissart in his own work and provides some of its most admired passages, notably the incident of the burghers of Calais.

Leblanc, MAURICE, see *Lupin, Arsène*. His sister Georgette Leblanc was the well-known actress and singer for whom several of Maeterlinck's plays were written.

Le Bossu, RENÉ, PÈRE (1631–80), author of a *Traité du poème épique* (1675) and of a *Parallèle de la philosophie de Descartes et d'Aristote*. His critical work was admired by Dryden, and quoted in Congreve's *The Double Dealer* and in Macaulay's *History of England*.

Le Breton, ANDRÉ-FRANÇOIS (1708–79), the publisher of the *Encyclopédie* (q.v.).

Le Brun, CHARLES (1619–90), an eminent painter and decorator of the period of Louis XIV, rector of the Academy of Painting and Sculpture, and director of the Gobelins factory. He was employed on the decoration of the Louvre and Versailles, and was for a time the dictator of French art.

Lebrun, PONCE-DENIS ÉCOUCHARD (1729–1807), known to his contemporaries as *Lebrun-Pindare*, of a family of Paris tradesmen, a lyric poet, author of *Odes* collected in an edition of 1811, which earned him in his day a great reputation, though they are little more than rhetorical exercises. Among the best of these were two odes on the Lisbon earthquake of 1755, an ode (addressed to Voltaire, 1760) evoking the shade of Corneille in favour of Corneille's destitute niece,

and the odes addressed to Buffon. He was an ardent supporter of the Revolution and wrote an ode *Sur le vaisseau 'Le Vengeur'* (a French man-of-war which in 1794 allowed itself to be sunk by the British rather than surrender). He was also a skilful writer of epigrams, which he made the vehicle of literary criticism.

Le Cardonnel, LOUIS (1862–1936), poet, born at Valence (Drôme), strongly influenced by Roman Catholicism. He frequented Symbolist circles in Paris between 1881 and 1890, became a Roman Catholic, and in 1896 was ordained priest without, however, having to undertake any definite parochial duties. His works include *Poèmes* (published 1904, written between 1881 and 1890), *Carmina Sacra* (1912, religious poems), and *De l'une à l'autre aurore* (1924), which contains several war poems.

Leclercq, THÉODORE (1777–1851), born in Paris, was the author of *Proverbes dramatiques* (1820–30) often performed in the *salons* of the Restoration period. They were lively, subtly-observed sketches of contemporary, ultra-Royalist society. He was for a time (*c.* 1802) in England with his friend Fiévée (q.v.), also in Hamburg, where his *proverbes* entertained the small colony of *émigrés* which had settled there.

Leconte, SÉBASTIEN-CHARLES (1865–1934), a disciple of Leconte de Lisle, was the author of *La Tentation de l'homme* (1903), *Le Sang de Méduse* (1905), and other poetic collections.

Lecocq, CHARLES, see *Angot, Mme*.

Le Conte, see *Valleran Le Conte*.

Leconte de Lisle, CHARLES-MARIE-RENÉ (1818–94), leader of the Parnassian poets (see *Parnassiens*) was born on Reunion Island, where his father, a former surgeon in Napoleon's armies, had gone from Normandy and become a planter. His mother, a cousin of the poet Parny (q.v.), belonged to the island. In 1837 he came to France, studied law at Rennes, and began to write. In 1843 he revisited Reunion Island but from 1846 he lived in Paris. *Fouriérisme* (q.v., a system of social reform) had his sympathies for a time, when he was on the staff of Fourierist reviews. The 1848 Revolution roused his enthusiasm, but it also ruined his family (the abolition of slavery ruined many colonial planters) and his private allowance ceased. Several years of struggle, and of disillusionment with political events, followed, during which he subsisted inadequately on journalism, translations, and private tuition, but still devoted himself mainly to poetry and published his most famous collections—*Poèmes antiques* (1852), *Poèmes et poésies* (1855), *Poèmes barbares* (1862). (In 1872 and 1874 respectively the *Poèmes et poésies* were divided between augmented editions of *Poèmes antiques* and *Poèmes barbares*.) During this time, too, his house became the recognized meeting-place for his disciples (the poets, in 1866, of *Le Parnasse contemporain*). Poverty forced him to accept an Imperial pension in 1864. In 1872 his circumstances were further eased when he became librarian (a sinecure post) to the Senate. His later publications included *Les Érinnyes*, a tragedy based on the *Oresteia* of Aeschylus (performed and published 1873), and *Poèmes tragiques* (1884). The *Derniers poèmes* (1895) were published posthumously.

In *Poèmes antiques* the poet's inspiration is largely Greek and reflects his friendship with the Hellenist Louis Ménard (q.v.). He depicts prehistoric, pagan Greece, the beauty of Greek art and thought, the various stages of Greek civilization (*La Source, Niobe, Hélène, Khiron*). But he has also (*Bhagavat, La Vision de Brahma*) been inspired by Indian (Buddhist) thought and religion (cf. the many translations and treatises, by Burnouf and other orientalists, published from the 'forties onwards). The *Poèmes barbares* (i.e. *barbare* in the sense of non-Greek or non-Indian) are inspired by Egyptian or Nordic mythology (*Néférou-Ra, Le Voile d'Isis; Vision de Snorr*) or biblical history (*Qaïn*); or they are nature poems, depictions of exotic scenery and of jungle life (*La Fontaine aux lianes, Le Jaguar*). Both collections are typical of the formal perfection and the visual rather than emotive beauty which characterize the Parnassian poetry. They achieve, to a remarkable degree, the effect of immobility, sometimes the static archaeological beauty of ancient Greece, or again the intense stillness of the jungle with the wild beasts crouching, ready to spring, or sleeping, gorged with their prey. In addition, choice of subject and treatment are frequently dictated by the poet's own embittered, pessimistic, and atheistic outlook on life (cf. also *Foreign Influences on French literature*, para. 23).

Lecoq, MONSIEUR, who figures in novels by Émile Gaboriau (q.v.), is perhaps the earliest of the famous detectives of literature. As a young man he was so appalled at his talent for inventing perfect crimes that in self-defence he decided to exercise it on the side of law and order. The character of M. Lecoq was also used (e.g. in *La Vieillesse de Monsieur Lecoq*, 1878) by the once popular but now forgotten *roman-feuilletoniste* Fortuné Du Boisgobey (1821–91).

Lecouvreur, ADRIENNE (1692–1730), an actress eminent especially in tragic parts, noted for her adoption of the simple and natural as opposed to the declamatory style. By her charm, intelligence, modesty, and good sense she contributed to raise the social position of actresses in France. She was the mistress of Maurice of Saxony, the most brilliant warrior of his day, who deserted her for the duchesse de Bouillon. Some mysterious circumstances which preceded her death (shortly after this rupture) gave rise to the unfounded rumour that she had been poisoned by her rival. Voltaire, who was her friend, addressed an epistle to her (1723) and also wrote an elegy on her death, indignantly censuring the Church for refusing her burial. She is the subject of a play by Scribe and Legouvé.

Leczinski (or more correctly **Leszczynski**), STANISLAS (1677–1766), king of Poland from 1704 to 1709, when he was obliged to leave the country. In 1718 he was allowed to settle in France and in 1725 his daughter Marie became the wife of Louis XV. After failing to re-establish himself as King of Poland in 1733 he renounced his kingdom in return for the duchies of Lorraine and Bar. His court was at Lunéville. He patronized letters and the arts, and left a monument in the fine Place Stanislas at Nancy, the capital of Lorraine.

Le Dain or **Le Daim**, OLIVIER NECKER, *known as*, of Flemish origin, valet, barber, and counsellor of Louis XI; he was hanged in 1484. He figures in Scott's *Quentin Durward* and, very slightly, in Hugo's *Notre-Dame de Paris* (q.v.).

Ledru-Rollin, ALEXANDRE-AUGUSTE (1807–74), politician. He was a member of the Provisional Government in 1848.

Lefebvre, FRANÇOIS-JOSEPH, one of Napoleon's marshals (see *Maréchal de l'Empire*).

Lefebvre, GEORGES (1874–   ), one of the most distinguished modern historians of Revolutionary France, which he has studied from the point of view of social, economic, and agrarian conditions. His works include: *Les Paysans du Nord pendant la Révolution française* (1924), *La Révolution française* (1930; 1951), *Napoléon* (1935), *Les Thermidoriens* (1935), &c.

Lefèvre or **Lefèvre-Deumier,** JULES-ALEXANDRE (1797–1857), minor poet and novelist, a friend of Soumet (q.v.) and a contributor to *La Muse française* (q.v.). He is remembered less by his writings than as a figure of the dawning Romantic Movement (see *Romantisme*). *Sir Lionel d'Arguenay* (1834, a novel), *Œuvres d'un désœuvré* (1842, verse and prose), *Poésies* (1844), and *Le Livre du promeneur* (1854), prose poems, are examples of his work. In later life he inherited a large fortune, lived handsomely, and patronized the arts.

Le Fèvre de la Boderie, GUY (1541–98), is remembered as a friend of Amyot, Baïf, and Ronsard (qq.v.) and a fine specimen of Renaissance humanist. A scholar, learned in oriental languages and religious doctrines, he kept a taste for poetry 'au milieu des études les plus arides'. His own poetical works include: *L'Encyclie des secrets de l'Éternité* (1571); *La Galliade ou la révolution des arts* (1578); *Hymnes ecclésiastiques* (1578).

Lefèvre d'Étaples, JACQUES (1450–1537), also known by the Latin name of *Faber Stapulensis*, whence *Stapoul*; humanist, born at Étaples in Picardy. He was one of the early students of Greek, stimulated by making the acquaintance in Italy of Pico della Mirandola and Ficino. He edited the *Ethics*, *Politics*, and *Logic* of Aristotle, disregarding the works of the medieval commentators. He applied the same method of rational interpretation of actual texts to the New Testament. He became the centre of the Humanist movement in France and also one of the leaders of *Évangélisme* (q.v.). He made the first complete translation into French of the Bible (1523–30). François Ier appointed him tutor to his third son.

Lefranc, ABEL-JULES-MAURICE (1863–1952), scholar and critic, author of much-prized studies of Rabelais (whom he edited), Marguerite de Navarre, Calvin, &c. He also, in various writings, summed up in *A la découverte de Shakespeare* (1945–50, 3 vols.), maintained that Shakespeare's plays were written by William Stanley, 6th Earl of Derby.

Le Franc, MARTIN (c. 1410–61), secretary to popes Felix V and Nicolas V and holder of various preferments, author of a poem *Le Champion des Dames* inspired by the *Roman de la Rose*, but attacking its author Jean de Meung and taking up the defence of women with the same medley of allegory and erudition as we find in the earlier work. The poem, completed in 1442, was printed in 1485. The neglect which it suffered at the court of the Duke of Burgundy, to whom a fine manuscript copy had been sent, provoked the author to write a *Complainte du livre du Champion des dames à son auteur*; it shows the author's dignity and independence, though his claims as a poet are not high.

Le Franc de Pompignan, see *Pompignan*.

Légataire universel, Le, a comedy by Regnard, produced in 1708.

Géronte is a rich old man, ill and on the verge of the grave, surrounded by a host of greedy prospective heirs. Chief among these is his nephew Éraste, who, provided that he can secure the bulk of the inheritance, has been promised the hand of Isabelle. Géronte's intention of leaving large legacies to two relatives is cunningly defeated by Crispin, Éraste's valet, who successively impersonates the relatives, and by his outrageous conduct infuriates the old man against them. When Géronte faints before making a will and is thought dead, Crispin impersonates him and dictates to the notary a will in favour of Éraste (with handsome legacies to himself and the maid-servant he intends to marry). Géronte recovers, and the conspirators are much embarrassed, but extricate themselves by assuring Géronte that he dictated the will while in a trance. By a mixture of suasion and bullying he is induced to ratify the will, and rascality triumphs. The play is immoral, but gay and sparkling.

Légende de Saint Julien l'Hospitalier, La, the second of Flaubert's *Trois Contes* (q.v.).

Légende des siècles, La, epic poems in three series (1859, 1877, and 1883) by Victor Hugo. They include some of his finest verse.

In a succession of scenes from different epochs the poet sets out to portray man's spiritual and historical development. He begins with idyllic pictures of the Creation and the early days of Biblical history (*Le Sacre de la femme*; *Booz endormi*), passes fairly rapidly across oriental, Greek, and Roman antiquity, lingers over medieval times (*Le Mariage de Roland*; *Le Petit Roi de Galice*; *L'Aigle du casque*, &c.) and, after paying slight attention to the 16th, 17th, and 18th centuries, arrives at the 19th century, after the Revolution has brought Liberty and made the people conscious of moral progress (*Jean Chouan*; *Les Pauvres Gens*). He concludes with several visions of the future and the Day of Judgement (*Pleine mer, Plein ciel, La Trompette du jugement*, &c.).

The poems of the 2nd and 3rd series do not alter or extend the scheme of the *Légende*. They are perhaps on a less consistently high level than those of the first series. Hugo's intention had been to make two further collections, *La Fin de Satan* and *Dieu*, the completion and crown of the whole work. In the first, the forces of evil were to be annihilated by the angel Liberty (thus giving scope for a number of poems on the Revolution, neglected in the *Légende* itself). The theme of the second was human nature seeking after light and coming finally to the conception of God as Love. They were published posthumously (1886 and 1891 respectively, both incomplete) and contain writing of a remarkable visionary quality.

Légende napoléonienne, La. To the France of 1815, exhausted by long wars and weary of despotism, the Allied conquerors seemed almost like deliverers. The next few years brought disillusionment: the terms of the 1815 treaty were humiliating, and the hard-won liberties of the Revolution disappeared under the restored Monarchy. As a result, in many quarters the memory of the despot who had brought his country to the verge of ruin began to fade. In its place evolved the legend of the 'soldat de la Révolution', the incarnation of the Revolutionary ideals of liberty, the hero who had restored France from chaos to order and who would, but for the hostility of Europe, have brought peace and liberty to the world. To this was added the sentimental picture of the lonely father, sorrowing on a rock in the Atlantic for the son torn from him by Allied persecutors. The legend grew, especially after Napoleon's death in 1821, when the companions of his exile returned with stories of the years of captivity. It was fostered in various ways, such as the *chansons* of Béranger (e.g. his *Souvenirs du peuple* in *Chansons inédites,* 1828) or some of Hugo's poems (e.g. *Ode à la Colonne,* written and published (*Journal des Débats*) 1827; *Lui,* written 1828, in *Les Orientales,* 1829; *Napoléon II,* written 1832, in *Les Chants du crépuscule,* 1835; and *Ode à l'Arc de Triomphe,* in *Les Voix intérieures,* 1837); and, not least, by the sheets of coloured pictures (*images d'Épinal,* q.v.) which circulated among the people (cf. also the picture of Napoleon given by the devoted old soldier in Balzac's *Le Médecin de campagne,* q.v.). In 1833 the government of Louis-Philippe, as a gesture of goodwill, once more erected a statue of Napoleon on top of the Column in the Place Vendôme. (The original statue had been replaced by an enormous fleur-de-lis during the Restoration.) In 1840 the remains of Napoleon were brought back from St. Helena and enclosed in a tomb at the Invalides (15 Dec.). Hugo called this 'la fête d'un cercueil exilé qui revient en triomphe', though Lamartine (26 May 1840, when funds for the 'translation des cendres' were voted) had deplored 'cette religion napoléonienne: ce culte de la force que l'on veut ... substituer dans l'esprit de la nation à la religion sérieuse de la liberté'. In 1848 the newly-organized Bonapartist party founded newspapers with such names as *Le Petit Caporal* and *La Redingote grise* (an allusion to Napoleon's famous grey overcoat), and used the *légende* and the magic name of Napoleon as political propaganda to capture the working-class vote for Prince Louis-Napoléon (later Napoleon III).

[The novel *Les Déracinés,* q.v., by Maurice Barrès, contains a short character sketch of Napoleon and an appreciation of what the *légende napoléonienne* had signified for succeeding generations and all types of men.]

Léger, ALEXIS SAINT-LÉGER (1889–   ), whose eloquent, stylized verse is written under the pseudonym of SAINT-JOHN PERSE, was born in Guadeloupe and educated in France. His career in the Diplomatic Service ended in 1940 when he was dispossessed by the Vichy Government. He went to the U.S.A., where he still lives. After *Éloges* (1911), a collection of early, mainly Symbolist verse, his output includes a long poem *Anabase* (1924), in which the conqueror who opens up new territory, halts awhile, and departs again for the unknown may symbolize man, the eternal uncertain wanderer in search of himself; also *Pluies, Vents, Neiges, Exil, Poème à l'étrangère*, all in *Œuvre poétique* (1953). As with Claudel, who influenced him, travel and a sense of vast land- and sea-scapes count for much in his work. He often employs Claudel's poetic form, the *verset* (q.v.).

Léger, Vie de Saint, one of the earliest surviving French poems, probably of the second half of the 10th century. It consists of forty *sixains* of octosyllabic verses. The author is not known.

Légion d'honneur, a non-hereditary order, instituted by Napoleon while still First Consul (decree of 29 Floréal, an X—i.e. 19 May 1802) as a reward for military and civilian services, and still continuing. The first investiture took place on the Champ-de-Mars (q.v.) on 14 July 1804, some months before Napoleon's coronation as Emperor.

There are five classes (in ascending order) —Chevalier, Officier, Commandeur, Grand-Officier, Grand-Croix. The last of these was at first called 'Grand-Aigle', after the original design of the medal, which on one side bore the effigy of 'Napoléon Empereur des Français' (later replaced by the head of the Republic), and on the other the Imperial Eagle (later replaced by two tricolour flags) and the words 'Honneur et Patrie' (which it still bears). The medal is a star with five double points, with oak and laurel leaves filling the interstices, and surmounted by a wreath of oak and laurel leaves.

Napoleon also founded *maisons d'éducation de la Légion d'honneur*, educational establishments for girls, daughters or other blood relations of members of the *Légion d'honneur*, and with paying and non-paying places. Some of these schools still continue,

the most important being at Saint-Denis. Mme Campan (q.v.) had much to do with the idea in its early stages.

Légion étrangère, the name of regiments of the French army based in Algeria and composed mainly of foreigners, though for the most part officered by the regular French Army. It was created in 1831 by the law authorizing the formation of a *légion étrangère* to be recruited in France from persons of non-French birth and sent to Algeria. This first Foreign Legion was ceded to Spain in 1835 but another was formed in the same year and again sent to Algeria, and from the original one regiment it expanded rapidly. It was sent wherever the French were fighting: to the Crimea (1854), Italy (1859), Mexico (1863), Indo-China (*c.* 1875 and again within recent memory), and has also fought in France. To some extent it continues the tradition of the foreign mercenaries introduced into their armies by the early kings of France. At the outbreak of the Revolution about one-quarter of the French Army consisted of foreigners—Swiss, Germans, Irish, Swedes, Hungarians, &c., and between then and the law of 1831 the practice of allowing, at times inviting, foreigners to serve had not completely died out.

The foreign soldiers of the *Légion étrangère* are volunteers, enlisted for limited but renewable periods, and often refugees from their own country. If identity papers are not in order no questions are asked. Frenchmen can also be enrolled, *as foreigners*, which means they must have some special reason for sinking their identity. The life is hard and exacting, often adventurous, though hardly the glamorous, romantic life depicted by Ouida in *Under Two Flags*.

Législateur du Parnasse, Le, a term used to designate Boileau.

Législative, La, see *Assemblée législative*.

Légitimistes, the name, after the July Revolution, for the supporters of the elder (Bourbon) branch of the royal family (cf. *Bourbon*; *Chambord, comte de*; *Orléanistes*; *Révolution du 29 juillet*).

Le Goffic, CHARLES (1863–1932), poet and novelist, at times also dramatist, of Breton life. His poetical works include: *Amour breton* (1889), *Le Bois dormant* (1889–1900), collected with others in *Poésies complètes* (1933). *Le Crucifié de Kéraliès* (1892) is typical of his novels, which are of a dramatic character.

Legouis, ÉMILE (1861–1937), born at Honfleur, literary historian and critic, for long Professor of English at the Sorbonne, and one of the finest English scholars of his day. With his colleague Louis Cazamian (q.v.) he wrote a history of English literature (1924) which has become a standard work. He also published studies of the great poets of the periods in which he was particularly interested, e.g. Wordsworth (1896), Chaucer (1910), Spenser (1923). His *Défense de la poésie française à l'usage des lecteurs anglais* (1912) should be noted.

Legouvé, GABRIEL-MARIE-JEAN-BAPTISTE (1764–1812), author of didactic and descriptive verse, of which *Le Mérite des femmes* (1801) is the best remembered, and of historical tragedies, seldom mentioned: *La Mort d'Abel* (1792), *Étéocle* (1799), *La Mort de Henri IV* (1806).

Legrand, MARC-ANTOINE (1673–1728), an actor at the *Comédie-Française*, wrote several short comedies which were played at that theatre between 1707 and 1727. *Le Roi de Cocagne* (1718, verse, see *Cocagne*) was popular, also *Le Galant coureur ou l'Ouvrage d'un moment* (prose). The latter is said to have inspired Marivaux's *Jeu de l'amour et du hasard*.

Leipzig, Battle of (16–18 October 1813), resulted in a shattering victory of the combined forces of the Sixth, or General Coalition (q.v.) over the French under Napoleon. Shortly afterwards, the Allied Armies invaded France (January 1814) and by 30 March they were before Paris (see *Paris, Treaty of*).

Lekain, HENRI-LOUIS CAIN, *known as* (1728–78), a tragic actor, who took leading parts in many of Voltaire's tragedies. He left interesting memoirs.

Le Laboureur, LOUIS, see *Epic poetry*.

Lélia (1833), a novel by George Sand (q.v.).

Lélian, Pauvre, an anagram of 'Paul Verlaine', see *Poètes maudits, Les*.

Lemaire de Belges, JEAN (*c.* 1473–d. before 1525), born in Hainault (a province of Belgium, whence his name), was one of the last and best of the *rhétoriqueurs* (q.v.). Attached as secretary or chronicler to various princely houses (notably of Margaret of Austria and Anne of Brittany), he travelled a great deal, visiting Italy thrice. He thus came under the influence of Italian literature (Dante, Boccaccio, Petrarch). His works reveal his interest in music, sculpture, and painting (he was concerned in the building of the Church of Brou, q.v.); also the influence of certain Latin authors, such as Ovid. They include epistles and miscellaneous allegorical poems, and the *Illustrations de Gaule*, a long compilation of fabulous narratives relating to the origins of the French (who are traced back to Hector of Troy); it is written in harmonious prose, interspersed with quotations from Latin and Greek poets, and contains many picturesque passages. Some of his best verses and ideas are contained in *La Concorde des deux langages*, i.e. those of France and Italy, an allegory in which he urges the spiritual harmony of the two nations.

Le Maître, ANTOINE (1608–58), a member through his mother of the Arnauld (q.v.) family, an eloquent and successful advocate who retired to Port-Royal in 1638.

Lemaître, FRÉDÉRICK (1800–76), French actor, particularly celebrated during the Romantic period. He played with the clown Deburau (q.v.) at the *Théâtre des Funambules*, turned the melodrama *L'Auberge des Adrets* (1823) from a failure into a success by burlesquing the part of Robert Macaire (q.v., incidentally endowing caricaturists of the period with a famous character), and later played leading roles in some of the Romantic dramas, e.g. *Ruy Blas* (q.v.).

Lemaître, JULES (1853–1914), for many years dramatic critic of the *Journal des Débats* (q.v.), was celebrated for his brilliant, impressionistic, often ironical articles. They were published in collected form: *Les Contemporains* (vols. 1–7, 1885–99; vol. 8, 1918), *Impressions de théâtre* (vols. 1–10, 1888–98; vol. 11, 1920). His dramatic works, overliterary and only moderately successful, included the comedies *Révoltée* (1889), *Le Député Leveau* (1891, a political satire),

Mariage blanc (1891), and *L'Aînée* (1898). He also published collections of short stories, including *Sérénus, histoire d'un martyr* (1886), *Dix contes* (1889), and *Contes blancs* (1900).

Le Maître de Saci, LOUIS-ISAAC (1613–84, *Saci* is an anagram of *Isaac*), younger brother of Antoine Le Maître, one of the solitaries of Port-Royal, the learned and prudent director of the community after Singlin (q.v.), and a leading Jansenist. He was imprisoned in 1666 in the course of the persecution of that sect and remained for two years in the Bastille. There he translated the O.T. from the Vulgate, having previously taken the principal part in the translation of the N.T. known as the *Nouveau Testament de Mons* (see *Bible, French versions*). His Bible (published 1672–95) replaced the ancient versions written in antiquated language (the Protestant versions being suspect). Saci also translated the *Imitation of Jesus Christ* (1662). Nicolas Fontaine (q.v.) in his *Mémoires* records a conversation of great literary interest, *L'Entretien* [de Pascal] *avec M. de Saci sur Épictète et Montaigne.*

Lemercier, NÉPOMUCÈNE (1771–1840), dramatist, author of several mediocre tragedies of which one, *Agamemnon* (1797, verse), was considered a masterpiece in its day. He is better remembered as the creator of French historical comedy with *Pinto ou la Journée d'une conspiration* (1800, prose). Its theme was the revolution of 1640 which drove the Spaniards out of Portugal; and Pinto, the chief character, bore some resemblance to Figaro. *La Panhypocrisiade ou le Spectacle infernal du seizième siècle* (1819), by this author, half epic, half verse-drama, and mainly satirical in intention, was called by his contemporary Charles Nodier 'ce chaos monstrueux de vers étonnés de se rencontrer ensemble'.

Lemerre, ALPHONSE (1838–1912), the publisher associated with the Parnassian poets. He published *Le Parnasse contemporain* (1866, 1871, 1876) and it was at his bookshop in the Passage Choiseul that the young poets of the movement held their gatherings. The firm and the bookshop still exist.

Lemierre, ANTOINE-MARIN (1723–93), poet, author of descriptive poems after the manner of Thomson's *Seasons, Les Fastes* and *La Peinture*; and of tragedies, *Hypermnestre*

(1758), *Térée* (1761), *Guillaume Tell* (1766), *Barnevelt* (1790), &c., none of them of much merit.

Lemoine, JEAN, CARDINAL (c. 1250–1313), prelate and theologian. He founded (c. 1302) the Collège Lemoine, one of the early colleges of the University (see *Universities*, para. 4).

Lemonnier, CAMILLE (1845–1913), novelist and art critic, a Belgian. He wrote in French and with other writers connected with the review *La Jeune Belgique* shared the aims of the French symbolists (see *Symbolisme*) and stimulated a revival of Belgian letters. Besides criticism, his works include: *Contes flamands et wallons* (1873) and several novels which range from naturalistic studies of the dregs and slaves of civilization (*Happe-chair*, 1886; *Madame Lupar*, 1888; *Un Mâle*, 1892, the most typical) to lyrical, at times rhapsodical, descriptions of country life (*Au cœur frais de la forêt*, 1899; *Le Vent dans les moulins*, 1900; *Le Petit Homme de Dieu*, 1903).

Le Moyne, PIERRE, LE PÈRE (1602–72), a Jesuit, author of an epic poem, *Saint Louis ou le héros chrétien* (1653, 1658).

Le Nain, three brothers, LOUIS (1593–1648), ANTOINE (1598–1648), MATHIEU (1607–77), born at Laon, painters of genre pictures of humble life and rustic scenes.

Le Nain de Tillemont, see *Tillemont*.

Lenclos, ANNE DE, *known as* NINON DE (1620–1705), a woman famous for her *liaisons* with some of the most distinguished men of her day (including Saint-Évremond), and for the charm, wit, virile intellect, and probity with which in her later years she acquired consideration. Her *salon* was then frequented by men of letters (Boileau, La Fontaine, Racine, Molière, and others), 'libertins' (q.v.), artists, and members of high society. Mme de la Fayette and Mme de Maintenon were among her friends. There is an interesting appreciation of her in Saint-Simon under the year 1705, and Mlle de Scudéry has depicted her as Clarisse in her *Clélie*. Her letters have been published; also a slender volume of sketches by her, *La Coquette vengée* (1659). The youthful Voltaire was presented to her in her old age, and she, with discernment, left him a small legacy to buy books. She was the subject of many anecdotes and one of these has endowed the French language with a proverb. The marquis de La Châtre, her lover, on leaving her for the army, obtained from her a written promise (*billet*) that she would be faithful to him. Her first infidelity occasioned her gay exclamation, 'Le bon billet qu'a La Châtre!', an expression which has become proverbial for an illusory promise.

Lenéru, MARIE (1875–1918), born at Brest of a family with long naval rather than literary traditions, spent her life mainly in Brittany with occasional stays in Paris. She kept a remarkable diary (1922, posth.), begun in 1886 as a task imposed on her by her mother when she was still a normally healthy, very lively-minded child. In 1889 it became irregular and in 1890 stopped wholly, for she had become completely deaf and was also for a time threatened with total blindness. The blindness was averted and in 1893 the diary was resumed. It now became the refuge of a character isolated by her affliction, secretly a prey to the most bitter depression and resentment, but stoically, almost arrogantly, determined to meet the world smiling and—for the diary was clearly intended for future readers—to let the world know what that determination had cost. She read ferociously, developed her critical faculty and her literary style, met and corresponded with many distinguished men of letters, and in time won a certain measure of success as a dramatist with, e.g., *Les Affranchis* (1911) and *Le Redoutable* (1912), plays which are interesting but somewhat lifeless. It is as the diarist that she remains.

Lenet, PIERRE (d. 1671), a lawyer of Dijon, a supporter of the prince de Condé in the Fronde. He wrote memoirs of that period.

Lenormand, HENRI-RENÉ (1882–1951), dramatist, born in Paris, author of interesting, somewhat gloomy plays which exploit the Freudian theories of the Unconscious. A feature of his technique is the use of *tableaux* (i.e. successions of very short scenes which occupy only one part of the stage, the remainder being blacked out for the time being). His best-known play *Les Ratés* (1918) traces the physical and spiritual downfall of an unsuccessful author and his mistress, a second-rate actress. They cannot accept happiness unthinkingly, and gradually succumb to mis-

fortune. The man acquiesces in the woman's shameful ways of earning money and is tortured by his failure to console either her or himself. He takes to drink, kills her, and commits suicide. Other plays by Lenormand are *Le Temps est un songe* (1919), *Le Simoun* (1920), *Le Mangeur de rêves* (1922), *L'Homme et ses fantômes* (1925), *Le Lâche* (1926).

Le Nôtre, ANDRÉ (1613–1700), the designer of the gardens of Versailles.

Léonard, NICOLAS-GERMAIN (1744–93), poet, an imitator of the idylls of Gessner, and of Tibullus and Propertius, author of *Idylles et poèmes* (1771–87), which occasionally show sincere melancholy and emotion, and of the romance *Thérèse et Faldrui* (1783).

Leonardo da Vinci (1452–1519), the great Italian painter, sculptor, and engineer, accepted service under Louis XII in 1507 and died in France under François Ier.

Léonins, Vers, Latin verses of which one hemistich rhymes with the other. The name is said to be derived from a certain Léon, canon of Saint-Victor in Paris in the 12th century, who set the fashion of such verses. In early French poetry the term is also used of lines in which the final rhyme is found again within the line.

Le Play, PIERRE-GUILLAUME-FRÉDÉRIC (1806–82), social reformer, founder of an international society for the practical study of social economics; author of *Les Ouvriers européens* (1855), a comparative study of typical family budgets of workers in different industries; *La Réforme sociale* (1864); *L'Organisation de la famille* (1871), &c. His doctrine was intrinsically religious, based on the need for maintaining a parental form of authority in industry as well as in the home.

Lépreux de la cité d'Aoste, Le (1811), a tale by Xavier de Maistre (q.v.).

Leprince de Beaumont, MARIE, MME (1711–80), wrote over seventy books for children, mainly collections of moral, instructive tales. She married unhappily in 1743 and about two years later went to London. There she remained for seventeen years, became a governess, published some of her books (her *Éducation complète*, 1753, was intended 'à l'usage de la famille de la princesse de Galles'), and remarried. From 1764 she lived in Switzerland. Her best-known collections were *Le Nouveau Magasin français, ou Bibliothèque instructive* (1750–5) and the *Magasin des enfants* (1757), both published in London. (See also *Children's reading*.)

Leroux, GASTON (1868–), author of popular detective novels, e.g. *Le Mystère de la chambre jaune*, *Le Parfum de la dame en noir*, in which he created Rouletabille, an amateur detective known to students of detective fiction. Joseph Rouletabille, so nicknamed from his bullet-shaped head, is a young journalist and crime reporter who uses his reasoning powers to solve a mystery while the police are still scratching their pates.

Le Roux, PHILIBERT-JOSEPH, see *Dictionaries and Encyclopedias* under date 1718.

Leroux, PIERRE (1797–1871), born in Paris, philosopher, economist, and idealistic social reformer. To support his family he broke off his education at the *École polytechnique* and became a journeyman printer (when he invented an apparatus to lighten compositors' work). In 1824, with Paul-François Dubois (1793–1874), he founded *Le Globe* (q.v.) and shared that journal's *Saint-Simonien* phase in 1831. In 1841 he founded the *Revue indépendante* (q.v.) with Louis Viardot (1800–83) and G. Sand (q.v.). The latter's novels at one period were strongly influenced by his vaguely pantheistic religion of humanity, expounded in obscure fashion in *De l'humanité, de son principe et de son avenir* (1840) and, to some extent, in an earlier work, *Du Christianisme et de ses origines démocratiques*, reprinted (1838) as *De l'égalité*. In 1843 he founded a printing business to put his socialist ideas into practice, but it failed. He was ineffective as a socialist Deputy to the Constituent and Legislative Assemblies of 1848 and 1849; and after the *coup d'état* (q.v.) of 2 December 1851 he retired to Jersey, where he wrote a socialist poem *La Grève de Samarez* (1863–4).

Le Roux de Lincy, ADRIEN-JEAN-VICTOR (1806–69), born in Paris, medievalist and bibliographer, sometime librarian at the Bibliothèque de l'Arsenal (q.v.). He published studies of medieval literature and of the early history of Paris, also *Le Livre des proverbes français* (1842–59, 2 vols.), still one of the best collections of French proverbs, with an interesting introductory essay on their history and their use in literature. The arrangement is by series, according to subject, but in alphabetical order following the leading word within each series, and there is also an index of leading words.

Le Roy, ÉDOUARD (1870–1954), Catholic (anti-Thomist) philosopher, was Professor of Philosophy at the Collège de France (q.v.) from 1921 to 1941, in succession to Bergson, whose inspiration is strongly apparent in his thought. His publications include: *L'Exigence idéaliste et le fait de l'évolution* (1927), *Les Origines humaines et l'évolution de l'intelligence* (1928), *La Pensée intuitive* (1930), all three the book form of lectures delivered at the Collège de France; also the collected articles and lectures, more specifically religious philosophy, of *Essai sur la notion du miracle* (1906), *Dogme et critique. Études de philosophie et de critique religieuse* (1907), *Le Problème de Dieu* (1929).

Leroy, JEAN, see *Satire Ménippée*.

Le Roy, LOUIS (1510–77), humanist, author of a translation (with commentary) of the *Politics* of Aristotle, of translations of Plato, and of political writings.

Lesage or **Le Sage**, ALAIN-RENÉ (1668–1747), of modest Breton origin, dramatist and novelist, spent a quiet and honourable life supporting himself and his family by unremitting literary work. In his last years he retired to the canonry of his son at Boulogne-sur-Mer. He began his literary career with translations from the Spanish, but first achieved success both as dramatist and novelist in 1707 (at almost forty) with his gay comedy *Crispin rival de son maître* and the romance *Le Diable boiteux* (qq.v.). In 1709 he produced his comedy *Turcaret* (q.v.), an audacious satire on the world of the financiers. Thereafter he quarrelled with the Comédie-Française, having a poor opinion of the grand style of acting, and wrote singly or in collaboration some hundred pieces for the Théâtre de la Foire. These were farces or comedies of manners, often in an oriental setting, interspersed with lyrics sung to popular airs (*comédies à vaudevilles*). The first two volumes of his great picaresque romance, *Gil Blas* (q.v.), appeared in 1715, the third in 1724, the fourth in 1735. The romance *Les Aventures de M. Robert Chevalier, dit de Beauchêne* (a real person; a story in the main of the wars between the English and the French in Canada, of buccaneers and Red Indians) was published in 1732, and three other picaresque novels, *Don Guzman d'Alfarache*, *Estevanille Gonzalès*, and *Le Bachelier de Salamanque*, appeared in 1732, 1734, and 1736 respectively. Of these the last is perhaps the best, and its theme has some analogy to that of *Gil Blas*: its hero, Don Chérubin, travels about the world in the character of a tutor and introduces the reader to his pupils and their parents. Lesage also wrote some minor pieces of fiction, *La Valise trouvée* and the Lucianic *Une Journée des Parques*. But none of the above is comparable in quality to the author's chief work.

The charm of Lesage lies in the good humour with which he depicts the failings and absurdities of human nature (he reserved his bitterness for the financiers alone), his power of vivid and dramatic presentation, the extraordinary animation of his narrative, and the fluidity and precision of his style. The principal reproach that can be addressed to him is a certain lack of moral elevation; there is little or nothing of the finer sentiments, such as love or filial affection, in his work. He was not adequately appreciated by his contemporaries; Voltaire disliked him. Sainte-Beuve ranks him as a satirist with Fielding and Goldsmith, below Cervantes and Molière. Saintsbury regards the novel of Lesage as the immediate parent of that of Fielding and Smollett.

Lescot (pron. as if *Lèss-co*), PIERRE (*c.* 1510–78), the first of the three famous architects of the French Renaissance (the other two being Philibert Delorme and Jean Bullant, qq.v.). Lescot, the son of a magistrate, was wealthy, learned, and an ecclesiastic, with a gift for drawing and architecture, and was invited by François Ier to design the palace of the Louvre. He submitted to Henri II the grandiose plan which, in its general lines, was eventually carried out, and spent a great part of his life supervising the beginning of the construction. He was celebrated by Ronsard.

Lescurel, JEHANNOT DE, a 14th-century poet, author of *ballades* and *rondeaux*, of whom nothing is known.

Lespinasse (pron. as if *Lèss-*), JULIE-JEANNE-ÉLÉONORE DE (1732–76), illegitimate daughter of the comtesse d'Albon, was a woman of keen intelligence and passionate sentiment. She became in 1754 companion to Mme du Deffand (q.v.), who was now blind, but in 1764 parted from her in consequence of a quarrel. Many frequenters of Mme du Deffand's *salon* (including d'Alembert, Turgot, and Condorcet) now deserted it for that of Mlle de Lespinasse, which became a meeting-place of the *encyclopédistes*. D'Alembert was her devoted friend (he and she are two of the three characters in Diderot's *Le Rêve de d'Alembert*); and she had lovers, first a Spaniard, the marquis Gonsalvo de Mora, who died in 1774; and secondly the comte de Guibert, who had written an essay on military tactics and appears to have been a showy mediocrity. Her passionate love-letters to the latter have been published.

L'Espine, JEAN DE, see *Jean de l'Espine*.

Lespy, JULIEN, see *Jodelet*.

Lesseps, FERDINAND DE (1805–94), French diplomat, to whose initiative the piercing of the Suez Canal was due (completed 1869). He was also one of the chief promoters of the Panama Canal scheme (see *Panama, L'Affaire du*).

L'Estoile, PIERRE TAISAN DE (1546–1611), a lawyer who recorded month by month in a *Registre-Journal* memorable events of the reigns of Henri III and Henri IV, as well as many occurrences of minor importance, current epigrams, and topical sonnets; a work of much interest and historical importance. Saintsbury regards him as the nearest approach to a French Pepys.

Le Sueur, EUSTACHE (1616–55), painter, notably of religious pictures (a series of the Life of St. Bruno) and landscapes, showing deep sentiment and serious thought.

Leszczynski, see *Leczinski*.

Le Tellier, MICHEL (1603–85), minister of war under Louis XIV, father of Louvois (q.v.). His funeral oration was delivered by Bossuet.

Letourneur, PIERRE (1736–88), published translations, in 1758 of Richardson's novels, in 1769 of Young's *Night Thoughts*, and in 1777 of Ossian. But his chief work was his translation of Shakespeare in twenty volumes

(1776–83)—a prose version, conscientiously close, but lacking all the magic of Shakespeare's verse, and not free from occasional misinterpretations (see for instance Lady Macbeth's 'Stand not upon the order of your going', which becomes 'N'attendez pas ses ordres pour vous retirer'). Letourneur thus contributed in a measure (with Ducis, Laplace, qq.v., and others) to the influence that English literature exerted on the pre-Romantic movement in France in the later 18th century. The admiration for Shakespeare which Letourneur expressed in an introduction increased the resentment which Laplace's translation had already awakened in Voltaire, and provoked the latter's famous letter to the *Académie* of 1776.

Letters, see *Correspondances littéraires*.

Lettre à d'Alembert sur les spectacles, a polemical treatise by J.-J. Rousseau, published in 1758, on the question of the morality of the drama.

Theatres were prohibited at Geneva by the authorities and in France they were looked on with disfavour by the Church. The drama had been austerely denounced by Bossuet and actors were treated with cruel harshness by the clergy. Voltaire, the principal dramatic author of his day, had asked d'Alembert, in his forthcoming article in the *Encyclopédie*, on *Geneva*, to plead the cause of the theatre, and this d'Alembert had done. Rousseau shared the view that the drama might with advantage be abolished, and in his *Lettre à d'Alembert* he sets forth his case at length. He argues, with ingenious illustrations, that the matter dramatically presented, while it can never be morally beneficial (in spite of old saws about pity and terror), may be actively pernicious, since the drama often represents vice in an attractive form. On the other hand, the attendant conditions of dramatic performances, such as the waste of time and money, are uniformly bad. These influences would be especially unfortunate in the simple, unsophisticated society of Geneva. The *Letter* contains a notable criticism of Molière's *Le Misanthrope*. D'Alembert replied in a *Lettre à J.-J. Rousseau*.

Lettres à l'inconnue (1873), the letters written by Prosper Mérimée to Mademoiselle Jenny Dacquin (qq.v.).

Lettres anglaises, or *Lettres sur les Anglais,* see *Lettres philosophiques*.

Lettres champenoises, Les, or *Correspondance politique, morale et littéraire* (1817–25), a literary review published as a miscellany, at irregular intervals, so as to evade censorship. It numbered Dumas *père*, Gautier, and Hugo, as well as other young Romantic writers, among its contributors (see *Romantisme*).

Lettres de cachet, the name, in pre-Revolutionary France, for letters sealed with the king's privy seal and usually directing the imprisonment or exile without trial of the persons named in them. They were used especially to confine persons whose conduct was likely to bring discredit on their families. The practice was much abused during the 17th and 18th centuries. These letters were also known as *lettres closes* to distinguish them from the *lettres patentes* written on State business, which were sealed with the Great Seal and counter-signed by a Secretary of State. One of Mirabeau's (q.v.) best-known treatises was his *Des Lettres de cachet et des prisons d'État*, written during his imprisonment at Vincennes and published at Hamburg in 1782. It expounds his theories of constitutional monarchy.

Lettres de Dupuis et Cotonet, Les, by A. de Musset, a satire of *le romantisme* (q.v.), first published in the *Revue des Deux Mondes* (1836, 1837, 1838), purported to be written by two provincial worthies who were puzzled by the literary terminology of the day. The first, and best known, letter is a witty description of the plain man's efforts to distinguish between classicism and romanticism. Finally he decides with relief that romanticism is merely a matter of adjectives run wild.

Lettres de Maximilien Robespierre ... à ses commettants, see *Défenseur de la Constitution*.

Lettres de mon moulin, see *Daudet, Alphonse*, para. 2.

Lettres du comte de Mirabeau à ses commettants, see *Courrier de Provence*.

Lettres d'une Péruvienne, by Mme de Graffigny, published in 1747, a series of forty-one letters purporting to be written by a young Peruvian lady brought to France when her country is conquered by the Spaniards. Her comments on French manners and customs are combined with a mild element of romance. After rejecting the advances of her amiable and love-stricken French protector and remaining faithful to the Peruvian lover from whom she has been separated, she discovers that the latter has transferred his affections to a Spanish lady. The work helped to popularize the epistolary novel.

Lettres d'une religieuse portugaise, see *Lettres portugaises.*

Lettres d'un voyageur, see *Sand, George,* para. 5.

Lettres du Sépulcre, see *Assises de Jérusalem.*

Lettres écrites de France et d'Italie, the letters written by Paul-Louis Courier (q.v.) to his family and friends between the years 1787 and 1812 and first published in his *Œuvres complètes* (1829–30). They contain interesting descriptions of French society in Milan and Rome and of the writer's army experiences, as well as correspondence about his classical studies. The letters to his women friends and, latterly, to his wife are good reading, sometimes models of their kind, e.g. the ones to his cousin Mme Pigalle, a lady whose pregnancies followed one another with great rapidity. The tone is lively, affectionate, bantering, and sometimes, suddenly, more serious: 'Mais savez-vous ce qui m'arrive de ne plus rire? Je deviens méchant. . . . Je rêve nuit et jour aux moyens de tuer des gens que je n'ai jamais vus, qui ne m'ont fait ni bien ni mal.'

Lettres écrites de la montagne, a series of nine letters, published in 1764, in which J.-J. Rousseau defended himself forcibly and at great length against the attacks made on him and his religious doctrines by his enemies at Geneva in Tronchin's *Lettres écrites de la campagne.*

Lettres familières, see *Patin, Gui.*

Lettres juives, see *Argens.*

Lettres normandes, Les (1817–20), one of the better-known literary reviews of the Restoration period, edited by Léon Thiessé (1793–1854), wittily written, and published

as a miscellany, at irregular intervals, so as to evade censorship. It favoured the maintenance of the classical traditions of French literature as opposed to the new theories introduced by the Romantics (see *Romantisme*).

Lettres persanes, by Montesquieu, published in 1721, a collection of imaginary letters written and received by two Persians who visit Paris about the end of the reign of Louis XIV. In 1754 Montesquieu added some further letters and at his death he left a number of corrections to be made in the text.

The letters, in which the Persians record what they observe and the reflections to which the observations give rise, form a satirical review of French contemporary society and social and political institutions, covering a great variety of subjects, from Louis XIV himself and later the Regent and their methods of government, through the Church and its sectarian quarrels, the magistrature and the University, the financiers and Law's system, to the poets, gamblers, Lotharios, and so forth whom they encounter. A series of letters (133–7) describing a visit to the University library contains pungent criticisms on the various categories of French literature. Some letters are of a wider scope, dealing with such matters as war, international law, and the causes of depopulation; these show the author's preoccupation with grave questions, and his powerful and original mind. Interspersed among the more serious letters are a number concerned with the affairs of the seraglio which one of the Persians has left behind him, giving a picture, voluptuous or repulsive according to taste, of the ardent passions, intrigues, and tragedies of life in an oriental harem.

The work admirably illustrates the spirit that prevailed widely in France in the early 18th century.

Lettres philosophiques (frequently referred to by the author in his correspondence as LETTRES ANGLAISES), a series of twenty-four letters by Voltaire, the outcome of his residence in England, 1726–8, the greater part of them probably written in 1729–31 and published in 1734. Ten editions were published by 1739; an English version appeared in 1733, before the first French edition. A twenty-fifth letter on the *Pensées* of Pascal is unconnected with the visit to England. The *parlement* immediately ordered the work to be burnt as scandalous and disrespectful, and the author to be arrested. It was then that Voltaire sought refuge at Cirey in the house of Mme du Châtelet. In the Kehl edition the letters are dispersed under various headings of the *Dictionnaire philosophique* and in the *Mélanges littéraires*. They have, however, been separately reprinted in their original form.

The letters discuss various aspects of English life, and these are made the occasion for the ironical comparison and criticism of French institutions. The first four deal with the Quakers. The author was evidently much impressed by a sect that paid more attention to the simple moral and spiritual precepts of Christ than to dogma and ritual. These are followed by three letters on the Anglican Church, the Presbyterians, and the anti-Trinitarians respectively. Next come two letters admiring the English system of government and tracing its history; then one on trade, and one on the inoculation of small-pox. After these come letters on Lord Bacon and Locke, four on Newton (whom Voltaire compares with Descartes) and his physical, optical, and mathematical discoveries. The author then turns to literature, discussing in succession English tragedy (Shakespeare, Dryden, Addison), comedy (Wycherley, Vanbrugh, Congreve), noble authors, the poetry of Rochester and Waller, the satirists (Swift, Butler, and Pope, incidentally showing his aversion to Rabelais), the respect shown in England for men of letters, and English learned societies. He occasionally ventures on French translations of passages from the authors he discusses (e.g. of Hamlet's soliloquy and of part of *Hudibras*).

In the letter on Pascal, Voltaire criticizes a large number of the *Pensées*, protesting in particular against the pessimism that humiliates and degrades human nature and human intelligence.

Lettres portugaises, a series of five letters written by a Portuguese nun of the convent of Beja in the province of Alemtejo, said to be a certain Marianna Alcaforado, to her lover, a French officer, Bouton de Chamilly, comte de Saint-Léger, later a maréchal de France, who had made her acquaintance during the Portuguese war with Spain of 1661–8 and had deserted her. They were published in 1669 in a French version announced as a translation, though the claim has more than once been made, and refuted, that the translator, the vicomte de Guilleragues (q.v.), was in fact the author. The manner in which the woman gives expression to her sorrow, shame, and reproaches is remarkable for its literary quality. The letters gave rise to imitations and supposed replies were subsequently published. An English translation by Sir Roger l'Estrange appeared in 1678. There is an account of Chamilly's career in Saint-Simon under the year 1703.

Lettres Provinciales, see *Pascal.*

Lettres sur les Anglais, see *Lettres anglaises.*

Lettre sur les aveugles à l'usage de ceux qui voient, a short philosophical treatise by Diderot, published in 1749. The author discusses the ideas and methods of reasoning of those born blind, as an illustration of the principle that all knowledge is relative to the extent of our sensory experience. The argument for religion drawn from the marvels of Nature is of little force, he holds, for the blind. He bases himself in particular on the case of the blind mathematician Nicholas Saunderson (1682–1739), who was professor of mathematics at Cambridge, citing an imaginary life of him by Dr. Inchlif. The atheistic and materialistic tendency of the treatise was made a pretext for imprisoning Diderot.

Lettre sur les spectacles, see *Lettre à d'Alembert sur les spectacles.*

Leurs figures (1902), Part III of the trilogy *Le Roman de l'énergie nationale* by Maurice Barrès (q.v.). It turns on the Panama (q.v.) scandal.

Le Vau, LOUIS (1612–70), the architect who carried out for Louis XIV the first enlargements of the château of Versailles.

Le Vavasseur, LOUIS-GUSTAVE (1819–96), minor poet, wrote *Poésies fugitives* (1846), *Dix mois de révolution* (1849), *Farces et Moralités* (1850), &c. An earlier collection, *Vers* (1843), has—but doubtfully—been attributed to Baudelaire. The two authors were friends.

Le Vayer, FRANÇOIS DE LA MOTHE, see *La Mothe Le Vayer.*

Lévi, ÉLIPHAS, see *Constant, l'abbé A.-L.*

Lévis, FRANÇOIS-GASTON, CHEVALIER, and from 1784 DUC, DE (1720–87), the last commander of the French troops in Canada, where he was sent in 1756 with Montcalm (q.v.). He took command after the latter's death at the fall of Quebec (1759), but was unable to reconquer any of the territory lost to the British and eventually returned to France.

Lévizac, L'ABBÉ JEAN-PONT-VICTOR LA-COUTZ DE, see *Dictionaries and Encyclopedias,* under date 1807.

Lévy-Bruhl, LUCIEN (1857–1939), sociologist. His chief work was *La Morale et la science des mœurs* (1903). He also wrote: *Les Fonctions mentales dans les sociétés inférieures* (1910); *Le Surnaturel et la nature dans la mentalité primitive* (1931).

L'Hermite, TRISTAN, see *Tristan.*

Lhomond, L'ABBÉ CHARLES-FRANÇOIS (1727–94), the first French grammarian to compile a Latin grammar in his mother tongue: *Éléments de la grammaire latine* (1780).

L'Hôpital, MICHEL DE (1505–73), humanist and chancellor of France (1560–8), author of Latin poems and of a treatise *de la Réformation de la justice,* an orator famous for his vigorous eloquence and his tolerance and fairness. Ronsard addressed to him the longest of his Pindaric odes (on the history of poetry).

Liaisons dangereuses, Les (1782), see *Laclos, Choderlos de.*

Libertins, the name given to the freethinkers, sceptics, or Pyrrhonians of the 17th and early 18th centuries. They were the intellectual descendants of Rabelais and Montaigne, refusing to be bound by the doctrines or the moral conventions of orthodox religion. Many of the more erudite among them (e.g. Naudé) wrote in Latin, as being a safer medium for the expression of their particular form of religious epicureanism, or irreligion, or at times blasphemy. Their views were exposed and denounced by the Jesuit Père Garasse (*La Doctrine curieuse des beaux esprits,* 1623) and by Père Mersenne

(*L'Impiété des déistes,* 1624), who accused them of atheism and dissipated living. They were also repeatedly combated by Bossuet, Bourdaloue, Pascal, &c. The accusations against them were partially true, and became increasingly so, with one result that the word 'libertin' lost its earlier sense of a freethinker in matters of religion and came to signify an ill-liver, debauched and contemptuous of sexual morality. In real life, noblemen such as Saint-Évremond and La Fare were among the *libertins,* also poets such as Théophile de Viau and Chaulieu, and many other men of letters. They prepared the way for Voltaire and the *encyclopédistes.* In literature, typical *libertins* are Molière's Don Juan or, an 18th-century example, Valmont in Choderlos de Laclos's *Les Liaisons dangereuses.*

Librairie, La. The government concerned itself with the book-trade from the early days of printing. The printers and booksellers of Paris formed a corporation, closely restricted in numbers, minutely regulated and supervised, and originally a dependency of the University. In 1521 an ordinance of François Ier required all books to be licensed before printing, with the University as authorizing body. An ordinance of 1535 (partly relaxed the following year) forbade under pain of death the printing of any book whatever. An ordinance of Charles IX in 1563, and further edicts during the next two centuries (including a royal declaration as late as 1757), confirmed under the severest penalties the prescriptions against unlicensed printing. The *privilège* or licence to print had another, earlier, object than to repress dangerous ideas: it was an exclusive licence intended to protect author and publisher against piracy. The political importance of the *privilège* dates from the religious disputes of the 16th century, and the University exercised its censorship chiefly in this connexion. In 1653 the function was transferred to four salaried royal censors, under the chancellor of the realm. The only books licensed were those guaranteed by a censor to contain nothing contrary to religion, the Government, or morals. The custom of granting general licences to particular authors was abolished in 1659 and the abolition was reaffirmed in 1686 (though bishops retained their right to licences without prior censorship). The censors increased in number as literature developed. There were eighty-two by 1751 when Malesherbes (q.v.) became *directeur de la librairie* under the chancellor, and 121 twelve years later. The function was then unpaid (except after twenty years' service), but carried certain advantages. The list of censors was revised from time to time by the chancellor. In addition, special censors selected *ad hoc* for their supposed competence in the subject-matter were occasionally charged with the scrutiny of particular works. Thus we find Rousseau's *Lettre sur les spectacles* submitted to d'Alembert, and comedies by Palissot to Diderot. An author might on occasion ask that a particular censor should be assigned to him. Books produced by the royal press (such as Buffon's *Histoire naturelle*) were, as might be expected, exempt from censorship.

(2) Sometimes, while a formal *privilège* was refused a *permission tacite* was granted, or a verbal promise not to prosecute the printer was given by the lieutenant of police. The *permission tacite*, though officially recorded, differed from the *privilège* in not being printed in the work itself. It was especially employed out of concern for the interests of French printers when a work contained subversive opinions, unsuitable for publication with express royal authority. Without this compromise a book would be printed abroad and smuggled into the country; and a very large number of unauthorized books by French authors were in fact printed in Holland or Switzerland. In some cases, also, the *permission tacite* extended to the introduction into France of a work printed abroad. The *privilège* and the *permission tacite* were both revocable. A notable instance of the tacit relaxation of the law was the continued printing of the *Encyclopédie* in Paris after its *privilège* had been revoked, thanks to the favour shown to the enterprise by Malesherbes.

(3) Several clandestine presses existed in Paris in the 18th century and often produced works bearing the imprint of some foreign town, such as Amsterdam or The Hague. The authorized booksellers were restricted, for convenience of inspection, to the University quarter. In consequence, many unauthorized bookvendors, known as *colporteurs*, sprang up, carrying books to other quarters of the city and even setting up shops in privileged localities, such as the precincts of royal palaces, where they were exempt from inspection. They became a means of disseminating illicit works from abroad or from clandestine presses.

(4) The repression of illicit printing and of the contraband trade, as well as the inspection of the recognized presses and book-shops, fell within the province of the lieutenant of police, acting under the instructions of the *directeur de la librairie* but with power himself to authorize certain minor works. The two functions were united from 1763 to 1776 in the person of Gabriel de la Sartine (1729–1801).

(5) But while the grant of *privilèges* rested with the chancellor and his delegate, the *directeur de la librairie*, three bodies possessed or arrogated the right of condemning works already published. These were (1) the Sorbonne, (2) the Church (i.e. either the bishops or the assembly of the clergy), (3) the *parlement*. The first was important in the days of the great religious controversies, for the Sorbonne had the duty of maintaining the purity of the doctrine of the Church; but in the 18th century public interest in these questions lapsed and the Sorbonne was discredited. The second, though active, had no effective power and could only appeal to the King, who would refer the question to the *parlement*. This last body had real and ostensibly formidable powers. Any work might be denounced to it, and the advocate-general would be charged with the duty of prosecuting. A work condemned might be seized, its sale prohibited, and the author imprisoned or exiled. The *parlement* even claimed to include in its condemnation the censor who had authorized the publication (as in the case of Helvétius's *De l'esprit*). But these powers were found in practice to be of little avail in restricting the dissemination of the works concerned.

(6) In fact the whole system, originally adopted to check the spread of the doctrines of the Reformation, proved ineffectual in the 18th century with its new conceptions of liberty and criticism, and was finally recognized to be useless and out of date. As exercised it was inconsistent, alternating between severity and indulgence, often unjust, and often at variance with the law. Its repressive measures served largely to advertise the works against which they were directed.

The liberty of printing was expressly recognized in 1789, and the system of the *privilège* was abolished in 1793.

(7) Until the Revolution the control of the *directeur de la librairie* extended to the newspaper and periodical press, and appears to have been less indulgent: Fréron, the critic of the *encyclopédistes* in his *Année littéraire*, was not always impartially treated. [For censorship and the periodical press after the Revolution see *Press, Development of.* Cf. also *Censorship, Dramatic.*]

(8) So far as the book-trade was concerned, control was in some measure re-established during the Consulate and (from 27 Sept. 1800) books were subjected to examination, and possible suppression, by the police before being distributed. An imperial decree of 5 February 1810 intensified its severity. References inimical to the dignity of the Throne or the interests of the State (elastic terms) were forbidden; and a *directeur général de l'imprimerie et de la librairie* was created, with powers of examination, confiscation, and suppression before the printing stage was reached. Moreover the police still retained the powers conferred on them in 1800 and the situation might, and frequently did, arise of a book being passed for printing by the censor but prohibited by the police before publication. This happened to Mme de Staël's *De l'Allemagne*, which was approved, with modifications, by the *directeur général* but confiscated before publication by the *Ministre de la Police*, who ordered the author to leave a country whose air did not suit her ('il m'a paru que l'air de ce pays-ci ne vous convenait pas'). Napoleon's first abdication ended this state of affairs; and in 1815 the *acte additionnel à la constitution* guaranteed full freedom of publication for any matter running to more than twenty pages. The book trade was thus finally freed from control. The law still provided, however, and still provides, for prosecution after publication on grounds of offences against public morals (see, for instance, *Madame Bovary*).

Libraries, see the group of entries beginning with *Bibliothèque de l'Arsenal.*

Libri-Carucci, COUNT GUGLIELMUS-BRUTUS-ICILIUS-TIMOLEON ['Libri the book-thief'] (1803–69), born in Florence, of an old family, a mathematician, scholar, and bibliographer who 'n'avait qu'un malheur: il était essentiellement *voleur*' [PH. CHASLES]. In 1830, following on political troubles, he came to France from the University of Pisa. He settled in Paris, published valuable treatises, acquired influential friends and high academic distinction, was naturalized French (1833), and eventually was appointed to inspect libraries and archives throughout France. About 1845 rumours spread that whenever he visited a library some valuable book or document disappeared. In 1848 police reports were discovered which had been suppressed by his friend Guizot (q.v.), with proof that he had for years been systematically pillaging the libraries he visited. He had word of the discovery and made off to London (with a large case of books). His trial, *in absentia*, was notable for the intervention of friends, e.g. Mérimée, who refused to believe in his guilt, but he was sentenced by default to ten years' solitary confinement. He remained some fifteen years in London, and married twice (an Englishwoman the second time). He amassed a fortune, for he found unsuspecting purchasers, including the famous collector Lord Ashburnham, for his stolen treasures. Many items, however, were traced and repurchased by the French Government. He died at Fiesole.

Lichtenberger, ANDRÉ (1870–1940), social historian, author of *Le Socialisme utopique* (1898), on socialism in the 18th century, and *Le Socialisme et la Révolution française* (1898). He also wrote fiction, notably *Mon Petit Trott* (1898), a highly popular children's book which is also a study of child psychology (the sensitive child in a world of warring grown-ups).

Ligne, CHARLES-JOSEPH, PRINCE DE (1735–1814), Belgian by birth, a general in the Austrian service, a man of culture and wit, who knew Voltaire, Mme de Staël, and other literary personages of his time, as well as many of the rulers (Frederick II, Catherine II, Marie-Antoinette, &c.). His miscellaneous prose works (*Mélanges militaires, littéraires, sentimentaires,* 1795–1811) and his Letters contain interesting portraits and narratives, and place him high among French authors. The *Mélanges* include a notable treatise on gardens entitled *Coup d'œil sur Belœil* (the name of his property in Belgium). Mme de

Staël published a good selection from the thirty volumes of the *Mélanges*.

Lignon, Le, a river (a small tributary of the Loire) in the Forez district of the Lyonnais, whose banks are the scene of d'Urfé's pastoral, *L'Astrée* (q.v.). The name is sometimes used to signify an Arcadia.

Ligue, La, an association founded in 1576, with the approval of Henri, third duc de Guise (1550–88, see under *Guise*), to defend the Roman Catholic religion against the Calvinists. Guise, known as *le Balafré*, who had taken a prominent part in the massacre of Saint Bartholomew, became its leader, and he was mentioned as a possible successor of the childless Henri III in preference to the Protestant Henri of Navarre. The Guises came to an understanding with Philip II of Spain, open hostilities between the *Ligue* and the Protestants broke out, and finally the duc de Guise became an overt rebel against the royal authority. In 1588 Henri III —who had been driven from Paris as the result of the fighting of 12 May known as the *Journée des barricades*— caused him to be assassinated, and was in turn himself assassinated in 1589 by a Dominican friar of the name of Clément. The Ligue, now under the leadership of the duc de Mayenne, the Balafré's brother, was defeated by Henri IV at Arques (near Dieppe) in 1589 and at Ivry (near Évreux) in 1590, and became unpopular owing to its relations with Spain; the conversion of Henri IV to the Roman faith finally brought it to an end in 1594.

Ligue de la patrie française, a body founded in 1899 during the Dreyfus (q.v.) case. It typified all that was bigoted, anti-Semitic, and reactionary in public life.

Ligue des droits de l'homme, a body founded during the Dreyfus (q.v.) case at the time of the Zola trial. The counterpart of the preceding, it was intended to safe-guard the rights of citizens.

Ligue des Patriotes, a league founded (1882) by Paul Déroulède (q.v.) to avenge the Prussian defeat of France in 1870. Its motto—'France quand même'—had, underneath, the dates '1870-18 . . . ', the blank figures being left until the date of 'la Revanche' could be inserted. Other objects of the League, which for a time supported

the Boulangist movement (see *Boulanger*), included revision of the constitution and a plebiscitary republic with a forceful leader.

Ligue du bien public (1465), a league formed against Louis XI by a number of powerful nobles, e.g. the Dukes of Brittany and Burgundy, the heads of the Houses of Alençon, Armagnac, Lorraine, &c. Its ostensible purpose was the public weal, to right wrongs and end oppression, but in fact it was out to oppose encroachment on feudal independence. The King entered into an alliance with the *bourgeoisie* (of Paris especially), arrested the rising by a show of military force, and ended it by negotiating separately with the leaders.

Liguistes, members of *la Ligue* (q.v.).

Limbes, Les, a title selected, but then rejected, by Baudelaire (q.v.) for *Les Fleurs du mal*.

Lindor, a popular 18th-century name for the type of love-sick Spaniard who serenades his mistress with a guitar.

Lingendes, JEAN DE (? 1580–1616), man of letters and poet, one of Mlle de Scudéry's circle; author of sonnets and light verse, e.g. *Les Changements de la Bergère Iris* (1605), and of translations from Ovid (*Épîtres*, 1615).

Linguet, SIMON-NICOLAS-HENRI (1736–94), see *Annales politiques, civiles et littéraires, Les.*

Lison, La, the name of the engine in Zola's novel of railway life *La Bête humaine* (q.v.).

Liszt, FRANZ (1811–86), Hungarian pianist and composer, of interest from the point of view of French literature for his connexion with the Romantic writers and artists during the years he spent in Paris (*c.* 1840). His liaison with the comtesse d'Agoult (q.v.) was of this period.

Lit 29, Le, a short story by Maupassant, first published (1884) in *Gil Blas*; a grimmer treatment of the *Boule-de-suif* (q.v.) theme.

Literary academies. These were founded, from the time of Louis XIV, in many provincial towns; some, e.g. at Arles, Soissons, Nîmes, Marseilles, were affiliated to the Académie française (q.v.). Some of Montesquieu's earliest works were papers read to the academy of Bordeaux. The academy of

Dijon first brought into notice the literary talent of J.-J. Rousseau (q.v.).

Literary correspondences, see *Correspondances littéraires.*

Literary Isms. French literary history of the 19th and early 20th centuries abounds in *isms*, new literary gospels propagated by small groups and schools who do not rely on creative effort alone but found reviews, issue manifestoes, and choose for themselves a label which will synthetise their aims. Some of these developed into 'movements' which enlarged the whole field of literature by introducing new conceptions of poetry, for poetry and *isms* seem to be naturally akin, but also of drama and the novel (cf. *Romantisme*; *Réalisme*; *Naturalisme*; *Symbolisme*; *Surréalisme*). Some, if less fundamentally important, are memorable because they enriched literature, again particularly poetry, with new aspects of vision, new matter for the poet to handle, and new techniques (cf. *Unanimisme*; *Cubisme*; *Fantaisiste, Le Groupe*). Some, perhaps, are remembered for the poets associated with them rather than for their intrinsic value (cf. *École romane*; *Humanisme*; *Naturisme*); others, e.g. *Dadaïsme*, because they engendered more lasting movements, or even because they announced their existence with a sound and fury which have not yet completely subsided (again cf. *Dadaïsme*; or *Futurisme*; *Simultanéisme*).

There were, too, some ephemeral groups and doctrines to which labels equally ephemeral were attached and which barely survived their first appearance on the literary horizon. They were the proliferative offspring of Symbolism and have a certain interest as period pieces. The list begins with the *Instrumentisme*, or *Instrumentation verbale* (c. 1887), of René Ghil, one of the early theorists of Symbolism. The same poet's *Scientisme* (c. 1888) had a metaphysical bias and could only be expressed in long poems. The *Magnificisme*—a self-explanatory label— of Saint-Pol Roux dates from about 1890, and so does the *Magisme* of J. Péladan, in which Wagner and occultism both had a share. The basis of *Anarchisme* (practised about 1891 by Gide amongst others) was the cult of the individual. The form of violent, explosive lyricism associated particularly with Verhaeren was sometimes known as

Paroxysme. Ésotérisme coincided (*c.* 1895) with a vogue for spiritualism, theosophy, and the occult. The back-to-Nature, back-to-mankind, back-to-the-land movements found their chief theorists and poets in *Naturisme* and *Humanisme* (qq.v.), but the doctrines which inspired this type of poetry were also (*c.* 1897) called *Jammisme*, from Francis Jammes, one of their earliest exponents, and they were also (*c.* 1910) very much behind the gentle, rather wistful poetry of *Intimisme*. *Synthétisme* (*c.* 1901) implied a poetry of synthesis, of small details assembled to make a panoramic whole. *Néo-romantisme* (*c.* 1905) was a mixture of science, religion, and emotion. The labels *Intégralisme* (*c.* 1902), *Néo-Mallarmisme* (*c.* 1904), *Impulsionnisme* (*c.* 1904), *Musicisme* (*c.* 1906), *Sincérisme* (*c.* 1909), *Intensisme* (*c.* 1910), *Floralisme* (*c.* 1911) covered a number of doctrines which all, in one way or another, stressed the importance of inspiration and spontaneity. Some, e.g. *Néo-Mallarmisme, Musicisme*, considered rhythm, the natural rhythm of poetic utterance, a prime factor; others, e.g. *Impulsionnisme*, wrapped themselves in philosophical arguments. This latter group is said to have consisted of a leader and one disciple (and it is on the leader, Florian Parmentier's, *Histoire des lettres françaises de 1885 à 1914* that the present article is largely based). *Somptuarisme* (*c.* 1903) was concerned with the jewelled effect to be produced in both verse and prose. *Aristocratisme* was launched about 1906. *Druidisme*, for which Max Jacob was responsible, and *Effrénéisme* belong to the years around 1909; so, also, do *Visionnarisme* and *Primitivisme* (so called to distinguish its essential tranquillity from the destructive spirit of *Futurisme*, q.v.), as well as *Subjectivisme, Spiritualisme* (not so much occult as anti-fleshly), and *Totalisme*.

The list closes, in 1913, with *Dynamisme*, which stood for strength, spontaneity, and free play of the imagination and would have no truck with the intellect. The era itself, in which these minor, barely-remembered poetic groups flourished, ended with the outbreak of the 1914–18 war. One movement, *Surréalisme* (q.v. and cf. also *Dadaïsme*), dominated the years between the 1914–18 and the 1939–45 wars. *Populisme*, in the novel, *c.* 1929 (cf. *Dabit, Eugène*), held that fiction should be written for the people, about the people. A *Prix du roman populiste* was established, and *romans populistes* are still being written. An outstanding movement of recent years, *Existentialisme* (q.v. and see *Sartre, Jean-Paul*), though primarily philosophical, has had notable repercussions on the novel and the drama. In poetry (*c.* 1945) the *Lettrisme* of Isidore Isou, once more a matter of sound and typography, had a brief vogue.

Littérature (two series, 1919–21 and 1922–4), the best known of the reviews associated with *Dadaïsme* (q.v.).

Littérature anglaise, Histoire de la, see *Taine*, para. 5.

Littré, ÉMILE (1801–81), positivist, savant, and lexicographer, born in Paris, studied medicine but had to give this up to earn money by scientific and learned journalism. He edited medical journals, also edited and translated Hippocrates. He was a disciple of Comte (q.v.), without accepting any of Comte's later, mystical or political, teachings. After Comte's death he signified for many people the incarnation of atheism and materialism, and his election to the Académie française (q.v.) in 1873 drove Mgr Dupanloup (q.v.) to resign rather than accept him as a colleague.

Littré remains famous particularly as philologist and lexicographer. His *Dictionnaire de la langue française* (see *Dictionaries and Encyclopedias*, under date 1863–72) is said to be 'perhaps the greatest dictionary ever compiled by one man' (*Enc. Brit.*). Printing began in 1859, and there can be few more interesting pictures of a life centred on the completion of one task than his reminiscences of the eleven years until publication was completed (see his *Études et Glanures*, 1880). Yet it was at this time that he gave some of his night hours to writing the study of Comte (*Auguste Comte et la philosophie positive*, 1863) which he considered as one of the three great works of his life, the others being the Dictionary and his translation of Hippocrates.

His other philosophical and philological works include: *Analyse raisonnée du Cours de philosophie positive d'Auguste Comte* (1845); *Application de la philosophie positive au gouvernement des sociétés* (1849); *Conservation, révolution et positivisme* (1852); *Histoire de la langue française* (1862); *La Science au point de vue philosophique* (1873), also a notable article on *Les Origines organiques de la morale* (1870, in the *Revue de philosophie positive* which he founded in 1867).

Liturgical Plays, see *Religious writings.*

Lives of Saints, see *Saints, Lives of.*

Livre d'amour, Le, see *Sainte-Beuve.*

Livre de la Terre Sainte, see *Terre Sainte.*

Livre de mon ami, Le (1885), romanticized autobiography by Anatole France (q.v.).

Livre d'Eracles, see *Terre Sainte.*

Livre des douleurs, Le (1840), by Balzac. The 'Études philosophiques' section of Balzac's *Comédie humaine* (q.v.) was first published (as such, for some of the tales had already appeared in reviews or in other collected volumes) in four series (called *livraisons*), each of five volumes, between 1835 and 1840. The fourth livraison was entitled *Le Livre des douleurs*, after a tale which Balzac projected but never wrote.

Livre des manières, a moral treatise attributed to Étienne de Fougères, bishop of Rennes from 1168 to 1178, who had been chaplain to Henry II of England. The author addresses his admonitions and censures to all classes of society—kings, clerics, knights, merchants, and villeins, and shows unusual compassion for the miserable lot of these last.

Livre des masques, Le (1896; 1898), criticism by Remy de Gourmont (q.v.).

Livre des métiers, see *Métiers de Paris.*

Livre des quatre dames, see *Chartier, Alain.*

Livre des trois vertus, see *Christine de Pisan.*

Livre du Conquest, see *Terre Sainte.*

Livre jaune, the French equivalent of the English 'Blue Book'.

Livre mystique, Le (1835), by Balzac, a volume of three tales—*Louis Lambert, Séraphita, Les Proscrits*—all greatly influenced by his reading of Swedenborgian and other forms of mystical philosophy. They were later included in the 'Études philosophiques' section of *La Comédie humaine* (q.v.).

Livry, a town in the Forest of Bondy, some miles east of Paris, of whose abbey Christophe de Coulanges, Mme de Sévigné's beloved uncle, was prior. Mme de Sévigné stayed there and wrote of it so frequently that Horace Walpole called her *Notre Dame de Livry.*

Lodi, a town in northern Italy (Lombardy), scene of Bonaparte's first famous victory— 10 May 1796—over the Austrians, during the first Italian campaign (cf. *Caporal, Le Petit*).

Loeve-Veimars (Weimars), FRANÇOIS-ADOLPHE (1801–54), born in Paris of German-Jewish parentage, a man of letters of wide rather than profound culture, wrote literary and (spirited) dramatic criticism for the *Revue de Paris,* the *Revue des Deux Mondes,* and *Le Temps* (qq.v.) between about 1825 and 1840. In later life he gave up literature for a diplomatic career. His translations of Wieland, Hoffmann, Heine, &c., and his *Histoire de la littérature allemande* (1826) helped to make German literature better known in France. *Népenthès* (1840) contains selections of his tales and articles.

Logique de Port-Royal, La, an educational work, by Pierre Nicole and Antoine Arnauld, see *Port-Royal.*

Logos, see Appendix I, § H (ii).

Loi Falloux, La, see *Falloux.*

Loi Peyronnet, La, see *Peyronnet.*

Loire, La, one (the longest) of the four great rivers of France. It rises in the Massif Central above Le Puy at the foot of the peak called Le Gerbier-de-Jonc (in the Department of Ardèche) and tumbles rapidly down to the plain at Roanne, where it becomes slower, and wider, with a sandy bed. It flows roughly north-west past Nevers to Orleans, then south-west, through a fertile plain and the country famous for the *châteaux de la Loire,* to Tours and Saumur. After Saumur, when it flows through southern Brittany, it becomes narrower; and it enters the Atlantic shortly after Nantes, between Paimbœuf (left) and Saint-Nazaire (right). Its main tributaries, which give their names to departments, are the Allier, the Cher, the Indre, the Vienne, and the Maine (cf. also *Lignon;* and see Appendix II).

Lois de Minos, Les, a tragedy by Voltaire published in 1773. It celebrated the dismissal of the *parlement* of Paris (1770). Its performance was prohibited.

The scene is Gortyn in Crete, where the ancient cruel laws of Minos are enforced by a superstitious and intolerant priestly caste. These laws require that a maiden, Astérie, a captive from the neighbouring tribe of the Cydonians, shall be sacrificed to the *manes* of dead heroes. King Teucer, a humane and enlightened man, determines to save her, and, after discovering that Astérie is in fact his lost daughter, overthrows the priests and the ancient system, assumes sole power, and establishes the rule of justice.

Loisy, L'ABBÉ ALFRED-FIRMIN (1857–1940), modernist theologian and exegetist. He was dismissed from the professorial staff of the Institut catholique de Paris (q.v.) in 1894 because of unorthodox views and from 1909 to 1932 held the chair of the History of Religions at the Collège de France (q.v.). Besides *L'Évangile et l'Église* (1902) and *Autour d'un petit livre* (1903), his most notable works include: *Études bibliques* (1901), *Le Quatrième Évangile* (1903), *Les Évangiles synoptiques* (1907–8), *La Religion* (1917), *La Morale humaine* (1923), &c.

Longepierre, HILAIRE-BERNARD DE (1659–1721), dramatic author and hellenist, wrote a tragedy *Médée* (1694) of some merit, also *Sésostris* (1695), *Électre* (1702). He took part in the quarrel of the Ancients and the Moderns, writing in 1687 a *Discours sur les Anciens* against Perrault (q.v.).

Longueville, ANNE-GENEVIÈVE DE BOURBON, DUCHESSE DE (1619–79), sister of the Grand Condé, a woman of great charm and distinction, who married the duc de Longueville, a descendant of Dunois and a widower with a daughter (later duchesse de Nemours, q.v.) only a few years younger than herself. A strong mutual affection bound her for a time to La Rochefoucauld (q.v.), and it was under the influence of a complicated series of motives, personal and political, among which was La Rochefoucauld's restless ambition, that she took a prominent part in the *Fronde* (q.v.). Remorse after these civil disturbances led her to seek spiritual guidance at Port-Royal (q.v.), of which she became an ardent supporter. In early life she was a frequenter of the Hôtel de Rambouillet (q.v.).

Longwood, Napoleon's villa on St. Helena.

Lorenzaccio, an historical drama (5 acts, prose) by Alfred de Musset, published in 1834 in *Un Spectacle dans un fauteuil* (q.v.). It was first produced in 1896 at the Théâtre Sarah Bernhardt, with Bernhardt in the title-role.

The young Lorenzo de' Medici (Lorenzaccio) has planned to rid Florence of its vicious despot, his cousin Alexander de' Medici. To succeed he must gain the confidence of Alexander by himself embracing a life of debauchery, but the day comes when he realizes that vice is for him no longer a disguise but his true nature. He keeps to his plan, and assassinates his cousin because, he says, this murder is all that remains to him of virtue; and he even knows a few moments of exaltation after the deed is accomplished. But almost at once he lapses into despondency, and making no attempt at defence he falls at the hands of his cousin's avengers. His horror as he probes into the dark places of his own character is sometimes compared with that of Hamlet faced with his own inaction.

Loret, JEAN (17th c.), author of *La Muse historique*, a collection of weekly letters or gazettes in burlesque verse which he addressed to his patroness, the duchesse de Longueville (q.v.), recording the events of the day, from 1650 to 1665.

Lorette, a term often used during the July Monarchy and the Second Empire for the rank and file of the *femmes entretenues*. Rooms in newly-built dwellings in the neighbourhood of Notre-Dame de Lorette, a well-known Paris church, were said to be let cheaply to these ladies of easy virtue until the plaster dried.

L'Orme, MARION DE, see *Delorme.*

L'Orme, PHILIBERT DE, see *Delorme.*

Lorrain, Le, see *Claude le Lorrain.*

Lorrain, JEAN [pseud. of Paul Duval] (1856–1906), born at Fécamp, a minor but fervent Symbolist (see *Symbolisme*) in his poetry and novels, biting rather than vague in his day-by-day literary journalism. His poetic output includes: *Le Sang des dieux* (1882), *La Forêt bleue* (1883), *L'Ombre ardente* (1897),

often inspired by ancient and medieval legends; also *Brocéliande, Yanthis, Prométhée,* poetic dramas which were typical of the productions at the *Théâtre de l'Œuvre* (q.v.) about 1900. His *Monsieur de Phocas* (1899) is also sometimes mentioned as typical of the 'morbid' Symbolist novel.

Lorrains, Geste des, see *Garin le Loherain.*

Lorris, GUILLAUME DE, see *Guillaume.*

Lot, FERDINAND (1866–1952), medieval scholar, philologist, and historian, for long a professor at the Sorbonne and the École pratique des hautes études (qq.v.). His many valuable studies of the origins of French literature and civilization include: *Les Derniers Carolingiens* (1891), *Études sur le règne de Hugues Capet et la fin du Xᵉ siècle* (1903), *Étude sur le 'Lancelot' en prose* (1918), *La Fin du monde antique et le début du moyen âge* (1927; 1951).

Loterie nationale. State-promoted lotteries are a recognized source of public revenue in France, and the stalls of ticket-vendors (small employment of many an honest widow) are a familiar sight at street corners. The lottery was introduced into France from Italy during the Renaissance. An edict of 1539 shows that its possibilities as an extra source of income appealed to François Iᵉʳ, but the practice was frowned upon by the *parlement* and until about the year 1700 lotteries were promoted privately for amusement and to collect money for charity, a fashion much loved by the *Précieuses* (q.v.). At the court of Louis XIV they were a favourite method of distributing gifts and largesse on special occasions such as weddings or the visit of foreign royalties. It was Louis XIV, too, who in 1700 reintroduced the system of State-controlled public lotteries. He and his successors used the proceeds particularly for benevolent purposes, such as restoring and building churches, e.g. Sainte-Geneviève (later the Panthéon, q.v.) and La Madeleine.

The *loterie royale* was too useful a source of revenue to be discarded for more than a short time during the Revolution, when it was renamed *Loterie nationale*. It continued throughout the Empire and the *Restauration* (and provided subjects for famous caricaturists, e.g. Daumier, Gavarni, Henri

Monnier), but was prohibited by law in 1836. Private lotteries still continued. They were usually promoted for charity, but sometimes they represented individual attempts to raise funds. When, for instance, Chateaubriand fell on evil days he tried unsuccessfully to get rid of his property of *La Vallée aux loups* (q.v.) by promoting a lottery.

In 1933 (law of 31 May) the *Loterie nationale* was re-established. The money raised is earmarked for such purposes as pensions for ex-servicemen or compensation for the victims of disasters.

Lothaire, born 941, son of Louis IV *d'Outre-Mer*, was King of France from the latter's death in 954 till his own death in 986. He belonged to the *Carolingien* (q.v.) dynasty.

Loti, PIERRE [pseud. of Julien Viaud] (1850–1923), novelist, of Protestant parentage, was born and brought up, by his widowed mother and his aunts, at Rochefort. He entered the navy—one way of seeing the world—and his novels and travel books, some forty volumes in about thirty years, were written when his duties as a naval officer allowed.

Three novels of Breton life are now considered his masterpieces, tales of the sailors who leave home each February for the fishing in Iceland waters, not to return until autumn; of the eternal struggle between man and the sea, and the anxiety and heartbreak of wives and parents— *Mon Frère Yves* (1883), *Pêcheur d'Islande* (1886), *Matelot* (1893). But Loti first won his very considerable reputation with idealized romances of sentimental adventure, variations on the theme of loving and sailing away, framed in a languorously tropical or oriental setting. The first, and perhaps the best, was published anonymously (*Aziyadé*, 1879). The scene was mainly Constantinople. Then came: *Le Mariage de Loti*, first called *Rarahu* (1880, scene Tahiti); *Le Roman d'un Spahi* (1881, Senegal); *Madame Chrysanthème* (1888, Japan); *Fantôme d'Orient*, a sequel to *Aziyadé* (1892, again Constantinople), &c. *Ramuntcho* (1897), though set in the Basque country, was of the same type. These novels are written, and so is Loti's purely travel literature, in an impressionistic, sensuous, but simple and musical style. The

descriptions convey atmosphere rather than pictorial detail, and are nostalgic, autumnal, of the past or what must pass, seldom gay or sunlit. The travel books include: *Jérusalem* (1895), *Le Désert* (1895), *L'Inde (sans les Anglais)* (1903), in which Loti ridiculed the Cook's tourists he met on his travels; *Vers Ispahan* (1904); *Un Pèlerin d'Angkor* (1912). Three semi-autobiographical works, *Le Roman d'un enfant* (1890), *Prime jeunesse* (1919), and *Un Jeune Officier pauvre* (1923), are also of interest. After his death selections from Loti's voluminous diary were edited by his son S. P. Loti-Viaud—*Journal intime de Pierre Loti* (1928–30, 2 vols.).

Louis Ier LE DÉBONNAIRE (also called *le Faible* or *le Pieux*), born 778, was the son of Charlemagne by his second wife. He succeeded his father in 814 as King of the Franks and in the same year was proclaimed Emperor of the West. He died in 840. He had three sons by his first wife: Lothaire, d. 855, who succeeded him as Emperor (see *Verdun*), Pépin King of Aquitaine, d. 833, and Louis *le Germanique*, d. 876; and one son, Charles *le Chauve* (who succeeded him as King of the Franks) by his second wife. He was a weak ruler, excessively devout, and was more than once deposed by his three elder sons, who united in their jealousy of Charles *le Chauve* but then quarrelled among themselves when their father was restored to the throne. He was one of the *Carolingien* (q.v.) dynasty.

Louis II LE BÈGUE, born 846, was King of France from the death of his father Charles *le Chauve* (877) till his own death in 879. He belonged to the *Carolingien* (q.v.) dynasty.

Louis III, born 860, became King of France in 879 on the death of his father Louis *le Bègue*. He shared the throne with his brother Carloman, who reigned alone after he died in 882. They belonged to the *Carolingien* (q.v.) dynasty. Carloman was succeeded by Charles *le Gros*.

Louis IV D'OUTRE-MER, born *c.* 921, the son of Charles *le Simple* (q.v.), was taken to England by his mother after his father died (hence 'd'Outre-Mer') and brought up at the court of King Athelstane, but he was later recalled to France. He was crowned King of France in 936 and reigned till his death in 954. He belonged to the *Carolingien* (q.v.) dynasty.

Louis V LE FAINÉANT, born 966, succeeded his father Lothaire as King of France in 986 and himself died (possibly poisoned by his wife) in 987. The *Carolingien* (q.v.) dynasty ended with him.

Louis VI LE GROS (sometimes also called *le Batailleur* because he was a great fighter), born in Paris 1081, succeeded his father Philippe Ier as King of France in 1108 and reigned till his own death in 1137. He belonged to the *Capétien* (q.v.) dynasty.

Louis VII LE JEUNE, born 1120, King of France from the death of his father Louis VI in 1137 till his own death in 1180. (One of the *Capétien*, q.v., dynasty.)

Louis VIII LE LION, born 1187, son of Philippe II (Philippe-Auguste) and Isabella of Hainault, was King of France from his father's death in 1223 till his own death in 1226. (One of the *Capétien*, q.v., dynasty.)

Louis IX, Saint, born 1215, was King of France from the death of his father Louis VIII in 1226 until his own death, on the fourth Crusade, in 1270. His mother, Blanche of Castille, had acted as Regent until he attained his majority. He belonged to the *Capétien* (q.v.) dynasty. (See also *Joinville*.)

Louis X LE HUTIN, born *c.* 1290, became King of France in 1314 on the death of his father Philippe *le Bel* and reigned till his own death in 1316. He belonged to the *Capétien* (q.v.) dynasty.

Louis XI, born 1423, succeeded his father Charles VII as King of France in 1461 and reigned till his own death in 1483. This astute monarch's reign was notable for his conflict with Charles *le Téméraire*, for the extension of the royal dominions, for the encouragement he gave to the early art of printing, and for the establishment of a postal service. He was a *Capétien* king, of the *Valois* branch (qq.v.). (See also *Commines*.)

Louis XII, LE PÈRE DU PEUPLE, born 1462, son of Charles d'Orléans and grandson of Louis d'Orléans the brother of Charles VI, came to the throne in 1464 on the death of Charles VIII and reigned till his own death in 1515. He invaded Italy to assert his claim

to the duchy of Milan. He was a *Capétien* king, of the *Valois* branch (qq.v.).

Louis XIII, LE JUSTE, born 1601, became King of France when his father, Henri IV, was assassinated in 1610. His reign lasted till his death in 1643, but the real rulers of the country were first his mother Marie de Médicis and then Richelieu. He married (1614) Anne of Austria and had two sons, Louis XIV and Philippe d'Orléans, father of the Regent (see *Régence*). He belonged to the *Bourbon* branch of the *Capétien* dynasty (qq.v.).

Louis XIV LE GRAND (*le Roi Soleil*), born 1638, succeeded his father Louis XIII as King of France in 1643 and reigned till his own death in 1715. Until he attained his legal majority (1651) his mother, Anne of Austria, acted as Regent, with Mazarin (q.v.) as chief Minister. After Mazarin's death in 1661 he governed as an absolute monarch, a masterful and ambitious ruler. His reign was largely a period of wars and conquests, conducted by great military captains (Turenne, Condé, Catinat, Vendôme, &c.), and ending in the economic prostration of the country. But it is even more famous for his encouragement of literature and art. Corneille, Racine, Molière, La Fontaine, Boileau, Bossuet, Fénelon, La Bruyère, La Rochefoucauld, Girardon, &c., are among the great names of the time.

Louis XIV's *Mémoires*, drawn up from his notes by Pellisson or some other secretary, and intended for the education of the Dauphin, include a narrative of his reign during the years 1661–8 and many letters of the subsequent period to 1694. They testify to the dignity and seriousness of his character and show him judicious and well intentioned in his earlier years, though later despotic and at odds with public opinion. Voltaire's *Siècle de Louis XIV* (q.v.) is a celebrated account of his reign.

He was married in 1660 to the Infanta Maria Theresa of Spain, by whom he had one son, Louis the *Grand Dauphin* (q.v.). After Maria Theresa's death (1683) he married, secretly, Madame de Maintenon (q.v. See also *La Vallière*, *Montespan*; and, for some of his principal ministers, *Colbert*, *Louvois*, *Fouquet*).

He belonged to the *Bourbon* branch of the *Capétien* dynasty (qq.v.).

Louis XV LE BIEN-AIMÉ, born 1710, third son of Louis duc de Bourgogne, was King of France from the death of his great-grandfather Louis XIV in 1715 till his own death in 1774 (see *Grand Dauphin*; *Régence*). His reign was notable for unsuccessful wars and the degradation of the court, but it was made illustrious by some of the greatest names in French literature, Voltaire, Rousseau, Montesquieu, the *encyclopédistes*, &c. He belonged to the *Bourbon* branch of the *Capétien* dynasty (qq.v.).

Louis XVI, born 1754, was the second of four sons of the Dauphin Louis (1729–65), who predeceased his father Louis XV. The first son died in 1771. The third and fourth were Louis XVIII and Charles X (qq.v.). He married Marie-Antoinette (q.v.) in 1770, and in 1774 succeeded his grandfather Louis XV as King of France. The *Assemblée législative* (q.v.) deprived him of his powers in August 1792 and on 21 January 1793 he was beheaded (see *Revolutions*). He belonged to the *Bourbon* branch of the *Capétien* dynasty (qq.v.).

'Louis XVII', son of Louis XVI and Marie-Antoinette, born 1785, died in prison 1795. He never reigned (see *Orphelin du Temple*).

Louis XVIII. Louis-Stanislas-Xavier (1755–1824), grandson of Louis XV, left Paris in 1791 on the same night as his brother Louis XVI and his family. The Royal party took the route through Varennes and were caught. He followed another route, reached Brussels, and from there went to Coblenz. He commanded the *armée des émigrés* (q.v.) and later fomented Royalist conspiracies against Napoleon. After the peace of Tilsit (q.v.) he took refuge in England, where he lived, pensioned by the British Government, till 1814. After Napoleon's first abdication (11 April) he returned to France, and on 3 May 1814 entered Paris as King Louis XVIII. (For his supporters he had been Louis XVIII since the death of the Dauphin in 1795.) He fled from Paris when Napoleon returned from Elba in 1815, remained at Ghent during the Hundred Days, and was restored to the throne for the second time after Waterloo. He had no children and was succeeded by his brother Charles X (q.v.,

and see also *Charte, La*). He belonged to the Bourbon branch of the *Capétien* (q.v.) dynasty.

Louis, LE DOCTEUR, see *Guillotine*.

Louis Capet, the 'civil' name of Louis XVI, see *Capétiens*.

Louis de Bourbon, Chronique de, see *History* (medieval period).

Louise, an opera, see *Charpentier, Gustave*.

Louis Lambert (1832–3), one of the *Études philosophiques* of Balzac's *Comédie humaine* (q.v.). Louis Lambert, a youthful prodigy of humble birth, receives an education at the Collège des Oratoriens at Vendôme thanks to a chance encounter with Mme de Staël (q.v.). In later life he becomes a distinguished mathematician and philosopher and, in Paris, belongs to the circle of journalists and artists described in *Illusions perdues* (q.v.). His sanity becomes overclouded. He suffers from delusions of abnormality followed by intervals of transcendent, sublime clarity, and after fearful sufferings dies on the eve of his marriage. The description of his early years at the Collège at Vendôme is said to be in part autobiographical. (See also *Livre mystique, Le*.)

Louis LE GERMANIQUE (806–76), third son of Louis *le Débonnaire* and father of Charles *le Gros* (qq.v.).

Louis-Napoléon, see *Napoleon III*.

Louison, a comedy (2 acts, verse) by Alfred de Musset (q.v.). It was produced at the Comédie-Française on 22 February 1849, published separately later in that year, and included in the 1853 edition of *Comédies et Proverbes* (q.v.). A young duke's affections stray to Louison, a country girl, his mother's god-daughter, brought into his household, decked up, and renamed 'Lisette'. But Lisette remains simple and virtuous, prefers her country lover, and contrives to open the duke's eyes to his real love, for his wife.

Louis-Philippe (1773–1850), born in Paris, King of the French from 1830 to 1848, succeeded his father Philippe Égalité as duc d'Orléans (see *Orléans*) in 1793. At the Restoration he returned to France from a very modest life in exile. He became the hope of the Opposition Party, and in 1830, after the *Révolution du 29 juillet* (q.v.), liberals and republicans united to place him on the throne as a constitutional monarch. He accepted a revised version of 'la Charte' (q.v.), re-established the tricolour flag, and affected democratic manners, taking pains to divest his court of royal splendour, and modelling his life on that of any prosperous citizen and family man. During his reign industry flourished, the middle classes became the dominating influence in French politics, and the prosperous bourgeois became a favourite object of satire and caricature (cf. *M. Prudhomme*). He pursued a foreign policy of peace at any price and at home refused, latterly, to introduce any liberal or electoral reforms. In 1848, after the *Révolution du 24 février* (q.v.) and his abdication, he took refuge in England. For the two years until his death he lived as the comte de Neuilly at Claremont, in Surrey.

He had married princesse Marie-Amélie de Bourbon in 1809 and had eight children. His great-great-grandson (through his eldest son Ferdinand-Philippe, duc d'Orléans, b. 1810, d. 1842) is Henri, comte de Paris, born 1908, the present Pretender.

Loup, Saint (d. 479), a famous Bishop of Troyes. He defended Troyes against Attila and the Huns (451).

Lourdes (1894), by Zola (q.v.), the first novel of his trilogy *Les Trois Villes*.

Loustalot, or **Loustallot**, ÉLYSÉE (1761–90), by profession a barrister at Bordeaux then in Paris, became an ardent Revolutionary, well known both as an orator and a journalist, and respected for his noble character and high ideals. His articles were mainly responsible for the success of the paper *Les Révolutions de Paris* (q.v.).

Lousteau, ÉTIENNE, in Balzac's *Comédie humaine* (q.v.), the corrupt journalist who strips Lucien de Rubempré of his illusions (see *Illusions perdues*). He also appears in *La Muse du département*, *Les Comédiens sans le savoir*, &c.

Louvel, LOUIS-PIERRE (born 1783, executed 1820), a working saddler, assassin (1820) of the duc de Berry (q.v.). He was an anti-Royalist fanatic bent on exterminating the Bourbons.

Louvet de Couvray, JEAN-BAPTISTE (1760–97), revolutionary and member of the *Convention nationale*, and author of a licentious novel *Les Amours du Chevalier de Faublas* (q.v.).

Louvois, MICHEL LE TELLIER, MARQUIS DE (1641–91), the great war minister of Louis XIV, an administrator of remarkable capacity, who completely reorganized the French army (as Colbert did the finances) of the period. He shared the ministry of war with his father, Michel Le Tellier, from 1662 to about 1677, after which he occupied the position alone. By encouraging the king's inclination for war and by instigating religious persecution, he exerted a pernicious influence during his tenure of power. His policy was in constant conflict with that of Colbert (q.v.) and there was a keen rivalry between the two ministers. Louvois was largely responsible for the devastation of the Palatinate (1689).

Louvre, Le, on the right (i.e. north) bank of the Seine in Paris, an ancient palace of the kings of France, said to be on the site of a hunting-lodge of Dagobert I (628–38) (*Louvre* is from the Late Latin *lupara*, which appears to mean 'a place or equipment for hunting wolves'). Here Philippe-Auguste built a fortress in 1204; it was greatly enlarged by Charles V, who surrounded it with a moat, then rebuilt under François Ier and Henri II (Pierre Lescot being the architect), and enlarged successively by Catherine de Médicis, Henri IV (to designs by Androuet du Cerceau), Richelieu, and Louis XIV (who built the Colonnade designed by Claude Perrault). The junction of the Louvre with the Tuileries (q.v.) was completed in 1857. See also *Louvre, Musée du*.

Louvre, Musée du, housed in the former royal palace (see above), the principal art museum in France, containing a number of collections, of which the most important are those of pictures and sculpture. The private collections of the kings of France form the nucleus of the former, which dates from the Renaissance, and particularly from François Ier, who imported a number of paintings from Italy, including the Monna Lisa (*la Joconde*) by Leonardo da Vinci. Louis XIV added largely to it (Colbert bought many of the pictures and drawings which Charles I had collected), and it was immensely increased by the spoils of conquest during the wars of the Revolution and the Empire (after the fall of Napoleon, the allies caused 5,000 works of art to be restored to their former owners). Since then it has been added to by purchase and bequests. The sculptures, like the pictures, come in part from royal collections; many are the fruit of archaeological missions.

Louÿs, PIERRE [pseud. of Pierre Louis] (1870–1925), novelist and poet, born in Ghent of French parents. He was educated in Paris, became a disciple of the poet Heredia (q.v.), whose youngest daughter he married, and made friends among the Symbolists. With André Gide, Henri de Régnier, and Paul Valéry he founded two of the more exclusive literary reviews— *La Conque* (1891) and *Le Centaure* (1896). In 1894 he published *Chansons de Bilitis*, prose poems 'd'amour antique', so-called translations from the Greek of a poetess contemporary with Sappho but in fact one of the most successful literary hoaxes of the 19th century, which deceived even scholars. His wide reputation in his own day rested on *Aphrodite: mœurs antiques* (1896), a novel of courtesan life in ancient Alexandria, a graceful mixture of licentiousness and erudition, with a continuing attraction for illustrators and fine binders. Another, less elegant, work of the same type was *Les Aventures du roi Pausole* (1900). Later critics often give first place to his novel *La Femme et le pantin* (1898), a study of the progressive break-up of a man who becomes the creature of a worthless woman. His *Poésies* (1927, posth.) include *Astarté*, twenty-five 'poèmes sur la femme et sur l'eau', said at their best to recall Baudelaire. His diary, covering the years of adolescence, is also of interest (*Journal intime 1882–91*, 1929, posth.).

Lovenjoul, see *Spoelberch de Lovenjoul.*

Lowe, SIR HUDSON (1769–1844), the English general who was governor of St. Helena during Napoleon's exile and was said by the ex-Emperor's sympathizers to have discharged his duties with exceptional harshness and suspicion.

Loyal Serviteur, Le (Jacques de Maille), see *Bayard.*

Luce de Lancival, JEAN-CHARLES-JULIEN (1764–1810), gave up an ecclesiastical career to write mediocre tragedies on conventional models. *La Mort d'Hector* (1809), sometimes mentioned, was moderately successful because it found favour with Napoleon.

Lucien Leuwen (1894, posth.), by Stendhal (q.v.), an uncompleted novel of life under the July Monarchy. He had considered various titles for it. One, *Le Chasseur vert*, was used when the first chapters were published in 1855 in a volume of his *Nouvelles inédites*. Another, *Le Rouge et le Blanc*, was given to an edition published in 1929.

Leuwen the elder, a rich banker and an ironically tolerant father, is a pillar of *juste-milieu* (q.v.) society. Lucien is his son, a hero whose youthful, idealistic Republicanism ends in expulsion from the *École Polytechnique*, after which his attitude to life is indeterminate. He resigns himself to a military career and is stationed at Nancy, where his wealth and charm make him welcome, despite his political upstartism, in the decayed ultra-Royalist *salons*, and where he experiences a violent passion, shared but unacknowledged by her, for the young Mme de Chasteller, a widow. A far-fetched episode shatters his passion and ends his military career before he has had the energy to seduce Mme de Chasteller or the common sense to override politics and insist on marriage.

In Paris he resumes life half-heartedly and enters Government service; and the second part of the novel (which Stendhal had intended to call *Le Rouge et le Blanc*) depicts bureaucratic circles, with an excursion to the provinces during an election. A final section, never written, would have followed Lucien on official duties to Italy (like Stendhal himself); Mme de Chasteller would have reappeared in his life, and the end would have been happy.

The book, which is dear to *Stendhaliens*, moves more slowly, is much less tautly written, than either *Le Rouge et le Noir* or *La Chartreuse de Parme*. It can be absorbing reading for those who appreciate its quiet realism.

Luçon, ÉVÊQUE DE, a title by which Richelieu is sometimes referred to in the early part of his career.

Lucrèce (1843), a tragedy, see *Ponsard, François*.

Lucrèce Borgia (1833), a prose drama by Victor Hugo.

By Lucretia's orders five young nobles who have insulted her are poisoned at a banquet. She comes to gloat over her revenge and finds Gennaro, their friend, an orphan of unknown parentage who has for some time been persecuted by her inexplicable fondness for him. Gennaro tells her that he, too, was at the banquet and has drunk of the poisoned wine. Lucretia, distracted, tells him that he is himself a Borgia. She implores him to drink an antidote and escape, but at that moment the dying Maffio calls to Gennaro to avenge him. Gennaro stabs Lucretia. As she falls her last cry reveals her secret: 'Ah!. . . tu m'as tuée! — Gennaro! je suis ta mère!' (see also *Drouet, Juliette*).

Lugné-Poë, AURÉLIEN-FRANÇOIS (1869–1940), actor and producer, acted at the *Théâtre Libre* (q.v.), then at the *Théâtre d'Art*, becoming Director of this in 1893 and changing its name to *Théâtre de l'Œuvre* (q.v., and see *Theatre of the 19th and 20th centuries*). He wrote interesting reminiscences (*La Parade*, 1931–3, 3 vols.).

Lulli, JEAN-BAPTISTE (1633–87), a Florentine by birth, whom Louis XIV appointed superintendent of music at court. He composed the music of numerous ballets for which Benserade (q.v.) wrote the libretti, and prepared several *comédies-ballets* in collaboration with Molière (*La Princesse d'Élide*, *L'Amour médecin, M. de Pourceaugnac, Le Bourgeois gentilhomme*). He established opera as an art in France when he obtained a *privilège* for it in 1672.

Lumière, the brothers AUGUSTE (1862–1954) and LOUIS (1864–1948), industrial scientists and inventors, born at Besançon, the sons of a photographer, were themselves among the pioneers of modern photographic technique and of colour photography, and the fathers of the modern cinematograph. Their exhibition of moving pictures, in the Grand Café in Paris (Boulevard des Capucines) on 28 December 1895, was the first of its kind ever presented to a paying audience. The charge for admission was one franc. The elder brother, Auguste, who by this time had already turned to medicine and biological science, became one of the most distinguished biologists of his day.

Lundis, Les, see *Causeries du Lundi*.

Lunéville [near Nancy], **Treaty of** (9 Feb. 1801) between France and Austria, marked the withdrawal of Austria from the Second Coalition (q.v., and see *Amiens, Peace of*).

Lupin, ARSÈNE, gentleman crook, and at times also detective, the hero in novels of crime and detection by Maurice Leblanc (1864–1925), e.g. *Arsène Lupin* (1907); *Arsène Lupin contre Sherlock Holmes* (1908); *Arsène Lupin, gentleman cambrioleur* (1914), &c.

Lustucru, a character in popular rhymes and songs, a credulous simpleton whose name may have come from *l'eusses-tu cru?* (LITTRÉ).

Lutèce (L. *Lutetia*), (1) the ancient name for Paris, first mentioned by Caesar (cf. *Seine*). The emperor Julian refers to it as Φίλη Λευτεκία; (2) see *Nouvelle rive gauche, La*.

Lutrin, Le, a mock-heroic poem in six cantos by Boileau, of which the first four cantos were published in 1674, the last two in 1683.

The subject of the poem was suggested by a dispute which had arisen between the treasurer and the precentor of the Sainte-Chapelle in Paris about the position of a *lutrin* or lectern in the choir of the chapel. The poet develops this in epic style, relating first the wrath of the treasurer (a high ecclesiastical dignitary) whose functions the precentor has been usurping; the plot to reduce the latter to obscurity by restoring to its place a huge lectern which used to overshadow his seat; the execution of the project by night; the fury of the precentor, who refers the matter to the Chapter, and the removal of the lectern; the appeal of the treasurer to the Sibyl 'Chicanery'; the meeting of the rivals with their respective supporters in a bookshop and the fierce battle in which they hurl the works of authors ancient and modern at each other (an occasion for some of the author's satirical sallies); the triumph of the treasurer by a stratagem, and the final reconciliation.

Luxembourg, François-Henri, duc de (1628–95), son of the comte de Boutteville (a noted duellist), a maréchal de France, and one of the great generals under Louis XIV, victor at Fleurus (1690), Steinkerque (1692), and Neerwinden (1693). From the number of captured colours that he sent to Paris, he was known as the *Tapissier de Notre-Dame*.

Luxembourg, Madeleine-Angélique de Neufville-Villeroi, duchesse de (1707–87), duchesse de Boufflers (q.v.) by her first marriage. Her husband, the maréchal de Luxembourg (1702–64), distinguished at Fontenoy and other battles, was J.-J. Rousseau's host at Montmorency. Mme de Luxembourg's *salon* in the latter part of the 18th century was frequented by the best society and was regarded as a school of refinement and good manners.

Luxembourg, Palais du, in Paris, built by Marie de Médicis in 1615–20 on a site once owned by François de Luxembourg, prince de Tingry. It was bequeathed by her to Gaston d'Orléans, from whom it passed to his two daughters, La Grande Mademoiselle (whose marriage with Lauzun was projected there) and the duchesse de Guise. The duchesse de Berry, daughter of the Regent, resided there during the Regency. It was a prison during the Revolution. Under the Empire it became the Palace of the Senate and was later the scene of many State trials, including that of Maréchal Ney (see *Maréchal de l'empire*). During the Second Empire and the Third Republic it was again the Palace of the Senate. Under the Fourth Republic it became the seat of the Conseil de la République (q.v.).

The precincts of the Luxembourg in the 17th century were an Alsatia or asylum of thieves and vagabonds, who were driven out by Colbert's orders. The Jardin du Luxembourg ('ce doux jardin des paisibles méditations'), one of the pleasantest and most famous of Paris parks, has many literary and artistic associations.

Luxembourg, Théâtre du, until 1946 known as the *Théâtre de l'Odéon*, was built in 1782 by order of Louis XVI as the official home of the Comédie française (q.v.). During the Revolution, when the Comédie française suffered disorganization, it was closed for a time but reopened after the Terror, and from 1796 it was known as the Théâtre de l'Odéon, a reference to the covered theatre built at Athens by Pericles for the musical competitions. At this date the intention was to include opera in the theatre's repertory. In 1799 (the year in which the Comédie française were installed in their present building in the rue Richelieu), and again in 1818, it was partially destroyed by fire.

Since 1946 the Théâtre du Luxembourg has become the second home of the Comédie française, utilizing the same company and the same repertory. It is known as the *Comédie-Française (salle Luxembourg)*.

From 1873 until recent years the 'Galeries de l'Odéon', the covered arcades extending along three sides of this theatre, formed part of the premises of a firm of publishers and booksellers and were a favourite haunt of book-lovers. Books lined the walls or were piled enticingly on long trestle tables, and the assistants, in rubbed grey cotton dustcoats, fitted unobtrusively into the background.

Luynes, Charles-Philippe d'Albert, duc de (1695–1758), a descendant of the connétable de Luynes who was a favourite of Louis XIII, and grandson by his mother of Dangeau (q.v.). He was a courtier who frequented the circle of Marie Leczinska, consort of Louis XV, and left memoirs in the form of a day-by-day chronicle of all that occurred at court, including much minute record of ceremonial, diversified by anecdotes, some of considerable interest. The memoirs cover the period 1715–57.

Lycanthrope, Le, see *Borel, Petrus*.

Lycée, Le, an institution founded in Paris in 1786 by the *philosophes*, where lectures (a sort of university extension course) were given on literature (by La Harpe, who published them under the title *Lycée*), history (by Marmontel), and mathematics (by Condorcet), as well as on philosophy, chemistry, physiology, natural history, &c. After 1803, when the name 'lycée' 'was employed for secondary schools (see *Lycées and Collèges* below), it was known as *L'Athénée* (*Athénée royal* during the Restoration). It lost stand- and finally disappeared in 1848, but during its last twenty years its lecturers none the less included such names as Auguste Comte, Benjamin Constant, Geoffroy Saint-Hilaire (qq.v.).

Lycées and Collèges. The term *lycée* has been used since Napoleon's day for a State-maintained secondary school, whereas *collège* denotes an institution for secondary education maintained by a local authority (though possibly State-aided), or, more commonly, an independent denominational, usually Roman Catholic, school (cf. *Écoles libres*).

The early medieval *collèges* were founded in Paris and also, subsequently, in the provinces as hostels for needy students attending courses at the University. Later, in order to exercise more control over the students, teaching was organized within the colleges. By the middle of the 14th century several famous colleges of the University were already in being, e.g. the Sorbonne, the Collèges de Navarre and de Montaigu (qq.v. and see *Universities*, A); some sixty colleges were founded before 1500. From the 16th century onwards secondary education was greatly developed and many teaching institutions were founded by the religious orders, particularly the Jesuits (e.g. Collège de Clermont, q.v.) and, somewhat later in the field, the Oratorians (e.g. Collège de Juilly, f. 1638). These, together with the colleges of the University, were for the most part suppressed during the Revolution. Some of the colleges run by the religious orders were resuscitated after 1806, as *lycées*, the name adopted for the secondary schools under Napoleon's system of unified State education. To begin with, the lycées, which were run on semi-military lines, were established only in the principal towns. In the smaller towns it was left to the municipality to provide for secondary education by founding and supporting *collèges*.

The Head of a lycée is the *proviseur*; of a collège, the *principal*. In a lycée the staff, appointed and paid by the State, may be either *professeurs agrégés* (see *Agrégation*) or *professeurs licenciés* (i.e. possessing only their university degree).

Famous Paris lycées include: the Lycée Condorcet (founded 1804, known in early days as Lycée Bonaparte); Lycée Henri IV (founded 1804 as Lycée Napoléon); Lycée Louis-le-Grand (which succeeded the former Collège de Clermont, q.v., and see also *Prytanée*); Lycée Saint-Louis (founded 1820 on the site of the ancient Collège d'Harcourt).

Lyons, Lyric school of, in the 16th century, see *Scève*.

Lyric poetry

[NOTE. The authors, movements, &c., referred to in this article receive fuller mention under separate headings.]

FROM THE MIDDLE AGES TO THE RENAISSANCE

(1) The lyric genre in French poetry appears to have originated in Provence, where the material prosperity of the 11th and 12th centuries favoured the growth of culture (see *Troubadours*). Here it reached its zenith from about the middle of the 12th century. The marriage of Eleanor of Aquitaine, herself a grand-daughter of an early troubadour, to Louis VII in 1137 had a powerful influence in bringing the literary culture of the South into Northern France, an influence continued by the courts of Eleanor's daughters, Marie de Champagne and Aelis de Blois. The earliest songs in the French of the north (*langue d'oïl*) that have survived date from the second half of the 12th century and show a high degree of technical development and similarity in form and sentiment to the lyrical poems of the South. These, based on elaborate systems of interlaced rhymes and strophes and having courtly love, a noble passion involving suffering and endurance (see *Amour courtois*), for their principal theme, were imitated by such poets of the North as Conon de Béthune, the Châtelain de Coucy, Blondel de Nesle, Gautier d'Épinal, Thibaud de Champagne, and Gace Brulé. Lyrics also grew up, of a more popular and bourgeois character, in which poets (most of them anonymous) sang of love and springtime, of good cheer or social satire, or discoursed of their lives and sufferings. Notable among the authors of these are Rutebeuf the poet of Paris, Jean Bodel, Adam de la Halle, and Colin Muset. The various types of lyric bore different names and gradually evolved, and their precise character is not always clearly known: see *Chansons à danser* (for *rondels, ballettes,* and *virelais*); *Chansons à personnages* (for *aubes* and *pastourelles*); *Chansons de toile*; *Romances*; *Rondeaux*; *Lai*; *Virelai*.

(2) The following period, to the end of the Hundred Years War, was not a fertile one. Its principal poets are Guillaume de Machaut (b. *c.* 1300), Eustache Deschamps

(b. *c.* 1341), Christine de Pisan (b. 1364), Alain Chartier (b. 1385), and Charles d'Orléans (b. 1394). It was now that the *rondeau* and the *ballade* were developed, and there was an endeavour to maintain the tradition of courtly poetry. The latter part of the 15th century is made illustrious by the great name of Villon, an author of a different order, a poet of death, a satirist, and a realist. The interval between Charles d'Orléans and the first poets of the Renaissance was filled by the *rhétoriqueurs*, the least poetic of all the French schools of poetry; the best of them was Jean Lemaire de Belges.

THE RENAISSANCE

(3) Clément Marot (b. 1496), though a disciple of the *rhétoriqueurs*, opened a new era, in which false taste was corrected by the study of the ancient literatures of Greece and Rome, of the literature of the Italian Renaissance, and, in the case of Marot himself and some others, of the Scriptures (see *Évangélisme*). Marot, in a few isolated pieces, was perhaps the first French poet to adopt from Italian models the form of the sonnet, to which Du Bellay and Ronsard later gave so wide a vogue. Mellin de Saint-Gelais, representing especially the Italian influence, is another notable figure of this transitional period. In the first half of the 15th century we have the small but remarkable school of Lyons poets (see *Scève* and *Louise Labé*). Then came Ronsard (1524–85) and the *Pléiade*, who boldly sought their inspiration in Pindar, Horace, and Anacreon, carrying to a pedantic excess their imitation of the ancients, but widening and elevating the sphere of poetry, introducing into it a new element of sincerity, passion, and enthusiasm, and amplifying its vocabulary.

FROM THE POST-RENAISSANCE TO THE PRE-ROMANTIC YEARS

(4) A reaction followed, heralded by Desportes and preached by Malherbe (1555–1628), who rejected the linguistic innovations and other excesses of the Pléiade and gave a more intellectual cast to poetry, aiming at clear, restrained, precise, and vigorous expression. Boileau, the great literary critic of the 17th century, carried on the teaching of reform, condemning what was precious (in poets such as Voiture), extravagant, or burlesque (e.g. Théophile, Scarron),

and insisting on the pursuit of the natural and true, with the aid of reason and common sense and of the canons of beauty laid down by the ancients. But the effects of this teaching are to be seen in other spheres than the poetic. In general, and not forgetting the mystical and baroque efflorescence of the late 16th and early 17th centuries typified by, for example, La Ceppède or Jean de Sponde, or the lyric note so often present in La Fontaine, the spirit of the 17th and 18th centuries was opposed to poetry. The genres (epic, didactic verse, odes, elegies, light verse, &c.) were carefully maintained and versifiers were numerous, but the prevailing opinion was that anything worth saying would be better said in prose. The elegant pieces of light poets such as Chaulieu and the charming verses of Voltaire are perhaps among the best and most typical productions, in their kind, of the two centuries. Many clever epigrams were also written.

(5) It is only late in the 18th century that the first considerable poet appears, namely André Chénier (b. 1762). In his love of antiquity, his faith in reason, his conception of a philosophical and didactic poetry, he was the last of the classics. He also, by his unwonted depth and sincerity of emotion (e.g. in the *Élégies*), heralded a 19th-century poetic revival which in its first stages assumed the aspect of a rebirth of lyric poetry, and which developed with and out of the Romantic Movement. He was followed during the pre-Romantic years by two minor poets, Millevoye and Chênedollé, in whose work an occasional hint of the new lyric note is also unmistakable.

FROM THE ROMANTIC MOVEMENT TO THE PRESENT DAY

(6) The four major poets of the Romantic Movement—Hugo, Lamartine, Musset, and Vigny—had each his own strongly-marked individuality, but all four had the great Romantic theme in common—the self in relation to what is universal, to love, nature, and death. All four were essentially lyric poets, writing what French literature had not known for some 200 years, verse dictated by emotional necessity. Such direct utterance needed greater freedom of prosody and diction than the restraints imposed by the 17th century had allowed, and this was won largely thanks to Hugo's battles over the

caesura, *enjambement, alternance des rimes* (qq.v.), &c. Hugo himself, from being the leader of the Romantic poets, lived to become the visionary genius whose lyricism, e.g. in *Dieu, La Fin de Satan*, was more apocalyptic and elemental than personal. (In this connexion cf. *Verhaeren*, one of the Belgian poets associated with *Symbolisme*.)

(7) Three poets of the Romantic period who also call for mention are Marceline Desbordes-Valmore, Sainte-Beuve, and Gérard de Nerval. The first wrote love poems which were sincere, and artless, and plaintive. Sainte-Beuve's *Poésies de Joseph Delorme* (1829), intimate verse of quiet streets, small happenings, and undramatic sorrows, were modelled on English poetry. Some years later the realistic note already apparent in it was to become transcendent in quality and at times sinister, or macabre, in Baudelaire's poems of Paris, and to approach the banal with Coppée. Sainte-Beuve's freedom of technique and its influence on Hugo give him an added interest. Gérard de Nerval's sonnet *El Desdichado* (see *Chimères, Les*) is one of the enduring poems of French literature.

(8) The beginnings of a reaction against the intensely subjective emotion of the Romantics can be seen towards the middle of the century in Gautier's delicate *Émaux et Camées* and in Banville, whose agile mastery of the art of versification has sometimes obscured his very real merit as a poet. Indeed, until about the eighties it might seem as if lyric utterance had been stifled by the Parnassian conceptions of an impersonal, scientific, or philosophical poetry, by the doctrine of *l'art pour l'art* (q.v.), and by an insistence on form which entailed suppression of much of the prosodic freedom introduced by the Romantics (cf. *Parnassiens*). But seen in retrospect the setback was only temporary. Beneath the surface preoccupation with form, the whole poetic subsoil was changing, so much so that from, roughly, the last twenty years of the 19th century the lyric cannot be considered as a separate genre: the case is rather that the later development of French lyric poetry is neither more nor less than the progress of French poetry as a whole, in the light of changing conceptions of the very nature of poetic content and the poetic medium.

(9) The change had been anticipated as early as 1828 by a critic (Charles de Rémusat)

writing in *Le Globe* (q.v.), who said: 'C'est le moment d'en finir avec tous les genres de convention. . . . La poésie en est réduite à sa forme naturelle et primitive, la poésie lyrique.' One poet, Baudelaire, forms the bridge between past and future; and in his prose writings he too is keenly alive to the artificiality of attempts to confine poetry within genres (cf. *Epic poetry*, para. 5). In formal beauty his *Fleurs du mal* (1857), published nine years before the first issue of *Le Parnasse contemporain*, are as serene, unadventurous, and controlled as any Parnassian poetry. His direct, often resentful and blasphemous, emotion harks back to the Romantics. But when he dwells on his own lassitude, or probes the uneasy depths of his own soul, he enlarges the whole poetic field.

(10) Moreover, by emphasizing the *correspondances* between nature and the arts (in his famous sonnet *La Nature est un temple . . .*) Baudelaire brought the quality of evocation to poetry. He pointed the way to the Symbolists' efforts to communicate by suggestion and analogy rather than by description, hence to their preoccupation with the prosodic means (*vers libérés, le vers libre*, qq.v.) of making poetry more vague, fluid, musical and mysterious, and hence also to their idealism. The latter usually took the form of an escape into medieval or mystical legend (and is perhaps somewhere behind the Christian idealism of later poets who had strong affinities with Symbolism, e.g. Claudel, Jammes, Le Cardonnel).

(11) And at a further remove, it is from Baudelaire's influence on three more immediate precursors of Symbolism—Verlaine, Mallarmé, and Rimbaud—that the main currents of modern French poetry derive. Verlaine, for instance, made the necessary lyricism of poetry, its spontaneity, simplicity, and singing quality, more apparent. His influence may be discerned in the poetry of, for example, the Symbolists Gustave Kahn, Albert Samain, Francis Vielé-Griffin, the early Moréas, the early Henri de Régnier, the early Francis Jammes, &c., and it has perhaps some responsibility through Laforgue for the fantasy, gaiety, and irony of the *Cubistes* and *Fantaisistes* who were writing about 1911 (cf. for instance *Apollinaire, Guillaume; Jacob, Max; Klingsor, Tristan; Toulet, Paul-Jean*).

(12) For Mallarmé the evocative quality

of poetry coincided more closely with its emotive power. In his difficult poetry of allusion rather than of analogy or symbols the reader must not so much divine the poet's meaning as participate in his sense of creative inspiration; and he must work hard if he is to experience this rare pleasure. From this poetry the direct line of descent was to be to Valéry and 'pure' poetry.

(13) With the third poet, Rimbaud, imagery and association (and dissociation too, the *alchimie du verbe*) are all-important, and the path is set for a poetry that is visionary or even mystical, yet sensuous and even robust (e.g. Claudel), or so completely visionary and oneiric as to seem hardly more than the fragmentary outcrop of some unconscious deposit, e.g. the poetry of *Surréalisme* at its most extreme. One of the finest modern poets, Paul Éluard, wrote some of his best poetry during his surrealist phase. (For another precursor of *surréalisme* cf. *Lautréamont*.)

(14) Paragraphs 5–13 above attempt only the barest sketch of poetic development since the revival which began with *le Romantisme*. Between the main lines come various small groups, some reacting against one or all of the new tendencies, others forming a link between them. These groups and the poets connected with them are described under, for example, *École romane*; *Humanisme*; *Unanimisme*; and see also *Literary Isms*.

(15) Attention may be drawn finally to the three reviews—*L'Occident*, founded 1901, *Vers et Prose*, founded 1905, and *La Phalange*, founded 1906—which represented the main tendencies in early 20th-century poetry. The

reviews associated in the preceding century with the Romantics, the Parnassians, and the Symbolists are mentioned in the articles devoted to these movements.

Lys dans la vallée, Le (1836), a novel, one of the *Scènes de la vie de campagne* in Balzac's *Comédie humaine* (q.v.). The time is the Restoration period, the scene mainly a small château in the midst of a verdant valley in Touraine. Mme de Mortsauf, the heroine, is married to a returned *émigré* whose health and character have been undermined by privation. She devotes her life to her two delicate children and to hiding her husband's weaknesses from the outside world. Félix de Vandenesse, his thwarted childhood not far behind him, and his chivalrous timidity still unmarred by experience, falls in love with Mme de Mortsauf at a ball. Later, he gets to know her, a deep sympathy springs up between them, and he becomes an *habitué* of the château. Mme de Mortsauf refuses to become his mistress, but with all the white heat of purity keeps his devotion at an unbearable pitch. He leaves for Paris and, partly through her influence, enters court circles. Mme de Mortsauf hears that he has formed a liaison with Lady Arabella Dudley. She loses all will to live and dies after a painful illness. From a letter she leaves Félix learns that, though for the sake of her husband and children she had refused to yield to it, her passion had been no less strong than his own.

Lys rouge, Le (1894), by Anatole France (q.v.), a novel of contemporary manners. The scene for part of the time is Florence.

M

Mabillon, JEAN (1632–1707), a Benedictine monk of St. Maur (see *Maurists*), author of *De re diplomatica* (1681, with supplement 1704), in which he created the science of Latin palaeography and laid down the principles for the critical study of medieval archives. He also wrote in 1691 a *Traité des études monastiques* and was author or editor of many Maurist publications. Colbert offered him a gratuity and a pension in re-

spect of his *De re diplomatica*, but Mabillon declined these, saying that he needed nothing.

Mably, GABRIEL BONNOT, ABBÉ DE (1709–85), moralist and historian, born at Grenoble, brother of Condillac and secretary for a time of the cardinal de Tencin, was author of *Entretiens de Phocion sur le rapport de la morale avec la politique* (1763), of interesting *Observations sur l'histoire de France* (1765),

De la législation ou principe des lois (1776), and of other works of political philosophy. He developed communistic theories with originality and courage, tracing social evils to the creation of landed property and the resulting inequality between members of a State.

Macaire, the title of one of the less important *chansons de geste*, relating to the misfortunes of Blanchefleur, consort of the emperor Charlemagne, who is traduced by the traitor Macaire and is obliged to flee to Constantinople until her innocence is finally established. It is interesting as containing an early form of the legend of the *chien de Montargis* (q.v.).

Macaire, ROBERT, the personage immortalized *c.* 1830 by the cartoons of Daumier (q.v.). He was a cad and a magnificent booster, an inventor with no inventions, a doctor with no patients, a company-promoter with no companies, sarcastic, and an exploiter of fools. His stooge Bertrand (whom Daumier pictured as scraggy as Macaire was well covered) usually accompanied him. Daumier did not create these two figures. They were originally the villains in *L'Auberge des Adrets* (prod. 1823), a melodrama by three authors (Benjamin Antier, Saint-Amand, and Paulyanthe). The part of Robert Macaire, who played havoc in a lonely inn and when arrested shouldered Bertrand with responsibility for his crimes, was created with gusto by the celebrated Romantic actor Frédérick Lemaître. In 1834 Lemaître and Antier in collaboration produced *Robert Macaire*, a comedy-sequel to the melodrama.

Macdonald, JACQUES - ÉTIENNE - JOSEPH - ALEXANDRE, one of Napoleon's marshals (see *Maréchal de l'Empire*).

Macette, in Régnier's 13th Satire, a hypocritical old woman, a prototype of Tartuffe.

Machaut, GUILLAUME DE, see *Guillaume*.

Machine infernale, an explosive contraption used with criminal intent to destroy life or property. The 'machine infernale de la rue Nicaise' refers to a Royalist conspiracy to assassinate Bonaparte on 24 December 1800 (3 nivôse An IX) as he was passing the rue Nicaise (since disappeared) on his way from the Tuileries to the Opera. The explosion was badly timed and Bonaparte was unhurt, but a number of people were killed, many more were injured, and some fifty houses were damaged. A *machine infernale* was again used, by Fieschi (q.v.), in an attempt to assassinate Louis-Philippe; and again, by Orsini (q.v.), in an attempt to assassinate Napoleon III.

Machine infernale, La (1934), a tragedy on the Oedipus theme by Jean Cocteau (q.v.).

Mackeat, AUGUSTUS, see *Maquet, Auguste*.

Mac Orlan, PIERRE [pseud. of Pierre Dumarchais] (1883–   ), author of humorous tales, e.g. *Le Rêve jaune* (1913), *La Bête conquérante* (1914), and of novels of adventure, often with an exotic element, and with pirates, and occasionally the Devil, prominent among the characters (*Le Chant de l'équipage*, 1918; *La Cavalière Elsa*, 1921; *La Vénus internationale*, 1923, &c.).

Macquart, the name of one of the two families from which the characters in Zola's *Rougon-Macquart* (q.v.) novels are descended.

Macquer, PHILIPPE, see *Dictionaries and Encyclopedias*, under date 1766 (*Dict. des arts et métiers*).

Madame, employed without addition of a name, was the courtesy title from the 17th century of the eldest daughter of the king or of the dauphin, or of the wife of *Monsieur*, the king's eldest brother. At the court of Louis XIV it was used, in the last sense, of the duchesse d'Orléans. The title 'Madame Royale', for the king's eldest daughter, was also used, e.g. Madame Royale the daughter of Louis XVI, later duchesse d'Angoulême (cf. *Orpheline du Temple*). *Mesdames*, or *Mesdames de France*, were the daughters of the royal house, distinguished by their names, e.g. Madame Adélaïde, 1732–1800, the eldest daughter of Louis XV, and her sister Madame Victoire, 1733–99, who left France during the Revolution (1791) and died at Trieste.

Madame Bovary (1857), a novel by Flaubert, set in Normandy, near Rouen.

Emma Rouault, a small farmer's daughter, is brought up in a convent, which she leaves with her head stuffed with sentimental religiosity and dreams of a life full of luxury and Byronic lovers. She marries Charles Bovary, a country doctor, and finds life in a little town with a loutish, if adoring, husband very unlike the glamorous pictures in novels. Her dreams look like being realized when she becomes the mistress of a local squire, but he soon abandons her. Her next lover, a lawyer's clerk, finds her too romantically exacting. Meantime she has fallen heavily into debt and her creditor threatens to reveal everything to her husband. In despair, she makes use of an infatuated chemist's assistant to procure some arsenic, with which she poisons herself.

Flaubert's object in *Madame Bovary* was to show his unbalanced, romantically-minded heroine at odds with her environment. He paints a flat, devastating picture of a petty provincial town (he names it 'Yonville') and the local worthies. Chief among these is M. Homais, the apothecary, type of the self-satisfied country busybody, who never opens his mouth without making a speech, is ready to settle the affairs of the world at any moment, and prides himself on being anti-clerical and *voltairien*.

Madame Bovary was first published in 1856 in the *Revue de Paris*, and upset readers' susceptibilities even though cuts had been made by the editor. Flaubert was prosecuted, together with the part-proprietor and the editor of the journal, for offences against public morals, but after a trial which was a literary sensation of the day he was acquitted.

Madame Chrysanthème (1888), a novel of Japan by Pierre Loti (q.v.).

'Madame Déficit', a contemptuous nickname for Marie-Antoinette. The people held her and her extravagance largely responsible for the disastrous state of the national finances.

Madame de la Chanterie, by Balzac, see *Envers de l'histoire contemporaine, L'*.

Madame Firmiani, by Balzac, one of the 'Scènes de la vie privée' of his *Comédie humaine* (q.v.).

Madame Mère, LAETITIA RAMOLINO (1750–1836), mother of Napoleon (see *Bonaparte family*). He brought her to Paris in 1799 when he became First Consul. She was a Corsican of great beauty and fine character. She kept aloof from court intrigues and after Napoleon's death devoted herself to good works.

Madame Putiphar (1839), by Petrus Borel (q.v.), a novel.

Madame Sans-Gêne (1898), a comedy of love and intrigue at the court of Napoleon, by Sardou (q.v.) and Émile Moreau (1852–1922). The chief character is the maréchale Lefebvre whose nickname was 'Madame Sans-Gêne' (see *Maréchal de l'Empire*, under *Lefebvre*).

Madame Thérèse ou les volontaires de 92 (1863), one of the popular *romans nationaux* by the collaborators Erckmann-Chatrian (q.v.).

'Madame Véto', i.e. Marie-Antoinette, see *Véto*.

Madeleine Férat (1868), an early novel by Zola, of the same realistic type as *Thérèse Raquin* (q.v.). He wrote it first as a play but could not get it accepted, so expanded it into a novel. As a play, it was produced several years later at the *Théâtre Libre* (q.v.).

Madelin, LOUIS (1871–1956), historian, author notably of a 16-volume narrative history of French life and politics under Napoleon (*Histoire du Consulat et de l'Empire*, 1937–54). It contains vivid descriptive passages as well as solid information. An earlier work by this author, *Fouché* (1901), was much praised.

Mademoiselle, a title used without addition of a name to signify the first princess of the blood royal while unmarried, or the daughter of *Monsieur*, the king's brother. For 'la Grande Mademoiselle' see *Montpensier*.

Mademoiselle de Maupin (1835), a novel by Théophile Gautier. D'Albert, a young poet, discontented and in love with love, finds the embodiment of his dreams in Théodore. Rosette, his mistress, loves Théodore. And Théodore, the charming young squire who comes riding out of the wood, is Mademoiselle de Maupin. There is much confusion, but by the time 'Théodore' sets out on further adventures everyone has been made happy, in pagan fashion. The novel is long and diffuse. Its true theme, physical beauty, is well served by the sensuous descriptive writing. It has a period interest. The subject scandalized the public of its day; and the preface was one of the first manifestoes of *l'art pour l'art* (q.v.).

Mademoiselle Fifi, the name-tale of a collection (1882) by Maupassant (q.v.), an episode of the Franco-Prussian war. A French prostitute shoots a Prussian officer (called 'Mademoiselle Fifi' because of his effeminate appearance) who has insulted the French flag. The local curé hides her in the belfry of his church, where she remains till the enemy troops have left the district.

Mademoiselle Irnois, one of the best of Gobineau's (q.v.) *nouvelles.*

Madrigal, a short poem, often addressed to a lady, expressing a tender sentiment or ingenious compliment.

Maeterlinck, MAURICE (1862–1949), Belgian poet, dramatist, and essayist, born at Ghent, gave up the Bar for literature and after 1890 lived mostly in France. He was a figure in the Symbolist movement (see *Symbolisme*) both in France and in Belgium. In 1889 and 1896 he published collections of verse (*Serres chaudes* and *Douze chansons*), but he made his reputation with his vague, allegorical, and romantic plays, mostly produced at the *Théâtre de l'Œuvre* (q.v.), the nursery of the Symbolist drama, and with essays: semi-scientific philosophical meditations on Nature and on insect life.

His best-remembered plays include: *La Princesse Maleine* (1889), *Pelléas et Mélisande* (1892), doubly successful because of Debussy's music, *Intérieur* (1894), *La Mort de Tintagile* (1894), *Monna Vanna* (1902), *L'Oiseau bleu* (1909), a fairy play; and *Le Bourgmestre de Stilmonde* (1919), a drama, written partly as propaganda, of the 1914–18 war. Others were: *Les Aveugles* (1890), *Alladine et Palomides* (1894), *L'Aglavaine et Sélysette* (1896), *Ariane et Barbebleu* (1901), *Joyzelle* (1903). Even the titles were typically Symbolist.

His essays include: *Le Trésor des humbles* (1896), *La Sagesse et la destinée* (1898), *La Vie des abeilles* (1901), *L'Intelligence des fleurs* (1907), *La Mort* (1913). The idea of death was constantly present in his work together with, in later years, an interest in mysticism and occultism.

Magasin des enfants, Le (1757), see *Leprince de Beaumont, Mme.*

Magasin pittoresque, Le (1833–73), a popular illustrated journal (weekly to begin with, costing 10 centimes), the first of its kind in France, with articles on agriculture, architecture, commerce, history, literature, science, travel, &c. It had a brilliant list of contributors and illustrators.

Magdebourg, Centuries de, an ecclesiastical history written in the 16th century by a number of Protestant divines, who styled themselves 'Centuriatores Magdeburgici'; there were thirteen volumes, one for each century.

Magisme, see *Literary Isms.*

Magnificisme, see *Literary Isms.*

Magnin, CHARLES (1793–1862), man of letters and critic (especially dramatic critic on the *Globe* and the *Revue des Deux Mondes*), and author of *Les Origines du théâtre en Europe* (1838), *L'Histoire des marionnettes* (1852), &c. He was noted for learning and good taste.

Magny, OLIVIER DE (1529?–60?), poet, of Cahors, a follower of Ronsard and a successful author of familiar odes and sonnets, written in an easy style. He formed part of a mission sent to Rome, where he had the company of Du Bellay; his *Soupirs* are modelled on the *Regrets* of the latter poet (though published before them, in 1557). He also published collections entitled *Amours* (1553), *Gayetez* (1554), and *Odes* (1559).

Magny, see *Dîners Magny.*

Mahomet (in the 1743 edition **Le Fanatisme ou Mahomet,** a tragedy by Voltaire, produced in 1742. The author in 1745 dedicated the play to Pope Benedict XIV.

The scene is Mecca, after Mahomet (who is represented as a cruel and unscrupulous impostor) has established his power at Medina.

Two children, Séide and Palmire, captured from the supporters of the old religion, have been brought up in his camp; but the girl, Palmire, has been recaptured from him and kindly tended by the aged Zopire, sherif of Mecca. Séide and Palmire love one another; but Palmire has attracted the passion of Mahomet, who demands her surrender. Now Séide and Palmire are in fact the children of Zopire, though neither they nor he know it. Mahomet, under pretence of negotiations, comes to Mecca and contrives that Séide, whom he hates, shall first kill Zopire and then die of poison, so that he may himself secure Palmire. Séide, who has had the murder presented to him as an act of religious vengeance and as the condition of his obtaining Palmire, with deep reluctance carries it out, thus unwittingly slaying his own father. The true position now comes to light, and Séide rouses the citizens against Mahomet. But his effort is short-lived, for he has been poisoned and now dies; and Mahomet triumphantly points to his death as proof of the divine support for his own cause. Yet he is robbed of the fruit of his crime, for Palmire takes her own life.

Maigret, le Commissaire, see *Simenon, Georges.*

Mail, Jeu de, an open-air game in which a box-wood ball was driven with a mallet (*mail*) through a ring suspended above the ground in a long alley. The object was to do this in the fewest number of strokes. It is to this game that Pepys refers in the following passage (2 Apr. 1661): 'To St. James's Park, where I saw the Duke of York playing at Pelemele, the first time that I ever saw the sport.'

Maillet or **Mailliet,** MARC DE (1568–1628), minor poet, one of the household of Marguerite de Valois (q.v.), author of *Poésies à la louange de la regne Marguerite* (1611 and 1612); *Poésies . . . dédiées à madame de Jehan* (1616), *Épigrammes* (1620). He is said to have been an eccentric Bohemian, vain and quarrelsome, a butt for many of his fellow writers.

Maimbourg, LOUIS, LE PÈRE (1610–86), a Jesuit ecclesiastical historian, whose *Histoire de la Ligue* was translated into English by Dryden at the request of Charles II (1684). Among his other works were an *Histoire des Croisades* (1675) and *Histoire du Calvinisme* (1682).

Mainard, FRANÇOIS, see *Maynard.*

Maine, LOUIS-AUGUSTE DE BOURBON, DUC DU (1670–1736), elder son of Louis XIV and Mme de Montespan. He was legitimated,

and by royal decree of 1714 declared heir to the crown in default of princes of the blood. He lost under the Regency the commanding position which Louis XIV had sought to give him after his death.

Maine, LOUISE DE BOURBON, DUCHESSE DU (1676–1753), granddaughter of the great Condé and wife of the duc du Maine (q.v. above); a restless and ambitious woman who took a leading part in the 'conspiracy' of the Spanish ambassador Cellamare against the Regent (1718), in consequence of which she suffered a temporary imprisonment. She was famous for the literary and political *salon* which she maintained at Sceaux, from 1700 to 1750, the best known, but not from a literary or philosophical standpoint the most important, of the time. Among the distinguished persons who frequented it were the cardinal de Polignac, the président de Mesmes, Chaulieu, Fontenelle, Voltaire. See also *Launay (Mlle de).* The duchesse du Maine (sometimes helped in the composition by persons of her court) wrote in verse *Divertissements de Sceaux.*

Maine de Biran, MARIE-FRANÇOIS-PIERRE GONTHIER DE BIRAN, *known as* (1766–1824), one of the most important figures in the history of 19th-century French philosophy, was born at Bergerac, in Périgord, a doctor's son. He spent most of his life there, though in youth he served for a short period (ended by ill health) in the king's bodyguard, and between 1797 and his death he played a part in politics which entailed frequent stays in Paris. But he suffered physically and spiritually from the fret of city life and was his most complete self in the country.

He began as a sensationalist, a disciple of Condillac and the *idéologues* (qq.v.) and in matters religious a sceptic, and he ended by holding doctrines which were the direct opposite and by subscribing to the Roman Catholic faith. His importance lies in the fact that the influence of foreign philosophers (e.g. Scottish or German) played no part in his changed views: these were the outcome of independent thinking and of long, deliberate, psychological observation of his innermost personality and the workings of his own mind. It was in fact with Maine de Biran that psychology and introspection entered into French philosophy.

In a treatise on *L'Influence de l'habitude sur la faculté de penser* (1803) he drew a distinction between what he called *passive* habits, i.e. sensations and impressions which become dulled with repetition, and *active* habits, i.e. those which are conscious, and willed. The effect of this, which was borne out by his later writings (notably, *Mémoire sur la décomposition de la pensée*, 1805; *Considérations sur les rapports du physique et du moral*, 1811; also *Les Perceptions obscures*, 1807–10), was that he maintained the importance of man as a reflective being whose soul, or *ego*, resides in the will, who is not formed solely by external circumstances but is free to exercise intellectual and moral choice, and whose best path to an understanding of the truth lies through observation and study of his own, even his own hidden, personality.

The difficult stages by which this thinker came to accept belief in the existence of a supreme reality, a Divine force external to man, namely God, as a necessity, can be followed in his intensely interesting *Journal intime* (1927, 2 vols., posth.), one of the outstanding examples of French introspective literature.

Maine-Giraud, le manoir de, a small country property near Angoulême inherited by Alfred de Vigny (q.v.). He led a secluded life there from 1846 to 1853.

Mainet, see *Berthe aux grands pieds*.

Maintenon, Françoise d'Aubigné, marquise de (1635–1719), granddaughter of Agrippa d'Aubigné (q.v.), born of Protestant parents at Niort where her father was a prisoner (she was born in prison). She grew up in poverty and dependence. She renounced Protestantism in 1648, and in 1652 married the paralytic poet Scarron (q.v.) as an alternative to the convent. Her sprightly and amiable character obtained for her admission to good society, but Scarron's death (1660) left her once more in poverty, except for a pension which she received for some years from the queen mother (Anne of Austria). In 1669 she was entrusted with the education of the children of Louis XIV and Mme de Montespan. About 1674 she replaced the latter as the royal mistress, and about 1684 after the death of the queen (Marie-Thérèse) was secretly married to the king. She took the name of Maintenon from a property which she bought and which the king erected into a marquisate. She was a modest, discreet, intelligent woman, capable of great self-control, and inclined to piety; her influence on the policy of Louis XIV, which has been variously estimated, does not appear to have been in fact very great; she appears, for instance, to have done nothing to mitigate the harsh treatment of her former co-religionists after the Revocation of the Edict of Nantes. One memorial of her influence is to be seen in Saint-Cyr, which she induced the king to found as a convent school for daughters of poor gentlemen and to place under her direction. Her *Lettres*, besides being written with a concise correctness and fitness of style which rank her little below Mme de Sévigné, reveal the good qualities of her character and her knowledge of human nature. They deal not only with personal matters, but with matters of Church and State, and include detailed instructions for the education of the girls at Saint-Cyr (cf. *Esther*; *Athalie*).

Mairan, Jean-Jacques de (1678–1771), physicist, mathematician, and astronomer, member of the three *académies*, wrote, somewhat after the manner of Fontenelle, works which combined scientific knowledge with literary skill.

Maire de Paris. Sylvain Bailly (q.v.), who was executed in 1793, was the last mayor of Paris. Since that time, for reasons of history, politics, and administration, the organization of municipal administration in Paris has been exceptional. At the present day there are mayors—who are centrally appointed—in each of the *arrondissements* (administrative districts) into which the city is divided, and who discharge certain minor administrative functions. Otherwise, with the exception of police powers (see *Police*, para. 3), the municipal responsibilities which would normally be the lot of the elected mayor of a large town are exercised by the centrally appointed *Préfet* of the *Département de la Seine* (see also *Commune*).

Maire du Palais, under the Merovingian (q.v.) kings of France, the head of the royal household (the *major palatii*, or *major domus regiae*) and eventually, as the importance of the office gradually increased, of the notables and officials of the kingdom. The Maire du

Palais nominated the dukes and counts who represented the royal authority in the country, administered the royal domains, and in the king's absence presided over the royal tribunal and commanded the royal army. In the 7th century the Maire du Palais is no longer chosen by the king but by the notables. After the death of Dagobert I (639) the Maire du Palais becomes the real ruler of the country, the kings being known as *rois fainéants*. The most notable holders of the office were three ancestors of Charlemagne: (1) Pépin d'Héristal, who ruled France with vigour from 687 to 714; (2) his son Charles Martel (714–41), an active and successful warrior, named 'Martel' for the way he 'hammered' his enemies, famous for his campaigns against Saracen invaders from Spain, especially for his great victory over them near Poitiers in 732; (3) his son and successor Pépin le Bref, so named on account of his short stature, who in 751, with the support of the Church, deposed the last of the Merovingian kings and usurped the throne. He died in 768. The war that he carried on for seventeen years with Waïfre, Duke of Aquitaine, is perhaps reflected in the *chanson de geste* (q.v.) of *Garin le Loherain* (q.v.). Pépin le Bref was father of Charlemagne (q.v.).

Mairet, JEAN (1604–86), born at Besançon, author of tragedies and tragicomedies, notably *Sylvie* and *Silvanire* (pastoral tragicomedies performed in 1626 and 1630 and *Sophonisbe* (tragedy, 1634). His chief claim to be remembered is that it was he who really introduced the unities in French drama, applying them substantially in *Silvanire* and formulating their theory two years later in a preface to the same play (the doctrine had previously been briefly enunciated by Ronsard and Jean de la Taille). His *Sophonisbe* (q.v.), on the theme of the Sophonisba of Roman history, is generally regarded as the first French play to conform to the rules of tragedy, by reason of its nobility of style, refinement of sentiment, simplicity of theme, respect of the unities, and exclusion of the comic element. Mairet violently attacked Corneille's *Le Cid*. He was protected by Richelieu and was for a time one of the *cinq auteurs* (q.v.) who wrote dramas under his direction.

Maison de Molière, La, a name for the Comédie-Française (q.v.).

Maison dorée, see *Café Hardy*.

Maison du berger, La, by Alfred de Vigny, one of the best-known poems of the posthumous collection *Les Destinées* (1864). It was written, and first printed (in the *Revue des Deux Mondes*), in 1844. The poet is disgusted with the world and an industrial civilization. He will turn to Nature, but not alone, for Nature is cruel and unmoved by suffering humanity. He wishes only to look at life and Nature through the eyes of his loved one and he invites her to share his solitude in the *maison du berger* (i.e. the movable hut used by shepherds when their flocks are on distant pastures).

Maison du chat qui pelote, La, one of the 'Scènes de la vie privée' in Balzac's *Comédie humaine* (q.v.).

Maison Nucingen, La, one of the 'Scènes de la vie parisienne' in Balzac's *Comédie humaine* (q.v., and see *Nucingen*).

Maison rouge, La, under the monarchy of pre-Revolutionary days was one of the companies of the King's Household Guard, so called because of the brilliant red cloak which was part of the uniform.

Maison Tellier, La (1881), the name-tale of a collection by Guy de Maupassant, a masterpiece of irony which the author considered equal, if not superior, to *Boule-de-suif* (q.v.). One evening in a small seaside town in Normandy the local worthies arrive at Mme Tellier's brothel, their regular meeting-place, sanctified by usage, to find it closed. Mme Tellier has gone to a village some way inland, taking 'ces dames' with her, to attend her niece's First Communion. The women have a highly successful outing. They frolic in the country, at the ceremony they are lusciously overcome by memories and emotion, and on the next day they return home refreshed and in riotous spirits. The windows are unshuttered and la Maison Tellier reopens to its overjoyed clients.

Maistre, JOSEPH DE (1753–1821), moralist and Christian philosopher, elder brother of the following, was born of French parents at Chambéry, then capital of the Duchy of Savoy (which at this time, and until conquered by the French in 1792, was a possession of the Kings of Sardinia). After studying at the University of Turin he entered the magistracy, married, and lived in Savoy. In 1793 he refused to swear allegiance to the French Republic and fled to Switzerland. His sentiments at this period were expressed (anonymously) in *Lettres d'un royaliste savoisien* (1793) and *Considérations sur la France* (1796, in which he treated the Revolution as a divine purification). In 1803 he was appointed Sardinian envoy to Russia, a difficult mission thanks to his king's reluctance to provide him with subsistence or official backing. He won the respect of the Russian court, but had to leave the country in 1817 because of his Jesuit sympathies. He went first to Paris and then to Turin, where he died. His works, admirably clear and vivacious in style, embody the Catholic reaction against the doctrines of the *philosophes,* the nationalist and monarchist views of the *ultras* (q.v.), and his opposition to the progress of physical science. Besides *Les Soirées de Saint-Pétersbourg* (1821, q.v.), his masterpiece, they include *Essai sur le principe générateur des constitutions politiques* (1810: God is the generating force of constitutions, society is of divine origin, so, too, is the monarchy, a necessity which has evolved from society. Hence the monarch's sovereignty is absolute and his duty is to support the Papal supremacy); *Du Pape* (1819, asserting Papal infallibility); *L'Église gallicane* (1820). His voluminous correspondence (included in *Œuvres complètes,* 1884-7) contains amusing warnings to his daughter against the danger of being too clever: 'Une coquette est plus aisée à marier qu'une savante; car, pour épouser une savante, il faut être sans orgueil, ce qui est très rare; au lieu que pour épouser une coquette, il ne faut qu'être fou, ce qui est très commun.' It was Joseph de Maistre who wrote 'Toute nation a le gouvernement qu'elle mérite'.

Maistre, XAVIER DE (1763–1852), novelist, brother of the preceding. An exile after the French occupation of Savoy (1798), he followed his brother to Russia, served in the Russian army, and rose to be a general. He married a Russian and lived mainly in Russia, where he died, except for travels in Savoy, Italy, and France between 1826 and 1839. He was over seventy when he first visited Paris. He wrote the charming *Voyage autour de ma chambre* (1794, q.v.), followed

in 1825 by the *Expédition nocturne autour de ma chambre*; also tales: *Le Lépreux de la cité d'Aoste* (1811), *Les Prisonniers du Caucase* (1825), *La Jeune Sibérienne* (1825).

Maître Cornélius, one of the 'Études philosophiques' in Balzac's *Comédie humaine* (q.v.).

Maître de forges, Le (1882), a sentimental novel, dramatized in 1883, by Georges Ohnet (q.v.), a best-seller of French 19th-century fiction. The nobly-born heroine is jilted by her ducal fiancé and marries the rich ironmaster Philippe Derblay, who has all the virtues except an apostrophe in his name. She treats him with shameful arrogance but is worn down by his cold politeness and in the end comes adoringly to heel.

Maîtres d'autrefois, Les (1876), collected art criticism by Eugène Fromentin (q.v.).

Maîtres des Requêtes, under the monarchy, magistrates whose function it was originally to receive and report on petitions presented to the king. Later, under Louis XIV, the above duty having been transferred to the minister for war, they were charged with a variety of special judicial functions, especially that of assisting the royal council in its judicial capacity. The office could be sold or inherited.

Malade imaginaire, Le, a *comédie-ballet* by Molière, produced in 1673, his last play.

   Molière returns once more to mockery of the medical profession, which 'knows everything about disease except how to cure it'. Argan imagines himself to be ill, and credulously submits himself to the endless medicaments prescribed by doctors Purgon and Diafoirus. A slight show of insubordination on his part, encouraged by the arguments of his sensible brother, calls down on his head a ludicrous imprecation from Purgon, whose long words terrify Argan almost to death. He is even determined that his daughter shall marry the son of Diafoirus, a pedantic medical student, because he wants to have a doctor in his family, though the daughter's affections are set elsewhere. His second wife, who makes a show of devotion to him, but is really interested only in his property, hopes to drive the daughter into a convent. Argan is induced to feign death, to prove his wife's affection. It reveals instead her heartless self-interest and the devotion of his daughter. The play ends with a ballet representing, in macaronic Latin, the burlesque admission of a doctor by the Faculty of Paris.

Malbrouk s'en va-t-en guerre, the first line of an old French song wrongly confused since the 18th century with the campaigns of the great Duke of Marlborough. It is said to go back to a much older song about the duc de Guise, and possibly even, before that, to have a remotely Arabic or Spanish origin. Malbrouk (or Malbrouck, or Malbrouc, or Malpronc), who may have been a crusader, goes off to the war; he may return at Easter or at the Trinity. His lady mounts to the top of the tower, sees his page returning, and learns that her lord is dead. The song was sung as a lullaby by a nurse to one of Marie-Antoinette's children, took the queen's fancy, and became popular. There are more than twenty couplets. Beaumarchais introduced the tune—which resembles 'We won't go home till morning'—into his *Mariage de Figaro*. [See HARVEY, *Comp. to Eng. Lit.*]

Maldoror, the demonic hero of Lautréamont's (q.v.) *Chants de Maldoror*.

Mal du siècle, Le, the imaginative (and subjective) melancholy, sometimes a gentle lassitude, sometimes despairing and violent, which characterized early 19th-century sensibility and was especially associated with *le Romantisme* (q.v.).

Mâle, ÉMILE (1862–1954), art historian, author of studies of medieval and religious art in France which are among the most valuable works of their kind (*L'Art religieux du moyen âge en France*, 1922; *L'Art religieux après le concile de Trente*, 1932, &c.).

Malebranche, NICOLAS (1638–1715), an exact contemporary of Louis XIV, born in Paris, theologian, scientist, and philosopher, entered the order of the Oratorians and the priesthood, but never held any cure or educational post, devoting himself to meditation and the composition of religious and philosophical works of which he published a considerable number (*La Recherche de la Vérité*, his principal work, 1674–5; *Conversations chrétiennes*, 1676; *Traité de la nature et*

de la grâce, 1680; *Méditations chrétiennes*, 1683; *Traité de morale*, 1684; *Entretiens sur la métaphysique et la religion*, 1688; &c.). An admirer of the method and physics of Descartes, Malebranche parted company with him in his metaphysical conceptions, and was equally a disciple of St. Augustine. He did not distinguish between the realms of faith and reason, but held that divine reason surpassed the imperfect reason of man. He advanced an original solution of the Cartesian dualism of spirit and matter: denying the action of matter on spirit and spirit on matter, he found in God the source of our notions of the material world and the sole and universal cause, operating the movements of external objects and of our ideas so as to produce correspondence between the two; at the same time he maintained, in some degree, the freedom of the will. His doctrine, with its tendency towards pantheism, was contested by the Jansenist Arnauld and others, and was disapproved by Bossuet, so that Malebranche was involved in much controversy; but he attracted many important admirers and disciples, including Leibniz. An English version of his *Recherche de la vérité* appeared in 1694. He was one of the best prose writers of the 17th century.

Malesherbes, CHRÉTIEN-GUILLAUME DE LAMOIGNON DE (1721–94), an enlightened administrator and a man of high character and integrity, who was *directeur de la librairie* (i.e. of the book-trade, see *Librairie*) from 1750 to 1763, under his father (Guillaume-Henri de Lamoignon) the chancellor, and a minister under Louis XVI with Turgot. While endeavouring to be strictly equitable between the various parties, he did much to soften the rigour of the censorship of books (for which he was responsible), being an advocate of the liberty of the press (see his *Mémoire sur la liberté de la presse*, 1790) and at heart in sympathy with the ideas of the *philosophes*. This sympathy was manifested especially in regard to the publication of the *Encyclopédie*; he also took great interest in the publication of Rousseau's *Nouvelle Héloïse* and *Émile*. Malesherbes defended Louis XVI before the Convention and was guillotined.

Maleville or **Malleville,** CLAUDE DE (1597–1647), lyric poet, one of the original members of the *Académie*. He wrote a sonnet on *La Belle Matineuse* in which he was thought to have excelled even Voiture's sonnet on the same subject.

Malezieu, NICOLAS DE (1650–1729), a man of wide learning appointed tutor to the duc du Maine and teacher of mathematics to the duc de Bourgogne, but noted chiefly as the organizer of *divertissements* for the duchesse du Maine's court at Sceaux. He wrote occasional pieces of little importance.

Malfilâtre, JACQUES-CHARLES-LOUIS DE (1732–67), born in Normandy, a poet of some promise who died young and unrecognized ('La faim mit au tombeau Malfilâtre ignoré', wrote Gilbert); author of satires and odes and of *Narcisse dans l'île de Vénus* (1769).

Malherbe, FRANÇOIS DE (1555–1628), poet, born at Caen in Normandy, entered the service of the duc d'Angoulême, governor of Provence, and spent twenty years in that province. He was recommended to Henri IV (1605) by du Perron and became official poet, remaining in favour under the Regent, Louis XIII, and Richelieu. He is especially known as a censor of earlier poets and the school of Ronsard, checking the decadence and increasing frivolity seen in Desportes; a purist in style, standing for strength and conciseness of diction as against the unbridled facility of the Pléiade, for sobriety and clearness and avoidance of mere ornament, for intellectual as opposed to emotional poetry. He condemned hiatus and *enjambement* (qq.v.) and approved of rigid rules as regards the caesura, elision, and rhyme (qq.v.); he also excluded the use of Latinisms and dialectal words, and other innovations of the Pléiade, in favour of the common Parisian speech; he prescribed accurate grammatical constructions in the interest of clearness and precision of meaning, but at the expense of many useful terms and of happy though irregular turns of phrase. He himself wrote comparatively little, choosing mainly high political themes for his lyrics (*Prière pour le roi allant en Limousin, Pour le roi allant châtier la rébellion des Rochelois, &c.*), and paraphrasing the Psalms. His verses, while lofty in tone, clear, concise, and vigorous, show as a rule lack of inspiration. He was slow in composition; it is related that he

spent three years on his stanzas on the death of the présidente de Verdun, so that when they were presented to console her husband he was already consoled and remarried and had died. He translated in prose the *De beneficiis* of Seneca and the 33rd Book of Livy. His literary opinions may be gathered from his commentary on Desportes and his letters to his friend Peiresc. Racan and Maynard (qq.v.) were his disciples, and Racan wrote a life of him. There are many anecdotes about him (mostly based on Racan) in Tallemant des Réaux's *Historiettes* (xxix). (See also *Dupérier, François*.)

Malheur d'Henriette Gérard, Le, (1860), a novel by Philippe Duranty (q.v. and see *Réalisme*). A provincial family persecute their daughter into marrying a rich old man. On her wedding-day she learns that the young clerk whom she really loved has drowned himself. She turns on her husband so violently that he has a stroke. She nurses him with competent, untender efficiency till he dies, then, equally competently, ensures that her family get no share in the fortune she inherits. Her courage (which only failed her at the crucial moment when she tried to run away on a pouring wet night and was driven back by her wretched state), and her insolent defiance of her parents, are well rendered. The young man is a weakling, the old man a pathetic dotard, knocked silly by passion. There are good scenes of squabbling family life.

Malibran, MADAME, *née* MARIA-FÉLICIA GARCIA (1808–36), born in Paris, a famous operatic contralto with a voice of exceptional range. She sang to enthusiastic audiences in all the capitals of Europe, and died while singing at a festival in Manchester. Musset's famous *Stances à la Malibran* were addressed to her. Her father was the famous Spanish tenor Manuel Garcia. Her younger sister, Pauline (1821–1910), also a singer, married Louis Viardot (1800–83), man of letters and Spanish scholar, and was a friend of Turgenev.

Mallarmé, STÉPHANE (1842–98), poet, born in Paris, went at twenty—from the lycée of Sens—to England and remained two years teaching French and studying English. While in London he married (1863) a young German governess whom he first knew at

Sens. On his return to France he held posts as English master in provincial schools (Tournon, Besançon, Avignon) and, after 1873, in Paris (lycées Condorcet, Janson de Sailly, Rollin). He retired in 1893 and lived until his death at Valvins, on the Seine near Fontainebleau.

Schoolmastering was his means—only less uncongenial than any other—of securing a livelihood. In fact, his life both before and after retirement was devoted almost exclusively to poetic creation (for him, an agonizing struggle), or to meditating or talking, occasionally to writing, about the poetic function. His output, nearly at a standstill by the end of his life, included: about sixty shorter poems and sonnets, usually first printed in reviews, notably in *Le Parnasse contemporain* of 1866; three fragments of a dramatic poem *Hérodiade* (*Ouverture*, posth., a monologue by Herodias's nurse; *Scène*, first published in *Le Parnasse contemporain* of 1869, a dialogue between the nurse and Herodias; *Cantique de saint Jean*); the long eclogue *L'Après-midi d'un faune* (1876), one of his most famous works, which inspired Debussy's *Prélude à l'Après-midi* . . . ; writings on style and aesthetics, with some prose poems, collected (1897) in *Divagations*; *La Musique et les Lettres* (1895), the Taylorian lecture delivered by him at Oxford in March 1894; a preface to the reprint (1876) of the original French edition of Beckford's *Vathek* (q.v.); and (1877) a *Petite Philologie à l'usage des classes et du monde: Les mots anglais*, rarefied beyond the ordinary run of school textbooks. The Pléiade edition (1945) of his *Œuvres complètes* includes the poems and prose published in his lifetime in *Poésies* (1887) and *Vers et Prose* (1893), also some fragments of a prose tale *Igitur ou La Folie d'Elbehnon*.

In spite of his early affinities the *monde visible* of the Parnassiens (q.v.) was not Mallarmé's. He believed that a poem should suggest rather than describe, and that words, as the poet employs them, have an evocative content beyond their everyday significance. His efforts to evoke an ideal beauty led him to use elaborate symbols and metaphors and to experiment with rhythm and syntax (e.g. by means of transposition, inversion, omission of the verbs and subordinate clauses which carry a reader forward with the writer's intention). They also, with his

theories of the 'musicality' of poetry, and of music and poetry as alternative aspects of the pure idea itself, made him a great poetic force in his own day and a notable influence on his successors. His influence over the younger poets began after Huysmans's praise of *Hérodiade* in *A rebours* and the essay devoted to him by Verlaine in *Les Poètes maudits* (qq.v., both 1884). It was most strongly exercised through his talk, though no written record of this exists. On Tuesday evenings between 1885 and 1894 poets and other writers in Paris—foreign as well as French, and many themselves destined for fame—congregated regularly at his flat (89 rue de Rome) to listen to talk which seems to have fallen like Divine utterance upon their ears. 'Sa pensée jaillissait de son âme à ses lèvres, toute formée, toute splendide, définitive.' [A. Poizat, *Le Symbolisme, de Baudelaire à Claudel* (1924).]

Some of Mallarmé's poems and prose writings are so obscure (the adjective 'hermetic' is frequently applied to them) as to defeat determined study. An extreme example is his last poem *Un Coup de dés jamais n'abolira le hasard*, first printed in May 1897 in the review *Cosmopolis*. The size of the type and the arrangement of the words on the (double) page are continually varied in an attempt both to produce the effect of a musical score and to reproduce the 'subdivisions prismatiques de l'idée'. But others, e.g. the sonnets, passages from *Hérodiade* and the *Faune*, have a rare, evocative beauty which can be apprehended if not always comprehended; which make him 'the crown and conclusion of the Symbolist Movement' (Bowra, *Heritage of Symbolism*); and which will always leave some readers silent before 'l'éruptif multiple sursautement de la clarté, comme les proches irradiations d'un lever de jour' [Pref. to *Un coup de dés*].

Mallet du Pan, JACQUES (1749–1800), man of letters and journalist, born in Geneva, an honest and courageous editor of the *Mercure de France* (see *Mercure galant*), and a defender of constitutional monarchy. In 1792 (spring) he left France to work for the interests of the *émigrés* in foreign countries. His *Considérations sur la nature de la Révolution de France* (1793) are of this period. Driven from Switzerland he took refuge in England

(1798), and from London (where he died) published the *Mercure britannique*, which was hostile to Republican France and the policy of the *Directoire*.

Mallet du Pan was one of the noteworthy writers of the Revolutionary period, possessed of political penetration and good sense, with a vigorous and ironic style. His *Mémoires et Correspondance*, published posthumously (1852) and highly praised by Sainte-Beuve, include letters of advice to the Bourbon (q.v.) family.

Malleville, CLAUDE DE, see *Maleville*.

Malmaison, on the outskirts of Paris, was in the Middle Ages a lepers' colony dependent on the Abbey of Saint-Denis. Early in the 17th century a country house was built there which in 1799 was bought by the Empress Josephine, then 'la générale Bonaparte'. She did much to enlarge and improve it, and during the Consulate it was Bonaparte's favourite residence. After the divorce (see *Napoleon*) the Empress Josephine remained at Malmaison with her children until her death in May 1814. The house passed into other hands, then fell into disuse. Eventually it was bought by the French financier and philanthropist Daniel Osiris (1828–1907), who restored and presented it (1904) to the nation. It is now a museum of the Napoleonic era, one of the most touching and evocative of French historical monuments.

Malot, HECTOR (1830–1907), is remembered particularly as a writer of children's stories. His great success was *Sans famille* (1878), the adventures of a foundling boy. *Romain Kalbris* (1869) and *En famille* (1893) were also much read.

Malraux, ANDRÉ (1901–   ), novelist and essayist. Psychology has little part in his novels of action, and the characters themselves have less interest and less dynamic force than the political and philosophical beliefs by which they are swept along. *Les Conquérants* (1928) and *La Condition humaine* (1933, q.v.) are about Communism in China. The first is set in Canton in the summer of 1925, the second in Shanghai in spring 1927. *L'Espoir* (1937), of a more documentary nature, is about the Spanish civil war of 1936 (in which the author took part). His other novels are: *La Voie royale* (1930); *Le Temps du mépris* (1935), and *Les Noyers de*

l'Altenburg (1945), though the last is a series of dialogues rather than a novel.

The three volumes of this writer's *Psychologie de l'art* (1948–50), on the psychological bases of art throughout the ages, are among the outstanding modern writings on art and aesthetics.

Malte, Chevaliers de, an order of military monks, known in England as the Hospitallers of St. John of Jerusalem, which had its origin in an earlier community, founders of a hospital and church in Jerusalem. The order was developed in the 12th century. After the recapture of Jerusalem by the Moslems the order was centred successively in Rhodes and Malta. The latter island it successfully defended, under its grand master La Vallette, against the Turks in 1565, and continued to govern until Napoleon occupied it in 1798.

Mamamouchi, the name given by Molière in *Le Bourgeois Gentilhomme* (q.v.) to an imaginary Turkish dignitary of his invention.

Mamelles de Tirésias, Les (1918), a 'drame surréaliste' by Guillaume Apollinaire (q.v.).

Mamelouks de la Garde, Les, a native mounted corps formed by Bonaparte in Egypt (*c.* 1798). From this corps, in 1804, was formed a company of the Imperial Guard, about 250 strong, who always wore oriental dress (though a few officers and n.c.o.s were French). The Mamelouks were dispersed in 1815 after Napoleon's abdication and many were massacred at Marseilles during the *Terreur Blanche* (q.v.) which followed the Restoration. [The Mamelukes, from the Arab. *Mamlūk* = slave, were originally the Turkish and Circassian slaves from whom the Ayoubite sultans of Egypt, descendants of Saladin, drew their bodyguard. They rose to positions of great dignity and eventually became masters of Egypt, Mameluke Sultans reigning from 1254 to 1517. When Bonaparte landed in Egypt in 1798 the country was governed by twenty-four Mameluke Beys under the Turkish viceroy. The French victories destroyed their power and those of them who remained were massacred (1811) by the Pasha Mohammed Ali.]

Mancini, see *Mazarin's nieces*.

Mandrin, LOUIS (1724–55), a celebrated leader of brigands. He was broken on the wheel.

Manekine, La, a *roman d'aventure* by Philippe de Beaumanoir (q.v.), written between 1270 and 1280. There are versions of the story in other languages. The earliest known form of it is in a *Vita Offae primi* probably written at St. Albans at the end of the 12th century.

A king of Hungary has promised his wife on her death-bed that he will only marry a woman resembling herself. He is urged by his barons to remarry, but the only woman found to comply with this condition is his own daughter Joïe. Joïe, revolted by the idea, cuts off her left hand. The king orders her to be burnt alive, but the seneschal from pity sends her adrift in a boat. She is carried by the boat to Scotland, where the king of Scotland gives her shelter, names her Manekine (for she will not say who she is), and despite his mother's opposition marries her. During his absence Joïe gives birth to a son, but the old queen substitutes for the letter announcing this to the king another missive saying that she has given birth to a monster. The king orders her to be carefully tended until his return. But again the queen substitutes an order that she is to be burnt alive. Once more the seneschal saves her and sends her adrift in a boat, which carries her to the mouth of the Tiber. After seven years the king discovers her in Rome, where her penitent father also appears. By a miracle the severed hand reappears in a fountain and by the Pope's prayer is reunited to the arm.

Manet, ÉDOUARD (1832–83), one of the first and most famous of the French Impressionist painters (see *Impressionnisme*), though he never exhibited with them. He was also very closely associated with his writer-contemporaries. He frequented the Parnassian reunions at the offices of the publisher Lemerre (see *Parnassiens*). Baudelaire encouraged him in his early days. He knew Mallarmé well, painted one of the best-known portraits of him, and illustrated the first edition of *L'Après-midi d'un faune*. Zola, whom he also painted, was another friend.

Manette Salomon (1867), a novel of artist life by E. and J. de Goncourt (qq.v.). The four contrasted types of the book—

Anatole Bazoche, Chassagnol, Garnotelle, and Coriolus—meet first as young art students. Bazoche, a typical Bohemian and a clown by nature, has great facility without application or any true creative gift. He loves animals, and when art fails becomes a keeper in the Zoological Gardens. Chassagnol, a theorist and a bore, ends by living on his wife and continuing to theorize. Garnotelle is a conventional success, wins prizes, becomes a fashionable portrait-painter, and marries a foreign princess. Coriolus, a genuine artist, is rich and a modernist, therefore suspect. He marries a beautiful Jewish model, Manette Salomon, and watches her ruin his life. Her relations fill the house; she grows increasingly avaricious and will only let him paint what will sell.

The book is a successful example of the nervous impressionistic manner in which these authors conduct a novel across a succession of tableaux and conversations. Notable passages are the opening picture of Paris viewed from the *Jardin des Plantes*, and the description of the stay made by Coriolus, Bazoche, and Manette at Barbizon, the artists' colony in the Forest of Fontainebleau.

Manières, Livre des, see *Livre des Manières*.

Manifeste des cinq contre 'La Terre'. This was a public repudiation—which the authors later regretted—of Zola's *Naturalisme* (q.v.), and a denunciation (provoked specially by his novel *La Terre* which was at the time being published serially) of his obscenity. It appeared in *Le Figaro* of 18 August 1887 over the signatures of five of Zola's former disciples: Paul Bonnetain (1858–99), Gustave Guiches (1860–1935), Lucien Descaves, Paul Margueritte, and J.-H. Rosny (qq.v.).

Manifeste du Surréalisme (1924), by André Breton (q.v., and see *Surréalisme*).

Mannequin d'osier, Le, see *Bergeret, M.*

Manon Lescaut (pron. as if *Lèss-cô*), **Histoire du chevalier des Grieux et de,** a romance by the abbé Prévost, first published in 1731 as the 7th vol. of his *Mémoires d'un homme de qualité*, reprinted two years later (when it was seized by the authorities), and published separately from

1753 onwards. The work proved immensely successful.

The chevalier des Grieux, when seventeen, meets by accident a young girl, Manon Lescaut, who is about to be made a nun against her will, and with whom he falls desperately in love and elopes. There follows the story of a blind and overmastering passion, which leads him through a series of unhappy adventures and reduces him to the basest expedients in order to obtain the means of supporting her and himself. It even triumphs over the repeated infidelities of Manon, who, though gentle and affectionate, is entirely devoid of moral sense. At last, with the connivance of des Grieux's respectable father, Manon, to the despair of her lover, is deported to New Orleans. He succeeds in accompanying her and for a time lives with her there in comparative happiness, until it comes to light that they are not married, as had been pretended. Whereupon she is allotted to the governor's nephew, who has fallen in love with her.

Des Grieux and Manon flee on foot from the colony, but Manon soon succumbs to fatigue and dies in the desert. Thereafter, it is indicated, religious sentiment and the punishment he has suffered recall des Grieux to greater dignity and fortitude.

Important secondary characters are Tiberge, des Grieux's faithful sensible friend; Manon's rascally brother; and des Grieux's father.

Mansard or **Mansart,** JULES HARDOUIN- (1645–1708), the principal architect in the employment of Louis XIV from 1670 onwards. His works include the palace and chapel of Versailles, the dome of the Invalides, the Place Vendôme.

His great-uncle François Mansard (1598–1666) was likewise a famous architect, who gave his name to the *mansarde* or mansard roof, i.e. a roof of which each face has two slopes, the lower steeper than the upper.

Manuel des péchés, see *Religious Writings* (medieval period).

Manzoni, ALESSANDRO (1785–1873), Italian poet and novelist, author of the famous novel *I Promessi Sposi* (1825–7), was leader of the Romantic Movement in Italy and an influence on the movement in France (see *Foreign Influences on French Literature,*

para. 18). Many of his works were translated into French by his friend Fauriel (q.v.). It was in his memory that Verdi composed his *Requiem.*

Mapah, Le, the name—compounded of the first syllables of *mater* and *pater*—assumed by Ganneau (?1805–51), a sculptor, who ran through a fortune and then, some time about 1835, founded a synthetic religion called *Évadisme* [i.e. Eve + Adam]. It exalted woman, and preached the perfect equality and eventual fusion of the sexes, since 'le véritable Dieu', the sum and symbol of humanity, must contain in himself both the male and the female principle and was thus both *père* and *mere*. Ganneau also held that the French nation, the 'Christ-peuple', had had its Golgotha at Waterloo. In his filthy lodging ('notre grabat apostolique') in the Île Saint-Louis he used to model figures, dubiously symbolic of the mysteries of his religion, which he sent to the various Deputies and Pairs de France. He also addressed encyclicals and manifestoes to the Pope, notably one announcing his own advent and requesting the Pope to vacate the Holy See in his favour. His activities were denounced to the magistrates of Paris, but the matter was dropped, rather than create a stir, when the heavily-bearded Mapah, in sacerdotal garb of working-man's blue blouse, sabots, and an immense grey felt hat, appeared for questioning.

Maquet, AUGUSTE (1813–88), born in Paris, remembered as having collaborated with Dumas *père* in writing historical novels. His share amounted to supplying the historical framework or the bare bones of a plot. In youth, when he called himself 'Augustus Mackeat', he belonged to the younger Romantics led by Gautier and Petrus Borel (qq.v. and cf. *Bousingo; Jeunes-France*). He wrote some novels and plays on his own. Of the latter, *La Maison du baigneur* (1856) is sometimes mentioned.

Marais, Le. (1) An ancient quarter of Paris, stretching up from the Right Bank of the Seine and originally a marshy area which was not drained till late in the Middle Ages. The present Place des Vosges (originally Place Royale, created by Henri IV, celebrated by Corneille in one of his early comedies, and scene of many duels) may be regarded as the centre. Besides the Bastille and the Hôtel des Tournelles, the quarter included many famous houses, such as those of Richelieu, Mme de Sévigné, Ninon de Lenclos. For its connexion with the history of the theatre see *Theatres and Theatre Companies*.

(2) A name given partly in derision to a large, floating group of the centre party in the *Convention nationale* (q.v.). They sided with Montagnards or Girondins (qq.v.), or with Montagnards and Girondins (see *Plaine*).

Marais, MATHIEU (1664–1737), a Parisian bourgeois whose *Journal* contains some interesting anecdotes and comments on literary events of his day. He collaborated with Bayle in the preparation of the latter's dictionary.

Marana, GIOVANNI PAOLO (1642–93), an Italian who lived latterly in France and was pensioned by Louis XIV. His *L'Espion dans les cours des princes chrétiens ou mémoires* [by 'un envoyé secret de la Porte'] *pour servir à l'histoire de ce siècle depuis 1637 jusqu'à 1682* (1684, 6 vols.), written in French and in effect a series of newsletters, was a model for Montesquieu's much more sparkling *Lettres persanes* (q.v.).

Marana, Les, one of the 'Études philosophiques' of Balzac's *Comédie humaine* (q.v.).

Marat, JEAN-PAUL (1743–93), born near Neuchâtel (Switzerland), was one of the most fiery Revolutionary journalists and believed himself to be the apostle of Liberty. A man of encyclopedic knowledge, a doctor by profession, partly educated in Edinburgh, he became a Deputy to the *Convention nationale* (q.v.) and a leader of the Montagnards (q.v.). It is sometimes held that the virulence of his articles in *L'Ami du peuple*, a journal which he founded and edited, prepared the way for the sudden outbreak of popular violence known as the September massacres (see *Revolutions*, Ia, 2–5 Sept. 1792). On 13 July 1793 he was assassinated in his bath by Charlotte Corday (q.v.).

Marbode, see *Lapidaires*.

Marcadé, EUSTACHE, see *Mystères*.

Marcel, the chief character, who is at the same time the narrator, in Proust's *A la recherche du temps perdu* (q.v.). The novel is half finished before we learn that he is called Marcel. We never learn his surname. In many respects his life resembles that of Proust himself (q.v.).

Marcel, ÉTIENNE (c. 1317–58), a draper, provost of the merchants of Paris, who played an important part about 1355–8 as leader of the democratic party in Paris against the regent Charles during the captivity in England of Jean II. He was killed in 1358 when about to deliver Paris to the King of Navarre, in spite of the latter's alliance with the English.

Marcel, GABRIEL (1889–   ), contemporary philosopher and dramatist, also critic of literature, music, and the drama. His philosophical writings include interesting fragments of spiritual and philosophical autobiography—*Journal métaphysique* (1928) —written between 1913 and his conversion to Roman Catholicism in 1929; also *Être et avoir* (1935), *Homo viator* (1945), and (1925) an article entitled *Existence et objectivité*, in the *Revue de métaphysique et de morale*, which is said to have introduced the term *existentialisme* into the vocabulary of French philosophy. (This author himself professes a form of what is called 'existentialisme chrétien'.) His plays, usually dramas of conscience, include: *Le Quatuor en fa dièse* (1920); *Le Cœur des autres* (1921); *L'Iconoclaste* (1923); *Un Homme de Dieu* (1925); *Le Chemin de crête* (1936); *Le Dard* (1938).

Marcelin, pseudonym of Émile-Marcelin-Isidore Planat, see *Vie parisienne, La*.

Marcellin, REMY, one of the original *félibres* (q.v.).

Marchand, LOUIS-JOSEPH-NARCISSE (1791–1876), valet to Napoleon, was born in Paris of a respectable family. His mother was one of three *berceuses* (cradle-rockers) employed for Napoleon's son, the Roi de Rome (q.v.). He himself was twenty when he became one of Napoleon's personal domestic staff, accompanying him on his campaigns (Germany, then Russia) and becoming his principal *valet de chambre* after the first abdication (1814) when Constant, the then holder of the office, took fright and made off.

Thereafter Marchand was continually with Napoleon—in Elba, on the return through France to Paris, at Waterloo, and finally all through the years in St. Helena. Napoleon, on his death-bed, created him *comte* and entrusted him with his will. Back in France, Marchand married the daughter of one of Napoleon's generals (in this following his master's death-bed advice). He was respected on all sides, was one of the escort sent to fetch Napoleon's remains from St. Helena, and at the ceremony of the *Retour des cendres* had one of the first places in the procession (see *Légende napoléonienne*). He received honours from Napoleon III and remained faithful to him after the fall of the Second Empire. He left memoirs, written with sincerity, unpretentiousness, and devotion, and covering the period from 1811, when he entered Napoleon's service, to Napoleon's death in 1821. Volume I (1952) ends with Napoleon boarding the *Bellerophon* after his second abdication. Volume II (1955) describes the years of exile, and Napoleon's death.

Marchant, GUYOT, see *Danse macabre.*

Mardoche, a narrative poem by Alfred de Musset, in *Contes d'Espagne et d'Italie* (1830, q.v.).

Mardrus, DR. JOSEPH - CHARLES - VICTOR (1868–1949), a medical man, and an orientalist whose most notable work was a translation of the *Arabian Nights—Mille Nuits et une nuit* (1898–1904, 16 vols.), much fuller and more colourful than that of Galland (q.v.; see also *Delarue-Mardrus, Lucie*).

Mare au diable, La (1846), by George Sand, a tale of rustic life. Germain, a widowed young farmer, proposes to remarry. He sets off with one of his three children in tow to pay court to an eligible widow in the next village. With him also goes Marie, a young girl whom he has undertaken to escort to her first situation. The party lose their way in the mist near a lake reputed to be enchanted. When they have to spend the night as best they can under the trees Marie's cheerful good sense makes Germain think he might go farther and fare worse for a wife. Next day they continue their journey, Marie to her new master (from whose obnoxious attentions she soon flees), and Germain to meet, and quickly dislike, the widow. The

tale moves to its obvious conclusion and Germain and Marie have a good, old-time country wedding.

Maréchal, in the Middle Ages, a high military officer subordinate originally only to the Connétable. At first, in primitive times, there was only a single maréchal, but the number was increased. There were also maréchaux in the provinces under the feudal princes, thus Villehardouin (q.v.) was maréchal de Champagne.

In 1788 there were twenty maréchaux de France. The dignity was suppressed during the Revolution (1793) but revived by Napoleon, with the title maréchal de l'Empire (see below). After the second restoration (1815) the title once more became maréchal de France. The number of marshals was gradually reduced and after 1870 there were no new promotions till that of General Joffre in 1916.

Maréchale d'Ancre, La (1831), an historical drama by Alfred de Vigny (q.v. and see *Concini*).

Maréchal de l'Empire. Art. VI of the *senatus consultum* of 18 May, 1804 (28 floréal, An XII), the law inaugurating the Napoleonic Empire, revived the ancient dignity of maréchal de France (see above) by providing for the creation of a certain number of maréchaux de l'Empire, to be selected from the most distinguished generals or former generals of the army. An Imperial Decree of 19 May announced the first eighteen promotions, increased later to twenty-five.

These grand dignitaries were Napoleon's chosen band—his brothers in arms, in command of army corps at the famous battles of his campaigns, or his representatives sent to administer conquered territories. He listened, if he did not defer to, their advice and he alternately bullied them or humoured their rivalries and jealousies. They were the nucleus of his imperial aristocracy, and as such he loaded them with dignities and favours, created duchies and principalities for them, insisted on their maintaining a grand way of life, and from the revenues he confiscated provided them with the wherewithal to do so; and he even, upon occasion, selected their wives.

For the most part the marshals had begun

life before the Revolution as professional soldiers; others had forsaken their original callings to enlist in the Revolutionary armies and had risen rapidly from the ranks. They came mainly of good bourgeois or petit-bourgeois stock, a few were of noble birth, and contrary to the general belief very few, possibly only Augereau, Lannes, and Ney, were of very humble origin. After, in some cases even before, Napoleon's first abdication (which some of them strongly counselled) the large majority swore fidelity to the restored monarchy, receiving honours and office from Louis XVIII both then and after 1815—and also from Charles X and Louis-Philippe. Barely a third rallied to Napoleon during the Hundred Days. With the Second Restoration some of these few suffered the severest penalty for their defection (e.g. Ney); most of the others were gradually restored to favour.

The following list of promotions is in two groups, namely, (a) the first eighteen promotions, in alphabetical order, and (b) the seven later promotions, in order of date. An asterisk in the first group denotes the honorary marshals, i.e. those who were promoted as a reward for former services and who were already members of the Senate (an office to which Napoleon frequently appointed his generals).

THE FIRST EIGHTEEN

AUGEREAU, CHARLES-PIERRE-FRANÇOIS (1757–1816), created duc de Castiglione (one of his famous victories) 1808, born in Paris. His father was a domestic, his mother a fruit-vendor. He enlisted in 1774 and had already led an adventurous life, in the army, and later as an army instructor and fencing-master in Italy, when he joined the Garde nationale (q.v.) in Paris in 1790. By 1793 he was a full general in the revolutionary armies. In 1797 after the Fructidor (q.v.) coup d'état he was sent to command the Army of Sambre-et-Meuse. He abandoned Napoleon in 1814, but shortly before Waterloo he wavered in his allegiance to the Monarchy. After the Second Restoration he was placed on the retired list without pay. He died suddenly six months later.

BERNADOTTE, JEAN-BAPTISTE-JULES (1763–1844), son of an attorney at Pau, was destined for the law but enlisted in 1780. He fought brilliantly with the Revolutionary armies, rising from n.c.o. to general between 1790 and 1794. He was created Prince de Pontecorvo in 1806. In 1810 the Diet of Stockholm elected him heir to the throne of Sweden. He adopted the interests and the religion of his new country—and at this time took the name of Charles-Jean—and in 1813 fought with the Sixth Coalition against the French at Leipzig. He refused to join the coalition of 1815. In 1818 he became King Charles XIV of Sweden. His wife was Désirée Clary of Marseilles, sister-in-law of Joseph Bonaparte and an early love of Napoleon. The reigning Swedish dynasty is descended from him.

BERTHIER, LOUIS-ALEXANDRE (1753–1815), born at Versailles, prince de Neuchâtel (1806), de Wagram (1809), son of a high-ranking army officer, was himself an army officer by profession before the Revolution, at one time in America. He was a commanding officer in the Garde nationale in Paris in 1789 and chief of staff to Lafayette (q.v.) in 1792. After a period of suspension (he was suspect as a Royalist) he was allowed to serve as a volunteer in 1793 and by 1795 was a general in the Revolutionary armies. In 1814 he accepted the monarchy. He followed Louis XVIII to Ghent in 1815 but went on to Bamberg in Bavaria and there died of a fall from the palace window (thought to have been suicide).

BESSIÈRES, JEAN-BAPTISTE (1768–1813), created duc d'Istrie 1809, was born at Prayssac (Lot), son of a barber-surgeon, and held a commission in the Garde nationale first there and later (1792) in Paris. Thereafter he was with the Revolutionary armies and was promoted general in 1802. He was killed in battle in Saxony.

BRUNE, GUILLAUME-MARIE-ANNE (1763–1815), came of a legal and military family at Brive-la-Gaillarde (Corrèze), went to Paris to study law but wasted his time. He turned printer and journalist of sorts, frequented extreme Revolutionary circles and finally found his vocation in the Revolutionary army. He was promoted general in 1797. He offended Napoleon in 1807 and was placed on the retired list. He held a command again in June and July 1815, in the Midi, but surrendered Toulon to the Royalists and was returning to Paris when he was murdered, very brutally, at Avignon.

DAVOUT, LOUIS-NICOLAS (1770–1823),

duc d'Auerstadt 1808, prince d'Eckmühl 1809, born at Annoux (Yonne), son of an army officer, began his own army career as a gentleman cadet at the *École militaire* in Paris. When his enthusiasm for the Revolution got him into trouble in 1791 he gave up his commission in the regular army for one in the Revolutionary volunteers. He was Napoleon's Minister of War during the Hundred Days. He organized the defence of Paris after Waterloo and then commanded the army when it retired behind the Loire. Thereafter he was deprived of his rank and pay and lived under police surveillance. He was restored to his position in 1817.

JOURDAN, JEAN-BAPTISTE (1762–1833), the victor of Fleurus, was born at Limoges, son of a barber-surgeon. He joined the army in 1778, retired six years later, married and set up as a draper. In 1789 he had a commission in the local *Garde nationale*, then he became an officer in the Revolutionary armies. He rallied to the Monarchy in 1814 and in 1815 was president of the court martial appointed to try maréchal Ney.

*KELLERMANN, FRANÇOIS-CHRISTOPHE (1735–1820), created duc de Valmy on promotion, was born of a legal family at Strasbourg. He already held high army rank when the Revolution broke out. He was the hero of Valmy but some months afterwards was declared suspect by the Convention, degraded, and put in prison. He was very soon reinstated in his command. He was one of the first members, and soon became President, of the Senate (q.v.).

LANNES, JEAN (1769–1809), duc de Montebello 1808, was born at Lectoure (Gers), the son of a stable-lad, and was apprenticed to a dyer before enlisting (1792) in the Revolutionary armies. One of Napoleon's most devoted generals, he was mortally wounded at the battle of Essling.

*LEFEBVRE, FRANÇOIS-JOSEPH (1755–1820), duc de Dantzig 1808, born at Rouffach (Haut-Rhin), was a miller's son and threw up work in a lawyer's office to enlist in 1773. In the Senate, in 1814, he voted for the downfall of Napoleon. His wife, originally a washerwoman, was the prototype of Madame Sans-Gêne in the play of that name (q.v.).

MASSÉNA, ANDRÉ (1758–1817), duc de Rivoli 1808, prince d'Essling 1810. (The French army was in full retreat at Essling,

a village in Germany, when a bridge broke and Masséna's action averted disaster.) He was born at Nice, at that time Italian, a grocer's son, and early orphaned. He was a ship's lad in a merchant vessel from 1771 to 1775 but then enlisted in the French army. He retired in 1789, married, and lived (and apparently engaged in smuggling) at Nice. Then he joined the Revolutionary armies with commissioned rank and via the local *Garde nationale*. He was naturalized French during the First Restoration (1814).

MONCEY, BON-ADRIEN JANNOT DE (1754–1842), duc de Conegliano 1808, was born at Moncey (Doubs), the son of a barrister at Besançon. He was destined for the law, but enlisted in 1769 aged fifteen, persisted against family opposition in remaining in the army, and had obtained his commission before the Revolution broke out. In 1814 he took part in the unsuccessful defence of Paris against the Allies and later reassembled his troops and led them to Fontainebleau (q.v.), where Napoleon signed his first abdication. He was degraded and for a time imprisoned for refusing to preside at the court martial appointed to try maréchal Ney, but before long his rank and dignities were restored to him.

MORTIER, ÉDOUARD-ADOLPHE-CASIMIR-JOSEPH (1768–1835), duc de Trévise 1808, was born at Le Cateau (Nord), the son of a sailcloth merchant who was a *député du Tiers État* to the *États Généraux*. He was destined for a commercial career, and well educated at the Collège des Anglais at Douai, but his preferences were with the army. From 1789–91 he served in the local (Dunkirk) *Garde nationale*, then entered the Army of the Revolution with the rank of captain. In 1814 he took part in the defence of Paris but had to surrender and fell back on Fontainebleau. He was ill during the Hundred Days. In later years he played a part in politics and was in Russia as French Ambassador. He was fatally injured in 1835 when the Fieschi (q.v.) 'machine infernale' exploded.

MURAT, JOACHIM (1771–1815), prince 1805, roi de Naples 1808, married Caroline Bonaparte, Napoleon's sister, 1800. One of Napoleon's most brilliant and audacious generals, he was born at La Bastide-Fortunière (now La Bastide-Murat) near Toulouse, the son of a prosperous innkeeper, and originally destined for the Church. He had to leave the seminary at Toulouse in bad odour, was ill received at home, and enlisted (1787). In 1799 Bonaparte promoted him general on the field of Aboukir. Towards the end of the Empire he intrigued unsuccessfully with Austria and England. In 1815 he offered his services to Napoleon but was forbidden to come to Paris. Later he had to abandon his kingdom. He was tracked down by Royalists and shot.

NEY, MICHEL (1769–1815), 'le brave des braves', duc d'Elchingen 1808, prince de la Moskova 1813, the most famous of the marshals and the most popular with the troops. He was born at Sarrelouis (Moselle), a wheelwright's son, enlisted in 1788 and by 1799 was a full general in the Revolutionary armies. In 1814 he was one of those who strongly counselled Napoleon to abdicate and was charged by him (with Marmont and Macdonald) to negotiate with Alexander of Russia. He then swore fidelity to the restored monarchy but when, in 1815, he was sent to check Napoleon's advance he joined forces with him instead. At Waterloo he led heroic but unsuccessful, and disastrously costly, charges against Wellington's troops. In August the same year he was arrested, tried for treason by the *Chambre des pairs* (after a court martial had declared itself incompetent to try him), convicted (6 Dec.), and shot (7 Dec.). Of the marshals who at this date were also *pairs de France*, two voted for his death—Marmont and Victor.

*PÉRIGNON, CATHERINE-DOMINIQUE (1754–1818), comte 1808, marquis de 1817, born at Grenade (Haute-Garonne) of a family of landed gentry, had been an army officer by profession before the Revolution. In 1789 he was a colonel in the local *Garde nationale*. In 1791 he was elected Deputy to the *Assemblée nationale* but resigned his seat (1792) to return to active service. He rallied to the Bourbons in 1814 and retired to his property in the Haute-Garonne during the Hundred Days.

*SÉRURIER, JEAN - MATHIEU - PHILIBERT (1742–1819), comte 1808. He was born at Laon (Aisne) where his father had a post in the Royal Stud. He was first commissioned in 1755, retired with the rank of major in the spring of 1789, and returned to active service in 1791. He was suspect as a Royalist in 1792 and degraded, but was soon reinstated and rose rapidly in the Revolutionary armies.

He was Governor of the Invalides at the time of Napoleon's first abdication (1814) and before the Allies arrived he burnt over 1,000 flags captured from the enemy and deposited there.

SOULT, NICOLAS-JEAN DE DIEU (1769–1851), duc de Dalmatie (1808), was born at Saint-Amans-Labastide (Tarn), a lawyer's son. He enlisted in 1785, was a corporal when the Revolution broke out, and a general by 1799. He fought against Sir John Moore at Corunna. In 1814 he accepted the Bourbons but rallied once more to Napoleon during the Hundred Days and fought at Waterloo. He lived in exile in Germany from 1816 to 1819 but was then allowed to return to France. His rank and honours were restored and he lived to hold government office, to be Ambassador extraordinary to London for the Coronation of Queen Victoria, and to be promoted maréchal-général de France (1847).

THE SEVEN LATER PROMOTIONS

VICTOR, CLAUDE-VICTOR PERRIN, *called* (1766–1841), duc de Bellune 1808. He was born at Lamarche (Vosges), a lawyer's son, and began his soldiering career as drummer in an artillery regiment (1781). He served in the *garde nationale* and then made his way up the ranks of the Revolutionary armies, becoming a full general in 1797. He was promoted maréchal after the battle of Friedland (1807). He accepted the Bourbons in 1814, was with Louis XVIII at Ghent during the Hundred Days, and re-entered Paris with him in July 1815.

MACDONALD, JACQUES-ÉTIENNE-JOSEPH-ALEXANDRE (1765–1840), duc de Tarente, 1809 (shortly after being promoted maréchal on the field of Wagram). He was born at Sedan, the son of a Scottish Jacobite who had taken service with Louis XV after the '45. The army was his career. He fought with the *Légion irlandaise*, in Holland, and then (1786) transferred to a French regiment. By 1795, aged thirty, he was a full general. In 1814 he was the last of the marshals to swear allegiance to the restored monarchy and he refused any form of service during the Hundred Days.

MARMONT, AUGUSTE - FRÉDÉRIC - LOUIS VIESSE DE (1774–1852), duc de Raguse 1809. He was promoted maréchal after the battle of Wagram. An army officer's son, born at

Châtillon-sur-Seine, he passed through the *École d'artillerie* at Châlons-sur-Marne into an artillery regiment and at Toulon in 1793 was remarked by Bonaparte and made his aide-de-camp. He fought brilliantly throughout the Revolutionary and the Napoleonic wars but his conduct after the fall of Paris in 1814 was disloyal to the point of treachery and made Napoleon's abdication inevitable. He was with Louis XVIII in Ghent during the Hundred Days and held various official and diplomatic posts after the second Restoration. In 1830 he accompanied Charles X (q.v.) to England and never returned to France. He died in Venice. In his memoirs (posth., 1856–7) he attempted to justify his conduct in 1814.

OUDINOT, NICOLAS-CHARLES (1767–1847), duc de Reggio 1809, was promoted maréchal after the battle of Wagram. He was born at Bar-le-Duc (Meuse), a brewer's son, and enlisted in 1784. He was one of the most daring of the marshals, a tough foot-soldier who had fought his way up the ranks and had a faculty for getting himself severely wounded (thirty-five times altogether) that was only excelled by his powers of survival. He accepted the restored monarchy in 1814 and remained faithful to it.

SUCHET, LOUIS-GABRIEL (1770–1826), son of a Lyons silk-merchant, began his military career in that city as a lieutenant in the *Garde nationale* (1791) and by 1799 was a general in the Revolutionary armies (the army of Italy). He was promoted maréchal (1811), and duc d'Albufera (1812), as a reward for services in the Peninsula. He accepted the Bourbons in 1814, then rallied to Napoleon during the Hundred Days. For a period after the Second Restoration he was deprived of his dignities.

GOUVION-SAINT-CYR, LAURENT (1764–1830), son of a butcher and tanner at Toul (Meurthe-et-Moselle), became an artist and taught drawing in Paris, enlisted in the Revolutionary army in 1792 and was a full general by 1799. He was created comte de l'Empire in 1808 and promoted maréchal in 1812 during the Russian campaign, but though a brilliant general he was never very popular with Napoleon. In 1815 he commanded the army sent against Napoleon at Orléans but was abandoned by his troops and made his escape to Boulogne. He was Minister of War under Louis XVIII, who

created him marquis, and was responsible for various army reforms.

PONIATOWSKI, JOSEPH-ANTOINE, PRINCE (1762–1813), born at Warsaw, was the son of a Polish officer and a nephew of Stanislas Augustus, King of Poland. After holding commands in the Austrian and then the Polish army he commanded the first Polish Legion in the French army (1807) and later (from 1812) the Polish corps. He was promoted maréchal in 1813 before the battle of Leipzig. Four days later he covered the French retreat and when harried by the enemy spurred his horse into the River Elster in an attempt to cross and was drowned.

Some of Napoleon's marshals left memoirs, interesting mainly from the point of view of military tactics or military history. Those of Gouvion-Saint-Cyr are frequently mentioned; those of Marmont are of more general interest.

Marengo, a village in north Italy (Piedmont) where Bonaparte won his crowning victory over the Austrians (14 June 1800) in the campaign against the Second Coalition (q.v.).

Marguerite d'Angoulême or **d'Alençon** or **de Navarre** (1492–1549), by birth duchesse d'Angoulême, sister of François Ier and wife first of the duc d'Alençon and after his death of Henri d'Albret, King of Navarre; by the latter marriage she was ancestress of the line of Bourbon kings. She was a woman of high character, intelligent, broad-minded, affectionate, eager for spiritual liberty yet devoutly religious. She learnt Latin, Italian, and Spanish, and studied Hebrew. She admired Plato and encouraged the translation of his dialogues. She supported *évangélisme* (q.v.) and protected, at her court of Navarre, the enlightened men whom the theologians persecuted, such as Lefèvre d'Étaples, Marot, Des Périers, and Calvin. Her chief work was the *Heptaméron* (q.v.). Her poetry in spite of a few pieces of merit, is less well known; it includes the *Miroir de l'âme pécheresse, Chansons spirituelles* published by a member of her household under the title of *Marguerites de la Marguerite des princesses*, and some mystical poems of her last years. Her plays (*Comédie à dix personnages*, 1542; *Comédie jouée à Mont-de-Marsan en 1547*, &c.) were edited by V.-L. Saulnier in 1946 (*Théâtre profane*).

Marguerite d'Anjou (1429–82), daughter of King René d'Anjou (q.v.). She became Queen of England in 1444 on her marriage (at Nancy) to Henry VI.

Marguerite d'Autriche (1480–1530), daughter of the emperor Maximilian. She married first the infante John of Spain, and secondly, in 1501, Philibert II of Savoy, in whose memory, after his death, she erected the church of Brou (q.v.). She was regent of the Netherlands, 1507–30, and negotiated the peace of Cambrai in 1529.

Marguerite d'Écosse, Margaret of Scotland (1424–44), daughter of James I of Scotland, first wife of Louis XI. See under *Chartier, Alain.*

Marguerite de Savoie (1523–74), daughter of François Ier, sister of Henri II, wife of Philibert-Emmanuel of Savoy; she wrote verses and was a patroness of the young school of poets headed by Ronsard.

Marguerite de Valois (1553–1615), daughter of Henri II and Catherine de Médicis, wife of Henri of Navarre (Henri IV), who, after they had long been in fact separated, divorced her for political reasons in 1599. She wrote poems (helped in some cases by her secretary Maynard, q.v.) and memoirs, the latter addressed to Brantôme for the purpose of helping him in the composition of his *Dames illustres,* and containing a vivid account of the massacre of St. Bartholomew and many other interesting passages. Her letters are in the same clear precise style as her memoirs.

Marguerites, Les trois, frequently referred to in the literary history of the 16th century, are: (1) *Marguerite d'Angouléme,* or *d'Alençon,* or *de Navarre* (1492–1549), q.v.; (2) *Marguerite de Savoie* (1523–74), q.v.; (3) *Marguerite de Valois* (1553–1615), q.v.

Margueritte, the brothers PAUL (1860–1918) and VICTOR (1867–1942), novelists. They wrote in collaboration between 1896 and 1908, notably a series of socio-historical novels of 1870–1: *Une Époque:* I *Le Désastre* (*Metz 1870*), 1898; II *Les Tronçons du glaive* (*Défense nationale 1870–71*), 1901; III *Les Braves Gens* (*Épisodes de 1870–71*), 1901; IV *La Commune* (*Paris–Versailles, 1871*), 1904; also the very popular children's books *Poum* (1897); *Zette, histoire d'une petite fille* (1903).

In earlier life Paul Margueritte—whose reminiscences, *Mon Père* (1884), may also be noted—signed the *Manifeste des cinq* (1887, q.v.), repudiating Zola's doctrines. Thereafter for a time he took Russian novelists, then coming into fashion, for his models in, for instance, *Pascal Géfosse* (1887), *La Force des choses* (1890), &c.

Maria Chapdelaine (1916, posth.), a tale of French-Canadian life by L. Hémon (q.v.).

Mariage de Figaro, ou la Folle Journée, Le, a comedy in prose by Beaumarchais, accepted by the Comédie-Française in 1781, but not publicly produced until 1784 owing to the royal veto, though it was widely read and performed in private in the interval. It was immensely popular.

The play is in substance a sequel to *Le Barbier de Séville* (q.v.). The Comte Almaviva has been for three years married to Rosine, has tired of her, and though jealous of her fidelity gives rein to his own licentiousness. The comtesse, though she still loves her husband, shows a dangerous romantic inclination. Figaro, now installed as the comte's door-keeper, is in love with the honest, merry Suzanne, the comtesse's maid, and is about to marry her. The comte favours the project, provided that it can be made to conform with his own designs on Suzanne. The essence of the plot lies in the struggle for the possession of Suzanne between the comte on the one hand, supported by feudal privilege and the machinery of the law (in the person of the absurd magistrate, Brid'oison), and Figaro on the other aided by the wits and the loyalty of his fiancée. Everything conspires to thwart the comte and render him ridiculous; Chérubin, a young page and budding libertine, in love with the comtesse, constantly serves to embroil the situation by arousing the comte's jealousy. The Bartholo and Bazile of the *Barbier de Séville* reappear as subsidiary characters. The culmination comes when the comtesse, impersonating Suzanne, takes her place at a twilight assignation which Suzanne has given to the comte, whose infidelity is thus exposed, while Figaro is left triumphant, and with him the cause of honourable marriage.

The comedy, which is highly animated, gay, and witty, had an important political side. By the bitter epigrams with which its gaiety is interspersed, by its audacious derision of the institutions and privileges of the old régime (summed up in a famous monologue by Figaro, v. iii), it was the echo of the popular feeling of the moment.

Mariage forcé, Le, a one-act comedy in prose by Molière, produced in 1664.

This trifling piece was prepared in great haste for an entertainment given by the king at the Louvre.

Sganarelle, a middle-aged bourgeois, has decided to marry, and has obtained the hand of the youthful Dorimène. His satisfaction is changed to uneasiness when he learns that the young lady has accepted him only to get her liberty and his money. He decides to take advice as to the probability of her remaining faithful to him. The absurd conversations between him and the two philosophers whom he consults (Pancrace the Aristotelian and Marphurius the Pyrrhonian), imitated from Rabelais, bring him no comfort; and after overhearing a conversation between Dorimène and her lover, he decides to renounce the marriage. But Dorimène's brother gives him the choice between marrying her and fighting him, and Sganarelle, who has no stomach for a duel chooses the less disagreeable alternative.

Mariamne, the wife of Herod the Great, executed by him in a fit of jealousy; the subject of tragedies by Hardy, Tristan l'Hermite, and Voltaire.

Mariana, Juan de (1532–1624), a Spanish Jesuit, who taught theology at Rome and Paris, wrote a Latin treatise *De Rege et regis institutione* (1598) in which, after discussing the organization of society, the duty of leaders to people and people to leaders, the circumstances in which regicide was permissible, and the best means of getting rid of tyrants, he went on to speak with approval of the assassination of Henri III by Jacques Clément. The work was thought to have inspired the assassination of Henri IV by Ravaillac. (See also *Marianne*.)

Marianne, a familiar name, after about 1854, for the republican form of government and, by extension, for the French Republic. It was the password of a secret society formed (in the departments of the West and directed from London by a central committee) after the *coup d'état* of 1851 with the object of overthrowing the government and re-establishing the Republic. Members underwent an elaborate ceremony of introduction and initiation, one of the questions asked being 'Connaissez-vous Marianne?' Various suggestions as to its origin have been made, e.g. that the name is a mystical translation of the words 'République démocratique et sociale'; that it may have had some connexion with the Jesuit historian Juan de Mariana (q.v.); or—with some measure of support—that its origin goes back to the Terror and a republican *fête* held at Montpellier, when the Goddess of Reason was impersonated by a 'Marianne', the local term for a woman of easy virtue. The incident was seized upon by adversaries of the Republic and the name, applied to the Republican Government, was not allowed to drop. It had reached Paris at the time of the 1848 Revolution.

Marianne, La Vie de, a romance by Marivaux, published in eleven parts, 1731–41.

The story is that of the life, narrated by herself, of a girl of unknown but apparently good birth (her parents having been killed by robbers on a journey and their infant child having been saved and brought up in the house of a *curé*). The vicissitudes of her life place her under the protection of M. de Climal, a hypocrite who makes pretence of piety and tries to seduce her. An accident brings her into contact with Valville, a young man of quality, who falls in love with her and she with him. Valville turns out to be the nephew of M. de Climal who, to punish her for her rejection of his advances, withdraws his support. Marianne now finds another protectress, who is presently discovered to be the mother of Valville and to be intent upon a different marriage for him, whence further complications. And so through a long series of incidents and obstacles, including Valville's temporary infidelity, Marianne, in whose character virtue is pleasantly blended with a little coquetry, passes to her final union with her lover. Her reactions to each event are minutely analysed with all the author's knowledge of the female heart, and we are given a picture of Parisian and conventual manners. A twelfth (concluding) section of the work, in which Marianne is restored to her distinguished family, was supplied by a continuator, Mme Riccoboni.

Richardson, in his *Pamela*, was thought to have been inspired by *Marianne*, but this is now denied.

Marie, ou l'Esclavage aux États-Unis, a novel by G. A. Beaumont de la Bonninière (q.v.).

Marie-Antoinette (1755–93), daughter of Francis I, Emperor of Austria, and Maria Theresa; consort of Louis XVI, whom she encouraged to resist the Revolution. She was condemned to death by the Revolutionary Tribunal and executed, two days later, on 16 October 1793.

Marie de France, a late 12th-century poetess, about whom little that is certain is known. She appears to have been born in France and to have done much or all of her literary work in England. She was a woman of culture, knowing Latin and English besides French. It has been conjectured (*English Historical Review*, vol. xxv) that she was a natural daughter of Geoffrey Plantagenet and consequently half-sister of Henry II, and abbess of Shaftesbury 1181–1215. She wrote a number of *lais* (q.v.), poems of love and adventure, fairies and marvels, which preserve a mysterious and romantic character attributed by some critics to Celtic originals. They were dedicated to a 'noble king', probably Henry II. Among her principal lays were: *Lanval* (the story, in which Arthur figures, of a poor knight who is secretly loved and enriched by a fairy; of this we have an English version in the 14th-century *Sir Launfal*); and *Frêne* (the touching story of a patient Griselda, who as a child was exposed in an ash-tree, whence the name), of which there is an English 14th-century version, the *Lai le Freine*. *Chèvrefeuille* is a slight episodic story of Tristram and Iseult. A cleft stick bearing Tristram's name placed in the queen's path as she passes through the forest brings about a brief meeting between the lovers. Marie also wrote a collection of Aesopic fables (based on the lost English version of a collection attributed to King Alfred), which she said was called *Esope*. This, in one or two late manuscripts, occurred in the form *Isopet* (or *Ysopet*), which became the usual name for medieval collections of fables.

Finally she made a French version of the legend of the Purgatory of St. Patrick.

Marie de Médicis (1573–1642), niece of the Grand Duke of Tuscany, consort of Henri IV from 1600 (after his divorce from Marguerite de Valois). She was regent 1610–17.

Marie Donadieu (1904), a novel by Charles-Louis Philippe (q.v.).

Marie Stuart, see *Mary Stuart*.

Marie Tudor (1833), by Victor Hugo, an historical drama (prose, in three 'journées'), with little fidelity to history. The queen's Italian lover, Fabio Fabiani, has seduced Jane, the adopted daughter, soon to be wife, of the worthy craftsman Gilbert. Fabiani knows that Jane is really the daughter, who disappeared mysteriously in infancy, of the Earl Talbot and thinks that in certain eventualities he might save his own fortunes by marrying her. When his intrigues miscarry he caps them with murder. There is a scene of great suspense in the last act, or 'journée', when a prisoner, who may be either Fabiani or Gilbert, but whose identity will not be known till all is over, is conducted to execution watched by Jane and the queen. The latter had engineered the arrest and is now overcome by events.

Marignan (Italian *Melegnano*), near Milan, scene of the defeat of the Swiss by the French under François Iᵉʳ in 1515 (referred to more than once by Rabelais, and the subject of a famous song by the musician Jannequin) and of the Austrians in 1859.

Marigny, JACQUES CARPENTIER (17th c.), a supporter of Cardinal de Retz in the Fronde (q.v.), famous for his satirical *mazarinades* and humorous songs and parodies.

Marinetti, FILIPPO TOMMASO (1878–1944), Italian poet, novelist, and critic, born in Alexandria, educated in France, lived mainly in Italy (Milan). He kept in touch with advanced literary circles in Paris and was the founder of a short-lived but clangorous poetical movement—*futurisme* (q.v., *c.* 1909–12). He wrote much in French, e.g. *La Conquête des étoiles* (1902, an epic poem), *Destruction: Poésies lyriques* (1904), *La Ville charnelle* (1908, poems of Africa), *La Bataille de Tripoli* (1912).

Marinisme. The Italian poet Giovanni Battista Marino had to flee from Italy in 1615. He found refuge until 1622 in France at the court of Marie de Médicis where he was called 'le Cavalier Marin'. He wrote *Adone*, a long poem in French, published in France in 1623 with a preface by Chapelain (q.v.). His style, admired and imitated in 'precious' circles, was characterized by extravagances and conceits. It came to be known as *Marinisme* (see *Gongorisme*).

Marion de Lorme (1831), a poetic drama by Victor Hugo. Marion de Lorme, the courtesan (see *Delorme, Marion*), loves, and is loved by, Didier, who is unaware of her identity. Didier and the marquis de Saverny, another of her admirers, are arrested for fighting a duel in defiance of a royal proclamation, inspired by Richelieu, making duelling a crime punishable by hanging. Marion sacrifices herself to M. de Laffemas, a magistrate, to procure Didier's escape. But Didier has learnt who she is and rejects her help, preferring death. The scenes are laid at Blois and in the Château de Nangis, belonging to the Marquis de Saverny's uncle. The characters include Louis XIII and Richelieu. The latter, who attends Didier's execution, speaks from behind the curtains of his litter.

This play was written in 1829, before *Hernani* (q.v.), but the Censor vetoed its production. Censorship restrictions ended with the July Revolution (1830), but the author then chose to delay production till 1831. Didier became a prototype for many romantic heroes of the eighteen-thirties.

Maritain, JACQUES (1882–), contemporary Catholic philosopher and man of letters. He was at first a disciple of Bergson, but in the early years of the 20th century he became a Roman Catholic and has since been one of the foremost French representatives of the form of religious teaching known as Neo-Thomism (see *Thomisme*) which finds it possible to reconcile philosophical speculation with belief in a divine origin of the universe. His works include: *La Philosophie bergsonienne* (1914), an indictment of Bergsonism as the root of all modern intellectual heresy; *Art et scholastique* (1920); *Saint Thomas d'Aquin apôtre des temps modernes* (1923); *Réflexions sur l'intelligence* (1924); *Trois Réformateurs* (1925), a denunciation of Luther, Descartes, and Rousseau; *Frontière de la poésie* (1926); *Primauté du spirituel* (1927); *Religion et culture* (1930); *Court traité de l'existence et de l'existant* (1947).

Marivaudage, see under *Marivaux*.

Marivaux, PIERRE CARLET DE CHAMBLAIN DE (1688–1763), born in Paris of a Norman family, dramatist and novelist. His comedies (in prose), which have as a rule love for their subject, are concerned in general with the trifling incidents, psychological rather than external, of courtship, such as arise from jealousy, pique, or misunderstanding, amid a sybaritic society such as Watteau and Boucher illustrated in their paintings. Their charm and light romantic fancy made Marivaux extremely popular for a time, but he outlived the period of his vogue. His first success was the dramatic fantasy *Arlequin poli par l'amour* (1720). Among his best plays may be mentioned *La Surprise de l'amour* (1722), *La Double Inconstance* (1723), *Le Jeu de l'amour et du hasard* (1730), *Les Sincères* (1739) (qq.v.); as well as *Le Legs* (1736), *Les Fausses Confidences* (1737), and *L'Épreuve* (1740). Marivaux wrote two novels, *La Vie de Marianne* (q.v., 1731–41) and *Le Paysan parvenu* (q.v., 1735–6), both left unfinished, notable for their delicate analysis of sentiment and the realistic picture they give of middle-class society; they perhaps influenced Fielding's *Joseph Andrews*. He did some more serious writing, on ethical and literary subjects, in his *Spectateur français* (1722, modelled on Addison's *Spectator*), &c. The term *marivaudage*, coined from his name, is used to signify the analysis of the delicate sentiments of the heart and the subtle, affected style used by Marivaux to this end in his comedies.

In his early days Marivaux was a frequenter of the *salons* of Mme de Tencin and Mme de Lambert, a supporter of La Motte and the 'Moderns' in the quarrel with the 'Ancients', and the author of an *Iliade travestie* (1717). He was admitted to the *Académie* in 1742.

Marlotte, a village on the southern edge of the Forêt de Fontainebleau, a celebrated artists' colony during the 19th century.

Marly, a splendid country house midway between Versailles and Saint-Germain, erected by the architect Mansart for Louis XIV, who had chosen the locality as a place of rest and comparative solitude. On either side of it were small pavilions for members of the royal suite. A pump, the celebrated *Machine de Marly*, was constructed to raise water from the Seine in such abundance as to form a river and cascades in the gardens. The estate was sold and the buildings demolished in the Revolution.

Marmier, XAVIER (1809–92), man of letters and critic, particularly well read in foreign literature. His works include: *Histoire de la littérature en Danemark et en Suède* (1839), *Chants populaires du Nord, traduits en français* (1842), &c., also some travel literature and a few novels, now forgotten.

Marmont, AUGUSTE-FRÉDÉRIC-LOUIS VIESSE DE, one of Napoleon's marshals (see *Maréchal de l'Empire*).

Marmontel, JEAN-FRANÇOIS (1723–99), born in Limousin, a man of wide but second-rate literary talent, a friend and disciple of Voltaire. He was the author of some forgotten tragedies (*Denys le Tyran*, 1748; *Aristomène*, 1749), of serious comedies (*La Bergère des Alpes*, 1766; *Sylvain*, 1770), of comic operas, among them *Zémire et Azor* (q.v., 1771, for which Grétry composed the music), and of a light comedy *L'Ami de la maison*; also of *Contes moraux* (collected in 1761 and 1789–92 after appearing one by one in the *Mercure*), slight tales with a moral intention, agreeably told, and of two mediocre historical romances, *Bélisaire* (q.v., 1766), which was condemned by the Sorbonne on account of a chapter on toleration (the censure serving only to render that body ridiculous and to advertise the book), and *Les Incas* (1777), in which Las Casas figures as defender of the Indians. Marmontel was, moreover, the principal contributor of the literary articles in the *Encyclopédie*. These were collected in *Éléments de littérature* (1787) and furnish an idea of literary taste in the 18th century. But his interesting and for the greater part agreeable *Mémoires d'un père* were the best thing he wrote, containing some good sketches of the *encyclopédistes*. He was, thanks to the protection of Mme de Pompadour, appointed editor of the *Mercure* in 1758. He was a member from 1763, and later, from 1783, perpetual secretary, of the *Académie*, succeeding d'Alembert. (For his satirical poem *Polymnie* see under *Gluck*.)

Marmousets, small grotesque sculptured figures on monuments; a nickname given to the bourgeois councillors of Charles VI. These were exiled by the duc de Bourgogne during the king's insanity, in spite of the efficiency of their administration.

Marne, Les Taxis de la. This refers to the crucial period early in the 1914–18 war when the retreating French 5th and 6th armies and the British Expeditionary Force made a stand at the River Marne against the German sweep on Paris and, on 5 September, launched a counter-attack. The offensive was maintained by rushing up reinforcements from the other French armies. Some of these troops were so exhausted when they reached Paris on their way that General Galliéni, then Military Governor, requisitioned all the Paris taxis and had the reinforcements driven up to the front. The German order to retreat was given on 9 September.

Marneffe, Mme, a character in Balzac's novel *La Cousine Bette* (q.v.).

Marolles, MICHEL, ABBÉ DE (1600–81), born in Touraine, instructor and literary secretary for many years of the princess Marie de Gonzague, future queen of Poland, an indefatigable scribbler of indifferent translations in verse and prose of the Latin poets, the Scriptures, and the Roman breviary. The bulk and badness of the translations which he inflicted on his contemporaries made him something of a comic figure in literature, but he did valuable work as a collector and cataloguer of engravings. He left memoirs.

Marot, CLÉMENT (1496–1544), poet, born at Cahors in Quercy, the son of Jean Marot (q.v., a Norman who had settled and married in the south). When his father entered the service of Anne of Brittany, Clément accompanied him to Paris. He became a law clerk and a member of the Basoche and of the Enfants sans souci (qq.v.), for whom he composed one of his early *ballades*. About 1518 he was appointed *valet de chambre* to Marguerite d'Alençon, the future Queen of Navarre. After the death of his father (1526) he succeeded to his place in the service of the king. In 1532 he published a collection of his early verse, the *Adolescence Clémentine*. He then began his metrical translations of the

Psalms, probably at the instance of his protectress, Marguerite of Navarre. Her *Miroir de l'âme pécheresse* (1533) contained a translation of Psalm vi by Marot. He was already suspect to the theologians, having in 1525 suffered imprisonment in the Châtelet for breach of the Lenten fast, and when the affair of the 'placards' (q.v.) in 1534 provoked repressive measures against the Lutherans he took refuge in Italy, at Ferrara (whose duchess was the Lutheran Renée de France) and later at Venice. After a time he was allowed to return, on making abjuration of his errors. In 1538 he published his *Œuvres* and in 1539 dedicated to the king the translations of thirty Psalms, which, in spite of his abjuration, he continued to write and published in 1541. He was obliged in consequence once more to leave the country and betook himself to Geneva, where he received encouragement from Calvin. A further edition of his Psalms, including twenty additional translations, was published in 1543. But his conduct was unacceptable at Geneva (he is said to have played backgammon on Sunday) and he withdrew first to Savoy, then to Italy. He died at Turin in 1544.

He combined an affectionate, cheerful, hare-brained, and yet in some measure religious disposition with intellectual independence. He wrote a great variety of poems, some of considerable length, such as *Le Temple de Cupidon* (an allegory after the manner of the *rhétoriqueurs*) and *L'Enfer* (a description of his captivity in the Châtelet); but the great majority are shorter pieces, epistles (mostly in decasyllabic couplets, including the *Coq-à-l'âne*, q.v.), eclogues, *rondeaux, chansons*, elegies, *ballades*, some three hundred epigrams, besides the translations of the Psalms. In most of his poems he is essentially a court poet, light, subtle, graceful, amusing with an artificial simplicity, neither sentimental nor passionate. But his wit, when directed against his enemies, could be mordant, as is seen in his epigrams. Inspired by the movement of religious reform, he was a keen critic of the theologians of the Sorbonne, the papacy, and the friars. His early poetry, in the use of allegories and other conceits, shows the influence of the *rhétoriqueurs* (q.v.), whom he regarded as his masters. Another side of his literary taste is to be seen in the fact that he pub-

lished in 1527 an edition of the *Roman de la Rose* and in 1533 an edition of Villon. He had some knowledge of the Latin classics (as early as 1530 he translated part of Ovid's *Metamorphoses*) and this knowledge was increased as a result of his exile in Italy; we find him subsequently adapting Virgil's Fourth Eclogue and translating epigrams of Martial. In Italy also he became acquainted with the sonnet, of which he wrote a few examples, being one of the first French poets to adopt it. He was thus a poet of the transition from the medieval tradition of allegorical didactic verse to the new spirit of the 16th century. His translations of the Psalms were much admired by his contemporaries and are remarkable for their 'sober and solemn music' (Saintsbury) and for the variety of metrical combinations that they display. His work in general, though not that of a poet of the first order, by its sincerity, refinement, and deliberate art shows the first influence of the Renaissance. Among noteworthy pieces may be mentioned his two epistles to the king, another to Lyon Jamet, the epigram on the death of Semblançay, the ballade of 'frère Lubin', the rondeau to a creditor.

For a time Marot was regarded by contemporary poets as pre-eminent among themselves (an obscure rhymer, François Sagon, alone attacked him in 1537). His fame, after his death, was eclipsed by that of the *Pléiade* (q.v.), but, later on, under Louis XIII, Ronsard was in turn condemned, and Marot came once more into favour, and under Louis XIV earned the praise of Boileau: 'Imitez de Marot l'élégant badinage.' His work had some influence on English 16th-century poets, notably on Spenser in his eclogues.

Marot, JEAN (d. 1526), a mediocre poet of the school of the *rhétoriqueurs* (q.v.), born at Caen in Normandy, settled for a time at Cahors, in the south, where his son, the far more famous Clément Marot, was born. About 1506 he became secretary to Anne of Brittany, and accompanied Louis XII on his two expeditions to Italy. He wrote descriptions of these in verse (including a lively account of the adventurers from various parts of France who joined the army in the hope of plunder), besides miscellaneous short poems.

Marquis, see *Duc.*

Marquis de Villemer, Le, a novel (1862, dramatized 1864) by George Sand (q.v.).

Mars, ANNE-FRANÇOISE-HIPPOLYTE BOUTET, *known as* MLLE (1779–1847), actress, born in Paris of theatrical stock, a famous member of the Comédie-Française during the Consulate and the Empire and for many years afterwards. She was most successful in comedy, particularly in the plays of Molière and Marivaux. Sainte-Beuve refers to her 'ingénuité habile'. She was said to have all the gifts—beauty, intelligence, talent, and a voice which never lost its fresh, youthful quality. She continued on the stage till 1841.

Marsay, HENRI DE, a constantly recurring character in Balzac's *Comédie humaine* (q.v.).

Marseillaise, La, the French national anthem, was written on 25 April 1792 by Rouget de Lisle (q.v.), then a captain of Engineers at Strasbourg. The news of the French declaration of war against Austria had reached the city and the mayor was entertaining some of the officers destined to take part in the campaign. He deplored the absence of a national anthem and called upon Rouget de Lisle to compose one. The young officer is said to have improvised the song, both words and music, during that evening, though his authorship of the music has been questioned. By June the 'Chant de guerre pour l'armée du Rhin' (as it was first called when published at Strasbourg) had made its way to the south. In July the *fédérés* who had marched from Marseilles to Paris sang it as they massed in the Place de la Bastille (see *Révolutions*, Ia: 10 Aug. 1792). The Parisians adopted it and renamed it *La Marseillaise*. It was sung by official order on the battlefield of Valmy after the first victory of the Revolutionary armies, and thenceforward it became the national anthem though it was suppressed for a time by Napoleon and again after the Restoration.

Of Rouget de Lisle's original six stanzas the first and the sixth are the best known:

> Allons, enfants de la patrie!
> Le jour de gloire est arrivé!
> Contre nous de la tyrannie
> L'étendard sanglant est levé. (*bis*)
> Entendez-vous, dans les campagnes,
> Mugir ces féroces soldats?

> Ils viennent jusque dans nos bras
> Égorger nos fils, nos compagnes! ...
> Aux armes! citoyens, formez vos bataillons!
> Marchons! marchons, qu'un sang impur
>   Abreuve nos sillons!

> Amour sacré de la Patrie!
> Conduis, soutiens nos bras vengeurs!
> Liberté, Liberté chérie!
> Combats avec tes défenseurs. (*bis*)
> Sous nos drapeaux, que la victoire
> Accoure à tes mâles accents;
> Que tes ennemis expirants
> Voient ton triomphe et notre gloire!
> Aux armes, etc.

At a later date, a seventh stanza, called the 'Children's stanza', was added.

Marsillac, PRINCE DE, see *La Rochefoucauld.*

Martial d'Auvergne (*c.* 1430–1508), poet and miscellaneous writer, author of *Vigilles de Charles VII* written on the death of that king in 1461, a long poem mainly in quatrains of short lines and divided into 'Psalms' and 'Lessons', containing some pleasant passages; also of *Arrêts d'amour* (*c.* 1460–5), a prose collection (with verse prologue) of imaginary lawsuits on questions of gallantry. This was reprinted at least thirteen times between 1525 and 1537. The cases submitted for judgement contain some picturesque details of contemporary manners. Martial also composed a *Danse macabre des femmes* (see *Danse macabre*).

Martin, a character in Voltaire's *Candide* (q.v.).

Martin, SAINT (d. *c.* 396), a Pannonian soldier of the Roman army in Gaul, who became a disciple of Saint Hilary (Bishop of Poitiers) and an earnest apostle among the poor. He was noted for his charity, and the well-known story of his dividing his cloak with a beggar is a favourite subject in ecclesiastical art. His popularity led to his appointment to the bishopric of Tours.

Martin, HENRI (1810–83), historian, born at Saint-Quentin, part and later sole author of a mediocre history of France (1833–6 and 1837–54) which gave much space to Celtic and druidic origins and the unbroken continuance of the Celtic spirit.

Martin du Gard, ROGER (1881–   ), novelist (Nobel Prizewinner in 1937), was born at Neuilly-sur-Seine and in 1906 finished a training at the École des Chartes (q.v.) which may have influenced his approach to the craft of fiction. He published his first novel, *Devenir*, in 1909, the year of the founding of the *Nouvelle Revue Française* (q.v.), with which he was for long closely associated. His reputation was made by, and rests on, *Les Thibault* (q.v., 1922–40), a *roman-cycle*. His other novels include: *Jean Barois* (1913), which introduces the Dreyfus (q.v.) case and portrays characters at grips with problems of morals and religion; *La Confidence africaine* (1931); and *Vieille France* (1933), a ferociously realistic study of country life. The sardonic comedy *Le Testament du Père Leleu* (1920) is also a picture of country life.

Martin le Franc, see *Le Franc*.

Martinozzi, see *Mazarin's nieces*.

Martyrs, Les, ou le Triomphe de la religion chrétienne (1809), by Chateaubriand (q.v.), a prose epic in twenty-four Books, designed as a pendant to *Le Génie du christianisme* (q.v.) to show Christianity triumphing over paganism. The time is the 3rd century, during the Emperor Diocletian's persecution of the Christians.

The narrative follows the loves of two young Greeks, Eudorus, a convert, and the maiden Cymodocea, a pagan. We learn in Bk. 3 that both are destined by God as sacrifices so that other Christians may be saved. Bks. 4–11 are the story of Eudorus's earlier life and adventures in Germany, Gaul, Egypt, and Rome. Bk. 12 resumes the main narrative. Cymodocea, for love of Eudorus, becomes a Christian. The two are married, but events separate them. After many vicissitudes they are reunited in Rome only to suffer persecution and death. Triumph crowns their martyrdom, for in the arena in which they have perished the victorious Emperor Constantine proclaims Christianity as the official religion of the Roman Empire.

The work, tedious as a whole, contains some stirring evocations of the past; and Augustin Thierry (q.v.) dated his vocation as a historian from his schoolboy reading of the description in Bk. 4 of a battle between Romans and Franks.

Marx, KARL HEINRICH (1818–83), social critic and revolutionary, was born of Jewish-turned-Lutheran descent at Trier in the Rhineland, a lawyer's son. He studied law, then philosophy, and was strongly influenced by Hegel and the Hegelian philosophy of history, at Berlin. In 1842–3, at Cologne, he edited the *Rheinische Zeitung*. This was suppressed on account of its radicalism and he then (1843) found work in Paris on a German paper. In 1845 he was expelled from Paris. He went to Belgium where, at the invitation of the London centre of the Communist League, he wrote the famous *Manifesto of the Communist Party* (published in London a few weeks before the outbreak of the 1848 Revolution—the *Révolution du 24 février*, see *Revolutions*, III—but not known in France till June of that year). He was expelled from Belgium on 23 February 1848; went straight to Paris; to Cologne (spring 1848), where he founded and edited the *Neue Rheinische Zeitung*, and whence he was expelled, partly on account of a violent article about *les journées de juin* (1848, q.v.); to Paris once more, a very unwelcome visitor; and a month later (August 1849) to London, where he was joined by his wife and family and where he remained, for the most part in conditions of acute poverty, till his death. (His two eldest daughters married French socialists.)

(2) Marx's years in Paris (1843–5) were his most important formative period. He soaked himself in history (notably the causes of the failure of the French Revolution), philosophy, political economy, and social reform (e.g. Saint-Simon, Fourier, Cabet, Proudhon, qq.v., and the collectivist Constantin Pecqueur, 1801–87, among the French reformers). He made French and foreign contacts and friends who shared his own awareness of the contemporary social ferment. He joined a Communist group of factory workers and artisans. And it was now that he parted company with the Hegelian doctrines and formulated the materialistic conception of the historical process and the belief in revolutionary communism and the importance of the proletariat which have extended their influence beyond politics to the literature of the 20th century. The *Manifesto* is the culminating work of this period. He also, in 1844, wrote a critique of Hegel's *Philosophy of Right*. In 1847 he published *La Misère de la*

philosophie, a harsh attack on Proudhon's *Philosophie de la misère* (1846). The essays and studies of the *German Ideology*, written in collaboration with Friedrich Engels in 1846, include a study of the social significance of Eugène Sue's (q.v.) novel *Les Mystères de Paris*. (Marx's admiration of Balzac and Stendhal may be noted; he projected but never wrote a study of Balzac as the analyst of bourgeois society.)

(3) Marx of the London years is primarily Marx the moving spirit of the First International Working Men's Association (1863) and Marx the author of *Das Kapital* (only Vol. I was published—1867—in his lifetime); but his studies of events in France call for mention here, namely (*a*) two pamphlets written shortly after his arrival in London, *The Class Struggle in France 1848–50* and *The Eighteenth Brumaire of Louis Bonaparte*, both written in German, the one contributed to the *Neue Rheinische Zeitung* in 1850, the other to a New York review, *La Révolution*, in 1852; and (*b*), in 1871, another pamphlet, later entitled *The Civil War in France*, an account of the rise and fall of the *Commune* (q.v.) and its historical significance in the process of working-class emancipation.

Mary Stuart, later Mary Queen of Scots (1542–87), daughter of James V of Scotland and Marie de Guise, betrothed in childhood and later (1558) married to François II. From 1548 she was brought up at the French court. After the death of François II (1560) she returned to Scotland. See under *Ronsard, Chastelard*.

Mascarille, a type of clever impudent valet in the comedies of Molière (*L'Étourdi, Le Dépit amoureux, Les Précieuses ridicules*).

Mascaron, Jules (1634–1703), born at Marseilles, Bishop of Tulle and later of Agen, an Oratorian and a noted preacher, contemporary of Bossuet but inferior to him in the style of his eloquence. He pronounced funeral orations on Turenne (1675), Anne of Austria, and Henrietta of England (daughter of Charles I).

Masculine, Feminine, lines and rhymes. In French prosody a feminine line is one that ends in *e* mute, or in *e* mute followed by *s* or *nt*. All lines which end otherwise are masculine. A feminine rhyme is one that couples two feminine lines; and a masculine rhyme couples two masculine lines. The last syllable of a feminine line does not count for metrical purposes.

Of the following lines the first pair are masculine, the second feminine:

Des intérêts du Ciel pourquoi vous chargez-vous?
Pour punir le coupable a-t-il besoin de nous?
Laissez-lui, laissez-lui le soin de ses vengeances:
Ne songez qu'au pardon qu'il prescrit aux offenses.   (Molière)

The earlier poets such as Villon followed no system in the arrangement of the two kinds of rhyme. Octavien de Saint-Gelais (q.v.) was among the first to adopt, in his translation of Ovid's *Heroides*, the practice of alternating masculine and feminine rhymes. Clément Marot also followed it in many of his psalms. Later, after Ronsard, this alternation became the rule.

Masque de fer, L'Homme au, the name given to a man who was imprisoned first at Pignerol (in 1679), then in the Bastille, where he died in 1703. His identity was concealed by a black velvet mask with iron hinges. He was probably a diplomatic agent of the name of Matthioli, arrested for treason by order of Louis XIV. The story (in the memoirs of the duc de Richelieu) that he was a twin brother of Louis XIV is discredited.

So persistent was the rumour that Monmouth had survived his supposed execution in 1685 that Voltaire thought it necessary to deny in his *Dictionnaire philosophique* (1764, under the heading *Anecdote sur l'homme au masque de fer*) that he was the Man in the Iron Mask.

Masséna, André, one of Napoleon's marshals (see *Maréchal de l'Empire*).

Massenet, Jules-Émile-Frédéric (1842–1912), born at Saint-Étienne (Loire), a celebrated musical composer in his day, studied at the Paris *Conservatoire de musique* and returned there in later life as Professor of Composition. His works include the operas *Manon* (1884) and *Werther* (1892), also a number of orchestral suites.

Massillon, Jean-Baptiste (1663–1742), born at Hyères in Provence, a member of the Oratorian order, Bishop of Clermont-

Ferrand from 1717, a famous preacher who achieved immediate success when he came to Paris in 1699, at which time Bourdaloue (q.v.) was ending his career. There was no thunder in his eloquence, but gentle persuasiveness, and some rhetorical affectation, which exerted a remarkable influence on his audiences. He avoided dogma almost entirely, confining himself to ethics and subtle psychological analysis; he was approved by the *philosophes*. His funeral orations (on Louis XIV and other members of the royal family) were less admired than those of Bossuet, though they are happy in their exordiums; as when, after surveying in silence the magnificent pomp of the funeral of Louis XIV, Massillon began, 'Dieu seul est grand, mes frères!' His sermons (except the funeral oration on the Prince de Conti) were not printed in his lifetime. He was admitted to the *Académie* in 1719 (see also *Carême*).

Massimilla Doni, one of the 'Études philosophiques' of Balzac's *Comédie humaine* (q.v.). Though slight as regards narrative it is often mentioned as an exposition (in the form of a running commentary on Rossini's opera *Mosé in Egitto*) of Balzac's views on music and the effect of passion on creative ability.

Massis, Henri, see *Agathon*.

Matamore, a character of Spanish comedy, who boasts of his imaginary exploits against the Moors. He appears as a character in *L'Illusion comique*, by Corneille.

Mateo Falcone, a short story of Corsican life by Prosper Mérimée, first published (1829) in the *Revue de Paris*, later included in *Mosaïque* (1833).

Mathieu or **Matheolus,** author of Latin *Lamentationes*, an attack on women, of the end of the 13th century; it was translated in 1371 or 1372 by Jehan le Fèvre in a French version which long remained popular.

Mathieu, Anselme, one of the original *félibres* (q.v.).

Mathiez, ALBERT (1874–1932), historian, author of many works on the French Revolution, and noted particularly for his studies of Danton, Robespierre (who was for him the hero of the Revolution), and the periods of and immediately after the Terror.

Mathilde, PRINCESSE (1820–1904), daughter of Jérôme Bonaparte (see *Bonaparte Family*) and niece of Napoleon I. She married, and later (1845) separated from, a Russian, Count Demidoff. During the Second Empire her friendship with her cousin Napoleon III gave her a fairly influential position. She enjoyed collecting writers and artists in her *salon* in Paris or her country house at Saint-Gratien. Flaubert, Gautier, Edmond de Goncourt, and Sainte-Beuve were among her favoured guests (cf. Flaubert's *Correspondance générale*; the *Journal des Goncourt*, &c.).

Matière et Mémoire, one of the chief works of the philosopher Henri Bergson (q.v., esp. paras. 3 and 4).

Matines brugeoises, a popular rising against the patricians of Bruges (the latter supported by the French governor, Jacques de Châtillon) on 18 May 1302. Many French knights were murdered in their beds. Cf. *Sicilian Vespers*.

Matisse, HENRI (1869–1954), French painter, sculptor, designer, and engraver. He was the leader of the group of Post-Impressionists known as 'Les Fauves' (see *Impressionnisme*).

Mauclair, CAMILLE, pseudonym of Séverin Faust (1872–1945), novelist, poet (*Sonatines d'automne*, 1895; *Le Sang parlé*, 1904), essayist, literary and art critic. In his novel *Le Soleil des morts* (1898), a picture of the young literary circles of the period, the character Calixte Armel is drawn from Mallarmé (q.v.). The essays and critical studies in *Éleusis* (1894), *L'Impressionnisme* (1904), *Princes de l'esprit* (1920: on Delacroix, Flaubert, Mallarmé, Poe, &c.) are of interest, as are also his souvenirs (*Servitude et grandeur littéraires*, 1922).

Maucroix, FRANÇOIS (1619–1708), poet, canon of Rheims, the devoted friend during fifty years of La Fontaine. He wrote epigrams, madrigals, and other lyrics; also translations from Greek and Latin authors, notably Plato and Cicero.

Maufrigneuse, a pseudonym occasionally used by Guy de Maupassant (q.v.).

Maugérard, JEAN-BAPTISTE (1735–1815), a book-thief, a precursor of Libri (q.v.), was originally a Benedictine monk of the congregation of Saint-Vannes de Verdun. He left the cloister (of Saint-Arnoul, near Metz) during the Revolution at the time of the *Constitution civile du clergé* (q.v.), was in Paris for a while, then lived as an *émigré*, in Germany. He was a man of learning, with a great knowledge of manuscripts and incunabula and their whereabouts. This knowledge he increased, but at the same time he put it to dubious use, by going around visiting monastic libraries in the parts of the Rhineland which became French territory during the Revolutionary wars (e.g. by the treaties of Campo Formio, 1797, and Lunéville, 1801). He professed to be a member of a commission charged with the classification and conservation (which seems for him to have connoted *confiscation*) of documents which had now become French national property; and in 1802 he was in fact given a government mission to seek out books and manuscripts in the departments formed out of the Rhineland provinces. He thus acquired a collection of treasures with which he enriched other libraries, notably the *Bibliothèque nationale* (q.v.) in Paris, though some of these had to be restored after 1815. In the process he lined his pockets effectively. He purchased land, and in Metz, where he lived on a government pension after 1808, he owned a house and a vineyard.

Maupassant, GUY DE (1850–93), famous short-story writer, also novelist and literary journalist, belonged to Normandy by birth, education, and sympathies. After army service in 1870–1—rich experience for one who was to write, for example, *Boule-de-suif* (q.v.) and *Mademoiselle Fifi* —he became a Government office clerk, conscientious if never zealous or ambitious (*Ministère de la marine*, 1872–8; *Ministère de l'instruction publique*, 1878–82). His main energies were reserved for outdoor pursuits —boating, fishing, shooting—and for hard discipline, under Flaubert's guidance, in the writer's craft. (He describes this discipline in his preface to *Pierre et Jean*, q.v.) Flaubert, whose feeling for his apprentice was one of delight in his talent combined with affection born of old family friendship, introduced Maupassant to literary circles. There the young writer met Zola and the other writers, Zola's disciples, with whom in 1880 he formed the *groupe naturaliste*

(see *Naturalisme*) of *Les Soirées de Médan* (q.v.), short stories of the Franco-Prussian war (q.v.). *Boule-de-suif*, his own contribution to the volume, made him a celebrity almost overnight, and by 1882 he could safely abandon the Civil Service for literature. During ten prodigiously successful years he made a lot of money and spent it luxuriously and extravagantly. His appearance was misleadingly robust. In fact, his health had early been undermined by dissolute living; and this, combined with continual overwork and mental strain, finally achieved his ruin. From 1890 his reason began to fail. His last eighteen months were spent in a mental home in Paris, following an attempt at suicide in December 1891. Between 1880 and 1890 he had contributed regularly to periodicals and published one volume of verse (*Des Vers*, 1880), three collections of travel sketches (*Au soleil*, 1884; *Sur l'eau*, 1888; *La Vie errante*, 1890), sixteen volumes of short stories, and six novels. *Histoire du vieux temps* (1879) was a one-act comedy in verse.

His tales were often published first in periodicals (*Le Gaulois*, *Gil Blas*, &c.), sometimes under a pseudonym, e.g. Joseph Prunier, used for his first tale, *La Main d'écorché* (1875, in the *Almanach de Pont à Mousson*), Guy de Valmont, Maufrigneuse. The majority have Normandy farm, peasant, or small-town life and characters for their subjects; or small tradespeople and petty officials in Paris. A few depict the more fashionable world to which success introduced him. Some recount episodes from the Franco-Prussian war; and in others the elements of mystery, hallucination, and horror of death predominate (e.g. *Le Horla*, *L'Auberge*, *Sur l'eau*— the tale, not the travel-sketches, *La Morte*, *L'Endormeuse*). Typical collections published in his lifetime were: *La Maison Tellier* (1881, q.v.), *Mademoiselle Fifi* (1882, q.v.), *Contes de la bécasse* (1883), *Les Sœurs Rondoli* (1884), *Miss Harriet* (1884, q.v.), *Contes du jour et de la nuit* (1885), *Toine* (1885), *Yvette* (1885), *Monsieur Parent* (1886), *Le Rosier de Madame Husson* (1888), *L'Inutile Beauté* (1890). His excellence as a *conteur* was due to his narrative style—simple, direct, realistic, dispassionate to the point of irony—and to his habit of presenting just, and no more than, the necessary incident or detail of character, custom, or atmosphere. Narratives, incidents, and characters belong for the most part, but not invariably (see, for instance, *Miss Harriet*), to a material, sometimes brutally sensual, life in which the finer feelings have small place. As a prose stylist he was said by Anatole France to possess 'les trois grandes qualités de l'écrivain français, d'abord la clarté, puis encore la clarté et enfin la clarté'.

His six novels—less tautly objective than the short stories—were: *Une Vie* (1883, a woman's lonely life, in Normandy: deception and disillusionment are her sole experiences); *Bel-Ami* (1885, q.v., a study of a careerist); *Mont-Oriol* (1887); *Pierre et Jean* (1888, q.v., a study of jealousy, usually accounted his finest novel); *Fort comme la mort* (1889: an ageing man's existence is disrupted by his hopeless love for a young girl); *Notre Cœur* (1890).

[In the Conard edition of Maupassant's *Œuvres complètes* (Paris: 1907–10, 29 vols.) separate tales can be found by reference to the index in the last volume.]

Maupeou (pron. as if *Maupou*), RENÉ-NICOLAS DE (1714–92), chancellor of France under Louis XV, famous for his expulsion of the *parlements* (q.v.) and substitution of *conseils du roi*, which were received with general disfavour and ridicule.

Maupertuis, the 'fort repere', or stronghold, of Renard the fox in the *Roman de Renart* (q.v.).

Maupertuis, PIERRE-LOUIS MOREAU DE (1698–1759), scientist, a captain of cavalry who gave up a military career for the study of natural science. He was the first in the *Académie des Sciences* to defend the principles of Newton, and the first Frenchman to be made a member of the Royal Society of London. He was a member of a mission sent in 1736 to measure a degree of the meridian in Lapland and so verify the shape of the earth as indicated by Newton (cf. *La Condamine*), and was appointed by Frederick II in 1740 director of the Academy of Science of Berlin. He was a worthy man with certain foibles, of no great scientific ability. Voltaire, while residing at Berlin, quarrelled with him, and Voltaire's lampoon, entitled *Diatribe du Docteur Akakia*, ridiculing Maupertuis on the occasion of a scientific dispute between the latter and the German mathematician Koenig, contributed to the final separation between Voltaire and Frederick.

Mauprat (1837), by George Sand, a romantic novel, high in the class of readable bad books, on the eternally enthralling theme of a brute (Bernard de Mauprat) transformed by love. The Mauprat family consists of the elder branch (Tristan and his eight sons who terrorize the countryside from their feudal stronghold of La Roche Mauprat and have brought up their orphaned cousin Bernard to be as brutish as themselves) and the younger (Hubert de Mauprat and his daughter Edmée, well living and well loved). Edmée is kidnapped by her wicked uncles but helped to escape by Bernard, much surprised at his own softer impulses. In return she promises never to marry unless she marries him. The *Maréchaussée* (an earlier form of mounted constabulary) attack La Roche Mauprat and kill or banish its inhabitants, except Bernard who is welcomed into the home of Edmée and her father. The two try to tame and educate him, a despairing task but finally successful when his passion for Edmée drives him to co-operate. One day while Bernard and Edmée are out hunting Edmée is mysteriously shot and nearly dies. Bernard is tried for attempted murder. His former violent nature tells against him but last-minute evidence clears him triumphantly. Edmée decides that she can now safely marry him; and it is towards the end of their long, happy marriage that Bernard sits down to tell the tale.

Edmée's wild ride with Bernard through the forest before she is attacked is a well-known episode of French literature.

Mauriac, FRANÇOIS (1885–   ), born at Bordeaux, one of the foremost contemporary French novelists (awarded the Nobel Prize for literature in 1952), also dramatist and critic. His chief novels up to 1939 include: *Le Baiser au lépreux* (1922); *Genitrix* (1923); *Le Désert de l'amour* (1925); *Destins* (1927); *Le Nœud de Vipères* (1932); *Le Mystère Frontenac* (1933); *Les Chemins de la mer* (1939); *Thérèse Desqueyroux* (1927, q.v.), perhaps his finest, with its continuation *La Fin de la nuit* (1935); *Les Anges noirs* (1936). Since 1939 *La Pharisienne* (1941) and *Le Sagouin* (1950) call for mention.

With few exceptions (e.g. *Le Nœud de Vipères*, which is longer, and an impressive study of avarice and family discord, and *Le*

Mystère Frontenac, which is largely the story of Mauriac's own family), these novels are psychological studies, short, and rapidly-moving, written from the standpoint of the author's fervid Roman Catholicism. The scene is almost invariably Bordeaux or the surrounding country, the wine-growing districts or the hot, sandy, pine-covered 'Landes' which stretch along the Atlantic coast, the 'climat complice des cœurs perdus ou avides de se perdre' [CLOUARD, *Litt. franç.* (1949), ii]. The characters, beneath an exterior of ordered, wealthy respectability, are the helpless victims of disordered, uneasy passions which the author explores into their most murky recesses. Such passions are continually at war with, or may indeed, he suggests, be the obverse side of, the religion which purifies the human heart; and this conflict between sensuality and religion is exploited to form the dramatic interest of the books.

Mauriac's plays are: *Asmodée* (1938), *Les Mal Aimés* (1945), *Le Passage du malin* (1948). His chief critical studies include: *Le Roman* (1928), *Vie de Jean Racine* (1928), and the more recent *Trois Grands Hommes* [Molière, Rousseau, Flaubert] *devant Dieu* (1947). He has also published a *Vie de Jésus* (1936); and at intervals since 1934 he has issued collections, entitled *Journal*, of articles contributed originally (daily) to *Le Figaro*: reminiscences, jottings, literary and musical criticism, political and polemical articles, &c. They represent, says their author, a 'journal semi-intime;—comme une transposition, à l'usage du grand public, des émotions et des pensées quotidiennes suscitées en nous par l'actualité'. Volumes I–III (1934–40) belong to the years 1932–40 (spring); volumes IV and V (1950, 1953), mainly political, to the period September 1944 to December 1947. Mauriac's clandestine writings under the pseudonym 'Forez', between later 1940 and 1944, belong to the literature of the French Resistance Movement, which is beyond the scope of the present *Companion*.

Maurists, or *Congrégation de Saint-Maur*, a congregation of French Benedictine monks, named after St. Maurus (6th c.), the legendary founder of the Benedictine rule in France. The Maurist congregation was established in 1618 with a view to the reform of the Benedictine order. But it became famous for the learning and literary industry of its members even more than for their monastic zeal. Under the impulse of its first superior-general, Dom Grégoire Tarisse, it carried out an immense amount of historical and critical work in connexion with patristic and biblical literature, monastic and ecclesiastical history, collections of documents, palaeography, and other branches of technical erudition. Some of its members travelled widely in France and Italy, examining the contents of the libraries in Benedictine monasteries. Instructions compiled about 1648 for their guidance in examining, copying, and collating manuscripts included a warning which holds good for present-day research workers: 'Et ne sommeillez pas quand vous serez dans le travail, car, si vous n'estes extrêmement vigilant et sur vos gardes, vous passerez asseurément beaucoup de petites pièces sans vous en appercevoir.'

The chief house of the Congrégation de Saint-Maur was at Saint-Germain-des-Prés in Paris. Mabillon and Montfaucon (qq.v.) were among its distinguished members. (See also *Histoire littéraire de France*.)

Mauritius, see *Île de France*.

Maurois, ANDRÉ (1885–   ), born at Elbeuf, man of letters and novelist (*Bernard Quesnay*, 1926; *Climats*, 1929; *Le Cercle de famille*, 1932, &c.). After his experiences as a liaison officer with the British forces during the 1914–18 war he wrote an entertaining and subtly observed study of an English officers' mess, *Les Silences du Colonel Bramble* (1918), followed by *Les Discours du Docteur O'Grady* (1922), a similar work. His reputation as an interpreter of the English spirit was confirmed by essays on English writers (*Quatre études anglaises*, 1927, and *Magiciens et Logiciens*, 1935); *Le Côté de Chelsea* (1929), an amusing *pastiche* of Proust; three short tales entitled *L'Anglaise* (1933), and the *Histoire d'Édouard VII et son temps* (1933), to which must be added the highly successful romantic biographies *Ariel ou la vie de Shelley* (1923), *La Vie de Disraëli* (1927), *La Vie de Lord Byron* (1930). His other works include biographical studies of Lyautey (1931), Voltaire (1935), and Chateaubriand (1937), and, more recently, a fine study and appreciation of Proust (*A la recherche de*

Marcel Proust, 1949) and lives of George Sand (*Lélia*, 1952) and of Hugo (*Olympio*, 1954). He has also published popular histories of England (1937) and of the United States (1947), as well as various collections of essays and lectures dating from his years in the latter country, as a professor at Princeton, during the 1939–45 war.

Maurois, whose name was originally Émile Herzog, comes of a family of industrialists who moved from Alsace to Elbeuf after the Franco-Prussian war. His *Mémoires* (1948) are interesting reminiscences of his early life at home and at the lycée of Rouen, where 'Alain' was his master (see *Chartier, Émile-Auguste*).

Maurras, CHARLES (1868–1952), poet, essayist, and journalist, in later life mainly a political and polemical writer. He was born at Martigues (Provence) and educated at Aix-en-Provence. At seventeen he began his literary career in Paris. He contributed essays and criticism to reviews, and not only wrote poetry but, with Jean Moréas, Maurice du Plessys, and others, and with encouragement from Mistral (q.v.), founded the *École romane* (q.v.), a group of poets in reaction against *Symbolisme* (q.v.). Within the next fifteen years he published *Le Chemin de Paradis* (1894), nine philosophical tales illustrating the pagan conception of life; *Anthinéa : d'Athènes à Florence* (1901), travel sketches, mostly of Greece; *Les Amants de Venise* (1902), a study of George Sand and Alfred de Musset; and *L'Avenir de l'intelligence* (1905), a collection which contains the essay on women writers, frequently mentioned, *Le Romantisme féminin*. (The later critical studies, *Barbarie et Poésie*, 1925, may also be mentioned at this point.) All these works showed a love of antiquity, and of the restraint and grace of classical culture, and a profound distaste for the romantic (*read* emotional) approach to life; and for a time Maurras exercised a considerable influence on thought and criticism. This was distorted by his increasing absorption in politics and his reactionary attitude. He had become a monarchist after the Dreyfus (q.v.) case, about 1899. He helped to found the *Action française* (q.v.) group, and after conducting (1901, in the *Gazette de France*) an *Enquête sur la monarchie* which created much stir he became moving spirit and

editor, with Léon Daudet (q.v.), of the notorious, extreme monarchist paper *L'Action française* (1908–44). The articles he wrote for it were often signed 'Criton'. *Au signe de Flore* (1931) contains his political reminiscences of these years. [Maurras was arrested in September 1944 and in January 1945 was tried and condemned to penal servitude for life. He was released on health grounds in 1952 and died shortly afterwards. The fact that he was stone-deaf for the greater part of his life is sometimes suggested as an explanation of his bitter fanaticism.]

Maury, JEAN SIFFREIN, ABBÉ (1746–1817), ecclesiastical writer and politician, a member of the *assemblée constituante*, where he defended the throne and the Church and in consequence was made a cardinal by Pius VI (1794), when he had left France. He returned to France in 1804. In 1810 he was created Archbishop of Paris by Napoleon, and held the office till 1814 despite the Pope's express prohibition. His *Essai sur l'éloquence de la chaire* (final ed., 1810) stands out among his other works. He recognized the high quality of Bossuet's sermons and justly appreciated Bourdaloue, and he was himself, in various *Éloges* and *Panégyriques*, a highly skilled, harmonious, but somewhat frigid orator.

Maximes (1665), by La Rochefoucauld (q.v.); and (1746) by Vauvenargues (q.v.).

Maximes des saints, see *Fénelon* and *Quietism*.

Mayenne, CHARLES DE LORRAINE, DUC DE (1554–1611), brother of Henri, third duc de Guise (see *Guise*), leader of the Ligue (q.v.) after the latter's death, defeated by Henri IV at Ivry in 1590.

Mayeux, the personage created first in *Le Fossé des Tuileries* (1831), a farce by Dumanoir, Mollien, and Lhéris, and made generally known by the caricatures of C.-J. Traviès (q.v.). He typified the petty-bourgeois who came into his own during the reign of Louis-Philippe. According to the Mayeux saga developed in the illustrated satirical journals he was born on 14 July 1789 while his father was attacking the Bastille, and was named successively Messidor – Napoléon – Louis – Charles – Philippe

Mayeux. He was a hunchback, bumptious, conceited, loose-living, the hero of comic and preposterous adventures, and a zealous patriot.

Maynard (Mainard), FRANÇOIS (1582–1646), born at Toulouse, a poet, the favourite disciple (with Racan) of Malherbe. After being secretary to Marguerite de Valois (q.v.) he spent most of his life as a magistrate at Aurillac. He was at his best in his epigrams, of which the following celebrated stanza, directed at an author's lack of perspicuity, is a good example:

> Si ton esprit veut cacher
> Les belles choses qu'il pense,
> Dy-moy, qui peut t'empêcher
> De te servir du silence?

But Maynard generally sacrificed vigour to a laborious correctness. One or two of his odes (*La Belle Vieille*; *Alcippe, reviens dans nos bois*) deserve notice. He was one of the original members of the *Académie*

Mayor of the Palace, see *Maire du Palais.*

Mazarin (GIULIO MAZARINI, 1602–61), son of a Sicilian employed as agent by the Colonna family, in early manhood doctor of laws, captain of infantry, diplomat, came into prominence as papal agent in 1630 by securing a truce between France and Spain. He was sent to Paris as papal legate in 1634, attracted Richelieu's notice, entered the French service, and was made cardinal. He became prime minister of France after the death of Richelieu, and retained his functions under Louis XIV by the favour of the regent Anne of Austria, in spite of his intense unpopularity (see *Fronde*). He may have been secretly married to Anne of Austria.

Mazarin, aided by the zeal and skill of his librarian Gabriel Naudé (q.v.), was a great collector of books, and from 1643 his splendid library of theological and historical works—some 40,000 volumes—was open to the public. But in 1651, during the *Fronde*, the *parlement* ordered his books to be sold. By 1660 he had managed to reconstitute his library and on his death he bequeathed it to the nation as part of a college which he had also willed should be founded in his memory (see *Bibliothèque Mazarine*; *Collège des Quatre Nations*).

Mazarin's nieces. Mazarin had numerous nieces, daughters of his sisters (married respectively to Girolamo Martinozzi and Lorenzo Mancini). Of these nieces he brought several to Paris in 1648 and 1653 and procured for them great marriages.

(1) LAURE MANCINI married in 1651 the duc de Mercœur, grandson of Henri IV and Gabrielle d'Estrées, and was mother of Vendôme, the famous general. She died at the age of nineteen.

(2) ANNE-MARIE MARTINOZZI married in 1654 the prince de Conti, brother of the Grand Condé, became a Jansenist and devoted herself to piety.

(3) LAURE MARTINOZZI married in 1656 Alphonse d'Este, heir of the duke of Modena, and was for twelve years regent of Modena after her husband's death. Her daughter married the Duke of York (James II).

(4) OLYMPE MANCINI. There was for a time a boy-and-girl affection between Louis XIV and her, which came to nothing; she married in 1657 Prince Eugène de Carignan, of the house of Savoy, who was created comte de Soissons. She was mother of Prince Eugene, the famous general, who in co-operation with Marlborough won the battles of Oudenarde and Malplaquet.

(5) MARIE MANCINI. Louis XIV fell deeply in love with her and proposed to Mazarin that he should marry her. The cardinal was opposed to the match and removed his niece from the court; the king's marriage to the Infanta put an end to the episode. Marie Mancini in 1661 married Prince Colonna, was unhappy, and left him.

(6) HORTENSE MANCINI, a woman of remarkable beauty and charm, was sought in marriage by Charles II (then in exile) and by other royal personages. Her uncle married her in 1661 to the son of the maréchal de la Meilleraye, leaving them the bulk of his vast fortune on condition that they should take his name: she is consequently known as the duchesse de Mazarin. Her husband was a jealous crank and made his wife's life intolerable. She presently ran away from him and her adventurous wanderings took her to Italy, Savoy, and finally England, where she shone at the courts of Charles II and James II, together with her fellow exile and admirer, Saint-Évremond, and where she died in 1699. The memoirs which bear her

name were probably written by the abbé de Saint-Réal from materials supplied by her or from her dictation.

(7) MARIE-ANNE MANCINI was married in 1662 (after Mazarin's death) to the duc de Bouillon, a gallant soldier, nephew of Turenne. She had literary tastes and was a patroness of men of letters, notably of La Fontaine. But she was hostile to Racine and procured the temporary failure of his *Phèdre*. She visited her sister in England in 1687.

Mazarinades, the name given to the very numerous pamphlets and satires, in prose and verse, issued against Cardinal Mazarin at the time of the *Fronde*. The name was sometimes extended to all satires published on the occasion of the conflict in question.

Mazas, a prison in Paris, built between 1845 and 1850 and demolished in 1898. It was designed solely for prisoners sentenced to solitary confinement. (The Place Mazas, its site, was named after Mazas 'le Brave', a hero of Napoleon's armies killed at Austerlitz.)

Meaulnes, see *Grand Meaulnes, Le*.

Meaux, évêque de, Bossuet, who occupied the see from 1681 till his death. He was also nicknamed *l'Aigle de Meaux*. See also *Condom*.

Méchant, Le, a comedy by Gresset, produced with much success in 1745.

'Le Méchant', Cléon by name, is a cynical and perfidious mischief-maker, who delights in provoking quarrels and trouble among others, and making himself feared and hated, for the amusement it gives him. He sets about spoiling the intended marriage of Valère and Chloé, by calumny and other devices. But the love of Valère, aided by the counsels of the firm and upright Ariste and the perspicacity of Chloé's maid, upsets his schemes and he is exposed. He goes off unabashed. The play has for its background a vivid picture of the soulless society of the *salons* of the period. There is evidence that this society saw nothing repulsive in the chief character of the play.

Médan, see *Soirées de Médan*.

Médecin de campagne, Le, a novel by Balzac, first published in 1833, and in 1846

placed among the 'Scènes de la vie de campagne' of his *Comédie humaine* (q.v.).

Benassis, a doctor, after unhappy experiences in love and in the world of Paris, has set up in practice in the mountainous, isolated region of the Grande Chartreuse, near Grenoble. An enlightened reformer, he has transformed a cretinous half-starved village into a healthy, self-supporting, and progressive community of which he is now the *Maire*. In the course of rural rides with le commandant [Major] Genestas from the garrison at Grenoble he tells how the transformation was effected and expounds his (i.e. Balzac's own) views on politics, religion, &c., on contemporary social conditions and how to better them. He introduces Genestas to various local characters, among them two old soldiers, Gondrin, sole survivor of the pontoneers of the Beresina (see *Moscow, Retreat from*), and Goguelat, one of the Imperial Guard, both still fanatically devoted to 'l'Empereur'. Goguelat is the village story-teller, and in one memorable scene, at night, in a candle-lit barn, and perhaps typical of many in real life at this period (about 1829), he keeps his audience enthralled with his fantastic biography of Napoleon, as naïve and highly coloured as an *image d'Épinal* (q.v., and see *Légende napoléonienne*).

Médecin malgré lui, Le, a comedy in prose by Molière produced in 1666. The plot was probably suggested in part by the fabliau *Le Vilain Mire* (q.v.).

Géronte has a daughter Lucinde who, being foiled by her father's opposition in her wish to marry Léandre, her penniless suitor, pretends to have been suddenly afflicted with dumbness. Her doctors having failed to cure her, Géronte sends out his servants to try to find one with special qualifications. They light on Martine, who is trying to think of some way to pay out her husband, a woodcutter, who has beaten her. This husband, Sganarelle, having been servant to a doctor, has retained some smattering of medical terms. She declares to Géronte's servants that Sganarelle is just the man they want, but that he is a whimsical fellow who will deny his miraculous powers unless they use their sticks to him. Sganarelle, well beaten, finally consents to attend Lucinde, and finding no difficulty in imposing on Géronte and earning his fee by the use of a little medical jargon, takes kindly to his new role. Bribed by Léandre, he introduces the latter as his apothecary. Lucinde at once recovers her speech—with such vigour that Géronte entreats Sganarelle to make her dumb again; this Sganarelle cannot do, but he offers to make Géronte deaf instead (a touch borrowed from Rabelais). Lucinde escapes with Léandre, and Géronte is reconciled to their marriage when he learns that Léandre has inherited his uncle's fortune.

A much-quoted phrase occurs in this play. When Sganarelle, holding forth learnedly about Lucinde's symptoms, refers to the heart as being on the right side and the liver on the left, and Géronte remarks that he thought it was the other way about, Sganarelle replies airily: 'Oui, cela était autrefois ainsi; mais nous avons changé tout cela.'

Médée, the first tragedy written by Corneille, produced in 1635.

It is modelled on the plays on the same subject by Euripides and Seneca. Jason is at Corinth, about to wed Creusa, daughter of Creon, king of Corinth, and to desert Medea. The play presents the vengeance of Medea, who destroys Creusa and her father by means of a poisoned robe, and slays her own children because Jason loves them. This early drama, though better than any of its kind that had preceded it, falls short of the dignity and simplicity that Corneille attained in his later tragedies. It contains the famous reply of Medea in the passage:

Votre pays vous hait, votre époux est sans foi:
Dans un si grand revers que vous reste-t-il?
— Moi!
Moi, dis-je, et c'est assez . . .

Médicis, see *Catherine de Médicis* and *Marie de Médicis.*

Méditations poétiques (1820), a collection of twenty-four odes and elegies by Lamartine, and his first published work. The publisher's advertisement called them 'the tender outpourings of a soul abandoned to its vague inspirations'. This collection included the two famous poems *Le Lac* and *L'Isolement.* In the former the poet is alone by the lac du Bourget (near Aix-les-Bains) where he had been the previous year with

'Elvire' (q.v.), now dying in Paris. How intense the lovers' happiness had been then as they listened to the rhythmical beat of the oars upon the water! Then, they had called upon Time to stand still. And now? Time has swept on, but love itself must linger in this place.

L'Isolement was written a year after Elvire's death. The poet, alone in a world where 'un seul être vous manque et tout est dépeuplé', now dreams of a mystical reunion in another world. He calls upon the north wind to sweep him, like a withered leaf, towards 'ce bien idéal que toute âme désire'.

Other well-known poems in this collection are *Le Soir, Le Vallon, L'Automne.*

Méhul, Étienne-Nicolas (1763–1817), famous French composer of operas, comic operas, and ballets, wrote the music for some of the great Revolutionary songs, e.g. the *Chant du départ* (q.v.), *Chant des victoires, Hymne du 9 Thermidor,* &c. On Easter Sunday 1802, at the Pontifical High Mass in Notre-Dame which marked the official return to the Christian religion and which was attended in state by the First Consul Bonaparte, the music was under the direction of Méhul and Cherubini (q.v.).

Meilhac, Henri (1831–97), born in Paris, was the author, in collaboration with Ludovic Halévy (q.v.), of drawing-room comedies, e.g. *Froufrou* (1869), which has moments of real pathos, *La Petite Marquise* (1874); and of the libretti, as gay and amusing as the music itself, for Offenbach's operettas *La Belle Hélène* (1865), *La Grande-Duchesse de Gérolstein* (1867), *La Vie parisienne* (1867), &c.

Meillet, Antoine (1866–1936), philologist, author of valuable studies in the field of linguistics and comparative grammar, e.g. *Introduction à l'étude comparative des langues indo-européennes* (1903), *Dialectes indo-européens* (1908), *Linguistique historique et linguistique générale* (1921), *Esquisse d'une histoire de la langue latine* (1928), &c.

Meilleure des républiques, La [i.e. Louis-Philippe]. After the July Revolution (1830) when Louis-Philippe accepted the crown it is said that La Fayette, as Commandant of the *Garde nationale,* embraced him and exclaimed, 'Voilà la meilleure des républiques!'

Meister, JACQUES-HENRI (1744–1826), Swiss man of letters. He was in Paris from 1770 to 1789 and was a friend of Diderot and d'Holbach. He contributed to Grimm's correspondence and continued it from 1773 to 1790.

'Mélanges', the French equivalent (e.g. *Mélanges de philologie offerts à Ferdinand Brunot*) for the type of collection known elsewhere as *Festschrift*, or as *Homage Studies*; essays, the work of colleagues and former students, in honour of a scholar of exceptional distinction.

Mélanide, a sentimental comedy (*comédie larmoyante*) in verse by La Chaussée, produced in 1741.

The comte d'Ormancé has clandestinely married Mélanide and has had a son by her. His family have repudiated the marriage and forcibly separated the couple. The comte is later led to believe that his wife and son are dead. Eighteen years later he again falls in love, this time with a girl of humble birth, whose mother welcomes so distinguished a match for her daughter. But he has a rival, favoured by the girl herself, in the young Darviane, who is in fact the comte's son, though neither knows his relation to the other. The play turns on the conflict in the father's mind when this is revealed, for he has forgotten Mélanide and at first hates and repudiates the son who is his rival. But Mélanide now appears and wins back her husband's heart; Darviane falls at the comte's feet, and father and son are reconciled.

Mélicerte, a pastoral play by Molière, of which only two acts were written. These were performed in 1666. The theme is taken from the *Grand Cyrus* of Mlle de Scudéry. The plot is trifling—two shepherdesses in love with a youthful shepherd who loves another—but the form is graceful.

Mélisande, the heroine of Maeterlinck's *Pelléas et Mélisande* (q.v.).

Mélite, a comedy by Corneille, produced in 1629, of some interest as the author's first play.

Éraste is in love with Mélite, but his love is not returned. He introduces his friend Tircis (who professes himself superior to any tender passion) to the lady, and the two fall mutually in love. Éraste devises a cruel revenge: Tircis has a sister, Chloris, who is betrothed to Philandre; Éraste fabricates a letter from Mélite declaring herself in love with Philandre, and this he gets delivered to Philandre. Thus, to ruin the prospects of Mélite and Tircis, he ruins equally those of the latter's sister; for Philandre allows himself to be seduced from his allegiance to Chloris, and shows Tircis the supposed letter from Mélite. Tircis falls into despair, and a report of his death is brought to Mélite, who faints at the news. Éraste is told that both Tircis and Mélite have died of grief, and remorse drives him crazy, so that he believes himself dead and in hell. However, all is cleared up: Tircis and Mélite are reunited, and Chloris, who repudiates the inconstant Philandre, is awarded to the penitent Éraste.

Melmoth réconcilié (1835), one of the 'Études philosophiques' of Balzac's *Comédie humaine* (q.v.). Balzac was much influenced in his early years by the Gothic romances of the Irish writer Charles Robert Maturin, which were translated into French about 1820 and widely read. Maturin's 'Melmoth the Wanderer' sold his soul—a transferable bargain—to the devil in return for long life. He discovered all the ennui and horror of diabolic omnipotence but could find no one, however sunk in misfortune, who did not shrink from relieving him of his pact. The Melmoth of Balzac's fundamentally cynical tale had no such difficulty at a time (the Restoration period) when 'notre civilisation . . . depuis 1815, a remplacé le principe Honneur par le principe Argent'. He exchanged souls with Castanier, a swindling cashier on the brink of ruin and discovery, then died an edifying death. Castanier, again, found a bankrupt stockbroker prepared to accept any pact; and he in his turn passed on the bargain.

Mélodrame [melodrama], a form of sensational drama with incidental music (and sometimes ballet) which may have evolved from *pantomime dialoguée* (q.v.). It filled the second-class theatres of Paris (*les théâtres du boulevard*) during the first thirty years of the 19th century and quickly penetrated to other countries. (It was played on the

London stage from 1802.) Interest depended on violent incident and exaggerated sentiment; and virtue almost invariably won a last-minute triumph over vice. The music was intended to indicate character or emphasize the action.

The best-known and most prolific of early authors of melodrama was Guilbert de Pixerécourt (q.v.). His plays were frequently adapted from novels, both French and foreign, e.g. *Les Mystères d'Udolphe* (1798), from Mrs. Radcliffe's *Mysteries of Udolpho*, and *Victor ou l'Enfant de la forêt* (1798) and *Cœlina ou l'Enfant du mystère* (1801), from novels by Ducray-Duminil (q.v.). About the middle of the century melodramas by Philippe d'Ennery and Frédéric Soulié (qq.v.) were popular. At the present day, in France as in other countries, stage melodrama has been largely superseded by sensational screen dramas.

Mélusine, a fairy of French folk-lore, the water-sprite of the fountain of Lusignan in Poitou, and the legendary ancestress and tutelary spirit of the house of that name. She consented to marry Raimond of Poitou on condition that he should never see her on a Saturday, on which day she resumed her mermaid-like shape. Her husband broke the compact, whereupon she fled. The legend was adapted in a prose romance by Jean d'Arras (*c.* 1387; translated by A. K. Donald for the E.E.T.S.) and was subsequently further developed.

Memnon, a philosophical tale by Voltaire, published in 1749. *Memnon* was also the title of the first draft of Voltaire's *Zadig* (q.v.).

Memnon conceives the idea of being perfectly wise, abjuring the love of women, avoiding excesses of food and drink, living within his means and on good terms with his neighbours. Yet within a few hours he is beguiled by a woman, gets drunk, loses an eye in a quarrel, and is ruined by the bankruptcy of a creditor. In a vision a celestial spirit explains to him that perfect wisdom is impossible in this imperfect world, and that (short of recovering his eye) he may yet live with moderate happiness provided he will abandon his silly project.

Voltaire subsequently prefixed these lines to the tale:

Nous tromper dans nos entreprises,
C'est à quoi nous sommes sujets;
Le matin je fais des projets,
Et le long du jour des sottises.

Mémoires de deux jeunes mariées, one of the 'Scènes de la vie privée' of Balzac's *Comédie humaine* (q.v.).

Mémoires de Trévoux, see *Journal de Trévoux.*

Mémoires d'outre-tombe (1849–50), the autobiography of Chateaubriand, one of the masterpieces of French literature, written between 1811 and 1841. In later life, when Chateaubriand was in financial difficulties, he sold the manuscript to a syndicate on condition that it should not be published till a year after his death. It came out by instalments during 1849–50. The first complete text was published in 1948.

The *Mémoires* are in four sections, subdivided into books. The first section covers the author's early years, his military career, travels, life in exile, and return to France (1768–1800); the second, his literary career (1800–14); the third, his political career (1814–30); and the last, the years of retirement (1830–*c.* 1840). The first books, which contain reminiscences of childhood and a description of the beginning of the Revolution, are considered incomparably the finest. Other noteworthy passages are the character-sketches of Napoleon (§ 3) and the descriptions of travel in Germany, Italy, and Central Europe (§ 4). But the whole work abounds in memorable and often self-revealing passages, such as portraits of contemporaries, coloured invariably by the writer's emotions; or the many remarkable descriptions of experiences and personal sensations.

Mémoires du diable (1837–8), a sensational novel by Soulié (q.v.).

Mémoires d'un fou, a fragmentary work by Flaubert, partly autobiographical, written when he was seventeen and published posthumously. (It can be found in his *Œuvres de jeunesse inédites* (Conard), vol. i.) It is interesting as a record of his first encounter with the Mme Schlésinger—here called 'Maria'—who was the Mme Arnoux of *L'Éducation sentimentale* (q.v.).

Mémoires d'un homme de qualité (1728–31), see *Prévost, l'abbé.*

Mémoires d'un médecin : Joseph Balsamo (1846–48), an historical novel by Dumas *père* (q.v., and cf. *Cagliostro*).

Mémoires pour servir à l'histoire de France sous Napoléon (1823), see *Montholon, comte de.*

Mémoires secrets, see *Duclos* and *Bachaumont, Louis Petit de.*

Mémoires sur la Bastille (1783, published in London), by the political writer Simon-Nicolas-Henri Linguet (see *Annales politiques, civiles et littéraires*), an eloquent, arresting indictment of the system of *lettres de cachet* (q.v.) and of the treatment meted out to prisoners in the Bastille. Linguet himself had been in the Bastille from September 1780 till May 1782.

Memoirs (including **Autobiographies** and **Journaux intimes**). For the purposes of the present *Companion* it has been thought preferable to give references to memoirs, autobiographies, and *journaux intimes* under one heading. Division cannot always be clear-cut, but so far as possible they have been assembled in four groups:

A. Memoirs of interest mainly or wholly as social and political history (see also *History*);

B. Reminiscences of literary, artistic, theatrical, &c. life—a type which developed considerably during the 19th century;

C. Works termed variously *memoirs, souvenirs, autobiographies*, in which the author is, and expects his readers to be, interested chiefly in himself or himself in relation to events. This class, too, is very much a 19th-century phenomenon. So, again, is

D. The diary, that form of self-confession and self-exploration, or psychological autobiography, which in French literature is termed 'journal intime'.

A. MEMOIRS (HISTORICAL AND POLITICAL)

1. *Covering various periods down to c. 1750*

See Antin, duc d'; Argenson, marquis d'; Aubigné; Bassompierre; Brantôme; Bussy-Rabutin; Castelnau; Catinat; Caylus, marquise de; Choisy; Commines; Conrart; Dangeau; Du Bellay, Guillaume; Duclos;

Duguay-Trouin; Du Hausset; Épinay; Fontaine, Nicolas; Fontenay-Mareuil; Forbin; Gourville; Gramont, Antoine de; Gramont, comte de; Hénault; Jeannin; Joinville; La Châtre; La Fare; La Fayette, Mme de; La Noue; La Rochefoucauld; Launay, Mme de; Lenet; L'Estoile; Louis XIV; Luynes; Marguerite de Valois; Mazarin's nieces (for duchesse de Mazarin); Monluc; Montpensier; Motteville; Nemours; Pontis; Retz, cardinal de; Richelieu, cardinal de; Richelieu, duc de; Rohan; Saint-Simon, duc de; Sully; Tallemant des Réaux; Tavannes; Turenne; Vieilleville; Villars; Villehardouin.

2. *Post 1750*

See Abrantès, duchesse d'; Arago; Beaumarchais; Bernis; Besenval; Broglie; Campan; Canrobert; Carême; Caulaincourt; Clairon; Genlis; Gourgaud; Guizot; Haussonville; Hugo; Las Cases; Latude; Lauzun (duc de Biron); Marchand; *Maréchal de l'Empire* (end); Marmontel; Ménard; Morellet; Napoleon I; Poincaré, R.; Récamier; Rémusat, Mme de; Rœderer; Roland, Mme; Staël; Tocqueville; Vidocq; Viel-Castel; Villemain. [The memoirs of the above-mentioned have often been published separately, sometimes posthumously; or, for the earlier centuries, they may be found in the *Collection des mémoires relatifs à l'histoire de France* by Petitot and Monmerqué (1819–29) and in the *Nouvelle Collection des mémoires pour servir à l'histoire de France* by Michaud and Poujoulat (1836–8)].

B. MEMOIRS (LITERARY, ARTISTIC, THEATRICAL, ETC.)

See Ancelot, Mme; Antoine; Berlioz; Chasles; Copeau; Daudet, A.; Du Camp; Dumas *père*; Goncourt (Journal des); Halévy, L.; Houssaye; Léautaud; Mauclair; Raynaud; Véron.

C. WORKS THAT ARE MAINLY AUTOBIOGRAPHICAL

See Arago; Chateaubriand; Colette; France; Gide; Lamartine; Maurois; Michelet; Musset, A. de; Quinet; Renan; Rousseau, J.-J.; Sand; Schlumberger; Stendhal; Vallès; Verlaine.

D. JOURNAUX INTIMES

See Amiel; Barrès; Bashkirtseff; Baudelaire; Bloy; Constant; Delacroix; Du Bos; Gide; Green; Guérin, Eugénie de; Guérin,

M. de; Lenéru; Loti; Louÿs; Maine de Biran; Régnier, Paule; Renard, J.; Vigny.

Mémorial de Sainte-Hélène (1822–3), by the comte de Las Cases (q.v.).

Ménage, GILLES (1613–92), scholar and man of letters, born at Angers, a frequenter of the Hôtel de Rambouillet, whose principal works were of a philological character. He was the author of *Origines de la langue française* (1650, completed 1694), an etymological work of value; of *Miscellanea* (1652), a collection of satires and other pieces in Greek, Latin, and French; of observations on the *Aminta* of Tasso (1655); of a translation, with commentary, of Diogenes Laertius; of etymologies of the Italian language; &c. He was quarrelsome and had controversies with Bouhours, Cotin, and others. Mme de Sévigné owed much to his instruction in her youth. The Vadius of Molière's *Les Femmes savantes* is supposed to be modelled on him. In spite of his merit he was never a member of the *Académie*. *Menagiana* is a collection of his sayings, observations, anecdotes, and miscellanies, prepared by him and published in 1693 after his death. His *Requête des Dictionnaires* is a witty criticism of the *Académie* containing some sound advice.

Ménagier de Paris, Le, a prose work written between 1392 and 1394 by a rich elderly *bourgeois* of Paris for the education of his young wife, in matters both of morals and of domestic economy, ranging in fact from religious duties to cooking-recipes. It throws an interesting light on the life of the rich middle classes at this period. Cf. *La Tour Landry.*

Ménalque, a character in *Les Caractères* by La Bruyère (q.v.); also in Gide's (q.v.) *Les Nourritures terrestres* and *L'Immoraliste.*

Ménard, LOUIS (1822–1901), one of the first group of *Parnassien* (q.v.) poets, author of *Prométhée délivré* (1844), an epic, a free version of the ancient myth; also of collected *Poèmes* (1855). But he is more memorable as a scholar and thinker (*Rêveries d'un païen mystique,* 1876, prose and verse), a Hellenist whose pagan attitude to life influenced his contemporaries (for instance, his friend Leconte de Lisle, q.v.). In 1848 he had taken an active part in the June insurrections

(les 'journées de juin', see *Republics*, para. 2, of which he left interesting and moving reminiscences in *Prologue d'une révolution* (1849).

Mendès, CATULLE (1842–1909), Parnassian poet, also novelist, playwright, and man of letters, born at Bordeaux, lived in Paris after 1859. He was for a time married to Théophile Gautier's daughter Judith (q.v.).

He founded the *Revue fantaisiste* (1861, Feb.–Nov., see *Parnassiens*), and poems by him were included in *Le Parnasse contemporain*. *Poésies* (1892), *Poésies nouvelles* (1893), and *Choix de poésies* (1925) are his collected poetical works. His plays, written alone or in collaboration, were his most successful work (*La Reine Fiammette*, 1889; *Médée*, 1898, &c.), and he wrote many novels (e.g. *Les Folies amoureuses*, 1877, a title indicative of their character). His *Légende du Parnasse contemporain* (1884) and *Rapport sur le mouvement poétique français* (1902) are studies—still valuable—of 19th-century French poetry.

Mendiant ingrat, Le (1898–1920, 8 vols.), the Journal of Léon Bloy (q.v.).

Ménechmes, Les, a comedy by Regnard, produced in 1705. The theme, the complications arising from the resemblance of two brothers who are mistaken for one another, is taken from the *Menaechmi* of Plautus. In the French play one of the brothers is an unsophisticated provincial who comes to Paris to receive a sum of money which he has inherited; the other is an unscrupulous adventurer who sets about securing the inheritance for himself as well as the hand of the woman whom his brother was about to marry.

Ménestrel, originally a paid servant or functionary in a household, extended to include *jongleurs* (q.v.) in the permanent employ of a prince or noble, then restricted to these, then extended to *jongleurs* in general. The secure position of the *ménestrel* in permanent employment made him free to devote himself to literary creation and thus favoured the transformation of the ancient type of *jongleur*, an amuser of the public, into the author or man of letters.

There was a corporation of *ménestrels* of Paris organized with statutes from 1321.

The example was imitated, but much later, in other cities.

Ménestrel de Reims, see *History* (medieval period).

Ménippée, Satire, see *Satire Ménippée.*

Menteur, Le, a comedy by Corneille, produced in 1643, adapted from *La Verdad sospechosa* of Alarcón.

Dorante, who has left the law-school of Poitiers and come to Paris to take up the profession of arms, is a young man of gallant character spoilt by an amazing propensity for telling lies. On every occasion, with light-hearted unconcern, he draws on a fertile imagination to recommend himself, or to escape from a quandary, or merely from love of romancing. To win favour with a lady he represents himself as just returned from the wars; to avoid an unwelcome betrothal he bamboozles his father with a fantastic tale of a previous marriage; he becomes embroiled with a rival by the story of a purely imaginary serenade; and so forth. He finally becomes hopelessly entangled by mistaking the name of the lady he is courting, and only extricates himself by transferring his favour to the other. It is proof of the author's art that he retains the reader's sympathy for his hero.

The success of this play led Corneille shortly to produce a sequel, *La Suite du Menteur,* imitated from a comedy of Lope de Vega. Although the hero and his valet in the sequel bear the same names as in *Le Menteur,* there is no real relation between the two plays, for in the sequel the hero is a model of generous self-denial, who refuses to liberate himself from imprisonment on a false charge by giving evidence that will incriminate a friend, and is even prepared to surrender to him the lady to whom he is bound by a mutual attachment.

Mérat, ALBERT (1840–1909), minor Parnassian poet (see *Parnassiens*), author of poems collected in *Les Chimères* (1866), *Les Villes de marbre* (1874), *Au fil de l'eau* (1877), *Poèmes de Paris* (1880), *Vers le soir* (1900), &c.

Méraugis de Portlesguez, a metrical romance of the early 13th century by Raoul de Houdenc. It belongs to the Arthurian cycle. Méraugis and Gorvain Cadrut are young knights who both love Lidoine, the former for her worth, the latter for her beauty. A tribunal of ladies, presided over by Queen Guinevere, awards her to Méraugis, on condition that he prove himself deserving of her, in a quest for Gauvain (Gawain), who has been absent from Arthur's court for a year. He sets off, accompanied by Lidoine, meets with the usual magical adventures, finds Gauvain, and ultimately returns successful. The complicated tale of the adventures is skilfully told, and is one of the most agreeable of its kind. The poem is also noteworthy for its discussion of abstract love themes.

Mercadet (1840), a drama adapted by d'Ennery (q.v.) from Balzac's play *Le Faiseur* (1830), was produced in 1851. It is a powerful, realistic study of a speculator.

Mercier, LOUIS (1870–1935), poet, of peasant extraction, was born and spent most of his life near Lyons. Such inspiration as his verse showed came from religion or the humble, familiar objects of daily life, e.g. in the collections *Voix de la terre et du temps* (1903), *Le Poème de la maison* (1909), *Les Pierres sacrées* (1919).

Mercier, LOUIS-SÉBASTIEN (1740–1814), dramatist and critic, author of domestic *drames* (q.v.) in prose, spoilt by sentimentality, moralizing, and pretentious style: *Jeunesse* (1768, based on Lillo's *George Barnwell*), *Le Déserteur* (1782, a protest against war and the rigours of military law), *La Brouette du vinaigrier* (1784, a plea for social equality); and of some historical dramas; also of a *Nouvel Essai sur l'art dramatique* (1773) and *De la littérature et les littérateurs* (1778), in which he preached the Romantic revolt against Classical drama and the unities. He also left an interesting *Tableau de Paris,* a very long work combining topography with descriptions of various classes of citizens, anecdotes, and short essays on all sorts of matters, from political events to mushrooms; and a Dictionary of Neologisms, see *Dictionaries and Encyclopedias,* under date 1801.

Mercier de la Rivière (1720–93), one of the physiocrats or *Économistes* (q.v.), author of *L'Ordre naturel et essentiel des sociétés politiques* (1767).

Mercœur, ÉLISA (1809–35), a poetess of the Romantic Movement (*Œuvres,* 1843, 3 vols.).

Mercure de France, Le.

(1) See *Mercure galant*.

(2) A famous literary and artistic review (monthly, and still existing), founded in 1890 by Alfred Vallette and a group of writers who had contributed to the early Symbolist review *La Pléiade*. It was at first particularly associated with *Symbolisme* (q.v.) but made a feature of printing original work by writers of all schools and nationalities. Its great period was about 1900.

Mercure du XIXᵉ siècle, Le (1823–30),

a literary review (ed. Henri de Latouche, q.v.) which opposed the extreme Romantic doctrines. Senancour (q.v.) was a contributor.

Mercure galant, Le,

a periodical founded in 1672 by Donneau de Visé (1638–1710, also author of farces and vaudevilles, and a critic, sometimes acrimonious, of Molière). It contained news of court and literary circles, literary criticism, sonnets, madrigals, &c., combining politics and literature in a light and agreeable form suited to a wide public. It appeared irregularly, then monthly from 1678, and was highly popular, enjoying the favour of Louis XIV, though attacked from certain literary quarters. (It was dismissed by La Bruyère as 'immédiatement au-dessous de rien'.) In 1724 it became the *Mercure de France*, with a greater literary scope, and assumed a semi-official character. Its editor was now appointed by the Government and its profits were devoted to pensions for men of letters. Its distinguished contributors included Thomas Corneille, Raynal, and Marmontel (editors), and La Harpe, Chamfort, and Voltaire (who contributed some light pieces). Immediately before the Revolution the management was in the hands of the publisher Panckoucke. Its literary features continued during the Revolutionary era, when its name was changed for a time to *Le Mercure français*, but it was little molested. It was suppressed by Napoleon in 1811 but reappeared after his fall and was a favourite periodical with the constitutional party during the early Restoration years. Publication ceased in 1820.

This periodical was the subject of Boursault's (q.v.) comedy *Le Mercure galant* (1683), later called *La Comédie sans titre*.

Mercuriale, see under *Daguesseau*.

Méré, ANTOINE GOMBAUD, CHEVALIER DE (1610–85), moralist, a friend of Guez de Balzac and a man of acute intelligence if a somewhat pedantic writer, a self-professed arbiter of good manners and the usages of the *honnêtes gens*. His *Lettres*, published 1682, include anecdotes and tales (among others an adaptation of the *Ephesian Matron* of Petronius), and are chiefly remembered for those addressed to his friend Pascal, whom he counselled to adopt an *esprit de finesse* in polite society rather than the bludgeoning tactics of logic. His *Conversations* with the maréchal de Clérambault and his *Maximes* were published in 1669 and 1692 respectively; his *traités—De la vraie honnêteté, De l'éloquence et de l'entretien, De la délicatesse,* &c.— appeared (1701) after his death.

Mère coquette, La,

a comedy in verse by Quinault, produced with great success in 1665.

The elderly Cremante wishes to marry Isabelle, the daughter of Ismène, a middle-aged coquette. Ismène, who thinks herself a widow, her husband having been carried off by the Turks eight years before, would like to marry Acante, Cremante's son. But the young people love one another. Laurette, a rascally maid-servant, perfidiously brings about a rupture between the young lovers, in order to favour the designs of their elders. But the unexpected return of Ismène's husband, aided by the abiding love of Acante and Isabelle, defeats the plot.

Mère coupable, La (1792),

a play, see *Beaumarchais*.

Mère l'Oye, Contes de ma, see *Perrault*.

Mère-Sotte, see *Enfants sans souci*.

Meriadeuc, see *Chevalier aux deux épées*.

Mérimée, PROSPER (1803–70), novelist, also archaeologist and historian, born and educated in Paris, was a great-grandson of Mme Leprince de Beaumont (q.v.) and the son of Léonor Mérimée (1757–1836), a mediocre but cultivated artist who was Perpetual Secretary of the Académie des Beaux-Arts. He studied, but never practised, law, preferred literature, and was for a time attracted, though not carried away, by *le romantisme* (q.v. and cf. *Stendhal*, his close friend). His active literary career began with a successful hoax, *Le Théâtre de Clara Gazul* (q.v., 1825, anon.), six short plays masquerading as translations from the writings of 'Clara Gazul', a fictitious Spanish actress. Next, under the pseudonym of Hyacinthe Maglanowich, came another hoax, *La Guzla* (1827, q.v.), translations, so-called, of Illyrian national songs and poems. *La Jacquerie* (dramatic sketches set in feudal times) and *La Famille de Carvajal* (a drama of incestuous love), published anonymously in 1828, were followed, still anonymously, by the *Chronique du règne de Charles IX* (1829, q.v.), one of the early French historical novels inspired by Scott (see *Foreign Influences on French Literature*, para. 20). It is comparable in quality to Vigny's *Cinq-Mars* and Hugo's *Notre-Dame de Paris* (qq.v.).

(2) Between 1829 and 1850 Mérimée contributed, usually to the *Revue de Paris* or the *Revue des Deux Mondes*—and seldom now anonymously—the works which place him enduringly among the French masters of the short or long-short story. (For individual titles, details of book-form collections, &c., see para. 4.) They are masterpieces of economic, objective narrative, with understatement and an ironic sense of humour keeping the passion and cruelty which more often than not are their themes well under control (hence perhaps their appeal for English readers. Mérimée knew England, as he did Spain, well and had many English friends.)

(3) After 1830 Mérimée's official career took preponderance, at least outwardly, over his creative work. From 1834, as Inspector General of Historical Monuments, he presented vigorous reports, the outcome of long, tiring tours of inspection, on the need for preserving and classifying ancient monuments (e.g. *Voyage dans le midi de la France*, 1835, on ecclesiastical architecture; *Voyage dans l'ouest de la France*, 1836; *Voyage en Corse*, 1840; *Rapport sur les monuments historiques*, 1843, &c.). He was a Senator during the Second Empire (q.v.), prominent at court (largely owing to his long-standing friendship with the Empress Eugénie and her mother) and in literary circles. After 1854, and perhaps because this year had seen the unhappy end of his long intimacy with Mme Valentine Delessert (a cultured, artistic woman whose husband was the Paris *Préfet de Police* under the July Monarchy), his creative impulse withered. He died at

Cannes after some years of miserable ill health.

(4) The first book-form collection of his tales was *Mosaïque* (1833). It included such well-known titles as *Mateo Falcone*, *L'Enlèvement de la redoute*, *Tamango*, *La Partie de Trictrac*, *Le Vase étrusque* (qq.v.). *Colomba* (q.v.) gave its name to a volume of three tales in 1841 (the first French edition), the other two being *Les Âmes du Purgatoire* and *La Vénus d'Ille* (q.v.). *Nouvelles*, in 1852, contained, notably, *Carmen* (q.v.), of an excellence somewhat swamped by Bizet's opera, *Arsène Guillot*, and two translations from Pushkin—*La Dame de pique* and *Le Hussard*. *Dernières Nouvelles* (1873), a posthumous collection, contained *Lokis*, a fantastic horror-tale (it had appeared in the *Revue des Deux Mondes* in the year of Mérimée's death), also *La Chambre bleue* (see *Eugénie, Empress*), &c. A longer story, *La Double Méprise*, not in any of the above collections, published in 1833 after the first chapters had appeared in the *Revue des Deux Mondes*, was possibly intended as a novel to begin with. A short comedy, *Les Deux Héritages* (q.v.), was published in 1853.

(5) Mérimée's later works included studies of and translations from Russian literature (he was a friend of Turgenev), also historical writings, e.g. *Histoire de don Pèdre Ier, roi de Castille* (1848), *Les Faux Démétrius* (1853), an episode from 16th-century Russian history. Seven fully annotated volumes of his interesting *Correspondance générale*, ed. M. Parturier, have been published to date (1954), reaching the year 1855. Various earlier editions of his correspondence include (1881) two volumes of letters written between 1850 and 1870 to his friend Antonio Panizzi (q.v.), the Director of the British Museum, the *Lettres à une inconnue* (1873), letters he wrote at almost daily intervals to Mlle Jenny Dacquin (q.v.) from 1831 till very shortly before his death, and his correspondence between 1838 and 1870 with the Delessert family (1931).

Merlin, a prophet and magician, whose name first occurs in the *Historia regum Britanniae* of Geoffrey of Monmouth, where he is identified with Ambrosius, a boy with a gift of prophecy of whom Nennius tells a tale in his *Historia Britonum*. According to Geoffrey it is thanks to Merlin's magic that

Uther Pendragon is enabled to approach Igerna in the shape of her husband Gorlois, duke of Cornwall, and become the father of Arthur. Merlin's prophecies occupy the seventh book of Geoffrey's *Historia*.

In the trilogy composed by Robert de Boron (see *Perceval*) Merlin forms the link between the early history of the Grail and the days of Arthur. The prose versions that followed these poems developed Merlin's part in the story. It is he who advises the foundation (by Uther) of the Round Table, and his intervention and counsel constantly influence the course of events. Finally he falls in love with Niniane, to whom he reveals the secret of magic. This is the end of the sage, for Niniane lays a spell on him and keeps him in a tower in the forest of Brocéliande. Merlin tells Gawain as he rides by that his voice will be heard no more.

Merlin l'enchanteur, (1860, 2 vols.), a long allegorical work in poetic prose by Edgar Quinet (q.v.).

Mérope, a tragedy by Voltaire, composed in 1736, produced in 1743, based on Hyginus's version of the legend of Merope. Voltaire was also acquainted with Maffei's tragedy on the same subject. The play was well received and the enthusiasm of the audience inaugurated the practice of calling a successful author before the curtain at the close of his play.

Mérope is the widow of Cresphonte, king of Messenia, who has been killed, it is supposed by brigands, but in fact by Polyphonte. Two of her sons have also been killed; the third, Égisthe (the Aepytus of the Greek legend), has been carried off to safety by the old man Narbas, and has been brought up without knowledge of his parentage; Mérope is ignorant of his fate. Polyphonte aspires to the throne of Messenia, and to strengthen his claim wishes to secure the hand of Mérope and the death of Égisthe, if he can be discovered. Mérope refuses indignantly to marry the man who seeks to usurp the rights of the royal line. A young man is brought in from the frontier who has slain another youth, according to his own statement in self-defence. Mérope is inclined to think, from his resemblance to Cresphonte, that he is her son, but the account he gives of himself discredits this supposition. On the other hand evidence is found that the youth he has killed was Égisthe. Polyphonte uses the presumed death of Égisthe to press his suit, and Mérope consents to marry him if she is allowed with her own hand to kill the murderer of her son; but she intends to take her own life immediately after. The captive is brought to the altar, but as she is about to plunge the dagger in his breast, the old man Narbas intervenes and reveals that he is in fact Égisthe, and that Polyphonte was the slayer of Cresphonte. Égisthe siezes the sacrificial axe and cuts down Polyphonte; the people rally to Mérope and her son, and Égisthe is recognized king.

There is an interesting discussion of Voltaire's treatment of the legend in Matthew Arnold's introduction to his own play *Merope*.

Mérovingiens, a dynasty of Frankish kings, so named from Mérovée (d. 458), the grandfather of Clovis I (q.v.), the chief of the Salian Franks, who defeated Syagrius the Roman governor and became king of all the Franks. After the death of Mérovée his kingdom, according to the Frankish custom, was divided among his four sons, but was later reunited under Clovis I. It was again divided among the latter's three sons into Austrasia, the eastern part, comprising the territories between the Meuse and the Rhine; Neustria, the north-west, comprising those between the Meuse and the Loire; and the south, including Burgundy. The dynasty remained in control of the country until the death of Dagobert I in 638, when the power passed into the hands of the *Maires du Palais* (q.v.). The Merovingian kings were brutal and barbarous chiefs of pillaging bands, few of them exercising any real government and administration of their kingdom. Their history (until they became nonentities) is an appalling record of family feuds, assassinations, and other crimes. The outstanding kings of the dynasty, besides its founder, Clovis, were Chilperic I (king of Neustria, 561–84), who showed some literary and artistic ambitions and even proposed to reform the alphabet, and Dagobert, king of Austrasia from 622, and of all France from 628, till his death in 638. He caused the Salic Law (q.v.) to be revised and founded the abbey of Saint-Denis.

Merrill, STUART (1863–1915), poet, of French descent on his mother's side, was born in the U.S.A. near New York, and brought by his parents to Paris in early childhood. Thereafter, except for occasional visits to the United States, he lived in France. He was closely associated with the Symbolist Movement, and the poems of *Les Gammes* (1887) and *Les Fastes* (1891), written at this period, are largely experiments in versification and in the *orchestration* of verse (see *Symbolisme*). A later collection, *Les Quatre Saisons* (1900), belongs to a socialist phase of his career. The lyrics of his last, and best, collection, *Une Voix dans la foule* (1909), were on a deeper note. Merrill also published *Petits Poèmes d'automne* (1895) and (in New York) *Pastels in Prose* (1890), translations from French poets of the second half of the 19th century.

Mersenne, MARIN, PÈRE (1588–1648), theologian, philosopher, and mathematician, correspondent of scientists all over Europe, friend and correspondent of Descartes, though not in any special degree his disciple. He discovered the laws governing the vibration of a stretched string.

Merteuil, MME DE, Valmont's partner in corruption, an even more corrupt character than himself, in *Les Liaisons dangereuses* by Choderlos de Laclos (see *Laclos*).

Merveilleuses, a name about 1797 for fashionable women who adopted the Greek styles of dress which can be studied in prints and caricatures of the *Directoire* (q.v.) period, e.g. those of Carle Vernet (cf. *Incroyables*; *Muscadins*).

Méry, FRANÇOIS-JOSEPH-PIERRE-AGNÈS (1797–1866), journalist and man of letters, born in Marseilles, came to Paris in 1824 and contributed to *Le Nain jaune* (q.v.) and other journals. With his compatriot Auguste Barthélemy (1796–1867) he published successful satirical pamphlets in verse, e.g. *Les Sidiennes* (1825), *La Villéliade, ou prise du château de Rivoli* (1826), a comico-heroic poem, and notably, after the July Revolution (q.v.), a weekly series, *La Némésis*, of invective verse. Lamartine's *Ode à Némésis* is a reply to one number of this which attacked him for prostituting his poetical gifts to politics.

Méry's many works include an epic poem, *Napoléon en Égypte* (1828), several plays and vaudevilles (alone or in collaboration), novels, and a number of lively short stories which deserve to be remembered. *La Chasse au chastre* (1853, q.v.) is one of the best of these.

Meschinot, JEAN (c. 1420–91), a poet of the school of the *rhétoriqueurs* (q.v.), employed in the military service of successive dukes of Brittany. He was the author of poems on moral, satirical, and love themes; also of political poems directed against Louis XI (*Innocent feint, tout fourré de malice*), and of a political allegory entitled *Les Lunettes des princes*.

Mesdames, see *Madame*.

Mesmer, FRIEDRICH ANTON (1733–1815), an Austrian doctor who originated the theory of animal magnetism or mesmerism. His thesis *De Planetarum influxa* sought to establish that the stars, by means of a force which permeated the universe, had an influence upon beings living upon the earth. Later, identifying this force with magnetism, he experimented in healing, by stroking the body with a magnet. He next claimed to be able to communicate the force himself and to heal by laying on of hands. He came to Paris in 1778, lectured, and held healing séances in luxurious, mysteriously-lit surroundings; and excited such a furore, despite accusations of charlatanism from the medical faculty, that the Government offered him a life annuity—not accepted—for his secret. His scientific pretensions were discredited later, and he died, forgotten, in Germany. His influence on Balzac may be noted. (Cf. *Gall*; *Lavater*.)

Message, Le, one of the 'Scènes de la vie privée' of Balzac's *Comédie humaine* (q.v.).

Messe de l'athée, La, one of the 'Scènes de la vie privée' of Balzac's *Comédie humaine* (q.v.).

Messidor, the tenth month of the Republican Calendar (q.v.). It ran from 20 June to 19 July.

Méténier, OSCAR, see *Alexis, Paul*.

Métiers, Livre des, a 13th-century collection of the regulations of trade guilds, by Étienne Boileau (q.v.).

Métra, François or (?) Olivier (*c.* 1714-86), was the anonymous author of a *Correspondance littéraire et secrète* published in Holland (1774-93) and reprinted with some alterations in London from 1787 under the title *Correspondance secrète politique et littéraire, ou Mémoires pour servir à l'histoire des cours, des sociétés et de la littérature en France depuis la mort de Louis XV.* It consists of gossipy comments, professing to be inside information, on political and literary events. Little is known about the author. He is said to have been a banker, at one time a correspondent of the King of Prussia, who got into trouble and fled to Holland, where he compiled his 'correspondance' from material supplied to him from Paris.

Metric system. In 1790 the *Assemblée constituante*, at the instance of Talleyrand (q.v.), decided that France should have an over-all system of weights and measures, thus ending the confusion due to variations, as between provinces, in systems and nomenclature. The new system was to be based on a scientifically measured unit (by later decision a fraction of the quadrant of the terrestrial meridian). Various scientific commissions were set to work, to frame the system, to determine the value of the basic unit (by measuring the arc of the meridian between Dunkirk and Mont Jany, near Barcelona), and to determine nomenclature. Following reports of these bodies a law of 10 December 1799 fixed the value of the basic unit, named *mètre*, at one ten-millionth part of the quadrant of the terrestrial meridian (i.e. 39·37 inches); and in 1801 the new system was officially introduced. A law of 4 July 1837 made it compulsory, to the exclusion of other systems, from 1 January 1840. It is now the official system in several other countries.

The *mètre*, the basic unit, is the unit of length. The other fundamental units are those of

(*a*) weight—*gramme*, i.e. the weight of a cubic centimetre of distilled water at the maximum density;

(*b*) surface—*mètre carré*;

(*c*) volume—*mètre cube*;

(*d*) capacity—the *litre* (one *décimètre cube*), used for liquids and grains, and the *stère* (one *mètre cube*) used for solids, such as firewood.

Métro, Le (LE MÉTROPOLITAIN DE PARIS), the system of underground electric railways which constitutes the main form of public passenger transport in Paris. The first line was opened in July 1900. By about 1950 there were fourteen lines zig-zagging in every direction seldom very far beneath, and occasionally above, street level. At some stations passengers can effect a *correspondance* from one line to another, a change which usually entails a very long walk. There are few seats in comparison with, for example, the London underground railways, but a solid mass of standing passengers can be accommodated.

Métromanie, La, a comedy in verse by Piron (q.v.), produced with much success in 1738. The theme is the good-humoured ridicule of poets (including the author himself) and poetasters, the hero being made at once comical and attractive.

Lucile is the daughter of Francaleu, a rhymester who tries to inflict his verses on anyone whom he can induce to hear them. Damis, a young man who has been sent to Paris to study law, has turned poet instead. His friend Dorante successfully woos Lucile with poems written by Damis, confesses the fraud, and retains her heart.

Francaleu seeks to marry Lucile to Damis, whom he admires as a brother poet, while he views Dorante with disfavour because the latter will not listen to his verses. But Damis has been carrying on an exchange of love verses in the *Mercure* with an unknown authoress, has pledged himself to her, and rejects Lucile. This unknown authoress turns out to be Francaleu himself (a hit at Voltaire who, with others, had been taken in by the verses of a certain Mlle de La Vigne, in reality the rhymester Desforges-Maillard). Dorante is reconciled to Francaleu and marries Lucile, while Damis remains the devotee of the Muses.

Metternich-Winneburg (1773-1859), CLEMENS WENZEL LOTHAR, PRINCE, the famous Austrian diplomat, and son of a diplomat, was born at Coblentz. His far-sighted policy was largely responsible for the overthrow of Napoleon. For more than thirty years after the Congress of Vienna (1814-15, q.v.) his diplomacy aimed at maintaining stability in Europe and the supremacy of Austria. He died at Vienna.

Meudon, CURÉ DE, Rabelais (q.v.).

Meung, JEAN DE, see *Jean de Meung.*

Meunier d'Angibault, Le (1845), by George Sand (q.v. para. 3), a novel of country life in which happily-timed catastrophes overcome obstacles of rank and fortune. A rich and avaricious farmer withdraws his opposition to his daughter's marriage with a poor but high-principled miller, and a proletarian but proud young lover listens to his heart and consents to marry an aristocratic but penniless widow. Stolen treasure bequeathed by a beggar to the miller, we learn in the last chapter, is to be used for founding a small community in which life will be simple, work hard, and profits shared.

Meyerbeer, JACQUES *or* GIACOMO (1791–1864), operatic composer, a German Jew by birth, highly popular in his own country, in Italy, and in France. His greatest successes—*Robert le diable* (1831), *Les Huguenots* (1836), *Le Prophète* (1849)—were composed for the Paris Opera and first performed there.

Meyerson, ÉMILE (1859–1933), one of the more important modern French philosophers, an anti-empiricist. His works include *Identité et Réalité* (1908), a fundamental statement of his views that, for example, hypothesis is a necessary preliminary of research; *De l'explication dans les sciences* (1921); *La Déduction relativiste* (1925); *Du cheminement de la pensée* (1931), an examination of various modern physical and mathematical conceptions of the nature of the universe.

Meysenbug, MALWIDA VON, see *Rolland, Romain; Monod, Gabriel.*

Mézeray, FRANÇOIS EUDES DE (1610–83), historian, born near Falaise in Normandy, author of a celebrated history of France down to 1598, published 1643–51, of especial interest in its later portion. He also wrote an *Abrégé chronologique* (1667) and a treatise *De l'origine des Français* (1682). He was admitted to the *Académie* in 1648, and succeeded Conrart as its perpetual secretary. He received a pension from Mazarin, which he subsequently lost in part, and finally altogether, under Colbert, in consequence of his criticism of the system of taxation.

Michaud, JOSEPH (1767–1839), publicist and historian, came to Paris from Savoy during the Revolution (1791), took to journalism, and was more than once in trouble over his freely expressed Royalist sympathies. His chief work, *Histoire des Croisades* (1812–22), which was a much enlarged and elaborated version of a preface ('Tableau historique des trois premières croisades') written for Mme Cottin's novel *Mathilde* (1805), did much to arouse interest in medieval history. He again augmented it (edition of 1840–1) after, at the age of sixty-two, visiting the scenes of the Crusades, when he wrote the interesting *Correspondance d'Orient* (1833–5). Michaud was associated with his brother Louis-Gabriel (1772–1858) in the publication of the *Biographie universelle* (q.v.).

Michaux, Henri (1899–), one of the most individual of contemporary French poets, born in Belgium, was educated partly, and lives, in France. The earliest of his many collections of poems and prose-poems belong to adventurous years of travel and by no means easy living, e.g. *Qui je fus* (1927), *Écuador* (1929), *Mes Propriétés* (1929), *Un Barbare en Asie* (1932). His later output includes *Voyage en grande carabagne* (1936), *Au pays de la magie* (1942), *Liberté d'action* (1945), *Épreuves, exorcismes* (1946). At its best the dialectical flight from reality which characterizes his work becomes a novel form of lyricism. It can be studied in his three volumes of selected poems, *Espace du dedans* (1944), *Ailleurs* (1948), *La Vie dans les plis* (1950).

Michel, FRANCISQUE-XAVIER (1809–87), born in Lyons, historian, wrote on various aspects of medieval life, e.g. *Chroniques anglo-normandes* (1836–40); *Théâtre français du moyen âge* (1839); *Recherches sur le commerce, la fabrication et l'usage des étoffes de soie d'or . . . pendant le moyen âge* (1852–4); *Les Écossais en France et les Français en Écosse* (1862), &c. It was Michel, in 1837, who edited the newly discovered Oxford manuscript of the *Chanson de Roland.*

Michel, GEORGES-ÉPHRAÏM, see *Mikhaël, Éphraïm.*

Michelet, JULES (1798–1874), historian, born in Paris, knew poverty in childhood, and toil, for his father was a printer beset by ill-fortune and needed the boy's help in the business. His parents sacrificed much to educate him but he repaid them brilliantly at school and at the university. In 1826 he became Professor of Ancient History at the *École préparatoire* (see *École normale supérieure*). He also taught philosophy, but before long he devoted himself wholly to medieval and modern history and began writing a history of France, his life's work. In this his appointment (1831) as Keeper of the National Archives afforded him endless opportunities for research among original documents.

L'Histoire de France is the most famous example of 19th-century romantic narrative history, a resuscitation of the past, picturesque, subjective, declamatory at times, but of high literary value. Underlying it is the philosophical conception that history is fundamentally a matter of the geographical distribution of peoples, with consequent racial distinctions, interactions, and antagonisms. This theory gives rise to the celebrated 'Tableau' in the second volume, describing France province by province, and seeing in physical and geographical features the influences responsible for variations in the character of the natives. The first six, and most famous, volumes of the History (1833–43) comprise the period from the Celtic origins to the Renaissance. Volume ii has a brilliant evocation of the Middle Ages, volume v a moving study of Saint Joan of Arc.

From 1838 Michelet held the Chair of History at the Collège de France. His ardent democratic sympathies were increasingly evident in his lectures, and he interrupted the sequence of his History to write the seven volumes of *La Révolution française* (1847–53) which depict, with imaginative insight and democratic fervour, men, moods, and events in France between 1789 (*États généraux*) and 1794 (fall of Robespierre). Other works of this period include: *Du prêtre, de la femme et de la famille* (1845, a pamphlet) and *Le Peuple* (1846).

Michelet was one of many who saw in the February (1848) Revolution the realization, and in the events of 1849–51 the end, of their dreams of liberty. His refusal to swear allegiance to the Second Empire lost him his posts at the Archives and the Collège de France. Thereafter he lived quietly in the country, completed his History (*Renaissance et temps modernes*, 1855–67, 11 vols., from the

Renaissance to the reigns of Louis XV and XVI), wrote *La Bible de l'humanité* (1864, q.v.), on the history of religion, and developed an interest in natural science which inspired several works in a lyrical vein: *L'Oiseau* (1856); *L'Insecte* (1858); *La Mer* (1861); *La Montagne* (1868). His earlier historical writings include: *Précis de l'histoire moderne* (1827); *Histoire romaine* (1831); *Introduction à l'histoire universelle* (1831); and *Principes de la philosophie de l'histoire* (1827), a translation of *La Scienza nuova* of the Italian philosopher Vico, whose theories, like those of Herder, had greatly influenced him. His reminiscences of childhood and adolescence (*Ma Jeunesse*, 1884) and his *Journal* (1888) of the years 1818–29 are of great interest.

Michel Strogoff, see *Verne, Jules*.

Micromégas (1752), a tale by Voltaire, possibly begun as early as 1739 and completed in Berlin. The theme is the relativity of all dimensions and the insignificance in the universe of the earth and mankind. The idea is derived from Cyrano de Bergerac's *Histoire comique* and Swift's *Gulliver*.

Micromégas, an inhabitant of the star Sirius, 120,000 feet tall, accompanied by an inhabitant of Saturn, 6,000 feet tall, visits the Earth. They converse with a party of philosophers just returned from the Polar regions whom they discover in the Baltic (see *Maupertuis*). They hear with horror of the massacres in which futile quarrels have engaged the human race, mere insects as they regard its members. They are surprised to find that while the philosophers have accurate information on physical questions such as the distance of the stars, they can only give vague and conflicting answers when asked what is meant by 'soul' and 'spirit', and are amused to hear the theologians maintain that the whole universe exists for the benefit of man. In the Saturnian, who draws erroneous inferences from what he observes, Voltaire satirized Fontenelle.

Midi, Canal du, see *Colbert*.

Mignard, PIERRE (1610–95), a distinguished painter of the reign of Louis XIV, head of the Académie de Peinture. His works include the famous fresco, *La Gloire des bienheureux*, on the cupola of the Val-de-Grâce (q.v.)

which inspired Molière's poem *La Gloire du Val-de-grâce*; also portraits of Molière, Mme de Sévigné, and Mme de Grignan.

Migne, JACQUES-PAUL (1800–75), theologian, editor of a large number of theological works, especially the great *Patrologiae cursus completus*, a collection of patristic writings (Latin series, 1844–55; Greek series, 1856–61) numbering over 300 volumes.

Mignet, FRANÇOIS-AUGUSTE (1796–1884), historian, born and educated at Aix-en-Provence, came to Paris in 1821 with his friend Adolphe Thiers (q.v.), became a political journalist (liberal), and in 1830 helped to found the *National* (q.v.), the newspaper associated with the July Revolution. After this he gave up politics for history, his great interest, and was appointed Keeper of the Archives at the Ministère des Affaires étrangères, a post which facilitated his researches. His works—clear, sober, and factual—include: *Histoire de la Révolution française* (1824, still recommended for study); *Négociations relatives à la succession d'Espagne sous Louis XIV* (1835–42, a collection of diplomatic documents, with a notable introduction) and other studies of Spanish and French relations; *Marie Stuart* (1851); and the interesting *Mémoires historiques* (1843), papers read between 1836 and 1843 before the *Académie des sciences morales et politiques*, of which he was Secretary.

Mikhaël, ÉPHRAÏM, pseudonym of Georges-Éphraïm Michel (1866–90), born at Toulouse, a young Symbolist writer (see *Symbolisme*) whose poems, first printed in small reviews, were collected in *L'Automne* (1886). He also wrote poetic dramas, notably the lyrical drama *Briséis* (1892, in collaboration with Catulle Mendès, q.v.).

Milet, JACQUES (c. 1428–66), author of the *Mystère de la destruction de Troye la grant* (1450–2), a work containing some 30,000 verses, much admired by contemporaries.

Mille et une nuits, Les, title of the first French translation (1704–17) of the *Arabian Nights*, see *Galland, Antoine*. The fuller translation of 1898–1904, by Dr. J.-C. Mardrus (q.v.), was entitled *Mille nuits et une nuit*.

Millet, JEAN-FRANÇOIS (1814–75), an artist famous for his studies of peasant life. He lived and worked mainly at Barbizon.

Millevoye, CHARLES-HUBERT (1782–1816), poet, born at Abbeville (Somme), was for a time a bookseller's clerk in Paris. He published *Poésies* (1800) and thereafter won literary prizes and some celebrity, notably with *Élégies* (1814, in 3 books) which were a faint anticipation of Romantic melancholy and response to nature. *La Chute des feuilles* and *Le Poète mourant* from this volume are favourite anthology pieces. His *Œuvres* (1814–16, 5 vols.; re-edited and augmented 1865, with a preface by Sainte-Beuve) reprinted the *Élégies* and also included an epic poem, *Charlemagne à Pavie*, translations of Virgil's *Bucolics*, and *Ballades et Romances*, again of a Romantic turn.

Millevoye, a consumptive, was himself a *poète mourant* for many years.

Milly, the small family property near Mâcon, where the poet Lamartine spent his youth. It came into his possession about 1830 and was sold by him in 1861 when he was in money difficulties. It is often described in his writings, e.g. in the poems *Milly ou la Terre natale* (*Harmonies poétiques et religieuses*) and *La Vigne et la Maison*, also in his autobiography, *Les Confidences*.

Milosz, OSCAR VENCESLAS DE LUBICZ (1877–1939), poet, a Lithuanian by birth but naturalized French in 1930, came to Paris with his parents and was educated there. Between 1919 and 1928 he was Resident Minister for Lithuania in Paris. His works, characterized by a mystical religiosity, include: poems (*Le Poème des décadences*, 1899; *Les Sept Solitudes*, 1906; *Les Éléments*, 1911; *La Confession de Lémuel*, 1920; *Poèmes, florilège 1895–1927*, 1929); works in prose and verse published between 1910 and 1927 and termed variously *romans*, *mystères*, *philosophie*; also collections of Lithuanian tales and fables.

Mimi, the consumptive heroine of Murger's (q.v.) *Scènes de la vie de Bohème*.

Mimi Pinson (1843), a tale by Alfred de Musset, see *Pinson, Mademoiselle Mimi*.

Minerve française, La, a literary and political miscellany, published irregularly to evade the censorship, was founded in 1818 by a group of writers, including Béranger and Benjamin Constant (qq.v.) who had contributed to *Le Mercure de France* (see *Mercure* *galant*). Its objects were the spread of knowledge, the furtherance of a liberal spirit, and the breaking down of political and literary prejudices. It was a prosperous and influential publication but succumbed eventually to the censorship (1820).

Minerve littéraire, La (1820–2), a literary review edited by Mme Dufresnoy (1765–1825), woman of letters and minor poetess. It was opposed to the new literary doctrines of the Romantics (see *Romantisme*). Senancour, usually considered a precursor of the Romantic Movement on account of his novel *Obermann* (q.v.), contributed criticism of a 'fort peu romantique' nature.

Minotaure (1933–8), a literary review, published works by the *Surréalistes* (see *Surréalisme*). There were eleven numbers.

Miomandre, FRANCIS DE (1880–   ), contemporary novelist, author of *Écrit sur de l'eau* (1908); *Le Veau d'or et la vache enragée* (1917), a good example of his many novels of Provence; *Direction Étoile* (1937), a fantasy with the Paris Métro (q.v.) for setting; &c.

Mirabeau, HONORÉ-GABRIEL DE RIQUETTI, COMTE DE (1749–91), born at the Château de Bignon, near Sens, eldest son of the following and a member of the petty nobility of Provence, was one of the great Revolutionary statesmen and orators. As a youth he led a violent and immoral life, fettered by debts and continually in revolt against the harsh control of his father, who more than once had him imprisoned by means of *lettres de cachet* (q.v.). During one such period, at the Fort de Joux, near Pontarlier, he met (*c.* 1775), and eventually escaped to Holland with, Marie-Thérèse de Ruffey, the young wife of the septuagenarian marquis de Monnier. In spring 1777 the lovers were arrested. He was sent to the prison of Vincennes (q.v.), she to a convent at Gien. He wrote to her almost daily from prison, letters which are a mixture of passion, literary criticism, hints for the care of the health during pregnancy, advice on the best way of making the hair grow (it should be washed every day, in *tepid* water if there is any fear of catching cold, and *of course* it should be dried afterwards!), plans for a future career, and fulminations against his father. (These *Lettres écrites du donjon de Vincennes* 1792, several times re-edited, also

included letters to his father and to family friends.) While at Vincennes, too, Mirabeau studied prodigiously and wrote numerous essays on politics and finance, the best known including *Des Lettres de cachet et des prisons d'état* (1782), *Dénonciation de l'agiotage* (1787), &c.

His public career, with the way thus prepared, began (May 1789) when he was returned to the *États Généraux* (q.v.) as *Député du Tiers État* for Aix-en-Provence. His notoriety, and a reputation for venality, had preceded him, but from the outset he imposed himself upon his fellow-Deputies by his powers of oratory, his political genius, and his remarkable gift for clarifying the most complicated situation in a few words. From May to July 1789 his *Lettres du comte de Mirabeau à ses commettants*, a vivid, almost day-to-day account of the Revolution, kept his electors in touch with events. He also founded and edited *Le Courrier de Paris* (q.v.).

Mirabeau had very definite views on the necessity for a constitutional government, with the rights of the people fully recognized, but with the king at its head. The fact that in 1790 he was receiving payment from court sources has caused it to be said that his enormous debts, due to his dissolute life, had something to do with his conviction. In any case, his popularity gradually waned, although until the last he could, by sheer force of oratory, carry his way against the most reluctant Assembly. His death on 2 April 1791, the violent result of excesses of work and pleasure, caused general consternation and he was given a public funeral. In later years opinion turned against him and his remains were removed from the Panthéon.

He was a man of imposing physical stature and (at first sight) repellent ugliness. His face was swollen and pitted with smallpox, his carriage ungainly, and his manner gauche. But he had a beautiful voice and, when he chose, such charm that he could soon make people forget their first sentiments of repulsion. His chief writings and speeches are contained in *Œuvres de Mirabeau: Les Écrits; les Discours* (1912 and 1921, ed. L. Lumet).

Mirabeau, VICTOR DE RIQUETTI, MARQUIS DE (1715–89), father of the more famous comte de Mirabeau (see above), combined the feudal chief with the revolutionary theorist. He was an ardent opponent of the *philosophes* and a supporter of religion, at the same time an enemy of priests and financiers, and an advocate of social reforms. The liberal views expressed in his *Théorie de l'impôt* (1761) caused him to be imprisoned and then banished to his country estates. In 1756 he published *L'Ami des hommes ou Traité de la population*, and in 1763 *La Philosophie rurale*, treatises of political economy supporting the view of Quesnay (q.v.) that the wealth of a nation resides in its land. He was a close friend of Vauvenargues.

Miracles, medieval dramas, in which the chief incident is the miraculous intervention of the Virgin Mary or of a saint. The chief surviving examples are contained in a collection of forty *Miracles de Notre-Dame par personnages*, probably of the 14th century. They are little dramas (1,000 to 3,000 lines) relating to the life of the nobility, of the people, or of ecclesiastics, or based on religious or national legends, generally painful and melodramatic in character and realistic in details, all marked by the intervention of the Virgin to save the penitent who appeals to her. In spite of the devout character of these Miracles, the Church is treated in them with great freedom, and ecclesiastics (including the Pope), as well as kings and emperors, are frequently shown in an unfavourable light. The authors of these Miracles are unknown and their subjects are drawn from various sources. They are written in rhymed octosyllabic couplets, each speech ending with a short line rhyming with the first line of the following speech. A short sermon, usually in prose, forms part of the majority. *Miracles* seem usually to have been performed by fraternities known as *puys* (q.v.) at solemn festivals in honour of the Virgin.

Miracles de la Sainte Vierge, see *Religious Writings* (medieval period).

Miracles de Notre-Dame, see *Miracles.*

Mirame, see *Richelieu, Cardinal de.*

Mirari vos, a Papal Encyclical of 15 August 1832 signifying disapproval of Lamennais (q.v.), his writings, and his claims for liberty of conscience and of the Press.

Mirbeau, OCTAVE (1848–1917), author of *Le Jardin des supplices* (1898), *Le Journal d'une femme de chambre* (1900), *Les Vingt-et-un Jours d'un neurasthénique* (1901). He also wrote one notable play (*Les Affaires sont les affaires*, 1903), a bitter satire on an unscrupulous financier who deals ruthlessly with his financial associates and with his family.

Mirèio (1859), an epic of rural life (in the Provençal language) by the poet Mistral (q.v.), usually considered his masterpiece.

Mirèio (Provençal for 'Mireille') loves a penniless basket-maker, but her parents, wealthy farmers, refuse to countenance this. She sets off on foot on a pilgrimage to the tiny church of Les Saintes-Maries-de-la-Mer, across the solitary plain of the Camargue, hoping that a miracle may dispel her parents' wrath and restore her happiness. Her parents and Vincent, her lover, follow and find her dying of exhaustion and sunstroke.

The story was used by Gounod for his opera *Mireille*.

Miroir de Mariage, see *Deschamps.*

Misanthrope, Le, a comedy by Molière, produced in 1666.

The plot is very slight and the play is little more than a finished portrait of Alceste, an honest cantankerous gentleman, exasperated by the perfidies and flatteries, and even the minor hypocritical conventions, of polite society, who sets himself uncompromisingly to attack them. Contrasted with him we have a courtier (of whose bad verses Alceste does not hesitate to tell him his frank opinion), a couple of ridiculous fops, and his friend Philinte, an intelligent man who admits the corruption of society, but prefers to accept its rules and make the best of them. By a stroke of the author's genius, Alceste is in love with Célimène, a back-biting coquette: he is conscious of her faults but cannot break his chains. The other female characters are Arsinoé, a pretended prude, who designs to capture Alceste for her husband and with whom Célimène has an entertaining passage of arms (III. v); and the gentle, sincere Éliante. The heartlessness of Célimène is exposed, but Arsinoé fails to win Alceste. The latter, finally infuriated by his defeat in a lawsuit where he has justice on his side, decides to abandon society and live in solitude. Even now he asks Célimène to accompany him, but she cannot renounce the world, and Alceste departs in indignation.

The play was not very successful, but was admired by persons of judgement. Boileau considered it Molière's greatest comedy. It suggested certain scenes for Wycherley's *The Plain Dealer*.

Misérables, Les (1862), a novel by Victor Hugo. In the year 1815 Jean Valjean is released after nineteen years of penal servitude. Once a slow-witted, kindly peasant (condemned for stealing a loaf of bread to feed his starving nephews), he is now an astute criminal. He attempts to rob the saintly Monseigneur Myriel, but meets with such kindness that his heart begins to soften. Unfortunately, another theft, no sooner committed than it fills him with remorse, renders him liable for rearrest and a life sentence.

Calling himself 'Monsieur Madeleine', he sets up in business in a small town in Northern France. He flourishes, becomes mayor, and is revered as the benefactor of the countryside. He is kind to Fantine, an unfortunate woman of the town, and promises to rescue her illegitimate daughter Cosette from foster-parents living near Paris, the rascally inn-keeper Thénardier and his wife. At this moment he learns that a prisoner at the local assizes is charged with being the wanted criminal Jean Valjean. After a struggle of conscience he attends the trial and confesses his identity. He is placed in the custody of Javert, a police-agent who has for some time suspected him. Once again he is sent to the convict settlement at Toulon, but within a year he escapes in such a manner that his death is presumed. Now he fulfils his promise to Fantine, and rescues Cosette. He takes her—a half-starved, terrorized child—to Paris and lives in semi-hiding. Cosette grows into a care-free creature for whom the past is a blank and who never questions that Jean Valjean is her father. One day Javert the police-agent, now also in Paris, meets and recognizes Jean Valjean. After an exciting chase Valjean escapes with Cosette to a convent where he remains for some years as gardener, while Cosette is educated by the nuns. Once again, as 'Monsieur Fauchelevent', he ventures into the world. Cosette is now a beautiful young girl and Valjean is, seemingly, a venerable citizen. They live

on money hidden by Valjean in former days. Cosette falls in love with a young student, Marius, who has left a wealthy home to become a democrat. Marius is wounded fighting at the barricades during the July Revolution (see *Revolutions*, II and IIa). Jean Valjean secures his body and escapes with him through a manhole into the great sewer of Paris. After a terrifying progress he emerges, deposits the unconscious Marius at his grandfather's house, and disappears. Marius's grandfather consents to his marriage with Cosette, thinking her to be the daughter of the respectable 'Monsieur Fauchelevent'. After the marriage Jean Valjean tells Marius that he is an ex-convict and not Cosette's father. Marius, shocked, and knowing neither the whole story nor the fact that he owes Jean Valjean his life, acquiesces in the old man's plan to disappear gradually from their lives. Eventually, his eyes are opened and there is a happy reconciliation, but in the meantime Jean Valjean, sorrowing for Cosette, has lost the will to live, and his death follows.

This synopsis leaves several complications of the plot untouched, e.g. the reappearance of Javert and Jean Valjean's struggles to elude him; the after-career of the Thénardiers and their connexion with Marius; the touching episode of the gay, heroic little guttersnipe Gavroche; the secret society of Marius's student friends, &c. The book is made still more unwieldy by the continual insertion of long historical, political, or sociological dissertations. Interesting ones are the description of the battle of Waterloo (in the 2nd part); the study of the end of the Restoration period and the figure of Louis-Philippe (3rd part); the famous description of the Paris sewers (5th part); and numerous pictures of Paris and Parisian underworld life.

Miserere, see *Charité and Miserere*.

Miss Harriet, the name-tale of a collection (1884) by Guy de Maupassant, developed from an earlier version, *Miss Hastings*, published in 1883 in *Le Gaulois*.

An artist on holiday in Normandy finds himself the only other lodger at an inn with an elderly English spinster, a gauche, grotesque creature who gradually thaws under his attentions. Suddenly, one day, he realizes that she has taken his casual, amused kindness

and semi-flirtatious teasing as meant seriously. At dinner that evening he tells the innkeeper that he must leave the next day. Later,
having gone out for a walk, he turns from
a few moments' hearty kissing of a farm
servant to discern Miss Harriet running dis-
tractedly off into the dusk. Next morning
she does not appear. Later in the day her
body is found in the well.

Missions. In literature dealing with the
Restoration years (i.e. those following
1815) the reference is usually to one of the
practices adopted by the Church to bring
about a return to religion. Small bands of
priests of the re-established Jesuit Order (see
Jésuites) used to settle for some weeks in
various parts of the country, holding services
and meetings. Books containing the atheistic
and philosophical doctrines of the 18th
century were burnt, and new churches were
founded to expiate the crimes of the
Revolution.

Mississippi Company, see *Law.*

Mistral, FRÉDÉRIC (1830–1914), Provençal
poet, is perhaps best remembered as the
leader (in association with Joseph Roumanille, q.v.) of the mid-nineteenth-century
movement ('le Félibrige', q.v.) for the revival of the Provençal language and literature. He was born in Provence of wealthy
farming stock, and acquired from his mother
a great knowledge of Provençal customs
and legends. His original writings (in
Provençal) included *Mirèio* (1859, q.v.), a
poem of rural life; *Calendau* (1867), the ex-
poits of a Provençal fisherman; *Lis Isclo
d'or* (1875), lyrics; *Nerto* (1884), a narrative
poem based on a medieval legend; *Lou
Pouèmo dóu Rose* (i.e. *Le Poème du Rhône,*
1897); and *Lis Oulivado* (1912), songs of the
olive-harvest). He spent many years compiling *Le Trésor du Félibrige* (1878–86), a
dictionary of Provençal words, proverbs,
legends, &c.

Except for a stay in Paris in 1858 Mistral
lived almost wholly in Provence. His
example and encouragement did much to
promote a revival of Catalan literature.

Mithouard, ADRIEN (1864–1919), author
of symbolical and religious poetry: *Le
Récital mystique* (1893), *Le Pauvre Pêcheur*
(1899), *Les Frères marcheurs* (1902); and of
Le Tourment de l'unité (1901), *Traité de*

l'Occident (1903), *Les Pas sur la terre* (1908),
Les Marches de l'Occident (1910), collected
essays, often first published in the review
L'Occident (q.v.) which he helped to found.
The general theme of these was the cultural
and aesthetic importance of Western Europe
with, as its centre, France.

Mithridate, a tragedy by Racine, produced
in 1673, based on the history of Mithridates
VI, the great enemy of Rome, with considerable alteration of the facts.

The scene is Nymphaeum in the Tauric
Chersonese. The aged Mithridates has become enamoured of Monime, a young
Greek lady of Ephesus, has obtained her
consent to marriage, and has sent her the
royal diadem as pledge. She has come to
Nymphaeum. Called away to resist Pompey,
Mithridates has been defeated and is reported
killed. Of his two sons (by different mothers)
Pharnaces favours the Romans, Xiphares
inherits his father's undying hatred of them.
Both are in love with Monime. Pharnaces,
whom Monime hates, at once on the report
of his father's death presses his suit and demands an immediate marriage. Monime
appeals to Xiphares for protection. A quarrel breaks out between the brothers, and
at that moment Mithridates unexpectedly
arrives. He hears of Pharnaces' action and
is incensed thereby, but remains ignorant
that Xiphares also loves Monime. To test
Pharnaces, he expounds to his two sons his
great project for the invasion of Italy itself;
Pharnaces is to marry a Parthian princess
and thus secure the Parthian alliance. From
this Pharnaces endeavours to dissuade his
father, while Xiphares eagerly supports it.
The king orders Pharnaces to start immediately for Parthia. Pharnaces demurs, thus
confirming his father's suspicions, and is
arrested. He thereupon reveals that Xiphares
also loves Monime. Mithridates, at first
incredulous, discovers from Monime herself, by a stratagem, that it is true and that
she returns Xiphares' love. She now refuses
to marry the king, preferring death. At this
moment Pharnaces provokes a mutiny and
leads a Roman force against his father. The
latter sends poison to Monime to take, but
hard pressed by the Romans stabs himself.
Xiphares drives the Romans back and rescues
the dying king, who has only time to save
Monime's life by a counter-order, to bless

Xiphares, and bestow Monime on him, before he dies.

Monime is one of the most charming female characters in Racine's plays, tender and modest, yet proud and intrepid when her honour is threatened.

Mockel, ALBERT (1866–1945), Symbolist poet and critic, a Belgian, lived until *c.* 1890 at Liège, where he founded *La Wallonie,* the well-known Symbolist review (q.v., and see *Symbolisme*). Thereafter he lived in Paris. His works include: *Chantefable un peu naïve* (1891), a 'symphonic' poem in *vers libre,* and *Propos de littérature* (1894), studies of Symbolist poets.

Modeste Mignon (1844), one of the 'Scènes de la vie privée' of Balzac's *Comédie humaine* (q.v.). In the year 1829 Modeste Mignon and her blind mother remain at Le Havre with the faithful M. and Mme Dumay while M. Charles Mignon is overseas seeking to rebuild his bankrupt fortunes. The romantic Modeste writes under an assumed name to the famous poet Canalis. Canalis is blasé and tired of anonymous adorers, but his secretary, Ernest de la Brière, uses his name on an impulse and replies to Modeste, and soon love-letters are exchanged. Modeste contrives to see her correspondent 'Canalis' (in reality Ernest). She tells him that her father is on his way home with a large fortune and advises him to visit M. Mignon in Paris and get his consent to their marriage. The real Canalis, learning what has happened, regrets having let slip a fortune. M. Mignon, having heard the whole story from Ernest, who would gladly marry Modeste without a portion, invites the real and the sham Canalis to Le Havre so that Modeste may choose her own husband. A third suitor is the impoverished duc d'Hérouville, a well-meaning nonentity. Modeste is furious with Ernest for having tricked her but she is soon impelled to contrast his genuine worth and lovableness with the egotism and cynical parade of Canalis. The tale ends with Canalis firmly tied again to the apron-strings of an elderly mistress, the Duke rebuffed as a suitor but kept as a friend, and Modeste and Ernest looking forward to a long and happy wedded life. Balzac is at his best in describing the Mignons' family circle, the evening whist parties, and the atmosphere of pro-tective affection which surrounds his headstrong young heroine.

Mohl, JULES (1800–76), an orientalist of German birth (Stuttgart), studied and lived in France and later adopted French nationality. He was Professor of Persian at the Collège de France (q.v.), also editor and translator of Firdusi (*Le Livre des rois,* 1838–78). In 1847 he married Mary Clarke (q.v.), an Englishwoman living in Paris, a well-known intellectual hostess of her time.

Moineau, GEORGES, see *Courteline, Georges.*

Moïse, a famous poem by Alfred de Vigny, contained in his *Poèmes antiques et modernes* (1826, q.v.). He wrote it in 1823.

Moissy, ALEXANDRE-GUILLAUME MOUSLIER DE (1712–77), born in Paris, man of letters of little merit but sometimes mentioned as one of the earliest writers of *proverbes dramatiques* (q.v.), usually with intent to instruct young persons, e.g. *Les Jeux de la petite Thalie ou Nouveaux petits drames dialogués sur des proverbes propres à former les mœurs des enfants et des jeunes personnes depuis l'âge de cinq ans jusqu'à vingt* (1769). His own mœurs left something to be desired, for he was a furious gambler. He died in poverty.

Molé, La Conférence, a political and debating society in the form of a miniature parliament constituted in 1832 by the statesman Louis-Mathieu Molé (1781–1855) with the object of training young barristers for political life. In 1877 it was merged with a similar society, the *Conférence Tocqueville,* and became the *Conférence Molé-Tocqueville.*

Molière, JEAN-BAPTISTE POQUELIN, *known as* (1622–73), the great comic dramatist, was born in Paris, the son of Jean Poquelin, a well-to-do upholsterer attached to the court, who ended his life in poverty. Molière (to use the theatrical name that he adopted in 1644) was educated at the Jesuit Collège de Clermont (where, according to modern scholarship, he did *not* receive lessons in philosophy from Gassendi). In 1643, in association with Joseph and Madeleine Béjart and some others, he founded the *Illustre Théâtre* in Paris and became an actor. The company having been financially unsuccessful left Paris and toured the provinces from 1645 to 1658; Molière composed for it slight pieces or sketches for improvised comedies in the Italian manner, of some of which the titles survive and in two cases (*Le Médecin volant* and *La Jalousie du Barbouillé*) the doubtful text. His first plays of some importance were *L'Étourdi* (1655) and *Le Dépit amoureux* (1656; for the plot of these plays and those mentioned below, see under their titles). In October 1658 his company settled in Paris in the Théâtre du Petit-Bourbon (part of the Louvre, cf. *Comédie-Française*), granted to him by the king. Here was produced in 1659 Molière's earliest comedy of manners, *Les Précieuses ridicules*, the first of a number of plays in which he held up to ridicule the various types of folly, oddity, pedantry, or vice which he observed in the society around him. It was very successful. In 1660 it was followed by *Sganarelle* and in 1661, after the company's transfer to the Palais-Royal, by *Dom Garcie de Navarre* (a failure) and *L'École des maris*. In the same year 1661 he hurriedly prepared, for a splendid entertainment which Fouquet was to give for the king at his country mansion of Vaux, *Les Fâcheux*, the first of the *comédies-ballets* (q.v.) which proved very popular at court and which form a considerable proportion of his works. In 1662 he married Armande Béjart, a younger sister of the Madeleine Béjart above mentioned (and *not* her daughter); the marriage was not a happy one. Later in the same year appeared *L'École des femmes*, notable for its important psychological element; it was much attacked and showed that while Molière had many friends and supporters, including the king himself and Boileau, he also had many enemies, especially rival authors, whom his unsparing ridicule had called up. Against the latter he defended himself in the *Critique de l'École des femmes* and the *Impromptu de Versailles* (both 1663). In 1664 appeared *Le Mariage forcé* and *La Princesse d'Élide*, and three acts of *Le Tartuffe* (or possibly a three-act version), one of his greatest masterpieces, were performed. In consequence of the opposition of the devout (see under *Tartuffe*) the public performance of the play was long prohibited. The interdict was finally removed in 1669 and the comedy proved extremely successful despite its condemnation by Bourdaloue and adverse criticism by Bossuet. Meanwhile Molière had produced *Dom Juan* (1665); this too gave rise to

violent attacks, and it was removed from the repertory. Then followed *L'Amour médecin* (1665); *Le Misanthrope* (another masterpiece) and *Le Médecin malgré lui* (1666); three slighter pieces in the winter of 1666–7, *Mélicerte*, *Pastorale comique*, and *Le Sicilien*; and *Amphitryon* (1668). Molière's company had been passing through hard times, but this last play met with considerable success. It was followed in the same year by *L'Avare* and *George Dandin*; by *Monsieur de Pourceaugnac* in 1669; *Le Bourgeois gentilhomme* and *Les Amants magnifiques* (part of the *Divertissement royal*) in 1670; *Psyché* (not wholly by Molière), *Les Fourberies de Scapin*, and *La Comtesse d'Escarbagnas* in 1671; *Les Femmes savantes* in 1672; and *Le Malade imaginaire* in 1673. During the performance of this last comedy Molière, who was taking the part of Argan, fell mortally ill and died soon after. Some difficulty was made by the clergy about his interment, and he was buried at night without pomp.

Molière may be said to have created modern French comedy by giving it a serious basis, where there had previously been little but farces and comedies of intrigue on Italian or Spanish models. His genius lay in his ability to combine profound observation of human nature in its complexity and in its foibles with the power of presenting these in their amusing aspect, that is to say short of the point where they turn to tragedy (though some of his greatest comedies reach the boundary). His lighter pieces, on the other hand, shine by their gaiety and absurdity. He was thus a master both of high comedy and farce. (Yet he is said by his familiars to have been of a melancholy humour.) He has, moreover, left a gallery of portraits of a wide variety of types of 17th-century society: noblemen of the court and provinces; doctors, lawyers, merchants, and their wives; servants and peasants (it is singular that financiers are not included). The theme of his more serious comedies as a whole is the exposure of hypocrisy and affectation in all their forms. He borrowed framework and episodes of plays from many sources, but these borrowings are no more than the rude materials which he converted into works of art. His comedy differs from that of Shakespeare, broadly speaking, in that he took types, rather than individual characters, as his subject. He has been criticized for defects of literary style, which were frequently due to hasty composition. Boileau reproached him for descending to buffoonery. His plots are slight and his denouements are often clumsy or conventional; for he was less interested in these than in the exposition of character. The English dramatists of the Restoration, D'Avenant, Dryden, Wycherley, Vanbrugh, &c., borrowed freely from Molière's plays, though his finer qualities were beyond their imitation.

Molinet, Jean (1435–1507), chronicler and poet, born in the Pas-de-Calais, entered the service of the dukes of Burgundy and became the continuator (to 1506) of the chronicle of Chastellain (q.v.). He was also a poet of the school of the *rhétoriqueurs* (q.v.) highly esteemed by his contemporaries, and author of a treatise, *L'Art de rhétorique* (i.e. poetry as then understood).

Molinier, Auguste, see *Sources de l'histoire de France.*

Molinistes, followers of Luis Molina (1535–1600), a Spanish Jesuit, whose teaching aimed at conciliating free will with the doctrines of grace and divine prescience. The Molinists in France, who included the Père de la Chaise (q.v.), confessor of Louis XIV, were in conflict with the Jansenists in the latter part of that monarch's reign.

For the followers of Molinos, known also as *Molinosistes,* see *Quietism.*

Monarchie de juillet, La [the July Monarchy], the reign of Louis-Philippe (q.v.), which began (1830) after the July Revolution and ended (1848) with the February Revolution (see *Revolutions,* II, IIa; III, IIIa).

Moncade, the hero of *L'Homme à bonnes fortunes* by Baron (q.v.). Also the name of the hero in d'Allainval's *L'École des bourgeois.*

Moncey, Bon-Adrien-Jannot de, one of Napoleon's marshals (see *Maréchal de l'Empire*).

Moncrif, François-Augustin Paradis de (1687–1770), a witty writer, popular in his day, a friend of Voltaire, secretary to d'Argenson and later reader to the queen. He was the author of comedies, tales, and pleasant *chansons*; his *Aventures de Zéloïde et d'Amanzarifdine* (1714) was an Indian

tale, and his *Histoire des chats* (1727) an erudite pleasantry.

Mondain, Le, a satire in verse by Voltaire, in praise of the luxury of the age, published in 1736. In the *Défense du Mondain* (1737) the author protested against the hypocritical censure of pleasure.

Monde comme il va, Le, see *Babouc.*

Monde où l'on s'ennuie, Le, a comedy, see *Pailleron.*

Mondory, Guillaume Desgilberts (17th c.), the chief actor in the company known as the *Comédiens du Prince d'Orange* which produced Corneille's earlier plays (see *Theatres and theatre companies,* para. 2). He was noted for the energy and grandeur of his acting. One of his most successful parts was Herod in Tristan's *Marianne.*

Monet, Claude-Oscar, French Impressionist painter, see *Impressionnisme.*

Money. The money of account, that is to say the terms in which values and monetary transactions were recorded, was in France completely distinct, from the 10th to the 18th century, from the money in actual circulation. The origin of this money of account (as indeed ultimately of the English £ s. d.) was the division by Charlemagne of the pound of silver (*libra argenti, livre*) into 20 *solidi* (*sols, sous*), and each *solidus* into twelve *denarii* (*deniers*). Though there were originally coins corresponding to these *sols* and *deniers,* from the time of the Capetian kings the terms *livres, sols,* and *deniers* ceased to signify their original weights of bullion, and the coins actually minted were given a great variety of names, such as *franc, écu, denier, liard* (see para. 5). The value of these coins, however, was defined by the government of the day in terms of *livres, sols,* and *deniers* of the money of account (which retained their primitive relation to each other), and this system prevailed until the Revolution.

(2) But the money of account after the break-up of the Carolingian empire was not uniform over France, and the *livres, sols,* and *deniers* are spoken of under various designations, Parisis, Tournois, Angevins, Poitevins, &c. Of these the first two were the most important, the *livre tournois* (originally current at Tours) being in general use in the south

of France, while the *livre parisis* prevailed in the domains of the Capetian kings. After the incorporation of Languedoc in the royal territory, these two moneys of account were retained side by side, the *livre parisis* and its subdivisions being valued one-fourth higher than the *tournois*. The *livre parisis* gradually went out of use and was finally abolished by Louis XIV (1667); after this the *livre tournois* was alone retained.

(3) In the course of its history the *livre* was subjected to a fairly continuous process of depreciation. What the precise weight of Charlemagne's *libra argenti* was is not known, but from a value of perhaps some 7,000 grains of silver the *livre* fell to less than one-fourth of this by the time of Louis IX, and by the 18th century to the value of about 70 grains. The reason of this depreciation is to be found chiefly in the advantage that the kings derived from assigning an ever higher value, in terms of the money of account, to particular weights of bullion constituting the currency of their realm, thus facilitating the discharge of their obligations. The counterpart of this appreciation of the currency was, of course, the depreciation of the money of account in terms of bullion.

(4) The distinction between currency and money of account was swept away at the Revolution and replaced by the modern system under which the mint merely impresses a stamp on bullion to authenticate the weight of the coins it strikes, charging (except in the case of token coins) only the expense of so doing. A law of 28 Thermidor An III (15 Aug. 1795), which introduced the decimal system into French currency, reintroduced the franc as a currency unit, divided into 10 *décimes* and the *décime* into 10 *centimes*. It was a silver coin, its weight being fixed at 5 grammes (77 grains) with a fineness of nine parts silver to one of alloy. This system was confirmed by another law of 17 Germinal An XI (7 April 1803). Neither weight nor fineness varied much during the 19th century, though under Napoleon III the fineness was a little less.

(5) The following monetary terms occur more or less frequently in French literature:

Franc, the name given to various coins from early times. Under Jean le Bon it was a gold coin bearing the legend 'Francorum Rex' (whence its name), equivalent to the *livre tournois*. It was reintroduced as a silver coin under Henri III, worth 20 *sols* or a *livre*. From that time until the Revolution the term *franc* was used as the equivalent of *livre* of the money of account;

Agnel or *Mouton*, a gold piece first struck under Louis IX, with the *Agnus Dei* on the obverse, worth ten *sols*;

Salut, a gold coin first struck by Charles VI, worth 25 *sols*, so named because the Angelical Salutation (Annunciation) was represented on the obverse;

Écu, a gold coin first issued by Philippe de Valois, worth 20 *sols* or a *livre*. The king is represented on it holding a shield sown with *fleurs de lis*. The *écu d'or* was repeatedly appreciated. The silver *écu* dating from the 16th century was worth 3 *livres*;

Teston, a silver coin issued under Louis XII bearing for the first time the king's head on the obverse (whence its name). It was worth 10 *sols*. *Testons* were issued during the succeeding reigns but discontinued from the time of Henri III;

Denier, a coin of silver or base metal corresponding to the *denier* of the money of account. The name was also at different times applied to a variety of other coins;

Liard, a small coin first issued under Charles VI, worth 3 *deniers*;

Louis, or *louis d'or*, a gold coin with the king's head on the obverse, first issued under Louis XIII. It was worth 20 *livres* or more before, and 20 *francs* after, the Revolution. During the First Empire it had Napoleon's head on the obverse and was called a *napoléon*;

Maille, a small coin worth half a *denier*;

Marc, the measure adopted in the 11th century in place of the *livre* of 12 oz. for stating weights of bullion; it contained 8 oz. or 4,608 grains.

Pistole, originally a Spanish gold coin, of the same value as the *louis d'or*.

The expression frequently met with in 17th-century literature, 'placer l'argent au denier dix' or 'au denier douze', means 'to put money out at interest at the rate of one-tenth or one-twelfth of the capital sum'.

Mon Frère Yves (1883), a novel of Breton fishing life by Pierre Loti (q.v.).

Monge, GASPARD (1746–1818), born at Beaune, celebrated French geometrician and physicist, a founder of the École polytechnique and one of the first professors at the

École normale supérieure (qq.v.). He was with Bonaparte on the expedition to Egypt, and later received many honours at his hands. With the Restoration he fell into disfavour. He left Memoirs.

Monime, the heroine of Racine's *Mithridate* (q.v.).

Moniteur de Gand, see *Journal universel.*

Moniteur universel, La Gazette nationale ou Le, a daily paper of liberal trend, modelled on the English newspapers. It was founded in November 1789 by the publisher Panckoucke (q.v.). It reproduced official documents, reported the discussions in the *Assemblée nationale*, and was noted for the excellence of its articles on home and foreign politics and on literature. (La Harpe was one of its first editors.) Thanks to a skilful habit, early acquired, of tempering its views to those of the Government, it outlasted the Revolution. Under the Consulate it acquired a semi-official status which it preserved until the later years of the Second Empire. During the First Empire Napoleon ordered it to be read aloud at mealtimes in the *lycées*, so that the younger generation might absorb the Napoleonic ideas. He also found it a convenient medium for sounding public opinion. In 1830 it was the paper selected for publication of the *ordonnances* which suppressed the liberty of the Press and provoked the July Revolution (see *Revolutions, II*). In later years it widened its scope on the non-political side, lowered its price, doubled its size, and acquired a distinguished circle of contributors who included Dumas *père*, Gautier, Mérimée, Musset, and Sainte-Beuve (qq.v.). It fell into disgrace with the Government in 1868 and was replaced by the *Journal officiel* (q.v.).

Monluc or **Montluc,** BLAISE DE LASSERAN-MASSENCÔME, SEIGNEUR DE (1502–77), born in Gascony, a captain who fought in nearly all the wars from 1521 till his death (taking part in five pitched battles, seventeen assaults, and eleven sieges) and became *maréchal de France* in 1574. Reduced by a severe wound to inactivity, he wrote and constantly revised his historical memoirs, entitled *Commentaires* (in emulation of Caesar), intended in part as a manual of instruction to young officers. Monluc is not

concerned with the broader aspects of war but with minor operations, stratagems, and desperate assaults. His work gives a vivid picture not only of the warfare of the time, but of the author himself, a cool, brave, ardent soldier, mildly vainglorious, cruel, but no religious fanatic. His description of his defence of Sienna against the Imperialists in 1556 is especially noteworthy.

Monnier, HENRI (1799–1877), author, actor, also—and best-remembered as—caricaturist, the creator of M. Joseph Prudhomme (q.v.). He contributed to *Le Charivari* and similar satirical journals.

Monod, GABRIEL (1844–1915), historian, notably of the Merovingian epoch (*Études critiques sur les sources de l'histoire mérovingienne*, 2 vols. 1872–85). When the École des hautes études (q.v.) was founded he and A. Rambaud (q.v.) were given the task of organizing the historical side. He wrote a valuable sketch of the progress of historical studies in France, and the evolution of historical method, for the first number of the *Revue historique*, which he founded. His studies of Renan, Taine, and Michelet in *Les Maîtres de l'histoire* (1894) should also be mentioned.

As a young man he travelled and studied in Germany and Italy, when he met and married Olga Herzen, daughter of the Russian anarchist and a ward of the German socialist refugee Malwida von Meysenbug, who was by that time living in Italy (cf. *Rolland, Romain*). He was a keen supporter of Dreyfus (q.v.) at the time of *l'Affaire.*

Mon oncle Benjamin (1841), a novel, see *Tillier, Claude.*

Monseigneur, at the court of Louis XIV, and after, a title used to signify the dauphin.

Monselet, CHARLES (1825–88), born at Nantes, came to Paris in 1846 and became a critic, for some time dramatic critic, on *Le Figaro* (q.v.). In 1854 he published a small volume of poems *Les Vignes du Seigneur*. Otherwise his collected writings include: *Statues et statuettes contemporaines* (1851); *Les Oubliés et les Dédaignés. Figures littéraires de la fin du XVIIIᵉ siècle* (1857; contains studies of Linguet, Mercier, and the gourmand Grimod de la Reynière); *Les Tréteaux du Sieur Charles Monselet* (1859); *De Montmartre* à *Séville* (1865), &c. They are admirably typical of the minor literary journalism of the Second Empire, witty, entertaining, accomplished, fruit of no small amount of reading and research and sometimes well worth disinterring.

Monsieur, a title used without addition of a name to signify the king's eldest brother.

Monsieur Croche, anti-dilettante, see *Debussy.*

Monsieur de Camors (1867), a novel by Octave Feuillet (q.v.).

Monsieur de Phocas (1899), a novel by Jean Lorrain (q.v.).

Monsieur de Pourceaugnac, a *comédie-ballet* by Molière produced in 1669, a light farcical work; it formed part of the 'Divertissement de Chambord' of that year.

Orgon, a Paris citizen, has arranged to marry his daughter Julie to the provincial Pourceaugnac, his lawyer at Limoges, whom neither he nor his daughter has ever seen. Her lover Éraste determines to defeat the project. Pourceaugnac arrives in Paris, Éraste claims acquaintance with him, and lures him to the custody of doctors who treat him for lunacy. Orgon is led to believe that Pourceaugnac is heavily in debt, Pourceaugnac that Julie is an immodest hussy. Two women claim to be already married to Pourceaugnac and he is threatened with prosecution for bigamy. He is thankful to escape from Paris, and Éraste wins Julie by pretending to have rescued her from an attempt by Pourceaugnac to carry her off. The play contains a famous satirical representation of a consultation between doctors.

Monsieur Féli, the name by which Lamennais (q.v.) was affectionately known to his intimates.

Monsieur Le Trouhadec saisi par la débauche (1923), a farcical comedy by Jules Romains (q.v.).

Monsieur Parent, the name-tale of a collection (1886) by Maupassant (q.v.).

Monsieur Véto, i.e. Louis XVI, see *Véto.*

Monsoreau, see *Montsoreau* and *Dame de Monsoreau, La.*

Monstrelet, ENGUERRAND DE (d. 1453), a Burgundian, continuator of Froissart's chronicle down to 1444. His work was in turn continued to 1461 by Mathieu d'Escouchi.

Montagnards, Les, members of the extreme revolutionary party (*la Montagne*) in the *Convention nationale* (q.v.), so named because they occupied the highest benches (cf. *Marais*; *Plaine*), and led at various times by Danton, Marat, and Robespierre, particularly Robespierre. They believed, in opposition to the more federal policy of the Girondins (q.v.), that complete centralization of government was necessary for the survival of the Revolution and the successful prosecution of the Revolutionary wars. From being a small group at the outset they finally numbered more than a third of the *Convention*. They overthrew the Girondins, directed the policy of the Jacobins (q.v.), instituted the Terror, and finally participated in the fall of Robespierre. But after this it was not long before they were victims of the Thermidorian reaction (see *Revolutions,* Ia, July 1794–Sept. 1795; cf. also *Commune,* I).

Montaigne, MICHEL EYQUEM DE (1533–92), essayist, born at the château de Montaigne in Périgord, was the son of Pierre Eyquem, a merchant and mayor of Bordeaux. He was taught Latin as a child before French, but was never a Hellenist. He was sent to college at Bordeaux, but profited little by the instruction there (his father being opposed to any constraint in his education), though we learn that he acted in the Latin plays of Buchanan and other professors of the college. He became a magistrate of the *parlement* of Bordeaux, where he had La Boétie (q.v.) as his colleague and friend. After the death of his father (1568) Montaigne retired from the magistracy to a life of occupied leisure in his château, and soon began (1572) the composition of his *Essais.* The first two books of these were published in 1580. He then travelled, partly in search of health (he suffered from stone), in Germany and Italy. He kept a journal of his voyage, which has been published. In 1581 he was elected mayor of Bordeaux, retaining the position till 1586 and showing vigilance and discretion in the difficult times of the Ligue's activity. The fact that he declined, on relinquishing office, to go in person to

Bordeaux (where the plague was raging) to surrender the keys of the city as custom required, has been the subject of unfavourable comment, but not by his contemporaries. A much enlarged edition of the first two books of the *Essais*, together with the third book, was published in 1588. Until his death he continued to annotate and amplify in manuscript a copy of this edition. This annotated text has since been published. In the religious strife of his time Montaigne was a supporter of the royal authority, but without fanaticism, and he recognized Henri de Navarre as the legitimate heir to the throne. His moderation and wisdom caused him to be sought as an intermediary by both parties. For his adoptive daughter, Marie de Gournay, who edited his works, see under her name.

The remarkable work known as his *Essais* was begun in the modest form of a sort of commonplace-book in which, reading and meditating in the library which he has described (III. iii), he noted memorable maxims and examples that he came across in ancient authors (especially Plutarch), together with his comments thereon. It was developed into a collection of studies of the human mind, 'vain, divers et ondoyant', in all its manifestations, as gathered both from self-examination and from observation of the society around him and the opinions and prejudices of authors of all countries and ages. His writings, if examined in their chronological order, reveal a striking evolution in his thought. In the first stage we find him aiming at a stoical indifference to death, suffering, and worldly misfortune, basing himself especially on the philosophy of Seneca and the model of Cato of Utica. In the second stage he passes through a phase of scepticism. Montaigne had translated for his father a Latin work on *Natural Theology* by Raymond of Sebonde (d. 1432), a Spanish professor of medicine at Toulouse, who undertook to prove all the articles of the Christian religion by natural reason. Now, in ch. xii of his second book, under the strange guise of an *Apologie de Raimond Sebond*, Montaigne, by a vast collection of instances drawn from all sources, shows the utter fallibility of the human mind and its inability to know anything with certainty. Judgement he concludes must be suspended. 'Que sais-je?' is the motto he adopted in

1576. From this Pyrrhonian attitude Montaigne in the third stage (seen in a few essays of Book II and Book III) proceeds to a personal philosophy, not based on the doctrine of the Stoics, but of an epicurean tendency and founded on his own experience of life. Virtue now consists for him in an orderly and harmonious exercise of all the human faculties. In religion he may be described as a tolerant deist, though outwardly a Catholic.

In the course of the *Essais* Montaigne draws a vivid picture of himself, physically, morally, and intellectually. He was tall but inactive, with a loud voice and good digestion, gay, talkative, and frank, without memory, a dreamer, a vagabond, detesting all obligations, incontinent, unsuited for marriage or paternity. He writes usually in an easy familiar style (though capable on occasion of lofty eloquence) and in a vigorous racy language, with freshness and gaiety and many apposite and entertaining illustrations and quotations, passing abruptly from idea to idea, frequently digressing from the main thread. Sainte-Beuve says that his style may be described as 'une épigramme continuelle ou une métaphore toujours renaissante'. At whatever page the work is opened the reader will find some wise thought expressed in a vivid and memorable form. There is no systematic composition; the arrangement of themes is haphazard, and the subjects dealt with in a chapter have often little connexion with its title. An amusing example of his lack of method is his chapter 'Des coches' (III. vi).

Among the many more serious and instructive essays may be mentioned those on consolation in public calamities ('De la physionomie', III. xii), on education ('De l'institution des enfants', I. xxv), on repentance ('Du repentir', III. ii), on conversation ('De l'art de conférer', III. viii), and on the thought of death ('Que philosopher c'est apprendre à mourir', I. xix).

Montaigne's work was admired by his contemporaries and by the following generations; more than a hundred editions of it have been published. It was the basis of the philosophical expansion of the 17th century. But it was regarded as questionable by the Church, and placed on the Index in 1676. It was translated into English by Florio (1603) and later (1685) by Charles

Cotton. It was quoted (in *The Tempest*) by Shakespeare (who perhaps owned the copy of Florio now in the British Museum), and was drawn upon by Webster, Marston, Burton, and Browne. It was the foundation of the English essay, as developed by Bacon, Cowley, Temple, and Dryden.

Montaigu, Collège de, see *Collège de Montaigu.*

Montalembert, CHARLES-FORBES-RENÉ, COMTE DE (1810–70), publicist, historian, and orator, was born in London of an *émigré* father and a Scots mother. He completed his education in Sweden, where his father was French Ambassador after the Restoration (see *Restauration*). After his father's death he used the distinguished position he had inherited, together with his own great intellectual and oratorical powers, to fight for liberal Catholicism, especially in regard to education and the limits of Church participation in secular affairs. He was a famous associate of Lamennais and Lacordaire (qq.v.) in the days of *L'Avenir* (q.v.), though like Lacordaire he remained in the Church when Lamennais left it. During the Second Empire he was a leader of the militant Catholics.

His writings, of more religious and literary than historical merit, include a *Vie de sainte Élisabeth de Hongrie* (1836) and a study of monachism as a factor in medieval Western civilization, *Histoire des moines d'Occident depuis saint Benoît jusqu'à saint Bernard* (1860–77, 7 vols.).

Montargis, Chien de, see *Chien de Montargis.*

Montausier, CHARLES DE SAINTE-MAURE, DUC DE (1610–90), a man of upright character, who rendered service to his country and his king (Louis XIV) and was eventually chosen to supervise the upbringing of the Dauphin. He frequented the Hôtel de Rambouillet (q.v.) and after a fourteen years' courtship married Julie d'Angennes, daughter of the marquise de Rambouillet (see *Guirlande de Julie*). He was possibly the original of Alceste in Molière's *Le Misanthrope* (q.v.).

Montbéliard, GUÉNEAU DE, see *Buffon.*

Montcalm de Saint-Véran, LOUIS-JOSEPH, MARQUIS DE (1712–59), French general, born near Nîmes, one of the great figures of French colonial history. He was sent in 1756 to defend the French-Canadian colonies against the British, and had some initial success (see *Carillon*), but the British strengthened their forces and launched the series of attacks which led eventually to the conquest of Canada. In 1759 Montcalm was besieged in Quebec by General Wolfe. The battle of the Heights of Abraham (12 Sept. 1759) ended the siege. Wolfe was killed outright. Montcalm was mortally wounded and succumbed two days later. The capitulation of Quebec followed in another four days.

Montchrétien, ANTOINE DE (*c.* 1575–1621), dramatist and economist, son of an apothecary of Falaise in Normandy, a man of active intelligence and turbulent spirit, whose career was a singular one. He was left for dead in a youthful brawl and obtained a large indemnity, supported a lady of good family in a lawsuit with her husband and, when she became a widow, married her; he was obliged to leave France as the result of a duel, visited England and Holland, studied their industries and commerce, and thereafter wrote a remarkable work, which inspired Richelieu and Colbert, the *Traité de l'économie politique* (1615, he is credited with the invention of the name of the science). In some of his ideas he follows earlier writers, notably Bodin. He proceeds from a detailed study of concrete industries and trades (e.g. the manufacture of hats or the cod and herring fisheries) to general rules of policy, showing himself a retaliatory protectionist in the circumstances in which France found herself when he wrote, but with aspirations to free trade. (The work was republished by Funck-Brentano in 1889.)

A year or two after this Montchrétien founded steel-works in France. He joined the insurrection of the Huguenots in 1621 and was killed in an affray. In his earlier years he published six tragedies on classical, biblical, and historical themes: *Sophonisbe* (published in 1596); *La Reine d'Écosse* (or *L'Écossaise*, on the death of Mary Stuart), *Les Lacènes* (on the fortitude of Cleomenes, king of Sparta, prisoner of Ptolemy), *David* (on the story of David and Bathsheba), *Aman* (on the story of Haman, Esther, and Ahasuerus), all published in 1601 (in an edition which included the long poem

Susane ou la Chasteté on the subject of Susanna and the elders); *Hector* (1604). He retained the chorus, which gave scope to his pronounced lyrical gift. Montchrétien also wrote a *Bergerie* (1601), a pastoral play in prose and verse, an early work in this kind (see *Pastoral*), confused and monotonous; it presents Arcadian lovers in various attitudes, disdainful, or rejected, or inconstant.

Mont des Oliviers, Le, by Alfred de Vigny, one of the poems in the posthumous collection (1864) *Les Destinées*. The subject is the Agony in the Garden. It was written in 1843 except for the conclusion, added in 1863, which is Vigny at his most bitterly stoical.

Monte-Cristo, see *Comte de Monte-Cristo*.

Montégut, ÉMILE (1825–95), born at Limoges, came early to Paris, joined the *Revue des Deux Mondes* in 1847, and became a distinguished critic on this and other reviews. His solid, well-informed articles on foreign (English and American) literature and, later, on contemporary French writers were particularly appreciated. His works include: *Libres opinions morales et historiques* (1858); *Essais sur la littérature anglaise* (1883); *Nos Morts contemporains* (1884); *Écrivains modernes de l'Angleterre* (1885–92); *Mélanges critiques* (1887), &c., also translations of Emerson, Macaulay, and Shakespeare.

Montespan, FRANÇOISE-ATHÉNAÏS DE ROCHECHOUART, MARQUISE DE (1640–1707), mistress of Louis XIV after La Vallière. She was a woman of taste, who encouraged Quinault, Racine, and Boileau. Her sons by Louis XIV were the duc du Maine (q.v.) and the comte de Toulouse.

Montesquieu, CHARLES DE SECONDAT, BARON DE (1689–1755), political philosopher, born at the château de la Brède near Bordeaux of a good Guyenne family, entered the magistrature, inherited a fortune in 1716, and in the same year was admitted to the *académie* of Bordeaux, where he gave various dissertations on political and scientific subjects. In 1721 he published (anonymously) his *Lettres persanes* (q.v.) which gave him a wide reputation, and in the following years some political treatises and slight political tales (such as the *Dialogue de Sylla et*

d'Eucrate, q.v.) and more trivial prose poems (such as *Le Temple de Gnide*, q.v.). In 1727 he was admitted to the *Académie française*. He travelled about Europe, part of the time with Lord Chesterfield, and spent the years 1729–31 in England. He then settled at La Brède, and in 1734 published his *Considérations sur les causes de la grandeur des Romains et de leur décadence* (q.v.). In 1748 appeared his *Esprit des Lois* (q.v.), his chief title to fame, introducing a new method in the study of social institutions, and envisaging the ideal of a liberal and beneficent government and the removal of the abuses of the French monarchical system. He defended the book in his *Défense de l'Esprit des lois* (1750), containing in its third part some of his best writing. His failing eyesight then restricted his work. He left unfinished an *Essai sur le goût dans les choses de la nature et de l'art*, which appeared under the heading 'Goût' in the *Encyclopédie*.

Montesquieu was a man of simple habits and happy temperament, devoted to his family, kindly and benevolent, a good citizen not only of France but of the world. His works show much erudition; his usual style was sober and grave, with an occasional tendency to affectation.

Montesquiou [Montesquiou-Fezensac], COMTE ROBERT DE (1855–1921), born in Paris, the descendant of an ancient French family, poet, aesthete, and highly cultivated man of letters, well known in both the literary and the fashionable worlds. His luxurious habits and grotesque mannerisms inspired many anecdotes and are said to have given the novelists Huysmans and Proust (qq.v.) the idea of their characters Des Esseintes and Charlus (qq.v.). His association and exchange of correspondence with Proust are probably his most lasting claim to be remembered. He wrote: *Les Chauve-Souris* (1892), *Le Chef des odeurs suaves* (1893), *Les Hortensias bleus* (1896), *Les Perles rouges* (1899), precious and elaborately symbolical poetry; *Roseaux pensants* (1897), *Autels privilégiés* (1898), essays; *Les Pas effacés* (1923, 3 vols., posth.), memoirs, &c.

Montfaucon, formerly outside the walls of Paris between La Villette and the Buttes-Chaumont, celebrated as a place of execution in the Middle Ages.

Montfaucon, BERNARD DE (1655–1741), scholar, served as a soldier under Turenne in Germany, and subsequently entered the Maurist community of Benedictines, working in various abbeys and at Rome on the study of manuscripts. His chief publication was *Palaeographia Graeca* (1708), which did for the science of Greek palaeography what Mabillon's *De re diplomatica* had done for Latin palaeography. His other writings include editions of Athanasius and Chrysostom, *L'Antiquité expliquée et représentée en figures* (1719–24), and *Les Monuments de la monarchie française* (unfinished, 1729–33).

Montfleury, ANTOINE JACOB, *known as* (1640–85), actor and comic dramatist, rival and enemy of Molière. His best-known comedies were *L'École des jaloux* (q.v., 1664), *La Femme juge et partie* (1669), and *La Fille capitaine* (1672). His last work was *La Dame médecin* (1678).

Montfleury, ZACHARIE JACOB, *known as* (1600–67), father of the preceding and also an actor. He was in the company at the Hôtel de Bourgogne. In Rostand's play *Cyrano de Bergerac* (q.v.) he is ordered off the stage by Cyrano, an incident which may have happened in real life. Molière disliked and ridiculed him (in *L'Impromptu de Versailles*).

Montgolfier, JOSEPH (1740–1810) and his brother ÉTIENNE (1745–99), inventors of the air-balloon (lifted by heated air), first successfully employed to carry a passenger in 1783.

Montherlant, HENRI DE (1896–   ), contemporary novelist, essayist, and dramatist. His earlier works, mainly novels and essays, exalt war, sport, bull-fighting, and the cult of the body, e.g. *Le Songe* (1922), *Les Bestiaires* (1926), novels; *Aux fontaines du désir* (1927), *Mors et vita* (1932), *La Petite Infante de Castille* (1929), essays and travel sketches. His later novels include *Les Célibataires* (1934), a study of three decayed noblemen who live together and have neither two sous nor one pleasant characteristic between them; it is realistic, ironical, and not without some underlying commiseration; *Les Jeunes Filles, Pitié pour les femmes, Le Démon du bien, Les Lépreuses,* a series (1936–9) written mainly in the form of correspondence between a successful, sensual novelist

and a handful of obstinately adoring women. It had something of a *succès de scandale.*

Montherlant's more recent reputation rests on his dramatic works, in which the interest is partly religious, partly historical, e.g. *La Reine morte* (1942), *Malatesta* (1946), *Le Maître de Santiago* (1947), *La Ville dont le prince est un enfant* (1951), *Port-Royal* (1954).

Montholon, CHARLES-TRISTAN, COMTE DE (1783–1853), one of Napoleon's generals, his aid-de-camp during the Hundred Days and his companion during the whole period of exile in St. Helena. On returning to France he published (in collaboration with General Gourgaud, in St. Helena till 1818) the *Mémoires pour servir à l'histoire de France sous Napoléon* (1823), based on notes dictated by Napoleon. A later work was *Récits de la captivité de Napoléon à Sainte-Hélène* (1847, 2 vols.).

Montijo, COMTESSE DE. Maria Kirkpatrick y Grevigné (1794–1879) married the 7th comte de Montijo (1784–1839), a Spanish grandee, and had two daughters. The elder married the Duke of Alba, the younger married (1853) Napoleon III (see *Eugénie, Empress*). Mme de Montijo is also remembered as a friend of Mérimée (q.v.). Their correspondence, published in 1930 (2 vols.), is an interesting chronicle of the Spanish and French social and political scene between 1839 and 1870.

Montjoie or **Montjoie-Saint-Denis,** the medieval war-cry of the French. 'Montjoie' in this sense occurs in the *Chanson de Roland* ('Munjoie escriet, c'est l'enseigne Carlun'). Much has been conjectured about the name 'Montjoie', as, for instance, that it signified the banner given by Pope Leo III to Charlemagne, and was derived from *Mons Gaudii,* the Vatican hill.

Montluc, BLAISE DE, see *Monluc.*

Montmartre, a district in the north of Paris, a centre of artistic and literary cabarets. The name is perhaps derived from *Mons martyrum,* the hill where Saint Denis (q.v.) and his companions suffered martyrdom.

Mont-Oriol (1887), a novel by Maupassant (q.v.).

Montparnasse, a district in Paris on the south (left) bank of the river which to some extent corresponds to Montmartre in the north as a centre for artists and for cabaret life. It was once a *butte*, or small hill, outside the city walls, where the university students of the 17th century used to go to declaim their verses, and which they named *Butte du Mont Parnasse*.

Montpensier, LOUISE D'ORLÉANS, DUCHESSE DE (1627–93), generally known as 'la Grande Mademoiselle', daughter of Gaston d'Orléans, brother of Louis XIII. She took an active part on the side of Condé in the troubles of the second *Fronde* (q.v., 1652), showing bravery and decision. She had aspired to marry some reigning prince (Charles II or the Emperor), but finally when forty-two fell in love with Lauzun, a Gascon gentleman and an adventurer. The king, who had at first consented to their marriage, withdrew his approval and imprisoned Lauzun for ten years; after which they were, it is believed, secretly married. But Lauzun, who had been lavishly enriched by her, showed gross ingratitude, and they separated. Mademoiselle left interesting and vivacious *Mémoires* and wrote some indifferent romances, *La Relation de l'île imaginaire* and *La Princesse de Paphlagonie*, published under the name of Segrais (q.v.).

Montre, the yearly assembly of the *Basochiens* (see *Basoche*), which took the form of a fancy-dress procession and often included dramatic performances, such as farces or moralities.

Mont-Saint-Michel, a rocky island crowned by a monastery, connected in recent times by a mole to the north coast of France (near Avranches). It held out for seventy years against English attacks in the Hundred Years War. During part of this time Du Guesclin (q.v.) was captain of the Mount. Here Louis XI instituted the order of knights of Saint-Michel.

Montsoreau, CHARLES DE CHAMBES, COMTE DE (1549–1619), remembered as the assassin of Bussy d'Amboise (q.v., and see *Dame de Monsoreau, La*).

Montreux, see *Nicolas de Montreux*.

Montyon, JEAN-BAPTISTE-ANTOINE, BARON DE (1733–1820), philanthropist, founder of prizes for works of moral value and for acts of virtue (1782), to be distributed by the *Académie française* (q.v. and cf. *Prix littéraires*).

Moralité, a form of dramatic representation current in the later Middle Ages, of which the purpose was, in principle, didactic, and in which use was made of allegory, by the personification of abstractions such as Vice, Virtue, Conscience, and Waste; but the frequent introduction of comic elements and of burlesque scenes from everyday life brought the *moralité* into close proximity to the *farce*, from which it is not always distinguishable. A typical edifying *moralité* was *Bien-avisé et Mal-avisé* (about 8,000 lines), in which Bien-avisé and Mal-avisé set out together but soon separate. The former follows *Reason* who leads him to *Faith*, and so he goes on from one to another, to *Contrition, Confession, Prayer, Chastity, Honour*, and finally, in the care of Good-End, goes to Heaven. Mal-Avisé meets as many evil companions in his wanderings—*Laziness, Debauchery, Despair*, &c.—and by Evil-End is brought to Hell. Other examples of this type of *moralité* were the very long *L'Homme juste et l'homme mondain*; *L'Homme pécheur*, in which a young man yields to all the vices, but ends by repenting and dies in a state of grace; *La Condamnation de Banquet*, in which *Gout, Dropsy*, and other diseases fall upon the feasters; *Charité*; *Les Blasphémateurs*, &c. But sometimes the theme was a simple parable, such as that of the Prodigal Son. For examples of satirical moralities, see *Coquillart, Baude, Gringore, Aveugle et le Boiteux, L'*.

Moralités légendaires, Les (1888) poetic prose narratives by Jules Laforgue (q.v.).

Morand, PAUL (1888–   ), born in Russia, educated in various places including Oxford, a widely-travelled diplomat as well as novelist. His novels and tales include *Tendres Stocks* (1921), with a preface by Proust; *Ouvert la nuit* (1922); *Fermé la nuit* (1923); *Lewis et Irène* (1924); *Rien que la terre* (1926), &c. For the most part they are impressionistic studies of night life in the Europe of between the wars and vary in little except their geographical setting. *France la doulce* (1934) is an amusing satire of the cinema world.

Moréas, JEAN, the name adopted by Iannis Pappadiamantopoulos (1856–1910), poet. He was born in Athens of Greek parentage but was wholly French by culture and tastes, and lived in Paris after 1870. He was at first an ardent Symbolist, contributing to small reviews and known in such groups as the *Hydropathes* and the *Zutistes* (qq.v., and see *Symbolisme*, para. 3): his two collections of sonnets and lyrics *Les Syrtes* (1884) and *Les Cantilènes* (1886, and see *Cantilène*) belong to this phase. The first shows the influence of Verlaine both in spirit and technique, the second the Symbolist love of medieval and archaic terms. After a third collection, *Le Pèlerin passionné*, published in 1891, Moréas, from being the champion of the Symbolist movement, reverted gradually to a more classical inspiration. With Charles Maurras and Ernest Raynaud as disciples he launched the *École romane* (q.v.), a return to the Greco-Roman roots of French culture, to subjects taken from antiquity and to greater restraint of form. *Le vers libre*, for instance, which he had employed with great skill in earlier collections, was banished from the later poems of *Poèmes et sylves, 1886–1896* (1907), the collection representative of this period. It contains *Énone au clair visage* and *Ériphyle*, frequently mentioned among Moréas's works. In his final phase he became on the whole soberly classical in theme, form, and style, and wrote his finest poems, notably the lyrics collected in *Les Stances* (1899, bks. i–ii; 1901, bks. iii–vi; 1920, posth., bk. vii).

Moreau, FRÉDÉRIC, the hero of Flaubert's novel *L'Éducation sentimentale* (q.v.).

Moreau, GUSTAVE (1826–98), painter, much admired at the time of the Symbolist Movement (see *Symbolisme*). His works 'désespérées et érudites' moved Des Esseintes, the hero of Huysmans's novel *A rebours*, to 'longs transports' . . . 'jusqu'au fond des entrailles'. His elaborate, symbolical, highly complicated and often perverse paintings can be studied at the Musée Gustave Moreau in the house he occupied in Paris.

Moreau, HÉGÉSIPPE (1810–38), minor Romantic poet, born in Paris, is remembered chiefly by the collected poems of *Le Myosotis* (1838). The best are of country life (Moreau was educated, and employed as a proof-reader, at Provins, near Paris), but the bitter *Ode à la faim* is a reminder that his life of dissipation and increasing poverty ended in the workhouse. His prose *Contes à ma*

sœur (1851, posth.) are sometimes mentioned. (*Œuvres complètes*, 1890, posth.)

Moreau, JEAN-VICTOR (1763–1813), a volunteer who became a famous general in the Revolutionary armies. Hohenlinden (1800, q.v.) was one of his victories. Ambition led him to take part in Royalist conspiracies against Napoleon (1804). He was arrested, sentenced to two years' imprisonment, and when the sentence was changed to exile went to the U.S.A., where he remained till 1813. He then returned to Europe to fight for the Russians against France. He was mortally wounded in action.

Morée, Livre de la conqueste de la princée de la, a chronicle of the French principality in the Morea from 1204 to 1305, written by a French inhabitant of that country, an eyewitness from about 1295 of what he relates. It throws an interesting light on the life of the French knights who had established themselves in Greece.

Morellet, L'ABBÉ ANDRÉ (1727–1819), economist and man of letters, known in the salons of the *philosophes* (q.v.), contributed articles on, mainly, theology and metaphysics to the *Encyclopédie*. He visited Italy in early life with a private pupil and was in England as the guest of Lord Shelburne in 1772. A member of the *Académie française* (q.v.) from 1785, he worked steadily on the *Dictionnaire* (see *Dictionaries and Encyclopedias* under date 1694) and during the Revolution managed to preserve the copy, ready for the printer, of a new edition. He himself was ruined by the Revolution and had to subsist on literary hack work, e.g. translating English novels. He was one of the first members (1803) of the *Institut de France* (q.v.).

His works include: the witty, polemical *Petit Écrit sur une matière intéressante: La Tolérance* (1756); *Manuel des inquisiteurs* (1762), a digest of the *Directorium inquisitorum* of Nicolas Eymeric (1320–99, the Inquisitor General of Aragon), a book which had aroused his horrified indignation when he found it in an Italian library; a translation of Beccaria's *Traité sur les délits et les peines* (1765), a work much read by the *Encyclopédistes*; *Mélanges de littérature et de philosophie au XVIII* siècle (1818, 4 vols.), his own selection of his best writings. He projected, but never carried through, a Dictionary of Commerce.

Morellet also left *Mémoires* (1822, 2 vols.), of interest as a study of pre-Revolutionary and Revolutionary France. They reveal a dry yet often engagingly light-hearted personality, and a philosopher who found compensation for his many misfortunes in 'le bonheur inestimable . . . d'avoir été toute ma vie un particulier obscur, . . ; d'avoir été le maître de mes travaux, de mes loisirs; de m'être toujours soustrait à la servitude d'une tâche commandée pour un temps fixe, aussi libre, aussi indépendant que peut le désirer l'homme de lettres le plus ami de l'indépendance et de la liberté'.

Morelly, ——, an 18th-century political theorist of whose life nothing is known. His memory is kept alive by *Naufrage des îles flottantes ou Basiliade* (1753) and *Le Code de la Nature* (1755), two audacious works in which he anticipated Rousseau and to some extent the early communism of Babeuf or the doctrines of *Fouriérisme* (qq.v.) by his contention that man is naturally good and that private property and the errors of the legislator are the root of all evil. The former work is a philosophical epic, in prose, purporting to be the translation of a poem by the Indian Bidpai. The *îles flottantes* are the prejudices which stand in the way of man's happiness, and the *Basiliade* is the reign of the philosopher king who restores the laws of nature in his kingdom. In the first three parts of the second work, the *Code de la Nature*, the author examines existing conceptions of politics and morals, then (pt. 4) sets out in full his own proposals for a code of laws for a model society.

Moreri, LOUIS (1643–1680), lexicographer, see *Dictionaries and Encyclopedias*, under date 1674.

Morice, CHARLES (1861–1919), one of the first of the Symbolist poets, a friend of Verlaine and Mallarmé (qq.v.), and usually referred to as one of the theorists of *symbolisme* (q.v.). His *La Littérature de tout à l'heure* (1889) was on the need for vagueness in poetry, for great thoughts to be veiled rather than clearly expressed.

Morin, BENOÎT, see *Dictionaries and Encyclopedias*, under date 1802.

Morin, SIMON (*c.* 1622–63), an illuminist with a large following who came to believe that he was Christ reincarnated and called himself *le Fils de l'Homme*. He was twice imprisoned in the Bastille, recanted each time and was released, but began again. Finally he was tracked down and arrested (a matter in which Desmarets de Saint-Sorlin, q.v., had some part), condemned, and burnt alive.

Mornay, see *Duplessis-Mornay*.

Morny, CHARLES-AUGUSTE-LOUIS-JOSEPH, DUC DE (1811–65), the natural son of Queen Hortense (mother of Napoleon III) and the comte de Flahaut (son of Mme de Souza, q.v.). He led the world of fashion *c.* 1840, and in 1851 helped to engineer the *coup d'état* (q.v.). Thereafter, with his brother's influence he became a brilliant political figure in Second Empire Paris. He still shone as a dandy and, less reputably, as a speculator. In 1856–7 he was in Russia as French Ambassador. He is one of the chief characters in Daudet's *Le Nabab* (q.v.).

Mort Artu, see *Perceval*.

Mort de César, La. (1) An early French tragedy, on the Senecan model, by Jacques Grévin (q.v.), produced in 1561. The first two acts, by monologue and declamations, present respectively Caesar and the conspirators. In the third act Calpurnia, who in a dream has seen Caesar murdered, entreats him to stay at home, but Decimus Brutus perfidiously eggs him on. The fourth act contains a narrative of the assassination; in the fifth, the conspirators appear before the Roman public, followed by Mark Antony.

(2) A tragedy by Voltaire, produced in 1731. There is no female character. The play shows the influence of Shakespeare on Voltaire's early dramatic writing.

Mort de Pompée, La, a tragedy by Corneille, based on part of Lucan's *Pharsalia*, written in the winter of 1642–3.

Pompey has been defeated at Pharsalia and is fleeing to Egypt. Ptolemy and his advisers discuss how he shall be received, and in spite of Cleopatra's opposition decide on his assassination. Pompey is killed. Caesar arrives in Egypt and reproves the deed. Ptolemy then proposes to assassinate Caesar, lest he should raise Cleopatra to the throne. Cornelia, Pompey's widow, reveals the plot to Caesar. Ptolemy is killed in battle, Cornelia is freed, and Cleopatra crowned. The noble bearing of Cornelia in face of Caesar, and the subjugation of the latter by Cleopatra's charms are further elements in the play.

Mort de quelqu'un (1911), a novel by Jules Romains (q.v.), the first *unanimiste* novel (see *Unanimisme*).

Mort du Loup, La, a poem by Alfred de Vigny. It was written in 1838, first published in the *Revue des Deux Mondes* in 1843, and included (1864) in the posthumous collection *Les Destinées*. Man has a lesson to learn from the wolf which, when cornered by the huntsmen, licks its wounds and dies silently. ('Seul le silence est grand; tout le reste est faiblesse.')

Mort d'un chêne, La, a long elegiac poem, a favourite choice for anthologies, is contained in the *Odes et Poèmes* (1844) of Victor de Laprade (q.v.).

Mortier, ÉDOUARD-ADOLPHE-CASIMIR-JOSEPH, one of Napoleon's marshals (see *Maréchal de l'Empire*).

Mortsauf, MME DE, the heroine of Balzac's novel *Le Lys dans la vallée* (q.v.).

Mosaïque (1833), the title of Mérimée's first collected volume of *nouvelles*, see under *Mérimée* (para. 4).

Mosca, COUNT, a character in Stendhal's novel *La Chartreuse de Parme* (q.v.).

Moscow, The Retreat from, was the disastrous end of Napoleon's Russian campaign of 1812. After the battle of Borodino (7 Sept. 1812) the French army occupied Moscow (14 Sept.). The city was practically empty, and on the following day it was three-parts destroyed by a fire said to have been prepared by the Russians before their departure. Napoleon was further disconcerted by the Russian refusal to negotiate; and after five weeks of hesitation he abandoned his plan of wintering in Moscow and ordered a retreat. On 19 October, with a fortnight's provisions in hand, the French army left Moscow. It had to make its way across devastated country, and starvation, allied to the severe Russian winter, took a fearful toll of the troops. Arrived at last at the River Berezina they found themselves hemmed in by three Russian armies, and unable to cross because a sudden thaw had loosened the ice. After twenty-four hours' labour the pontoneers managed to construct two narrow bridges, and a confused mass of men, horses, and vehicles fought their way across under fire from the Russians, those who were fortunate reaching the other bank over the bodies of their comrades (25–29 November). When the Russian campaign began the French army numbered some 400,000 men. By the end 380,000 had been lost, 90,000 in the retreat from Moscow alone. Of Napoleon's Old Guard only 1,500 remained. The most famous description of the retreat from Moscow is Tolstoy's, in *War and Peace*. In French literature, old Goguelat's description in Balzac's *Le Médecin de campagne* (q.v.) may be recalled.

Moskova, Bataille de la, see *Borodino*.

Motin, PIERRE (? 1566–1610), cabaret poet, a disciple and friend of Régnier, reputed in his day for his amorous and licentious verse, to be found in contemporary collections such as *Le Parnasse satyrique, Le Cabinet satyrique*, &c. Boileau ridiculed him (*Art poét.* iv. 3940).

Motteville, MME DE (1621–89), née Françoise Bertaut, a niece of Bertaut the poet, married when eighteen to the octogenarian M. de Motteville. After his death and that of Louis XIII she was for twenty-two years lady-in-waiting, as well as friend, of Anne of Austria. She was also well acquainted with Henrietta Maria of England. She left interesting memoirs of the period of Anne of Austria's regency and Mazarin's power, including a valuable account of the *Fronde* (q.v.), and passages relating to the revolution in England and the exiled Stuarts.

Mouchefrin, one of the seven young *déracinés* in the novel *Les Déracinés* (q.v.) by Maurice Barrès.

Mouhy, CHARLES DE FIEUX, CHEVALIER DE (1701–84), one of the forgotten novelists of the 18th century, a prolific writer whose least bad work is said to have been the six-volume *La Mouche ou les aventures de Bigand* (1736). He was for a time paid by Voltaire to send him news from Paris. He also left an *Histoire du théâtre français depuis son origine jusqu'en 1780* (1780, 3 vols.).

Mounet-Sully, JEAN SULLY MOUNET, *known as* (1841–1916), famous tragic actor, one of the company of the Comédie-Française. His brother PAUL (1847–1922) was also an actor at the Comédie-Française but of less standing.

Mounier, EMMANUEL (1905–50), Personalist philosopher, came to the Sorbonne from Grenoble via the University of Lyons in 1927 and passed the *Concours d'agrégation* (q.v.) in Philosophy in 1928. In 1932 he abandoned all thought of an academic career and founded the review *Esprit* as the organ of a new movement, a form of moral and social philosophy known as *Personnalisme* (q.v.). His life thenceforward was bound up with his review and the activities resulting from it. He suffered hardship during the 1939–45 war and was at one time imprisoned by the Vichy government. In 1944 he returned to Paris and resumed publication of *Esprit*, suppressed since 1941. Mounier is said to have been for his followers very much what Péguy (q.v., one of his influences) had been for an earlier generation. His outstanding works include: *La Pensée de Charles Péguy* (1931); *La Révolution personnaliste et communautaire* (1935), articles contributed to *Esprit* between 1932 and 1934; *Manifeste au service du Personnalisme* (1936); *Traité du caractère* (1946); *Qu'est-ce que le Personnalisme?* (1947); *Le Personnalisme* (1949).

Mousket, PHILIPPE, see *History* (medieval period).

Mouton Blanc, Le, a tavern in the Place du cimetière Saint-Jean in Paris frequented by 17th-century authors.

Moyen de parvenir, Le, see *Béroalde.*

Mugnier, L'ABBÉ ARTHUR (1853–1944), a Benedictine priest who for many years had care of the souls of one of the most fashionable congregations in Paris (the church of Sainte-Clotilde, in the Faubourg Saint-Germain) and who was, much more than this, a man of piety, wisdom, and learning. He was friend and spiritual adviser of many writers of the late 19th and early 20th centuries and in more than one case was instrumental in effecting their conversion or return to the Roman Catholic Church. His influence over Huysmans (q.v.) is one notable example of this. He was the model

for the abbé Gevresin, spiritual director of the character Durtal (q.v.) in Huysmans's novel *En route.*

Mule du Pape, La, the most famous of Alphonse Daudet's (q.v.) tales of Provence, one of the *Lettres de mon moulin*. There is, says the author, an old saying 'Comme la mule du Pape qui garda sept ans son coup de pied', and he has consulted his *bibliothèque des cigales* for the explanation. A small boy, an *arriviste* from his early years, won the favours of the good Pope Boniface of Avignon by lavishing endearments in public on the latter's much-cherished mule though in private he teased and provoked her unmercifully. He was sent to Rome for his education, and the mule bided her time. He grew up and came back, and secured for himself a fine post close to the Pope's person. On the day of his installation in office he turned up confident and bedecked for the ceremony. As he went forward to the platform he stopped before his old 'friend' the mule, who seized her opportunity and in one mighty kick let fly the stored-up rancour of seven years.

Mule sans frein, La, a verse romance (1,136 lines) of the 13th century belonging to the Round Table group, dealing with an episode in the life of Gauvain (Gawain).

A damsel arrives at the court of Arthur riding on a mule with a head-stall but without bit. Brought before the king she declares that she has been robbed of the bit and will give herself to whatever knight will recover it, and moreover will lend her mule to guide him. Keu (Kay) undertakes the adventure but soon returns terrified by the perils he meets with. Gauvain then takes his place and by his courage and loyalty achieves the quest.

Muller, CHARLES, and **Reboux,** PAUL, see *Pastiche.*

Multiple Splendeur, La (1906), collected poems by Verhaeren (q.v.).

Murat, AMÉLIE (1888–1940), author of love and nature (Auvergne) poems: *D'un cœur fervent* (1909), *Bucoliques d'été* (1920), *Le Sanglot d'Ève* (1923), *Chants de minuit* (1927), &c.

Murat, JOACHIM, one of Napoleon's marshals, see *Maréchal de l'Empire.*

Muret (latinized as **Muretus**), MARC-ANTOINE DE (1526–85), a learned humanist of the French Renaissance, born at Muret near Limoges. He taught the classics in various places, including Paris (where he had as pupils Scévole de Sainte-Marthe, Jacques Grévin, and Vauquelin de la Fresnaye) and Bordeaux (where Montaigne was his pupil); edited Latin authors, and wrote letters, orations, and a play on Julius Caesar (1544), in elegant Latin. He also wrote a *Commentaire* on the *Amours* of Ronsard, explaining the mythological allusions in these poems.

Murger, HENRY (1822–61), novelist, born in Paris, had a scanty education, then tried his hand at painting and literature. (He was encouraged by a tenant in the building where his father, a German, was concierge.) He wrote some verse, collected in *Poésies* (1855), but his talent was for poeticized, sentimental descriptions of humble life or of the rackety, precarious existence led by the artists and writers (like himself) who people his best, and best-remembered, work *Scènes de la vie de Bohème* (published serially in 1848 in *Le Corsaire*, q.v.; dramatized in 1849; published in book form in 1851; the story of Puccini's opera *La Bohème* in 1896). His other works, usually variations on the same theme, include *Les Buveurs d'eau* (1854), *Scènes de campagne* (1857), and a one-act comedy *Le Bonhomme Jadis* (1852).

Muscadins, a name for the gilded youth (dandies, perfumed with musk) who took part in anti-Jacobin manifestations during the *réaction thermidorienne* (q.v., and see *Revolutions*, Ia, under July 1794–Sept. 1795). It is said to have been applied first at Lyons in 1793 to the youths who resisted the troops of the Convention. (Cf. *Incroyables*; *Merveilleuses*.)

Muse du département, La, one of the 'Scènes de la vie de province' in Balzac's *Comédie humaine* (see *Parisiens en province, Les*).

Musée Carnavalet. This, the *Musée historique de la ville de Paris*, created in 1866, occupies the fine Renaissance Hôtel Carnavalet (near the former Place Royale, q.v.) which was bought for the purpose by the Municipality of Paris. Its collection of portraits, prints, porcelain, *bibelots*, costume, &c., make it one of the most interesting,

and most live, of French museums, notably for the Revolution and Empire periods. The Hotel Carnavalet (named after a former owner Mme de Kernevenoy, known as Carnavalet) was the residence of Mme de Sévigné from 1677 till her death in 1696.

Musée Grévin, a museum of waxworks in Paris. It was created, on the model of Madame Tussaud's but including mainly contemporary personages, by Alfred Grévin (1827–92), a caricaturist noted for gay sketches of Parisian life.

Muse française, La (1823–4), a short-lived but famous literary review associated with the early days of le *Romantisme* (q.v.), founded by Alexandre Guiraud, Alexandre Soumet, Émile Deschamps (qq.v.), and other, younger, writers, among them Victor Hugo and Alfred de Vigny. It published many of the Romantic manifestoes and made a point of fostering new talent. Nearly all the great figures of the Romantic Movement contributed to it.

Muse historique, La, see *Loret*.

Muset, COLIN, see *Colin*.

Musette, a character in Murger's *Scènes de la vie de Bohème*. The *Chanson de Musette*, which she sings, was Murger's best poem.

Muséum d'histoire naturelle, see *Jardin des Plantes*.

Musical Controversies. There was a resounding dispute about 1752 concerning the comparative merits of French and Italian music. In this J.-J. Rousseau and Grimm took a prominent part on the side of the Italians (the latter in his *Petit Prophète de Boemischbroda*). There was a renewal of musical controversy during the period 1774–80 between the supporters of Gluck and Piccini, of which there are echoes in the literature of the day (Sauvigny, *Les Piccinnistes et les Gluckistes*, Chabanon, *L'Esprit de parti ou les Querelles à la mode*, comedies); see also *Gluck*, *Gluckistes*.

Musicisme, see *Literary isms*.

Musset, ALFRED DE (1810–57), poet, novelist, and dramatist, born and educated in Paris (his father was a Government official), took to literature after one or two attempts to study law and medicine. Sainte-Beuve (q.v.), scenting a new talent, introduced him to Charles Nodier and Victor Hugo, thus to the Romantic *cénacles* (q.v.)—a new atmosphere for a young dandy, used to fashionable *salons*.

His first published work was a very free translation of De Quincey's *Opium Eater* (*L'Anglais mangeur d'opium*, 1828). In 1830 came his first collection of poems, *Contes d'Espagne et d'Italie*. It contained narrative poems at times reminiscent of Byron, also a 'Ballade à la lune' which brought anathemas upon his head because he compared the moon to a dot over an 'i'. It was followed in 1833 by the first of the series entitled *Un Spectacle dans un fauteuil* (q.v.), the dramatic poems, verse and prose comedies, and *proverbes dramatiques* which, after the failure of *La Nuit vénitienne* (q.v.) when produced on the stage, he wrote expressly for armchair consumption. The second series was published in 1834. *Rolla*, another Byronesque poem, was also published in 1833, in the *Revue des Deux Mondes*, and in the same year the poet met, and fell passionately in love with, the novelist George Sand (q.v.), who was six years his senior. The two went to Italy, where first (at Genoa) George Sand went down with fever, when Musset was bored and neglected her for other women, then Musset (at Venice) fell dangerously ill. George Sand called in a young Italian doctor, Pietro Pagello. Between them, she and he nursed Musset devotedly back to life, but she became Pagello's mistress. Musset returned to Paris in March 1834 broken in spirits and enfeebled in health. He described the episode later in his autobiographical novel *Confession d'un enfant du siècle* (1836, q.v.) and made a fantastic satire of it, and of *le Romantisme* (q.v.), in *Histoire d'un merle blanc* (1842). George Sand and Pagello returned in the summer of 1834 but Pagello was already fading out of the picture and was dismissed back to Venice in September. The relationship between Musset and George Sand was resumed, and broken, and the two tore at each other for some months till the final break in March 1835.

Between his return to Paris and the year 1843 Musset produced some of his finest work—lyrics, the bulk of his comedies and *proverbes* (short comedies written to illustrate the truth of proverbial sayings), and the best

of his *nouvelles* (e.g. *Emmeline*, *Frédéric et Bernerette*, &c.). The lyrics, among them *Le Souvenir* and *Les Nuits*, qq.v., are distinguished by their music and a genuine passion which puts him in the front rank of French poets. The lyric note re-echoes in his comedies, which hold their own in French literature by their wit, grace, and dramatic quality. To this period also belong the well-known *Stances à la Malibran* (written on the death of the great singer Mme Malibran, 1808–36) and the verses in praise of Molière, *Une Soirée perdue* (1840). After 1843 his output declined, and by 1852, the year he was elected to the *Académie française*, it had practically ceased. His manner of life was disastrous, to health and character, and he was only forty-seven when he died.

Musset is usually classed with Hugo, Lamartine, and Vigny as one of the four great figures of the Romantic Movement; and he does, even more directly than his three contemporaries, communicate his self (the 'moi' of the Romantics) and his sufferings in his poetry. On the other hand, after the exaggerated and at times hardly serious Romantic mannerisms of his early writings he took pains to dissociate himself from what he called (in the *Lettres de Dupuis et Cotonet*, q.v.) the 'rhyming school' of Hugo and his followers.

After 1834 his writings were usually published first in the *Revue des Deux Mondes* (q.v.). The chief collected editions of his works published in his lifetime were: *Poésies complètes* (1840) and *Premières poésies*. *Poésies nouvelles* (1852, 2 vols.); *Nouvelles* (1840), and *Comédies et proverbes* (1840, q.v.).

Musset, PAUL DE (1804–80), brother of Alfred de Musset (see above), man of letters, author of *Lui et Elle* (1859), an account, thinly disguised, of the episode of his brother's trip to Italy with George Sand (1833–4), of their rupture, partial reconciliation, and final separation. It constitutes a bitter attack on George Sand in reply to her *Elle et Lui*. Paul de Musset also wrote a biography of his brother (1877), and his *Monsieur le Vent et Madame la Pluie* (1860) was for long a small classic of children's literature.

Mystère Frontenac, Le (1933), a semi-autobiographical novel by Mauriac (q.v.).

Mystères, in English 'Mysteries', are medieval religious dramas having their origin in the liturgical plays, and representing scriptural scenes. From an early date they were performed in churches on high festivals. The name (perhaps derived from *ministerium* confused with *mysterium*) had at first a somewhat wide sense of 'function' or 'representation', and only in the second half of the 15th century came to be applied almost exclusively to dramas concerned with the central mysteries of the Christian religion, such as the Nativity and the Passion, though occasionally used in this sense in the 14th century. For early examples of such representations see under *Religious writings*. There was a great development of this form of drama in the 14th century, all over France, through the agency of various confraternities, somewhat similar to the *puys* (q.v., and see *Confrérie de la Passion*). An example of these 14th-century Mysteries is contained in what appears to be the repertoire of the confraternity of Paris, a manuscript of the Bibliothèque Sainte-Geneviève; it includes the Nativity, the play of the Three Kings, the Passion, and the Resurrection.

The early part of the 15th century witnessed a further extension and evolution of these dramatic performances: an increased prominence was given to the person of the Virgin Mary and to a realistic presentation of the sufferings of Christ. The performances became very elaborate, involving a large number of actors (ordinary citizens, members of the fraternities, or professional actors), a vast stage including many scenes, and rich costumes, and lasted over several days. There was no limit of time or place to the incidents represented, which were taken from the O.T., the N.T., the apocryphal scriptures, the 'Legenda Aurea', &c. Buffoonery was included, and contemporary life was realistically presented, the nobility and clergy being unfavourably depicted. The style of writing was in general vulgar and prolix, without literary pretension. The rhymed octosyllabic verse was the fundamental metre, but many others were employed. An important feature, constantly appearing in the prologue or opening of the Mystery, was the *Procès de Paradis* (inspired by Ps. lxxxv. 10) in which the allegorical figures of Justice and Mercy, Peace and Truth, plead before God the cause which is

resolved in the sacrifice of Our Lord. The performance had popular edification as its object; it was also an act of piety, sometimes designed to avert pestilence, or as a thanksgiving. The cost, to the extent that it was not recouped by the charge made to spectators, was borne by the fraternities, the municipalities, the ecclesiastical authorities, or private individuals, in varying proportions. The performances, announced some time before by a *cry* or solemn proclamation about the city, were witnessed by large crowds and excited great enthusiasm; they were made the occasion of a general holiday. The most important and famous Mysteries of the 15th century were: the *Passion of Arras*, probably by Eustache Marcadé, a learned ecclesiastical functionary of Corbie in Picardy, who died in 1440, dealing with the life of Christ from the Nativity to the Ascension; and that by Arnoul Greban (organist and choirmaster of Notre-Dame, later canon of Le Mans, a man of erudition and poetic gifts) of the middle of the 15th century, covering the same events—a work, taken as a whole, of considerable power. It was rehandled and added to by an Angevin doctor, Jean Michel, who had it sumptuously performed at Angers in 1486; its performance occupied four days. Simon Greban, brother of Arnoul, collaborated with him in a very long Mystery (60,000 lines), one of several entitled *Actes des Apôtres*, which follows the twelve Apostles all over the world in a monotonous series of preachings, conversions, miracles, imprisonments, and martyrdoms. We hear of this being performed as late as 1540 by the *Confrérie de la Passion* (q.v.). The *Mistère du Viel Testament* was another notable example of the class. Two 15th-century Mysteries dealing with profane subjects were the *Mystère du siège d'Orléans* (the deliverance of that city by Joan of Arc) and the *Destruction de Troye la grant* (1450–52), by Jacques Milet. It is uncertain whether the latter work was ever performed.

The performance of Mysteries was brought to an end in Paris by an edict of the *parlement* in 1548, and gradually ceased throughout France. This form of drama had by then fallen into disfavour except among the illiterate: it was condemned by the pious as irreverent, and by the cultured as out of harmony with the new spirit of the Renaissance. It was attacked moreover by the Protestants as a profanation of the Bible. The performance of Jodelle's *Cléopâtre*, inaugurating a new dramatic era, followed the edict of 1548 after an interval of three or four years.

Mystères de Paris, Les (1842–3), a sensational novel of the Parisian underworld, probably the best remembered of many such by Eugène Sue (q.v., and cf. *Marx, Karl*, para. 2).

N

Nabab, Le (1877), a novel by Alphonse Daudet, and a good study, often based on real people, of Second Empire society. The 'nabab' is Bernard Jansoulet, the son of Provençal peasants. He had worked at odd jobs until his thirtieth year, then gone to Tunis and made a fortune. The novel opens thirty years later when he returns to France, a very rich man, with several millions still unrealized in Tunis. He is vulgar, yet likeable in his exuberance and his loyalty to his humble origins; shrewdly ready to disburse vast sums, and ask no awkward questions, in order to further his social ambitions, yet for all his experience innocently certain that the world will be as delighted at his romantic fortunes as himself; and thus destined to become the prey of flatterers and swindlers. He establishes himself with great pomp in Paris, determined to cut a figure in society and to enter politics. A former associate of his Tunis days, now a rich Paris banker and his enemy, plots to entangle him in a shady company-promoting scheme, at the same time making it impossible for him to obtain money from Tunis. He is elected Deputy for Corsica, but when his enemies spread libellous stories about his private life the election is annulled and his sycophantic friends flee before his disgrace and approaching ruin. His end is pitiful. In his private box at a theatre which exists on his generosity he finds himself scorned and avoided by his sometime followers. He tries to defy them, but the blow is too heavy and he dies of an apoplectic seizure.

Nabis, Les, a group of French Post-Impressionist painters (see *Impressionnisme*). At the time they banded themselves together they were art-students, so inflamed and exalted by their ideas that Henri Cazalis (the poet Jean Lahor, q.v.) christened them *Nabis* (prophets), from the cabbalistic Hebrew. They held their first exhibition in 1891.

Nadar [pseud. of Félix Tournachon] (1820–1910), a figure in Parisian life under the Second Empire, was in turn journalist, caricaturist, photographer (his collection, *Panthéon-Nadar*, of portrait-photographs of celebrities was well known), and aeronaut. The first exhibition of the group of artists who became known as the *Impressionnistes* (q.v.) was held in his studio in 1874. As an aeronaut he experimented hazardously with an immense balloon 'Le Géant', constructed to his own design, and during the Franco-Prussian war was head of an observer corps in Paris which studied enemy movements from captive balloons.

Nadaud, GUSTAVE (1820–93), born at Roubaix, wrote popular light verse, which is still quoted occasionally: *Chansons* (1849; 1867; 1875, &c.); *Contes, proverbes, scènes et récits en vers* (1870), &c.

Naigeon, JACQUES-ANDRÉ (1738–1810), man of letters and *philosophe*, friend of Diderot, of whom he wrote a *Mémoire* besides publishing his works (1798), and an associate of d'Holbach in his anti-religious writings. He edited Montaigne's *Essais* (1802), with a commentary.

Nain de Julie, see *Godeau*.

Nain jaune, Le, a newspaper with Bonapartist sympathies, founded in 1814, after the first Restoration, was noted for its caricatures and for lively, satirical articles which seized the ridiculous element in persons and events, irrespective of party. The name was again given to a short-lived paper of similar character founded in 1863 by Aurélien Scholl (q.v.).

Naissance du Chevalier au Cygne, see *Chevalier au Cygne.*

Namouna (1833), an oriental poem by Alfred de Musset, in *Un Spectacle dans un fauteuil* (q.v.).

Nana (1880), by Émile Zola, one of his *Rougon-Macquart* novels. Nana is the daughter of Gervaise, the laundress, in *L'Assommoir* (q.v.). She goes on the stage and leads a life of luxurious and for a time very profitable vice, all of which provides the occasion for detailed descriptions of this side of Second Empire society.

Nanine ou le préjugé vaincu, a sentimental comedy in decasyllabic verse by Voltaire, produced in 1749, of little interest except as an early example of this type of drama. The theme of the play had already been treated by La Chaussée in his adaptation of Richardson's *Pamela.*

The comte d'Olban, won by the beauty and amiable qualities of Nanine, a girl of lowly birth, who humbly returns his love, decides to defy social prejudice and to marry her, breaking off from the haughty ill-tempered *baronne* to whom he is in some sort pledged. The course of true love is temporarily interrupted by the interception of a letter, in ambiguous terms of affection, from Nanine to a man suspected to be her secret lover, but presently revealed to be her lost father.

Nanteuil, CÉLESTIN (1813–73), celebrated book-illustrator, took part in the Romantic Movement and illustrated books by Romantic writers (e.g. Victor Hugo's *Notre-Dame de Paris*).

Nanteuil, ROBERT (1630–78), pastel-portraitist and engraver, remembered specially as the latter. His portrait of Mazarin is well known.

Napoleon. NAPOLÉON BONAPARTE, EMPEROR NAPOLEON I (1769–1821), born at Ajaccio, was a Corsican of Italian descent and patrician origin but a French citizen by birth, for he was born two weeks after Corsica came under French domination. From the age of nine he was educated in France (Autun, and the military colleges of Brienne and Paris). In 1785 he was commissioned lieutenant in an artillery regiment. His promotion in the Revolutionary

armies was rapid: in October 1795 his prompt action saved the situation when the *Convention* was attacked by insurgents, and 1796 found him, aged twenty-seven, in Northern Italy as general in command of the campaign against Austria. With the triumphant finish of this (see *Rivoli; Campo Formio*) he became one of the great military heroes of the day. He kept himself in the public eye by his conquest of Egypt, then a dependency of the Sublime Porte, in 1798. His aim was to make the Egyptian expedition the successful preliminary to the destruction of British supremacy in India. It failed, thanks largely to Nelson's naval victory at Aboukir (1–2 Aug. 1798), and he profited by a crisis in home politics to abandon it and return to France with his fame still high. A month later he engineered the *coup d'état* of 9 November ('le dix-huit brumaire'), and under the new government which resulted he became First Consul. He had supreme authority in both internal and external policy and could rule as a dictator. After an interval during which, by his successful military campaigns, he achieved the break-up of the Second Coalition (q.v.) and thus increased his power, he was elected Consul for life (1802), and by the Senatus-Consultum of 18 May 1804, confirmed by plebiscite, he constituted himself Emperor. At his coronation on 2 December 1804 (at Notre-Dame, with the Pope Pius VII present to celebrate the Mass) he crowned himself Emperor Napoleon I and his wife, Joséphine de Beauharnais (q.v.), Empress Josephine. Interesting pictures of life at the Imperial Court—very unlike the courts of the *ancien régime*—can be found in, for example, the *Mémoires* of Mme de Rémusat (q.v.). Napoleon had no children by the Empress Josephine, and with the object of founding a dynasty he divorced her in 1809 and married (1 April, 1810) the Archduchess Marie-Louise of Austria. Their son, the Roi de Rome (see next and *Aiglon, L'*), was born on 20 March 1811.

At home, Napoleon restored order and unity to France, and showed a genius of which the effects still remain in reconstructing the internal economy of the country, e.g. local and central government, financial, judicial, and legal systems, Church government, secondary and university education, &c. He also instituted many works of public utility and architectural embellishment. He was ruthless in crushing conspiracies, real or imaginary (cf. *Enghien, duc d'*), and he established drastic systems of espionage and censorship (cf. *Press, Development of*, para. 8). Externally, his reign belongs to the history of Europe. By 1810, after a practically unbroken succession of military campaigns (1805–9), he had formed a Napoleonic Empire which, with its confederate or vassal states, covered most of Europe excluding Russia: and out of this he had distributed princedoms and kingdoms to his kinsfolk and favourites. But he had not gained command at sea, nor, after Trafalgar (1805), could he hope to do so; and by persisting with the Spanish campaign in the teeth of solid national resistance, as well as with the economic blockade of Britain (see *Blocus continental*), he had sown the seeds of final disaster. His ill-fated Russian campaign followed in 1812, his defeat at Leipzig by the General Coalition (q.v.) in 1813. In 1814, after the Allied invasion of France and the capitulation of Paris (31 March), he abdicated unconditionally (6 April). He was allowed to retain the title of Emperor and the sovereignty of the island of Elba, to which, on 20 April, he went. Ten months later (1 March 1815) he escaped and landed, with 700 soldiers, on the French coast between Cannes and Antibes. Via Grenoble, Lyons, Autun, Avallon, and Auxerre, amid wildly increasing enthusiasm, he made his way to Paris where, on 20 March, the people and the soldiers carried him in triumph to the Tuileries. The restored Bourbon king, Louis XVIII, had left the previous day to take refuge in Belgium.

But enthusiasm was not general. The bourgeoisie supported him reluctantly in spite of his introduction of liberal government (see *Acte additionnel aux constitutions de l'empire*); the Royalists of the west, which was an ancient centre of disaffection (see *Vendée*), rose against him; and the General Coalition at once re-formed, this time in order to destroy, finally, 'an enemy and disturber of the peace of the world'. At the battle of Waterloo (18 June 1815) the French army was routed. Napoleon again abdicated (22 June). On 29 June he went to the port of Rochefort with the idea, which he eventually abandoned, of going to America. He decided to claim the protection of the British government and on 15 July he boarded H.M.S. *Bellerophon*. He was not allowed to land in England and a Bill was hurriedly enacted 'for the more effectually detaining in custody Napoleon Buonaparté' [56 Geo. III, c. 22, repealed 1950 by the Statute Law Revision Act 1873 (36–37 Vic. c. 91)]. On 7 August, off Plymouth, he was transferred to the flagship *Northumberland* in which he was transported to the island of St. Helena. There, from 15 October, he interned. In failing health, with a handful of devoted followers for company, he lived for six years in his villa of Longwood, subjected to the closest supervision, mainly occupied in composing and dictating his memoirs. He died, of a disease of the stomach thought at that time to be cancer, on 5 May 1821.

The Napoleonic Empire ended in 1815. At the International Congress held in Vienna between November 1814 and June 1815 the Allied Powers repartitioned Europe and left France, brought by Napoleon to a state of physical and military collapse, territorially smaller than before the Revolution. Yet there were signs within the next ten years that the *Légende napoléonienne* (q.v.) was forming. One of the earliest was the wide popularity of the *Mémorial de Sainte-Hélène* (1822–3), the account of Napoleon's life in exile by Las Cases (q.v.), who shared it till 1818. Other 'memoirs' (only those by French authors are here selected for mention), compiled partly from notes dictated by Napoleon and also from their own records of his conversation and of life on St. Helena, include those of Gourgaud and Montholon and of General Bertrand (qq.v., and see also *Caulaincourt; Marchand*).

Napoleon's Correspondence was edited and published during the Second Empire (1858–70) by order of Napoleon III. There are twenty-eight volumes, covering the periods 1793–1808 (vols. 1–17) and 1809–15 (vols. 18–28), plus three volumes (29–31) of works dictated at St. Helena. His will and various notes on St. Helena make up a final (32nd) volume. His numerous proclamations and Orders of the Day call for mention because of their definite literary value as models of their kind: nervous, terse, to the point and, upon occasion, magnificently inspiring. Nevertheless, his influence on French literature was bad and shackling. He cold-shouldered Chateaubriand and exiled

Mme de Staël (qq.v.), the two foremost writers of the day; he expected to impose his will upon thinkers and writers as he did upon his ministers and generals; he disliked independence of spirit and freedom of speech; he forbade eloquence in politics and in the pulpit; he controlled the newspapers almost out of existence. And he said to Benjamin Constant: 'Je ne hais point la liberté. Je l'ai écartée, lorsqu'elle obstruait ma route; mais je la comprends, j'ai été nourri dans ses pensées.' (See also *Bonaparte family*; *Maréchal de l'Empire*; *Napoleonic aristocracy*.)

Napoleon II. JOSEPH-FRANÇOIS-CHARLES (1811–32), born in Paris, only son of Napoleon I and Marie-Louise of Austria, proclaimed 'Roi de Rome' while still in his cradle. Although he was recognized as the Emperor Napoleon II by the Government at the time of Napoleon's second abdication (1815) he never reigned. He had left Paris in 1814 with his mother, and the remainder of his life was passed, as duc de Reichstadt, with his grandfather, the Emperor of Austria, in Vienna at the castle of Schönbrunn. He died of phthisis. He is the hero of Rostand's poetic drama *L'Aiglon* (q.v.).

Napoleon III. CHARLES-LOUIS-NAPOLÉON BONAPARTE (1808–73), born in Paris, was the third son of Louis Bonaparte, King of Holland, a younger brother of Napoleon I. By his mother, Queen Hortense (Hortense de Beauharnais), he was a grandson of the Empress Josephine. After the fall of the First Empire his mother, now separated from her husband, took him to live at the château d'Arenenberg, in Switzerland.

As a young man he served in the Swiss Federal armies and he was later involved in Carbonarist conspiracies (see *Carbonari*). After the death of Napoleon's son, the duc de Reichstadt, he was Bonapartist Pretender to the throne of France and made two abortive attempts to overthrow Louis-Philippe (q.v.). On the first occasion (1836) he was deported to the U.S.A. but managed to return to Europe a year later and from London published (1838) *Les Idées napoléoniennes* in which he spoke of his duty to realize the social reforms dreamed of by Napoleon I. The second time he was tried and sentenced to life imprisonment in the fortress of Ham (near Péronne in Northern France). In 1846 he escaped disguised as a mason (see *Badinguet*) and reached London, remaining there till the February Revolution (1848, see *Revolutions*, III), when he returned to France.

In June 1848, and again in September, he was elected to the *Assemblée constituante* (q.v.). By 10 December 1848 'the Great Emperor's nephew' had attracted such a large following, especially in the provinces, that he was elected Prince-President of the Republic with a very large majority over the other candidates. He increased his power with the *coup d'état* (q.v.) of 2 December 1851, then introduced several reactionary measures, and initiated successful propaganda for the re-establishment of the Empire. On 2 December 1852 he was proclaimed Emperor, with the title of 'Napoléon III' (see *Republics* (2); *Empire, Le Second*). In January 1853 he married the beautiful daughter of the comte de Montijo, a Spanish nobleman who had fought with the armies of Napoleon I (see *Eugénie, Empress*).

Napoleon III was in continual ill health during the later years of his reign, which may have accounted for his vacillating policy both at home and abroad. On the outbreak of the Franco-Prussian War (q.v.) in 1870 he accompanied his armies as Commander-in-Chief. After Sedan (q.v.) he was for some months a prisoner in the palace of Wilhelmshöhe, near Cassel, in Germany. Eventually he joined the Empress Eugénie and their son Prince Eugène ('le Prince Impérial', q.v.), in exile at Chislehurst, near London, where he died.

Napoleon, PRINCE, see *Bonaparte family*, s.v. *Jérôme*.

Napoleonic aristocracy. To maintain the dignity of his Empire Napoleon surrounded himself with a court and instituted many titled offices which necessitated elaborate rules of precedence between those holders who ranked as *Grands Dignitaires de l'Empire*, those who were *Grands Officiers*, and so on, in descending scale. In 1808 (by a decree of 1 March) he systematized these by creating the *noblesse impériale*, a peerage, in some cases hereditary, with a hierarchy of *ducs, princes, barons, comtes*, and *chevaliers* (for members of the *Légion d'honneur*, q.v.) into which *Grands Dignitaires, Grands Officiers*, &c., were all fitted. (See also *Noblesse*.)

Napoléon le Petit (1852), by Victor Hugo, a history (in four books, prose) of the period between December 1848 and April 1852 (see *Napoleon III*). From beginning to end it is a rhetorical indictment of Napoleon III. 'Je me lève devant lui', the author said, 'comme le remords en attendant que tous se lèvent comme le châtiment.' The work was written in Brussels in 16 days and published in London (see *Hugo, Victor,* paras. 5 and 8).

Napoleon's marshals, see *Maréchal de l'Empire.*

Napol le Pyrénéen, see *Peyrat, Napoléon.*

Narcissus, see *Romans d'antiquité.*

Natchez, Les (1826), a prose epic in twelve books, by Chateaubriand (q.v.). He wrote it in England between 1794 and 1799 with the intention, which he abandoned, of making it part of *Le Génie du Christianisme* (q.v.). It is a continuation of the history of René after he leaves his sister Amélie in France and of Chactas after the death of Atala (see *René; Atala*). The Natchez, after whom a town founded in 1716 by the French on the Mississippi to the north-west of New Orleans was named, were a tribe of American Indians. They revolted against the French colonists and were in their turn nearly exterminated (*c.* 1730).

National, Le, a daily paper founded by Thiers, Mignet, and Carrel (qq.v.) in 1830 shortly before the publication of the *ordonnances* of Charles X which abolished the liberty of the Press. A protest drafted by Thiers, and signed by the editors of several other papers, was issued from the *National*'s offices and did much to provoke the July Revolution (see *Revolutions*, II, IIa). In the first years of Louis-Philippe's reign *Le National* stood for a constitutional monarchy on the English model. Later, it objected to the king's policy of peace at any price and became Republican. The *coup d'état* of December 1851 terminated its existence.

Nattier, JEAN-MARC (1685–1766), a distinguished portrait-painter.

Naturalisme. After 1865 the documentary and scientific aspects of the novel were still more heavily emphasized, and *réalisme* (q.v.) developed into *naturalisme* (*c.* 1865–*c.* 1895). This was largely due to Taine's determinist philosophy of the influence of 'la race, le milieu, et le moment' on the formation of character; to his theory, also, that the novel should be a form of human case-history, amply documented with facts throwing light on the antecedents and circumstances of the characters. As a result, the novel became more brutal. It concentrated on the lowest side of human nature, and its characters were frequently pathological cases at the mercy of their inherited criminal and vicious instincts. Another result was the doctrine that the novel, to be a faithful study of human nature, should dispense with action, because the majority of existences were uneventful.

The theories were little more than an exaggerated form of *réalisme*. The difference between the two movements lay in the pseudo-scientific character given to the naturalistic movement by its leader, Émile Zola. He proposed to apply to fiction the methods of observation and experiment advocated by the physiologist Dr. Claude Bernard (q.v.) in the *Introduction à l'étude de la médecine expérimentale*, a book which created a stir on its publication in 1865. He drew a false analogy between the functions of the scientist and the novelist, and in 1880, when the movement was in full swing and he had written several novels illustrative of his theories, he produced *Le Roman expérimental*, which stands as the manifesto of *le naturalisme*. It was in great part a naïve transposition of Bernard's treatise, made by substituting the word 'romancier' wherever the other work uses 'médecin'.

In the extreme naturalistic novel (e.g. Zola's *Rougon-Macquart* series, q.v.), the author proceeds by experiment and analysis, from hypotheses to demonstration. He selects his situation and endows his characters with conflicting temperaments which are in every case shown to be the outcome of heredity and environment. He then by the accumulation of detail proceeds to a logical demonstration that given this situation and these temperaments the struggle must have one inevitable conclusion. Thus *naturalisme* came to imply that the novelist's art, besides being the faithful reproduction of Nature, necessitated as it were the laboratory methods of the natural scientists. The theory was carried to an extreme by Zola, but it coloured the work of all the writers of his school. Among these the outstanding names are Alphonse Daudet, Guy de Maupassant, and Joris-Karl Huysmans. The last two were among the five disciples who formed the *groupe de Médan* (see *Soirées de Médan, Les*). Flaubert (especially with *L'Éducation sentimentale*) and Edmond de Goncourt are also often termed *naturalistes* (and in fact the theory of *documentation* in the novel was largely due to the brothers Goncourt), but they occupied a position apart from the extreme naturalist campaign. The typical naturalistic novel in which nothing happens is Henry Céard's *Une Belle Journée* (q.v.).

Reaction against the *roman naturaliste* was evident before 1890. Besides a growing conviction among public and authors alike that monotony and naturalism were becoming synonymous, other influences were at work —the decline of positivism, new trends in philosophy (e.g. the theories of Bergson, q.v.), a reawakening interest in religion, the appearance of the psychological novel (see *Bourget, Paul*), also the repercussions of the Symbolist movement in poetry (see *Symbolisme*). In 1883 the critic Brunetière had published *Le Roman naturaliste*, a severe criticism of the naturalistic movement. In 1887 five of Zola's own disciples issued a manifesto protesting against the falseness of his doctrines and the deliberate obscenity of his work. Zola himself was finding *Les Rougon-Macquart* a depressing task; Maupassant's novels were becoming psychological (and his characters were moving upwards in the social scale); Daudet's irrepressible good humour made it difficult for him to remain in the gloomy naturalistic depths; and Huysmans was turning to religion. In 1891 one of the questionnaires beloved of French journalists was circulated to sixty-four prominent writers who were asked whether they thought *le naturalisme* was dead or dying. One, Paul Alexis (q.v.), sent a frantic telegram 'Naturalisme pas mort. Lettre suit', but the general trend of the replies was that the movement was incurably moribund.

Naturalism also influenced the theatre, first through the dramatization of works by the brothers Goncourt and by Zola, and still more effectively through the plays of Henry Becque and, between 1887 and 1896, the work of the *Théâtre-Libre* (q.v.).

Naturisme, a poetic movement, began about 1895 as a reaction against the Symbolist fogs and general lack of contact with real life (see *Symbolisme*). The *naturistes* (with Paul Fort, Francis Jammes, the comtesse de Noailles, and Saint-Georges de Bouhélier prominent among them) wished to return to Nature—not to *Naturalisme* (q.v.). They wrote of rustic life and of everyday joys and sorrows, of social energy, social justice, and universal brotherhood.

Nau, JOHN-ANTOINE [pseud. of Antoine Torquet] (1860–1918), poet and novelist, was born in San Francisco of French parentage but brought to live in France at the age of three when his father died. For a time he sailed before the mast, then he gave this up but still travelled. The exotic element is conspicuous in his work, which includes the novels *Cristobal le poète* (1912) and *Thérèse Donati* (1921) in which background and atmosphere, of Algiers and Corsica respectively, are picturesquely conveyed; also the poems collected in *Au seuil de l'espoir* (1897), *Vers la Fée Viviane* (1908), and *En suivant les goélands* (1914).

Naudé, GABRIEL (1600–53), a man of learning, friend of Guy Patin (q.v.), librarian to the cardinal de Bagni in Italy, and subsequently to Richelieu and Mazarin (he persuaded the latter to open his library to the public, but the *Fronde* intervened). His best known and most important work was probably the *Apologie pour les grands personnages faussement soupçonnés de magie* (1625). His *Advis pour dresser une bibliothèque* (1627) was translated into English by John Evelyn (1661). He was the author, also, of historical works, of *Mascurat* (1649), a dialogue in defence of Mazarin, and of a *Jugement de tout ce qui a été imprimé contre le cardinal de Mazarin*, containing a mass of miscellaneous information on all sorts of subjects.

Naundorff, CHARLES, one of the best known of the 19th-century 'faux dauphins' (cf. *Orphelin du Temple, L'*).

Nautilus, Le, the submarine in *Vingt mille lieues sous les mers*, by Jules Verne (q.v.).

Navarre, see *Collège de Navarre*; *Marguerite d'Angoulême (de Navarre)*.

Necker (pron. as if *Neckère*), JACQUES (1732–1804), a banker born at Geneva who settled in

Paris and directed the finances of France with honesty and wisdom from 1776 (after the fall of Turgot) to 1781, when his famous *Compte rendu* or report on the finances led to his resignation. He was once more in office in 1788–9 (after the fall of Loménie de Brienne) on the very eve of the Revolution; and again in 1789–90. His *Éloge de Colbert* appeared in 1773, and his work on *La Législation et le commerce des graines* in 1775.

Necker's wife was Suzanne Curchod (1739–94), the daughter of a Swiss Protestant pastor, whom Gibbon in his youth had wished to marry. She came to Paris and married Necker in 1764, and her *salon* from that time was frequented by men of letters. Lacking the easy grace of the true Parisian woman, she showed on the other hand, in her conversation and some miscellaneous writings, intelligence, rectitude, and kindliness, coupled with some haziness of thought and errors of taste. She was a friend and admirer of Buffon and tells us much about him. Her daughter was the famous Mme de Staël (q.v.).

Necker de Saussure, MME ALBERTINE (1766–1841), daughter of the Swiss physicist and geologist Horace-Bénédict de Saussure (1740–99), was a cousin by marriage and an intimate friend of Mme de Staël. Her *Notice sur le caractère et les écrits de Mme de Staël* (1820) is her best-remembered work, but she also translated Schlegel's (q.v.) lectures on the drama, and at one time her treatise on children's education and the position of women was much read and praised (*L'Éducation progressive, étude du cours de la vie*, 1828–32, 3 vols.).

Némésis, La, see under *Méry.*

Nemo, le capitaine, hero of *Vingt mille lieues sous les mers,* by Jules Verne (q.v.).

Nemours, MARIE DE LONGUEVILLE, DUCHESSE DE (1625–1707), step-daughter of the duchesse de Longueville (q.v.), author of interesting memoirs relating to the period of the *Fronde.* The Duke of York (the future James II, then in exile) at one time proposed to marry her, but the project was not approved by the regent, Anne of Austria.

Nennius (*fl. c.* 800), the traditional author, but probably only the reviser, of the Latin *Historia Britonum,* one of the sources on

which Geoffrey of Monmouth (q.v.) drew for his *Historia Regum Britanniae,* and interesting for the account it purports to give of the historical Arthur. Nennius lived on the borders of Mercia and was a pupil of Elbod, Bishop of Bangor.

Néo-impressionnistes, see *Impressionnisme.*

Néo-Mallarmisme, see *Literary Isms.*

Néo-romantisme, see *Literary Isms.*

Néo-Thomisme, see *Thomas Aquinas, Saint.*

Nepveu, ANDRÉ, see *Durtain, Luc.*

Néricault, PHILIPPE, see *Destouches.*

Néron (Nero), the chief character in Racine's *Britannicus* (q.v.).

Nerval, GÉRARD DE [pseud. of Gérard Labrunie] (1808–55), author, was born in Paris. While his father, a doctor, campaigned with Napoleon's armies, he had a country upbringing with cousins, in the district to the north of Paris still remembered by its old name of Valois (Compiègne, Senlis, and Villers-Cotterets are situated in it); and for mental food he had the run of his uncle's library of occult books. Later, he attended the Lycée Charlemagne, in Paris, and in time became one of the *Jeunes-France* (q.v.) led by Théophile Gautier and Petrus Borel. Like them he was a *bousingo* (q.v.), with revolutionary sympathies and influenced by German romanticism. At twenty he published a translation of *Faust* (1828), which Goethe himself praised and on which Berlioz drew freely for *La Damnation de Faust*; and his writings indicate that between (probably) 1831 and 1838 his life was profoundly affected by his love for an actress, Jenny Colon. He also, about this time and later, travelled in Germany and Austria and in the Near East (*Voyage en Orient,* 1851; *Loreley: Souvenirs d'Allemagne,* 1852), and formed lasting vagabond habits. Eventually he was to drift through life with no settled abode, relying on the casual hospitality of friends or the odd sleep in a café. In 1841 he had his first mental breakdown. Some months in a private asylum restored his balance for a time, but his latter years were spent continually on or over the verge of insanity. One winter's morning, shortly after he had, supposedly, recovered from a relapse, his body was found hanging to a railing in the rue de la Vieille Lanterne—in the old quarter of Paris—one of his favourite haunts.

His considerable output, usually first contributed to reviews, consisted of poetry (both original and in translation, and including political and satirical verse); prose (literary and dramatic criticism, essays and portrait sketches, and, notably, short stories), also attempts at dramatic authorship. Works collected and published in book form during his lifetime include: *Les Illuminés, ou les Précurseurs du socialisme* (1853), studies of Cagliostro, Restif de la Bretonne, &c.; *Petits châteaux de Bohème* (1853), prose and poetry, including some early 'Odelettes' and five sonnets entitled *Le Christ aux oliviers* which later formed part of the twelve sonnets *Les Chimères* (q.v.) appended to *Les Filles du feu* (see below); *Contes et Facéties* (1853), which include *La Main enchantée* (first entitled *La Main de gloire* and published in a periodical miscellany of 1832), a typical 'young Romantic' piece of jocose Gothic with a historical background and a hand, newly severed from a corpse, that performs blood-curdling antics; *Les Filles du feu* (1854), tales (with the sonnets *Les Chimères* appended) which include his masterpiece, *Sylvie* (q.v.), a simple, beautiful evocation of early days and early love in the country; *La Bohème galante* (1855), prose, including criticism, and poetry; *Le Rêve et la vie* (1855). This last collection, of prose and poetry, contains *Aurélia*, a remarkable record of his visions and the various phases of his mental derangement which has earned Gérard de Nerval a place as a precursor of much of the consciously hallucinatory writing of modern times. The matter is delirious, the language lucid to a degree that led Gautier to characterize the work as 'la Raison écrivant les mémoires de la Folie sous sa dictée'.

The first collected edition of Gérard de Nerval's writings was published between 1867 and 1877 (Michel-Lévy *frères*, 6 vols.).

Nervèze, (?) ANTOINE (?) GUILLAUME-BERNARD (*c.* 1570–?), a man of letters and novelist in whom the *précieux* style can be seen at its most exaggerated (*Les Amours de Filandre et de Marizée*, 1603; *Les Aventures guerrières et amoureuses de Léandre*, 1608, &c.).

Nesle, Tour de and **Hôtel de.** The *Tour de Nesle*, originally known as the Tour Hamelin from the name of the *prévost* of Paris at the time of its construction, was a large tower standing at the eastern extremity of the wall of medieval Paris where it reached the left (south) bank of the Seine. It was demolished in 1663. The site is now occupied by the Institut de France (q.v.). In the 13th century a sieur de Nesle built in proximity to the Tour Hamelin the *Hôtel de Nesle*, a spacious residence, which then gave its name to the adjacent tower. It was associated with the legendary crimes of Marguerite de Bourgogne (*c.* 1290–1315), queen of France and Navarre, and gave Dumas *père* the subject of his historical drama *La Tour de Nesle* (q.v.).

The *Hôtel du Petit-Nesle*, where Benvenuto Cellini resided during much of his stay in Paris (1540–5), was part of the premises of the Hôtel de Nesle, but distinct from the main building, and stood on the town wall.

Nettement, ALFRED (1805–65), man of letters and publicist, and a politician of strong Roman Catholic and Royalist views. His works include: *Histoire de la révolution de juillet* (1833); — *de la Restauration* (1860–6); — *de la littérature française sous la Restauration* (1852) and ... *sous la royauté de juillet* (1854). From 1858 he edited *La Semaine des familles*, a weekly.

Neustria, see *Mérovingiens*.

Neveu de Rameau, Le, a character-sketch in the form of a dialogue, by Diderot, written, it is believed, between 1761 and 1774. The work was first made known through a German translation by Goethe, then printed in 1823 from a copy of the manuscript. It was finally printed from the manuscript itself in 1891 and is the most characteristic of Diderot's works.

The subject, a nephew of the French composer Rameau (q.v.), is an original, a crack-brained parasite, who combines laziness and sensuality with a passion for music and a gift of mimicry, and is utterly frank in his depravity. The dialogue gives astonishing vigour and animation to the portrait, at the same time throwing light on the corruption of contemporary society. This nephew of Rameau's was a real person, of whom L.-S. Mercier has also left a picture.

Newspapers and periodicals, see *Press, Development of the.*

Ney, MICHEL, the most famous of Napoleon's marshals (see *Maréchal de l'Empire*).

Nicaise, L'ABBÉ CLAUDE (1623–1701), antiquarian, a native of Dijon, pursued his interests in France and Italy and for over twenty years maintained a correspondence with Leibniz, Huet, Bayle, &c.

Nicaise, rue, see *Machine infernale*.

Nicolas, Jeu de saint, see *Bodel*.

Nicolas de Montreux (b. 1561), dramatist and novelist who wrote under the pseudonym 'Ollenix de Montsacre'; a gentleman of Maine, author in early life of a number of mediocre tragedies and comedies (*Le Jeune Cyrus, Annibal, Cléopâtre, Joyeuse,* &c.), and later of a long pastoral romance, *Les Bergeries de Juliette* (1585–93), of other romances (e.g. *Les Chastes et Délectables Jardins d'Amour,* 1594) of a moral tendency, and of pastoral plays: *Athlette* (1585), *Diane* (1592), *Arimine* (q.v., 1596). In 1601 he published two further plays, *Sophonisbe* and *Joseph le chaste*.

Nicolas de Troyes (16th cent.), a saddler, native of Troyes, living at Tours, who left in manuscript a collection of short tales, *Le Parangon des nouvelles nouvelles,* of which the first part is lost and the second was in part printed in 1867. The majority of the surviving tales are borrowed from Boccaccio, the *Cent nouvelles nouvelles,* the *Quinze joyes de mariage,* &c. The remainder, though agreeably told, are of no special literary merit.

Nicole, the outspoken servant in Molière's *Le Bourgeois gentilhomme* (q.v.).

Nicole, PIERRE (1625–95), born at Chartres, moralist and theologian, one of the learned solitaries of Port-Royal (q.v.). He collaborated in the *Logique de Port-Royal* with Antoine Arnauld (q.v.), whom he helped and sought to moderate in many religious controversies. He was author of *Essais de morale et instructions théologiques* (first vol. 1671), a work much admired by Mme de Sévigné; of *Les imaginaires, ou Lettres sur l'hérésie imaginaire* (from 1664) after the manner of Pascal's *Provinciales,* designed to show that the pretended Jansenist heresy was a matter of little importance; and of *Les Visionnaires, ou seconde partie des Lettres sur l'hérésie imaginaire* (1667) directed against Desmarets de Saint-Sorlin (who had attacked Jansenism). A sentence in this last work bitterly condemned novelists

and dramatists, provoking an acrimonious reply from Racine (1666). Nicole took a large part in drafting (with Arnauld) *La Perpétuité de la Foi de l'Église catholique touchant l'Eucharistie,* directed against the Protestant doctrine (1669–76). He followed Arnauld into exile, but soon made his accommodation and obtained permission to return.

Nicolette, see *Aucassin et Nicolette*.

Nicomède, one of Corneille's most remarkable tragedies, produced in 1651.

Nicomède returns from his conquest of Cappadocia to the court of his father, Prusias, king of Bithynia. He encounters the hostility of his stepmother Arsinoé (who desires to see her own son Attale succeed to the throne), of the king (ruled by his wife), and of Flaminius the Roman ambassador (who rules both king and queen and has recently procured the death of Hannibal, a refugee at their court). Moreover, his half-brother, Attale, is his rival for the hand of Laodice, queen of Armenia. He meets all intrigues with magnanimous prudence and cool irony; and when his enemies make a last effort to ship him off a prisoner to Rome, even wins the help of Attale to defeat it.

Nicot, JEAN, see *Dictionaries and Encyclopedias,* under date 1606.

Niepce, JOSEPH-NICÉPHORE (1765–1833), the inventor of photography, see under *Daguerre*.

Ninon de Lenclos, see *Lenclos*.

Nisard, DÉSIRÉ (1806–88), literary historian and critic, born at Châtillon-sur-Seine (Côte-d'Or), began as a political journalist on the *Journal des Débats* and the *National* (qq.v.). During the July Monarchy and the Second Empire he held various academic and government appointments, e.g. Professor of French Eloquence at the Sorbonne (after Villemain, q.v.), Director—responsible for several administrative reforms—of the École normale supérieure (1857–67). His criticism, reactionary, was marked by an uncompromising distaste for the Romantics (see *Romantisme*) and the belief that few works of merit had appeared in French literature after the 17th century. After *Histoire de la littérature française* (1855–61), his chief work, his writings included: *Poètes latins de la décadence* (1834, early studies); *Mélanges d'histoire et de littérature* (1868); and *Nouveaux, mélanges . . .* (1886).

Nitouche, sainte, a popular term for a person who affects an air of excessive innocence, a facetious adaptation of 'n'y touche'.

Nivelle de la Chaussée, see *La Chaussée*.

Nivôse, the fourth month of the Republican Calendar (q.v.). It ran from 21 December to 19 January.

Noailles, COMTESSE MATHIEU DE [*née* princesse Anna-Élisabeth de Brancovan] (1876–1933), born in Paris of Rumanian and Greek ancestry and one of the outstanding French women writers of the last half-century, belonged to the poetic group known as 'la Nouvelle Pléiade' (q.v.). Her poetical output is at its most characteristic in *Le Cœur innombrable* (1901), which contains beautiful descriptions of French landscape (particularly that of the Île-de-France), and in *L'Ombre des jours* (1902) and *Les Éblouissements* (1907), where the themes are love of life and youth, travel, and the East. It is classical in form but strongly romantic, often pagan, in spirit, and intensely subjective in its sense of personal communion with Nature. The poems of her later life, which include two notable collections, *Les Vivants et les morts* (1913) and *Les Forces éternelles* (1920), as well as *Poème de l'amour* (1924) and *L'Honneur de souffrir* (1927), are on a more melancholy note. Her prose output includes the diffusely sensuous novels *La Nouvelle Espérance* (1903), *Le Visage émerveillé* (1904), *La Domination* (1904).

Nobel Prize for literature, see *Prix Nobel*.

Noble, the lion, in the *Roman de Renart* (q.v.).

Noblesse, La. The aristocracy of pre-Revolutionary France originated in the *noblesse de parage* (i.e. by birth) of feudal times, based on the possession of land ('Point de seigneur sans terre') and carrying with it, in addition to other privileges and exemptions, the right of direct male succession. By about the 12th century the *ducs*, *comtes*, &c. (see *Duc*), of Charlemagne's creation were no longer removable officials but the highest ranks of a growing class of hereditary land-owners, warriors (*la chevalerie*) for whom the possession of lands was indispensable if they were to meet the heavy expenses of knightly life. The king was at the head of the hierarchy, which extended downwards through *ducs*, *comtes*, and *vicomtes* (the *grands feudataires* who took their titles—e.g. duc de Bourgogne—from their domains or provinces, where they exercised sovereign authority), to the *seigneurs*, usually called *sire*, or *baron*, and the *chevaliers*, and below these (a 13th-century extension) to the *écuyers*, who were called *gentilshommes* and became the country gentry. This hereditary *noblesse* was further extended from the 13th century, when the French kings began to issue *lettres de noblesse* ennobling rich commoners. Philippe *le Hardi* is said to have done so first when he ennobled his goldsmith. Alternatively, offices were bestowed which carried with them entitlement to noble rank.

By the 16th century some of the hereditary rights and privileges of the nobility had disappeared but many remained, such as exemption from taxation, or vested right to certain high offices, and led to abuse (cf. *Privilégiés*). By the 16th century, too, the *noblesse d'épée* had come into being, so called because, to begin with, military service over a specified period counted as entitlement to hereditary noble rank. Here, with the years, the tendency was to confine military promotion solely to the *noblesse d'épée*.

Other categories of hereditary aristocracy which evolved during the 16th and 17th centuries were, notably, the *noblesse de robe*, conferred on holders of high judicial or legal office, and in a smaller way the *noblesse municipale* or *de cloche*, conferred on magistrates or municipal officials. Again the possibilities of abuse were many, for traffic in titles was a means of procuring revenue. Moreover, in some cases when the families of the original *ducs* and *comtes*, whose rank had been the badge, so to speak, of their functions, became extinct the same rank, but without any accompanying office, was conferred on lesser nobles who were favourites of, or a possible source of profit to, the king.

During and still more after the reign of Louis XIV a distinction between *noblesse de cour* and *noblesse de province* led to much abuse. The former lived for a great part of the year at court and tended to secure all the high offices, while the latter remained in the country, often, if they belonged to the lesser nobility, in poverty and precluded by the very circumstances of their birth from following any but a military career.

All forms of hereditary titles and offices were abolished by decree of the *Assemblée constituante* (q.v.) in January 1790. Napoleon reintroduced some of the old titles when he created his Napoleonic aristocracy (q.v.). The pre-Revolutionary aristocracy was revived during the Restoration and the *noblesse impériale* was maintained. Titles were again abolished by decree in 1848 but re-established in 1852.

Nodier, CHARLES (1780–1844), novelist and miscellaneous writer, one of the fathers of *le romantisme* (q.v.), was born and educated at Besançon, where his father was mayor. In early life he was a librarian there but occasionally he visited Paris seeking other employment. On one trip (1803) he spent thirty-six days in prison for having written and circulated a rhymed pamphlet (*La Napoléone*, 1802) disrespectful to Napoleon. Between 1807 and 1809 he was literary assistant to the eccentric Sir Herbert Croft and Lady Mary Hamilton, near Amiens (see *D.N.B.*). In 1813, at Laibach, in Illyria, then in French occupation, he combined the duties of municipal librarian, editor of the *Télégraphe illyrien* (a tetraglot newspaper), and secretary to Fouché (q.v.). After 1814 he settled with his wife and daughter Marie (cf. *Arvers, Félix*) in Paris, contributed to the *Journal des Débats* (q.v.), and from 1824 was librarian of the *Bibliothèque de l'Arsenal* (q.v.). Here his *salon*, described in lively fashion in the *Mémoires* of Dumas *père*, was one of the famous Romantic *cénacles* (q.v.).

Nodier, a prolific author, was at his most typical in novels, e.g. *Le Peintre de Salzbourg, journal des émotions d'un cœur souffrant* (1803, much influenced by Goethe's *Werther*); *Jean Sbogar* (1818, q.v.); *Thérèse Aubert* (1819, q.v.), and in half fairy, half fantasy tales which had a strong foretaste of Romantic extravagance, e.g. *Smarra ou les Démons de la nuit* (1821); *Trilby, ou le lutin d'Argail* (1822); *L'Histoire du roi de Bohème et de ses sept châteaux* (1830); *Mademoiselle de Marsan* (1832); *La Fée aux miettes* (1832, set, like *Trilby*, in Scotland); *Inès de las sierras* (1837). (Cf. *Foreign Influences on French Literature*, para. 20.)

He also wrote poetry (*Essais d'un jeune barde*, 1804) and at least one melodrama (*Le Vampire*, 1820). His miscellaneous writings include criticism, entomology, and lexicography, e.g. *Bibliographie entomologique* (1801); *Dictionnaire raisonné des onomatopées françaises* (1808); *Questions de littérature légale* (1812); *Mélanges de littérature et de critique* (1820); *Dictionnaire universel de la langue française* (1826); *Mélanges tirés d'une petite bibliothèque* (1829); *Rêveries* (1832, containing essays significant of their period, e.g. *Des types en littérature, Du fantastique en littérature*); *Souvenirs de la jeunesse* (1832), &c.

Noël, MARIE (1883–), author of *chansons* (often written with musical accompaniment) and lyrics of religious inspiration, e.g. in the collections *Les Chansons et les heures* (1920), *Les Chants de la Merci* (1930).

Noëls, medieval lyrical pieces connected with the feast of the Nativity. Of the few that have survived, one is by Adam de la Halle (q.v.).

Noëls bourguignons, see *La Monnoye*.

Nœud de Vipères, Le (1932), a novel, see *Mauriac, François*.

Nohant, Château de, in the ancient province of Berry, the home of George Sand (q.v.) who was often called 'la bonne dame de Nohant'.

Nollet, JEAN-ANTOINE, ABBÉ (1700–70), physicist, who developed and popularized by his lectures and writings the methods of experimental science, substituting observation and experiment for deductive reasoning.

Nonnotte, CLAUDE-FRANÇOIS, ABBÉ (1711–93), a Jesuit, published (1762) *Les Erreurs de Voltaire* in which he undertook to point out Voltaire's errors of historical fact. As a result he was involved in controversy with, and frequently ridiculed by, Voltaire.

Normands, Geste des, see *Wace*.

Norpois, LE MARQUIS DE, in Proust's *A la recherche du temps perdu* (q.v.), a conventional diplomat of the old school. His habit of elaborate discourse, without ever committing himself, is admirably conveyed. His friendship with Marcel's father and his liaison—sanctified by long years—with Mme de Villeparisis (q.v.) make him a link between the *Swann* and the *Guermantes* (qq.v.) sides of Marcel's life.

Nostradamus, MICHEL DE NOSTRE-DAME, *known as* (1503–66), astrologer and physician, born at Saint-Remy in Provence. Catherine de Médicis summoned him to the court and he was physician to Charles IX. He was the author of a book of prophecies, written in quatrains obscure in style, entitled *Centuries* (1555) which had a wide vogue. We find Mme de Sévigné referring to it (11 Mar. 1676). It was finally condemned by the Pope. There is an allusion to Nostradamus in the opening scene of Goethe's *Faust*; also in Pepys's Diary, under 3 February 1667.

Notables, Les, members of the Privileged Orders (see *Privilégiés*) in the France of the *ancien régime*. In times of difficulty the king could at will consult a specially-convoked *Assemblée des Notables*. The most celebrated of these assemblies was held in February 1787, on the advice of the king's Minister of Finance, Calonne (1734–1802), when the Notables refused to agree to proposals for taxation which would touch both the privileged and the unprivileged orders. This was the first stage in a crisis which ended with the summoning of the *États généraux* (q.v.).

Notes sur l'Angleterre (1872) by Taine, see under *Taine, Hippolyte*.

Notes sur Paris. Vie et opinions de M. Frédéric-Thomas Graindorge (1868) by Taine (q.v.), studies, at times ironical, of Parisian life under the Second Empire. M. Graindorge, whom Taine makes his mouthpiece, is a Frenchman who had left Paris at the age of twelve and returned thirty-five years later. In the interval he had been educated at Eton and the University of Heidelberg, then gone to America where he made a fortune out of canned pork. The chapters 'Aux Italiens' and 'Tête-à-tête', by Taine the lover of Mozart and Beethoven, are of great interest.

Notre cœur (1890), a novel by Maupassant (q.v.).

Notre-Dame de Paris (1831), a novel of 15th-century Paris, by Victor Hugo.

Claude Frollo, archdeacon of Notre-Dame, becomes enamoured of Esmeralda, a gipsy dancer, the favourite of the idle Parisian crowds. He employs Quasimodo, the grotesque, hunchback bell-ringer of Notre-Dame, whom he has succoured and befriended, to kidnap her. Esmeralda is rescued by Phœbus de Châteaupers, Captain of the Royal Archers. She falls in love with him, taking him for a hero rather than the loose-living braggart that he is, and agrees to meet him secretly. Frollo follows her to the rendezvous, stabs Phœbus before her eyes, and escapes, leaving her to be arrested and sentenced to death for his crime. Quasimodo, whom one casual act of kindness has made her slave, snatches her from the scaffold itself and brings her secretly to sanctuary in the Cathedral. Frollo so engineers matters that the band of gipsies, beggars, and malefactors to whom Esmeralda belongs (cf. *Cour des miracles*) learn of her hiding-place and determine to rescue her. They make a midnight attack upon the Cathedral (one of the most dramatic scenes of the book) and are repulsed by Quasimodo, single-handed. Meantime Frollo, in disguise, has persuaded Esmeralda to fly with him. Suddenly she recognizes him and chooses to be denounced to the authorities rather than yield to his threats. Frollo, enraged, goes off to find the officers of the guard, leaving Esmeralda in charge of a half-mad woman whose daughter had been kidnapped by gipsies some years previously. Suddenly the woman sees by an amulet the girl is wearing that Esmeralda is her daughter. At this moment the archers arrive. After almost superhuman efforts they wrest Esmeralda from her mother, leaving the old woman dying on the pavement. From one of the towers of Notre-Dame Quasimodo, in despair, sees Esmeralda's body swinging to and fro on the gallows. He turns and discovers Frollo gloating over the same scene. With one movement he dashes him from the balustrade to the cobblestones far below. One day, in the vault where criminals' corpses are flung, Quasimodo's skeleton is found beside that of Esmeralda.

Another character in the book is Pierre Gringoire, a travesty, antedated, of Pierre Gringore (q.v.). He helps Frollo to abduct Esmeralda the second time, and afterwards rescues Esmeralda's pet goat, a creature of enticing ways and many tricks.

Despite numerous historical and topographical digressions, *Notre-Dame de Paris* presents a vivid picture of medieval Paris. People and houses swarm, ant-like, round the *Île de la Cité*, the nucleus from which Paris has spread to both banks of the river; and the Cathedral itself dominates all the characters in the book.

Nourritures terrestres, Les (1897), by André Gide, prose and verse fragments of great sensuous and musical appeal, counsel addressed to a non-existent youth Nathanaël. He is exhorted to live fully, in and for the moment, to abandon doubt and preoccupation with disciplined morality, to let desire and impulse be his justification for action, to be *disponible*, ready to accept *all* experiences and sensations (for to choose is to renounce all that one might have chosen); and ultimately to make self-emancipation the way to self-realization.

The character Ménalque, invoked in the course of the book as a mentor, also occurs in Gide's novel (or *récit*) *L'Immoraliste*. (For *Les Nouvelles Nourritures* see *Gide*, para. 6.)

Nouveau, GERMAIN (1852–1920), poet, self-styled **Humilis**, led a Bohemian existence which included a stay in London with Rimbaud (q.v.). Later, he was influenced by Verlaine (the Verlaine of *Sagesse*, q.v.) and became a devout Roman Catholic. His *Poèmes d'Humilis* (1911) were written after his conversion. *Poésies d'Humilis et vers inédits* is a posthumous collection (1926).

Nouveaux lundis (1863–70), by Sainte-Beuve, see *Causeries du lundi*.

Nouvelle, a somewhat vague literary term for a short piece of fictitious narrative, generally in prose, which critics have distinguished from the *roman* (see *Novel*) in that it deals artistically with a single situation, usually taken from everyday life, or a single aspect of a character or a contrast of characters which it throws into strong relief, leading up to a more or less dramatic or unexpected issue. It may be of a comic or a tragic nature.

Elements of the *nouvelle* may be seen in early *lais* (such as some of those of Marie de France) and in the *fabliaux*, in the tales of eastern origin found in the *Roman des sept sages*, and in some other early narratives in verse or prose. (The process of transition from verse to prose as the natural vehicle for realistic narrative in general may be seen in *Aucassin et Nicolette*.) But there appears to be no direct continuity of development of the *nouvelle* from the *lai* and the *fabliau*. A closer relation may perhaps be seen in the realistic and dramatic descriptions of incidents of married life in the 15th-century satire *Les Quinze Joyes de mariage* and in some of Antoine de la Sale's works (notably the *Réconfort de Madame de Fresne* and the final episode of *Petit Jehan de Saintré*). Finally the *nouvelle* properly so called takes shape (under Italian influence) in the *Cent Nouvelles Nouvelles* (1462), where we find a marked advance on the *fabliau* in comicality and dramatic force, and to a less extent in realism, and in the detached, ironical attitude of the narrator. Other works of the same period and the end of the 15th century partaking of some of the features of the *nouvelle* are the *Arrêts d'amour* of Martial d'Auvergne and the remarkable little tale of *Jehan de Paris*; while a 16th-century example of the genre is the *Nouvelles Récréations* attributed to Despériers. From the 16th century the *nouvelle* ranged from the *Heptaméron* of Marguerite de Navarre to the fully developed masterpieces of Voltaire in the 18th century. In the 19th century the terms *nouvelle* and *conte* (q.v.) were often used interchangeably. Flaubert and Maupassant, for instance, used the word 'conte' (e.g. *Trois Contes*; *Contes du jour et de la nuit*). Authors of this period include: Charles Nodier, with half-fanciful, half-fairy tales (e.g. *La Fée aux miettes, Le Chien de Brisquet*); Alfred de Musset, with the delicate sentiment of *Frédéric et Bernerette, Mimi Pinson*, &c.; Alfred de Vigny, whose three tales in *Servitude et grandeur militaires* are small classics; Méry, whose tales were slight, but often witty and light-hearted; Mérimée, who introduced an objectivity and forceful economy of construction rivalled by few of his successors except Maupassant, whose short tales are some of the most perfect examples of purely objective writing in French literature; Gobineau, whose *Nouvelles asiatiques* or his excellent *Mademoiselle Irnois*, or *Adélaïde*, are too often forgotten; and another master of the short story, Anatole France.

Nouvelle France, La, the name by which the French-Canadian territory in the valley of the St. Lawrence river was known in the days of the early French settlers (17th century).

Nouvelle Héloïse, Julie ou la, a romance by J.-J. Rousseau, composed at Montmorency in 1756–8, published in 1761, 'an attempt to rehabilitate human nature in as much of the supposed freshness of primitive times as the hardened crust of civil institutions and social use would allow' (Morley). The narrative is told in the form of letters. See *Houdetot, Mme d'*.

Saint-Preux is a youthful tutor in the house of Julie's father, the baron d'Étanges. He and Julie fall deeply in love, but the pride of Julie's father excludes all hope of their marriage, and they yield to their mutual passion. Remorse soon follows; Saint-Preux is saved from suicide by the generous intervention of Lord Edward Bomston, an English nobleman, who offers the couple an asylum on his estate, and when this is refused, places Saint-Preux on the ship in which Admiral Anson is setting out for his voyage round the world; Julie obeys her father's behest and marries the elderly, benevolent, judicious foreigner, baron Wolmar. Saint-Preux returns after some years, and is invited by Wolmar to stay with them. Julie has confessed to her husband her previous relations with Saint-Preux (which in fact he knew already) and he thinks it wiser to regulate than to oppose their mutual attachment, by trusting to their loyalty to himself; he moreover decides to make Saint-Preux tutor to his children. We have now a picture of orderly, virtuous, contented family life, in which Julie and Saint-Preux bravely struggle against a renewal of their passion. Julie endeavours to make Saint-Preux share in her religious devotion, and encourages him to marry her cousin. Her untimely death brings the narrative to an end. She dies confessing the survival of her love.

In addition to the romantic story, the work contains an ideal picture of a happy, prosperous countryside, which its readers could contrast with the misery that prevailed among the peasantry of France; also a notable invective (placed rather oddly in Lord Edward's mouth) against the social privileges of high rank when the latter is not accompanied by corresponding worth, and a letter (also by Lord Edward) on the subject of suicide.

La Nouvelle Héloïse was immensely successful (seventy-two editions were published between 1761 and 1800) and exerted a great influence, by reason both of the sentimental drama of the first part and of the example of conjugal fidelity in the second. It may be said to have effected a sort of moral revolution in the empty dissipated life of the society of the day.

Nouvelle Revue, La (1879–1926), a political and literary review founded by Juliette Adam (q.v.).

Nouvelle Revue Française, La, a famous 20th-century French review of literature and the other arts, came definitely into being, after a false start in November 1908, in February 1909. Its founders included Jean Schlumberger, Jacques Copeau (later associated, with the *N.R.F.* backing him, with the Théâtre du Vieux Colombier, q.v.), and André Gide, who became the moving spirit. They were united in feeling that the symbolist aesthetic (see *Symbolisme*) was inadequate for what the younger generation had to say, but it was only as time went on that their own objects emerged at all clearly. They upheld the importance of literary method, of sensibility, and of what they termed *esprit*—of, in fact, the enduring aesthetic values independent of intellectual and moral prejudices or of fashions in writing. They were anxious to encourage new trends and obscure authors, and before long added a publishing business to their other activities (the 'maison d'éditions de la nrf', still continuing, under Gaston Gallimard).

The influence of the *Nouvelle Revue Française* was particularly strong—in the fields of criticism, the theatre, and the novel—during the years immediately before and after the 1914–18 war; and an impressive list can be made of 'little-known' authors whom it printed in its early days, e.g. Claudel, Giraudoux, Péguy, Valéry, Gide himself. It failed in literary perceptiveness in 1913 when it refused Proust's *A la recherche du temps perdu* (q.v.), but by 1917 the failure was made good and the literary rights of Proust's work were bought from the publisher Grasset.

The *Nouvelle Revue Française* lost its intellectual independence during the 1939–45 war and in the end (1943) ceased to appear. (One special number, 'Hommage à Gide, was produced in autumn 1951.) In 1953 *La*

Nouvelle Nouvelle Revue Française began publication.

Nouvelle Rive gauche, La, the chief Symbolist review (founded 1882, weekly) in the early days of the movement (see *Symbolisme*), and better known, from 1883, as *Lutèce*. It lasted till 1886 and printed work by Paul Adam, Jules Laforgue (*Les Complaintes*), Jean Moréas, H. de Régnier (qq.v.), and others.

Nouvelles à la main, see *Nouvellistes*.

Nouvelles de la République des Lettres, see *Bayle*.

Nouvelles ecclésiastiques, see *Jansénius*.

Nouvelles Nourritures, Les (1935), by André Gide (q.v. para. 6).

Nouvelles Récréations et joyeux devis, see *Des Périers*.

Nouvellistes, the name given to persons who, in the 17th century, before the development of the Press, assembled at various points in Paris, to hear, communicate, and discuss the news of the day. There are references to them in La Bruyère, Montesquieu, &c. The collection of news for persons of importance eventually became a paid profession. Manuscript records of news with comments (i.e. news-letters), known as 'Nouvelles à la main' or 'Gazettes à la main', were also clandestinely circulated, even after the establishment of printed gazettes. They were often of a satirical and propagandist character, and sometimes in verse. See *Loret*.

Novalis [pseud. of Friedrich Leopold Freiherr von Hardenberg (1772–1801)], a German imaginative writer who had an influence upon *le romantisme* (q.v.) in France. His fragmentary output consisted of poetry, tales, and an unfinished novel, in all of which a mystical, semi-philosophical, often fantastic strain is noticeable. (See also *Foreign influences on French literature*, para. 20.)

Novel, The [Note: See under separate headings for fuller details of authors and works mentioned below. Cf. also *Foreign influences on French literature*.]

THE WORD 'ROMAN'

(1) The French word for a novel, *roman*, comes from the Old French (c. 10th century) *romanz* (pop. L. *romanice*, adv.) which at first signified the vernacular, and from the 12th century a work, more often told orally than written, in the vernacular as opposed to Latin. (Latin was the language of the written literature to be found, say, in the monastic libraries, the *Homilies*, *Lives of Saints*, &c.) By the 14th century *romanz* or *roman* was applied more specifically to the romances of chivalry or antiquity (see *Romans courtois*), which were usually, though not invariably, in verse (cf. *Lancelot*). By the 16th century, as a result of the introduction of printing (1470 in Paris), a reading public had developed, for whom the word *roman* had come to denote any prose narrative written around the exploits of its hero. From the 17th century onwards it was used in the sense which still largely holds, of a prose work of imagination, usually of considerable length, portraying characters and actions representative of real life. (See also *Conte*; *Nouvelle*.)

MIDDLE AGES TO LATE SIXTEENTH CENTURY: INFLUENCES AND PRECURSORS

(2) These remote ancestors of the modern novel, the verse *romanz* or *romans*, are lengthy, episodic narratives woven round highly idealized themes of love and women; and it was mainly to audiences of women that they were read aloud, not, as the *chansons de geste* (q.v.) had been, sung. Lovers are separated, encounter danger, monsters, and marvels, at home or in foreign lands (where the Crusades take them), and finally reach happiness or, occasionally, disaster (the *romans d'aventure*). The knight of chivalry performs feats of endurance and prowess, described at prodigious length, to prove his love for his mistress. His love is a refined, disciplined sentiment (*amour courtois*) which his mistress, usually a married woman, accepts and (sometimes cruelly) tests, but all too seldom rewards.

(3) The *romans courtois*, especially those known as the *romans bretons*, were often reproduced in 16th-century prose compilations, but with the sentimental element lessened, because tastes had changed with the times. The idealistic *romans courtois* had been designed for a knightly, feudal society. With the 15th-century dissolution of this society the taste for fictional entertainment spread from courtly to bourgeois circles and a more cynical, matter-of-fact, and earthy

type of narrative developed, as seen in the *Fabliaux* (verse) and in the prose tales of, for example, *Les Quinze Joyes de mariage*. Conduct is here on a lower level: the clergy (for now the Church was losing its authority) are venal; men eat, drink, and make love coarsely, while women are inconstant if not frankly lecherous, and lovers are more often under their mistresses' beds than adventuring among marvels. (Cf. also the satire of the later parts of the *Roman de Renart*; or the second part of the *Roman de la rose*, which is cynical and derides women, in contrast to the glorification of *amour courtois* in the first part.)

(4) This reaction was a notable step forward in development, because, whether by straightforward description or burlesque, such tales convey an illusion of real life (cf. again the lifelike dialogues of another 15th-century collection, the *Cent nouvelles nouvelles*). Adventures and episodes are indeed still of prime importance, but they are interludes in the daily life of real men and women, even if the characters themselves are rarely convincingly differentiated. (The vivid description and character-drawing of the latter part of Antoine de la Sale's *Petit Jehan de Saintré*, 1456, are exceptional.) In the 16th century various minor writers depict rustic scenes, or bourgeois society, or country-house life (e.g. Noël du Fail, Guillaume Bouchet, Jacques Yver). One genius—Rabelais—combines the fantastic extravagances of Gargantua and Pantagruel with a vivid representation of the life of all classes of the people, evoked by innumerable slight but precise touches. This was the first sustained work of prose fiction in that the successive books continue the chronicle from father to son; it might also be termed the first philosophical novel, for Rabelais's exceptional genius played over life itself, in all its manifestations.

(5) From the late 15th century the great popularity of translations from foreign literature undoubtedly helped to make love the central theme of fiction—love the passion, rather than the idealistic love of chivalrous romance or love the Platonic sentiment favoured by such writers as Marguerite de Navarre, Antoine Héroët, or Maurice Scève. Boccaccio's *Decameron* was known, and an influence, even before it was first translated in 1485. His *Filocopo* was partly

translated in 1531. His *Fiammetta* (tr. 1532), a tale of a married woman who falls in love with a stranger and is deserted by him, would appear to have influenced if not inspired *Les Angoysses douloureuses qui procèdent d'amour*, by the 16th-century authoress Hélisenne de Crenne, a work which is a distinct signpost on the way to the novel of sentimental analysis. Other works translated from the Italian (and seldom only once) include the romance of Eurialus and Lucretia, by Aeneas Sylvius (Pope Pius II); the *Novelle* of Bandello (which became the *Histoires tragiques*, 1565, of Belleforest); Tasso's *Aminta* (1573), and several other pastoral romances and tragicomedies. Translations from the Spanish —the *Amadis*, translated by Herberay des Essarts, 1540–8, in particular—gave new life to the tales of chivalrous and romantic love (hence the *romans courtois* in the prose compilations). Some are still more interesting from the point of view of the future because they showed love as a sombre passion (e.g. the *Carcel de Amor* and the story of the love of Arnalte and Lucenda, byDiego de San Pedro), or debated the relative culpability of man and of woman in cases of lapse from virtue (the *Jugement d'amour* of Juan de Flores).

SEVENTEENTH AND EIGHTEENTH CENTURIES: CONSOLIDATION AND PROGRESS

(6) During the 17th and 18th centuries the novel develops as a separate literary genre. Develops; or, more exactly, it assimilates and consolidates the formative influences of the previous centuries. Its great period of expansion will be the 19th century; but the ways by which it reaches this are clearly discernible early in the 17th century.

(7) There is, first, the sentimental tale, which follows the course of true love, whether simple or tortuous, to a happy ending; which meets the reader's desire for a story (i.e. for plot, which now, though rambling, and interrupted by subsidiary plots, comes definitely into the picture, with a young girl rather than a married woman for heroine); and which is not of necessity concerned with verisimilitude. D'Urfé provides a first landmark with *L'Astrée* (1607–28), a sentimental, etherialized, precious, and interminably episodic work (5 volumes, 12 books, and over 5,000 pages), clearly inspired by the Spanish and Italian pastoral romances. Its success strengthened the vogue associated

with the little world of the Hôtel de Rambouillet for long, unreal, insipid, heroic-sentimental works in which fine ladies and gentlemen of the court were thinly disguised by pastoral or classical settings (Gomberville, Mlle de Scudéry, La Calprenède are the authors). In *L'Astrée* itself, however, the shepherds and shepherdesses are individuals, whose shades of sentiment are indicated, and the very number of personages introduced emphasizes the sense of the complications and interplay of passions. The vogue was ridiculed by Sorel (*Le Berger extravagant*, 1627–8) and later by Boileau (*Dialogue des héros de roman*, q.v., not published till after Mlle de Scudéry's death), and petered out. Then for a time the love-story *qua* story goes to ground. It re-emerges in the 18th century, with an element of irregular passion to emphasize a moral purpose—a feature that has come to stay—and very much hampered by philosophical and didactic trappings, in Rousseau's *Nouvelle Héloïse* (1761, an early French novel in letter-form). It is simple, lyrical (as Rousseau too had been), and pathetic, and brings in nature (again as Rousseau had done, but this time in an exotic setting), with Bernardin de Saint-Pierre (*Paul et Virginie*); and eventually reaches Gothic realms and a delicious, swooning sensibility. On its way it has been touched by both English and German influence.

(8) Then again, there is the type of (equally formless) narrative which deliberately reacts against sentimental invention and is concerned to create an atmosphere of real life by its depiction of society (more often bourgeois, or frankly low, than aristocratic), scenes, and manners, e.g. Sorel's *Francion* (1623), Furetière's *Roman bourgeois* (1666), Restif de la Bretonne's *Paysan perverti* (1775), Diderot's *La Religieuse* (1796, posth.). Even when the narrative is picaresque, and here also we have Spanish influence (*Lazarillo de Tormes*, known in the 16th century; *Don Quixote*, current reading in the 17th century; *Don Guzman d'Alfarache*, adapted by Lesage in 1732), the crowded background of thieves, vagabonds, travelling comedians, and wayfaring, hand-to-mouth life will still be realistic (e.g. Scarron's *Roman comique*, 1651; Lesage's *Gil Blas*, 1715–35). Even, again, in the pseudo-oriental, licentious tales or the philosophical romances fashionable in the 18th century

(e.g. those of Crébillon or Voltaire), the satire is aimed at contemporary manners.

(9) The illusion of real life is possibly at its strongest in a small number of 17th- and 18th-century narratives which constitute yet a third type, concerned with human problems and the analysis of sentiment. To some extent these continue the narrative of sentimental adventure, but they have been stripped of extraneous matter and have in them the purest stuff of the novel. The adventures now are those of the soul at grips with the cruel, dangerous, and no longer idealistic passion of love, emerging victorious, at tragic cost (*La Princesse de Clèves*, 1678); disintegrating under its ravages (*Manon Lescaut*, 1731); playing with it deliberately and fiendishly (*Les Liaisons dangereuses*, 1782); or, less sombrely, merely underestimating its force and observing itself caught in the toils (*Marianne*, 1731–41). The last work is long, and loosely constructed, but all four have in common a quality of close interest in human nature that makes them true precursors of modern psychological fiction.

NINETEENTH AND TWENTIETH CENTURIES: THE MODERN NOVEL.

(10) With the introduction of printing the novel had come into its own as a separate genre. In the 19th century its exuberant and self-conscious development was encouraged by an avid novel-reading public—due this time to the spread of education and to the reviews and serialized fiction in the daily and periodical press—and took the form of prolonged bursts of creative energy alternating or at times proceeding side by side with phases of concentration on technique. The result was a vastly enlarged conception of what constitutes the appropriate form and matter of fiction.

(11) Between about 1800 and 1850 creative genius was particularly evident. Chateaubriand, Senancour, and Benjamin Constant portrayed the state of mind of individuals whose emotions, whether love or spiritual loneliness, mean more to them than outward events (*René*; *Obermann*; *Adolphe*; and cf. *Romantisme*). Directly or indirectly they inspired a long line of novels of introspection and self-revelation, beginning with Musset's *Confession d'un enfant du siècle* and Sainte-Beuve's *Volupté*. Their contemporary,

Mme de Staël, evoked the loneliness of the woman who dares to be unconventional (*Corinne*; *Delphine*). Incidentally, too, she paved the way for the *roman à thèse*. She also to some extent, but Chateaubriand to a very much greater, developed the exotic element introduced by Bernardin de Saint-Pierre.

(12) The two great novelists of the period were Balzac and Stendhal. Balzac's genius had the universal quality which defies classification because succeeding ages find in it new sources of inspiration. His *Comédie humaine*, at all times great story-telling, contains studies of life and character that can be described variously as historical novels (*Les Chouans*) or as novels of ideas (*La Cousine Bette*; *Le Père Goriot*), illustrating the devastation wrought by vice or exaggerated passion. Crime fiction and the *roman noir* (the novel permeated by the influence of one sinister character) owe much to his master-criminal Vautrin, or to *La Rabouilleuse*. His method of linking the great divisions of his work (the 'Scènes de la vie privée', 'Scènes de la vie de province', &c.) or the tales within those divisions by reintroducing the same character in roles of varying importance, foreshadows the 20th-century *roman-fleuve* or *roman-cycle*. The famous exposition of his plan for the *Comédie humaine* may have led to the emphasis on form which with some later writers took the place of true creative ability. He was one of the few contemporaries who appreciated Stendhal, a writer of less universal genius but whose penetrating, scrupulously objective studies of character and motives (*Le Rouge et le noir*; *La Chartreuse de Parme*) bore fruit, about 1890 (see para. 18), in the novel of psychological analysis.

(13) From about 1830 George Sand went steadily on, combining sentiment, passion, melodrama, and, in her second phase, ideology. *Indiana* and *Lélia* depicted the passionate woman defying convention; *Mauprat* was the brute tamed by a good woman's love; *Le Compagnon du Tour de France* and *Le Meunier d'Angibault* were idealistic socialism. The eternally popular true-love story also flourished, sometimes well spiced with licentiousness or satire, or serving as a lively portrait of contemporary society (Paul de Kock and Alphonse Karr are typical authors), sometimes sugary (e.g. Lamartine's *Graziella*). Heroines died

piteously, with their beauty unravaged, of broken hearts, but the novel of sensibility, abounding in tears, fainting fits, and hysterics, languished after the disappearance early in the century of such writers as Mme de Genlis, Mme de Souza, and Mme de Duras. A passing phase of extravagant romanticism was exemplified in novels and tales by Théophile Gautier (with exceptions such as his *Capitaine Fracasse*, a picaresque novel, and the lyrical, and unique, *Mademoiselle de Maupin*). Several years later it was again reflected in some of Barbey d'Aurevilly's novels and tales (e.g. *Les Diaboliques*) and in Villiers de l'Isle-Adam (*Claire Lenoir*; *Contes cruels*). Melodramatic extravagance was the keynote of the *romans-feuilletons* of Frédéric Soulié and Eugène Sue. The latter was one of the first French novelists of the underworld.

(14) The historical novel, also, came to the fore between 1800 and 1850, inspired by Scott (translated in 1822). Alfred de Vigny's *Cinq-Mars* (1826) came first. Balzac's *Les Chouans*, Mérimée's *Chronique du règne de Charles IX*, Hugo's *Notre-Dame de Paris* followed; and the vogue continued throughout the century. Dumas *père* exploited French history as the background for innumerable adventure stories. Barbey d'Aurevilly combined history with fantasy (*L'Ensorcelée*; *Le Chevalier des Touches*). Flaubert reconstituted Carthage (*Salammbô*). The Hugo of later years combined history with sociology (*Les Misérables*; *Quatre-vingt-treize*). Authors of straightforward historical novels of the Napoleonic wars, the Restoration period, the Franco-Prussian war, &c., included the Alsatian collaborators Émile Erckmann and Alexandre Chatrian; George Esparbès; the brothers Paul and Victor Margueritte, and Zola, whose *La Débâcle* concentrated mainly on the disaster of Sedan. In the 20th century Anatole France's fine novel of the Revolution, *Les Dieux ont soif*, should be noted, also the two 'Verdun' volumes of Jules Romains's *Les Hommes de bonne volonté*.

(15) Novelists between 1850 and *c.* 1890 were preoccupied with questions of form, technique, and the function of the novel. The Positivist spirit of the age, a reaction against earlier idealism, manifested itself in the novel in *le réalisme* and *le naturalisme* (qq.v; and cf. in poetry *les Parnassiens*). The

réalistes were determined to represent life as it is, not as it is very unlikely to be, lived. They set themselves to *document* their novels, which implied at the least the minute depiction of everyday life practised by, for example, Champfleury and Ernest Feydeau, and to some extent by Daudet (but never to the exclusion of his natural sympathy, fancy, and exuberance). Documentation at its extreme signified the unrelieved portrayal of drunkenness, vice, and squalor or, it might be, disease and abnormality (cf. the brothers Edmond and Jules de Goncourt; also Zola's *Thérèse Raquin*). Flaubert, who dominates the period, is not the outstanding *réaliste*, but the exception which glorifies the rule. Flaubert—who objected to having any classifying adjective applied to him—was not out to make the novel illustrate a particular theory. His laborious care for documentation, his objectivity and realism (i.e. exclusion of extraneous matter and sentiment) resulted from his view of the novel as an impersonal work of art. *Madame Bovary* and *L'Éducation sentimentale* are among the great novels of French literature: they also happen to be great realistic novels.

(16) The tendency of the *réalistes* to photographic and formless representation of life was exaggerated by the *naturalistes*, with Zola at their head. *Le naturalisme* was, moreover, influenced by the determinism of Taine and by contemporary interest in heredity and experimental physiology. Zola alone put his theories rigorously into practice (see *Rougon-Macquart, Les*; cf. also *Céard, Henri*; *Huysmans, J.-K*; *Maupassant*).

(17) Between about 1890 and 1913 no literary giants had appeared (though Proust was already at work, cf. para. 22) to change the course of evolution, but in a quiet way the novel was expanding its province by reflecting and exploiting contemporary interests and ideologies. It took little from Symbolism (q.v.), but it absorbed new humanitarian (and later psychological) ideas from the Russian writers. Psychology and idealistic philosophy replaced Positivism as its intellectual background.

(18) About 1890, after one strangely isolated precursor in Fromentin's *Dominique* (1863), the novel of psychological analysis developed. Its chief concern was with human character and the gradual, cumulative process by which habits are formed; and its

affinities can thus be traced back to the 17th century (see para. 9 above). More immediately, it derived from Stendhal and the critic Taine. Paul Bourget was for long the recognized leader in this kind; Maupassant has at least one excellent example (*Pierre et Jean*), and heightens the effect by his naturalistic technique; and one early novel by Gide, *La Porte étroite*, is a masterpiece.

(19) Some writers made philosophy, psychology, religion and religious experience, or vague or sentimental humanitarianism the staple of their work, and had an appeal which still remains for small circles, e.g. Élémir Bourges; J.-K. Huysmans (in his later phase); Édouard Estaunié; Charles-Louis Philippe. Others were successful in combining an exploitation of similar themes with just sufficient realism and attention to contemporary life and agitations to ensure wide popularity if not lasting renown, e.g. Paul Adam; René Bazin; Octave Feuillet; Octave Mirbeau; Marcel Prévost. The two outstanding novelists of the period were Maurice Barrès and Anatole France. Elegance, sophistication, and style, rather than any overriding creative energy, characterized the work of both, but their reputations underwent too severe an eclipse for some years after they died.

(20) The beginnings of the exotic novel have already been mentioned (paras. 7, 11). Balzac's 'Scènes de la vie de province' were early regionalism and were followed by George Sand's idylls of country life (*La Mare au diable*; *François le champi*). Next came Ferdinand Fabre's fine studies of clerical life in the Cévennes, and Daudet's and Jean Aicard's sketches of Provençal life; and from about 1870 to the present day regionalism and the exotic novel have flourished and expanded. One after another a long succession of novelists has put the Far East or the international scene, the French colonies or the French provinces, on the literary map, depicting landscapes, customs, superstitions, and characteristics with a fidelity both realistic and informed, and often, in more recent times, suiting style and methods of description to an age that sees life on the screen of the cinema, or beneath the wings of an aeroplane, or over the rim of a cocktail glass (see, for instance, *Loti*; *Farrère*; *Tharaud*; *Larbaud*; *Morand*; *Bazin*; *Boylesve*; *Giono*). The strictly exotic and regional novel, as

distinct from the novel which merely abounds in local colour, usually subordinates the general to the particular, and sacrifices universal human interest to atmosphere or to its own mixture of geography or topography and social history. Moving exceptions are Loti's tales of Breton fisherfolk (e.g. *Pêcheur d'Islande*) or Louis Hémon's tale of French-Canadian life *Maria Chapdelaine*.

(21) Development was again remarkable between 1913 and 1939 (the limit of this survey). The *roman-fleuve* came into being, and reflected social history, as Balzac had done. But the 20th-century writers employed a looser framework and at times relied more upon *reportage* than on plot. In some cases the social panorama was seen through the eyes of one character, or one family group (e.g. Romain Rolland's *Jean-Christophe*, R. Martin du Gard's *Les Thibault*, G. Duhamel's *Pasquier* chronicles). In others it usurped the stage and the personages of the book filled only minor or passing roles (J. Romains's *Les Hommes de bonne volonté*). The novel of psychological analysis became the novel of interior conflict, the adventures of the soul beset by religious, moral, and political uncertainties and by the uneasy preoccupation with sin, and sex, and the growing sense of 'la part du diable' which were characteristic of the period (e.g. works by Gide; Lacretelle; Mauriac; Radiguet); and some authors (e.g. Gide; Mauriac) developed an economy of form and style admirably befitting the poignancy of their subject. Political ideals and a concern for the human condition itself were predominant in the vigorous novels of André Malraux. A woman novelist, Colette, was unique in her subtle exploration of physical sensitivity. The need to escape from a dreary or terrifying reality, another feature of the inter-war years, was met by, among others, Cocteau and Montherlant. The rapid growth in France as in other countries of the detective novel and the psychological thriller (see *Simenon*) is another aspect of escapism. Montherlant's biting study *Les Célibataires* continued the realist tradition. So, too, did the *romans populistes* which made their appearance in the 'twenties (cf. *Dabit, Eugène*), but without bitterness or concentration on the sordid.

(22) Taken by and large these novels represented no radical departure from existing conventions. In 1913 two works appeared which led to change, the second to greater changes of content and of form than had taken place at any time since 1850, if not in the whole history of the novel. Alain Fournier's *Le Grand Meaulnes* introduced the novel of fantasy, situated in the strange, luminous world which hovers between dream and reality. Proust's *Du côté de chez Swann* (followed between 1913 and 1923 by the other parts of *A la recherche du temps perdu*) invaded the hitherto unexplored realms of instinct and intuition (here the influence of Bergson is noticeable), of the intimate places and hidden cankers of the soul, and the dark, uneasy world of the subconscious. (The last of these was to become yet darker and more uneasy as the theories of Freudian analysis gained currency.) An effect of both novels was to make objectivity and chronological plot disappear and technique expand to suit a new, amorphous content. In the novel of fantasy, which as the years passed was particularly open to the influence of *Surréalisme*, this became disjointed and as unselective as dreams themselves. Or (with Giraudoux for instance) it reached almost mystifying heights of imagery and paradox. The novel which derived from Proust was long, discursive, and infinitely complicated. Proust's aim had been to convey the stratification of the conscious, and the sense of a reality which is both synthetic and simultaneous, in which space and time, sensation and apperception, are all one. It lent itself to various technical innovations; and it was with these, rather than with any fresh creative outburst, that the period 1913–39 ended. Gide's experimental novel *Les Faux-Monnayeurs* is one example. With Proust's Marcel the reader, unaware of what he is heading for, reaches the moment at which the novelist's inspiration is born, and at the same time (with Marcel in his other role of Narrator) he watches himself approaching this moment. With Gide, whose character Édouard is himself writing a novel called *Les Faux-Monnayeurs* and keeping a diary as he proceeds, the reader is allowed to share in the creative process.

(23) A final factor which cannot be discounted in the evolution of modern French fiction is the influence of foreign writers and of foreign theory, both creative and critical. The type of *littérature engagée* which springs

from deliberate subordination of aesthetic to political theory may be referred to in passing but is beyond the present limit.

Novembre, a tale by Flaubert, one of his youthful works. It can be found in his *Premières Œuvres* (1914–20).

Nucingen, BARON FRÉDÉRIC DE, in Balzac's *Comédie humaine* (q.v.), a repulsive Jewish financier from Alsace who laid the foundations of his wealth by speculating on the outcome of the battle of Waterloo. He figures notably in *La Maison Nucingen*, *Le Père Goriot* (his wife, Delphine, was one of Goriot's two daughters), *Splendeurs et Misères des courtisanes*, and *César Birotteau* (qq.v.).

Nuits, Les, four lyrics, among the masterpieces of Alfred de Musset, dialogues between the poet and his Muse. He dwells upon the anguish he had suffered through disappointed love, but in the end prefers to relive his sufferings rather than forget them. The poems appeared first in the *Revue des Deux Mondes*—*La Nuit de mai* and *La Nuit de décembre* in 1835 (15 June and

1 Dec.), *La Nuit d'août* in 1836 (15 Aug.), and *La Nuit d'octobre* in 1837 (15 Oct.).

Nuit vénitienne, La, ou Les Noces de Laurette, by Alfred de Musset, a one-act comedy in prose, a failure when produced in December 1830. It was published the same month in the *Revue des Deux Mondes*, and again in 1834 in the second series of *Un Spectacle dans un fauteuil* (q.v.).

Numa Roumestan (1881), a novel by Alphonse Daudet, is an interesting study of the contrast between the French of the North and the *gens du Midi*. A typical *méridional* (q.v.) comes to study law in Paris and is carried from triumph to triumph by his exuberant temperament and his overwhelming oratorical force. Finally he becomes Minister of Education. Unfortunately he cannot realize that in the eyes of the cold, realistic Northerners with whom he comes in contact, promises exact fulfilment; and his expansiveness nearly ruins both his private and his public life. Provençal life and the Provençaux in Paris are vividly described.

O

Obermann (1804), a famous pre-Romantic Movement novel—in letter-form—by Senancour (q.v. and see *Romantisme*). Over a long period of years the hero writes to a friend, describing his state of soul, the melancholy, ennui, sense of frustration, and inability to rouse himself to any kind of active life, that afflict him. There is no plot, though at times the pages are overshadowed by an unhappy love affair. The hero's surroundings, a remote Alpine valley, and at one time the Forest of Fontainebleau, play a great part in his letters, but they are seen always through his melancholy.

After Senancour's death his book appealed increasingly to generations tortured by the 'désordre des ennuis'. Its influence can be seen in, for example, Balzac's *Le Lys dans la vallée*, Sainte-Beuve's *Volupté*, or George Sand's *Lélia*.

Obey, ANDRÉ (1892–   ), actor-manager and dramatist. His works, produced by the

Compagnie des Quinze (q.v.), with which he was associated, include: *Le Viol de Lucrèce* (1931), which treats the story of the rape of Lucretia in the manner of Greek tragedy, with a chorus and commentators; *Noë* (1931), the Deluge from the point of view of those in the Ark; and *La Bataille de la Marne* (1932). A tragicomedy, *La Souriante Madame Beudet* (1921), on a theme resembling that of Flaubert's *Madame Bovary* (q.v.), was written in collaboration with Denys Amiel (q.v.).

Oblat, L' (1903), by Joris-Karl Huysmans (q.v.), the last of his novels of religious experience.

Occident, L' (1901–   ), one of the most representative literary, mainly poetical, reviews of the early 20th century, founded by Adrien Mithouard (q.v.). Others associated with it included Francis Jammes, Charles Morice, Francis Vielé-Griffin, and Tancrède de Visan (qq.v.).

Oceano Nox, a famous poem by Victor Hugo (in *Les Rayons et les ombres,* q.v., 1840), a lament for sailors lost at sea, without even a humble stone in some churchyard to keep their memory alive. Tristan Corbière's (q.v.) defiant, ironical treatment of the same theme (*La Fin,* in *Les Amours jaunes,* 1873) is often contrasted with this.

Ode, a lyric poem in stanzas that are similar in respect of the number and arrangement of the lines they contain, of which, as a rule, some are long, others short. The ode was first introduced under that name into French poetry by Ronsard, who imitated both Pindar and Horace; but it may be said to have had its germ in the songs and psalms of Clément Marot. It is not always easy to discriminate between the ode and the *chanson,* but a distinction may be drawn between the serious ode (heroic, religious, philosophic, satirical, &c.) and the light ode (*odelette,* song, or *vaudeville*).

Odéon, Théâtre de l', see *Luxembourg, Théâtre du.*

Odes et ballades (1826), by Victor Hugo. This collection includes the earlier *Odes* (1822) and *Nouvelles Odes* (1824), and was itself enlarged in 1828. Some of the *Odes* are intimate and domestic, more are political, celebrating events of the restored monarchy, e.g. *Le Sacre de Charles X.* The *Ballades,* e.g. *Le Géant, La Fiancée du timbalier,* are already picturesque and romantic (see *Romantisme*). The preface to this collection is one of Hugo's first Romantic manifestoes.

Odes funambulesques (1857), see under *Banville, Théodore de.*

Odette (de Crécy), in Proust's *A la recherche du temps perdu* (q.v.), appears first as the Mme Swann seen occasionally on his walks at Combray by the child Marcel. Earlier in life she had been a demi-mondaine of the Second Empire (the mysterious 'dame en rose' who visited Marcel's worldly uncle Adolphe, the 'Mlle de Sacripant' painted by the young artist Elstir) and a protégée of the Verdurins (q.v.), to whose *salon,* then in its infancy, she introduced Charles Swann. Swann, whose mistress she became, married her to secure a future for Gilberte (q.v.), their daughter. [All this, pieced together by Marcel in later life, is recounted in the section entitled *Un Amour de Swann,* which forms almost a small novel in itself. It begins late in the first volume and takes up most of the second (*Du côté de chez Swann,* pts. i and ii).]

When Marcel's life becomes linked with the Swann *ménage* through his early love for Gilberte, his friendship with Swann, &c., he observes Odette profiting by the Dreyfus (q.v.) Affaire and the admiration of her men friends to form a *salon* and establish her position in the 'monde élégant'. After Swann's death Odette marries M. de Forcheville, a former lover. We last meet her at the reception described in the final volume (*Le Temps retrouvé,* pt. ii). In old age, with her disintegrating charms miraculously held together, she has become the mistress of the duc de Guermantes (q.v.).

Œdipe, (1) a tragedy by Corneille, produced in 1659. It is based on the *Oedipus Tyrannus* of Sophocles, of which the subject is the discovery by Oedipus, king of Thebes, not only that he has unwittingly killed Laius, the late king, whose widow Jocasta he has married, but worse than this, that he is actually the son of Laius and Jocasta. Corneille spoils the simple grandeur of the original tragedy by adding a complication: he invents the character of Dirce, daughter and heiress of Laius, whose love affair with Theseus, prince of Athens, occupies a considerable part of the play. In Act III, sc. 5 there is a famous declaration of belief in the freedom of the will.

(2) The first tragedy written by Voltaire, produced in 1718. He inserted (it is said on the insistence of the actors) a slight romantic element in the original story, by introducing Philoctetes, an old lover of Jocasta, and causing him to be suspected of the murder of Laius. The play contains some polemical allusions to political and religious questions.

Œil-de-bœuf, an antechamber in the palace of Versailles, adjoining the king's bedroom, where the courtiers awaited the king; it was so named in the reign of Louis XV from an oval window in one of the walls, made in 1701.

Œnone, the nurse in Racine's tragedy *Phèdre* (q.v.).

Œuvre, L' (1886), one of Zola's *Rougon-Macquart* (q.v.) novels, makes Claude Lantier, son of the laundress Germaine of *L'Assommoir* (q.v.), the chief character, but otherwise neglects the general thesis (heredity) of the series. Lantier, brought up at Plassans, in Provence, inherits a little money and becomes an artist in Paris. When his great picture *Plein air* is exhibited at the *Salon des Refusés*, its revolutionary treatment of light and colour excites derision, but it also initiates the *École de plein air*, and when imitated, well watered down, makes the success of several mediocre painters. Lantier sacrifices everything—fortune, his wife Christine, their child—to his art. He becomes impotent before his own theories and in the end commits suicide.

The novel is an interesting picture of artist life and the early days and doctrines of the Impressionists. Lantier is frequently identified with an amalgam of Manet and Cézanne (cf. Manet's picture *Déjeuner sur l'herbe*). Sandoz, Lantier's friend, who is writing a long, interconnected series of social and psychological novels, is a mouthpiece for Zola's theories of his own Rougon-Macquart novels.

Œuvre, Théâtre de l'. This, known for the first three years of its existence as the *Théâtre d'Art*, was founded (1890) in Paris by the poet Paul Fort (q.v.) in reaction against naturalism in the theatre (cf. *Théâtre Libre*). Symbolist dramas, e.g. by Maeterlinck (q.v.), were produced, or scenic adaptations of poems (by Laforgue, Mallarmé, Rimbaud, and others). Young artists, e.g. Gauguin, Bonnard, Vuillard, painted the scenery and illustrated the programmes. From 1892 to 1929, with Lugné-Poë (q.v.) as director and chief actor, and now known as the *Théâtre de l'Œuvre*, it did much for the development of the modern theatre and to encourage young or unknown, and also foreign, dramatists.

Œuvres et les hommes, Les (1860-1909), collected criticism by Barbey d'Aurevilly (q.v.).

Offenbach, Jacques (1819-80), the composer (to the libretti of H. Meilhac and L. Halévy, qq.v.) of the operettas *Orphée aux enfers* (1858), *La Belle Hélène* (1864), *La Vie parisienne* (1866), *La Grande-Duchesse de Gérolstein* (1867), &c. Few reminiscences or social histories of the Second Empire (1852-70) leave him unmentioned, for his infectiously gay and melodious works seem to have been a musical manifestation of its pleasure-loving ironic spirit. He was born at Cologne, the son of a German-Jewish father, but Paris was his home from 1833 when he arrived to study at the Conservatoire, and he later adopted French nationality. He was a violoncellist to begin with, playing in the orchestra of the Opéra-Comique, and also making his name as a virtuoso at private recitals. From 1850 to 1855 he led the orchestra of the Comédie-Française. After that he leased a small theatre, the Bouffes Parisiens (1855), to produce his own operettas, which were unfailingly successful. He died three months before the production of his last, and most lasting, work, *Les Contes d'Hoffman* (1880), based on Hoffmann's (q.v.) *Phantasiestücke*. The libretto was by two minor dramatists, Jules Barbier (1825-1901) and Michel Carré (1819-72).

Ogier, FRANÇOIS, see under *Schelandre*.

Ogier de Danemarcke, the hero of a *chanson de geste* (q.v.), the *Chevalerie Ogier de Danemarcke*, of the 12th century which forms part of the 'Doon de Mayence' cycle; of a rehandling of part of this by Adenet le Roi (q.v.), the *Enfances Ogier*; and of many exploits related in the Charlemagne romances. In the main story Ogier is at Charlemagne's court, a hostage for his father. He gains the king's favour by his exploits in Italy. His son having been killed by Charlemagne's son in a quarrel, Ogier in a fury kills the queen's nephew and would have killed the king himself but for the intervention of the knights. He is pursued, besieged, and at last imprisoned. He is released to fight against the Saracens.

Ogier is identified with a historical warrior, the Frankish Autgarius, who fought against Charlemagne and was then reconciled to him. 'Danemarcke' perhaps signifies, not Denmark, but the marches of the Ardennes. Nevertheless, as Holger Danske, Ogier became a Danish national hero and a subject of Danish folk-song.

Ohnet, GEORGES (1848-1918), author of *Serge Panine* (1881), *Le Maître de forges* (1882, q.v.), *La Comtesse Sarah* (1883), *La Grande*

Marnière (1885), &c., snobbishly sentimental novels (also usually dramatized) which made him the best seller of the 19th century and aroused the disgusted wit of critics. Anatole France in *Le Temps*, in an article headed 'Hors de la littérature', said: 'Il a sa puissance, sa vertu et sa magie: tout ce qu'il touche devient aussitôt tristement vulgaire et ridiculement prétentieux.' Jules Lemaître, in the *Journal des Débats*, began: 'J'ai coutume d'entretenir mes lecteurs de sujets littéraires: qu'ils veuillent bien m'excuser si je leur parle aujourd'hui des romans de M. Georges Ohnet.'

Oiseau bleu, L' (1909), a play by Maeterlinck (q.v.).

Oiseaux s'envolent et les fleurs tombent, Les (1893), a novel by Élémir Bourges (q.v.).

Olim, Les, name given to certain registers in which were entered the enactments of the *parlement* of Paris, from 1254 to 1318.

Olimpie, a tragedy by Voltaire, produced in 1764.

Cassandre, king of Macedonia, having killed Alexander the Great and, as he believes, his widow Statira, has saved and protected their daughter Olimpie, who is ignorant of her parentage. Filled with remorse and loving Olimpie, who returns his love, he is about to marry her. Antigone, a rival king, penetrates the secret of Olimpie's birth, and a fierce struggle arises between the two kings for her hand. Meanwhile Statira, who has in fact survived and has hidden herself as a priestess in the temple of Ephesus, recognizes her daughter and is revolted by the projected marriage with Cassandre. Thinking him about to overcome Antigone, she takes her own life and with her dying words orders Olimpie to marry Antigone. Olimpie, torn between love and duty, immolates herself on her mother's pyre.

Olive, see *Du Bellay*.

Olivet, see *Fabre d'Olivet*.

Olivet, L'ABBÉ PIERRE-JOSEPH THOULIER D' (1682–1768), man of letters, translator, and grammarian. He was at one time tutor to Voltaire and in later life 'received' him into the *Académie française* (q.v.). He carried Pellisson's (q.v.) *Histoire de l'Académie française* down to the year 1700 (1729).

Olivetan, PIERRE ROBERT, *known as* (d. 1538), author of a translation (1835) of the Bible. See *Bible (French Versions of the)*.

Olivier, in the *chansons de geste* (q.v.), one of the Twelve Peers of Charlemagne and the bosom friend of Roland. His early exploits are related in the *chanson* of *Girard de Viane* (q.v.). He is the son of Renier and nephew of Girard, the unruly and formidable sons of Garin de Monglane (q.v.). War breaks out between the emperor and the brothers, and they are besieged in Vienne. Olivier, with his sister Aude, is among the defenders, and Roland among the besiegers. Roland falls in love at first sight with Aude and tries to carry her off, but she is rescued by Olivier. A duel is appointed between Olivier and Roland, to settle the issue of the war. This, after prolonged fighting and much chivalrous conduct, is stopped by divine intervention, the heroes swear eternal friendship, and Aude becomes the promised bride of Roland, a promise destined never to be fulfilled. Olivier accompanies Charlemagne in the 'Pèlerinage à Jérusalem', and figures in the fights with the giants Fierabras and Ferragus (qq.v.). He plays an important part in the tragedy of Roncevaux (see *Roland, Chanson de*). He is now the faithful companion of Roland, and when they find themselves surrounded by the Saracens in overwhelming numbers urges him in vain to sound his horn and recall Charlemagne. He is killed fighting heroically.

The chief characteristic of Olivier in the *chansons* is that his valour is tempered with moderation and common sense, in contrast with the impetuous fury of Roland.

The duel of Roland and Olivier was rehandled by Victor Hugo in the *Légende des siècles*.

Olivier de la Marche, see *La Marche*.

Olivier le Dain, see *Le Dain*.

Ollé-Laprune, LÉON (1830–99), philosopher, author of *De la certitude morale* (1880), *Le Prix de la vie* (1885), *La Philosophie et le temps présent* (1895), &c. His philosophy of belief was an influence on later, neo-Catholic philosophers such as Blondel (q.v.).

Ollenix de Montsacré, see *Nicolas de Montreux*.

Olympie, see *Olimpie* above.

Olympio, the name under which Victor Hugo personified himself in his poem *Tristesse d'Olympio* (see *Rayons et les ombres, Les*). It is frequently applied to him.

Ombre, Lai de l', see *Lai de l'Ombre*.

O'Meara, BARRY EDWARD (1786–1836), born in Ireland, was naval surgeon on board H.M.S. *Bellerophon* in July 1815 and the following month was authorized to go with Napoleon to Saint Helena as his physician. He was there for three years but quarrelled with Sir Hudson Lowe (q.v.) and was recalled. A French translation of his reminiscences of Napoleon in exile was published in Paris in 1822.

Ondine, see *Giraudoux*; *La Motte Fouqué*.

O'Neddy, PHILOTHÉE, pseudonym (an anagram) of Théophile Dondey (1811–75), one of the *Bousingos* (q.v.) who created some stir about 1830 (cf. *Gautier, Théophile*, and *Borel, Petrus*). His poems *Feu et Flamme* (1833) are typical of the writings of the later, frenetic, Romantics (see *Romantisme*). He also wrote short stories and a prose-and-verse romance of chivalry, *L'Histoire d'un anneau* (1842). Later he became a dramatic critic.

On ne badine pas avec l'amour (1834), a comedy in three acts by Alfred de Musset, first published in the *Revue des Deux Mondes* of 1 July 1834 and included later in that year in the second series of *Un Spectacle dans un fauteuil* (q.v.). It was produced at the Comédie-Française in November 1861.

Perdican is only too ready to comply with his uncle's wishes and marry his cousin Camille, but she refuses him consistently. To punish her he pretends to fall in love with Rosette, a village girl, and even decides to marry her. At this Camille's resistance breaks. She is discovered by Perdican and the two, in a scene of reconciliation, pledge their love. A sudden cry reveals that Rosette had overheard the lovers from a hiding-place. She dies. Perdican and Camille part, unable to build their happiness upon such a sacrifice. In spite of the introduction of comic characters, and a chorus of villagers who comment on events, the gay note of Musset's other comedies is lacking in this piece.

On ne saurait penser à tout, a *proverbe* (one act, prose) by Alfred de Musset (q.v.), closely based on an earlier *proverbe* by

Carmontelle (q.v.), *Le Distrait*. It is about a marquis who is young, charming, and in love, but so absent-minded that he forgets to propose. It was printed as a *feuilleton* in the daily paper *L'Ordre* in June 1849 after having been performed in May at a charity matinée (for which it was written) and then at the Comédie-Française. It was included in the 1853 edition of *Comédies et Proverbes* (q.v.).

Onuphre, the pious hypocrite in La Bruyère's *Caractères* (q.v.).

Opéra, Théâtre de l', see *Académie nationale de musique*.

Opéra-Comique, a form of drama set to music. It differs from grand opera by alternating spoken dialogue with music. It had its origin in the *comédies à ariettes*, comedies or farces interspersed with lyrical passages sung to music specially composed, and which the players of the *Théâtre de la foire* obtained the right of performing about 1713 (see *Theatres and theatre companies*, para. 5). The principal authors who wrote for these players were Le Sage, Piron, Favart, and Sedaine. Despite competition, suppressions, and interruptions, the players of the *foire* persisted, with public support, and in 1762 combined with the Italian actors then at the Hôtel de Bourgogne, under the official title of *Comédie italienne*, paying an annual tribute of some fr. 40,000 to the Opéra for their privilege. The Italian element gradually disappeared, surviving only in the name of the Boulevard des Italiens. From 1780 the company was known officially as the *Opéra-Comique*, and in 1783 it moved to the Salle Favart, on the site which it occupies today. The *Opéra-Comique* is subsidized by the State.

Opinions de Jérôme Coignard, Les (1893), by Anatole France, see *Rôtisserie de la Reine Pédauque, La*.

Oraisons funèbres. Famous preachers of funeral sermons include Bossuet, Fléchier, Mascaron, and Massillon (qq.v.).

Orateur du genre humain, L', see *Cloots, Anarcharsis*.

Orateur du peuple, L', a newspaper founded in late 1789 or early 1790 by Stanislas Fréron, son of Élie Fréron (q.v.) of *L'Année littéraire*. It lasted till July 1795. The younger Fréron (1754–1802), a Deputy to the *Convention nationale* in 1789, was for a time a disciple of Marat and conducted his journal on violently revolutionary lines to begin with. After the fall of Robespierre (July 1794) he changed his own politics and those of his paper and became an equally violent reactionary. In 1802 he went with General Leclerc's expedition to San Domingo but succumbed almost at once to the climate (see *Toussaint Louverture*).

Oratoire, Congrégation de l', a congregation of priests founded in France in 1611 by cardinal Pierre de Bérulle, on the basis of the earlier foundation (1564) in Rome by St. Philip Neri. Its aim was the instruction and sanctification of the clergy, and it was an important feature in the counter-reformation, designed to meet the need for educated priests. Malebranche and Massillon were among its members. It came to number some seventy-five establishments in France, as well as several teaching institutions which played an important part in the education of the laity (see under *Lycées and collèges*).

Orbigny, CHARLES DESSALINES D', see *Dictionaries and Encyclopedias*, under date 1841–9.

Ordonnances of 26 July 1830. See *Révolution du 29 juillet*; *Press, Development of*, para. 9.

Oresme, NICOLAS (d. 1382), a Norman, professor of theology, Bishop of Lisieux, chaplain and councillor of Charles V, author of important translations (from a Latin text) of certain treatises of Aristotle (1370–77) including the *Ethics* and *Politics*. He also wrote a famous *Traité des monnaies*, in which he condemned the debasement of coinage, and treatises on cosmography and astronomy (which he distinguished from astrology).

Oreste, a character in Racine's *Andromaque* (q.v.).

Oreste (1750), one of three plays written by Voltaire (q.v. para. 2) in competition with Crébillon.

Orgon, a character in Molière's *Tartuffe* (q.v.).

Oriane, see *Guermantes*.

Orientales, Les (1829), an early collection of lyrics by Victor Hugo, mainly on oriental themes, and conveying, vividly, the author's conception of the East, its heat, languor, and underlying savagery. Their bold imagery, and striking effects of rhythm, sound, and colouring, were new to French versification. Notable poems in the collection are: *Le Feu du ciel*, *Clair de lune*, *Les Djinns*, *Grenade*, *Sara la baigneuse*, *Mazeppa*.

Oriflamme, said to be from L. *aurea flamma*, 'golden flame', a small red three-pointed banner of the abbots of Saint-Denis (q.v.), which, when the abbey passed into the hands of the kings of France, became the French royal banner. See also *Montjoie*.

Origines de la France contemporaine, Les (1875–94), by Hippolyte Taine (q.v.), an historical study, in six volumes, of pre-Revolutionary France (vol. i, *L'Ancien Régime*), of the Revolution (vols. ii, iii, iv, *L'Anarchie*, *La Conquête Jacobine*, *Le Gouvernement révolutionnaire*), and of Napoleon, and Napoleonic and post-Napoleonic France (vols. v, vi, *Le Régime moderne*). Two long studies (in vol. vi) of the state of the Church and of education in 19th-century France were to have been followed by further general surveys of the social scene, the position of the family, &c., but the author died before he could complete the full work he had planned.

In the two last volumes the pictures of the rigidly organized, semi-strangulated France of the Napoleonic era are of great interest. The first four volumes, however, and especially the three on the Revolution, are most generally read.

Taine's fame as a historian rests upon this book, though later historians have found his documentation incomplete and unmethodical, and have criticized him, despite his avowed conception of history as a science to be studied objectively, for having allowed his anti-Revolutionary convictions to lead him into unwarranted generalizations. (His conservative sympathies had been intensified in 1871 by his horror at the events of the *Commune*, q.v.) As literature, however, if not as history, the work is highly readable, with characteristically brilliant and eloquent similes and passages of description or of psychological interpretation of events and characters.

Origines du Christianisme, Les

(1863–83, 7 vols.), a study of the origin and development of the Christian tradition, by Renan (q.v.).

Orléanistes. After the February Revolution (see *Revolutions*, III; IIIa) the Monarchist party was divided into *Légitimistes* (q.v.) and *Orléanistes*. The latter, supporters of the younger—Orléans—branch of the Royal family, hoped to place on the throne the comte de Paris, grandson of Louis-Philippe (q.v.).

Orléans, a name borne by younger princes of the blood royal from the 14th century, when Charles VI of France made the Duchy of Orléans an appanage of the Crown (1392) and bestowed it on his brother Louis. There were three branches of the House of Orléans:

(a) The Valois-Orléans branch, which began with the Louis (1371–1407), duc d'Orléans, mentioned above. His grandson (by his son Charles, duc d'Orléans, the poet, see *Charles d'Orléans*) became Louis XII of France. His great-grandson (by his second son Jean, duc d'Angoulême) became François Ier. This branch ended with the death of Henri III in 1589 (see *Kings of France*; *Valois*).

(b) The first Bourbon-Orléans branch, whose only male representative was the duc Gaston d'Orléans (1608–60), third son of Henri IV and Marie de Médicis, brother of Louis XIII, and father of *la Grande Mademoiselle* (q.v.).

(c) The second Bourbon-Orléans branch, descended from Philippe duc d'Orléans (1640–1701), through his second wife, the Princesse Palatine (q.v.); his first wife was Henriette d'Angleterre (q.v.). He was the second son of Louis XIII and Anne of Austria, and only brother of Louis XIV. Notable members of this branch include:

(i) Philippe duc d'Orléans (1674–1723), son of the foregoing, Regent during the minority of Louis XV (see *Régence*);

(ii) Louis-Philippe-Joseph (1749–93), the great-grandson of the Regent, a cousin of Louis XVI, and father of King Louis-Philippe Ier. He threw in his lot with the Revolution from the very outset, may have been no stranger to the agitations which culminated in the fall of the Bastille (q.v. and cf. *Palais-Royal*), and is often accused of having financed revolutionary groups.

He took the name of 'Philippe-Égalité', by which he is remembered, when he became Deputy for Paris in the *Convention nationale* (autumn 1792); and he voted in the *Convention* for the death of Louis XVI. He himself died on the scaffold (6 Nov. 1793);

(iii) Louis-Philippe, son of Philippe-Égalité. He became Louis-Philippe Ier (q.v.), King of the French, in July 1830. His great-great-grandson Henri, comte de Paris (b. 1908) is the present Pretender.

Orléans, DUCHESSE D', see *Palatine*.

Orme du mail, L', see *Bergeret, M.*

Orondate, the principal hero of La Calprenède's novel *Cassandre*. The father of the maréchal de Villars was nick-named Orondate on account of his romantic mien.

Oronte, in Molère's *Le Misanthrope* (q.v.), a courtier, called 'l'homme au sonnet'.

Orosius Tubero, see *La Mothe Le Vayer*.

Orphée (1928), by Jean Cocteau (q.v.), a 'tragédie en un acte et un intervalle', a modern treatment of the Orpheus story.

Orphée aux Enfers (1858), a comic opera by Offenbach with libretto by Meilhac and Halévy (qq.v.).

Orphelin de la Chine, L', a tragedy by Voltaire, produced in 1755.

Genghis Khan, the Mongol, has conquered China and slain the emperor and five of his sons. An infant son survives, entrusted by the dying emperor to Zamti, a mandarin, who conceals the child. Genghis demands the child's surrender, and Zamti, to save him, substitutes his own son for the prince and gives him up. But Zamti's wife Idamé, unable to bear the sacrifice of her child, rushes forward and declares the cheat. Now Genghis, when an obscure warrior, had loved Idamé, and loves her still. There ensues in consequence a struggle between Genghis (who seeks to obtain the surrender of the prince and of Idamé herself by threatening the death of her husband and child), and Zamti and Idamé, who prefer death to shame and disloyalty. Their courage and fidelity at last win the admiration of Genghis and teach the conqueror to conquer himself.

Orphelin du Temple, L', Louis-Charles de France, born 1785, the second son of Louis XVI and at first called duc de Normandie. He became Dauphin when his elder brother died (1789). He was imprisoned with his parents in the Temple (q.v.) in August 1792. After his father's death (when, for the *émigrés* and the foreign Powers, he became Louis XVII) he was taken from his mother and placed in the charge of the guard Simon, a cobbler. He is said to have died in prison, of a scrofulous affection, in 1795, though the circumstances were not free from mystery. Some people believed that his escape had been procured and a sickly child substituted for him.

Of some thirty pretenders ('faux dauphins') during the first half of the 19th century the best known were Charles Naundorff (d. 1845), a Prussian clockmaker, whose claim was taken to the French courts and gained credence in some quarters, and Mathurin Bruneau, a peasant from Normandy. Others included an American missionary to the Indians and a British subject, a lunatic.

Orpheline du Temple, L', Marie-Thérèse de France ('Madame Royale', 1778–1851), daughter of Louis XVI and Marie-Antoinette. She was imprisoned with her parents in the Temple (q.v.) in August 1792. In 1795 the *Directoire* handed her over to the Austrians in exchange for eight French prisoners. In 1799 she married the duc d'Angoulême (1775–1844), son of the comte d'Artois, who took the title of Dauphin when his father became Charles X. She returned with the Royal Family to Paris at the Restoration but accompanied her husband into exile again after the July Revolution (see *Revolutions*, II, II*a*) when, with his father, he abdicated in favour of the duc de Bordeaux, more usually remembered as the comte de Chambord (q.v.). Sainte-Beuve's (q.v.) *Lundi* of 3 November 1851 has a sympathetic study of her.

Orsini, FÉLIX (1819–58), Italian conspirator, condemned and executed for having tried to assassinate Napoleon III (q.v.) in January 1858. The Emperor was unharmed but the *machine infernale* (q.v.) did much damage among the crowd.

Ossian, a legendary 3rd-century Gaelic warrior and bard. In 1762–3 a Scottish man of letters, James Macpherson (1736–96), published long epic poems which purported to be translations from the Gaelic of Ossian but were later declared to be a hoax. They were, however, much admired at the time both at home and abroad. In France, where a first translation, by Letourneur, appeared in 1777, they were, like '*Les Nuits* d'Young' (Young's *Night Thoughts*), one of the strong foreign influences of the pre-Romantic era. Their wild, romantic qualities served to emphasize Mme de Staël's distinction between 'les littératures du Nord' and 'du Midi'. They were again translated in 1810 (with a preface by Ginguené, q.v.) and more than once imitated.

Otage, L' (1911), a drama by Claudel (q.v.).

The action takes place between 1812 and 1814. Sygne and her cousin Georges are the last members of the ancient family of Coufontaine, ruined by the Revolution. Georges rescues the Pope (who has been Napoleon's captive in France) and brings him to the derelict Abbey of Coufontaine where Sygne now lives. The escape is discovered by Turelure, a creature of low birth and vile character, an ex-Revolutionary who has become Napoleon's man and local Préfet. He is willing to keep silence if Sygne will marry him. Sygne is pledged to her cousin but sacrifices love and honour to save the Pope. The last act opens in 1814, shortly before Napoleon's first abdication. Turelure now exacts a further sacrifice from Sygne. If she can persuade Georges to make over all his Coufontaine rights to the son born of her marriage, Turelure, now Préfet de la Seine and a man of power, will hand over Paris to Louis XVIII. Georges arrives as the king's envoy to treat with Turelure and after a painful interview with Sygne he signs the necessary deed. He attempts to shoot Turelure but Sygne intercepts the bullet and dies. Georges is also killed. Turelure receives Louis XVIII and the Allied Sovereigns in front of the bier on which the two corpses have been placed. Claudel's two further dramas *Le Pain dur* (1913–14) and *Le Père humilié* (1916) continue the history of the Coufontaines in the 19th century.

Othon, a tragedy by Corneille, produced in 1664, one of his less successful plays. The theme is drawn from the *Histories* of Tacitus.

The scene is Rome in the time of the emperor Galba, and the play represents the conflict for the succession to the throne between Piso and Otho, the selection of Piso, the rising of the Praetorians in favour of Otho, and the murder of Galba, Piso, and the consul Vinius. The author has complicated the historical narrative with court intrigues regarding the marriages of Camilla, niece of Galba, and Plautina, daughter of Vinius. These ladies are assigned, in a bewildering succession of rapid changes, first to one suitor, then another.

Oton, SIRE DE GRANSON [Grandson], was the medieval French poet imitated and translated by Chaucer, who called him 'Graunson flour of hem that make in France'. He is mentioned by Froissart as having fought at the siege of La Rochelle (1372) in the army of the Earl of Pembroke. After this he was in England. Some years later he played an important part at court in his own country of Savoy and died (1397) in a duel defending himself against a charge of complicity in the murder of the Count of Savoy. He married (1365) Jeanne Alamand the daughter of Humbert, seigneur d'Aubonne et de Coppet (see *Coppet*).

Oudinot, NICOLAS-CHARLES, one of Napoleon's marshals (see *Maréchal de l'Empire*).

Ozanam, FRÉDÉRIC (1813–53), critic and literary historian, born in Milan of French parentage, came to Paris (1831) from Lyons for his university education, became known by his writings on foreign literature, and eventually (1844) succeeded Fauriel (q.v.) in the Chair of Foreign Literature at the Sorbonne. He was a man of much piety, a founder of the Society of Saint Vincent de Paul (q.v.), and a fine, poetical speaker, whose lectures at Notre-Dame were part of the religious life of Paris in the mid-19th century. His writings were intended to show religion glorified by history. His masterpiece is said to be *Les Poètes franciscains en Italie au XIIIe siècle* (1852).

P

Pagello, PIETRO (1807–98), the Italian doctor summoned by George Sand to attend Alfred de Musset in Venice in 1834. See under *Musset*.

Pagnol, MARCEL (1895–   ), contemporary dramatist, author of the satirical comedy *Topaze* (1928, q.v.); also of *Marius* (1929), *Fanny* (1931), and *César* (1936), popular comedies of life in Marseilles; &c.

Pailleron, ÉDOUARD (1834–99), dramatist, born in Paris, is remembered by *Le Monde où l'on s'ennuie* (1881), a lively satire of a world in which 'culture' is an amusement for society women, and political and literary honours depend on skilful wire-pulling. His other successes, more short-lived, include: *Le Monde où l'on s'amuse* (1868), *Les Faux Ménages* (1869), *L'Âge ingrat* (1879). His young girls were drawn with skill and sympathy.

Pain dur, Le (1913–14), by Claudel, the second of the trilogy which begins with *L'Otage* (q.v.).

Pairs, Les Douze, or Paladins, of Charlemagne, the principal warrior companions of the Emperor, are differently named in various *chansons de geste* (q.v.). In the *Chanson de Roland* (q.v.), perhaps the most authoritative record of them, they are Roland, Olivier, Gérin, Gérier, Bérengier, Otton, Samson, Engelier, Ivon, Ivoire, Anséis, Girard.

In the early 13th century there were in fact 'Twelve Peers of France' forming a Court of Peers, six ecclesiastical and six lay, which in 1202 declared King John of England deprived of Normandy and his other fiefs in France. These peerages were subsequently suppressed, but the dignity was revived; and it continued, though without its former importance, till the Revolution. Saint-Simon the memorialist, for example, was *duc et pair*.

There were again *pairs de France* between the Restoration (1814) and the February Revolution (1848, see *Revolutions*, III, IIIa), when France had a constitutional monarchy with a two-chamber system of government. These peers, the members of the Upper

House, were created by the king, the dignity (one highly coveted by the *arrivistes*) being for life or hereditary as he chose (but for life only after 1831).

Pairs de France, see *Pairs, Les Douze,* above.

Païva, La, who is frequently mentioned in literary reminiscences and correspondence of the later 19th century, was Thérèse Lachmann, a Russian Jewess of humble birth (b. Moscow 1819) who left her first husband, a tailor, and turned up in Paris about 1840. There she moved up the ranks of 'la galanterie' and became known in artistic circles. In 1849 she married, but soon left, a rich Portuguese, the marquis de la Païva. She retained his name but lived, still in Paris, with a very wealthy Prussian and kept open house for writers, artists, and musicians. Some time in the seventies she became suspect of political intrigue and had to leave Paris.

Paix aux Anglais, see *Comedy.*

Paix du ménage, La, one of the 'Scènes de la vie privée' of Balzac's *Comédie humaine* (q.v.).

Paix perpétuelle, Projet de, see *Saint-Pierre, Charles-Irénée,* and *Rousseau, J.-J.*).

Paladins, see *Pairs, Les Douze.*

Palais-Bourbon, in Paris. This was the seat of the *Conseil des Cinq-Cents* in 1795, of the *Corps législatif* under Napoleon, of the *Chambre des Députés* after the Restoration and again during the Third Republic. Under the Fourth Republic it became the seat of the *Assemblée nationale* (q.v.). It occupies the site of a dwelling on the left (south) bank of the Seine constructed originally (*c.* 1728) for the daughter of Louis XIV and Mme de Montespan. Its north (quai d'Orsay) side is directly opposite the Place de la Concorde and, beyond that, the Église de la Madeleine, being connected with them by the Pont de la Concorde and thus forming one of the finest examples of perspective in Paris (This is partly thanks to the addition, in 1808, of a Corinthian, and purely decorative, façade designed specially to match the Église de la Madeleine: the entrance is on the south side, from the Place du Palais-Bourbon.)

Palais-Royal, in Paris, a palace and gardens (surrounded by arcades) with many social, political, and literary associations. It occupies a quadrilateral site flanked (west) by the Théâtre-Français and fronting (south) on to the rue Saint-Honoré. It was constructed about 1636 for Richelieu and known first as the Palais Cardinal. Its gardens were open to the public, and soon became a place of popular resort. Corneille made it the scene of one of his early comedies; and at a later date Louis XIV placed one of its halls at the disposal of Molière's company of actors, who remained there till Molière's death.

Richelieu bequeathed his palace to Louis XIII. In 1643 Anne of Austria, the king's widow, went to live there with the five-year-old Louis XIV and his brother Philippe I, duc d'Orléans, to whom he gave it in 1692. As the residence of the Orléans family it was a notorious place of revelry under Philippe I's son (the Regent, q.v.) and his great-grandson Louis-Philippe-Joseph, later Philippe-Égalité (q.v.). The latter began the construction of the arcades on three sides of the garden, hoping to make money by renting them as shops and dwellings. Throughout the Revolution and the early years of the 19th century these arcades remained as temporary wooden constructions, the *galeries de bois*, with shops and cafés on the *rez-de-chaussée* and restaurants and gaming-houses above, while the top floors were lived in. The cafés were hotbeds of political agitation, both Revolutionary and counter-Revolutionary (cf. *Desmoulins, C.*), and the upper stories were the haunt of gamesters and prostitutes. (There are good descriptions in, for example, Anatole France's *Les Dieux ont soif* and Balzac's *Illusions perdues,* qq.v.) The name was 'Palais-Égalité' from 1792 to 1799, and 'Palais du Tribunat' from 1799 to 1807 because the *Tribunat français,* a legislative assembly created in 1799, sat there. The *galeries de bois* were demolished by Louis-Philippe (q.v., King of France from 1830), who lived at the Palace from 1814 till he moved to the Tuileries, and spent much money on restoring and completing it. During the *Commune* (q.v., 1871) it was in great part burnt, but it was again restored. The main buildings are now in Government occupation. The gardens are a place of repose and recreation, the small dark shops of the stone arcades which have replaced the *galeries de bois* are a lure for collectors of postage-stamps and *antiquités,* the dwellings above are still inhabited, or coveted, by writers and artists.

Palaprat (pron. as if *-pra*), JEAN (1650–1721), dramatist, born at Toulouse, remembered especially for his collaboration with Brueys in *L'Avocat Pathelin* (1706), an adaptation of the original 'Pathelin' (q.v.), and in other comedies and farces, of which the best was *Le Grondeur* (1691).

Palatine, CHARLOTTE-ÉLISABETH DE BAVIÈRE, PRINCESSE (1652–1722), born at Heidelberg, was the second wife of the duc d'Orléans, brother of Louis XIV (who treated her abominably), and mother of the Regent, Philippe d'Orléans. Her father was a grandson of James I and she herself was a cousin of George I. Her letters (translated for the most part from the German) are a valuable source of information on the court of Louis XIV, which she saw from the standpoint of a foreigner. They show her a woman of sturdy outspoken character, simple, sensible, and humorous, and contain much that is interesting and entertaining, including keen criticisms of Louis XIV and Mme de Maintenon (whom the princess detested), references to the exiled Stuarts, William III, his successors, and the Duke of Marlborough, and observations on curious points of manners.

Palinod, a medieval poem containing refrains, such as the *rondeau* (q.v.), and especially a poem in honour of the Immaculate Conception. See *Puy*.

Palissot de Montenoy, CHARLES (1730–1814), generally known as *Palissot*, dramatist, author of *Les Originaux ou le Cercle* (1755), a light comedy in which he caricatured various social types, including some which recalled Rousseau, Mme du Châtelet, and Voltaire himself; of *Petites lettres sur les grands philosophes* (1757); of *Les Philosophes* (1760), a comedy modelled on *Les Femmes savantes*, a somewhat coarse attack on the *Encyclopédistes* and a considerable success in spite of the anger of the philosophical party; and of *Les Courtisanes* (1782), a comedy of social satire. He also wrote *La Dunciade* (1764), a satirical poem, and *Mémoires sur la littérature* (1771). In later life he drew nearer to the party he had attacked, and he appears to have remained on good terms with Voltaire.

Palissy, BERNARD (*c.* 1510–*c.* 1589), a celebrated potter, born near Agen in humble circumstances. He was a man of scientific and inquiring spirit, self-educated, who devoted many years, in the face of destitution and disappointments, to experiments in enamels and in the production of high-relief ware. His success in this is the basis of his fame and procured for him the protection of Catherine de Médicis and the connétable de Montmorency. But he also wrote works on natural science readable today for the impression they give of the author's strong and elevated character, and his love of nature: *Recette véritable par laquelle tous les hommes de la France pourront apprendre à multiplier . . . leurs trésors* (1563), *Discours admirable de la nature des eaux et fontaines . . .* (1580). The latter includes, in the section entitled 'De l'Art de terre', a vivid account of Palissy's early struggles. He died in the Bastille, imprisoned for his Protestant religion.

Palma-Cayet, PIERRE-VICTOR (1525–1610), chronologer royal under Henri IV, author of records of his reign entitled *Chronologie novénaire* and *Chronologie septénaire*.

Palmes académiques, an order instituted in 1808 as a reward for academic merit. There are two classes: *Officier d'Académie* and *Officier de l'Instruction publique*.

Paludes (1896), see under *Gide*.

Pamphile et Galatée, a 13th-century version by Jean Bras de Fer of a 12th-century Latin poem (*Pamphilus*), a dialogue on love (*amour courtois*, q.v.).

Panama, L'Affaire du. In 1881 a company was promoted (largely by the vicomte Ferdinand de Lesseps, 1805–94, of Suez Canal fame) to finance the piercing of a canal across the Isthmus of Panama, thus uniting the Atlantic and Pacific Oceans. Its failure in 1889, a notorious French scandal of the nineties (the background of the novel *Leurs figures* by Maurice Barrès, q.v.), revealed widespread official corruption and abuse of funds. [The Panama Canal was completed in 1914 by American enterprise.]

Panard, CHARLES-FRANÇOIS (1674–1765), a very prolific writer of songs, *vaudevilles*, and comic operas of a moral and sentimental cast. He was an easy versifier and excelled in the couplet and song rather than in the drama. None of his work was of sufficient merit to be remembered today.

Panckoucke, the name of a distinguished family of publishers, originally of Bruges, later of Lille, of the 18th and 19th centuries. The members whose names most often occur were:

ANDRÉ-JOSEPH (1700–53), born and remained at Lille. He wrote burlesque poems, which were sometimes attacks on Voltaire, and compiled various manuals and dictionaries, notably one of proverbs, see *Dictionaries and Encyclopedias* under date 1748;

CHARLES-JOSEPH (1736–98) his son, and the most famous of the family. He came to Paris in 1760 and acquired various periodicals including the *Mercure* and the *Journal des savants*, and in 1789 created the *Moniteur universel*. The *Encyclopédie méthodique* was his conception. He treated authors liberally; and Boswell (under the year 1755) refers to him as deserving of the same praise as Dr. Johnson had bestowed on the Scottish publisher Millar, for that he had 'raised the price of literature'. See *Dictionaries and Encyclopedias*, under dates 1767–74 and 1781–1832; see also *Suard*;

CHARLES-LOUIS-FLEURY (1780–1844), son of Charles-Joseph. He continued the family business and edited and published various large-scale works (see *Dictionaries and Encyclopedias*, under date 1812–22).

Pangloss, Maître, a character in Voltaire's *Candide* (q.v.).

Panizzi, ANTONIO [afterwards Sir Anthony] (1797–1879), an Italian political exile, an advocate, who settled in England in 1823. He found friends, and his remarkable administrative abilities led to his being appointed (1831) to the staff of the British Museum where, as Keeper of Printed Books from 1837 to 1856, he reorganized the Library and the Reading Room and set in hand a complete revision of the Catalogue. He and Mérimée (q.v.) became warm friends after early official contacts, and some of Mérimée's most delightful letters were written to him (*Lettres à Panizzi, 1850–1870*, 1881).

Pantagruel, by Rabelais (q.v.); published under the pseudonym of Alcofribas Nasier (anagram of his own name) late in 1532 or in 1533, the first Book to appear of his great

work, though the second in the chronological order of the story (see *Gargantua*). The title is taken from the name of a devil mentioned in Simon Gréban's mystery of the *Actes des Apôtres*, whose role is to fill the throats of drunkards at night with salt, and the first conception of the hero is of a being who induces thirst in others, a notion which recurs at intervals in this Book. The work had its origin in the extraordinary success of a recently published chap-book *Les Grandes et Inestimables Cronicques du . . . geant Gargantua*, a fantastic romance concerning a giant created by the enchanter Merlin and transported to England, where he overcomes the enemies of King Arthur. This suggested to Rabelais the idea of producing a story of the same character. He makes Pantagruel the son of Gargantua and endows him with enormous strength and a stupendous capacity for meat and drink. But Rabelais is not consistent, and Pantagruel at times loses these gigantic characteristics; in the later Books they disappear almost entirely. His birth and childhood (in parody of the *chansons de geste*) are attended by marvellous incidents. He then goes a round of the universities of France, ending with that of Paris. At Orléans he meets with the Limousin scholar, whose Latinized mode of speech is ridiculed in a famous chapter. In Paris, where he installs himself, he visits the library of the abbey of Saint-Victor and we have the satirical catalogue of the books which it contains. He receives from his father a letter of advice on the studies that he should pursue (which reveals the author's enlightened views on the subject of education and also expresses admirably the ideals of the early French Renaissance). He next makes the acquaintance of Panurge, a cunning and audacious rogue, who becomes his constant attendant. On the model of Merlin Coccai's *Baldus*, Pantagruel is provided by the author with companions symbolizing various qualities: as Panurge symbolizes cunning, so Epistemon stands for knowledge, Eusthenes for strength, and Carpalim for speed.

Pantagruel is recalled from Paris to his country Utopia, which has been invaded by the Dipsodes. With his companions he sets out for this country, which lies in the Far East, and, aided by the stratagems of Panurge, destroys the invaders and conquers the kingdom of the Dipsodes. The only casualty on his side is Epistemon, who has his head cut off, but, recovering, relates his experiences in hell, where he has seen the great heroes of antiquity, the knights of the Round Table, and various popes, set to the most incongruous occupations.

Twelve years after the appearance of the second instalment of the story (*Gargantua*, q.v.), in 1546, Rabelais published the TIERS LIVRE . . . DU NOBLE PANTAGRUEL. It differed widely in character from the two Books that had preceded it. Pantagruel's gigantic attributes now (except on rare occasions) drop out of sight, and he figures as a serene, sensible, and good-humoured prince. Panurge has been transformed into a fluent and pusillanimous buffoon. The scene at the outset (as at the end of the preceding Book) is Utopia, but soon shifts to Touraine. The Prologue reflects the political circumstances of the moment, the strenuous efforts then being made to secure the kingdom against the threatened attack of Charles V. After some remarks on the superiority of peaceful colonization over violent conquest, and a brilliant apology for borrowing and lending by Panurge (who has been made lord of Salmigondin and has prodigally wasted its revenues), the question arises whether Panurge would do well to marry. This is the subject of a series of inquiries—by opening Virgil at hazard and by consulting an old witch, a dumb man (who answers by signs), an old French poet (Raminagrobis), a philosopher, and the fool Triboulet. It proves impossible to obtain the opinion of Bridoye, the judge, for he has been called upon to defend before the *parlement* his practice of deciding cases by throw of dice. The various inquiries having proved inconclusive, it is decided to consult the oracle of the *Dive Bouteille* (Holy Bottle) and a fleet is equipped for the purpose. This gives occasion for a disquisition on the virtues of the herb Pantagruelion (hemp).

The question of women and marriage (the principal matter of this Book) had long been the subject of much discussion in France, and two friends of Rabelais, André Tiraqueau (see under *Rabelais*) and Amaury Bouchard, had taken part in it by their writings on opposite sides. Rabelais does not show himself favourable to the cause of women.

Of the QUART LIVRE, the prologue and eleven chapters appeared in 1548, the complete Book in 1552. It relates the adventures of Pantagruel and his companions on their way to consult the oracle, and testifies to Rabelais's interest in recent voyages of discovery to North America. The fleet sets out for Cathay via the North-West passage. On the voyage occurs the famous meeting with a ship carrying a cargo of sheep and the bargaining between Panurge and Dindenault the sheep-merchant. There is a vivid picture of a storm at sea. Various islands are visited whose inhabitants provide material for satire. The episodes of the Papefigues (condemned to misery for having mocked the Pope's image) and the Papimanes (devotees of the Pope and the Decretals) reflect, in their outspoken hostility to Rome, the attitude of the French court just before the Book appeared. Among other subjects of satire are the institution of the Lenten fast and the greed and idleness of the monks (Gastrolatres). To the Book Rabelais added a 'Briefve declaration' or glossary of obscure words used in the course of it.

In 1562, nine years after Rabelais's death, sixteen chapters of the CINQUIÈME LIVRE appeared under the title *L'Isle sonnante*, and the whole Book in 1564. The doubt whether the work is authentic or not has been referred to under *Rabelais*. However this may be, the Book shows a marked decline in quality and interest, and, particularly towards the end, consists largely of translations and imitations. It conducts the travellers to the temple of the *Dive Bouteille*, where they receive from the priestess Bacbuc the oracle 'Trinch' (i.e. 'Drink'). The principal episodes are those of the 'Isle sonnante' (where bells ring all day and the inhabitants are ecclesiastics of various grades in the form of birds), and that of the Chats-fourrez and their archduke Grippeminaud, a crude satire on the administration of justice.

Pantagruelion, see *Pantagruel* (*Tiers livre*).

Pantalon-Phœbus, see under *Desfontaines*.

Panthéon, Le (in the Place du Panthéon, on the Left Bank of the Seine, near the Sorbonne), is one of the famous edifices of Paris, the (secular) burial-place of famous Frenchmen to whom a national funeral has been given. It was built originally (1757–90) as a church, with funds obtained largely by means of a *loterie nationale* (q.v.), to replace the then wellnigh derelict collegiate church of Sainte-Geneviève. It is in the shape of a Greek cross, and of enormous proportions. It was barely finished when the *Assemblée constituante* decreed (1791) that it should be used solely for the purpose it now serves, that the words 'Aux grands hommes la Patrie reconnaissante' should be carved over the portal, and that its name should be changed from *Église Sainte-Geneviève* to *Panthéon français*. Mirabeau, who had just died, was the first 'grand homme' to be buried there, and there, too, not long afterwards, the remains of Voltaire and Rousseau were transferred. Attempts were made, notably in 1821 during the reign of Louis XVIII, to restore it to its original purpose as a place of worship but these were not lasting. Since Hugo was buried there in 1885 after a spectacular funeral there has been no question of change.

Panurge, see *Pantagruel*. The name is derived from the Greek πανοῦργος, resourceful, crafty (so used by Aristotle of the fox), or wicked, knavish (so used by Aristophanes).

Papadiamantopoulos, JANNIS, see *Moréas, Jean*.

Papefigues, see *Pantagruel* (*Quart livre*).

Papimanes, see *Pantagruel* (*Quart livre*).

Paquebot Tenacity, Le (1920), a play, see *Vildrac, Charles*.

Paraclet, Le, the convent founded by Abélard (q.v.), of which Héloïse became abbess.

Paradoxe sur le comédien, see *Diderot*, para. 4.

Parallèle des anciens et des modernes, see *Perrault*.

Parallèlement (1889), a collection of poems, see *Verlaine*.

Paranymphe, in the University of Paris in old times, the friend of a candidate for the licence in theology or medicine who accompanied him during his examination and solemnly complimented him on his admission. The word is also used of this complimentary discourse.

Parc aux Cerfs, at Versailles, the notorious seraglio of Louis XV, so called, it is said, because the house bought for the purpose stood in a district long since built over, used by Louis XIII as a sort of deer-farm.

Paré, AMBROISE (1517–90), surgeon, born near Laval on the Mayenne, devoted his life to the improvement of surgical science. He first effected the ligature of arteries and veins (his chief title to fame) and among many distinguished patients cured the duc de Guise (*Le Balafré*) of his wound in the head. He wrote a number of surgical treatises, beginning in 1545 with his *Méthode de traiter les plaies faites par harquebutes*; his treatises were written in French, which angered the medical faculty. He also left an interesting autobiographical work, *Apologie et voyages*. He is said to have been devout and modest in character, always ending reports of cases he had cured with the words 'Je le pansai, Dieu le guérit'.

Parents pauvres, Les. Two of the 'Scènes de la vie parisienne' of Balzac's *Comédie humaine* (q.v.) are united under this title, namely, *La Cousine Bette* and *Le Cousin Pons* (qq.v.).

Parfaict, FRANÇOIS (1698–1753) and his brother CLAUDE (1705–77), joint authors of important records of the French drama.

Parfaicte Amye, La, see *Héroët*.

Pari de Pascal, Le, see *Pascal*, para 3.

Paris (1898), the third novel of Zola's (q.v.) trilogy *Les Trois Villes*.

Pâris, Les frères, financiers under the Regency and Louis XV, the four sons, Antoine, Claude, Joseph (known as *Pâris-Duverney*, 1684–1770), and Jean, of an innkeeper in the Dauphiné. They showed their financial ability in the commissariat of the French army in Flanders, and after the collapse of Law's system in 1720 were entrusted with the national finances. Pâris-Duverney, the best known of the brothers, incurred the enmity of cardinal Fleury and was imprisoned 1726–8, but was favoured by Mme de Pompadour. He protected and enriched Beaumarchais.

Pâris, FRANÇOIS DE (1690–1727), a Jansenist deacon who repudiated the papal bull *Unigenitus* (1713) condemning Jansenist propositions (see *Jansenius*). He continued his life of rigorous austerity in the poor quarter of the Faubourg Saint-Marceau, devoting himself to the people. After his death the belief grew among the Jansenists that miraculous cures were worked at his tomb in the cemetery of the Église Saint-Médard and that these were accompanied by convulsions symptomatic of the violent struggle between life and death for the body of the sick person. Crowds flocked daily to the tomb. They fell into trances, prophesied, spoke in strange tongues, and indulged in various, often unseemly, forms of religious ecstasy, contortionism, and convulsionism which caused them to be called the *convulsionnaires de Saint-Médard*. The manifestations were such that in 1732 the cemetery was officially closed; and on the gates some wag is said to have written: 'De par le roi, défense à Dieu De faire miracle en ce lieu.' But for long years afterwards the *convulsionnaires* continued their practices furtively. In the late 19th century the cemetery (where Nicole, q.v., was also buried) was turned into a small public square.

Paris, GASTON (1839–1903), one of the foremost medievalists of the 19th century, educated in Paris and in Germany, succeeded his father Paulin Paris (1800–81, himself a pioneer in medieval scholarship) in the Chair of Medieval French at the Collège de France and held it for nearly forty years. His published works (including innumerable articles in learned journals) are an index to his wide range of literary, critical, and philological interests. They include: *Histoire poétique de Charlemagne* (1865); *La Poésie au moyen âge* (1885 and 1895, 2 series, in which he discusses the origins of the *chansons de geste*, q.v.); *La littérature française au moyen âge* (1888); *Mélanges linguistiques* (1905), &c., also many critical editions of medieval romances.

Paris, Treaty of (30 May 1814), followed the Capitulation of 30 March to the Allied Armies of the Sixth, or General, Coalition (q.v.). The Allies entered Paris on 31 March, and on 6 April Napoleon, from Fontainebleau, abdicated and Louis XVIII was proclaimed king (see *Restauration*). By this treaty France returned to the territorial limits of January 1792 and lost her colonial gains.

The Treaty of Paris of 20 November 1815 (following Waterloo, Napoleon's second abdication, and the second Restoration of the Monarchy) was framed in accordance with the resolutions of the Congress of Vienna (q.v.) and stiffened the terms of the 1814 treaty.

Parisienne, La (1885), a play by Henri Becque (q.v.). Clotilde, the chief character, plays elegant acrobatics with a husband, a lover who is jealous of the husband, and a second lover brought in to maintain equilibrium.

Parisiens en province, Les. Two of the 'Scènes de la vie de province' of Balzac's *Comédie humaine* (q.v.) are united under this title, namely *L'Illustre Gaudissart* (q.v.) and *La Muse du département*.

Parlamente, the name under which Marguerite de Navarre figures in the *Heptaméron* (q.v.).

Parlement, an offspring of the *curia regis* or royal court, gradually developed and specialized from the days of Louis IX as the supreme judicial assembly, next after the *conseil d'état* or king's council. In time there came to be eight *parlements*, those of Paris, Toulouse, Bordeaux, Rouen, Aix, Grenoble, Dijon, and Rennes; Pau and Metz were added later. The *parlement* of Paris was the most ancient; its jurisdiction extended over half of France, and it comprised 200 magistrates. These sat in general assembly only to consider the gravest questions of State, such as the verification and registration of the king's edicts required to give them force of law. The *parlement* was divided into separate benches to deal with ordinary suits and with appeals from lower jurisdictions (see *Bailli*). A special bench, known as *la Tournelle*, dealt with criminal cases. The *parlements* of the other cities comprised fewer magistrates but were organized on the same plan. A *parlement* included, besides presidents and *conseillers*, magistrates known as the *parquet*, viz. a *procureur général* and *avocats généraux* and their deputies, whose business it was to defend the interests of the king and State; when the king presided in person at a sitting of the *parlement*, they knelt in the centre of the hall, on the *parquet*, whence their name. The *parlements* and subordinate magistratures had control of the police. The officials of the *parlements* were irremovable; their offices were hereditary and might be purchased. In general, when the *parlement* is spoken of, without further designation, the *parlement* of Paris is meant.

For the important part played by the *parlement* in the first *Fronde*, see under that word. As a political institution the *parlement* never exerted a more unfortunate influence than in the 18th century. As a privileged society of hereditary lawyers, it was naturally a stubborn opponent of reform in administration, and of new ideas in philosophy. Nevertheless, as the chief seat of opposition to a corrupt court it enjoyed popularity. The *parlements* of Paris and the provinces were suppressed by chancellor Maupeou in 1771 but reconstituted amid general rejoicing by Louis XVI on his accession in 1774.

Par les champs et par les grèves, see under *Flaubert*; also *Rocher du Grand-bé*.

Parloir aux bourgeois, see *Hôtel de ville*.

Parmentier, ANTOINE-AUGUSTIN (1737–1813), born at Montdidier, near Amiens, the French agriculturist and chemist who turned the French into a nation of potato-eaters. During the Seven Years' War he was with the army and was more than once taken prisoner. In the course of long, hungry spells of captivity he discovered the virtues of the potato as an article of diet. Thereafter he devoted his energies, with royal encouragement, to popularizing this vegetable among a people who had hitherto thought of it as fit only for animal fodder and as a possible cause of leprosy. After the Revolution he was called upon to reorganize the army health services. He wrote various treatises on potatoes, grains, bread and bread-making, and other forms of rural and domestic economy. In the early chapters of Erckmann-Chatrian's (q.v.) *Histoire d'un paysan* there is an interesting picture of country peasants faced with starvation when the wheat crop fails, and being saved because one more enlightened than the others has planted his field with potatoes.

Parmentier, JEAN (1494–1529), born at Dieppe, navigator and poet, who wrote a few stirring *chants-royaux* and a rhymed exhortation to his company when discouraged on a long voyage to the East Indies.

Parnasse contemporain, Le. Recueil de vers nouveaux (1866; 1871; 1876), see *Parnassiens.*

Parnasse satyrique, a collection of licentious verse, published in 1622. The best known among the authors was Théophile de Viau (q.v.), who was imprisoned and banished in consequence.

Parnassiculet contemporain, Le (1867), see *Pastiche.*

Parnassiens, Les, a group of poets who, after 1860, represented in poetry the scientific and positivist spirit of the age and its reaction against *Romantisme* (q.v., and cf. *Réalisme* and *Naturalisme* in fiction and the drama). To begin with, they were associated with the *Revue fantaisiste* (1861), a poetry review founded by Catulle Mendès (q.v.); the *Revue du progrès moral, littéraire, scientifique et artistique* (1863–4), founded by Xavier de Ricard (q.v.), which had political tendencies and favoured scientific poetry; and *L'Art* (1865–6), which voiced the doctrines of *l'art pour l'art* (q.v.). At intervals during 1866 the publisher Alphonse Lemerre (q.v.) issued the first series (in eighteen fascicules) of *Le Parnasse contemporain,* poems by members of the group, hence the name *Parnassiens.* The second, prepared during 1869, was delayed by the Franco-Prussian War and published in 1871. The third, in three volumes, appeared in 1876 but had lost much of its original character.

The Parnassian poetry was objective, impersonal, and restrained, where the Romantic poetry had been self-revealing and lyrically expansive. It confined itself to descriptions of nature, remarkable for their static, pictorial quality ('impassibility'), and often introducing an exotic element; or to evocations of a historic (mostly Greco-Roman) or archaeological past; or it attempted to convey philosophical conceptions, often pessimistic (see *Foreign Influences on French Literature,* para. 23). It was, or aimed at being, impeccable in form. Technical liberties, such as Hugo had introduced, were rejected. Rhythm was of supreme importance.

The great precursor of the Parnassians was Théophile Gautier, the apostle of *l'art pour l'art.* Care for the art of versification makes

Théodore de Banville another precursor; and the classic perfection of Baudelaire's finest poems, and the fact that he contributed (*Nouvelles Fleurs du mal*) to the first series of *Le Parnasse contemporain*, must also be mentioned.

The undoubted leader of the group was Leconte de Lisle (q.v.). It formed round him, met in his house, accepted his doctrines unquestioningly; and his *Poèmes antiques* and *Poèmes barbares* are in all aspects typical Parnassian poetry. Other Parnassians were Sully Prudhomme (q.v.), whose most Parnassian verse attempted to describe philosophic and scientific systems and was his least successful poetry; and José-Maria de Heredia (q.v.), whose sonnets *Les Trophées*, immobilizations of fugitive moments from past history, are the perfect expression of the Parnassian ideals of serene images and measured rhythms. François Coppée (q.v.) began as a Parnassian. Léon Dierx, Louis Ménard, Albert Mérat (qq.v.), &c., were *minores*: while youthful contributors to *Le Parnasse contemporain* were Anatole France, Mallarmé, and Verlaine.

Parny, ÉVARISTE-DÉSIRÉ DE (1753–1814), poet, born in the Île Bourbon (Île de la Réunion) in the Indian Ocean. He was author of *Poésies érotiques*, elegies on the vicissitudes of his loves, showing some measure of sincerity as well as simplicity and elegance and, in places, an exotic descriptive talent which anticipates Leconte de Lisle (q.v.). His later and longer poems are inferior. Voltaire addressed him as 'Mon cher Tibulle'.

Paroles d'un croyant (1834), by Lamennais (q.v.), a work of Christian apologetics, famous in its day and still of poetic value. It is written in a sweeping, apostrophic style, closely modelled on the Bible in language, use of parable, and division into verses. Its emotional appeal was so strong that compositors are said to have been hindered by their tears as they set up the type. The underlying idea is that democracy has its source in the Gospels; men should unite in forming a Utopian republic in which religion and mutual love will suffice to guide their conduct. The work and its author were condemned by the Pope.

Paroxysme, see *Literary Isms.*

Partage de midi (1906), a play by Claudel (q.v.).

Partenopeus de Blois, a 12th-century metrical romance (see *Romans d'aventure*) of which there are two 15th-century English versions.

The story is similar to that of Cupid and Psyche, with the roles reversed. Partenopeus (i.e. Parthenopaeus, a name taken from the myth of the siege of Thebes) is borne by enchantment to a magnificent palace where he enjoys the love of the lady Melior on condition that he shall not seek to see her. At last one night he turns the light of a lamp upon her, with results disastrous for both lovers. But after many sufferings and experiences, Partenopeus gains the lady's hand.

Partie de chasse de Henri IV, La, a historical comedy, one of the first of its kind, in prose, by Collé (1709–83, q.v.). The main theme is the frustration of a double intrigue by the insidious Concini to overthrow the minister Sully and to rob an honest miller lad of his fiancée. One episode (based on the old English legend of the Miller of Mansfield and Henry II) shows the king familiarly hobnobbing with his humbler subjects. This was considered lacking in respect to royalty and caused the play to be prohibited under Louis XV. It was not produced till 1774, after Louis XVI had come to the throne.

Partie de tric-trac, La, by Prosper Mérimée, a short story of remorse and its ravages in a man who cheats at the gaming-tables to provide money for his mistress. It appeared first (1830) in the *Revue de Paris* and was included in 1833 in *Mosaïque* (see *Mérimée*, para. 4).

Parure, La, a short story by Guy de Maupassant, first printed (1884) in *Le Gaulois*, and included in 1885 in the collection *Contes du jour et de la nuit*.

A young civil servant and his wife are invited to an official reception. The wife borrows a diamond necklace for the occasion from a rich friend and loses it on the way home. The distraught couple find and purchase an exact duplicate which they return, saying nothing; and payment over the years reduces them to a coarse, spiritless poverty from which there is no escape. One day the wife meets the friend, tells her the story, and learns that the original necklace had been paste.

Pascal, BLAISE (1623–62), philosopher and physicist, born at Clermont-Ferrand in Auvergne, the son of Étienne Pascal, a magistrate and an ardent student of science and mathematics. As a boy he showed a precocious taste for mathematics, rediscovering many of the propositions of Euclid, and writing when only sixteen years old an *Essai sur les coniques* (i.e. on conic sections); during the years 1642–52 he developed the first calculating machine. He came under Jansenist influence in 1646, but retained his interest in scientific matters (taking part especially in experiments connected with the Torricellian tube and the weight of the atmosphere) and leading a somewhat worldly life; but his *Préface d'un traité du vide*, his *Prière pour le bon usage des maladies*, and his *Lettre sur la mort de M. Pascal père*, of the period 1648–51, show his profoundly religious disposition. The *Discours des passions de l'amour*, discovered in the 19th century and doubtfully attributed to Pascal, is assigned to a slightly later date. In 1654, after a period of discouragement and repeated meditations, he underwent a mystical experience which effected his definite conversion to a religious life. He recorded his devotion in an ecstatic prayer which he always henceforth carried about with him and of which the text survives. He now, in 1655, took up his residence at Port-Royal (q.v.) and thereafter published nothing further in his own name.

(2) The two works by which he is famous date from these remaining years of his life (he died at the age of thirty-nine). Attacks by the Jesuits on the Jansenist cause and on Antoine Arnauld (q.v.) led to the publication in 1656–7 of eighteen *Lettres de Louis de Montalte à un Provincial de ses amis et aux RR. PP. Jésuites sur la morale et la politique de ces Pères*; they were composed by Pascal and are known as his *Lettres provinciales*. They deal with two subjects: divine grace, and the ethical code of the Jesuits. Pascal's views on the former are also to be found in his *Écrits sur la grâce* of uncertain date. Against the relaxed morality which the Jesuits were said to teach, he makes a vigorous appeal to public opinion by means of quotations from Jesuit works and by dialogues in which Jesuits are made, by their admissions, to cast discredit on themselves. The *Lettres provinciales*, written with polite irony and the utmost simplicity, lucidity, and objectivity, were an enormous success and dealt the Jesuits a blow from which they never recovered. The work was placed on the Index and was ordered by the Royal Council to be burnt (1660).

(3) Pascal conceived during his last years the idea of writing an *Apologie de la religion chrétienne*; but the work was never completed, and we have only the *Pensées*, fragments varying from mere subject-headings to developed expositions, which he wrote down in preparation for it. The general scheme that he had in view is known: to conquer incredulity by confounding the rational basis of that incredulity and by showing the impotence of reason in metaphysical matters. For reason, suspended between two infinities which it cannot grasp, and therefore unable to seize the whole, can know nothing but 'some appearances in the midst of things'. Faith, on the other hand, is not contrary to reason but above it. We must venerate the Christian faith, for the story of the Fall and the Redemption alone explains the contradictions of human nature (the baseness of man contrasted with the grandeur of his aspirations). Moreover, its truth is attested by the miracles and the prophecies (to which Pascal devotes much attention). Faith finally is desirable because it gives true happiness. Even if man cannot attain to certainty in religious belief, his reason must force him to accept the Christian mode of life, for by so doing he hazards only a few years of chequered pleasure against an infinity of future happiness ('le pari de Pascal'). But faith comes only by grace: to obtain this one must discipline the body to the outward observances of Christianity. The spirit of the *Pensées* may be summed up in the words, 'C'est le cœur qui sent Dieu et non la raison: voici ce que c'est que la foi: Dieu sensible au cœur.' The work is notable for its acute analysis of human character, for many striking sayings, and for its combination of powerful and persuasive reasoning with passionate devotion. It combines also the style of the philosopher with that of the lyric poet, the latter seen especially in his contemplations of infinity ('Le silence éternel de ces espaces infinis m'effraie') and of the Christian mystery. The *Pensées* were imperfectly published in 1670, the 'authentic

text'—a difficult matter to establish—at various dates and by various editors since Faugère's (q.v.) edition of 1844. The importance attached to the work in the 18th century may be gathered from Voltaire's *Remarques sur les pensées de M. Pascal* and the fact that Condorcet thought it worth while to reprint it with criticisms.

(4) Pascal, whose health had all his life been precarious, died, after sufferings aggravated by self-mortification, in Paris in 1662. Both by the profoundness of his thought and the perfection of his style he was one of the greatest of French prose writers.

Pasdeloup, JULES-ÉTIENNE (1819–87), orchestral conductor, instituted (1861) the Concerts Pasdeloup, popular Sunday concerts of classical music. They came to an end in 1884 but were revived some thirty years later and still continue (cf. *Colonne*; *Lamoureux*).

Pasquier, ÉTIENNE (1529–1615), a learned jurist and miscellaneous writer, born in Paris. In 1565 he pleaded the case of the university of Paris against the Jesuits, to whom it desired to deny the right of teaching. He wrote poems in Latin and Greek, but is especially famous for his *Recherches de la France* (of which the first book appeared in 1560 and the whole in 1621); in this he assembled much miscellaneous information relating to the history of France, its literature, and the university of Paris, all told in a pleasant ingenuous style, without pedantry. The work favours toleration and condemns religious wars, and is especially hostile to the claim of the Vatican to interfere in French affairs. Pasquier is also remembered for his *Lettres* (1586 and 1619), disquisitions on many learned subjects. His *Catéchisme des Jésuites*, an attack in dialogue form on that body, appeared in 1602.

Pasquier, see *Chronique des Pasquier*.

Passepartout, the valet in Jules Verne's (q.v.) *Le Tour du monde en quatre-vingts jours*.

Passerat, JEAN (1534–1602), born at Troyes, humanist and poet, a professor at the Collège de France, a collaborator of Jean Leroy in the *Satire Ménippée* (q.v.), and a witty railer, whose gaiety sometimes conceals his bitter indignation at the horrors of the times. Among his pleasant lighter pieces may be mentioned

Le Premier Jour de mai, a *chanson*, and the villanelle *J'ai perdu ma tourterelle*. He lost an eye at tennis in his youth, and became completely blind in 1597.

Passeur, STÈVE (1899–   ), contemporary dramatist. His works include: *L'Acheteuse* (1930); *Je vivrai un grand amour* (1935), his greatest success, a psychological drama, set in the 17th century; *Le Témoin* (1936); *La Traîtresse* (1946), &c.

Passion d'Arras, de Semur, de Sainte Geneviève, &c., see *Mystères*.

Passion de Clermont, see *Religious Writings*.

Pasteur, LOUIS (1822–95), famous French chemist and biologist, one of the great benefactors of mankind. The modern science of bacteriology, the practice and conception of curative and preventive inoculation against virus diseases, and the introduction of antiseptic and aseptic methods into surgery derive almost wholly from his researches and discoveries. After his most dramatic discovery, the virus of rabies, he began (1885) to inoculate human beings against hydrophobia and treated persons from all parts of the world. The Institut Pasteur, in Paris, for the prosecution of scientific research, was founded in his honour in 1888. The method of Pasteurization, or heat treatment of liquids, by which bacterial action is nullified, is named after him.

Pastiche, a form of literary exercise or amusement which consists in reproducing not only an author's style and mannerisms but also his mode of thought and his approach to his subject. It is often ironical, and tends to become parody if the irony is tinged with caricature. At the other extreme a *pastiche* is sometimes passed off as the work of the author imitated, and succeeds so well that it joins the ranks of literary hoaxes (see *Hoaxes and forgeries*). Although the form has been increasingly practised by 19th- and 20th-century French writers it is no more new in French than in other literatures. The *Cabinet satirique*, a collection of licentious verse, published 1618, contains several examples, and one of the articles in Marmontel's (q.v.) *Éléments de littérature* was on *Pastiche*. Balzac's *Contes drolatiques* are 19th-century *pastiches* of Rabelais. A thin little volume entitled *Le Parnassiculet contemporain* (1867), largely the work of Paul Arène and Alphonse Daudet (qq.v.), was more parody than *pastiche* of *Le Parnasse contemporain* (q.v.), published a year earlier, but parody of a high order. In 1885 *Les Déliquescences d'Adoré Floupette* (q.v.) were so convincingly *décadentes* and *symbolistes* that some critics took them seriously. Other excellent examples of the art can be found in the amusing, irreverent, occasionally coarse verses of *La Négresse blonde* (1909) by Georges Fourest; the *Anthologie du pastiche* by L. Deffoux and P. Dufay (2nd edit. 1926); *A la manière de . . .* , by P. Reboux and Ch. Muller, a collection of brilliant *pastiches* of mainly 19th-century French authors but also of Racine and of English writers, e.g. Kipling and Conan Doyle (latest edition 1950); the *Pastiches et mélanges* (1919) of Proust (q.v.); or the more recent *Exercices de style* (1947) of Raymond Queneau in which one small incident is recounted in ninety-nine different manners.

Pastoral romance and drama had their true beginning in France in the latter part of the 16th century, for the *Jeu de Robin et de Marion* (q.v., *c.* 1283) of Adam de la Halle was an isolated literary phenomenon and Amyot's translation of *Daphnis and Chloe* no more than a preparatory influence. The pastoral came to France from Italy and Spain. Sannazaro's *Arcadia*, Tasso's *Aminta*, and Guarini's *Pastor Fido* were translated from the Italian, and the *Diana* of Montemayor from the Spanish, between 1544 and the end of the century. We find traces of this Italian influence in the poets of the *Pléiade*, and Belleau wrote a *Bergerie*, which however is no more than a pastoral frame for a number of complimentary poems. The first true pastoral works of this period are probably the *Ombres* of Nicolas Filleul, a poet of Rouen, performed in 1566, and the *Pastorale amoureuse* by Belleforest (1569), a dramatic eclogue with four characters, imitated from the Italian or Spanish. In 1585 Nicolas de Montreux (q.v.) began the publication of his *Bergeries de Juliette*, a monotonous pastoral romance, of which he issued sequels from time to time, supplemented by *Athlette*, a pastoral drama. This was followed by his further pastoral dramas

Diane (1594) and *Arimine* (q.v., 1596). Among the many writers of pastoral dramas who now appeared may be mentioned Montchrétien (q.v.), who published a *Bergerie* (1600) in prose and verse, and Nicolas Chrestien des Croix (*Les Amantes ou la grande pastourelle*, 1613). These early works deal monotonously with the loves and jealousies of shepherds and shepherdesses (chaste or passionate), complicated by the interference of satyrs and magicians, by oracles and judgements of Druids, and by the intervention of deities such as Diana, Pan, and Cupid. They consist largely of long tirades and laments, and there is little dramatic action. They are written in verses of eight, ten, or twelve syllables. Hardy (q.v.), who adopted the line of ten syllables, introduced more action and liveliness in the five pastoral dramas that he published (1623–8); they are in fact simple comedies of love and rivalry, with some addition of the mythical and marvellous (such as the intervention of oracles and satyrs, of Cupid or Pan). The various parts of *L'Astrée* (q.v.), the long sentimental romance in pastoral form by Honoré d'Urfé, appeared between 1607 and 1627. French pastoral drama reached its zenith about the end of this period. Among the works of this kind then produced were the *Bergeries* (printed 1625) of Racan, the *Sylvie* and *Silvanire* (*c.* 1625–9) of Mairet, and the *Amaranthe* (1631) of Gombauld, all in Alexandrines. They still include the old features, satyrs (whose discomfiture furnishes the comic element), oracles, judgement scenes, disguises, and recognitions; but they show a transition towards comedy by the omission of the more outrageous and unnatural incidents, and by greater delicacy and elegance of style and treatment. The *Folies de Cardenio* (1629) and the *Inconstance d'Hylas* (1630), by Pichou and Mareschal respectively, were based on *L'Astrée*. After 1631 pastoral drama shows a decline and a reversion to the earlier type; but before long it fades out, losing itself in comedy, tragi-comedy, or musical drama, to which it had served as a preparation. In 1629 Sorel's *Berger extravagant*, a long parody of *L'Astrée*, had contributed to display the absurdity of much of the pastoral writing. Lisis, for instance, prepares to throw himself (like Céladon in *L'Astrée*) into the Lignon at the first cruel word of his mistress, but takes the precaution to send word to three nymphs to be ready to pull him out, 'car que sçay-je si elles y viendroient si on ne les avertissait; car je ne sçay nager'. Molière wrote some pastoral comedies, notably *Mélicerte* (1666) and *Les Amants magnifiques* (1670), but his more typical attitude was that of M. Jourdain, 'pourquoi toujours des bergers?'

Pastorale comique, La, a *comédie-ballet* composed by Molière for a royal festival at the end of 1666. Only part of the text is extant.

Pastourelle, see *Chansons à personnages*.

Pâté et de la Tarte, Farce du, see *Farce*.

Pathelin, La Farce de maistre Pierre, the most famous of the ancient French farces, composed *c*. 1470, by an unknown author. It is in octosyllabic couplets. ('Pathelin' is the spelling in the first editions. 'Patelin' prevailed in the 16th century.)

Pathelin, a rascally lawyer, tricks the foolish draper Joceaume out of a piece of cloth. When Joceaume comes to Pathelin's house for payment, Pathelin, with the help of his wife Guillemette, feigns illness and in his delirium talks nonsense in half a dozen dialects and finally in Latin. Meanwhile Joceaume has discovered that he is being robbed of his sheep by his shepherd, Aignelet, whom he hales before the judge. Aignelet enlists Pathelin's services as advocate. Joceaume, confused at seeing the rascal Pathelin in court, mixes up his two complaints, against the shepherd and against the lawyer, keeps recurring to the loss of his cloth, and is recalled to the business of the moment by the judge in the famous phrase, 'Revenons à ces moutons'. Aignelet, who to every question replies, on Pathelin's advice, by merely bleating, is discharged as an idiot. But the tables are turned on Pathelin when, in reply to his demand for his promised fee, Aignelet merely bleats.

The farce was adapted by Brueys and Palaprat (qq.v.) in *L'Avocat Pathelin* (1706).

Patin, GUI (1602–72), born in Picardy, physician, dean of the faculty of medicine 1650–2, a man of an original and satirical turn of mind, who has left lively letters containing much curious information about his times, and occasionally some good literary judgements. He was ahead of his age in preferring a healthy diet to the use of drugs. He detested apothecaries, as well as monks and Jesuits (see also *Renaudot*). His letters reveal the intolerant and pedantic attitude of the faculty in his day.

Patriote français, Le (July 1789–June 1793), a journal, founded by Brissot (q.v.), which set out to be 'libre, impartial et national'. It contained good, commented reports of proceedings in the *Assemblée nationale*, and its later numbers are particularly interesting as a picture of the conflict between *Girondins* and *Montagnards* (qq.v.).

Patriotes, see *Ligue des Patriotes, La*.

Patru, OLIVIER (1604–81), an advocate, the chief representative of forensic eloquence in the 17th century, and a noted authority on style and literary taste, was a friend of Vaugelas, Balzac, Perrot d'Ablancourt, Boileau, and La Fontaine. He was admitted to the *Académie* in 1640, and his speech of thanks to that body initiated the custom of formal harangues on such occasions. His *Plaidoyers* were published, otherwise he wrote little; some of his letters have merit.

Paul et Virginie, a romance by Bernardin de Saint-Pierre, first published in vol. iv of his *Études de la Nature* in 1787. The author called it a *pastorale*, but it is a tale of passion with didactic digressions.

Paul and Virginie, two fatherless children, are brought up in poverty and innocence, far from society and its corruption, amid the tropical scenery of the Île de France (Mauritius). They love one another from their infancy. Virginie, to the despair of both, is recalled to France by a harsh and wealthy aunt. There she is miserable, and after two years returns to the Île de France. But her ship is wrecked on the island and she herself is drowned before the eyes of Paul. (She could have been saved if she had been willing to strip her clothes off and jump into the raging sea with the naked sailor who tried to rescue her, but she repulsed him with dignity and awaited inevitable death with 'une main sur ses habits, l'autre sur son cœur'.) Paul dies of a broken heart two months later, a melancholy moral of the imperfection of human life when it departs from nature. Although excessively sentimental, this little work contains many charming passages, especially the descriptions, in which Rousseau's influence can be seen, of an idyllic life in strange surroundings. It had an immense vogue, was translated into many languages, and still retains its popular fame. Bonaparte considered it the language of the soul, and he pensioned and decorated the author.

Paulet, MLLE, see *Paulette*.

Paulette, La, an annual tax of one-sixtieth of the price of a judicial or financial office, in consideration of the payment of which, under the *ancien régime*, the holder of the office acquired a full right of property in it. The name was derived from that of CHARLES PAULET, a financier under Henri IV, the first farmer of the tax. He was father of MLLE ANGÉLIQUE PAULET (1592–1651), a prominent member of the circle of the Hôtel de Rambouillet (q.v.), who was known as *la lionne* from her character and the colour of her hair, and to whom some of Voiture's most entertaining letters are addressed.

Paulhan, JEAN (1884–   ), critic and essayist, editor of the *Nouvelle Revue Française* (q.v.) from 1925 to 1940 in succession to Jacques Rivière (q.v.), and of the *Nouvelle Nouvelle Revue Française* from 1953. His publications include: *Entretiens sur des faits divers* (1930), *Les Fleurs de Tarbes* (1941), &c.

Pauline, the heroine of Corneille's *Polyeucte* (q.v.).

Paul-Louis, vigneron, see *Courier, Paul-Louis*.

Paume, Jeu de, the game known to us as tennis. A distinction was made between *courte paume*, played in an enclosed court, and *longue paume*, played in an open space. The *Jeu de Paume* at Versailles was the enclosed court where, on 28 June 1789, the deputies of the *tiers état* took an oath not to disperse until they had given France a constitution.

Pauvre diable, Le, a satire in verse on the Horatian model by Voltaire, published in 1758, directed mainly at the literary profession, with incidental ridicule of Fréron, Le Franc de Pompignan, and other authors.

Pavie. Pavia, in Lombardy, where François Ier was defeated by the imperial army and taken prisoner in 1525. It was from there that the king wrote to his mother: 'De toutes choses il ne m'est demeuré que l'honneur et la vie qui est sauve.'

Pavie, VICTOR (1808–86), was born, and for most of his life managed the family printing business, at Angers. He studied law in Paris, frequented Romantic circles (see *Romantisme*), and made many lasting friendships, notably with Sainte-Beuve (q.v.). His *Œuvres choisies* (mainly verse, criticism, and articles on history and archaeology contributed in the first place to local papers) were published in 1887.

Pavillon, ÉTIENNE (1632–1705), minor poet, of amiable character but no distinctive merit; a member of the *Académie*.

Pavillon, NICOLAS (1597–1677), Bishop of Alet (near the Spanish frontier), a firm and prominent supporter of the Jansenists during their persecution.

Paysan du Danube, Le, the title of a fable by La Fontaine which has become the synonym for a rough but forcible critic. (An untutored peasant under Roman domination protests against the corrupt officials with a vigour that reaches Rome itself and produces changes for the better.)

Paysan parvenu, Le, a romance by Marivaux, published in 1735–6, the story of Jacob, a sturdy young peasant from Champagne who, coming to Paris, makes his way in the world thanks to his good looks, becomes a farmer-general of taxes, and marries a countess. The work is a counterpart of the author's *Marianne* (q.v.), with a man in place of a woman as the principal character. Like *Marianne*, it was left unfinished. It may have influenced Fielding in *Joseph Andrews*.

Paysan perverti, Le (1775); ***Paysanne pervertie, La*** (1776), novels by Restif de La Bretonne (q.v.).

Paysans, Les (1844), by Balzac, a long, somewhat disconnected novel, is one of the 'Scènes de la vie de campagne' of his *Comédie humaine* (q.v.). It turns on the intrigues which in the end drive General de Montcornet to sell his property. The period is *c.* 1825; the peasants who engineer the intrigues are the crafty, surly inhabitants of the Morvan, a district in Burgundy.

Pays d'élections and **pays d'États,** see *Fiscal system*.

Peau d'Ane, one of the fairy-tales of Charles Perrault (q.v.), originally in verse.

A fair and virtuous princess, to avoid a criminal marriage, escapes from her father's court under the protection of a fairy, her face disguised with soot, and with an old ass's skin for dress. She wanders far away, but with her sluttish appearance the only place she can obtain is that of a drudge on a farm. She lives alone in a hovel and there she sometimes comforts herself by secretly resuming her beauty and gay clothes. On one of these occasions, a prince who is out hunting looks from curiosity through the keyhole of the hovel and discovers her. He inquires who lives there and is told 'Peau d'Ane'. He falls ill from love of her, and nothing will cure him but he must have a cake made by Peau d'Ane. His whim is humoured, but as he eats the cake, he comes upon a ring which has slipped off Peau d'Ane's finger. The prince will now only marry the woman whose finger the little ring will fit. All the women of the kingdom try it on in vain. Finally Peau d'Ane is brought in, amid the derision of the courtiers. The ring fits her finger, she becomes once more a beautiful princess, and her royal birth is revealed.

Peau de chagrin, La (1831), a novel by Balzac, one of the 'Études philosophiques' of his *Comédie humaine* (q.v.). A magic piece of shagreen has power to grant its owner's wishes, but with every wish granted the leather shrinks and the owner's life is shortened.

Pêcheur d'Islande (1886), a novel of Breton fishing life by Pierre Loti (q.v.).

Pécuchet, see *Bouvard et Pécuchet.*

Pédauque, Reine, see *Rôtisserie de la Reine Pédauque.*

Péguy, CHARLES (1873–1914), essayist and poet, born at Orleans in humble circumstances, was brought up by his widowed mother, a chairmender, and his grandmother. Scholarships took him to the Collège Sainte-Barbe in Paris, then to the École normale supérieure (q.v.), which he left without taking his degree. In 1900, after having run a socialist bookshop for some years, he founded, and was the moving spirit of, the *Cahiers de la quinzaine* (q.v., 1900–14,),

a periodical publication of highly individual character. At first an ardent socialist, with strong anti-clerical convictions, he was by the end of his life a keen patriot and nationalist, also—though he remained outside the Church—a fervent, almost mystical Catholic. His changing convictions were at all times reflected in his writings. He died in action leading his company at the battle of the Marne.

Nearly all Péguy's output appeared first in the *Cahiers* and consisted until the last four years of his life mainly of polemical prose, the titles most frequently mentioned being: *Notre Patrie* (1905; the reflections of an ordinary citizen who returns to Paris from a week-end in the country to find the air heavy with international crisis and the menace of German invasion. His sense of threatened happiness quickens his understanding of what France and French culture mean to him); *A nos amis, à nos abonnés* (1909) and *Notre jeunesse* (1910), both about the Dreyfus case and its enduring, unforgettable effect on Péguy's generation; *Victor-Marie, comte Hugo* (1911). His poetical writings are dominated by his intense veneration for St. Joan of Arc, whose gradual awakening to her vocation forms the theme of his three dramatic poems *Le Mystère de la Charité de Jeanne d'Arc* (1909), *Le Porche du mystère de la deuxième vertu* (1912), and *Le Mystère des Saints Innocents* (1912). An embryo version of the first of these, *Jeanne d'Arc*, had already been published in 1897. The collections called *Tapisseries—de sainte Geneviève* (1912) and *de Notre-Dame* (1913)—are also characterized by his love of Orleans and the country of the Loire. The latter contains the *Présentation de la Beauce* [the fertile plain which extends as far as the eye can see from Chartres] *à Notre-Dame de Chartres. Ève* (1914), a very long poem, contains the famous 'Prière pour nous autres charnels' with its litanical repetition and variation of the first line 'Heureux ceux qui sont morts pour la terre charnelle'. Constant repetition and variation of words and phrases are features of Péguy's style, both in prose and poetry.

Peintre de Salzbourg, Le, see *Nodier.*

Peiresc, NICOLAS-CLAUDE FABRI DE (1580–1637), born in Provence, magistrate, antiquarian, and naturalist, a friend of Malherbe, and a correspondent of the learned men of all Europe.

Péladan, JOSÉPHIN (1859–1918), man of letters and playwright, author of *Le Vice suprême* (1884), *La Décadence esthétique* (1888–98), essays, and *Les Fils des étoiles* (1895), *La Prométhéide* (1895), *Le Prince de Byzance* (1896), &c., mystical dramas. He was associated with some of his contemporaries about 1888 in a revival of Rosicrucianism and called himself Sâr (i.e. High Priest) Péladan. He founded the *Théâtre de la Rose-Croix* (1890) in opposition to the naturalism of the *Théâtre Libre* (q.v.).

Pelé, the rat, in the *Roman de Renart* (q.v.).

Pèlerinage de Charlemagne à Jérusalem, a *chanson de geste* (q.v.) in alexandrines, probably of the 12th century, notable for the grotesque element in it, a departure from the severe grandeur of the *Chanson de Roland*. Charlemagne, irritated by his wife's indiscreet praise of Hugo, emperor of Constantinople, sets off to see for himself whether her praise is justified. He goes first to Jerusalem, where he acquires various precious relics; then visits Hugo at Constantinople. The visit gives occasion for some crudely comic incidents and leads to the conclusion that Charlemagne's queen was much mistaken in her estimate of Hugo.

Pèlerin passionné, Le (1891), collected poems by Moréas (q.v.).

Peletier, JACQUES (1517–82), *known as* PELETIER DU MANS, born at Le Mans, mathematician and poet, who inspired Ronsard and du Bellay with their first ideas of poetic reform. His views on the subject were expressed in a preface to his translation of the *Ars Poetica* of Horace (1545) and in his own *L'Art poétique* (1555). He figured in Ronsard's original list of members of the *Pléiade* (q.v.).

Pelléas et Mélisande (1892), by Maeterlinck (q.v.), one of the best known of the Symbolist dramas. It became even better known after 1902 when Debussy set it to music. It is about two ill-fated lovers—Mélisande, a frail, mysterious maiden, found weeping in the forest by Golaud, a king's son, who marries her, and Pelléas, brother of Golaud. Mélisande talks with

Pelléas by a fountain and loses her ring, the gift of Golaud, in the water. Golaud's jealousy mounts. He surprises the lovers taking a last farewell of each other and kills Pelléas. He seeks forgiveness, too late, from Mélisande. Mélisande dies.

Pellerin, JEAN (1885–1920), wrote Fantaisiste (q.v.) poems of modern life, collected in *La Romance du retour* (1921), *Le Bouquet inutile* (1923), &c.

Pellisson, PAUL (1624–93), born at Béziers, man of letters, secretary to Nicolas Fouquet (q.v.), and an eloquent advocate in his favour at the time of Fouquet's disgrace. Pellisson was imprisoned for five years in the Bastille, but was then released by Louis XIV and made his historiographer. He wrote a short *Histoire de l'Académie française*, in the form of a letter to a friend, relating its inception and early proceedings down to 1652. This work is praised by Sainte-Beuve as one of the most finished and agreeable pieces of French writing. It won for its author a seat in the *Académie*. (Cf. *Olivet, l'abbé d'*.)

Peltier, JEAN-GABRIEL (1765–1825), born at Nantes, founded and edited the celebrated anti-Revolutionary journal *Les Actes des apôtres* (q.v.). After the fall of the monarchy (1792) he fled to England and there edited *L'Ambigu*, a paper at first anti-Revolutionary and subsequently anti-Napoleon. He remained in England after the Restoration but returned to Paris to die.

Pensées de Pascal, see *Pascal*.

Pensées philosophiques (1746), see *Diderot*, para. 2.

Pensées sur l'interprétation de la nature (1754), see *Diderot*, para. 2.

Pépin d'Héristal and **Pépin le Bref,** see *Carolingiens*.

Perceforest, a vast prose romance of the 14th century, in which the author seeks to link the legends of Alexander and of Arthur. Alexander, after his conquest of India, is driven by a storm on to the coast of Britain. He makes one of his followers (called Perceforest because he has killed a magician who lives in an impenetrable forest) king of the land. Perceforest institutes an order of knights of the Franc Palais. Under his grandson the Grail is brought to England. Among the numerous adventures recounted is that of the 'Belle au bois dormant' or the Sleeping Beauty. The work was first printed in 1528 and was translated into Italian in 1531, which attests its popularity.

Perceval. In its earliest form the story of Perceval was a primitive folk-tale. A boy brought up by his widowed mother in ignorance of chivalry comes by chance to the king's court, becomes a doughty knight, slays the man who killed his father, rescues a damsel from her enemies and marries her, and recovers his mother. Into this simple tale Chrétien de Troyes (q.v.), in his *Perceval* or *Conte del Graal*, introduced the matter of a *graal* or mysterious dish which Perceval had seen in a castle, but of which he had failed to ask the significance. To the quest of this *graal* and of the bleeding lance which he had seen on the same occasion Perceval devotes himself; but Chrétien left his poem unfinished. The story was continued by various other poets, and in these continuations the *graal* took on a character apparently not contemplated by Chrétien—that of the dish in which Joseph of Arimathea had received the blood of the Saviour on the Cross, brought, according to developments of the legend, to the castle of Corbenic in Great Britain, the approach to which was unknown.

Late in the 12th or early in the 13th century Robert de Boron or Borron, a poet of Franche-Comté, composed a trilogy— *Joseph d'Arimathie, Merlin, Perceval,* in which he developed the early story of the Holy Grail and linked it with the Arthurian tradition. He thus brought together two distinct strata of legend, Merlin (q.v.), with his knowledge of the past and the future, serving as a connecting link. Of the trilogy only the first poem and part of the second survive.

Of the story as a whole or of its parts various prose versions followed in the 13th century. The principal one, generally known as the 'Vulgate' Version, is an immense cycle composed between 1225 and 1230, containing five 'branches' (*L'Estoire del Saint Graal, Merlin, Lancelot del Lac, Queste del Saint Graal,* and *Mort Artu*). In it Perceval is ousted by Galaad (Galahad), son of Lancelot. The work has been improbably attributed to Walter Map, who was archdeacon of Oxford under Henry II. It was the favourite reading of the French nobility down to the time of Louis XI (witness Froissart).

The story has been treated in other languages than French: in German the *Parzifal* of Wolfram von Eschenbach (and cf. Wagner's opera *Parzival*), and in the Welsh Mabinogi *Peredur*. In English we have, before Malory, the 15th-century *Sir Percyvelle of Galles* and two pieces both dealing with the early story of the Grail, *Joseph of Arimathie* (14th c.) and the *History of the Holy Grail* by Henry Lovelich (15th c.).

Perceval de Cagny, Chronique de, see *History* (medieval period).

Perdican, hero of *On ne badine pas avec l'amour* (q.v.), by Alfred de Musset.

Père de famille, Le, see *Diderot*, para. 4.

Père Duchesne, Le (1790–4), a Revolutionary journal (two series of 8vo pamphlets, 355 numbers in all), founded by Hébert (q.v.). It appeared three times weekly and contained articles notorious for their foulmouthed violence though by no means illwritten. It was widely read among the poorer people.

'Le Père Duchesne' appears to have been a stock character of the *Théâtre de la Foire* (q.v.), to whom were gradually attributed any opinions or anecdotes which could not be uttered openly. He was pictured in a vignette at the head of Hébert's paper, at first with a pipe in his mouth and a shag of tobacco in his right hand, later with moustaches, and two pistols in his belt, and with the tobacco replaced by an axe which he was brandishing over the head of a kneeling *abbé* (the abbé Maury, q.v.). The motto beneath the vignette was: 'Je suis le véritable Père Duchesne, foutre.' One article usually filled each number, the heading being *La Grande Joie du Père Duchesne sur* or *La Grande Colère du . . . contre* the particular object of attack; and Hébert left few personalities or events untouched.

Before Hébert started his paper the name 'Père Duchesne' had already been used for another, much less violent, pamphlet-series, the *Lettres bougrement patriotiques du Père Duchesne* (1790–2), and it was revived for one of the short-lived papers founded in 1848.

Péréfixe, HARDOUIN DE BEAUMONT DE (1605-71), Archbishop of Paris and historian, author of a life of Henri IV written for Louis XIV. He was the son of a steward in cardinal de Richelieu's service and was chosen in 1644 by the Regent to be tutor to the young king. It was he who, as archbishop, forbade in 1667 the performance of Molière's *Le Tartuffe*.

Père Goriot, Le (1834), by Balzac, one of the 'Scènes de la vie privée' (and one of the key-novels) of his *Comédie humaine*. Eugène de Rastignac (q.v.) has come to Paris to study law. He is ambitious, impatient of poverty, and determined to conquer Paris society. His fellow boarders at the dingy Maison Vauquer include the mysterious Vautrin and a retired merchant, M. Goriot. Vautrin advises Rastignac to use all means of advancement, even crime, and unfolds a plan for a murder leading to marriage with a rich heiress. Rastignac is about to consent when Vautrin is arrested and turns out to be *Trompe-la-Mort*, a long-wanted criminal (see *Vautrin*). Le père Goriot, obviously poverty-stricken, is the butt of the boarding-house, for no one believes his story that the baronne Delphine de Nucingen and the comtesse Anastasie de Restaud are his daughters. But Rastignac meets Anastasie, the younger daughter, at a ball and learns that Goriot's story is true. This adoring father had given up his great wealth to his two children, who are now ashamed of him and only visit him if they think they can bleed him still further. Out of pity Rastignac attaches himself to the old man and at the same time, as a stepping-stone to a career, makes Mme de Nucingen his mistress. Old Goriot falls mortally ill after a last desperate effort to pay Anastasie's debts and avert a scandal. Dying, he calls piteously for his daughters, but only Rastignac and Bianchon, a medical student, are beside him, and Rastignac sells his watch to pay for the lonely burial. The book ends with Rastignac looking down on Paris from the heights of the cemetery of Père-Lachaise. The great city lies beneath him like a monster, only to be conquered after the most cynical struggle; and with the words 'A nous deux maintenant!' he turns to begin the fight.

Père humilié, Le (1916), by Claudel, the third play of the trilogy which begins with *L'Otage* (q.v.).

Père Joseph, Le, see *Éminence grise*.

Père-Lachaise, Cimetière du, a famous cemetery in Paris, see *La Chaise, Père François de*.

Péret, BENJAMIN (1899–), author of *surréaliste* works—*Immortelle maladie* (1924), *Le Grand Jeu* (1928), *De derrière les fagots* (1934), *Trois cerises et une sardine* (1937), &c. (see *Surréalisme*).

Périchole, La [La Perricholi], a peasant girl found singing in the streets of Lima who became a famous actress and singer—famous also for her adventures—of 18th-century Peru. In Mérimée's short comedy *Le Carrosse du Saint Sacrement* (1830; see *Théâtre de Clara Gazul*), she is the *comédienne* who aspires to be a great lady off as well as on the stage, the cajoling, resourceful mistress of the Viceroy, as temperamental and impetuous in her devotions as in her loves. In Offenbach's operetta *La Périchole* (1868, with libretto by Meilhac and Halévy) she is still the street singer, betrothed to a fellow singer and a prey to the Viceroy's attentions. [She is one of the characters whose history is related in Thornton Wilder's novel *The Bridge of San Luis Rey*.]

Pérignon, DOMINIQUE-CATHERINE, one of Napoleon's marshals (see *Maréchal de l'Empire*).

Pernelle, MME, in Molière's *Tartuffe* (q.v.), the mother of Orgon.

Péron, FRANÇOIS (1775-1810), French naturalist and sea-voyager, was serving in the army at the outbreak of the Revolution and taken prisoner. In captivity he became interested in history and travel and on his release studied medicine. Between 1800 and 1804 he was attached as zoologist to a scientific, largely hydrographic, expedition to the Southern Hemisphere, under Captain Nicolas Baudin (1750-1803). On his return to France, when he brought with him a large and valuable collection of animals, he wrote one of the well-known books of French travel and discovery, *Voyage de découverte aux terres australes* (1811-16).

Perrault, CHARLES (1628-1703), poet and critic, of a good *bourgeois* family of Paris, a man of much originality and versatility and of amiable character, employed by Colbert as adviser in matters of art and letters. He was a member of the *Académie* from 1671, and is chiefly famous for the part he took in support of the Moderns in the 'querelle des anciens et des modernes' (q.v.). This quarrel he revived by his poem on the *Siècle de Louis le Grand* (1687) in which he set Régnier, Malherbe, Molière, Rotrou, and others above the poets of Greece and Rome. His *Parallèle des anciens et des modernes*, lively dialogues making fun of the pedants (but betraying his own ignorance of classical antiquity), appeared from 1688 to 1697. His *Préface* to an epic poem *Saint Paulin* attacking the *Art poétique* of Boileau was published in 1686. In 1694 Perrault published an *Apologie des femmes* in reply to Boileau's *Satire X*. His *Histoires et contes du temps passé, avec des moralités. Contes de ma mère l'Oye*, a collection of fairy-tales, no doubt based on French popular tradition and told with simplicity and charm, appeared in 1697 over the name of his son aged ten (a few separately before this date). It contained *La Belle au bois dormant, Le Petit Chaperon rouge, La Barbe-bleue, Le Maître Chat ou le chat botté, Les Fées, Cendrillon ou la petite pantoufle de verre, Riquet à la houppe*, and *Le Petit Poucet*, all in prose. *Grisélidis, Peau d'Ane*, and *Les Souhaits ridicules*, in verse, were added in later editions.

Perrault's *Contes* were translated into English by Robert Samber (1729) and were discussed by Andrew Lang in *Perrault's Popular Tales* (1888). His *Les Hommes illustres qui ont paru en France pendant ce siècle* was published 1696–1701.

CLAUDE PERRAULT (1613–88), brother of the above, physician, architect, translator of Vitruvius, and designer of the colonnade of the Louvre, also took part in the controversy of the Ancients and Moderns; as did likewise another brother,

PIERRE PERRAULT, a receiver-general (d. 1680).

NICOLAS PERRAULT, a third brother (1611–61), was a theologian and a Jansenist.

Perrette, the day-dreaming milkmaid in La Fontaine's fable *La Laitière et le pot au lait*. She carries her milk to market on her head, skips with pleasure at the thought of the money she will make, and upsets the pail.

Perrichon, M., see *Voyage de M. Perrichon, Le.*

Perrin, CLAUDE-VICTOR, one of Napoleon's marshals, see *Maréchal de l'Empire.*

Perrin Dandin, the judge in Racine's *Les Plaideurs* (q.v.).

Perrot d'Ablancourt, see *Ablancourt, Nicolas Perrot d'*.

Personnalisme. (1) The philosophic system —also called *Neo-criticism*—of Charles Renouvier (q.v.), who made his conception of the individual as a being free to choose and to act the basis of his conception of the universe. He expounded it in, notably, *Le Personnalisme* (1903).

(2) A movement founded in 1932 by Emmanuel Mounier (q.v.), later more often described as a moral and social philosophy, and sometimes compared with Existentialism and Marxism as one of the three modern philosophies of existence. It had its origins in the disquiet experienced by Mounier and many of his (the inter-war) generation at the spiritual and political apathy of an age which seemed to them menaced with the total wreck of civilization. The apathy, in their view, could be combated by a new approach to the problems of existence, one less exclusively moralist and economic than the philosophies of the universities or the theologians proposed; and more concrete, because based on the individual's *sense of his responsibility* as a being free to choose and to act in a universe which he takes for granted.

Mounier's *Personnalisme* was already widely established by 1939. Its influence increased in other countries as well as France after 1944. It is Christian but, though in France much tied up with young Catholic groups, not denominational. It is also lay, in the sense of economic and political (its tendencies are left-wing), because 'la Révolution sera économique ou ne sera pas. La Révolution sera morale ou ne sera pas'. Its tenets were first expounded in the review *Esprit*, which Mounier founded for the purpose and which has remained its organ. They can also be studied in Mounier's *Manifeste du personnalisme* (1936) and other works; and in *Mounier et sa génération. Lettres, carnets et inédits* (1956).

Pertharite, a tragedy by Corneille, produced in 1653. It was a complete failure.

The sentiments expressed were, Voltaire says, extravagant or feeble, the versification in general poor, and even the names of the characters, Edvige, Grimoald, Unulphe, repellent.

Pertharite, king of the Lombards, has been driven from his throne by Grimoald; he is reported to be dead by the usurper, who though betrothed to Edvige, sister of Pertharite, falls in love with Pertharite's wife Rodelinde, and hopes to win her hand. The latter resists a marriage that she regards as criminal, but is at last brought to consent to it on the strange condition that Grimoald will add crime to crime by killing her son. Pertharite returns and is declared an impostor by Grimoald. But when the latter discovers that Pertharite only wishes to recover his wife, struck by his magnanimity, he abandons the kingdom to him, and abides by his pledge to Edvige.

The failure of this play was the occasion of Corneille's withdrawal for seven years from dramatic composition.

Pétain, HENRI-PHILIPPE (1856–1951), maréchal de France (1918), was one of the great French generals of the 1914–18 war. He organized the defence of Verdun (q.v.) in 1916, restored the morale of the army when it was dangerously low, and was one of the leaders of the offensive against Germany which ended in 1918 with the Armistice of 11 November. But in June 1940, as *Président du Conseil*, he demanded the armistice with Germany which brought the (at any rate open) participation of France in the 1939–45 war to an end. In July 1940 he was invested with full constitutional and legislative powers by the *Assemblée nationale*. He assumed the title and functions of Head of the State and from the seat of government at Vichy pursued a collaborationist policy with Germany. After the Liberation of France he was tried (1945) and condemned to death, a sentence altered to life-long imprisonment. His place of confinement until very shortly before his death was a fort on the Île d'Yeu, off the west coast of France.

Pétaud, Roi, the name formerly given to the chief of the community of beggars in France, facetiously derived from the Latin *peto*, I beg. His authority over his subjects was slight and 'la cour du roi Pétaud' was proverbial for an assembly where every one

wishes to command or speak at once (cf. *Tartuffe* I. i: 'On n'y respecte rien, chacun y parle haut, Et c'est tout justement la cour du roi Pétaud'). The term was sometimes applied to the court of Louis XV.

Pétion de Villeneuve, JÉRÔME (1756–94), a prominent Revolutionary writer and politician, born at Chartres, was elected Mayor of Paris in 1791. He escaped after the downfall of the *Girondins* (his party) in 1793 but committed suicide after months of wandering.

Petit Chaperon rouge, Le, one of Perrault's (q.v.) *Contes de ma mère l'Oye*, the tale of Red Riding Hood.

Petit Chose, Le (1868), a semi-autobiographical novel in two parts by Alphonse Daudet. The first follows fairly closely the early years of Daudet and his brother Ernest, called Daniel and Jacques Eysette in the book. The second, after the two brothers come to Paris, is almost purely fiction. Both fall in love with Camille, the daughter of a porcelain-manufacturer. She loves Daniel. Jacques becomes entangled with an actress and dies. Daniel, who had meant to write, renounces his ambition for a solid mercantile career in his father-in-law's factory.

Petit de Julleville, LOUIS (1841–1900), medieval scholar, studied the origin and development of the theatre in France, beginning with the Mystery Plays. He was also general editor of the eight-volume *Histoire de la langue et de la littérature françaises des origines à 1900* (1896–9), which is still a standard work.

Petit-Dutaillis, CHARLES (1868–1948), medieval historian. He made a special study of the feudal systems of France and England.

Petite Fadette, La (1848), a tale of rural life by George Sand (q.v.).

Petites Affiches, Les (f. 1751), a journal composed in the main of advertisements of all kinds, law notices, &c. It was developed (with modifications of form and title) during the 18th century, but it had its prototype in the sheets published by Renaudot (q.v.) in the 17th century, containing extracts from the registers of his *Bureau d'adresse*. The *Petites Affiches* contained information on current literary subjects and are of bibliographical and historical interest.

Petites Écoles de Port-Royal, Les, see *Port-Royal.*

Petites Misères de la vie conjugale. Several tales collected under this title are among the 'Études analytiques' of Balzac's *Comédie humaine* (q.v.).

Petit-Jean, a character in Racine's comedy *Les Plaideurs* (q.v.).

Petit Jehan de Saintré, Histoire du, a prose romance by Antoine de la Sale (q.v.), published *c.* 1456. Jehan de Saintré, a young page at the Court of Jean le Bon (1350–64), obtains the favour of a lady, vaguely named as the Dame des Belles Cousines, who devotes herself to educating him as a perfect knight and shows a growing affection for him, which he returns. The first part of the work is largely a veritable manual of conduct and chivalry, and we hear much of the etiquette of tourneys and of blazons and trappings. Saintré becomes an accomplished knight, fighting against the Saracens, and famed all over Europe. But his resolve to leave the lady for a while in order to win fresh laurels provokes her resentment. During his absence a rich and burly monk, Damp [an early form of *Dom*] Abbé, has little difficulty in supplanting him as her lover, and on his return he is frigidly received. He is even subjected to the disgrace of being forced to wrestle with the monk in her presence and being defeated. The signal revenge which he takes on the monk and the humiliation of the lady before the court bring the story to a close. The three main characters, the knight, the lady, and the monk, are sharply drawn, though some lack of consistency may be detected in the first two; and the closing scenes are strikingly depicted. If we disregard the didactic element and the details of the expedition against the Saracens, we have here the first French realistic novel. In the supplanting and defeat of Saintré by the *bourgeois* monk we may see the author's reluctant testimony to the passing of feudal chivalry.

Jehan de Saintré was a historical character of the 14th century, regarded, according to Froissart, as the best French knight of the day; he fought and was taken prisoner at the battle of Poitiers (Froissart, ch. 144).

Petit Philosophe, Le (1760), a comedy by Poinsinet (q.v.).

Petit Pierre, Le (1918), one of four books of romanticized autobiography by Anatole France (q.v.).

Petit Poucet, Le one of Perrault's (q.v.) *Contes de ma mère l'Oye,* the tale of Tom Thumb.

Petits Châteaux de Bohème (1853), prose and poetry by Gérard de Nerval (q.v.).

Petit Traité de versification (1923), see *Romains, Jules.*

Petit Traité de versification française (1872), see *Banville, Théodore de.*

Petrarch, see *Foreign influences on French literature,* para. 2.

Peuples et civilisations, an historical series, see *Appendix I,* § H (ii).

Peyrat, NAPOLÉON (1809–81), a Protestant pastor, friend of Lamennais and Béranger (qq.v.), wrote a work on French protestantism which is still remembered—*Histoire des pasteurs du désert depuis la révocation de l'édit de Nantes jusqu'à la Révolution française, 1685–1789* (1842–3, 2 vols.). He also published *L'Arise, romancero religieux, héroïque et pastoral* (1863), poems which included a fine romantic ode—*Roland*—written in early life when he styled himself 'Napol le Pyrénéen'.

Peyronnet, La Loi, a bill introduced in December 1827 by the comte de Peyronnet, one of Charles X's ministers. The measures it proposed would have destroyed any liberty remaining to the Press and the book-trade (cf. *Press, Development of*). Public resentment inspired many petitions to the king, including one from the *Académie française* (q.v.). The debate on the bill (which was eventually withdrawn) was notable for a speech by Royer-Collard (q.v.): 'Plus d'écrivains, plus d'imprimeurs, plus de journaux', such, he protested, would be the régime of the Press and would elevate man 'jusqu'à l'heureuse innocence des bêtes'.

Phalange, La (1) (1836–43), see *Phalanstère, Le*; (2) (1906–14), a literary review, which continued the traditions of Symbolisme (q.v.) but also sponsored new writers. Contributors included Apollinaire, Jammes, and Vielé-Griffin (qq.v.).

Phalanstère, Le, a journal founded about 1833, the first organ of the *Fouriéristes* (q.v.). It advocated the 'fondation d'une phalange agricole et manufacturière, associée en travaux et en ménage'. It was succeeded by *La Phalange* (1836–43), a fortnightly, and *La Démocratie pacifique* (1843–51), a daily.

Pharamond, the legendary ancestor of the Merovingian dynasty (see *Mérovingiens*) of the kings of France, supposed to have reigned from 420 to 428 and to have had a son Clodion who may have been the father of Mérovée; but his name is not found in trustworthy chronicles. He is the subject of a historical romance by La Calprenède (q.v.).

Phébus, in such expressions as *parler Phébus,* a manner of speaking or writing which is rendered obscure by refinement and conceits. There are examples of this in the heroic romances of Mlle de Scudéry, La Calprenède, &c.

Phèdre, a tragedy by Racine, produced in 1677, based on the *Hippolytus* of Euripides and to some extent on that of Seneca, with some modifications (notably in the introduction of the character Aricie). The play, a very powerful drama, shocked the audience of the day by its presentment of extreme passion, but the theory no longer holds that it was initially unsuccessful because of an organized cabal in favour of Pradon's (q.v.) rival play *Phèdre et Hippolyte.*

Hippolyte, son of Thésée and the Amazon Antiope, is at his father's court at Troezen. Thésée has long been absent on some unknown adventure, and Hippolyte is about to set out to seek him; he dreads his growing love for Aricie, a princess of royal Athenian blood but of a family hostile to Thésée, held captive at the court. Phèdre, wife of Thésée, conceals a guilty passion for Hippolyte. A report that Thésée is dead reaches Troezen. Phèdre, on the pretext of taking leave of Hippolyte, reveals her passion to him and he repels it with horror. In the midst of her humiliation comes the news that Thésée is alive and is returning. On his arrival Phèdre retires with a few words of guilty confusion. Hippolyte, no less perturbed, asks his father's permission to withdraw from the place where Phèdre is living. Thésée, shocked by this strange reception, seeks the explanation. Œnone, the old nurse

and confidant of Phèdre, who has encouraged her to give rein to her passion, accuses Hippolyte to Thésée of dishonourable advances to her mistress. Thésée, in his furious indignation, calls on his protector, the god Neptune, to destroy Hippolyte. The latter denies the charge, and, while hinting that the guilt is elsewhere, refrains from accusing Phèdre; he declares his own love for Aricie. Phèdre's miserable passion is now intensified by jealousy of Aricie; distraught by love, remorse, and jealousy, she curses the nurse who has led her on. Aricie, to whom Hippolyte has confessed his love and who returns it, boldly asserts his innocence to Thésée and warns him of his error. Thésée, shaken in his belief of his son's guilt, is about to interrogate the nurse further, when he learns first of her suicide, then of the death of Hippolyte by the intervention of the god whom he has invoked (see *Théramène*). Phèdre, who has taken poison, dies confessing the innocence of Hippolyte and her own guilt.

Phèdre et Hippolyte, see *Pradon.*

Philaminte, a character in Molière's *Les Femmes savantes* (q.v.).

Philémon et Baucis (1685), a poem by La Fontaine (q.v.) about the famous couple in classical mythology to whom the gods came in disguise and were received with kindness. As a reward their dwelling was transformed into a temple, of which they became priest and priestess. They lived to be very old, and at their death—together, as the gods had consented—were changed into trees: 'Baucis devint tilleul, Philémon devint chêne.'

Philidor, see *Danican.*

Philinte, a character in Molière's *Le Misanthrope* (q.v.).

Philipon, CHARLES (1800–62), lithographer, caricaturist, and journalist, born in Lyons, came to Paris, where he died, in 1823. He founded and edited *Caricature* (1830) and *Le Charivari* (q.v., 1832), satirical journals celebrated, and often prosecuted, for their cartoons. These ridiculed the bourgeoisie and the July monarchy, particularly Louis-Philippe who, from the shape of his head, was often represented as a pear. On one occasion Philipon, when prosecuted, appeared in his own defence. To suggest the absurdity of basing a prosecution on a chance resemblance he made four lightning sketches and handed them to the jury. The first might have been a head of Louis-Philippe, but it was also very like a pear. The other three showed a series of witty transformations as the result of which the last was neither more nor less than a pear. Here, he asked the jury to remark, were four sketches of pears. Was a man to be imprisoned for having drawn a pear which also chanced to resemble the king? He lost his case, but sold his sketches for a very considerable sum.

Philippe I, born 1053, was king of France from the death of his father Henri I in 1060 till his own death in 1108. He belonged to the *Capétien* (q.v.) dynasty.

Philippe II [PHILIPPE-AUGUSTE], born 1165, succeeded his father Louis VII in 1180 and reigned till his own death in 1223. One of the greatest of the early French kings, he did much to achieve national unity and to expel the English. His reign was also one of the landmarks in the development of Paris and of the University. He belonged to the *Capétien* (q.v.) dynasty.

Philippe III LE HARDI, born 1245, succeeded his father Louis IX as king of France in 1270 and reigned till his own death in 1285. He belonged to the *Capétien* (q.v.) dynasty.

Philippe IV LE BEL, born 1268, succeeded his father Philippe III in 1285 as king of France and reigned till his own death in 1314. He was also, by his marriage with Jeanne de Navarre, king of Navarre. The first recorded meeting of the *États généraux* (q.v.) took place in his reign. He belonged to the *Capétien* (q.v.) dynasty.

Philippe V LE LONG, born 1293, second son of Philippe IV, became King of France and Navarre in 1316 and reigned till his death in 1322. He belonged to the *Capétien* (q.v.) dynasty.

Philippe VI (PHILIPPE DE VALOIS, born 1293, son of Charles de Valois and grandson of Philippe III) was the first of the Valois branch of the Capetian kings of France (see *Capétiens*; *Valois*). He became king in 1328, after the death of Charles IV, when it was decided that a woman could not occupy the throne of France (see *Salic Law*). He reigned until his own death in 1350.

Philippe, CHARLES-LOUIS (1874–1909), novelist, born at Cérilly (Allier), was a cobbler's son, largely self-educated. He came to Paris and became known to Barrès (q.v.), who procured him a small municipal employment. He earned a pittance, but had leisure to write. *Bubu de Montparnasse* (1901), his first success, was a study of the dregs of humanity in Paris in which the influence of Tolstoy and Dostoevsky has been variously recognized (e.g. in the small clerk's effort to redeem a prostitute). His gift for realistic description infused with a sympathy which at times borders upon sentimentality is also marked in later novels, studies of seamy town types or of the humble people of his own province (Bourbonnais) and, primarily, of poverty. Such are *Le Père Perdrix* (1903), *Marie Donadieu* (1904), *Croquignole* (1906), *Charles Blanchard* (1913, unfinished, based on his father's early life).

Philippe de Beaumanoir, see *Beaumanoir*.

Philippe de Champagne, see *Champagne*.

Philippe de Novare (d. *c.* 1265), miscellaneous author, a man of Lombard origin who spent most of his life in Cyprus. His very varied writings include, besides poems amatory and pious, his memoirs, and an *Estoire* (interspersed with satirical topical songs) on the long war (1228–43), in which he took part, between the emperor Frederick II and Philippe d'Ibelin for the regency of Cyprus; also a treatise of jurisprudence (the *Livre de forme de plait*); and an ethical treatise, the outcome of his experience and meditations, *Des quatre temps de l'âge d'homme*. The *Estoire* received a continuation (1243–1309) known as the *Gestes des Chiprois* by Gérard de Montréal.

Philippe de Thaon or **Thaün** (*fl.* early 12th c.), an Anglo-Norman cleric, author of the earliest *Bestiaire* (q.v.). He also wrote a *Comput* or ecclesiastical calendar, and a *Lapidaire* or description of precious stones, both accompanied by mystic or fabulous features and moralizations.

Philippe-Égalité, see under *Orléans*.

Philomena, see *Romans d'antiquité*.

Philomneste junior, see *Brunet, Pierre-Gustave.*

Philosophe inconnu, Le, see *Saint-Martin, Louis-Claude de.*

Philosophe sans le savoir, Le, a prose comedy by Sedaine, produced in 1765, his masterpiece.

M. Vanderk is a man of good family whom circumstances have made a merchant, and who, in spite of his noble birth (which he conceals under an assumed name), is proud of his beneficent occupation. His home is represented as a happy and orderly one. He is about to marry his daughter to a magistrate. On the eve of the wedding his son, hearing another young man abusing all merchants as scoundrels, challenges him, and the duel is to be fought on the wedding day. The father tries ineffectually to prevent it and is left in dread of the issue. The first report is that the son has been killed, but it presently appears that after a first encounter, the adversaries have been reconciled, and the day ends in happiness. The play, a typical *drame bourgeois*, is simply and smoothly conducted, with some pleasant subsidiary characters. In its scenic effects and its loose handling of the unity of time it anticipates the Romantic drama (see *Romantisme*).

Philosophes, Les, a term used without great precision to designate the literary men, scientists, thinkers of the 18th century, widely different in their individual tendencies, who were united by their belief in the sovereign efficacy of human reason, and in their desire to overthrow the ancient institutions and beliefs that offered obstacles to its effective supremacy. Circumstances that favoured the development of this doctrine were on the one hand the weakening of the Church through sectarian dissensions (quarrels of Jesuits and Jansenists, of Bossuet and Fénelon), and on the other the discredit of absolute monarchy by the disastrous wars and ruinous and unequal taxation of the end of the reign of Louis XIV. The philosophical method of Descartes, with its exaltation of reason, the worldly scepticism of the *libertins* (q.v.) or free-thinkers, the popularization of science by Fontenelle, the direct and erudite attack on dogma by Bayle, the influence of English Deism, all contributed to prepare the intellectual path of the *philosophes*.

The movement against old creeds, institutions, and abuses was moderate and restrained in the first half of the 18th century, a period dominated by Montesquieu and Voltaire (in the earlier phase of his activity). It proceeded with increasing energy in the second half with the emergence of Diderot, Rousseau, Buffon, Condillac, Turgot, and Condorcet (qq.v.), and the development of Voltaire's attack. The *Encyclopédie* (q.v.), the great engine of intellectual revolution in which all the energies of the *philosophes*, however divergent their individual views, were gathered together, appeared between 1751 and 1766. Other prominent *philosophes*, besides those mentioned above, were d'Alembert, Morellet, d'Holbach, Marmontel, Helvétius, and Raynal (qq.v.). They were attacked from many sides: in the *Journal de Trévoux* by the Jesuits, in the *Nouvelles ecclésiastiques* by the Jansenists, in the satires of Laurent Gilbert (q.v.), in the satirical drama *Les Philosophes* by Palissot; their works were publicly burnt by order of the *parlement*; and many of them were imprisoned for the expression of their views (Voltaire, Diderot, Marmontel, Morellet). But their official opponents were divided, Jansenists against Jesuits, ministers against *parlements*; many important personages and subordinate officials were won over to the views of the *philosophes*, and the director of literary censorship at the critical period, Malesherbes, was in sympathy with them. It is not surprising that in these conditions their doctrines established themselves in France and contributed to the Revolution, by discrediting the Government, the magistrature, and the Church, and setting an example to the people by their own rebellious attitude.

Philosophes, Les, a comedy by Palissot (q.v., and cf. *Poinsinet*).

Phlipon, MLLE, see *Roland, Mme.*

Phocas le jardinier, a poetic drama by Vielé-Griffin (q.v.); not to be confused with the novel *Monsieur de Phocas* by Jean Lorrain (q.v.).

Physiocrates, see *Économistes.*

Physiologie du goût (1825), by Brillat-Savarin (q.v.).

*Physiologie du mariage, ou Médita-
tions de philosophie éclectique sur
le bonheur et le malheur conjugal*
(1828), by Balzac but first published anonymously, collected studies of marriage and
passion, some satirical, some coarsely facetious, some with a pseudo-sociological
interest. At a later date the author placed
them among the 'Études analytiques' of his
Comédie humaine (q.v.).

The word *Physiologie*, which often occurs
in titles of non-scientific literature between
roughly 1830 and 1840, denotes collections
of sketches of characters, types, and callings,
seldom profound, often humorous or
satirical, and providing good material for
book-illustrators.

Pibrac, GUY DU FAUR DE (1529–84), born
at Toulouse, magistrate and moralist, a man
of classical culture and distinguished career,
who narrowly escaped death under Henri II
for his bold advocacy of religious toleration,
and who, as one of the three envoys of
Charles IX, defended the Gallican church at
the Council of Trent (1562). Pibrac is famous
as the author of 126 quatrains (the first fifty
published in 1574) of decasyllabic verses
rhyming *a b b a*, in which he urges, with
simple sincerity, a manly and practicable
virtue ('le plus ennuyeux mortel qui ait
jamais écrit', Anatole France). The quatrains
were long regarded as a code of wisdom and
gentlemanly conduct, and knowledge of
them as a necessary part of a liberal education. Gorgibus, in Molière's *Sganarelle*, recommends them as reading to his daughter.

Picard, LOUIS-BENOÎT (1769–1828), born in
Paris, son of an advocate, was an actor (but
renounced this calling on his election to the
Académie française in 1807), theatre-manager,
and author of numerous vaudevilles and
comedies. The latter were popular and contain many amusing sketches of provincial
life and manners in the early nineteenth
century: *La Petite Ville* (1801), *Les Provin-
ciaux à Paris* (1802), *Les Marionnettes* (1806),
Les Ricochets (1807), *Les Deux Philibert*
(1816).

Picasso, PABLO RUIZ BLASCO (1881–), one
of the foremost, and most discussed, painters
and sculptors of modern times, a founder
(with Georges Braque, b. 1882) of the
Cubist movement in art and closely asso-

ciated about 1908 with the Cubist writers
(see *Cubisme*; also *Apollinaire*, whose *Les
Peintres cubistes*, 1913, includes a study of his
work; also *Salmon, André*, &c.). At a later
date he was associated with the Surrealist
Movement. He was born at Malaga and
brought up in Barcelona. Since 1904 he has
lived and worked mainly in France.

Piccini, Piccinistes, see *Gluck*.

Picciola (1836), a novel by Saintine (q.v.).

Pichat, MICHEL (1790–1828), poet and
dramatist. His tragedies on the classical
model, *Léonidas* (1825) and *Guillaume Tell*
(1830), were praised in their day.

Pichegru, CHARLES (1761–1804), a Revolutionary general, conqueror of Holland, who
later conspired with 'Georges' *Cadoudal*
(q.v.) to overthrow Napoleon and restore
the monarchy (1803). The plot was
discovered and the ringleaders were condemned to death. Pichegru died (in all
probability committed suicide) in prison.

Pichot, AMÉDÉE (1795–1877), man of letters
and translator. He did much to popularize
English literature at the time of the Romantic movement, translated works by Byron,
Shakespeare, Scott, Dickens, &c.; published
a *Voyage historique et littéraire en Angleterre et
en Écosse* (1825), and edited the *Revue britannique* for some years from 1839.

Pichou, — DE (1597–1631), a mediocre
dramatist who enjoyed the favour of
Richelieu; author of *Les Folies de Cardenio*
(a tragicomedy or novel in dialogue from
Cervantes) and *Les Aventures de Rosiléon*
(from *L'Astrée*), both of 1630. Pichou was
assassinated.

Picrochole, see *Gargantua*.

Pierre de Langtoft (*fl.* 14th c.), a canon of
Bridlington in Yorkshire, who composed
shortly after 1311 a summary of the history
of England to the death of Edward I in
9,000 French alexandrines.

Pierre et Jean (1888), a novel, usually
considered his best, by Guy de Maupassant.
It is a study of jealousy and suspicion.
Pierre and Jean are the sons of a retired
Parisian jeweller M. Roland, living at Le
Havre. Pierre is a doctor, a nervous, un-
steady character. Jean, the younger, a placid

nature, is a lawyer. Both love the widowed young Mme Rosémilly, who seems to prefer Jean. Suddenly Jean inherits a fortune from M. Maréchal, an old family friend. Pierre, who gets nothing, is puzzled, jealous, then seized by suspicion of his mother's one-time adultery. She reads his thoughts, and both live in torture. Rage finally masters him when he learns that Mme Rosémilly has consented to marry Jean, and he blurts out his suspicions to his brother. Jean, alone with his mother, learns that Pierre had guessed correctly. He will, he decides, rid the family of a disquieting presence and continue his life as if nothing had happened. He manœuvres Pierre into a post of doctor on a transatlantic liner; and the book ends as the ship departs with the miserable Pierre on board.

Maupassant's preface to *Pierre et Jean* is celebrated. He develops his theories of the novel and the novelist's function and describes how Flaubert (q.v.) taught him to see and to write.

Pierre Faifeu, Légende joyeuse de maître, the verse narrative of the exploits of a rascally student of Angers of the type of Villon, written by an Angevin priest, Charles Bourdigné (1527). Bonaventure des Périers devoted one of his *Nouvelles* (XXIII) to an anecdote of Pierre Faifeu.

Pierre Grassou, one of the 'Scènes de la vie parisienne' of Balzac's *Comédie humaine* (q.v.).

Pierre le Lombard (*c.* 1100–*c.* 1160), known as *Magister sententiarum*, born at Novara, theologian, was appointed Bishop of Paris in 1159. He wrote between 1145 and 1150 his *Sententiae*, a collection of opinions of the Fathers on the subject of God, the creation, redemption, and the nature of the sacraments. The work was very popular and became a theological textbook.

Pierre l'Ermite (d. 1115), a gentleman of Picardy, who first followed the career of arms and then became a monk. He preached the first crusade, and led a multitude of followers into Asia Minor (1096). Nearly all these died or were killed at the siege of Nicaea before the regular crusaders arrived; but Peter survived and accompanied these crusaders eastwards in 1097. He was cer-

tainly present at the siege and countersiege of Antioch in 1098, but his later history is uncertain.

Pierre Nozière (1899), one of four works of romanticized autobiography by Anatole France (q.v.).

Pierrette one of the 'Scènes de la vie de province' of Balzac's *Comédie humaine* (q.v.).

Pierrot, a typical character in French pantomime, thievish and greedy, artless and without moral sense; dressed in loose white garments, with his face whitened.

Pigal, EDMÉ-JEAN (1794–1872), humorous artist and lithographer. His sketches of everyday working-class life were popular about the end of the Restoration period and his work is said to be a useful source for studying the history of women's costume.

Pigalle, JEAN-BAPTISTE (1714–85), sculptor, remembered by his statue of Prince Maurice of Saxony, a bust of Voltaire, and a Mercury (in the Louvre).

Pigault-Lebrun, CHARLES-ANTOINE-GUILLAUME PIGAULT DE L'ÉPINOY, *dit* (1753–1835), born at Calais, author of lively, licentious novels, widely read about 1800 (the favourite reading of old Miss Crawley in Thackeray's *Vanity Fair*). *L'Enfant du carnaval* (1792), *Mon Oncle Thomas* (1799), *La Folie espagnole* (1799), *M. de Kinglin* (1801), *Tableaux de la société* (1813) are some titles. During a riotous, dissipated youth this author returned to Calais on one occasion to find that his disgusted father had published a notice of his death. Thereafter he called himself Pigault-Lebrun. At one period he was a travelling comedian and himself wrote moderately successful comedies. In later life (1806–24) he combined the professions of Customs Inspector and novelist.

Pilon, GERMAIN (1539–90), a sculptor who enjoyed the favour of Charles IX and Catherine de Médicis, famous especially for his tombs of François Ier and Henri II at Saint-Denis, and for a group of the Three Graces.

Pimbesche (Pimbêche), Comtesse de, a character in Racine's *Les Plaideurs*, a typical inveterate litigant.

Pinson, Mademoiselle Mimi, the Parisian *grisette*, or shop-girl, heroine of a short story of this name by Alfred de Musset, is a typical figure of the student *vie de Bohème* portrayed by Musset, Murger, and Gautier (qq.v.) among others. She leads a gay, hand-to-mouth existence, pawns her one frock to help a starving friend, and a few hours later, having by some means obtained a few spare sous, may be seen with the same friend devouring ices in a café.

Pinte, Dame, a hen, in the *Roman de Renart*.

Pipe-en-bois, the nickname of Georges Cavelier, leader of a band of Paris students during the Second Empire (1852–70) who systematically hissed plays by any author whom they suspected of Imperialist leanings. He is said to have organized the demonstration which caused the Goncourts' (q.v.) play *Henriette Maréchal* to be withdrawn from the Comédie-Française after six performances. The play's acceptance in the first instance was rumoured to have been due to the princesse Mathilde's (q.v.) interest in the authors.

Pipelet, La Mère and her husband, the two concierges, characters so well remembered from Eugène Sue's (q.v.) *Mystères de Paris* that 'Pipelet' as a term for concierge has passed into the language. They suffered a succession of amusing mishaps at the hands of one of the other characters, the young artist Cabrion.

Piramus et Tisbé, see *Romans d'antiquité*.

Piron, ALEXIS (1689–1773), born at Dijon, a light witty poet, author of many keen epigrams, besides verse tales, satires, &c., not free from coarse buffoonery; also of comedies, *La Métromanie* (q.v., 1738), his best-known work, *Les Fils ingrats* (1728), *Arlequin Deucalion* (1722, a witty farce in which, to comply with the interdict on the employment of more than one actor by the *Théâtre de la Foire*, the author takes as his subject Deucalion re-creating mankind after the flood), &c. Piron's election to the *Académie* in 1753 was vetoed by Louis XV on account of a licentious *Ode à Priape*, written by him in his youth and since regretted. An anecdote illustrates the character of the man. The wealthy Voltaire condoled with Piron on the fact that he was not rich. 'Cela est vrai,' Piron replied, 'mais je m'en moque; et c'est comme si je l'étais.' Piron had a formidable

gift of repartee, in which he is said to have worsted Voltaire himself. There was a profound antipathy between the two men.

Pisan, CHRISTINE DE, see *Christine*.

Pisançon, ALBÉRIC DE, see *Alexandre le Grand*.

Pithou, PIERRE, see *Satire Ménippée*.

Pitoëff, GEORGES (1886–1939), actor and producer, born at Tiflis, studied law in Paris then went on the stage and from 1919 had his own company. He produced many Italian, Russian, Norwegian, and English plays in translation. His wife Ludmilla Pitoëff (1896–1951) was a notable Saint Joan in Shaw's play.

Pixérécourt, RENÉ-CHARLES GUILBERT DE (1773–1844), the 'Corneille des boulevards', born at Nancy, was in Paris after 1793. He was a prolific author of comedies, comic operas, vaudevilles, and, particularly, melodramas, a type of play then new, and which he popularized on the French stage (see *Mélodrame*). Between 1798 and 1835 more than a hundred of his dramas and melodramas were produced in the *théâtres des boulevards* (the secondary theatres) in Paris. Among the most successful were *Victor ou l'Enfant de la forêt* (1798) and *Cœlina ou l'Enfant du mystère* (1800). Many of his plots were taken from successful novels of the day, both French and foreign.

Placards, Affaire des, a famous incident in the early phase of the Reformation movement. On 18 October 1534 Paris was found placarded with denunciations of the Mass. This gave rise to general indignation and many Protestants were arrested and executed. Among those who fled from Paris at this time were Clément Marot and Calvin.

Place de la Concorde, a famous open space in Paris, to the north-west of the Jardin des Tuileries, created by Louis XV, at first adorned by a statue of that king and known by his name. Under the Revolution it was known as the 'Place de la Révolution', a statue of Liberty was erected there, also the guillotine on which Louis XVI, Marie-Antoinette, Mme Roland, and many others perished. Its name was changed after the Terror to Place de la Concorde, by one of the last decrees of the *Convention*. It became Place Louis XV after the Restoration and

Place de la Concorde again in 1830. Around it are eight statues representing the chief towns of France. The one of Strasbourg was shrouded in crape from 1870 to 1918.

Place de l'Hôtel de ville, see *Grève, Place de.*

Place des Vosges, see the following article.

Place Royale, the present-day Place des Vosges, in the historic Marais quarter of Paris, a residential square which even now has lost little of its 17th-century architectural unity. Construction began—from plans of Androuet du Cerceau—under Henri IV, who at one time contemplated living in the *pavillon du roi* which, with the *pavillon de la reine,* occupied the site, on the north side, of the ancient *Hôtel des Tournelles* (q.v.). During the 17th and 18th centuries the Place Royale became a centre of fashion and culture (cf. *Précieux, Précieuses*). Richelieu lived there; Mme de Sévigné was born there (Hôtel de Coulanges) and afterwards lived near by, at the Hôtel (now Musée) Carnavalet; the courtesan Marion Delorme (q.v.) lived there. It was a frequent scene of duels, and the setting of an early comedy, *La Place Royale,* by Corneille. Nineteenth-century residents included Victor Hugo (at No. 6, now the Musée Victor-Hugo, from 1833 to 1848), Théophile Gautier, and Alphonse Daudet.

Place Vendôme, a large and stately square in Paris, originally projected by Richelieu, and in part constructed under Louis XIV. An equestrian statue of that king by Girardon stood in the centre and the square was called 'Place Louis-le-Grand'. The statue was overthrown in the Revolution. In 1806 the 'Colonne de la Grande Armée' was erected in the centre, in imitation of Trajan's Column in Rome, the bronze bas-reliefs being made from cannon captured from the enemy. On the summit stood a statue of Napoleon. The column was thrown down in the Commune and reconstructed in 1873.

Plaideurs, Les, a farcical comedy by Racine, produced in 1668. The central idea, of a judge with a mania for judging, is derived from the *Wasps* of Aristophanes. The play is an amusing satire on French legal procedure, with allusions to corrupt judges, false witnesses, pompous advocates, and absurd sentences. Some of Racine's friends,

including Boileau and La Fontaine, collaborated in its preparation.

Perrin Dandin is a magistrate whose passion for his profession has driven him crazy, so that his son has to keep him locked up. Chicaneau, a *bourgeois,* and the comtesse de Pimbesche are no less ardent litigants. Dandin, shut up in his house, tries to hear their case first from a garret window, then through the air-hole of his cellar. He is induced to exercise his judicial functions over the members of his household. His dog has been caught eating a capon and is tried with all the formalities; there are absurd speeches for the prosecution and defence by two of Dandin's servants. The dog is sentenced to the galleys, but the appearance of the orphan puppies moves the judge's compassion. Dandin's son, by a stratagem of legal procedure, wins the hand of Chicaneau's daughter. The proverbial saying 'Point d'argent, point de suisses' comes from this play.

Plaine, La, the deputies (numerically the strongest element of the assembly) who occupied the middle benches in the *Convention nationale* (q.v.), between the *Girondins* and the *Montagnards.* They sided intermittently with both parties (cf. *Marais*).

Plaisirs et les jours, Les (1896), see Proust.

Planche, GUSTAVE (1808–57), born in Paris, was literary and art critic on the *Revue des Deux Mondes* after 1831 and at times contributed to, or edited, other journals, notably the *Journal des Débats* and the *Chronique de Paris* (founded by Balzac in 1836). Published collections of his articles—many on English literature—include: *Portraits littéraires* (1836–49, 4 vols.), *Nouveaux Portraits littéraires* (1854), *Études sur les arts* (1855–6), &c. His criticism, bitter and hard-hitting in general and even more so when dealing with the Romantics, made him many enemies.

Plantin, CHRISTOPHE (1514–89), born near Tours, a famous printer, established at Antwerp.

Plassans, in Zola's *Rougon-Macquart* (q.v.) novels, the Provençal town in which his Rougons and Macquarts originated. In reality it was Aix-en-Provence. It is the setting of the first and some other volumes of the cycle.

Pléiade, La, a name taken from that given to the seven most eminent Greek tragic poets of the reign of Ptolemy II (derived from the seven stars of the constellation the Pleiades), and applied in Ronsard's day to a group of poets of his 'Brigade' or circle. It was composed (according to a passage in Ronsard's works) of Ronsard himself, du Bellay, Pontus de Tyard, Baïf, Jodelle, Belleau, and Peletier. For the last of these, contemporaries substituted Dorat (though he was a poet of no eminence), as the great humanist who inspired the school. The literary revolution effected by the *Pléiade* consisted in the abandonment of the medieval poetical tradition, its popular and frivolous subjects and finicking forms, and the founding of a new poetry. This was to be based on a profound study of the Greek, Latin, and Italian literatures (notably Homer, Pindar, Horace, and Petrarch) and the substitution of classical and Italian models and of noble and aristocratic themes for those of the 15th century. The *Pléiade* was animated by a lofty idea of the role of the poet. It further aimed at a remodelling of the French language, enriching it by borrowing from or imitating Greek and Latin (e.g. it introduced the word 'patrie'), by the use of old French, technical, and dialectal terms, and by the development of existing words (e.g. making verbs from substantives). It substituted Greek mythology for national and Christian tales in poetical allusions. Du Bellay, who in his *Défense et illustration de la langue française* (q.v., February 1549–50) was the first spokesman of the school, and Ronsard, its greatest poet, laid down precepts for versification, dealing with caesura, enjambment, the use of masculine and feminine rhymes, inversion, hiatus, &c., of which the best were subsequently adopted by Malherbe. The *Pléiade* gave its proper pre-eminence to the alexandrine (although Ronsard wrote the *Franciade* in decasyllables). See also *Sonnet*.

The subsequent eclipse of the *Pléiade* was due to its excessive erudition, its too servile imitation of the classics, and the artificial character of much of its poetry.

Pléiades, Les (1874), a novel by Gobineau (q.v.).

Plessis, FRÉDÉRIC (1851–1941), poet, one of those who followed in the wake of the *Parnassiens* (q.v.). His output was collected in *La Lampe d'argile* (1886); *Vesper* (1887), &c.

Plessys, MAURICE DU, see *Du Plessys*.

Plon-plon, a familiar name for Prince Napoleon Bonaparte, see *Bonaparte family*, s.v. *Jérôme*.

Plowert, JACQUES, a pseudonym used upon occasion by Paul Adam (q.v.).

Pluche, NOËL-ANTOINE, ABBÉ (1688–1761), a popularizer of scientific knowledge. His *Spectacle de la Nature* (1732) was very widely read.

Pluche, Dame, a character in Alfred de Musset's *On ne badine pas avec l'amour* (q.v.).

Plume, La (1889–1904, fortnightly), one of the earliest Symbolist reviews (see *Symbolisme*), soon extended its scope and became an excellent guide to all new trends in literature and art. It frequently devoted a whole number to one author or one movement, and published original work by Mallarmé, Moréas, and Verlaine. Maurice Barrès, Anatole France, and Charles Morice (qq.v.) were among its literary critics.

Plutarch, see *Amyot*.

Pluviôse, the fifth month of the Republican Calendar (q.v.). It ran from 20 (or 21 or 22) January to 19 (or 20 or 21) February.

Poème moral, see *Religious Writings* (medieval period).

Poèmes antiques (1852), the first collected volume of poetry published by Leconte de Lisle (q.v.). The preface contained the Parnassian doctrines in germ.

Poèmes antiques et modernes (1826) by Alfred de Vigny, the collection which made his reputation. Two famous items are the narrative poem *Éloa* (q.v.) and *Moïse*. In the second, Moses, alone on a mountain-top overlooking the Promised Land, sinks under the solitary grandeur of his position as the man chosen of God to lead the people. He cries to God for release ('Vous m'avez fait vieillir puissant et solitaire, Laissez-moi m'endormir du sommeil de la terre'). Vigny republished this collection in 1837, dividing it into three books—*mystique*, *antique* (biblical and Greek antiquity), *moderne*—and adding ten poems.

Poèmes barbares (1862), see *Leconte de Lisle*.

Poèmes saturniens (1866), see *Verlaine*.

Poèmes tragiques (1884), by Leconte de Lisle (q.v.), the last collection published in his lifetime.

Poète mourant, Le, a well-known elegy by the poet Millevoye (q.v.).

Poètes maudits, Les (1884), by Verlaine (q.v.), short critical and biographical studies, with plentiful quotations, intended to stimulate interest in six poets who were, he considered, not sufficiently appreciated, namely, Tristan Corbière, Marceline Desbordes-Valmore, Villiers de l'Isle-Adam, Stéphane Mallarmé, Arthur Rimbaud, and 'Pauvre Lelian' (Verlaine's anagram of his own name). The phrase 'Poètes maudits' may be a reference to Baudelaire's *Bénédiction*, the first poem of *Les Fleurs du mal*. In this, the poet is described as an object of hatred for his mother and 'l'instrument maudit' of God's ill-will from the moment of his birth, a target all through life for contempt and persecution. Yet he is serene and untouched, a child, intoxicated with the sun, playing with the wind, gay as the birds are gay; a man, able to bless God who sends suffering 'Comme un divin remède à nos impuretés', and who keeps a place for the Poet 'Dans les rangs bienheureux des saintes Légions'.

Poil de Carotte (1894), the tale of a lonely child in the country, by Jules Renard (q.v.).

Poincaré, HENRI (1856–1912), born at Nancy, a famous mathematician and savant of the 19th century. Some of his books reached beyond a purely scientific public, e.g. *La Science et l'hypothèse* (1902), *La Valeur de la science* (1906), *Science et méthode* (1908). They were translated into several languages.

Poincaré, RAYMOND (1860–1934), politician and statesman, a cousin of the preceding, was President of the French Republic from 1913 to 1920. He left memoirs of much interest for the study of political and European history of the period leading up to and during the 1914–1918 war (*Au service de la France*, 1929–33). They begin with *Le Lendemain d'Agadir* [i.e. after 1911] and end (vol. x) with *Victoire et armistice*.

Poinsinet, ANTOINE-ALEXANDRE-HENRI (1735–69), dramatist, a man of very simple character whose credulity made him the butt of many practical jokes, author of comic operas, comedies, and tragedies. He is especially remembered for his *Le Cercle* (1764), a one-act prose comedy ridiculing the social life of contemporary Paris, successful for its portraits of personages who were immediately recognized; it imitated *Les Originaux* by Palissot, and perhaps *Les Mœurs du temps* by Saurin. In an earlier comedy, *Le Petit Philosophe* (1760), written in *vers libres* (q.v.), he had parodied Palissot's *Les Philosophes*.

Poirier, Monsieur, see *Gendre de Monsieur Poirier, Le*.

Poisons, Affaire des, see *Chambre ardente*.

Pois pilés, which signifies a *purée*, or mixture, was the name often applied, from the 16th century onwards, to joint performances given in Paris by the *Confrérie de la Passion*, the *Basochiens*, and the *Enfants sans souci* (qq.v.), at which the programmes were made up of sacred mysteries, followed by profane farces and *soties* (q.v.).

Polexandre, a heroic romance by Gomberville, published in 1632–7 in five volumes, his chief work, and much admired at the time, even by La Fontaine.

Alcidiane, queen of an 'inaccessible island', is so beautiful that many kings of distant lands, on the sight of her portrait, ask her hand in marriage. Alcidiane, offended, sends her knight Polexandre to chastise their presumption. The reader is accordingly taken about the world through a long series of adventures. Incidentally descriptions of the sea and its tempests are first introduced into French literature in this work.

Police. The word 'police' in French is used to signify not only a police force or police forces but also the various directions in which police activities are exercised and, further, the powers (both administrative and executive) by means of which these activities are defined, delimited, organized, regulated, and controlled by the responsible central and local authorities.

(2) Under the *ancien régime* the responsibility for maintaining order in the realm was entrusted to *baillis, sénéchaux, prévôts,*

and similar officers, operating frequently through the *maréchaussée* (a form of mounted constabulary). In Paris, where responsibility lay partly with a municipal functionary, the *prévôt des marchands*, Louis XIV created the office of *Lieutenant-Général de police*. Gabriel-Nicolas de la Reynie (from 1667 to 1697) and Marc-René Voyer d'Argenson (from 1699 to 1718) were the first holders. They established eleven *bureaux*, or divisions, e.g. religion, morals, public safety, and laid down general lines for the maintenance of order.

(3) For a time during the Revolution police responsibilities were divided among committees. A *Ministère de la police générale* was established in 1796 (cf. *Fouché*), but at a later date its functions were returned to the *Ministère de l'Intérieur*. In Paris the office of *Lieutenant-Général de police* was suppressed but it was in effect revived under Napoleon's (then First Consul Bonaparte) administrative reforms of 1800, when he created the office of *Préfet de police*. Since then, for reasons of history, politics, and administration, the City of Paris has remained in an exceptional position. The *Préfet de police* has full police powers, with autonomous police forces under his control. He also has a large measure of responsibility in the *Département de la Seine*, in which Paris is situated (cf. *Maire de Paris*), and the control of Police Forces in certain adjoining Departments.

(4) Present-day police powers and activities in France fall roughly into the two classes of *police administrative*, or *générale*, and *police judiciaire*. The first is concerned with the general maintenance of state security (internal and external), with public order and safety, with hygiene, decency, traffic control, &c. The second is a plain-clothes criminal police corresponding roughly to the English Criminal Investigation Department. In both cases the central authority for the country as a whole (except as regards the *police générale* in Paris, where the *Préfet de police* is directly responsible to the Minister of the Interior) is the Department of the Ministry of the Interior known as the *Sûreté nationale* (q.v.) and divided into nine Directorates.

(5) Local responsibility for the *police générale* (except for the *Renseignements généraux*, the branches concerned with information, frontier and passport control, &c., and the *Surveillance du territoire*, con-cerned with counter-espionage) lies normally with the Prefects of Departments and the Mayors of *Communes*. Police forces are recruited, organized, and controlled variously according to whether they are the *police rurale* of the country districts or the *police municipale* of the towns. The day-to-day duties of the former are carried out by the rural policemen (*gardes-champêtres*) and in a larger way by the *gendarmerie nationale* (q.v.). The locally-recruited *police municipale* may be reinforced—and in *communes* above a certain number of inhabitants (Paris again excepted) are replaced—by the *police d'État*, State-recruited security forces which are controlled by the *Sûreté nationale*.

(6) The *police judiciaire* is concerned variously with the investigation and repression of crime, vice, fraud, conspiracy, drug offences, &c. Though its central administration, as stated above, is the responsibility of the *Sûreté nationale*, the regional *brigades* (i.e. mobile detachments, squads) through which it operates take their orders solely from the judicature.

(7) It may be added, as an aid to readers of French detective fiction, that an *agent*, or *sergent de ville*, is a municipal (uniformed) policeman; an *inspecteur* corresponds to the English 'police-sergeant', particularly a detective sergeant; a *tribunal de simple police* is a police court; a *commissaire de police* is a police superintendent (who has both uniformed police of the *police générale* and plain-clothes detectives of the *police judiciaire* attached to his station, called *commissariat de police*, and under his control); the operative headquarters in Paris of the *police judiciaire* is familiarly known as the '*P.J.*' or as the *Quai des Orfèvres*, the latter name being due to its situation in the part of the *Palais de Justice* which forms the corner of the Quai des Orfèvres and the Place Dauphine.

Polichinelle, a name apparently adapted from Neapolitan dialectal *polecenella*, equivalent to Italian *pulcinella*. The latter word is the diminutive of *pulcina*, a chicken; and *polecenella* is diminutive of *polecena*, the young of the turkey-cock. Alternatively it has been conjectured to be the corruption of the name of an Italian comedian. The character of *Pulcinella* is stated by Italian authors to have been invented, about the year 1600, for the Neapolitan impromptu comedies, to imitate the peasants of Acerra, a town near Naples. Transferred to France as *Polichinelle*, the character was subsequently degraded to that of a marionette, hook-nosed, with a hump before and behind, mocking, boastful, and quarrelsome. Our *Punch* has a similar derivation. Polichinelle figures early in the first interlude of Molière's *Le Malade imaginaire*.

Polignac, JULES-AUGUSTE-ARMAND-MARIE, COMTE, later PRINCE, DE (1780–1847), born in Versailles, was with the *émigrés* in youth. A Royalist and Catholic of the most reactionary type, he was in prison (1804–13) for his part in the Cadoudal-Pichegru (qq.v.) conspiracy, returned to Paris with the Bourbons in 1815, and in 1816 was entrusted with a mission to the Pope (who created him a *Prince romain*). He was French Ambassador in London from 1823–9; and as Foreign Minister, then *Président du Conseil*, to Charles X (1829–30) was held largely responsible for the latter's repressive policy. He fled during the July Revolution (1830, q.v.) but was arrested. When his life-imprisonment was commuted to exile in 1836 he retired for some years to England. In 1845 he published *Études historiques, politiques et morales* and *Réponse à mes adversaires*.

Politiques, Les, the name given to a party, formed under François II and Charles IX, consisting of moderate men such as Mi hel de l'Hôpital (q.v.) who were equally opposed to the extreme Huguenots and fanatical Catholics, supported the monarchy, and endeavoured to put an end to the wars of religion.

Politiques et moralistes du XIXᵉ siècle (1891–1900, 3 series), critical studies by Émile Faguet (q.v.).

Politique tirée de l'Écriture Sainte (1709, posthumous), by Bossuet (q.v.).

Polyeucte, a tragedy by Corneille, produced in 1641 or early 1642. The substance of the story is contained in the *Vitae Sanctorum* of Surius, a German monk of the 16th century.

Polyeucte, husband of Pauline, daughter of Felix, the governor of Armenia under the emperor Decius, is the friend of Néarque, a Christian, and is himself about to accept Christian baptism when the play opens.

Pauline is disquieted by a dream in which she has beheld her former lover Severus, whom she believed to be dead, and seen her husband killed by her father. Polyeucte is baptized. Severus, who is in fact alive and is now the favourite of the emperor, arrives to do sacrifice in the town, hoping to claim Pauline for his bride. He sees Pauline, who still loves him, learns that she is married, and honourably renounces her. Polyeucte and Néarque attend the sacrifice and revile the pagans. Néarque is executed. Polyeucte, imprisoned, desires martyrdom, and surrenders Pauline to Severus. Pauline at first has not loved her husband, but her admiration for him now turns to love. She refuses Severus, because her husband will have owed his death to him, and Severus nobly determines to save Polyeucte. But the weak and time-serving Felix, afraid that Severus will denounce him to the emperor if he shows leniency to his son-in-law, orders the latter's execution. Pauline is converted to Christianity by the sight of her husband's martyrdom. Severus upbraids Felix for sacrificing Polyeucte in order to save himself. Felix declares himself also converted.

Polymnie (1819), a satirical poem by Marmontel, see under *Gluck*.

Pomme de Pin, La, the name of a classic tavern in Paris, referred to by Villon, Rabelais, Régnier; somewhat resembling the 'Mermaid' of the Elizabethan poets. It stood in the rue de la Juiverie in the Cité.

Pompadour, ANTOINETTE POISSON, MARQUISE DE (1721–64), a woman of the rich middle class, mistress of Louis XV. She was an intelligent patroness of literature and art, but the influence that she exercised over politics for some twenty years (especially in matters of war and foreign affairs) was less fortunate. It was she who said to Louis XV, 'Après nous le déluge!'

Pompée, see *Mort de Pompée, La*.

Pompignan, JEAN-JACQUES LE FRANC, MARQUIS DE (1709–84), an erudite magistrate and a poet of some merit, author of a tragedy *Didon* (1734), of a satirical opera *Prométhée* directed against Voltaire, of an ode on the death of his master, J.-B. Rousseau, and of *Poésies sacrées*. He was admitted to the *Académie* in 1760, where he declaimed against the *encyclopédistes*, but was thereafter undeservedly overwhelmed by Voltaire's ridicule.

Pomponne, SIMON, MARQUIS DE, see under *Arnauld d'Andilly.*

Poniatowski, JOSEPH-ANTOINE, PRINCE, one of Napoleon's marshals, see *Maréchal de l'Empire.*

Pons, SYLVAIN, see *Cousin Pons, Le.*

Ponsard, François (1814–67), dramatist, born at Vienne (Dauphiné), is remembered with Émile Augier (q.v.) as a leader of the *école du bon sens,* a movement in the theatre which marked a reaction against the exaggerations of the Romantic drama, though it profited by the broader conception of the dramatic art which the Romantics had introduced (see *Romantisme*). His first, and striking, success was the classical tragedy *Lucrèce* (5 acts, verse), produced in 1843 (with the actress Rachel in the name-part) shortly after the failure of Hugo's *Les Burgraves*. His other tragedies, all in verse, included *Agnès de Méranie* (1846) and *Charlotte Corday* (1850). *Horace et Lydie* (1850), a slight, one-act comedy, took its subject from an ode of Horace. *L'Honneur et l'argent* (1853) and *La Bourse* (1856), dramatic comedies in verse, satirized the mid-nineteenth-century worship of money. *Le Lion amoureux* (1866), an historical comedy (also in verse), was a lively representation of society under the *Directoire* and remained popular for many years.

Ponson du Terrail, PIERRE-ALEXIS, VICOMTE DE (1829–71), born at Montmaur, near Grenoble, novelist, a roman-feuilletonist and best-seller who produced some thirty to forty volumes a year. His stock character, Rocambole, went through countless adventures, told, with a serene, often ludicrous, disregard for plot and style, in twenty-two volumes of *Les Exploits de Rocambole* (1859) and many sequels.

Pont-Allais, JEAN DU, see *Jean de l'Espine.*

Pont-au-Change, the name later given to the Grand Pont (see *Cité*), when in the 12th century money-changers were established there by the king.

Pontigny, Les Décades de, the yearly gatherings, mixture of a retreat and a summer school, instituted about 1905 by the critic and professor Paul Desjardins (1859–1940) at his home, the former Cistercian Abbey of Pontigny, in Burgundy. There were several every summer, each lasting ten days, down to 1939. The purpose was study, and free discussion of topics of spiritual, cultural, and academic interest, and for many years the *Décades* were a 'rendez-vous d'intellectuels' from France and many foreign countries.

Pontis (pron. as if —*iss*), LOUIS DE (1583–1670), a military officer who after some fifty years of service ended his long life as a solitary of Port-Royal. He left interesting memoirs, though these were actually written, it is said, by another hand.

Pont-Neuf, Le, connecting the western end of the Île de la Cité (see *Cité*) in Paris with the right and left banks of the Seine. It was begun (1578) by Henri III and completed (1607) by Henri IV, of whom, halfway across, there is a large equestrian statue.

This was the first bridge in Paris which was not lined with shops. It was for long a bustling popular resort, a mixture of a fair and a market, where at any time of day might be seen: 'deux chevaux blancs, le perruquier et la femme enceinte'. There are allusions in 17th-century literature to the *chansonniers* or *colporteurs* of the Pont-Neuf. In the 18th century the term was used colloquially to signify a song or popular air; thus the Président des Brosses speaks of Rousseau's *Le Devin du village* as nothing more than 'un lampon [satirical couplet] et un pont-neuf'.

Pont-Sainte-Maxence, GUERNES DE, see *Thomas Becket.*

Pontus de Tyard, see *Tyard.*

Populisme, see *Literary Isms.*

Poquelin, see *Molière.*

Porte étroite, La (1909), by André Gide, a fine but painful example of the studiedly simple type of novel, in structure and telling, that he styled *récit* (see *Gide*, para. 4).

There is no reason why Alissa, the chief character, should not marry Jérôme, her cousin, except, in the first place, her fear that marriage may profane love. This fear soon turns to a form of exacerbated religious scrupulosity against which Jérôme can make no headway. The holiness for which she strives entails mortification of spirit and flesh, turning her back on love, joy, human contacts, finally on life itself. Jérôme tells the tale, with the aid of quotations from Alissa's diary from which it would seem that with less high-souled diffidence on his part her scruples might have collapsed.

Porthos, one of the heroes of *Les Trois Mousquetaires* (q.v.), by Dumas *père*.

Porto-Riche, GEORGES DE (1849-1930), dramatist, became known with *La Chance de Françoise* (1889), a one-act comedy produced at the *Théâtre Libre* (q.v.). He was an innovator of the so-called *théâtre d'amour*, i.e. dramas of psychological analysis, which studied the relations between men and women in love. His greatest successes were *Amoureuse* (1891, q.v.), *Le Passé* (1898), and *Le Vieil Homme* (1911), a domestic tragedy of a woman torn between her husband and her son. His first play was the historical drama *Un Drame sous Philippe II* (1875).

Portraits contemporains, by Sainte-Beuve, see *Critiques et Portraits littéraires*.

Portraits de femmes, by Sainte-Beuve, see *Critiques et Portraits littéraires*.

Portraits littéraires, by Sainte-Beuve, see *Critiques et Portraits littéraires*.

Port-Royal, a Cistercian convent in the Vallée de Chevreuse to the south-west of Paris, founded in 1204. At the beginning of the 17th century discipline in this, as in other convents, was much relaxed, until it was energetically re-established by its young abbess Jacqueline Arnauld (q.v.), known by her religious name as Mère Angélique de Sainte-Madeleine, during the period from 1608. In 1625 the nuns migrated thence to larger premises in Paris, distinguished as 'Port-Royal de Paris' from the older foundation thereafter known as 'Port-Royal des Champs'. In 1634 Du Vergier de Hauranne (q.v.), abbé de Saint-Cyran, became director of the convent and introduced into it the austere moral and theological conceptions of Jansenism (see *Jansenius*), of which the convent became the centre and symbol.

(2) Meanwhile the deserted premises of Port-Royal des Champs had been occupied by a group of solitaries holding Jansenist ideas, who, when some of the nuns returned from Paris (1648), moved to a neighbouring hill. Here and in the vicinity they founded some small schools (*les Petites Écoles de Port-Royal*), which became famous for the excellent education they gave. Jansenists of Port-Royal such as Antoine Arnauld, Nicole, and Lancelot (qq.v.) prepared educational works of high quality. Of these the most important were *La Logique ou l'art de penser* (1661), by Arnauld and Nicole, originally intended for the young duc de Chevreuse; the *Grammaire générale* (1660), by Arnauld and Lancelot, on the art of speech and its various parts, irrespective of a particular language; the *Jardin des racines grecques* (1657), a versified Greek dictionary by Lancelot and de Saci; and *Nouvelles méthodes* of learning Greek, Latin, Italian, and Spanish, by Lancelot. The young Duke of Monmouth appears to have been placed for a time at one of these schools. Racine was a famous pupil.

(3) The most celebrated name associated with Port-Royal is that of Pascal (q.v.). Arnauld was the most important of its later leaders. Its chief enemies were the Jesuits, who were afraid of losing their monopoly of education and spiritual direction. They impugned certain doctrines attributed to Jansenius and procured their condemnation by the Pope (Innocent X, 1653), the censure of Arnauld by the Sorbonne, the closing of the schools of Port-Royal, the dispersion of the solitaries, and the prolonged persecution of the nuns. These obstinately refused to sign a 'formulary' condemning the doctrines attributed to Jansenius, and had many supporters in high places, even among the clergy. Some were removed to other convents (cf. *Arnauld d'Andilly, Angélique*); then all were reunited at Port-Royal des Champs but kept in a state of sequestration. An accommodation was reached in 1668 when Clement IX became Pope, and a truce (*la paix de l'Église*) followed for some ten years; but the persecution was then resumed as a result of the king's annoyance at the revived popularity and influence of the Jansenist community. Arnauld was driven into exile, and from 1679 the convent was forbidden to accept any novices, and was consequently doomed to extinction. Before this came about, however, in its natural

course, the abolition of Port-Royal was decreed by papal bull in 1708, the remaining nuns were forcibly removed in 1709, and the buildings were razed to the ground in 1710. Even the remains of those buried in the precincts were dug up and dispersed in 1711.

(4) The importance of Port-Royal lies perhaps less in the Jansenist doctrines that its followers advocated than in the general spirit in which it combated irreligion, its austere conception of life, which exercised a very widespread influence. Port-Royal did much to disseminate knowledge of the Scriptures among the public, undertaking a new translation of them into the vernacular (see *Le Maître de Saci*). Cartesianism, which reconciled the philosophic ideas of the day with religion, appears to have attracted some of the Port-Royal leaders (notably Arnauld, but not Pascal).

(5) Racine wrote an admirable *Abrégé de l'histoire de Port-Royal*. In more recent times we have the important works of Sainte-Beuve (see the following article) and Augustin Gazier (*Histoire générale du mouvement janséniste*, 1922) on the subject. *La Grande Mademoiselle* (q.v.) describes a visit to Port-Royal in June 1657.

Port-Royal (1840–59), Sainte-Beuve's greatest work of re-creative criticism, the published form of lectures delivered in 1837–8 at the Academy of Lausanne (see *Sainte-Beuve*; and see under separate headings for persons and works mentioned in this article). There are six books.

Bk. I. *Origine et renaissance de Port-Royal.* This outlines the early history of the convent and narrates in detail the reforms effected at the beginning of the 17th century by Mère Angélique de Sainte-Madeleine. The whole Arnauld family are described, the characters of Saint François de Sales and the abbé de Saint-Cyran are contrasted, and an examination of contemporary doctrines of *la grâce* leads to various literary digressions, notably a study of Corneille and of *Polyeucte*, and of religious dramas by other 17th-century authors.

Bk. II. *Le Port-Royal de M. de Saint-Cyran.* This is largely a study, individually and as a group, of the solitaries who established themselves to begin with at Port-Royal des Champs. Their many literary, philosophic, and social connexions give rise to studies of Guez de Balzac, Jansenism, Descartes, the duc and duchesse de Luynes (who built a château in the neighbourhood), &c.

Bk. III (in two parts). *Pascal.* This, one of the high spots of the whole work, is a study of Pascal, his life, death, and works. The digressions, equally famous, are studies of Montaigne and of Molière (especially of *Tartuffe*).

Bk. IV. *Écoles de Port-Royal.* The main theme—education at the *petites écoles* established by the solitaries, and of the books used for teaching—leads to portraits of the masters and pupils and of the abbé de Rancé.

Bk. V (in two parts). *La Seconde Génération de Port-Royal.* Sainte-Beuve now moves to the years from 1660 to 1669. He describes the death of Mère Angélique de Sainte-Madeleine, and the renewed persecution culminating in the dispersal of the nuns, studies Mère Angélique de Saint-Jean, a later abbess, and Nicole, as well as persons connected with Port-Royal in a more literary or worldly fashion, such as La Fontaine (cf. *Captivité de Saint Malc, La*), Mme de Sablé, or Mme de Longueville.

Bk. VI (in two parts). *Le Port-Royal finissant.* This covers the long, last years of persecution and final destruction (1679–1711). Arnauld is studied at length, and Boileau as his friend and defender. The second part is devoted almost wholly to Racine, his connexion by birth and upbringing with Port-Royal, his education at one of the *petites écoles*, his break and later reconciliation with the institution, after which he wrote *Esther* and *Athalie*, and then his death. A long study of *Athalie* forms the crown and conclusion of 'cette histoire . . . modestement commencée à la journée du Guichet' (q.v., 1609).

The long, meandering masterpiece of criticism-*fleuve* which has thus traversed an epoch is the work of Sainte-Beuve the poet, penetrating 'le mystère de ces âmes pieuses', and of Sainte-Beuve the seeker after truth, who found, as he proceeded, that poetry disappeared, for 'la religion seule s'est montrée . . ., et le christianisme dans sa nudité'. But the poetry lingered in his approach, in what he termed his 'procédé de peintre, . . . plein de retouches et de revisions, . . . de scrupules et de repentirs, cheminant petit à petit'; and in his style, described by Taine in a characteristically metaphorical passage as 'ne se lassant pas de poursuivre le contour complexe et changeant, la frêle et fuyante lumière qui est le signe et comme la fleur de la vie'.

Portugaises, Lettres, see *Lettres portugaises.*

Pot-bouille (1882), one of Zola's *Rougon-Macquart* (q.v.) novels. It is a cross-section of life—a round of adultery and seduction and their gloomy, at times obscene, consequences—in a block of flats in the centre of Paris.

Pougens, MARIE-CHARLES-JOSEPH DE, see *Dictionaries and Encyclopedias,* under date 1819.

Pourceaugnac, see *Monsieur de Pourceaugnac.*

Pour et Contre, Le, a literary periodical conducted by the abbé Prévost (q.v.) from 1733 to 1740. It included information on English literary productions, from Shakespeare and Dryden to Rochester and Savage. In form it resembled the periodicals of Addison, Steele, and Johnson.

Pour et le Contre, Le, a poem by Voltaire, published in 1722, in which he advances the arguments for and against Christianity, but with a strong tendency towards Deism.

Pourrat, HENRI (1887–   ), novelist, especially of the Auvergne country (*Gaspard des montagnes* 1922, &c.).

Poussin, NICOLAS (1594–1665), born near Les Andelys in Normandy, a great historical and landscape painter, among whose works (now chiefly in the Louvre) are *Le Déluge, Moïse sauvé des eaux, L'Enlèvement des Sabines.* His *Correspondance* was published in 1824.

Prades, L'ABBÉ DE (1720–82), one of the *Encyclopédistes* (q.v.), who in 1751 sustained before the Sorbonne, for the licentiate in theology, a thesis which, though admitted at the time, was subsequently found to throw doubt on the credibility of the Christian miracles. The thesis was condemned by the *Parlement,* and de Prades, threatened with arrest, withdrew to Berlin. The affair contributed to the suppression of the first two volumes of the *Encyclopédie* in 1752.

Diderot wrote a *Suite de l'Apologie de l'abbé de Prades* (1752).

Pradon, NICOLAS (1632–98), an obscure tragic poet, brought into notoriety by his *Phèdre et Hippolyte* (1677), which he was induced by the cabal hostile to Racine to compose in rivalry with that author's *Phèdre.* It was produced two days after Racine's play. The best of his other tragedies, which lack poetry and colour, is perhaps *Régulus* (1688).

Prairial, the ninth month of the Republican Calendar (q.v.). It ran from 20 May to 18 June.

Pré-aux-Clercs, a meadow in front of the Abbey of Saint-Germain-des-Prés in Paris, used in the Middle Ages as a sort of playground of the University. The ownership of the land was a subject of dispute between the Abbey and the University, which gave rise to violent affrays.

Précellence du langage françois, see *Estienne.*

Précieuses ridicules, Les, a one-act comedy in prose by Molière, produced in 1659. In this play for the first time Molière held up to derision the absurdities of contemporary society, though he endeavoured to avoid offence by distinguishing in the preface between the 'véritables précieuses' and their imitators.

Madelon and Cathos, daughter and niece of Gorgibus, a *bourgeois* from the provinces, are infatuated admirers of the affected manners and speech of Parisian society (though Madelon is more romantic than her pedantic cousin). They reject with scorn the suitors who crudely propose marriage to them without the circumlocutions and preparatory adventures described in the Scudéry romances. The rejected suitors contrive that their valets, who are likewise inclined to ape persons of condition, shall visit the ladies in the guise of the marquis de Mascarille and the vicomte de Jodelet. An amusing scene follows in which the ladies are delighted by the extravagant language and exaggerated dress of their visitors, which they take for the height of fashion, and are correspondingly chagrined and humiliated when the impostors are exposed.

Précieux, Précieuses, see *Rambouillet, Hôtel de* ; *Pure, abbé de,* and *Somaize. L'esprit précieux* was in origin the pursuit of elegance and distinction in manners, style, and language, devising new and metaphorical expressions, avoiding low or barbarous words, and pursuing clearness and precision. Brunetière has defined it as an 'Esprit de mesure et de politesse qui dégénère trop vite en un esprit d'étroitesse et d'affectation'. At its best *préciosité* was delicacy of taste and sentiment, of manners and language.

Préfet de département, the executive head (appointed centrally) of a *département* (q.v.), an important civil office created by Napoleon in 1800 as part of his reorganization of local government in France, and still continuing. Similarly, there is a *sous-préfet*, also centrally appointed, for each *arrondissement*. The *Préfet* of a department has police powers except in the *Département de la Seine*, in which Paris is situated. There is a special office of *Préfet de police* for Paris (see *Police*).

The *préfet*, his wife *la préfète*, and the *sous-préfet* figure largely in 19th-century French fiction from Balzac and Stendhal to Anatole France.

Préfet de la Seine, see the preceding article.

Préfet de police, see *Police.*

Premiers lundis (1874–5), selected early criticism by Sainte-Beuve, published posthumously, see under *Causeries du lundi.*

Prémontrés, Ordre des [Premonstratensians], an order of regular canons founded in the 12th century by St. Norbert at Prémontré near Laon, so called because the site of their original house is said to have been prophetically pointed out to St. Norbert.

President

(1) The office of President of the French Republic did not exist during the first republican era (1792–1804).

(2) THE SECOND REPUBLIC (1848–52). The President elected (by the people, for a term of four years) under the provisions of the Constitution of 4 November 1848 (see *Republics*, para. 3 ; also *Revolutions*, IIIa; *Constitutions*) was Louis Napoleon Bona-

parte (see *Napoleon III*), who governed practically as a dictator after the *coup d'état* of 2 December 1851 and in December 1852 was proclaimed Emperor Napoleon III.

(3) THE THIRD REPUBLIC (1870–1940). In the spring of 1871 the newly elected *Assemblée nationale* (see *Republics*, para. 4) proclaimed the statesman Adolphe Thiers (q.v.) *Chef du pouvoir exécutif de la République Française* and under a law of August of the same year he was officially designated President of the Republic. There were in all fourteen Presidents of the Third Republic (elected by both Chambers voting as one for a period of seven years, and vested with executive powers), as follows:

THIERS, Adolphe (1797–1877), in office 1871–3. Resigned.

MAC-MAHON, Maréchal de (1808–93), in office 1873–9. Resigned.

GRÉVY, Jules (1807–91), in office 1879–87 (re-elected 1885). Resigned.

CARNOT, Marie-François-Sadi (1837–94), in office 1887–94. Assassinated.

CASIMIR-PÉRIER, Jean (1847–1907), in office 1894–5. Resigned.

FAURE, François-Félix (1841–99), in office 1895–9.

LOUBET, Émile (1838–1920), in office 1899–1906.

FALLIÈRES, Armand (1841–1931), in office 1906–13.

POINCARÉ, Raymond (1860–1934), in office 1913–20.

DESCHANEL, Paul-Eugène-Louis (1855–1922), in office 1920. He resigned within a few months for reasons of health.

MILLERAND, Étienne-Alexandre (1859–1943), in office 1920–4. Resigned.

DOUMERGUE, Gaston (1863–1937), in office 1924–31.

DOUMER, Paul (1857–1932), in office 1931–2. Assassinated.

LEBRUN, Albert (1871–1950), in office 1932–40 (re-elected 1939). Resigned July 1940.

(4) THE FOURTH REPUBLIC (1947–   ). The first President, M. Vincent Auriol (1884–   ), held office from his election in January 1947 till 1954. His successor, M. René Coty (1882–   ), was elected in November 1953 and assumed office in January 1954. Election, again for a term of seven years, is by the *Assemblée nationale* and the *Conseil de la République* voting in joint session.

Présidente, La, the name given (it is said by Flaubert) to Mme Apollonie-Aglaé Sabatier, a well-known beauty of the mid-19th century, at one time an artist's model, who was friend of many writers and artists and loved by some. The Sunday evening gatherings at her flat are often mentioned in literary correspondence of the period. She was idealized by Baudelaire and inspired some of his most beautiful poems (*Hymne*; *Que diras-tu ce soir*, &c.).

Presles, RAOUL DE (*c.* 1270–*c.* 1330), jurist and one of Charles V's councillors, author of translations from the Bible and of the *De Civitate Dei* of St. Augustine, also of the *Songe du Verger*, a polemical work largely on the conflict between pope and king.

Press, Development of the.

PRE-REVOLUTION

(1) The periodical and daily Press in France originated in the 17th century, with Renaudot's *La Gazette* (q.v.), a weekly, founded in 1631, with Loret's (q.v.) *La Muse historique*, a 'Gazette burlesque', also weekly, and with the activities of the *Nouvellistes* (q.v.). To a great extent the foundations of the modern periodical Press, catering for divers types of readers, were laid before the Revolution.

(2) Initial development was slow. As with the book-trade, a licence to print—the *privilège* granted by the *Directeur de la Librairie* (see *Librairie*)—was required and the few licences granted created a virtual monopoly for the journals which enjoyed them. Political journals were subject to censorship, but this was frequently evaded, e.g. by printing and circulating them clandestinely; by printing them abroad and introducing them to subscribers in France; or by claiming that they were devoted to a subject (such as medicine) exempt from censorship. The liberty of the Press was a burning subject almost from the beginning. It was openly discussed by Condorcet (*Fragments sur la liberté de la presse*, 1776) and in 1778 it was advocated in a decree of the Parlement.

(3) Other typical periodicals and reviews founded before the Revolution include: *Le Mercure galant*, 1672, *Le Journal de Paris* and *Les Annales politiques, civiles, et littéraires*, 1777, *Le Journal des savants*, 1665, *L'Année littéraire*, 1754, *Le Journal de Trévoux*, 1701, and *Le Pour et contre*, 1733 (qq.v.).

REVOLUTION

(4) Development was rapid in the months preceding the Revolution. Louis XVI, when convoking the *États Généraux*, had decreed that information and memoranda relative to the state of the country should be submitted to the Keeper of the Seals. This provoked a flood of pamphlet literature (with such titles as *Avis aux bonnes gens*, *Manière de s'assembler*, *Considérations sur les intérêts du tiers état*, &c.) too strong for any control by licensing or censorship. With the opening of the *États Généraux* in May 1789 numbers of new journals came into being, political for the most part, and often founded by the pamphleteers of the previous year. They were termed indiscriminately *gazette*, *journal, bulletin, chronique, feuille,* &c. Publication was daily, weekly, three or four times weekly, or at irregular intervals. They were designed to keep the country informed of events, to report proceedings in the *Assemblée nationale*, and to serve as mouthpieces for party leaders. Their size varied: a daily might be four quarto pages (sometimes printed in double columns); the others were more often anything from two to five pages octavo. Some included literature and gossip in their scope, but many were little more than news-sheets, often ill-written, at times obscene, containing personalities and diatribes rather than informative criticism. They were circulated to subscribers, or sold by street-vendors (*colporteurs*), who outvied one another in shouting their wares and were a source of trouble to the Municipality as potential disturbers of the peace.

(5) Freedom of the Press was assured by Art. 11 of the 'Déclaration des droits de l'homme', and confirmed by the Constitution of 1791. But as the Revolution proceeded it became increasingly frequent for a journal, in the person of its editor, printer, or vendor, to be denounced and prosecuted for expressing opinions calculated to undermine the order established by law. Many journals had to suspend publication temporarily while their editors were in prison or in hiding; and for those of Royalist or constitutionalist sympathies freedom to publish ended when the monarchy fell in 1792. Their type was dispersed and their editors

were pursued by the Revolutionary Tribunal as enemies of liberty. From the fall of the Girondins (1793) to that of Robespierre (1794) the Press was virtually controlled by the Jacobins, and some journals were openly or clandestinely subsidized by the *Comité de salut public*.

(6) Typical papers founded at this time include: *Les Actes des apôtres, Le Courrier de Provence, La Gazette nationale* (better known as *Le Moniteur universel*), 1789; *L'Ami du Roi, des Français, de l'ordre et surtout de la vérité*, 1790; *La Quotidienne*, 1792 (qq.v.)— all Royalist or liberal, and mainly counter-revolutionary; and *L'Ami du peuple, Les Annales patriotiques et littéraires, Le Courrier des départements, Le Journal de Perlet, L'Orateur du peuple, Le Patriote français, Les Révolutions de Paris, Les Révolutions de France et de Brabant*, founded 1789; *Le Père Duchesne*, founded 1790; *Le Défenseur de la Constitution*, founded 1792 (qq.v.)—papers of from moderate to violent revolutionary or republican complexion. The famous *Journal des Débats* (q.v.) was also founded in 1789.

DIRECTOIRE

(7) The principle of the freedom of the Press was again enunciated in general terms in Art. 353 of the Constitution of 5 Fructidor, An III (22 Aug. 1795), which inaugurated the *Directoire*. But the many new, counter-revolutionary journals (e.g. *L'Accusateur public*) born of the *réaction thermidorienne* (see *Revolutions*, Ia, July 1794) soon abused their liberty and quarrelled with their opponents, while journals of all parties combined to attack the *Directoire* and hamper its efforts at peaceful government. A law of April 1796, the first of its kind in France, made it a penal offence to agitate by means of the periodical Press for the overthrow of the Government or the restoration of the monarchy. This proved ineffective, and after the *coup d'état* of 4 September 1797 (le 18 Fructidor, called 'La Saint-Barthélemy des journalistes') the Government took drastic action. The editors and printers of several journals were accused of conspiring against the internal security of the Republic with intent to restore the monarchy, and their arrest was ordered. Some were condemned to imprisonment or deportation (to the Île d'Oléron); their presses were destroyed; and finally a law was passed,

equivalent to the reimposition of censorship, subjecting all periodical publications to strict police surveillance (and possible suppression) for a period of twelve months.

CONSULATE AND EMPIRE

(8) Napoleon effectively deprived the Press of its little remaining liberty. In 1800 he suppressed all but thirteen out of seventy-three political papers produced in the Paris region and forbade the creation of any new ones. The survivors were allowed to continue only under severe police control exercised through a Press Bureau. Certain topics, e.g. religion, were prohibited or could only be treated on certain lines. In the provinces control was exercised by departmental *préfets*. Further, specially appointed censors supervised the tone of any journal disliked by Napoleon, who even, upon occasion, nominated journalists to editorial staffs to write articles specified by himself. (He followed this course with the *Mercure de France* because Chateaubriand, reviewing a book in its columns, had denounced tyrants.) At times, too, he dictated the manner in which profits were to be employed. In 1810 he issued a decree re-establishing the censorship of the periodical Press and of books; and in 1811 he reduced the number of tolerated political papers from thirteen to four, namely *La Gazette de France, Le Journal de l'Empire* (i.e. *Le Journal des Débats* renamed), *Le Journal de Paris*, and *Le Moniteur universel* (qq.v.). The result of his policy was that news unfavourable to the Government remained unpublished until its truth was so certain, and so generally known, that publication had become unnecessary. Periodicals concerned solely with literature, art, science, commerce, &c., were tolerated if they published no article capable of being interpreted as unfavourable to the Government.

RESTORATION

(9) In the post-Restoration years the struggle for liberty of the Press continued fiercely, but with the July Revolution (1830) ended temporarily in victory. The battle was not easily won. The Charter granted by Louis XVIII on his restoration guaranteed full liberty, but in fact, for several years to come, 'la liberté selon la Charte' was severely restricted by laws hotly debated on their passage through both Chambers.

Royal sanction was made necessary for the publication of even remotely political journals (daily or otherwise); and pamphlets of less than twenty pages were subjected to censorship. This regulation was frequently evaded by the issue of publications, in the nature of miscellanies, at irregular intervals (e.g. *La Minerve française*, *Le Conservateur*, qq.v.).

(10) The restrictions were lifted by three constructive laws passed in 1819. Full freedom of publication (subject to certain preliminary guarantees, financial and otherwise) was accorded to newspapers and other periodicals, the censorship was abolished, the duties and responsibilities of editors and printers were defined. A year later, however, and again during the reign of Charles X (1824–30), censorship over the periodical Press was re-established in more reactionary fashion than ever. Matters came to a head with the *ordonnances* of 26 July 1830, which entirely suppressed the liberty of the Press. Resentment was so hot that *Le National* and *Le Temps* (qq.v.), with several other journals, issued a signed protest calling upon the nation to resist; and the ensuing disaffection led to the July Revolution and the overthrow of the legitimist dynasty.

(11) Daily and other papers founded between 1815 and 1830 include: *Le Constitutionnel*, *Le Globe*, *Le Journal universel ou Moniteur de Gand* (founded at Ghent during the Hundred Days), *Le Nain jaune* (qq.v.). The period was fertile in new conceptions of politics, philosophy, religion, and aesthetics; and their discussion in daily papers and periodical reviews by statesmen, historians, and men of letters made the Press a powerful factor in the movement of ideas.

(12) There was also a great development in the predominantly literary press. Many new reviews were founded, in which a threefold object can be discerned—to publish original work by both known and unknown authors; to provide a survey of contemporary foreign as well as French literature; and in their literary criticism to interpret and emphasize the connexion between the new spirit in literature and the progressive ideas of the day. The chief literary reviews are roughly of three types. First come those of the classical school, edited by liberals or monarchists brought up on the pseudoclassicism of the 18th century, and on the

whole hostile to the ideas of, for example, Chateaubriand and Mme de Staël (qq.v.). They are represented by *Les Lettres normandes*, *La Minerve française*, *La Minerve littéraire* (qq.v.). At the opposite extreme are the reviews founded and supported by the ultra-Romantics (in part the younger generation of writers, in part the returned *émigrés*), and reflecting the Romantic ferment. Typical of these were *Les Lettres champenoises*, *Les Annales de la littérature et des arts*, *La Revue de Paris* (to some extent), and, above all, *Le Conservateur littéraire* and *La Muse française* (qq.v. and see *Romantisme*). Last come the reviews of a rationalist tendency founded by the political party known as the *doctrinaires* (q.v.), for whom the literature of every age was one expression of its social and political development. The most widely read were *Les Archives philosophiques* and *La Revue française* (qq.v.). They welcomed the new theories in literature in so far as these agreed with the views of the editors. (The famous *Revue des Deux Mondes* (q.v.) was founded in 1829 but did not at once develop its literary side.)

THE JULY MONARCHY

(13) With the advent of Louis-Philippe in 1830 the Press regained a freedom not effectively impaired in 1834 and 1835 by one law controlling the activities of street-vendors of pamphlet literature and another dealing with slander, seditious writings, &c. It became less important politically. In 1848, for instance, it was only indirectly responsible for the fall of the monarchy; more was effected by *banquets* (q.v.) and general mass-indignation.

(14) The period saw the development of the idealistic, socialistic, and humanitarian Press, reflecting the ideas of Lamennais and Leroux, the *Saint-Simoniens*, and the *Fouriéristes* (qq.v.); of the satirical and cartoonist Press (see *Charivari*); of the feminist press, with the *Gazette des femmes* (1836–7 and 1841–3), edited solely or mainly by women, and *Le Miroir des dames* (founded 1841), a fortnightly; and of the *roman-feuilleton* (q.v.) or novel by instalments, whose presence often determined the success or ill-success of a paper. At this time, too, the chronicle-writers or columnists made their appearance (e.g. Jules Janin; Mme Émile de Girardin, qq.v.), while a subscription to the monthly

Journal des enfants, founded 1831, became a popular New Year's gift for children. The outstanding innovation (1836), was the cheap Press, which relied largely on advertisements for its income (see *Presse*; *Siècle*). At first the older papers objected strongly to the practice but they soon followed suit, opened their columns to advertisements, reduced their subscription rate from 80 to 40 francs: and increased their circulation. In 1835 some 70,000 people had subscribed to newspapers published in Paris and throughout the country, the population at that date being *c.* 35,000,000. By 1836 there were 200,000 subscribers to daily papers published in the Paris region alone.

1848 AND THE SECOND REPUBLIC

(15) After the February Revolution the Provisional Government put an end to the system of laws and penalties regulating the conduct of the Press. Universal manhood suffrage was in the air, and newspapers, now no longer a luxury of the bourgeoisie, were founded to voice the opinions of the many political parties. Typical ones, all founded in 1848 and destined to a short life, were *La République française*, *L'Assemblée nationale*, *L'Événement* (qq.v.), and *Le Représentant du peuple* (founded by Proudhon). There was also a crop of papers devoted to topical satire and caricatures, or to sensational news and gossip; and semi-political journals for women readers included *La Voix des femmes*, *La Politique des femmes*.

(16) Louis Napoleon became President of the Republic in December 1848. He soon reintroduced the laws which had been repealed and (by a law of 1850) made signature of political articles obligatory. He was ineligible for re-election as President, and it is of interest to find him recognizing the propaganda value of the Press and launching what amounted to a Press campaign in 'inspired' journals (*Le Constitutionnel* among others) to prepare public opinion for the *coup d'état* of 2 December 1851 by which he seized control of the government (see *Republics*, para. 3) and, a year later, his transformation of himself from Prince President of the Republic into Hereditary Emperor of the French.

THE SECOND EMPIRE

(17) The *coup d'état* had entailed wholesale suppression of newspapers and the compul-sory or voluntary exile of their editors. By decrees of February 1852 the daily and other periodical Press was once more subjected to police control; a rigorous system of taxes, preliminary deposits, and obligatory authorization and supervision of papers of political or economic character was re-instituted; and the Government took power, as a measure of public security, to suspend or suppress any paper which contravened the law. In such cases preliminary warning was necessary. Official censorship was not re-imposed, but the effect of the decrees was to make each editor his own censor. Political papers practically ceased to exist, only eleven being allowed to continue, and in any case freedom of comment was rendered impossible for many years to come. In compensation, many existing papers developed their literary, dramatic, musical, and art criticism; new papers arose solely devoted to these features or to cartoons and non-political news; and the illustrated press also increased (see *Charivari*; *Figaro*; *Nain jaune*; *Temps*; *Univers*; *Vie parisienne*). *Le Petit Journal*, founded 1863 and costing only one sou (cf. the 'penny paper'), brought the daily paper within reach of all classes. It supplied miscellaneous information and gossip, ran a *roman-feuilleton*, and soon had a record circulation. In 1868 the repeal of the law requiring authorization before publication caused a host of new journals to appear, all of an anti-Empire tendency (e.g. *La Lanterne*, *Le Rappel*, *Le Réveil*, qq.v.).

1870 AND AFTER

(18) Although several new, mainly short-lived, papers came into being with the fall of the Second Empire the Press was virtually under military control during the Franco-Prussian war and the Siege of Paris, and freedom of comment was not immediately regained. Many leading journals suspended publication while the Prussians occupied Paris; others followed the Government and were printed at Tours or Bordeaux. In Paris the Military Governor used his emergency powers to suppress some of the more violent Republican papers and prohibit new ones. This created strong opposition and the 'liberty of the Press' became a cry of the insurrectionists in March 1871. A few weeks later, however, the *Commune* (q.v.) in its turn suppressed some of the more out-

spokenly disapproving Conservative papers and created new papers with old, Revolutionary-period, titles revived.

(19) After the defeat of the *Commune* successive governments busied themselves with legislation concerning the position and conduct of the Press; and in 1881 a bill conceived in a thoroughly liberal spirit was enacted and, with little alteration in later years, has since regulated the periodical Press (and the book trade). Its main features were that the liberty of printers and booksellers was safeguarded; full comment and criticism were permitted, but nothing might be published that constituted a political misdemeanour or an offence against the public safety; and any official correction of misstatements had to be given prominent insertion, free of charge. In exceptional circumstances, such as time of war, freedom of publication might be limited and a press censorship introduced, as happened during the 1914–18 war. (Both before and after the outbreak of the 1939–45 war the freedom of the Press was controlled and restricted by a number of special decrees.)

(20) During the years before the establishment of the Third Republic the newspapers had reflected the various party struggles concerning the form of government (monarchy or a republic) to be adopted by the country. Some new political papers achieved a wide circulation (e.g. *Le XIXe Siècle*, *La République française*) and a number of the older party papers continued. Towards the turn of the century the bitter feuds of the Dreyfus (q.v.) Affair encouraged a polemical tendency in journalism, well exemplified by *L'Action française* (q.v.) on the one side and *L'Aurore*, which was Clemenceau's paper, on the other. Thanks partly to the law of 1881, and perhaps still more to the development of the rotary press, which made production both easier and cheaper, the turn of the century also witnessed the increasingly rapid growth of the cheap sensational Press devoted primarily to the supply of 'news', political and general, home and foreign, written and photographed. Parisian papers with exceptionally large circulations were: *Le Petit Parisien*, 1876; *L'Écho de Paris*, 1883; *Le Matin*, 1884; *Le Journal*, 1889. Easier production and transport, again, favoured the development of a highly influential, more solidly political

provincial Press such as *La Gironde*; *Le Phare de la Loire*; *La Dépêche de Toulouse*; *Le Journal de Rouen*, &c. There was also, as in other countries, a vast expansion of the cheap sporting, feminine, and other press which needs no further mention in the present context. For literary reviews of the period see under *Symbolisme*; *Lyric poetry*, para. 15; also *Nouvelle Revue Française*; *Revue . . .*, &c.; and *Appendix* I, § G.

Pressburg [today Bratislava]. The Treaty of Pressburg (27 Dec. 1805), between the French and the Austrians, followed Napoleon's victory at Austerlitz (q.v.).

Presse, La, a daily paper of democratic sympathies, founded in 1836 by Émile de Girardin (q.v.), the originator of the cheap daily Press in France. It soon acquired a large circulation and a distinguished band of contributors (including Balzac, Dumas *père*, Gautier, George Sand, and Hugo). It had both a *roman-feuilleton* and a scientific *feuilleton*. During the Second Empire it was noted for its good foreign correspondence. When the century ended its circulation was one of the largest of the time.

Pretenders, see *Chambord, comte de*; *Louis-Philippe Ier* (last para.).

Prétextes (1903) and ***Nouveaux Prétextes*** (1911), by André Gide (q.v.), criticism.

Pretintaille, LA MARQUISE DE, in a satirical *chanson* by Béranger (q.v.), the aristocrat of the *ancien régime* who never in any circumstances forgets her quarterings.

Prêtre de Némi, Le (1885), one of Renan's *Drames philosophiques* (q.v.).

Prévert, JACQUES (1900–   ), contemporary author of humorous, and satirical, prose and poetry (*Paroles*, 1946; *Histoires*, 1951, &c.).

Prévost, ANTOINE-FRANÇOIS, L'ABBÉ, later known as *Prévost d'Exiles* (1697–1763), novelist, born at Hesdin in Artois, the son of a provincial official. He was educated by the Jesuits with a view to an ecclesiastical career, entered the army, then returned to the Jesuits, then rejoined the army, then entered the Benedictine congregation of Saint-Maur, pronouncing his vows (as he declares) with internal reservations. His dual temperament and his taste alternately for a monastic and a worldly life unfitted him for the Maurist austerities, and in 1728 he fled from the cloister, relying on a papal brief which he had obtained permitting his transfer to Cluny. But the formalities were not completed, and Prévost, finding himself in a dangerous position, fled to Holland and England, returning to France only in 1734. His life was spent in arduous literary work. His first romance, *Mémoires d'un homme de qualité*, appeared in 1728–31. This was followed in 1732–9 by *Le Philosophe anglais ou les mémoires de Cleveland*, a romance of love and startling adventure concerning a supposed natural son of Oliver Cromwell who becomes king of a tribe of South American Indians; the work shows in germ some of the ideas later found in the political philosophy of Rousseau. In 1733 Prévost started the literary periodical *Le Pour et Contre*, interesting for the publicity it gave to works of English literature. In 1735–40 appeared *Le Doyen de Killerine*, another romance of adventure, of which an Irish ecclesiastic is the hero and furnishes the title. He was once more exiled in 1741 for a short time in consequence of his part in a scandalous publication. The last twenty years of his life were occupied with vast compilations (such as an *Histoire générale des voyages*) and translations (and see *Dictionaries and Encyclopedias* under date 1750). His translations or adaptations of Richardson's novels appeared as follows: *Paméla* in 1742, *Clarisse Harlowe* in 1751, and *Grandisson* in 1755–8. By these, as also by the second and third romances mentioned above, Prévost popularized in France the knowledge of English literature and of the English character as he conceived it. He also wrote some further novels of less importance, *Histoire d'une Grecque moderne* (1741), *Mémoires d'un honnête homme* (1745), &c.

His most notable work, by which alone he is generally remembered, *L'Histoire du chevalier des Grieux et de Manon Lescaut* (see *Manon Lescaut*) had been issued in 1731 as vol. vii of the *Mémoires d'un homme de qualité*. When republished separately in 1733 it created a great sensation, and though ordered to be seized, was immensely successful. This success it owed to the simple and realistic description of a man's overmastering passion for an unworthy woman, effacing all sense of honour, dignity, and duty, com-

bined with adventurous incident, and a moral and edifying development. (Changes in a revised edition of 1753 tended to emphasize the moral aspect.) Prévost is said, but the fact is uncertain, to have died under the scalpel of a village surgeon, when under an attack of apoplexy.

Prévost, MARCEL (1862–1940), born in Paris, novelist, had numerous successes with 'society' novels of a type popular at the end of the 19th century. He specialized in feminine psychology. *L'Automne d'une femme* (1893), *Les Demi-vierges* (1894), and a series called *Lettres à Françoise* (1902–28) are typical of his output.

Prévost-Paradol, LUCIEN-ANATOLE (1829–70), born in Paris, a well-remembered Second Empire journalist, was one of a number of brilliant students, about 1850, who turned their backs on an academic career on leaving the École normale supérieure (cf. About, Edmond; Taine). He was on the *Journal des Débats*, then founded a weekly, the *Courrier du Dimanche*, which was suppressed for hostility to the Government. His attitude softened when the Second Empire policy became more liberal, and in 1870 he went to Washington as Ambassador, his mission being to assure the United States that Europe was at peace. But the Franco-Prussian war broke out soon after his arrival; he considered himself disgraced, and committed suicide.

His firm moral and political convictions and lucid, ironical style are exemplified in *De la Liberté des cultes en France* and others of the articles and book reviews collected in *Essais de politique et littérature* (1859–63). His other publications included *Études sur les moralistes français* (1864), *Quelques pages d'histoire contemporaine* (1861–6), &c.

Prévôt (L. *praepositus*), under the *ancien régime*, a royal agent exercising political, judicial, military, and financial functions over a small area (*châtellenie*), functions which in feudal times conflicted with those of the feudal lords. The powers of the *prévôts* were further restricted (*c.* 1190) by the institution of the *baillis* (q.v.) and *sénéchaux*, their hierarchical superiors with jurisdiction over a larger area. The *prévôt de Paris* exercised the royal authority over the city. His official seat was the Châtelet (q.v.).

Prie, MARQUISE DE (1698–1727), mistress of the duc de Bourbon, minister of Louis XV at the beginning of his reign. A clever, ambitious, and seductive woman, she exercised a considerable influence on affairs until the overthrow of the duc de Bourbon in 1726.

Prière sur l'Acropole, La, see *Souvenirs d'enfance et de jeunesse.*

Prière sur la Tour Eiffel, La, see *Juliette au pays des hommes.*

Primat, see *Grandes Chroniques.*

Primitivisme, see *Literary Isms.*

Prince Impérial, Le, title of Napoléon-Eugène-Louis-Jean-Joseph Bonaparte (1856–79), only son of Napoleon III and the Empress Eugénie. He went with his mother to England at the fall of the Second Empire (1870) and was educated at the Royal Military Academy at Woolwich. In 1879 he was allowed to take part in the British expedition against the Zulus and was killed in battle.

Princesse de Babylone, La, an oriental tale by Voltaire, published in 1768.

The princess wanders about the world in company with a wise phoenix and in pursuit of her lover, visiting different countries from China to England. This gives the author an opportunity for comparing and criticizing their customs and beliefs.

Princesse de Clèves, La, a novel by Mme de La Fayette (q.v.), published in 1678 under the name of Segrais (q.v.).

Mme de Chartres, in the time of Henri II, marries her daughter to the prince de Clèves for worldly reasons. The princess, a woman of the highest character, does not love her husband (who is passionately devoted to her) but is scrupulously loyal to him. The duc de Nemours, an Admirable Crichton, falls in love with her, and she returns his affection, but endeavours from a sense of duty to conceal her feelings from him. At last, hoping to be strengthened and supported in her virtue, she avows the situation to her husband. Their mutual esteem is increased, but his life is embittered by jealousy and he dies of a broken heart. The princess retires to a convent, and her life is short. The work aroused great interest, but Mme de Clèves's

avowal to her husband did not commend itself to public opinion in general.

Nathaniel Lee's play *The Princess of Cleve,* founded on the above, was acted in 1681, printed in 1689. An English version of *La Princesse de Clèves* appeared in 1688.

Princesse d'Élide, La, a *comédie-ballet* by Molière, produced in 1664. It was composed for a festival at Versailles and was begun in verse but, time pressing, was completed in prose.

The prince of Elis is celebrating games in the hope that one of the young princes of Greece will win the heart of his daughter. But she professes to be averse to marriage and to disdain all men. Euryale, prince of Ithaca, who is in love with her, adopts a stratagem: unlike the other suitors, he professes to be indifferent to her, and she is in consequence much piqued. To provoke him, she tells him that she has determined to give her hand to the prince of Messenia. He retorts by declaring to her his love for her cousin Aglante. Her jealousy is now aroused, and when she finds him, in appearance, actually asking her father for Aglante's hand, she can resist no longer, and surrenders rather than that he should marry her cousin.

Princesse lointaine, La (1895), a poetic drama by Edmond Rostand (q.v.).

Princesse Maleine, La (1889), one of the first Symbolist dramas, by Maeterlinck (q.v.).

Prisonnière, La (1923), the fifth section of Proust's novel *A la recherche du temps perdu* (q.v.). Originally it formed the third part of the fourth section (*Sodome et Gomorrhe*).

Privilège, see *Librairie.*

Privilégiés, Les. At the outbreak of the Revolution there were two parties in France —the *Privilégiés* (the majority of the nobility and the upper ranks of the clergy) and the *Non-Privilégiés* or *Tiers État* (q.v.). The *Privilégiés* possessed the greater share of the wealth of the kingdom and at the same time held innumerable hereditary rights by which they both levied and avoided taxation. The same division prevailed in the *États Généraux,* when the *Non-Privilégiés* became the *Parti des réformes.*

Prix Goncourt, see *Prix littéraires.*

Prix littéraires. To the foreigner who studies the annual *Guide des prix littéraires* (some 1,000 of them) available for award in France and French-speaking countries it seems as if any young French author may reasonably hope to win one of these at some time or another in his career. The value in terms of money actually handed over may be small, but the effect on his reputation and, indirectly, on his sales may be considerable. Nor is he restricted in his choice of subject, for besides imaginative literature the field includes aviation, education, gastronomy, opera, philosophy, psychology, rural economy, sport, and wine.

The prizes which create most stir are those awarded for the best works of imaginative literature, usually novels. First come the *Prix Goncourt*, founded 1903 (see *Académie Goncourt*), and two similar prizes awarded at the same time of year (December), the *Prix Femina*, founded 1904 by the reviews *Femina* and *Vie heureuse*, and the *Prix Théophraste Renaudot*, founded 1926 by newspaper editors. Other prizes for novels are the *Prix de la Renaissance*, founded 1921, the *Prix Interallié*, founded 1930, and the *Prix du Quai des Orfèvres*, founded 1946, the most important of a number of prizes awarded for the best detective novel. The *Académie française* alone has over 100 prizes at its disposal, among them being the *Grand Prix de littérature* for works of prose or poetry of outstanding literary value of form and content, the *Grand Prix du roman*, usually awarded to a young novelist, and the *Prix Montyon* (the highest in monetary value) for a work of elevated character and moral utility. The other *académies* which make up the *Institut de France* (q.v.) also award several prizes each year, usually for works of a more specialized character. The *Société des Gens de lettres* (q.v.) awards various prizes for fiction, poetry, criticism, &c.; and the many other prizes founded by individuals or societies include a *Prix Rivarol* for the best work written in French by a foreigner, a *Prix Denyse Clairouin* for the best French translation of an English work, and a prize (*Broquette-Colin*) to be awarded yearly to the author of a work—philosophy, politics, or general literature—'jugé susceptible d'inspirer l'amour du vrai, du beau et du bien'. (See also *Grand prix des meilleurs romans du demi-siècle*; *Prix Nobel*.)

Prix Nobel. By December 1956 the Nobel Prize for Literature, established in 1901 under the will of the Swedish chemist Alfred Bernhard Nobel (1833–96), had been awarded to the following French authors: Sully Prudhomme (1901), Frédéric Mistral (1904), Romain Rolland (1915), Anatole France (1921), Henri Bergson (1925), Roger Martin du Gard (1937), André Gide (1947), François Mauriac (1952), Albert Camus (1957). In 1911 it was awarded to the Belgian writer Maurice Maeterlinck.

Procès de Paradis, see *Mystères*.

Procope, Café, see *Café Procope*.

Procurateur de Judée, Le, one of Anatole France's finest short stories (in *L'Étui de nacre*, 1892).

The aged statesman Pontius Pilate is discussing old times, particularly his years in Judea, with a friend. The friend mentions one 'Jesus the Nazarene' who had been crucified for some crime or another. Does Pontius Pilate remember? But the name strikes no answering chord in Pilate's memory.

Profession de foi du Vicaire savoyard, see *Émile*.

Progrès de l'esprit humain, Tableau historique des, see *Tableau historique*.

Promenades littéraires (1904–27), collected criticism by Remy de Gourmont (q.v.).

Prométhée mal enchaîné, Le (1899), a *sotie* by André Gide (q.v.).

Propos d'Alain, see *Chartier, Émile-Auguste*.

Proscrits, Les, one of the 'Études philosophiques' of Balzac's *Comédie humaine* (q.v.).

Prose (pour Des Esseintes), a poem by Mallarmé, of interest for his aesthetic theories. The dedication 'pour Des Esseintes' is Mallarmé's acknowledgement of Huysmans's admiring references to him in *A rebours* (q.v.). The poem appeared first in 1885 in *La Revue indépendante* (q.v.) and in 1887 was included in *Les Poésies de Stéphane Mallarmé*.

Protesilaus, see *Huon de Rotelande.*

Proudhon, Pierre-Joseph (1809–65), publicist and social reformer, was born at Besançon in poor circumstances. After some schooling at the Collège de Besançon he went to work with a firm of printers (as compositor, then proof-reader) and continued to educate himself. In 1839 he won a three years' scholarship to Paris and took up economics. His first work of note, a treatise, was an attack on property (*Qu'est-ce que la propriété?*, 1840). It began with the famous paradox 'La propriété, c'est le vol', and went on to maintain that the theory of property was a denial of the fundamental principles of justice, liberty, and equality, because it enabled one set of men to exploit the labour of others. Property was only justifiable when it resulted from work and was shared by all in a society so organized that the rights of the individual were equitably maintained.

After a spell managing his own printing-business at Besançon, followed by commercial employment at Lyons, Proudhon settled in Paris (1847) hoping to live by his pen. He was now a well-known writer on social questions (*Avertissement aux propriétaires,* 1842, another treatise on property; *Système des contradictions économiques ou Philosophie de la misère,* 1846, denouncing Utopian reformers). After the February (1848) Revolution he represented the Department of the Seine in the *Assemblée constituante* but in 1849 his journalistic violence earned him three years in prison, after which he retired into private life. In 1858 a new work *La Justice dans la Révolution et dans l'Église* attacked Church, State, and other public institutions so fiercely that it was confiscated and he had to flee to Brussels to escape imprisonment. Hardship undermined his health and he died three years after his return (1862) to Paris.

Proudhon's writings, which had considerable influence upon socialist thinkers of the later 19th century, were vigorous, dialectical, full of diatribe, paradox, and destructive criticism, and without any of the utopianism or mysticism of the *Saint-Simoniens* or *Fouriéristes* (qq.v.). Besides those mentioned above they included: *De la création de l'ordre dans l'humanité* (1834); *Confessions d'un révolutionnaire* (1849); *La Théorie de l'impôt* (1861); *La Guerre et la Paix* (1862, studies of might and right); *Du Principe de l'art et de sa destination sociale* (1865), &c.

Proust, Marcel (1871–1922), novelist, whose title to fame is his long work *A la recherche du temps perdu* (1913–27, q.v.), was born, and died, in Paris. He seldom left it except for holidays—spent with relations at Illiers, near Chartres (in childhood), or at Normandy sea-side resorts—or for short literary and artistic pilgrimages. His father, Dr. Adrien Proust (d. 1903), was a professor on the Faculty of Medicine. His mother (d. 1905), whom he adored and depended on, was of Jewish descent.

He was educated at the Lycée Condorcet, did a year's military service at Orléans (1889–90), and for two years (1891–3) studied law and political science. Violent asthma, which had first attacked him when he was ten, precluded any regular profession: in any case his own wish was to write. He contributed to literary reviews and was part-founder of one (*Le Banquet,* 1892, 8 numbers). In 1896 he published *Les Plaisirs et les jours,* an elegantly-produced little collection of short stories, sketches, and poems, with illustrations by the fashionable painter Madeleine Lemaire, musical settings by Reynaldo Hahn, and an amiable preface by Anatole France. It was received indulgently; and one or two of the stories are interesting anticipations of his great work. Other writings of these earlier years, often first contributed to *Le Figaro,* were collected in *Pastiches et mélanges* (1914) and call for mention as evidence of his witty talent for stylistic imitation.

For some years, when health permitted, Proust seems to have devoted most of his ambition and ingenuity to his social career and to securing introductions. Charm, wit, and wealth helped him. This snobbish phase was to yield immense profit, for the world of the *salons,* the still more rarefied stratospheres to which he penetrated, became the setting of his book. [*A la recherche du temps perdu* is not autobiography, but in many ways Proust is his character Marcel and his own life is transposed to form the matter of his novel.]

Proust was from early years a neurotic. His neurosis was no doubt complicated by his asthma, and in all probability further aggravated by the inner conflict due to his homosexual tendencies and his efforts to conceal them—an abnormality in his own life which led him, in his novel, to treat the subject of perversion at very great length. As time went on his health deteriorated and he stayed more at home, entertaining largely and writing occasionally for periodicals. He began to translate Ruskin (*La Bible d'Amiens*, 1904; *Sésame et les lys*, 1906), whose ideas on art and architecture influenced his own. [Another influence which may be mentioned here and which is noticeable in Proust's approach, in his novel, to the theme of time, was that of Bergson.] After his mother's death he lapsed into almost complete invalidism and led the life of a recluse. If he went out at all, or if friends were summoned to visit him, it was usually at night. He spent most of his time in bed, writing feverishly, in a room lined with cork to exclude noise. All windows were tightly shut and the air was thick with inhalants. He kept up a constant correspondence with friends, but his pattern of life was broken only at rare intervals when he was well enough to visit the country or the sea (and then always with a closed window between him and the land- or sea-scape).

During these years his writing was something of a mystery for his friends, but he himself now had the idea of his novel and, too, the fear that he might not live to finish it. From papers found after his death it appears that he first wrote substantial fragments of a novel *Jean Santeuil* (published posth. 1952, 3 vols.), which was the germ, at times the bare bones, at times as much as a first draft, of *A la recherche du temps perdu*. (Other fragments, similarly retrieved, and bearing the same relation to the later work, were collected and published in 1954 together with *Contre Sainte-Beuve*, the profoundly interesting study, which gives the volume its title, of the critical practice of Sainte-Beuve and of Proust's own, opposed, theories of intuitive criticism.) But from 1910 he was definitely at work on *A la recherche du temps perdu* itself. He finished it in its first form in 1912. The first volume, *Du Côté de chez Swann*, appeared in 1913. From then until the moment of his death in 1922, and though latterly in constant suffering, he never ceased to revise and expand his manuscript and his proofs. The complete work

consists of seven sections: *Du Côté de chez Swann*, *A l'ombre des jeunes filles en fleurs*, *Le Côté de Guermantes*, *Sodome et Gomorrhe*, *La Prisonnière*, *Albertine disparue*, *Le Temps retrouvé*. (For details and dates of publication see *A la recherche du temps perdu*, § iv.)

Du Côté de chez Swann made little stir at first, but gradually it attracted readers both in France and abroad. In 1920 the award of the *Prix Goncourt* (q.v.) for *A l'ombre des jeunes filles en fleurs* marked Proust as the outstanding novelist of the year. By the time he died it was clear that the writer whom few had taken seriously to begin with was one of the great novelists of the 20th century. His fame and influence have only grown with the years.

Provençal poetry, Influence of, see *Troubadour*; *Lyric Poetry*. For the 19th-century revival of Provençal language and literature see *Félibrige*.

Proverbes, or **proverbes dramatiques,** short dramatic sketches composed to illustrate, or 'point', a proverb. The genre originated in the *salons* of the 17th and 18th centuries and had been preceded (under Louis XIII) by the fashionable *jeu des proverbes*, a sort of parlour-game in which a general conversation in proverbs had to be kept going as long as possible. Then, for the private theatricals which were a feature of the *salons*, short *proverbes dramatiques* were written, sometimes with the scenes and dialogues only roughly indicated and amplification left to the performers. At first these resembled charades in that the audience had to guess what proverb was in question. Later authors did not exact this measure of co-operation from the audience: the proverb illustrated was disclosed at once as the title, and was also spoken as the closing words, of what was in effect a short, usually one-act, comedy.

(2) A small collection of 'Proverbes' by a Mme Durand was printed at the end of the 17th century, and about the same time Mme de Maintenon was composing *proverbes* (not printed till 1829) for performance by the young ladies of Saint-Cyr (q.v.). The great vogue for this type of entertainment was in the middle of the 18th century and ended, with the society in which it flourished, with the Revolution. Collé (q.v.) wrote comedies and proverbs for the private theatre of the

duc d'Orléans. Carmontelle (q.v.), in all but chronological time, was very much the creator of the genre with the slight pieces contained in his *Proverbes dramatiques* (1768–87). These, too, were written for the duc d'Orléans. He had several imitators, and the memoirs of Mme de Genlis contain many references to performances in contemporary *salons*. Edifying *proverbes* were written to provide instruction for the young, e.g. those of Moissy (q.v.) published in 1769 or the ones included by Mme de Genlis in her *Théâtre à l'usage des jeunes personnes* (1779–80). Occasionally, too, in the years immediately preceding the Revolution, *proverbes dramatiques* were performed publicly in the theatres.

(3) After 1815 *proverbes* were again often read or performed in the Restoration *salons*. The most popular, the *Proverbes dramatiques* (published 1820–30) of Théodore Leclercq (q.v.), are excellent little sketches of ultra-Royalist circles. Antoine-Marie, baron Roederer (1782–1865), son of Roederer the economist and politician (see *Roederer, Pierre-Louis*), wrote *Comédies, proverbes et parades* (1824–5), and Hyacinthe [Henri] de Latouche (q.v.) also wrote one or two (e.g. *On fait ce qu'on peut et non pas ce qu'on veut*). In the middle of the century Octave Feuillet (q.v.) wrote *Scènes et proverbes* (1851), some of them on a satirical note. But by this date Alfred de Musset, the perfect master of the genre, moved to imitation in the first place by the work of Carmontelle, had transformed the *proverbe*. In his hands, what had been a passing entertainment became a high form of art, the purest, most delicate comedy, kept eternally fresh by its blending of wit, sentiment, gaiety which borders at times on sadness, and poetry (e.g. *On ne badine pas avec l'amour*; *Il faut qu'une porte soit ouverte ou fermée*).

Proverbes au vilain, Proverbes au comte de Bretagne, medieval collections of homely proverbs, some of them interesting for the light they throw on the life of the period; of the type of 'Ne sont pas tous chevaliers qui en cheval montent'.

Proverbes français, Le Livre des (1842–59), see *Le Roux de Lincy*.

Provinces, Les Anciennes. Electorally, and for various purposes of local government and what may be called administrative classification, the Frenchman is a man of his *département*, i.e. of one of some ninety areas into which, for these purposes, France has been divided since the Revolution. As an individual, he is still more likely to consider himself a man of his *province*, with customs, tastes, idiosyncrasies of language and physique, territorial loyalties, that differentiate him from his fellows from another province.

A department—which was, to begin with, an administrative circumscription and now corresponds also to a political, economic, and to some extent moral reality—is usually part of one of the so-called *anciennes provinces*, much larger areas which were abolished by the Revolution (or, from the way its boundaries run, it may, but this only very rarely, take in bits from two or three of these larger areas). The word *province* only passed into the language of administration about the 14th century, and though it came to be employed frequently in royal, and from the 17th century in common, parlance it seems to have had no very precise or consistent administrative significance. Yet the entities represented by the term *anciennes provinces* are tied up historically and ethnically with the evolution of the French as a nation.

The provinces, so called, go back to the cities of Ancient Gaul. Out of these, via the Romans' partitioning of their conquered territories into seventeen *provinciae* (cf. *Provence*) there evolved under the Merovingian and Carolingian dynasties the *duchés* and *comtés* of pre-feudal and then (during the period of strife and anarchy that followed the death of Charlemagne) of feudal France (see *Mérovingiens*; also *Carolingiens*; *Noblesse*). At the height of the feudal period many *duchés* and *comtés* were in fact separate kingdoms and principalities, domains which, with the offices attached to them, had been appropriated as their hereditary right by the great military and land-owning warriors. They had their own customary laws, their own administrative and often monetary systems, their own languages, and at need the smaller proprietors or fiefs provided the *seigneur*, whose vassals they were, with an independent army (cf. the word *hommage*).

To begin with, the Kingdom of France was one such feudal kingdom like another.

Hugues Capet, the first Capetian king (987–96), ruled his own domain directly (at that time it corresponded very roughly to what later came to be known as Île-de-France), but he was accepted by the other great warriors as their suzerain ruler, the military chief to whom they paid homage, who could call upon them for service. Moreover, he and his successors possessed a mystical significance in that they were anointed, i.e. consecrated in their office by the Church; and since, further, they took the precaution of having their eldest sons anointed during their own lifetime they succeeded in making the monarchy hereditary. They also—a great step forward—about the 14th century acquired the exclusive right of making war and from this proceeded to organize their own standing armies. This progressive consolidation of the monarchy was accompanied by what is known as the *progrès du domaine royal*, a process of conquest and annexation, or of acquisition by death, marriage, purchase, or barter, by which the vassal states and some frontier territories were absorbed into the Crown property and from which, more immediately, the *anciennes provinces* derive.

When these new possessions were beyond reach of the king's immediate government they had to be brought within fiscal, judicial, and other systems (see *Fiscal systems*; *Intendant*; *Parlement*) which were extended or improvised to meet the needs of particular services and which were often complicated and incoherent, necessitating division into purely artificial areas. For military purposes, by the 16th century, division was into *gouvernements généraux*, and these were the areas that most nearly preserved the outline of the territories absorbed. Governors were sent to them whose sole function at first was to command the king's forces stationed there to defend frontiers and fortified places, but in time the governor became the direct representative of the king, the *gouverneur et lieutenant général du Roy* and of the *états de la province* (which the king might speak of as *nos provinces*). In an early 18th-century geographical primer used in the Collège Louis-le-Grand, which proceeded by question and answer, the question 'Comment divisez-vous la France?' occurs, to which the pupil is supposed to reply, 'En trente provinces, qui sont autant de gouvernements'.

At the beginning of the 17th century, by which time the monarchy was firmly consolidated, there were twelve *grands gouvernements*, or provinces, namely: Auvergne, Bourgogne, Bretagne, Champagne, Dauphiné, Guyenne (in which the *duché* of Gascogne had been included since 1052), Île-de-France, Languedoc, Lyonnais, Normandie, Picardie, Provence. Between then and 1789 new 'provinces' were annexed or ceded to the *domaine royal* (e.g. Alsace, Artois, Franche-Comté, French Flanders, 1678; Lorraine, 1766; Corsica, 1768), or old ones were split up (some into such small units that their names are barely remembered) and the number of *gouvernements* was nearly trebled (though the functions of the *gouverneur* became more purely decorative in the 18th century as the number and powers of the *intendants*, the king's provincial inspectors of justice, police, and finance, an office instituted by Richelieu in 1636, increased. By 1789 there were over thirty areas called *intendances*, and these, too, were often termed *provinces*).

The *esprit de province*, however, had resisted partitioning and dismemberment. Indeed, it became all the stronger after 1750 as the monarchy weakened its own authority by a series of capitulations to the growing though largely unjustifiable pretensions of the *parlements* (q.v.) and the provincial *états* (see *Fiscal system*), privileged bodies which claimed to represent local custom and law. When 1789 came, the Revolutionaries, who considered that provincial privilege and particularisms had helped to ruin France, were suspicious of the provinces and of provincialism, identifying both with sectional and vested interests. In their eyes, the *esprit de province* would, if allowed to persist, militate against national unity and was thus an additional reason for abolishing existing institutions and for entirely reorganizing the administrative and territorial bases of the country's government. The first step towards reorganization was taken by a law of 22 December 1789 establishing the principle of the creation of departments. The outlines which these should follow occasioned much dispute but finally they were kept in geographical relation to the *gouvernements généraux*. There were variations, but the approximate relationship is indicated in Appendix II, Map 1.

Provinciales, Lettres, see *Pascal.*

Prudhomme, M. JOSEPH, the personification of the banal, prosperous bourgeois under the July monarchy, able by his large stomach and loud voice to impose himself and his platitudes on any assembly. He was the creation of the caricaturist Henry Monnier (q.v.) who spent twenty years developing him from his first, lightly-sketched appearance in *Scènes dessinées à la plume* (1830). In 1852, when the type was disappearing, Monnier made a play of him (*Grandeur et Décadence de M. Joseph Prudhomme*), and in 1857 he recorded his life and sayings (*Mémoires de M. Joseph Prudhomme*).

Prunier, JOSEPH, a pseudonym occasionally used by Guy de Maupassant (q.v.).

Prytanée. During the Directory and the Consulate the Collège Louis-le-Grand, formerly Collège de Clermont (q.v.) and subsequently Lycée Louis-le-Grand, became the *Prytanée* (so called after the *Prytaneum* of Greek antiquity, the public or 'town' hall in which the hearth of the State was maintained and where honoured guests were entertained). Lectures were given and it became a form of boarding-school, intended as the nucleus of a reorganized educational system, on lines proposed by Napoleon's brother Lucien Bonaparte. To some extent it was the germ of the Napoleonic *lycées* (see *Lycées and collèges*).

Prytanée national de La Flèche (founded *c.* 1760), a military school for officers' sons at La Flèche on the Loir near Le Mans. It replaced a famous college founded by Henri IV in 1603 and given by him to the Jesuits (the college where Descartes was educated from 1604 to 1612).

Psalms, The. For names of authors who translated or paraphrased the Psalms, see under *Religious writings* (paras. 6, 7).

Psalters, see *Bible (French versions of the).*

Psichari, ERNEST (1883–1914), professional soldier and novelist, a grandson of Renan (q.v.), born in Paris, died on active service. His novels were militaristic and—he was a convert to Roman Catholicism—semi-mystical in character. In *L'Appel des armes* (1913) two members of a military expedition in the Sahara discover how far the glories of a soldiering life outweigh its trials. In *Le Voyage du centurion* (1915), the study of a religious conversion, the setting is again military life in Africa.

Psyché, a *comédie-ballet* in *vers libres* (q.v.) by Molière, Quinault, and Corneille, produced in 1670. The greater part of acts II–V was written by Corneille; the old poet, who had suffered a rebuff in his *Tite et Bérénice*, showed here that he could still write exquisite verse. Molière wrote the prologue, act I, and the first scene of act II and act III, and planned the whole.

The play is an adaptation of the fable of Cupid and Psyche from the *Golden Ass* of Apuleius; La Fontaine had recently given a version of it in his *Amours de Psyché et de Cupidon.* Venus, jealous of the beautiful maiden Psyche, has sent Cupid to make her fall in love with some unsightly monster. But Cupid has himself fallen in love with her. He has transported her to a beautiful palace, and there he courts her and wins her heart, but she does not know who he is. Psyche's jealous sisters instil suspicions in her mind, and she presses her lover to reveal himself, against his warning of the dire consequences. She insists, palace and lover disappear, and Psyche is subjected to cruel hardships by the angry Venus. However, the hard heart of the goddess is at length melted by her sufferings and constancy, and the lovers are reunited among the immortals.

Psyché (1841), a narrative poem by Victor de Laprade (q.v.), an early example of many poems written about this time on subjects from antiquity (cf. *Leconte de Lisle*; *Ménard, Louis*; *Parnassiens*).

Psychologie de l'art (1948–50), see *Malraux, André.*

Publiciste parisien, Le; Publiciste de la République française, Le, see *Ami du peuple.*

Puce de Mme Des Roches, La, the subject of a celebrated collection of verses in French, Latin, and other languages by magistrates and men of learning (such as Passerat, Scévole de Sainte-Marthe, Joseph Scaliger, Odet de Turnèbe), written on the occasion of the discovery of a flea on the breast of Catherine Des Roches (q.v.) at an evening party at Poitiers in 1579, at the house of her mother.

Pucelle, La, abbreviation of *La Pucelle d'Orléans*, Jeanne d'Arc (q.v.), the subject and title of: (1) an epic poem by Chapelain (q.v.) in twenty-four cantos; (2) a mock-heroic poem by Voltaire, published in 1755, an unseemly burlesque, containing a good deal of licentious matter.

Puget, PIERRE (1622–94), sculptor and painter of the period of Louis XIV.

Pulchérie, a tragedy by Corneille on an historical theme, produced in 1672 and described by him as an 'heroic comedy'. The play is of little interest and was unsuccessful.

Pulchérie, daughter of the Roman emperor Arcadius, has succeeded to the throne. She loves Léon (then an obscure soldier) but will only marry him if the Senate elect him emperor, among the various competitors for the position. Later her ambition and reluctance to share the throne with one who, she fears, will be her master cause her to change her mind, and to choose as her husband the aged senator Marcian, on condition that he is to be her husband in name only.

Pure, L'ABBÉ MICHEL DE (1634–80), author, remembered for the ridicule he suffered in Boileau's satires, on account of a libel he was thought by Boileau to have circulated, though he appears to have been a quiet, harmless man. He wrote a tragedy *Ostorius* (1659); miscellaneous works showing a certain erudition, and a novel, *La Prétieuse ou le mystère des ruelles* (1656–8) in which, in the course of conversations and arguments on the subject of marriage, the different types of *précieuse* are defined.

Purgon, a character in Molière's *Le Malade imaginaire* (q.v.).

Puvis de Chavannes, PIERRE (1824–98), born in Lyons, painter, a famous master of 19th-century decorative art. His mural paintings are in the Sorbonne and the Panthéon in Paris and in other official buildings in France. His idealistic, poetical work was much esteemed by the Symbolists (see *Symbolisme*).

Puy or **Pui,** a name given to medieval fraternities of *jongleurs* (q.v.) and ordinary burghers at Arras and other towns of Northern and Western France, which held contests at which lyric poets competed. The name is perhaps derived from *puy* = an eminence, signifying the raised stage on which the judges and the president of the contest sat and the competitors recited their verses, or from Le Puy-en-Velay, where such contests, at first in honour of the Virgin Mary, are said to have originated; other derivations have also been suggested. The institution appears to date from the 12th century and the greater part of the poems submitted were of a religious character. It is possible that early dramatic pieces such as the *Jeu de la feuillée* (q.v.) were played by such fraternities. The *Miracles de Notre-Dame* (see *Miracles*) were probably written for a Parisian *puy*. The *puy* of Rouen was known as the *puy des Palinods*; it was founded in the latter part of the 15th century in honour of the Immaculate Conception and was devoted to poems on that subject. There were other such *puys* at Caen and Dieppe.

Pyat, FÉLIX (1810–99), born at Vierzon, a revolutionary and an idealistic social reformer who flourished, in and out of prison, and in the wake of the *Fouriéristes* (q.v.), between 1830 and 1848. Dramas by him, championing the rights of the people, were moderately successful but quickly forgotten (e.g. *Une Révolution d'autrefois*, 1832; *Le Chiffonnier de Paris*, 1847). He lived in exile in England during the Second Empire.

Pyrenees, Treaty of, concluded in 1659 on an island in the Bidassoa between France (whose plenipotentiary was Mazarin) and Spain. France restored many of her conquests to Spain, but acquired Roussillon and Cerdagne on the Spanish border and territory in Artois and Flanders. Louis XIV was to marry Maria Teresa, the Infanta, who renounced her claim to the Spanish crown provided that she received a dowry of 500,000 crowns, which in fact Spain was unable to pay. (Cf. *Collège des Quatre Nations*.)

Pyrrhus, one of the main characters in Racine's tragedy *Andromaque* (q.v.).

Q

Qaïn [Cain], by Leconte de Lisle (q.v.), one of his *Poèmes barbares* (1862).

Quadrilogue invectif, see *Chartier, Alain.*

Quai des Orfèvres, see *Police,* para. 4.

Quai d'Orsay, i.e. the French Foreign Office (*Ministère des affaires étrangères*), so called because it is on the part of the Seine embankment (Left Bank) known as the Quai d'Orsay.

Quarante, Les, the forty members of the *Académie française* (q.v.).

Quarante-cinq, Les (1848), a historical romance (*c.* 1584) by Dumas *père* (q.v.), a sequel to *La Dame de Monsoreau* (q.v.).

Quartier latin, the name given to the university quarter of Paris, on the Left Bank of the Seine. It covers an area stretching roughly upwards from the Seine to the Montagne Sainte-Geneviève and from the rue du Bac on the west to the rue Cardinal-Lemoine on the east. It used also to be called the *Pays latin.*

Quasimodo, the hunchback bell-ringer of Notre-Dame, in Victor Hugo's historical novel *Notre-Dame de Paris* (q.v.).

Quatre-Bras, the crossroads near Waterloo (q.v.), the agreed point of junction for Wellington's and Blücher's forces.

Quatre Évangiles, Les, see *Zola.*

Quatremère de Quincy, ANTOINE-CHRYSOSTOME (1755–1849), see *Dictionaries and Encyclopedias,* under date 1788–1825.

Quatre offices de l'ostel du Roy, Dit des, see *Deschamps, Eustache.*

Quatre temps de l'âge d'homme, see *Philippe de Novare.*

Quatre vents de l'esprit, Les (1881), by Victor Hugo, the last collection of his poems to be published in his lifetime. It was so named because of its division into four books—satiric, dramatic, epic, and lyric—the forms that the poet's inspiration had always taken.

Quatre-vingt-treize (1873), by Victor Hugo, an historical novel of Royalist insurrections during the Revolution. The insurgents—*les blancs*—wage a guerrilla war, with a mixture of savagery and superstition, in Brittany and the Vendée (q.v.). Their leader is the marquis de Lantenac. His nephew Gauvain leads the Republican forces, *les bleus.* The Republican troops have adopted the three children of a refugee peasant woman. The Royalists, by order of their leader, capture these children and use them as hostages. Gradually the Royalists are defeated, and nineteen of them, including their leader, take refuge in an old fortress that forms part of the ancestral home of the Lantenac family. They escape by a secret passage, leaving the children in an inaccessible part of the château, to which they have set fire. The *bleus* make unavailing attempts to rescue the children. Suddenly the marquis, who has in his pocket the only key to the burning wing, returns, rescues the children, and gives himself up. He is condemned to the guillotine, but Gauvain, whose admiration for his uncle's bravery has transcended his loyalty, comes to his cell, helps him to escape, and takes his place. When the substitution is discovered a special court of three sits in judgement upon Gauvain and the casting vote for his death is given by one of the chief characters of the book, Cimourdan. The one human strain in this fanatical revolutionary, an ex-priest, has been his devotion to his former pupil Gauvain. Now, in the conflict between theories and affections, his theories win, but as soon as Gauvain has been guillotined he shoots himself.

The book has some notable passages, e.g. the descriptions of the forests of Brittany and the Vendée, where the ground is mined with subterranean passages and refuges known only to the natives; or, when the scene shifts to Paris, the imaginary conversation between Danton, Robespierre, and Marat, followed by a meeting of the *Convention nationale* (q.v.).

Queneau, RAYMOND (1903–   ), contemporary author (novels and verse) and critic. See also *Pastiche.*

Quérard, JOSEPH-MARIE (1797–1865), bibliographer. He compiled, notably, *La France littéraire ou Dictionnaire bibliographique des savants, historiens et gens de lettres de la France, ainsi que des littérateurs étrangers qui ont écrit en français, plus particulièrement pendant les XVIIIe et XIXe siècles* (10 vols., 1827–39 and 2 supplementary vols. 1854–64). *Les Supercheries littéraires dévoilées* (5 vols., 1845–56) is a dictionary of apocryphal and pseudonymous writers. (*La littérature française contemporaine*, 1827–49, 6 vols., by Louandre, Bourquelot, and Maury, continued Quérard's *La France littéraire*.)

Querelle des Anciens et des Modernes, a dispute which developed in the latter part of the 17th century between the advocates of imitation of the literature of classical antiquity and the champions of progress, new ideas, and self-sufficiency. Desmarets (q.v.) was one of the first supporters of the Moderns, defending in a series of writings the choice of a Christian national hero in his epic *Clovis*. His doctrine was summarily condemned by Boileau in the *Art poétique* (q.v.), but the dispute was taken up by Charles Perrault and his brothers. Charles Perrault in his *Siècle de Louis le Grand* (1687) and his *Parallèle des anciens et des modernes* (1688–97) definitely maintained the superiority of modern writers, as representatives of the maturity of the human intellect. He was supported by Fontenelle. The opposite cause was upheld by La Fontaine in his *Épître à Huet*, by La Bruyère in his *Caractères*, and by Boileau in his *Discours sur l'Ode* (1693) and *Réflexions sur Longin* (1694). The dispute died down, and Boileau, in a letter to Perrault (1700), recognized, within certain limits, the equality in literary merit of the 17th century to any period of antiquity. See also *Classicisme, Du Bos, Houdar de La Motte,* and *Dacier, Mme.*

Que sais-je?, see Appendix I, § H (ii).

Quesnay, FRANÇOIS (1694–1774), a physician and political economist, founder of the group of the physiocrats or *Économistes* (q.v.). He was protected by Mme de Pompadour. He contributed articles on *Fermiers* and *Grains* to the *Encyclopédie*, and was author of *Le Tableau économique* (1758) and *Le Droit naturel* (1765).

Quesnel, PASQUIER (1634–1719), regarded by the Jesuits as the chief of the Jansenists after the death of Antoine Arnauld (q.v.), was author of *Réflexions morales sur le Nouveau Testament* (1671, re-edited 1699), a work of great popularity which provoked papal condemnation by the Bull *Unigenitus*; its whole trend was hostile to the Jesuit teaching.

Quesnes de Béthune, see *Conon de Béthune.*

Quiberon, a small peninsula on the southwest coast of Brittany, was in July 1795 the scene of a disastrous attempt at a Royalist insurrection. A party of *émigrés* escorted by an English squadron landed there and was joined by insurgents from the Vendée under the leadership of Cadoudal (q.v.). They were met by General Hoche (q.v.) and his forces and driven back into the peninsula and the sea. The efforts of the English squadron to cover the re-embarkment were futile. Many were drowned. Others, hoping to save their lives, attempted to surrender, but Hoche had orders to take no prisoners. This failure, and the loss of over 1,200 lives, left bitter feelings among the Royalists.

Quicherat, JULES-ÉTIENNE-JOSEPH (1814–82), younger brother of the following, one of the foremost French archaeologists of the 19th century, also historian, author of *Procès de condamnation et de réhabilitation de Jeanne d'Arc* (1841–9); *Histoire de Sainte-Barbe* (1860–4), a work of importance for the history of education in France; *Mélanges d'archéologie et d'histoire* (1885–6).

Quicherat, LOUIS-MARIE (1797–1884), philologist. He compiled Latin–French and French–Latin dictionaries, wrote on Latin and French versification and on music, and also published *Mélanges de philologie* (1879).

Quietism, a form of religious mysticism, originated prior to 1675 by Miguel Molinos (1640–96), a Spanish priest, consisting in passive devotional contemplation, with extinction of the will and complete abandonment to the Divine Presence. Quietism was advocated in France by Mme Guyon (Jeanne-Marie Bouvier de la Motte-Guyon, 1648–1717), a mystic, but was vigorously condemned by Bossuet, to whom any relaxation of the will and personal energy in the pursuit of virtue was repugnant. Mme Guyon's ideas were in part supported by Fénelon in his *Explication des Maximes des Saints* (1697); Bossuet's views were stated in his *Instruction sur les états d'oraison* (1697) and *Relation sur le quiétisme* (1698). Molinos was arrested by the Roman Inquisition in 1685 and two years later was sentenced to perpetual imprisonment. Mme Guyon was imprisoned from 1695 to 1703. The Quietist doctrine was condemned by Innocent XII in 1699. There is a good deal about Quietism in Shorthouse's novel *John Inglesant*.

Quinault, JEANNE-FRANÇOISE (*c.* 1700–83), a clever actress, remarkable also for her taste and judgement in literary matters. Her house was a centre of literary and philosophical society (d'Alembert, Diderot, &c.). Voltaire addressed a number of letters to her.

Quinault, PHILIPPE (1635–88), son of a Paris baker and educated by Tristan l'Hermite, a dramatist who with Thomas Corneille occupied the interval in the history of French drama between the zenith of Pierre Corneille and the rise of Racine. His most successful tragedy was *Astrate, roi de Tyr* (q.v., 1664; it was ridiculed by Boileau) His other chief tragedies were *La Mort de Cyrus* (1656) and *Amalasonte* (1657). In the plots of all these the element of love predominates. Of his comedies, which show greater talent, *La Mère coquette* (q.v., 1665) was very successful. *L'Amant indiscret* (1654) supplied Dryden with some touches for his adaptation of Molière's *L'Étourdi*. After 1670 Quinault devoted himself to opera, and wrote libretti for the composer Lulli, introducing dramatic action in the old *ballets*. His principal operas were *Cadmus et Hermione* (1673), *Alceste* (1674), *Atys* (1676), *Persée* (1682), *Phaéton* (1683), *Roland* (1685), and *Armide* (1686).

Quincampoix, rue, a street—one of the oldest—in Paris, near the Bourse, in which John Law (q.v.) established his bank in 1716; often mentioned in connexion with Law's financial schemes.

Quinet, EDGAR (1803–75), historian, mainly interested in the philosophy of history, was born at Bourg-en-Bresse. After travels in Greece, Italy, and Germany, and a period as Professor of Foreign Literature at Lyons, he was appointed to the Chair of Language and Literature of Southern Europe at the Collège de France (1842). Here (cf. his friend Michelet, with whom he wrote *Les Jésuites*, an attack on ultramontanism) his views on matters political and educational led to the suppression of his lectures. He was a Deputy to the *Assemblée nationale* in 1848 and again after 1870 (having spent the years following the *coup d'état* of 1851 in exile in Belgium and Switzerland). He was an idealistic patriot, fundamentally religious for all his anti-clericalism, and a worker in the cause of educational freedom. His autobiographical fragment, *Histoire de mes idées* (1855), is an interesting account of his early years.

His many historical, philosophical, and religious writings include: *Idées sur la philosophie d'histoire* (1827, a translation, with a prefatory *Essai*, of Herder's *Philosophie der Geschichte*); *L'Allemagne et la révolution* (1831, a prophetic study of the Prussian menace to France); *Les Révolutions d'Italie* (1848–52); *Histoire de la Révolution* (1865); also *Le Génie des religions* (1842), one of a contemplated series of works which would have formed a universal history of religious and social revolutions. It describes the religions of antiquity and the civilizations associated with them; the development of the idea of a Divinity before whom all men are equal, and the emergence, out of this idea, of democratic theories of political equality. The work is a witness to the keen mid-nineteenth century interest in oriental studies.

Quinet also published several poetical works, heavy reading for the most part, semi-philosophical, obscurely symbolical and allegorical, but showing a powerful imagination. Some of them may have influenced Rimbaud (q.v.). *Ahasuérus* (1833), one of the earliest, is a dramatic epic, in dialogued prose, in which the Wandering Jew of legend incarnates humanity's march across the ages. It consists of a Prologue, four *journées*, and an Epilogue. The *journées* (*La Création*; *La Passion*; *La Mort*—the period from the Middle Ages to the end of the known world —and *Le Jugement dernier*) are linked together by *interludes*. Among the others were: *Napoléon* (1836), verse; *Prométhée* (1838), verse; *Les Esclaves* (1853), a verse-drama, with Spartacus for hero; and *Merlin l'enchanteur* (1860), prose.

Quinquina, Le, a poem by La Fontaine, published in 1682. *Quinquina* is the cinchona bark, from which quinine is derived. Its value as a febrifuge was learnt by the Spaniards from the Indians of South America, and it was introduced into Europe in the 17th century. The poem relates the opening of Pandora's box and the dissemination of the evils that afflict mankind, the worst of them being fever; the virtues of the remedy are then described.

Quinze joyes de mariage, Les, a work formerly attributed to Antoine de la Sale, but probably by an ecclesiastic of somewhat earlier date (early 15th century).

It is a satirical description of the tribulations to which marriage exposes a man, who is likened to a fish which, seeing other fishes imprisoned in a net, is not satisfied till it likewise gets inside and then can never get out again. His tribulations are attributed to the failings of his wife, such as her frivolity, avarice, infidelity, love of fine clothes, of bullying while posing as a martyr. In spite of division into fifteen heads the work shows a lack of systematic treatment. Under each head the wife betrays much the same defects, and the husband is the victim of much the same misfortunes, which generally resolve themselves into impoverishment, complete subjection, and reduction to imbecility. The husband is a poor creature from the outset, weak, credulous, and stupid. The merits of the work are the lively, realistic illustrations of everyday life, the incidents of a pilgrimage, the wife's cajoleries, her plottings with her gossips, the conspiracy in which these and even the confessor join to convince the husband that his eyes misled him when he found his wife with her lover. The work was translated into English as *The Fifteen Comforts of Matrimony* (1682).

Quinze-Vingts, Hospice des. In the Middle Ages this present-day national hospital for the blind was a hospice for blind paupers and beggars, who made it a flourishing self-governing community. Founded originally by Louis IX (*c.* 1260), it is said (doubtfully) to have been intended for 300 (*quinze* × *vingt*) crusaders released by the Saracens after their eyes had been put out.

Quotidienne, La, a daily paper, outspokenly anti-Revolutionary, founded in 1792. It existed precariously till 1797, when it ceased publication and was revived only at the return of the Bourbons in 1814. It was Royalist and Legitimist throughout the Restoration and the July monarchy, widely read both in Paris and the provinces in ecclesiastical and ex-*émigré* circles. La Harpe and Fontanes (qq.v.) were early contributors. In 1847 it was amalgamated with two other papers.

R

Rabbe, ALPHONSE (1786–1830), a publicist and hack historian in his lifetime, also a friend of some of the Romantic writers, left a remarkable *Album d'un pessimiste*, first published in 1835. It contains essays and meditations (with such titles as *Philosophie du désespoir*; *Horreur*; *L'Enfer d'un maudit*) written under the mental and physical stress of a painfully disfiguring infection contracted in his youth.

Rabelais, FRANÇOIS (1494?–*c.* 1553), physician, humanist, and satirist, born near Chinon in Touraine, probably at La Devinière, a farm-house belonging to his family. His father was a lawyer of Chinon.

Nothing is known of his early years. In 1520 he was a member of the Franciscan convent of Fontenay-le-Comte in Bas-Poitou, and there remained till 1524 and was ordained priest. During this period he showed his humanistic tastes, studied Greek (receiving encouragement from Budé and incurring the persecution of his monastic superiors), and obtained a reputation for learning among his friends, who included André Tiraqueau (q.v.). In 1524 he obtained permission to remove to the Benedictine convent of Maillezais, through the protection of Geoffroy d'Estissac, Bishop of Maillezais. Of this wealthy and enlightened prelate Rabelais became the secretary, travelling with him about his estates in Poitou and making the acquaintance of men of learning. He left Poitou about 1528 and probably spent the next two years visiting various provincial universities and perhaps studying medicine in Paris. He now abandoned the cowl and betook himself to Montpellier, where in December 1530 he received the degree of bachelor of medicine, and in the following year lectured on Hippocrates and Galen. In 1532 he settled at Lyons, then a centre of great literary activity, and published in that year editions of the medical letters in Latin of the Ferrarese physician Manardi, of the *Aphorisms* of Hippocrates, and of the *Lucii Cuspidii Testamentum* (a Latin document which was subsequently discovered to be a fabrication). In November of the same year he was appointed physician to the municipal hospital of Lyons. He thrice visited Rome (1534, 1535–6, 1548–50) as physician to his friend and protector, Cardinal Jean du Bellay, forfeiting his appointment at the hospital by his absence without leave. On the second of these visits, by a *Supplicatio pro Apostasia*, he obtained from the Pope absolution for his breaches of ecclesiastical discipline. In 1540–1 he was at Turin, in attendance on Guillaume du Bellay, Governor of Piedmont, the cardinal's brother. In 1550 he was appointed to two livings, Meudon near Paris and Jambet near Le Mans, but appears to have discharged personally the duties of neither. Nothing further is known of his life. He died before 1 May 1554.

Rabelais was held in high regard by his contemporaries as an eminent physician, as a pioneer of humanism, and as the author of an entertaining book. It is in this last capacity that he is chiefly known to posterity. He published *Pantagruel* (q.v.), the first instalment of his great work, late in 1532 or in 1533; *Gargantua* (q.v.) in 1534; the *Tiers Livre de Pantagruel* in 1546; part of the *Quart Livre* in 1548 and the whole Book in 1552. The authenticity of the Fifth Book is questionable; it certainly contains work by other hands and was perhaps worked up from fragments and imperfect or rejected drafts left by Rabelais at his death. The first sixteen chapters of it, under the title of *L'Isle sonnante*, appeared in 1562, the whole Book in 1564. For a summary of the contents of these Books see under *Gargantua* and *Pantagruel*.

The work does not form a single artistic whole. Composed at intervals over twenty years, it varies greatly in character as the spirit moved the author or circumstances prompted; it is loosely held together by a thread of narrative and abounds in digressions. We have in the first two Books the fantastic tale of a family of giants, written (so Rabelais tells us) in moments of relaxation for the solace of the sick, though occasion is taken to expose the author's views on education, the monks, and the theologians. In the Third Book the fantastic features are abandoned and we pass to a series of amusing and dramatic discussions of the questions of the day. The Fourth and Fifth Books take us on a voyage to Cathay and provide occasion for satire and propaganda suited to the political views of the French court. The interest of the whole lies in the vivid picture it gives not only of French society in the early days of the Renaissance but also of the Protean author himself: his enthusiastic humanism, his love of life in all its manifestations and hatred of asceticism, his interest in knowledge of all kinds, above all his contempt for monkery and scholasticism. He was an enlightened reformer of education (witness the systems he drew up for Gargantua and Pantagruel). His description of the abbaye de Thélème (in *Gargantua*) is inspired by confidence in the essential rightness of human instincts. His precise attitude to religion is a question of some difficulty. He was undoubtedly a supporter of the earlier evangelical Reformers, but was repelled by the rigidity of Calvin. His writings suggest that for dogma and forms of religion of any kind he had little sympathy. He is above all a realist, and carries on and develops the doctrine of Jean de Meung, the cult of uncorrupted nature. The passages of gross indecency, the physiological and medical obscenities that (especially in the first two Books) offend the modern reader, must be explained partly as the outpourings of the irrepressible jester writing for a coarse and outspoken society, but in part, also, as a realist's presentation of life in all its activities, or indeed a humanist's, who believes that no aspect of life is contemptible or should be concealed.

Rabelais's picture of French society includes all conditions of men: rustics at their labours and games, artisans, merchants, monks, country gentlemen, and professional men, particularly doctors and lawyers. Sketches of the latter and their proceedings are especially rich and varied. The university world, professors and students, its solemnities and diversions, its quarrels and jargon, are very fully depicted.

Rabelais's style has rare qualities of vividness, harmony, and strength. The wealth of his vocabulary is extraordinary; he adopts dialectal terms and invents new words. He is perhaps at his best in dialogues and snatches of conversation. He draws largely on his knowledge of the classics, weaving quotations and reminiscences into his text so naturally as at times almost to defy detection.

The work aroused the anger of the theologians and was condemned by the *parlement*. In 1542 Rabelais issued a revised edition of the first two Books. In this he attenuated the various insulting references to the theologians, but the hostility of the Sorbonne was unabated and *Gargantua* and *Pantagruel* were once more condemned in 1543. The Fourth Book was condemned in 1543, Rabelais's friend Tiraqueau being one of the judges. But Rabelais had the ear of the king and the more enlightened classes. He wrote no other original work of any importance, his *Prognostication Pantagrueline*, published under the pseudonym Maistre Alcofribas in 1533, being no more than a facetious forecast of events in the coming year, a parody of popular almanacks of the kind. In later ages he has been variously judged. Molière borrowed from him, Voltaire and later Balzac imitated him; but many saw ground for censure in his obscenities. His work was soon known in England (for instance to Gabriel Harvey, John Donne, and Francis Bacon), and various later English authors (such as Sterne) were indebted to him. The first three Books were translated by Sir Thomas Urquhart (two being published in 1653, the third in 1693); the last two by Peter Anthony Motteux in 1693–4.

Rabouilleuse, La (1840), by Balzac, one of the 'Scènes de la vie de province' of his *Comédie humaine* (q.v.). It follows *Pierrette* and *Le Curé de Tours* as the third tale of the trilogy *Les Célibataires*. The brothers Bridau are contrasting characters. Joseph, the younger, a painter of genius, sacrifices himself to care for his mother. She is far more devoted to Philippe, the elder, a debauched cad and profligate since his career as an army officer was cut short by the fall of Napoleon. The Bridau affairs reach such a pass, thanks to Philippe's continual excesses and crimes, that Mme Bridau goes from Paris to the provincial town of Issoudun in hopes of raising money from her wealthy brother, M. Rouget, whom she has not seen since her girlhood. Joseph goes with her. Their attempt fails, for M. Rouget, although he has so far managed to keep the final disposal of his fortune in his own hands, is led by the nose by his housekeeper and mistress Flore Brazier (La Rabouilleuse) and her lover Max Gilet, a third member of the household. Gilet, also a former officer of Napoleon's army, has, like Philippe Bridau, become a gangster in civil life. Max and Flore plot to get hold of M. Rouget's fortune but are beaten at their own game of criminal intrigue when Philippe Bridau, a much stronger antagonist than his mother or Joseph, arrives. Philippe provokes a duel, kills Max, and gets the old man and Flore into his power. Now nothing but a heartless, calculating monster, he persuades M. Rouget to marry Flore and make over his wealth to her. He then causes Rouget's death by indirect methods, marries Flore himself and thus secures the money. He throws in his lot with the Royalists, regains a high position in the army, and aspires to a title and—if he can get rid of his wife—a rich marriage. His dying mother begs him to help his brother Joseph whom, earlier in the book, he had robbed. His cold, insulting refusal reaches her on her death-bed and finally opens her eyes to his hateful character. Meanwhile Flore, as he had planned, is dying of drink and vice. But from now on his plans miscarry, his evil character is recognized or suspected, he speculates and loses heavily during the July revolution, has to return to active service, and is killed. His artist brother inherits what wealth he leaves.

Notable passages in this gloomy but powerful book are the descriptions of the enforced deterioration in the Bridau way of life, of the parsimonious household of M. and Mme Hochon (Mme Bridau's godmother) at Issoudun, and of the malicious, gossiping inhabitants of that town. [*Rabouilleur, rabouilleuse*, is dialect for the person who, in fresh-water crayfishing, troubles the water, thus causing the fish to rise and get caught in the nets. Flore Brazier had acted as *rabouilleuse* for her uncle in childhood.]

Racadot, one of the seven young *déracinés* in the novel *Les Déracinés* (q.v.) by Maurice Barrès.

Racan, HONORAT DE BUEIL, SEIGNEUR DE (1589–1670), poet, born on the borders of Anjou and Maine of a military family, was page to Henri IV and later entered the army, but his rusticity hindered his career and at the age of thirty-nine he retired to his estates in Touraine. He was, within somewhat narrow limits, a true poet, a lover of rural nature and a disciple of Malherbe (of whom he wrote a life), though neglectful of the latter's rigid rules. He was author of *Stances sur la retraite* (c. 1618, a fine poem on the theme of Horace's *Beatus ille qui procul negotiis*), one or two other good lyrics, and *Bergeries*, a sort of pastoral comedy (1625, previously produced as *Arthénice* in 1619) containing graceful and harmonious verse but poor on the dramatic side. In his later years he paraphrased the Psalms in a great variety of metrical forms.

Rachel, or **Mademoiselle Rachel,** the stage name of ÉLISABETH (known familiarly as ÉLISA) FÉLIX (1820–58), a celebrated tragic actress of Jewish descent, born in Switzerland. As a young girl she was a street-singer. She had her first triumph in 1838 as Camille in Corneille's *Horace*. She played Corneille and Racine, and was also particularly successful as Adrienne Lecouvreur in the play of that name by Scribe and Legouvé (qq.v.). Sainte-Beuve in a contemporary article notes the revival of the Comédie-Française under her influence. She visited England in 1841.

Rachilde [pseud. of Mme Alfred Valette, *née* MARGUERITE EYMERY] (1860–1953), literary critic and author of some sixty novels (most of them daring in a ninetyish manner). With her husband she founded *Le Mercure de France* (q.v.), one of the best-known French literary reviews, famous for its connexion with the Symbolist movement. Her memoirs (*Quand j'étais jeune*, 1948) give an interesting picture of the Symbolist milieu.

Racine, JEAN (1639–99), dramatist, was born at La Ferté-Milon near Soissons in what is now the department of the Aisne;

his father held the office of *procureur* in his bailiwick. Racine was soon left an orphan in the care of a Jansenist grandmother and from 1655 was educated at the schools of Port-Royal, where he acquired, besides the Jansenist doctrines, a wide knowledge of Greek and Latin literature. In 1658, having already shown, by some odes on the scenery of Port-Royal, his poetic vocation, he went to the Collège d'Harcourt in the University of Paris. From this time Port-Royal and the profane world contended for him. Racine frequented the society of actors, wrote an ode on the marriage of Louis XIV (*La Nymphe de la Seine*, 1660), was protected by Chapelain, and obtained a small pension. His family removed him to Uzès, in Languedoc, to the care of an uncle who was himself a cleric, with a view to his adopting an ecclesiastical career, but in 1662 he returned, published further odes, and was on more or less friendly terms with Boileau (who exercised a valuable influence over him), Molière, for a time, and La Fontaine. In 1664 Molière produced Racine's first tragedy, *La Thébaïde* (for the subjects of this and other plays by Racine see under their titles), followed by *Alexandre le Grand* (1665), which, although not masterpieces, made their author famous. The latter play was shortly withdrawn by Racine from Molière's theatre and transferred to the Hôtel de Bourgogne, whence arose a breach between the two authors. Racine now quarrelled definitely with Port-Royal, intervening with acrimony in the quarrel between Nicole (q.v.) and Desmarets on the side of the latter. His *Andromaque* (1667) rivalled Corneille's *Le Cid* in its success, and in 1669, after the appearance of his comedy *Les Plaideurs* in 1668, he challenged the older dramatist on his own ground with the political play *Britannicus*. The contest was repeated in 1670, and the younger poet was held the victor, when his *Bérénice* and the *Tite et Bérénice* of Corneille appeared almost simultaneously, though the story is now doubted that this was by the contrivance of the duchesse d'Orléans (Henriette d'Angleterre, q.v.). Racine's other great plays followed: *Bajazet* (1672), *Mithridate* (1673), *Iphigénie* (1674), *Phèdre* (1677). He was admitted to the *Académie* in 1673. But he had, from the days of *Alexandre*, always had critics and enemies. A rival *Iphigénie* was hastily concocted by inferior poets to damp the success of Racine's play; an influential cabal contrived that his *Phèdre* should be opposed by the *Phèdre et Hippolyte* of the obscure Pradon. Racine now decided to abandon the theatre; he repented of his dramatic writing and was reconciled with Port-Royal. He married in 1677 and was in the same year appointed by Louis XIV his historiographer, together with Boileau. He took his new duties seriously and accompanied the king on journeys and campaigns. (There is some gentle mockery of the 'two poets' employed in this capacity in Mme de Sévigné's letters.) In 1689 and 1691 Racine wrote at Mme de Maintenon's request the two religious dramas *Esther* and *Athalie* for performance by the young ladies of the school of Saint-Cyr. His later writings include four *Cantiques spirituels*; a memorandum on the sufferings of the people which was said by his son Louis Racine (see the following) to have brought him into royal disfavour; and an *Abrégé de l'histoire de Port-Royal* (published in part in 1742 and wholly in 1747), but he wrote nothing further for the theatre.

The tragedies of Racine follow in their main features those of Corneille : in their observance of the unities, in their concentration on the exposition of character, in the acute spiritual conflicts that they display, and in the exclusion of everything irrelevant to the main theme. But they differ from Corneille's tragedies in certain important respects. Instead of presenting the will as triumphing over instinct and circumstance, they show it as feeble and vacillating (here Jansenist influence may be suspected); the interplay of conflicting motives leads to the final solution. Racine's characters are more real and human than Corneille's. The 'majestic grandeur' of Corneille gives place to the 'sublime and touching charms' of Racine (Valincour). The choice of so many themes from Greek originals points to the influence of Hellenism in Racine's education. His style is simple and natural, smooth and polished, less oratorical than Corneille's. His most striking characters are women: Phèdre, Andromaque, Hermione, Monime, Roxane, Athalie. Racine 'inaugurated the literature of the passions of the heart' (Brunetière); but love and women in his plays, it has been pointed out, are subversive and anti-social

forces, leading not to heroism but to forgetfulness of duty, unhappiness, and crime. He was widely criticized in his own day for what was regarded as the crude realism of his dramas (notably *Phèdre*), the interplay of common, if intense, passions in characters of no exceptional grandeur. La Bruyère said of Corneille and Racine that 'celui-là peint les hommes comme ils devraient être, celui-ci les peint tels qu'ils sont'.

While Corneille was soon appreciated in England, Racine was at first less favourably received, and it was not till the beginning of the 18th century that adaptations of his plays (*Phaedra and Hippolitus*, 1706, by Edmund Smith; *The Distrest Mother*, 1712, from *Andromaque*, by Ambrose Philips) met with considerable success.

Racine, LOUIS (1692–1763), poet, son of the preceding. He was educated by the Jansenists and wrote didactic poetry of little merit (on *La Grâce*, 1720, and *La Religion*, 1742, his chief work), also pious, but sometimes less than veracious, memoirs of his father, and essays on poetry and the dramatic art. He translated Milton's *Paradise Lost* into French prose.

Racine et Shakspeare (1823, 1825), two pamphlets by Stendhal in defence of *le Romantisme* (q.v.), appeared first in the *Paris Monthly Review*, nos. 9 and 12. Stendhal, whose particular concern was with the drama, defined *romantisme* as the element in literature which satisfies a continually changing criterion of beauty. All great writers, he declared, had been romantic in their day, becoming classic only with the lapse of time. Racinian and Shakespearian tragedy could both be termed romantic, the first because it depicted the passions, the second because it treated the catastrophic events of history and laid bare the workings of the human heart. Shakespearian tragedy, because unhampered by the unities of time and place, was more truly romantic: it could emphasize the eternal theme of tragedy, change of heart, and thus more easily follow the psychological development of the characters. Romantic tragedy of the future, he concluded, should spread the action over several months and several happenings. It should, further, be written in prose so as to secure perfect freedom of expression.

The chapter 'Le Rire' in this work is largely a study of comedy.

Radiguet, RAYMOND (1903–23), an author who died aged twenty, having already written two brilliant novels of psychological analysis, *Le Diable au corps* (1923), a study of adolescence forced to a precocious maturity in time of war, and *Le Bal du comte d'Orgel* (1924) which, from its analogies of situation and treatment, might be termed a sort of latter-day *Princesse de Clèves* (q.v.). A remarkably clear, confident, penetrating style is a feature of both works.

Ragotin, see *Roman comique*.

Ragueneau, CYPRIEN or FRANÇOIS (d. 1654), pastry-cook, actor, and poet. He carried on the former trade in Paris about 1640–50, but failed in it no less than as a poet. He joined nomadic companies of actors (including it is said that of Molière) in some humble capacity. He was celebrated by Rostand in *Cyrano de Bergerac*.

Rains, Chronique de, see *History* (medieval period).

Rais, GILLES DE, see *Retz*.

Raison, Fêtes de la, were instituted during the Revolution as part of a movement to eradicate Christianity. The first was held in Notre-Dame in November 1793. The church was draped inside so as to disguise whatever might recall the Catholic faith. A small temple was erected with the inscription 'A la Philosophie' and, on either side, a bust of Voltaire and of J.-J. Rousseau. An actress from the Opera played the part of the Goddess of Reason and emerged from her temple to receive the homage of the people.

Raison par alphabet, La, the title given by Voltaire to later editions of his *Dictionnaire philosophique portatif* (see *Dictionaries and Encyclopedias*, under date 1764).

Raison raisonnante, La, an expression used by Taine (q.v.) to signify the dogmatic and pedantic disquisitions, verging on the sermon or the political harangue, to be found in much of the later 18th-century drama, notably in La Chaussée and Diderot, and even in Voltaire.

Rambaud, ALFRED (1847–1905), historian, author of *Histoire de la civilisation française des*

origines à nos jours (1885–7) and of many studies of foreign (especially Russian) and French colonial history. He was joint editor, with Ernest Lavisse (q.v.), of an *Histoire générale du IVe siècle à nos jours* (1891–1900).

Rambouillet, Château de, some twenty miles south-west of Versailles, originally belonged to the Angennes family (see the article below). François Ier died there. The estate passed into the hands of the comte de Toulouse, and later of Louis XVI, and at the Revolution became national property. (It is now the French 'Chequers'.)

Rambouillet, Hôtel de, in Paris (on part of the site of the present Palais-Royal), the intellectual centre of the best Parisian society in the first half of the 17th century. It was the town house of Catherine de Vivonne, marquise de Rambouillet (1588–1665), born in Rome, a kindly intelligent woman, serious and learned without being pedantic, who had been married when only twelve years old to Charles d'Angennes, later marquis de Rambouillet. There, over a period stretching from about 1618 to 1650, and with her daughter Julie d'Angennes (who became duchesse de Montausier), she used to receive, besides many persons of high rank, most of the eminent writers and wits of the day, including Malherbe, Racan, Gombauld, Conrart, Vaugelas, Chapelain, Voiture, Saint-Évremond, La Rochefoucauld, the Scudérys, Ménage, Costar, Mme Cornuel; even Bossuet appeared there, and Corneille for a time. The conversation was on every kind of subject—the news or scandal of the day, the latest literary event (the relative merits, for instance, of Voiture's sonnet on Uranie and Benserade's sonnet on Job), points of ethics, the precise character of certain sentiments, or the meaning of certain words. Mme de Rambouillet was known in her circle as Arthénice, an anagram of Catherine. Her *salon* (though not the first of its kind) set the example for many others, such as those of Mme de Sablé and Mme de Longueville. Its influence on French literature, an influence which was at its zenith 1642–8, has been variously estimated. It brought into fashion preciosity, that is a delicacy of thought and of the language used to express it, which checked and disciplined what was spontaneous and coarse. It thus had a clarifying but narrowing tendency. This quality was in time carried to excess, for instance in the cult of the periphrasis in place of the proper name for a thing. The *précieuses*, as the ladies were called who practised it, were ridiculed for their pedantry and affectation, and Boileau, Racine, and Molière reacted against it. But some of the locutions of the *précieux* have survived (such as 'travestir sa pensée') and their practice helped to simplify spelling. See also *Somaize* and *Guirlande de Julie*.

Rameau, JEAN-PHILIPPE (1683–1764), born at Dijon, lived in Paris from 1721 and died there. For long an organist by profession, he became famous in middle life as a composer of operas, ballets, and music for harpsichord, and as the author of important treatises on the theory of music, e.g. *Traité de l'harmonie* (1722), *Nouveau système de musique théorique* (1726), &c. He received a pension from Louis XV and held an appointment at court. See also *Neveu de Rameau*.

Raminagrobis, see *Pantagruel* (*Tiers livre*).

Ramond de Carbonnières, LOUIS-FRANÇOIS (1755–1827), born at Strasbourg, a geologist and pioneer in the study of mountains, translated W. Coxe's *Sketches of the natural, civil, and political state of Swisserland* (1779), adding original chapters of his own (1781), and was also author of *Observations faites dans les Pyrénées* (1789) and *Voyages au Mont-Perdu* (1801), containing remarkable descriptions of mountain scenery.

Ramus, see *La Ramée*.

Ramuz, CHARLES-FERDINAND (1878–   ), novelist, lived for long in Paris but later returned to his native Switzerland. His novels of French-Swiss country life include: *Aline* (1905); *Les Circonstances de la vie* (1907); *Jean Luc persécuté* (1909); *Vie de Samuel Belet* (1913); *Le Règne de l'esprit malin* (1917); *Terre du ciel* (1918), called *Joie dans le ciel* in later editions; *Les Signes parmi nous* (1920); *La Grande Peur dans la montagne* (1926), &c.

Rancé, L'ABBÉ ARMAND-JEAN LE BOUTHILLIER DE (1626–1700), son of a president of the Chambre des Comptes, held various benefices, including the abbacy of La Trappe (q.v.). He withdrew from worldly life in 1657 (in consequence, according to a doubtful story, of the death of the duchesse de Montbazon, whose lover he was), retired to this abbey in 1662, and reformed it, introducing there a rule of great austerity. Chateaubriand (q.v.) wrote a life of him (*Vie de Rancé*, 1844).

Randon, GABRIEL, see *Rictus, Jehan*.

Raoul (or **Rodolphe**), duc de Bourgogne, became King of France when the *Carolingien* (q.v.) King Charles III, *le Simple*, was deposed for the second time (923). He reigned till he died in 936. He came after Robert I, whose daughter he had married.

Raoul de Cambrai, a *chanson de geste* (q.v.) of the 12th century, one of the *Doon de Mayence* (q.v.) cycle, interesting for the light it throws on feudal sentiment. Raoul, having been awarded by the king the estate of Herbert of Vermandois, invades the territory and sacks and burns the town of Origny, with its convent and its nuns. Bernier, one of Herbert's grandsons, and squire of Raoul, faithful in his feudal allegiance, follows his lord and sees his mother burnt before his eyes. Bernier renounces his allegiance only when Raoul strikes him down for lamenting these calamities, and later he kills Raoul. But thereafter he is ever tormented by his broken oath, and spends his life in distant pilgrimages, seeking to allay his conscience; till one day Geri, uncle of Raoul, kills him where he himself had killed his lord.

Raoul de Houdenc, a 13th-century poet, author of didactic allegories, the *Songe d'Enfer* (see *Religious Writings*) and the *Roman des ailes de la courtoisie* (a description of the chivalrous virtues), and of a *roman breton*, *Méraugis de Portlesguez* (q.v.).

Raoul de Presles, see *Presles*.

Raphaël (1849), a short novel by Lamartine (q.v.), the romanticized account of his love for the 'Elvire' (q.v.) of many of his poems. In this she is called by her own name Julie.

Rapin, NICOLAS (1540?–1608), a gentleman of Poitou who fought at Ivry in the army of Henri IV, a poet of the school of Ronsard, and a collaborator in the *Satire Ménippée* (q.v.). He wrote in French and in Latin (*Les Plaisirs du gentilhomme champêtre, augmentés de quelques nouveaux poèmes et épigrammes*, 1583, &c.).

Rapin, RENÉ, known as *le père Rapin* (1621–87), a literary critic of merit, a Jesuit, author of *Réflexions sur la Poétique d'Aristote* (1674). This work is referred to in Congreve's *The Double Dealer*; it had been translated into English by Rymer in the year in which it appeared and was highly commended by Dryden. Rapin also wrote a *Traité de la manière d'écrire l'histoire*.

Rapin de Thoyras, PAUL DE (1671–1725), historian, a Huguenot who withdrew to Holland after the revocation of the edict of Nantes and accompanied William of Orange to England. He was author of an *Histoire d'Angleterre* (1724) to the revolution of 1688, which was translated by Nicholas Tindal (1723–31).

Rappel, Le, a newspaper, a favourite of the working classes, representing the extreme opposition, was founded in 1869, the last year of the Second Empire. Its first number contained a stirring letter from Victor Hugo, then still in Guernsey, appealing for the 'rappel de la liberté par le réveil de la France'. It continued into the 20th century.

Raspail, FRANÇOIS-VINCENT (1794–1878), chemist and politician, born at Carpentras, was educated at the Seminary of Avignon. After 1815 he developed Republican sympathies, refused to enter the Church, and came to Paris where he gave lessons and studied science. He very quickly made his name in the field of organic chemistry, but after 1830, and again in and after 1848, his activities were frequently more political than scientific, and of an advanced revolutionary character. He served a long sentence in prison in the early years of the Second Empire, then lived in Belgium. He returned to France in 1869. He sat in the Chamber as Deputy for Lyons, then for Marseilles, but owed his position rather to his past career than to his political force.

Rastignac, EUGÈNE DE, one of the chief characters in Balzac's *Comédie humaine* (q.v.), belonged to the impoverished provincial nobility. He came to Paris from near Angoulême in 1819 to study law and stayed at the Pension Vauquer, where he met Goriot and the ex-convict Vautrin (see *Le Père Goriot*). In *Illusions perdues* and *Splendeurs et Misères des courtisanes* (qq.v.) his fortunes were to some extent linked with those of Lucien de Rubempré, Vautrin's protégé. In *L'Interdiction, La Peau de chagrin* (q.v.), *Une*

Fille d'Ève, La Maison Nucingen, La Cousine Bette (q.v.), &c., he appears at other stages of his career, pursuing riches, becoming a successful politician and a peer of France, and finally marrying the daughter of his first mistress, Mme de Nucingen, herself a daughter of old Goriot.

Ratisbonne, LOUIS (1827–1900), minor Parnassian poet (see *Parnassiens*) and a translator of Dante, was also a popular writer of tales and poems for children. They were moral, gentle, pleasing, and not without humour, e.g. *La Comédie enfantine* (1860).

Ravachol, —, 19th-century revolutionary and anarchist, one of a group who believed in propaganda by deed (i.e. bomb-throwing). He was denounced and arrested in 1892, and at his trial made an impassioned attack on the 'bourgeois' exploitation of the poor.

Ravaillac, FRANÇOIS (1578–1610), the assassin of Henri IV.

Ravaisson [**Ravaisson-Mollien**], FÉLIX (1813–1900), philosopher, one of the first French philosophers to react against the eclecticism of Cousin (q.v.). His works, in which the influence of Maine de Biran (q.v.) is strongly recognizable, include: *De l'habitude* (1838), his doctor's thesis; *Essai sur la métaphysique d'Aristote* (1837–46), one of the great philosophical treatises of the 19th century; and also a remarkable *Rapport sur la philosophie en France au XIXᵉ siècle*, written for the Great Exhibition of 1867 and published in that year. The important feature of his philosophy—which is sometimes called Neo-criticism, or Neo-spiritualism —was that it found a purely scientific explanation of the universe inadequate and insisted on the need for spiritual belief.

Ravel, MAURICE (1875–1932), composer, born at Cibourne, near Saint-Jean-de-Luz, lived mainly, and died, in Paris. Like Debussy he had many associations with the Symbolist Movement in literature and the Impressionist Movement in painting. He wrote various suites for piano and for orchestra and set many poems, e.g. by Mallarmé, Verlaine, to music (also Aloysius Bertrand's prose poems *Gaspard de la nuit*).

Ravignan, LE PÈRE XAVIER DE (1795–1858), a noted French preacher during the

Restoration and the July Monarchy, a Jesuit. He initiated the famous practice of Lenten sermons for men only at Notre-Dame. His own were delivered between 1837 and 1846. He had given up what was already, when he was only twenty-seven, a brilliant career in the magistracy to enter the Church.

Ravisius Textor, see *Tixier de Ravisi.*

Raynal, GUILLAUME, ABBÉ (1713–96), historian, one of the *encyclopédistes*, author of a long *Histoire philosophique et politique des établissements et du commerce des Européens dans les deux Indes* (1772). Its essential theme is the doctrine of our moral obligations to the lower races. It contains, besides much entertaining information on a great variety of subjects, many disquisitions against religion, despotism, slavery, &c., probably supplied in part by Diderot. It encouraged the revolutionary ardour of Toussaint Louverture among others. The work was suppressed by an order of the Council in 1772 and the author was in 1775 obliged to leave the country; but the work was widely read, some thirty editions appearing (with numerous additions from time to time) between 1772 and 1789. Raynal began in 1747 a literary correspondence with various German sovereigns which from 1753 was continued by Grimm (q.v.). In 1791 Raynal reproved the National Assembly for its errors and intolerance. His remonstrance was disregarded and his property was confiscated, so that he died in extreme poverty. He was a fellow of the Royal Society of London. Among the letters of the poet Cowper is one (7 May 1778) devoted to the praise of Raynal. Horace Walpole, after having commended his work as 'the most amusing book that tells one everything in the world', found the author himself a tiresome bore, and pretended to be deaf to escape his importunities.

Raynal, PAUL (1885–   ), dramatist, made his name with *Le Maître de son cœur* (1920), a drama of love and jealousy, and *Le Tombeau sous l'Arc de Triomphe* (1924). This 'modern tragedy', as the author calls it, of the 1914–18 war, contrasted the miseries of the trenches with the comfort and security—
—which could at that time still be counted upon—of the civilians at home.

Raynaud, ERNEST (1864-1936), poet, in his youth an ardent Symbolist, at a later date helped to found the *École romane* (q.v., 1890), a movement opposed to some of the Symbolist doctrines. He was also in at the beginnings of the *Mercure de France* (q.v.). His poetical output includes the collections *Le Signe* (1887), *Chairs profanes* (1889), *Les Cornes du faune* (1890), *La Tour d'ivoire* (1899), &c. His reminiscences, *La Mêlée symboliste* (1918-23, 3 vols.) are full of interest.

Raynouard, FRANÇOIS (1761–1836), born at Brignoles (Provence), was distinguished during his lifetime for his studies in medieval French language and literature (*Des Troubadours et des cours d'amour*, 1817; *Lexique roman*, 1838). He also wrote *Les Templiers* (1805), a tragedy which was one of the successes of the Parisian stage during the Empire, perhaps owing to Talma's acting (q.v.). From 1817 Raynouard was Perpetual Secretary of the *Académie française.*

Rayons et les ombres, Les (1840), a collection of lyrics, the last of his first period, by Victor Hugo (q.v.). It contains some of his most famous poems, e.g. *Ce qui se passait aux Feuillantines vers 1813*, memories of childhood; *Tristesse d'Olympio* (q.v.); *La Statue*; *Oceano Nox* (q.v.); and *Fonction du poète*. In the last of these Hugo indicates his conception, elaborated in later life, of the poet as prophet, not the man of destiny as Lamartine (q.v.) conceived him, but the seer who recognizes those events of daily life which are destined to become historic, and who reads the fate of peoples in the sky.

Réaction thermidorienne, La, the period of reaction that followed the downfall of Robespierre on 27 July 1794 (the *Journée du 9 Thermidor,* q.v. and see also *Revolutions,* Ia). It ended with the establishment of the *Directoire* in October 1795.

Réalisme, Le, a movement in the French novel, at its height between 1850 and 1865. It reflected the interest of a progressively positivist and scientific age in material facts, and the general distaste for the vague enthusiasms of the Romantics (see *Romantisme*). The latter had called for 'la liberté dans l'art': the new slogan was 'la sincérité dans l'art'.

Stendhal, to some extent, and Balzac had been forerunners. Stendhal had maintained that the actions of his characters proceeded logically from the numerous small factors that composed their natures and influenced their motives (though it is to be noted that Stendhal's factors were moral rather than material). Balzac, who claimed for his novels a sociological value as studies of society, was more truly a precursor; and the theory of *documentation* which played a strong part in both the realistic and the naturalistic novel may be said to have derived from the scrupulous exactitude with which he set the stage for his stories. He made his characters known by his detailed observation of the material facts of their existence, the houses they lived in, their habits of life, the journeys they took, or their complicated business transactions. These aspects of Balzac and Stendhal were emphasized in essays by the critic and philosopher Taine (q.v.), who was himself one of the great forces behind *Réalisme* and *Naturalisme*. [The terms *Réalisme* and *Naturalisme* are often confounded, but although the two schools had much in common the doctrines of the extreme *naturalistes* went farther than those of the *réalistes*; see *Naturalisme*.]

The *réalistes* owed a more immediate debt to the painter Courbet (q.v.), who introduced realism into art before it was applied to literature. From 1848 onwards he had announced his intention of painting only the modern and the vulgar. His theories attracted a number of artists and writers, and were transposed from art to literature by Champfleury (q.v.), the novelist, who became the leader of the movement and wrote a number of now more or less unreadable novels, as well as *Le Réalisme* (1857), a manifesto of the new doctrines.

The aim of the intransigent realists was to give a scrupulous reproduction of life in all its aspects. The novel was to represent 'history that might have happened' (said the brothers Goncourt, q.v., and cf. Balzac's sociological conception of the novel). As such, it should be documented as a work of history would be, with the same careful regard for truth. Every fact, every detail of background, must be recorded without softening, or exaggeration, or incidental description, and without any care for style. Imagination and sensibility, love of form, the perfect rendering of sounds, sights, and colours, the effort to convey an idealized,

unreal beauty, no longer counted. Complicated plots, catastrophic events, or shattering passions, were falsifications of the truth. Subjects should be taken from contemporary, everyday life, and preferably from lower-class, petty-bourgeois or industrial life, where a more naked reality was to be found.

When Flaubert's novel *Madame Bovary* (q.v.) first appeared (in the *Revue de Paris* in 1856, in book form in 1857) it was hailed as a triumph of *réalisme* (and equally, at a later date, of *naturalisme*: Flaubert himself objected to such labels) because of its close observation of life, and because the action formed an unavoidable sequence of cause and effect due to the natures of the characters themselves. The book's greatness as a work of art was seldom noticed, or noticed only in negative fashion when some of the extreme *réalistes* decried it for being too carefully written. Another, more truly realistic novel was *Germinie Lacerteux* (1865), by Edmond and Jules de Goncourt, though this again by its style—the nervous, impressionistic style which these authors made peculiarly their own—differed from the ordinary realistic output. It exemplified the *réalisme* which believed that the general, in this case vice and debauchery and the demoralization of the working classes, could most vividly be realized from the close study of an exaggerated form of the particular, the particular being a servant, the victim of an abnormal form of hysteria, who sinks through drink, theft, vice, and the most brutal debauchery, and finally dies of consumption. Other *réalistes* were Ernest Feydeau (q.v.) with *Fanny* (1858), and Duranty (q.v.), who later called himself a *naturaliste*, with *Le Malheur d'Henriette Gérard* (1860, q.v.). At the hands of the extremist the realistic novel, when it was not merely the unselective accumulation of monotonous events, became the laborious depiction of vice, ugliness, and squalor. This feature was to be intensified by the *naturalistes*.

Réaumur, RENÉ-ANTOINE FERCHAULT DE (1683–1757), physicist and naturalist, born at La Rochelle, is remembered as the inventor of the Réaumur thermometer, which divides the interval between the freezing point of water (Réaumur: zero; Cent.: zero; Fahr.: 32°) and the boiling point into 80 equal parts (as against Cent.: 100;

Fahr.: 180). He also carried out researches on the manufacture of steel, lead, and porcelain, on artificial incubation, and on methods of preserving eggs. As a naturalist his interests were fish, bird-life, and insects; he published *Mémoires pour servir à l'histoire naturelle des insectes* (1736–42). Buffon, his younger contemporary, who showed some contempt for insects as subjects of study, extended this contempt unjustly to Réaumur.

Rebell, HUGUES [pseud. of Georges Grassal] (1867–1905), born at Nantes, wrote poetry (*Chants de la pluie et du soleil*, 1894); and novels, usually with elaborate historical settings and said to be reminiscent of those of Pierre Louÿs, e.g. *La Nichina* (1897, Venice during the Renaissance), *La Femme qui a connu l'Empereur* (1901), *La Saison à Baïa* (1901).

Reboux, PAUL, and **Muller,** CHARLES, see *Pastiche.*

Récamier, JEANNE-FRANÇOISE, MME, *née* Bernard (1777–1849), was born at Lyons, the daughter of a solicitor. In 1793 she married the rich and elderly Paris banker Récamier. She was a woman of great beauty, charm, and tact, who inspired many passions and had the gift of transforming them into devoted friendships. During the Napoleonic period and the Restoration the most eminent figures in literature and politics met in her *salon*. She was Mme de Staël's closest, perhaps her only, woman friend and for a time (*c.* 1815) was worshipped in vain, and to his own great exasperation, by Benjamin Constant (q.v.). From 1819, after some reverses of fortune, she lived, still in Paris, in rooms at l'Abbaye-aux-Bois, a convent with which was combined a sort of select *pension*. Here she continued her *salon*. Its acknowledged and cherished hero was Chateaubriand (q.v.), round whom her life from henceforward revolved. It was here that friends and admirers collected to listen to him reading passages from 'work in progress', his *Mémoires d'outre-tombe* (q.v.). The years passed. Chateaubriand died in 1848, Mme Récamier, by now totally blind, ten months later. Her *Souvenirs et correspondance* were edited by her niece Mme Lenormand. Two famous portraits of her, by David and by Gérard, may be recalled.

Recherche de l'absolu, La (1834), one of the 'Études philosophiques' of Balzac's *Comédie humaine* (q.v.). Balthazar Claes, the respected head of an old family of Flemish weavers, and for years a devoted husband and father, suddenly develops a passion for scientific research. In his zeal to find the 'absolute', the philosopher's stone which will convert all it touches to wealth, he ruins himself and his family. His wife dies after having struggled to save him from himself. His daughter, a firmer character, takes charge and restores the family fortunes for a time, but eventually she too is powerless. Balthazar dies a victim to his mania, leaving the family to face disaster.

Recherche de la vérité, La (1674–5), by Malebranche (q.v.).

Recherches de la France (1560–1621), by Étienne Pasquier (q.v.).

Reclus, ÉLISÉE (1830–1905), geographer and revolutionary, had to leave France in 1851 because of his Republicanism. He travelled in Europe and America, observed conditions, and wrote about his travels, and became a Communist. He returned to France in 1857 but was exiled after the Commune (q.v., 1871). The *Géographie universelle*, his claim to academic remembrance, was written abroad and published from 1875 to 1894.

Reclus de Molliens, see *Charité and Miserere.*

Recueillement, a famous sonnet by Baudelaire, in the 'Spleen et idéal' section of *Les Fleurs du mal* (1857).

Recueillements poétiques (1839), poems by Lamartine. It contains *La Vigne et la maison*, his last poetic masterpiece, in which he describes the home of his childhood (cf. *Milly*).

Redon, ODILON (1840–1916), French painter and lithographer (he illustrated Flaubert), one of those associated with Symbolisme (q.v.). He is mentioned in Huysmans's *A rebours* (q.v.).

Réflexions sur Longin, by Boileau, published in 1694. The author takes a succession of passages from the Greek treatise known as *Longinus on the Sublime* (of which he had published a translation) and uses them as texts of dissertations in which he defends against Charles Perrault the merits of the ancient classical authors, Homer and Pindar in particular.

Réfractaires, clergy who in 1791 refused to take the oath of allegiance to the *Constitution civile du clergé* (q.v.). In the later years of the Revolution they were tracked down ruthlessly and were liable to deportation if not summary execution.

In the mid-nineteenth century the term 'réfractaire' was sometimes used (e.g. by Louis Veuillot, Jules Vallès, qq.v.) to denote the journalistic hacks, hangers-on of literary circles, failures who had expected to reach the top of the tree without sacrifice or hard work and were ending their days in embittered poverty.

Régale, Droit de, the right, claimed by the kings of France, to the revenues of archbishoprics and bishoprics during any vacancy of those sees, together with the right to nominate to benefices dependent on them. This was the subject of a violent dispute between Louis XIV and Innocent XI (1677–82).

Régence, La, a term applied in particular to the regency (1715–23) of Philippe duc d'Orléans, nephew of Louis XIV, during the minority of Louis XV. It was a period of profligate reaction from the moral austerity of the latter years of Louis XIV and of liberal reaction from his political absolutism. It was marked by the disastrous fiscal experiment of Law (q.v.).

The other important regencies in French history were those of Anne de Beaujeu during the minority of her brother Charles VIII (1483–91), that of Marie de Médicis during the minority of Louis XIII (1610–21), and that of Anne of Austria during the minority of Louis XIV (1643–61; he attained his legal majority in 1651 but in fact remained in tutelage until Mazarin died, in 1661).

Régie, La. An industry is said to be *mise en régie* or *mise sous la régie* [from the verb *régir*] when it is controlled or monopolized by the State. (Cf. *tabacs de la Régie*: the tobacco monopoly in France goes back to 1674. It was abolished at the Revolution but re-established later and is now regulated by law.)

Regnard, JEAN-FRANÇOIS (1655–1709), comic dramatist, born in Paris, of a well-to-do *bourgeois* family, was long regarded as the nearest successor to Molière. He travelled extensively, and was taken by corsairs (1678) and held captive at Algiers till ransomed, an incident treated in his romance *La Provençale*. His *Voyage en Laponie* is likewise an account of his experiences. He wrote comedies first for the *Italiens*, and from 1695 for the Comédie-Française; of these the best known are *Le Joueur* (1696, q.v.), *Le Distrait* (1697), *Démocrite* (1700, q.v.), *Les Folies amoureuses* (1704, q.v.), *Les Ménechmes* (1705, q.v.), *Le Légataire universel* (1708, q.v.). Regnard was no moralist, but depicted a corrupt world with boundless gaiety, in a rich, picturesque, and lively style and in excellent verse. He also wrote some verse epistles and satires and other minor pieces.

Régnier, HENRI DE (1864–1936), poet and novelist, born at Honfleur (near Le Havre), came of a family whose interesting ancestral associations he sometimes used in his novels. He studied for the diplomatic service but gave this up to write both poetry and prose. He quickly became celebrated as a poet of *Symbolisme* (q.v.), and for his musical, supple employment of *le vers libre* (q.v.). The lyrics and *odelettes* collected, from the small reviews in which they were first printed, in *Poèmes anciens et romanesques* (1890), *Tel qu'en songe* (1892), *Jeux rustiques et divins* (1897) are typical of this phase. His poetry of later years returned to classical forms, with themes chosen mainly from antiquity, e.g. *Les Médailles d'argile* (1900), sonnets dedicated to André Chénier (q.v.); *La Sandale ailée* (1906), or *Le Miroir des heures* (1911). In *La Cité des eaux* (1902) he wrote of the deserted splendours of Versailles. Other, later, collections were: *1914–1916; poèmes* (1918) and *Vestigia flammae* (1921), which contains the tenderly evocative *Te souviens-tu, ô Roméo?* His earliest collections —*Lendemains* (1885), *Apaisement* (1886), *Sites* (1887, sonnets), *Épisodes* (1888)—had been faintly reminiscent of the *Parnassiens* (q.v.).

In the second half of his life Henri de Régnier, by now one of the most distinguished writers of the day, published several successful novels and tales. Some, in 17th-

and 18th-century settings, were written with an elaborate libertinism and in a highly decorative, precious style, e.g. *La Canne de jaspe* (1897, tales); *La Double Maîtresse* (1900), his best-known novel, which also had a psychological interest; *Les Rencontres de M. de Bréot* (1904). Others in a modern setting included: *Le Mariage de minuit* (1903), which used comte Robert de Montesquiou (q.v.) as a model for one of its characters, and *Les Vacances d'un jeune homme sage* (1903), an indulgent, amused, and highly sophisticated picture of provincial life and of calf-love.

Henri de Régnier married, in 1896, Marie, second daughter of the poet José-Maria de Heredia (q.v.) and herself an author (see *Houville, Gérard d'*).

Régnier, MATHURIN (1573–1613), satirist, born at Chartres, a nephew of Desportes (q.v.). He visited Italy several times, notably in the suite of the Cardinal de Joyeuse, the French envoy at the papal court (1593), but his dissolute habits hindered his advancement, in spite of his easy-going good-humoured temper. His interest in manners and characters led him to write his *Satires*, poems (in alexandrines) after the manner of the satires of Horace and Juvenal, compared by Sainte-Beuve to Flemish paintings. The first collection of these appeared in 1608. In them he describes with vigorous and amusing traits the physician, the poet, the hypocrite, the Gascon adventurer, &c. His ninth satire shows him in vigorous revolt against the peddling reforms of Malherbe and the purists. His general philosophy is that of Montaigne, that everything varies with the point of view of the individual, and that each should follow what his own reason or his situation dictates. The *Satires* raised Régnier to a high position in the public esteem, even in that of Malherbe, and later of Boileau; they prepared the way for Molière. Régnier also wrote some elegies and lyrics of less importance, but showing command of other metres besides the alexandrine.

Régnier, PAULE (1888–1950), was the author of one moderately successful novel, *L'Abbaye d'Évolayne* (1933), and some others (*Octave*, 1913; *La Vivante Paix*, 1924; *Les Filets dans la mer*, 1949) which did not pass unnoticed. Her *Journal*, published in 1951,

a year after her death by suicide, is more likely to preserve her memory.

She had been left badly deformed by an illness in infancy. She was poor, after an upbringing in easy circumstances that were badly reduced by the depredations of a fraudulent man of business a few years after her father's death in 1902. Her instinctive love of literature had received no encouragement from her parents, but she began to write when she was about twenty. She also, about 1912, formed a deep friendship, which on her side turned to unhappy love, with a man of her own age, a poet, who was killed in battle in 1915. She never got over his death. After her mother died in 1926 she lived alone. Her books made some literary contacts for her but she was poor, deformed, and sensitive, and seldom followed them up. She became more and more of a solitary, reading, writing, a prey to spiritual perplexities which conflicted with her desire for faith, increasingly overwhelmed by the material struggles of existence; and gradually she lost the will to live. The last entries in the diary were written the night before she died.

Régnier-Desmarais, FRANÇOIS-SÉRAPHIN (1632–1713), grammarian and poet, one of the *académiciens* principally concerned in the preparation of the 1694 (the first) edition of the *Dictionnaire de l'Académie française* (see under *Dictionaries and Encyclopedias*); author also of a *Traité de la grammaire française* (1705) which was both highly praised and severely attacked. His *Poésies françaises, italiennes, latines et espagnoles* were published in 1707–8.

Regrets, see *Du Bellay.*

Reichstadt, DUC DE, see *Napoleon II.*

Reinach, JOSEPH (1856–1921), politician and publicist, born in Paris, campaigned vigorously in the Press against *Boulangisme* (1889, q.v.) and in support of Dreyfus (1894, see *Dreyfus, L'Affaire*).

Reinach, SALOMON (1858–1932), brother of the foregoing, philologist, archaeologist, and art historian who wrote many valuable works on all these subjects. He was custodian of the national museum of Saint-Germain-en-Laye and head of the *École du Louvre* (for the study of the general history of art).

Reine Margot, La (1845), an historical romance by Dumas *père*. It introduces the massacre of St. Bartholomew.

Réjane, GABRIELLE-CHARLOTTE RÉJU (1857–1920), born in Paris, was one of the leading French actresses (in light comedy) between 1880 and her retirement in 1915. She was a memorable Madame Sans-Gêne in Sardou's (q.v.) historical comedy of this name and a 'provoking and irresistible' Clotilde in Henri Becque's *La Parisienne* (q.v.). She played with equal success in London, the U.S.A., and other countries.

Relations des Jésuites. The early Jesuit missionaries in Canada had to furnish yearly reports of their activities to their Superior-General in Quebec, who used them as material for the *Relations de ce qui s'est passé en la Nouvelle France* which he sent back to Paris to be printed and circulated (1632–72, and later editions). These *Relations* are of the greatest interest and are sometimes the only source for the early history of Canada.

Religieuse, La, a romance by Diderot, written in 1760, published in 1796. It had its origin in a mystification of which M. de Croismare, a credulous and charitable gentleman, was the victim. His friends Diderot and Grimm sent him a series of letters purporting to be addressed to him by an unfortunate nun (a real person), who had protested against her vows obtained by duress, imploring his protection.

The story is that of a girl whose parents have exhausted their means in endowing her elder sisters and condemn her to be a nun. It describes the cruel treatment by which she is forced to take the veil, the sufferings to which she is subjected in the cloister, her transfer to a convent under a dissolute superior, her escape and subsequent misfortunes.

Religieuse portugaise, see *Lettres portugaises*.

Religious oratory. For the 17th century, the great age of religious oratory in France, see *Bossuet, Bourdaloue, Fléchier, Massillon, Mascaron*. There was some revival of religious oratory in the 19th century, particularly the first half, see *Lacordaire, Dupanloup, Frayssinous, Ravignan*.

Religious writings and the religious element in French literature. (NOTE: The authors referred to in this article receive fuller mention under separate headings.)

MEDIEVAL PERIOD

(1) A church song, the *Séquence de sainte Eulalie*, is one of the earliest extant writings in French (*c.* 880). For early translations and imitations of parts of the Scriptures see under *Bible, French versions of the*. The earliest French text based on the Bible is a 10th-century poem, *La Passion de Clermont*, in octosyllabic quatrains. Religious writings in prose and verse are frequent from the 12th century: apocryphal narrations and legends, many with an origin in the early Eastern Church, about the Virgin Mary, Judas, Pilate, and a multitude of saints and martyrs (see *Saints, Lives of*). Notable poems about the Virgin Mary are the *Miracles de la Sainte Vierge* (*c.* 1220), a compilation by Gautier de Coincy (*c.* 1177–1236), a Benedictine monk, of instances of the Virgin's mercy to humble sinners: and the *Tombeur de Notre-Dame*, the story of a poor *jongleur* who devotes his skill as an acrobat to the service of the Virgin (cf. Anatole France's tale *Le Jongleur de Notre-Dame*, 1892, in *L'Étui de nacre*).

(2) Didactic works of Christian ethics were also numerous. Hélinand, a monk of noble family, wrote (*c.* 1195) eloquent *Vers de la mort* adjuring the worldly to think of the life hereafter. The *Poème moral* (13th c.) is a sincere exhortation, accompanied by many examples (including the life of St. Thaïs), to renounce the vanity of worldly joys. (See also *Besant de Dieu*; *Dîme de pénitence*; *Charité* and *Miserere*.) Some of these works took dialogue form: thus in the *Débat du corps et de l'âme* (12th c.), in couplets of six-syllabled verses, a soul reproaches the body, from which it has recently been separated, for causing its damnation, and the body retorts. (See also *Trois morts et des trois vifs, Dit des*.) Others were allegorical, such as the strange *Songe d'enfer* of Raoul de Houdenc, in which Lucifer is seen devouring usurers and other sinners. The *Somme des vices et des vertus* or *Somme le Roi* (1279), dedicated by a Dominican named Laurens to Philippe le Hardi, an encyclopedic treatise on Christian ethics, throws interesting light on social conditions in the 13th century. The *Manuel des péchés* by

William of Wadington, in Norman French of the 13th century, similarly illuminates English customs. It was adapted in English, under the title *Handling Synne*, by Robert Manning of Brunne in the same century.

(3) Thirteenth-century literature also contains a number of religious and edifying tales, such as *Barlaam et Josaphat*, the *exempla* taken from the Latin sermons of Jacques de Vitry, and the story of the *Chevalier au barisel* (qq.v.).

(4) The drama in France, as in England, had in its earliest phase a close relation with the Church through the gradual secularization of the liturgical plays performed at Christmas and Easter in the churches or their precincts. Originally written in Latin and performed by the clergy, they were as time passed transformed into vernacular plays by lay societies. Little of these early liturgical plays has survived. They dealt with such themes as the Annunciation, the Nativity, the Resurrection, or the raising of Lazarus. The earliest in which French (Provençal) is mingled with Latin in the text is the play of *L'Époux* ('Sponsus'), which dramatizes (in verse) the parable of the Wise and Foolish Virgins, and dates probably from the 11th century. In the 12th century we have the important *Jeu d'Adam*, written in Anglo-Norman eight-syllabled verse (with stage directions in Latin) and representing the Fall, the death of Abel, and the prophets of the Redemption. A later dramatic poem, also in Anglo-Norman, dealt with the Resurrection and presented apocryphal incidents connected with Longinus and Nicodemus, and finally with the Three Marys, to whom angels announce that the Lord is risen. Besides dramas connected with the principal events related in Holy Scripture, other religious plays represented incidents in the lives of saints. Of these, the *Jeu de saint Nicolas* (the patron of scholars and a favourite theme) referred to under *Bodel* is an example, though it was partly of a profane character. (See also under *Rutebeuf* for the *Miracle de Théophile*; and under *Miracles*; *Mystères*; *Confrérie de la Passion* for the further development of religious drama in the 14th and 15th centuries; and see *Noëls*; *Bible, French Versions*.)

Sixteenth and Seventeenth Centuries

(5) The Reformation added theology to the field of French literature. Calvin's French version (*Institution de la religion chrétienne*, 1541) of his earlier *Institutio religionis christianae* was the first theological work to be written in French and inspired many others. It also counts as an early formative influence on French prose style.

(6) Among post-Reformation poets those of the *Pléiade*, though primarily pagan in inspiration, turned at times to the Bible, e.g. Joachim du Bellay's *Monomachie de David et de Goliath* (1560), Remy Belleau's paraphrases of Ecclesiastes and the Song of Solomon, or *Les Amours de David et de Bethsabée* in his *Bergeries* (1572) or, like Ronsard in his *Discours*, defended the Catholic faith against the Protestant reform. The great poet of French protestantism was Agrippa d'Aubigné (*Les Tragiques*, 1616; *La Création*, written c. 1630). *La Semaine*, a grandiose, immensely long biblical epic by du Bartas describing the Creation of the world, appeared in 1578 and provoked a reply by Christofle de Gamon, also entitled *La Semaine*, in 1609. Other 17th-century authors of religious epics included, notably: Montchrétien, Saint-Amant, Desmarets de Saint-Sorlin, Godeau, and Le Moyne. Many poets, following the example of Clément Marot, wrote paraphrases of the Psalms, and religious canticles, e.g. Bertaut, Desportes, Malherbe (16th c.), and Godeau and Racan in the 17th century. Some were men who in their youth had chosen very different subjects. Two 16th-century religious poets, La Ceppède and Sponde, have appealed to the 20th-century interest in metaphysical and baroque verse.

(7) Du Vair, the humanist, wrote prose paraphrases of Psalms as well as meditations on books of the Scriptures. Other religious writers of importance were Pierre Charron and Saint François de Sales, as also the great preachers and ecclesiastical authors of the reign of Louis XIV (Bossuet, Bourdaloue, Fléchier, Massillon, and Fénelon) ; and the 17th century is remarkable for the emergence of Port-Royal and the Jansenists, above all of Pascal.

(8) In the field of drama, between Buchanan's *Baptistes sive calumnia* (1540) and Racine's *Esther* (1689) and *Athalie* (1691), the Bible provided subjects for Théodore de Bèze (*Abraham sacrifiant*, 1550), Jean de la Taille (*Saül le furieux*, 1572), Des Masures

(three *Tragédies saintes*, 1566), Robert Garnier (*Sédécie ou Les Juives*, 1583), Montchrétien (*David*, 1601; *Aman*, 1601), and Du Ryer (*Saül*, 1642; *Esther*, 1644). The conflict between paganism and Christianity is the theme of Corneille's tragedies *Polyeucte* (1641–2) and *Théodore* (1645).

NINETEENTH AND TWENTIETH CENTURIES

(9) Religious writings had been no feature of the 18th century, though *Le Journal de Trévoux* (1701–57), the organ of the Jesuits, and *Les Nouvelles ecclésiastiques* (1728–1803), the organ of the Jansenists, were among the earliest French periodicals. Religious sentiment revived, and could once more be openly expressed, after the *Concordat* (q.v.) of 1801, ratified 1802, gave Roman Catholicism official status as the national faith. Chateaubriand's work of Christian apologetics, *Le Génie du Christianisme*, was published aptly in 1803. It had been anticipated, to some extent, in 1801 by Ballanche's *Du Sentiment considéré dans son rapport avec la littérature et les beaux-arts*. Chateaubriand's more stimulating, more poetical, work did much to awaken the enthusiasm for medieval piety and *le merveilleux chrétien* which characterized the early phases of the Romantic Movement.

(10) During the Restoration years, in the writings of Joseph de Maistre and of Bonald, theories of Papal infallibility and the Divine origin of monarchical authority combined to form a political philosophy. About the same time Lamennais, perhaps the most remarkable Christian writer of the 19th century, published his famous *Essai sur l'indifférence en matière de religion* (1817–23), followed some years later by the impassioned *Paroles d'un croyant* (1834), which advocated Christianity and mutual love as the guiding principles for a democracy. After this he broke with the Church. Three of his contemporaries, Lacordaire, l'abbé Gerbet, and Montalembert, who were at one time his disciples at La Chesnaie, or associated with him in *L'Avenir* (q.v.), were also religious writers of some note. The first, like Mgr Dupanloup, also a contemporary, is better remembered as a preacher.

(11) Nineteenth-century developments in philosophic thought, in journalism, and in biblical and literary criticism and history, again widened the significance of the term 'religious writings'. This came to include, for instance, the work of a long line of spiritualist philosophers which begins with Maine de Biran and continues by way of Lachelier, Ravaisson, Fouillée, and Édouard le Roy to such living writers as Gilson (on Thomism and medieval philosophy), Maritain (on Neo-Thomism), and Gabriel Marcel on what has been called Christian Existentialism, see *Existentialisme*). It also embraces Roman Catholic essayists and journalists, from Veuillot, in the mid-nineteenth century, a particularly fiery specimen, to Bernanos in the twentieth (and cf. the militantly Catholic and Royalist standpoint of Barbey d'Aurevilly's essays and reviews, collected in *Les Œuvres et les hommes*). Renan is an outstanding figure in the field of biblical and literary criticism and history, if only, in the present connexion, for the respect and sympathy for orthodox religion in which he clothed his inability to accept it. (Cf. *Loisy* in more recent times.) Ozanam, too, should be mentioned; also Quinet (e.g. his *Le Génie des religions*, 1842), and the less well remembered Ernest Hello. The influence of religious sentiment on 17th-century French literature was studied by Sainte-Beuve in his *Port-Royal* (1840–59), and on French literature as a whole by the abbé Bremond (*Histoire littéraire du sentiment religieux en France*, 1916–33).

(12) In purely creative writing the religious element is apparent early in the 19th century in Chateaubriand's prose epic *Les Martyrs* and in Lamartine's poetry. Later, some of the poems of Hugo's *Légende des siècles* have biblical subjects (e.g. *Booz endormi*). Religious sentiment and emotion are the very essence of poems by Péguy and Claudel, and are strongly present in the work of such younger poets as P.-J. Jouve, or Patrice de la Tour du Pin, or Pierre Emmanuel. Many of Claudel's later essays, too, are commentaries on the Bible (see, for instance, *Accompagnements*, 1949; *Une Voix sur Israël*, 1950). In the drama of the period religious sentiment counts for little, though here again Claudel may be mentioned, e.g. *L'Annonce faite à Marie*, *L'Otage*, and *Le Soulier de satin*; as well as, much more recently, Montherlant's *Le Maître de Santiago* and *Port-Royal*. Claudel also stands out, as before him the novelist J.-K. Huysmans, among several French writers of the later 19th and the early

20th centuries (e.g. Paul Bourget, Léon Bloy, Charles du Bos, Max Jacob, Francis Jammes, Louis le Cardonnel, Verlaine) who found matter for literature in their conversion from religious apathy or positive disbelief to active acceptance of the Catholic faith. A final, and paradoxical, name for mention is that of André Gide, for few writers can ever have clothed their religious unease, or their apologia for acts and sentiments running counter to religious teaching, in language so fundamentally reminiscent of the Bible. (Cf. also *Novel*, para. 21.)

Remarques sur la langue française (1647), see *Vaugelas*.

Rémusat, CHARLES, COMTE DE (1797–1875), son of the following, politician and author of works on philosophical and miscellaneous subjects (e.g. English politics and history), including *Essais de philosophie* (1842), *Abélard* (1845), *L'Angleterre au XVIIIᵉ siècle* (1856), *Channing* (1857), *Philosophie religieuse* (1864), *John Wesley et le méthodisme* (1870), &c.

Rémusat, CLAIRE-ÉLISABETH GRAVIER DE VERGENNES, COMTESSE DE (1780–1821), daughter of an aristocrat who died on the scaffold, became lady-in-waiting to the Empress Josephine while the latter was still Madame Bonaparte, and in 1809 followed her into retirement. Her *Mémoires* (1879) and *Lettres. 1804–14* (1881), edited by her grandson, are a valuable picture of life at the court of Napoleon from the days of the Consulate until shortly before the divorce. The anecdotes and character sketches of Napoleon, the Bonaparte relations, and Talleyrand are particularly interesting.

Rémusat, JEAN-PIERRE-ABEL (1788–1832), born in Paris, a celebrated orientalist and Chinese scholar, was interested from boyhood in everything to do with China but at first studied and practised medicine. He was able to devote himself wholly to oriental studies after the second Restoration (1815) and held the Chair of Chinese specially created for him at the Collège de France. Besides many philological studies he left interesting *Mélanges asiatiques* (1825–6); *Mélanges d'histoire et de littérature orientales* (1843, posth.).

Renaissance, The, a term which seems not to have been employed before the 17th century, signifies, in its connexion with French literature, the great revival that took place in the 16th century under the influence of Greek and Latin models, to the gradual exclusion of the medieval tradition. Under the pressure of a narrow dogmatic theology and of scholastic philosophy the inspiration of the Middle Ages had by the end of the 15th century become exhausted: a cynical materialistic spirit prevailed; poetry in general was light and frivolous, devoid of grandeur, and complicated and artificial in form. The reaction is thought by some to have been in part occasioned by the successive invasions of Italy, between 1494 and 1525, by Charles VIII, Louis XII, and François Iᵉʳ; these, by bringing the French into contact with Italian culture and Italian humanists, led to a refinement of taste and a better understanding of the works of classical antiquity—notably Aristotle and Plato. The movement was powerfully supported by men of learning like Lefèvre d'Étaples, who visited Italy, Guillaume Fichet, and Robert Gaguin (qq.v.), and by the arrival of Greek professors such as Hermonymus and Lascaris. The *Decameron* of Boccaccio and the *Cortegiano* of Castiglione had already been translated and were widely read; and the sojourn of Petrarch himself at Avignon and Paris had not been without some preparatory influence. The new spirit was especially fostered at the courts of François Iᵉʳ and his sister Marguerite, where poets, artists, and men of learning enjoyed protection. The study of the humanities, *disciplinae humaniores*, as distinct from the formal logic and barbarous Latin of the scholastics, had already to a limited extent been adopted at the University of Paris before the end of the 15th century; the printing of Greek books began in Paris in 1507.

(2) The new humanism had as its exponents Budé, Estienne, Rabelais, Amyot, among many others; in 1530 François Iᵉʳ founded the Collège de France for the study of the ancient languages, outside the jurisdiction of the theologians. The first effects of the new influence on literature may be traced in some degree in the poetry of Clément Marot and Maurice Scève; then in a more revolutionary fashion in the work of Ronsard and the *Pléiade*, a school with a definite creed and programme—the imita-

tion of antiquity in French, a language which they claimed was equal to the task. The century of the Renaissance saw a vast change in the character and capacity of French literature, largely as a consequence of the work done by these men. The language was greatly extended and enriched (though somewhat indiscriminately), and new forms of literary expression were devised, or established: the alexandrine, the sonnet, the drama, the essay.

(3) At first the humanists of the Renaissance and the leaders of the Protestant Reformation went hand in hand, but after the affair of the *placards* (q.v., 1534) their paths diverged: Reformation became Calvinism, which was opposed to free inquiry in pursuit of truth. The first confidence and enthusiasm of the Renaissance presently gave place to the scepticism of Montaigne. There followed in literature, under Henri IV and Louis XIII, a period of transition leading to the great age of Louis XIV. It was marked by a certain relaxation of the previous ardent revolutionary effort, a consolidation as it were of what had been gained. The essential basis of the Renaissance, the imitation of classical models, was retained, but Malherbe, reacting against the early exuberance of the new school of poets, defined and preserved what was good in their innovations. Hardy gave animation to the Senecan tragedies of Jodelle and others. Vauquelin and Régnier gave form to satire. Du Vair, Du Plessis-Mornay, and François de Sales developed the moral discourse.

Renan, ERNEST (1823–92), historian, Hebrew scholar, philologist and critic, born at Tréguier (Brittany). He was educated for the priesthood, first at the local ecclesiastical college, later at clerical seminaries in Paris, notably (from 1843) the important seminary of Saint-Sulpice. There his philological and critical study of the Semitic languages (before long he was teaching as well as learning Hebrew) and of biblical texts led him to question the divine inspiration of the Bible and, from that, the fundamental doctrines of orthodox, revealed religion. The outcome of a period of spiritual crisis was that he was unable to take his vows, and in 1845 he left Saint-Sulpice. He became a pupil-teacher, *au pair*, in a private school, enduring considerable hardship in order to

study for the degree of 'agrégé de philosophie' of the École normale supérieure (q.v.), which he obtained in 1848. He was already a distinguished Semitic scholar; and essays contributed by him at this period to the *Revue des Deux Mondes* and the *Journal des Débats* (qq.v.) are among his collected *Études d'histoire religieuse* (1857) and *Essais de morale et de critique* (1859). His *Souvenirs d'enfance et de jeunesse* (1883, q.v.) are reminiscences of these early years; and the notes and memoranda of the *Cahiers* and *Nouveaux Cahiers de jeunesse* (posth. 1906 and 1907) are interesting pointers to the formation of his views on religion and literature, especially literary criticism.

(2) In 1849 a visit to Rome to work on his doctoral thesis *Averroès et l'Averroïsme* (1852) awakened his interest in antiquity and the arts, though it was not till 1865, in Athens, that the sense of the classical past invaded him with full force. In 1851 he was appointed to the Manuscript Department of the Bibliothèque nationale (q.v.) and devoted himself chiefly to biblical studies. In 1860–1 he headed a Government archaeological expedition in Phoenicia and Palestine, then remained to visit the scenes of Gospel story. The trip was overshadowed by the death of his sister, his continual stay and companion, who had gone with him. *Ma Sœur Henriette*, written for private circulation at the time (published 1895), is a moving testimony to his grief at her loss.

(3) On returning to France he was appointed (1862) Professor of Hebrew at the Collège de France (q.v.). His public lectures delivered in fulfilment of the requirements of the post were on the part played by the Jews in the history of civilization. They were considered unorthodox in tendency and suspended by Government order. His chair itself was suppressed after the publication (1863) of the *Vie de Jésus*, the first volume of his long-projected work (it took twenty-five years to write) *Les Origines du Christianisme* (1863–83). This is a study of the origin of the Christian tradition in the beliefs of a small Jewish sect, the gradual emergence of a monotheistic doctrine, the founding of the Church and its triumph over Greek, then Roman opposition. The treatment is critical, from the standpoint (following the example of German scholarship) of biblical exegesis. But it is also biographical and psychological

in so far as the approach is through the figures of the founders of Christianity. The value of the work as a scientific study has been disputed, but it caused an undeniable sensation when first published. This was particularly so with the *Vie de Jésus*, for beneath an enchanting, lyrical picture of the carpenter's son growing to maturity amid the flowers of the Galilean country-side lay a rationalization of the fundamental belief in the divinity of Christ.

(4) The subsequent volumes of *Les Origines . . .* were: *Les Apôtres* (1866), *La Vie de saint Paul* (1869), *L'Antéchrist* (1873), *Les Évangiles* (1877), *L'Église chrétienne* (1879), *Marc-Aurèle* (1881), and an index-volume (1883). *Saint Paul* and *Marc-Aurèle* are the most notable, as indicating the development both of the Christian faith and of Renan's own philosophic viewpoint. The later *Histoire du peuple d'Israël* (1887–93, 5 vols.) calls for mention here as being in a measure a prelude to the *Origines . . . .*

(5) In 1870, after the Revolution (see *Revolutions*, IV and IV*a*), the Provisional Government reinstated Renan at the Collège de France, of which, in 1883, he became head. By this time his wide-ranging erudition and literary knowledge, the persuasive force of his reasoning and of his style, and the controversy that any new book by him was almost certain to provoke, had made him a famous literary personality. He was, with Taine (q.v.), the foremost representative of French thought in the later years of the Second Empire, and for the generation reacting—*c*. 1870–80—against the cheerless positivism of earlier years his intellectual appeal was enormous. It combined three elements: a romantic (and from his origin Celtic) spiritualism; a materialism which recognized that the future of the world lay in the progress of science; and a reluctance to deny a place to an ideal towards which the universe is striving. His attitude is already discernible in the essays—written as early as 1848—of *L'Avenir de la science* (1890, q.v.). In *Dialogues et fragments philosophiques* (1876) and his very interesting *Examen de conscience philosophique* (1888) it is clear. In the *Drames philosophiques* (1878–86, q.v.) the 'haute impartialité philosophique qui ne s'attache exclusivement à aucun parti' has become a form of intellectual dilettantism.

(6) Renan's correspondence, e.g. with his sister Henriette between 1842 and 1845, and with his friend Marcelin Berthelot (q.v.) over the long period 1847–92, is of great interest. His *Œuvres complètes* (ed. H. Psichari, to be completed in 10 vols.) have been in course of publication since 1949.

Renard, JULES (1864–1910), novelist, belonged by family and upbringing to the rather isolated district of Burgundy known as Le Morvan, where craggy, wooded hills make for difficult cultivation and dour inhabitants. He was educated at Nevers and Paris, then struggled (in Paris) to live by his pen and by private teaching. Marriage in 1888 brought some financial relief. His position in advanced literary circles was assured when (1890) he joined the original staff of the *Mercure de France* (q.v.), chief among Symbolist reviews. He was also an early member of the Académie Goncourt (q.v.).

His writings have few of the characteristics usually associated with Symbolisme (q.v.). His ironic humour, and rare but acidulously keen gifts of observation and description, were often exercised (perhaps as the reaction of an exacerbated sensibility) on human nature in its meanest, sourest, and most rebarbative aspects. Sympathy and poetic feeling did break through at times, e.g. in *Poil de Carotte* (1894), the work which made his name. It is the tale of the sufferings (till he learns the painful art of self-preservation) of a dreamy, sensitive child in the country, bullied by his mother and neglected by his father. It was dramatized (one act) in 1900 and has also been adapted for cinema. (*Les Cloportes*, 1919, posth., written *c*. 1888, and *Sourires pincés*, 1890, had contained it in germ.)

Other works by Jules Renard were: *L'Écornifleur* (1892, dramatized 1903 as *Monsieur Vernet*, 2 acts), a study of a scrounger, who profits by M. and Mme Vernet's credulous admiration for their 'literary' friend to make shameless abuse of their hospitality; *Coquecigrues* (1893); *Le Vigneron dans sa vigne* (1894); *Les Philippe* (1898); *Les Bucoliques* (1898), *Nos Frères farouches* (1908), sketches and pen portraits (the reverse of sentimentalized) of country, village, and peasant or (*Histoires naturelles*, 1896) animal life; also some one-act plays in the naturalistic tradition (*Le Plaisir de* rompre, 1898; *Le Pain de ménage*, 1899; *Huit jours à la campagne*, 1906). His *Œuvres complètes* (1925–7, 9 vols., Bernouard) contain his *Correspondance inédite, 1880–1910* and his *Journal inédit, 1887–1910*. The *Journal* has many notes on contemporary literary events and personalities together with interesting, at times painful, pictures of family life in the country where Renard spent each summer. (Latterly he became *maire* of Chitry-les-Mines, his home town.) It is also a constant revelation of a bitter, dissatisfied character for whom life had few rose-coloured moments.

Renart, JEAN, a remarkable French poet (probably from the Île-de-France) who, early in the 13th century, wrote with great charm and delicacy romances of adventure such as the *Lai de l'ombre, Guillaume de Dole, L'Escoufle* (qq.v.), and perhaps *Galeran de Bretagne*. They are notable for the vivid sketches of domestic life and the little portraits of characters which they contain.

Renart, Roman de, see *Roman de Renart.*

Renart le Bestourné, a poem by Rutebeuf (q.v.), a bitter satire in which Renart, no longer the jolly rascal of the earlier *Roman de Renart*, now symbolizes the mendicant friars. He gets control of Noble the lion, to the detriment of the realm.

Renart le Contrefait, see *Roman de Renart.*

Renart le Nouvel, see *Roman de Renart.*

Renaud de Montauban or **Les Quatre Fils Aymon,** a *chanson de geste* (q.v.) of the late 12th or early 13th century, one of the *Doon de Mayence* (q.v.) cycle. Renaud and his three brothers, sons of Aymon de Dordogne, escape from the Emperor's court after Renaud has killed Charlemagne's nephew in an affray. A long war follows, in which the brothers are beleaguered and endure great sufferings with fortitude until Charlemagne is prevailed on by his paladins to make terms. Under these the brothers are pardoned on condition that Renaud goes to Palestine and his wonderful horse Bayard is surrendered. Bayard by the Emperor's order is thrown into the river, with a millstone tied about his neck, but disengages himself and escapes. Renaud, after further exploits, meets his death while helping, as

a simple workman, the building of the shrine of St. Peter at Cologne. Charlemagne, it may be noted, plays an inglorious part: he is dishonourable and revengeful, and is fooled by the enchanter Maugis; the sympathy of the author and his readers is with the rebels, but the latter are finally brought to repentance.

Renaud figures as Rinaldo in the *Orlando Innamorato* of Boiardo and *Orlando Furioso* of Ariosto. During the German occupation of Belgium (1940–4), a modern dramatic version of the story, entitled *Les Quatre Fils Aymon*, banned in Brussels by the Germans because of the sympathy it showed for resistance to authority, was performed 'underground' in villages to enthusiastic audiences.

Renaudin, one of the seven young *déracinés* in the novel *Les Déracinés* (q.v.) by Maurice Barrès.

Renaudot, THÉOPHRASTE (1586–1653), publicist, born at Loudun, a physician of original and enlightened views, remembered as the founder of the first French newspaper, *La Gazette* (q.v.). He was also, or at least posed as, a philanthropist, who set up an institution in Paris for the gratuitous distribution of medicine to the sick poor, thereby incurring the fierce hostility of the Faculty of Medicine, led and represented by Gui Patin (q.v.), who described Renaudot as *nebulo hebdomadarius*. Renaudot was also accused of usury, because he founded the first *mont-de-piété* or pawnshop, for the benefit of the poor. He was the inventor, moreover, of the *Bureau d'adresse et de rencontre*, an advertising centre, where anyone wishing to sell or buy anything, to give or obtain employment, or to obtain information, could make known his wants. These advertisements were published in successive sheets, the prototype of the later *Petites Affiches* (q.v.). Lectures on various subjects were also given at the *Bureau d'adresse*.

René, by Chateaubriand, a tale of great poetical beauty, first included in *Le Génie du christianisme* (1802, q.v.) and published separately in 1805.

René is a romantic, melancholy youth, brought up, as Chateaubriand himself had been, in the deepest solitudes of nature with only the close companionship of an adored sister, Amélie. She, realizing that her love for René is a more than sisterly affection, takes desperate refuge from her passion in a convent. René learns the reason for her flight on the day she takes her vows. Grief and horror drive him to the wilds of America. He meets an aged Indian, Chactas (cf. *Atala*), and a missionary, Père Souël, and tells them his story.

René incarnates all the vague, unsatisfied yearnings, the world-weariness, the passion for nature in its most melancholy and terrifying aspects, that typify the early phases of *le romantisme* (q.v.). It introduced the *mal du siècle* into French literature, and for years to come 'René, c'est moi!' (said by Sainte-Beuve) was the sentiment of countless young men.

[Like *Atala*, this tale had originally been intended by Chateaubriand to form part of *Les Natchez*, q.v.]

René d'Anjou, DUC D'ANJOU and COMTE DE PROVENCE (1408–80), titular king of Naples, the two Sicilies, and Jerusalem, known as 'le bon roi René' ('whose large style agrees not with the leanness of his purse', Shakespeare, *2 Hen. VI*, I. i), was a devotee of knight-errantry, tilting, and hunting, and a patron of poets and musicians. His court at Aix-en-Provence is described in Scott's *Anne of Geierstein*. He was himself a poet of no great originality. His best poem is *Regnault et Jehanneton*, in which, in the form of a pastoral, he celebrated his love for his second wife, Jeanne de Laval. He also wrote a treatise on *Tournois* and a romantic work in verse and prose, the *Livre du cueur d'amour espris*. His daughter Marguerite d'Anjou was the wife of Henry VI of England.

Renée Mauperin (1864), a novel by E. and J. de Goncourt (q.v.), one of their first, and most successful, 'impressionistic' novels (cf. *Écriture artiste*). The petted, attractive, impetuous young heroine is too spontaneous, too credulous, a disturbingly incalculable member of her rich conventional family. Her brother Henri, a calculating, pushing young man, for long carries on a liaison with a rich neighbour's wife, then becomes engaged to the daughter. Renée, shocked and disgusted when she learns of this, stirs up trouble so successfully that Henri has to fight a duel and is killed. Remorse drives Renée into a decline. She dies;

and the bereft parents seek consolation in travel.

Renoir, PIERRE-AUGUSTE (1841–1919), French painter, one of the first Impressionists (see *Impressionnisme*). A tailor's son, he began work in a Paris factory, painting porcelain, and gradually managed to earn enough money to study art.

Renouvier, CHARLES (1815–1903), philosopher, came to Paris from Montpellier, his birthplace. His system of Neo-criticism, or *Personnalisme*, by giving a place to moral liberty and freedom of choice, made a rigidly scientific conception of the universe untenable. It can be studied in, for example, his *Essais de critique générale*, one of the most important philosophical works of the 19th century. Between their first publication (1854–64) and 1897 they were revised and augmented, and new essays were added, until finally they filled thirteen volumes. The subjects are Logic, Psychology, the Principle of Nature, and the Philosophy of History. His other works, hardly less important, include: *La Science de la morale* (1869); *Les Dilemmes de la métaphysique pure* (1901) and its sequel *Histoire et solution des problèmes métaphysiques* (1901), and, a final statement of his doctrines, *Le Personnalisme* (1903). In his early years he had to some extent been influenced by Comte (q.v.), but his thought was opposed to the doctrines of Positivism and his own influence was considerable about 1870–90 when Positivism was losing ground. He founded two famous journals, *L'Année philosophique* (1867–9) and *La Critique philosophique* (1872–9). The latter contained articles on politics and religion as well as on philosophy.

Republican calendar. This was introduced by a law of 5 October 1793 and officially discontinued from 1 January 1806, having lasted for twelve years, two months, and twenty-seven days. On its introduction it was antedated from 22 September 1792 (the day of the Proclamation of the Republic), thus the first year of the Republic ran from 22 September 1792 to 21 September 1793. The object was to make a definite break with the Gregorian Calendar (introduced in 1582) and the Christian tradition, by which the year had begun on 1 January and followed the festivals of the

Church (see *Year, Beginning of the*). The year now began on 22 September (the autumn equinox) and consisted of twelve months of thirty days each. These in their turn were divided into three *décades*, or periods of ten days, instead of the former weeks. The re-arrangement left five intercalary days (six in a leap year) which were called *sansculottides* and observed as national festivals. The chronology of the Calendar was the work of Romme (q.v.), the mathematician.

Nomenclature was also changed. The eponymous saints of the Gregorian calendar gave way to metals, plants, agricultural instruments, and so on. The task of renaming the months was entrusted to the poet Fabre d'Églantine (q.v.), then a member of the *Convention nationale*. He gave them their seasonal significance, as follows:

Vendémiaire, Brumaire, Frimaire, the autumn months of vintage, mist, and frost; *Nivôse, Pluviôse, Ventôse*, the winter months of snow, rain, and tempest; *Germinal, Floréal, Prairial*, the spring months of seed-time, flowers, and meadows; *Messidor, Thermidor, Fructidor*, the summer months of harvest, heat, and fruit. The days were named after their numerical order:

Primidi, duodi, tridi, quartidi, quintidi, sextidi, septidi, octidi, nonidi, décadi (the day of rest).

Republics

THE FIRST REPUBLIC

(1) A Revolutionary Municipal Government was set up in Paris in 1789 after the Fall of the Bastille (14 July), but the monarchy lasted nominally until August 1792. On 21 September 1792 the *Convention nationale*, meeting for the first time, decreed the abolition of the monarchy and proclaimed the Republic. This first republican era lasted officially until the Senatus-consultum of 18 May 1804, by virtue of which the First Consul, Napoléon Bonaparte, received the title of Napoléon Ier, Empereur des Français. It falls into three periods: *Convention, Directoire*, and *Consulat* (qq.v.; and for further details see *Revolutions*, I, Ia).

THE SECOND REPUBLIC

(2) This was proclaimed on 25 February 1848 and lasted officially until 2 December 1852, when it gave way to the Second Empire (q.v.). It was humanitarian and pacific in its ideals, but its leaders (see *Revolutions*, IIIa) were enthusiasts and theorists with no practical experience of government and were soon divided amongst themselves. Some wished to improve existing conditions, others to establish a new social order. The socialists had the upper hand at first, but at the elections for a Constituent Assembly (April 1848) the country showed its dislike of their measures, notably of the establishment of the *ateliers nationaux* (q.v.). In June the proposed re-organization of these ateliers provoked republican and socialist discontent which culminated in insurrection and savage street fighting (23–26 June, 'les journées de juin'). The Government declared Paris in a state of siege, suppressed the insurrection with difficulty, and took such severe reprisals that the progress of republicanism was arrested for many years to come. The reactionary spirit triumphed and the class struggle became marked, between *bourgeoisie* and peasants on the one hand and industrial workers on the other. All three orders found grounds for discontent with the Republic. The *bourgeoisie* thought they lost money by it and the peasants suspected it of having designs on their property. The industrial workers had lost faith and the outcome of the situation was that Bonapartism profited.

(3) The Constitution voted (4 Nov. 1848) by the Constituent Assembly provided for a legislative assembly and for a President of the Republic with executive power, both to be elected by universal manhood suffrage. Meanwhile the Bonapartist party came forward, with Prince Louis Napoleon Bonaparte (see *Napoleon III*) as candidate for the presidency. The *parti de l'ordre* supported it (the largest party in the country, standing for re-establishment of 'moral order' and including *légitimistes, Orléanistes*, qq.v., and Catholics). In December 1848 Louis Napoleon was (easily) elected Prince-President. In the Assembly, on 20 December, he swore fidelity to the Republic, the Assembly, and the Constitution. In fact, he spent the next three years in paving the way for the *coup d'état* (q.v.) of 2 December 1851 by which he abolished the Legislative Assembly (elected May 1849). He followed this by a plebiscite on a limited franchise (14–21 Dec. 1851), when the electorate by an overwhelming majority empowered him to frame a new constitution (14 January 1852),

thus consolidating him in a position of absolute authority. A second, and still more emphatic, plebiscitary vote (20 Nov. 1852) ratified a senatus-consultum of 7 November re-establishing 'the imperial dignity in the person of Louis Napoleon'; and on 2 December 1852 the new emperor was proclaimed 'Napoléon III, empereur héréditaire des Français'. [The events leading up to and during 1848 are described in Flaubert's *Éducation sentimentale* and in Louis Ménard's *Prologue d'une Révolution*. Hugo's *Histoire d'un crime* (q.v.) is also of interest, and the *Souvenirs et idées* of George Sand, perhaps less well known, carry the picture beyond 1851.]

THE THIRD REPUBLIC

(4) This was proclaimed in Paris (at the Hôtel de Ville) after the Révolution du 4 septembre 1870 (see *Revolutions*, IV, IVa) and came to an end seventy years later. During its first few months the country was kept going by an improvised Government of National Defence (Gouvernement de la Défense Nationale, 4 September 1870–17 February 1871), sitting partly in Paris and partly in delegation at Tours (cf. *Gambetta*). Paris, besieged by the Germans, was cut off from the rest of France from late September 1870 till the end of January 1871. On 18 January the King of Prussia was proclaimed German Emperor in the Hall of Mirrors at Versailles. On 28 January Paris capitulated. While peace terms were being negotiated the revolutionary movement known as the *Commune* (q.v.) broke out, lasting from 18 March till 28 May. The Peace Treaty was signed (Frankfurt, 1 May 1871) by a Government which had been elected some three months previously and which functioned as a National Assembly until three constitutional laws, generally known as the Constitution of 1875, definitely consolidated France as a republic. (The seventy-four-year-old Adolphe Thiers, q.v., was the first President: the last was Albert Lebrun, see *Presidents of the French Republic*.) For some time after 1871 the restoration of the monarchy had been a possibility. The spread of republicanism, and division among the monarchists themselves (see *Chambord, comte de*), had finally destroyed this. In 1877 a political crisis resulted in the triumph of parliamentary democracy.

(5) Between *c.* 1880 and the outbreak of the 1914–18 war France was shaken internally by such happenings as the Boulangist Movement (see *Boulangisme*), the Panama (q.v.) Scandal (1888–92), and the tremendous political and spiritual emotions excited by the Dreyfus (q.v.) case (1894–1906, esp. 1897–9). The period was also marked by

(*a*) the conflict between Church and State, at its most intense perhaps in matters of education (a law of 1882 made primary education free, compulsory, and lay), and culminating in the law of 9 December 1905 (the *Loi de la séparation*) by which the Roman Catholic Church was disestablished and disendowed (cf. *Concordat*);

(*b*) the rapid growth of socialism, Trade Unionism and Syndicalism, with marked repercussions on economic, political, and intellectual life. The C.G.T. (*Confédération Générale du Travail*), French equivalent of the Trades Union Congress, was formed in 1895. Jaurès (q.v.), the famous socialist and orator, won respect and reverence at home and abroad and his assassination on 31 July 1914 was regarded as a disaster by all parties;

(*c*) the vast growth of the informational daily and periodical Press.

(6) Externally, France's colonial expansion (in the eighties and nineties) was notable, also her restoration to the position of a great European and world Power. An alliance was concluded with Russia in 1892; the *Entente cordiale* with Great Britain in 1904. The years immediately before 1914, especially after the Agadir (q.v.) crisis of 1911, were clouded for France as for other European countries by the growing menace of German expansionism.

(7) During the 1914–18 war concentration on the war effort involved a truce—at first—to internal disputes and a progressive disruption of the country's ordered economy. (The war as a factor in accelerating and intensifying changes in the social fabric was studied by Proust in the last volume of *A la recherche du temps perdu*, q.v., a work of great interest generally for the social history of the Third Republic.)

(8) The post-1914–18 war years in France (again as in other countries) were dominated by the anxieties of the precarious international situation, reflected in daily life in general discontent, political and spiritual malaise and instability (all, increasingly,

with their counterpart in literature, cf. *Gide, Proust*). In 1922 a split in the Trade Union Movement led to the formation of the C.G.T.U. (*Confédération Générale du Travail Unitaire*) with a definitely communist bias. Literature showed a growing tendency to become tied to political (for the most part communist) doctrines (cf. *Surréalisme*). At the opposite extreme the rabid nationalist and monarchist party of the 'Action Française' (q.v.), or other violently right-wing organizations, had many adherents. Internal division and discontent were emphasized by the fact that attempts by successive governments to introduce long-overdue measures of social reform were hampered by international crises and the urgent need, from the point of view of national defence, to increase productivity.

(9) On 3 September 1939 France, following Great Britain, declared war on Germany. In May 1940 the Germans overran Holland and Belgium and broke through, as in 1870, at Sedan. By 16 June they had entered Paris, which the French Government had already left. The Head of the Government (M. Paul Reynaud) resigned and was succeeded by Marshal Pétain (aged eighty-four), who signed the Armistice of 22 June between France and Germany. On 9 and 10 July the Chamber of Deputies and the Senate, sitting together as a National Assembly (see *Assemblée nationale*) at Vichy (though in the enforced absence of some of their number), voted a revision of the Constitution of 1875 which gave him special powers. These he used to constitute himself executive and legislative head of the French State. The Republic which ended thus by implication rather than by direct action had outlasted any régime since 1789.

(10) *A la recherche du temps perdu* has been mentioned (para. 7). Other novels depicting the social and political scene during the Third Republic include: the trilogy entitled *Le Roman de l'énergie nationale* by Maurice Barrès; the *Jean-Christophe* cycle (especially the volumes *La Maison* and *La Foire sur la place*) by Romain Rolland; and the several volumes of Roger Martin du Gard's *Les Thibault* and Jules Romains's *Les Hommes de bonne volonté* (qq.v.). Cf. also *Naturalisme*; *Press, Development of*, paras. 18–20; *Symbolisme*; *Theatre of the 19th and 20th centuries*, paras. 5, 6.

THE FOURTH REPUBLIC

(11) This form of government came into being after the 1939–45 war. The Constitution was promulgated on 27 October 1946, the Republic was officially inaugurated on 1 January 1947, and on 16 January the first President, M. Vincent Auriol, was elected. This Constitution provided for a Parliament of two elected bodies, with legislative power vested solely in one, the *Assemblée nationale*, sitting in what was formerly the Chambre des Députés (see *Palais-Bourbon*). The other body, the *Conseil de la République*, unlike the former Senate, was given only consultative powers. Its members were still called *Sénateurs*.

République, Six livres de la, see *Bodin*.

République française, La. (1) A daily, typical of many papers founded immediately after the February Revolution (1848) to air the new doctrines of socialism. It stood for 'la liberté, le progrès, et l'ordre', for free education, electoral reform, and the improvement of the working man's lot. George Sand and the political economist Bastiat (qq.v.) wrote for it.

(2) The organ (founded 1871) of Gambetta's (q.v.) parliamentary group, and sometimes called *Le Journal des Débats de la démocratie*. At a later date many of its contributors became members of the Government.

Réquisitionnaire, Le, one of the 'Études philosophiques' of Balzac's *Comédie humaine* (q.v.).

Rességuier, BERNARD-MARIE-JULES, COMTE DE (1789–1862), a minor figure, but sometimes remembered, of the very early days of the Romantic Movement (see *Romantisme*). He wrote verse and one novel (*Almaria*, 1835). After 1830 (see *Révolution du 29 juillet*) he lived quietly in the country, devoting himself to literature and to the fortunes of the legitimist party (see *Légitimistes*).

Restauration, La, the period in French history which followed the restoration of the Bourbons to the throne after the fall of Napoleon and the end of the Empire. There were, in fact, two Restoration periods: the first, from Napoleon's first abdication in April 1814 till his return from Elba in March 1815; the second, after the Hundred

Days, Waterloo, and Napoleon's second abdication in July 1815. This ended with the July Revolution (1830) and the fall of the Bourbon monarchy.

Restif or **Rétif de la Bretonne**, NICOLAS-EDME (1734–1806), novelist, the son of a peasant and himself a working printer, wrote some 250 volumes of realistic, didactic romances, of little literary merit, but intended to be edifying, which preserve for us many features of the life of the peasantry and of the women of the humbler classes in the 18th century. His principal works were *Le Paysan perverti* (1775), the tragic tale of a young peasant corrupted by the evil influences of Paris, *La Paysanne pervertie* (1776), *La Vie de mon père* (1779), *Les Contemporaines* (1780–5), *Monsieur Nicolas* (1796–7). Parts of these show considerable power of observation and his work was admired by contemporaries, though marred, in some opinions, by melodrama, obscenities, and a coarse style.

Retour de l'enfant prodigue (1907), see *Gide*.

Retour des cendres, see *Légende napoléonienne, La*.

Retté, ADOLPHE (1863–1930), Symbolist poet, edited two early Symbolist reviews, *La Vogue* and *L'Ermitage*, and wrote much about the theories of *Symbolisme* and *le vers libre* (qq.v.). One notable essay on rhythm in poetry, first published in the *Mercure de France* (q.v.), was later included in his reminiscences, *Le Symbolisme* (1903). His published collections of verse include *Une belle dame passa* (1893); *L'Archipel en fleurs* (1895); *Campagne première* (1897), and the more exclusively nature poems of *Lumières tranquilles* (1901) and *Dans la forêt* (1903). In later life, after his conversion to Roman Catholicism, he wrote a good deal of sentimental religious prose; also further reminiscences.

Retz or **Rais**, GILLES DE (*c.* 1396–1440), maréchal de France, who fought by the side of Joan of Arc against the English. Later he engaged in necromancy, kidnapped children, and murdered them. He was tried and executed. His name is connected with the story of Blue Beard in the local traditions of Brittany, where he had estates (though he

had only one wife, Catherine de Thouars, who left him).

Retz, PAUL DE GONDI, CARDINAL DE (1614–79), born at Montmirail in Brie of a family that came originally from Florence, a man who, without the least vocation for an ecclesiastical career, became coadjutor to his uncle, Archbishop of Paris, from 1644, his successor from 1653 to 1662, and cardinal from 1652. Without any definite political aim other than to become himself a minister of Louis XIV, but loving cabals and conspiracies for their own sake, he played an active and important part in the troubles of the Fronde (q.v.), at first as an opponent of Mazarin and the queen, later as a moderator and negotiator. He was imprisoned after the Fronde, but escaped and was pardoned in 1662 on condition of relinquishing his archbishopric. He was highly esteemed and defended by Mme de Sévigné and was fond of her daughter (though she did not return his affection). He wrote when a young man an account of the *Conjuration de Fiesque* (1655), the conspiracy of Fiesco of Genoa against Andrea Doria; but is remembered especially for his remarkable *Mémoires* (not published until 1717), a lucid and vivacious if unreliable account of the vicissitudes of his career and of the political events with which he was concerned; they have given rise to various estimates of their author. They contain many interesting and incisive portraits (Condé, Turenne, &c.), and aphorisms worthy of La Rochefoucauld.

Revanche, La, see *Patriotes, La Ligue des*; also *Boulanger*.

Rêve, Le (1888), one of Zola's *Rougon-Macquart* (q.v.) novels is, unlike most of the series, in an idyllic strain. A foundling (a Macquart, abandoned at birth by her mother) is brought up in the shadow of a northern cathedral by a tender-hearted childless couple. She dreams of saints and legends, of a rich, highly-born lover who will come to her out of the past, and weaves her dreams into the resplendent church embroideries which her guardians have taught her to make. Reality comes sadly. The lover appears, but is torn away by his proud father. She remains, to die, with her embroidery, her dreams, and her grief; and consent, when it does come, is too late.

Rêve de d'Alembert, Le, see *Diderot*, para. 2.

Rêve de Pascal, Le, see *Pascal*, para. 1.

Réveil, Le, one of the best remembered of the extreme opposition journals founded in 1869, the last year of the Second Empire.

Revenons à nos moutons, a proverbial phrase taken (slightly modified) from *Pathelin* (q.v.).

Reverdie, see *Chansons à personnages*.

Reverdy, PIERRE (1889–), modernist poet, associated first with *Cubisme* (q.v.) about 1917, when he founded a short-lived review *Nord-sud*, and then with *Surréalisme* (q.v.). Rimbaud's (q.v.) influence is strongly perceptible in his poetry (*Les Épaves du ciel*, 1924; *Flaques de verre*, 1929, &c.).

Rêveries du promeneur solitaire, Les, ten meditations written by J.-J. Rousseau in his last years and published posthumously (1782).

They are reflections on various phases of his life, including many biographical details, and showing a calmer spirit than the dialogues entitled *Rousseau juge de Jean-Jacques*. The *Rêveries*, notably the third (in which he relates his early years and mental development) and the fifth (in which he describes his sojourn on the island of Saint-Pierre in the Lake of Bienne), contain some of his most charming pages.

Reviews, see *Revue . . . .*

Révolte des anges, La (1914), a novel by Anatole France (who thought it contained some of his finest writing). A number of angels tire of their heavenly existence and determine to live as ordinary men and women in Paris. Their adventures afford scope for sharp social satire.

Revolutionary Calendar, see *Republican Calendar*.

Revolutions. Between 1789 and 1939 there were four major French revolutions:

I. THE REVOLUTION OF 1789, as the result of which monarchical absolutism was shattered. This was the most overwhelming of the four and is always referred to as 'la Révolution' or 'la Révolution française', with no further distinguishing adjective. The monarchy fell in August 1792, and in September 1792 the Republic was proclaimed. The Revolutionary era ended in November 1799, when the Consulate came into being. The Republic ended in 1804, when the First Consul Bonaparte became the Emperor Napoleon I. For the chief events of the Revolutionary period see below (I*a. Révolution française: Sequence of Events*); cf. also *Republics*; and for the royal family at the outbreak of the Revolution see *Bourbon*.

II. THE JULY REVOLUTION, in 1830. The elder branch of the Bourbons, which had been restored to the throne in 1814, was overthrown and Louis-Philippe, duc d'Orléans, became king (see II*a. Révolution du 29 juillet*).

III. THE FEBRUARY REVOLUTION, in 1848. The Orléans monarchy was overthrown and the Second Republic proclaimed. The latter in its turn gave way to the Second Empire (see III*a. Révolution du 24 février*; also *Republics*; *Second Empire*).

IV. THE SEPTEMBER REVOLUTION, in 1870. The Second Empire was overthrown and the Third Republic established (see IV*a. Révolution du 4 septembre*; *Republics*).

I*a.* RÉVOLUTION FRANÇAISE:
SEQUENCE OF EVENTS

1789

5 May. The *États généraux* (q.v.), convoked to decide upon reforms of taxation, meet at Versailles and at once disagree: the nobles insist that each order (see *Privilégiés*; *Tiers État*) should deliberate separately; the *Tiers État* holds that reform is possible only if the three orders deliberate and vote in common.

17 June. The *Tiers État*, now self-entitled *Assemblée nationale*, constitutes itself the controlling body for purposes of taxation.

20 June. The *Tiers État* (*Assemblée nationale*) is excluded by royal command from the building intended originally for meetings of the combined orders but in which for over six weeks the orders have been meeting separately. It retires to the *Salle du Jeu de Paume* and swears (*Serment du Jeu de Paume*) not to dissolve until it has framed a constitution.

23 June. The king addresses a specially convoked session of the combined *États généraux*. He refuses to abolish the distinction

between the *Privilégiés* and the *Tiers État*, declares that the latter's recent decisions are null, and orders the whole assembly to disperse and to resume sittings on the following day in order to consider a programme of ineffective reforms which he has offered. The *Tiers État* (*Assemblée nationale*) refuses to obey, and Mirabeau defies the king in the famous utterance: 'Nous sommes ici par la volonté du peuple et . . . on ne nous arrachera que par la force des baïonnettes.'

9 July. The *Assemblée nationale*, now reinforced by a majority of the clergy and a minority of the nobility, calls itself *Assemblée constituante* and sets to work to frame a constitution. This signifies the finish of the absolute monarchy.

12 July. In Paris a harangue by Camille Desmoulins (q.v.) inflames the revolutionary spirit (cf. *Palais-Royal*).

14 July. The people attack and take the Bastille (q.v.). A revolutionary municipal government is established in Paris (see *Commune*). At Versailles the *Assemblée constituante* undertakes the drafting of the *Déclaration des droits de l'homme* (q.v.).

15 July. The king is received at the Hôtel de Ville by the newly-appointed Mayor of Paris (Bailly, q.v.). He adopts the tricolour flag (see *Tricolore*) and agrees to the new order.

27 August. The *Assemblée constituante* votes the *Déclaration des droits de l'homme*, which the king, holding to his right of veto, refuses to sanction till 5 October.

5 October. Public discontent has been aggravated by shortage of food, notably bread. A crowd, mainly women, marches from Paris to Versailles and brings the royal family back by force to the Tuileries.

16 October. The *Assemblée constituante* removes from Versailles to Paris.

1790
14 July. The first *Fête de la Fédération* (q.v.). The king and the nation swear fidelity to the new order.

1791
21–24 June. Various causes, e.g. the confiscation of the *biens nationaux* and the *constitution civile du clergé* (qq.v.), have increased the king's hostility to the *Assemblée*. The royal family attempt to escape (21 June), are arrested at Varennes, and brought back

to Paris (24 June). The *Assemblée*'s decree (22 June) suspending the king from his functions splits the Revolutionary party into Republicans (at this date the minority) and Constitutional Monarchists.

15 July. The *Assemblée constituante* refuses the Republicans' petition for the trial of the king and uses armed force (17 July) to suppress opposition.

3 September. The Constitution—the first written constitution in French history—is voted by the *Assemblée constituante* (see *Constitutions*).

14 September. The king swears to uphold the constitution and is re-established on the throne as a constitutional monarch. Both Royalists and extreme Republicans dislike the constitution.

1 October. The *Assemblée législative* succeeds the *Assemblée constituante* and is at first predominantly in favour of a constitutional monarchy.

1792
20 April. The *Assemblée législative*, by declaring war on Austria, forestalls the attack of Austrian and Prussian forces (see *Coalitions*) bent on re-establishing the king's authority. This is the beginning of the Revolutionary Wars, which in turn will lead to the Napoleonic wars.

10 July. The *Assemblée* declares 'la patrie en danger' as the result of increasing pressure on the Revolutionary armies by foreign forces plus the *Armée des émigrés* (q.v.). National defence is organized and recruiting thrown open.

General discontent grows, largely caused by the king's refusal to sanction the *Assemblée*'s decrees. The movement to depose the king gathers strength.

10 August. The fall of the monarchy. The people of Paris, aided by provincial detachments of the *Garde nationale* (q.v.), the citizen defence army created during the Revolution, and especially by the detachment from Marseilles (cf. *Marseillaise*), attack and take the royal palace of the Tuileries. The royal family—the king, the queen, their daughter Madame Royale, aged fifteen, the Dauphin, aged eight, and the king's sister Madame Élisabeth—take refuge with the *Assemblée législative*. The *Assemblée* deprives the king of his powers, itself

assumes executive functions, and summons the country to elect a *Convention nationale* with a view to framing a new constitution. The royal family are imprisoned in the Temple and a temporary Revolutionary government is formed with Danton (q.v.) at its head (cf. *Commune*).

2-5 September. The continuing defeats of the Revolutionary armies are attributed to Royalist treason. The people, incited by Marat (q.v.), invade the prisons and massacre over 1,200 prisoners ('the September massacres').

20 September. The Revolutionary army of the North, under Dumouriez and Kellermann, defeats the Prussians at Valmy.

21 September. The *Assemblée législative* is succeeded by the *Convention nationale*. As one of its first acts the *Convention* decrees the abolition of the monarchy.

22 September. The first day of the Republic. Now the period of struggle begins between the different Republican factions (see *Convention nationale*; *Girondins*; *Montagne*; *Jacobins*; *Cordeliers*; *Robespierre*).

— October: The *Comité de sûreté générale* is established.

1793
21 January. Execution of Louis XVI after a trial lasting from 11 December 1792 to 20 January 1793. From now on the power of the *Montagnards*, the extreme Revolutionary faction in the *Convention nationale*, increases.

11 March. *Tribunal révolutionnaire* established.

6 April. *Comité de salut public* established.

31 May-2 June. The struggle between the parties ends with an organized insurrection in the *Convention nationale* and the overthrow of the *Girondins*, with the arrest or flight of their leaders.

13 June. Assassination of Marat by Charlotte Corday.

— July. Advent of Robespierre (q.v.) to full power.

10 August. Celebrations in Paris inaugurate the new constitution voted by the *Convention nationale* on 23 June and accepted by the country. The same evening the Convention renders the constitution void by deciding not to dissolve until the Revolutionary Wars are ended.

17 September. The *Convention* passes the *loi des suspects* (repealed 4 Oct. 1795) ordering the arrest of all persons suspected of disloyalty to the Revolution. Beginning of the Terror (see *Terreur*).

5 October. A decree of the *Convention nationale* introduces the Republican Calendar (q.v.).

10 October. A Revolutionary Government is established by decree of the *Convention nationale*. The supreme authorities are the Convention, its commissaries, the *Comité de sûreté générale*, the *Comité de salut public*, and the *Tribunal révolutionnaire*.

16 October. Execution of Marie-Antoinette after a trial lasting three days.

31 October. Execution of a number of *Girondins*, including their leader, Brissot (q.v.). Further trials and executions of *Girondins* take place during the next few months.

1793-4
During this winter the Revolutionary armies are victorious in the field. At home Robespierre's policy is hampered both by the extremists (Hébert and the *Hébertistes*, q.v.) and the moderates (Danton and his party).

1794
13-15 March. Hébert and the *Hébertistes* are arrested and (24 March) guillotined.

30-31 March. Danton, Fabre d'Églantine, Camille Desmoulins, and their followers are arrested and (5 April) guillotined.

5 May. The *culte de l'Être Suprême* is instituted. Opposition to Robespierre becomes marked.

10 June [le 22 prairial, An II]. The *loi du 22 prairial* renders the trial of suspects a purely nominal procedure and the Terror reaches its height. Opposition to Robespierre grows.

27 July [le 9 thermidor, An II]. Downfall of Robespierre. On the following day he and his followers, including Saint-Just and Couthon (qq.v.), are guillotined.

1794 (August)-1795 (October)
[The fourteen months after the fall of Robespierre are known as *la réaction thermidorienne*. During them the extreme democratic party loses strength and 'moderates' who had escaped the guillotine return to Paris.]

12 November. The *club des Jacobins* is closed.

May (1795). There are a number of abortive Royalist insurrections in the provinces, where they are suppressed with great cruelty (see *Terreur blanche*), and in Paris.

22 August. The *Convention nationale* has proceeded with its work of reorganizing the social and educational structure of France and now presents a new constitution providing for government by a *Directoire* (q.v.).

The Revolutionary armies are still victorious and the frontiers of France are extended.

5–12 October. Resentment at the prolonged existence of the *Convention* has culminated in attacks by insurrectionists, notably on 5 October (le 13 vendémiaire, An IV), one of the most bloody risings of the Revolutionary era. The armed defence organized by the young General Napoléon Bonaparte is successful.

26 October [le 4 brumaire, An IV]. The *Convention nationale*, meeting for the last time before dissolution, decrees a general amnesty for anti-revolutionary acts, with the exception of deported priests, *émigrés*, *vendémiaires* (see above). It also abolishes capital punishment; and the *Place de la Révolution*, scene of so many executions, is renamed *Place de la Concorde*.

1795 (October)–1799 (December)

The Government of the *Directoire*, which has now replaced the *Convention nationale*, is feeble and divided in itself. Famine and bankruptcy threaten. At the same time a certain section of *nouveaux riches*, profiteers, and returned nobility (see *Incroyables*; *Muscadins*) scandalizes the country by its profligacy. The foreign wars are continued as a means of exploiting the people. Lesser republics on the French model are formed in the conquered territories of Holland, Switzerland, and Italy. Other states of Europe become alarmed. Bonaparte comes to the fore. (See also *Press, Development of*, para. 7.)

By November 1799 the internal and external policy of the *Directoire* has brought the country to the brink of disaster. Bonaparte sees his opportunity and on 9 November 1799 (le 18 brumaire, An VIII) seizes the military command of Paris. On the day after this *coup d'état du dix-huit brumaire* a provi-

sional Government is set up. A new Constitution, the result of a plebiscite of the electorate, and promulgated on 13 December 1799 (le 22 frimaire, An VIII), establishes the *Consulat* (q.v.), with Bonaparte as First Consul. With this the period of the Revolution comes to an end and Bonaparte's dictatorship begins (see *Napoleon*).

IIa. RÉVOLUTION DU 29 JUILLET 1830

Discontent with the government of Charles X (q.v.) came to a head in 1829 when the king dissolved the Chamber of Deputies for protesting against his reactionary policy. The electorate showed its feelings by returning a new Chamber with a much larger opposition party. Thereupon the king disregarded the theory of ministerial responsibility and issued ordinances (26 July 1830) which again dissolved the Chamber, ended representative government by changing the electoral law, and violated the Charter of 1814 (see *Charte, La*) by abolishing the liberty of the Press. This minor *coup d'état* provoked immediate resistance among journalists, politicians, and the Parisian populace. Street rioting began on 27 July and turned to fighting, which lasted for three days (*les trois glorieuses*) until the 29th. Charles X, who had retired to Rambouillet, then abdicated in favour of his grandson the duc de Bordeaux (later known as the comte de Chambord, q.v.), the posthumous son (1820) of the duc de Berry (q.v.). At this stage the Orleanist faction of the opposition, exploiting a victory largely won by the Republicans, successfully engineered the establishment of a constitutional monarchy, and on 7 August Louis-Philippe, duc d'Orléans (q.v.), was proclaimed king. A charter voted by the Chamber of Deputies the same day, and accepted by the king, replaced the charter of 1814.

IIIa. RÉVOLUTION DU 24 FÉVRIER 1848

This began on 22 February 1848 as manifestations of discontent at the Government's refusal, backed by a display of military force, to allow a patriotic banquet (see *Banquets*) to be held in Paris. Renewed insurrections took a serious turn on the night of 23 February, and on 24 February the king (Louis-Philippe) abdicated in favour of his ten-year-old grandson, the comte de Paris. The insurgents, rejecting the comte de Paris, invaded the Chamber of Deputies and demanded a provisional government. This, when constituted, was headed by the poet Lamartine (q.v.) and included the savant François Arago (q.v.), the politician Alexandre-Auguste Ledru-Rollin (1807–74), and, before long, the republican socialist Louis Blanc (q.v.). The Second Republic was proclaimed on 25 February and the country proceeded to elect an *Assemblée constituante* (q.v., and see also *Republics*).

The February Revolution had direct causes in the country's discontent with the government of Louis-Philippe (notably its refusal to accord any measures of democratic reform), and in acute food shortages (1845–7) which had already occasioned risings in the provinces. In a wider sense it was the manifestation of socialistic ideas and ideals which had for some years been fermenting in France and in Europe generally; and it was a symptom of the growing consciousness, among a working class partly created and now menaced by industrialism, of the importance of the individual worker's rights to work and social security.

IVa. RÉVOLUTION DU 4 SEPTEMBRE 1870

This was a bloodless revolution. Dissatisfaction with the Second Empire (q.v.) had led to a recrudescence of republican sentiment which came to a head during the first month of the Franco-Prussian war (q.v.). After the defeat of Sedan (1 September 1870) the Empire crumbled. On 4 September a crowd, headed by the republican leaders Gambetta (q.v.) and Jules Favre (1809–80), interrupted the session of the *Corps législatif* (which was debating how best to carry on the government of the country), then proceeded to the Hôtel de Ville and proclaimed the Third Republic. A Government of National Defence was constituted, composed of Deputies for the Department of the Seine, all of them moderate Republicans, and with General Trochu, the Military Governor of Paris, as President (see *Republics*).

Révolutions de France et de Brabant, Les (1789–91 and, as *La Semaine politique*, 1791–2), a weekly founded by Camille Desmoulins (q.v.). It was widely read because of his stirring and eloquent articles. It had some illustrations, in the form of vignettes and mainly caricatures.

Révolutions de Paris, Les (1789–94), one of the most widely-read journals of the Revolution, founded by Louis-Marie Prudhomme (1752–1830), a publisher and journalist who had come from Lyons to Paris. It was an excellent guide to public opinion. Each number was a small pamphlet of about 50 pages octavo with topical engravings. After France was divided into *départements* (q.v.) in 1790 these engravings took the form of small maps of the different departments. Fervently idealistic articles by Élysée Loustalot (q.v.) largely made the success of this paper.

Revue. For reviews other than those mentioned below, and associated with particular periods or trends in French literature, or with particular individuals, see *Foreign Influences on French Literature*, para. 16; *Lyric poetry*, para. 15; *Nouvelle Revue Française*; *Parnassiens*; *Press, Development of*; *Romantisme*; *Surréalisme*; *Symbolisme*, &c. See also the contemporary publications mentioned in Appendix I, § G.

Revue blanche, La (1891–1903), a literary and dramatic review, founded by Alexandre Natanson, published work by Mallarmé, Henri de Régnier, Vielé-Griffin (qq.v., and see *Symbolisme*). It was one of the first reviews to introduce Ibsen and Tolstoy to French readers. Debussy was its musical critic. The literary and dramatic criticism, of a very high order, was written by Léon Blum (q.v.).

Revue britannique, La (1825–1902). Originally, this review published translations and abstracts of articles from English reviews. Later its scope widened to include original work in English and other foreign languages. Amédée Pichot (q.v.) was its editor from 1835 to 1877.

Revue critique d'histoire et de littérature, La, a learned review founded in 1866 by Paul Meyer and Gaston Paris. It ran till 1935.

Revue de métaphysique et de morale, one of the best-known contemporary French philosophical periodicals (a quarterly), founded 1893.

Revue de Paris, La, a review, mainly literary, founded by Dr. Véron (q.v.) in 1829. One of its aims was to secure recognition for unknown writers. It also initiated the practice (for literary reviews) of publishing novels in serial form. It was killed by the cheap press in 1845. Benjamin Constant, Alfred de Musset, Alfred de Vigny, and Sainte-Beuve (qq.v.) were early contributors. The *Revue de Paris* of the present day was founded in 1894.

Revue des Deux Mondes, La, founded in 1829 as a review largely devoted to home and foreign affairs, was acquired in 1831 by François Buloz (1803–77), who developed its literary and philosophical sides and made it one of the foremost periodicals of its kind in Europe. Its early contributors included Balzac, Hugo, Musset, George Sand, Alfred de Vigny, and Sainte-Beuve. It is still one of the best-known French literary reviews, appearing every two months.

Revue encyclopédique, La, a popular literary and scientific review, founded in 1819 by Jullien de Paris. It contained notes, criticism, abstracts, and some bibliographical features. It lasted till 1833. Another *Revue encyclopédique* founded in 1894 became the *Revue universelle* and, from 1907, *Larousse mensuel* (see *Larousse*).

Revue fantaisiste, La, see *Parnassiens*.

Revue française, La (1823–30), an organ of the *doctrinaires* (q.v.) and one of the best-remembered reviews of the Restoration period. It was founded on the English model by Guizot (q.v.) and devoted to philosophy, history, moral and political economy, and criticism. The quotation on its front page was 'Et quod nunc ratio est, impetus ante fuit'.

Revue indépendante, La (1884–95), a fortnightly review of literature and the arts and also, at first, of politics, existed throughout four series. The third (1886–9) was the famous series when, edited by Éd. Dujardin and Félix Fénéon (qq.v.), it became a leading Symbolist review (see *Symbolisme*). Barrès, Laforgue (Parisian chronicles), Mallarmé (dramatic criticism mainly, and see *Prose pour des Esseintes*), Moréas, Téodor de Wyzewa (articles on the Russian novel) were contributors.

Revue parisienne, La (1840). Balzac was part founder and sole editor of this review. There were only three numbers. His contributions included tales, a savage attack on Sainte-Beuve's *Port-Royal* (q.v.), and a long, discerning, and appreciative study of Stendhal's *La Chartreuse de Parme* (q.v.).

Revue philosophique de la France et de l'étranger, one of the leading French philosophical journals, founded 1876 by Théodule Ribot (q.v.).

Revue universelle, see *Revue encyclopédique*.

Revue wagnérienne, La (1885–8), a literary and musical review founded by Éd. Dujardin (q.v.) and others, and devoted specially to making Wagner better known not only as a composer but as a poet and the creator of a new form of art. It was supported by Mallarmé and several other Symbolist writers (see *Symbolisme*). Mallarmé's contributions included sonnets and an article on Wagner (*Richard Wagner, rêveries d'un poète français*).

Rey, MARC-MICHEL (18th c.), a publisher at Amsterdam, who printed most of the works of J.-J. Rousseau and d'Holbach.

Reybaud, MARIE-ROCH-LOUIS (1799–1879), man of letters and publicist, is remembered as the author of the satirical novel *Jérôme Paturot à la recherche d'une position sociale* (1843, q.v.) and its sequel *Jérôme Paturot à la recherche de la meilleure des républiques* (1848). Otherwise he wrote mainly on social economics and had a brief political career which ended after December 1851 (see *Coup d'état*). He was at one time a *Saint-Simonien* (see *Saint-Simonisme*).

Reynaud, JEAN (1806–63), a 19th-century philosopher whose chief work, *Terre et ciel* (1854), influenced Victor Hugo.

Rhadamiste et Zénobie, a tragedy by the elder Crébillon, produced in 1711, regarded as his masterpiece.

The plot is complicated and singular. Zénobie, daughter of Mithridate, king of Armenia, is loved by three men. The first is her cousin Rhadamiste, son of Pharasmane (brother of Mithridate). His father being opposed to the marriage, he, before the play begins, has carried her off, and when pursued, has stabbed her from jealousy and thrown her body into the Araxes, a treatment which she has survived, though this is not known. After the play opens, Rhadamiste, in the guise of a Roman ambassador, discovers her, an unrecognized prisoner, at the court of Pharasmane, and from a sense of duty she once more flies with him, though meanwhile Arsame, another son of Pharasmane, has fallen in love with her and she with him. Her third lover is Pharasmane himself, who pursues the fugitives and kills Rhadamiste, not recognizing in him his son. Horrified, when he discovers it, by the crime he has committed, he yields Zénobie to Arsame, but bids the pair withdraw beyond the reach of his fierce jealousy.

Rhétoriqueurs. The term *rhétorique* was applied in the latter part of the 15th century to poetry as opposed to prose. The *grands rhétoriqueurs* (a term said to have been first used by Coquillart, q.v.) were the principal poets of a school of that period, which occupied the interval between Charles d'Orléans and Clément Marot (Villon, however, is outside it). The characteristics of the school (of which tendencies can be found in the preceding period with Machaut and others), shown in a greater or lesser degree by its various members, were: a lack of sincere emotion; neglect or contempt of nature, an undiscriminating admiration of Latin literature, an inclination to moralize on outworn themes (largely taken from Jean de Meung's *Roman de la Rose*), and the frequent employment of allegory, dreams, symbols, and mythology for didactic purposes. The types of poems that they affected were the *doctrinal* (purely didactic), the *débat*, the *complainte* or *déploration* (dirge), the *testament*, the *blason* (the minute description of the qualities of an object). The *rhétoriqueurs* paid special attention to metrical technique and complication of rhyme, and greatly elaborated the forms of verse (Molinet enumerates nineteen of these); they were pretentious and claimed an intellectual mastership in France.

The school, which throve particularly in Burgundy, included the following among its principal poets (some of them were known also as chroniclers): Georges Chastellain, Jean Molinet, Jean Meschinot, Olivier de la Marche, Guillaume Crétin, Jean Marot, Pierre Gringore, Jean Bouchet, and (the best of them) Jean Lemaire de Belges (qq.v.).

Rhin, Le (1842, 2 vols., revised and aug-

mented in 1845), by Victor Hugo, a work based on long descriptive letters written to his wife during his visits to the Rhineland in 1839 and 1840. He padded it with history and legend (notably the medieval *Légende du beau Pécopin et de la belle Bauldour*, which he invented himself), then added a conclusion of much topical and political interest (cf. *Rhin allemand, Le*)—a historical study of the balance of power in Europe since the early 17th century, with a proposal of his own for a policy of mutual aid and concession on the part of France and Germany designed to lead to an alliance of the two countries and thus to peace in Europe.

Rhin allemand, Le, a satirical poem by Alfred de Musset, included in *Poésies nouvelles* (1841), in reply to a provocative *Hymne du Rhin* (1840) by the German poet Nicolas Becker, in which the first words of each stanza were (in the French translation), 'Ils ne l'auront pas, le libre Rhin allemand'. An earlier reply, *La Marseillaise de la paix*, by Lamartine, and on a more dignified, humanitarian note, had been published in the *Revue des Deux Mondes* of 28 May 1841. (Cf. Hugo's *Le Rhin* above.)

Rhône, Le (Lat. *Rhodanus*), the river by which Latin civilization penetrated from the Mediterranean up to the Lugdunum (the present-day Lyons, the second city of France) of the Romans. It is the second in length of the four great rivers of France (cf. *Garonne; Loire; Seine;* and see Appendix II). It issues from the Rhône glacier in the Valais (Switzerland), flows into one end of the Lake of Geneva and emerges at the other, at Geneva, only reaching French territory about 12 miles farther on. It then flows violently, through deep, narrow gorges, south and then westward, between the Jura and the Alps, becoming wide, and more calm, before Lyons, by which time it has received, notably, the Ain, from the Jura, and (at Lyons) the broad, beautiful, more placid Saône, its main tributary (which has risen in the Vosges and been joined in Franche-Comté by the Doubs). From Lyons, by now very broad, with many islands, its flow is south between the Cévennes and the Alps. It receives the Gier, the Ardèche, the Gard, &c., on its right, from the Massif Central, and the Isère, the Drôme, the Durance, &c., on its left, from the Alps; and it passes Vienne, Valence, Avignon, Tarascon, and Arles. Shortly before Arles it forks to become the Rhône delta, and its various branches (Grand Rhône, Petit Rhône, Rhône mort, Rhône vif), which enclose the famous nature reserve of the Camargue, a vast, reedy expanse of salt marshes, enter the Mediterranean at different points on the Golfe du Lion. The great Mediterranean port of Marseilles (Massilia, the colony founded in 600 B.C. by the Phocaean traders) is joined to the Rhône by a canal.

Rhumbs (1926), by Paul Valéry (q.v.), a collection of *pensées*, aphorisms, &c., so called in reference to the navigational sense of the word *rhumb* or *rumb*, i.e. the angular distance between two successive points of the compass. Valéry says: 'Comme l'aiguille du compas demeure assez constante tandis que la route varie: aussi peut-on regarder les . . . applications successives de notre pensée . . . comme des écarts définis par contraste avec je ne sais quelle constante dans l'intention profonde et essentielle de l'esprit.'

Rhyme, see *Alternance des rimes; Masculine, feminine lines and rhymes; Rimes croisées, embrassées, équivoquées, mêlées, plates, riches, suffisantes.*

Ribot, THÉODULE (1839–1916), a philosopher, and notably a psychologist, of far-reaching influence. He held that psychology, more particularly experimental psychology, which owes its existence as an independent science in France to him, should be studied objectively, as were the natural sciences, and had nothing to do with metaphysical inquiry into the nature of the human soul. His ideas were much influenced by such 19th-century English philosophers as Hartley, J. S. Mill, Herbert Spencer, Bain, &c., whom he studied in *La Psychologie anglaise contemporaine* (1870), a work with an important introduction. Another work of great interest was his *Essai sur l'imagination créatrice* (1900). In 1876, the year in which the English journal *Mind* was founded, he founded the important *Revue philosophique de la France et de l'étranger*.

In later life his work lay particularly in the field of psychopathology.

Ricard, LOUIS-XAVIER DE (1843–1911), man of letters and author of *Les Chants de l'aube* (1862) and other collections of poetry, is chiefly remembered as having been, with Catulle Mendès (q.v.), one of the two founders of the Parnassian group of poets. The young writers who formed the group met in his mother's (the marquise de Ricard's) *salon*, and *Le Parnasse contemporain* was published after reviews he had founded (e.g. *L'Art*), and in which the Parnassian doctrines were first formulated, had failed (see *Parnassiens*). In later life he lived mainly in the Midi and divided his interests between political journalism and a movement for decentralizing literature.

Riccoboni, LODOVICO (1677–1753), an Italian actor and playwright, published in 1743 a *Traité de la réformation du théâtre*, a contribution to the dispute on the question whether theatrical performances are desirable. See *Lettre à d'Alembert.*

Riccoboni, MARIE-JEANNE (1713–92), *née* Laboras de Mézières, daughter-in-law of the preceding, novelist, author of sentimental romances, *Ernestine, Le Marquis de Crécy*, &c., including a continuation of Marivaux's *Marianne.*

Richard I, Cœur de Lion (1157–99), King of England 1189–99, was the author of two extant *serventois*, one of which, of considerable length and some historical interest, was written during his imprisonment. It laments his fate: he says in the course of it,

N'est pas merveille, se j'ai le cuer dolent,
Quant mes sires tient ma terre en torment.

Richard Cœur de Lion, see *Sedaine.*

Richard de Fournival, see *Bestiaires.*

Richelet, CÉSAR-PIERRE (1631–98), grammarian and lexicographer, see *Dictionaries and encyclopedias*, under date 1680.

Richelieu, ARMAND DU PLESSIS, CARDINAL DE (1585–1642), son of a gentleman of Poitou, the great minister of Louis XIII. He first came into prominence as Bishop of Luçon at the *États Généraux* of 1614–15, entered the Council of the queen mother about 1616, and became principal minister in 1624. He effected the ruin of the Protestant cause in France, consolidated the autocratic power of the monarchy, and extended the boundaries of France at the expense of the house of Austria. He left a *Testament* *politique,* which depicts his character and policy, and *Mémoires,* which are not by him but by other hands, though they reproduce in part his own reports to the king. These, and his letters and State papers, testify to his remarkable political ability rather than to literary talent. Nevertheless Richelieu interested himself in literature. He founded the *Académie française* (q.v.). He employed five authors, of whom Corneille was one, to write plays under his direction (see *Cinq auteurs*), and himself composed (with more or less assistance from Desmarets) the tragicomedy *Mirame,* a play of no merit, which he caused to be produced in a hall of the Palais-Royal specially built for the purpose, where later Molière's company gave its performances.

Richelieu's invitation to the *Académie* to formulate criticisms of Corneille's *Le Cid* may have been due partly to disapproval—because the play exalted the chivalrous customs of Spain, with which France was at war, and justified the duel—and partly to literary jealousy. This view has, however, been questioned in recent years.

Richelieu, ARMAND, DUC DE (1696–1788), grand-nephew of the cardinal de Richelieu, maréchal de France; he fought at Fontenoy and commanded the land forces which captured Port-Mahon in 1756, but was especially famous for his gallantries. Memoirs of his life, depicting the depraved courts of the Regent and of Louis XV, were drawn up from his notes by Jean-Louis Soulavie (1753–1813), a literary abbé of doubtful reputation; the authenticity of parts of the memoirs is questionable.

Richepin, JEAN (1849–1926), poet and dramatist, became known with *Les Chansons des Gueux* (1876), poems about tramps and vagrants in which he employed the cant of this class with much verbal dexterity. *Les Caresses* (1877), *Les Blasphèmes* (1884), and *Interludes* (1922) were of much the same type. His real success came from his dramatic works, usually in verse: *La Glu* (1883), *Nana Sahib* (1883), *Le Flibustier* (1888), *Par le glaive* (1892, a heroic drama) and *Le Chemineau* (1897, a drama of country life which for a time rivalled Rostand's *Cyrano de Bergerac,* q.v., in popularity).

Richeut, the title of the earliest extant *fabliau* (q.v.), composed about 1170.

Richeut is a successful and unscrupulous courtesan, skilled in the art of duping her lovers. She educates her son Samson so well that he becomes as great a scourge to women as she is to men. Samson sets out on his adventures, a prototype of Don Juan, but the reputation he earns gives umbrage to his mother, and she succeeds, by humiliating him, in proving the superior cunning of women.

Rictus, JEHAN [pseudonym of Gabriel Randon] (1867–1938), wrote the poems and ballads of Parisian low life collected in *Soliloques du pauvre* (1897); *Les Doléances* (1899); *Les Cantilènes du malheur* (1902); *Le Cœur populaire* (1914). They were slangy, elliptic, sincere, and often genuinely moving.

Ridadondaine, La, a name given to the *Théâtre de la Foire.*

Rideau cramoisi, Le (1874), one of the tales in Barbey d'Aurevilly's *Les Diaboliques* (q.v.).

Rigaud, Hyacinthe (1659–1743), portrait-painter, who left fine portraits of Louis XIV, Boileau, Bossuet, La Fontaine, &c.

Rigolboche, the stage name of Marguerite Badel, a favourite variety actress of mid-19th-century Paris. She was associated specially with the Délassements-Comiques, a theatre which, like the Funambules (q.v.), disappeared during the large-scale building operations of the Second Empire.

Rimbaud, ARTHUR (1854–91), a poet of precocious genius and violent, unstable character, began writing at fifteen and abandoned literature some five, or possibly ten, years later. At thirty-seven, after years as a trader, at times an explorer, at Harar and in the interior of Abyssinia, he died unaware that he had become a master for the Symbolists. He now counts as one of the strongest influences on modern, and not only French, poetry (see *Symbolisme, Surréalisme, Claudel,* &c.).

(2) He was born at Charleville in the Ardennes, and brought up, with his brother and sisters, by his mother, a dour woman of peasant stock. The father, an able army officer whose intellectual ability Rimbaud may have inherited, had forsaken the home. Rimbaud was star pupil at the Collège de Charleville, but in August 1870, excited by

the outbreak of the Franco-Prussian war and by revolutionary ideas, and rebelling against his repressive family environment, he ran away to Paris. He was arrested at the station for travelling without a ticket, and sent back to his family. Ten days later he ran away again, to Belgium, on this occasion writing some of his first original poems, and again had to return home; while a second flight to Paris (it lasted a fortnight) coincided with the Prussian entry of 1 March 1871. After this he was at home again, a defiant, unruly adolescent, devouring the public library, writing poetry, and already forming his poetic doctrine, the *théorie du voyant*. He determined that the poet, to get beyond good and evil, and express the inexpressible, must develop his creative faculty by experimenting with evil and with self-induced states of delirium. In the late summer of 1871 he sent some verses to Verlaine (q.v.), who invited him to Paris, whereupon in a burst of enthusiasm he composed *Le Bateau ivre* (q.v.), perhaps his finest poem. In Paris, where he arrived at the end of September, he met other poets, who admired his work but disliked his boorishness and arrogance. Verlaine, however, had formed a passionate attachment for him. In summer 1872 the two poets left Paris to lead a dissolute existence first in Brussels, then in London. Rimbaud sickened of the life and the relationship and returned alone to France more than once. The end came at Brussels in July 1873, after a drunken quarrel, when Verlaine fired at Rimbaud and wounded him. Verlaine went to prison, Rimbaud back to Charleville. At one time when he was at home before the break Rimbaud began, and now he finished, *Une Saison en enfer*, a work variously interpreted as his submission to, and continued denial of, religion. It consists of nine fragments (prose and poetry) of remarkable psychological retrospection and of desperate spiritual confession and self-examination. In the last—*Adieu*—the poet abandons the hells he had deliberately entered in search of experience. The work, published at Rimbaud's expense in October 1873, was poorly received and he burnt the manuscript and his papers. In 1874 he again visited England, this time with the poet Germain Nouveau (q.v.). He was in London and, for some months, Reading, where he taught French; and perhaps, during this period, wrote some of the prose poems of *Les Illuminations*. By 1875 he may—but this is not certain—have definitely abandoned literature for a life of action. For five years he wandered: in Germany and Italy in 1875 (with a further encounter with Verlaine at Stuttgart); with the Dutch army in Batavia in 1876 (deserting the moment he could); in Europe again in 1877–8 (as interpreter-manager with a circus for part of the time); in Cyprus in 1879. In 1880 he found employment in Aden with a firm of coffee exporters and was sent by them to Harar (not yet, at that date, part of Abyssinia). In time he set up on his own as trader and explorer, travelling in the interior and at one time trafficking in arms. The life was hard and he spared no effort to make money. He wrote home constantly but never mentioned literature. In May 1891 he was transported from Aden to Marseilles, in agony, with a neglected tumour on the knee. His leg was amputated and at the end of July he managed to get home to Charleville. In late August his sister Isabelle had to take him back to the hospital and there, on 10 November, he died. He was said by his sister to have been converted at the end, i.e. converted to active acceptance of the faith (Roman Catholicism) in which he had been nurtured.

(3) While he was in Abyssinia his fame had grown in Paris, thanks to Verlaine's essay on him in *Les Poètes maudits* (q.v.) and to the publication, also by Verlaine (who had the manuscript from him at Stuttgart), of *Les Illuminations* (1886, in the Symbolist review *La Vogue*). As published by Verlaine this work consisted of poems and prose poems. In the light of later research it appears that *Les Illuminations* proper consists only of prose poems and two poems in *vers libre* (q.v.), and that the other verse items were extraneous material. The work shows how strongly Rimbaud had been influenced by his early reading of Baudelaire, as well as by works on illuminist and occult philosophies, or the semi-mystical writings of Ballanche (q.v.).

(4) Rimbaud went farther than any poet before him in the exploration of the subconscious and, technically, in experimenting with rhythm and the use of words as units, without syntactical relationship, purely for their evocative and sensational value. He himself said, 'J'écrivais des silences, des nuits, je notais l'inexprimable. Je fixais des vertiges.'

(5) A first collected edition of Rimbaud's works was published in 1898 (*Œuvres de Rimbaud*) by his brother-in-law Paterne Berrichon. The complete edition by Jules Mouquet and Roland de Renéville was published in 1946 in the *Bibliothèque de la Pléiade* series. A lost work by him, *La Chasse spirituelle* (q.v.), said to have been written in early 1872 or late 1871 and to have been his greatest, engendered one of the outstanding literary frauds of modern times.

Rimes croisées, in French prosody, the alternation of masculine and feminine lines to produce an *abab* rhyme-scheme. (See also *Alternance des rimes*.)

Rimes embrassées, in French prosody, the alternation of masculine and feminine lines to produce an *abba* rhyme-scheme. (See also *Alternance des rimes*.)

Rimes équivoquées, in French prosody, a form greatly favoured by the *rhétoriqueurs* (q.v.) and praised even by Du Bellay in the *Défense et Illustration* (q.v.). The rhyming syllables are identical in spelling and sound but the words which, in various combinations, they make up have a punning sense.

Rimes mêlées, in French prosody, verses which rhyme haphazardly, according to the poet's fancy, except that the rule for the alternation of masculine and feminine rhymes is observed. They occur frequently in the light verse, madrigals, fables, chansons, &c., of the 17th century. When—as in La Fontaine's *Fables* or the choruses of Racine's *Athalie* and *Esther*—the stanzas consisted of lines of differing length ending in *rimes mêlées* they were said to be in *vers libres* or *vers irréguliers*. [Note the distinction between this free verse of the 17th century and *le vers libre* (q.v.) of the Symbolists.]

Rimes plates, see *Alternance des rimes*.

Rimes riches, in French prosody, rhyming syllables in which both the accented vowels and the consonants preceding them are identical in sound. The preceding consonant is called the *consonne d'appui*. This rhyme was much practised by the *rhétoriqueurs* and was again in favour during the 19th century. It can easily become over-elaborate and monotonous. It contrasts with

rimes suffisantes, in which the *consonnes d'appui* are not identical.

Rimes suffisantes, in French prosody, rhyming syllables in which, contrary to *rime riche* (q.v.), the consonants preceding the accented vowels are not identical.

Rimes suivies, see *Alternance des rimes*.

Riquet, the name of M. Bergeret's dog in Anatole France's *Histoire contemporaine* (q.v.).

Riquet à la houppe, one of Perrault's (q.v.) *contes*; also the title of a fairy play (1885) by Théodore de Banville (q.v.).

Rire, Le, see *Bergson, Henri* (para. 7).

Risorgimento (Ital. word = *resurrection*), the mid-19th-century movement which resulted in Italy's liberation from Austria, her recognition (1861) as an independent kingdom (in which ultimately all the small Italian states and kingdoms were united), and, finally (1870), in the end of the temporal power of the papacy. In 1858 Napoleon III came to the aid of Italy against the Austrians, who were defeated decisively at Magenta (1860).

Rivalités, Les. Two 'Scènes de la vie de province', in Balzac's *Comédie humaine* (q.v.), are united under this title, namely, *La Vieille Fille* and *Le Cabinet des antiques*.

Rivarol, ANTOINE DE (1753–1801), man of letters, journalist, and pamphleteer, was the son of a Provençal schoolmaster and had an Italian grandfather. He was educated for the Church but gave this up to come to Paris (1777), where he became celebrated for his learning, wit, and brilliant conversational powers, and where his dissipated worldly life hindered his literary work. Yet he had serious aspirations and was capable of elevated thought. His translation of Dante's *Inferno* (1783) was praised, and his *Discours sur l'universalité de la langue française* (1784, containing the famous saying 'Ce qui n'est pas clair n'est pas français') won a prize from the Academy of Berlin, praise from Frederick the Great, and a small pension from Louis XVI. His many amusing literary and political satires delighted all but his victims—e.g. *Le Chou et le navet* (1782, against Delille); *Le Petit Almanach de nos grands hommes, année 1788*; *Petit Dictionnaire* *des grands hommes de la Révolution* (1790). The most pungent satires of the royalist journal *Les Actes des apôtres* (q.v.), if not actually from his pen, were reports of his sayings. He left France in 1792, was in Brussels till 1794, then went to England and was respectfully welcomed by Pitt and Burke. But he did not stay. The fogs dismayed him. There was no conversation. The men were phlegmatic, the women (with 'deux bras gauches') unattractive. He left for the exiles' colony at Hamburg (q.v.) and remained there until 1800. During this time a Hamburg publisher wrung from him the *Discours préliminaire du nouveau dictionnaire de la langue française* (1797, a study on the dissolving social effect of contemporary philosophy, and perhaps his best work), the first instalment of a vast treatise and dictionary intended to present the human mind through the evolution of language, particularly the French language. The remainder of the book, like too many works projected by Rivarol, existed only in his conversation, but existed so vividly that whole fragments are reported in the reminiscences of his friends. He died at Berlin, where during his remaining months he had enjoyed a life that recalled the brilliance of the former *salons* of Paris. Five volumes of his *Œuvres complètes* (in fact very incomplete) were published in 1808, and his *Pensées inédites* were published in 1836. More recent selections from his writings are the *Œuvres choisies de Rivarol* (1882) and *Collection des plus belles pages de Rivarol* (1906).

Rivière, JACQUES (1886–1925), critic, essayist, and novelist, one of the literary personalities of his generation, became Secretary of the *Nouvelle Revue Française* (q.v.) in 1910 and Director in 1919. His published works include: *Études* (1911) and the posthumously published *Nouvelles Études* (1947), collected criticism (literary, art, and music) and essays (those on the novel are of exceptional interest); *Marcel Proust* (1924); *De la sincérité envers soi-même* (1926); one complete novel (*Aimée*, 1922) and one not much more than sketch of another (*Florence*, published posthumously in 1935). His correspondence between 1905 and 1914 with his friend Alain-Fournier, whose sister Isabelle he married, is the exchange of ideas and experiences between two developing young

intellectuals of the early 20th century (4 volumes, 1926–8). His correspondence with Claudel (between 1902 and 1914, published in 1926) is largely concerned with his return, under Claudel's influence, to active acceptance of Roman Catholicism. *Marcel Proust* [the great influence of his later years] *et Jacques Rivière, correspondance (1911–22)* was published posthumously in 1955.

Rivoli, a village in Northern Italy, on a plateau not far from Mantua, the scene (14 January 1797) of Bonaparte's most brilliant victory over the Austrians during his first Italian campaign. He gained the mastery of Northern Italy and marched on Vienna (see *Campo Formio*).

Robert I, born *c.* 865, second son of the Robert le Fort, comte d'Anjou, from whom the *Capétien* (q.v.) dynasty remotely stemmed, was elected King of France in 922 by the nobles who refused to submit to the authority of Charles III le Simple. He died a year later (923) fighting against his rival. His grandson Hugues Capet was the first Capetian king.

Robert II le Pieux, born *c.* 970, was King of France from 996 to 1031, in succession to his father Hugues Capet (see *Capétiens*).

Robert de Blois, see *Chastiement des dames*.

Robert de Boron, see *Perceval*.

Robert de Clary, see *Crusades*.

Robert le Diable, the subject of a legend (which originally had no connexion with Normandy) according to which a childless woman obtains a son by praying to the Devil; the son is strong and wicked and lives a lawless life, but finally repents of his misdeeds and is reconciled with the Church. The tale was attached to Robert, sixth Duke of Normandy, father of the Conqueror, about whom many legends gathered on account of his violence and cruelty. It was the subject of a French medieval romance, of which there were various versions, and also English versions. It was also the theme of one of the *Miracles de Notre-Dame* (q.v.). It is embodied in the English 15th-century metrical romance 'Sir Gowther'. In the 19th century Scribe (q.v.) wrote the libretto for Meyerbeer's *Robert le Diable* (1831, the opera described in Balzac's *Gambara*).

Robert le Fort (d. 866), from whom the *Capétiens* (q.v.) stemmed, comte d'Anjou from 864. He defended his territory with great valour against the Normans (hence *le Fort*), and was killed by an arrow when attacking them. His eldest son Eudes and his second son Robert were both kings of France. Robert (Robert I) was the grandfather of Hugues Capet (q.v.).

Robespierre, FRANÇOIS - MAXIMILIEN - JOSEPH DE (1758–94), who was one of the great leaders of the French Revolution, and also one of its great orators (cf. *Danton*; *Mirabeau*), was born at Arras. He was educated in Paris at the Collège Louis-le-Grand (see *Collège de Clermont*) and on his return to Arras practised at the bar until, in 1789, he was elected *Député du Tiers État* for Arras to the *États Généraux*. As leader of the *Jacobins* (q.v.) he emerged into full prominence after the fall of the monarchy (1792). He led the Montagnards (q.v.) in the *Convention nationale*, was a member of the *comité de salut public*, and chief organizer of the Terror, which he used as a political instrument and during which he exercised a virtual dictatorship. He was attacked in the *Convention* on 27 July 1794 (*la journée du neuf thermidor, An II*) and overthrown. The following day he was executed.

There has been more controversy about Robespierre than about any other figure of the Revolution. The people trusted him, and named him 'l'Incorruptible' because of the integrity of his private life and his rigid, and logical, adherence to his democratic ideals (cf. *Seagreen Incorruptible*).

Robinet, JEAN-BAPTISTE-RENÉ, see *Dictionaries and Encyclopedias* under date 1777–83.

Robin et Marion, see *Jeu de Robin et de Marion*.

Rocambole, the hero of many novels by Ponson du Terrail (q.v.).

Rochefort [Rochefort-Luçay], HENRI DE (1830–1913), political journalist, in early life held a minor clerical post at the Hôtel de Ville in Paris but was dismissed. He then (like his father) wrote vaudevilles and took to journalism. He contributed to *Le Nain jaune* and *Le Figaro* (qq.v.) and in 1868 founded *La Lanterne* (q.v.), a weekly in which he consistently, with both wit and venom, attacked the Government and Napoleon III. After the first numbers he was prosecuted but escaped to Belgium, where for a time he continued his paper. In 1869 he was elected Deputy for Paris. After the September Revolution (1870, see *Revolutions*, IV) he was a member of the Government of National Defence and for a time a Deputy to the *Assemblée nationale*. He described his own varied career, which included further arrests, and deportation, and the founding of two other papers, *La Marseillaise* (1869) and *L'Intransigeant* (1880), in *Les Aventures de ma vie* (5 vols. 1896–8).

Rocher du Grand-Bé, Le, the rocky islet off Saint-Malo where Chateaubriand was buried, at his own wish, in 1848. [*Bé* is an ancient Breton word for 'tomb'.] Flaubert visited it some years later and described it in a famous passage of *Par les champs et par les grèves* (ch xi):

'L'île est déserte; une herbe rare y pousse où se mêlent de petites touffes de fleurs violettes et de grandes orties. Il y a sur le sommet une casemate délabrée avec une cour dont les vieux murs s'écroulent. En dessous de ce débris, à mi-côte, on a coupé à même la pente un espace de quelque dix pieds carrés au milieu duquel s'élève une dalle de granit surmontée d'une croix latine. Le tombeau est fait de trois morceaux, un pour le socle, un pour la dalle, un pour la croix.

'Il dormira là-dessous, la tête tournée vers la mer; dans ce sépulcre bâti sur un écueil, son immortalité sera comme fut sa vie, déserte des autres et tout entourée d'orages. Les vagues avec les siècles murmureront longtemps autour de ce grand souvenir; dans les tempêtes elles bondiront jusqu'à ses pieds, ou les matins d'été, quand les voiles blanches se déploient et que l'hirondelle arrive d'au delà des mers, longues et douces, elles lui apporteront la volupté mélancolique des horizons et la caresse des larges brises. Et les jours ainsi s'écoulant, pendant que les flots de la grève natale iront se balançant toujours entre son berceau et son tombeau, le cœur de René devenu froid, lentement, s'éparpillera dans le néant, au rythme sans fin de cette musique éternelle.'

Rochers, Les, the country house and estate

of Mme de Sévigné (q.v.), a short distance south of Vitré, in Brittany.

Rocroi, in the Ardennes, the scene of a famous battle in which the Grand Condé in 1643, being then twenty-two years of age, defeated the Spanish army.

Rod, ÉDOUARD (1857-1910), novelist and critic, of Swiss origin, was educated in Switzerland. He lived in Paris for some years from 1878, then from 1886 was a professor at Geneva. He wrote over forty novels. Some early ones were naturalistic (e.g. *Palmyre Veulard*, 1881; *La Femme d'Henri Vanneau*, 1884) but the majority were psychological studies. Struggles of conscience, ill-fated passionate entanglements, or general moral problems were the themes of, for example, *Le Sens de la vie* (1889), *Les Trois Cœurs* (1890), *Le Message du Pasteur Nauche* (1898), *La Vie privée de Michel Teissier* (1893), *L'Ombre s'étend sur la montagne* (1907). He was influenced, while in France, by the vogue for the Russian novel, e.g. in *La Course à la mort* (1885), in which the narrator observes himself slipping discontentedly into futility. *Études sur le XIXᵉ siècle* (1888) and *Les Idées morales du temps présent* (1892) are collected criticism.

Rodenbach, GEORGES (1855-98), a Belgian poet and novelist (born at Tournai) who did much, with Verhaeren and Maeterlinck, to extend the Symbolist Movement (see *Symbolisme*) to Belgium. After graduating in law he went to Paris, about 1876, for further studies, frequented the small poetic groups (e.g. *les Hydropathes*, q.v.), and published his first collections of verse, including *Les Foyers et les champs* (1877), *Les Tristesses* (1879). Some years later he returned to practise at the bar in Brussels but gave this up for literature, and after 1887 he lived in Paris. Other collections of his poems are: *La Jeunesse blanche* (1886); *Le Règne du silence* (1891); *Les Vies encloses* (1896); *Le Miroir du ciel natal* (1898). They contain musical, gently melancholy descriptions of landscapes and life in the villages and old towns of Belgium. His best-known novel, *Bruges-la-morte* (1892), was dramatized in 1901 as *Le Mirage*.

Rodilard, 'bacon-gnawer', a name used by La Fontaine to designate the cat. Rabelais has the adjective 'rodibilardicque', adapted from 'rodilardus', a word invented by Calenzio.

Rodin, FRANÇOIS-AUGUSTE-RENÉ (1840-1917), sculptor, born in Paris in modest circumstances, had to support himself for many years by the ancillary crafts of sculpture, e.g. moulding, chiselling, &c. His first masterpiece (1877, *L'Age d'airain*) created a scandal, more than once the fate of his enormous, architecturally conceived works, but it was eventually bought by the State. By 1900 he was himself very much a national monument. The Hôtel Biron, with its beautiful garden, in which he lived from 1907 till his death, is now the Musée Rodin. The Austrian poet Rainer-Maria Rilke (1875-1926) was Rodin's secretary during the years he lived in Paris and was profoundly influenced by him.

Rodogune, a tragedy by Corneille, produced in late 1644 or early 1645, based on a passage in Appian. The author preferred this play to all his other works.

The scene is Seleucia. Demetrius Nicanor, king of Syria, has been captured by the Parthians. Cleopatra his queen, a woman of ruthless ambition, believing him dead, has married his brother Antiochus, and sent away his twin sons to Egypt. Antiochus has been killed, and Nicanor, angered by Cleopatra's second marriage, has set out for Syria announcing his intention to marry Rodogune, sister of the Parthian king. Cleopatra, to avoid being dispossessed of her throne, has killed Nicanor in an ambush and taken Rodogune captive. She has recalled her two sons from Egypt, intending to declare which is to inherit the crown. The two sons, Antiochus and Seleucus, both fall in love with Rodogune, but each is prepared to renounce crown and princess in favour of the other. Cleopatra tells them she will cede the crown to whichever undertakes to kill her hated rival Rodogune; Rodogune tells them she will marry whichever will kill his mother Cleopatra. Presently, however, she confesses her love for Antiochus and withdraws her stipulation. Cleopatra, dissembling her intentions, pretends to accept their marriage and to grant Antiochus the crown; but she kills Seleucus and prepares a poisoned nuptial cup for Antiochus and Rodogune. She drinks from the poisoned cup to reassure Antiochus and falls dead.

Rodolphe, a character in Eugène Sue's *Les Mystères de Paris*; in Murger's *Scènes de la vie de Bohème*, and in Flaubert's *Madame Bovary*.

Rodrigue, the hero of Corneille's *Le Cid*.

Rodrigues, OLINDE (1794–1851), born in Bordeaux, economist, a prominent *Saint-Simonien* (q.v.).

Rœderer, PIERRE-LOUIS (1754–1835), politician and economist, also historian and man of letters, a very able journalist. He was born at Metz, a magistrate's son, and at the age of twenty-five was already a prominent figure there, a counsellor of the *parlement*, known for his liberal principles. He was elected a Deputy to the *Assemblée constituante* and in Paris played an active part in public affairs during the Revolution, and even more during the Consulate and the Empire, when Napoleon was quick to appreciate his great mental energy and his exceptional financial and administrative ability. After 1815, his public career ended, he turned to the study of the 17th century, reconstructed in his own house a *salon* in imitation of the *Hôtel de Rambouillet* (q.v.), and compiled *Mémoires pour servir à l'histoire de la société polie en France* which he printed privately but circulated widely in 1835 and which did much to stimulate interest in 17th-century society.

In *Chronique de cinquante jours, du 20 juin au 10 août 1792* (1832), he gives a good picture of the critical period of the flight of the Royal family from Paris and their subsequent capture. His *Journal*, published 1909, is useful for the study of Napoleon. (See also *Proverbes*, para. 3.)

Rœmerspacher, one of the seven young *déracinés* in the novel *Les Déracinés* (q.v.) by Maurice Barrès.

Rohan, ÉDOUARD, PRINCE and CARDINAL DE (1734–1803), see *Cagliostro* and *Collier, L'Affaire du*.

Rohan, HENRI, DUC DE (1579–1638), of a noble Breton family, the principal military leader of the Protestant faction in France in the civil wars of the reign of Louis XIII, in which he played a brave, arduous, and unsuccessful part. He was exiled to Venice, but after a time returned to favour and held high military command in the war against the Imperialists of 1635. He died of wounds in 1638. He wrote *Mémoires* of the period 1610–29, of considerable historical interest; also *Le Parfait Capitaine*, an abstract of Caesar's *Gallic War*, with observations; and a political treatise *De l'intérêt des Princes et États de la Chrétienté*.

Roi Candaule, Le, by André Gide (q.v.), a drama, produced in 1901 and published in 1904.

Roi de Rome, Le, see *Napoleon II*.

Roi des montagnes, Le (1857), a tale by Edmond About (q.v.).

Roi d'Yvetot, Le, a song by Béranger (q.v.), included in *Chansons morales et autres* (1815), about the genial, easy-going ruler of a small contented country.

> [Il] n'agrandit point ses États,
> Fut un voisin commode,
> Et, modèle des potentats,
> Prit le plaisir pour code.

It was sung first at *Le Caveau* (q.v.) about 1813, when France was wearying of Napoleon's despotism and ambition. [From the 14th to the 16th centuries the lords of the territory of Yvetot, in Normandy, were exempted from duties of vassalage to the Crown and were themselves called 'rois'.]

Roi s'amuse, Le (1832), a poetic drama by Victor Hugo. (Verdi adapted the plot for his opera *Rigoletto*, 1851.)

Triboulet, the hunchback jester of François Ier, has brought up his adored only daughter in secret. The king and his court discover her existence and the king seduces her. Triboulet in despair plots to have the king murdered while he is pursuing his amours in disguise in a low quarter of the city. He goes at midnight, as arranged, to fetch the sack containing the king's corpse. Just as he is about to throw the sack triumphantly into the Seine the stitches give way and a flash of lightning illumines the face of his daughter. The girl, still in love, had contrived to take her seducer's place as victim.

Rois en exil, Les (1879), a novel by Alphonse Daudet (q.v.). It is set in the years after the downfall of the Second Empire and contrasts the reckless life of one section of society with the dignity and devotion to duty of a few individuals. The king and queen of Illyria, driven from their country by a revolution, live in exile with their son, a child of congenitally feeble constitution. At first the exiled court maintains its etiquette and a semblance of its former glory, but the king is thankful to be quit of the cares of monarchy and plunges into a dissipated, extravagant life in which his associates are mainly other fallen royalties. He loses all respect for his rank, and even pawns the crown jewels and traffics in Illyrian decorations to pay for his follies. Finally he abdicates in favour of his son, on whom the queen centres her aspirations for the future. The boy is blinded in a shooting accident, becomes still more frail, and the last hopes of a Royalist restoration in Illyria have to be abandoned.

Rois fainéants, a name given to the kings of the *Mérovingien* (q.v.) dynasty after the death (639) of Dagobert, when, his successors being minors, the power passed into the hands of the *Maires du Palais* (q.v.). The kings thereafter were allowed no share in the government, until in 751 Pépin le Bref deposed Childéric III and usurped the throne.

Roi Soleil, Le, Louis XIV.

Roland, in the *chansons de geste* (q.v.), son of a sister of Charlemagne (Berte or Gilain) and, according to one version, of Milon d'Angers, a humble seneschal, with whom she makes a runaway match. Roland is the legendary hero of many feats of arms. He is represented as proud and impetuous; but his character softens at the approach of death. For the story of Roland and Olivier and of the betrothal of Roland to Olivier's sister Aude, see under *Olivier*. The *Chanson de Roland* (q.v.) relates his last great battle and his death. His sword was called Durendal.

Roland was an historical character, warden of the marches of Brittany under Charlemagne; he accompanied the Emperor in the Spanish campaign which ended in the destruction of the French rearguard by the Basques at Roncevaux in 778. He figures as Orlando in the poems of Boiardo and Ariosto. In medieval English literature he appears in *Sir Firumbras* and *Roland and Vernagu*.

Roland, MARIE-JEANNE PHLIPON, MME (1754–93), born in Paris, the daughter of Gatien Phlipon, an engraver, married in 1780 Jean-Marie Roland de la Platière (see the following). A woman of high intelligence, sincerity, and a generous enthusiasm, a lover of nature and literature, an ardent admirer of J.-J. Rousseau, she was the inspirer of the Girondins, much of their policy being hatched in her *salon*. She hated Danton and Robespierre, and the enmity of the Montagnards brought her to the guillotine. As she mounted the scaffold she cried 'O liberté, que de crimes on commet en ton nom!'—one of the famous apostrophes of history. She left interesting *Mémoires* and letters, and from prison wrote a spirited *Appel à l'impartiale postérité*, first published in 1795 and several times re-edited.

Roland de la Platière, JEAN-MARIE (1734–93), economist and politician, held government office during the Revolution. On hearing of his wife's death (see the preceding article) he killed himself.

Rolland, ROMAIN (1868–1944), novelist, playwright, essayist, also historian and critic of music and painting. He was born at Clamecy, in Burgundy, and had a somewhat intense childhood, influenced by his widowed mother, by music, and by solitary reading. He was sent to the Lycée Louis-le-Grand, in Paris, and from there proceeded to the École normale supérieure, passing the *concours d'agrégation* (q.v.) in history in 1889. After this he spent two years, of great spiritual and cultural importance in his development, in Rome with a fellowship at the French School of Archaeology and History. Tolstoy's teachings of joy through suffering had already found him receptive. In Rome he made friends with the aged Malwida von Meysenbug, a German of Huguenot descent, a socialist who had settled in Italy after various wanderings (see also *Monod, Gabriel*). Her wide circle of friends had included Wagner and Nietzsche, and her talk of these men, and of Goethe and Beethoven, awakened Rolland's sympathy with the struggles of genius, and his lifelong conviction that spiritual freedom must transcend all bonds of race, religion, caste, or prejudice.

He returned to Paris (1895) to teach history at the École normale and the history of music at the Sorbonne (1900–12). By this time he had begun to write on music (*Histoire de l'opéra en Europe avant Lulli et Scarlatti*, 1895; the essays on *Musiciens* d'autrefois and Musiciens d'aujourd'hui, not published till 1908, &c.), and for the theatre (three poetical tragédies de la foi: Saint Louis, 1897; Aërt, 1898; Le Triomphe de la raison, 1898, and three dramas of the Revolution: Les Loups, 1898; Danton, 1900; Le 14 juillet, 1902). He had a sudden success in 1903 with a lyrically written life of Beethoven, followed later by similar, equally successful, studies of Michelangelo (1908) and Tolstoy (1911). During the Dreyfus (q.v.) case he was in close sympathy with Péguy (q.v.), campaigning with him for a revision of the verdict and afterwards collaborating in the famous Cahiers de la quinzaine (q.v.). The friendship cooled in later years, but before then several issues of the Cahiers had been devoted to publishing his most famous work Jean-Christophe (q.v., 1906–12). This long roman-fleuve (q.v.) is both the study of a musical genius of German birth who makes France his second country and the expression of Rolland's views on the fundamental kinship between the two races.

When the 1914–18 war broke out Rolland was living in retirement in Switzerland. He remained there, doing work in keeping with his international sympathies, and in 1915 published Au-dessus de la mêlée, a pamphlet appealing to intellectuals in allied and enemy countries alike to agitate for peace. It provoked resentment in many quarters. For some years after this he was a rallying-point for pacifist intellectuals. He also became interested in Buddhism and communism. This gradual evolution of his thought can be followed in, for example, the essays collected in Les Précurseurs (1919), Quinze ans de combat (1919–1934) (1934), Par la Révolution, la Paix (1935), Essai sur la mystique et l'action de l'Inde (1929–30, 2 parts and 3 vols.).

In 1919 Rolland, who had been awarded the Nobel Prize for Literature in 1916, turned again to fiction in addition to his writings of other kinds. He published Colas Breugnon (1919), sketches of Burgundian peasant life; Clérambault: histoire d'une conscience libre pendant la guerre (1925), of interest as theory rather than as a work of literature; Pierre et Luce (1925); and L'Âme enchantée (1922–33, 7 vols.). This, like Jean-Christophe, is a roman-fleuve, but with a woman as central figure (1. Annette et Sylvie, 1922;

2. L'Été, 1923; 3. Mère et fils, 1927, 2 vols.; 4. L'Annonciatrice, 1933, 3 vols.). The Cahiers Romain Rolland, in course of publication, contain correspondence of great interest, e.g. with the composer Richard Strauss, and with Malwida von Meysenbug.

Rollin, CHARLES (1661–1741), historian, rector of the University of Paris (1694), then principal of the Collège de Beauvais (1699), but obliged to retire in 1712 on account of his Jansenist views. He was the author of a valuable Traité des Études (1726–8), of an uncritical Histoire ancienne (1730–8), and of an equally uncritical Histoire romaine, of which he completed eight volumes before his death.

Rollinat, MAURICE (1853–1903), a poet of the transition from the Parnassiens to Symbolisme (qq.v.). The collections Dans les brandes (1883) and Paysages et paysans (1899) are calm descriptions of Nature and of country life. Les Névroses (1883) and L'Abîme (1886) are more often morbid or despairing.

Romains, JULES [the pseudonym adopted by Louis Farigoule] (1885–   ), poet, playwright, essayist, and novelist, born at Saint-Julien-le-Chapteuil, a village in the Cévennes, was brought up from infancy in Paris, where his father was a schoolteacher. From the Lycée Condorcet he proceeded to the École normale supérieure and passed the concours d'agrégation (q.v.) in philosophy in 1909. His literary career began about 1908 when he was associated with (though never a member of) the Abbaye (q.v.) community. They printed his Vie unanime (1908), the poems in which he first expressed the convictions which underlie all his writings (as well as the writings of the unanimiste group of poets which he founded shortly afterwards, see Unanimisme), that men cannot at all times be regarded as separate individuals; the individual may at any moment be merged in the group, and the spirit of man become one with a greater spirit that infuses whole cities ('Comment savoir si j'ai un cœur qui a aimé Quand la foule remue et que je suis en elle?'; 'Nous cessons d'être nous pour que la ville dise "Moi"'). The Petit Traité de versification (1923), by J. Romains in collaboration with G. Chennevière, can be mentioned here: a discussion of the *unanimiste* innovations in prosody. Other volumes of poetry by Romains include: *Un Être en marche* (1910); *Odes et Prières* (1913); *Europe* (1916); *L'Ode génoise* (1925); *L'Homme blanc* (1937). *Choix de poèmes* (1948) is a good representative collection of his poetry.

This author's creative output, however, has consisted far more of novels, tales, and plays than of poetry. Apart from what may be called their philosophical message these works are characterized by brilliance, irony, fine powers of observation and description, a lively, if heavy, sense of the burlesque, a facility and encyclopedic knowledge that at times border on the superficial, and also a remarkable gift, particularly noticeable in *Les Hommes de bonne volonté* (novel), his principal work, for holding the reader's attention through long passages of *reportage*. The most notable titles are: PLAYS: *L'Armée dans la ville* (1911); *Cromedeyre-le-vieil* (1920), an isolated mountain village returns suddenly to primitive customs; *Knock ou le Triomphe de la médecine* (q.v., 1923), farce; *M. Le Trouhadec saisi par la débauche* (1923); *Le Mariage de M. Le Trouhadec* (1925). In the first two (both in verse) the theme of group emotion is treated seriously, at moments lyrically. The last three, originally produced and played by Jouvet (q.v.), are among the most successful farcical comedies of modern times. All form part of the seven volumes of the author's *Théâtre* (1924–35). TALES: *Le Bourg régénéré, conte de la vie unanime* (1906), in which an incidental discovery gives a village a sense of its own entity and of new and continuing life. *Le Vin blanc de la Villette* (1914), tales and scenes of humble life in Paris; *Donogoo-Tonka* (1920, also dramatized), with a political imposture becoming matter for *l'unanimisme*. NOVELS: *Mort de quelqu'un* (1911), about the unconscious bond created between persons even remotely affected by the death and funeral of an insignificant railway employee; *Les Copains* (1913), *unanimisme* in terms of broad farce; *Psyché* (*Lucienne*, 1921, *Le Dieu des corps*, 1928, *Quand le navire*, 1929), a lavishly amorous novel with excursions into psychophysiological phenomena, and *Les Hommes de bonne volonté* (q.v., 1932–47), the generic title of twenty-seven novels which present a panorama of

French life and thought between 1908 and 1933.

Roman à tiroirs, a novel constructed as a series of episodes with no, or no very apparent, connecting thread (e.g. *Gil Blas*, q.v.). A character in Balzac's *La Maison Nucingen* speaks of having spent the hours from six till midnight telling the company 'une aventure à tiroirs'.

Roman bourgeois, Le, a novel by Furetière (q.v.), published in 1666, offering a strong contrast to the romantic literature of his day. Instead of gentlefolk disguised as shepherds or warriors and named Céladon or Artamène, we have a group of *bourgeois* from the Place Maubert in Paris, bearing such names as Vollichon, Charroselles (under which Charles Sorel is caricatured), and Mlle Collantine; magistrates, advocates, merchants, shopkeepers, sacristans, and their wives and daughters. The novel is without general plot. Instead we have incidents and scenes from the lives of these people, their love affairs, quarrels, elopements, lawsuits, marriage contracts; their characters, their dress, the dishes they eat. The principal element in the first book of the work is the courtship of Javotte, the daughter of Vollichon (a swindling lawyer, 'all whose possessions, except his bad reputation, are ill gotten') by a young *bourgeois* who apes the man of fashion. The second Book is concerned with the loves of Charroselles, an unsuccessful writer, and Mlle Collantine, the daughter of a police official. They both have a craze for litigation, and do not cease from suing one another even after marriage. This part of the work was imitated by Racine in *Les Plaideurs*. All is told with simple realism (though without charm or gaiety), giving a picture of *bourgeois* life such as we find in a novel of Balzac, but without the drama.

Romance, a French term sometimes used to signify a class of medieval songs, in stanzas each followed by a refrain, telling some simple love story, generally in dramatic form. See *Chansons à personnages*.

Romance languages [in French, *les langues romanes*], a generic or collective name for the group of languages descended from Latin, chief among these being French, Provençal, Italian, Spanish, Portuguese, and Rumanian. The French word *roman* and, via the French, the English *romance*, are derived from the Old French *romanz*, the equivalent of the popular Latin adverb *romanice, romanice loqui* meaning 'to speak in the manner of the Romani' in the conquered countries in which Rome had established her authority. In Old French, *romanz*, treated as a substantive, at first denoted the vernacular in both its spoken and its written form as opposed to the language of the Germanic invaders, and then (much more commonly) it denoted the vernacular as opposed to Latin, whether Classical Latin or Low.

For the manner in which the French language developed out of this vernacular see *French Language* (and cf. *Romania*).

Romanceros. The Spanish *romanceros* (plur. of *romancero*, a collection of romances) were collections of national and folk literature. El Cid Campeador, the partly historical, partly mythical hero of Spain, is the hero of most of them (and see *Cid, Le*). Many were translated into French, or imitated, in the early 19th century, e.g. *Les Romances du Cid* (1814 and 1823), translated by Creuzé de Lesser, and in the *Études françaises et étrangères* (1828) of Émile Deschamps. (See also *Foreign Influences on French Literature*, para. 17.)

Romances sans paroles (1874), lyrics by Verlaine. This collection contains some of his most musical and best-known verse.

Roman comique, Le, an unfinished romance by Scarron, the first volume of which appeared in 1651, the second in 1657. It is the lively account, with some coarse buffoonery interposed, of the adventures and love affairs of the members of a travelling company of actors. Some of these are well drawn: Le Destin (a young man of good family who has joined the company) and Mlle de l'Estoile (a lady whom he has rescued from a persecutor), the old players La Rancune and Caverne, the comical little lawyer Ragotin, who has attached himself to the troupe and (after the manner of Hardy and Molière) composes plays for them and is the butt of all the Company and the victim of ludicrous misadventures. The tavern life of the period is vividly depicted. The work throws a valuable light on the conditions in which provincial touring companies lived and worked in the 17th

century. It was completed by an anonymous continuator under the title of *Suite d'Offray* (but Offray was only the editor).

Roman-cycle, a term used in modern fiction for a series of self-contained but interrelated novels, a form of saga, concerned with a central character or family (e.g. Duhamel's *Salavin* series, or his *Chroniques des Pasquier*). The term probably harks back to the *cycles* (see *Cycle*) of the *chansons de geste*.

Roman d'Alixandre, see *Alexandre le Grand*.

Roman de la Poire, a medieval allegorical verse romance, in which a lover is besieged by Love in a tower, an imitation of the *Roman de la Rose* (q.v.).

Roman de la Rose, a poem in octosyllabic couplets, of which the first portion (some 4,000 lines) was written probably in the first half of the 13th century by Guillaume de Lorris (q.v.), and the remainder (some 18,000 lines) about the years 1275–80 by Jean de Meung (q.v.).

The first part is an 'Art of Love', after the model of Ovid, but in which love is the courtly gallantry of the day (*amour courtois*, q.v.) and the form is an elaborate allegory. The author relates a dream in which Oiseuse (Idleness) admits him to a garden where, amid trees, flowers, and birds, the company includes such personages as Déduit (Pleasure), Liesse, Doux Regard, Richesse, Largesse, and the god of Love himself. He discovers a beautiful rose-bud, and desires to pick it. He falls victim to the god of Love, who lays his commands upon him (the code of courtly love) and tells him of the sufferings and alleviations of his service. The lover's efforts to reach the Rose are encouraged or repelled by various other allegorical personages, representing the lady's impulses or the influences on her mind; Bel Accueil (Courtesy), Danger, Male Bouche (Slander), and so forth. Thwarted in his attempts, he is dissuaded by Reason from further efforts. Then Pity and Venus intervene and he is allowed a kiss. But Male Bouche raises an outcry, the Rose is more strictly guarded, walls are built round her, and a duenna is set to watch her. Here the poem of Guillaume de Lorris ends. Whether the poet intended to carry the story further is a matter of conjecture.

The poem was continued by Jean de Meung in a very different strain. The earlier portion had been an allegory, not devoid of picturesque quality, designed for the amusement of an aristocratic audience. This allegory now sinks into comparative insignificance, a pretext for an encyclopedic discourse, addressed to a more general public, written from a *bourgeois* standpoint, and in many passages with a coarse realistic vigour and vividness. The allegory is indeed continued and the lover's difficulties are prolonged. The siege of the fortress is undertaken. Faux Semblant (Hypocrisy, usually found, it is declared, in the guise of a friar) comes to the support of love and overcomes Male Bouche. The duenna is won over to the lover's interests; Nature intervenes on the same side; the fire-brand of Venus drives away Danger, Shame, and Fear; and the rose is won. But between the successive incidents are inserted long digressions in which the author, by quotations or imitations, incidentally shows his familiarity with the ancients, Plato, Aristotle, Livy, Cicero, Sallust, Virgil, Horace, Lucan, and others; more recent authors are also invoked, such as Boethius, Roger Bacon, John of Salisbury, and Abélard. The themes of these digressions (which show a bold and independent spirit) cover almost the whole field of medieval thought: satires on women (a reaction against their glorification in troubadour poetry), attacks on the magistrates, the hereditary nobility, and the mendicant friars, disquisitions on the origin of society and of the royal power, on property, pauperism, and marriage, on the relations of nature and art, on hallucinations and sorcery, and on the physical sciences. When the allegory brings Nature on the scene to preach obedience to her laws we have the essence of Jean de Meung's doctrine: everything that is contrary to nature is vicious and this is the criterion by which social institutions may be judged. By this we may determine true nobility, true wealth, and true love.

The popularity of the poem is attested by its survival in a large number of manuscripts, and by the influence it exerted particularly on the poets of the 14th and 15th centuries. No fewer than forty editions were printed by 1538, one by Marot in 1527; and even

Ronsard and Baïf, in spite of their condemnation of the medieval authors in general, praised Jean de Meung. The latter expressed, in his criticism of those in power, much that the humbler people were thinking, at a time when they were suffering from the exactions and robberies of their feudal chiefs; while, in setting up Nature as the sovereign guide, he showed himself animated by the true spirit of the Renaissance and a forerunner of Rabelais. Jean de Meung's attack on women provoked the indignation of Christine de Pisan (q.v.), who found a vigorous supporter in Jean Gerson (q.v.), and a regular controversy between the supporters and adversaries of the satirist ensued early in the 15th century. In English, the *Romaunt of the Rose*, attributed to Chaucer, but probably only in part written by him, is a translation, with amplifications, of the poem by Guillaume de Lorris and of portions of the continuation.

Roman de l'énergie nationale, Le, a trilogy by Maurice Barrès. The respective parts are *Les Déracinés* (1887, q.v.), *L'Appel au soldat* (1900, q.v.); *Leurs figures* (1902, q.v.).

Roman d'Eneas, see *Romans d'antiquité.*

Roman de Renart, a group of versified tales, of which the earliest and best were composed by different authors, for the most part unknown, between *c.* 1175 and *c.* 1205. These present human society, with a gay absurdity and occasional flashes of a mild and genial satire, under the guise of various animals, of which Renard the fox is the most prominent. The other principal figures are Noble the lion, Ysengrin the wolf, Brun the bear, Tibert the cat, Chantecler the cock, and Tiercelin the rook, each provided with a wife and each marked by his peculiar animal characteristics. Their various adventures are the subject of the tales. One of the best known is the *Jugement de Renart*: Dame Pinte the hen demands justice at the court of Noble the lion, against Renard for the death of Dame Coupée, one of her relatives, and not the first to suffer from Renard's tooth. Renard is sentenced to be hanged, but obtains a reprieve on condition that he ends his days in the Holy Land in expiation of his crimes. He starts on his way, but as soon as he reaches a safe distance, throws away his pilgrim's staff and heaps insults on the august assembly. Dame Coupée is venerated as a saint and martyr, and miracles are performed at her tomb. The incidents of the trial, in which the animals display their characters, make an amusing little comedy. The general theme of the tales, so far as they have one, is the conflict of wit and cunning with brute force. The best of them (they vary greatly in merit) show narrative and dramatic skill, wit, and delicacy of touch. Their origin is partly in Greco-Roman fables, but to a greater extent in the general popular traditions of Europe. The *Roman de Renart* had a direct precursor in the Latin *Ysengrimus* completed at Ghent in 1148; the two poems are similar in spirit, and certain episodes are common to both.

(2) Further branches of the *Roman* continued to be produced in the first half of the 13th century, but these are generally inferior in invention. In some, earlier episodes are rehandled; in others, the animals lose their distinctive characteristics and are merely names for human beings; in some Renard himself does not figure at all. The satire becomes more bitter, and Renard, from being an agreeable rascal, becomes a personification of Evil.

(3) The popularity of this group of works gave 'renard' to the French language as the ordinary word for a fox, in place of the older 'goupil'. A Flemish version of the group, no longer extant, was translated and printed by Caxton in 1481. Goethe wrote a free translation, *Reineke Fuchs*, in 1794. Chaucer's *Nun's Priest's Tale* appears to be developed from one of the episodes in the *Roman*.

(4) In the second half of the 13th century two further works related to the *Roman de Renart*, the *Couronnement de Renart* and *Renart le Nouvel*, were produced. The first is a bitter and melancholy criticism of contemporary society, Renard (who contrives to be proclaimed king in place of Noble the lion) being presented as the embodiment of hypocrisy, cupidity, and other vices. The second poem, by Jacquemart Gelée, a poet of Lille, is a long and chaotic satirical allegory, interspersed with songs, and directed especially against the clergy and religious orders. It relates various phases of a conflict between Noble the king and Renard accompanied by personified vices, and ends

with their reconciliation. A third allegory, *Renart le Contrefait*, by an anonymous writer, an unfrocked cleric of Troyes, appeared early in the 14th century. This somewhat incoherent work presents Renard sometimes in the comical character of the early tales, sometimes allegorically as the source of current abuses, sometimes again condemning the vices that are their cause. The author introduces discourses on all sorts of subjects, displaying his erudition. See also *Renart le Bestourné*.

(5) Editions of the *Roman de Renart* include one by Ernest Martin (Strasbourg, 1882–7) and one (in course of publication since 1948) by Mario Roques.

Roman de Rou, see *Wace*.

Roman de Thèbes, a poem composed by an unknown author about the middle of the 12th century, one of the principal French epics dealing with antiquity (see *Romans d'antiquité*). It consists of some 10,000 octosyllabic verses in rhyming couplets, and tells the story of Oedipus, followed by that of Eteocles and Polynices and the siege of Thebes. In this latter part the author follows in its main lines the *Thebaid* of Statius, adding a sentimental element in episodes of his own invention, such as the falling in love of Parthenopacus and Antigone, and all sorts of military incidents. The poem ends with the intervention of Theseus to secure the burial of the besiegers who have fallen on the field, the destruction of the city, and the death of Creon.

Roman de Troie, a poem of some 30,000 octosyllabic verses in rhyming couplets, by Benoît de Sainte-Maure (q.v.), probably written *c.* 1160 and dedicated to Eleanor of Aquitaine. It relates the legendary history of Troy from the Argonauts to the death of Ulysses after his return home from the siege. It thus forms part of the 'romans d'antiquité' (q.v.). The narrative is based on the pretended record of Dares Phrygius and Dictys Cretensis, who claimed to have fought in the Trojan war on the Trojan and Greek sides respectively. It makes Hector rather than Achilles the principal hero of the story. It depicts antiquity in many respects under the guise of the feudal society of the 12th century, and adds episodes of gallantry (the author appears to have been the first to invent the story of Troilus and Cressida, whom he calls Briseida). But the main interest lies in the elaboration of lyrical monologue and the analysis of various types of love. The poem was extremely popular and was widely diffused, translated, and imitated.

Roman des Sept Sages, see *Sept Sages* and *Dolopathos.*

Roman d'un jeune homme pauvre, Le (1858), a novel by Octave Feuillet (q.v.).

Roman expérimental, Le (1880), Zola's statement of the aims of *Naturalisme* (q.v.).

Roman-feuilleton, a novel published in instalments as part of a daily paper. Novels were first serialized (about 1830) in the fortnightly and monthly periodicals. The first *roman-feuilleton* was a translation of the 16th-century Spanish picaresque romance *Lazarillo de Tormes* (q.v.), of which a few chapters appeared in the newspaper *Le Siècle* (q.v.) from 5 August 1836. Two months later the same paper began publication of Balzac's *La Vieille Fille.* Other papers quickly followed suit, notably *La Presse* (q.v.), and 1836 to 1850 was a flourishing period. The masters of the art were Eugène Sue, Frédéric Soulié, Balzac, Dumas *père,* and, in a less degree, George Sand (qq.v.). The *romans-feuilletons* made the success of many papers; Eugène Sue is even said to have been released from imprisonment on one occasion so that publication of his novel might continue without break. Drawings of the period show people in the provinces collecting in one another's houses for a reading of the *roman-feuilleton* on the day the newspapers arrived. For the most part *roman-feuilletonistes* wrote from one day to another with no preconceived plan, piling up the intrigue and breaking off each day's instalment at a moment of suspense. Eugène Sue spoke of writing the *Mystères de Paris* by instinct, with no idea where he was going.

Roman-fleuve, a continuous series of novels, of which each one may be complete in itself, following the life and spiritual development of one character or group of characters. In his preface to *Jean-Christophe* (q.v.), which is typical of the genre, Romain Rolland says: 'Jean-Christophe m'est apparu comme un fleuve; . . . il est, dans le cours des fleuves, des zones où ils s'étendent, semblent dormir, . . . ils n'en continuent pas moins de couler et changer . . . .' (Cf. *Roman-cycle.*)

Romania, a quarterly review founded in 1872, and still continuing, for the study of the Romance languages and literatures. Paul Meyer and Gaston Paris were the original editors. The first article in the first number (by Gaston Paris) studied the history of the word *roman* and of words derived from it (cf. *Romance languages*).

Romanische Bibliothek, ed. Wendelin Foerster (Halle, 1888–1926, 24 vols.), an important series of medieval French and Anglo-Norman texts.

Romans bretons, or **Romans de la Table Ronde,** poems written, for the most part in octosyllabic couplets, *c.* 1150–1250, relating to the 'matière de Bretagne', that is to say, recounting adventures of which the scene is a 'Brittany' that includes Cornwall, Wales, and Ireland, and the characters are 'Breton', such as those of Arthur and his knights or of Tristram and Iseult. There is no evidence that the legends related in them in fact originated in Brittany properly so called. Geoffrey of Monmouth (q.v.) in his fabulous *Historia Regum Britanniae* (1135) had given considerable space to tales of Merlin and Arthur. This had been translated into French by Wace as early as 1155, and appears to have been the source of inspiration of Chrétien de Troyes and other authors of *romans bretons,* who drew on their imagination for much of the remainder. Eleanor of Aquitaine (wife of Louis VII and subsequently of Henry II) had brought into the feudal society of Northern France and of England something of the more refined spirit of the South, and prepared it to welcome a type of poetry strongly contrasting with the *chansons de geste,* particularly in the position it assigned to women (see *Amour courtois*). For the principal authors of *romans bretons* see *Marie de France; Chrétien de Troyes; Thomas; Boron.* See also *Lancelot; Tristan; Perceval* (for the Grail legend); *Galaad; Guinglain; La Mule sans frein; Méraugis.*

Prose adaptations of some of these were produced in the 13th century and again when the printing-press first came into use (late 15th and early 16th centuries). See also *Bibliothèque bleue.*

Romans courtois, a term used to designate various types of medieval romances, such as the *romans bretons*, the *romans* or *cycle de l'antiquité*, and miscellaneous tales of adventure known as the *romans d'aventure* (qq.v.). They are nearly all in verse, in octosyllabic couplets with a few exceptions, and were destined to be read aloud, not sung. They are thus sharply distinguished from the *chansons de geste*, and were intended for a more limited and refined audience; their main purpose was to set up an ideal of cultivated and sentimental life.

Romans d'antiquité, a group of medieval metrical romances of which the subjects are drawn from the writings of ancient Latin authors ('matière de Rome la grant', in the words of Jean Bodel, q.v.). The chief of these were the romances of the late 11th to the early 13th century dealing with *Alexandre le Grand*, and the *Roman de Troie* and *Roman de Thèbes* (qq.v.), both of the 12th century. Of about the same date is *Eneas*, a travesty of the *Aeneid*, in which the sentimental and marvellous elements are expanded and the influence of Ovid is shown. Minor poems of this group, also inspired by Ovid, are *Piramus et Tisbe*, *Narcissus*, and *Philomena* (i.e. the story of Philomela and Procne, perhaps by Chrétien de Troyes).

Romans d'aventure. In a general sense a *roman d'aventure* is the type of fictional narrative in which the element of adventure predominates over that of sentiment. The term *romans d'aventure* is also applied in a narrower sense to a group of romances which developed and attained great popularity in the 12th–13th centuries, most of them in verse, a few in prose or in mingled prose and verse, resembling the *romans bretons* in that they dealt with love and chivalry, but differing in that the scene is not 'Brittany' but in various lands. They make no claim to be historical but are fictions, designed solely to please. Their sources are to be found in antiquity or in the East, in Celtic myth or popular tradition. They are in general written in harmonious verse (as a rule the octosyllabic couplet) and present a refined civilization, for unintentionally they throw much light on the manners of the day. With some exceptions they exalt the role of women, for whose entertainment they were, unlike the *chansons de geste*, principally in-tended. They include such works as *Ipomedon*, *Partenopeu*, the *Lai de l'ombre*, *Guillaume de Dole*, *Aucassin et Nicolette*, *Le Châtelain de Coucy*, *Guillaume de Palerme*, *Floire et Blancheflor*, and *Robert le Diable* (qq.v.). The above are in verse with the exception of the *chante-fable* (so named by the author) *Aucassin et Nicolette* which is partly in prose, partly in verse. Among prose romances of this class we have the *Conte du roi Constant l'empereur* and *Le Roi Flore et la belle Jeanne*.

Romantic drama, see *Romantisme*.

Romantisme, Le, a new spirit which made itself felt in French literature towards the beginning of the 19th century and found full expression a few years later in the Romantic Movement. The spirit was by no means confined to French literature (see *Foreign Influences on French Literature*, paras. 10–20), but its manifestations in other countries fall outside the province of the present *Companion to French Literature*. [NOTE: Authors and works referred to in this article receive fuller mention under separate headings.]

(1) The outstanding characteristic of 18th-century French literature had been the primary importance it attached to reason, and to clarity and objectivity in both the conception and the expression of ideas. About the turn of the century, almost imperceptibly at first, but with the change gradually imprinting itself upon men's consciousness, literature became a matter of senses and emotions. Nature, hitherto an almost unremarked background, emerged as something of which men were palpitatingly aware, to some extent because of its intrinsic beauty, still more as something in which they saw their own moods and questionings reflected. Restlessness, strange melancholies, dreamings and discontents, unaccountable upsurges of happiness, waves of unreasoning emotion, all found their counterpart in Nature. A leaf drifts soundlessly to earth, from the lake the sedge is withering, from the mountain slopes the bronze confusion of cowbells descends upon the breeze; and the early 19th century stands entranced in melancholy before the prospect, then turns to brood upon the endless 'whys' and 'whithers' of existence, to sink under the *mal du siècle*.

(2) Several influences had combined to bring this about: the writings of J.-J.

Rousseau (d. 1778); the political upheaval of the Revolution (1789), with its inevitable intellectual reverberations; the chaotic educational system of the succeeding years; the unsettled world in which the young generation grew to maturity; the return of the *émigrés*, with minds broadened and receptivity deepened by contact with other nations; the discovery of novel beauties, far removed from the French canons, in foreign literatures; the revival of interest in the Middle Ages; and, finally, the works of the two great precursors of the Romantic Movement, Chateaubriand and Mme de Staël. The one by his creative writings (e.g. *René*, *Atala*) incarnated the essence of the young Romantic spirit; the other by her criticism (*De la littérature* and *De l'Allemagne*) interpreted foreign literature to her fellow countrymen and emphasized the distinction, then novel, between Romantic and Classical literature. Though the word *romantisme* was not employed before 1822, and *romantique* served both as noun and adjective, the theory of *romantisme* came into being with Mme de Staël.

(3) The *mouvement*, or *école*, *romantique* gave practical expression to the new spirit by recognizing that the conventions governing classical literature—the drama especially, to begin with—were too rigid to allow the free play of moods and sensations. Its nucleus, the first of the romantic *cénacles* (q.v.), was the *salon* of Charles Nodier, then Keeper of the *Bibliothèque de l'Arsenal* (q.v.), where a number of authors, young in years or in spirit, used to meet (1823) to discuss literature and read their works. Writers to be seen there included the poets Lamartine (infrequently), Vigny, and Hugo, all of whom had already published first works (Lamartine's *Méditations poétiques*, 1820; Vigny's *Poèmes*, 1822; Hugo's *Odes*, 1822) strongly permeated by the new spirit and, in Hugo's case, heralding an astonishing new poetic force. Later comers were Alfred de Musset and Dumas *père*.

(4) The Romantic theorists claimed, through their spokesman, Hugo, that there should be *liberté dans l'art* (cf. *Réalisme*), and that they should be free in their choice and treatment of subject and in their choice of words. If correct thought, perfection of style, the dramatic conventions, or the classical standards of the beautiful, hampered the true representation of life, with its mingling of the sublime and the grotesque, the old rules must be abolished. The poet's mission was to relate the colours and harmonies of Nature to his own changing moods, to lay bare his innermost self: if he was to achieve this object the vocabulary must be enlarged and the rules of versification relaxed.

(5) The Romantic doctrines were frequently expounded in literary reviews associated with the movement, e.g. *La Muse française* (q.v., and see *Press, Development of*, para. 12). But the most famous manifesto was Hugo's preface to his drama *Cromwell* (1827); and it was in the theatre that the great Romantic battles were fought. The notable dates are the production of Dumas *père*'s prose drama *Henri III et sa cour* (1829), of Vigny's adaptation of *Othello* (1829), and, particularly, of Hugo's lyrical drama *Hernani* (1830). After these striking and unexpected successes the Romantics were no longer upstarts: they were a conquering force. Yet, apart from the lasting technical innovations which it introduced, many of them, such as freedom of language and of versification, applying equally to poetry, the Romantic drama did not, in fact, wear very well. It was unwieldy, and slow-moving, and plays which interrupted their action to introduce historical, philosophical, or literary disquisitions lost in dramatic intensity.

(6) In other branches of literature the influence of *le romantisme* was more dynamic. The preoccupation with the self produced a note of lyrical expansiveness that dominated the poetry of the period and resounded in many of the novels, e.g. those of George Sand. It also, in its more uneasy aspects, reflected or produced such early psychological novels as *Obermann*, by Senancour, *Adolphe*, by Benjamin Constant, and *Volupté*, by Sainte-Beuve, which were partly autobiographies, largely dissections of the authors' souls.

(7) Like all great creative and revolutionary movements the Romantic Movement had its excesses and its decadent offshoots. The yearnings for the Infinite, the eternal questionings, led to a morbid preoccupation with death, the horrors of the tomb, and beyond. Or, again, the step was short from belief in the glorification of the individual—usually a sardonic, Byronic

creature of superior intelligence, whose very crimes were grander than the virtues of ordinary mortals—to contempt for the bourgeois and the desire to shock. Thus the genre of frenetic romanticism began. Vampirism, lurid crimes, so-called Satanism, flourished in the days of the *bousingos* (q.v.), the wild young Romantics of the thirties, but it was an extravagance that exhausted itself with the years. Théophile Gautier, once the most truculent of the Romantics, was to find in later life that his loudly-proclaimed theories of 'l'art pour l'art' led him far away from the individual to the serenely Parnassian verse of *Émaux et Camées*. Among the minor, fiery figures some died young, others took to respectability and journalism. A few later survivals have a place in literature almost as anachronisms (cf. *Barbey d'Aurevilly*). On the other hand, though *romantisme* and *classicisme* provide seemingly eternal subjects for controversy, the grand Romantic figures—Chateaubriand, Hugo, Lamartine, Vigny, the Musset of *Les Nuits*—are now established classics of French literature.

(8) The concern of the present *Companion* is with the Romantic Movement in French literature and drama, but this movement had its counterparts in music and painting. Gautier (see para. 7) began his career as an art student and he approached literature at all times with an artist's eye. Berlioz, who (in France) dominated the Romantic Movement in music, was as strongly influenced by Shakespeare and Goethe as were his literary contemporaries. Géricault and Delacroix were the outstanding Romantic painters, and the latter's *Journal* shows the part played in his life by literature and music. Next to these two come the many painters and engravers, e.g. Devéria, Johannot, Nanteuil, Scheffer, whose illustrations were an almost inseparable feature of the books by Romantic writers. This aspect of the movement is interestingly studied in *Les Vignettes romantiques*, by Champfleury (q.v.).

Rome (1896), the second novel of Zola's (q.v.) trilogy *Les Trois Villes*.

Rome, Naples et Florence en 1817 (1817), see *Stendhal*, para. 2.

Rome, rue de, a street in Paris, near the Gare Saint-Lazare, where the poet Mallarmé

lived during his Paris years. It was in his apartment in this street that he entertained his friends on Tuesday evenings, the famous 'mardis de la rue de Rome'.

Romme, GILBERT (1750–95), mathematician, a Deputy to the *Convention nationale* during the Revolution, was responsible for the chronology of the Republican Calendar (q.v.). He also presented the *Convention nationale* with a work compiled by himself and collaborators who included Daubenton, Parmentier, and Lamarck (qq.v.), a gently innocent little almanac describing an agricultural product or implement for each day of the year. Names were sometimes altered in the interests of patriotism: a variety of plum became 'la prune de citoyen' with a footnote 'ci-devant de Monsieur'.

Roncevaux, see *Chanson de Roland*.

Rondeau, a poem (in its typical form) of thirteen lines—either of eight syllables or of ten syllables with caesura after the fourth—on two rhymes, forming three strophes, successively of five, three, and five lines. The second and third of these strophes are supplemented by a refrain consisting of the first word or words of the first strophe. The rhyme can be patterned variously, as shown below (R indicates the refrain, which does not rhyme with any other line):

    a b a b a, a b a R, a b b a a R
or
    a a b b a, a a b R, a a b b a R
etc.

Villon, Marot, Voiture, Voltaire, Musset, were among the masters of this verse-form.

The *rondeau redoublé* is composed of six quatrains rhyming alternately a b a b and b a b a, of which the last is followed by a refrain consisting of the first word or words of the poem.

Rondel, a poem consisting of two quatrains and a *cinquain*, on two rhymes only, and rhyming as follows (the capitals indicate refrains):

    A B B a   a b A B   a b b a A

The best poems in this form are by Charles d'Orléans (q.v.).

Rondet, see *Chansons à danser*.

Ronsard, PIERRE DE (1524–85), poet and humanist, of a good family of the Vendômois, the central figure of the French poetical Renaissance. His father served with distinction in Italy under Louis XII and François Ier, and was, moreover, a man of letters. Ronsard became a page at court and in 1537–9 visited Scotland in the suite of the two successive French queens of James V (Madeleine de France and Marie de Guise), and also attended the humanist Lazare de Baïf on a mission to a religious conference at Haguenau. But, owing to incipient deafness, he withdrew about 1541 to the study of letters, coming under the influence of Peletier and Dorat (qq.v.) and being led by them to pursue the reform of French poetry through the study of Greek and Latin literature. For the story of Ronsard's meeting with du Bellay see under the name of the latter. For five years Ronsard, with du Bellay and the young Baïf, studied at the Collège de Coqueret under Dorat. His first ode appeared among the *Œuvres poétiques* of Peletier in 1547. His *Odes* (first four Books) were published in 1550, the collection of sonnets entitled *Amours* (and the fifth Book of the *Odes*) in 1552, a reprint of the *Amours* with a commentary by Muret and four additional odes (including the famous *Mignonne, allons voir si la rose*) in 1553, his *Bocage* in 1554, his *Hymnes* in 1555–6. These, with additions, were republished in his collected *Œuvres* in 1560.

(2) Ronsard's *Odes* and *Amours* were received with enthusiasm by the cultured, and, after a time, by the court. The arrogance with which he and du Bellay announced their new doctrines had offended Mellin de Saint-Gelais, the leader of the old school, but a reconciliation was effected. By 1560 Ronsard had probably reached the summit of his fame. He enjoyed the protection of Charles IX and his sister Marguerite, and the admiration of Mary Stuart, who later sent him a present from her imprisonment. He occupied the position of court poet, and before long was granted an annual stipend besides two priories in Vendômois and Touraine. In 1561–3 appeared his chief political poems, of which more below, and in 1565 his *Abrégé de l'art poétique français*, as well as his *Élégies, Mascarades, et Bergeries*, lyrical pieces for court entertainments, dedicated to Queen Elizabeth, and including poems addressed to herself, to Dudley, and to Cecil. The four books of his unfinished

epic, the *Franciade*, appeared in 1572. After the death of Charles IX (1574) Ronsard gradually withdrew from court to a retired and studious life, in great part spent in his priories. To his latter years we owe the collection of *Sonnets pour Hélène*, first published in the 1578 edition of his *Œuvres*. He died in 1585 at his priory of Saint-Côme in Touraine.

(3) For the general character of the poetical revolution of which Ronsard was the central force see under *Pléiade*. He made his first public contribution thereto by his *Odes*, introducing great lyrical poetry on the model of Pindar, assuming for the poet a lofty role, celebrating important events and distributing praise and blame to the great. The Odes were intended to be sung, generally with stringed accompaniment, and we have the airs prepared for them by composers of the day, among them Janequin and Certon; certain metrical peculiarities, such as the alternation of masculine and feminine rhymes, are the outcome of this intention. The defect of his Pindaric odes was the excessive and indiscriminate imitation of their prototype, the immoderate use of mythology, metaphors, and other pedantry. Ronsard soon abandoned this phase of his writing, and turned to Horace as his chief model in the *ode grave* (moral, satirical, literary, political, or encomiastic). For the *ode légère* (erotic, bacchic, or rustic) he found models not only in Horace, Catullus, Ovid, and (for a time) Petrarch, but also in Anacreon. The collection of imitations of Anacreon known as the *Anacreontea*, first published by H. Estienne in 1555 as being the work of Anacreon himself, aroused Ronsard's enthusiasm. It is on the light ode and the sonnet that his fame is especially founded, and the poems that are most remembered are free from his early pedantry. It is in these especially that he introduced a new rhythm into French poetry.

(4) Of the women principally celebrated in his love poems, the Cassandre of the *Amours* was Cassandre Salviati, the daughter of a Florentine banker settled in France; the lady maintained a chaste reserve and remained for the poet an inspiration of ideal love. Who the Marie of the sonnets was, except that she was an Angevin peasant girl who died young, is not known. Hélène was Hélène de Surgères, a maid of honour of Catherine de Médicis. The *Hymnes* celebrating the king

and other high personages, of little interest to the modern reader, are of importance as showing Ronsard's adaptation of the alexandrine to moral and philosophical subjects, narratives, and allegories. The *Franciade* was his not very fortunate attempt at an epic. It relates the legend of Francus, son of Hector of Troy, the fabled progenitor of the French kings. It was written (at the request, it is said, of Charles IX) not in alexandrines but in decasyllabic verse, and was discontinued at the death of the king. His political poems, the *Institution pour l'adolescence du Roi très chrétien*, in which he treats of the reciprocal duties of kings and subjects, the *Discours des misères de ce temps* (i.e. of the period of the wars of religion), and *Remontrance au peuple de France*, urging the nation to rally round the king in the struggle with the Huguenots, contain some of his best and most natural work, in which patriotic ardour overcomes his erudition and produces some of his most eloquent alexandrines. The *Sonnets pour Hélène* of his later years, perhaps in some measure provoked by the rivalry of a new and rising court poet, Desportes, include some of his most perfect poems, among others the famous *Quand vous serez bien vieille*.

(5) Ronsard continued to be admired for some fifty years after his death; but he was condemned by Malherbe and his poetry fell into strange neglect and contempt. The best of his doctrines were adopted by the 17th century, but he himself was remembered chiefly for his defects. His popularity was not revived until the 19th century. Among the many editions of Ronsard's works and treatises concerning him, special mention may be made of those of Paul Laumonier.

Roonel, DAN, in the *Roman de Renart* (q.v.).

Roquefort, JEAN-BAPTISTE BONAVENTURE DE, see *Dictionaries and Encyclopedias*, under date 1829.

Roquelaure, GASTON-JEAN-BAPTISTE, MARQUIS and later DUC DE (1617–83), lieutenant-general and master of the wardrobe, celebrated at the court of Louis XIV for his witticisms.

Roqueplan, NESTOR (1804–70), a well-known *boulevardier* of the Second Empire. He was a journalist, part founder (1854) of *Le Figaro* (q.v.), sometime theatre manager,

but mainly wit, leader of fashion, and a typical 'dandy'.

Roscel[l]in or **Roscel[l]inus** (d. after 1121), a native of Northern France, and a famous scholastic philosopher, chief founder of Nominalism. Abélard was for a time his pupil.

Rose, Roman de la, see *Roman de la Rose*.

Rose-Croix, Frères de la, see *Rosicrucians, Rosicrucianism*.

Rose-Croix, Théâtre de la, see *Péladan*.

Rosicrucians, Rosicrucianism. Many 17th- and 18th-century illuminists, who were often moral and religious reformers beneath a cloak of occultism, called themselves *Rosicrucians*, claiming various forms of secret and magical knowledge, such as the transmutation of metals, the prolongation of life, and power over the elements and elemental spirits [O.E.D.]. They professed to belong to a society or order which had originated in the 15th century, when one Christian Rosenkreuz brought the secret wisdom of the East back with him to Germany from a pilgrimage. It is uncertain whether the order itself ever existed, but the esoteric, semi-occult, semi-religious philosophy of Rosicrucianism became prominent in Germany after 1615, when the poet and religious writer Andreae (1586–1654) published a *Confessio Roseae Crucis*. It aroused interest in France in the 18th century, when it had a supposed connexion with Freemasonry, and in the 19th century it influenced such widely differing writers as Balzac (e.g. his *Études philosophiques*) and, later, the Symbolists (cf. *Villiers de l'Isle-Adam*, *Joséphin Péladan*). Rosicrucians in France were known as *Frères de la Rose-Croix*.

Rosier de Madame Husson, Le, the name-tale of a collection (1888) of stories by Maupassant (q.v.).

Rosine, the heroine of Beaumarchais's *Le Barbier de Séville* (q.v.), who reappears as the Comtesse Almaviva in his *Le Mariage de Figaro* (q.v.) and *La Mère coupable*.

Rosny, BARON DE, the name by which Sully (q.v.) was known during the early part of his career.

Rosny, J.-H. [collective pseudonym of the brothers JOSEPH-HENRI ('Rosny aîné', 1856–1940) and SÉRAPHIN-JUSTIN ('Rosny jeune', 1859–1948)], novelists, who wrote usually in collaboration. Some of their novels had a contemporary interest, e.g. *Nell Horn, de l'armée du Salut* (1886), London life; *Le Bilatéral* (1887), anarchist circles in Paris; *Le Termite* (1890) and *La Fauve* (1899), Parisian literary and theatrical life. Others, their best known, had prehistoric or semi-scientific settings, e.g. *Vamireh* (1892), *Eyrimah* (1895), *La Guerre au feu* (1911), *Le Félin géant* (1920, by Rosny aîné alone).

Rossbach, a village in Saxony, scene of the famous battle in 1757 in which the army of Frederick the Great defeated the French (under the maréchal de Soubise) and the Imperialists.

Rossini, GIOACCHINO ANTONIO (1792–1868), the Italian opera-composer, lived a great part of his life, and died, in Paris. For eighteen months from 1820 he was director of the Théâtre Italien (the Opéra-Comique, q.v.). Thereafter he held the post specially created for him of Premier Compositeur to the king (he wrote a one-act opera *Il Viaggio a Reims* for the coronation of Charles X in 1825 and used it later in *Le Comte Ory*). His most famous opera, *Il Barbiere di Siviglia,* after Beaumarchais (q.v.), was produced in Rome in 1816. *Guillaume Tell,* to a French libretto, his last opera and his intended master-piece, was produced in Paris in 1829.

In France, Rossini's fame and influence extended beyond music (on which his influence was very strong) to literature and also to the social world, where his wit, irony, and at times buffoonery were much appreciated, and his Saturday night receptions were crowded to suffocation. Balzac and Stendhal stand out among his admirers. The former refers to him particularly in the two 'Études philosophiques' *Massimilla Doni* (q.v.) and *Gambara.* Stendhal's *Vie de Rossini* (1823), for long the main source for biographers, is an anecdotal work (in the manner of *Promenades dans Rome*), with long analyses of the operas, and full of interesting and, like his *Racine et Shakspeare* (q.v.) of the same period, fundamentally Romantic music and literary criticism.

Rostand, EDMOND (1868–1918), poetic dramatist, won sudden fame in 1897 with the heroic comedy *Cyrano de Bergerac* (q.v.) and followed this with *L'Aiglon* (1900), an historical drama based on the life of Napoleon's son (see *Napoleon II*). A later work, *Chantecler* (1910, q.v.), an allegorical drama, was less successful but is sometimes said to have contained his best writing. His earlier dramas were: *Les Romanesques* (1894), *La Princesse lointaine* (1895), *La Samaritaine* (1897).

Rostand, JEAN (1894–   ), son of the foregoing, a biologist who has also made a name for himself as an essayist and moralist, a writer of great talent and sincerity, who does not hold it possible for belief in a spiritual explanation of the universe to persist in the face of a full comprehension of modern biological science. His outstanding works of a lay character include: *L'Aventure humaine* (1933–5), *Le Journal d'un caractère* (1931), *Pensées d'un biologiste* (1939), *La Vie et ses problèmes* (1939).

Rostand, MAURICE (1891–   ), elder son of Edmond, dramatist (e.g. the verse-dramas *La Gloire,* 1921; *Le Secret du sphinx,* 1924, &c.). He has also published verse and novels.

Rôtisserie de la Reine Pédauque, La (1893), a celebrated philosophical romance (cf. *Voltaire*) by Anatole France.

We are in the 18th century. The abbé Coignard, a learned cleric, combines a liberal humanism with a profound and ingenuous piety. He loves women. He sustains himself in misfortune with the bottle of wine and the *Consolations* of Boethius drawn from his cloak pocket. He steals diamonds, but when they prove false and unsaleable he recognizes the manifestation of God's will to preserve him from sin. Preferment continually passes him by.

In return for food and drink at the Reine Pédauque, a tavern, he becomes tutor to Jacques Ménétrier, known as 'Tournebroche' ('turnspit'), the proprietor's son (and the narrator of the book). With his pupil he undertakes to translate Greek papyri for M. d'Astarac, an eccentric occultist who lives in a dilapidated château, in a mystical world of sylphs and salamanders. In a pavilion in the grounds lives Mosaïde, supposedly a centenarian scholar, learned in the cabbalistic mysteries of the Old Testament (see

Cabbala), actually an absconding Portuguese banker. With him is Jahel, no salamander as at first imagined, but his flesh-and-blood niece, beautiful, and free with her charms. There is a brawl in Paris, after which the abbé, his pupil, and a rakish marquis, enamoured of Jahel, flee the city, taking Jahel with them. They are pursued and overtaken by Mosaïde, who stabs the abbé, thinking him to be Jahel's abductor. The abbé's death is edifying. The marquis and Jahel continue their journey and Jacques Tournebroche returns to Paris, to become a bookseller.

Les Opinions de Jérôme Coignard (1893), nominally a collection made by Jacques Tournebroche of the abbé's reflections on life, is a vehicle for Anatole France's sharp criticism of contemporary life and politics.

Rotrou, JEAN DE (1609–50), dramatist, born at Dreux, author of tragedies, tragicomedies, and comedies showing a marked advance in their style and romantic quality on those of Hardy. He was the friend of Corneille and his only rival in his day. Molière drew freely on his comedies. He was one of the five authors who wrote plays under the direction of the cardinal de Richelieu (see *Cinq auteurs*). His first play, *L'Hypocondriaque ou le mort amoureux*, appeared in 1628, before he was twenty, the tragedy *Hercule mourant* in 1634; but his best works date from his later years: the tragedies *Saint Genest* (1646), *Venceslas* (1647), and *Cosroès* (1649); the tragicomedies *Laure persécutée* (1627) and *Don Bernard de Cabrère* (1648); and the comedies *Les Sosies* (1636) and *La Sœur* (1645). The plots of these are given under their titles. Rotrou drew his themes from many sources, among others from Spanish authors, notably Lope de Vega (e.g. in *Laure persécutée* and *Saint Genest*) and Francisco de Rojas (in *Venceslas*). He died at an early age at Dreux, where he held the office of *lieutenant civil*, having refused to leave his post during an epidemic.

Roucher, JEAN-ANTOINE (1745–94), poet, author of *Les Mois* (1779), a descriptive poem after the model of Thomson's *Seasons*, showing love of nature and including some good lines, but soon relapsing into the commonplace. Roucher was guillotined on the same day and the same scaffold as André Chénier.

Rouet d'Omphale, Le, one of the poems in Bk. ii of Hugo's *Les Contemplations* (q.v.); the title, also, of a symphonic poem (1871) by the composer Saint-Saëns. [Hercules, in classical mythology, was for three years the slave of Omphale, queen of Lydia. She set him to work to spin, while she assumed his tiger's skin and his club.]

Rouge et le Blanc, Le, see *Lucien Leuwen.*

Rouge et le Noir, Le (1831), the first in order of date of Stendhal's two most famous novels (cf. *Chartreuse de Parme, La*), depicts the French social order under the *Restauration* (q.v., 1814–30).

Julien Sorel, a carpenter's son, combines a sensitive, noble spirit with boundless but calculating ambition. Under the Empire he might have won glory with Napoleon's armies (*le rouge*). As it is, only the Church (*le noir*) offers possibilities of advancement, by means of intrigue and hypocrisy, to a youth without birth or fortune. [This is only one of various suggested explanations of the title. Another is that *le noir* signifies the forces of clerical reaction, while *le rouge* stands for republicanism or liberalism.] As first step in his career he becomes tutor to the children of M. de Rênal, mayor of Verrières, and dares himself to seduce the virtuous Mme de Rênal. Having succeeded, he falls as much in love with her as she with him—a flash of sensibility. To avoid gossip he leaves the Rênal household for the seminary at Besançon. Here, though unpopular, he does brilliantly and in time is sent to Paris as secretary to the marquis de la Mole. Again triumphing over disadvantages he obtains his employer's confidence, the consideration of the household and its frequenters, and the lively interest, soon turning to love, of Mathilde, the marquis's arrogant daughter. It suits his ambition to respond, and he seduces her. More in love than ever she insists on marriage. To avoid scandal her father arranges for Julien to be ennobled and commissioned in the army. Wedding preparations go forward. At this point the marquis gets a letter from Mme de Rênal denouncing Julien as a monster who employs seduction as a means to advancement. Julien, in a cold fury, decides that only Mme de Rênal's death can satisfy his honour. He returns to Verrières, finds her in church, praying, and fires at her twice. He is arrested, and despite the efforts of both Mathilde and Mme de Rênal (repentant and only slightly injured) his condemnation follows. He goes to the scaffold undaunted, resigned to having lost his fight with destiny, overcome by no regrets. Mme de Rênal dies, heart-broken. Mathilde, in macabre imitation of a 16th-century ancestress, procures Julien's head and gives it a magnificent burial—a melodramatic incident thought by some critics to be out of keeping with the rest of the novel.

Stendhal is said to have found the germ of his plot in the career of Antoine Berthet, a labourer's son, whose trial for attempted murder was reported in the *Gazette des Tribunaux* for 1827.

Rouget de Lisle, CLAUDE-JOSEPH (1760–1836), born at Lons-le-Saulnier (Jura), a very minor poet and musician, but immortal as the author of the French national anthem (see *Marseillaise*).

After an only moderately successful military career, once interrupted by imprisonment because of his lukewarm Republican sympathies, he retired from the army in 1796 and thenceforward supported himself meagrely by copying music. He was pensioned by Louis-Philippe, and on 14 July 1915 his name was honoured posthumously and his ashes were transported to the Panthéon (q.v.). His *Chants français* (1825) were settings of songs by various authors. His other works—poems, comedies, and essays—are now forgotten.

Rougon-Macquart, Les (1871–93), the generic title of the cycle of twenty novels written by Émile Zola (q.v.) to illustrate his pseudo-scientific theory of the naturalistic novel (see *Naturalisme*). He described the series as 'l'histoire naturelle et sociale d'une famille sous le Second Empire' and intended it to form a study of the recurrence and development of transmitted characteristics (mainly vicious) over five generations of one family, the Rougon-Macquarts.

The opening volume, *La Fortune des Rougon*, introduces various members and generations of the Rougons, the legitimate branch, and the Macquarts, the low-class, illegitimate branch. The latter have sprung from the amours of the mentally unbalanced Rougon grandmother, Adèle, with a drunken smuggler. Thus attention is directed at the outset to the 'heredity' theme.

The plot of this volume is concerned with the happenings of the years 1848–52 and with politics, class-warfare, and intrigues in the small Provençal town of Plassans (actually Aix-en-Provence) where the family lives. During the *coup d'état* (q.v.) of 1851 the greedy, ambitious Pierre and Félicité Rougon intrigue surreptitiously with their dissolute half-brother Antoine Macquart, and manage so to exploit events that they secure for themselves power and social position. Their son Eugène, in Paris, becomes a Senator of the Second Empire (see *Son Excellence Eugène Rougon*).

In later volumes of this cycle the scene shifts about the country, and up and down the social scale. In *La Curée, Une Page d'amour, Pot-Bouille, Au bonheur des dames, L'Argent*, it is the bourgeois world of tradespeople and financiers. In *Le Ventre de Paris* it is *Les Halles*, the great provision-market of Paris. *L'Assommoir, Germinal*, and *La Bête humaine* depict the victims of industrialism in the slums of Paris, in the mines, on the railways. *Nana* is the story of a prostitute. Politicians, artists, the Church, the army, doctors are the chief characters in *Son Excellence Eugène Rougon, L'Œuvre, La Débâcle, La Conquête de Plassans, La Faute de l'abbé Mouret, Le Docteur Pascal*. *La Terre*, a prolonged study of greed, concupiscence, and bestiality in peasant life, roused five young authors of Zola's day to protest against his obscenity. *La Joie de vivre* and *Le Rêve* portray a milder variety of country life. In *Le Docteur Pascal*, which closes the cycle, the plot turns on a love-affair between the ageing Dr. Pascal and his young niece, Clotilde, but the book is mainly interesting as a summary of preceding history and an exposition of the Rougon-Macquart theme. It is prefaced by a family tree with a brief case-history attached to each name. This is supposed to have been compiled by Pascal, who had renounced a promising career to write a great work on heredity, based on the hereditary dispositions of his own family. It is in this novel that Antoine Macquart catches fire when in a drunken sleep and dies of spontaneous combustion, leaving only a spot of grease and a few ashes on the floor!

The titles and dates of publication of the twenty novels of this cycle are given below. The asterisks denote works summarized under separate headings:

La Fortune des Rougon (1871), *La Curée**
(1872), *Le Ventre de Paris** (1873), *La Conquête de Plassans** (1874), *La Faute de l'abbé
Mouret** (1875), *Son Excellence Eugène Rougon** (1876), *L'Assommoir** (1877), *Une Page
d'amour** (1878), *Nana** (1880), *Pot-Bouille**
(1882), *Au bonheur des dames** (1883), *La
Joie de vivre* (1884), *Germinal** (1885),
L'Œuvre* (1886), *La Terre* (1887), *Le Rêve**
(1888), *La Bête humaine** (1890), *L'Argent**
(1891), *La Débâcle** (1892), *Le Docteur
Pascal* (1893).

Rouletabille, JOSEPH, crime reporter and
amateur detective, see *Leroux, Gaston.*

Roumanille, JOSEPH (1818–91), Provençal
poet, a leader of the *félibres* (q.v., and see
also *Mistral, Frédéric*). His works (written
in Provençal) included *Li Margarideto* (i.e.
Les Pâquerettes, 1847), *Li Flour de Sauvi* (*Les
Fleurs de sauge*, 1859). He also edited a collection of Provençal poetry *Li Prouvençalo*
(1852).

Roumieux, LOUIS (1829–94), Provençal
poet, author of comedies; a mock-heroic
poem *Jarjaiado* (1878); and various poetic
collections, some humorous, including:
La Rampelado [*Le Rappel*] (1868) and *Li
Couquilho d'un roumieu* [*Les Coquilles* (mis-
prints) *d'un pèlerin*] (1890–94), a punning
allusion to his work as a proof-reader, for
long his means of livelihood.

Rousseau, HENRI [LE DOUANIER ROUS-
SEAU]. The self-taught artist Henri Rousseau
(1844–1910) was nicknamed thus because he
had been employed in the *octroi* (a form of
local customs or toll-collection service) outside Paris before, about 1885, becoming a
professional painter. The design and simpli-
fication of his portrait groups and scenes from
exotic nature had a remarkable primitive
quality which was derided in his lifetime but
which brought him posthumous fame.

Rousseau, JACQUES (1630–93), a court artist
under Louis XIV. He left France in 1681 on
account of his Protestant faith but later
became a Catholic and returned. He died in
London, where he had come in 1690 to
decorate Montagu House and Hampton
Court.

Rousseau, JEAN-BAPTISTE (1671–1741), regarded as one of the chief poets of his age, a
man of arrogant temper and caustic humour,

who was sentenced to banishment in 1707 on
account of some defamatory verses attributed
(probably unjustly) to him, and spent thirty
years in miserable exile. A collection of his
odes and other poems, mostly panegyrical
or drawn from the Scriptures, which show
good workmanship rather than vigour and
inspiration, was published in 1723; his best
work is perhaps seen in his satirical epigrams
and in one or two of his imitations of the
Psalms. Rousseau's prolonged misfortune
finally gained the compassion even of his
enemies, who included Voltaire.

Rousseau, JEAN-JACQUES (1712–78), philosopher, born at Geneva, the son of a watchmaker. His mother died when giving him
birth. His father was a man of restless and
unstable character who gave his son little or
no education, but read romances with him,
developing prematurely the child's sensibility and imagination. When Jean-Jacques
was ten, the father left his home and family
in consequence of a quarrel. After a short
period of schooling the boy was set to work
first with a notary, then with an engraver.
With neither was he happy; in 1728 he left
Geneva, wandered about the country, and
found a protectress in Mme de Warens
(q.v.), a woman of charitable and affectionate disposition but indifferent moral
character. Her protection, first at Annecy
then at Chambéry in Savoy, extended, with
interruptions, for some dozen years. Under
arrangements made by her he was admitted
at Turin into the Roman Catholic Church
(he reverted to Protestantism in 1754, having
never been at heart a Catholic). It was at
Turin that his taste for music was first
awakened, and he subsequently studied it
with ardour. After a period of vagabond
existence, in the course of which he took
service as a lackey and gave music lessons,
he returned to Mme de Warens, who from
1738 gave him a home in a small farm-
house, Les Charmettes, near Chambéry. Here
for the first time he devoted himself to
methodical reading of history, philosophy,
science, and mathematics. The part of his
Confessions relating to this period of his life
contains serious misstatements, and it is open
to question how far his idyllic account of his
relations with Mme de Warens is tinged with
imagination.

(2) After an unsuccessful experiment as a

private tutor at Lyons, Rousseau finally left Mme de Warens about 1742 and betook himself to Paris, carrying with him a new scheme of musical notation, from which he hoped to derive the means of sustenance. He entered into literary society, and was for a short time secretary to the French Ambassador at Venice, the comte de Montaigu, with whom he quarrelled, then returned to France (1744). He now formed a lifelong liaison with Thérèse Levasseur, a coarse and stupid servant-girl, with whom he appears to have lived for many years contentedly, until her affection turned to aversion. He sent her five children (who may possibly not have been his) to the Foundling Hospital, and later claimed that he did so in their interests. He was first brought into literary prominence by the two *Discours* (q.v.) that he wrote in 1750 and 1754 on themes propounded by the Academy of Dijon, *Si le rétablissement des sciences et des arts a contribué à épurer les mœurs* and *L'origine et les fondements de l'inégalité parmi les hommes*. The consideration of these themes formed a crisis in Rousseau's life (see *Vincennes*), revealing to him the conviction, confirmed by his own experience, that man is originally and by nature virtuous, free, and happy; that he has been corrupted by society, the source of property, inequality, and despotism; and that in order to restore him to some measure of happiness, it is necessary to return to nature so far as practicable (for Rousseau recognized that existing institutions must be retained because 'la nature humaine ne rétrograde pas'). This doctrine is at the root of his subsequent works: the *Lettre à d'Alembert sur les spectacles* (1758), in which he defended the prohibition at Geneva of dramatic performances as fostering the vices of society; *Julie ou la Nouvelle Héloïse* (q.v., 1761), in which the natural relations of man and woman are reconciled with the social order; *Émile* (q.v., 1762), in which he expounds his theory of a natural education and (in the passage entitled *Profession de foi du vicaire savoyard*) his idea of a natural religion; and *Du contrat social* (q.v., 1762), the ideal organization of an ideal society.

(3) Rousseau's two Discourses were widely read; his pastoral operetta *Le Devin du village* (played before the court in 1752) was also successful. He supported himself principally by copying music. In 1755 he wrote

the article on *Économie politique* in the *Encyclopédie*. In 1756 he settled at *l'Ermitage* (q.v.), the small house in the Forêt de Montmorency (north of Paris) placed at his disposal by Mme d'Épinay. There he wrote his letter to Voltaire protesting against the pessimistic doctrine of the latter's poem on the Lisbon earthquake of 1755. Having quarrelled with Mme d'Épinay (and with his friends Grimm and Diderot) he transferred himself at the end of 1757 to a cottage at Montmorency, where he received much friendly hospitality from the maréchal de Luxembourg and his wife. It was here that he wrote or completed the *Lettre à d'Alembert* (q.v.) on theatrical performances (1758), the *Nouvelle Héloïse* (q.v.) in which he was influenced by his unhappy passion for Mme d'Houdetot (q.v.), *Émile*, and *Du contrat social* (qq.v.). But *Émile* incurred the censure of the Sorbonne and the *parlement*; Rousseau was threatened with arrest and left France for Switzerland (1762). Persecution by the Genevan and Bernese authorities drove him to Motiers in the Val-Travers near Neuchâtel (territory belonging to the King of Prussia). Here he stayed for three years, receiving kindness from Frederick's Scottish governor, George Keith, 10th Earl Marischal, and making the acquaintance of Boswell, whom he urged to visit Corsica, with the consequences that are well known. From here he issued his dignified reply (1763) to the charge of the Archbishop of Paris, Christophe de Beaumont, regarding *Émile*; also his *Lettres écrites de la Montagne* (1764) in reply to the attack made on him in the *Lettres écrites de la campagne* written by the procurator-general Tronchin in support of Rousseau's Genevan enemies. This work was condemned by the *parlement* in 1765. The clergy of Neuchâtel having now joined the troop of his persecutors, Rousseau, after a short stay on the island of Saint-Pierre in the lake of Bienne (charmingly described in the fifth of his *Rêveries*), removed to England (1766), where David Hume procured him an asylum at Wootton in Derbyshire. The British Government granted him a pension of £100. But he quarrelled with Hume and left England after eighteen months; he had suffered all his life from an ailment perhaps of nervous origin and from morbid sensitiveness, and he was now the victim of persecution mania. He returned to France in

1767, befriended by the elder Mirabeau and by the prince de Conti. After a period of wandering he settled in Paris in 1770, partly supporting himself once more by copying music (he refused to draw his British pension), and remained there till 1778; he then accepted from the marquis de Girardin a little house at Ermenonville near Senlis (cf. *Girardin, marquis de*), where he died in the same year.

(4) Rousseau's *Confessions* (q.v.) were composed between 1764 and 1770 and cover his life down to 1766; they were published posthumously. They are supplemented by three dialogues written in 1775–6, *Rousseau juge de Jean-Jacques*, in which he exposes the cruelty and bad faith of his persecutors with an exaggeration savouring of mania, and by the *Rêveries du promeneur solitaire* (q.v.); both these works were published posthumously. Rousseau also wrote, among other minor works, some of the articles on music in the *Encyclopédie*, a *Lettre sur la musique française* (1753, maintaining the superiority of Italian music), and a *Dictionnaire de Musique* (1767). Among his minor political writings may be mentioned his abstract and criticism of the abbé de Saint-Pierre's *Projet de paix perpétuelle* by means of a federation of Europe. The abstract was published in 1761, the whole work in 1782. It has been translated into English by C. E. Vaughan (1917) and by E. M. Nuttall (1927). His *Correspondance générale* (1924–34) fills twenty volumes.

(5) The chief importance of Rousseau lies in the fact that, though a philosopher himself and sharing with the *philosophes* their hatred of the old order of oppression and intolerance, he was yet the principal adversary of 18th-century philosophy in some of its dominant characteristics. Whereas the latter was in the main critical, atheistic, materialistic, based on reason, the philosophy of Rousseau was constructive, deistic, and based on sentiment. Recovering from his early failings and arguing from his own spiritual experience, he was led to condemn society, to preach the return to nature, to maintain the existence of God, conscience, personal virtue (as distinct from social benevolence), and the immortal soul. His writings, marred here and there by provincialisms and faults of taste, have an eloquent and lyrical character unusual in 18th-century literature; they manifest his highly developed sensibility and sympathy with nature. Some of his most charming passages are descriptions of Swiss scenery, of simple family life, or the work of the farm. He left his imprint on French literature, introducing the picturesque element and the reverie, and was a precursor of the Romantic Movement (see *Romantisme*). Sainte-Beuve says of him that he endowed the French language with a continuous force, a firmness of tone, and a solidity of texture that it had not previously known, perhaps his most certain achievement.

(6) 'Rousseau', said Johnson to Boswell, 'is a very bad man.' BOSWELL. 'Sir, do you think him as bad a man as Voltaire?' JOHNSON. 'Why, Sir, it is difficult to settle the proportion of iniquity between them.' None the less Rousseau profoundly influenced many English writers, from the author of *Sandford and Merton* to Wordsworth. Byron has some sympathetic stanzas on him in Canto III of *Childe Harold's Pilgrimage*.

Rousseau juge de Jean-Jacques, see *Rousseau, Jean-Jacques, para. 4.*

Rousseau, PIERRE-ÉTIENNE-THÉODORE (1812–67), French landscape painter, one of the Barbizon (q.v.) school. He lived mainly, and died, at Barbizon and was called 'le Grand Refusé' because his works were so often unsuccessful at the *Salons*.

Roussel, ALBERT-CHARLES-PAUL-MARIE (1869–1937), French composer of symphonies, ballet-music, &c., among them *Le Festin de l'araignée* (1913), *Bacchus et Ariane* (1931), &c. He had many connexions with the poets and poetry of his day.

Roustan, a Mameluke presented to Napoleon in Egypt and brought back by him as his personal attendant. Napoleon took Roustan everywhere and lavished favours, exotic clothes, and money on him. But Roustan fled from Fontainebleau at the time of Napoleon's first abdication (1814). He died in 1845.

Rouvier, MAURICE (1842–1911), French statesman, born at Aix-en-Provence. He was Premier and Minister of Finance at the time of the Boulangist agitation (see *Boulanger*) and from then until 1906 was in and out of office. His longest period out of office was one of nearly ten years after the Panama Scandal (q.v.).

Roux, PAUL, see *Saint-Pol-Roux.*

Roxane, the heroine of Racine's *Bajazet* (q.v.).

Royaumont, Abbaye de, near Pontoise (Seine-et-Oise), a Cistercian abbey founded in 1228 by Louis IX. It had fallen into ruins but was restored about 1930 and transformed into the Foyer de Royaumont, a residential hostel providing tranquil working conditions for writers and artists. At intervals since 1945 it has been used, on the lines of the former *décades* at Pontigny (q.v.), as a meeting-place for discussion groups. The concerts given during the summer in the restored chapel are a feature of Parisian musical life.

Royaumont, SIEUR DE, PRIEUR DE SOM-BREVAL, the pseudonym under which *L'Histoire du Vieux et du Nouveau Testament représentée avec des figures et des explications édifiantes tirées des Saints Pères* was published in 1670. The work, sometimes called the *Bible de Royaumont,* consists of translated selections (with numerous plates) from the Old and New Testaments, probably by Le Maître de Sacy and/or Nicolas Fontaine (qq.v.).

Royer, CLÉMENCE (1830–1902), philosopher and scientist. She was the first French translator (1869) of Darwin's *Origin of Species.*

Royer-Collard, PIERRE-PAUL (1763–1845), philosopher and statesman, also one of the noted parliamentary orators of his day, came to Paris from the small town of Vitry-le-François (near Châlons-sur-Marne) and by the age of twenty was already practising at the bar. He was at first a partisan of the Revolution, but his enthusiasm cooled. He went into retirement during the Terror and studied philosophy. In 1811 he was appointed Professor of the History of Philosophy at the Sorbonne and brought a rare force of eloquence, argument, and clear exposition to his lectures. His political career began after the Restoration when he became a leader of the *doctrinaires* (q.v. and cf. *Guizot,* also *Peyronnet, la loi*). His influence declined after the July Revolution (q.v., 1830), though he still retained his standing in the educational world.

Royère, JEAN (1871–   ), poet and critic, a disciple of Mallarmé and 'la poésie pure';

founder of *La Phalange* (1906–   ), an important post-Symbolist review; author of the poetic collections *Exil doré* (1898), *Eurythmies* (1904), *La Sœur de Narcisse nue* (united in *Poésies,* 1924), *Orchestration* (1936), &c., and of collected essays and critical studies: *Clartés sur la poésie* (1925), *Frontons* (1932), *Le Point de vue de Sirius* (1935); *Mallarmé* (1927), *Le Musicisme: Boileau, La Fontaine, Baudelaire* (1929). He gave the name *Musicisme* to his doctrines of the relative values of language, sonority, and rhythm in poetry.

Royou, L'ABBÉ THOMAS, see *Ami du peuple, L'.*

Rubempré, LUCIEN DE, the hero of Balzac's *Illusions perdues* (q.v.).

Rudel, JAUFRÉ, PRINCE DE BLAYE, a Provençal poet of the 12th century, author of a famous song celebrating distant love ('amor de lonh'). This gave rise to the legend that he had fallen in love with the Countess of Tripoli, on the reports of her brought by pilgrims; had set sail for the East to see her, but had fallen ill on board ship and had been carried dying to an inn at Tripoli. The countess, apprised of his coming, came to him and took him in her arms, where he died. The legend is referred to in Petrarch's *Trionfo d'amore,* in Swinburne's *Triumph of Time,* and in Browning's *Rudel and the Lady of Tripoli.*

Rudler, GUSTAVE (1872–1957), the first Marshal Foch Professor of French Literature in the University of Oxford (1919–49). His work on Benjamin Constant (q.v.), the man, author, and politician, is especially notable, e.g. the critical edition (1919) of *Adolphe* and the many studies which preceded and followed it, beginning with *La Jeunesse de Benjamin Constant (1767–1794)* (1909), his doctoral thesis (which, a signal honour, was 'crowned' by the *Académie française*), and continuing with articles contributed to reviews. *Les Techniques de la critique et de l'histoire littéraires en littérature française moderne* (1923), *Michelet historien de Jeanne d'Arc* (1925–6, 2 vols.), also editions of Racine (*Mithridate,* 1943) and Molière (*Le Misanthrope*), stand out among his other publications. The introduction to *The French Mind* (Oxford, 1952; studies in his honour by colleagues and former pupils; with a bibliography) bears witness to the respect and esteem he inspired alike as scholar and teacher.

Ruelle, the part of their bedroom in which, in the 16th and 17th centuries, ladies of quality, reclining in bed or on a couch, received their visitors.

Rulhière, CLAUDE DE (*c.* 1735–91), historian and writer of light verse, was in Russia as secretary to the French minister at the time of the revolution of 1762 which placed Catherine II on the throne. Of this revolution he wrote an agreeable anecdotic narrative. He was charged in 1768 by the French Government to write an account of the Polish troubles of that time for the instruction of the Dauphin; this work, which is Rulhière's chief title to be remembered, remained (unfinished) in manuscript until published by Napoleon in 1806, as *Histoire de l'anarchie de Pologne et du démembrement de cette république.* Another important work by Rulhière was his *Éclaircissements historiques sur les causes de la Révocation de l'Édit de Nantes* (1788). This also was written at the request of the Government, in support of the favourable attitude of Louis XVI towards the Protestants. Rulhière had a considerable gift for epigram and light verse. His verse epistle on *Les Disputes* was inserted by Voltaire in his *Dictionnaire philosophique.* He was admitted to the *Académie* in 1787.

Rute, MME DE, the name by her third and last marriage of the novelist and woman of letters Marie-Lætitia-Studolmine Wyse (1831–1902), previously comtesse Rattazzi, and before that Mme de Solms. She was born at Waterford, County Cork, a daughter of Sir Thomas Wyse (q.v.) and his wife Lætitia Bonaparte (a daughter of Lucien Bonaparte). She was not recognized as a Bonaparte by Napoleon III and had to leave France, where she lived after her first marriage, in 1853, and a second time in 1864 after the publication of her novel *Les Mariages de la Créole.* She lived finally in Savoy. *Bicheville* (1865) was a novel of Florence. *Si j'étais reine* (1868) was in part autobiographical. Her brother was the *félibriste* William Bonaparte Wyse (q.v.).

Rutebeuf, a 13th-century French poet and *jongleur* (q.v.) who lived a wretched life in

Paris, always destitute and in debt, frequenting the company of gamblers and the humbler classes of society. His poetic work shows remarkable versatility, satiric force, eloquence, and a lyrical gift. He wrote *fabliaux* (q.v.), satires, and *débats* (q.v.), but also (perhaps on commission) a life of Saint Elizabeth and other pious works. His satire is directed against all classes, against the king himself (Saint Louis, for the favour he shows to monks and friars), against the Pope, against nobles, officials, merchants, and lazy workmen. His *Miracle de Théophile* is a short religious drama in a variety of metres on the theme of an ambitious priest who sells his soul to the Devil, repents, and is saved by the Virgin Mary. Literature with Rutebeuf begins to direct public opinion and to take on more of a journalistic character; for instance, he vigorously supported Guillaume de Saint-Amour (q.v.), a doctor of the University of Paris, in the University's quarrel with the religious orders. He showed much technical skill as a versifier, employing in the main octosyllables in stanzas of a various number of lines, variously rhyming.

Ruy Blas (1838), a poetic drama by Victor Hugo, set in 17th-century Spain.

Don César de Bazan, a gay but honourable rascal, has squandered his fortune and disappeared, ostensibly to the Indies. His actual whereabouts, with a troop of bandits, are known only to his relative Don Salluste de Bazan, an enemy of the Queen. Don Salluste's valet, Ruy Blas, more truly noble at heart than any grandee, worships the queen from a distance. His master, discovering this, plots to avenge a fancied insult by making the queen fall in love with a valet. He introduces Ruy Blas at court as his long-lost relative Don César, threatening him with dire punishment if he refuses to play his part. Some months later the pseudo-Don César has become the chief grandee at the court, using his influence with the king for the good of the people; and he has won the queen's love. A false letter (from Don Salluste) begs the queen to come to 'Don César's' house at midnight. The rightful Don César nearly upsets the plot by arriving unexpectedly (down the chimney), but Don Salluste gets him out of the way. The queen arrives, and Ruy Blas tries to effect her escape, but Don Salluste enters by a secret door and insults her by revealing her lover's identity. Ruy Blas kills Don Salluste, then poisons himself at the queen's feet.

Ruy Gomez de Sylva, Don, a character in Victor Hugo's *Hernani* (q.v.).

S

Sabatier, MME, see *Présidente, La.*

Sabbathier, FRANÇOIS, see *Dictionaries and Encyclopedias,* under date 1766–1815.

Sablé, MAGDELEINE, MARQUISE DE (*c.* 1599–1678), a famous *précieuse* (q.v.), a woman of intelligence and sound judgement (to whom Arnauld sent his *Logique* for criticism), whose literary *salon* had an importance almost rivalling that of the Hôtel de Rambouillet and contributed to the production of the *Maximes* of La Rochefoucauld. The last part of her life was spent at Port-Royal, in semi-solitude. Her letters have been published, and *Maximes et Pensées diverses* (1678, not all by her hand).

Sac au dos, the short story contributed by J.-K. Huysmans to *Les Soirées de Médan* (q.v.).

Sacy, Le Maître de, see *Le Maître de Sacy.*

Sacy, ANTOINE-ISAAC SILVESTRE DE (1758–1838), born in Paris, was one of the great orientalists of the late 18th and early 19th centuries. He was Professor of Arabic at the École des langues orientales and of Persian at the Collège de France and, later, became head of both institutions. He was one of the founders (1822) of the *Société asiatique,* and from 1833 was Keeper of Oriental Manuscripts at the Bibliothèque nationale as well as Perpetual Secretary of the Académie des Inscriptions et Belles-Lettres.

Sacy, SAMUEL-USTAZADE SILVESTRE DE (1801–79), born in Paris, son of the orientalist (see above), was one of many distinguished critics and political journalists associated with the *Journal des Débats* (q.v.). His articles were collected in *Variétés littéraires, morales et historiques* (1858).

Sade, DONATIEN - ALPHONSE - FRANÇOIS, COMTE (generally known as MARQUIS) DE (1740–1814), was the author of licentious and obscene writings which have given his name to *Sadism.* The son of a diplomat, he fought in the Seven Years War, married at the age of twenty-three, and led a life of criminal debauchery which ended compulsorily about 1772 when he was condemned to death by the *parlement,* a sentence altered by the king to imprisonment. He occupied his captivity—first at Vincennes but mainly in the Bastille—in writing (*Justine ou les malheurs de la vertu; Juliette ou les prospérités du vice; La Philosophie dans le boudoir,* &c.). The Revolution freed him and he became a fairly zealous Revolutionary. After 1794 he busied himself with the publication of his works. The personalities in his pamphlet *Zoloë et ses acolytes* (1801) offended Bonaparte, who had him confined as a lunatic in the Charenton (q.v.) asylum, where he died.

As recently as 1957 the French courts upheld a decision of 1814 that publication of works by the marquis de Sade should be banned. Some 20th-century critics, however, have stressed his importance as a precursor of Nietzsche's Superman, and as a psychologist and analyst a century ahead of his time; they contend, also, that his qualities of style and his influence on 19th-century writers (Lamartine and Baudelaire among others) give him a place in literature.

Sagesse (1881), a collection of poems by Verlaine (q.v.).

Sagesse, De la, see *Charron.*

Sagon, FRANÇOIS (16th c.), an obscure poetaster who in 1537 scurrilously attacked Clément Marot, giving rise to a literary controversy in which Marot was triumphant.

Saint-Amand, JEAN-ARMAND (1797–1885), dramatist, part author of *L'Auberge des Adrets,* see *Macaire, Robert.*

Saint-Amant, MARC-ANTOINE DE GÉRARD, SIEUR DE (1594–1661), poet, born at Rouen, the son of a naval officer. He was the boon companion of the comte d'Harcourt, whom he accompanied on his campaigns and sea-voyages and in a mission to England in 1643, and later a follower of Marie de Gonzague, Queen of Poland. He was a freethinker and a remarkable poet, vivid and realistic, especially in his songs of the tavern. He was the author of picturesque, some of them burlesque, lyrics and of a long and tedious epic on Moses, *Moïse sauvé* (1653). The bizarre and whimsical quality of some of his verse is seen in his well-known sonnet *Les Goinfres* and in the longer poem *La Solitude*. He was one of the original members of the *Académie*, but was condemned by Boileau.

Saint-Amour, GUILLAUME DE (*fl. c.* 1250), a secular doctor in the University of Paris who took a leading part in the struggle of the University (1250–56) against the admission of the mendicant friars to the Society of Masters of the University. He was cited before a bench of prelates for contumacy on account of a work *On the Perils of the Last Times*, which was finally condemned by the Pope (1256).

Saint-Arnaud, JACQUES LEROY DE (1801–54), maréchal de France, born in Paris, a famous army commander and an able administrator. He was Minister of War at the time of the *coup d'état* (q.v.) of 2 December 1851 and largely responsible for its success. He died during the Crimean war. A contemptuous nickname for Boulanger (q.v.) was 'Saint-Arnaud de café-concert'.

Saint-Aubin, Horace de, the pseudonym most frequently employed by Balzac (q.v.) before he wrote under his own name. The works—mainly bad sensational novels—of 'Horace de Saint-Aubin' filled sixteen volumes in a collected edition of 1836–40.

Saint-Barthélemy, La, the massacre of Huguenots ordered by Charles IX at the instigation of his mother Catherine de Médicis and her advisers, carried out in Paris on the festival of St. Bartholomew, 24 August 1572. There were similar massacres in many provincial towns. Among notable victims were Coligny and La Ramée (qq.v.).

Saint-Barthélemy des journalistes, see *Press, Development of*, para. 7.

Saint-Cyr, a small town near Versailles, one-time site of (*a*) the *Institut de Saint-Cyr* and, later, (*b*) the *École spéciale militaire de Saint-Cyr*.

The *Institut des filles de saint Louis* or *Institut de Saint-Cyr* was founded (1686) by Mme de Maintenon and Louis XIV as a convent school for young ladies of noble birth but small means. It was for performance by these pupils of Saint-Cyr that Racine's *Esther* and *Athalie* (qq.v.) were written. The establishment was closed by the Revolutionary Government in 1793. In 1803 Bonaparte, then First Consul, transferred his newly created military college from Fontainebleau to what had been the convent school at Saint-Cyr, where it remained until the 1939–45 war. (It is now in Brittany.) This college, for the training of officers in infantry and cavalry regiments, is comparable with Sandhurst in England. A distinctive feature of the uniform of these military cadets is the hat, of shako type with a cockade of white plumes (the *panache*) in front. The passing-out ceremony is known as *triomphe*.

Saint-Cyr, see *Gouvion Saint-Cyr*.

Saint-Cyran, ABBÉ DE, see *Du Vergier*.

Saint-Denis, Abbaye de, a famous abbey, a few miles north of Paris, founded by the Merovingian king Dagobert in 626, burial-place of Saint Denis (q.v.) and of the French kings.

Saint-Esprit, Ordre du, an order of knighthood inaugurated by Henri III on 1 January 1579, comparable to the great orders of the Garter and of the Golden Fleece. It subsisted till the Revolution and was revived under the Restoration. The insignia of the Order included the *Cordon bleu* (q.v.).

Saint-Évremond or **Saint-Évremont,** CHARLES DE SAINT-DENIS, SIEUR DE (1613–1703), man of letters. He belonged to a good Norman family and at first followed a military career, but was obliged to leave France in 1661 in consequence of his *Lettre sur le Traité des Pyrénées* of 1659 in which he condemned Mazarin's treaty with Spain. He spent most of the remainder of his life in England at the courts of Charles II, James II, and William III. A man of sceptical and epicurean temperament, one of the most distinguished of the *libertins* (q.v.), he wrote with light, sober, witty elegance short disquisitions on many subjects, literary and other, and his literary criticism had considerable influence in England, where he was on intimate terms with courtiers such as Buckingham and writers such as Hobbes, Waller, and Cowley. Among many other essays he wrote one on English comedy. His *Réflexions sur les divers génies du peuple romain* (1663) is a pioneer work as making the study of ancient manners and mentality part of history, but incomplete and unequal. A good example of his lighter ironic style is to be seen in his *Conversation du maréchal d'Hoquincourt avec le P. Canaye*. His *Comédie des Académistes* (1643) is a satirical comedy in which the persons satirized—the principal members of the original *Académie* together with Mlle de Gournay—figure under their own names. Saint-Évremond was buried in Westminster Abbey. Some of his essays were translated into English from time to time (with a character of Saint-Évremond by Dryden in a collection of 1692). His works, with a life by Des Maizeaux, appeared in an English translation in 1714.

Saint-Exupéry, ANTOINE DE (1900–44), aviator and author, trained as a military pilot after failing his naval entrance. Some years later he became one of the pioneer civil pilots on colonial, trans-desert, and transcontinental lines and at this time made his name as a writer with *Courrier-Sud* (1928) and *Vol de nuit* (1931). Next, he was by turns test pilot and journalist. In 1939, about eighteen months after a serious flying accident in Guatemala, he was mobilized. He had also, in 1939, published the novel—or collection of sketches—*Terre des hommes*. When the Germans overran France in June 1940 he reached North Africa with his unit, was demobilized the following month, and in December went to New York. *Pilote de guerre* (1942; first published in New York, in English, as *Flight to Arras*) describes his experiences of May and June 1940. In 1943 he managed to return to North Africa and ultimately to rejoin his unit (by this time attached to the American Forces). He was well beyond flying age, and crippled as a result of accidents, but as a concession he was allowed to undertake a limited number of reconnaissance missions. Eight were success-

ful, but he failed to return from the ninth (July 1944), which was to have been the last.

The works already mentioned are Saint-Exupéry's direct transmutation into literature of his experiences, physical and spiritual, of flying. His other writings include: *Lettre à un otage* (New York, 1943), propaganda of a very high order, *Le Petit Prince* (New York, 1943), a much profounder work than the children's tale it professes to be, though among the best of these; and *La Citadelle* (1948, posth.), an uncompleted, more philosophical, work begun in 1936; meditations in the desert which constitute, for some, a modern Bible of humanism.

Saint-Gelais, MELLIN DE (1487–1558), poet, nephew of Octovien de Saint-Gelais (q.v.), was a man of good education, who knew not only Latin but Greek; he was also a musician. After a long sojourn in Italy, he became a priest, almoner to the king, and keeper of the library at Fontainebleau. He wrote light verses (*rondeaux*, madrigals, &c.), showing grace and mastery of language, on frivolous themes for ladies of the court, also some lively epigrams. He was one of the first to introduce the sonnet, and the spirit of the Italian Renaissance generally, from Italy into France. Saint-Gelais also wrote a tragedy, *Sophonisbe*, from the Italian of Trissino, performed in 1559. When Ronsard, with his new poetic theories, first came forward, there was some conflict between him and the old poet, but a reconciliation was effected.

Saint-Gelais, OCTOVIEN *or* OCTAVIEN DE (1468–1502), courtier and prelate (Bishop of Angoulême from 1495), and a poet of the school of the *rhétoriqueurs* (q.v.), was born at Cognac in the Angoumois. Besides *ballades*, *rondeaux*, &c., he wrote an erotic poem, *Histoire de Eurialus et Lucresse*; a long allegory, *Le Séjour d'honneur*, in which he draws instruction from his own life and human life in general; a translation of the *Heroides* of Ovid, and a particularly bad version of the *Aeneid*.

Saint Genest, Le Véritable, a tragedy by Rotrou, performed in 1646, imitated from a play by Lope de Vega. This is one of the finest of Rotrou's dramas. Genest, a favourite actor of the Emperor Diocletian, is directed to perform before him a play representing the obstinacy and martyrdom of a Christian. Genest has himself felt impelled to adopt the new faith, and, as he prepares his part, a voice from Heaven encourages him in his resolve. The play is performed, and in the course of it Genest, abandoning his assumed character, boldly in the face of emperor and court professes himself a Christian. He cheerfully meets the torture and execution to which Diocletian condemns him.

Saint-Georges de Bouhélier [pseud. of Stéphane-Georges de Bouhélier-Lepelletier] (1889–1942), *Naturiste* poet and dramatist (see *Naturisme*). He wrote *Chants de la vie ardente* (1902), *Romance de l'homme* (1912), and other collections of verse characterized by ideals of universal brotherhood and resentment of social injustice. *Le Carnaval des enfants* (1910), a verse-drama, probably the best known of his many plays, is a mixture of religious symbolism and social satire.

Saint-Germain, LE COMTE DE, a mysterious 18th-century adventurer who was introduced *c.* 1740 at the court of Louis XV where he ingratiated himself with the king and Mme de Pompadour. He was a man of wealth (he had apparently inexhaustible stores of precious stones and ready money), wit, and address, who pretended to have lived in past centuries and to have vast, occult sources of information on all subjects. He may have been a spy, and was possibly of Portuguese-Jewish origin.

Saint-Germain, Faubourg, see *Faubourg Saint-Germain*.

Saint-Germain-des-Prés, a famous abbey in Paris on the left (south) bank of the Seine, founded in 558 by Childebert I, a Merovingian king, son of Clovis I. It was the burial place of Childebert himself and of many of the kings and queens of the Merovingian dynasty. It became the chief house of the Benedictine Congrégation de Saint-Maur (see *Maurists*), and Montfaucon and Mabillon (qq.v.) worked there. Only its church (rebuilt in the 11th–12th centuries) now remains.

St. Helena, the small island in the Atlantic, a British possession, to which Napoleon was exiled in October 1815. He died there on 5 May 1821.

Saintine, XAVIER, the name taken by Joseph-Xavier Boniface (1798–1865), a novelist and dramatic author (the latter usually in collaboration with better-known writers). He is remembered by the graceful, sentimental tale *Picciola* (1836), one of the successes of its day, in French and in the many languages into which it was immediately translated. A prisoner's captivity is solaced, and his resentful character softened, by his love for a plant that suddenly appears in the courtyard outside his cell. A sickly wavering tendril at first, struggling towards the light, it becomes a hardy growth under his care.

Saint-John Perse, see *Léger*.

Saint-Just, LOUIS DE (1767–94), an able and fanatical lieutenant of Robespierre and, like him, a theoretician of the Revolution and a man of rigid principles. He was a leader and one of the chief orators of the *Montagnards* and a member of the *Comité de salut public* (q.v.). He was executed with Robespierre.

Saint-Lambert, JEAN-FRANÇOIS, MARQUIS DE (1716–1803), poet and *encyclopédiste*, author of *Les Saisons* (1769), a poem modelled in general design on Thomson's *Seasons*; in it nature is described from both a romantic and a philosophic standpoint and rustic life is praised, but without Thomson's sincere emotion. The poem met with much success, but was condemned as flat and tedious by some good judges, such as Grimm, Diderot, and Mme du Deffand. Saint-Lambert is also remembered as the successor of Voltaire in the affections of Mme du Châtelet, and as the rival of J.-J. Rousseau in those of Mme d'Houdetot.

Saint-Lazare, Prison de. This Paris prison, demolished *c.* 1935, was in the first instance a lepers' hospital, built *c.* 1100. By the early 17th century it was no longer required for its original purpose and became the headquarters of the *Congrégation des Prêtres de la Mission*, a religious order founded by St. Vincent de Paul and known also as *Lazaristes*. (Cf. the religious and military order of St. Lazarus founded in Jerusalem in the early 12th century. The knights, 100 in number, all of noble birth, devoted themselves to caring for lepers and were usually lepers themselves.) In the later 17th century one part of Saint-Lazare became a house of detention for loose-living young men of good family. During the Revolution it was sacked by the people and, later, used as a prison. Here André Chénier wrote his *Ïambes* and *La Jeune Captive*. Still later it became a prison for female delinquents and prostitutes.

Saint-Loup, MARQUIS [ROBERT] DE, nephew of the duc de Guermantes, in Proust's *A la recherche du temps perdu* (q.v.). Marcel (q.v.) first meets him at Balbec, a seaside resort, when he comes from the neighbouring garrison at Doncières to visit his great-aunt Mme de Villeparisis at the hotel where Marcel and his grandmother are also staying. The young men become friends and through Saint-Loup Marcel is introduced to the duchesse de Guermantes. Eventually Saint-Loup marries Gilberte (q.v.) Swann. He also, during the years before his death in action in the 1914–18 war, succeeds his uncle Charlus in the affections of the violinist Morel.

Saint Malc, Captivité de, see *Captivité.*

Saint-Marc Girardin [the name taken by Marc Girardin] (1801–73), born in Paris, a distinguished critic—anti-Romantic—and publicist associated for over forty years with the *Revue des Deux Mondes* and the *Journal des Débats* (qq.v.). He was also Professor of French Poetry at the Sorbonne from 1833 to 1863 and large crowds attended his lectures on the treatment of the passions in dramatic literature. (*Cours de littérature dramatique*, 1843–68, 5 vols. The study ranges from Greek drama to the 19th century but dwells at length on the 17th century.) His other works include: *Essais de littérature et de morale* (1845); *Souvenirs de voyages et d'études* (1852–3); *Souvenirs et Réflexions politiques d'un journaliste* (1859, his *Journal des Débats* articles); *La Fontaine et les fabulistes* (1867); *Étude sur Jean-Jacques Rousseau* (1870), and numerous pamphlets. He was active in politics during his last years.

Saint-Martin, LOUIS-CLAUDE DE ['le philosophe inconnu'] (1743–1803), philosopher and mystic, an illuminist (see *Illuminisme*), was born at Amboise. His first work, *Des Erreurs et de la vérité* (1775), was influenced by his association with Martines de Pasqually (1715–91), a Portuguese Jew prominent in the history of freemasonry. Before reading it Voltaire said: 'S'il est bon, il doit contenir cinquante volumes in-folio pour la première partie, et une demi-page pour la seconde.' After reading it he said: 'Je ne crois pas qu'on ait jamais rien imprimé de plus absurde, de plus obscur, de plus fou et de plus sot.' Saint-Martin's later, very obscurely-written works were influenced by the writings (some of which he translated) of Jakob Boehme (1575–1624), the German shoemaker-theosophist. They include: *L'Homme de désir* (1790), *Le Crocodile, poème épico-magique en CII chants* (1794), *Le Nouvel Homme* (1796), *Le Ministère de l'homme-esprit* (1802).

Saint-Maur, Congrégation de, see *Maurists.*

Saint-Médard, Convulsionnaires de, see *Pâris, François de.*

Saint-Pavin, DENIS SANGUIN DE (1600–70), a poet of the *libertin* (q.v.) school, author of polished verse, including sonnets and epigrams, showing some boldness of thought and vivacity. His father was seigneur of Livry and lived in the neighbourhood, and Saint-Pavin thus came into relations with Mme de Sévigné, to which there is reference in her letters. The abbacy of Livry passed to the Saint-Pavin family after the death of her uncle Coulanges.

Saint-Phlin, one of the seven young *déracinés* in the novel *Les Déracinés* (q.v.) by Maurice Barrès.

Saint-Pierre, BERNARDIN DE, see *Bernardin.*

Saint-Pierre, CHARLES-IRÉNÉE, ABBÉ DE (1658–1743), economist, born in Normandy of a noble family, author of many projects of political and economic reform, some of them absurd, others showing clear vision, if somewhat pedantically framed. Among them was a *Projet de paix perpétuelle* (1713), of which Rousseau wrote an abstract, supplemented by a criticism. He wrote *Annales politiques* or memoirs of the reign of Louis XIV; his outspoken criticism of that monarch's administration in his *Discours sur la Polysynodie* (1718, on the use of councils in government) caused him to be expelled from the *Académie*. He became an active member of the *Club de l'Entresol* (q.v.). His projects were all designed for the welfare of mankind, showing hatred of war and despotism; he was a utilitarian before Bentham. Montesquieu regarded him as his master, but in general he was treated as a dreamer and by many as a bore. He invented the word *bienfaisance*.

Saint-Pierre, EUSTACHE DE (*c.* 1287–*c.* 1371), a burgher of Calais, celebrated for his courage and devotion to his fellow citizens on the occasion of the surrender of the town to Edward III (1347).

Saint Pierre et le Jongleur, see *Fabliaux.*

Saint-Pol-Roux, pseudonym of Paul Roux (1861–1940), minor Symbolist poet who was also known as 'Saint-Pol-le-Magnifique'. His works, often obscurely written, include the three collected volumes of *Les Reposoirs de la Procession* (1893–1907): *La Rose et les épines du chemin, De la colombe au corbeau par le paon, Les Féeries intérieures*; also *La Dame à la faulx* (1899), a dramatic poem with three speakers—a Man, a Woman, and Death.

Saint-Preux, see *Nouvelle Héloïse.*

Saint-Réal, CÉSAR, ABBÉ DE (1639–92), author of various historical works, including the remarkable *Histoire de la conjuration des Espagnols contre Venise* (an episode of 1618), on which Otway based his *Venice Preserv'd*. The work was published in 1674 and an English translation appeared in the following year.

Saint-Saëns, CAMILLE (1835–1921), French organist and composer of operas, symphonic poems, and chamber music.

Saint-Simon, CLAUDE-HENRI DE ROUVROY, COMTE DE (1760–1825), from whom the system of social philosophy known as *Saint-Simonisme* (q.v.) was named, was born in Paris of a younger branch of the family of Saint-Simon the memorialist. At eighteen he went to America and fought in the War of Independence. He was home again by the Revolution but kept apart from it. He speculated successfully in *biens nationaux* (q.v.), travelled, married, and lived extravagantly. Both his marriage and his fortune came to an end and from about 1808 until he died his circumstances bordered on destitution.

He had at all times pursued vague political and scientific studies, and was so convinced of their importance that his valet had orders to waken him every morning with the words 'Souvenez-vous, Monsieur le Comte, que vous avez de grandes choses à faire'. In time he evolved a theory of the necessity for a reorganization of society which would give the controlling share in government to industrialists and scientists instead of to the military and property-owning, or the clerical, classes. True Christianity, he held, was a social religion of love and charity, not a matter of doctrine; each man's duty was to strive, in a society framed to that end, for the betterment of his poorer brethren.

Saint-Simon's principal writings were: *Lettres d'un habitant de Genève à ses contemporains* (1802); *Réorganisation de la société européenne* (1814); *L'Industrie* (1816) and *L'Organisateur* (1819), two short-lived periodicals in which he propounded industrialism as a political force; *Le Système industriel* (1821); *Le Catéchisme des industriels* (1823–4); *Le Nouveau Christianisme* (1825).

Saint-Simon, LOUIS DE ROUVROY, DUC DE (1675–1755), whose father, of an old but inconsiderable family of the Vermandois, had been made *duc et pair* (i.e. member of a sort of honorary grand council of the kingdom) by Louis XIII, was maintained in those functions by Louis XIV and retained his father's excessive sense of their dignity and importance. He served in the army but resigned his commission in 1702, in consequence of what he regarded as his unduly slow promotion. This and his pride alienated the favour of the king, but he nevertheless thereafter lived at court, hoping to secure high office. He obtained the favour of the duc de Bourgogne, and when the latter became heir to the throne formed part of the cabal which discussed the future constitution. He advocated a reform of the government in the direction of a constitutional monarchy in which the nobility should play an important role. The death of the duc de Bourgogne was a severe blow to Saint-Simon. He attached himself, however, to the duc d'Orléans and with more capacity might have played a part of importance in the Regency. But a special mission to Madrid in 1722 to fetch the Infanta (betrothed to Louis XV) was his only success. After the death of the Regent (1723) he retired from court, and occupied himself largely with the preparation of his *Mémoires*. He had contemplated writing these since 1694, when he was nineteen, and had then begun recording his observations. About 1730 he secured a copy of the unpublished *Journal* of Dangeau (q.v.), and on the basis of this (which he criticized as unduly favourable to Louis XIV), of his notes, and of his remarkable memory, he composed between 1740 and 1750 his voluminous record of the later years of Louis XIV (from the siege of Namur in 1692) and of the period of the Regency. A supplement to the death of Fleury is unfortunately lost. The manuscript after his death was claimed by his creditors, and was in 1760 sequestrated by the State. The first authentic edition was not published until 1829–30, but even this was imperfect. A correct edition was published between 1879 and 1928 (Collection des Grands Écrivains de la France).

Saint-Simon was a little man of sickly appearance, with a pointed turned-up nose, of violent temper and narrow intelligence, with an antipathy to knaves and hypocrites. He was a pious but not intolerant Catholic, excessively occupied with his importance as *duc et pair*, detesting Louis XIV and an administration conducted by *bourgeois* to the detriment of the old nobility. His *Mémoires* are not the work of a critical and accurate historian. He aims at the truth, but he mingles facts with gossip, and impartiality, he admits, is beyond him. The defeat of his political ambitions embittered him and warped his judgement, but it intensified the vividness of his picture of the court of Versailles and the brilliancy of his portraits. These form a gallery extending from the king himself, through the chief members of the royal family, Mme de Maintenon, Vendôme, Fénelon, and other great generals and prelates, to a host of minor characters, often sketched in a few pungent words. One or two English men and women are included, such as Sir Richard Temple and Elizabeth Hamilton. He was no less successful in depicting crowded scenes and dramatic incidents, and in evoking the physical environment, the galleries and terraces of Versailles. The effect of his descriptions is enhanced by his observation of minute points, the narrow gold braid on a red velvet cushion at a ceremony, a Swiss soldier's bare arm thrust suddenly from his truckle-bed amid the scene of consternation

at the death of the Dauphin (1711). Sainte-Beuve selects, as showing the maximum of searching observation and brilliant expression, the descriptions of this latter scene and of the *Lit de Justice* in 1718, when the duc du Maine was degraded to the rank of an ordinary peer. Another characteristic description is that of the visit of the king to the camp at Compiègne in 1698. The memoirs are much occupied, not only with the great events of the time, but with marriages and other incidents in high society, with genealogies, with the minute description of ceremonies (e.g. the homage rendered by the duc de Lorraine), and with points of etiquette, such as the *droit du tabouret* (q.v.). The author does not appear to be greatly interested in literature, but a few words here and there show appreciation of Racine, La Fontaine, La Bruyère, &c. Saint-Simon writes in a rich and varied, at times passionate style, incorrect in its impetuosity, with a copious and expressive vocabulary.

Saint-Simonisme, a system of social philosophy inaugurated by the comte de Saint-Simon (q.v.) and continued after his death (1825) by his disciples (*Saint-Simoniens*), particularly by Armand Bazard (author of *L'Exposition de la doctrine saint-simonienne*, 1828–30), Barthélemy-Prosper Enfantin (known as *le père Enfantin*) and Olinde Rodriguez (qq.v.). They held meetings in Paris and the provinces, used *Le Globe* (q.v.) as their official organ, and within six years developed the *Saint-Simonien* theories far beyond their confused beginnings. They had a far-reaching influence on the thought of their own and succeeding generations.

They believed that history had alternated, with the spirit of the time, between negative *états critiques* (war and antagonism) and constructive *états organiques* (obedience and association), and that hope for the future lay in the spirit of association. To bring this about they advocated the abolition of hereditary rights, the introduction of social equality and the disappearance of the exploited classes, the furtherance of education, and the emergence of a state in which finance and industry would be on a level with science and art, with work as the touchstone of merit. ('A chacun selon sa capacité, à chaque capacité selon ses œuvres.') They also, in advance of their time, believed in disarmament and the protection of the rights of small peoples: and it was Enfantin who first suggested the piercing of the Suez Canal.

The *Saint-Simoniens* also had a religious side based on doctrines of fraternity and love. They formed themselves into a 'collège', later called an 'église', and introduced a form of sacerdotalism with Bazard and Enfantin as 'les pères suprêmes'. They lived as a community in a house in the centre of Paris (1829) till dissension arose, when Bazard and others seceded and the remnants of the community followed Enfantin to Ménilmontant, then a suburb of Paris (1831). They adopted a symbolical dress consisting of white trousers (love), a red waistcoat (work), and a violet-blue tunic (faith), which signified that their creed was based on love, fortified by work, and enveloped by faith. The tunic also symbolized fraternity and mutual help, for it buttoned up the back and could not be put on without assistance. This costume is often mentioned in writings of the time.

Life ran less smoothly at Ménilmontant, partly because of confusion between the theories of female emancipation and community of property. Also, Enfantin's ideas became increasingly mystical. He decided that *le père suprême* must have a holy bride, and sent envoys in search of a female Messiah. (It has been said that Lady Hester Stanhope was one possible choice, that she was interviewed at Jerusalem but declined the honour.) Meantime the authorities had become uneasy and the sect was finally disbanded in the interests of public morals.

In later years many former *Saint-Simoniens* made practical use of their theories of group association and became successful promoters of joint-stock companies or schemes of industrial development.

Saint-Sorlin, DESMARETS DE, see *Desmarets de Saint-Sorlin.*

Saint-Sulpice, the name of a seminary for priests founded in the rue du Vieux-Colombier in Paris in 1635. Fénelon received priestly orders there. It showed bitter antagonism to the Jansenists, and is frequently referred to in the memoirs of Saint-Simon. There is a good deal about the seminary in later days in Renan's *Souvenirs d'enfance et de jeunesse* (q.v.).

Saint-Victor, Abbaye de, the Abbey of the Canons Regular of St. Victor, was situated on the left (south) bank of the Seine in Paris, where the Halle aux Vins now stands. Guillaume de Champeaux (q.v.) developed it in the 12th century from the chapel of Saint-Victor when he retired there after his conflicts with Abélard. By the 16th century its library was considered the richest and most important in France. During the reign of François Ier (1515–47) it was thrown open to students, the only library where they were free to come and work. Rabelais used it, and in *Pantagruel* c. vii he ridiculed the titles of some of the books. The Abbey was suppressed in 1790 and the library dispersed. The manuscripts found their way to the Bibliothèque nationale (q.v.) and the books, or many of them, to the Bibliothèque de l'Arsenal (q.v.).

Saint-Victor, PAUL, COMTE DE (1825–81), born in Paris, man of letters and dramatic critic on several papers, notably *La Presse* (q.v.). His chief work was a study of the origin and development of the drama, *Les Deux Masques* [i.e. Tragedy and Comedy] (1880–3). This examines (vols. 1, 2) the classical drama in relation to the age which produced it and the influence of Greek mythology, then continues (vol. 3) with Shakespeare and the drama down to Beaumarchais (q.v.).

Also calling for mention are the collected essays (subjective but stimulating), *Hommes et Dieux* (1867), particularly those on *Les Comédiens de la Mort, L'Argent, Manon Lescaut.*

Sainte-Barbe, Collège, see *Collège Sainte-Barbe.*

Sainte-Beuve, CHARLES-AUGUSTIN (1804–69), critic, born at Boulogne-sur-Mer, was brought up by his widowed mother (his father died before he was born) and an aunt, who both strained their slender resources to enable him to continue his education in Paris after 1818. He studied medicine for over three years from 1823, including one year as a hospital extern, but from 1824 he combined it with literary journalism on the newly-founded *Globe* (q.v.). After 1827 literature claimed him altogether. His *Globe* articles included many sympathetic appreciations of the young Romantics (see *Romantisme*).

Some, collected, formed the *Tableau histo-rique et critique de la poésie française et du théâtre français au XVI* *siècle* (1828), which put the Romantics effectively on the literary map by tracing their affinity with Ronsard and the Pléiade (qq.v.). A review early in 1827 of Hugo's *Odes et Ballades* won him the friendship of both Hugo and Hugo's wife. The relationship with Adèle Hugo turned to a passion which killed his friendship with Hugo, went far to cool his sympathy with the Romantic Movement, and left him for many years a prey to emotional stress and profound spiritual disquiet. He traversed phases of Saint-Simonism and of sympathy with Lamennais (qq.v.); and religious doubt at this time may have been the first cause of his interest in Port-Royal (q.v.). In 1837, for the sake of distraction, he went to lecture for a year at Lausanne and made Port-Royal his subject. *Port-Royal* (q.v., 1840–59) is the book form of these lectures and one of his masterpieces of re-creative literary criticism.

(2) From 1829 Sainte-Beuve was a regular critic on the *Revue de Paris*, and from 1831 (when he left the *Globe*) also on the *Revue des Deux Mondes*. His articles for these two reviews form the basis of his *Critiques et Portraits littéraires* (q.v., 1832; 1836–9), col-lections which in their turn were the nucleus of the three series *Portraits littéraires, Portraits de femmes*, and *Portraits contemporains*. Some of his early articles were also included in the posthumous *Premiers lundis* (1874–5, see *Causeries du lundi*). Soon after the February Revolution (1848, see *Revolutions*) he re-signed a pleasant, unexacting post at the Bibliothèque Mazarine (q.v.), held since 1840, and accepted a temporary professorship at the University of Liège. The twenty-one lectures he delivered (winter 1848–9) re-sulted in another notable work, *Chateaubriand et son groupe littéraire* (published 1861), a study of the man (not wholly admiring), his work, and his literary circle during the First Empire. The preface deserves special mention as a fine proclamation of the faith of a man of letters.

(3) During this half of his career his output was creative as well as critical. He published *Vie, Poésies et Pensées de Joseph Delorme* (1829, q.v.) and *Les Consolations* (1830), two collections, the first especially, of intimate, reflective verse; with what has been criticized as questionable taste he printed *Le Livre*

d'amour, love-poems addressed to Mme Adèle Hugo, for private circulation (pub-lished posthumously), and he also published a long, to some extent autobiographical, novel *Volupté* (1834, q.v.), of interest to students of introspective fiction.

(4) The second half of his career began when he returned to Paris in 1849 and accepted an offer from Dr. Véron (q.v.) to review, in his own fashion and with almost complete free-dom in his choice of books, for the *Constitu-tionnel*. This was the beginning of the famous *Lundis*, literary *causeries* which he contributed weekly to the *Constitutionnel*, then to the *Moniteur*, and lastly to the *Temps*, between 1849 and 1869. They appeared every Mon-day. Every Friday one went to the printer. Every Sunday, at the offices of the news-paper, Sainte-Beuve corrected the proofs. The change, a few months before his death, from the *Moniteur*, the official Government organ of the Second Empire, to the *Temps*, a journal of the Republican Opposition, emphasized his political progress from a too-complacent support of the Second Empire in its early days to open disapproval of its reactionary policy, particularly in questions of religion and education. His earlier, pro-Government attitude had earned him official rewards and some unpopularity, e.g. in 1854 he was appointed Professor of Latin Poetry at the Collège de France (q.v.) but was unable to lecture because of hostile manifestations. (The lectures were published in 1857, entitled *Étude sur Virgile*.) Between 1858 and 1861 he lectured at the École normale supérieure (q.v.) on medieval and 16th-century French literature. His appoint-ment as a member of the Senate in 1865 eased his financial circumstances during his last years of failing health and, in the end, great suffering.

(5) But above all, the Sainte-Beuve of the years after 1849 was the 'father of modern criticism', the writer who most strikingly typifies the 19th-century development, for which he was largely responsible, of profes-sional criticism from a minor to at its best a major form of the literary art. He had a conception, novel and stimulating in his day if well-worn now, that criticism should be re-creative rather than dogmatic; that the critic should provide data of the formative in-fluences on an author's character, e.g. physio-logical inheritance, environment, family

circumstances, education, love and friendships, early and later sympathies, &c., and
then leave his readers to draw conclusions
for themselves (cf. 'Corneille' in *Portraits
littéraires*, or 'Chateaubriand' in the *Nouveaux
Lundis*). The carefully documented monographs of the *Lundis* and the earlier *Portraits*
are the practical expression of his theories.
They are, moreover, an illustration of the
astonishing range of his reading and of the
breadth of view which enabled him to approach widely differing authors, not French
alone. Between them, they cover not only
the great figures down to, and in some cases
during, Sainte-Beuve's own day but also
many lesser figures (important influences, in
his eyes, on thought, and the most profitable
approach to the study of any literary age).
They are still an indispensable guide to
French literature, particularly to 17th-cen-
tury literature.

(6) Sainte-Beuve has at times been reproached with unfairness to his contemporaries, and
there seems to be little doubt that his reservations, or his judgements, were at times
influenced by temperamental distastes, at
times, even, by a nervous jealousy of creative
exuberance. But it is also the case that for
Sainte-Beuve, for whom literature was 'une
religion ardemment embrassée dès l'enfance',
what mattered above everything else was
truth. So far as the realistic writers were concerned, for instance (see *Réalisme*), he more
than once made it clear (e.g. in *La Tradition
en littérature*, in the *Lundis*) that he found
their work on the whole lacking in charm,
overweighted, and thus neither poetically nor
historically true; that he accepted it reluctantly, and only because it was less untrue,
and more courageous, than the literature
blessed by official opinion.

(7) Publication of Sainte-Beuve's *Correspondance générale* (edited and fully annotated
by J. Bonnerot), which stands high in interest
among literary correspondences of the 19th
century, began in 1933.

Sainte-Geneviève, École de, a medieval
school at Paris, belonging to the collegiate
church of Sainte-Geneviève on the south
bank of the Seine, outside the jurisdiction
of the Bishop of Paris. Abélard's teaching
there brought it great fame. At one time
early in the 13th century it assumed a position almost of rivalry to the University, the

abbot of Sainte-Geneviève conferring *licences
ès arts* on students in its territory.

Sainte-Marthe, CHARLES DE (*c.* 1512–55),
poet, author of *Poésie française* (1540), in
which he treated Platonic themes in the form
of *rondeaux* and epigrams. He was the uncle
of Scévole de Sainte-Marthe (see below).

Sainte-Marthe, SCÉVOLE DE (1536–1623),
humanist and poet, born at Loudun in
Poitou, a poet of the school of Ronsard and
the Pléiade, who wrote in both Latin and
French, and was honoured by Ronsard in a
dedication as 'excellent poète'.

Sainte-Maure, BENOÎT DE, see *Benoît de
Sainte-Maure.*

Sainte-Palaye, see *La Curne de Sainte-
Palaye.*

Sainte-Pélagie, in Paris, originally founded
(under Louis XIV) as a convent-refuge for
women, was used as a prison from the Revolution onwards. Its inmates were mainly
debtors and political offenders, especially the
too-outspoken men of letters and journalists.
It no longer exists.

Saintré, Petit Jehan de, see *Petit Jehan de
Saintré.*

Saints, Lives of. Throughout the Middle
Ages (from the 10th to the 13th cc.) lives of
saints occupied an important place among
the subjects treated by French poets. They
are a more archaic form of literature than
the *chansons de geste* (q.v.), and a clear influence on these. Many were founded on or
inspired by Latin texts, others (such as that
of St. Brendan, q.v.) on Celtic legends, or on
the stories of contemporary martyrs (such as
St. Thomas à Becket). After a first phase
when they had a strictly religious character,
they soon came, as a rule, to be destined for
more popular audiences, parishioners or
pilgrims assembled at shrines or church doors
on festivals. They were composed and recited
principally by clerks, though lay poets also
(such as Rutebeuf, q.v., who wrote a life of
Sainte Marie l'Égyptienne) are among their
authors; and similarly lives of saints came to
be included among the pieces that *jongleurs*
recited. See, as examples of the best-known
lives, *Alexis, Thomas Becket, Brendan.*

Saisnes, Chanson des, see *Bodel, Jean.*

Saison en enfer, see *Une Saison en enfer.*

Salacrou, ARMAND (1899–   ), contemporary dramatist. His plays are a mixture of tragedy, comedy, and ironical farce, often with a streak of poetry. In *L'Inconnue d'Arras* (1935) a man learns of his wife's infidelity and shoots himself. The three acts represent what passes through his mind during the minute he takes to die. *La Terre est ronde* (1938) is a drama of religious fanaticism, set in the Italian Renaissance. His other plays include: *Le Casseur d'assiettes* (1925); *Atlas Hôtel* (1931); *Un homme comme les autres* (1936); *Histoire de rire* (1939); *Le Soldat et la sorcière* (1945); *Les Nuits de la colère* (1946), a drama of the Resistance; *L'Archipel Lenoir* (1948).

Salammbô (1862), a novel of ancient Carthage, by Gustave Flaubert (q.v.). The time is after the first Punic war, when Carthage was besieged by the unpaid mercenaries. Their leader is Mathô, a superb Libyan giant, who loves Salammbô, priestess in the temple of the goddess Tanit, and daughter of Hamilcar, the Carthaginian leader. Mathô enters Carthage by stealth and steals from Salammbô's guardianship the sacred veil of Tanit. For a time the fate of Carthage is in the balance and the High Priest commands Salammbô to retrieve the stolen treasure. Salammbô goes to Mathô's tent and gives herself to him in return for the veil. The mercenaries are defeated. Mathô is tortured to death and the grief-stricken Salammbô dies soon after.

In *Salammbô* Flaubert gave full rein to the romantic side of his nature, his love for the voluptuous and the gorgeous. But in his evocation of the historical background he also showed a meticulous care for historical and archaeological exactitude which cost him years of labour and for some critics weakened his book.

Salavin. Louis Salavin is the hero of *Vie et Aventures de Salavin* (1920–32), five complete novels by Georges Duhamel (q.v.). Under a shabby, unobtrusive, rather clumsy exterior he is nerve-racked, full of fears and ambitions, diffident to a degree, yet ever at the mercy of overriding impulses. In *Confession de minuit* (1920) he loses his small clerk's job because one day he yields to an impulse to touch his employer's fat red ear with his finger. In *Deux Hommes* (1924) failure is spiritual, when he makes and loses a friend because he cannot respond generously to simple devotion. In *Le Journal de Salavin* (1927), in diary form, he is a prey to agonies of self-disgust which lead to the resolve to become a saint. An effort to stamp out dishonesty around him, a first step in a pitifully farcical martyrdom, only results in his dismissal from employment with a fraudulent dairy company; and he again comes to grief when he flees home to live in chastity and seek grace in organized religion. A year later (in *Le Club des Lyonnais,* 1929) he seeks grace through politics rather than through faith, but his experiences with a group of communists intensify his sense of spiritual failure. He determines that change of soul will never come in Europe, and *Tel qu'en lui-même* (1932), the final volume, finds him in Tunis, nominally running a gramophone shop. At the native hospital, daily, he performs sickening menial tasks which others seek to avoid and at home he undertakes to reform his nauseous young Arab servant, who shoots him. His wife, a devoted, inarticulate creature, from the beginning a figure in the background, is sent for and gets him back to Paris, but they have barely arrived when he dies. It is left to the reader to decide how nearly the blundering would-be saint had approached spiritual perfection.

Salel, HUGUES (*c.* 1504–53), poet, a Gascon, almoner to François Ier, author of an early translation into verse of the *Iliad* (bks. i–xii, completed by Amadis Jamyn, q.v.), and of *blasons* (q.v.) and other occasional pieces.

Salente, the French name for the country of the Salentini in Calabria, who claimed to have originally come from Crete under the guidance of Idomeneus. Here Fénelon, in his *Télémaque,* placed his ideal republic.

Sales, SAINT FRANÇOIS DE, see *François de Sales, Saint.*

Saliat, PIERRE, a 16th-century translator of Herodotus (*Les Neuf Livres des histoires*).

Salic law, the code of law, written in Latin, of the Salian Franks. It includes a statement that a woman can have no portion in the inheritance of Salic land. It was supposed, wrongly, to be in virtue of this law that women were held to be incapable of succeeding to the throne of France (see *Valois*).

Sallo, DENIS DE (1626–69), founder of the *Journal des savants* (q.v.).

Salmasius, see *Saumaise, Claude de.*

Salmon, ANDRÉ (1881–   ), author of poetry and novels which are a mixture of fantasy and realism, simplicity and irony, in the Cubist manner (see *Cubisme*), e.g. *Les Féeries* (1907), *Le Calumet* (1910), *Prikaz* (1919), *Peindre* (1922), *Tendres Canailles* (1913, a novel of the Latin Quarter underworld), *La Négresse du Sacré-Cœur* (1920), *L'Entrepreneur d'illuminations* (1921). He was one of a group which included Guillaume Apollinaire, Max Jacob (qq.v.), and, in art, Picasso, and is also known as a critic of modern art.

Salomé (1893), a drama in one act, in French, by Oscar Wilde. It was produced in Paris in 1896 when Wilde was in Reading Gaol. The composer Richard Strauss made an opera of it (produced in Dresden in 1909) and used the text as the libretto for a French version. But he got into difficulties over adapting his music to the—to him incomprehensibly variable—stresses of the French silent E and consulted Romain Rolland, who annotated his music and explained that the *E muet* was 'moins un son, qu'une résonance, un écho de la syllabe précédente, qui vibre, se balance et s'éteint doucement dans l'air' [in *Richard Strauss et Romain Rolland: Correspondance* (*Cahiers Romain Rolland 3*), 1951].

Salomon et Marcoul, Dialogues de, dialogues perhaps of Eastern origin in which, to each wise saw propounded by Solomon, Marcoul, a grotesque character, objects in a sentence of vulgar common sense. Two of the sayings are quoted by Rabelais (I. xxxiii). There is a version of the dialogues in the O.E. *Salomon and Saturn.*

Salon

A. In the sense of an assembly held regularly (generally on one or more days of the week) in a private house, presided over by the lady, or sometimes the master, of the house and frequented by a more or less constant company.

(1) These *salons* reached their chief development in the second half of the 18th century. There were the *salons* of high society, such as that of the maréchale de Luxembourg (duchesse de Boufflers by her first marriage);

the *salons* of the great financiers such as Samuel Bernard, which by their sumptuous hospitality sought to attract the nobility; and the intellectual *salons*, of chief concern here, where persons interested in literature, art, philosophy, or politics, assembled for conversation and discussion. The 17th-century prototype of the intellectual *salon* was that of the marquise de Rambouillet (q.v.). After an eclipse during the latter part of the reign of Louis XIV and the first years of the 18th century, when Versailles and the courts of the princes gathered all Paris society about them, a host of new *salons* sprang up, each with its special characteristics, largely dependent on the taste and temperament of the hostess.

(2) The institution is of importance for the influence it enabled women to exert. In its early days it favoured the growth of polite manners, delicacy of sentiment, and purity of language, and had a salutary effect after the social disorganization of the civil wars. The *salons* of the later 18th century formed a power in the State, independent of the official authorities; in them, the intellectuals of the day met, talked, appreciated each other, and realized their strength as a party. Sometimes the *salons* degenerated into coteries, mutual admiration societies, or centres of intrigue, creating or destroying reputations, promoting admissions to the *Académie*, and so forth, and fostering a literature that was witty, luminous, and instructive, but impersonal and colourless.

[For some of the most famous *salons* and centres of pre-Revolutionary society see under: *Cornuel*; *Delorme*; *Du Deffand*; *Épinay*; *Geoffrin*; *Helvétius*; *Holbach*; *Lambert*; *Lespinasse*; *Maine, duchesse du*; *Necker*; *Palais-Royal*; *Sablé*; *Staël*; *Suard*; *Temple*; *Tencin*; and cf. *Dorat*; *Roederer*.]

(3) By about 1792 the society in which the *salons* had thrived had largely dispersed. The few *salons* of the Revolutionary era were less sophisticated, less urbane, and more political. The *Girondins* (q.v.), for instance, came into being in the *salon* of Mme Roland. During the Consulate and the Empire politics and literature met again when the marquise de Condorcet reopened her *salon*, or when Mme de Staël was suffered to remain in Paris (cf. also *Coppet*). Napoleon, moreover, encouraged his officers to marry and their wives to open *salons*. But though the institution

was revived the great days of the *salon* as a formative influence on culture and taste had ended. Some 19th-century *salons* may none the less be noticed (see the following paragraphs; and see separate headings for fuller details of persons mentioned), since references to them occur frequently in contemporary memoirs and correspondence (and in fiction the *salon* plays a notable part, e.g. in Balzac in the 19th and in Proust in the 20th century).

(4) One brilliant hostess of Napoleon's Empire was the duchesse d'Abrantès (q.v.) while her husband was Military Governor of Paris. She entertained a mixed company—the army, the diplomatic corps, bankers, newly-enriched industrialists, with an element of literature. Mme de Montesson, who had been married to the duc d'Orléans, grandson of the Regent (see *Régence*), and whom Napoleon had chosen to organize his court at the Tuileries, revived an aristocratic past in her *salon*. Social distinctions were finely drawn and she accompanied her guests to the door only if she did not mean them to be readmitted. Returned *émigrés* were among her company and were to be found, also, in Mme de Genlis's rooms at the Hôtel de l'Arsenal (cf. *Bibliothèque de l'Arsenal*), where they were entertained with *proverbes dramatiques* (q.v.). Reading, acting, and music were features of the then young Mme Récamier's *salon* in the rich house specially decorated for her. Here many English *en passage* could be seen, e.g. Fox, Lord and Lady Holland, but the element of the opposition was too strong for Napoleon's liking. Her *salon* was again a centre after the Restoration (1815), and in its last phase, after 1830, it became more than anything else a shrine for Chateaubriand and a place of pilgrimage. Mme de Staël's *salon* between her return to Paris in 1814 and her death in 1817 was 'un miroir où se peint l'histoire du temps'. The Duke of Wellington was a visitor.

(5) During this Restoration period Nodier's *salon* at the Bibliothèque de l'Arsenal was the first of the Romantic *cénacles* (q.v. and see *Romantisme*), where youth and enthusiasm breathed new life into literature. Some years later the second *cénacle* met at Victor Hugo's home in the rue Notre-Dame-des-Champs. At this time, too, on Saturday evenings at the Jardin des Plantes, the naturalist Cuvier used to entertain scientists and writers, and his attractive stepdaughter Sophie Duvaucel was the life and soul of the company (cf. Nodier's daughter Marie at the Arsenal). Stendhal, Mérimée, the artist Delacroix, and for a time the young naturalist Jacquemont were among the younger guests. *Their* rounds also included Mme Ancelot's *salon*, where poets, social reformers, and historians might be found listening to recitations by the young actress Rachel. (This *salon* began during the Restoration and continued well into the Second Empire. It was sometimes called 'une porte d'entrée de l'Académie française'.) On Wednesday evenings the turn was for the baron Gérard's studio. Balzac, too, came here.

(6) During the July monarchy two Englishwomen, Mary Clarke (q.v. and see next paragraph) and her mother, became firmly established among the intellectual hostesses of Paris society. Literature, journalism, and politics rubbed shoulders in the *salon* of Mme Émile de Girardin (q.v. and cf. also her mother, Mme Sophie Gay), herself a woman of letters. Guizot and *doctrinaire* (q.v.) politics reigned in the *salon* of the Russian princesse de Lieven; and the atmosphere was again mainly political at the princesse Belgiojoso's, frequented by Mignet, Augustin Thierry, and Alfred de Musset amongst others. Another foreigner, whose gatherings attracted outstanding Roman Catholic personalities (e.g. Lacordaire, Montalembert), was the Russian Mme Schwetchine, a convert to Roman Catholicism who lived in Paris between 1825 and 1857 and took an active part in religious and educational controversies.

(7) Literary and artistic *salons* of the Second Empire included that of Mme Xavier de Ricard, where the young poets (the later *Parnassiens*, q.v.) met, and that of the princesse Mathilde, with Flaubert, Gautier, the brothers Goncourt, Sainte-Beuve, and many other great literary figures among the company. Artists, writers, and musicians were collected in more Bohemian fashion by Mme de Païva and Mme Sabatier (see *Païva, La*; *Présidente, La*), and by the young Mme Nina de Callias, daughter of a barrister at Lyons and one-time wife of a journalist. She entertained and befriended many young geniuses or would-be geniuses, among them Verlaine. The atmosphere and

the conversation were heavier at Mme d'Agoult's Sunday afternoons, where older poets and men of letters, as well as historians, philosophers, and all the Second Empire opposition met, and where Thiers would lecture brilliantly and epigrammatically on any question put to him. At Mme Mohl's (the former Mary Clarke, see preceding paragraph) the 'élite des hommes du jour', French and foreign, are said to have assembled and to have been refreshed with tea and biscuits.

(8) Of the *salons* of the later 19th century, some were literary and artistic, some political, some musical, some elegant; in most of them one particular figure was the centre of attraction, e.g. Dumas *fils* in the very strictly ruled *salon* of Mme d'Aubernon (herself a brilliant talker), Anatole France in that of Mme Arman de Caillavet (frequented by the young Proust), Jules Lemaître in that of Mme de Loynes, where the temper was strongly anti-Dreyfus at the time of the *Affaire* (q.v.). Proust described some of these *salons* in articles contributed to *Le Figaro* between 1900 and 1905 (collected in *Chroniques*, 1927); and in *A la recherche du temps perdu* (q.v.) he conveyed an even better idea of the *salons* of this period, e.g. his description of 'le petit clan' of Mme Verdurin or of the company entertained by Mme de Villeparisis.

B. In the sense of periodic exhibitions of work by living artists.

(1) The first such exhibition in France was organized by the Académie Royale de Peinture et de Sculpture at the instigation of Colbert (q.v.) and held in 1667 in one of the large rooms (a *salle*, or *salon*) in the royal palace of the Louvre (q.v.). Between 1667 and 1795 there were exhibitions at irregular intervals, with stretches when they were biennial or annual. They were resumed biennially after the Revolution and became annual after 1849. The right to exhibit was at first limited to the forty members of the Académie Royale. Since the middle of the 19th century there has been a selection committee, and the *Salons* are now held in the Grand Palais des Champs-Élysées. In the course of time the use of the word *salon* extended to other art exhibitions, e.g. the Salon des Indépendants, Salon d'automne, &c. (and cf. *Impressionnisme*), and then to

exhibitions of different types, e.g. Salon de l'automobile.

(2) Diderot's (q.v.) *Salons*, the accounts of nine exhibitions held between 1759 and 1781 which he contributed to Grimm's (q.v.) *Correspondance littéraire*, inaugurated the genre of art criticism in France; while Baudelaire's (q.v.) *Salons* of 1845, 1846, and 1859 mark its progress in the 19th century.

Salpêtrière, La, a famous hospital in Paris, was erected during the reign of Louis XIV (*c.* 1650) on the site of an arsenal and saltpetre works dating from the reign of Louis XIII. One part of the earlier building still exists. In the first place this institution was a prison for vagrants, beggars, and prostitutes, later also for lunatics, and it was notorious for filth and vice. It is famous in literature as the prison to which Manon Lescaut (q.v.) was sent. One part of the building, called 'La Force', was used for political prisoners during the Revolution and it was there that some of the worst of the September massacres (1792) took place. The present-day Salpêtrière is both a hospital, which also specializes in the treatment of mental diseases, and a public-assistance institution for the care of aged and incurable persons.

Samain, ALBERT (1858–1900), poet, born at Lille, was a small clerk in Paris, poor and consumptive, who gave his spare time to literature. He helped (1891) to found the *Mercure de France* (q.v.) and in 1893 published *Au jardin de l'infante*, a collection of sonnets and elegiac verse of great beauty which brought him sudden renown. A later volume, *Aux flancs du vase* (1898, short poems of Greek antiquity), was less successful. Another, posthumous, collection *Le Chariot d'or* was published in 1901. He had also written some tales (*Contes*, 1903) and a poetic drama in two acts, *Polyphème* (produced at the Théâtre de l'Œuvre in 1904 and published in 1906). His verse showed much Symbolist influence but he belonged to no one school.

Saman, MME DE, see *Allart, Hortense*.

Sambre-et-Meuse, L'Armée de, the most famous of the armies that defended French territory during the Revolution. Under Jourdan (q.v.) it won the important victory of Fleurus in June 1794.

Sand, GEORGE, nom de plume of Lucile-

Aurore Dupin, baronne Dudevant (1804–76), novelist, born in Paris. Her father, an army officer and a descendant of the Maréchal de Saxe, died when she was very young. Her childhood upbringing at her paternal grandmother's country property (later hers) of Nohant was on Rousseauesque lines, with a background of quarrels between her grandmother and her mother (whom the former never forgave for 'inveigling' her son into marriage). After a convent education in Paris she was again at Nohant, running wild, reading Rousseau, Byron, Shakespeare, Chateaubriand ('Il me sembla que René c'était moi'), watching her grandmother die. Thereafter (1822) she married the baron Dudevant, a retired army officer. Two children, Maurice and Solange, were born, but by 1831 she was, with her husband's acquiescence, in Paris, enjoying an independent, trousered, life and trying to earn money by writing. She collaborated at first with Jules Sandeau (q.v.), under the pseudonym 'Jules Sand', publishing articles and a novel, *Rose et Blanche* (1831). Then, writing alone, and for the first time as 'George Sand', she published the novel *Indiana* (1832, q.v.), first of many successes. Over the next forty years she produced a rapid succession of novels, tales, biographical and critical essays, and, later, dramatic works. Her literary output, which falls roughly into three periods, usually echoed whatever men or ideas were foremost in her personal life. Renan (q.v.) called her 'la harpe éolienne de notre temps'.

(2) The first period was signalled at the outset by a liaison—of which her version was *Elle et lui*, 1859—with Alfred de Musset. It was characterized by the novels *Indiana* (1832), *Valentine* (1832), *Lélia* (1833), *Jacques* (1834), *Mauprat* (1837, q.v.), and was romantic *par excellence*. Her theme was passion, and the right of the individual to follow his, or rather her, heart and defy conventional morals: it was 'l'amour', as she said of *Indiana*, 'heurtant son front aveugle à tous les obstacles de la civilisation'.

(3) Towards 1840 (by which time she was legally separated from her husband, having kept the children) came a phase of enthusiastic, uncritical fervour for the various *isms* of the day and their exponents, e.g. humanitarianism (Pierre Leroux), Christian socialism (Lamennais), Republicanism. It was reflected in, for example, *Spiridion* (1839, a mystical

hotchpotch), *Les Sept Cordes de la lyre* (1840), *Le Compagnon du Tour de France* (1840, q.v.), *Consuelo* (1842, q.v.), *Le Meunier d'Angibault* (1845, q.v.), &c. But she also began to write the simple, idyllicized romances of country life which keep her fame alive (*La Mare au diable*, 1846; *La Petite Fadette*, 1848; *François le champi*, 1850, qq.v.).

(4) Political journalism claimed her for a time during the 1848 Revolution, but thereafter her life was passed mainly at Nohant and her writing, in her own words, became 'plus sobre et mieux digérée'. She kept open house for her friends, diverted herself with a miniature theatre, and came to be known as 'la bonne dame de Nohant'. She wrote as vigorously as ever—several plays, produced occasionally but seldom successful; letters (e.g. to Flaubert) of great literary interest (*Correspondance*, 1882–4); and many novels of country or social life. She was not only an effortless writer: she was a born story-teller, with a lyrically descriptive style which could often carry off her most astonishing flights of imagination.

(5) Besides the works mentioned, her output (105 volumes in the Michel Lévy collected edition) includes: *Lettres d'un voyageur* (1834–6), impressions of her early years in Paris and of her ill-fated trip to Italy in 1833–4 with Alfred de Musset when she nursed him through an illness but deserted him for the doctor she had called in (see under *Musset*); *Un Hiver à Majorque* (1841), describing her stay on the island with Chopin during the first stages of their nine years liaison; *Histoire de ma vie* (1854–5, 4 vols.; she is born at the end of the second volume, and the fourth contains interesting appreciations of her contemporaries); also many other novels, e.g. *La Comtesse de Rudolstadt* (1843), a poor sequel to *Consuelo*; *Le Péché de M. Antoine* (1847); *Les Maîtres Sonneurs* (1852); *L'Homme de neige* (1856); *Les Beaux Messieurs de Bois-Doré* (1858); *Le Marquis de Villemer* (1860); *Mademoiselle de Quintinie* (1863), &c.

Sandeau, JULES (1811–83), a writer most frequently mentioned as the collaborator of more famous authors. He had one success to his sole credit, namely *Mademoiselle de la Seiglière* (1848, dramatized in 1851), a novel of the conflict between love and aristocratic birth. The more realistic *Sacs et parchemins*

(1851), a study of business life, and *La Roche aux mouettes* (1871), a tale for young people, are also remembered. In his earlier days as a law student he collaborated with the baronne Dudevant (i.e. George Sand, q.v.) in the novel *Rose et Blanche ou la comédienne et la religieuse*, published in 1831 under the pseudonym Jules Sand. In later life he was part author, with the dramatist Émile Augier, of *Le Gendre de M. Poirier* (1853, q.v.).

Sandras, COURTILZ DE, see *Courtilz*.

Sangrado, Le Docteur, the quack doctor in *Gil Blas* (q.v.). He had two universal remedies—hot water and blood-letting.

Sans-culottes, in the beginning a contemptuous name given by the aristocrats to the Revolutionaries (1789) because these had taken to wearing trousers instead of breeches. Applied by the Revolutionaries to themselves it became synonymous with *patriot*.

Sans-culottides, see *Republican Calendar*.

Sanseverina, La, the Duchess de Sanseverina, in Stendhal's novel *La Chartreuse de Parme* (q.v.).

Sans famille (1878), the tale of a foundling child, by Hector Malot (q.v.).

Sanson, CHARLES (1740–93) and HENRI (1767–1840), son and father, the official executioners in Paris during the Revolution. The father beheaded Louis XVI, the son beheaded Marie-Antoinette. Fabricated memoirs of the family were published in 1862.

Santé, La, founded in the 13th century by Marguerite de Provence, widow of St. Louis, as a hospital for overflow patients from the Hôtel-Dieu (q.v.), was used in later centuries as an annexe of the prison of Bicêtre (q.v.) and like that institution had many lunatics among its inmates. In the mid-19th century all the mental cases were transferred to Bicêtre, since when La Santé has been a prison for, mainly, offenders serving short-term sentences.

Santerre, ANTOINE-JOSEPH (1752–1809), head of a Paris brewery, commandant of the *Garde nationale* in Paris during the last days of the monarchy, was responsible for the custody of the royal prisoners in the Temple.

Santeuil, JEAN, the chief character in Proust's (q.v.) unfinished novel *Jean Santeuil,* an early version of *A la recherche du temps perdu,* published posthumously in 1952 (3 vols.).

Santeul, JEAN (1630–97), author of Latin liturgical hymns and other sacred poems in Latin which attained a certain reputation.

Sanxon, MAÎTRE JEHAN, a 16th-century translator of Homer (into French verse).

Sapho, the name under which Mlle de Scudéry depicted herself in *Le Grand Cyrus,* and by which her contemporaries frequently referred to her.

Sapho (1884), by Alphonse Daudet, one of his most naturalistic novels (cf. *Naturalisme*). It is a study (in some ways comparable to *Manette Salomon* by *les frères* Goncourt or *La Femme et le pantin* by Pierre Louÿs) of the gradual moral and spiritual collapse of a young artist who comes to Paris from Provence, forms a liaison with the model Sapho, and is completely subjected to her.

Sarasin (also spelt SARRASIN, SARAZIN, and SARRAZIN), JEAN-FRANÇOIS (1603–54), poet, prose-writer, and wit; author of *ballades* and other light verse, and of a well-written historical essay, *La Conspiration de Wallenstein* (c. 1645). He was banished by Mazarin in 1647 for some satirical verses.

Sarcey, FRANCISQUE (1827–99), gave up teaching for journalism and became one of the best-known and soundest dramatic critics of the second half of the 19th century, contributing a weekly column for over thirty years to *Le Temps* (collected in *Quarante ans de théâtre,* 1900–2). He was not a profound critic, but his good sense, independent judgement, and understanding of the theatre were renowned.

Sardou, VICTORIEN (1831–1908), born in Paris, was the author of comedies and historical dramas characterized by complicated plots and skilful construction. They lacked life, and his success was not lasting, though for a time it rivalled that of his predecessor Scribe (q.v.), on whom his technique was modelled. The most notable were: *Les Pattes de mouche* (1860), *Nos Intimes* (1861), and *La Famille Benoîton* (1865), comedies of manners; *Rabagas* (1872), a political comedy, and *Divorçons* (1880), vaudeville. *Fédora* (1882), revenge in a Russian setting, with Bernhardt in the title-role, *Tosca* (1887), the melodrama used by Puccini for his opera, *Patrie* (1869) and *Thermidor* (1891), historical dramas, and *Madame Sans-Gêne* (1893), an historical comedy, were also successful. The principal character of the last-named was the laundress who married François-Joseph Lefebvre, the miller's son who joined the Revolutionary armies and ended as one of Napoleon's marshals and duc de Dantzig (see *Maréchal de l'Empire*).

Sarment, JEAN (1897–   ), contemporary playwright. In *Le Mariage d'Hamlet* (1922) Hamlet, Polonius, and Ophelia have come to life again and intend to live peacefully. Hamlet is bored with Ophelia and leaves her. Later, he falls in love with her again but kills Polonius, after which he is stoned to death by peasants. Other plays by this author include, notably, *Le Pêcheur d'ombres* (1921) and *Les Plus Beaux Yeux du monde* (1925).

Sarrasin, JEAN-FRANÇOIS, see *Sarasin*.

Sarrasine, one of the 'Scènes de la vie parisienne' in Balzac's *Comédie humaine* (q.v.).

Sarrazin, JEAN, see *Crusades*.

Sartine, GABRIEL DE, see *Librairie*.

Sartre, JEAN-PAUL (1905–   ), born in Paris, contemporary philosopher, novelist, and dramatist, the most active exponent, since about 1943, of the form of philosophy known as *Existentialisme* (q.v.). In 1928 he passed the *concours d'agrégation* after three years at the École normale supérieure (q.v.), then taught philosophy in *lycées* in the provinces and in Paris until 1944, with one interval to study philosophy in Berlin and another (1939–41) when he was on active service and a prisoner of war. Literature and philosophy have been his profession since 1944. His published works include: ESSAYS (PHILOSOPHICAL AND CRITICAL)—*L'Imagination* (1938), *L'Imaginaire* (1940), *Esquisse d'une théorie des émotions* (1940), *L'Être et le Néant* (1943), *L'Existentialisme est un humanisme* (1947), *L'Engrenage* (1948), *Baudelaire* (1947), *Situations*, I, II, III (1947, 1948, 1949); NOVELS —*La Nausée* (1938), one of a list of twelve novels selected in 1950 for the award of the *Grand Prix des meilleurs romans du demi-siècle* (q.v.), *Le Mur* (1939, short stories), and *Les*

Chemins de la liberté (I. *L'Age de raison*, 1945; II. *Le Sursis*, 1945; III. *La Mort dans l'âme*, 1949; to be completed with IV. *La Dernière Chance*); PLAYS—*Les Mouches* (1942), *Huis-clos* (1944), *La Putain respectueuse* (1946), *Morts sans sépultures* (1946), *Les Mains sales* (1948), *Le Diable et le Bon Dieu* (1951), *Nekrassov* (1956). His plays, like his novels, are usually a means of conveying his philosophical ideas, but they are also very good theatre and have been successful when produced.

Satire. The medieval literature of France was prolific in satirical writings both in verse and prose; some directed at all ranks of society (such as the *Livre des Manières* of Étienne de Fougères, *c.* 1170), some at particular classes, such as women (e.g. the *Dit de Chichevache*, q.v.), clerics, or villeins; some of a political character, directed for instance at England or papal Rome. Many of the *fabliaux* (q.v.) and of the plays performed by the Basoche (q.v.) were of a satirical character. The most important and sustained satires of this early period are the *Roman de Renart* and the second part of the *Roman de la rose* (qq.v.).

Satire is a feature so frequently occurring in French literature from Villon and Clément Marot onwards that only some of the most important satirical works and authors can be mentioned as illustrations: Rabelais, the Huguenot writers such as d'Aubigné, the *Satire Ménippée*, Henri Estienne (author of the *Apologie pour Hérodote*), Régnier, Boileau, La Bruyère, and, dominating all the satirists of the pre-Revolutionary era, Voltaire (q.v.). André Chénier's *Ïambes*, written while he was in prison in 1794, were inspired by his horror at the excesses of the Revolution. Auguste Barbier also wrote *Ïambes* (1832) satirizing contemporary politics and morals.

The pamphlets (in prose) in which Paul-Louis Courier satirized the Church and the Restoration monarchy were none the less biting for being written with grace and an air of geniality; and the satire of Béranger's *chansons*, of the same period, was also clothed in geniality. Victor Hugo's *Les Châtiments* (q.v.), one of the greatest collections of satirical and invective verse in French literature, was directed at the Emperor Napoleon III after the *coup d'état* (q.v.) of 2 December 1851. Anatole France, in more recent times, satirized the contemporary scene, and modern civilization, in such novels as *L'Histoire contemporaine* and *L'Île des pingouins* (qq.v.).

Satire bernesque, a type of satire, named after the Italian poet Berni (1490–1536), consisting in a picture or caricature of manners, marked by grotesque detail, startling strangeness of comparisons, bold paradox, verve and fantasy. Examples are to be found in the works of Régnier and Sygognes.

Satire Ménippée, a satirical pamphlet in prose and verse, parodying the assembly of the *États généraux* in 1593, and expressing the views of the party that opposed the Ligue (q.v.) and its Spanish allies and supported the claims of Henri IV. The full title of the work is *De la Vertu du Catholicon d'Espagne et de la Tenue des États de Paris*. The work was published in 1594 and was written by Jean Leroy, a canon of Rouen, with collaborators: Jacques Gillot (b. *c.* 1560), Nicolas Rapin (q.v.), Pierre Pithou (1539–96), Jean Passerat (q.v.), Florent Chrétien (1540–96), men of the middle class—functionaries, lawyers, ecclesiastics, and men of learning. It comprises three parts: an introduction in which two charlatans (cardinals from Spain and Lorraine) sing the praises of the panacea Catholicon, followed by a burlesque description of the opening procession of the assembly and of the allegorical tapestries with which the hall of the assembly is hung. The second part, after a catalogue of the chief *Ligueurs* (in which their failings are not overlooked), contains imaginary speeches by various real personages and by a representative of the third estate. Lastly we have some miscellaneous satires and epigrams, notable among them *Le Trépas de l'âne ligueur* by Gilles Durant (1550–1615). The work as a whole is written in a lively mocking vein; the first six speeches are amusing caricatures of what the several speakers might have said, but the speech of d'Aubray, representing the third estate, written by Pithou and the most important element in the work, is a solemn and eloquent indictment of the Ligue, the central element in the composition. The satire was published at the favourable moment of the Ligue's defeat and was immensely successful.

In the title the word 'satire' reproduces the senses of the Latin *satura*, either a mixture of prose and verse, or a satirical writing; while *Ménippée* is from the name of the Cynic philosopher Menippus of Gadara (3rd c. B.C.), who wrote satires in this form.

Satires of Boileau, twelve satires in verse, composed at various dates from 1660 onwards. Boileau used to read them to his friends and they became famous before they were published. The first seven appeared in 1666, the eighth and ninth in 1668, the tenth (composed in 1692) in 1694; the eleventh was composed in 1698; the twelfth, composed in 1705, caused some scandal among the theologians; the king forbade its publication, and it did not appear until after Boileau's death in 1711.

Boileau found models for his satires in those of Horace, Juvenal, Persius, and Régnier. Their importance lies in the fact that they helped to found literary criticism in France. The author constitutes himself the judge of literary reputations, condemning in particular the affectations of writers of the 'precious' school such as Cotin, the extravagant romances of Mlle de Scudéry, the frigid epic of Chapelain, the mild tragedies of Quinault; contrasting with them the work of Racine, Molière, and La Fontaine. He thus helped to form the public taste. Some of the 'Satires' deal with moral subjects, such as Satire V, on what constitutes true nobility; Satire XI on honour. These are somewhat heavy and commonplace; but Satire VI, on the dangers of the city (after Juvenal's third satire), and Satire X, a diatribe against women (after Juvenal's sixth satire), contain passages of powerful realistic painting. In Satire IX, regarded by some as the best, he draws his own literary portrait and makes his defence, with incidental hits at his contemporaries. Satire XII, *sur l'Équivoque*, on ambiguity in religion, written from the Jansenist standpoint, was his last work.

The literary *Satires* show insight, good sense, and caustic wit, and are written with the precision and vigour of a skilful artist.

Saül, title of: a mock tragedy (1763) by Voltaire (q.v., para. 4); a tragedy in five acts (verse) by Lamartine, written in 1818 in an attempt to distract his mind when he was grieving over the death of Mme Julie Charles. He offered it to Talma, who refused it, but he was often invited to read it in the *salons* he frequented; a tragedy (1822) by Soumet; a drama (1904) by André Gide (q.v., para 4).

Saül le furieux, a tragedy by Jean de la Taille, published in 1572.

The general theme is the mystery of divine Providence, under which man appears at times to suffer unjustly. The tragedy traces the progressive humiliation of the proud spirit of Saul, culminating in his despair and death.

The sequel, *La Famine ou les Gabaonites* (1573), shows the curse on Saul extending to his children and grandchildren. The famine which is devastating Israel is to be relieved only when his sons and the sons of his daughter have been delivered to the Gibeonites, with whom Saul has broken faith.

Saumaise, CLAUDE DE (1588–1653), known also by the Latinized form of his name *Salmasius,* born at Semur in Burgundy, a Protestant and an eminent scholar, a professor at Leyden University when Charles II was living at The Hague. He was commissioned by Charles to draw up a defence of his father and an indictment of the regicide government. This took the form of a Latin *Defensio regia pro Carolo I* (1649). Milton was ordered by the Council to reply to it and in 1651 produced his Latin *Pro populo anglicano defensio.* Saumaise wrote other works of Latin scholarship. It was he, at the age of nineteen, who discovered in the Palatine Library at Heidelberg, and first copied, the famous 10th-century manuscript collection of Greek poetical epigrams since known as the *Palatine Anthology.*

Saurin, BERNARD-JOSEPH (1706–81), dramatist, author of *Spartacus* (1760), a successful philosophical tragedy, composed largely of declamations on liberty and humanity; *Blanche et Guiscard* (q.v., 1763), a tragedy on the theme of James Thomson's *Tancred and Sigismunda*; and *Béverlei* (1768), a *tragédie bourgeoise* on the career of a gambler, founded on Edward Moore's *The Gamester* and written in *vers libres* (q.v.). Saurin also wrote a successful one-act prose comedy, *Les Mœurs du temps* (1760), from which Poinsinet perhaps partly drew his *Le Cercle.* Saurin received financial support from Helvétius and was on friendly terms with Voltaire. He was a member of the *Académie.*

Sauvage, CÉCILE (1883–1927), poetess, a schoolmaster's daughter and later a schoolmaster's wife, spent her life in Provence and was first encouraged to write by Mistral (q.v.). Her poems of maternal love (in *Œuvres de Cécile Sauvage,* 1929, posth.) have been particularly praised.

Savoir [born **Posznanski**], ALFRED (1883–1934), a dramatist of Polish origin, author of satirical comedies and farces which include: *La Huitième Femme de Barbe-bleue* (1921); *Banco* (1922) and *La Grande Duchesse et le garçon d'étage* (1924), the inter-war world; *Lui* (1929), a mysterious stranger's impact on a Swiss resort; *La Petite Catherine* (1930), 18th-century Russia and the court of Catherine the Great; *La Voie lactée* (1933), theatre life, &c.

Savonnerie, La, was originally a soap-works, situated on the north bank of the Seine, near the then village of Passy. In the 17th century it became a State factory for the manufacture of carpets in the oriental style and for a time pauper children were trained there as carpet-weavers. In the early 18th century it was merged with the *Gobelins* (q.v.).

Saxe, MAURICE DE (1696–1750), MARÉCHAL DE FRANCE, natural son of Augustus II, Elector of Saxony, a great and successful general in the French service, victor at the battle of Fontenoy (1745). The novelist George Sand (q.v.) was descended from him on her father's side.

Saxons, Chanson des, see *Bodel, Jean.*

Scaliger, JOSEPH JUSTUS (1540–1609), the greatest scholar of the Renaissance, born at Agen, the son of Julius Caesar Scaliger (q.v.). Joseph Scaliger revolutionized ancient chronology by his edition of Manilius, his *De Emendatione Temporum,* and his reconstruction of the chronicle of Eusebius.

Scaliger, JULIUS CAESAR (1484–1558), born at Riva on the Lake of Garda, a scholar who settled in France as physician to the Bishop of Agen after twenty years (according to his own account) of a condottiere's life in Northern Italy. He came into prominence by polemical writings against Erasmus. He wrote a long Latin treatise on poetics (1561), a dogmatic exposition of the classical rules of literary perfection; and a philosophical work, *Exercitationes* on the *De sub-tilitate* of the Italian philosopher Cardano.

Scapin, a type of resourceful rascally valet, taken from Molière's *Fourberies de Scapin* (q.v.).

Scaramouche, adaptation of the Italian *scaramuccia* meaning 'skirmish', a stock character of the old Italian farce, a cowardly and foolish boaster, who is constantly cudgelled by Harlequin. The character was intended to ridicule the Spanish don, and was dressed in Spanish costume, usually black. The clever impersonation of the part by Tiberio Fiorillo (d. *c.* 1694), who came to Paris with his company in 1655 and to London in 1673, made it popular in France and England.

Scarmentado, Histoire des voyages de, a philosophical tale by Voltaire, published in 1756. Its theme was later developed in *Candide* (q.v.).

Scarmentado, son of a governor of Candia, relates his travels about the world, including England at the time of the Gunpowder Plot. He witnesses the stupidity and cruelty and especially the religious intolerance of mankind, repeatedly escaping death with difficulty and being finally enslaved by negro pirates because his nose is of a different shape and his hair of a different colour from theirs.

Scarron, PAUL (1610–60), burlesque writer, son of a Paris magistrate, immobilized and deformed by rheumatism from the age of thirty. He received a pension from the queen, Anne d'Autriche. In 1652, when over forty, he married the youthful Françoise d'Aubigné, the future Mme de Maintenon. His *Recueil de quelques vers burlesques* appeared in 1643, *Typhon* (a burlesque mythological poem) in 1644, *Virgile travesti* (a parody of Virgil, which was never finished) in 1648–52. He also wrote comedies, of which *Jodelet, ou le Maître valet* (see *Jodelet*) and *Don Japhet d'Arménie* (q.v.) are the best known, and *Nouvelles tragi-comiques*, among which *La Précaution inutile* and *Les Hypocrites* inspired Sedaine and Molière. His *Roman comique* (q.v., 1651), an unfinished romance, is his most important work. It is written in a gay, simple, unaffected style, and occasional passages of delicate romance combine in it with a realistic picture of

turbulent life. It is the prototype of Gautier's *Le Capitaine Fracasse* (q.v.). Scarron rebelled against the artificiality and preciosity of current literature, and his burlesque writing helped to discredit the grand style (mythological and heroic) in prose and poetry.

Sceaux, see *Maine, duchesse du.*

Scènes de la vie de Bohème, see *Murger, Henry.*

Scènes de la vie privée; . . . de la vie de province; . . . de la vie parisienne; . . . de la vie politique; . . . de la vie militaire; . . . de la vie de campagne, the subdivisions of the ÉTUDES DE MŒURS in Balzac's *Comédie humaine* (q.v.).

Scève, MAURICE (*c.* 1510–*c.* 1564), poet, born at Lyons. He acquired fame when a student at Avignon by discovering there the tomb of Petrarch's Laura. His *Délie, object de plus haulte vertu* (q.v.), a long poem in obscure and learned dizains on sublimated love, appeared in 1544. He also wrote *La Saulsaye*, an eclogue on rustic life on the banks of the Saône. Scève was leader of a school of poetry at Lyons (a city of great literary activity in the 16th century, much under Italian influence, especially that of Petrarch and Bembo); this school included Pernette du Guillet and Louise Labé (qq.v.).

Scévole, a tragedy by Du Ryer, probably produced in 1644, published in 1647, regarded as the author's masterpiece. It continued to be acted till 1775.

The play is developed from the legend told by Livy of the Roman Mucius Scaevola, who, when Porsena, the Tuscan king, was besieging Rome to restore the Tarquins, made his way to the enemy camp and attempted to kill Porsena, subsequently showing his indifference to death by thrusting his right hand into the fire until it was consumed.

The scene is the camp of Porsenne before Rome. Porsenne is represented as a sagacious and generous ruler, with whom is contrasted the overbearing and ungrateful Tarquin. Junie is a Roman maiden captive in the enemy camp, loved both by Porsenne and his son Arons, and by Scévole, who has saved the life of Arons. The essential action of the play consists in the various influences that act on Porsenne: the proof of Roman bravery in the defence of the bridge by Horatius Cocles; Junie's appeal to Porsenne to raise the siege and the advice of Arons in the same sense; the heroism of Scévole after his unsuccessful attempt on Porsenne's life; the growing hostility between Porsenne and Tarquin. These lead finally to the pardon of Scévole and the abandonment of the siege, and the generous surrender of Junie by Arons to Scévole.

Schelandre, JEAN DE (*c.* 1585–1635), dramatist, a gentleman of Verdun, who died of wounds fighting under Turenne; author of a long tragedy *Tyr et Sidon* (q.v., 1608), in two parts, remodelled as a tragicomedy in 1628 under the influence of Hardy (q.v.). The author spent some time in London, where, in 1611, he dedicated to James I a ridiculous poem entitled *Stuartide*, tracing the king's genealogy to Astraea and Banquo. He may have known Shakespeare. The preface to his tragicomedy, written by François Ogier, a learned ecclesiastic, contains a vigorous defence of the irregular drama as against the servile imitation of the ancients; also of the combination of tragic and comic elements in a single drama, as resembling real life.

Scherer, EDMOND (1815–89), critic, born in Paris of Swiss extraction, and a Protestant till he lost his faith, had studied, taught, and written on philosophy and theology until in middle life he turned to literature and foreign languages. From 1861 he edited *Le Temps* (q.v.). His works in volume form include *Mélanges de critique religieuse* (1860), *Mélanges d'histoire religieuse* (1864) and—his articles from *Le Temps*—*Études critiques sur la littérature contemporaine* (1863–95, 10 vols.). These are valuable criticism and discussions of critical theory by a writer whose aim was to observe 'le caractère essentiellement relatif de la vérité'. Moral prejudices biased his judgement of such writers as Chateaubriand, Baudelaire, and Gautier.

Schiller, JOHANN CHRISTOPH FRIEDRICH VON (1759–1805), German poet, dramatist, and philosopher. See *Foreign Influences on French Literature*, paras. 18, 19.

Schlegel, AUGUST WILHELM VON (1767–1845), German scholar, translator of Shakespeare and Calderón and, later, of Hindu literature, and critic. He was a friend of Mme de Staël (q.v.), tutored her children, and travelled with her in Europe. His views on the distinction between the classical and the romantic in literature no doubt helped to form hers. His Berlin (1801) and Vienna lectures on the drama, in which he propounded these views, were translated by Mme Necker de Saussure (q.v.) and published (*Cours de littérature dramatique*) in 1809 and 1814, in Paris. In Paris also, in 1817, he published a comparison (in French) of the *Phèdre* of Racine and of Euripides, not favourable to Racine. These works were widely read and did much to make French critical theory more independent of the older conventions.

Schlésinger, MME MAURICE, *née* ÉLISA FOUCAULT (1810–88), is said to have been the one woman whom Flaubert loved, for all that the affection was platonic. She was the Mme Arnoux of *L'Éducation sentimentale* (q.v.), the Émilie Renaud of the first version of this work, and also the Maria of the early autobiographical fragment *Mémoires d'un fou* (q.v.). Her husband was a music publisher in Paris.

Schlumberger, JEAN (1877–), novelist and critic, one of the founders of the *Nouvelle Revue Française* (q.v.). His novels include *Un Homme heureux* (1920), *Le Camarade infidèle* (1922), *Saint-Saturnin* (1931). His reminiscences—*Éveils* (1950)—contain interesting descriptions of family life of the seventies and eighties in Alsace and in Normandy, of the emotions aroused by the Dreyfus case, and of the early days of the *Nouvelle Revue Française*.

Schmucke, WILHELM, the old musician, friend of Pons, in Balzac's novel *Le Cousin Pons* (q.v.).

Schneider, HORTENSE (1838–1920), the famous French comic-opera star of the Second Empire. Her singing and her personality helped to make the success of Offenbach's (q.v.) *La Belle Hélène, Barbe-Bleue, La Grande-Duchesse de Gérolstein,* &c.

Scholl, AURÉLIEN (1833–1902), a wellknown wit and journalist of Second Empire days whose talk and writings—e.g. in *Le Nain jaune* (founded by himself), *Le Figaro, L'Événement*—sparkled with the celebrated *esprit du boulevard.*

Schwetchine, MADAME, see *Salon*, para. 6.

Schwob, MARCEL (1867–1905), born at Chaville, near Paris, of an old family of Jewish intellectuals, was, like his contemporary Remy de Gourmont (q.v.), an essayist and critic of wide-ranging erudition and at the same time an imaginative writer; and he too was associated with the early days of the Symbolist *Mercure de France* (q.v.). As a scholar, his interests lay chiefly in classical and medieval studies (particularly the language and times of Villon) and in philology. He was also, from childhood, fluent and exceptionally well read in English and German. An early education in Nantes, where his father owned an influential provincial newspaper, was followed by *lycée* and university in Paris, then by research and literary journalism. His career was cut short by a serious operation in 1895. Thereafter his creative energies were hampered by pain and physical disability till he died, and his reputation was confined to a comparatively small circle.

His works include *Étude de l'argot français* (1889), *Le Jargon des coquillards en 1451* (1890), scholarly studies; *Moll Flanders*, translated from Defoe (1893); *Spicilège* (1896), critical and philosophical essays, including studies of Villon, Meredith (whom he introduced to French readers), R. L. Stevenson, and trends in modern fiction; *Les Vies imaginaires* (1896), imaginative reconstitutions of the lives and backgrounds of characters encountered in his reading; *Cœur double* (1891), *Le Roi au masque d'or* (1892), *Mimes* (1894), *Le Livre de Monelle* (1894), *La Croisade des enfants* (1896), tales, sometimes realistic, more often ornate or morbid, and influenced by Symbolism. Many are based on oriental, classical, or medieval legend (e.g. *La Croisade* . . .). The wraith-like children in *Monelle*, their fantasies and sudden cruelty, are remarkable in an otherwise somewhat incoherent book. His *Œuvres complètes* were published between 1927 and 1930 (10 vols.).

Scribe, EUGÈNE (1791–1861), born in Paris, a prolific and probably the most successful French dramatist of the first half of the 19th century. His great gifts of plot-construction and stage-craft (which he himself considered the essential qualities in playwriting) contrasted with the over-literary drama of the Romantics (see *Romantisme*),

and his sound craftsmanship influenced many later dramatists. But his plays were lifeless and superficial, the characters seldom more than types subordinated to the artifices of his plots, and for this reason his reputation faded very quickly. His output (more than 300 plays written alone or in collaboration) consisted mainly of vaudevilles and comedies of manners—excellent, light-hearted pictures of bourgeois life—but also included historical and political comedies. Among the best-remembered are the vaudevilles *Une Nuit de la Garde Nationale* (1815) and *Le Solliciteur* (1817); the comedies *Le Mariage de raison* (1826), *Le Mariage d'argent* (1828), *La Camaraderie ou la courte échelle* (1837), *Une Chaîne* (1841, his best work), *Bataille de dames* (1851); and the historical comedies *Bertrand et Raton* (1833) and *Le Verre d'eau* (1842). Scribe was noted for his generous attitude towards his collaborators.

Scudéry, GEORGES DE (1601–67), dramatist, born at Le Havre (his father, a magistrate, had migrated from Provence), a ruffling soldier and vainglorious writer, a prolific author of tragedies, tragicomedies, and comedies, marked by abundant imagination, excessive rhetoric, extraordinary incidents and situations. His chief works include the *Comédie des Comédiens* (1635, in which a company of actors is staged, as later in Corneille's *Illusion comique*), the tragicomedy *L'Amour tyrannique* (1638), which Richelieu supported as a rival to *Le Cid*, and the prose tragicomedy *Axiane* (1643). Scudéry took a prominent part in criticizing Corneille's *Le Cid*. His epic *Alaric* (1654), 11,000 verses dedicated to Queen Christina of Sweden, incurred the ridicule of Boileau. He took some part in the composition of his sister Madeleine's romances.

Scudéry, MADELEINE DE (1607–1701), novelist, sister of the above, well-educated, intelligent, an acute observer, plain and virtuous, author (with some assistance from her brother) of two famous and very long romances, *Le Grand Cyrus* (1649–53, in Bk. x of which she partly depicts herself as 'Sapho', by which name she was known to her friends) and *Clélie* (1654–60) (qq.v.). These temporarily had a great success, for the characters are portraits of persons of the author's society or of her time, travestied as Greeks, Romans, or Persians. The conversations introduced in the story are the best part and contain sound ideas on the education of women and other subjects; these conversations were extracted and separately published. But they lack freshness and life, and the works as a whole are quite unreadable today; they were severely condemned by Boileau from 1665, though it may be noted that they were admired by Mme de Sévigné. They were translated into English and we find Pepys checking his wife for her long stories out of 'Grand Cyrus' (12 May 1666). Mlle de Scudéry's earlier and less famous romance *Ibrahim* (1641, q.v.), published like her two later works under her brother's name, relates the story of a Christian who, having fallen into the hands of the Turks, becomes the Sultan's favourite, assumes the name of Ibrahim, and after countless victories and adventures recovers the noble Italian lady, Isabel, whom he has loved throughout. Mlle de Scudéry's later works include, besides *Almahide ou l'Esclave reine* (1660–3, a story of the Moors in Spain) and other forgotten romances, a discourse *de la Louange et de la Gloire* (1671) with which she won the prize for eloquence founded by Guez de Balzac. Mlle de Scudéry's house was a gathering-place of literary society on Saturdays, her famous 'samedis'.

Scythes, Les, a tragedy by Voltaire produced in 1767.

The play sets in contrast the Scythians, primitive and poor, but equal and free, with the highly sophisticated Persians, slaves of the great king, wealthy but corrupt. Sozame, a Persian general, has, with his daughter Obéïde, sought refuge among the Scythians from the persecution of Athamare, heir to the Persian throne, who has tried to carry off Obéïde. After long residence in Scythia, Obéïde has consented to marry Indatire, a young Scythian, but she has in fact given her heart to Athamare. The latter, now king of Ecbatana, comes to Scythia in the guise of friendship, hoping to recover Obéïde. He finds her just married to Indatire, kills the latter in single combat, and is himself captured and his Persian bodyguard defeated. Required by Scythian custom to kill with her own hand the slayer of her husband, Obéïde takes her own life.

Seagreen Incorruptible, The (i.e. Robespierre, q.v., whom the people called 'l'Incor-

ruptible'). According to Belloc (Introduction to the Everyman edition, 1905, of *The French Revolution*) Carlyle's constantly recurring epithet is based on a misreading of *one* phrase of Mme de Staël's, namely 'that the prominent veins in Robespierre's forehead showed greenish-blue against his fair and somewhat pale skin'. (The quotation is from Belloc: he does not specify the source.) In *Considérations sur la Révolution française* (1818, ii. 140) Mme de Staël says of Robespierre: 'Ses traits étoient ignobles, son teint pâle, ses veines d'une couleur verte; . . . , et sa contenance n'avoit rien de familier', and in the same year her English translator rendered this almost word for word: 'His features were mean, his complexion pale, his veins of a greenish hue; . . . , and his countenance had nothing familiar'. If Belloc had this in mind the question is not so much of a misreading as of a combination of words that fired Carlyle's imagination, and his venom.

Sebillet (or **Sibilet**), THOMAS (c. 1512–89), author of an *Art poétique français* which shows signs of the transition from the age of the *rhétoriqueurs* to the poetry of the Renaissance; also of a translation of the *Iphigenia at Aulis* of Euripides. Sebillet regards 'divine inspiration' as the true essence of poetry, and rhyme and other artificial adornments as mere outward adjuncts.

Sebonde, RAIMOND, see under *Montaigne.*

Secrétan, CHARLES (1815–95), a Swiss philosopher and moralist who was closely associated with the 19th-century philosophical movement in France and who himself recognized the influence of Maine de Biran (q.v.) on his own thought. His works include: *La Philosophie de la liberté* (1849, 2 vols.), *Le Principe de la morale* (1883), *La Civilisation et la croyance* (1887).

Secrets de la princesse de Cadignan, Les, one of the 'Scènes de la vie parisienne' of Balzac's *Comédie humaine* (q.v., and see *Cadignan, Princesse de*).

Sedaine, MICHEL-JEAN (1719–97), born in Paris, dramatist, began life in poverty as a stonemason. He combined wit with a kindly, honest, and independent character. His best plays were *Le Philosophe sans le savoir* (q.v., 1765), a *drame bourgeois* without the pathos and moralizings of La Chaussée and Diderot; and *La Gageure imprévue* (1768), a light one-act comedy of society after the manner of Marivaux. Sedaine also wrote the libretti of a number of comic operas (or dramas interspersed with songs), in which he introduced, alongside of gaiety, a pathetic element. The characters are generally working folk and peasants. The themes are often taken from La Fontaine. Among the best known are *Rose et Colas* (1764), *Les Sabots* (1768), *Le Déserteur* (1769, a more ambitious attempt to combine tragic and comic elements). In his *Richard Cœur de Lion* (1784), on that monarch's imprisonment and liberation through Blondel, occur the indifferent verses which Grétry's music has rendered famous:

> O Richard, ô mon roi,
> L'univers t'abandonne:
> Sur la terre il n'est que moi
> Qui s'intéresse à ta personne.

Sedan, on the Meuse, near the Belgian frontier, a centre of Protestant printing and learning in the 17th century, was the scene of a crushing military disaster for the French during the Franco-Prussian war (1870–1, q.v.). One part of the army, under General MacMahon, had fallen back on Châlons and was rejoined by the Emperor Napoleon III. The principal army, under General Bazaine who had replaced the Emperor as Commander-in-Chief, was at Metz, unable to make its way out. The best course for the Army of Châlons would have been to move back on Paris, but feeling in Paris was running high and the Emperor was urged to move to the relief of Metz if a revolution was to be avoided. After a delay which killed any chance of success the Army of Châlons set out, still hesitating, for Metz. The German Command, discovering the movement, diverted two of its armies marching on Paris to encircle the French, surprised MacMahon's forces on 30 August and encircled them at Sedan on 1 September, keeping them under heavy shell-fire all day. The French cavalry's heroic efforts to make a way for the infantry were vain, and at five o'clock in the afternoon Napoleon III ordered the white flag to be hoisted. The Germans exacted unconditional surrender; the capitulation was signed the following day; and the Emperor himself was taken prisoner with a large army. [Zola's *La Débâcle* has a vivid description of the battle.]

In May 1940, during the 1939–45 war, Sedan was again the scene of a German break-through.

Sée, EDMOND (1875–   ), playwright and critic, whose comedies of manners recall the classical comedy of the 18th century (e.g. *La Brebis*, 1896; *L'Indiscret*, 1903; *Saison d'amour*, 1918; *La Dépositaire*, 1924). His *Théâtre français contemporain* (1928) is a guide to the development of the modern French drama.

Ségalen, VICTOR (1878–1919), author of *Stèles* (1914), prose poems in the Chinese manner; *Les Immémoriaux* (1907), *D'après René Leys* (1923), novels of Tahiti and China, &c. He was a ship's doctor and knew the countries he wrote about.

Segrais, JEAN REGNAULT DE (1624–1701), man of letters, born at Caen in Normandy, was for twenty-four years secretary to the duchesse de Montpensier (q.v.), and allowed his name to appear as author of two romances by her. He was a friend of Mme de La Fayette, and two of her novels, *Zaïde* and *La Princesse de Clèves*, similarly were published under his name. He translated Virgil's *Aeneid* and *Georgics* into French verse, and wrote a pastoral poem *Athis*, and some eclogues, of more elegance and smoothness than true poetical feeling; also a collection of short tales, *Les Divertissements de la princesse Auréliane*, the princess being la Grande Mademoiselle.

Ségur, SOPHIE ROSTOPCHINE, COMTESSE DE (1799–1874), born at St. Petersburg, wrote many children's books which, although they belong to an era of moral tales, are still remembered and read. Her *Œuvres* in twenty volumes were published in 1930–2. The most popular titles include: *Nouveaux Contes de fées pour les petits enfants* (1857), *Les Petites Filles modèles* (1858), *Les Vacances* (1859), *Mémoires d'un âne* (1860), *François le bossu* (1864), *Les Malheurs de Sophie* (1864), *Le Général Dourakine* (1864), *Un Bon Petit Diable* (1865). (See also *Children's reading*.)

Seignobos, CHARLES (1854–1942), historian. His works include: *Histoire de la civilisation* (1884–6), *Histoire politique de l'Europe contemporaine*. *Évolution des partis et* *des formes politiques (1814–1914)* (1924, 2nd ed.), *Histoire sincère de la nation française* (1933), a combination of erudition and readability which is an excellent introduction to French history, &c. Seignobos was an outstanding example of the late 19th-century school of historians who brought scientific methods to the study of history. His *Introduction aux études historiques* (1897, in collaboration with C.-V. Langlois) was for long an indispensable handbook.

Seillière, ERNEST - ANTOINE - AIMÉ - LÉON, BARON (1866–   ), moralist, sociologist, and critic, educated in France (École polytechnique) and Germany (Heidelberg), became prominent early in the present century with a philosophy that he termed *Imperialism*, namely : rational imperialism, a form of individualism restrained by reason, and the only true source of energy; and irrational imperialism, a form of moral romanticism, in essence a revolt of sentiment or instinct against reason. He expounded his theories time and again, but notably in the four volumes of *La Philosophie de l'impérialisme*. (i) *Le Comte de Gobineau et l'Aryanisme historique* (1903), racial imperialism; (ii) *Apollôn ou Dionysos* (1905), the individual, as represented by Nietzsche; (iii) *L'Impérialisme démocratique* (1907); (iv) *Le Mal romantique* (1908), irrational imperialism : a study of five generations of romantics beginning with Rousseau and going on to Fourier and Stendhal (treated at length) and to 19th-century thought in general.

Seine, La [Lat. *Sequana*], the third in length of the four great rivers of France (cf. *Garonne*; *Loire*; *Rhône*). In the days of the Roman conquest of Gaul it formed a barrier between Latin civilization and the barbarian north, and by giving France her capital, Paris, it became the river most intimately associated with the historical and cultural development of the French nation. (Paris, chosen early in the 6th century by Clovis, founder of the Merovingian dynasty, as his capital, grew out of a small island known in the time of Julius Caesar as *Lutetia*, and inhabited by the Parisii. It was a flourishing trading centre, a river port, and linked by two bridges to the other cities of Gaul. The town developed up the slopes of the hills on the river-banks.)

The river rises in the middle of the plateau of Langres, to the north-west of Dijon, and flows north-west, and then west and south, and again north-west, till it enters the English Channel between Le Havre and Honfleur. Its estuary begins at Quillebeuf. After Paris, where already it is not very much above sea-level, it becomes lazy and winding, so winding that it nearly doubles its length. Its chief tributaries include, on the right, the Aube, the Marne, the Oise (swollen by the Aisne); and on the left, the Yonne, the Loing, and the Eure. All except the Loing give their name to *départements* (q.v.). Troyes before Paris, and Rouen after, are the largest towns on its banks besides Paris itself. (See Appendix II; cf. also *Grève, Place de*; *Hôtel de ville*; *Prévôt*.)

Seize, Le Grand, see *Café* (CAFÉ ANGLAIS).

Seize, Les, a demagogic committee of the Ligue (q.v.) in Paris, which from 1587 assumed a revolutionary authority in the City. In 1591 they hanged Brisson, president of the *parlement*. They were overthrown in 1594 when Henri IV entered Paris.

Semaine, La (1578), see *Du Bartas*.

Semaine politique et littéraire, La, see *Révolutions de France et de Brabant*.

Semaine sanglante, La (21–28 May 1871), the last week of the *Commune* (q.v.).

Semblançay, JACQUES DE BEAUNE DE (1457–1527), treasurer of François Ier, executed for malversation, though probably innocent. Clément Marot has an epigram on the fortitude with which he met his death.

Sénac de Meilhan, GABRIEL (1736–1803), man of letters, son of Jean Sénac, physician to Louis XV, held provincial administrative posts until the Revolution. He emigrated in 1791, and after visiting various places in Europe—Russia, Hamburg, Venice—and usually succeeding in finding some benevolent protector, he settled in Vienna, where he died. His most important writings were: *Considérations sur l'esprit et les mœurs* (1787, in which he depicted worldly society in the last years of Louis XVI); *Du gouvernement, des mœurs et des conditions en France avant la Révolution* (1795, a political treatise of some merit); *Portraits et caractères des personnages* *distingués de la fin du XVIIIᵉ siècle* (1813). His short novel in letter form, *L'Émigré* (1797, q.v.), passed unnoticed in his day but has been praised, deservedly, since then.

Senancour, ÉTIENNE PIVERT DE (1770–1846), whose *Obermann* (1804, q.v.), like Chateaubriand's *René* (q.v.), inspired several novels of romantic introspection, was born in Paris in comfortable circumstances and destined for a church career. He cut free from this and went to Switzerland, where the majesty of the scenery intensified his bent for *rêverie*, already encouraged by early reading (e.g. Rousseau, Bernardin de Saint-Pierre, the Goethe of *Werther*), and where he dreamed of settling in a remote valley alone with Nature and his soul. He also, in 1790, made an unhappy marriage which had practically ended when he returned to Paris in 1794. In later years the son and daughter of this marriage lived with him, and at one time he had his wife's illegitimate son on his hands. In Paris he drifted on, enfeebled in body, a prey to neurotic melancholy, spiritual disillusionment, and an inability to bestir himself. Once he thought he had found a soulmate in a Mme de Walckenaer (sister of a friend, and the 'Mme Del★★' of *Obermann*), at another time he experimented with drugs and intoxicants. He had some money, soon spent, from his parents (d. 1795). For two years *c.* 1800 he was tutor to the grandson of the Mme d'Houdetot known to Rousseau (q.v.). Thereafter he relied chiefly on his pen for subsistence, and on hack work, e.g. articles for an encyclopedia, political and historical journalism, some criticism, rather than on his creative writings. These latter included *Rêveries sur la nature primitive de l'homme* (1799), on man's need to find the guiding principles of conduct in an understanding of his own nature and instincts rather than in religious dogma; *Obermann* (1804, q.v.), a novel—or usually so called—in letter-form, and his lasting title to fame; an embryonic form of it, *Aldomen*, had been published in 1795; *De l'amour considéré dans les lois réelles et dans les formes sociales de l'union des deux sexes* (1805), a semi-philosophical treatise; the *Libres Méditations d'un solitaire inconnu* (1819), a work of Christian philosophy which he himself considered important, and another, inferior, novel in letter-form *Isabella* (1833). After 1833 his slender income was supplemented by a pension.

Senancour's reputation in France and his now established position as a precursor of the Romantic Movement owed much in the first place to Sainte-Beuve's appreciative criticism (preface to second edition of *Obermann*, 1833, and articles in the *Lundis*, q.v.). Matthew Arnold made him known to English readers (in the poems *Obermann*, 1852, *Obermann once more*, 1867, and the essay 'Obermann' first printed in *The Academy*, 9 Oct. 1869).

Senate

(1) DURING THE CONSULATE AND THE FIRST EMPIRE (1799–1814) the *Sénat conservateur* was the most important of the legislative bodies created by the *Constitution de l'an VIII* (1799, see *Consulat*). It issued decrees, known as *sénatus-consultes*, but, like the other bodies, it did very much what Napoleon wanted. The majority of its members (who were life-members) were, or could be, nominated by Napoleon. The office of *sénateur* was a high-ranking and lucrative dignity often bestowed on Napoleon's generals, and he drew largely on the Senate for his imperial aristocracy. In April 1814, at the invitation of the Allies, the Senate voted a Provisional Government and declared the reign of Napoleon at an end. It was abolished by the Charter of 4 June 1814 (see *Charte, La*), but about two-thirds of its members became members of the new Upper House, the *Chambre des Pairs*.

(2) UNDER THE SECOND EMPIRE (1852–70) the *Sénat français* was the Upper House of the legislature (the lower being the *Corps législatif*). Its functions were determined, and its members nominated, by the Emperor Napoleon III.

(3) UNDER THE THIRD REPUBLIC (1875–1940) the *Sénat français* was again the Upper House (the lower now being the *Chambre des Députés*). Its functions were determined by law (the constitutional laws of February and July 1875). At first it had some life-members and after 1884 all its members were (indirectly) elected, for fixed periods. (See also *Conseil de la République*.)

Sénecé, ANTOINE BAUDERON DE (1643–1737), minor poet, born at Mâcon, son of a magistrate, author of some agreeable verse tales, besides madrigals, epistles, epigrams, &c.

Sept Cordes de la lyre, Les (1839), a novel by George Sand (q.v.).

September Revolution (4 Sept., 1870), see *Revolutions*, IV, IV*a*.

Septembriseurs, the instigators of the September massacres (2–5 Sept. 1792. See *Révolutions*, I*a*). Marat (q.v.) was one of the most prominent.

Sept Sages, Roman des, a collection of oriental tales, popular in the Middle Ages, derived from those of the Indian philosopher known as Syntipas or Sindabar. The seven sages, to defend the king's son against an accusation brought by a jealous stepmother, each relate a tale designed to show the perfidy of women; the queen retorts with seven tales calculated to discredit the sages. From the Latin version of this collection there is an anonymous French prose version of the second half of the 12th century. See also *Dolopathos*.

Sequana, the Latin name of the River Seine (q.v.).

Séraphita, one of the 'Études philosophiques' of Balzac's *Comédie humaine* (q.v.). The scene is Norway at the end of the 18th century.

Serées, Les, see *Bouchet, Guillaume*.

Sergents de La Rochelle, Les Quatre. Four young sergeants of the line—Bories, Goubin, Pomiers, and Raoulx—members of the *Charbonnerie* (q.v.), a secret political society, were incited by *agents provocateurs* and attempted (1822) to foment a republican uprising at La Rochelle. They were arrested there, tried, condemned, and executed in Paris (the last execution to take place on the Place de Grève, q.v.). Their youth, and the circumstances of their arrest and trial, excited public sympathy.

Serment(s) de Strasbourg, an oath of mutual support (*sacramentum firmitatis*), and of alliance against their brother Lothaire, sworn by Louis le Germanique and Charles le Chauve (sons of Louis le Débonnaire and grandsons of Charlemagne), in the presence of their respective armies assembled at Strasbourg in 842, prior to the Treaty of Verdun

the following year by which the Carolingian Empire was divided among the three brothers. The oath was sworn in French by Louis le Germanique, so as to be understood by the army of Charles le Chauve, and, similarly, in German, by Charles; then, in a modified form (*sacramentum fidelitatis*), it was sworn by the followers of Louis (in German) and by those of Charles (in French). Both texts are given in a (Latin) history of the dissension between the sons of Louis le Débonnaire, written by one of the earliest French chroniclers, Nithard (*c.* 790–858), who was a grandson of Charlemagne. The French text is of great philological interest as the earliest extant document in the French language.

Serment du Jeu de Paume, see *Paume, Jeu de*.

Sermon joyeux, a mock sermon, at first delivered in medieval churches, especially in France, during the revelries in connexion with the Feast of Fools (see *Fête des Fous*). Like this it was later expelled from the church and became secularized. The *sermon joyeux* might take a satirical form, often directed against women, and be in verse. The comic element lay especially in the contrast between the pious passages from the Scriptures or liturgy and the ribaldry that was intermingled.

Serres, OLIVIER DE (1539–1619), Seigneur de Pradel in the Vivarais, a Protestant and a favourite of Henri IV, author of a *Théâtre d'agriculture et ménage des champs* (1600), on the management of rural property. He introduced the culture of the silk-worm in France. Arthur Young records, under date 20 August 1789, a visit to what had been his estate of Le Pradel.

Serres chaudes (1889), collected poems by Maeterlinck (q.v.).

Sertorius, a tragedy by Corneille, produced in 1662.

The theme is the historical struggle of Sertorius in Spain against the senatorial army under Pompey, the assassination of Sertorius by his lieutenant Perpenna, and Perpenna's execution by Pompey. Corneille has introduced two female characters, Aristie, the divorced wife of Pompey, and Viriate, queen of Lusitania. But Sertorius, in his choice between Aristie and Viriate, and

Viriate, in making her choice between Sertorius and Perpenna, are actuated less by love than by policy, and the play remains essentially political. The most interesting scene is that of the meeting between Pompey and Sertorius (III. ii), when Pompey tries to persuade Sertorius to lay down his arms, while Sertorius on the other hand proposes that Pompey and he shall unite against Sulla.

Sérurier, JEAN-MATHIEU-PHILIBERT, one of Napoleon's marshals, see *Maréchal de l'Empire.*

Serventois (*Sirventes*, and more often encountered in this form, in Provençal), a medieval lyric, very like the *chant royal* (q.v.) in form, of serious character, moral, satirical, or political, in couplets; apparently so called because originally composed by or for servants of great lords. The name was later applied in particular to poems in honour of the Virgin Mary.

Servitude et grandeur militaires (1835), by Alfred de Vigny, a collection of three tales illustrating the devotion to duty and the self-sacrifice of Napoleon's armies. The titles are: *Laurette, ou le cachet rouge*; *La Veillée de Vincennes*; and *La Vie et la mort du capitaine Renaud, ou La Canne de jonc*. The last, familiar as *La Canne de jonc*, takes the form of reminiscences by an old officer in Napoleon's Imperial Guard. At one time he had spent some weeks as a prisoner on board H.M.S. *Victory* under Admiral Collingwood. On another occasion he was an uneasy witness of an interview between Napoleon and the Pope when the latter was held prisoner at Fontainebleau. The talk was one-sided—on Napoleon's part braggadocio and bluster and a long discourse which moved Napoleon himself to admiration and self-pity. His listener's only comments were 'Commediante!' and, when the Emperor's fury intensified, 'Tragediante!'

Servitude volontaire, Discours de la, see *La Boétie.*

Sévère, a character in Corneille's *Polyeucte* (q.v.).

Séverine, pseud. of CAROLINE RÉMY (1855–1929), by her second marriage Madame Guebhard, probably the outstanding French woman journalist of her day. She was born in Paris in modest but comfortable circumstances and after a first, unhappy, marriage met Jules Vallès (q.v.), who introduced her to journalism. She edited her own paper, *Le Cri du peuple*, then gave it up to become a free-lance journalist. She was an excellent reporter, much loved and read by the people. Papers of all complexions employed her but allowed her to follow her own, decidedly left-wing, sympathies. She left an autobiography, *Line* (1921), and some volumes of collected articles.

Sévigné, MARIE DE RABUTIN-CHANTAL, MARQUISE DE (1626–96), letter-writer, daughter of the baron de Chantal, a gallant soldier and a noted duellist, and granddaughter of Mme de Chantal who founded the Order of the Visitation. Bussy-Rabutin (q.v.) was her first cousin. She was left an orphan when very young (her father was killed fighting against the English near La Rochelle, 1627), and was brought up by her uncle Christophe de Coulanges (d. 1687), abbot of Livry, to whom she remained devotedly attached. She was a woman of culture, who knew Latin, Spanish, and Italian; she showed familiarity with Tasso, Ariosto, and Ovid's *Metamorphoses*, and interest in Josephus and Tacitus. Among her instructors were Chapelain and Ménage (qq.v.). She frequented the Hôtel de Rambouillet (q.v.) for a time in the period of its decline. In 1644 she married the marquis de Sévigné, an agreeable man but a faithless husband, who squandered their fortune and was killed in a duel in 1651, leaving her with a son, amiable, witty, and devoted, but prodigal of money and without solidity of character, and a daughter, considered a great beauty, but cross-grained and cold-hearted. The daughter in 1669 married the comte de Grignan, whom his duties as Lieutenant-Governor of Provence retained in the South. Her passionate devotion to this daughter, from whom she was thus separated for long periods and who, moreover, was not in full sympathy with her mother, was at once the chief joy and the chief torment of Mme de Sévigné's life. This was mainly spent in Paris (her house from 1677, the Hôtel Carnavalet, see *Musée Carnavalet*, was near the old Place Royale, q.v.) or at her country house (Les Rochers) near Vitré in Brittany; but she was sometimes with her uncle at the abbey of Livry near Paris, and occasionally with her daughter in Provence. Mme de Sévigné was a woman of great charm, witty, intelligent, with an expansive friendliness, outwardly cheerful and courageous if at times given to serious and melancholy reflection. A playful imagination constantly pervades her letters. She was an intimate friend of Mme de La Fayette (q.v.). The *Letters* for which she is famous were published after her death, the first collection (thirty-one letters) in 1725, much enlarged in later editions (1735-54 and subsequently); that of the *Grands Écrivains de la France* is the best, supplemented by the *Lettres inédites* published by Capmas. The majority of the letters are addressed to her daughter. They give an instructive and amusing picture of the life of the nobility of the day, at court, in the country, and in their social and domestic relations. They also illuminate the life and the character of the author herself, enjoying the society and diversions of Paris and occasionally Versailles, delighting in the natural beauties of Les Rochers; looking after her woods and rents, passing judgement on the books she reads, and pouring out her anxious affection for her daughter. She introduces us to interesting persons and events, such as the cardinal de Retz, the trial of Fouquet, the proposed marriage of Mademoiselle, the death of Vatel, Lauzun escorting James II's queen and infant son in their flight from England, a performance of Racine's *Esther* at Versailles. She has the gift of animating the incidents she relates, giving them the charm of little comedies. She shows observation of nature unusual in her day (as in her remark that the 13th June is late for the nightingale's song). She writes naturally but not carelessly, in a racy and picturesque style. Besides her own letters the collection contains a number from some of her friends, such as Mme de La Fayette, but especially from her proud and embittered cousin Bussy-Rabutin. Edward Fitzgerald collected materials for a dictionary of the *dramatis personae* of the letters, published in 1914 by his great-niece; this contains much that is useful to English readers.

Horace Walpole describes a visit to Livry in a letter of 3 April 1766.

Sèvres, a suburb of Paris on the south-west, famous for its manufacture of costly porcelain, removed from Vincennes to Sèvres in 1756 and shortly afterwards acquired by the State.

Seyssel, CLAUDE DE (1450–1520), born at Aix in Savoy, humanist and diplomat, Archbishop of Turin, author of *La Grant Monarchie de France* (1519), a work of political philosophy, in praise of the French constitution, and translator of Thucydides, Xenophon, and other ancient Greek authors.

Sganarelle, ou le Cocu imaginaire, a one-act comedy in verse by Molière, produced in 1660.

Célie, daughter of Gorgibus, a *bourgeois*, is in love with Lélie; but her father requires her to marry a richer suitor. By a chain of accidents and misunderstandings Sganarelle, another *bourgeois*, is led to believe that his wife loves Lélie; Lélie that Célie has married Sganarelle in his own absence; Mme Sganarelle that her husband loves Célie; and Célie that her lover is unfaithful to her. The misunderstandings are cleared up, and Célie's rich suitor is found to be already married.

SGANARELLE is also the name of other characters in Molière's comedies: Don Juan's pusillanimous servant, and the hero of *Le Médecin malgré lui*.

Shakespeare, see *Foreign influences on French Literature*, paras. 13, 18.

Sibilet, see *Sebillet*.

Sicilian Vespers, see *Vêpres Siciliennes*.

Sicilien, Le, ou L'Amour peintre, a *comédie-ballet* by Molière, in prose, produced in 1667.

Don Pèdre, a Sicilian, wishes to marry Isidore, a Greek slave, whom he keeps jealously shut up. But Adraste, a French gentleman, has seen her and fallen in love with her. By posing as a painter who is to paint her portrait he obtains access to her, and by another stratagem Isidore escapes from her master's house.

Siècle, Le, founded in 1836, one of the first cheap daily papers, had a circulation, unprecedented at the time, of 38,000, largely among small traders and the working classes. It supplied news, opinions ready-made, and a *roman-feuilleton*. It was pro-Revolutionary in politics when founded and, in so far as politics were allowed, succeeded in remaining democratic during the Second Empire. It continued into the 20th century.

Siècle de Louis le Grand, Le (1687), see *Perrault*.

Siècle de Louis XIV, Le, an historical work by Voltaire, begun in 1734, published at Berlin in 1751, republished with corrections in 1756 and 1768. An edition of 1763 contained as a supplement a *Précis du siècle de Louis XV*. Voltaire was well equipped for the task by his personal acquaintance with many of the survivors of the great age, by the personal inquiries that he carried out methodically, and by his wide reading of memoirs. The history is a solid piece of work, as accurate as was possible in the circumstances. It brings out clearly the great political problems of the day and the characters of the protagonists, the king, Colbert, Mme de Maintenon, &c. It is at the same time a history of the progress of civilization (with an incidental condemnation of aggressive war), eliminating, in contrast to Bossuet, the action of Providence. The plan of the work, by which the reign is treated under separate headings (political and military history, anecdotes of the court, internal administration, finance, ecclesiastical affairs) has been much criticized, as impairing the truth and interest of the narrative and giving it a singularly unimpressive conclusion.

Siècle de Louis XV, Précis du, see under *Siècle de Louis XIV*.

Siegfried et le Limousin (1922), a novel, and later a play (*Siegfried*), by Jean Giraudoux (q.v.). It is a study, on the whole gently satirical, of the German and the French mentality, the good and the bad points in each, and how each one might complement the other. A soldier is picked up on the battlefield by the Germans during the 1914–18 war, unconscious, naked, with no clue to his identity and, when his consciousness is restored, no memory. He is re-educated as a good German and becomes leader of the Weimar Republic. One day a French journalist is struck by a familiar ring in some of his writings and utterances and eventually discovers that 'Siegfried' is no other than the Frenchman Jacques Forestier, a native of the Limousin, and the friend of

his youth. When Giraudoux rewrote this novel as a play he tightened it up considerably and altered the ending. It was produced in 1929 and made his name as a dramatist.

Siéyès, L'ABBÉ EMMANUEL-JOSEPH (1748–1836), born at Fréjus (Provence), a noted politician during the French Revolution, published three celebrated pamphlets during the winter of 1788–9, before the meeting of the États Généraux: *Essai sur les privilèges*, *Délibérations à prendre dans les assemblées de bailliage*, and (the most famous) *Qu'est-ce que le Tiers État?* This was a forcible exposition of the sentiments and ambitions of the *bourgeoisie*, and a sketch of the means by which the *Tiers État* could secure its rights. It began with three questions and answers: 'Qu'est-ce que le Tiers État? *Tout.* Qu'a-t-il été jusqu'à présent dans l'ordre politique? *Rien.* Que demande-t-il? *A y devenir quelque chose.*' In 1799 Siéyès was associated with Bonaparte in the *coup d'état* of *le dix-huit brumaire* (q.v.).

Signoret, EMMANUEL (1872–1900), a poet of promise, who died young. His *Daphné* (1894), *Vers dorés* (1895), *La Souffrance des eaux* (1898) were republished in *Poésies complètes* (1908, with a preface by André Gide).

Sigogne, see *Sygognes*.

Si le grain ne meurt (1926), by André Gide (q.v.), the autobiography of his early life.

Silhouette, a portrait obtained by tracing the outline of a profile by means of its shadow and filling in the outline with black, or cut out of black paper. The word is derived from Étienne de Silhouette (1709–67), controller-general of finances for eight months in 1759. According to the usual account, the application of his name to this rough-and-ready type of portrait was intended to ridicule the petty economies introduced by Silhouette during his tenure of office. But Hatzfeld and Darmesteter take the expression 'à la silhouette' to refer to his brief tenure of office 'appliqué plaisamment à tout ce qui paraissait ephémère'; and Littré quotes a statement that Silhouette himself decorated the walls of his château at Bry-sur-Marne with outline portraits.

Sillonisme, a short-lived Christian democratic movement led by the publicist and social reformer Marc Sangnier (1873–1950), and having its organ and focus in *Le Sillon*, a paper founded by him in 1902.

Silvestre, PAUL-ARMAND (1838–1901), minor Parnassian poet (see *Parnassiens*) e.g. in *Rimes neuves et vieilles* (1862), *Gloire des souvenirs* (1872), *Les Ailes d'or* (1880), &c. He also wrote novels and some plays.

Simenon, GEORGES (1903–), novelist of Belgian birth (Liège), who writes in French and lived long in France but has for some years past been domiciled in the U.S.A. Since *Au Pont des Arches* (1920), his first published novel, he has produced a vigorous succession of works, rising from straight detective fiction, or popular or crime fiction with a psychological interest, to purely psychological novels, depending for plot and interest on the workings of the characters' minds and their reaction to the outside world. For the most part his characters belong to a vitiated, crapulous underworld, seldom described, but evoked with a remarkable sense of atmosphere and the sinister.

Simenon is one of the most widely read and widely translated of contemporary novelists, with an output that runs into hundreds of titles. In his earlier novels, now published (e.g. by Fayard or the Presses de la Cité) in such collected series as *Le Commissaire Maigret* or the *Collection Maigret*, he created the imperturbable Commissaire Maigret, the detective-superintendent of the *Police judiciaire* (see *Police*, para. 6), who relies on psychological intuition rather than scientific methods and who is by now one of the famous characters of detective fiction.

Other, more purely psychological, novels by Simenon include: *Le Pendu de Saint-Phorien*; *Les Volets verts*; *Pedigree*; *La Neige était sale*; *Tante Jeanne*; *Le Passage clandestin*. Novels of American life are also among his more recent work, e.g. *Trois chambres à Manhattan*; *La Jument perdue*; *Le Fond de la bouteille*.

Simon, RICHARD (1638–1712), Hebrew scholar, was expelled from the Oratorian Order for publishing an *Histoire critique du Vieux Testament* (1678) which contained unorthodox views. He wrote various works of biblical criticism and had incessant disputes with Bossuet and with the solitaries

of Port-Royal (qq.v.) over points of theology. He was an uncle of the geographer Bruzen de la Martinière (see *Dictionaries and Encyclopedias*, under date 1726–39).

Simon le pathétique (1918), a novel by Jean Giraudoux (q.v.).

Simultanéisme, one of the more ephemeral movements in modern poetry, an exaggerated mixture of *Cubisme* and *Unanimisme* (qq.v.). Typical writings are to be found in *La Trilogie des forces* (1908–14), collections of verse by H.-M. Barzun (q.v.), the leader of the movement, and *Naissance du poème* (1918), described by its author, Fernand Divoire (1883–), as a prose symphonique'. The aim is to produce an effect of simultaneity, not only of images, but of sounds which are supposed to represent the voice of man mingled with the voice of Nature and of the great cities.

Sincères, Les, a comedy by Marivaux, produced in 1739.

Ergaste and the marquise both pride themselves on their sincerity and always say what they think of everyone. This produces sympathy between them, and all promises well for their happy marriage, until Ergaste is so ill-advised as to reply with sincerity when questioned by the marquise as to the comparative charms of herself and Araminte; the marquise retorts with a sincere comparison between Ergaste and a rival admirer Dorante. They part in coolness, she to give her hand to Dorante, he to propose to Araminte, finding that less sincerity will promote happiness in marriage.

Sincérisme, see *Literary Isms*.

Singlin, ANTOINE (c. 1607–64), son of a Paris wine-merchant, became a priest and entered Port-Royal (q.v.) in 1637, where under the guidance of Saint-Cyran he became eminent as spiritual director of the nuns and solitaries and as a preacher; some of his sermons were published as *Instructions chrétiennes*. He played a part in the conversion of Pascal.

Singulari nos, a papal Encyclical of 15 July 1834 condemning Lamennais's (q.v.) *Paroles d'un croyant* as a book small in dimensions but immense in perversity.

Sirventes, see *Serventois*.

Sismondi, LÉONARD SIMONDE DE (1773–1842), historian and political economist, born and educated at Geneva, was the son of a Protestant pastor who lived with his family in Italy after the Revolution and took to farming. After publishing a *Tableau de l'agriculture toscane* (1801) Sismondi settled in Geneva (then French). He divided his time between writing (*L'Histoire des républiques italiennes du Moyen Age*, 1809–18, 16 vols.; *De la littérature du midi de l'Europe*, 1813, 4 vols., the expanded version of lectures delivered at Geneva in 1811) and frequenting Mme de Staël's (q.v.) circle at Coppet, which he often describes in his Correspondence, or accompanying her on her travels. He was also a friend of, and maintained an interesting correspondence with, the Countess of Albany, widow of the Young Pretender and mistress of the Italian poet Alfieri. In Paris between 1813 and 1815 he was welcomed in literary *salons* and during the Hundred Days caused his friends some astonishment by his enthusiastic support of Napoleon. His *Nouveaux principes de l'économie politique* (1819) is said to have influenced the Saint-Simoniens (q.v.). In 1819 he married an Englishwoman. He spent the rest of his life in Geneva, interested in religion and writing another long historical work (*Histoire des Français*, 1821–42, 31 vols.) which Sainte-Beuve recommended for its good sense to 'une lectrice douée de patience'. His correspondence with a wide circle of friends has been published at various dates.

Six, Les. The music for Cocteau's (q.v.) ballet *Les Mariés de la tour Eiffel* (1921) was composed jointly by six composers, his contemporaries: Georges Auric (1899–); Louis Durey (1888–); Arthur Honegger (1892–), of Swiss nationality; Darius Milhaud (1892–); Francis Poulenc (1899–), and Germaine Taillefer (1892–). For a time they were classed together as *le groupe des Six*, but their paths diverged later. Another composer associated with them, though not actually one of the group, was Erik Satie (1866–1925).

Smarh, the title of an early version (1839) of Flaubert's *La Tentation de saint Antoine* (q.v.).

Smarra ou les démons de la nuit

(1821), a nightmare-like tale by Nodier (q.v.).

Société de l'histoire de France, La, a learned society founded in 1833 by Guizot and other historians, and still continuing. Its object was to publish documents concerning the pre-Revolutionary history of France, e.g. chronicles, memoirs, registers, &c., and to maintain a periodical in connexion with its work (the *Annuaire* from 1837 to 1863, the *Bulletin* from 1863 onwards). In 1927 it absorbed the *Société de l'histoire contemporaine* (founded 1890). Human factors at times retarded publication. There is mention in the Society's *Notes et Documents* of 1884 of a M. Lacabane, a professor at the École des Chartes, whose edition of Froissart's *Chroniques* had long been 'attendue avec impatience', but 'en présence des difficultés, sa probité scientifique éprouvait des scrupules qui l'empêchaient de conclure' and another editor had to be found.

Société des anciens textes français, La, was founded in 1875 (with the medievalist Gaston Paris, q.v., as first president) on the model of the Early English Text Society to publish critical editions of French and Provençal texts of the Middle Ages. The 149 volumes published down to 1950 include such works as the *Roman de la Rose*, the *Roman de Troie*, and the *Recueil des Sotties*.

Société des gens de lettres, La, founded in 1838 by Louis Desnoyers (1802–68, novelist and man of letters) with the support of the most prominent literary men of the period, and still continuing, is primarily an authors' rights society in matters of copyright, publication, &c. It can also provide help in cases of necessity.

Société des textes français modernes, La. This was founded in 1905 by Gustave Lanson (q.v.) to publish critical editions of post-medieval texts.

Sociétés joyeuses, associations mainly of citizens and tradespeople, but at times including young men of good family, which existed in Paris and many provincial towns in the later Middle Ages for purposes of revelry and amusement. They were probably a lay survival of the *Fête des Fous* (q.v.) which had been banished from the cathedrals, and their members wore fools' dress, while their chief officers usually bore the title of *Prince des Sots*, or *Mère Sotte*. Their activities took the form of processions, or dramatic performances on temporary stages erected in the public squares, when farces, moralities, or *soties* (qq.v.) were performed and improvised verses recited, in which local happenings or personages were rudely satirized. The most famous of the *Sociétés joyeuses* was the *Enfants sans Souci* (q.v.) in Paris. Other well-known associations were the *Infanterie Dijonnaise* (whose chief was called *Mère Folle* or *Mère Folie*); *Les Connards*, at Rouen and Évreux (these were probably originally *Cornards*, from the two ears, or *cornes*, on their fool's caps); the *Suppôts* [followers, myrmidons] *du Seigneur de la Coquille*, at Lyons, whose members belonged to the typographical workers of the town [*coquille* = misprint]; and the *sociétés* of Amiens, Auxerre, Beauvais, and other towns of, mainly, Northern France.

Sodome et Gomorrhe. (1) The fourth section (i. 1921; ii. 1922) of Proust's *A la recherche du temps perdu* (q.v.); (2) The last drama (2 acts, prose) by Jean Giraudoux (q.v.) to be produced (1943) in his lifetime. It was published in 1946. It is a study, made all the more bitter by the brilliance and paradox of the dialogue, of enmity and incomprehension between the sexes. God will withhold His wrath from Sodom and Gomorrah if even one couple can be found there who are happy in the normal union of man with woman. Hopes centre on the couple Lia and Jean but they are dashed. The end of the world itself cannot still the dissension between these two.

Sœur, La, a comedy by Rotrou, performed in 1645, adapted from the Italian of J. B. della Porta.

Lélie, sent by his father to Constantinople to recover his lost mother and Aurélie his sister, on the way at Venice falls in love with Sophie, a girl of unknown parentage, marries her, returns, and passes her off as Aurélie. Trouble arises when his father proposes to marry the false Aurélie to an old gentleman, a complication which the ingenious valet Ergaste endeavours to avert. There are further complications when the mother returns from captivity and recognizes this Aurélie as in fact her daughter. But it turns out that Aurélie and another child had been

exchanged surreptitiously in infancy, and all is cleared up satisfactorily.

Sœur Philomène (1861), a novel by Edmond and Jules de Goncourt (q.v.).

Sœurs Rondoli, Les, the name-tale of a collection (1884) by Maupassant (q.v.).

Sœurs Vatard, Les (1879), a naturalistic novel by J.-K. Huysmans (q.v.).

Soirées de Médan, Les (1880), a volume of naturalistic short stories (see *Naturalisme*) by Émile Zola and five authors who were his disciples at that time: Paul Alexis, Henry Céard, Léon Hennique, J.-K. Huysmans, and Guy de Maupassant (qq.v.). Each story has a military setting because Zola's own contribution, *L'Attaque au moulin*, which it was agreed should come first and set the scene for the others, was an episode of the Franco-Prussian war. The other stories, in order of printing, were Maupassant's *Boule-de-suif* (q.v.), Huysmans's *Sac au dos*, Céard's *La Saignée*, Hennique's *L'Affaire du grand 7*, and *Après la bataille*, by Alexis. Zola's country home, where he entertained his friends, was at Médan, near Paris, hence the title of the volume.

Soirées de Saint-Pétersbourg, Les, ou Entretiens sur le gouvernement temporel de la Providence (1821, posth.), the chief work of Joseph de Maistre (q.v.), was written in Russia. It takes the form of dialogues, brilliant, witty, and often paradoxical, between a count (the author), a devout Russian senator, and a young French *émigré*. They discuss the place of evil in the scheme of Providence; suffering as the Divine punishment for sin; the efficacy of prayer; and the eventual certain triumph of the Catholic Church. The first dialogue contains a celebrated passage in defence of capital punishment. Were it not for 'le bourreau', the executioner, agent of the Divine will, order would give place to chaos.

Somaize, ANTOINE BAUDEAU, SIEUR DE (b. 1630), a 17th-century man of letters who took exception to Molière's ridicule of the Précieuses (see *Rambouillet*) and constituted himself their defender and historian. Very little is known of his life except that he was secretary to Marie Mancini (see *Mazarin's nieces*) and accompanied her to Rome. He wrote verse and satirical prose, a comedy, *Les Véritables Précieuses*, and a famous *Dictionnaire des Prétieuses* (1660, see *Dictionaries and Encyclopedias*, under date 1660). Doubt has been cast upon the value of the information he gives.

Sombreval, PRIEUR DE, see *Royaumont, sieur de.*

Sombreval, the ex-priest in Barbey d'Aurevilly's (q.v.) novel *Un Prêtre marié* (1851).

Somme des Vices et des Vertus, or *Somme le Roi,* see *Religious Writings,* para. 2.

Somptuarisme, see *Literary Isms.*

Son Excellence Eugène Rougon (1876), one of Zola's *Rougon-Macquart* (q.v.) novels.

Without either money or influence the ambitious Eugène Rougon went to Paris from Plassans, his native town in Provence, threw in his lot with the supporters of the Second Empire, and battered his way to power and social position. He became one of the chief ministers of state, then fell from power, but restored himself speedily by altering his political opinions. He was surrounded by parasites and for a time yielded to his passion for a mysterious half-Italian, 'la belle Clorinde'. The book contains many detailed, often satirical, not always accurate, pictures of court and political circles under the Second Empire.

Songecreux, see *Jean de l'Espine.*

Songe d'Athalie, Le. The reference is to Athalie's (q.v.) famous narration of her dream, in Racine's tragedy (said to have been one of Bernhardt's finest pieces of acting). Three times in succession, Athalie tells Abner and Mathan, she had been warned in a dream by her mother Jézabel (see 2 Kings ix) that the God of the Jews was about to take vengeance on her. On each occasion the apparition, 'comme au jour de sa mort pompeusement parée', had seemed to lean over her bed, but when 'moi, je lui tendais les mains pour l'embrasser' it changed to a clotted mixture of bones and blood-sodden flesh over which the dogs were quarrelling. And on each occasion it had been followed by another apparition, of a young, unknown boy, magnificently attired in Hebrew priest's robes, about to plunge a knife into her breast.

Songe d'Enfer, see *Religious Writings,* para. 2.

Sonnet, in French poetry, a poem composed of two quatrains and two tercets of any metre. In the regular form—but there are many irregular forms—the rhyme-scheme is as follows:

a b b a   a b b a   c c a   d a d.

It was introduced in France mainly by Du Bellay and Ronsard, though there are earlier examples of it in the works of Clément Marot, Scève, and Mellin de Saint-Gelais.

Sonnet des voyelles ('A noir, E blanc, I rouge, U vert, O bleu : voyelles, Je dirai quelque jour vos naissances latentes'), a sonnet by Rimbaud (written in 1871), was first printed in the chapter on Rimbaud in Verlaine's *Les Poètes maudits* (1884, q.v.) and was used later to illustrate the Symbolist doctrine of *correspondances* (see *Symbolisme*). It has been interpreted variously: as inspired by a coloured alphabet used by Rimbaud in childhood; by the alchemical colours (it was written when Rimbaud was studying magic); and as a deliberate piece of literary mystification.

Sonnets pour Hélène (1578), see *Ronsard,* paras. 2, 4.

Sopha, Le (1745), by Crébillon *fils* (q.v.), a licentious tale in an oriental setting, and at the same time a satirical picture of contemporary manners and morals.

Sophie, Lettres à, see *Mirabeau, comte de.*

Sophonisbe, the subject of tragedies by Mellin de Saint-Gelais, Montchrétien, Nicolas de Montreux, Mairet, Corneille, and Voltaire. The historical Sophonisba, daughter of a Carthaginian general, married Syphax, king of Numidia, and her influence drew him away from his alliance with Rome during the Second Punic War. Syphax was captured by Masinissa, an ally of Rome, and Sophonisba fell into Masinissa's power. Masinissa became enamoured of her and determined to marry her. But Scipio Africanus, dreading her influence, claimed her as a captive to be sent to Rome. Masinissa, to save her from captivity, sent her poison, which she drank without perturbation.

Mairet, in what is regarded as the first French classical tragedy, tried to redeem the rather inglorious role of Masinissa by making him take his own life over the dead body of Sophonisba. Corneille, who unsuccessfully attempted to compete in his play with Mairet, places Masinissa in a humiliating position towards Rome, that of a valet (as Voltaire says) 'qui s'est marié sans la permission de son maître'.

Sorbonne, La, a college, that is to say originally a hostel, for students of theology of the University of Paris, founded about 1257 by Robert de Sorbon, chaplain to Louis IX, with the view of helping poor scholars. It was at first designed to accommodate sixteen bursars, four from each 'nation', but was enlarged by supplementary benefactions. Further, the college took to admitting members other than bursars, from among the bachelors of theology, and such membership became an honorary distinction; it came, moreover, to be the practice (*c.* 1554) for the faculty of theology to hold its meetings on the premises of the college, especially for the consideration of alleged heresies. Thus 'la Sorbonne' was popularly adopted as the title of that faculty. From early times the Sorbonne (in the latter sense) played an important part in French history. In the 13th century it vigorously opposed the inroads of the mendicant friars. In 1393 fifty-four of its doctors were charged to give an opinion on the question how the papal schism might be ended. In the 15th century the Sorbonne showed bitter animosity against Joan of Arc. With greater enlightenment it erected the first printing-press in Paris. Later it played a prominent part by its hostility to the Jesuits, on their admission to France by Henri II, and by its support of the Ligue; it declared Henri III deposed and Henri IV incapable of reigning. It was prominent again in the great quarrel between the Jesuits and the Jansenists of the 17th century and was acutely divided on the subject of the Bull 'Unigenitus'. Its condemnation of Arnauld (q.v.) was the immediate cause of Pascal's (q.v.) *Lettres Provinciales*. It took a vigorous though ineffectual part in the attempts of the authorities to repress the philosophical movement of the 18th century, attacking for instance Montesquieu, Buffon, and Marmontel's *Bélisaire*.

It was suppressed in 1792. In 1821 its buildings (which had been reconstructed by Richelieu, who was buried in the new chapel) became the official headquarters of the reorganized University of Paris (see *Universities, A,* para. 4) and the seat of the faculties of theology, letters, and the sciences. (The faculty of theology was suppressed in 1885.)

The *Sorboniques, petite* and *grande,* were the final theses to be sustained for the doctorate of theology.

Sorel, AGNÈS (1422–50), mistress of Charles VII, said to have exercised a favourable influence on him during her short period of favour (1444–50). She was known as Mlle de Beauté, from the domain of Beauté-sur-Marne which the king gave her.

Sorel, ALBERT (1842–1906), historian, particularly noted for his studies of the French Revolution in relation to external politics. His great work was *L'Europe et la Révolution française* (1885–1904).

Sorel, CHARLES (1597–1674), novelist, author of the *Vraie histoire comique de Francion* (1622), an early example of the picaresque novel and a protest against the idealist romances of the *Astrée* type. The hero is a man of quality who is first seen, in the disguise of a pilgrim, pursuing Laurette, with whom he has fallen in love, to her husband's house, where after ludicrous incidents he ends the night in a vat with a broken head. The story of his early life, which he relates to a friend, and his subsequent turbulent adventures, when in the guise of a charlatan he sets off in pursuit of another love, furnish a realistic picture of the humbler, even the lowest, ranks of society: penniless poets, lawyers, pedants, bullies, schemers of both sexes. The work was extremely successful and much of it can still be enjoyed, for instance the opening description of village life and, still more, the later descriptions of life in a Paris college. In 1627 Sorel published *Le Berger extravagant,* in which he ridiculed the false rustic life depicted in *L'Astrée* (q.v.). The hero, Lysis, a sort of Don Quixote who has lost his wits through reading a multitude of pastoral romances, adopts the life and dress of a shepherd, and is involved in a series of grotesque adventures, until those who have, for their own amusement, encouraged his illusions, take pity on him and restore him to his senses.

Sorel, who appears as Charroselles in Furetière's *Roman bourgeois* (q.v.), also wrote some bibliographical works, *La Bibliothèque française* and *La Connaissance des bons livres*.

Sorel, GEORGES (1847–1922), social philosopher, an exponent of revolutionary syndicalism. In 1892 he gave up State employment as a civil engineer to devote himself to study and to publicizing his views. He was an anti-intellectualist, believing, roughly, that progress and social reform are effected by violence, and by the spirit of collective enthusiasm that violence engenders (hence the power of mob action and the general strike, and the relative unimportance of the ideologies, whether bourgeois or Marxist, which lead to violence). *Réflexions sur la violence* (1908) and *Les Illusions du progrès* (1908) are his chief works. Others (some partly published for the first time in the *Cahiers de la quinzaine*, q.v.) include: *Introduction à l'économie moderne* (1903), *La Décomposition du marxisme* (1908), and *La Révolution dreyfusienne* (1909).

Sorel, JULIEN, the hero of Stendhal's novel *Le Rouge et le Noir* (q.v.).

Sosies, Les, a comedy by Rotrou, produced in 1636, based on the *Amphitruo* of Plautus. The plot is the same as that of the *Amphitryon* (q.v.) of Molière, who imitated some of Rotrou's passages. 'Sosie' is the name of Amphitryon's servant.

Sotie, or **Sottie,** a kind of satirical farce, closely akin to the satirical *moralités* of the same—later medieval—period. *Soties* were played by those *sociétés joyeuses* (q.v., and see *Enfants sans souci*) who were also *confréries des sots*, secularized descendants of the earlier celebrants of the *Fête des Fous* (q.v.). The actors always wore fool's costume and took full advantage of it to give mordantly satiric parodies of society, manners, and political events. The characters were usually the Prince of Fools, the Mother Fool (played by a man), and their supporters.

One of the best-known *soties* was *Le Jeu du Prince des Sots et Mère Sotte*, by Pierre Gringore (q.v.), played in Paris on Shrove Tuesday 1512. It was designed to support by its satire Louis XII (represented by the Prince des Sots) in his quarrel of that time with

Pope Julius II (Mère Sotte, played by Gringore himself). Another typical *sotie, Les Trois Pèlerins* (c. 1521), attacked Louise de Savoie, the mother of François Ier, whom the people considered responsible for most of the misfortunes of her son's reign. Three devout pilgrims emerge from their retreat to see what is happening in the world. *Malice* meets them and tells them that everything is changed. The women govern and the men think only of pleasure. This picture of disorder so discourages the pilgrims that they go back to their cells.

André Gide (q.v.) in the 20th century described some of his satirical tales as *soties*.

Sots, see the preceding article; also *Enfants sans souci*.

Souday, PAUL (1868–1931), the official literary critic of *Le Temps* (q.v.) from 1912 to 1929, was a defender of the classical canons in literature and criticism. Besides three series of collected articles and reviews (*Les Livres du temps*, 1913–30), his publications include: *La Société des grands esprits* (1929); critical studies of Proust, Gide, Valéry (all 1927), and Bossuet (1929), and an edition (1927) of Voltaire's *Mémoires* with a preface 'Voltaire demi-urge' which caused remark.

Soufflot, JACQUES-GERMAIN (1714–80), architect. The Panthéon (q.v.) was built to his plans and, until he died, under his supervision.

Souffrances de l'inventeur, Les, the third of the three 'Scènes de la vie de province' which form the trilogy *Illusions perdues* (q.v.) in Balzac's *Comédie humaine*.

Soulaire, JEAN-LOUIS, see *Richelieu, duc de*.

Soulary, JOSEPH-MARIE, self-styled *Joséphin* (1815–91), poet, born at Lyons, wrote delicate verse, often in sonnet form. His best-known collection was *Sonnets humoristiques* (1858). Others included: *A travers champs* (1838); *Les Cinq Cordes du luth* (1838); *Éphémères* (1846).

Soulié, FRÉDÉRIC (1800–47), one of the earliest *roman-feuilletonistes* (see *Roman-feuilleton*), wrote at least forty gloomily sensational novels, best-sellers in their day, including *Les Deux Cadavres* (1832), *Les Mémoires du diable* (1837–8), *La Lionne* (1846), *La Comtesse de Monrion* (1847), &c.

He also wrote melodramas in collaboration with Dumas *père*.

Soulier de satin, Le (1925–8), by Claudel (q.v.), a long, impressive drama on the theme of God's grace. It was produced in a shortened version in 1943 with music by the Swiss composer Honegger.

Soult, NICOLAS-JEAN DE DIEU, one of Napoleon's marshals; see *Maréchal de l'Empire*.

Soumet, ALEXANDRE (1788–1845), minor poet and dramatist, wrote some didactic verse, e.g. *La Découverte de la vaccine* (1815) which won a prize from the *Académie française*, but he also frequented the Romantic *cénacles* (see *Romantisme*) and contributed to *La Muse française* (q.v.). His elegy *La Pauvre Fille* (1814) is remembered. The long *Divine Épopée* (1841), his life's work, enraptured his contemporaries. His tragedies had some life in them and some sense of the theatre, and at times herald the transition from classical to romantic drama (*Clytemnestre*, 1822; *Jeanne d'Arc*, 1825; *Les Maccabées*, 1827; *Une Fête de Néron*, 1829, &c.).

Soupault, PHILIPPE (1897–), poet and novelist, a *surréaliste* in the nineteen-twenties (see *Surréalisme*). His works include: *Rose des vents* (1920) and *Georgia* (1926), poems; and *Les Frères Durandeau* (1924) and *Dernières nuits de Paris* (1928), novels; also *Les Champs magnétiques* (1921) in collaboration with André Breton (q.v., and cf. also *Lautréamont*).

Sourches, LOUIS-FRANÇOIS DU BOUCHET, MARQUIS DE (1639–1716), of a family settled since the 12th century in the province of Maine, was appointed in 1664, after military service, *prévôt de l'hôtel du roi*, an office charged with the discipline of the royal court. His memoirs, covering the period 1681–1712, were not published in their entirety (except the years 1683–4, which are missing) until 1882 (a fragment had been published in 1836). They are of historical importance, both because the marquis de Sourches was exceptionally well informed and dispassionate in his narrative, and because they serve as a valuable check on the memoirs of Dangeau and Saint-Simon. The author's admiration for Louis XIV does not preclude criticism on occasion; he writes

in a simple natural style, without Saint-Simon's acrimony where he disapproves, and shows no predilection for scandalous anecdotes.

Sources de l'histoire de France, Les, an invaluable repertory of narrative sources for the history of medieval France, also of such indirect sources as letters, poems, &c. The first part, *Des Origines aux guerres d'Italie*, was published (1901–6, 6 vols.) by Auguste Molinier, and the work was continued by Henri Hauser, Émile Bourgeois, and Louis André. The texts are enumerated in groups according to their character (chronicles, lives of saints, and so on) for each successive period, and there are bibliographies.

Sous le soleil de Satan (1926), a novel by Georges Bernanos (q.v.).

Sous-offs (1889), a novel of army life by Lucien Descaves (q.v.).

Souvenir, a famous lyric by Alfred de Musset (first published in the *Revue des Deux Mondes* of 15 Feb. 1841), was written shortly after the poet had revisited the Forêt de Fontainebleau where once, before love had died, he had passed so many perfect hours with George Sand. He cherishes his memories, even though happiness was followed by suffering—'En est-il donc moins vrai que la lumière existe, Et faut-il l'oublier du moment qu'il fait nuit?' The same theme is treated in *Le Lac*, by Lamartine, and *Tristesse d'Olympio*, by Hugo.

Souvenirs d'égotisme, reminiscences by Stendhal (q.v.), published posthumously in 1892.

Souvenirs d'enfance et de jeunesse (1883), Renan's (q.v.) reminiscences of early life. They describe his childhood in Brittany and the Breton scene and legends; his early years in Paris preparing for, and at, the Seminary of Saint-Sulpice; the stages leading to his break with orthodox religion and his leaving the Seminary (one of the most interesting sections); the beginning of his new life, &c. The style is typical of Renan at his most limpid, supple, persuasive, and (e.g. the description of Talleyrand's deathbed return to the Church, in the section

'Saint-Nicolas du Chardonnet') gracefully ironic.

This work contains Renan's invocation to Athene, the *Prière que je fis sur l'Acropole quand je fus arrivé à en comprendre la parfaite beauté.* This was not composed on the spot. He saw the Acropolis for the first time in 1865 and brought a few notes home with him in an envelope marked 'Acropole. À emporter'; and from time to time, over the next ten years, he worked and reworked these into one of the famous passages of 19th-century French prose. It was first published in the *Revue des Deux Mondes* of 1 December 1876.

Souvenirs d'un homme de lettres (1888), reminiscences, with much about naturalistic circles, by Alphonse Daudet (q.v.).

Souza, MME DE [Adélaïde Filleul, marquise de Souza-Botelho] (1761–1836), born in Paris, wrote sentimental romances of the 18th-century aristocratic society of which she herself was a relic (cf. Mme de Genlis), notably *Adèle de Senanges* (1794, partly autobiographical), *Eugénie de Botelho* (1808). During the Revolution—her first husband, the comte de Flahaut, was guillotined in 1793—she joined the colony of *émigrés* at Mickleham, Surrey, and lived by her pen. Later, she moved to Hamburg (q.v.). In 1798 she returned to Paris and married the Portuguese ambassador, Joseph-Marie de Souza-Botelho, who settled there permanently. Her other novels include *Émilie et Alphonse, ou le Danger de se livrer à ses premières impressions* (1799), *Eugénie et Mathilde* (1811), *Mademoiselle de Tournon* (1820), *La Comtesse de Fargy* (1822), &c. She was the paternal grandmother of the duc de Morny (q.v.).

Spanish Influence on French literature, see *Foreign Influences* . . . .

Spectateur français, Le (1722), see *Marivaux.*

Spiridion (1839), a novel by George Sand (q.v.).

Spiritualisme, see *Literary Isms.*

Spleen de Paris, Le (1869), a posthumously published collection of fifty prose poems by Baudelaire.

Spleen et idéal, the first section of Baudelaire's *Les Fleurs du mal* (1857).

Splendeurs et misères des courti-

sanes (1839–47), a group of four 'Scènes de la vie parisienne' (see *Comédie humaine, La*), namely, *Comment aiment les filles; A combien l'amour revient aux vieillards; Ou mènent les mauvais chemins,* and *La Dernière Incarnation de Vautrin,* in which Balzac continues the adventures of Lucien de Rubempré (q.v., and cf. *Illusions perdues*). Lucien accompanies the abbé Carlos Herrera to Paris and soon discovers that his companion (who dominates the book) is the ex-convict Vautrin (q.v.). Stifling his scruples, Lucien leads a life of ambition and pleasure on money that Vautrin supplies. At the theatre he and the courtesan Esther Gobseck fall in love at first sight. Esther, compelled by Vautrin, becomes the Baron de Nucingen's mistress so that she may enrich Lucien, but the baron is such a vile creature that she commits suicide rather than remain with him. Unknown to herself she had been heiress to immense wealth, and after her death Lucien is arrested on suspicion of murder. Innocent, but terror-stricken, he confesses to his association with Vautrin, then hangs himself in his cell.

Spoelberch de Lovenjoul, VICOMTE CHARLES DE (1836–1907), a wealthy and erudite bibliophile of Flemish descent who amassed famous collections of books, manuscripts, autographs, and ana, notably those of Balzac, Gautier, Alfred de Musset, Sainte-Beuve, and George Sand, and bequeathed them to the Institut de France. He wrote *Lundis d'un chercheur* (1894) and compiled valuable bibliographical manuals, e.g. *Histoire des œuvres de Balzac* (1879 and subsequent editions), *Histoire des œuvres de Théophile Gautier* (1887).

Sponde, JEAN DE (1557–95), poet and humanist, a Protestant by birth and education who later became a Roman Catholic and who turned to the study of theology after an earlier career at court and in the magistracy. He wrote poetry which was occasionally included in 16th- and 17th-century collections but seldom published separately in his lifetime, when his importance was as a humanist and jurist and as a translator. His *Sonnets d'amour* and, more especially, such poems of religious experience as *Sonnets et stances de la mort,* the long poem *Stances du sacré banquet et convive de Jésus-Christ,* and the *Méditations sur les Pseaumes avec un essay de quelques poèmes chrestiens* are examples of the metaphysical trend in some of the late Renaissance French poetry. His *Poésies* were published in 1949; his *Méditations sur les Pseaumes* in 1954 (ed. A. M. Boase, who had already drawn attention to his work in an article in the *Criterion* in 1930).

Staal, Mme de, see *Launay, Mlle de.*

Staël, Anne-Louise-Germaine Necker, Mme de (1766–1817), was the daughter of the famous Genevan banker Jacques Necker (q.v.), who had married Gibbon's early love, the Swiss pastor's daughter Suzanne Curchod, and who became chief minister of Louis XVI. Her husband by her first marriage (1785) was the baron de Staël-Holstein (1749–1802), Swedish Ambassador in Paris, a man several years older than herself and for whom she had no affection. She had had three children by 1798, the date of her legal separation from him. The eldest, Auguste (1790–1827), edited his mother's *Œuvres complètes* in 1821. The second, Albert, born 1792, was killed in a duel in Sweden. The third, Albertine (1797–1833), married the duc Léonce-Victor de Broglie (q.v.).

From childhood upwards her mother's *salon* in Paris had been for Mme de Staël a sort of intellectual forcing-ground where she listened to the conversation of such men as Buffon, Diderot, Grimm, and Talleyrand. After her marriage her own *salon* was among the most celebrated of its day, both as a centre of intellectual activity and, in later years, as a meeting-place for those who shared her antipathy to Napoleon and the Empire. In 1792 she emigrated, spending some time in England and then retiring to Coppet (q.v.), a family property on Lake Geneva. In 1795 she spent nine months in Paris, but came under the suspicion of the *Directoire* and had to return to Coppet. In 1797 she re-established herself and her *salon* in Paris, but she incurred the disfavour of Napoleon, who exiled her in 1803, again in 1806, and finally, after the seizure of her book *De l'Allemagne* (q.v.), in 1810. On these occasions she travelled extensively in Germany, Italy, Austria, Russia, Sweden, and England, and her headquarters at Coppet became a centre of European culture. Her companions on many of her travels were the German writer August Wilhelm von Schlegel (q.v.), who acted as tutor to her

children; or Benjamin Constant (q.v.), with whom she had a stormy liaison lasting from 1794 to 1811, but, more than this, an intense intellectual sympathy. (So much so that Sismondi, q.v., another of her friends, said: 'On n'a point connu Mme de Staël si on ne l'a pas vue avec Benjamin Constant. Lui seul avait la puissance, par un esprit égal au sien, de mettre en jeu tout son esprit, de la faire grandir par la lutte, d'éveiller une éloquence, une profondeur d'âme et de pensée, qui ne se sont jamais montrées dans tout leur éclat que vis-à-vis de lui.') After the fall of Napoleon in 1814 she returned to Paris where, three years later, she died. She was buried at Coppet. In 1811, aged forty-five, she had married, secretly, the twenty-five-year-old Albert de Rocca, a Swiss officer; and it was to the one son of this marriage that Doudan (q.v.) was tutor.

Mme de Staël holds an important place in the history of French thought by her belief in *perfectibility*, i.e. in the doctrine that scientific material progress entails moral progress, and that the human race is advancing towards perfection. As a critic, she emphasized that judgement should be relative, not absolute, and should be based on a sense of history—views contrasting strongly with the rigid conventions which governed French literature in her day; and she drew a distinction between the *classical* literature of the South—an alien literature, transplanted into French soil—and the *romantic* literature of the North, with its roots in French soil. Because of these theories she stands with Chateaubriand (q.v.) as one of the great precursors of *Romantisme* (q.v.) and of modern criticism (see *Critics and criticism*, para. 7).

Her two most important works are *De la littérature considérée dans ses rapports avec les institutions sociales* (1800) and *De l'Allemagne* (1810, qq.v.). Her other works include: Novels, *Delphine* (1802) and *Corinne* (1807), qq.v. The leading theme of both is the fundamental solitariness of the intellectual woman, and they reflect the conflict in her own life between her thirst for fame and her longing for human affection; Memoirs, *Du caractère de M. Necker et de sa vie privée* (1804), *Dix années d'exil* (1821, written between 1810 and 1813; it contains many interesting comments, on Russia, for instance, and the Russian character); Political, Philosophical and Critical Treatises, *Lettres sur les ouvrages et le caractère de J.-J. Rousseau* (1788), *Essai sur les fictions* (1795), *De l'influence des passions sur le bonheur des individus et des nations* (1796), *Réflexions sur le suicide* (1813, written 1810), *Considérations sur les principaux événements de la Révolution française* (1818, written 1813 and 1816); also a number of tales written in early life and of plays written for the private theatre at Coppet. Some of these were published posthumously in *Essais dramatiques* (1821).

Stances à la Malibran, a poem by Alfred de Musset (q.v. and see *Malibran*).

Stapfer, PAUL (1840–1917), professor and critic, author of: *Shakespeare et l'antiquité* (1879–80); *Molière et Shakespeare* (1887); *Les Réputations littéraires* (1893–1901, contrasting studies of literary merit and the qualities that make for enduring fame or contemporary renown); *Récréations grammaticales et littéraires* (1909), &c.

Stapoul, see *Lefèvre d'Étaples*.

Stavisky, ALEXANDRE (1886–1934), a crook who obtained a footing in French government circles and engineered a large-scale financial swindle which was one of the scandals of the Third Republic. He disappeared after it was discovered and died in dubious circumstances.

Stello, by Alfred de Vigny (q.v.), published 1831 (15 Oct. and 1 Dec.) in the *Revue des Deux Mondes* and 1832 in book form, is a long dialogue, or series of *consultations*, between the poet Stello and the kindly but realistic 'docteur Noir'. Stello is prostrated with melancholy after one of the excursions, which he cannot resist making, into active life. Le docteur Noir enters, and seeks to convince him by means of anecdotes that the poet's duty is to preserve himself for his sacred mission, a solitary, well above the mêlée of daily life and politics. One of le docteur Noir's anecdotes is the germ of Vigny's play *Chatterton* (q.v.).

Stendhal, the pseudonym (now more familiar than his original name) of Henri Beyle (1783–1842), novelist and critic. Born and educated at Grenoble, he detested his early environment (Royalist and devout) and his father, Chérubin Beyle, an advocate who eventually sank the money his son should

have had in agricultural experiments. His mother died when he was seven.

(2) He was in Paris by 1799, with thoughts, soon abandoned, of the École Polytechnique. Influence procured him an army commission (1800) which took him to Milan. He recognized in Italy his spiritual home; he fell in love—unsuccessfully; and he began to study English. In 1802 he resigned his commission, spent some years mainly in Paris but could not afford a dilettante life, and in 1806 turned again to the army—the Commissariat branch. For some years victualling Napoleon's armies in Germany, Russia, and Austria constituted much of his work, and though never in the thick of the fighting he often endured severe hardship. In 1813 he left the army with his health impaired, largely through his own excesses. In 1814 he accepted the Restoration but refused office under the Bourbons. He scraped some money together and realizing his great ambition went to Milan. He stayed seven years in Italy (until he found himself suspected of espionage and had to leave), absorbed by art, music, literature, society, and a shattering, unrequited passion which he never forgot. ('L'amour', said Stendhal, writing his own obituary, 'a fait le bonheur et le malheur de sa vie.') During these years he published the *Vie de Haydn, de Mozart et de Métastase* (1814) and *Histoire de la peinture en Italie* (1817), both consisting largely of unacknowledged extracts from other authors, but interspersed with original critical comment; also *Rome, Naples et Florence en 1817* (1817; the first work published under his pseudonym of 'Stendhal').

(3) From 1821 to 1830 he was mostly in Paris, living frugally, writing, frequenting literary *salons* (e.g. Mme Ancelot's, q.v.). He published the well-known study *De l'amour* (1822, q.v.); the *Vie de Rossini* (1823); *Racine et Shakspeare* (1823, 1825, q.v., discussing classicism and romanticism); *Armance, ou quelques scènes d'un salon de Paris en 1827* (1827, his first novel); *Promenades dans Rome* (1829), and *Le Rouge et le Noir* (1830, q.v.), the first of his two enduringly famous novels. Under the July Monarchy (q.v.) he got himself appointed (1831) French Consul at Trieste and was soon transferred to Civitavecchia, a dreary, unhealthy little port, but only forty-five miles from Rome. He held this office until his death. He was an

efficient, not popular, consul when there, but boredom and poor health accounted for increasingly lengthy periods of leave spent in Paris or travelling. His death (from apoplexy) occurred during one visit to Paris. In 1837 he had composed his own epitaph, containing the words 'Visse, Scrisse, Amò'. The inscription on his tomb in the Montmartre cemetery reads 'Arrigo Beyle, Milanese, Scrisse, Amò, Visse'.

(4) The publications of his last ten years include: *Mémoires d'un touriste* (1838), travel impressions with frequent excursions into criticism; the novel of Italy *La Chartreuse de Parme* (1839, q.v.), which disputes the place as his greatest work with *Le Rouge et le Noir*; *L'Abbesse de Castro* (1839), a short novel; and several tales of 16th-century Italy contributed to reviews.

(5) As a writer Stendhal was not a conscious stylist. He set himself to express his thought, however complicated, with the utmost lucidity, sacrificing harmony and rhythm if necessary in the process. His ironical attitude to life was influenced by his study of the 18th-century sensationalists and *idéologues* (e.g. Condillac, Cabanis, Destutt de Tracy, qq.v.). He believed, briefly, that thought is a consequence of sensation, and that man's behaviour is governed by his passions, hence by his desire for happiness. We should, therefore, recognize without illusion that our actions—our virtues or our avoidance of vice—spring from interested motives: only hypocrisy or stupidity will attempt to explain them otherwise. He also considered that the most useful faculty a man could acquire was to be able to deduce character from observation and from analysis of motives. His beliefs were allied to what he himself called *Beylisme*—a worship of magnificent, all-conquering energy in the pursuit of happiness (whether the conquests were of love or of power). It had in it much that was fundamentally romantic; and for a time his *Racine et Shakspeare* (q.v.) linked him with the Romantic Movement, as did also his views that art and literature should depict passion, and that the *beau idéal*—the criterion of beauty—should change with the conditions and ideas of succeeding generations. But in general neither his attitude nor his writings had any appeal for a generation concerned with the delights, not the causes, of sensibility. Appreciation came towards the end of the century, thus fulfilling a prophecy of his own. Balzac and Gobineau (qq.v.) were rare in appreciating him before or shortly after he died, in 1842. Taine (q.v.), *c.* 1880, did much to awaken interest in him. And when literature turned to the psychological observation of life for its raw material he won a secure place among the great French novelists.

(6) The definitive edition of his works (Paris, Le Divan, 1927–37) fills 79 volumes. Besides those already mentioned it includes: *Vie de Napoléon* (first published in 1876); *Lamiel* (fragments of a novel, first published 1889); *Lucien Leuwen* (q.v.), an uncompleted novel, first published 1894; also three works of great interest for the study of a writer whose irony and sensuality often concealed a sensitive, wounded spirit—*Journal* (first published 1888; covers the years 1801–18), *La Vie de Henri Brulard* (first published 1890; romanticized autobiography, unfinished), *Souvenirs d'égotisme* (first published 1892; his life in Paris 1822–30; also unfinished).

(7) Stendhal visited England more than once, read much English, wrote—in French, which was translated—for English reviews, and had a habit of annotating his manuscripts or interpolating sentences in his *Journal* in English, cf. *Café Hardy*.

Stern, DANIEL, see *Agoult, comtesse d'*.

Strasbourg, Serment(s) de, see *Serment(s) de Strasbourg*.

Sturel, one of the seven young *déracinés* in the novel *Les Déracinés* (q.v.) by Maurice Barrès.

Style, Old and New, see *Year, Beginning of the*.

Suard, JEAN-BAPTISTE (1733–1817), man of letters, journalist, critic, belonging to the group of the *philosophes* (q.v.). He wrote much in the *Journal étranger*, *Gazette de France*, and *Lettres critiques*. His *Mélanges de littérature* appeared in 1803–5. His work includes translations from English. He was elected to the *Académie* in 1772, but his admission was postponed, owing to the influence of the court, till 1774. He was dramatic censor from 1777. His wife, *née* Panckoucke (q.v.), had a *salon* which was frequented by members of the philosophical party.

Suarès, ANDRÉ (1868–1948), born near Marseilles, of Jewish and Portuguese origin, an essayist and critic of wide reading and forceful and independent views. His publications include: *Images de la grandeur* (1900), *Voici l'homme* (1906), essays; *Wagner* (1899), *Musique et poésie* (1928), *Tolstoï vivant* (1911), *Trois hommes: Pascal, Ibsen, Dostoïevski* (1912), *Goethe le grand Européen* (1932), *Trois grands vivants: Cervantes, Tolstoï, Baudelaire* (1937), music and literary criticism; *Le Voyage du Condottiere* (*Vers Venise*, 1910; *Fiorenza*, 1932; *Sienne, la bien aimée*, 1932), geographical and spiritual travel; also some attempts at drama, e.g. *La Tragédie d'Élektre et d'Oreste* (1905), *Cressida* (1914).

Subjectivisme, see *Literary Isms*.

Subventionnés, Les, the term often used in speaking of the State-supported theatres in France, see *Theatres and theatre companies*, para. 9.

Suchet, LOUIS-GABRIEL, one of Napoleon's marshals, see *Maréchal de l'Empire*.

Sue, MARIE-JOSEPH, self-styled *Eugène* (1804–75), novelist, born in Paris, came of a distinguished line of doctors (his father took part in Napoleon's Russian campaign in 1812 as Surgeon-in-chief to the Imperial Guard and later published various works). He began his own career as a ship's surgeon, retiring in 1829 to write sea-faring novels (*Plik et Plok*, 1831; *La Vigie de Koatven*, 1833, &c.). Next came *Arthur* (1838), *Mathilde* (1841), *Le Morne au diable* (1842), &c., all moderately successful. He owed his immense popularity to sensational novels of Parisian low life, written with more exuberance than style, but showing a fertile, at times grandiose, imagination and strong dramatic sense; and containing a hotch-potch of contemporary ideals of social and democratic reform. Many of his characters have become familiar names, e.g. 'Rodolphe', the mysterious prince who haunts the Paris underworld in disguise, punishing evil and rewarding virtue, 'La Mère Pipelet (q.v.), 'Le Chourineur', the redeemed convict; 'Le Tortillard', the vitiated street-urchin (cf. *Gavroche*); and any paper publishing his novels as *feuilletons* was assured of a wide circulation. The following among his enormous output are still well known: *Les Mystères de Paris* (1842–3); *Le Juif errant* (1844–5); *Les Sept Péchés capitaux* (1847–9); *Les Mystères du peuple* (1849–56).

Suffren, PIERRE-ANDRÉ, BAILLI DE (1726–88), naval commander, distinguished in operations against the English in Indian waters.

Suite du Menteur, La, see *Menteur*.

Sully, MAURICE DE (d. 1196), Bishop of Paris, a preacher who seems originally to have composed some of his sermons in French. They were used as models by parish priests and are extant in many MSS. (often anonymous).

Sully, MAXIMILIEN DE BÉTHUNE, DUC DE (1559–1641), known earlier as *baron de Rosny*, the famous minister of Henri IV, who reorganized the finances of France by stringent economies and reform of abuses, and encouraged agriculture. He left memoirs (entitled *Économies royales*) drawn up under his supervision by his secretaries (1638), and addressed to himself, recalling his various actions. The last book of these is our authority for the celebrated scheme by which Henri IV hoped to establish perpetual peace through a sort of federation of the States of Europe, rearranged so as to involve a great reduction of the power of the House of Austria. The scheme, Sully asserts, had the warm support of Queen Elizabeth. It is discussed by Rousseau in his essay on Saint-Pierre's *Paix perpétuelle*.

Sully-Prudhomme, RENÉ-FRANÇOIS-ARMAND (1839–1907), Parnassian poet, born in Paris. His studies were first scientific, then legal, but on inheriting money he gave them up for literature and philosophy. He became one of the best known of the *Parnassiens* (q.v.), but to begin with he wrote gentle, sentimental, faintly melancholy lyrics—*Stances et poèmes* (1865; *Le Vase brisé* from this collection finds a place in most anthologies); *Les Épreuves* (1866); *Les Solitudes* (1869). Afterwards, the lyrical note was subordinated and he carried the Parnassian theories of impersonality to the extent of attempting to turn abstract scientific and philosophical systems into epic verse (*La Justice*, 1878; *Le Prisme*, 1884; *Le Bonheur*, 1888). In the end he wrote only prose (collected, with his poetry, in *Œuvres*, 1883–1908, 8 vols.). He was awarded the Nobel Prize for literature in 1901.

Supervielle, JULES (1884–   ), poet, novelist, short-story writer (and, more recently, dramatist), was born in Montevideo (cf. *Lautréamont, Laforgue*) of French parents who came from the Pyrenees. He was sent to Paris for his school and university years, then made Uruguay his permanent home (though he frequently returned to France and came to Paris to live after the 1939–45 war).

His work, as is natural, is coloured and enlivened by his familiarity with the South American scene. Over and above this his writing, whether prose or verse, has exceptional qualities of pure poetic feeling, freshness of vision, humour, and fantasy. The short stories, especially, show a very modern faculty for treating the fantastic in an everyday fashion, then, with one or two unobtrusive details, throwing the incongruous into relief, e.g. in *Le Bœuf et l'Âne de la crèche* (the Nativity, from the point of view of the two animals, and with all the reverent *naïveté* of a medieval sculpture), or the other tales (*L'Inconnue de la Seine, Les Boiteux du ciel*, &c.), including the name-tale, of the collection *L'Enfant de la haute mer* (1931); or in *L'Arche de Noé* (1938) and other tales. In *Le Petit Bois* (1947), the treatment of mythological legend (*Les Premiers Pas de l'univers, Orphée, Le Minotaure*) might invite a contrast with Kingsley's *Heroes* of a century earlier.

Besides the collections mentioned Supervielle's output (sometimes first published in South America) includes: *L'Homme de la Pampa* (1923), *Le Voleur d'enfants* (1926, dramatized 1948), *Le Survivant* (1928), novels; *Poèmes* (1919), *Débarcadères* (1922), *Gravitations* (1925), *Le Forçat innocent* (1930), *Les Amis inconnus* (1934), *La Fable du monde* (1938), *1939–1945* (*Poèmes*) (1945), poetry; *La Belle au bois* (1932), *Bolivar* (1936, with music by the composer Darius Milhaud), *La Première Famille* (1936), plays.

Supplément au voyage de Bougainville, see *Diderot*, para. 2.

Sur Catherine de Médicis, one of the 'Études philosophiques' in Balzac's *Comédie humaine* (q.v.).

Suréna, a tragedy by Corneille, produced in 1674, his last play.

Suréna, the Parthian general who has de-stroyed the army of Crassus, and Eurydice, daughter of the king of Armenia, are secretly in love with each other. But the king of Parthia designs that Eurydice shall be married to his son Pacorus, and, distrustful of the power of Suréna, to secure his loyalty offers him his own daughter in marriage. This offer Suréna declines, on the pretext that he is unworthy of the honour. The secret of Suréna and Eurydice is discovered. Suréna is assassinated and Eurydice is left dying of sorrow.

Sûreté, La, the shortened form of *Direction de la Sûreté nationale* (at one time *générale*), a department, divided into directorates, of the *Ministère de l'intérieur*. It has central police powers, i.e. responsibility within very wide limits for the organization and control in France, Algeria, and the oversea *départements* of services concerned with state security both internal and external (intelligence, counter-espionage, &c.), and with the maintenance of public order, safety, decency, hygiene, &c. (see *Police*, para. 4). It is sometimes known familiarly as the 'rue des Saussaies', from the street in which it is situated, and should not, by readers of detective fiction, be confused with the *Quai des Orfèvres*, the bureau or headquarters from which the *police judiciaire* in Paris set out to investigate crime (cf. *Police*, paras. 6, 7).

Suret-Lefort, one of the seven young *déracinés* in the novel *Les Déracinés* (q.v.) by Maurice Barrès.

Sur l'eau, a macabre tale by Guy de Maupassant (q.v.), included (1881) in the collection *La Maison Tellier*; also (1881) the title of a volume of notes and sketches which he wrote after a cruise in the Mediterranean.

Surprise de l'amour, La, a charming and characteristic comedy by Marivaux, produced in 1722. Lélio and the comtesse, who persuade themselves that they have each renounced all dealings with the other sex, are by circumstances thrown together. The play traces with wit and delicacy the development of their relations, from pretended indifference, through friendship, to mutual love, a progress assisted by the sprightly Colombine, the comtesse's attendant.

Surréalisme, an extremist movement in

which both writers and artists have taken part, evolved in Paris *c.* 1924 from the defunct *Dadaïste* movement (see *Dadaïsme*). It aroused interest, enthusiasm, scorn, or disgust for several years thereafter and extended to many other countries. (It had no connexion whatever with the literary movement known as *Réalisme*, q.v., and was in fact a negation of all that the *réalistes* held most important.)

In its early stages it represented an attempt to reach back to a pre-conscious, dream state, from which the chaotic, freakishly-concerted images that crowd the unconscious could be captured and, by a sort of 'pure, psychic automatism', expressed, unimpeded by any selective or critical faculty or by any aesthetic or moral principle (cf. *Écriture automatique*). It was strongly influenced by psychoanalytic theories and at one time appeared also to have some affinities with oriental mysticism, a similar idea of a point beyond reality, in which life and death, the real and the imaginary, the communicable and the uncommunicable, were one. But preoccupation with the Absolute seems to have been abandoned for attempts, possibly less taxing, to illumine objective reality by the elaborate assembling of haphazard images. In later years (*c.* 1926–7) many *surréalistes* confused revolutionary politics—i.e. communism—with a felt need for revolution and destruction of aesthetic or moral conventions in literature and art. A split developed within the movement and by about 1938 was threatening disintegration.

The movement was led by the poet André Breton (q.v.), whose manifestoes (1924, 1930, 1934) kept pace with his changing theories. Other writers prominently associated with it in its, and their, early days were Louis Aragon, Paul Éluard, Benjamin Péret, Philippe Soupault (qq.v.). Its precursors have been said to include Gérard de Nerval, Baudelaire, Rimbaud, Lautréamont (most consistently), and Apollinaire (qq.v.). Its literature can be studied in reviews (which appeared irregularly), e.g. *Littérature* (2nd ser., 1922–4), *La Révolution surréaliste* (1924–9), *Le Surréalisme au service de la Révolution* (1930–3), *Minotaure* (1933–8); in a *Petite anthologie poétique du surréalisme* (1934, ed. G. Hugnet); and in individual works (usually poetry or prose poems) such as *Les Champs magnétiques* (1921) by André Breton

and P. Soupault; *Une Vague de rêves* (1924) and *Traité du style* (1928) by L. Aragon; *Nadja* (1928, a novel) and *L'Union libre* (1931) by A. Breton; *Les Yeux fertiles* (1936) by P. Éluard.

Surréaliste as an adjective is frequently applied indiscriminately in the sense of *unusual*; and the literature produced in the heyday of the movement was often exaggerated and out to scandalize. But *surréalisme* as an attitude of mind has been accepted by its age. It recognizes and intensifies the element of surprise which the poet Apollinaire in 1917 (*L'Esprit nouveau*) called the distinguishing characteristic of modern poetry; and by its persistent awareness of an irreality concomitant with reality it has lent a new sharpness to creative perception. [Artists associated with the *surréaliste* movement include Picasso, Chirico, Max Ernst, Salvador Dali, and the photographer Man Ray.]

Surville, CLOTILDE DE, supposedly a French poetess, a contemporary of Christine de Pisan and Alain Chartier (qq.v.) and one of a hitherto unknown school of 'trouveresses' (see *Trouvères*). Her *Poésies* were published in 1803 but soon discovered, on internal evidence, to be a hoax. The supposed discovery aroused an excitement all the greater because it coincided with a revival of interest in the Middle Ages. The poems were said to have been transcribed from manuscripts at one time in his possession by the 'poetess's' descendant, the marquis Joseph-Étienne de Surville, an army officer with literary ambitions who fought with the *armée des émigrés* (q.v.) and was captured and executed during the *Directoire*. His papers were traced by one of his *émigré* friends, the vicomte de Vanderbourg, who had returned to France and was seeking a livelihood. He arranged for publication and added a circumstantial account of the supposed authoress. Although the authenticity of the poems was conclusively disproved, some critics maintained that a poetess Clotilde de Surville had actually existed.

Surville, MME LAURE, *née* Balzac (1800–71), the sister of Honoré de Balzac, and author of *Balzac, sa vie et ses œuvres d'après sa correspondance* (1858). Her husband was a civil engineer in State employment.

Suzanne et le Pacifique (1921), a novel by Jean Giraudoux (q.v.).

Swann, CHARLES, a key-character in Proust's *A la recherche du temps perdu* (q.v.). He appears first (vol. i, *Du Côté de chez Swann*) during Marcel's childhood holidays at Combray as the friendly owner of a neighbouring property. On visits to the grandparents he often talks kindly and stimulatingly to the child about art and literature. The grandparents accept him almost patronizingly as one of their own (comfortable, country, middle-) class. They have known his father, an Alsatian Jewish financier. They do not know, but gossip about, his wife. In Paris this same simple country gentleman is Swann, the wealthy, cultivated amateur of the arts, the member of the Jockey Club, who hobnobs at Twickenham with the Prince of Wales [some time in the 'seventies] and is welcomed—without his wife—in the exclusive society governed by the duchesse de Guermantes (q.v.). The Swann whose household Marcel frequents later in Paris is yet another person, affable to anyone who can further his wife's position in society. When Marcel last meets him at the princesse de Guermantes's evening party (the long description of this party in *Sodome et Gomorrhe* ii is a significant pause in the novel) he is a dying man. The Dreyfus (q.v.) Affair has stirred his racial sympathies and in some quarters has weakened his welcome. Some years after his death his daughter Gilberte (q.v.) marries into the Guermantes family.

[*Du Côté de chez Swann* (*Un Amour de Swann*) relates Swann's early history and his passion for Odette (q.v.), whom he eventually marries. It is the first of the many detailed studies of love and love's sufferings contained in the whole novel.]

Swedenborg [Swedberg], EMMANUEL (1688–1772), Swedish scientist, philosopher, and mystic, born in Stockholm, the son of a Lutheran bishop and professor of theology, studied at the university of Upsala, toured Europe, published Latin verses which were much praised, then returned to Upsala and a scientific career. His work in, for example, natural science and in physics was so brilliant and anticipated so many modern discoveries that he would have needed no further title to fame. In middle life, however, he turned increasingly to abstract speculation, and after 1745, when he first claimed to have been visited by God and to have conversed with angels and demons, he gave up scientific study and devoted himself to the mystical interpretation of the Scriptures. Thenceforward his life was spent between Sweden, Holland, and London, and he died in London.

His theosophic teaching proceeded from the belief that there are two worlds, both emanating from God, who is infinite love and infinite wisdom. One, the 'New Jerusalem', is the spiritual world to which man will one day be restored by a process of purification through divine love. It stands in the relation of cause and effect to the second world, the world of nature that we know, and there is in it a symbolic counterpart for all that is familiar to us in our world.

Swedenborg's mystical writings (e.g. *Arcana coelestia*, 1749–57; *De coelo et inferno ex auditis et visis*, 1758; *De nova Hierosolyma*, 1758; *Vera christiana religio, seu theologia novae ecclesiae*, 1771) were widely translated in Europe. Soon after his death his English followers were organized in London as the 'New Church', from which branches spread to the U.S.A. and other distant parts of the world. In France he influenced, directly or indirectly, many thinkers and writers, e.g. Ballanche, Balzac, the Symbolists (cf. the Symbolists' doctrine of *correspondances*). He was, further, one of a number of visionaries whose influence can be traced in the various forms of romantic, semi-religious, semi-mystical socialism that were a feature of the French scene in the years before 1848.

Sygognes, CHARLES DE BEAUXONCLES, SEIGNEUR DE (1560–1611), satirical poet, who had a chequered career in the army, at court, and as governor of Dieppe, was an imitator of the Italians (especially Berni) in his coarse and violent burlesque satires. He shows occasionally a quaint fancy in his evocations, as in his *Sonnet pour un solliciteur de procès*:

Petit rat de Brésil, qui vous a botiné?
Où allez-vous ainsi en robe de guenuche,
Les bras sur les rognons comme ceux d'une
    cruche?
Vous froncez le sourcil? Estes-vous mutiné?

Sylvestre II, see *Gerbert d'Aurillac*.

Sylvie, a tale by Gérard de Nerval (q.v.), first published in the collection *Les Filles du feu* (1854). The narrator hovers between a never very stable reality and a shifting world of reminiscences of his youth in the country near Paris known as *le Gâtinais,* in which lie such places as Chantilly, Senlis, and Rousseau's Ermenonville (q.v.), and where he had known a simple traditional life of dance and song. His passion for an actress fills the present, yet two loves of the past still hold him—Sylvie, who had married in the end a dull but unhesitant suitor, and Adrienne, who died. They had been, as he one day realizes, 'les deux moitiés d'un seul amour', a substance of which his later love was only a half-shadow, adored for what she evoked.

Symbolisme, Le, the most important movement in French poetry since 1850, with an influence that is still evident. It began about 1880, when the poems of Mallarmé (*L'Après-midi d'un faune,* 1876) and Verlaine (*Romances sans paroles,* 1874) were becoming known, and at first gained ground in the *décadent* circles (*c.* 1885, see *Esprit décadent*). It signified a departure from the traditional conventions governing both theme and technique in French poetry, and a reaction against the 'exteriorization' beloved of the *Parnassiens* (q.v.).

The Symbolistes wished to liberate the technique of versification in every way that would make for 'fluidity', a word much used at the time (see *Vers libérés* and *Vers libre*). Nothing was to be crystallized; the function of poetry was to evoke, not to describe; its matter was impressions, intuitions, sensations; reality was what one represented for oneself; and the poet's images should be symbols of his state of soul, inspired rather by latent affinities than by resemblances. To Baudelaire, who is recognized as having been its true precursor, the movement owed its theories of poetic music and the symbolic relations of scent, sound, and colour (cf. Baudelaire's sonnet *Correspondances*); and these combined with the prevailing cult for Wagner to produce the Symbolist conception of the essential 'musicality' of poetry. This was, briefly, that the theme of a poem could be, as it were, orchestrated and expanded by the choice of words having colour, harmony, and evocative power of their own.

Among many writers whose names come to mind (some of them as precursors) when Symbolisme is mentioned are: Mallarmé, Verlaine, Rimbaud, Jules Laforgue, Henri de Régnier, Jean Moréas (who first, in *Le Figaro* of 18 September 1886, proposed to replace the term *décadent* by *symboliste* and *symbolisme*), Tristan Corbière, Villiers de l'Isle Adam (qq.v.). Many Symbolist reviews were founded, the chief being *Le Mercure de France* (q.v.), which still exists, *La Conque, Le Décadent, La Plume, La Revue blanche, La Revue indépendante, La Revue wagnérienne, La Wallonie* (qq.v.). Other writings associated with the movement were Verlaine's *Art poétique* (in *Jadis et naguère,* 1884) and his studies of six *Poètes maudits* (1884, q.v.); Huysmans' novel *A rebours* (1884, q.v.); and the pastiches by Henri Beauclair and Gabriel Vicaire entitled *Les Déliquescences d'Adoré Floupette* (1885, q.v.). The two Symbolist critics were Remy de Gourmont and Marcel Schwob (qq.v.). Dramatic works by Symbolist authors were produced at the Théâtre des Arts and the Théâtre de l'Œuvre (qq.v.). In music the composer most closely associated with the movement was Debussy (q.v.). Painters allied to it by sympathy or style were Gauguin, Gustave Moreau, Odilon Redon, Puvis de Chavannes, Van Gogh.

The extreme Symbolist Movement, with Mallarmé as leader, reached its height about 1890. A few years later new schools, such as the *École romane* (q.v.), arose and in some cases heralded a modified return to classicism (see also *Literary Isms*).

Symphonie fantastique, La, a well-known work by the composer Berlioz (q.v.), sometimes described as the perfect musical equivalent of romanticism (especially in its fantastic element) in literature. It is in five sections or 'episodes in the life of an artist'. He wrote it after seeing and falling in love with the English actress Harriet Smithson, who played Ophelia in Paris in 1830.

Symphonie pastorale, La (1919), a *récit* by André Gide (q.v.).

Synthétisme, see *Literary Isms*.

Système de la nature, Le, a philosophical treatise by the baron d'Holbach (q.v.), published in 1770. He was helped in its composition to some extent by Diderot. Two years later the author issued a convenient résumé of the work entitled *Le Bon Sens, ou Idées naturelles opposées aux idées surnaturelles.* The original work was condemned by the *parlement.*

The treatise is a self-consistent and in some parts an eloquent defence of the materialist and determinist standpoint in philosophy. D'Holbach argues that man is nothing but a physical being so organized as to feel and think; that his supposed spiritual side is a false distinction, the soul nothing but the body considered relatively to certain of its functions; that man is governed only by the universal laws of matter and motion; that the freedom of the will is an illusion, and likewise the immortality of the soul; that the need for reciprocal conduct conducive to the happiness of society is the basis of morality;

and that the source of evil is an erroneous estimate of happiness, which can be corrected by proper education. The author passes to a vigorous attack on existing political institutions, and more elaborately on religion in general, of which he traces the origin to man's ignorance of the causes of physical phenomena, to his tendency to give an anthropomorphic form to the causes he imagines, and to the advantage taken of his credulity by priests. In general, he deprecates any attempt to go outside nature, of which man forms a part, into a realm peopled for us by chimaeras, in search of unattainable knowledge. The work, which is somewhat marred by declamation and repetition, was the culmination, in literary form, of the revolt against existing political and religious institutions.

T

Tabaret, Le Père, see *Gaboriau.*

Tabarin, the nickname of a certain Jean Salomon, a clown or merry-andrew who advertised the drugs sold by a charlatan named Mondor on the Pont-Neuf in Paris in the early 17th century. Sometimes Mondor and Tabarin appeared together in short sketches in which Tabarin took the part of servant. These dialogues and other *facetiae* were collected and had enormous success. He retired from the business in 1630.

Tableau historique des progrès de l'esprit humain, Esquisse d'un, a treatise of political philosophy by Condorcet, written in 1793-4 while he was under proscription, published posthumously in 1795.

This sketch of a larger and more detailed work is divided into ten epochs or chapters. In these the history of mankind is broadly traced from the dawn of the earliest societies, beginning with the growth of a learned and priestly caste and of primitive religions, through the Greek and Roman civilizations and the decline of the Roman empires, the rise of the Moslem religion and of Arab culture, the invention of printing and the geographical discoveries of the 15th-16th

centuries, the revolt led by Luther, to the conception of the rights of man worked out in the American and French revolutions. Much attention is given to the development of the sciences; and the liberation of mankind from tyranny and superstition is described as effected under the war-cry of 'Reason, toleration, humanity'. The last chapter contains a sketch of Condorcet's hopes for the future, under the headings of (1) the growth of equality between nations (the acquisition of independence by subject peoples, the abolition of the slave trade, &c.), (2) the growth of equality among the subjects of the same nation (equalization of the sexes, of wealth, of education, &c.), (3) the moral, intellectual, and physical improvement of mankind, which he believed capable of indefinite extension by better laws and institutions. The whole work shows a striking advance on the speculations of Montesquieu, in its conception of a history of the human mind, of a chain of cause and effect following a natural order.

Table ronde, Romans de la, see *Romans bretons.*

Tabouret, Droit du, the privilege accorded under the monarchy to ladies of princely or ducal rank to be seated in the presence of the king and queen. Attempts were frequently made to obtain an extension of the privilege, and it is repeatedly referred to by Saint-Simon and in other memoirs.

Tabourot, ÉTIENNE (1549–90), known as Tabourot des Accords, and sometimes also called 'le Rabelais de la Bourgogne', was a lawyer by profession, of Dijon, and a facetious writer and poet, author of *Les Bigarrures* (1582), *Les Touches* (1585), *Les Escraignes dijonnaises* (posth., 1614), &c., medleys of amusing anecdotes, tales, epigrams, also riddles and acrostics. He was also responsible for one of the earliest French rhyming dictionaries (see *Dictionaries and encyclopedias* under dates 1572, 1587).

Taches d'encre, Les, see *Barrès, Maurice.*

Taglioni, MARIA (1804–84), born in Stockholm, a famous ballerina at the Paris Opera between 1827 and 1847.

Tahureau, JACQUES (1527–55), born at Le Mans, a poet of the school of Ronsard, author of love lyrics on the Petrarchan model (one collection of which was entitled *Mignardises amoureuses de l'Admirée*) and of satirical dialogues (published 1562 and frequently reprinted till the end of the century).

Tailhade, LAURENT (1854–1919), poet and man of letters. His works include the sentimental and semi-religious verse of *Le Jardin des rêves* (1880) and *Vitraux* (1891), collected with additions in 1907 as *Poèmes élégiaques*; also the invective verse of *Au pays du mufle* (1891) and *A travers les groins* (1897), collected in 1904 as *Poèmes aristophanesques.*

Taille, see *Fiscal system.*

Taillefer, according to Wace (q.v.), a minstrel who sang before Duke William at the battle of Hastings—of Roland and Olivier and their death at Roncevaux. See *Chanson de Roland.*

Taine, HIPPOLYTE (1828–93), philosopher, critic, and historian, was born at Vouziers, in the Ardennes. After his father, a solicitor, died he was educated in Paris. He did brilliantly at the École normale supérieure (q.v.) but failed in the examination for the title of *agrégé de philosophie* (1851), his views being too daring for the reactionary examiners of a reactionary era. He taught for

a while in provincial schools, then fell back on private tuition and literary journalism for a living, and managed also to read voraciously (physiology, psychology, and mathematics) for his own ends, to take his doctor's degree in literature, and to visit the Pyrenees, Italy, and England. In 1864 he succeeded Viollet-le-Duc (q.v.) as Professor of Aesthetics and of the History of Art at the École des Beaux-Arts, a position he held, with one year's interruption in 1876–7, till 1883.

(2) By the time he was thirty, with his reputation already firmly established, his publications included: *Essai sur les Fables de La Fontaine* (1853), his doctor's thesis and in effect a study of 17th-century society and the court of Louis XIV; *Voyage aux Pyrénées* (1855, q.v.); *Essai sur Tite-Live* (1856); *Les Philosophes français du XIXᵉ siècle* (1857), and *Essais de critique et d'histoire* (1858). The first three were remodelled in subsequent editions, but even in their early form they contain in germ the theories of *la race, le milieu, et le moment* (see para. 5 below) with which Taine's name is lastingly associated. The fourth and fifth were the book-form of articles first published separately. The fourth, which became *Les Philosophes classiques du XIXᵉ siècle en France* in the revised (a third) edition of 1868, includes studies of Maine de Biran, Jouffroy, and Victor Cousin (qq.v.). The *Essais de critique et d'histoire* were more than once re-edited and augmented. Two studies, of Balzac and Stendhal, often mentioned in writings on 19th- and 20th-century French fiction, were among the additions.

(3) Taine (and Renan, q.v.) did more than any other writers of the period to mould the thought of the generation reaching maturity about 1870. Taine's importance lay in his theories of the interdependence of the physical and psychological factors which influence human development, and in his application of the principles of scientific investigation to the study of literature, history, and art. His theories, which owed much to Positivism, are expounded at length in *De l'intelligence* (1870, 2 vols.). Nature, he says, using the word in the sense of the inherent impulse which determines man's evolution, consists of a succession of events in the parallel development of the psychological (or moral) and the physical elements

in man. The psychological element he relates
to man's innermost sensations which, with
the images they provoke, constitute ideas;
while the physical element, he considers, corresponds to the external manifestations of
these sensations. Thus it should be possible to
explain and predict human personality in
terms of significant facts, their interrelation,
and what effects the combinations can be
expected to produce.

(4) To illustrate his theory Taine invites
his readers to think of a book printed with
an interlinear translation into another language. The book is Nature. The main text
represents the psychological element, and
the interlinear translation the physical. In
the opening chapters (which correspond
to the early development of man's personality) the translation, or physical element,
is clear and legible. The main text, or
psychological element, on the other hand,
is not evident and indeed does not begin to
show in the earlier pages. As the book, or
evolution of man's personality, proceeds,
the main text becomes clearer and stronger,
while the translation changes and deteriorates
until in the final chapters, although it continues to the end and there are still indications
that text and translation are related, it is
illegible. What, then, were the philosophers
to make of this book? The materialist, who
would start to read at the beginning and
there find only the interlinear translation,
would say that that alone was the language
of the book, whether the number of texts
eventually to be found printed on the page
was one, or two. The spiritualist, for whom
the workings of the mind and the will
cannot be wholly explained in terms of
physiological facts, and who would begin
at the end and read back, would admit that
a large portion of the book was indeed
printed in a second language. He would
nevertheless refuse to recognize in this anything but a mysterious juxtaposition of two
unrelated texts. Taine himself had no doubt
of the relationship: it was the interdepen-
dent one of original and translation: therefore at any moment one 'text' could be used
to explain, or to supplement gaps in, the
other.

(5) In the famous Introduction to the *Histoire de la littérature anglaise* (1863, 3 vols.)
Taine had already emphasized the importance, for historians and critics, of studying

the physical and psychological factors responsible for cultural and social development.
For instance, what, given such and such a
literature, or historical figure, were the
causes which determined its, or his, evolution? What was the dominant characteristic
(*faculté maîtresse*) of this literature, or this
man, and what forces had been at work to
condition it, or him, e.g. forces arising from
racial inheritance (*la race*), from physical,
social, and political environment (*le milieu*),
and from a combination of the momentum
(his '*vitesse acquise*') or driving force of development, of the age, and the moment of
time in which the literature or the historical
figure emerged (*le moment*)? The problem,
he said, was simply one of psychological
mechanics, to be solved by the same methods
of collection and analysis of significant facts
as would be employed in solving a problem
of physical mechanics: with this difference,
in regard to the psychological problem, that
the conditioning forces could not be
exactly measured or reduced to formulae.

(6) Such were among the views that
constituted Taine the theorist of *naturalisme*
(q.v.) and gave point to Zola's use of his
axiom 'le vice et la vertu sont des produits
comme le vitriol et le sucre' (*Litt. anglaise*) as
the epigraph for a second edition of *Thérèse
Raquin* (q.v.). They are also largely behind
the conscious development of the novel of
psychological analysis. But they do not by
any means represent the whole extent of his
thought. There are, for instance, passages in
De l'intelligence (Bk. I), on the manner in
which an unforeseen sensation can reawaken
an image long obliterated, which herald the
exploration of the unconscious to be found
in some of the greatest works of modern
fiction.

(7) Taine wrote at all times with unwavering conviction, pursuing his thought
with the controlled logic of a man with a
passion for abstract reasoning, and emphasizing it with metaphors so poetic as well as so
forcible that Paul Bourget (q.v.) wrote
paradoxically of his 'souci de doubler la
soie brillante de l'imagination avec l'étoffe
solide de la science'. At times he drove his
theories hard, e.g. to the detriment of his
famous historical work *Les Origines de la
France contemporaine* (1875–93, q.v.); or in
Notes [of a trip in 1861–2] *sur l'Angleterre*
(1872), when he concluded that English-

women owed their long teeth to a heavy meat diet and their large feet to their habit of tramping for miles across rain-sodden soil.

(8) His works other than those mentioned above include: *Nouveaux* and *Derniers Essais de critique et d'histoire* (1865 and 1894); *La Philosophie de l'art* (1885), the book form of lectures delivered at the École des Beaux-Arts, augmented in 1882 by other essays, some already published separately and some written after travel in Italy, e.g. *De l'idéal dans l'art*, &c.; *Notes sur Paris. Vie et opinions de M. Frédéric-Thomas Graindorge* (1868, q.v.); also the travel-sketches *Carnets de voyage: Notes sur la province* (1863–5) and *Voyage en Italie* (Naples, Rome, Florence, and Venice) (1866); *Étienne Mayran* (q.v.), an unfinished novel published posthumously; and (the only poetry he is known to have written) twelve sonnets dedicated to his three cats Puss, Ébène, and Mitonne. They were published in *Le Figaro* the day after his death.

(9) Novels which have interesting references to Taine's influence include *Les Déracinés*, by Maurice Barrès, and *Le Disciple*, by Paul Bourget (qq.v.).

Tallemant des Réaux, GÉDÉON (1619–92), born at La Rochelle, son of a rich *bourgeois*, author of a collection of anecdotal memoirs, arranged under the names of the notable persons of his time (besides a few under general headings), entitled *Historiettes* (376 in number). Tallemant is pre-eminently a scandalmonger, but many of his statements are borne out by independent evidence. The *Historiettes* give a valuable and amusing picture of French society from the time of Henri IV to the middle of the 17th century, and contain some biographical details of historical interest; many of them relate to men and women of letters, e.g. J.-L. Guez de Balzac, Corneille, Godeau, La Fontaine, Mme de Rambouillet, Mlle de Scudéry, Mlle de Gournay. The work was completed about 1659, except for notes subsequently added, but was not published till 1834.

Talleyrand-Périgord, CHARLES-MAURICE DE (1754–1838), born in Paris, a celebrated diplomat whose political genius, wit, urbanity, and venality are all remembered. As a young man, incapacitated from infancy by lameness, he had to enter the Church. His great financial and administrative abilities soon won him preferment despite his licentious tastes. He became Bishop of Autun in 1788. In 1789 he represented the clergy of his diocese at the *États Généraux*, joined the *Tiers État*, supported the *constitution civile du clergé* (see these names) and himself left the Church for a secular career. Between 1792 and 1794 he was engaged in dubious diplomatic activities in London, popular neither there nor in France. He went to America, amassed money, and was back in France by 1796, again winning power, and losing it by corrupt practices. He was associated with Bonaparte's *coup d'état* of 1799 (see *dix-huit brumaire, Le*); became the Emperor's trusted adviser; fell from power over foreign policy; by 1814 was receiving overtures from the Restoration party; was prominent in the negotiations before and after Napoleon's downfall; and represented France in 1815 at the Congress of Vienna (q.v.). During the Restoration he played a watching part and when he saw the increasing unpopularity of the Government of Charles X he entered into relations with the Orleans faction. As French ambassador in London after the *révolution du 29 juillet* (1830, q.v.) he did much to shape the future course of events in Europe. He retired in 1834. Napoleon had created him Prince of Benevento in 1806.

There is a well-known description in *Souvenirs d'enfance et de jeunesse* (q.v.), by Renan, of Talleyrand's death-bed reconciliation with the Church. Five long articles on him by Sainte-Beuve in the *Nouveaux lundis* have an added interest as revelations of the critic's own character, of his veneration for truth, and the conflict between his desire to appraise the diplomat's achievements and his contempt for Talleyrand the man.

Tallien, MME (1773–1835), *née* Thérèse Cabarrus, daughter of a Spanish financier, a woman of seductive charm, was married very young to the marquis de Fontenay (who divorced her) and then to the journalist Jean-Lambert Tallien (1767–1820), who had come to her aid when she took fright at the Revolution, tried to return to Spain, and was arrested. Tallien was one of the leaders in the overthrow of Robespierre (inspired it is said by his wife, who became known as 'Notre-Dame de Thermidor'). Mme Tallien was subsequently the mistress of Barras, a member of the *Directoire*, and during this period was queen of the mixed society that frequented the *salons* of the Luxembourg. She led the fashions in women's dress, introducing the audacious Greek mode. In 1805, having divorced Tallien, she married the comte de Caraman, later prince de Chimay.

Talma, FRANÇOIS-JOSEPH (1763–1826), celebrated tragic actor, born in Paris, forsook dentistry (his father's calling) for the stage (1787) and joined the company of the Comédie-Française. His first great part was in M.-J. Chénier's *Charles IX* (q.v.). During the first quarter of the 19th century he created the principal roles in all the famous tragedies of the day. He introduced many lasting reforms into methods of acting (less artificiality, less declamation) and production (period costume and scenery). He was one of Napoleon's intimate circle and performed at Erfurt under his auspices before a 'parterre de rois'. His *Mémoires* were published in 1826 and again in 1850.

Talon, OMER (1595–1652), a magistrate who took a prominent part in the *Parlement* at the time of the Fronde. He left memoirs (largely a collection of his own speeches and other documents) of historical interest.

Tamango, by Prosper Mérimée (q.v., para. 4), the tale of a revolt in a French slave-ship, printed in the *Revue de Paris* in 1829 and included in *Mosaïque* in 1833. The negroes who form the cargo massacre the white crew, then find themselves helpless in mid-ocean in a ship they are unable to navigate. One day an English frigate discovers an apparently abandoned hulk, but on it there is one barely live negro. This is Tamango, an African chief who had been captured by a trick and had then led the revolt. He is nursed back to health and taken to Jamaica, where he ends his days as a regimental cymbalist. He seldom speaks, but he drinks quantities of rum and dies finally in hospital of a chest complaint.

Tancrède, a tragedy by Voltaire, produced in 1760.

The scene is Syracuse in the year 1005, when the city had recovered its liberty but was threatened by the Moors who held the rest of Sicily. Civil strife among the nobles of Syracuse is to be settled by the marriage of Orbassan, one leader, with Aménaïde, daughter of another. Aménaïde, however, is secretly pledged to Tancrède, a Norman

knight born at Syracuse, but exiled and despoiled of his property, who has won glory fighting under the Eastern Empire. To escape the projected marriage she sends a message to Tancrède, whom she knows to be once more in the island. The message is intercepted in circumstances which make it appear that it was intended for the leader of the Moors, and Aménaïde is condemned to death for her crime. Tancrède coming unrecognized to Syracuse learns of her impending fate, and though broken-hearted by her supposed infidelity to himself, comes forward as her champion and defeats Orbassan, her accuser. Then by desperate deeds of valour he drives off an attack of the Moors, but is mortally wounded. It is only as he dies that he learns that Aménaïde's love for him has never failed.

Tapissier de Notre-Dame, Le, see *Luxembourg, François-Henri, duc de.*

Tarde, GABRIEL (1843–1904), philosopher and sociologist. His chief works, many of which were studies in criminology, include: *Les Lois de l'imitation* (1890), *La Logique sociale* (1895), *L'Opposition universelle* (1897), *La Criminalité comparée* (1898), *Études de psychologie sociale* (1898). Tarde preceded Bergson (q.v.) in the Chair of Philosophy at the Collège de France (q.v.).

Tardis, SIRE, the snail, in the *Roman de Renart* (q.v.).

Tartarin de Tarascon, the hero of three tales by Alphonse Daudet (q.v.), is a genial caricature of the Frenchman of the Midi, a type proverbially mercurial and exuberant, boastful, but so carried away by its own tall stories that it believes them. [Tarascon is a typical very small, hot, Provençal town, beautifully situated on the Rhône between Avignon and Arles. It is joined by a suspension bridge to Beaucaire, on the other side of the river.]

In *Tartarin de Tarascon* (1872), the first tale, this local hero finds that his prestige as a crack big-game hunter is tottering. Action alone can save him, and after elaborate preparations he sets off to shoot lions in the North African desert. He is fiercely armed and still more ferociously costumed, ready for any emergency, and more than a little uneasy since, indeed, an armchair adventurer who has never been farther away from home than Beaucaire is apt to cling to his creature comforts. But the desert, invaded by modern civilization, has become such a built-up area that all self-respecting lions have long since departed. He does shoot an aged, lethargic lion, the livelihood of two travelling showmen, and has to pay heavy compensation; he does acquire—in the sense that he cannot rid himself of—a broken-down camel; and he does himself become easy game for a bogus Montenegrin prince who despoils him. With the camel, and as nearly crestfallen as it is possible for him to be, the destitute Tartarin returns to Tarascon. To his astonishment he meets with an ovation from his fellow townsmen, for whom their hero in absence has become still more heroic. His spirits soar, and as he leaves the station he can be heard beginning the first of many subsequent sagas: 'Figurez-vous, qu'un certain soir, en plein Sahara....'

In *Tartarin sur les Alpes* (1885) he has become first President of the Tarascon mountaineering club (which climbs the local hillocks on its Sunday walks) and finds his supremacy threatened by a rival. He sets off for Switzerland, to plant the banner of the Tarascon club on the summit of the Jungfrau, and again survives astonishing adventures.

In *Port Tarascon* (1890) he heads an expedition of his fellow Tarasconnais to found a colony in a South Sea island. The enterprise fails, the island turns out to be a British possession, and His Excellency the Governor Tartarin, with his now rebellious colonists (but without his island wife), is repatriated in a British warship. Once back in France the great man is disowned by Tarascon. He removes across the river to end his days in Beaucaire.

Tartuffe, Le, a comedy by Molière. When a version in three acts was performed at Versailles in 1664 it provoked violent opposition from the devout, and the public performance was prohibited by the king. It was produced again under the title of *L'Imposteur* in 1667 with some alterations (Tartuffe himself now figuring as Panulphe), and its performance was again interdicted by the president of the *parlement*. The interdict was withdrawn in 1669 and thereafter *Le Tartuffe* was performed freely.

Tartuffe is an odious hypocrite, who under an assumption of extreme piety introduces himself into the household of the credulous Orgon. The latter, in spite of the opposition of his sensible brother-in-law Cléante and of his own son, proposes to marry his daughter against her will to the impostor, and actually makes over the whole of his property to him. His eyes are opened only when, by a device of his wife, Elmire, he witnesses an attempt by Tartuffe to seduce her. But Tartuffe is now owner of Orgon's house, orders the family out of it, and contrives the arrest of Orgon himself. The king, however, now interposes for the defeat of fraud, and Tartuffe is hauled off to prison. The outspoken family servant Dorine is one of Molière's best characters of this type.

Molière spelt the name, which he is said to have taken from Italian comedy, 'Tartuffe'. 'Tartufe' in the sense of 'faux dévôt' was admitted into the *Dictionnaire de l'Académie française* in 1694.

Tassart, FRANÇOIS, Maupassant's valet from 1883 to 1893, described his master's last years of failing health and reason in *Maupassant (1883–93)* (1911).

Tastu, MME AMABLE (*née* Voïart) (1798–1885), poetess, born at Metz, published *Poésies* (1826) and *Poésies nouvelles* (1834), collections of sentimental and elevating verse. She also wrote children's stories and educational books: *Le Livre des enfants* (1836–7), *Voyage en France* (1845), &c., and translated *Robinson Crusoe* into French (1835).

Taureau blanc, Le, an oriental tale by Voltaire, published in 1774, of the daughter of Amasis king of Egypt and her lover, King Nebuchadnezzar, who has been transformed into a white bull. It contains much mockery of Old Testament tales.

Tavan, ALPHONSE, one of the early *félibres* (q.v.).

Tavannes, GASPARD DE SAULX DE (1509–73), maréchal de France, who took a leading part in bringing about the Massacre of St. Bartholomew. His life was written by his son, Jean de Saulx, vicomte de Tavannes (1555–1629), an ardent *ligueur*, who fought at La Rochelle and had an adventurous career. Another son Guillaume (1553–1633) wrote his own memoirs.

Tavernier, JEAN-BAPTISTE (1605–89), a traveller who visited Turkey, Persia, and the Indies. His narrative (*Les Six Voyages de Jean-Baptiste Tavernier*, 1676) and that of Jean Chardin (q.v.) developed public interest in the East, of which we see evidence in Montesquieu's *Lettres Persanes*.

Taylor, ISIDORE-JUSTIN-SÉVERIN, BARON (1789–1879), patron of literature and the arts, archaeologist and philanthropist. He was director of the Théâtre Français at the time of the Romantic Movement and used his position to give the Romantic dramatists their chance (he produced Hugo's *Hernani*, q.v.). He himself wrote plays and, more memorably, the many volumes, beautifully illustrated by contemporary artists, of *Voyages pittoresques et romantiques de l'ancienne France* (1820–63).

Télémaque, a didactic romance, written by Fénelon for the edification of his pupil, the duc de Bourgogne, and surreptitiously published in 1699; a precursor of the political and philosophical tales of Marmontel and Voltaire.

The author relates the imaginary adventures of Télémaque (Telemachus), son of Ulysses, when he sets out from Ithaca in search of his father, who has been long detained on his return from Troy. He is accompanied by the goddess Minerva under the semblance of the wise old man Mentor, and meets with adventures that have no relation to the *Odyssey* but rather resemble those of a knight-errant, amid Greek surroundings charmingly described. With this story Fénelon combines precepts of physical and intellectual education, political utopias, and moral dissertations. Télémaque is shipwrecked on the island of Calypso, where he relates to her his earlier adventures in a number of countries round the Mediterranean. He is now exposed to the allurements of Calypso herself and her nymph Eucharis, to save him from which Mentor goes so far as to throw him into the sea. A Phoenician ship carries them to Salente, a city just founded by Idomeneus, and round this, with various episodes (including a visit to the Elysian Fields), the rest of the narrative revolves. Idomeneus entrusts the organization of the State to Mentor, who proceeds to create an ideal (if over-regulated) republic. This part of the work is in effect a treatise on government, especially as regards the high standard of political conduct required of a good king. Care for the welfare and happiness of his subjects is a king's first concern (a doctrine enforced by the picture of the sufferings in Hades of the kings who have abused their power). The author even asserts that the law is above the king, an audacious statement for a subject of Louis XIV. He repeatedly deplores the folly and cruelty of war. He has notable passages on the need for good faith in international relations and on the wise treatment of a conquered nation. He shows himself ahead of his times in his economic views and in his assertion that a suspect, however strong the suspicion, must be held innocent until proved guilty. The work is written in a harmonious, somewhat languid style, and it has been described as the first prose-poem in French, but its charm is marred by the incongruous medley of pagan fiction with the didactic Christian spirit. Reflecting as it did, intentionally or not, on the government of Louis XIV, it gave offence at court and contributed to bring Fénelon into disfavour. It may be said to have inaugurated the novel of religious and political allusion of which the *philosophes* made frequent use.

Tel qu'en lui-même. This title of one of Duhamel's *Salavin* (q.v.) novels is taken from the first line of Mallarmé's famous sonnet *Le Tombeau d'Edgar Poë* (q.v.).

Temple, Le, a fortified lodge, dating from the late 12th century, of the Knights Templars in Paris. It lay to the north-east of the city, in the district bounded today on the west by the rue du Temple and at that time outside the walls of Philippe-Auguste. The vast wealth of the Templars brought them into suspicion in France early in the 14th century, their property was seized, and many of them were executed. The Temple in Paris passed into the keeping of the Knights of St. John; many of the buildings were demolished, but an important part remained, including the celebrated 13th-century *Tour* or *Donjon du Temple*, originally destined to house the archives of the Order. Other buildings were added, such as the fine residence (17th c.) of the *Grand-Prieur de l'Ordre de Malte* which became, when inhabited by Philippe de Vendôme, the centre of the free-thinking society of the day (late

17th and early 18th centuries), including many distinguished men of letters, Chaulieu, La Fare, Campistron, Palaprat, and the youthful Voltaire. A later *Grand-Prieur*, Louis-François de Bourbon, prince de Conti (1717–67), a distinguished soldier and a protector of J.-J. Rousseau, Beaumarchais, and Florian, also had a *salon* where the best society, including men eminent in art and literature, used to assemble and where the young Mozart played before a brilliant company. The Temple was declared national property in 1790, and at the downfall of the monarchy (August 1792) Louis XVI and his family were imprisoned in the tower. The buildings finally disappeared early in the 19th century, and were replaced on the site (1857) by municipal gardens, the *Square du Temple*.

Temple de Gnide, Le, a prose-poem by Montesquieu, published in 1725, purporting to be translated from a Greek work. The narrator describes the temple of Aphrodite at Cnidos and its frequenters, a terrifying visit to the cave of Jealousy, and the restoring effect of the temple of Bacchus.

Temple du Goût, Le, a short work of literary criticism by Voltaire, published in 1733. It takes the form of an allegory in prose and verse, in which the author describes a visit to the temple of the god of Taste, and with gay wit and acute judgement distributes praise and blame (mostly the latter) among the writers of his own age and of the preceding century. Not even the greatest names in French literature, Corneille and Racine, Molière and La Fontaine, Bossuet and Fénelon, are spared from his discriminating criticism. He touches incidentally on music, architecture, and sculpture.

Temps, Le

(i) A daily paper devoted to progress in politics, literature, science, and industry, founded in 1829. It was particularly active in the struggle for the liberty of the Press, at its height in that year. It failed in 1842 for lack of funds. Guizot (q.v.) was one of its first editors.

(ii) *Le Temps* of later renown was founded in 1861 by the political journalist Auguste Nefftzer (1820–76) and proposed to follow an enlightened, progressive path in politics without being attached to any one party. It was suppressed during the *Commune*

(1871, q.v.) but revived directly afterwards, and for long remained one of the foremost French newspapers, with a consistently high standard of criticism, literary, dramatic, and musical, and of general writing. Of all French papers it most nearly resembled *The Times*. [After June 1940 *Le Temps* was printed at Lyons but by the end of 1942 it had ceased to appear. After 1945 it was replaced on the same high level, and with the same layout, by *Le Monde*.]

Temps retrouvé, Le (1927), the seventh and concluding section of Proust's *A la recherche du temps perdu* (q.v.). The beginning, which purports to be a hitherto unpublished extract from the *Journal des Goncourt* (q.v.), is an excellent example of Proust's talent for *pastiche*.

Tencin, CLAUDINE-ALEXANDRINE GUÉRIN, MARQUISE DE (1685?–1749), a woman of intellect and letters but of an unpleasant character, 'cupide, rapace, intrigante' (Sainte-Beuve), who in her later years, after a discreditable youth, presided with good judgement over a *salon* much frequented by the intellectuals of the period (including Montesquieu, Fontenelle, and Marivaux, and also Prior and Bolingbroke). She was protected by Dubois (through whom her worthless brother was made cardinal). She was the mother of d'Alembert, whom she barbarously exposed shortly after his birth on the steps of a Paris church. She wrote three romances: *Mémoires du comte de Comminges* (1735), a work of some merit (two lovers after many ordeals find one another in a Trappist convent, recognizing each other by their public confession of their sins); *Le Siège de Calais* (1739), an indifferent historical novel in which the simple narrative of Froissart is tricked out with episodes of modern gallantry; and *Les Malheurs de l'amour* (1747), a tragic love-story distantly resembling *La Princesse de Clèves*.

Tençon, see *Jeux partis*.

Tendre, Carte de, see *Carte de Tendre*.

Tentation de saint Antoine, La (1874), by Flaubert (q.v.). The saint, in the desert, remembers former temptations and is beset by new ones, the lusts of the flesh and the senses, or the onslaught of philosophic doubt. The work, a form of dramatic poem in prose, is remarkable for its beauty of style and language, and its imaginative power. Mallarmé (q.v.) called it 'un idéal mêlant époques et races dans une prodigieuse fête, comme l'éclair de l'Orient expiré'. The idea had been with Flaubert since childhood. It took definite shape at Geneva in 1845 when he saw Breughel's picture of the Temptation of Saint Antony. In 1849 he read a first version to his friends Louis Bouilhet and Maxime Du Camp (qq.v.), who advised him to burn the manuscript and forget about it. He did put the manuscript away, but he worked on it again some years later (when fragments were published in *L'Artiste*, a review), and in 1872 he completed the version published in 1874.

Ternaire, in French prosody, a form of three-line stanza, on one rhyme, which the poet Auguste Brizeux (1803–55, q.v.) claimed to have been the first to employ.

Terre, La (1877), a novel of (non-idyllic) farming and peasant life by Zola, one of his *Rougon-Macquart* (q.v.) series. It is perhaps the most extreme example of *Naturalisme* (q.v.) as he practised it (cf. *Manifeste des cinq contre La Terre*).

Terre Sainte, Livre de la, a 13th-century translation of the *Historia rerum transmarinarum* of Guillaume, Archbishop of Tyre, relating the proceedings of the Christians in the Holy Land to 1184; to which were added the Chronicle of Ernoul (see *Crusades*) and various continuations to 1275. The work is also known as the *Livre du Conquest, Estoire d'outre-mer*, or *Livre d'Eracles* (from the name of the Emperor Heraclius, mentioned in the opening sentence of the chronicle).

Terreur, La, the reign of terror which began in 1793, after the fall of the *Girondins* (q.v.), with the passing of a law ordering the arrest of everyone suspected of disloyalty to the Revolution. It ended with the fall of Robespierre on 27 July 1794 (le 9 thermidor, An II). Suspects were tried, and almost invariably condemned, by the *Tribunal révolutionnaire*, and during the worst period, after the passing of the *loi du 22 prairial*, An II (10 June 1794), they were executed *en bloc* without trial. One of the first victims was Marie-Antoinette (16 Oct. 1793).

At the height of the Terror there were 1,376 executions in Paris alone in forty-nine days. For the whole period there were nearly 20,000 executions throughout the country.

Terreur blanche, La, a term sometimes used for the period (*c.* 1795) of severe anti-Revolutionary measures taken in the provinces during the *réaction thermidorienne* (q.v.). More often, perhaps, it refers to the period after the second Restoration (1815), when Royalists in the South exercised bloody reprisals on Revolutionary 'traitors'.

Terza rima, a poetic measure of Italian origin (used by Dante in the *Divina Commedia*), in which the lines are grouped in threes, the middle line of each group rhyming with the first and third lines of the succeeding groups (*a b a   b c b   c d c*, &c.). It is as old in French poetry as Jodelle (q.v.). It was used by poets of the 19th century, especially by Théophile Gautier (q.v.). The lines in French *terza rima* are usually *alexandrins* (q.v.). In Dante they were eleven-syllabled.

Testament, Grand and **Petit,** see *Villon.*

Teste, MONSIEUR, the monster of the intellect who 'ne connaît que deux valeurs . . . le possible et l'impossible', a character first created by Valéry (q.v.) in *La Soirée avec Monsieur Teste*, originally published in 1895 in *Le Centaure*, a review. Thirty years later three further fragments were added to the original work, namely *Lettre d'un ami* (to Monsieur Teste); *Lettre de Madame Émilie Teste* (describing what it is like to be the wife of a 'mystique sans Dieu'); and *Extraits du Log-book de Monsieur Teste.*

Tête d'or (1890), by Claudel (q.v.), a symbolist drama.

Thaïs (1890), by Anatole France, a novel of 4th-century Egypt, based on the tale, in the *Golden Legend*, of the courtesan who became a saint.

Paphnuce, a voluptuous young Alexandrian noble, is converted to Christianity and becomes a fierce ascetic, revered by disciples, in the desert of the Thebaid. Visions assail him, of Thaïs the beautiful actress and courtesan of former days. Are they temptations of the devil or a message from God? He returns to Alexandria to win Thaïs for eternal life. She is not unready to listen to him, for she has begun to dread losing her beauty and to question the satisfactions of her present existence. But she interrupts talk of conversion to attend a banquet, taking Paphnuce with her. He listens with incredulous horror to philosophical discussions; and both he and Thaïs are sickened by the orgies which follow. Thaïs now longs to seek joy in renunciation and sorrow. Paphnuce takes her to a convent in the desert, then returns to the Thebaid, to find himself still pursued by visions of Thaïs which no mortification will banish. Meantime Thaïs has become a saint but is dying of her self-imposed privations. On learning this Paphnuce realizes that desire and pride alone had governed his conduct towards her. He hastens to the convent to conjure Thaïs back from death to a world of life, love, and beauty. The horrified Abbess turns him away, and Thaïs dies, her eyes lit by a vision of the eternal morning.

Thaon or **Thaün**, PHILIPPE DE, see *Philippe de Thaon*.

Tharaud, Les Frères (JÉRÔME, 1874–1953, and JEAN, 1877–1952), novelists and essayists, always spoken of together (cf. *les frères* Goncourt) because of their close collaboration. For some time Jérôme was a fellow student with Péguy (q.v.) at the Collège Sainte-Barbe and the École normale supérieure (qq.v.), then he taught French at the University of Budapest, while Jean was secretary to Barrès (q.v.). Their novels and tales, distinguished by a sober, forcible style, usually have a background of topical interest such as English imperialism in the Transvaal (*Dingley, l'illustre écrivain*, 1902, in which the influence of Kipling is noticeable), French colonization in North Africa (*La Fête arabe*, 1911; *Rabat ou les Heures marocaines*, 1918), or the Jewish problem (*Quand Israël est roi*, 1920; *Un Royaume de Dieu*, 1920).

Theatre of the 19th and 20th centuries, The. [After about 1830 it becomes impracticable to consider the development of the French theatre by genres. For the earlier period see under *Tragedy*; *Comedy*; *Tragicomedy*; *Drama*; also *Comédie-Française*; *Mélodrame*; *Romantisme*; *Theatres and theatre-companies*; *Vaudeville*. See also under separate headings for the authors mentioned.]

(1) The two main influences on the French theatre during the first half of the 19th century were Scribe (q.v.), who began writing about 1815, and the Romantic drama, at its height between 1830 and 1840. Scribe's influence was on technique. He emphasized the importance of dramatic construction and the need to entertain an audience and to hold its attention. His comedies and vaudevilles (*Le Solliciteur, Une Chaîne, Bataille de dames*) had a certain incidental value as pictures, or satires, of contemporary society, but their interest and their importance as innovations lies in their complicated plot, artifice, and action. They were well suited to their audience, which often lacked cultural background but always thirsted for entertainment, being largely composed of the uneducated newly rich, or of provincials or foreigners on holiday in the capital.

(2) The second, and more lasting, influence, the Romantic, was on the aesthetics of the dramatic art. The Romantic theorists held that observance of the unities mattered little, that tragedy and comedy, the sublime and the grotesque, should be mixed on the stage as they were in real life; also that accuracy of historical setting was of great importance. The ultimate triumph of their theories—for all that the stage success of the Romantic drama ended with the failure of *Les Burgraves*, q.v., in 1843—was fatal to the survival of conventional tragedy. Over and above this it can be seen in retrospect to have led to the emergence of the modern, intimate, play or drama of contemporary life, very much the *drame bourgeois* suggested by Diderot (see *Drame*) which shows a small group of characters—individuals rather than types—reacting to a given situation or problem. As developed during the second half of the nineteenth century, this was nearer comedy than tragedy, but comedy in a serious, often moralizing, vein. It portrayed and satirized contemporary society with the faithful attention to detail prescribed by the Romantics (cf. also *Réalisme*, in the novel) and had no hesitation in changing from broad comedy to tragedy or near-tragedy. In its later phases it was often solely concerned to study the effect of passion on character, where the less subtle, less sophisticated Romantic drama had been content to glorify passion (e.g. *Antony*, by Dumas *père*).

(3) Early examples of the move towards the drama in this more restricted sense were the comedies, or dramatic comedies, of

Ponsard (*L'Honneur et l'argent*, *La Bourse*) and Augier (*Maître Guérin*, *Les Lionnes pauvres*). They owed their solid construction to Scribe, but did not continue Scribe's fault of sacrificing life to artifice. In tenor they were far from romantic, for their authors represented the *école du bon sens*, which reacted against the exaltations of the Romantic drama and extolled the domestic virtues. They were often attacks on contemporary failings, e.g. the materialistic outlook of the Second Empire. With Dumas *fils*, the leading dramatic author of the Second Empire, the new drama came into its own. His plays (e.g. *Le Demi-Monde*, *Les Idées de Mme Aubray*) turned on the problems and misfortunes of persons condemned by birth or character to an insecure footing in society. They were *pièces à thèse*, strong pleas for social reform, but he never lost sight of the importance of plot, dialogue, and the need to hold his audience. A feature of his dramatic construction imitated by later authors was the introduction of a character, usually a family friend or counsellor, who at the outset of the play expounded the situation to be treated. At the end of the century Brieux (with *Blanchette* and *Les Trois Filles de M. Dupont*) and Hervieu (with *Les Tenailles*) were still writing *pièces à thèse*.

(4) The theatre of the Second Empire and the early years of the Third Republic was also represented by the plays of Pailleron (*Le Monde où l'on s'ennuie*), Gondinet (*Les Braves Gens*), Feuillet (*Le Pour et le contre*), and Barrière (*Les Filles de marbre*), which ranged from light comedy of manners to drama; and by Sardou, who followed Scribe and made plot the prime factor whether he wrote vaudevilles, comedies, or historical plays. Vaudeville, and, still more, burlesque or farcical comedy, in which the characters are whirled riotously through a succession of ridiculous situations, also flourished. The supremely successful example in this genre was *Un Chapeau de paille d'Italie*, by Labiche. Meilhac and Halévy were good seconds with gay, frothy comedies, e.g. *La Petite Marquise*, of Parisian life. This pair of authors also wrote the sparkling libretti for Offenbach's operettas, a new and very successful mixture of vaudeville and comic opera. The delightful comedies and *proverbes* of Musset, not intended for stage production when written,

were a genre in themselves. Love, as with Marivaux, was their essential element (*On ne badine pas avec l'amour*, *Fantasio*, *Le Chandelier*), but their superficial gaiety concealed a passion and pathos unattempted by the earlier dramatist. *Lorenzaccio* (1834), also by Musset, is probably the nearest French approach to Shakespearian drama.

(5) A new point in development was reached between 1880 and 1890 when Henry Becque (*Les Corbeaux*, *La Parisienne*) and the productions of Antoine's experimental theatre (see *Théâtre Libre*) brought the naturalistic movement from the novel to the stage (see *Naturalisme*). Action, plot, and dramatic construction now became outmoded, their places being taken by the 'slice of life' type of play in which nothing happened. About the same time—again reflecting trends in the novel—an increasing element of psychological analysis became apparent and this, together with the influence of Ibsen, gave rise to the *théâtre d'idées*, or problem play, best exemplified by the plays of François de Curel (*Les Fossiles*, *Le Repas du lion*). In these we are presented, objectively, with a problem of conscience. Sometimes, though not always, a solution is found by the characters themselves: the author imposes no theories of his own. Plays by Georges de Porto-Riche were less ideological, and analysed passion and the feminine heart. So, also, in a lighter, wittier vein did those of Donnay (*Amants*), Lavedan (*Le Marquis de Priola*), and Abel Hermant (*L'Esbrouffe*). Passion, of a more violent or uneasy character, is again the theme of plays by Bataille and by a number of his 20th-century successors such as Bernstein, Bourdet, Lenormand; and these dramatists often bring the Freudian theories of the Unconscious to the stage.

(6) The Symbolist Movement in literature (see *Symbolisme*) reached the stage about the nineties and produced the romantic, symbolical, and allegorical dramas of Maeterlinck (*La Princesse Maleine*, *Pelléas et Mélisande*) and, some years later, the mystical dramas of Claudel (*L'Annonce faite à Marie*). During the same years a passing revival of enthusiasm for poetic drama owed much to the success of Rostand (*Cyrano de Bergerac*) and, in a lesser degree, of Jean Richepin (*Le Chemineau*). The type of witty, light, drawing-room comedy intro-

duced by Meilhac and Halévy during the Second Empire was continued during the Third Republic by G.-A. de Caillavet and Robert de Flers (*L'Habit vert*) and Alfred Capus (*La Petite Fonctionnaire*). The farcical and satirico-farcical sketches of military, bureaucratic, and domestic life by Courteline *Le Train de 8h. 47*; *Boubouroche*) were masterpieces of their kind. The traditions of farce and vaudeville were maintained by Tristan Bernard (*L'Anglais tel qu'on le parle*) and Georges Feydeau (*La Dame de chez Maxim's*, *Occupe-toi d'Amélie*). The grotesque farce of *Ubu Roi* by A. Jarry had an interest for a restricted, more literary public. A particularly interesting feature of the more recent theatre is the tendency to treat themes from ancient tragedy in the intimate, almost casual manner of modern drama, e.g. the *Électre* of Giraudoux (perhaps the outstanding French dramatist of the first half of the 20th century), the *Antigone* of Anouilh, or Sartre's *Les Mouches*. (For other 20th-century dramatists see: *Cocteau*; *Marcel*; *Mauriac*; *Montherlant*; *Obey*; *Pagnol*; *Romains*; *Vildrac*, &c.)

Théâtre de Clara Gazul, Le, the first work published (1825, anon.) by Prosper Mérimée (q.v.) and one of the successful hoaxes of French literature. It purported to be translations of six short plays by a Spanish actress 'Clara Gazul'. Her portrait (i.e. a faked portrait of the twenty-two-year-old Mérimée wearing a mantilla) formed the frontispiece. The plays owe much to Calderón, while their semi-burlesque, semi-sympathetic treatment of Romantic theories of the drama is typical of Mérimée's lifelong, somewhat dilettante attitude to literature.

A second, augmented, edition (1830) contained *Le Carrosse du Saint-Sacrement*, a one-act near-masterpiece of irony, kindred in theme to Maupassant's tale *La Maison Tellier.*

Théâtre de la foire, see *Foire, Théâtre de la*; also *Theatres and theatre companies.*

Théâtre de la Rose-Croix, Le, see *Péladan.*

Théâtre Libre, Le, a subscription theatre founded by Antoine (q.v.), opened in 1887 with a programme of four one-act plays by naturalistic writers (*Jacques Damour*, from

one of Zola's tales, by Léon Hennique; *Mademoiselle Pomme*, a farce by Duranty and Paul Alexis; *Le Sous-Préfet*, by Arthur Byl; and *La Cocarde*, by Jules Vidal). It lasted for ten years and specialized in naturalistic drama, i.e. plays bringing a slice of life to the stage, with plots simplified to vanishing-point. The slices of life were usually drab representations of unrewarded virtue and unpunished vice and were known as *comédie rosse*. The settings—scrupulously exact reproductions from real life instead of, as hitherto, conventionally decorative—heightened the naturalistic effect; and acting became much less artificial. The Théâtre Libre had to close in April 1896, partly because of financial difficulties but also because the public had tired of unrelieved naturalism. But its innovations in methods of play-writing, stage-production, and acting had made the venture a landmark in the evolution of the modern theatre and for many young dramatists it had been the first step on the road to success.

Theatres and theatre companies

(1) In the 16th century there was only one permanent theatre in Paris, that on the site of the Hôtel de Bourgogne (q.v.) owned by the *Confrérie de la Passion* (q.v.), but from 1578 leased to professional actors. There were, however, theatrical performances, those at the annual fairs of Saint-Germain and Saint-Laurent held outside the city, and the more irregular ones in various colleges and other premises. [For earlier dramatic representations see under *Mystères, Moralités, Sotties, Farces.*]

(2) From about 1606 the company of the Hôtel de Bourgogne, headed by Valleran Le Conte, assumed a fairly permanent character and was known as the *Comédiens du Roi*. It left Paris for a time in 1622, but returned to the Hôtel de Bourgogne in 1628. During its absence, in 1622, 1624, and 1626, a company of French actors known as the *Comédiens du Prince d'Orange* was at the Hôtel de Bourgogne; it was directed by Lenoir, with Montdory as its principal actor. In 1629 this company was at Rouen, where Montdory received *Mélite* from the young Corneille; the play was subsequently produced in Paris, where the company had hired premises (the Hôtel d'argent) and finally (1634) established themselves in the

Marais quarter as rivals to the company of the Hôtel de Bourgogne.

(3) In 1658 Molière brought his company from the provinces to Paris and founded the *Théâtre du Petit-Bourbon* near the Louvre. It was transferred to the Palais-Royal in 1661. After Molière's death in 1673, the king decided that there should be only two companies of actors in Paris, one, the *Comédiens du Roi*, at the Hôtel de Bourgogne, the other at the playhouse in the rue Mazarine, whither Molière's company had now removed. The best actors of the Marais theatre were combined with those of Molière's company to form the company of the Mazarine, known later as the *Compagnie de Guénégaud*, from the site of the theatre in the rue Guénégaud. In 1680 a further fusion took place, the *Comédiens du Roi* from the Hôtel de Bourgogne and the *Compagnie de Guénégaud* being formed into one, which has survived as the Comédie-Française (q.v.).

(4) The already long-established company of Italian actors (see *Italiens*) then moved to the Hôtel de Bourgogne. They had been authorized to act improvised plays in their own tongue; but with increasing frequency and audacity they introduced scenes in French into their farces. They were expelled in 1697 on the pretext of the immorality of their representations and returned only after the death of Louis XIV (1716). Boileau, referring to the poverty of French comedy at this time, said: 'il valait mieux chasser les Français'. Marivaux entrusted to these clever actors the best of his comedies. Strolling players at the fairs of Saint-Germain and Saint-Laurent also entered into competition with the Comédie-Française. They were known, generically, as the *Théâtre de la Foire* and proved irrepressible. Their comic dialogue was gradually developed and improved in character, and Lesage wrote many comedies for them. In 1762 a combination was brought about between the players of the *Foire* and the *Italiens*; the joint companies specialized in comic pieces interspersed with songs, at first sung to popular airs (*comédies en vaudevilles*), later sung to music specially composed (*comédies à ariettes*), gradually developing into true comic opera (see *Opéra-Comique*). Typical examples were the plays of Sedaine and Favart. But they also produced other types of play, alongside of the privileged Comédie-Française.

(5) Thus, by the outbreak of the Revolution there were two principal theatres in Paris, the Comédie-Française, established from 1782 on the site of the later *Odéon* (q.v.), and that of the joint company of the *Italiens* and the *Théâtre de la Foire*, for a time at the Hôtel de Bourgogne and from 1783 on the *boulevards*. There were also three or four minor playhouses.

(6) In the provinces, as late as the 17th century, there were no theatres, and the companies of actors that perambulated them had to make use of any premises available (as depicted in the *Roman comique*, q.v.). These provincial companies, however, played a part of considerable importance in the history of the French theatre. They included some good actors, such as Montdory, and noteworthy plays were written for them, for instance some of Hardy's, and the earlier comedies of Molière. In the middle of the 18th century theatres sprang up in many provincial towns, Rouen, Lyons, Amiens, Montpellier, &c. Arthur Young comments (26 Aug. 1787) on the splendour of the theatre at Bordeaux, and (21 Sept. 1788) finds the theatre at Nantes twice the size of Drury Lane.

(7) Benches for distinguished spectators were allowed on the stage of the Comédie-Française until 1759, when they were removed at the instance of the comte de Lauraguais, who paid 30,000 francs compensation to the Company. Seats were introduced in the *parterre* or pit in 1782. In the 17th century, at Molière's theatre in the Palais-Royal, the price of single places at ordinary performances ranged from 15 *sols* in the *parterre* to 5 *livres* 10 *sols* in the *premières loges* or on the stage.

(8) During the Revolution several new theatres were established. The Comédie-Française itself split into two factions but the original company was eventually reconstituted by the Government and after May 1799 occupied its present quarters in the rue Richelieu. Napoleon kept a firm hold over the theatres, limiting their numbers and dividing the Paris ones into first- and second-class theatres. The latter, the *théâtres du boulevard*, presented plays of a more popular character, mainly vaudevilles, melodrama, and, in time, the new forms of drama (see *Theatre of the 19th and 20th centuries*). A maximum of two theatres was permitted in

the larger provincial towns and one in the smaller. Until 1864 no new theatre could be established without previous sanction.

(9) The Paris theatres of the present day are, broadly speaking, of three types: 'les subventionnés', i.e. the official, or state-subsidized theatres, namely, the *Comédie-Française* (*salle Richelieu*) and the *Comédie-Française* (*salle Luxembourg*), the *Opéra*, and the *Opéra-Comique*; the *théâtres du boulevard*; and a small number of *théâtres d'avant-garde*. The repertory of the first is mainly classical, with occasional, and increasingly frequent, excursions into modernity. The second type still caters for a wider public, and its productions are largely governed by the need for commercial success and the fact that the plays selected must contain star parts. The *théâtres d'avant-garde*, experimental theatres, encourage new dramatists and new forms of dramatic art and production. They are often sponsored by actor-producers, and may be said to have originated in 1887 with Antoine's *Théâtre Libre* (q.v.), which had successors in the *Théâtre de l'Œuvre*, the *Théâtre du Vieux-Colombier*, the *Théâtre de l'Atelier*, the *Théâtre de l'Athénée*, &c. (qq.v.).

Thébaïde, La, or **Les Frères ennemis,** a tragedy by Racine, produced in 1664 by Molière's company; this was Racine's first play. The theme is the conflict of the brothers Eteocles and Polynices for the throne of Thebes. Polynices is besieging Eteocles in the city. Jocasta, their mother, and Antigone, their sister, try in vain to reconcile them. Creon, brother of Jocasta, desiring to obtain the throne for himself, excites his nephews to their mutual destruction. The two brothers meet and fight. Haemon, son of Creon and lover of Antigone, tries to separate them and is killed, and the brothers slay each other. Jocasta has already taken her own life. Creon inheriting the throne proposes to marry his niece Antigone; she replies by killing herself. Creon, in remorse for his crime, also takes his own life.

Thèbes, Roman de, see *Roman de Thèbes.*

Thé chez Miranda, Le (1886), by Paul Adam and Jean Moréas (qq.v.), a novel sometimes remembered as a typical product of the early Symbolist era. The character Jacques Plowert gave Paul Adam his pseudo-nym for his *Petit Glossaire pour . . . l'intelligence des auteurs symbolistes.*

Thélème, Abbaye de, see *Gargantua.*

Théocrates, a politico-religious, ultra-Royalist party of the Restoration period (i.e. post-1815; and cf. *Ballanche*; *Bonald*; *J. de Maistre*). Their main thesis was that the social hierarchy, with its irregularities, was of Divine origin, therefore any attempt to limit the power or direct the actions of the monarch—God's representative—by man-made constitution was contrary to Nature. Further, restoration of the Monarchy entailed restoration of monarchical institutions, with consequent reversal of much Revolutionary legislation.

Another of this party's theories, that a Christian and Royalist literature could help to re-educate the people, helped to stimulate the interest noticeable at this period in chivalry and the Middle Ages—and thus contributed to the initially Royalist complexion of the Romantic Movement (see *Romantisme*).

Théodore, a tragedy by Corneille, produced in 1645, unsuccessfully.

The scene is Antioch. The Roman governor, Valens, a contemptible creature, has married the wicked Marcelle, a widow, mother of Flavie. Disappointed in her hope of marrying Flavie to Placide, her stepson, because the latter loves Théodore, a princess of the old race of Syrian kings and a Christian, Marcelle and Valens decide to condemn Théodore to prostitution and thus to ruin her in Placide's esteem. Théodore is rescued from her threatened fate by another lover, Didyme, a Christian, who secures her escape by changing clothes with her and taking her place; Didyme thus arouses the jealousy of Placide. Théodore surrenders herself and a conflict of generosity follows between her and Didyme. Finally Marcelle with her own hand kills them both, and Placide takes his own life.

Théophilanthropie, a rationalist movement which took its principles of the necessity of a belief in God for the conduct of life partly from Voltaire, partly from Rousseau, and, apparently, partly from freemasonry. It developed during the Directoire and numbered several scholars, politicians, and writers (e.g. Bernardin de Saint-Pierre, M.-J. Chénier) among its adherents. The weekly meetings for purposes of moral reading and the singing of specially composed hymns were attended by *théophilanthropistes* dressed in robes which symbolized the national colours. The movement petered out after 1801, when Roman Catholicism was re-established as the national religion of France.

Théophile, Miracle de, see *Rutebeuf.*

Théophile de Viau (1590–1626), generally referred to as *Théophile,* poet, born at Clairac in Guyenne, produced in 1617 the tragedy (with elements of pastoral and tragicomedy, printed 1623) *Pyrame et Thisbé,* which was very successful in spite of affectation and artificiality. In 1619 he was banished as a Huguenot and a free-thinker. He was pardoned in 1621, the year in which his *Œuvres* were first published (containing a free translation of the *Phaedo, Traicté de l'immortalité de l'âme ou la Mort de Socrate,* and his *œuvres poétiques*), but in 1623, after the republication under his name of *Le Parnasse satyrique* (q.v.), he was held responsible for the worst obscenities in that collection of licentious verse, was accused of being the leader of the free-thinkers, and was imprisoned and again banished.

Théophile opposed the strict doctrine of Malherbe in the matter of style: 'J'approuve que chacun écrive à sa façon.' His own work was often negligent and consequently unequal, and in general he wasted his talent. At his best, in such odes as *Le Matin* and *La Solitude,* and in spite of preciosities which led Boileau to condemn his affectation and insincerity, he showed a fine sense of beauty and an eye for, and love of, nature. The note of originality in *Le Corbeau* is strikingly modern, and the bitter sonnet *Ton orgueil peut durer* also calls for mention.

Théramène, in Racine's *Phèdre* (q.v.), the tutor and confidant of Hippolyte. The *Récit de Théramène* is the famous passage in this tragedy in which Théramène, who had accompanied Hippolyte on his doomed journey, returns and tells Theseus how his son died.

Thérèse Aubert (1819), by Charles Nodier (q.v.), a novel of unhappy love and the risings in the Vendée (q.v.). Sainte-Beuve's *Joseph Delorme* (q.v.) nourished his melancholy imagination on it.

Thérèse Desqueyroux (1927), a novel by François Mauriac. The heroine's marriage has been one of reason, arranged by wealthy landowning parents on both sides. But she is young and intelligent, stifled by life with a loutish husband, among unsympathetic relations. When suddenly an opportunity presents itself she yields to temptation and sets to work to poison her husband gradually, with arsenic. She is discovered, but the family conspire to prevent scandal and she is not committed for trial. After this she breaks away from a state of virtual imprisonment in her husband's home, persecuted and separated from her child, and goes to live in Paris. Her complex character, her longing for affection and understanding, her subtle attractiveness, her equally mysterious power of wreaking havoc in other people's lives, and her feeble attempts to refrain from doing so, are drawn with great sympathy by the author. *La Fin de la nuit* (1935) describes her last spiritual struggles and her mental and physical decay. She also figures in a chapter of *Ce qui était perdu* (1930) and in two of the stories collected in *Plongées* (1938).

Thérèse Raquin (1867), a novel by Émile Zola, a powerful psychological study written before he began his *Rougon-Macquart* series (q.v.). Thérèse Raquin and her lover Laurent murder her husband Camille, a weakling, and after an interval get married. Even before marrying they have each been a prey to nervous terrors, haunted by visions of Camille. They hope these will disappear when once they are together, but on the contrary their terrors increase. The corpse seems to be with them whenever they are alone, and what had been an overmastering passion, not stopping at crime, turns to loathing. To make matters worse, their scenes of terror and hate are enacted under the eyes of Camille's paralysed old mother, who thus comes to realize what had happened but is physically incapable of passing on her knowledge. In the end Thérèse and Laurent kill themselves; and the old woman sits, watching. (See *Taine,* para. 6.)

Thermidor, the eleventh month of the Republican Calendar (q.v.). It ran from 20 July to 18 August (see *Journée du 9 thermidor*).

Théroigne de Méricourt (1762–1817), a

Revolutionary heroine about whom many stories have collected. She was born in Belgium (at that time the Austrian Netherlands), and in 1785 she came to Paris with an elderly, not her first, protector. There her Revolutionary sympathies were soon awakened. At one time (*c.* 1790) she had a political *salon*. At another she was a leader of the people and tried to raise a women's army. She was particularly fierce and vindictive at the time of the fall of the Monarchy (1792). Later, in 1793, her extremism and her popularity waned rapidly and on one occasion she was set upon by women of the Jacobin party and whipped. Her reason failed and during her later years she was confined in the Salpêtrière (q.v.), where she died. She is said to have been beautiful. She was known variously as 'la belle Liégeoise' and 'l'Amazone de la Liberté'. Her real name was Anne-Josèphe Terwagne. She is the subject of a drama *Théroigne de Méricourt* (1902), by Paul Hervieu (q.v.).

Thésée. (1) a lyrical tragedy in five acts by Quinault with music by Lulli (qq.v.). It was produced for the first time in 1675 before Louis XIV at Saint-Germain-en-Laye; (2) a *récit* by André Gide (q.v.), published in 1946.

Thésée, see *Phèdre*.

Theuriet, Claude-Adhémar-André (1833–1907), a popular 19th-century novelist, especially when he wrote of country and small-town provincial life. His large output includes, notably, *Raymonde* (1877) and *Sauvageonne* (1880); also *Le Mariage de Gérard* (1875), *La Maison des deux Barbeaux* (1879), *Toute seule* (1880), &c. Some of these were dramatized. In earlier life he counted among the minor Parnassian poets (*Le Chemin des bois*, 1867; *Le Livre de la payse*, 1883, &c.).

Thibaud or **Thibaut de Champagne** (1201–53), poet, comte de Champagne and king of Navarre (1234–53), a man of varied activities, who took part in the crusade against the Albigenses. He is said to have loved the regent Blanche de Castille, who inspired some of his songs. He was a patron of men of letters and wrote poems of courtly love after the manner of the troubadours of Provence (see *Lyric poetry*); among these poems were *jeux partis* (q.v.).

Thibaud de Vernon, see *Alexis, Vie de saint*.

Thibaudet, ALBERT (1874–1936), born at Tournus (Saône-et-Loire), one of the foremost literary critics of the first half of the 20th century. He became prominent with *La Poésie de Stéphane Mallarmé* (1912 and, with additions and alterations, 1926). Studies of other authors followed, e.g. *Flaubert* (1922; 1935); *Paul Valéry* (1923); *Intérieurs: Baudelaire, Fromentin, Amiel* (1924); *Triptyque de la poésie moderne: Verlaine, Rimbaud, Mallarmé* (1924); *Stendhal* (1931). Latterly he was Professor of French Literature at the University of Geneva. His interesting but uncompleted *Histoire de la littérature française de 1789 à nos jours*, published posthumously (1936), groups authors by generations (1789; 1820; 1850; 1885; 1914–18) rather than—the more usual method—by epochs and literary affiliations. His other works, for the most part essays and reviews contributed in the first place to the *Nouvelle Revue Française*, can be found in *Réflexions sur la littérature, . . . le roman, . . . la critique* (1938–41).

Thibault, Les (1922–40), by Roger Martin du Gard (q.v.), one of the outstanding *romans-cycles* of 20th-century French fiction (cf. *Jean-Christophe*; *Les Hommes de bonne volonté*). It is in seven parts: *Le Cahier gris* (1922); *Le Pénitencier* (1922); *La Belle Saison* (1923); *La Consultation* (1928); *La Sorellina* (1928); *La Mort du père* (1929); *L'Été 1914* (1936); with an *Épilogue* (1940). We meet the brothers Antoine and Jacques Thibault, whose lives the book follows, when Antoine is a medical student and Jacques a schoolboy. They are motherless, and dominated, as is the book, till he dies, by their father, a zealous Roman Catholic sociologist and moral reformer, of pharisaic character. According to their temperaments they accept their prosperous middle-class environment and heritage, or rebel against it. Antoine becomes absorbed by his profession, yielding occasionally to affairs of the heart, but adhering to a strict, unquestioning conception of duty which simplifies the conduct of his life: he both faces responsibility (e.g. for his brother) and accepts the need for sacrifice (e.g. of his own interests to the demands of war and patriotism). He is gassed in 1917 and dies in November 1918.

Jacques is a misfit from the beginning, and all the more so after being confined in one

of the father's pet institutions, a peniten-
tiary for better-class young delinquents. He
has barely completed his university studies
when he decamps from home, to be discovered some years later by Antoine in
Switzerland leading a life of his own
choosing. He writes, and he is involved in
international socialist politics. The latter, and
his father's illness, bring him back to Paris
in the summer of 1914. The international
situation becomes daily more volcanic; in
his personal life he is once more beset by
hates and complexes; and he yields again to
his love for the sister of an old schoolfellow.
When war comes he refuses to fight and
manages to return to Switzerland. He undertakes to fly over the battlefields dropping
pacifist leaflets. He is shot down and captured, and his death is expedited by a
cowardly stretcher-bearer.

Other characters, and the contrast between
Catholic and Protestant milieux, play their
part, but on the whole the novel stands, or
falls, as a strictly objective and impersonal
narrative. It is unsparingly realistic, in the
19th-century manner, though the technique
is more modern in that before describing
events themselves the author shows their
effects and repercussions. The description of
the summer of 1914 in Paris, of the days
before mobilization, of the assassination of
Jaurès (q.v.), and, later, of the scenes on the
battlefield, approximate to social history: the
episodes of Antoine's professional career;
or his day-to-day record of his own painful
break-up until the moment comes to end
his life; or the merciless description (filling
nearly a whole volume) of M. Thibault's
lingering death from uraemia, resemble the
case-histories in medical textbooks.

Thibault, JACQUES-ANATOLE-FRANÇOIS, see
France, Anatole.

Thierry, AMÉDÉE (1797–1873), historian,
brother of the following, born at Blois.
In *L'Histoire des Gaulois jusqu'à la domination
romaine* (1828), his chief work, he studied the
Gauls as a nomad people; their development
wherever they settled; their conquest and
assimilation by the Romans, and the emergence of a new civilization.

Thierry, AUGUSTIN (1795–1856), historian,
born at Blois, educated there and in Paris.

He did much to stimulate the early 19th-
century enthusiasm for historical studies,
and to extend their scope by basing them
more thoroughly on contemporary documents, by going farther back in time, and by
devoting more attention to the part played
by the common people. He himself wrote
vivid, picturesque narrative, enlivened by
anecdote and local colour. (In the light of
later knowledge he was criticized for providing an insufficient basis of fact or for using
his sources indiscriminately.) He came to
history by way of scientific studies, of *Saint-
Simonisme* (q.v.), and of political, which
turned to historical, journalism (in *Le Censeur européen* from 1817 to 1820 and *Le Courrier de France* from 1820 to 1821). His two
most celebrated works were, *L'Histoire de la
conquête de l'Angleterre par les Normands*
(1825), a study of the Anglo-Saxon spirit of
liberty surviving invasion and emerging in
the system of parliamentary government,
and *Récits des temps mérovingiens*, a vivid
retelling of stories from the Chronicle of
Gregory of Tours, preceded by *Considérations sur l'histoire de France* (1840). This work
was published ten years after Thierry had
become totally blind and dependent on his
wife and secretaries for help in his researches.
Dix ans d'études historiques (1834), another
work, contains his journalistic writings and
has an interesting, in part autobiographical,
preface.

Thiers, ADOLPHE (1797–1877), statesman
and historian, born at Marseilles, educated
there and at Aix-en-Provence, came to
Paris (with Mignet, q.v.) in 1821 and soon
made a name as a political journalist and a
historian. Between 1823 and 1827 he published the first of his two famous works,
Histoire de la Révolution française. After the
July Revolution (1830) which, as one of the
founders of the newspaper *Le National*
(q.v.), he helped to bring about, he was one
of several historians in the Government. In
1840 he went into opposition over foreign
policy, retired, and wrote his second great
work, *Histoire du consulat et de l'empire*
(1845–62). He returned to active (republican
and anti-Imperialist) politics in 1863, led the
peace negotiations in 1871 (see *Franco-
Prussian War*), took a major share in planning economic and military reconstruction,
and was first President of the Third Republic.

His two works, models of clear-flowing narrative, are among the standard histories of the Revolutionary and immediately post-Revolutionary eras. He had a remarkable gift of clear exposition, particularly of financial and military situations.

Thomas, author of a 12th-century poem on Tristan (q.v.).

Thomas, ANDRÉ-ANTOINE, see *Dictionaries and encyclopedias*, under date 1890–1900.

Thomas, ANTOINE-LÉONARD (1732–85), miscellaneous writer of the *philosophe* school, author of odes of little merit, and of *Éloges*, academic discourses in praise of great men, such as Sully, Duguay-Trouin, and Descartes, in a style of pompous eloquence; also of an *Essai sur le caractère . . . des femmes dans les différents siècles* (1772). Thomas was a member of the *Académie*.

Thomas Aquinas, SAINT **(saint Thomas d'Aquin)** (1227–74) the greatest of medieval philosophers and theologians, was born in Italy, near Aquino, at the Castle of Rocca Secca. He was educated at Monte Cassino and Naples, then, after entering the Dominican Order, at Cologne under Albertus Magnus. He followed his master to Paris and there, while still below the prescribed age, was himself admitted to teach. He was on his way to the oecumenical council of 1274 at Lyons when he died. He was canonized in 1323 and declared a Doctor of the Church in 1567. His followers were known as *Thomists*.
    St. Thomas Aquinas 'represents in his writings, and notably in his *Summa Totius Theologiae*, the culmination of scholastic philosophy, the harmony of faith and reason' (HARVEY, *Comp. to Eng. Lit.*). In 1879, by the Papal Bull 'Aeterni Patris' of Leo XIII, Thomism (since then frequently termed *Neo-Thomism*) was adopted as the official philosophy of the Roman Catholic Church, one which reconciles philosophical speculation with belief in the Divine origin of the universe. (Cf. Gilson, Maritain.)

Thomas Becket, Vie de saint, a poem in monorhyme stanzas of five alexandrines, completed in 1174, by Garnier or Guernes de Pont-Sainte-Maxence, a wandering scholar. The author draws the facts of the life and death of Thomas à Becket mainly from two Latin lives of the saint, but he visited Canterbury in order to supplement and reconcile the information given by these. The poem shows great vigour and literary skill, as well as the enthusiastic devotion of the author to his subject. It is recorded that he frequently read his poem to the pilgrims assembled at the shrine of the saint.

Thomas l'imposteur (1927), a novel by Jean Cocteau (q.v.).

Thomisme, see *Thomas Aquinas, Saint.*

Thou, FRANÇOIS-AUGUSTE (1607–42), son of the following, was executed for complicity in the conspiracy of Cinq-Mars (q.v.).

Thou, JACQUES-AUGUSTE DE (1553–1617), historian, a magistrate, director of the royal library from 1593, author of a Latin *Historia sui temporis* (the period 1543–1607), published in five parts and 138 volumes between 1604 and 1620. The 5th part was completed by other hands. In it he showed a scrupulous justice and tolerance in his appreciation of the Reformation Movement and of the wars of religion which brought him into disfavour with Rome. The whole work was translated into French in 1734 (*Histoire de mon temps*). Parts had been translated earlier, e.g. the first fifty books by Du Ryer in 1659.

Thunder-ten-tronckh, the name of the Westphalian baron in Voltaire's *Candide* (q.v.).

Thyard, PONTUS DE, see *Tyard.*

Tiberge, in Prévost's *Manon Lescaut,* the faithful friend of des Grieux, a contrast to him in character, sensible and self-controlled.

Tibert, the cat in the *Roman de Renart* (q.v.).

Tiercelin, the rook in the *Roman de Renart* (q.v.).

Tiers État, the Third Estate of the realm in pre-Revolutionary France, the Commons who, in contra-distinction to the other two Estates (the clergy and the nobility, *les Privilégiés*, q.v.), had to sustain the main burden of taxation. At the États Généraux (q.v.) of 1789 the representatives of the clergy and the nobility were directly elected, while those of the Tiers État were elected at second remove by *ad hoc* electoral assemblies nominated by the middle- and lower-class voters. Regulations of January 1789 governing the composition of the États Généraux introduced the principle of double representation, i.e. two representatives of the Tiers État to one each of the other two Estates.

Tillemont (pron. *ll* as in *fille*), SÉBASTIEN, *known as* Le Nain de (1637–98), a learned French historian, a Jansenist, author of *Mémoires pour servir à l'histoire des six premiers siècles de l'Église* (1693–1712), a work praised by Gibbon for its accuracy, and of *Histoire des empereurs et des autres princes qui ont régné pendant les six premiers siècles de l'Église* (1690–1738). His secretary Tronchai has left *La Vie et l'esprit de M. de Tillemont*. He added Tillemont to his name from a small property which he owned and where ultimately he lived.

Tillier, CLAUDE (1801–44), journalist, pamphleteer, and novelist, spent much of his life at Nevers (in Nivernais, his native province), where he edited a daily paper. His pamphlets, mainly on politics and religion, and collected in *Œuvres* (1846), were written with vigour and irony. Among his novels the good-humouredly satirical *Mon oncle Benjamin* (1843) is still remembered.

Tilsit [E. Prussia], **Treaty of** (8 July 1807), between France, Russia, and Prussia. This followed the battles of Jena and Friedland (qq.v.) and marked the break-up of the Fourth Coalition (q.v.). The peace established was at the expense of Prussia. France and Russia formed a military alliance against Britain, the document being signed by Napoleon and the Tsar Alexander I after meetings held on a raft in the river Niemen.

Timocrate, see *Corneille, Thomas.*

Timon le misanthrope, see *Cormenin, vicomte de.*

Tinan, JEAN DE (1875–99), a minor figure of the Symbolist Movement. His *Document sur l'impuissance d'aimer* (1894), a piece of introspective writing, is sometimes mentioned. *Penses-tu réussir* (1897), *Aimienne* (1898) were exaggeratedly Symbolist novels (see *Symbolisme*).

Tiraqueau, ANDRÉ (*c.* 1480–1558), jurist, a man of vast learning, sometimes called the Varro of his century, came from Bordeaux to Paris in 1541 and was entrusted with important missions by François Ier and Henri II. He wrote treatises (in Latin) on civil law.

Tiron, Abbé de, see *Desportes.*

Tite et Bérénice, a tragedy by Corneille produced in 1670. The story is said to be untrue that the duchesse d'Orléans contrived for Corneille and Racine to work simultaneously on the same subject, each unaware of what the other was doing. Racine's play *Bérénice* (q.v.) was considered superior to that of Corneille.

Titus, who has just ascended the throne, is about to marry Domitia, daughter of Nero's general Corbulo. The unexpected arrival in Rome of Berenice, queen of Judaea, revives the ardent love of Titus for her and places him in great embarrassment. The situation is complicated by the fact that Domitia loves Titus's brother Domitian, and is loved by him. Finally Bérénice, recognizing that her marriage with Titus would endanger his position, decides to renounce her hopes and leave him. Titus on the other hand surrenders Domitia to his brother.

Tixier de Ravisi, known also as *Ravisius Textor* (15th–16th c.), of Nevers, professor at the Collège de Navarre (1500–24) and rector of the University of Paris, author of Latin dramatic dialogues (moralities and farces).

Toast funèbre (1873), a poem contributed by Mallarmé to a memorial volume, *Le Tombeau de Théophile Gautier*, published in 1873 on the first anniversary of Gautier's death (cf. *Tombeau d'Edgar Poë, Le*). Other contributors included Coppée, Heredia, Leconte de Lisle (qq.v.).

Tocqueville, ALEXIS-HENRI-CHARLES-MAURICE CLÉREL, COMTE DE (1805–59), an historian of enduring reputation, was born at Verneuil (Normandy) and educated at Metz, where his father was prefect, and in Paris. He studied law, and from 1830 to 1835 filled a post in the judicature at Versailles. After 1835 he lived on his private means, was politically active from 1839 (Deputy, and for some time Foreign Minister), then, following the *coup d'état* of 1851, left France, lived in Italy and Germany, and devoted himself wholly to writing.

His appointment at Versailles had been interrupted for a year in 1831 when he went on an official mission to the U.S.A. (with M. Beaumont de la Bonninière, q.v.) to study and report on the penal system (*Du système pénitentiaire aux États-Unis et de son application en France*, 1832, in collaboration). He had been impressed, in America, by the success with which the principles of liberty and equality evolved in the Old World had been applied to meet the needs of a new civilization governed by different ideals and different physical conditions. Soon after his return to France he set down his observations on the American people and the American political scene in *La Démocratie en Amérique*, first of two famous works. It is in two parts (1835 and 1840). His conclusions were that the trend of history was irresistibly towards equality; and that the future of France, indeed of the Western world, was bound up with the acceptance of democratic principles, these being the one effective means of avoiding submission to tyranny.

Tocqueville had always considered that the French Revolution, contrary to the view generally accepted of a violent social upheaval constituting a complete break with the past, had in fact demonstrated the continuity of history. Although its aims in the first place had been both equality and liberty (i.e. political freedom), the second aim had been dropped, leaving the people a prey for a government much stronger than the one they had abolished; and the administrative principles put into effect in 1800 were in the event those of the monarchy the Revolution had destroyed. He had hoped to write a work on these lines, in three sections: *l'ancien régime*; a history of the events of the Revolution itself; and a life of Napoleon. *L'Ancien Régime* (1856), the only section to be completed, and the author's second great work, was based upon long research into official and municipal records. It studies the social and political fabric of pre-Revolutionary France and seeks to explain why the Revolution broke out in France rather than any other European country, how it proceeded from the very society it wished to destroy, and why the collapse of the monarchy was so sudden and so complete.

Tocqueville's *Souvenirs* (1893) of the period 1848-9 contain good descriptions of the February Revolution and the *journées de juin* (qq.v.). Much of his correspondence (ed. at various dates, posthumously) is with English friends, notably Henry Reeve of *The Times*, John Stuart Mill, and Mrs. Grote, wife of the historian.

Toepffer, RODOLPHE (1799–1846), born at Geneva, a Swiss artist and man of letters who wrote in French. In *Voyages en zig-zag* (1844) he described, and himself illustrated, wanderings in Switzerland. *La Bibliothèque de mon oncle* (1832–4) and *Nouvelles genevoises* (1840) are collections of short stories. He was praised by Sainte-Beuve.

Toison d'or, Ordre de la, the order of the Golden Fleece, an order of knighthood founded in 1429 by Philippe le Bon, Duke of Burgundy. It became the principal order of knighthood of Austria and Spain. The origin of the Golden Fleece is the Greek myth of the Argonauts.

Tolérance, Traité sur la, a treatise by Voltaire on religious toleration, written at the time of the author's campaign for the vindication of Calas (see under *Voltaire*) and issued from Geneva in 1763.

In it the author claims that religious intolerance was unknown to the ancient civilizations, that it was not taught by Jesus Christ, and that it was condemned by some of the Fathers. He attributes the monopoly of religious fanaticism to the Catholics and especially the Jesuits.

Tombeau d'Edgar Poë, Le, a famous sonnet by Mallarmé ('Tel qu'en Lui-même enfin l'éternité le change'). It was first printed in *Edgar Allan Poe, A memorial volume*, published at Baltimore in 1876, the year after a monument had been erected on Poe's grave. (The date of the definitive version is 1887.) Mallarmé, like Baudelaire before him and Valéry after, rated Poe and his aesthetic theories very highly and he translated some of his poems.

Two other *in memoriam* poems by Mallarmé may be noted here: the sonnet 'Le temple enseveli divulgue par la bouche', contributed to a volume entitled *Le Tombeau de Charles Baudelaire*, published by subscription in 1895, and *Tombeau* ('Le noir roc courroucé que la bise le roule'), published in January 1897 for the first anniversary of the poet Verlaine's death. This is said to be the last sonnet Mallarmé wrote. (See also *Toast funèbre*.)

Tombeur de Notre-Dame, see *Religious Writings*, para. 1.

Topaze (1928), a satirical comedy by Marcel Pagnol (q.v.). A master in a seedy private school is dismissed for being too honest about his pupils' progress when a few sycophantic lies would be better policy. He finds employment as unwitting stooge to a local big-business crook and when in the end even his eyes are opened he masters his new job so thoroughly that he outwits his employer.

Torelli, GIACOMO, see *Andromède*.

Torquet, ANTOINE, see *Nau, John-Antoine*.

Tortillard, Le, a character in Eugène Sue's (q.v.) *Les Mystères de Paris*.

Tory, GEOFFROY (b. *c.* 1480), grammarian and king's printer. He developed typography and was the author of several translations of Greek authors; also of *Champfleury* (1529), in which he encouraged the practice of writing learned works in French and the improvement of the language, protesting, in anticipation of Rabelais, against its excessive latinization.

Tosca (1887), a play by Sardou (q.v.). Puccini's opera *Tosca* (1903) is based on it.

Totalisme, see *Literary Isms*.

Toulet, PAUL-JEAN (1867–1920), journalist, poet, and novelist, was born at Pau, of Creole origin (his parents, though French by ancestry, belonged to Mauritius). After some years' travel he settled (*c.* 1898) in Paris. There he made a name as a brilliant conversationalist and as the author of novels and tales (usually written first for *La Vie parisienne*) which, like his talk, were witty, libertine, cynical, and sometimes savagely ironical. The best-remembered are: *Monsieur du Paur, homme public* (1898), *Le Mariage de Don Quichotte* (1901), *Tendres Ménages* (1904), *Mon Amie Nane* (1905), *La Jeune Fille verte* (1920), and the *Contes de Béhanzigue* (1921, posth.).

His more enduring reputation rests on the highly-polished verses of *Les Contrerimes* (1921, posth.). In these, emotion has been crystallized in tranquillity and the irony is alternately sharpened or softened by fantasy. (The title refers to the unusual stanzaic form 8a 6b 8b 6a.)

Toulouse, Floral Games of, see *Jeux floraux*.

Toulouse-Lautrec, HENRY - MARIE - RAY -

MOND DE (1864–1901), French painter and lithographer, notably of scenes of circus and music-hall life. He came from Albi, near Toulouse, where there is a fine permanent collection of his work.

Tour de Nesle, La (1832), by Dumas *père*, an historical drama of medieval times and crimes. Every night the turret windows of the Hôtel de Nesle (a 13th-c. fortified tower and residence in Paris, see *Nesle, Tour de* and *Hôtel de*) are lit for revelry: every morning three corpses lie at the foot of the tower, victims of the secret debauches of the queen (Marguerite of Burgundy, d. 1315) and her two sisters-in-law. One victim is Gaultier d'Aulnay, brother of the queen's favourite. Another, who escapes, is Buridan, a soldier of fortune. Buridan reveals himself to the queen as her girlhood's lover and the father of the two sons she abandoned at birth. He gets himself appointed chief Minister, and plots to have the queen surprised in her tower with her favourite, the elder d'Aulnay. At the last moment he discovers that the supposedly dead children (rescued, and now arrived at manhood) of his youthful love-affair with the queen are none other than the brothers d'Aulnay. He rushes to forestall his own son at the meeting-place and perishes in his stead. (Cf. *Beauvoir, Roger de.*)

Tour du monde en quatre-vingts jours, Le (1873), see *Verne, Jules*.

Tour Eiffel, La, one of the famous sights of Paris, if not of the world, and now also one of the world's most powerful radio-transmitting stations, is a gaunt, lattice-work iron structure, erected (1887–9) in the Champ-de-Mars to the design of the engineer Gustave Eiffel (1832–1923) for the Exhibition of 1889. It tapers upwards to a height of 300 metres (984 ft.). The apex is crowned by a lantern. The topmost of three platforms which intersect the structure is within a short distance of the apex and is reached by lift.

This intrinsically hideous erection provoked much dismay and ridicule in its early days, but it is now an inseparable part of the Paris landscape and possesses a beauty of familiarity which defies aesthetic standards. The exile returns to it with affection. The tourist who reaches the highest platform can, if he have but eyes, see spread out below him two thousand years of history, art, and literature, of passion, politics and ambition, of strife, glory, disaster and renewal.

Tournachon, FÉLIX, see *Nadar*.

Tournelle, La, see *Parlement*.

Tournelles, Hôtel des, see *Hôtel des Tournelles*.

Toussaint-Louverture (1743–1803), negro statesman. In 1791 the present-day republic of Santo Domingo (the eastern half of the West Indian island of which Haiti forms the other half) was a French possession (San Domingo) with a population of whites, mulattoes (free, but without civic rights), and negro slaves. When the negroes were freed by the Constitution of 1791 the mulattoes were given the privileges of French citizens, but conflicts between the white and the coloured population led to the decree being revoked. A successful revolt of negroes and mulattoes against whites was headed by Toussaint-Louverture, and by 1801, after some years of turmoil, his remarkably intelligent administration had brought order and prosperity to the whole island (the French title having meanwhile been extended to cover Haiti, the other half). He asked for Bonaparte's approval of a form of constitutional government for the island as a French colony, with himself as Governor. Far from consenting, Bonaparte sent a military expedition under General Leclerc, first husband of Pauline Bonaparte (see *Bonaparte family*), to subdue the island and reinstitute slavery. After months of fierce resistance the negroes came to terms. Toussaint-Louverture laid down his arms but was captured by a trick and deported to France (June 1802). He was imprisoned in the Fort de Joux (Jura) and died, ten months later, of consumption. Wordsworth's sonnet *Toussaint, the most unhappy of men* was written in 1803.

[The negroes renewed the struggle ferociously, and in 1803 such remnants of the French expedition as had survived massacre, dirt, and disease evacuated San Domingo. General Leclerc himself had died of yellow fever. In 1804 the island declared its independence, reverting to the name of Haiti. Vicissitudes in later years led once more to a split between the Western (Haiti) and eastern (Santo Domingo) halves and the Independent Republic of Santo Domingo came into being in 1844.]

Toutain, CHARLES (16th c.), remembered as the author of an early tragedy *Agamemnon*, published in 1555.

Toute la lyre, posthumously published poetic collections by Victor Hugo: two series in 1888 (*L'Humanité*; *La Nature*) and one in 1893 (*La Pensée*).

Tout-Paris, Le, the name given during the Second Empire (1852–70) to a part of Parisian life made up of journalists, literary and aristocratic idlers, 'les dandys', and distinguished foreigners. Their haunts were the cafés, restaurants, and theatres situated in a limited stretch of boulevard near what is now the Place de l'Opéra.

Trafalgar. The victory of the British over the combined French and Spanish fleets at this famous sea-battle (21 Oct. 1805) gave Britain undisputed command of the sea, thus making it impossible for Napoleon to carry out his plan of invading England from Boulogne (cf. *Armée, La Grande*) and causing him to confine his plans to the Continent.

Tragédie bourgeoise, a name given by Diderot to a class of dramatic composition intermediate between heroic tragedy and purely comic comedy, based on situations such as may occur in ordinary middle-class life, and hardly distinguishable from the *drame* (q.v.).

Tragedy

[NOTE. Authors referred to in this article receive fuller mention under separate headings.]

(1) Apart from the tragic element in the Christian drama represented in the popular Mysteries, tragedy was first known in France in the form of translations from the Greek, at first into Latin, then into French (either direct from the Greek or through Seneca's Latin versions). In 1506 Erasmus printed in Paris Latin translations of the *Hecuba* and *Iphigenia* of Euripides. In 1537 Lazare de Baïf published a French translation in clumsy alexandrines of Sophocles' *Electra*. About 1539 Buchanan wrote at Bordeaux, for the students of the Collège de Guyenne, four Latin plays, *Medea* and *Alcestis*,

translated from Euripides, and *Baptistes* and *Jephthes*, derived from Biblical sources, the last a well-ordered dramatization of the story of the sacrifice of Jephthah's daughter. We know that the youthful Montaigne acted in several such plays. In 1546 the *Julius Caesar tragoedia* of Muret was performed, a frigid play on the classical model. In 1544 appeared a French translation of the *Hecuba* of Euripides by Guillaume Bochetel, far superior in quality to Baïf's *Electra*.

(2) The first original French tragedy was the *Cléopâtre captive* (q.v.) of Jodelle. It was acted in the presence of the king in 1552/3 and accompanied by a comedy *Eugène*, by the same author. These plays caused a great sensation. Jodelle also produced a tragedy *Didon*, with what success is not known. A considerable number of tragedies followed during the next twenty years, among which may be mentioned a *Médée* by La Péruse (*c.* 1553, from Seneca), *Sophonisbe* by Saint-Gelais (1559), *La Mort de César* by Grévin (1561). A somewhat different class of plays appear to draw their inspiration in part from the Mysteries, which it was sought to bring into harmony with the form of classical tragedy; such are *Abraham sacrifiant* (1550) by Théodore de Bèze, and three tragedies on the story of David by Desmasures (1566). The remarkable play *Saül le furieux* (q.v.) by Jean de la Taille (1572) and its sequel *La Famine, ou les Gabaonites* (1573) are tragedies of considerable power.

(3) These early tragedies have certain prevailing characteristics: a subject taken from mythology or Roman or Christian history; presentation of a tragic fact or situation rather than action (the essential scenes of conflict of characters or passions are avoided); little psychology; use of monologues by which characters reveal themselves; a chorus (to draw the moral, commiserate the victims, and divide the acts); dreams, maxims, much oratory; unity of time. The prevailing metre is the alexandrine couplet; the choruses are in a variety of shorter metres. The audiences for which the tragedies were composed were not popular but lettered and restricted, such as colleges and the court; after 1567 representations at court become rare. The most important of these early tragedians was Robert Garnier, who besides six tragedies, performed in 1568–82, produced the first tragicomedy, *Bradamante*

(based on Ariosto, a hybrid work, in which a theme of rivalry in love is transferred to characters of tragedy, and the ending is happy). Hardy, who composed tragedies and tragicomedies for the popular stage from *c.* 1593 to *c.* 1630, gave greater animation to French drama, gradually discarding the chorus, choosing romantic subjects, introducing in it a succession of adventures and some psychological development. Montchrétien and Théophile are other dramatists of this period, the latter noted for the artificial and affected style of his *Pyrame et Thisbé*. (It may be interesting to remark for purposes of comparison that Marlowe's *Edward II* was published in 1594, that *Hamlet* appeared probably in 1600–1 and *Macbeth* in 1605–6.)

(4) But a marked change in the character of French tragedy did not come about until the time of Mairet and Corneille, when there was a revival of tragedy after its temporary eclipse by tragicomedy and pastoral play. Mairet may be regarded as having introduced the 'unities', that is to say the doctrine that a play should consist of one main action, represented as occurring at one time (i.e. in one day or less), at one place. This doctrine was supposed to be based on Aristotle's *Poetics*, though in fact Aristotle speaks only of unity of time. The doctrine had been briefly formulated by Ronsard in his *Art poétique* (1565), and more substantially by Jean de la Taille in the preface to *Saül le furieux* (1572), and it had been largely observed by Jodelle and Garnier. It was then forgotten for half a century. Mairet (whose *Sophonisbe*, of 1634, is generally regarded as the first regular tragedy on the new classic stage) advocated in 1631 the unities of action and time (cf. also *Chapelain*); but as regards unity of place it was still customary to represent several different localities side by side on the stage (*décor multiple*). Corneille's *Le Cid* (1637) involves three scenes; but his *Horace*, *Cinna*, and *Polyeucte* (1640–2) one only. The single scene and the other unities become henceforth characteristic of classical tragedy (though some irregular pieces continue, e.g. Rotrou's). The unities are memorably defined by Boileau in his *Art poétique* (q.v.). The other principal features of the Cornelian tragedy are that the central interest is transferred from external events to the human heart, and that it possesses a well-knit plot, of

which the springs of action are psychological. The unities were important as tending to concentrate drama in moral action and development of character rather than in bodily movement.

(5) The principal tragedians, contemporaries of Corneille, were Rotrou (whose masterpieces were *Saint Genest, Venceslas,* and *Cosroès,* qq.v.), Du Ryer, Tristan (*Marianne*), Scudéry, La Calprenède, Cyrano de Bergerac (*La Mort d'Agrippine*), authors of very unequal merit. It may be noted that Corneille and others applied the term 'tragédie' to plays with a happy ending if the theme was lofty and the treatment serious. This period (*c.* 1637–45) was extremely productive in dramatic works. Besides the authors named above, a host of poets, such as Baro, Claveret, Colletet, Boisrobert, were producing plays that are now comparatively forgotten. Experiments were made in prose tragedies (e.g. Desmarets's *Érigone,* 1639; du Ryer's *Bérénice,* 1645), but this form did not become established.

(6) Racine, while accepting the dramatic system of Corneille, modified the treatment under the influence of his Hellenism and Jansenism; in particular he represents the human will as weak, swayed by human passions; the dominating motives are reduced to love and hatred; the principal role is given to women.

(7) The great examples of Corneille and Racine hampered the subsequent evolution of tragedy; their successors, instead of studying life afresh, drew from them certain formulas of the tragic art. On the other hand public taste tended away from psychological analysis towards sentiment, and at the same time was inclined to seek a moral purpose in drama. The only tragedians deserving even passing mention between Racine and Voltaire are Campistron, Longepierre, La Fosse, La Grange-Chancel, and Crébillon. Voltaire endeavoured to revive the great tragedy of the 17th century, with Racine for his chief model, sometimes seeking novelty in an exotic setting (*Alzire, L'Orphelin de la Chine*), in themes of national history (*Tancrède, Zaïre*), or in a philosophic thesis (*Mahomet*). La Motte in his prefaces suggested innovations, e.g. disregard of the three unities, but these seldom penetrated to his works. The adaptations of *Hamlet, Romeo and Juliet,*

King Lear, &c., by Ducis were attempts (carefully modified to suit French taste) to introduce Shakespearian tragedy. M.-J. Chénier, the outstanding tragic author of the Revolutionary era, popularized themes taken from national history (notably with *Charles IX,* q.v.). But in spite of the ephemeral success of mediocre works, largely due to the acting of Talma (q.v.), and of attempts at resuscitation and innovation more apparent in critical than in creative writings, tragedy on the strictly classical model became still more lifeless during the first half of the nineteenth century. The tragedies of Arnault, Baour-Lormian, Brifault, de Jouy, Legouvé, Lemercier, Luce de Lancival, and Raynouard, produced with varying success during the Empire and the Restoration, are now forgotten.

(8) Several factors contributed to the decline. Creative writing was undoubtedly stultified by severe dramatic censorship, though in any case the tragedy of this period lacked the essential quality of poetic inspiration. The champions of *le Romantisme* (q.v.) were fighting a winning battle against the conventions which governed classical tragedy, especially those which forbade the intermingling of any comic element, or which required action to be off-stage. Further, as time went on, classical tragedy lost its appeal. The post-Revolutionary theatre public was larger, more heterogeneous than formerly, composed of people accustomed to the excesses of the Revolution or born into the disturbed years which succeeded it. No longer an educated *élite,* they brought to the theatre a demand for incident rather than a trained faculty of critical and, fundamentally, literary appreciation. The result was that strict tragedy was gradually ousted by various forms of drama (see *Drame*), e.g. historical drama, melodrama, the Romantic drama (see *Romantisme*), and, later, drama of the type popularized by Dumas *fils.* The transition is noticeable after 1820 in some of the works of Casimir Delavigne and Alexandre Soumet (qq.v.), which keep to the form of classical tragedy but make use of intrigue and incident. For a moment in 1843 Ponsard's *Lucrèce,* a skilfully written tragedy on classical lines (including chorus and dream), filled the theatres, but its success was a dying flicker, due less to intrinsic merit than to

a momentary reaction in the public taste. [After 1850 it is not practicable to consider Tragedy as a separate branch of the French theatre, and the reader is referred to the article on the *Theatre of the 19th and 20th centuries.*]

Tragicomedy, a form of drama introduced from Italy and inaugurated in France by the *Bradamante* of Garnier (q.v.), published in 1582. It was developed in the second edition (1628) of the *Tyr et Sidon* of Jean de Schelandre (q.v.) and especially by Hardy. Tragicomedy, a term variously defined, provided an escape from the restrictions on pure tragedy; its features were usually a romantic subject (though the characters might be of the heroic kind suited to tragedy), a happy ending, startling but not dreadful adventures, the play of the ordinary passions. It does not, as its name would suggest, necessarily contain a comic element. It was irregular in structure, that is to say the unities were not respected. It became very popular and for a time, about 1628, together with pastoral drama, it almost ousted tragedy and comedy; it remained in favour till the middle of the century; during this period about two hundred of these dramas were composed (including those of Hardy). But from the time of *Le Cid* (1637) the distinction between tragedy and tragicomedy tended to become obscured. The best of the tragicomedies were perhaps *Don Bernard de Cabrère* by Rotrou and *Don Sanche d'Aragon* by Corneille (qq.v.) and some of the plays of Scudéry and du Ryer.

Tragiques, Les, a poem in about 9,000 alexandrines, by Agrippa d'Aubigné (q.v.), written when he was from twenty-five to thirty years old, but not published until 1616, though parts of it were in circulation as early as 1593.

It is a lyrical satire, inspired by fanatical Protestantism, powerful and violent, unequal, lacking in proportion and lucidity, but redeemed by the sombre splendour of many passages. It is divided into seven books: (I) *Misères*, a poignant exposition of the sufferings of the people and a denunciation of the tyrants who are responsible for them, especially the Jezebel, Catherine de Médicis; (II) *Princes*, a diatribe against her sons Charles IX and Henri III; (III) *La Chambre dorée*, an over-long attack on the administra-

tion of justice; (IV) *Feux*, a Protestant martyrology; (V) *Fers*, an account of the religious wars; (VI) *Vengeances*, an enumeration of historical instances of divine vengeance on tyrants; (VII) *Jugement*, an evocation of the Day of Judgement, the punishment of the reprobates and the bliss reserved for the faithful servants of God. The work has been justly described as the epic of Calvinism. With the other great Protestant epic (the *Semaine* of du Bartas) and with the tragedies of Garnier, it finally secured the position of the alexandrine as the metre of serious French poetry.

Trahison des clercs, La (1927), see *Benda, Julien.*

Train de 8h. 47, Le (1888), a collection of farcical sketches of military life by Georges Courteline (q.v.). The name-piece was dramatized.

Traité de la connaissance de Dieu et de soi-même (1722), a philosophical treatise written by Bossuet (q.v.) for his pupil the Dauphin. It leads by the study of man to the study of God. When first published it was said to be by Fénelon, but this was corrected in subsequent editions.

Traité de l'education des filles (1687), by Fénelon (q.v.), a work written at the request of the duchesse de Beauvilliers, a mother of eight daughters. Girls have reckless imaginations, which should be restrained. Novels, plays, and adventure stories are insufficiently solid diet for their empty heads. But philosophy and theology are equally unsuitable. A girl's education should fit her to become a pious, submissive spouse and a good housewife.

Traité du style (1928), by Louis Aragon, an essay on the principles of *surréalisme* (q.v.).

Traité du verbe (1886), an essay on poetic technique, by René Ghil (q.v.), one of the early symbolists.

Transnonain, Les Massacres de la rue. In 1834, discontent with the government of Louis-Philippe led to insurrectional movements in various parts of France. One at Lyons in April was suppressed with such violence that it was followed two days later in Paris by a fierce local insurrection in the neighbourhood of the Temple (q.v.). The odds against large detachments of armed troops were hopeless and the fighting was soon over, but after this one lot of troops broke into a house in the rue Transnonain, one of the network of small streets in which barricades had been erected, and murdered all the inhabitants, including old people and children.

Trappe, Abbaye de la, an abbey at Soligny near Mortagne in the department of Orne, founded in 1140. The monastic body connected with it, a branch of the Cistercian order, was reformed about 1664 by its abbot, Armand de Rancé (q.v.); it was noted for the extreme austerity of its rules, enjoining almost perpetual silence, severe manual labour, and general asceticism.

Travail (1901), a novel by Zola (q.v., para. 3), the second of his series *Les Quatre Évangiles*.

Travailleurs de la mer, Les (1866), a novel by Victor Hugo, dedicated to the Island of Guernsey, where the scene is laid.

Mess (fam. for 'Monsieur') Lethierry has two treasures, his adopted daughter Déruchette and his steamboat *Durande*, the first steamboat the Channel Islands have seen. The *Durande* is wrecked off the coast but her valuable engine is reported to be intact, and Déruchette promises to marry the man who can salvage it. Gilliatt, a fisherman who for years has worshipped Déruchette from a distance, sets out to accomplish this apparently impossible task, and many chapters are devoted to his superhuman efforts to dislodge the wreck. (An account of his fight with a giant octopus gives full play to Hugo's powerful imagination and his talent for vivid descriptive writing.) Gilliatt triumphs in the end, but finds on returning that Déruchette loves another man. Nobly, he helps her to marry where her heart is. The newly-wed couple set sail for England. Gilliatt, sitting on a rock to watch their vessel pass, allows the tide to rise slowly and engulf him.

Traviata, La (1853), an opera by Verdi, based on *La Dame aux camélias* by Dumas fils.

Traviès de Villers, CHARLES-JOSEPH [known as C.-J. Traviès] (1804–59), carica-

turist on the staff of Philipon's (q.v.) *Charivari*, *Caricature*, &c., was the creator of the hunchback Mayeux (q.v.). In this personage he satirized the vanity and stupidity of the lower middle classes during the July monarchy.

Trébutien, GUILLAUME-STANISLAS (1800–70), man of letters, is remembered as the friend of Barbey d'Aurevilly (q.v.) from their student days at Caen, and as the editor of Eugénie and Maurice de Guérin (qq.v.). He also edited old French texts and was something of an orientalist.

Trente, combat des or *Bataille des,* a poem in the form of a *chanson de geste* in alexandrines, of 1351, relating a combat between thirty Englishmen and thirty Bretons in the wars of Edward III.

Trésor, Livre du, an encyclopaedic treatise written in French by the Florentine, Brunetto Latini, Dante's teacher, c. 1265. Dante refers to it in the *Inferno* (xv. 119).

Trésor de la langue française, by Nicot, see *Dictionaries and Encyclopedias*, under date 1606.

Trésor de la langue grecque (1572), the *Thesaurus graecae linguae* of Henri Estienne, see *Estienne*.

Trésor de la langue latine, the *Thesaurus linguae latinae* (1532) of Robert Estienne, see *Estienne*.

Trésor des humbles, Le (1896), essays by Maeterlinck (q.v.).

Trésor du Félibrige, Le (1878–86), a dictionary of Provençal words and lore compiled by the poet Frédéric Mistral (q.v.).

Trésoriers de France, see *Fiscal system*.

Trévoux, a small town on the Saône, near Bourg (Ain). At one time it was the capital of the little principality of Dombes. A printing-press was established there in 1671 with a *privilège* granted first by Mme de Montpensier and continued, when Dombes became his, by the duc du Maine. It became one of the famous 18th-century centres for books printed outside Paris (see *Librairie*, paras. 1, 2). For the *Dictionnaire de Trévoux* see *Dictionaries and Encyclopedias* under date 1704. See also *Journal de Trévoux*.

Trianon, the name originally of a hamlet near Versailles where, in 1668–70 during the construction of the palace of Versailles, Louis XIV had a pleasure-house built, consisting of five single-storied pavilions. This was demolished in 1687 and a new and splendid single-storied building of wide extent was erected to the design of Mansart. This was known as the *Grand Trianon*.

The *Petit Trianon* was a separate pavilion in the vicinity erected by Louis XV in 1751, supplemented by a small country-house in 1766. It was handed over, with its elaborate gardens and dependencies, by Louis XVI to Marie-Antoinette for her private domain. There she discarded etiquette, kept cows, gave parties, and herself acted in musical comedies.

Triboulet, Le Fleurial, *known as* (d. *c.* 1536), court jester of Louis XII and François Ier. He is celebrated by Rabelais (III. xlv) and he is the chief character in Victor Hugo's drama *Le Roi s'amuse* (q.v.).

Tribulat Bonhomet, Le Docteur, the character created by Villiers de l'Isle-Adam (q.v.), embodies, at times in almost terrifying fashion, the complacent pseudo-scientific materialism of his age (the mid to later 19th century). His grotesque person, clothes (including 'une houppelande fermée et drapée sur ma poitrine comme mes grandes phrases le sont habituellement sur ma pensée'), and mentality are delineated with ironic care in *Le Tueur de cygnes* and *Claire Lenoir*, two tales in the collection (1887) to which he gives his name. He belongs to a company which includes M. Prudhomme, M. Homais, Bouvard and Pécuchet, and Ubu-Roi (qq.v.), and his name has to some extent passed into the language of French criticism.

Tribunal révolutionnaire, Le, was constituted by decree of the *Convention nationale* (q.v.) in March 1793 as a central court to try persons accused by the supreme Revolutionary authorities of counter-Revolutionary activities or attempts against the public safety. Judges, jury, and the Public Accuser (Fouquier-Tinville, q.v.) were nominated by the *Convention*.

Tricolore, Le Drapeau. The adjective *tricolore* is used to describe the French national flag or any emblem (flag, cockade, or rosette) consisting of the national colours (blue, white, and red). The three colours were adopted during the Revolution by joining the blue and red of the city of Paris to the white of royalty.

Trilby, le lutin d'Argaïl (1822), a *conte fantastique* by Charles Nodier (q.v.). It is set in Scotland (Argyll). A sprite, a sort of Lob-lie-by-the-fire, falls in love with a poor fisherman's wife. All goes well for a time, he keeps her hovel clean and her husband prospers. But the couple are uneasy, and have him exorcized. Now all luck departs from the house, the husband loses all his catches and the wife's brain gives way. The sprite is imprisoned in a birch-tree and Jeannie, the wife, commits suicide.

Triolet, a stanza of eight lines, of which the first is repeated after the third, and the first and second after the sixth, rhyming as follows (the capital letters indicate the lines that are repeated): A B a A a b A B.

Trissotin, a character in Molière's *Les Femmes savantes* (q.v.), a caricature of the abbé Cotin.

Tristan, the hero of medieval romance known in English as Tristram. The earliest extant poem about him is that which an Anglo-Norman named Thomas wrote about 1165–70; of this only a part survives. The theme had probably already been treated and in the hands of Thomas loses some of its primitive character. This is better preserved in the somewhat later poem by Béroul (probably a Norman), of which unfortunately much is lost. Two short poems survive (one of the late 12th, the other early 13th century) entitled *La Folie Tristan*, in which Tristan, disguised as a fool, relates to Mark the story of his love for Iseut. Chrétien de Troyes (q.v.) also wrote a poem on Tristan, which is not extant. Marie de France (q.v.) in her lay *Chèvrefeuille* dealt with an incident in the life of Tristan which is not in the Tristan story proper. Finally the legend was embodied in a long prose compilation called the *Prose Tristan*, written about 1230, where it is combined with that of Arthur, and Tristan and Lancelot are brought into rivalry.

The story is that of two lovers, Tristan and Iseut, wife of his uncle, king Mark. They are conscious of the tie of kinship and loyalty which binds them to king Mark, yet dominated by irresistible passion as the result of a love-philtre which they have drunk unawares. Béroul's poem traces with great penetration the development of this dramatic situation: the hard life of the lovers in the forest, at first borne light-heartedly; their growing uneasiness; Mark's pursuit of them with intent to kill, but his discovery of them asleep, their lips not touching, and a naked sword between them; and finally, when after three years the philtre has lost its power, their repentance and separation. Other versions of the legend end differently.

English versions of the story are *Sir Tristrem*, one of the earliest romances in the vernacular, and Malory's *Morte Darthur*; and it has furnished themes to modern poets, e.g. Matthew Arnold and Swinburne. The incident in the latter's *Tristram of Lyonesse* of the ship sent to fetch Iseult to the dying Tristram and reported to be returning with a black sail (as a signal of failure) was taken from Thomas's version of *Tristan*, where it is probably a classical echo from the story of Theseus.

Tristan, Flora (1803–44), writer, feminist, and revolutionary socialist, born in Paris. Her father, a Peruvian said to be descended from Montezuma, died when she was eight leaving her mother (because the marriage had been irregularly celebrated) with no provision and no legal claim to his money. At seventeen she went to work in a lithographer's business and made a disastrous marriage with her employer. She left him in 1825, taking her three children, but could not get legally free, and was persecuted by him, till 1839, when he tried to murder her and was sent to penal servitude. After leaving him she had gone to England in domestic service (followed by other visits, in other circumstances). She also went to Peru (1833) to seek help and recognition from her father's relatives; and she began to educate herself, to agitate for women's rights and divorce-law reform, to write, and to make contacts with social reformers, notably Fourier and some of the Saint-Simoniens (qq.v.). She travelled about France increasingly as her socialist activities developed, and she came to regard her struggle on behalf of the oppressed classes as a sort of apostolic mission. In 1843, a year before her death (at Bordeaux), she founded the *Union ouvrière*. Her published works include: *Pérégrinations d'une Paria (1833–1834)* (1834, 2 vols. out of four contemplated), semi-autobiographical, with an account of her Peruvian year, and *Promenades dans Londres* (1840), studies of English social conditions. She is said to have been beautiful, and of a romantic and violent character. One of her daughters was the mother of the painter Paul Gauguin.

Tristan l'Hermite, (1) Louis, at one time public executioner, *prévôt des maréchaux* (a sort of provost-marshal) under Louis XI, and one of the king's advisers. He figures in Scott's *Quentin Durward*; (2) dramatist, see below.

Tristan l'Hermite, François L'Hermite, *known as* (1602–55), dramatist, poet, and novelist. He took when twenty the name of Tristan, in memory of the famous Tristan l'Hermite with whom his family claimed connexion. He was poor, a gambler, and had ill health. His chequered youth in the service of the duc d'Orléans is represented in his *Page disgracié*, an autobiographical romance (1642–3). He was author of four notable tragedies: *La Mariane* (1636) on the love of Herod for Mariamne, whom he puts to death from jealousy (this play rivalled *Le Cid* in popular favour); *La Mort de Sénèque* (1644; the characters Seneca, Pauline, Poppaea, &c., are vigorously drawn, and the play is the finest Roman tragedy after those of Corneille and Racine); *La Mort de Crispe* (1645, Fauste, second wife of Constantine, conceals a guilty passion for her stepson Crispe, who loves his cousin Constance, and falls a victim to the jealousy of Fauste); *Osman* (printed 1656, the struggle of the Sultan with his janissaries, at first subduing them, then slain by them). Tristan's comedy *Le Parasite* (1654) introduced from Latin comedy the type of the parasite. His lyrics *Les Amours de Tristan* (1638) contain the ode *Le Promenoir des deux amants*.

Tristesse d'Olympio, by Victor Hugo, one of his most famous lyrics, in the collection *Les Rayons et les ombres* (q.v.). The poet revisits the scene of former happiness to find that Nature has pursued her changing course untouched by the emotions she has witnessed. He concludes that the past can remain with us only in memory. (Cf. Lamartine's *Le Lac* and Alfred de Musset's *Souvenir*.)

Tristesse verlainienne, a note of wistful, vague melancholy never far absent from the poetry of Verlaine (q.v.).

Triumvirat, Le, a tragedy by Voltaire produced in 1767, designed to hold up to abhorrence the cruel abuse of arbitrary power.

It presents Octavian and Mark Antony, the chief members of the triumvirate, at the moment of the proscriptions by which they sought to remove their principal enemies. Fulvia, divorced by Antony that he may marry Octavia, and the proscribed Sextus Pompeius, plot the assassination of the two triumvirs. The plot fails and Sextus is arrested. Octavian, awaking to a sense of his high role, pardons the conspirators, and though he had hoped to win Julia, Lucius Caesar's daughter, who loves Sextus, gives her up to Sextus.

Trivelin, a rascally valet, one of the stock characters of the old Italian comedy. The part was created in Paris in the mid-17th century.

Troie, Roman de, see *Roman de Troie*.

Troilus and Cressida, see *Roman de Troie*.

Trois Contes (1877), by Flaubert, three finely contrasted examples of his narrative art. The first, *Un Cœur simple*, is the uneventful life-story of Félicité who, at sixteen, became a domestic servant in a house at Pont l'Évêque, in Normandy. Her existence centred on her widowed mistress, the widow's children, her own sailor nephew, and a parrot. Time passed, and one after another death robbed her of them. She lived on (till one day, as the Corpus Christi procession was passing, she too died) in the empty, unsold, mouldering house, enfeebled in mind and body, pious as she always had been, but confusing the stuffed parrot before whom she knelt with the Holy Ghost to whom she prayed.

La Légende de Saint Julien l'Hospitalier is a medieval tale, jewelled in style like a stained-glass window (and Flaubert's inspiration may have come from a window in the cathedral at Rouen). The saint of the legend was a hermit who sought expiation for the blood-lust of his youth, and his crime of parricide, by ferrying people across a dangerous river. One stormy night he was summoned to transport a filth-ridden leper who then demanded the shelter of his hut, and of his bed, and finally the warmth of his naked body 'bouche contre bouche, poitrine sur poitrine'. Julian did all that he was asked, and the air became filled with sweetness, the roof disappeared as the firmament opened, and he found himself being carried to heaven in the arms of his Lord.

Hérodias is a sensuously ornate, yet realistic, evocation of a Biblical past and the worlds of Judaea and Rome. Herod the tetrarch and Herodias are feasting the proconsul Vitellius. The imprecations of the captive John the Baptist are heard from the cistern in the background. Salome dances, and receives his head as her reward. Later it is discarded, *objet lugubre*, among the remains of the banquet. It is retrieved by three of John's disciples who set out, carrying it, in the direction of Galilee. 'Comme elle était très lourde,' the tale ends, 'ils la portaient alternativement.'

Trois Glorieuses, Les, the three days' fighting (27, 28, and 29 July 1830) which culminated in the July Revolution (see *Revolutions*, II, IIa).

Trois morts et des trois vifs, Dit des, a religious didactic poem in dialogue form, of which the oldest version, by Baudoin de Condé, dates from before 1280; the theme is the meeting of three young noblemen with three corpses which rise and confront them. One has been a pope, another a cardinal, the third a papal notary. They warn the young men that these will soon be as they are, and that power, honour, and riches are worthless. A somewhat different version, presenting the incident as the vision of a hermit, was printed at the end of the 15th century. The legend was adopted in that century as a frequent subject for the decoration of churches. See also *Danse Macabre*.

Trois Mousquetaires, Les (1844), by Dumas *père*, one of the best of all cape-and-sword novels, based largely on the *Mémoires de M. d'Artagnan* by Courtilz de Sandras (q.v.).

The action takes place *c.* 1625, in the days of Louis XIII and Richelieu. D'Artagnan, a young Gascon—shrewd, brave, and hotheaded as Gascons proverbially are—comes to Paris to seek his fortune. He has an introduction to the Captain of the King's Musketeers, the picked body who act as

Royal Guard and are on terms of continual hostility with Richelieu's Guard. Barely arrived, he is involved in duels along with three Musketeers, Athos, Porthos, and Aramis. The first is a typical, polished aristocrat, the second a goodhearted braggart of huge physical strength, the third, only temporarily a soldier, means to enter the Church and already displays a Jesuitical subtlety.

The four companions (D'Artagnan is admitted into the *Corps des Mousquetaires* as the tale proceeds) have many adventures, the most exciting being when they protect the queen's honour against Richelieu's intrigues. In token of affection the queen (Anne of Austria) has given the Duke of Buckingham a set of diamond ornaments presented to her by the king. Richelieu discovers this and instigates the king to give a ball, when the queen will have to wear the diamonds. Through d'Artagnan's mistress the four companions learn of the queen's distress and set off at once for England. Athos, Porthos, and Aramis fall by the way, but d'Artagnan reaches the Duke of Buckingham, secures the diamonds, and returns them to the queen in the nick of time.

The villain of the book is 'Milady', a mysterious and beautiful spy in Richelieu's pay, who becomes d'Artagnan's deadly enemy. Through her machinations the Duke of Buckingham is assassinated and d'Artagnan's mistress poisoned. Years before, Milady had tricked Athos into marrying her. He thought her dead, but she had in fact married again, bigamously, then poisoned her husband for his money. In time the four companions discover her identity, and when she falls into their power they agree that she deserves no mercy. The story ends with her death.

There are two sequels to *Les Trois Mousquetaires*: *Vingt ans après* (1845) and *Le Vicomte de Bragelonne* (1848–50).

Trois Villes, Les (1894–8), a novel in the form of a trilogy (*Lourdes, Rome, Paris*), see Zola.

Trompe-la-Mort, a name given to Vautrin (q.v.), a character in Balzac's *Comédie humaine*.

Tronchin, the name of a Genevese family of French origin, remembered as friends of Voltaire as well as on their own account. JEAN-ROBERT TRONCHIN (1702–88), whom Voltaire met in 1754, was a banker and jurist who later became Fermier-Général in Paris. Voltaire bought Les Délices (q.v.) with his help in 1755 and soon entrusted him with the management of his financial affairs as well as with innumerable commissions such as buying wine, household goods, or plants and seeds for the garden. DR. THÉODORE TRONCHIN (1709–81), a cousin of Jean-Robert, and Voltaire's physician, was celebrated for his treatment of the nervous troubles induced by the artificial and dissipated life of Paris society in the latter half of the 18th century. He relied largely on exercise and fresh air. There is a good deal about him in the letters of Mme d'Épinay. FRANÇOIS TRONCHIN (1704–98), a brother of Jean-Robert, played a part in public life in Geneva and patronized the arts. Besides seeing them frequently Voltaire kept up a lively correspondence with these three and with other members of the family from 1755 until he died, though chiefly between 1755 and 1766.

Trophées, Les (1893), by J.-M. de Heredia (q.v.), one of the famous sonnet-collections of French literature.

Troubadours (the Provençal form of *trouveurs*, q.v.), the medieval poets who composed in the *langue d'oc* (q.v.) of Southern France. In the latter part of the 11th century they developed a lyric poetry in the Midi where conditions both social and physical (an easy peaceful life in a genial climate), in sharp contrast with those of Northern France, favoured its growth. It consisted of short songs, elaborate in form, concerned almost exclusively with love and the cult of woman (see *Amour courtois*). The famous troubadours Bertrand de Born (q.v.) and Bernard de Ventadour were received at the court of Eleanor of Aquitaine (who was the grand-daughter of Guillaume IX of Aquitaine, the earliest troubadour known to us, and the wife successively of Louis VII of France and Henry II of England), and through her influence and that of her daughters, who married the counts of Champagne and Blois, this Provençal poetry penetrated into Northern France and found imitators there. The literature of the South declined after the 13th century. See *Lyric poetry*; also *Rudel* (*Jaufré*) and *Jeux floraux de Toulouse*. For the revival of Provençal literature in the 19th century see *Félibrige*.

Trouvères or **Trouveurs**, the medieval poets who composed in the *langue d'oïl* (q.v.) of Northern France, authors of the *chansons de geste*, *romans bretons*, and court poetry (lyrics which show the influence of, but are by no means wholly derived from, the *troubadours*, q.v., the poets who composed in the *langue d'oc* of the Midi). The nouns 'trouvère' (*langue d'oïl*, nom. case) and 'troubadour' (*langue d'oc*, object. case) are derived from the verbs 'trouver' (*langue d'oïl*) and 'trobar' (*langue d'oc*), which originally meant 'to compose' (a poem) or 'invent'. The *trouvère* might at times also be a *jongleur* (q.v.), that is to say the *jongleur* might recite poems of his own composition. But he was more likely to be a person of good birth or high position, such as Conon de Béthune or Thibaud de Champagne (qq.v.).

Troyes, see *Nicolas de Troyes*.

Trubert et d'Autrognart, Farce de Maître, see *Deschamps, Eustache*.

Tuileries, La Comédie des (1635), see *Cinq auteurs, Les*.

Tuileries, Palais des, a former royal residence in Paris adjoining the Louvre (on the west side of the Place du Carrousel). Its construction was begun in 1564 by Philibert Delorme (q.v.) for Catherine de Médicis (on the site of an old tile-factory, whence its name) and extended from time to time. Later French kings, from Louis XIV, preferred Versailles or Saint-Cloud as a residence, but it was the scene of important events during the Revolution (Louis XVI, Marie-Antoinette, and the Dauphin had to return to it from Versailles in October 1789; its attack and seizure by the people of Paris on 10 August 1792 marked the fall of the monarchy). Napoleon I lived in it. So too did the restored Bourbons and, later, Napoleon III. It was burnt down by the *Communards* in 1871. Its charred ruins remained standing for many years, but eventually the Place du Carrousel and the Jardin des Tuileries were enlarged to cover the site.

Turcaret, a comedy by Lesage in prose, produced in 1709 with great success. It is a vigorous satire on contemporary society and especially on the financiers, who strove to prevent its performance.

It presents Turcaret, a heartless and unscrupulous revenue-farmer and usurer, indifferent to everything but the profit to be got from any transaction, a *parvenu* who has risen from menial service and abandoned his wife. But astute as he is in money matters, he is easily duped by the Baronne, a gay widow whom he is courting, herself the dupe of her pretended lover the Chevalier. The designs of the various parties are interrupted by the exposure of Turcaret (through the arrival on the scene of his wife and sister) and by his arrest. Meanwhile the Baronne and the Chevalier are themselves cheated by rascals in a lower grade, their own servants. Altogether a melancholy comedy, unrelieved by any honest character, and displaying the author's hatred of the social group that he depicts.

Turenne, HENRI DE LA TOUR D'AUVERGNE, VICOMTE DE (1611–75), maréchal de France, a grandson of William the Silent, one of the great captains of the wars of Louis XIV. By his successful campaigns of 1645–8 in Germany he made possible the Peace of Westphalia. During the Fronde, by defeating Condé, he recovered Paris for the king. His victory of the Dunes over the Spaniards in 1657 prepared the way for the treaty of the Pyrenees. He commanded French armies in the wars of 1667 and 1672. He was killed by a cannon-ball during a reconnaissance at Salsbach on the Rhine. He left some military memoirs. To him is attributed the saying, 'Dieu est toujours pour les gros bataillons'.

Turgot, ANNE-ROBERT-JACQUES (1727–81), a famous economist and administrator. He was of good Norman stock and was destined for the Church; but after ending his education at the Sorbonne he renounced an ecclesiastical career and entered the magistrature. From 1761 to 1774 he was *intendant* (q.v., and see *Fiscal system under the Monarchy*) of the *Généralité* of Limoges, one of the poorest and most backward districts in France, where he devoted himself to improving the lot of the humbler classes. After this he was Controller-general of finance till 1776. During his brief tenure of this office he sought to effect various reforms, the free importation and free circulation at home of corn, the suppression of the *jurandes* and *maîtrises* (the corporation of craftsmen which restricted the liberty of industry), and the remedying of various fiscal abuses. But these proposals, which he pressed uncompromisingly and injudiciously, provoked much hostility and brought about his fall. His *Réflexions sur la formation et la distribution des richesses* (1766) show him to have shared the views of Quesnay (q.v.) and the physiocrat school. He also published a large number of treatises, pamphlets, and articles, including translations of the idylls of Gessner. He contributed five articles to the *Encyclopédie*, of which those on *Étymologie* and *Existence* are the most noteworthy. He associated with the *philosophes*, d'Alembert, Condorcet, Helvétius, Mlle de Lespinasse, &c., and was esteemed by Voltaire; but with austere probity he protested against such of the new doctrines as did not commend themselves to his reason. He was also acquainted with Adam Smith, and their general economic views were in harmony. Condorcet, who was Turgot's faithful friend and admirer, wrote a life of him.

Turlupin, see *Gros-Guillaume. Turlupinade* was a term applied to the sort of poor jokes and plays on words popular during part of the 17th century and condemned by Molière and Boileau.

Turnèbe [Turnebus], ADRIEN (1512–65), a learned humanist, reader in Greek at the Collège Royal, and director of the royal printing-press, where he printed Homer. He was the father of Odet de Turnèbe (q.v.).

Turnèbe, ODET DE (1553–81), humanist and dramatist, son of Adrien Turnèbe (q.v.) and an advocate by profession. Before the end of his short life he was the author of one of the best of the early comedies, *Les Contens* (printed 1584). It is on the theme of two rivals for the hand of a girl, of whom one is favoured by the girl, the other by her mother. The former attains his object by disguising himself in a crimson cloak belonging to the latter; he is assisted by an old woman, a go-between of the type of the old bawd of *Celestina* (q.v.). The comedy is in prose.

Turoldus, see *Roland, Chanson de.*

Turpin (d. *c.* 800), Archbishop of Rheims, to whom was erroneously attributed a Latin chronicle *De Vita et Gestis Caroli Magni*, a fabrication of much later date. It purports to tell the exploits of Charlemagne in Spain and was probably written in the 12th century by some cleric as part of a guide-book for clerics visiting the shrine of St. James of Compostella. Turpin's legendary death at Roncevaux by the side of Roland is recounted in the *Chanson de Roland*.

Tyard or **Thyard,** PONTUS DE (1521–1605), poet and philosopher, a member of the *Pléiade* (q.v.), in later life Bishop of Chalon. As a young man he wrote a sequence of sonnets entitled *Erreurs amoureuses* (1549, 1554, and 1555), which are among the early examples of this form in French poetry. Later he wrote, in prose, *Dialogues philosophiques*, of a Platonic cast, and astronomical and other serious works.

Tyr et Sidon, a tragedy by Jean de Schelandre (q.v.) published in 1608, remodelled as a tragicomedy under the influence of Hardy in 1628. The tragedy shows some resemblances to Shakespeare's *Romeo and Juliet*, which Schelandre may have read, though he did not visit England until after his tragedy was written. It was probably never acted.

The scene is Phoenicia, where Tyre and Sidon are at war, and the sons of the kings of those cities have each been captured by the enemy. Belcar, son of the king of Sidon, has fallen in love with Meliane, younger daughter of the king of Tyre, and she with him. Eurydice, the nurse of Meliane's elder sister Cassandre, favours the loves of Belcar and Meliane, until she discovers that her favourite Cassandre cherishes a similar passion, whereupon she decides to help the latter and deceive Meliane. At this point the son of the king of Tyre, a prisoner in Sidon, is discovered in adultery and killed. His father, in vengeance, imprisons Belcar pending his execution on the morrow. Belcar, by the design of Eurydice, escapes on a ship, accompanied, not as he supposes by Meliane, but by Cassandre. Infuriated by the discovery of the cheat, he quits the ship in a boat, while Cassandre stabs herself and falls into the sea. Her body is washed ashore and found by Meliane, who is seen by her father as she draws the dagger from the wound. Suspected of killing her sister, Meliane maintains an obstinate silence (for she thinks herself deserted by her lover) and is put to death. The truth is now divulged by the nurse, and the king, driven crazy by his misfortunes, brings death upon himself.

In the tragicomedy the play ends happily, with the discovery of Meliane's innocence and the return of Belcar.

Tzara, TRISTAN (1896–   ), a Rumanian by birth, became known as a leader of the *dadaïste* group of writers and artists (see *Dadaïsme*). His writings include *La Première Aventure céleste de M. Antipyrine* (1916), *Sept Manifestes dada* (1924), *L'Homme approximatif* (1930).

U

Ubu Roi (1896), a satirical farce by Alfred Jarry (q.v.).

Ulm, a fortified town in Germany (Württemberg), where the Austrians capitulated to the French (20 Oct. 1805) during Napoleon's campaign against the Third Coalition (q.v.).

Ulm, rue d', the street in Paris, on the left bank of the Seine, near the Panthéon, in which the École normale supérieure (q.v.) is situated. The name of the street is often, by metonymy, used to designate the institution itself.

Ultramontanism, see *Gallicanism*.

Ultras, Les, the ultra-Royalist party after the Restoration (1815, see *Restauration*). They were uncompromising believers in absolute monarchy and the supremacy of the Church.

Unanimisme, a 20th-century poetic movement which owes much to the Whitman-esque doctrine of universal brotherhood as well as to more modern psycho-philosophical theories of group emotion. It was developed *c.* 1908–11 by Jules Romains and other young writers, e.g. René Arcos, Georges Chennevière, Georges Duhamel, Luc Durtain, Charles Vildrac (qq.v.), all of whom had their association with the *Abbaye* (q.v.) group, as well as other interests, in common. Its central idea is that collective sentiment cannot be focused in one representative type. The poet's task is, rather, to emphasize the *dispersive* element of man's soul, to show how the personality of the individual becomes merged in a greater soul which is that of the group, such as the church, or factory, or city ('Je cesse d'exister tellement je suis tout'). The emotions and activities of this greater soul are more powerful, less circumscribed, than those of the elements composing it, for it is both their sum and their essence: it emanates from them and they in turn are animated by it.

The *unanimistes* had their own, fairly recognizable, technique of versification, expounded in *Notes sur la technique poétique* (1910) by Duhamel and Vildrac, and in the *Petit Traité de versification* (1923) by Romains and Chennevière. Symbols and allegory and all unnecessary adornments were avoided, end-rhymes and even assonance were banished, and the rhythm was variable and strongly accented, suitable to the expression of 'la poésie immédiate'.

Un Caprice, a slight, sentimental comedy (one act, prose), by A. de Musset, of a husband inclined to stray, a timid, adoring wife, and a friend who saves the situation. It was published in the *Revue des Deux Mondes* in 1837 and produced in a Russian translation in the same year, and again some years later, at St. Petersburg. In 1840 it was included in the first edition of Musset's *Comédies et Proverbes* (q.v.). In 1847 it was produced with great success at the Comédie-Française, with the French actress Mme Allan Despréaux, who had played (in French) in the Russian production, in the cast. (See also *Un Spectacle dans un fauteuil*.)

Un Chapeau de paille d'Italie (1851), a farcical comedy (to be found in vol. i of his *Théâtre complet*) by Eugène Labiche (q.v.). Fadinard sets out in his pony carriage, across the Bois de Vincennes, to his wedding. He drops his whip and gets down to retrieve it. His pony meanwhile chews contentedly at a bunch of straw and poppies. This turns out to have been a Leghorn hat, a present from her husband to its owner, who has been flirting in a nearby thicket with a soldier. There are lamentations, and Fadinard, anxious to make good the loss, drives hastily back to Paris to go hat-shopping. He finds himself involved in several intrigues which all turn on a Leghorn hat trimmed with poppies. He runs from one place to another with, behind him, an ever-lengthening stream of interested or irate followers, including his own wedding party. After a ridiculous, inconsequent series of chases, evasions, and encounters, an identical hat is produced and all ends well.

Un Cœur simple, one of Flaubert's *Trois Contes* (q.v.).

Un Coup de dés, see *Mallarmé.*

Un Début dans la vie, one of the 'Scènes de la vie privée' of Balzac's *Comédie humaine* (q.v.).

Un Dîner d'athées, by Jules Barbey d'Aurevilly, one of the tales of *Les Diaboliques* (q.v.).

Un Drame au bord de la mer, one of the 'Études philosophiques' of Balzac's *Comédie humaine* (q.v.).

Une Belle Journée (1881), a naturalistic novel by Henry Céard (q.v.). A very ordinary woman, married to a very ordinary man, starts on a day's outing with her would-be lover, fully expecting that by the end of the day she will have allowed him to seduce her. During lunch her companion warms into a talkative vulgarity that causes her to change her mind. Meantime a drenching rain has set in, and the couple are imprisoned in the gloomy *cabinet particulier* of a shabby restaurant. Their boredom and distaste for each other's company increase, and they have nothing to do but look at old newspapers and exchange banal remarks (all of which are recorded for the reader). The evening is far advanced before they find a cabman willing to drive them back to the city through the rain.

As she prepares for bed in her own home Mme Duhamain draws from her day's outing the moral that the boredom of marriage is preferable to the boredom of adultery.

Une Double Famille, one of the 'Scènes de la vie privée' of Balzac's *Comédie humaine* (q.v.).

Une Fille d'Ève, one of the 'Scènes de la vie privée' of Balzac's *Comédie humaine* (q.v.).

Une Histoire sans nom (1882), a novel by Jules Barbey d'Aurevilly (q.v.).

Une Page d'amour (1878), by Zola, one of his *Rougon-Macquart* (q.v.) cycle. The story is of the ailing child who dies, finally, consumed with jealousy because she has sensed the passion which exists between her mother, the widowed Mme Grandjean, and Henri Deberle, the family doctor. The child's death effectively ends the relationship between the lovers. Perhaps the best passages of the book are the lyrical descriptions of its ever-present background—Paris at all times and seasons.

Une Passion dans le désert, one of the 'Scènes de la vie militaire' of Balzac's *Comédie humaine* (q.v.).

Un Épisode sous la Terreur, one of the 'Scènes de la vie politique' of Balzac's *Comédie humaine* (q.v.).

Une Saison en enfer (1873), by Rimbaud (q.v.), one of his most remarkable works. It is a mixture of verse and prose.

Une Ténébreuse Affaire (1841), one of the 'Scènes de la vie politique' of Balzac's *Comédie humaine* (q.v.).

The scene is the country near the château of Gondreville, once the property of the de Simeuse family but acquired during the Revolution by the upstart Malin, now a figure in the Napoleonic Empire. The extremely complicated plot turns on Royalist conspiracies engineered by the Simeuse family. They are aided by Michu, the gamekeeper, who, outwardly a ferocious Republican, is in fact loyal to his former masters, even to the point of murder, if necessary. The activities and methods of the two police agents Corentin and Peyrade provide the chief interest and make the book in many ways a precursor of modern detective fiction. In Pt. II there is an excellent description of a trial. Another good episode is when the marquise de Cinq-Cygne, Royalist as she is, makes her way in face of difficulties to the battlefield of Jena and begs the victorious Emperor's pardon for her two Simeuse cousins, who have been sentenced to penal servitude. Success rewards her audacity.

Corentin and Peyrade, the unlovable but astute servants of law and order, reappear several times in Balzac. They are the deadly enemies of Vautrin (q.v.).

Une Vie (1883), by Guy de Maupassant (q.v.), the first of his six novels.

Une Vieille Maîtresse (1851), a novel by Barbey d'Aurevilly (q.v.). M. de Marigny marries a young girl with whom, for all his Byronic past, he has fallen deeply and genuinely in love. For a while their life together is one of perfect felicity, but when Marigny's former mistress, Mme Vellini, reappears he finds that, struggle as he may, and though his real love is for his wife, La Vellini is in his blood and he is powerless to resist her. The story is told with d'Aurevilly's typical extravagance but it is continually preserved from bathos by the author's descriptive and evocative force. His drama unfolds, partly in an elegant drawing-room in Paris (about 1830) but mainly in an isolated manor on the wild coast of Normandy opposite the Channel Islands. It is followed, as by a chorus, now by aristocratic Parisian society and again by the villagers and fishermen on whose lives it has impinged.

Un Homme d'affaires, one of the 'Scènes de la vie parisienne' of Balzac's *Comédie humaine* (q.v.).

Unigenitus Dei Filius, title of the papal Bull of 1713 condemning one hundred and one propositions in the *Réflexions morales* of the Jansenist Quesnel (q.v.). See also *Jansenius*.

Unities, The, see *Tragedy*.

Univers, L', religieux, philosophique, politique, scientifique et littéraire, a Roman Catholic daily paper founded in 1833, came into the limelight some ten years later on account of the militant and virulent articles contributed by Louis Veuillot (q.v.). It was suppressed by imperial decree in 1860.

Université de France. This is not an institution for higher education. The term denotes the uniform system of state education in France (primary, secondary, and higher) and the officials responsible for its administration. Thus, for purposes of educational administration France is divided into sixteen regions (seventeen including Algiers), called *académies*, in each of which higher education is provided by a university (in the sense of institution). Each such university has at its head a *Recteur de l'université* who is at the same time *Recteur de l'académie*, i.e. the chief education officer for the *Académie* or region in which the university is situated. The *Ministère de l'éducation nationale* (formerly *de l'instruction publique*) is the central government department and the Education Minister for the time being is *ex officio* at the summit of the educational hierarchy.

The system had its origin in the *Université impériale* (q.v.) created by Napoleon. It has undergone many modifications but still preserves certain essential resemblances. The following—in alphabetical order—are the seventeen State universities: Aix-Marseille; Algiers; Besançon; Bordeaux; Caen; Clermont-Ferrand; Dijon; Grenoble; Lille; Lyons; Montpellier; Nancy; Paris; Poitiers; Rennes; Strasbourg; Toulouse.

Université de Paris, see *Universities*.

Université impériale. This name was given (in a decree of 17 March 1808) to the official hierarchy established by Napoleon for the administration and application of a state system of secondary and higher education. The first *Grand-Maître de l'université* (the highest-ranking official) was Fontanes (q.v.).

Universities

A. THE UNIVERSITY OF PARIS

(1) This was an outgrowth of the Cathedral School of that city, of which Guillaume de Champeaux (d. 1121) was the first important master. The school attained European fame from the teaching there of Guillaume's great pupil and adversary Abélard (q.v.), and drew many students to Paris. A university or *studium generale* (i.e. a school of general resort for students from all parts) gradually developed in the 12th century and a Society of Masters was formed probably about 1170. The University had its first written statutes and was recognized as a corporation early in the 13th century. It was under ecclesiastical

jurisdiction, exercised by the bishop and his chancellor, but the latter's effective power soon diminished. The organization in four 'nations' of the students in the faculty of arts and the institution of a rector elected by the united 'nations' followed by the middle of the 13th century. The rector gradually acquired the position of head, not only of the faculty of arts, but of the whole university. The 'nations' (not to be confused with those of the *Collège des Quatre-Nations*, q.v.) were named after the nationalities that predominated in each: the French, the Normans, the Picards, and the English; the last included the Germans and the students from north and east Europe.

(2) From the beginning of the 13th century the University included masters of three faculties, theology, law, and arts; medicine, though taught, was not recognized as a separate faculty till later. The University had from the first been pre-eminent as a place of study of theology, and Peter Lombard (*c.* 1100–*c.* 1160) had written his *Sententiae* in Paris (1150–2). From the 13th century its importance as a philosophical school also developed. An affray in which students were killed by the royal police caused the University to disperse itself in 1229 as a protest against this infringement of its privileges; the measure was successful and the privileges were confirmed. Masters and scholars returned in 1231 and the University was now placed directly under papal jurisdiction (by the Bull *Parens scientiarum*). Soon after this the emergence of the Mendicant Friars as educators and their claim to teach in the faculty of theology brought about an acute conflict, the University in 1253 expelling the friars, who appealed to the Pope. In this conflict, which lasted till 1255, Guillaume de Saint-Amour (q.v. and see under *Rutebeuf*) took a leading part. By the papal decision (Bull *Quasi lignum vitae*) the secular cause was technically defeated, but the participation of the regulars in University affairs was at the same time rigorously restricted. Moreover by this struggle the organization of the University was consolidated, while the seeds of Gallicanism were sown in it by the papal see's support of the mendicants. The relations between the University and the friars continued a subject of dispute until the 15th century.

(3) Before the 14th century the University and its constituent bodies possessed no buildings but held their meetings in churches or convents; the *Pré-aux-clercs* (q.v.) was in early times the only property in their hands. Teachers hired their own schoolrooms apparently until the 14th century. They were supported by benefices or by religious orders, or received fees from their students, though instruction was, in principle, gratuitous. The schoolrooms of the faculty of arts were concentrated about the rue du Fouarre (so named from the straw on which the students sat). The colleges were in origin endowed *hospicia* (the residences in which parties of students lived), the first founders of colleges seeking merely to provide board and lodging for poor scholars (bursars), though the head of the college took a gradually increasing part in education. The earliest college was the *Collège des dix-huit* (1180), founded by a Londoner on his return from a pilgrimage to the Holy Land for the support of eighteen students. For the college of the *Sorbonne* see under that name. Other colleges, important in themselves or memorable for their associations, include: the Collège de Navarre, de Montaigu, de Boncourt, de Coqueret (qq.v.); the Collège d'Harcourt, founded in 1280 (the Lycée Saint-Louis now occupies its site) by Raoul d'Harcourt, member of a great Norman family, an ecclesiastical dignitary and counsellor of Philippe le Bel; the Collège des Bons-enfants, founded in 1209 for 'treize povres escholiers', mainly choirboys of Paris; the Collège de Beauvais, where law was taught, &c. Gradually all students, not only bursars, came to reside in colleges, of which some sixty were founded before 1500. These disappeared before or during the Revolution, though some were later resuscitated in the form of other institutions (cf. *Lycées and Collèges*; *Collège Sainte-Barbe*).

(4) In the 14th century the University became increasingly subject to royal authority; it also became an organ of public opinion. In the conflict between the king and the papacy it sided with the king, playing for instance an important part at the Council of Constance (1414–15). But with the growth of its political influence, its intellectual and spiritual leadership declined. The lay character of the institution became more accentuated as its wealth increased (it acquired buildings and a library). The conservative spirit of the University as a whole and particularly of

the Sorbonne was out of harmony with the intellectual progress of the Renaissance, though some of the colleges supported the humanistic movement. A memorable outcome of this movement was the foundation by François Ier, at the instance of Guillaume Budé, of what became the Collège de France (q.v.), at first as part of the University but soon distinct from it, by the appointment of royal readers in Greek, Hebrew, Latin, and mathematics. In the 17th century the University entered on a period of decline, in spite of the attempt at reform in its organization made by Henri IV in 1598. Many colleges became impoverished and disappeared, though Richelieu enriched the Sorbonne and Mazarin founded the *Collège des Quatre-Nations* (1661, q.v.) and instituted his great library.

(5) As the University had been out of sympathy with the Renaissance, so its conservatism opposed the new movement of philosophical thought. It condemned Gassendi and was hostile to the teaching of Descartes. Under the absolute government of Louis XIV it became involved in the political and religious controversies of the century—Jansenists against Jesuits, Jesuits against Gallicans, and its educational force was thus dissipated. Indiscipline and venality were prevalent. Literature and the humanities were neglected and the leadership in these was transferred elsewhere: the *Académie française* was founded by Richelieu in 1635, the *Académie des Inscriptions* in 1663; the work of Mabillon and Montfaucon was carried on at Saint-Germain-des-Prés. Scientific teaching was likewise neglected. In the 18th century we again find the University hostile to the philosophical movement of the age, refractory to the ideas of Bacon, Newton, and Locke, the opponent of the *Encyclopédistes*. The need for a general reform of education was already widely felt on the eve of the Revolution, and when it came the old system was swept away. The colleges lost their revenues and their property was nationalized, while the suppression of the religious orders dispersed their personnel. The University itself was suppressed in 1793. When, in 1808, Napoleon established his *Université Impériale* (q.v.) the buildings of the Sorbonne were handed over for the purposes of the reorganized University of Paris, becoming its headquarters after 1821 and the headquarters of the *Académie de Paris* (see *Université de France*).

B. PROVINCIAL UNIVERSITIES

There were universities from an early age in a number of French provincial towns, as many as twenty-one on the eve of the Revolution: Toulouse, Montpellier, Orleans, Angers, Perpignan, Aix, Avignon, Orange, Valence, Bourges, Poitiers, Bordeaux, Besançon, Caen, Nantes, Strasbourg, Douai, Pau, Rheims, Dijon, and Nancy. Toulouse, the oldest, was founded in 1229 by the comte de Toulouse to combat the Albigensian heresy. The fame of Montpellier (founded in 1289) as a medical school was enhanced by the names of Rabelais and the great anatomist Vesalius (1514–64). Orleans (1305) was distinguished as a centre of juridical study; Bourges (1463) likewise for juridical humanism; the Collège de Guyenne (1472) at Bordeaux (where Buchanan taught and Montaigne was a pupil) for literature and philosophy. But these provincial universities of the pre-Revolutionary era were unequal in value and lacked uniformity of system.

Un Prêtre marié (1865), a novel by Jules Barbey d'Aurevilly (q.v.). Sombreval, the chief character, is a priest who forswore his vows during the Revolution and afterwards married.

Un Prince de la Bohème, one of the 'Scènes de la vie parisienne' of Balzac's *Comédie humaine* (q.v.).

Un Spectacle dans un fauteuil (1833 and 1834), two series of dramatic poems, comedies, and *proverbes* by Alfred de Musset (q.v.), so called because, when an early comedy *La Nuit vénitienne* failed on production in 1830, Musset decided henceforth to write only plays that could be read comfortably in an armchair by the fireside.

(2) The first series contained the dramatic poem *La Coupe et les lèvres* (the first of Musset's *proverbes*), the comedy (verse) *A quoi rêvent les jeunes filles* (q.v.), and also the oriental poem *Namouna*. Some years later Musset included these in *Premières Poésies*.

(3) The second series (in two volumes) contained (i) the historical drama *Lorenzaccio* and the comedy *Les Caprices de Marianne* (qq.v.), both prose; and (ii) *André del Sarto* (3 acts), another historical drama, first published in the *Revue des Deux Mondes* for April

1833 and produced at the Comédie-Française in 1848, *Fantasio, On ne badine pas avec l'amour*, and *La Nuit vénitienne* (qq.v.), in prose. In 1840 these, with another four comedies, formed the first edition of *Comédies et Proverbes* (q.v.).

Uranie. (1) For Voiture's sonnet to Uranie see under *Benserade*; (2) the name under which Mme du Châtelet is addressed in two verse epistles by Voltaire.

Urfé, HONORÉ D' (1567–1625), novelist, of an old family of the Forez (Lyonnais) and connected through his mother with the ducal house of Savoy, was an ardent supporter of the Ligue and after its defeat retired to the territories of the Duke of Savoy, where he held a distinguished position. He died in 1625 in the course of military operations between Savoy and Genoa. He wrote a pastoral drama (*Sireine*) and *Épîtres morales*, but is remembered for his vast prose romance *L'Astrée* (q.v.) published, part I in 1607, part II in 1610, part III in 1619, part IV posthumously in 1627; the conclusion was added by Balthazar Baro (1628, q.v.) from d'Urfé's notes. D'Urfé also wrote, by direction of Marie de Médicis, a long and complicated pastoral play called *Sylvanire* (1627).

Ursins, princesse des, see *Des Ursins*.

Ursule Mirouët (1841), one of the 'Scènes de la vie de province' of Balzac's *Comédie humaine* (q.v.). Ursule Mirouët, a sweet-natured, beautiful and gifted orphan, has been brought up from infancy by her adoring uncle Dr. Minoret, at Nemours. His friends the curé and a local magistrate, equally adoring, have helped with her education. Dr. Minoret's many, and detested, relations at Nemours, most of them town worthies, are jealous of Ursule and suspect her of scheming to displace them in her uncle's will. Thanks to successful economies and speculation Dr. Minoret has accumulated enough to leave Ursule a very considerable fortune on his death without touching the money legitimately due to his other relations. On his death-bed he tells Ursule of a letter which will guide her to this fortune, but he is overheard by a cousin who promptly steals the letter. Ursule, practically penniless, lives on very simply in Nemours, worshipped by her uncle's old friends and by the young Count Savinien de Portenduère. The latter's aristocratic, bigoted old mother had refused to allow his marriage with a humble orphan even though the Portenduères had only been saved from ruin by Dr. Minoret's help. Her obstinacy was indirectly responsible for Ursule's plight.

Balzac had recourse to supernatural agencies to produce a happy ending for this tale. First of all, Ursule's uncle appears to her several times in dreams and explains exactly how her cousin stole the letter. Thereafter pressure is brought to bear on the thief, who ends by confessing his guilt and restoring Ursule's fortune, after which he reforms and becomes a respected citizen of Nemours. Ursule and Savinien, their trials at an end, lead a happy married life in Paris.

Utrillo, MAURICE (1883–1955), a French painter famous for his pictures of Paris streets and houses, the Montmartre district especially. His mother and first teacher was the artist Suzanne Valadon (q.v.).

V

Vacances d'un jeune homme sage, Les (1903), a novel by Henri de Régnier (q.v.).

Vache à Colas, La, a nickname for the Huguenots. A poor man's cow was said to have strayed into a Protestant church near Chartres, or Orleans, during a service. The enraged congregation killed the beast, then made a collection to recompense the owner for his loss. A popular song was composed, ridiculing the episode, and sung in the streets on every possible occasion to annoy the Huguenots until in 1605 this was proclaimed an offence. 'Être de la vache à Colas' became a proverbial expression for 'to be a Huguenot'.

Vacherot, ÉTIENNE (1809–97), philosopher. He took some part of his beliefs from Cousin (q.v.), whom he succeeded in the Chair of Modern Philosophy at the Sorbonne, and some from Positivism, and attempted to combine a positivist with a metaphysical conception of the universe. His chief work was *La Métaphysique et la science* (1858, 3 vols.). He was Director of the École normale supérieure for many years, and had considerable intellectual influence at a time when Positivism was being replaced by a more idealist philosophy.

Vacquerie, AUGUSTE (1819–95), man of letters and critic, author of poems (*L'Enfer de l'esprit*, 1840; *Demi-Teintes*, 1845), comedies (*Souvent homme varie*, 1859), and topical essays (*Profils et grimaces*, 1856; *Aujourd'hui et demain*, 1875, &c.). He was much influenced by Victor Hugo, whose daughter Léopoldine married his brother.

Vadé, a pseudonym used by Voltaire: sometimes GUILLAUME VADÉ, sometimes Guillaume's cousin CATHERINE, who supplies an introduction to the *Contes de Guillaume Vadé* of 1764, and sometimes ANTOINE, Guillaume's brother, who figures as the author of a *Discours aux Welches* (see *Velche*) included in the *Contes*.

Vadé, JEAN-JOSEPH (1720–57), author of humorous verse, parodies, light comedies, in which he made free use of the coarse jargon of the fish-market. His *La Fileuse* (1752), a parody of the opera *Omphale* (of the same year), was a marked success. Beaumarchais in his *Le Mariage de Figaro* borrowed some ideas from Vadé's *Le Trompeur trompé*. His *La Pipe cassée*, a burlesque poem in four cantos, was at one time admired.

Vadius, a character in Molière's *Les Femmes savantes* (q.v.), supposed to be a caricature of Ménage (q.v.).

Vainqueur d'Austerlitz, Le, i.e. Napoleon, see *Austerlitz*.

Vair Palefroi, Le, a verse tale by Huon le Roi, of the 13th century.

A young knight, handsome and valorous, but poor, falls in love with the daughter of a rich lord, who refuses to grant him her hand. By the lady's advice, the knight asks the assistance of his wealthy uncle, who promises it, but, instead, treacherously obtains the lady for himself, to her despair. The knight has a fine grey (*vair*) horse, which the father borrows to carry his daughter to the wedding. As they ride through the forest the horse carries off the lady to the castle of the knight, who promptly summons a priest and marries her.

Valade, LÉON (1841–84), a minor Parnassian poet (see *Parnassiens*), was the author of: *A mi-côté* (1873); *L'Affaire Arlequin* (1882), in triolet-form, &c. He sometimes collaborated with Albert Mérat (q.v.).

Valadon, MARIA - CLÉMENTINE, called SUZANNE (1867–1938), mother and first teacher (in an attempt to counteract his alcoholism) of the painter Maurice Utrillo, and herself an artist of standing. She had followed other callings—dressmaking, acrobat in a circus, artist's model—before her own gifts were recognized.

Val de Grâce, Le, in Paris, on the left bank of the river, so called after a Benedictine convent moved to the site in 1621 by Anne of Austria. Between 1645 and 1665 she added a church as a thank-offering for the birth of her son (later Louis XIV, born in 1638). The first architect, François Mansard, died before the work was completed. The cupola is a famous Paris landmark (cf. *Mignard*). The convent was suppressed and used as a hospital-supply depôt during the Revolution. It became a military hospital under Napoleon and has so remained, with the addition since 1916 of a historical museum of the Army Medical Services.

Valentine (1832), a novel by George Sand (q.v.).

Valentinois, DUCHESSE DE, see *Diane de Poitiers*.

Valère, a character in Molière's *L'École des maris* (q.v.).

Valérien, Mont, the highest hill in the neighbourhood of Paris, on the north bank of the Seine, to the west, between Saint-Germain and Versailles. In pre-Revolutionary times it was a place of pilgrimage. A fort was built on it after 1830, as part of the system of defences surrounding Paris. It serves upon occasion as a prison for state offenders.

Valéry, PAUL-AMBROISE (1871–1945), poet, critic, and essayist, was born at Sète (formerly Cette), a small Mediterranean port near Montpellier and the eastern end of the Pyrenees. His father was French, his mother Italian. He went to school and to the university (studying law) at Montpellier, and in 1892 came to Paris. He had already met and made friends with André Gide and Pierre Louÿs (qq.v.). During his first years in Paris he was strongly influenced by the Symbolists, notably Mallarmé (a lasting influence). Some of his poems were printed in the smaller reviews, e.g. *La Conque,* and found admirers, but before long he turned from poetry to write two short prose works (also, in the first instance, published in reviews), the *Introduction à la méthode de Léonard de Vinci* (1895, in *La Nouvelle Revue*) and *La Soirée avec Monsieur Teste* (see *Teste*) in 1896 (in *Le Centaure* and augmented in later, separate, editions). He then turned his back upon creative writing altogether and for some fifteen years, in the leisure left him by his professional career—the War Office for three years from 1897, the secretariat of the Havas News Agency thereafter until 1922— he devoted himself to abstract speculation and study. In 1913 he was persuaded to collect some of his early poems for publication in volume form (*Album de vers anciens, 1890–1900,* 1920). Rehandling the early work stimulated him to write, partly as an exercise, what he intended as a closing poem for the volume. In fact, this alone took him four years. It was published separately (entitled *La Jeune Parque*) in 1917, and with *Charmes* (1922), a volume of further poems written between 1913 and 1922, so effectively made his name that after 1923 he depended on literature alone for a livelihood. At his death he had for twenty years been pre-eminent among contemporary French poets and men of letters, an *académicien* (see *Académie française*) from 1925 and Professor of Poetry (a chair created specially for him) at the Collège de France from 1937.

In *Introduction à la méthode . . .* and in *Monsieur Teste* Valéry had come to grips for the first time with the philosophical and metaphysical problems which fascinated him during his years of silence—problems of the nature of genius and the creative process (which led to an interest in linguistics); of the conflicting claims, for the creative artist, of emotion and intellect; of the universe, and man, and man's activities, in terms of Being and Not-being. (The idea of Being made possible by Not-being permeates Valéry's work. Monsieur Teste, the incarnation of the universal brain, existed in a realm of abstract, sterile contemplation of his own potentialities: to condescend to translate any one of these into action would have been to mar his perfection.)

Such problems were the stuff of Valéry's later writings, both his brilliant, graceful, and aphoristic prose and his poetry. The poetry is usually obscure; not, like Mallarmé's (q.v.), because it seems to be trying to express the inexpressible, but because it is quintessential. The matter of abstract speculation has been seized and worked upon as it were at white heat by the poet's sensuous faculties of emotion, imagery, and fantasy, then condensed into the mould of classical form. (Valéry's adherence to form was rigid; and within the traditional, often Racinian, form he made a subtle, intensely musical, use of inner assonance and alliteration.)

La Jeune Parque, mentioned above, is a long, difficult, symbolical and allusive, and mysteriously beautiful, poem which defies analysis. It may be the monologue of a young Fate torn between the serenity of the immortals and the conflicts and responsibilities, and also the dark ecstasies, of mortal life; or it may signify the mind struggling to free itself from the fetters of the body. Other outstanding examples of Valéry's later poetry are the *Fragments du Narcisse* and the famous *Cimetière marin,* the poet's soliloquy on the theme of death. The cemetery is the cemetery on the cliff-top at Sète, his birthplace, with the clear, changeless sky in which blazes the noonday sun for roof, and the sea, only momentarily stilled, scintillating below. Here the dead are at peace, having become one with the void: it is the living, inactive in contemplation, who may be sapped by the devouring worm. And the poet turns back to life, finding his stimulus in the fresh breeze which is now whipping the spray against the rocks.

After *Charmes,* which contained these poems and also the odes *La Pythie* and

Ébauche d'un serpent, Valéry wrote little more poetry. His prose included: two dialogues in Socratic form (some of his most beautiful writing), *L'Âme et la danse* and *Eupalinos ou l'Architecte* (1923: on dancing as the supreme expression of movement and architecture as the supreme expression of repose); five volumes of *Variété* (1924–44: the first two are perhaps the most satisfying), collections of critical essays and prefaces, or of jottings and aphorisms, on literature, philosophy, politics or near-politics (e.g. *La Crise de l'esprit*, in vol. I), education, &c., together with occasional addresses, e.g. at school prize-givings, which stand out as small masterpieces in the art of fulfilling official duties with grace, lightness, and sincerity; *Rhumbs* (1926, q.v.); *L'Idée fixe* (1932); *Regards sur le monde actuel* (1933); *Pièces sur l'art* (1934); *Mélanges* (1941); *Tel Quel* (1941–3). He also left an unfinished comedy *Mon Faust*, published in 1946.

Valincour, JEAN-HENRI DU TROUSSET, SIEUR DE (1653–1730), man of letters, friend of Boileau and Racine, Jansenist, historiographer to Louis XIV, member of the *Académie*.

Valjean, JEAN, ex-convict, chief character in Victor Hugo's novel *Les Misérables* (q.v.).

Vallée-aux-Loups, La, the house bought by Chateaubriand on his return from the Holy Land (1811). It was in the vicinity of Sceaux, near Paris. He spent several years there.

Valleran Le Conte (d. *c.* 1628), one of the earliest of the known French professional actors, leader of the company at the Hôtel de Bourgogne (see *Theatres and theatre companies*).

Vallès, JULES (1833–85), journalist and novelist, born at Le Puy-en-Velay (Auvergne), came of peasant stock, but his father had succeeded with great difficulty in becoming a provincial schoolmaster. He was sent to Paris in 1848 to try for the École normale supérieure (q.v.) and was soon caught up in revolutionary activities. After a term in prison (1853) he tried to earn money by journalism. His sketches of seamy bohemianism and street life (*Les Réfractaires*, 1865; *La Rue*, 1866) were first contributed to *Le Figaro*, *L'Événement*

(qq.v.), &c. After 1871 he was exiled for his part in the *Commune* (q.v.) and spent several years in England. He returned (1880) to Paris to left-wing journalism and finished his masterpiece *Jacques Vingtras*. This remarkable autobiographical trilogy (*L'Enfant*, 1879, *Le Bachelier*, 1881, *L'Insurgé*, 1886) relates—with the most searing resentment and exceptional vividness of sensation and recollection—his miserable childhood, his years of struggle for a livelihood, and his later years of active revolt. The dedication is 'A tous ceux qui nourris de grec et de latin sont morts de faim'. There is a notable description of the *Commune* in *L'Insurgé*.

Valmont, GUY DE, a pseudonym occasionally used by Guy de Maupassant (q.v.).

Valmont, VICOMTE DE, the chief character (and see also *Merteuil, Mme de*) in *Les Liaisons dangereuses* by Choderlos de Laclos (see *Laclos*).

Valmont de Bomare, JACQUES-CHRISTOPHE, see *Dictionaries and Encyclopedias*, under date 1764.

Valmy, a village in the Argonne where, on 20 September 1792, the French under Dumouriez and Kellermann stopped the advance of the Prussians under King Frederick William of Prussia. With this victory the success of the Revolutionary armies began and also, according to Goethe, who had accompanied his master the Duke of Weimar on the Prussian campaign, a new epoch in world history.

Valois, a royal family of France, a branch of the Capétiens (q.v.). It first ascended the throne in 1328. When Charles IV died in that year, he left only a daughter, and an assembly of nobles decided that the throne of France could not be occupied by a woman (see *Salic Law*). Thereupon the crown passed to Philippe de Valois (Philippe VI), son of Charles de Valois, brother of Philippe IV. The Valois line endured until the death of Henri III in 1589, and was followed by the Bourbon (q.v.) line (see also *Orléans*).

Valvins, a village near Fontainebleau, where the poet Mallarmé lived during the last years of his life.

Vandenesse, FÉLIX DE, a character in Balzac's (q.v.) *Comédie humaine.* He occurs notably in *Le Lys dans la vallée* (q.v.).

Van Gogh, VINCENT (1853–90), one of the outstanding artists of the French post-Impressionist school. He was of Dutch birth but lived mainly, and died (by his own hand), in France. Colour and rhythm are striking qualities in his work, which includes many landscapes of Provence.

Vanini, LUCILIO (1585–1619), an Italian philosopher and freethinker who called himself Giulio Cesare. He settled in Toulouse after travel in Europe and a spell in Paris. His *De admirandis naturae* (later translated into French as *Dialogues*), an ironical, antireligious work which influenced the *Libertins* (q.v.), was published in 1616, and censured. He was accused of practising black magic, condemned, and burnt at the stake after having his tongue cut out.

Van Lerberghe, CHARLES (1861–1907), born and educated at Ghent, author of *Les Flaireurs* (1890), a short prose drama; *Entrevisions* (1898) and *La Chanson d'Ève* (1904), poems. He was one of a number of Belgian writers (cf. *Maeterlinck, Verhaeren*) who took part actively or by sympathy in the Symbolist Movement (see *Symbolisme*) in France and fostered a similar movement in Belgium.

Varennes, in the Argonne, the village in which, on 22 June 1791, Louis XVI and his family were arrested in their flight from Paris.

Variété (1924–44), five volumes of collected essays by Paul Valéry (q.v.).

Varillas (pron. *ll* liquid), ANTOINE (1626–96), historian, author of an *Histoire de l'hérésie* (1686) and various other historical treatises, which have been criticized as containing many inaccuracies.

Varlet, THÉO (1878–   ), poet, also novelist and translator (e.g. of Robert Louis Stevenson and Kipling), born at Lille in northern France. His best verse is inspired by his love of the Mediterranean countries, Provence, Corsica, Sicily, &c. His poetic collections include: *Aux Libres Jardins* (1923); *Le Démon dans l'âme* (1924); *Paralipomena* (1926); *Ad astra et autres poèmes* (1930).

Vase brisé, Le, a well-known lyric by Sully-Prudhomme (q.v.), a favourite anthology piece.

Vase étrusque, Le, a short story by Prosper Mérimée (q.v., para. 4), first printed in 1830 in the *Revue de Paris*, then included (1833) in *Mosaïque.* A lover suspects his mistress of infidelity and discovers his mistake too late: he is committed to fight a duel and cannot in honour retreat. He is killed. His mistress, alone and heartbroken, does not long survive him.

Vatel, FRANÇOIS (d. 1671), steward to Fouquet and subsequently to the Grand Condé (qq.v.). Because he thought the fish would not arrive in time for a Friday's repast given at Chantilly to Louis XIV, he committed suicide. Mme de Sévigné gives an account of this in letters to her daughter of 24 and 26 April 1671.

Vathek, Beckford's Oriental tale, was written first in French and published simultaneously in Paris and Lausanne in 1787 in what should have been the original edition. It had, however, been preceded by an English translation published in London in 1786. Mallarmé (q.v.) discovered the French edition in the Bibliothèque nationale and had it reprinted in 1876 with a facsimile of the original title-page (including the royal Censor's approbation of 'une petite brochure écrite dans le goût des Contes Arabes'). He added a preface, an appreciation of this 'songe serein', borne by its rhythm beyond magic halls and oriental gardens to a poetic sphere where 'l'aile de péris et de djinns fondue en le climat ne laisse de tout évanouissement voir que pureté éparse et diamant, comme les étoiles à midi'.

Vauban, SÉBASTIEN LE PRESTRE, SEIGNEUR DE (1633–1707), a great military engineer and maréchal de France, born in Burgundy, who directed fifty-three sieges and fortified the frontiers of France. Towards the end of his life he published a *Projet de dîme royale* (1707, q.v.) advocating equality of taxation, thereby incurring the king's disfavour.

Vaucluse. The *fontaine de Vaucluse* immortalized by Petrarch was a spring (about 16 miles from Avignon), the source of the river Sorgue, a small tributary of the Rhône. It gave its name to a *département* (q.v.) which in 1793 replaced the former papal *enclave* made up of the Comtat d'Avignon (capital Avignon; a papal possession from 1274 until 1791 when it was annexed to France by decree of the *Assemblée nationale*) and the adjoining Comtat Venaissin (capital Carpentras; territory ceded in the first instance in 1229 to Pope Gregory IX by Count Raymond VII of Toulouse).

Vaudeville. For the origin and early history of the term see *Basselin, Olivier*. In the 17th and 18th centuries it was applied to the series of couplets, sung to some known tune, often introduced into the light comedies of the Théâtre de la Foire (see *Theatres and theatre companies*, para. 4). By the end of the 18th century, and as developed during the Empire and the Restoration period by the dramatist Scribe (q.v.), when it became very popular, vaudeville had come to mean a form of gay, light comedy of manners, partly farcical, partly topical (e.g. Scribe's *Une Nuit de la Garde Nationale*). Seldom longer than one act, or at most two, it was written in prose and rhymed couplets, interspersed with songs. The vaudevilles of this period, usually played at the Théâtre du Vaudeville (founded during the Revolution) or the Théâtre des Variétés, give an amusing picture of *bourgeois* and *petit bourgeois* life. (See also *Theatre of the 19th and 20th centuries*.)

Vaudois, *Waldenses*, adherents of a religious sect which originated in the South of France about 1170 through the preaching of Pierre Valdo (Valdus), a merchant of Lyons, who distributed his wealth to the poor and turned missionary. They rejected the authority of the Pope and various rites and doctrines, and were excommunicated and subjected to persecution (together with the Albigeois, q.v.). But they survived and eventually became a separately organized church, which associated itself with the Protestant Reformation and still exists. Their persecution by the duchess-regent of Savoy in 1655 led to Milton's sonnet *Avenge, O Lord, thy slaughtered saints*.

Vaugelas, CLAUDE FAVRE, SIEUR DE (1585–1650), grammarian, an original member of the *Académie française*, whose influence was powerful in determining the character of its early efforts to reform the French language. He was author of *Remarques sur la langue française* (1647), a record of decisions on particular points of diction, preceded by a preface in which the author explains his principle, viz. to adopt as guide the usage of the most judicious members of the court, in conformity with that of the most judicious writers of the day. He aimed at the avoidance of ambiguity and obscurity, at elegance without affectation, at ornament chastened by restraint. He did not attempt to fix the language for all time, but recognized that it was in a constant state of change. Vaugelas translated Quintus Curtius (published 1653).

Vauquelin, see *Wauquelin*.

Vauquelin de la Fresnaye, JEAN (1536–1606 or 1608), poet, born near Falaise in Normandy, a magistrate by profession, author of light verse (*Foresteries*, 1555, a work of his youth; *Idillies* under the influence of Desportes; some sonnets of merit; &c.); *Satyres françoises* (translations for the most part of Italian satires); and an *Art poétique* (1605) in verse, upholding in the main the doctrines of the *Pléiade* (q.v.), but showing esteem for the pre-Renaissance poets.

Vauquelin des Yveteaux, NICOLAS (1567–1649), poet, son of Vauquelin de la Fresnaye (q.v.), appointed preceptor of a son of Henri IV and Gabrielle d'Estrées, and later of Louis XIII; author of a verse *Institution du Prince*, and of odes and sonnets. He introduced Malherbe at court.

Vauquer, La Maison, the boarding-house kept by Mme Vauquer, in Balzac's novel *Le Père Goriot* (q.v.).

Vautrin, the master criminal who figures in several novels of Balzac's *Comédie humaine* (q.v.). His real name was Jacques Collin, but he was 'Trompe-la-Mort' to his fellow criminals and had many other aliases. Originally he had escaped to Paris from a wrongful imprisonment for forgery. He presided over an association of thieves and was for a time a boarder at the Pension Vauquer (see *Père Goriot*) with Eugène de Rastignac, to whom he gave some characteristic advice: 'Si j'ai encore un conseil à vous donner . . . c'est de ne pas plus tenir à vos opinions qu'à vos paroles . . . . Il n'y a pas de principes, il n'y a que des événements;

il n'y a pas de lois, il n'y a que des circonstances; l'homme supérieur épouse les
événements et les circonstances pour les
conduire.' He was discovered and rearrested,
but again escaped, and impersonated the
Spanish abbé Carlos Herrera, whom he had
murdered (see *Illusions perdues*). He took
Lucien de Rubempré to Paris and financed
his extravagances from the moneys of
the thieves' association. After Lucien's
suicide (see *Splendeurs et Misères des courtisanes*) he forsook his life of crime and, as
Saint-Estève, became head of the Sûreté. He
ended as Chancellor of Police and Public
Health in a small Italian principality and was
assassinated by a forger. The character of
Vautrin may have been partly suggested to
Balzac by the *Mémoires* of Vidocq (q.v.).

Vauvenargues, Luc de Clapiers, marquis
de (1715–47), ethical writer, born at Aix-en-
Provence, served for a time in the army, but
in 1743, after Dettingen, seeing little prospect
of advancement, resigned his commission.
He sought employment in diplomacy, but
an attack of small-pox ruined his health. He
thereafter lived in Paris, in poverty, devoting himself to literature, among a few
friends, including Marmontel and the elder
Mirabeau. He died when only thirty-two.
He was a man of high and generous character,
whose virtue and sincerity won the affection
even of such sceptics as Voltaire. His *Introduction à la connaissance de l'esprit humain,
suivie de réflexions et maximes* appeared in
1746, but attracted little notice until the
19th century. In three books he deals first
with the mind (imagination, reflection,
memory), next with the passions, thirdly
with the vices and virtues. There follow
some six hundred detached maxims and
reflections. In contrast to La Rochefoucauld,
who saw man exclusively under the domination of egoism and vanity, and to Pascal,
who stressed his intellectual impotence, he
discerns both good and evil in him, refuses
to denigrate human nature, and rehabili-
tates virtue (in which La Rochefoucauld
had seen little but hypocrisy). He finds in
the heart (by which he means spontaneous
impulse), rather than in the reason, the true
source of best thought and action ('les
grandes pensées viennent du cœur'), and in
the passions, properly guided, the springs of
moral energy. His writings, which include
minor essays and fragments of literary
criticism, breathe a serene and sympathetic
spirit.

Vaux, Madame Clotilde de (1815–46),
daughter of an army officer, was the victim
of an unfortunate marriage but as the law
then stood could obtain no redress by
divorce. Auguste Comte (q.v.) met and fell
violently in love with her in 1845, but
she was able to sublimate his passion into
an idealistic friendship. He made her the
patron saint of his Religion of Humanity.

She wrote *Lucie*, a short novel in letter
form published by *Le National* in 1845. The
theme, of personal tragedy due to the injustice of social conventions, was obviously
inspired by her own experiences. It was
treated with more restraint than George
Sand brought to similar tales. She also left an
unfinished novel, *Wilhelmine*. In this case
Positivist philosophy was to have brought
tranquillity to a heroine ravaged and degraded by romantic exaltation and the
struggle for social freedom.

Vaux-de-Vire, see *Basselin, Olivier*.

Vaux-le-Vicomte, near Melun (about
25 miles south-east of Paris), the splendid
château built (in the three years 1656–9, by
18,000 workmen) for Fouquet (q.v.). Le
Vau, Le Brun, and Le Nôtre (qq.v.) were
responsible for the architecture, decorations,
and gardens, as they were later for Versailles.
The tapestries were woven in a manufactory
specially installed in the neighbourhood (it
was transferred to Paris after Fouquet's
downfall and became the Gobelins, q.v.).
Fouquet entertained Louis XIV at Vaux-le-
Vicomte more than once. On the last occasion (17 Aug. 1661) Molière's comédie-ballet
Les Fâcheux (q.v.), his first work of this type,
was produced, having been written and rehearsed in a fortnight. The whole evening's
entertainment, banquet, spectacle, fountains,
and fireworks, displayed a pomp and magnificence that put the final spark to the king's
wrath that one of his subjects should outdo
him in splendour, and a fortnight later Fouquet was arrested. La Fontaine described this
last entertainment in a letter of 22 August
1661 to M. de Maucroix and after Fouquet's
arrest he wrote the *Élégie aux nymphes de
Vaux*. The château survived the Revolution

and remains one of the finest examples of 17th-century architecture.

Velche, or **Welche** from the German *waelsch* or *welsch*, meaning 'Italian' or 'French', used contemptuously as signifying 'ignorant', 'barbarian'; a word that Voltaire was fond of employing to designate his compatriots of the 18th century, which he regarded as a period of literary decadence. (Cf. *Vadé*.)

Velléda, the druidess in Chateaubriand's *Les Martyrs* (Bks. ix, x).

Venaissin, Comtat, see *Vaucluse*.

Venceslas, a tragedy by Rotrou, regarded as his most finished work, and imitated from the Spanish of Francisco de Rojas; performed in 1647.

Ladislas, a prince of ungoverned passions, son of Venceslas king of Poland, has conceived a violent hatred of Féderic, a gallant soldier, the king's favourite, whom he suspects of aspiring to the hand of Cassandre, a noble lady whom Ladislas has in vain pursued with dishonourable attentions. In fact Féderic's attitude to Cassandre is designed to cloak the courtship of the Infante, Ladislas's younger brother. Ladislas, unable to win Cassandre by dishonest methods, proposes marriage to her and is indignantly rejected. To escape his further persecution of her, the Infante and Cassandre decide to marry secretly forthwith. This comes to the knowledge of Ladislas, who, however, believes Féderic to be the intended bridegroom. Secreting himself in Cassandre's house on the wedding night, Ladislas awaits the bridegroom and stabs him as he enters, to discover too late that he has killed his brother. Cassandre demands vengeance and justice from Venceslas, who subordinates his love as a father to his duty as a king and orders Ladislas's execution. However, the intervention of the prince's sister and of Féderic, the clamour of the populace, and the consent of a mollified Cassandre, avert his death. Venceslas cedes the crown to his repentant son, as the only way of reconciling his duty and his affection.

Vendanges de Suresne, Les, a pastoral comedy by Du Ryer, produced *c.* 1633, published in 1635, interesting for its con-

temporary setting, and its scene on the banks of the Seine.

Polidor and Dorimène are lovers, but Polidor has a rival in Tirsis, and Dorimène in Florice. The wealth of Tirsis wins the support of Dorimène's father, and Tirsis and Florice seek by tricks to separate the lovers. But an inheritance brings riches to Polidor, and a duel with Tirsis puts an end to the latter's rivalry. Polidor and Tirsis combine to rescue Dorimène from a noble ravisher (who takes the place of the conventional satyr). Polidor and Dorimène are married, and Tirsis consoles himself with Florice. The manners are those of contemporary society, with satirical touches. The parents of the heroine quarrel, one favouring wealth, the other birth, as qualifications for their daughter's hand.

Les Vendanges de Suresnes is also the title of a comedy by Dancourt.

Vendée, Guerre de. After the death of Louis XVI a number of Royalist insurrections fomented by nobles and priests in the Vendée (a large area of Western France) led to a state of civil—very much guerrilla—war between Republican troops ('les bleus') and peasant armies ('les blancs'). This lasted intermittently from 1793 to 1796. The Vendéens were led by 'M. Henri' (de la Rochejaquelin), Cathelineau, Charette, Stofflet, and others and were ultimately pacified by General Hoche (q.v.). The victims of the Vendée far outnumbered those of the Terror. (Cf. *Quiberon* and *Chouannerie*.)

Vendémiaire, the first month of the Republican Calendar (q.v.). It ran from 22 September to 21 October.

Vendetta, La, one of the 'Scènes de la vie privée' of Balzac's *Comédie humaine* (q.v.).

Vendôme, LOUIS-JOSEPH, DUC DE (1654–1712), a great-grandson of Henri IV and Gabrielle d'Estrées, and an eminent general in the latter part of the reign of Louis XIV, distinguishing himself in the Netherlands, Spain, and Italy. He was defeated at Oudenarde (1708) by Marlborough and Prince Eugène.

Vendôme, Place, see *Place Vendôme*.

Vengeance d'Alexandre, see *Alexandre le Grand*.

Ventadour, see *Bernard de Ventadour.*

Ventôse, the sixth month of the Republican Calendar (q.v.). It ran from 19 February to 20 March.

Ventre de Paris, Le (1873), one of Zola's *Rougon-Macquart* (q.v.) novels. Florent, escaped from penal servitude for conspiracy during the February Revolution (1848, q.v.), returns to Paris. He finds work as an inspector at Les Halles, the great provision market of Paris, and lodges near by with his half-brother Quenu, proprietor of a flourishing delicatessen shop. Florent, a dreamer, takes to conspiracy again and his recapture soon follows, thanks in large measure to the ill-will of Mme Quenu.

Most of the characters have their place in the *Rougon-Macquart* pattern, but the real theme of the book is Les Halles. Zola's imagination runs riot as he describes the food, endows it, indeed, with life and a mysterious power of changing the nature of those who handle it continually. One celebrated passage describing the various sorts of cheese in the market has been called the 'symphonie des fromages'.

Vénus d'Ille, La, a *nouvelle* by Prosper Mérimée (q.v., para. 4), first printed in 1837 in the *Revue des Deux Mondes*. In a district of the Pyrénées-Orientales, where once Phoenician settlers may have been, a bridegroom lingers on the way to his wedding to play a match of long tennis. His diamond ring, which he will give to his bride, disturbs his grip, so he slips it on to the finger of a bronze Venus, a life-size statue of rare but sinister beauty still standing under the olives where it has recently been dug up. His match won, he hurries to the church, forgetting the ring. After the wedding he goes to retrieve it and finds to his horror that the bronze finger has closed and cannot be opened. He confides in one friend but otherwise says nothing. Next morning the young husband is found dead, an expression of agony on his face and his body marked as if he had been crushed in an iron embrace. The bride, half mad with terror, has a story of a mysterious visitor in the night. The diamond ring is on the floor.

Vêpres siciliennes, Les, a general massacre of the French in Sicily, on Easter Monday 1282 (during the reign of Philippe III), when the bells were ringing for vespers. In 1262 Pope Urban III had ceded Sicily as a papal fief to Charles d'Anjou, brother of Louis IX. The insurrection against the French was instigated by emissaries of Peter III of Aragon. The massacre is the subject of a tragedy (1821) by Casimir Delavigne (q.v.).

Vercingetorix (Vercingétorix), regarded by the French as one of the early heroes of their race, was a son of the king of the Arverni (inhabitants of what was later known as Auvergne) at the time of the invasion of Julius Caesar. A man of high and disinterested character (as Caesar himself recognizes), an ardent and energetic military commander, intelligent and eloquent, he became in 52 B.C. the centre of resistance to the Romans. He won an important victory over Caesar at Gergovia (in Auvergne), but was subsequently invested in Alesia (in Côte-d'Or) and obliged to surrender, and after six years' captivity at Rome was put to death by his conqueror.

Vercors, a thickly wooded plateau in the Alps (*départements* of Drome and Isère), the *Vertacomicorus pagus* of ancient France and a centre of the French Resistance Movement during the 1939–45 war; also the pseudonym of Jean Bruller (1902–   ), author of *Le Silence de la mer* (published clandestinely in 1942), a tale of the conflict between patriotism and personal sentiment.

Verdun [the *Verodunum* of the Romans], a small fortified town on the River Meuse, the seat of a bishop, has occupied a situation of prime strategical importance from the earliest days of European history. By the Treaty of Verdun (843) the Carolingian Empire was divided among the three surviving sons of Louis *le Débonnaire*. The youngest, Charles *le Chauve*, received, roughly, the territory west of the Rhine and the Rhône, stretching over to Spain and corresponding, again roughly, to modern France. Louis *le Germanique* obtained the territory east of the Rhine (plus, on the left bank, and 'à cause de l'abondance du vin' ['propter vini copiam'], the towns of Mainz, Speyer, and Worms) corresponding roughly to the modern Germany. Lothaire the eldest son's portion was a narrow middle strip extending roughly from the North Sea along the Rhine and the Rhône down to Italy.

During the Revolution Verdun was

occupied (1792) by the Prussians after only a few hours' resistance but evacuated after Valmy (q.v.). In 1870, this time after a two months' siege, it was again occupied by the Prussians. During the 1914–18 war it was violently besieged by the Germans (1916) and for ten months was the centre of the epic resistance, which later turned to an offensive, organized by Marshal, at that date General, Pétain. (Volumes 15 and 16 of *Les Hommes de bonne volonté* (q.v.), by Jules Romains, describe this period.)

Verdurin, M. and MME, leading characters in Proust's *A la recherche du temps perdu* (q.v.). They stem from the wealthy, cultivated *bourgeoisie* who throughout the whole novel are opposed to, but ultimately fuse with, the aristocracy typified by the Guermantes (q.v.). Their *salon*—though they would never admit this—is their ladder to social success. It is seen in early days, with its habitués ('le petit clan'), in *Du Côté de chez Swann* (pt. 2, *Un Amour de Swann*). In *Sodome et Gomorrhe*, ii, *salon* and habitués are rising in the world on the tides of aesthetic fashions. It is at Mme Verdurin's that Marcel (q.v.) hears the first performance of the Vinteuil septet and comes closer than ever before to understanding what life holds for him (*La Prisonnière*). On the same occasion the young violinist Morel is spurred on by Mme Verdurin to insult Charlus (q.v.), to whom he owes his professional and social success. (This is one of the most dramatic moments in the whole work.) In *Le Temps retrouvé*, ii, we find the Mme Verdurin of former days, after two widowhoods, enjoying a triumphant old age, with her *bourgeois* origins forgotten. She has married the widowed prince de Guermantes and become a queen of post-war Parisian society.

Vergniaud, PIERRE-VICTURNIEN (1753–93), born at Limoges, was famous for his speeches in the *Convention nationale* (q.v.) opposing the violent measures advocated by the Montagnards. He was arrested with his fellow Girondins in June 1793 and executed five months later.

Verhaeren, ÉMILE (1855–1916), chief among the Belgian poets associated with the Symbolist Movement (see *Symbolisme*), was born at Saint-Amand, near Antwerp (described in the poem 'Mon village' in *Toute la*

Flandre). He studied law at the University of Louvain and was called to the Bar at Brussels, but before long devoted himself to literature. From 1892, after some years of serious illness, he was keenly interested in social questions and formed hopes for a world of the future animated by a spirit of universal brotherhood. The war of 1914–18, and the German invasion of Belgium, destroyed these hopes. (The poems of *Les Ailes Rouges*, 1916, are a bitter indictment of war.) He met his death in a railway accident at Rouen.

His most notable poems are contained in *Les Flamandes* (1883), early poems in which the peasant life made familiar by the works of the Flemish painters is described in a realistic manner; in *Les Moines* (1886), memories of childhood and of visits paid to a neighbouring monastery; in *Les Soirs* (1887), *Les Débâcles* (1888), and *Les Flambeaux noirs* (1890), a trilogy with a pessimistic note unusual in his other poems, and showing great mastery of *le vers libre*; and in *Les Campagnes hallucinées* (1893), *Les Villages illusoires* (1895), *Les Villes tentaculaires* (1895), and *Les Images de la vie* (1899), *Les Forces tumultueuses* (1902), *La Multiple Splendeur* (1906), two further trilogies describing life in the country and the great industrial towns and the gradual extinction of the countryside by the forces of the machine age. Some of these are written with a violence and a sense of warring cosmic forces reminiscent of the later Hugo. The more peaceful collections, *Les Heures claires* (1896), *Les Heures d'après-midi* (1905), *Les Heures du soir* (1911), are mainly love poems dedicated to his wife. His other published works include: *Aux bords de la route*, *Les Apparus dans mes chemins* (1891), *Les Aubes* (1898), *Les Visages de la vie* (1899), *Les Rythmes souverains* (1910), *Les Blés mouvants* (1912), *Toute la Flandre* (1904–11), *Les Flammes hautes* (1917, posth.).

Vérité (1903, posth.), the third novel of Zola's series *Les Quatre Évangiles*.

Verlaine, PAUL (1844–96), who wrote some of the finest and most musical lyrics in the French language, was associated with the early Symbolists (see *Symbolisme*), at an earlier date with the *Décadents* (q.v.), and earlier still with the *Parnassiens* (q.v.). He was born at Metz but educated in Paris (Lycée Condorcet), where the family

lived after his father, an army officer, retired. At the university he made so little pretence of study that his father preferred
(1864) to find him regular employment,
an unexacting clerical post at the Hôtel de
Ville. This left time for frequenting cafés and
other haunts of those young writers and
artists from whom sprang the group of
Le Parnasse contemporain (q.v.); and the
Parnassian care for form and objectivity is
traceable in the early Poèmes saturniens and
Fêtes galantes (1866 and 1869 respectively).
The latter poems also recall the sophisticated
pastorals of the 18th-century painters (e.g.
Watteau, Lancret, Fragonard).

In 1867 Verlaine met and fell deeply in
love with Mathilde Mauté, a young girl too
timid by upbringing and instincts for their
marriage (1870) to succeed, even without
external complications. (Its legal end came in
1874.) His heavy drinking-bouts were one
complication. These became serious during
the winter and spring of 1870-1, when he
served for a time, while Paris was besieged,
in the Garde nationale (q.v.) or hung about,
unemployed, after the Commune (q.v.).
Another, the worst, was his complete subjection to the influence of the boy-poet
Rimbaud (q.v.). The two met first in 1871,
when Rimbaud came to Paris at Verlaine's
invitation; and in 1872 Verlaine forsook
wife, home, and employment and left
Paris with Rimbaud. They led a vagabond
existence (from which came the poems of
Romances sans paroles, 1874) in London and
Belgium. It was punctuated by drunken
quarrels, in the last of which, at Brussels,
Verlaine fired at Rimbaud, wounding him
in the arm. Two years of prison followed,
at Mons, during which Verlaine turned to
religion and was received into the Roman
Catholic Church. To his conversion, which,
if emotional, was wholly sincere at the time,
are due the poems of Sagesse (1881), among
his finest work. They are the broken prayers
of a repentant sinner, anxious but too
humble to believe that God's grace is meant
for him.

On leaving prison Verlaine spent nearly
two years in English schools (at Stickney, in
Lincolnshire, and at Bournemouth), teaching French, Latin, and drawing. Next, he
taught in a Roman Catholic school at
Rethel (Ardennes). Between 1878 and 1883
he tried to farm in the Ardennes, went to

England, and back to Paris, all in the company of Lucien Létinois, one of his Rethel
pupils, whom he termed his 'fils adoptif', and
to whom many of the elegies of Amour
(1888) refer. Létinois died suddenly in Paris,
of typhoid.

A second spell of rustic life (1883-5),
when his drunkenness had the upper hand,
ended with another prison sentence, this
time for attacking his widowed mother, who
had been keeping house for him. Thereafter
until he died, his life, in Paris, in poverty,
often dependent on Public Assistance for
shelter (described in Mes hôpitaux, 1891,
prose), was a series of lapses into debauchery
followed by what might equally be termed
bouts of repentance. The alternations can be
traced in his writings.

After the publication (1884) of Les Poètes
maudits (q.v., prose essays) he became a
leader for the younger Symbolists. In this
year, too, he published Jadis et naguère,
poems which form a transition between his
earlier, more objective, and later, intensely
personal, verse. The one-act comedy in an
18th-century setting, Les Uns et les autres, was
first printed in this.

Verlaine had a considerable influence on
French prosody. He did not countenance
all the Symbolist innovations, such as le vers
libre, but chose at most to employ the freed
alexandrine, vers libérés. He defined this in his
Art poétique (written 1871-3 and included
in Jadis et naguère), together with his conception of verse as essentially musical,
rhythmic, fluid, and evocative, unfettered by
rhyme and regularity ('De la musique avant
toute chose; Rien de plus cher que la chanson
grise Où l'Indécis au Précis se joint').

Besides those already mentioned his
works include: La Bonne Chanson (1870,
lyrics written for Mathilde Mauté before
their marriage); Parallèlement (1889); Dédi-
caces (1890, short poems, each dedicated to
a friend); Bonheur (1891); Chansons pour elle
(1891); Liturgies intimes (1892); Élégies
(1893); Odes en son honneur (1893), &c.; and,
among the prose, the autobiographical Mes
Prisons (1893) and Confessions (1895). The
last are reminiscences of his early years down
to the appearance of Rimbaud.

Verne, JULES (1828-1905), born at Nantes,
was the author of innumerable adventure
stories, which combined a vivid imagination

with a gift for popularizing science, and were the delight of young people in his own and many other countries. They were usually published first in the *Musée des familles* (founded in 1850), an early juvenile magazine. He came of legal and seafaring stock, was himself educated for the law, but refused to work seriously at anything but writing. His most popular tales include: *Cinq Semaines en ballon* (1863), his first success; *Voyage au centre de la terre* (1864), geology; *Les Aventures du Capitaine Hatteras* (1866), polar exploration; *Vingt mille lieues sous les mers* (1870), introducing the misanthropic Captain Nemo, a refugee Indian prince, and his submarine, the *Nautilus*; *Le Tour du monde en quatre-vingts jours* (1873), introducing Phileas Fogg who, accompanied by his imperturbable valet Passepartout, wins a wager to travel round the world in the then incredibly short space of eighty days; *Michel Strogoff* (1876), Russians and Tartars, &c. He also wrote a popular history of exploration from Phoenician times to the mid-19th century (*La Découverte de la terre*, 1878–80), and was successful in his work for the theatre. He died an old man, but he had long since worn himself out with writing.

Vernet, ANTOINE-CHARLES-HORACE [Carle] (1758–1836), born at Bordeaux, son of the following, a celebrated painter of portraits and of battle-scenes. A number of the famous portraits of Napoleon are by him. He was also a witty caricaturist of scenes from everyday life.

Vernet, CLAUDE-JOSEPH (1714–89), a celebrated landscape- and marine-painter, grandfather of the following.

Vernet, JEAN-ÉMILE-HORACE (1789–1863), born in Paris, grandson of the foregoing, was, like his father 'Carle' Vernet (see above), an historical painter, depicting events, particularly battles, from the Revolution onwards. One of his earliest commissions was the ornamental design for the Emperor Napoleon's letters of invitation to hunting-parties.

Véron, DR. LOUIS-DÉSIRÉ (1798–1867), a well-known Paris character about 1840–50. After qualifying as a doctor and making a fortune by exploiting a patent medicine he patronized literature and the arts. In 1829 he founded the *Revue de Paris* (q.v.). From 1831 to 1835 he was Director of the Opéra (q.v.). He bought *Le Constitutionnel* (q.v., a prominent daily) in 1844, restored its circulation (largely by developing the *roman-feuilleton*, q.v.), and used its influence to support Louis Napoleon (see *Napoleon III*) in 1852. He published interesting *Mémoires d'un bourgeois de Paris* (1853–5, 6 vols.). He was a noted *bon vivant* and a prey of caricaturists.

Versailles, Château de, originally built as a royal hunting-lodge or country-house by Louis XIII in 1624, was reconstructed and vastly enlarged by Louis XIV and became his principal palace. The first enlargement was begun about 1661 and completed about 1668 with Louis Le Vau (1612–70) as architect. No sooner was this finished than a second enlargement was undertaken, again with Le Vau as architect, though he did not live to see his work completed. The third enlargement was begun when Louis XIV, after the treaty of Nimwegen, decided to make Versailles the seat of his government; it was continued through the greater part of the remainder of his reign, being finished in 1710. Of this great extension Hardouin Mansart (q.v.) was the architect. The decoration of the interior was carried out by Le Brun (q.v.), who also designed the fountains and groups of statuary which form an important feature of the vast gardens. The latter were drawn out by André Le Nôtre (1613–70). The expenditure on Versailles and its dependencies during the reign of Louis XIV was of the order of one hundred million francs. The changes subsequently made there under Louis XV and Louis XVI were chiefly in the internal disposition of the apartments. See also *Trianon, Marly, Œil-de-Bœuf.*

Versailles et Paris, see *Journal de Perlet.*

Vers de la Mort, see *Religious Writings* (medieval period).

Verset, a modern verse-form, see *Claudel.*

Vers et Prose (1905–14), a literary review founded by Paul Fort (q.v.), of interest as a guide to French poetry of the early 20th century.

Vers libérés. About 1880 the Symbolists, inspired notably by Verlaine, introduced various new metrical forms or modifications of old ones. Their object, largely successful, was to free French versification from the classical conventions governing the length of the verse-line (12 syllables at most), employment of hiatus, fixed position of the caesura in the *alexandrin* (q.v.), value of the mute *e*, the cases in which *enjambement* (q.v.) was legitimate, the alternation of masculine and feminine rhymes, &c., all of which had been zealously reimposed by the *Parnassiens* (q.v.). This 'liberated verse' was, however, still syllabic; it still rhymed; and it is thus to be distinguished from the more sweeping innovation of *le vers libre* (described below), also due to the Symbolists.

Vers libre, Le, an innovation (*c.* 1880) in French prosody, due to the Symbolist reaction against Parnassian restraints on the technique of verse (see *Parnasse*; *Symbolisme*). Going beyond the *vers libérés* described above, it abandoned both the division of the verse line into a prescribed number of syllables and the use of regularly recurring metrical patterns; and it accepted rhythm, and division into rhythmical units, as the only essential basis of poetic form. Moreover, the *vers-libristes* held that this basic rhythm should be personal, proceeding from the poet's own impulse, varying according to subject and individual. Rhyme or assonance could be used, or not, at will, and frequently became merely an irregular melodic design in the rhythmic pattern. Stanzas, if any, had no fixed form but followed the shape, or length, of the thought they embodied. It is easy for *vers libre* to degenerate into a form of cadenced prose in which the rhythmic movement is a matter of style.

Who first employed this form, and what influence, if any, the poetry of the American Walt Whitman (*Leaves of Grass*) had on its development, are much-disputed questions. Two poems by Rimbaud (q.v.), *Marine* and *Mouvement*, said to have been written as early as 1872 or 1873, are in *vers libre*. Verlaine printed them as part of *Les Illuminations* in the little review *La Vogue* in May and June 1886. *Le vers libre* was again used in poems printed later in 1886 and in 1887 in the same review and in *La Revue indépendante* and *La Wallonie*, by Gustave Kahn, Jules Laforgue, Édouard Dujardin, and Moréas (qq.v.). The poetess Marie Krysinska (q.v.) claimed to have been the first writer of *vers libre* to get into print (in 1881) and some critics sup-

ported her. Other early *vers-libristes*—some only during a phase of their career—include Francis Jammes, Henri de Régnier, Émile Verhaeren, and Francis Vielé-Griffin.

Vers libres, the term used to denote the verse forms often employed in the 17th century by, for example, Corneille (*Agésilas*), Molière (in *Amphitryon*), and, notably, La Fontaine in the *Fables*. Here, alternation of masculine and feminine rhymes may occur between lines of varying length, and the length of the line, and the length of stanza, are so skilfully employed that metrical changes coincide with change of mood. The essential metrical basis is, however, still syllabic.

Vert-galant, Le, a term sometimes used to signify Henri IV, in allusion to his amorous adventures.

Vertot, RENÉ, L'ABBÉ (1655–1735), historian, author of a history of the knights of Malta, of an *Histoire des révolutions romaines*, &c. It is related that Vertot, having tardily received for the purpose of his history some notes on the siege of Rhodes, disregarded these, with the remark 'Mon siège est fait', which has become proverbial for persistence in some idea or resolution in spite of information that corrects it.

Vert-Vert (1733), a tale in decasyllabic verse by Gresset (q.v.). Vert-Vert is a parrot, the pampered favourite of a convent of nuns of Nevers; he is a highly decorous bird and learned in religious phrases. His fame causes him to be invited to visit a convent at Nantes. On the way he is corrupted by profane travelling-companions and picks up some shocking language; whereby the nuns on his arrival are scandalized. The penalties to which he is sentenced render him once more devout. He is restored to favour, but falls a victim to a surfeit of sweet-meats. Xavier de Maistre chose a couple of lines from the poem as the motto for his *Voyage autour de ma chambre* (1794, q.v.).

Vervins, a small town in northern France (Aisne) where, in 1598, Henri IV and Philip II of Spain signed the treaty which put an end to the Wars of Religion.

Vestris, GAETANO-APOLINO-BALTHAZAR (1729–1808), born in Florence, a famous dancer, made his début at the Paris Opera in

1748 and did not retire till 1781. He was almost equally renowned for his vanity, and considered that there were only three great men in Europe—Voltaire, Frederick the Great, and himself.

Véto, Le. The question of the need for continuing the king's 'véto', or royal prerogative of refusing assent to legislation, arose in the early days of the Revolution. The moderate party in the *Assemblée législative* wished to retain it, at any rate in a suspensive form: the patriots, backed by the Municipality of Paris, the newly-formed *Garde nationale* (q.v.), and most of the political journalists, wished to abolish it. The king's stubborn exercise of his prerogative increased his unpopularity and won him the nickname of 'Monsieur Véto', while Marie-Antoinette became 'Madame Véto'.

Veuillot, LOUIS-FRANÇOIS (1813–80), journalist, probably the most militant and virulent Roman Catholic writer of the 19th century, edited (from 1843, with intervals of suppression) *L'Univers religieux*, a prominent Catholic daily. Everyone who, in his opinion, undermined religion and morals, either by writing or by some other activity, was a *libre-penseur*—Héloïse, for instance, beloved of Abélard, 'a jade who should have been well trounced'; Alfred de Vigny (q.v.), author of the 'revoltingly immoral drama' *Chatterton*, and George Sand (q.v.). His chief writings, *Le Pape et la diplomatie* (1861), *Le Fond de Giboyer* (1863; and cf. *Augier, Émile*), *Le Parfum de Rome* (1862), *Les Odeurs de Paris* (1867), are collected in *Mélanges religieux, historiques et littéraires* (1857–75, 18 vols.) and *Derniers Mélanges 1873–7* (1908–9). His *Correspondance* (1883–1903) is of some interest.

Veyne, DR. FRANÇOIS-AUGUSTE, see *Dîners Magny*.

Vianney, JEAN-BAPTISTE-MARIE (saint), see *Ars, Le Curé d'*.

Viau, THÉOPHILE DE, see *Théophile de Viau*.

Viaud, JULIEN, see *Loti, Pierre*.

Vicaire, GABRIEL (1848–1900), wrote satirical light verse and was part-author with Henri Beauclair (q.v.) of *Les Déliquescences d'Adoré Floupette* (q.v.).

Vicaire savoyard, Profession de foi du, see *Émile*.

Vicomte de Bragelonne, Le (1848–50), the second sequel to *Les Trois Mousquetaires* (q.v.), by Dumas *père*. The novel as a whole flags, but some of the characters are exceptionally well drawn, e.g. the now ageing d'Artagnan.

Vicomte inversif, Le, see *Arlincourt, vicomte d'*.

Victoires, Fête des, a national festival held on 21 October 1794 (le 30 vendémiaire, An II) to celebrate the victories of the Revolutionary armies and the departure of foreign invaders from French soil. The hymn sung was the *Chant du départ* of M.-J. Chénier (q.v.).

Vidal de La Blache, PAUL (1843–1918), one of the first modern, scientific, geographers, author of *La Terre* (1883), *États et nations de l'Europe autour de la France* (1889), *Principes de géographie humaine* (1921, posth.); also of an inspiring introduction—*La France: Tableau géographique*—to the Lavisse (q.v.) *Histoire de France* (1903; it was reprinted separately in 1908) which was the equivalent for a later generation of Michelet's (q.v.) *Tableau de France* of seventy years earlier. He founded (1891) and edited the *Annales de géographie* and was responsible for the well-known *Atlas général Vidal de La Blache*.

Vidame (L. *vicedominus*), originally the person acting for the bishop in the service of his fiefs in such matters as justice and military service. From the 12th century such officers took their place in the feudal hierarchy.

Vidocq, FRANÇOIS-EUGÈNE (1775–1857), born in Arras, a baker's son, was an illustration in real life of the truth of the saying 'Set a thief to catch a thief'. After many years of adventure and crime he offered his services to the Government and was made head of a specially-created 'Brigade de la Sûreté' [*not* the Sûreté of the present day] composed of ex-criminals familiar with the practices, slang, &c., of the underworld. He retired in 1827 with a great reputation and a fortune, but lost the latter in an attempt to run a factory manned by ex-convicts. In later life he became a private inquiry agent and died finally in poverty. The *Mémoires de Vidocq* (1828, 4 vols.) are probably not by him. They were known to Balzac, who may have had Vidocq in mind in creating his master criminal Vautrin (q.v.).

Vie de Jésus, La (1863), the first volume of Renan's (q.v.) *Origines du Christianisme*.

Vie de Marianne, La, see *Marianne*.

Vie des anciens Pères, a collection of devout verse tales very popular in the 13th and 14th centuries, printed in 1486. It probably consists of two distinct works, one by a native of Picardy, the other by a native of Champagne. The first consists of little parables and paintings of manners, well told, without excess of piety and even with humour. The second contains tales of miracles and legends, showing a more ardently pious spirit. Some of the stories are drawn from Latin versions by St. Jerome or Rufinus of Lives originally written in Greek or Coptic.

Vie en fleur, La (1922), the last of four books of romanticized autobiography by Anatole France (q.v.).

Vieille Fille, La, one of the 'Scènes de la vie de province' of Balzac's *Comédie humaine* (q.v.).

Vieilleville, FRANÇOIS DE (1510–71), maréchal de France, a distinguished general, the subject of memoirs written by another hand, perhaps that of his secretary Vincent Carloix.

Viel-Castel, COMTE HORACE DE (1802–64), man of letters and historian, a great-nephew of Mirabeau, was the author of novels; a study of Marie-Antoinette and other studies of the Revolutionary era; and, particularly, of *Mémoires sur le règne de Napoléon III (1851–1864)*, published posthumously (1881–4, 6 vols.) and frequently mentioned as an entertaining picture of Second Empire society.

Vielé-Griffin, FRANCIS (1864–1937), poet; one of the early Symbolists (see *Symbolisme*), born in Virginia of French descent, was educated and lived permanently in France. His first collected poems, *Cueille d'avril* (1886), were influenced by *l'esprit décadent* (q.v.). Later, more robust, collections were inspired by the countryside of Touraine (*Les Cygnes*, 1887; *La Clarté de vie*, 1897; *La Partenza*, 1899; *Le Domaine royal*, 1923) or by the legends of antiquity, the Middle Ages, and Scandinavia (*Phocas le jardinier*, 1898, a poetic drama of early Christian persecution

and martyrdom; *La Lumière de la Grèce*, 1892; *La Légende ailée de Wieland le forgeron*, 1900; *L'Amour sacré*, 1906; *Voix d'Ionie*, 1914; *Couronne offerte à la Muse romaine*, 1923). He employed the *vers-libre* form with great success (e.g. in *Les Joies*, 1889).

Vie littéraire, La (1888–1950, 5 vols.), by Anatole France (q.v.), collected criticism.

Vienne, Congrès de. The Congress of Vienna, which opened in October 1814 after Napoleon's first abdication, ended in June 1815, having in the meantime reshaped the boundaries of the European states. Representatives, and some of the sovereigns, of the Coalition Powers (see *Coalition*) took part in it. French interests were upheld by Talleyrand (q.v.). Its decisions left France territorially smaller, if anything, than she had been before the Revolution.

Viennet, JEAN-PONS-GUILLAUME (1777–1868), born at Béziers, an indefatigable writer of fables, epistles, and satires, epic poetry (e.g. *La Franciade*, 1863), and epic dramas, all keeping lifelessly to classical models and seldom now mentioned. An *Épître aux Muses*, an attack on the Romantics (see *Romantisme*), brought him some fleeting celebrity. He also had a career in the navy and in politics. It was he, after the July Revolution (q.v.), who read the proclamation of Louis-Philippe to the people assembled before the Hôtel de Ville.

Vie parisienne, La, one of the first French weekly illustrateds, was founded in 1863 by Marcelin (pseud. of Émile-Marcelin-Isidore Planet, 1829–87, writer and book-illustrator), who contributed many articles himself. It was a typical product of the Second Empire, its most flourishing period, with a staff which included brilliant artists and writers but no professional journalists. Taine's *Thomas Graindorge* (see *Notes sur Paris*) appeared in it. Gustave Droz, Ludovic Halévy, Charles Monselet, P.-J. Toulet (qq.v.) were contributors. Matter and illustrations were amusing and witty, occasionally risky in tone. It continued, on a lower level, into the 20th century.

La Vie parisienne is also the title of one of Offenbach's (q.v.) most popular operettas (1866), with libretto by Meilhac and Halévy (qq.v.).

Vie, Poésies et Pensées de Joseph Delorme (1829), a volume, mostly of poems, supposedly by a friend of Sainte-Beuve who died young. In fact the author was Sainte-Beuve himself. In a prefatory memoir which contains much autobiography he pictures Joseph Delorme as a melancholy, misunderstood, ill-fated Romantic who died in obscure poverty. The poems, which show signs of Sainte-Beuve's feeling for the English Lake poets, were on a note, unusual for their time, which, together with prosodic innovations, influenced later poets, Baudelaire among them. They were gentle, reflective, intimate (at times almost prosaic) rather than highly imaginative, and described humble scenes and people, small streets in Paris, and uneventful lives.

Vies des dames illustres; ***Vies des dames galantes*** (2 vols.); ***Vies des hommes illustres et grands capitaines français*** (4 vols.); ***Vies des hommes illustres et grands capitaines étrangers*** (2 vols.), the nine volumes of *Lives* in Brantôme's (q.v.) memoirs.

Vies des hommes illustres, Les (1559, 2 vols.), see *Amyot*.

Vieux Célibataire, Le (1792), a comedy by Jean-François Collin d'Harleville (q.v.).

Vieux-Colombier, Théâtre du, a famous experimental theatre in Paris, run between 1913 and 1924 by the actor and producer Jacques Copeau (1878–1949, q.v.). New techniques of production and acting were encouraged, and plays were accepted for their interest as works of art rather than for their potential money-making qualities. It brought many new dramatists to the fore and also put on notable productions of old plays, e.g. the production of *Twelfth Night* (*La Nuit des Rois*). Dullin and Jouvet (qq.v.), well-known producers themselves at a later date, were with the original Vieux-Colombier company. (See also *Compagnie des Quinze*.)

Vieux Cordelier, Le, the most eloquent journal of the Revolutionary era, founded December 1793, and wholly written, by Camille Desmoulins (q.v.). There were seven numbers, published at five-day intervals, each bearing the motto 'Vivre libre ou mourir'. The whole series was an appeal for moderation, elaborating Machiavelli's saying printed at the head of the first number: 'Dès que ceux qui gouvernent seront haïs, leurs concurrens ne tarderont pas à être admirés.' The third number consisted almost wholly of quotations (possibly at second hand, see below) from Tacitus, cleverly strung together to form a severe indictment of the Revolutionary excesses. The fourth, which people stood in queues outside the booksellers' to buy, was the protest which eventually cost Desmoulins his life, against the excessive bloodshed of the Terror, and an appeal for the establishment of a *comité de clémence*. Desmoulins was arrested while he was correcting the proofs of the seventh, and last, number and was executed before it appeared. The famous closing phrase, 'Les Dieux ont soif' (Carlyle's 'The Gods are athirst', and the title, in 1912, of Anatole France's fine novel of the Revolution), is said—by Mathiez et Calvet, ed. *Le Vieux Cordelier*, 1936—to be one of many signs that Desmoulins made extensive use of the Scottish pamphleteer Thomas Gordon's *Tacitus* and the *Political Discourses* which precede it. (Thomas Gordon was the 'Silenus' of Pope's *Dunciad*.) These were translated by the French Protestant writer and theologian Pierre Daudé (1685–1754) in 1742, with subsequent editions, including one during the Revolution (1794). Gordon [*Tacitus, Works* (1728), II. i *Discourses*, 169] speaks of the priests of Mexico who were wont to cry . . . that the Deities were hungry. In the translation this becomes: 'Les Dieux ont faim! c'est ce que les prêtres . . . avaient coutume de crier . . . .' Desmoulins, with a sound rhetorical flair, changes *faim* to *soif*.

[It may be of interest to note here that a similar passage: 'Les prêtres faisoient dire à l'Empereur que les Dieux avoient faim'— occurs in another widely-read book of the period, the abbé Raynal's *Histoire des établissements et du commerce des Européens dans les deux Indes,* 1770 and subsequent editions. The quotation is from the 1780 (Geneva) edition, ii. 35.]

Vigée-Lebrun, MME ÉLISABETH (1755–1842), painter, remembered especially for her portraits, which include several of Marie-Antoinette.

Vignettes romantiques, Les, see *Champfleury*.

Vignon, MARIE-LOUISE (1888–   ), author
of nature and love poems, e.g. *Chants de
jeunesse* (1911), *Ciels clairs de France* (1922
and 1932), &c.

Vigny, ALFRED DE (1797–1863), poet and
novelist, sometimes called the 'intellectual'
of the Romantic Movement (see *Romantisme*
and cf. *Hugo, Lamartine,* and *Musset, Alfred
de*), was born at Loches (Touraine) and
brought up in Paris, in a family circle composed largely of returned *émigrés* with ultra-
Royalist sympathies. On leaving school,
where he was persecuted by his fellow
pupils, he obtained a commission in the
royal bodyguard. His army career was un-
distinguished, partly for lack of opportunity
(the glorious days of the army were ending),
but largely because he was temperamentally
unfitted for a life of action. He soon began
to write, some of his most famous poems
(e.g. *Moïse* and *Éloa,* in *Poèmes antiques et
modernes,* 1826, q.v.) dating from 1815, and
his historical novel *Cinq-Mars* (1826, q.v.)
being partly written when he was stationed
in the Pyrenees in 1824; and on his periods of
army leave he frequented Nodier's *cénacle*
(q.v.), which saw the first flowering of the
Romantic Movement. At this time he formed
a friendship with Victor Hugo. He left the
army in 1827 and settled in Paris. In 1825 he
had married Lydia Bunbury, the daughter of
a wealthy Englishman from Demerara. She
soon lapsed into invalidism, and her fortune
was a myth, but his marriage, and visits to
England, brought him many English friends.

(2) By this time Vigny's reputation had
been made by the *Poèmes antiques et modernes*
and still further established by *Cinq-Mars,*
and he was at the happiest and most fecund
period of his creative life. He frequented the
Romantic circles more rarely. Their noisy
expansiveness was uncongenial to his reserved nature, and his friendship with Hugo
was cooling off, largely owing to the latter's
jealousy at the success of his dramatic works.
These had begun with translations from
Shakespeare—*Shylock* (1828) and *Othello*
(1829)—and continued with *La Maréchale
d'Ancre* (1831), a long, complicated, historical
drama; *Quitte pour la peur* (1833), a short,
witty piece (not unlike the *proverbes* to come
later from Alfred de Musset) in which an
absentee husband returns to save his young
wife's honour and at the same time dis-

covers her charm; and *Chatterton* [i.e. the poet
Chatterton] (1835, q.v.), his masterpiece.
This had a striking success at the Théâtre
Français, possibly due in part to the acting
of Marie Dorval (q.v.) as Kitty Bell. Vigny
had an unhappy liaison with this actress for
many years. He broke with her finally in
1835 and thereafter wrote no more for the
stage. During this period he had also published collections of tales—*Stello* (1832,
q.v.), three tales which, like *Chatterton,*
illustrate the sufferings of oppressed and
unrecognized genius, and *Servitude et
grandeur militaires* (1835, q.v.), three episodes
of the Napoleonic wars.

(3) From 1835 until his death Vigny's life
was uneventful and increasingly melancholy.
His mother, whom he had nursed devotedly,
died in 1837 after a long illness. His wife's
hopeless invalidism called from him a selfless
care which, added to monetary worries and a
disinclination for the battles of life, led him
to withdraw from the world. He retired for
increasingly long periods, sometimes years,
to the manor of Maine-Giraud (near
Angoulême) which he had inherited. Except
for rare visits from intimate friends his life
was one of seclusion. His days were devoted
to nursing his wife or to managing his small
property. At nights, in the small turret-
chamber called by Sainte-Beuve his *tour
d'ivoire,* he wrote and read. His writing was
largely correspondence, and the *pensées,*
day-to-day jottings, and drafts of seldom-
completed works that form the interesting
Journal d'un poète (1867, posth.). During these
years he also wrote eleven poems collected
posthumously (*Les Destinées,* 1864) after
some had appeared in reviews in his lifetime.
These are noteworthy for the manner in
which the poet, starting with a concrete
image, develops a philosophical idea. They
all reveal stoical, somewhat bitter resignation to the world as a place of suffering, to
life as a process of abnegation, and to God,
if He exists, as the ruthless Divinity of the
Old Testament, of whom it is better to make
oneself independent. The most famous are
*La Bouteille à la mer, L'Esprit pur, La Maison
du berger, Le Mont des oliviers, La Mort du
loup* (qq.v.), *La Colère de Samson.*

(4) Vigny's sense of spiritual loneliness
was deepened by unsuccessful attempts to
enter politics. He returned to Paris in 1853
but still lived in an isolated fashion with few

outside interests except his duties as a member of the *Académie française* and his contacts with young writers in need of encouragement. His wife died in 1862 and he, already suffering from cancer, outlived her only a few months. Ten *Poèmes* which he had published anonymously in 1822 were afterwards added to *Poèmes antiques et modernes*; and *Daphné*, a short novel found among his papers at his death, appeared in 1912 in the *Revue de Paris*. A correspondence with a young woman called Augusta was discovered about 1950 and published in 1952 (*Lettres d'un dernier amour*).

Vilain Mire, Le, i.e. The Peasant Doctor, a *fabliau* which probably suggested to Molière the idea of *Le Médecin malgré lui*.

A peasant is in the habit of beating his wife, hoping thereby to keep her faithful. She seeks a remedy for her sorry plight. Two messengers of the king ask her for hospitality; they are on their way to England to fetch a doctor for the king's daughter, who has a fish-bone in her throat. She tells them they need not go so far, for her husband is the best physician in the world, though he will only display his skill after having been well beaten. The messengers seize the husband and carry him to the court, where a sound beating awakens the man's wit, and he cures the princess by making her laugh.

Vilain qui conquist paradis par plaist, Le, a *fabliau* (q.v.). A villein is refused admission to Paradise. Thereupon he maintains his claim against St. Peter, St. Thomas, and St. Paul by caustic references to their earthly lives; a curious example of the element of irreverence so often to be remarked in medieval devotion.

Vildrac, CHARLES MESSAGER (1882–   ), poet and dramatist, born in Paris, was (with Duhamel, q.v.) an original member of the Abbaye (q.v.) community of young writers and artists. His works, often reminiscent of the early ideals of this group, include: *Poèmes* (1905), *Images et Mirages* (1907, printed on the Abbaye press), *Chants du désespéré* (1920), verse characterized by a belief in friendship and in man's intrinsic goodness; a number of plays, mostly collected in two volumes of *Théâtre*; and also some stories for children (e.g. *L'Île rose, Les Lunettes du lion*), outstanding among modern

literature of their kind. His considerable reputation as a dramatist was made with a small masterpiece of character study, *Le Paquebot Tenacity* (3 acts, produced in 1920, printed in the author's collected *Théâtre*, 1943–8). Two ex-soldiers about to emigrate to Canada arrive from Paris at Mme Cordier's inn on the waterfront at Le Havre. Bastien, full of drive and self-confidence, is the moving spirit. Ségard, gentle and diffident, follows where he is led. They have to remain at the inn for a fortnight because the s.s. *Tenacity*, in which they are to sail, develops engine trouble. Each in his own way makes love to Thérèse the serving-maid. When sailing day comes it is the go-ahead planner Bastien who backs out at the last minute and elopes with Thérèse. Ségard, too diffident to speak when he might have won Thérèse, and too lacking in determination to renounce a project about which he had never been more than half-hearted, sets out in the *Tenacity* for Canada.

Villages illusoires, Les (1895), collected poems by Émile Verhaeren (q.v.).

Villa Médicis, see *École de Rome*.

Villanelle, a poem composed, in its typical form, of an indefinite number of tercets and ending with a quatrain, the whole containing only two rhymes, as follows:

aba   aba   aba...abaa

The first and third lines of the first tercet recur alternately as the third lines of the succeeding tercets, and together as the third and fourth lines of the quatrain.

Villars, LOUIS-HECTOR, DUC DE (1653–1734), maréchal de France, who commanded the French army at Malplaquet (1709) and won the victory of Denain (1712). He was admitted to the *Académie* in 1714, and is remembered in a literary connexion for his friendship with the youthful Voltaire, who frequented the château de Villars in the period 1718–24. His *Mémoires* were, at least in part, arranged after his death from his letters, dispatches, and other papers. The best edition is that of 1884–91 (Société de l'Histoire de France).

Ville, La (1893), by Claudel (q.v.), a poetic drama.

Villedieu, Catherine des Jardins, Mme de (1640–83), author of some thirty short novels (now forgotten, which had a considerable vogue in their day), besides other equally forgotten writings. The best of the novels is said to be *Mémoires de la vie de Henriette-Sylvie de Molière*.

Villehardouin, Geoffroy de, historian, born not later than 1152 near Troyes in Champagne, died *c.* 1212 in the East. He held the position of *maréchal* (q.v.) of Champagne and took part, as warrior, diplomat, and counsellor, in the Fourth Crusade, which was launched in 1202, after long preparations, for the recovery of the Holy Sepulchre (reconquered from the Christians by Saladin in 1187). Villehardouin was one of the negotiators with Venice for the transport of the Crusaders and his narrative of the negotiations and of the operations that followed (to 1207) is entitled *Conquête de Constantinople*. It is in part an explanation and defence of the diversion of the Crusade from its original purpose to a predatory excursion against the Greek Empire, which was, in the intention (never realized) of the barons, to serve as a base of further operations in the Holy Land. The candour and sincerity of the narrative in this connexion has been a matter of controversy. Villehardouin received various fiefs in the East and was made *maréchal* of Romania (i.e. the empire of the East). His narrative is a brief, precise, somewhat dry record of events, lit up by a few vivid passages describing striking scenes, e.g. the sailing of the crusaders from Corfù (ch. 60) and their first view of Constantinople (ch. 64). The work is important as one of the earliest examples of French prose and of French memoirs.

Ville lumière, La, i.e. Paris. The name is said to go back to the year 1470, when the *Recueil des lettres de Gasparin de Bergame* [Gasparinus Barzizius, 1370–1431, the Italian restorer of learning] was the first book to issue from the first printing-press established in France. The work was dedicated to Paris: 'De même que le soleil répand partout la lumière, ainsi toi, ville de Paris, capitale du royaume, nourricière des Muses, tu verses la science sur le monde.'

Villemain, Abel-François (1790–1870),

literary historian, critic, sometime politician, born in Paris. He had long been marked down as one of the most brilliant young scholars of his day when, at twenty-six, he became Professor of French Eloquence (and a famous lecturer on 15th-, 16th-, and 17th-century French literature) at the Sorbonne (1816–30). His career between 1830 and 1848 was largely political and he twice held office as Minister of Public Instruction.

His approach to literary criticism was novel for its day, being concerned mainly with literature in its relation to history (cf. Mme de Staël; and see *Critics and criticism*, paras. 7, 8) and with parallels between French and European literature (which, except German, he knew well). His chief works include: *Discours et Mélanges littéraires* (1823; containing noteworthy studies of Montaigne, Montesquieu, Fénelon, Pascal); *Nouveaux Mélanges historiques et littéraires* (1827); *Cours de littérature française* (1828; vols. 3–6 have a panorama of 18th-century literature); *Études de littérature anc'enne et étrangère* (1846); *Choix d'études sur la littérature contemporaine* (1857), &c. His *Souvenirs contemporains* contain interesting descriptions of events and opinion during the First Empire (particularly the Hundred Days) and the Restoration period (e.g. lectures and lecturers at the Sorbonne *c.* 1825 and the thirst for knowledge that sprang from idealistic conceptions of liberty; literary and political *salons*).

Villeparisis, the elderly Mme de, in Proust's *A la recherche du temps perdu* (q.v.), aunt of the duchesse de Guermantes, and somewhat *déclassée* by her long-standing liaison with the diplomat M. de Norpois. In her *salon* Marcel (q.v.) studies human nature and social climbers. Here, too, he realizes an ambition and is introduced to the duchesse de Guermantes.

Villequier, on the Seine, the place where Hugo's daughter Léopoldine and her husband were drowned on 4 September 1843 when out boating. One of the famous poems of *Les Contemplations* (q.v., in Bk. IV) is the elegy 'A Villequier'.

Villeroi, Nicolas de (1598–1685), maréchal de France, tutor to Louis XIV.

Villers-Cotterêts, a small town near Soissons and Compiègne. Its château was rebuilt as a royal residence by François Ier and it was there that he issued (10 Aug. 1539) one of the famous *ordonnances*, or decrees, of French history, the *ordonnance Guillelmine* (from Guillaume Poyet, *c.* 1474–1568, the celebrated jurist, who drafted it). In addition to certain civil and juridical reforms it made French the language of official records and usage.

Villes tentaculaires, Les (1895), collected poems by Émile Verhaeren (q.v.).

Villiers de l'Isle-Adam, PHILIPPE-AUGUSTE, COMTE DE (1838–89), novelist and dramatist, born at St-Brieuc (Brittany), belonged to an ancient, impoverished, and by his father's time eccentric, family steeped in traditions of grandeur and chivalry, and fervently Roman Catholic. After an education of sorts in Brittany he lived mainly in Paris, made literature the sole object of a vagabond existence, and suffered atrocious poverty which had only slightly lessened when he died. He is usually classed as a Symbolist. His writing, of undeniably poetic quality, is often obscure, ornate in language and rhythm, and heavily influenced by philosophical ideas and by all the *isms* in vogue in his day (occultism, spiritualism, Wagnerism, &c., and cf. *Foreign Influences on French Literature*, paras. 21–23, 25). But it is also characterized by its at times extravagantly romantic spirit (see *Romantisme*), exemplified, for instance, in the poetic drama *Axël* (1890, q.v.) or the earlier dramas *Elen* (1865) and *Morgane* (1866), or in the 'horrific' parts of *Claire Lenoir* (in the collection *Tribulat Bonhomet*, 1887, q.v.). Many of the *Contes cruels* (1883) and the *Nouveaux Contes cruels* (1888), too, belong to the horrific genre, though others, perhaps the best, are realistic, ironical, and much more tautly written.

Other works by this author include the dramas *La Révolte* (1870), earlier than, but with a theme resembling, Ibsen's *A Doll's House*; *Le Nouveau Monde* (1880), which won a prize for a play commemorating the centenary of the American Revolution; and a semi-scientific, semi-philosophical novel *L'Ève future* (1886).

Villon, FRANÇOIS (1431–?), poet, originally named François de Montcorbier (from the village on the borders of Burgundy where his father was born) or des Loges (probably the name of his father's farm), was himself born in Paris. He was brought up by Guillaume de Villon, chaplain of Saint-Benoît-le-Bétourné in Paris, whose name he assumed and who remained his kindly patron. He joined the University of Paris and became a licentiate and master of arts; he took part in the turbulent life of the students, frequented disreputable society, and fell into evil ways. In 1455 he killed in a quarrel an ecclesiastic, Philippe Sermoise. On Christmas Eve 1456 he, with some companions, broke into the Collège de Navarre and carried off 500 gold pieces. The *Lais* (i.e. 'legs', legacies) or *Petit Testament*, his earliest poem of which we know the date with certainty, was written precisely at this time. In it he represents himself as driven to leave Paris by the perfidy of the woman he loved, and facetiously bequeaths to each of his friends and enemies some worthless memento—a stolen duck, the sword and the breeches he has pawned, and to his false love his broken heart. He thus provided an innocent explanation of his flight from Paris, dictated by fear of arrest. He remained in exile for six years, probably wandering about France from town to town. We know that he visited Blois, where Charles d'Orléans received poets at his court, and took part in a poetic contest organized by the prince. There is some evidence that he was in prison at Orleans about 1457 or 1460. In 1461 we find him imprisoned at Meung-sur-Loire by order of the Bishop of Orleans, a captivity which lasted for many months and against the cruelty and injustice of which he never ceased to protest. It ended in October of that year with a general release from his prison when Louis XI passed through the town. Some time in 1461, in a fit of despair caused by ill health, destitution, and remorse, he had composed his *Testament*, a poem of some 2,000 lines, very different in sentiment and character from the *Petit Testament* of 1456. In it he reviews his life, his mistaken courses, his disappointments in love, and his sufferings, and expresses his horror of sickness, old age, the jail, poverty, and death. As in the *Lais*, and parodying the legal forms of a testamentary disposition, he makes a number of bequests, some pathetic, some ironical, some facetious, to various persons: his old mother and foster-father, comrades and women who have entered into his life, tavern-keepers, the executioner, jailers, police officers, and officials of the court with whom he has had dealings, and many others. By its mingled bitterness, melancholy, and humour, its sincerity and deep feeling, it contrasts strikingly with the insipid lyrics of his predecessors and with the moralizings of the *rhétoriqueurs* who followed him. Villon inserted in it a number of *ballades* and *rondeaux*, some written at an earlier date which he wished to have preserved, others written at the same time as the main poem; a few are left as legacies to various persons. These inset pieces include some of his best-known work, the *Regrets de la belle heaulmière*, the *Ballade des dames du temps jadis*, the *Contredits Franc Gontier* (q.v.), and the *oraison* for the soul of Jehan Cotar.

He had returned to Paris, and in the autumn of 1462 we find him twice more under arrest. In the second case he had been present at an affray in which a papal notary was wounded. For this he was sentenced to be hanged, a sentence which was quashed on appeal; but he was exiled from Paris for ten years 'in view of his evil life'. The death sentence evoked the moving poem or epitaph (*Ballade des pendus*), perhaps his finest work, beginning 'Frères humains qui après nous vivez', in which he sees himself swinging on the gibbet and appeals to God from the justice of men. Apart from a gay *ballade* on the success of his appeal, and another of thanks to the court, we hear no more of him. The date of his death is unknown. Rabelais has two anecdotes in which he is referred to, but for various reasons they are thought undeserving of credit.

Villon's surviving work amounts to no more than some 3,000 lines. It is almost entirely included in the *Lais* and the *Testament*. The principal other pieces are the *ballade* composed for the poetic contest above mentioned (*Je meurs de soif auprès de la fontaine*), the *Débat du cuer* [cœur] *et du corps de Villon*, and the epitaph composed under sentence of death. The *Lais* and the *Testament* (apart from the inserted poems) are in octosyllabic *huitains* (q.v.). The *Ballades en jargon* are some half-dozen pieces written in the cant or secret language of the Coquillards (q.v.), with some of whom Villon had relations. They are chiefly of philological interest. The *Repues franches* (literally 'free meals', sc. 'artful thefts') is a collection of little pieces

of verse, at one time attributed to Villon, in fact composed about the end of the century, relating various tricks and knaveries supposed to have been carried out by him and his associates. His connexion with these misdeeds is now regarded as purely legendary.

He found early imitators of his literary work in the poets Coquillart and Henri Baude (qq.v.) and in 1533 Clément Marot issued an edition of the 'meilleur poëte parisien qui se trouve'; but after the middle of the 16th century, Villon was in large measure forgotten until the 19th century. The *Ballade des dames du temps jadis* was translated into English by D. G. Rossetti and *La Belle Heaulmière* by Swinburne.

Vimeiro, a town in Portugal, north of Lisbon, where on 21 August 1805 Wellington, at the head of a British expeditionary force and Portuguese troops, defeated the French under General Junot (see *Abrantès, duc d'*). This gave the British a base in Portugal from which to continue the Peninsular war.

Vin blanc de la Villette, Le (1914), a collection of tales by Jules Romains (q.v.).

Vincennes, Château et Donjon de, on the outskirts of Paris, originally a royal hunting-box, was rebuilt as a fortified castle between 1328 and 1373, and the court was held there until Versailles took its place. Under Louis XIII persons imprisoned under *lettres de cachet* (q.v.) were sent to the dungeons, among them being Diderot and Mirabeau (qq.v.). In the summer of 1749 Rousseau (q.v., para. 2) was walking from Paris to Vincennes to visit Diderot, reading the *Mercure de France* to keep him from going too quickly in the heat, when his eye lighted on the subject proposed by the Académie de Dijon for the following year's literary contest and he had the sudden revelation of his *Discours sur les sciences et les arts*. It was at Vincennes, also, that Mirabeau's famous *Essai sur les lettres de cachet* (1784) was written. Prince Charles Edward Stuart was imprisoned there for a few days shortly after he escaped to France from Culloden, and in 1804 the duc d'Enghien (q.v.) was executed in the moat. Vincennes is now a fort and a barracks.

Vincent de Beauvais (d. *c.* 1264), a learned Dominican, who enjoyed favour at the court of Louis IX; author of the *Speculum* *majus*, an enormous Latin compilation of all the knowledge of the time. He is mentioned by Chaucer in the prologue to *The Legend of Good Women*. The *Speculum* was translated, about 1330, into French by Jean de Vignai.

Vincent de Lérins, Saint (d. *c.* A.D. 450), a religious who, after bearing arms in his youth, retired to the monastery of Lérins (on an island near Antibes) and became noted for his wisdom, piety, and eloquence. He was author of a *Commonitorium pro catholicae fidei antiquitate* in defence of the tradition of the Church, a work which was later repeatedly printed and translated. It contains the often quoted phrase, 'quod semper, quod ubique, quod ab omnibus, creditum est'.

Vincent de Paul, Saint (1576–1660), a shepherd-boy who became a priest, celebrated for his self-sacrificing labour and countless works of benevolence among the aged and the oppressed, as well as for his simple eloquence. He was the founder, in 1625, of the *Congrégation de la Mission*, known as the Lazarists (cf. *Saint-Lazare, Prison de*), and (in 1633) of the Sisters of Charity, and was canonized in 1737.

Voltaire expressed his predilection for Saint Vincent de Paul among the saints on account of his beneficence and humility (letter to the marquis de Villette, 4 Jan. 1766).

Vinet, ALEXANDRE (1797–1847), a Swiss, born at Ouchy (Lausanne) of French refugee origin, was both man of letters and theologian, holding chairs of theology and of French literature at the Academy [the small university] of Lausanne. His solid, somewhat dryly written, but penetrating criticism reflected a high sense of moral values and a sure appreciation of French literature. His judgement was highly esteemed by his fellow critics, e.g. Sainte-Beuve, Brunetière (qq.v.). Besides several works of a religious character his writings included *Études sur Pascal* (1848) and *Études sur la littérature française au XIXᵉ siècle* (1849–51, 3 vols.).

Vingt ans après (1845), an historical novel by Dumas *père*, continues the adventures of *Les Trois Mousquetaires* (q.v.).

Vingt mille lieues sous les mers, see Verne, Jules.

Vinteuil, a composer, in Proust's *A la recherche du temps perdu* (q.v.). His music (a sonata and a posthumous septet), and the emotions and reflections it inspires, are a constantly recurring feature of the novel's emotional and aesthetic background.

Vintras, PIERRE-MICHEL (1807–75), religious reformer and visionary, born at Bayeux, had been by turns tailor, domestic servant, and clerk to a wine merchant, and was in 1839 assistant manager of a cardboard factory, when he had his first visit from the Archangel Michael. After this he proclaimed himself the Prophet Elijah, reincarnated to reform the Church. He lived in an atmosphere of visions and miracles, instituted a new cult, celebrated a sacrilegious mass, and in 1850 was condemned by the Pope (Pius IX). He also made the authorities uneasy by his support of the *faux dauphin* Naundorf's (q.v.) claim to the throne of France. Official investigations into his activities were begun and he fled to London. He continued to preach the new Evangel, to work miracles, and to send inspiring messages to the faithful in various parts of France. In 1862 he returned and established himself at Lyons, where he died. [The brothers Baillard, who figure in Barrès's novel *La Colline inspirée*, q.v., were disciples of Vintras.]

Viol de Lucrèce, Le (1931), a play by André Obey (q.v.).

Viollet-le-Duc, EUGÈNE-EMMANUEL (1814–79), architect, born in Paris, is remembered especially, and not always kindly, as a restorer of medieval buildings. He also wrote many valuable works on architectural subjects, e.g. *Dictionnaire raisonné de l'architecture française du XIᵉ au XVIᵉ siècle* (1854, illustrated by himself); *Essai sur l'architecture militaire au moyen âge* (1854), &c.

Violon d'Ingres, see *Ingres*.

Virelai, a short poem, of which the form dates from the 14th century, on two (sometimes three) rhymes variously arranged. Two of the lines of the first stanza are repeated alternately as refrains in the course of the poem at intervals; the poem sometimes closes with the same two lines. A typical form of the *virelai*, of which there were many varieties, is that of Deschamps's *Sui-je, sui-je, sui-je belle?*:

$$A^{(1)} \ b \ b \ c \ A^{(2)}$$
$$b \ b \ c \ A^{(1)}$$
$$b \ b \ c \ A^{(2)}$$
$$b \ b \ c \ A^{(1)}$$

where $A^{(1)}$ and $A^{(2)}$ are two refrains on the same rhyme.

The origin of the word *virelai* is uncertain; it is probably a modification (under the influence of the word *lai*) of *vireli* (see *Chansons à danser*).

Vireli, see *Chansons à danser* and *Virelai.*

Viret, PIERRE (1511–71), a Swiss religious reformer, disciple of Lefèvre d'Étaples (q.v.), and author of many satirical pamphlets, *Le Monde à l'empire* (i.e. 'qui devient pire'), &c.

Virginie, see *Paul et Virginie.*

Visan, TANCRÈDE DE [pseudonym of VINCENT BIÉTRIX] (1878–1945), born at Lyons, was the author of poetry, and of essays and studies which make him one of the most interesting critics of his generation. His publications include: two prose works which fall into the category of novels, *Lettres à l'élue: confession d'un intellectuel* (1908) and *En regardant passer les vaches* (1924); two poetic collections, *Paysages introspectifs* (1904) and, a few years before he died, *Le Clair Matin sourit* (1938), both containing valuable introductory essays—'sur le Symbolisme' in the first case and 'Mon credo poétique' in the second; also numerous critical studies (sometimes first contributed to the reviews *Vers et Prose* and *L'Occident*), e.g. *Paul Bourget sociologue* (1908); *Colette et Bérénice* (1909); *Les Élégies et les sonnets de Louise Labé* (1910); *Le Guignol lyonnais* (1910); *L'Attitude du lyrisme contemporain* (1911), collected studies of Verlaine, Vielé-Griffin, Verhaeren, Maeterlinck, and others, of added interest for his remarks on poetic vision, *le vers libre*, &c.; *Un Homme de lettres: le comte Gobineau* (the preface to a 1913 edition of Gobineau's, q.v., *Nouvelles asiatiques*); *De la culture* (1921); *Essais sur la tradition française* (1921), which includes some of the above-mentioned; *Sous le signe du lion* (1935), and *Le Visage et le masque* (1942).

Visé, JEAN DONNEAU DE, see *Mercure Galant.*

Vision de Babouc, see *Babouc.*

Vision de Charles XI [of Sweden], *La,* by Mérimée, a tale of hallucination, in the form of a historical narrative. It appeared first in 1829 in the *Revue de Paris*, and was included in 1833 in the collection *Mosaïque* (see *Mérimée*, para. 4).

Visionnaires, Les, see *Desmarets de Saint-Sorlin.* For *Lettres sur les Visionnaires* see *Nicole. Les Visionnaires* is also the title of a novel (1933) by Julien Green (q.v.).

Visionnarisme, see *Literary Isms.*

Vitry, JACQUES DE, see *Jacques de Vitry.*

Vitry, PHILIPPE DE, see *Franc Gontier.*

Vivien, RENÉE [pseud. of Pauline Tarn] (1877–1909), poetess, born in London of an English father and an American mother, lived nearly all her life in Paris and wrote in French. Her musical, very sensuous verse, which shows the influence of Baudelaire, was written with great purity of form (sometimes in Sapphic metres) and usually on perverse themes (*Poésies complètes*, 1901–10, 12 vols.; 1934, 2 vols.).

Vivonne, CATHERINE DE, see *Rambouillet.*

Vogue, La, a well-known Symbolist (see *Symbolisme*) review (weekly, 32 numbers from 1886). It published *Les Illuminations* by Rimbaud, and some of Verlaine's *Poètes maudits* (q.v.). Other contributors were Paul Bourget, Édouard Dujardin, Félix Fénéon, Jules Laforgue, Villiers de l'Isle-Adam, Mallarmé. It was revived for a few numbers in 1889 by Gustave Kahn and Adolphe Retté and again in 1899 by Tristan Klingsor. (See also *Vers libre.*)

Vogüé, VICOMTE MELCHIOR DE (1850–1910), a novelist and man of letters whose studies of Turgenev, Dostoevski, and Tolstoy (*Le Roman russe*, 1886) stimulated interest in Russian novelists and indirectly influenced the French novel. Russian influence is apparent in his own idealistic novels, e.g. *Jean d'Agrève* (1897), *Les Morts qui parlent* (1899), *Le Maître de la mer* (1903). His quick sympathies and receptive understanding of a changing world were appreciated by younger writers.

Voie Royale, La (1930), a novel by André Malraux (q.v.).

Voir dit, see *Guillaume de Machaut.*

Voisenon, CLAUDE-HENRI, ABBÉ DE (1708–75), author of light verses and tales, popular in the *salons* of the time, a friend of Voltaire. He wrote *Le Sultan Misapouf et la princesse Grisemine.*

Voisin, La, see *Chambre ardente.*

Voiture, VINCENT (1598–1648), poet and letter-writer, son of a wine-merchant of Amiens, a man of brilliant social gifts covering more serious qualities of intellect. He was for a time in the service of Gaston d'Orléans (brother of Louis XIII), and later obtained an appointment at court; he visited Italy and Spain on political missions. He is best known as one of the principal habitués from about 1625 of the Hôtel de Rambouillet (q.v.), where he was esteemed for his wit and amusing conversation. His works consist of occasional verses written for that circle and of letters which show a pleasant wit and fancy, if also an excess of subtlety and conceits, and which contributed to the improvement of French prose. They contain here and there the same kind of amusing whimsical nonsense that we find in Charles Lamb's letters. Tallemant calls him 'le père de l'ingénieuse badinerie', but he could also write well on serious subjects, as for instance in his letter on the recapture of Corbie from the Spaniards (1636), a fine panegyric of Richelieu. For the famous dispute over the sonnets of Voiture and Benserade, see under the name of the latter. Voiture was an original member of the *Académie.* His writings were published posthumously. See also *Costar.*

Voix intérieures, Les (1837), lyrics by Victor Hugo, inspired partly by family, partly by national events. Well-known items in this collection are the lines *A Eugène Vicomte Hugo* (his brother, who died after several years spent in a mental home), *A l'Arc de triomphe, A Virgile, A des oiseaux envolés.*

Voland or **Volland,** MLLE SOPHIE, see *Diderot.*

Vol d'aigle, Le, signifies Napoleon's sudden escape from Elba in 1815 and his swift and triumphant march on Paris. (Cf. his proclamation dictated while crossing from Elba, and read by his officers to their men on landing: 'Soldats! nous n'avons pas été vaincus! ... La victoire marchera au pas de charge; l'aigle avec les couleurs nationales volera de clocher en clocher jusqu'aux tours de Notre-Dame!')

Vollichon, M. and MME, characters in Furetière's *Roman bourgeois* (q.v.).

Volney, CONSTANTIN, COMTE DE (1757–1820), the author, celebrated in his day, of a *Voyage en Syrie et en Égypte* (1787), and of *Les Ruines ou Méditations sur les révolutions des empires* (1791), a singular mixture of picturesque description with philosophical disquisition, suggested by the ruins of the past, on the origin and growth of social, political, and religious institutions. The author concludes in favour of the equality of all men before the law and the overthrow of despotism; while from a comparison of various religions, he infers the necessity of toleration and agnosticism in religious matters where truth is not verifiable.

Volpone. Ben Jonson's play of this name was adapted for the French stage in 1928 by Jules Romains and Stefan Zweig.

Voltaire, FRANÇOIS-MARIE AROUET, generally known as Voltaire (1694–1778), poet, historian, and philosopher.

LIFE AND PRINCIPAL WORKS

(1) Voltaire was born in Paris, of a family from Poitou. His father was a notary and later a minor official of the Chambre des Comptes. He was educated by the Jesuits at the Collège Louis-le-Grand, and at an early age became acquainted with the free-thinking and epicurean circle of the Temple (q.v.), which rebelled against the austerity of the last years of Louis XIV. He made the acquaintance of the aged Ninon de Lenclos (q.v.), who left him a small legacy. An attempt to wean him from frivolous society by sending him as page to the French ambassador in the Netherlands (1713) only resulted in an unfortunate love affair and his enforced return. During an eleven-month sojourn in the Bastille, in consequence of a pungent political lampoon, he completed his tragedy *Œdipe* (q.v.), produced with success in 1718 and printed in 1719 under the name of Voltaire (an approximate anagram of Arouet), by which he soon became known; he also worked at his epic on Henri IV,

which appeared as *La Ligue ou Henri le Grand* in 1723, and as *La Henriade* (q.v.) in 1728. Both *Œdipe* and the *Henriade* showed signs of the author's nascent political revolt. On his release he began once more to frequent the highest society, where his wit made him welcome. He received pensions from the court, speculated successfully, and became rich. In 1722 his *Le Pour et le Contre* appeared, a poem in support of deism, in the guise of arguments for and against Christianity. His tragedy *Marianne* was published in 1725. As the result of an altercation with the chevalier de Rohan, he was forced, after a further spell in the Bastille, to betake himself in 1726 to England, where he remained till early in 1729, learning English, reading Shakespeare, Milton, and the Restoration dramatists, making the acquaintance of Walpole, Congreve, Gay, Berkeley, and associating with Bolingbroke, Pope, and Swift. The chief literary fruit of his visit was the *Lettres philosophiques* (q.v.), published in 1734 (English version 1733). After his return to France he produced further tragedies, of which the more important were *Brutus* (1730, q.v.), *La Mort de César* (1731, showing Shakespearian influence), *Zaïre* (1732, q.v.); also his *Histoire de Charles XII* (1731, q.v.), his first attempt at history, and his *Temple du goût* (1733, q.v.), which provoked enmities among literary men.

(2) The publication of the *Lettres philosophiques* in 1734, 'the first bomb thrown at the *ancien régime*' (Lanson), exposed Voltaire to danger of arrest, and he left Paris; he established himself at Cirey, close to the frontier of Lorraine, at the house of the learned and intelligent Mme du Châtelet (q.v.), whose affection and protection he long enjoyed. His sojourn at Cirey, which lasted for ten years, was a period of great literary activity: he wrote a *Traité de métaphysique* about 1734 which was not published till later; the dramas *Alzire* (1736), *Mahomet* (1742), and *Mérope* (1743), qq.v.; *Le Mondain* (1736, q.v.), a satirical poem against the Jansenists, and the *Éléments de la philosophie de Newton* (same year), a popular exposition of the principal discoveries of Newton; and about the same time a philosophic poem, the *Discours sur l'homme*; and he worked at the *Siècle de Louis XIV* and the *Essai sur les mœurs*. He also devoted part of his time to scientific study and to physical

and chemical experiments, but his scientific work was defective and amateurish, for he lacked the necessary time and patience and was inclined to reject facts (e.g. fossils of fishes in the Alps) which appeared not to square with his theories. After 1743 (when Fleury died) he temporarily recovered some measure of favour at court, where he had powerful advocates (including Mme de Pompadour), though he was disliked and distrusted by the king (Louis XV). His *Poème de Fontenoy* (1745) constituted him a sort of official poet; he frequented Versailles and Fontainebleau, was made historiographer, and received a pension. He was admitted to the *Académie* in 1746. It was now that he wrote the philosophical tale *Zadig* (1747, q.v.) and the plays *Sémiramis* (1748), *Catilina* (1750), *Oreste* (1750)—these three in competition with Crébillon—but this period was on the whole one of sterility.

(3) In 1749 Mme du Châtelet died, and he sincerely mourned the loss of this good friend, though their liaison had been interrupted some time before. In 1750 he yielded to the pressing invitation of Frederick II and took up his residence at Potsdam. There he completed the *Siècle de Louis XIV* (1751, q.v.), continued work on the *Essai sur les mœurs*, which he had begun in 1740, and wrote, or completed, *Micromégas* (1752, q.v.). But Frederick and Voltaire could not get on together; a crisis was reached in 1753 and Voltaire left Prussia, after publishing his *Diatribe du Docteur Akakia* against his rival Maupertuis (q.v.), the president of Frederick's Academy of Science, and after a disagreeable incident at Frankfort, where he was subjected to the humiliation of being arrested and having his baggage searched. He now established himself for a time in Switzerland, at Lausanne in winter and in a property which he purchased near Geneva (*Les Délices*) in summer. *La Pucelle* (q.v.) appeared in 1755, but he disavowed its authorship; he wrote *L'Orphelin de la Chine* (a tragedy, 1755); his *Poème sur le désastre de Lisbonne* (1756), in which the terrible earthquake of 1755 in that city serves as a text for an attack on the doctrine of a free and benevolent Providence; and *Le Pauvre Diable* (a satire, 1758, q.v.). He also supported the *Encyclopédie* and wrote a number of articles for it, e.g. *Esprit*, *Grâce* (in their literary aspects). His relations with the Calvinists of Geneva were not harmonious;

and in 1760 he settled at Ferney, in French territory but close to the Swiss frontier, where he became master of a considerable estate and combined the life of a country magnate with immense literary activity. He was now very rich, thanks to his clever administration of his funds. In 1768, after vigorous reductions of expenditure, the budget of his establishment at Ferney was fixed at 40,000 livres a year, which provided for a staff of sixty servants and for twelve horses. His niece kept house for him, the ugly, vulgar, and extravagant Mme Denis, with whom it has become clear from correspondence recently discovered that he had been on most intimately affectionate terms since even before the break with Mme du Châtelet; and he was extremely hospitable, receiving distinguished guests of every nation. He had a host of adversaries (such as Fréron, Rousseau, Chaumeix, Pompignan, Monnotte) with whom he delighted to squabble; at the same time showing kindness and generosity in a multitude of cases of distress.

(4) Purely literary subjects hereafter occupied comparatively little of his time: *Tancrède* (1760, q.v.), his *Commentaire sur Corneille* (1764), his letter to the *Académie* against Shakespeare (1776); he was chiefly concerned with political, philosophical, and religious questions. His *Saül* (of which he denied the authorship), a mock tragedy in prose holding up to obloquy certain parts of the Old Testament connected with Saul, Samuel, and David, appeared in 1763; his *Dictionnaire philosophique* (see *Dictionaries and Encyclopedias*) in 1764; his deistic *Lettres de Memmius à Cicéron* in 1771. Some of his most effective work of propaganda is contained in his tales (called *romans*, but in reality merely the amusing vehicle for conveying his ideas on philosophical, religious, and political matters), dialogues, *facéties*, and private letters, of which a constant stream flowed from his pen during the last twenty years of his life. Of many of these (other than the private letters) he repudiated the authorship, but deceived no one. *Candide* (q.v.), his masterpiece among the tales, was published in 1759, *L'Ingénu* (q.v.) in 1767, *L'Homme aux quarante écus* (q.v.) in 1768, *Histoire de Jenni* (q.v.) in 1775. Other works of this kind not previously mentioned were *Babouc* and *Cosi Sancta* (written *c.* 1747), *Memnon* (1749), *Le Blanc et le noir* (1764),

Jeannot et Colin (1764), *La Princesse de Babylone* (1768), *Le Taureau blanc* (1774), qq.v. The dialogues, such as the conversation of *L'Intendant des menus avec l'abbé Grizel* on the excommunication of actors, are very vivid and realistic. It was during his residence at Ferney that, fired by his hatred of intolerance and injustice, he carried on to a successful issue his campaign for the rehabilitation of Jean Calas (q.v.), a Huguenot executed in 1762 on a false charge of murdering his son; a similar campaign for the rehabilitation of Sirven, another Huguenot, condemned on a somewhat similar charge; another in the case of La Barre, a youth decapitated for some trivial religious offence; and finally for the rehabilitation of the comte de Lally (q.v.), executed in consequence of the popular indignation at the loss of the French establishments in India, of which Lally was governor-general. He issued his *Traité sur la tolérance* in 1763. In 1778 the production of his last tragedy *Irène* (q.v.) was the occasion of his triumphal return to Paris. He was too ill to attend the Comédie-Française until the sixth performance, when he was acclaimed with the wildest enthusiasm and crowned with a wreath of laurel. A few weeks later he died (30 May 1778) in the house of the marquis de Villette on the quay which commemorates his name. The Church refused him burial, and this had to be carried out surreptitiously. His memory was avenged thirteen years later, when his remains were brought in triumph to the Panthéon.

CHARACTER AND OPINIONS

(5) Voltaire was a man of strangely varied characteristics: vain, irritable, vindictive, untruthful, sometimes servile; yet humane, generous, a good friend, and a passionate defender of the oppressed. Of the various forms of his literary activity, his philosophical propaganda is perhaps that by which he is best known. His views show a development during the course of his life, from the comparative optimism of his early days (seen for instance in *Babouc* and *Zadig*) to the pessimism of his later years (*Candide*). While affirming the existence of a Deity (e.g. in the *Sermon des cinquante*, 1761), he had little comprehension of religion and bitterly attacked the Christian faith (especially in its minor outward manifestations) with every resource

of wit and satire. His repeated war-cry was 'Écrasons l'infâme', apparently meaning by 'l'infâme' intolerant religious fanaticism, embodied in any dogmatic religion, but especially in Catholicism and its priesthood. In fact for him true religion consisted in the practice of virtue according to the conscience we have received from God, and this virtue he identified substantially with social justice. With this narrowness of spirit he combined extreme clearness of vision regarding the defective political organization and the practical abuses of his time, such as *lettres de cachet* and acts of religious intolerance. The dominant trait of his writings on political as well as on religious subjects is lack of respect for existing institutions and contempt for authority; he was thus a dissolvent influence and prepared the way for the Revolution. But he favoured the idea of government by a beneficent despot, a philosopher king. He aimed, not at a political upheaval, but at the transformation of political thought through rational criticism, which should bring the reign of humanity and justice.

LITERARY CHARACTERISTICS

(6) Voltaire's style is marked in general by simplicity, precision, brevity, and an appropriateness to the particular kind of writing in which he was engaged. His three principal historical works, on Charles XII and Louis XIV, and the *Essai sur les mœurs*, are carefully documented, rapid, luminous recitals of essential facts, tracing cause and effect, the parts played by the various actors, and their characters. But they are deficient in warmth and life and fail to resuscitate the ages they describe. In his tragedies he followed in the main the principles of the classic drama, though here and there we may trace the influence of Shakespeare (whom at one time he claimed, on the whole with justice, to have introduced to the Continent, but whom he subsequently condemned in his *Lettre à l'Académie* of 1776). But he is essentially a good playwright, aiming at scenic success rather than psychological study. He used many of his plays as vehicles for political or philosophical propaganda. Besides the tragedies named above (the best of which are perhaps *Zaïre*, *Mérope*, and *Alzire*), there are interesting features in *Olimpie* (1764), *Le Triumvirat* (1767), *Les Scythes* (1767), *Les Guèbres* (1769), and *Les*

Lois de Minos (1773), qq.v. His comedies are mediocre, for he lacked profundity of observation. The most successful were *L'Enfant prodigue* (1736) and *Nanine* (1749), qq.v., sentimental comedies. *L'Écossaise* (or *Le Café*, 1760) is a comedy in which his enemy Fréron is vilified as a starving journalist and cowardly calumniator. His philosophical tales, to the success of which reference has already been made, are marked by rapidity and sharp outline; they utilize trivial, comic, but vividly illustrative facts, substituting the striking concrete example for the abstract theory. Hence their appeal to all classes of readers. Their author had a gift of expressing better than anyone else what everyone was thinking.

(7) Voltaire was also an exquisite master of light verse, displaying his felicity of expression and lively wit in occasional trifles, epistles, satires, verse tales, &c. The *Épître à Boileau* and *Épître à Horace* are among his best later works; and these lines on Pindar illustrate his gift for gentle mockery:

> Sors du tombeau, divin Pindare,
> Toi qui célébras autrefois
> Les chevaux de quelques bourgeois
> Ou de Corinthe ou de Mégare;
> Toi qui possédas le talent
> De parler beaucoup sans rien dire;
> Toi qui modulas savamment
> Des vers que personne n'entend,
> Et qu'il faut toujours qu'on admire.

(8) His private letters, of which a vast number have been published, reveal the man in all his defects, and at the same time in his broad humanity, and are, in the opinion of some, his most characteristic writings; in them he is natural, lively, graceful, serious on occasion but soon reverting to gaiety. His general influence may be estimated from the fact that some fifty editions of his collected writings (apart from numerous editions of separate works) were issued in the hundred years from 1740. The most famous edition of the complete works was that printed at Kehl (in Baden), 1784-90, by the enterprise of Beaumarchais, who purchased for the purpose the type of the English printer Baskerville. Mention may also be made of the bibliography of Voltaire's works by G. Bengesco (1882-90) and the edition of his *Notebooks* by Th. Besterman (Genève, 1952).

Voltairien. The following definition is taken from the collected *Études et pensées* (1882) of Ernest Bersot (1816–80), philosophical writer and one-time director of the École normale supérieure.

'Un Voltairien est un homme qui aime assez à voir clair en toutes choses; en religion et en philosophie, il ne croit volontiers que ce qu'il comprend, et il consent à ignorer; il estime plus la pratique que la spéculation, simplifie la morale comme la doctrine, et la veut tourner aux vertus utiles; il aime une politique tempérée qui préserve la liberté naturelle, la liberté de la conscience, de la parole et de la personne, retranche le plus possible de mal, procure le plus possible de bien, et met au premier rang des biens la justice; dans les arts, il goûte par-dessus tout la mesure et la vérité; il déteste mortellement l'hypocrisie, le fanatisme et le mauvais goût; il ne se borne pas à les détester, il les combat à outrance.'

Volupté (1834), a novel by Sainte-Beuve (q.v.). The narrator, Amaury, a priest on his way to America, spends the voyage writing, for the spiritual benefit of a friend in France, the story of his life prior to taking orders. There is a confused background, in Brittany and Paris, of Royalist conspiracy during the Consulate; and Georges, Pichegru (qq.v.), &c., come into the picture. The long, rambling work is, however, chiefly interesting as the inner history of a character who is, or has been, a prey to melancholy, frustration, and introspection (cf. *Obermann*; *René*; *Adolphe*; *Confession d'un enfant du siècle*), and whose gross sensuality is continually at war with his more sensitive, spiritual, and intellectual nature. Eventually he finds sublimation in religion, enters a seminary, and, though only after almost mystical agonies of temptation, becomes a priest.

There is one approach to a dramatic moment at the end, when, shortly after being ordained, Amaury is called to administer the last rites to Mme de Couaën, the wife of his former friend and patron. She had been the object of his adoration at all times, no matter where his baser instincts led him—an adoration necessarily pure, for she had remained an unfailing model of wifely and maternal virtue.

This was Sainte-Beuve's only full-length work of fiction. Much of it can be recognized as autobiographical and he himself said he had drawn his characters and situations from real life.

Voyage, Le, and *Un Voyage à Cythère,* poems by Baudelaire (q.v.), in *Les Fleurs du mal.* The former, one of his finest poems, concludes the section 'La Mort' (and the whole series). The latter is in the section 'Le Vin'.

Voyage au bout de la nuit (1932), a novel by L.-F. Céline (q.v.).

Voyage autour de ma chambre (1794), the best-known work of Xavier de Maistre (q.v.), written during his early years of service with the Piedmontese army. It describes, with a delicate mixture of sentiment, humour, and exact observation, a period of temporary imprisonment in his quarters at Turin. The underlying idea is that circumscribed surroundings cannot rob us of happiness, which we must find in ourselves. The form of the book is said to have been influenced by Sterne's *Sentimental Journey.* (Cf. also *Vert-Vert.*)

Voyage aux eaux des Pyrénées, later called *Voyage aux Pyrénées* (1855), by Taine (q.v., para. 2), notes of a trip from Bordeaux through the Landes to Biarritz, from there to Luchon, and back to Toulouse. He says: 'Je me suis promené beaucoup; j'ai causé un peu; je raconte les plaisirs de mes oreilles et de mes yeux.' The eyes and the ears were those of a historian and philosopher; of a lover of nature; and an observer of human and animal life who missed neither the poetry nor the humour in what he saw.

Voyage de Monsieur Perrichon, Le, a farcical comedy by Eugène Labiche (q.v.), produced in 1860 and to be found in volume 2 (1889) of his *Théâtre complet.* M. Perrichon, a wealthy retired tradesman, sets off for a holiday in Switzerland with his wife and his daughter Henriette. They are followed by Armand and Daniel, friendly rivals for Henriette's affections. Armand's stock goes up when he rescues M. Perrichon, who falls off a horse. Daniel's soars when he lets M. Perrichon rescue *him,* from a well-stage-managed fall into a crevasse. Complications ensue, in gay, see-saw fashion. In the end the clever Daniel over-reaches himself and it is Armand who wins Henriette.

Voyage du jeune Anacharsis en Grèce, see Barthélemy, *l'abbé J.-J.*

Voyage d'Urien (1893), an early work by André Gide (q.v., para. 2).

Voyage en Orient (1851), travel notes by Gérard de Nerval (q.v.).

Voyelles, see *Sonnet des voyelles.*

Vrain-Lucas (1818–?), a clever literary forger of the second half of the 19th century. He was the son of a gardener at Châteaudun, and for many years managed to read and educate himself while following his father's calling. In 1852 he went to Paris. He found employment with a genealogist of fairly dubious repute, discovered that he had a talent for imitating handwriting, and turned this to profitable account. Within a few years' time he had imposed on the eminent mathematician Michel Chasles (1793–1880) to the extent of selling him some 7,000 letters, said to be either genuine autographs or genuine 16th-century translations of the originals. The 'writers' ranged from Cleopatra to Petrarch and Laura, to Madame de Maintenon, and to Pascal (a letter to the English scientist Boyle from which it appeared that Pascal, not Newton, had discovered the law of gravitation). Chasles maintained their authenticity in several heated discussions at the *Académie des sciences* but finally had to yield to evidence that he had been deceived. In February 1870 Vrain-Lucas was convicted of forgery, fined heavily, and sent to prison for two years. He came out, recommenced his old practices, and again went to prison. Daudet's novel *L'Immortel* was a satire of the Vrain-Lucas case.

W

Wace of Jersey (*c.* 1100–75), an Anglo-Norman poet, who was made a canon of Bayeux by Henry II; the author of long historical poems written to the order of noble patrons: the *Roman de Brut* or *Geste des Bretons* and *Roman de Rou* or *Geste des Normands.* The former, in octosyllabic verse, dedicated to Eleanor of Aquitaine, is based on the *Historia Regum Britanniae* of Geoffrey of Monmouth (q.v.), with the addition of much picturesque detail, including the story of the Round Table. The *Roman de Rou* (i.e. Rollo), a history of the dukes of Normandy, partly in monorhyme stanzas of alexandrines, partly in octosyllabic couplets, is based on Latin chronicles or from tradition, down to the battle of Tinchebrai in 1106. At this point Wace abandoned the work, being discouraged by the favour shown to his rival Benoît de Sainte-Maure (q.v.). Wace also wrote, in verse, lives of various saints.

Wagner, RICHARD (1813–83). Although operas by Wagner were performed in whole or in part in Paris as early as 1860 his music was barely appreciated in France till several years later. Baudelaire, meanwhile, had lauded him in various articles (e.g. in the *Revue européenne* and the *Presse théâtrale et musicale*) and remarked on affinities between his own theory of *correspondances* and Wagner's attempts to make his operas, or music-dramas, syntheses of music and poetry. The Symbolists made these theories of *correspondances* their own and for many of them Wagner became a master (see *Axël*; *Mallarmé*; *Revue wagnérienne*; *Symbolisme*). His influence was largely responsible for the Symbolists' *orchestrated* verse.

Wagram, a village in Austria, not far from Vienna, where Napoleon defeated the Austrians on 6 July 1809. By the Treaty of Vienna (14 October 1809) he consolidated this victory, depriving Austria of a large part of her territory and population and breaking up the Fifth Coalition (q.v.). At one time during the campaign (at Essling, when attempting to cross the Danube) the French army had narrowly escaped defeat.

Wairy, LOUIS-CONSTANT, *known as* CONSTANT (1778–1845), a Belgian hotel-keeper's son, came young to France and was in the service of Eugène de Beauharnais in

1799. In 1800 he became head *valet de chambre* to Bonaparte, then First Consul, and was his close personal attendant thereafter at all times—on campaign, on the retreat from Moscow (1812) and the return to Paris. But at the time of Napoleon's first abdication (1814) he abandoned him and it was Marchand (q.v.) who went with Napoleon to Elba.

Constant was in low water when he died, despite the high wages and many favours he had received from Napoleon. His Memoirs (1830–1, 6 vols.) were compiled, from his own story, by Charles-Maxime de Villemessant (1785–1852), a needy political journalist.

Waldenses, see *Vaudois*.

Waller, MAURICE WARLOMONT, *called* MAX (1866–95), a poet of Belgian nationality; founder and leader of *La Jeune Belgique* (Brussels, 1881–97), a review famous in the history of the 19th-century literary renaissance in Belgium. It was primarily sympathetic to the Parnassian ideals, but for a time many Belgian Symbolists (e.g. Maeterlinck, Rodenbach, Verhaeren, qq.v.) were contributors.

Wallonie, La (1886–92), a literary and artistic review (monthly) founded at Liège by the Belgian poet Albert Mockel (q.v.). It was the organ of the Symbolist Movement (see *Symbolisme*) in Belgium and published the first works of many French as well as Belgian Symbolists. The name is a reference to the former *Pays wallon*, roughly the south-eastern part of Belgium, with Liège in the centre.

Walter, ANDRÉ. For *Les Cahiers* and *Les Poésies d'André Walter* see *Gide*, para. 2.

Walter, JUDITH, the pseudonym used by Judith Gautier (q.v.) when she first published *Le Livre de jade*.

Warens, MME DE (1700–62), born at Vevey in Switzerland, famous as the protectress of J.-J. Rousseau from 1729 to about 1742. She had left her husband and was employed by the priests of Savoy in matters relating to the conversion of Protestants from Geneva; she was also, it appears, engaged in political espionage. She was a kindly benevolent woman, flighty and of easy morals, who mismanaged her affairs and was reduced to indigence before her death. Arthur Young,

under date 24 December 1789, relates his visit to her house, *Les Charmettes*, and gives the text of the certificate of her death.

Watelet, CLAUDE-HENRI, see *Dictionaries and encyclopedias*, under date 1792.

Waterloo, a village in Belgium, south of Brussels, near which on 18 June 1815 Napoleon (with a hastily collected army of some 100,000 men) was finally and decisively defeated by the United Army, which included British, Netherlander, Hanoverian, and Brunswickian forces, under the Duke of Wellington, and the Prussian army, under Blücher. Napoleon's object was to dispose of Wellington's army before the Prussians arrived. There had been a violent storm in the night and Napoleon delayed his attack until midday. The English withstood him throughout the afternoon. By two o'clock a first contingent of Prussians had arrived, and attacked Napoleon on the right. They were finally repulsed about 7 p.m., by which time nearly all the French infantry reserves had been used up. Napoleon then launched his famous Imperial Guard in a desperate attempt to break Wellington's squares. They were mown down by British fire as they tried to advance. At this point Blücher appeared with the main Prussian forces, taking Napoleon in the flank, and Wellington ordered a general advance. The exhausted French forces, attacked in front and on the flank, took panic and were routed, with the exception of the Guard, who resisted to the end (see *Cambronne, Mot de*). Although this battle is called Waterloo from the name of the village to the north of the battlefield, where Wellington had his reserves, the chief fighting took place between the farm of La Haie-Sainte, Wellington's advanced post, and the Plateau of Mont-Saint-Jean, where his troops were entrenched.

[French authors who have described Waterloo include: Stendhal, in *La Chartreuse de Parme* (q.v.); Victor Hugo, in Pt. ii of the poem 'L'Expiation' (in Bk. V of *Les Châtiments*, q.v.) and in *Les Misérables* (q.v.); Erckmann-Chatrian, in *Waterloo*, &c.]

Watteau, ANTOINE (1684–1721), born at Valenciennes in Hainault, came to Paris when eighteen. He was a famous genre painter, especially of *fêtes galantes* in a rustic setting (shepherds and shepherdesses in the fashionable costumes of the period), superficially gay and playful, but with an underlying melancholy. *L'Embarquement pour Cythère* is one of his best-known works.

Wauquelin or **Vauquelin**, JEAN (d. 1453), a native of Picardy; a compiler, translator, and copyist in the service of the Burgundian duke Philippe le Bon. He translated Geoffrey of Monmouth's *Historia regum Britanniae*, also the *Annales de Hainaut* of Jacques de Guise, and made prose adaptations of the old verse romances of *Girart de Roussillon* and *Alexandre le Grand*.

Weights and measures. Before the metric system was introduced at the Revolution a great variety of weights and measures were in use in different parts of France, and the same terms had not everywhere precisely the same meaning. Those which occur most frequently in French literature were the following, their signification being subject to local variations:

Long measure:

> *Pouce*, twelfth part of a *pied*, roughly an inch;
> *Pied*, a little more than an English foot;
> *Aune*, about $3\frac{1}{4}$ feet (cf. the English *ell*);
> *Toise*, 6 *pieds*;
> *Lieue*, league, very variable, about $2\frac{1}{2}$ miles.

Square measure:

> *Arpent*, a little more than an acre.

Capacity:

> *Boisseau*, about $\frac{1}{3}$ of a bushel;
> *Muid*, about 400 gallons.

Weight:

> *Livre*, about 1 pound.

Weil, SIMONE (1909–43), a writer on religion, philosophy, and sociology whose works and personality have aroused great interest since her death at the early age of thirty-four. She was born in Paris of (nonpractising) Jewish parentage. In 1931 she left the École normale supérieure (q.v.) as an *agrégée de philosophie* and thereafter taught philosophy in provincial *lycées*. This teaching career was interrupted at times by periods of ill health and still more by her political and sociological interests and her desire for firsthand experience of conditions, as, for instance, when she spent a year as a factory hand at the

Renault motor works in Paris, or when, in 1936, during the Spanish Civil War, she joined the International Brigade. After June 1940 she was in Unoccupied France, at Marseilles and—because the teaching profession had been closed to Jews—in the country, where she worked as a farm servant. She managed, however, to pursue her classical and philosophical interests and to explore her attitude to religious belief (her preference for a life guided and enriched by Christian inspiration, but not limited by acceptance of dogma, and her intense understanding of spiritual tribulation can be followed in *L'Attente de Dieu*, 1950).

In 1942 she accompanied her family to the U.S.A. and within a few months was able to come to London to work at the Headquarters of the Provisional French Government. But she ruined her health by privations (self-imposed lest her lot should be better than that of her compatriots in Occupied France). In April 1943 she was admitted to the Middlesex Hospital. From there, in August, she was moved to a sanatorium at Ashford, in Kent, where, a few days later, she died.

Publication of her many works has been proceeding since her death. *L'Attente de Dieu*, already mentioned, is a form of spiritual autobiography. Other titles include: *L'Enracinement* (1949), a long essay on the obligations of the individual and the State; *La Pesanteur et la Grâce* (1950), religious and philosophical meditations; *La Source grecque* (1953), translations from the Greek and studies of Greek thought; *Oppression et liberté* (1955), political and sociological studies, &c.; also three volumes (1951, 1955, 1956) of *Cahiers*, containing notes (obviously in view of future writings), *pensées*, and some literary criticism.

Weimars, see *Loeve-Veimars*.

Weiss, JEAN-JACQUES (1827–91), a brilliant political journalist, also a literary critic, with reactionary views. His works include: *Essai sur Hermann et Dorothée* (1865); *Essais sur l'histoire de la littérature française* (1865); *Le Théâtre et les Mœurs* (1889), &c.

Welche, see *Velche*.

Werthers, Die Leiden des jungen (1774), by Johann Wolfgang von Goethe, a semi-autobiographical novel founded on an episode of the author's youth. Werther, a young student, falls in love with Charlotte, who is betrothed to his friend Albert. He has no wish to betray his friend but he cannot conquer his passion. He absents himself, returns, and finds Charlotte married to Albert. He fancies that she is not entirely happy, but when one day he makes love to her she banishes him. Realizing that his passion is hopeless, he commits suicide.

This book, with its picture of will power destroyed by excessive sensibility and passion, and of a melancholy, appealing hero who turns to nature for an echo of his emotional storms, was one of the most important foreign influences on French literature about 1800 (see *Romantisme*; *Foreign Influences on French Literature*, paras. 10, 18, 20).

Wiener, FRANTZ, see *Croisset, F. de.*

Wilde, OSCAR (1854–1900). Wilde had many associations with French literary circles and spent most of his later life in France. He wrote his drama *Salomé* (q.v.) in French in the first instance.

William of Palerne, see *Guillaume de Palerne.*

William Shakespeare (1864), by Victor Hugo (q.v.), a biographical and critical study which he dedicated to England as a 'glorification de son poëte'. The work is apocalyptic in style but interesting as one of Hugo's emphatic pleas for a relative approach in criticism (cf. *Critics and criticism*, para. 7). Mention may also be made here of Hugo's preface of the following year (1865) for his son Jean-François-Victor Hugo's (q.v.) translation of the complete Works of Shakespeare. When first printed it was included in vol. xv of the translations. It moved up to vol. i when these were published in a second edition.

Willy, see *Colette.*

Wolff, PIERRE (1865–1930), dramatist. His works—popular successes of the *théâtre du boulevard*—include *Le Secret de Polichinelle* (1903); *L'Âge d'aimer* (1905); *Les Marionnettes* (1910); *Les Ailes brisées* (1920), &c.

Wolmar, BARON and JULIE DE, see *Nouvelle Héloïse.*

Wyse, SIR THOMAS (1791–1862), Irish politician and at one time British Minister in Greece, married (1821) Lætitia Bonaparte, a daughter of Lucien Bonaparte (see *Bonaparte family*) by his second wife Mme Joubenton (*née* Alexandrine de Bleschamp). For his daughter Marie-Lætitia-Studolmine Wyse see *Rute, Mme de.* For his son, the *félibriste* William Bonaparte Wyse, see the following article.

Wyse, WILLIAM BONAPARTE, or BONAPARTE-WYSE (1826–92), son of the above, was born at Waterford, co. Cork, and educated in England. He became associated with the *félibres* (q.v.) in 1859, settled at Avignon, and began to study the Provençal language and its literature. He published two collections of poetry: *Li Parpaioun blu* (*Les Papillons bleus*) (1868) and *Li Piado de la Princesso* (*L'Empreinte des pas de la princesse*) (1882).

Wyss, JEAN-RODOLPHE (1781–1830), a Swiss professor of philosophy and literature whose interest for English readers is that he wrote *The Swiss Family Robinson* (though the idea is said to have been his father's, Pastor Jean-David Wyss, 1743–1818). It was published in parts in 1812–13 and 1826–7, and translated almost at once from the original German into other languages. The French translation, entitled *Le Robinson suisse ou Journal d'un père naufragé avec ses enfants*, was later adapted and shorn of many pedagogical digressions by P.-J. Stahl (pseudonym of the well-known publisher and editor Hetzel).

Wyzewa, TEODOR DE (1862–1917), of Polish origin, an essayist and critic widely read in foreign literatures, was closely associated with the early days of *Symbolisme* (q.v.), notably in the *Revue wagnérienne* and the *Revue indépendante* (qq.v.), the typical and most influential organs of the movement. His articles on Wagner and *Symbolisme*, originally printed in the *Revue wagnérienne*, were collected in book form as *Nos maîtres* (1895). His later *Contes chrétiens* (1901) were written after his conversion to Roman Catholicism. An early novel, *Valbert* (1893), sometimes mentioned, has a hero who lives in a world of books and imagination and is terrified of real life.

Y

Year, Beginning of the. The year, in different parts of France, and at different times, was reckoned as beginning on a variety of dates, viz. 25 December, 25 March, Easter (mobile), and 1 January. The first of these systems, from 25 December (*style de la Nativité*), was widely used in medieval times, notably in parts of Southern France, in regions under the English domination, and in the Dauphiné. The *style de l'Annonciation*, under which the year began on 25 March instead of 1 January as in our modern year, was frequently used until 1564 in documents of the southern provinces and elsewhere, penetrating even to the north of France. The inconvenient system of reckoning the year from the mobile feast of Easter was in such wide use in France in the Middle Ages as to be known as the *style de France*; it had the consequence that the last ten days of March and the first twenty-four days of April, or some of these, might occur twice, or not at all, in a particular year. It was adopted by the royal chancellery probably under Louis VI, and its use gradually spread to the provinces from the 12th to the 14th centuries, remaining fairly general until 1564. The year beginning on 1 January (*style de la Circoncision*), adopted from Roman usage, was prescribed by an edict of Charles IX of January 1563/4, soon registered by the *parlements* of Toulouse and Bordeaux, but not till 1567 by that of Paris. It became general before long and remained in force until the adoption of the Republican Calendar (q.v.) in 1793. While that lasted, the year began on the day of the autumnal equinox (22 Sept.). From 1806 onwards, with the official re-establishment of the Gregorian calendar, the year was once more reckoned as beginning on 1 January.

Yonville, in Flaubert's *Madame Bovary* (q.v.), the country town in Normandy where most of the action takes place.

Young, ARTHUR (1741–1820), a Suffolk squire, experimental farmer, rural economist, and writer on agriculture. His many publications include surveys of agricultural, social, and political conditions, made during travel in England, Ireland, and France before the year 1793, when he was appointed secretary of the newly created Board of Agriculture. His *Travels in France* (1792), a work of the greatest value (an authority for historians) and also of lively interest, describes three journeys undertaken between 1787 and 1790, in the course of which he covered practically the whole country. It was translated into French in 1794, and 20,000 copies are said to have been printed by order of the *Convention nationale* (q.v.) for free distribution among the *communes* (small rural areas). Selections from his writings on agriculture were also published in translation in 1801, by order of the *Directoire* (*Le Cultivateur anglais*, 18 vols.).

Young, EDWARD (1683–1765). The long, gloomy, and didactic poem by which this English author is chiefly remembered, *The Complaint, or Night Thoughts on Life, Death, and Immortality* (1742–5), was translated into French by Letourneur (q.v.) in 1769, and like Macpherson's *Ossian* helped to bring romantic melancholy into French literature. It was called *Méditations de la nuit* and is frequently referred to as 'Les Nuits d'Young'.

Ys, a legendary buried city off the coast of Brittany (Finistère), said to have stood once (in the 4th or 5th century) on the edge of sea, protected by a dike with flood-gates of which the king held the only key. One night the king's daughter, after carousing with her lover, stole the key from her sleeping father and opened the flood-gates. The city was engulfed, but sometimes on a transparent morning, the legend says, the cathedral can be seen rising out of the water, its bells are heard, and the murmur of the priests intoning. The story was adapted (from a poem by a forgotten author Édouard Blau) by the composer Édouard Lalo (1823–92) for his opera *Le Roi d'Ys* (1888), and it inspired one of Debussy's best-known pianoforte compositions (a *Prélude*), *La Cathédrale engloutie*.

Ysopet, see *Marie de France*.

Yvain or **Le Chevalier au Lion,** a *roman breton* (q.v.) by Chrétien de Troyes (q.v.), of which we have an abbreviated English version in the 14th-century *Ywain and Gawain*. It was composed about 1173.

Yvain, a knight of Arthur's court, goes to the magic fountain of Brocéliande. Challenged by the knight who guards it, he slays him. The knight's widow, Laudine, at first filled with grief and the desire for vengeance, is gradually won over by her maiden Lunette to look with favour on Yvain, who, for his part, has been profoundly moved by the widow's beauty. Thus the seemingly impossible union is brought about. Shortly after their marriage they are visited by Arthur and his knights, and Yvain is urged by Gauvain not to sink into voluptuous sloth but to resume his knightly life. Laudine consents to his departure but appoints a day for his return; if he fails to come, he will lose her love. This in fact he does, forgetting his promise and the appointed day as he goes from tourney to tourney. A messenger from Laudine tells him that she renounces him and that he is never to return to her. Yvain is thunderstruck and filled with remorse. He goes about the world seeking adventures in the course of which he saves a lion from a dragon and wins the animal's devotion. Finally he obtains, though with difficulty, the pardon of Laudine.

The poem is remarkable for the subtle delineation of the complex character of Laudine, in both phases of the story—the transference of her affection from her dead husband to his slayer, recalling the celebrated theme of the Matron of Ephesus, and in the subsequent display of wounded pride when Yvain temporarily forgets her. Here as in the author's *Lancelot*, the man is absolutely dominated by the woman.

Yver, JACQUES (1520–72), a gentleman of Poitou, author of a collection of five tales of varied character, entitled *Printemps* in facetious contrast to his own name, published in 1572. The setting is what would now be called a house party in a country house in Poitou, and the pleasant description of this gives an idea of the mode of life and conversation of the wealthy classes of this period, while the last of the tales combines with its *esprit gaulois* some other aspects of contemporary society. There were twelve editions of the book by the end of the century.

Yvetot, see *Roi d'Yvetot*.

Yvette, the name-tale of a volume (1885) of short stories by Guy de Maupassant (q.v.). A *demi-mondaine*'s daughter grows up in her mother's house unaware of the true nature of her surroundings, an enigma by her innocent provocativeness to the familiars of the household. She learns the truth, pens a farewell note of outraged virtue for her mother 'la marquise', and tries to end her life by inhaling chloroform. She has sunk into a coma when she is discovered (as is also her note), and revived, by one of her most perplexed admirers. In the exhilaration of returning to life she is glad to have failed—and to fall. Which leaves her admirer more puzzled than ever.

Z

Zadig, a philosophical tale by Voltaire, first published in 1747 under the title of *Memnon, histoire orientale*, and in 1748 under the title of *Zadig*. Another tale which he entitled *Memnon* (q.v.) appeared in 1749.

Zadig, a young man well endowed by nature and fortified by a good education, is puzzled by the vagaries of his destiny. He rises to the highest offices but is unfortunate in love and, despite his wisdom and moderation, meets with a number of misfortunes. In a series of adventures he comes within an ace of being strangled in Babylon, roasted alive in Basra, impaled by bonzes in Serendip, and is actually enslaved in Egypt. In the remarkable penultimate chapter entitled 'L'Hermite' he is finally relieved of his perplexity by the angel Jesrad, who reveals to him that there is no evil in the world but some good arises out of it; and that there is no such thing as chance, but that all is trial or punishment, recompense or prevision. Zadig marries the queen whom he loves, becomes king, and adores Providence.

There are some sly hits, in the course of the story, at the clergy and Catholic dogma.

Zaïre, a tragedy by Voltaire, produced in 1732, one of his finest plays.

Zaïre, a Christian child carried off by the Turks at the capture of Caesarea, has been brought up in the seraglio at Jerusalem. The sultan Orosmane has fallen in love with her and is about to make her his consort. She returns his love. She had formerly as companion in captivity Nérestan, like herself carried off as a child, but since ransomed and taken back to France, then again captured and released on his promise to bring back from France the ransom of ten knights. He arrives just as the marriage of Zaïre is to be celebrated; but the ransom has exhausted his fortune and he surrenders himself a prisoner once more. The generous Orosmane refuses the ransom and gives liberty to a hundred prisoners. But he excepts from these Zaïre and the aged Lusignan, the last of the race of the French kings of Jerusalem. Zaïre, who has witnessed the disappointment of Nérestan, obtains from her lover the release of Lusignan. He is brought from his dungeon, aged and infirm, and Nérestan and Zaïre, his liberators, are presented to him. By certain signs he discovers in them his own lost son and daughter. Horrified to learn that Zaïre is a Moslem, he adjures her to become a Christian and she yields to his entreaty; the discovered relationship is to be concealed. Lusignan is dying, and Nérestan presses his sister to receive baptism secretly. She arouses the sultan's suspicions by asking for a postponement of the marriage. A letter from Nérestan is intercepted bidding her meet him, in terms which suggest to Orosmane a guilty connexion between Nérestan and Zaïre. Maddened with jealousy, he awaits her at the meeting-place and kills her with his dagger. Then he learns the truth from Nérestan and takes his own life.

Zamacoïs, MIGUEL (1866–1939), author of romantic dramas in verse: *Les Bouffons* (1907), the most successful; *La Fleur merveilleuse* (1910), &c.

Zamet, SÉBASTIEN (1549–1614), an Italian financier born at Lucca, who came to France with the Médicis and rose to favour and great wealth under Henri IV. He had two sons, one an ecclesiastic, Bishop of Langres

and at one time (1624–36) director of Port-Royal, the other a brave and pious soldier, active in warfare against the Huguenots.

Zélide, see *Charrière, Mme de.*

Zémire et Azor, an *opéra-comique* produced in 1771, of which Marmontel wrote the libretto and Grétry the music, on the theme of Beauty and the Beast. It was highly successful.

Azor is a Persian prince, deprived by a malignant fairy of the beauty of which he was too proud and condemned to bear the form of a monster till he should be loved by a woman in spite of his ugliness. Zémire is a maiden who, sacrificing herself to save her father, is won by the prince.

Zimmer, BERNARD (1893–   ), dramatist, author of (mainly) satires and farces with a grotesque element reminiscent of Jarry's (q.v.) *Ubu Roi*: *Le Veau gras* (1924); *Les Zouaves* (1925); *Bava l'Africain* (1926); *Le Coup du 2 décembre* (1928); *Le Beau Danube rouge* (1932).

Z. Marcas, one of the 'Scènes de la vie politique' of Balzac's *Comédie humaine* (q.v.). Zéphirin Marcas is young, gifted, and ambitious, but can make no headway against corruption.

Zola, ÉMILE (1840–1902), novelist, born in Paris, of Italian origin on his father's side, was brought up at Aix-en-Provence. When he was seven his father died, leaving little money. In 1858 he settled in Paris and from 1860 to 1865 he worked for Hachette, the publishers. At this time he contributed verse and short stories to periodicals. A collection of tales, *Contes à Ninon*, was published in 1864, and his first full-length novel, *La Confession de Claude*, in 1865. After this he supported himself by literary and art criticism and wrote the realistic novels *Thérèse Raquin* and *Madeleine Férat* (qq.v., both 1868). About this date he evolved a pseudo-scientific theory of the 'naturalistic' novel (see *Naturalisme*) which owed much to the philosophy of Taine (q.v.) and to the *Traité philosophique et physiologique de l'hérédité naturelle* (1847–50) of Dr. Prosper Lucas (1808–65) and the *Introduction à la médecine expérimentale* (1865) of Dr. Claude Bernard (q.v.). To illustrate his theory he wrote the *Histoire naturelle et sociale d'une fa-mille sous le Second Empire*, a cycle of twenty novels with the generic title of *Les Rougon-Macquart*, published between 1871 and 1893. (For a full description, with titles and publication dates of the several volumes, see under *Rougon-Macquart*.) He also elaborated it in *Le Roman expérimental* (1880) and in the studies and reviews collected in *Les Roman-ciers naturalistes* (1881) and *Le Naturalisme au théâtre* (1881).

(2) At times, in his naturalistic novels, Zola laboured documentation and scientific ex-position to the detriment of the works as fiction: at times, fortunately, he forgot his theories. His descriptions of vice and misery, if lurid and often revolting, are powerful ('C'est un colosse qui a les pieds malpropres, mais c'est un colosse', Flaubert, *Correspon-dance*, 18 Apr. 1880); and his books contain extravagantly lyrical descriptions of nature that are primarily romantic in inspiration. Few French novelists have so well conveyed the teeming, tumultuous life of Paris, and he brings a painter's eye to its long vistas, its skies, or river, through the changing seasons. He also draws a successful picture of France during the Second Empire. His characters move against a background of social history—financial enterprise, the in-ception of the great department stores, the changes in peasant life wrought by indus-trial development, the growing self-con-sciousness of the working classes, and, finally, the political, social, and military collapse of the era.

(3) The novels of his last years had little to do with naturalism. The trilogy *Les Trois villes*: *Lourdes* (1894), *Rome* (1896), *Paris* (1898), is concerned with social and religious problems. Another, incomplete, series *Les Quatre Évangiles*: *Fécondité* (1899), *Travail* (1901), which owed much to Fouriérisme (q.v.), *Vérité* (1903, posth.), and *Justice* (pro-jected, but never written), was inspired by humanitarian ideals. The author's four new evangels were Maternity, Work, Truth, and Justice.

(4) In 1898 Zola agitated for a revision of the Dreyfus (q.v.) verdict, and after the trial and sentence resulting from the publication of his letter *J'accuse* (q.v.) he spent a year in exile in England. His pamphlets of 1901, *La Vérité en marche* and *L'Affaire Dreyfus*, refer to the case, which also inspired *Vérité*, the third of the *Évangiles* mentioned above. He died of carbon monoxide poisoning—an accident, the chimney of his stove was blocked—in September 1902.

(5) His other critical writings include: *Mes Haines* and *Mon Salon* (both 1866), collected essays on realism in literature and in art (the former contains another of his often-quoted remarks: 'Une œuvre d'art est un coin de la création vu à travers un tempérament'); *Édouard Manet* (1867), a study; *Nos auteurs dramatiques* (1881), dramatic criticism. Several of his novels were dramatized, and he also wrote directly for the theatre (but with little success), e.g. *Madeleine Férat* (q.v.); *Les Héri-tiers Rabourdin* (1874), a comedy; *Le Bouton de Rose* (1878), a farce.

Zutistes, Les, a short-lived literary society remembered for its association with *les décadents* and the beginnings of the Sym-bolist Movement (see *Hydropathes*; *Sym-bolisme*).

APPENDIX I

POINTERS TO THE STUDY OF FRENCH LITERATURE AND ITS BACKGROUND

THE young student, adventuring on his first independent piece of research, wishes to know how to set about it and what books, which libraries, and which source-collections he should consult. The *Guide de l'étudiant en littérature française*, by E. Bouvier and P. Jourda (1936 and later editions), is at hand to help him, and he may also profitably consult *Les Techniques de la critique et de l'histoire littéraires en littérature française moderne*, by Gustave Rudler (Oxford, 1923). Far on, at the other end of the scale, the experienced research-worker will find all possible sources of documentation, national and international, compartmented and classified in one of the monuments of modern bibliographical scholarship, *Les Sources du travail bibliographique*, by L.-N. Malclès [Genève, vol. i (1950) *Bibliographies générales*; vols. ii, iii (1952) *Bibliographies spécialisées (Sciences humaines)*].

Midway between these two comes the Common Reader—a personage who may know and love the few in French literature but is less familiar with the many; who is, possibly, dismayed by bibliographical manuals, yet is not incurious and would welcome occasional guidance. The list printed below has been compiled with him, or her, in mind. It gives only *pointers*, and makes no pretensions to bibliographical completeness; and since limits—which imply no invidious distinction—had to be determined it has been confined almost wholly to French books and periodicals. The works mentioned should be available in this country at booksellers', or at or through national, students', or public libraries. Most of them are provided with bibliographies and notes which are themselves a stimulus to further reading.

The place of publication, when not specified, is Paris; the dates are those of first editions with, in square brackets, the latest edition (often revised and augmented) down to and including 1955. Asterisks refer to articles in the main body of the *Companion*.

A. LITERARY HISTORY AND CRITICISM

(i) Large-scale general and critical histories, from the origins to modern times, the work of specialists under general editors:

Histoire de la langue et de la littérature françaises des origines à 1900. Publiée sous la direction de L. Petit de Julleville.* 1896–9 [1899], 8 vols., with plates.

(This older but still valuable work is less useful for the post-1850 period. The 17th century begins with vol. IV, the 19th with vol. VII. The 1899 edition has an index of authors and works.)

Histoire de la littérature française. Publiée sous la direction de Joseph Calvet. 1931– .

    I. *Le Moyen Âge*, by R. Bossuat (1931).

    II. III. } *La Renaissance*, by R. Morçay (1933–5).

    IV. *Les Écrivains classiques*, by H. Gaillard de Champris (1934).

    V. *La Littérature religieuse de François de Sales à Fénelon*, by J. Calvet (1938).

    VI. *De Télémaque à Candide*, by A. Chérel (1933).

    VIII. *Le Romantisme*, by P. Moreau (1932).

    IX. *Le Réalisme*, by R. Dumesnil (1936) [1948].

(The plan, a series of monographs, not necessarily published consecutively, resembles that of the *Oxford History of English Literature*. The volumes are well supplied with chapter-bibliographies. The general editor was for long associated with the *Institut Catholique de Paris*★.)

Histoire de la littérature française illustrée. Publiée sous la direction de Joseph Bédier★ et Paul Hazard★. 1923 [1948–9], 2 vols.
 I. Origins to *c.* 1680.
 II. *c.* 1680 to the present day.

(This work is commonly known as *Bédier–Hazard*. The many fine illustrations, often reproductions from old prints and engravings, or from manuscripts, add to its interest. Each volume has full Tables of Contents. The second volume has the author-index.)

(ii) Histories confined to epochs or phases; also shorter histories, or manuals, by individual authors.

ADAM, ANTOINE. *Histoire de la littérature française au XVIIe siècle.* 1948–56, 5 vols.
I. *L'Époque d'Henri IV et de Louis XIII.*
II. *L'Époque de Pascal.*
III, IV. *L'Apogée du siècle: 1661–1677* [Boileau, Molière; Racine, La Rochefoucauld, Mme de Sévigné, &c.].
V. *La Fin de l'École classique: 1680–1715.*

(A balanced, scholarly presentment of the period, well served by clear, narrative form and the biographical and bibliographical footnotes; also by its layout. Each volume has an author-index.)

BRAUNSCHVIG, MARCEL. *Notre littérature étudiée dans les textes.* 1920–1 [1953], 2 vols.
 I. *Des origines à la fin du XVIIe siècle.*
 II. *Le XVIIIe et le XIXe Siècle* [to 1850].
—— *La Littérature française contemporaine étudiée dans les textes. 1850–1925.* 1926 [1950].

(These useful volumes, with generous selections from texts, are kept well up to date and the contemporary section is extended in the later editions. They contain general and specialized bibliographies, biographical and explanatory footnotes, author-indexes, full tables of contents, and much general information, though this is not always easy to find.)

CLOUARD, HENRI. *Histoire de la littérature française du symbolisme à nos jours.* 1947–9, 2 vols.
 I. *De 1885 à 1914.*
 II. *De 1915 à 1940.*

(With full Tables of Contents and an author-index in each volume, but no bibliography.)

GIRARD, MARCEL. *Guide illustré de la littérature française moderne (de 1918 à 1949).* 1949.

(An informative guide—no more than this, but useful—to contemporary authors and movements.)

JALOUX,★ EDMOND. *Introduction à l'histoire de la littérature française.* Genève, 1946, 2 vols.
 I. *Des origines à la fin du moyen âge.*
 II. *Le XVIe Siècle.*

(The author died leaving only these two volumes out of six contemplated. They are one of the most interesting approaches to the study of French literature; without index or bibliography but with a useful *Table chronologique* at the end of each volume.)

JASINSKI, RENÉ. *Histoire de la littérature française.* 1947, 2 vols.
 I. Origins to *c.* 1715.
 II. 1715 to the end of the 19th century.

(This is practical and factual, with informative introductory surveys for each period. Each volume has an author-index. No bibliography.)

LALOU, RENÉ. *Histoire de la littérature française contemporaine (1870 à nos jours).* 1940 [1946], 2 vols.

(By a contemporary literary critic and historian widely versed in English as well as French literature. A full guide to the period, plentifully and aptly pointed with quotations. There are footnotes, and the 1946 edition (vol. II) has an author-index.)

LANCASTER, HENRY CARRINGTON. *A History of French Dramatic Literature in the Seventeenth Century.* 1929–42, 9 vols.

I, II. (Pt. I) *The Pre-Classical Period: 1610–1634.*
III, IV. (Pt. II) *The Period of Corneille: 1635–1651.*
V, VI. (Pt. III) *The Period of Molière: 1652–1672.*
VII, VIII. (Pt. IV) *The Period of Racine: 1673–1700.*
IX. (Pt. V) *Recapitulation.*